THE RED HORSE

EUGENIO CORTI

THE
RED HORSE

A Novel

Translated from the Italian

IGNATIUS PRESS   SAN FRANCISCO

Origianal Italian edition:
Il Cavallo rosso
Tenth Edition 1995
Edizioni Arres, Milan
© 1983 Eugenio Corti

Cover art: *The Horse*
by the Ukranian artist Petro Hedeck

Cover design by Roxanne Mei Lum

© 2000 Ignatius Press, San Francisco
ISBN 0-89870-747-1 (HB)
Library of Congress catalogue number 99-73011
Printed in the United States of America

When [the Lamb] opened the second seal, I heard the second living creature say, "Come!" And out came another horse, bright red; its rider was permitted to take peace from the earth, so that men should slay one another; and he was given a great sword. . . .

When he opened the fourth seal, I heard the voice of the fourth living creature say, "Come!" And I saw and behold, a pale horse, and its rider's name was Death, and Hades followed him; and they were given power over a fourth of the earth, to kill with sword and with famine and with pestilence and by wild beasts of the earth.

Revelation 6:3–4, 7–8

CONTENTS

BOOK ONE

THE RED HORSE

PART ONE

I

The end of May 1940. Slowly advancing, side by side, Ferrante and his son Stefano were cutting the meadow. Behind them the small chestnut horse, tied to the cart, was waiting. It had already finished the entire pile of grass Stefano had put in front of it when they began the work. The horse had eaten eagerly, continually lifting and shaking its head to shrug off the bulky collar that was sliding along its neck. Now, without taking a step, it reached forth with its muzzle to tear off the leaves from the mulberry tree, where it had been left in the shade; it also tore at the bark of the more tender branches, which looked broken and white as tiny bones where the horse's teeth had left their mark.

From time to time Ferrante stood up, gave a half turn to the long handle of his scythe, resting the point on the ground; the blade was then parallel with his chest. The edge of the blade was rimmed with green foam, the living spirit of grass. With the whetstone made of an ox horn that hung from his waist, Ferrante first cleaned green slime from the blade, then sharpened it, alternating the two sides of the blade with a steady rhythm of the whetstone. Then, out of consideration for his father, the son stopped working and also turned his own scythe round and began to sharpen it in the same fashion.

He's a good worker, Ferrante thought, observing him while he carried out this operation. *He doesn't quit unless he has a reason, and he's never the first.*

Now I can outlast him, his son Stefano was thinking, in contrast, and he had a feeling of pride mixed with regret. *Only last year it was the other way around*, he reflected. He looked at his father out of the corner of his eye: robust, with his neck solidly planted between his shoulders like a tree trunk, and with a peppery mustache that covered almost his entire mouth, he certainly was not someone who inspired pity. *But he's practically fifty*, Stefano told himself. Realizing that his father had noticed his look, he slowly shifted his gaze, always sharpening the edge of his blade with the whetstone, and fixed his eyes on the cart road from Nomanella, his farm, up to the town of Nomana.

Ferrante guessed what had passed through his son's mind, so well did he know him. *Very good, my boy*, he thought. To break the silence he asked, obviously in the local dialect, "What's happening? Are you waiting for someone?"

"Yes, Father", Stefano answered. "I'm not sure, but Ambrogio could be coming."

"What Ambrogio, Riva?"

"Yes."

Ferrante was a bit surprised. "It's still May", he said. "Isn't today the last day of May?"

"Yes, Father."

"But doesn't your friend always return from school in the second half of June?"

"Normally, yes. In fact, because of the exams he would have had to return later this year, at the end of July or even in August. At least that's what he told me at Easter. But yesterday Giustina heard from the girls at the factory that he's going to arrive today, this afternoon."

"I see", Ferrante said vaguely.

"Maybe because of the war, the danger of war", Stefano suggested.

Ferrante reflected a moment in silence, and then he said, "If you young people only knew what a dirty thing war really is." And he shook his head several times with a gesture of no, no, meditatively. Several memories were flowing confusedly through his mind, among which one prevailed: an indescribably disagreeable sensation that he had experienced, more than twenty years ago now, listening to the lugubrious words of a comrade in the trenches, an infantryman like himself, while they waited to take off for one of those terrible assaults that were always announced as decisive ones, which later were never really decisive. He no longer remembered the words, but he remembered well that extraordinarily disagreeable sensation.

"Poor fellows", he concluded, incapable of completely expressing his own thoughts. "You'll find out that . . .", he continued, still saying no with his head.

Then he went back to handling the scythe energetically.

"In any case, there's still no war", Stefano said, also starting to mow again. "And while there's no war, there's hope."

Ferrante nodded, but he was thinking, *There's no war yet, no. But the others, they're already at war, the Germans, the French . . . Yes, the others. And in the cities, even in Milan, there are those bloody damned students and the rest of that mob who are staging prowar demonstrations. It was like that in 1915, too; it began that way.*

But he did not want to continue; he even forced himself not to think about the war, not to become obsessed with the topic.

So they both continued, interrupting their work only occasionally to sharpen the scythes, until they finished the square of grass they had set out to mow.

When they reached the end, they turned and went back together to the cart, from which Ferrante took the water bottle his wife had prepared, wrapped in green fig leaves. Without speaking, first the father and then the son drank from the bottle, between sighs of satisfaction. They took rakes from the cart and gathered together the cut grass, which smelled fresh, into green rows first and then into piles, which took some time. When they finished, they were again at the end of the mowed section.

At a sign from his father, Stefano went for the horse, waiting with its head up and its ears stiff, and started it walking vigorously as soon as he had it secured with the reins.

They began the loading: the young man on the cart distributing and arranging the growing heap of grass with the pitchfork; and the older man below, who kept hurling new forkfuls. Ferrante reserved the hardest work for himself. From the height of the cart, Stefano glanced occasionally toward the road that led to Nomana in case his friend Ambrogio appeared. From there he could see him come down the cart road from the beginning, where it turned off the main road that entered the town.

But instead of Ambrogio there appeared, very tiny on the road, his brother and sister, Pio and Isadora, who were returning from school, hand in hand. No doubt Pio had put his clogs in the lunch basket and was barefoot. *It's practically a vice*, Stefano thought, smiling. That way his mother was forced to wash his feet, as she did every afternoon, as well as the lunch basket.

Ambrogio's garden, or rather the garden of Ambrogio's father, the textile industrialist, who before becoming an industrialist had been a laborer (yes, he had come a long way)—that garden was like a backdrop for the two little children.

The garden was like many others in Brianza. From the cart Stefano could see others, at the very edge of Nomana, or on the opposite side, that is, toward the north, farther from the Beolco factories, where the hilly terrain—which there formed a large shallow hollow—rose toward the background of Alpine mountain ridges. They were nineteenth-century-style gardens, with evergreen foliage—yews, laurels, firs, holly trees, magnolias—which grew thickly together like a single splotch of dark green vertical brushstrokes. The old gardens, no less than the factories, at that time characterized the hill landscape of Brianza.

Finally, when all the grass was in the cart, Stefano poked the pitchfork into it with energy, letting himself slide down to one of the shafts of the cart— which made the horse start—and then he leapt to the ground. His father took hold of the short hemp rein, and they left: the cart went from the soft terrain to the white road, pulled along by the horse's strong and decided steps, until the moment they met up with Pio and Isadora, who immediately begged to be lifted up onto the cart.

Ferrante stopped the horse and, without speaking, gestured with his head to Stefano to allow them up. The two children were hurled, more than lifted, onto the heap of grass. Happily ensconced on it, side by side, they sat, their legs horizontal, their caps pulled down almost covering their eyes, the lunch basket beside them. The horse took off again amidst the happy chatter of the children and an occasional excited shout from Pio. Stefano walked behind the cart.

After a few minutes Stefano turned, alerted by an unexpected ringing of a bell: Ambrogio was coming on bicycle. Like Stefano—his old school friend—he was nineteen; he seemed especially euphoric at that moment: "Hi, there!" he shouted by way of greeting.

"Hi, Brogio!"

Ferrante, still walking beside the horse, and without letting go of the rein, turned to one side to greet the boy cordially. *This one,* he thought, *even if he is a student, is not one of those jerks asking for war. On the contrary . . .*

"Good afternoon, Signore Ferrante!" Ambrogio shouted back. He also greeted the two little children: "Hi, Isadora. And, you, Pio, little loafer . . ." And by that detail, the fact that he was taking an interest in the youngsters, Stefano could not help but notice, as on other occasions, that he did not behave like the peasants. Or the workers. In fact, everybody knew he was a *liceo* student.

"Stefano, today is my last day, God willing. No more school for the rest of my life. Can you imagine?" Ambrogio exclaimed, while he followed along on his bicycle in the middle of the road behind the cart. Unlike the peasants, he spoke in Italian.

"But . . . those exams you spoke of?"

"No more exams!" Ambrogio exclaimed, gesturing with one of his arms, given the impossibility of doing it with two. (*Something must have happened,* his friend was thinking, *to make him this effusive.*) "Of course . . . even I can scarcely believe it! Imagine, Stefano, we were on the point of doing our final review, a tremendous business—a regular nervous breakdown, seriously, I'm not kidding—when the news came that this year there are no exams. You understand? They gave us our grades right away, and everyone was sent back home on the thirty-first of May! When I think of those poor guys last year who had to spit blood to pass the exams."

"But why didn't you take the exams? The war? I mean, because of the threat of war?"

"Yes", Ambrogio said, suddenly less euphoric. "At least it seems so; it couldn't be for anything else."

"But what's happening? Are we really at war?"

"Don't know", Ambrogio answered. "I hope not." In a reflective tone, more suited to him, he added, "Of course, if war does come, we'll pay dearly for this present piece of luck . . ." They were silent for a spell.

"Well," Stefano said, repeating what he had said earlier to his father, "there's no war now. And while there's no war, there's always hope."

"Of course, it's always stupid, as they say, to bandage your head before it's broken", the other chimed in. "Besides, neither you nor I can do anything", and his face again shone with a smile.

"Do you know that Igino and the others from the first semester, Pierello, Giacomo di Contra, and Castagna, have all received their papers and must show up tomorrow at the district barracks?"

"Tomorrow? We heard about these papers at school. They left us students alone, on the other hand. Half the class is going, aren't they?"

"Yes, they've called the first semester of the year '21."

"Igino and Pierello", Ambrogio repeated, "tomorrow . . ."

Stefano nodded. "Pierello no longer works in the village. For the last six or seven months he's been working at the forge in Sesto, did you know?"

"Yes, he told me at Easter. Listen, I'm thinking, why don't we accompany them by car to the barracks? Should we?"

"Tomorrow? No, you know I can't tomorrow. It's a work day."

2

The cart entered the Nomanella farmyard. Nomanella was a small farm on two levels in the form of a U, open toward the south, that is, toward Nomana.

The western side was occupied by the stable, with its upper part for hay; the center area was taken up by the home of Ferrante, the owner, who had let the other side to a worker's family.

The farmyard was bordered in front by a row of fruit trees: three old cherry trees, with disproportionately robust trunks, and a younger and shorter fig tree, whose color broke the harmony of the whole. The cart road led into the farmyard between the worker's dwelling and the miserable fig tree.

On hearing the noise of the wheels, Stefano's grandmother and mother appeared at the door of the house. Both were dressed in black, as was usual among peasant women, with a handkerchief tied round their heads. His mother had the same big brown eyes as Stefano.

The two children leapt rapidly from the cart and ran toward her, who caressed them while she first exchanged greetings with Ambrogio, before fully paying attention to them. She expressed herself in dialect, the only language used in the village then: "Welcome, Ambrogio."

"Thank you, thank you, Mama Lucia."

"Have your studies been hard?"

The grandmother, attentive, with her toothless mouth half open, brought a finger to her forehead, as if to show that mental work was fatiguing.

"No. Besides, this time it has been even too easy: there were no exams."

"There were no exams?"

"Yes, a piece of incredible luck." Ambrogio pointed to Stefano as if to say, "I've explained it already to him." Stefano nodded.

Lucia smiled approvingly. "I'm happy for you."

The grandmother, Ferrante's mother, came up and took the young man's hand in hers, all too obviously pleased by his visit. She always acted this way. It did not seem real that he came to visit them, he, the son of the industrialist who provided work for so many people (they were in Brianza, where there was no aversion at all toward industrialists in those days). The old woman shook Ambrogio's hand several times. Forward in her affection, so different from the delicate manners of his mother.

Ferrante, meanwhile, was shouting and pushing the horse backward in order to get the cart next to the stable door. Then he untied the animal, which, with its harness on, went to drink from a tub close to the wall. It pulled out its dripping snout to breathe and looked around. Once it had drunk, the animal went through the stable door and, alone, reached its stall, separated from the cows by a thick wooden partition. Ferrante and Stefano were looking at it, pleased, without moving.

"Now . . . ?" the father said at last.

It was early evening, not yet sunset, time to milk the cows and carry out the late afternoon chores in the stable.

"Yes", the son answered. And grabbing up a large load of new grass with his pitchfork, he preceded his father into the lower part of the stable.

Ambrogio followed them. The stable gave off a light musty smell of the country, not disagreeable. The two dark-coated cows hurriedly separated one from the other and, with their necks and heads to the back, pulled their chains forcefully, ready to receive the grass that was coming. Stefano went between the animals and unloaded the grass in the iron crib in front of one of them, from which it immediately began to eat voraciously, while the other stuck out its head in vain to reach the food. The young man returned shortly with a second enormous load of grass on the pitchfork and unloaded it in front of the other cow; then he continued to fill the entire crib. Later he filled the chestnut horse's rack, of less capacity but higher. Ferrante, meanwhile, had tied the horse to the crib, freeing it from its trappings, which now were hanging from two sticks jutting out of the wall.

No one spoke: the sound of the three animals eating, the coming and going of the two peasants could be heard, as well as occasional kicking and bellowing of the only calf there, which, tied in the corner, had got to its feet and was also asking to be fed. Its legs were disproportionately long and its coat lighter than that of the cows (*Brand new*, thought Ambrogio), and it was wearing a basket of straw over its mouth to prevent it from eating the forage. Ambrogio knew that once the milking was over Ferrante would pour a measure of milk in a bucket and, not having a nursing bottle, would make the calf suck the milk by putting a finger in its mouth.

From the wall at the back—of an indefinable color, so dirty was it—in an old oleograph, Saint Anthony, who was shown next to a pig ("Saint Anthony of the little pig", the people called him), seemed to stand vigil over the small stable.

How nice this place is, Ambrogio thought, and for a moment he was about to fantasize, *this is the life I'd like to lead . . .* , but he immediately corrected himself: *The trouble is that this kind of work doesn't allow one to live as one ought.*

The grandmother entered the stable with two buckets: one small and dark, with water to wash the udders of the cows, and the other large and shiny, for the milk. Behind her came the little Pio laughing away: he was running around with his feet soaped up; no doubt he had escaped from his mother, Lucia, who was washing him. His mother appeared: the boy, after a few attempts, finding it impossible to flee, let himself be cornered; but his mother picked him up with affection, scolded him more with the severe expression on her face than with her voice. She took him in her arms, making sure the boy's feet, once again dirty, were away from her apron. From the door, the grandmother, in contrast, did not fail to shout at him: "For shame, you should get it, running off with soapy feet! You've made your mother have to wash you again! What will the gentleman say . . . ?"

Pio did not seem to be impressed by the gentleman. He was used to seeing him, so much so that on going by him, he tried to kick him in the chest with one dirty foot. Ambrogio hardly had time to back away. This time his mother gave him a slap on his behind and also said, "For shame, you should be spanked!" The boy replied with a guffaw.

"These children . . . !" the grandmother sighed, looking at Ambrogio and then at Stefano, who was going toward her to take the two buckets. "These children . . . !" she repeated.

"Is something the matter, Grandmother?" Ambrogio asked.

"It's about my work", Stefano said, winking at Ambrogio. "You know. Try not to wind her up."

"Of course it's about your work!" the grandmother replied. "About your work and your own good."

"How's that?" Ambrogio insisted.

"He's fixed on being a peasant. They need apprentices now in the factories in Beolco; and he, no, he wants to be a peasant. It was not what we talked about or agreed on."

"Well . . .", Ambrogio said. "The agreement was that he would help in the country only until he was fourteen or fifteen, and after that he'd go into a factory. And the truth is he is already nineteen."

"Not yet", Stefano corrected.

"It's a good trade, being a mechanic", the grandmother said, without handing over the buckets in order to delay a little. "Work with a future. Isn't that so, Signore Ambrogio?"

"Yes, of course", Ambrogio responded, who was completely serious on this point.

"Did you hear, Stefano?" the old lady exclaimed, triumphant that she had extracted that declaration. "You see how even your friend says so?"

"It can be a good trade, being a mechanic—everyone knows it", Stefano said, and added mockingly. "I've nothing against mechanics." And, serious once again, he added, "But the point is something else, and it's that I like the land. You know that, Grandmother. Come, give me the buckets."

"But it's for your own good, that I—that we—and your father first, tell you . . . Does this small parcel of land seem so much to you?" The grandmother, instead of handing him the buckets, looked at Ferrante, in whom she knew she had an ally, but he, however, as always in the presence of outsiders, did not intervene.

From a hole in the wall, next to the reproduction of Saint Anthony, a mouse peeped out; Ambrogio remembered having seen it in the same place during his last visit. The tiny animal tested the surroundings and then tucked itself away again, though not entirely: it left the point of its tiny nose visible, as if it had decided to form part of the group. The old lady insisted, "Stefano, times are changing. You know very well that the boys here, even peasants' sons, no longer work in the fields; too much work for too little profit. Only during the early evening, returning from the factory, do some of them help the old folks to get on with the land they have. Look at Giacomo di Contra and Luigino del Brivio, for example. You, too, if you like the land so much, could do the same." She addressed Ambrogio, "Isn't it true he could do the same as they do?"

Ambrogio agreed easily, smiling, while Stefano, although full of respect, showed that as far as he was concerned, the conversation was over. Then the grandmother gave him the two buckets, turned around, and left the stable, complaining to herself that the boy was so stubborn.

The milking was going to begin. Ambrogio, who had thought of staying, suddenly felt like leaving. "Well, goodbye, Stefano", he said without further ado. "It's been nice seeing you, but I can't stay today. Perhaps tomorrow. Goodbye, Signore Ferrante!"

"What, you're going?"

Stefano left the buckets on the ground and gestured with his head to his friend. "I'll see you out."

Outside the night air was fresh, pure. The sun in the west, already going down, lit up the whole horizon: the large amphitheater of the Alpine foothills. "Look," Ambrogio observed, "what a lovely color the mountains are this afternoon, especially the Grigne and Resegone, look."

"The what, the mountains?" Stefano shook his head. *Student interests*, he thought. "If you want to know the truth, I neither look at them nor think about them."

"Because they're always in front of you", Ambrogio said. "If you lived all year in a school, in the city, with only houses around you, walls, trolleys . . . Well, I've finished school today, forever!" Making this declaration, already repeated several times during the course of the afternoon, he felt a new joy. (To which he paid no attention, for happiness seemed obvious to him, almost obligatory. He did not know that the moments of happiness, infrequent even in youthful years, would be more and more infrequent during his lifetime.) He said to his friend, "What freedom!"

Stefano smiled. "Well, I'm going back to work. So long."

"So long."

On his way to his bicycle, which was against the wall, Ambrogio shouted out, "Wait a minute! You said Igino and Pierello were leaving tomorrow . . ."

"Yes, tomorrow."

"What time?"

18

"I don't know. I didn't ask."

"Listen, I'll go over and see Igino before dinner, no, right after. Why don't you come with me?"

"To town, this evening?"

"Yes, after dinner. Come on, we'll meet at Igino's at eight-thirty."

Stefano thought it over as he scratched his head. (*He does the same things as his father without realizing it*, Ambrogio noticed.) "All right", he finally agreed.

"See you later."

"Fine."

Once at his bicycle, a lightweight blue racer, Ambrogio lifted it with only one hand, turned it in the right direction, and mounted.

3

Ambrogio pedaled slowly toward his house. He was accompanied, from a nearby field, by the intermittent song of a quail. In the pauses of that lonely song, the evening's silence was punctuated by other rustic voices, very faint in general, to which the boy listened: my land, he thought, this is my land. How many times, locked between the oppressive walls of school, had he turned his thoughts to these places, to the place he had been born!

Suddenly he heard coming toward him along the road the sound of foot-steps, the unmistakable tread of clogs. He looked ahead curiously, but at that spot in the road, flanked by high hedges of mulberry and white hawthorn, there was a curve that blocked his view.

Who could that be? he wondered, full of curiosity. *Who can be coming to Nomanella at this hour? Perhaps someone coming to buy fresh milk. If not, who then? We'll know now.*

It was Giustina, the twenty-something-year-old sister of Stefano, the oldest of the four Ferrante children. Ambrogio met her head on in the middle of the curve; he braked and stood up. "Giustina! Hi!"

"Good afternoon", she answered, happy, looking at him and wondering if she should stop or not. She was wearing a black worker's apron. Her hair was chestnut brown, with braids gathered in a bun, held to the nape of her neck with a comb; she had the same big brown eyes as Stefano and their mother. The high clogs made her slender figure even slimmer. (Perhaps even too thin, looking back on it now.)

"How are you, Giustina?"

"Working . . .", she answered in dialect, accentuating her pretty smile.

"I see. Are you just coming back now?"

"We did an extra hour." She looked as if she were about to set off again.

"Are you going already?" Ambrogio asked regretfully. "Are you afraid I'll eat you?"

Giustina blushed to the roots of her hair. "No", she answered. "I know you, and I know you're clean, not just on the outside, but inside, too."

"That's out of Don Mario's books", Ambrogio immediately guessed. "It's a typical phrase of his. But spoken by Giustina I must admit it doesn't sound too bad."

The young woman smiled again, said, "Good evening", and left.

Before entering Nomana, the road, about a kilometer in length, went by Ambrogio's garden, or rather that of his father, the textile industrialist. As the ground level of the garden was several meters higher than that of the road, it was supported by an old wall, which had a sandstone balustrade over its central area; the rest was surrounded by a long myrtle hedge, from which thick branches of trees showed here and there, curving over the road. While cycling parallel to the wall, Ambrogio looked carefully at it, as he usually did. He noticed a few new water leaks, probably at spots where the tree roots were pushing out from within. *If one looks closely, everything breaks down, everything comes to an end*, he thought. *The old walls are like the lives of people, who also grow old and die.* But his life—he answered himself—was only beginning; up to now it had been only preparation. Now his real life was going to begin, next autumn, for example, at the university, where, above all, there would be girls . . . There were so many other things to think about instead of death! Thinking about the end was all right for . . . for the . . . old people, or might it be for the others, but not for him. The prospect of death made him smile, so far off it seemed to him. He did not dwell on these thoughts, since he was not given to daydreaming.

He looked up to see if one of his family was at the balustrade; there was no one. "Naturally. It isn't the time of day to come and enjoy the view of the mountains."

His brothers and sisters (six of them, all younger than he) were at home at that moment with his mother. Those who had returned from school were probably telling stories of their student life, and the two little ones listening, no doubt, most attentively. Only Manno, his orphan cousin who had always lived with the family, would be missing from dinner; he was two years older than Ambrogio and an architectural student. Manno was in Pesaro now, in the artillery officers' school: if war broke out, Manno would suddenly find himself up to his neck in it.

After skirting the garden, the cart road joined the main road, which from the north went to Nomana. At the juncture the garden wall formed a blunt angle in which a niche had been cut with a fresco of Our Lady of the Rosary holding the infant child in her arms, against a background of mountains (they clearly resembled the two Grigne and the Resegone); crowning the fresco was a legend in the form of an arc: *Regina sacratissimi rosarii, ora pro nobis.* Ambrogio bowed slightly, by way of a salute, and turned left to the main road, which at this height, at the entrance of the town, became cobbled. He pressed hard on the pedals, coasted along the west side of the garden, then along one doorless wall of his house, and at last, after another enclosure, came to a larger space enclosed by a small half-moon entranceway grating, the entrance to the garden.

From here the entire house could be seen, peaceful, ochre colored, with three floors, and at least a hundred years old. It looked a comfortable house, almost manorial, despite the fact that fifty years before it had been a textile factory, and then half factory and half living quarters. Only some twenty years before (when his father married) had it been transformed completely into their home. When Ambrogio was a child he had still seen the last manual looms in the granary. Only one still functioned, and it continued functioning until the worker who handled it retired, a pensioner with handlebar mustaches, playful with children, and extraordinarily simple (Ambrogio imagined that everyone must have been that way once), who assured them he still remembered when the women in Nomana wore fan-shaped silver ornaments in their hair.

"And the men? What did the men wear on their heads?" the children would ask him, though they already knew the answer.

"The men? Perhaps a louse or two", he would answer. And one did not really know if he was telling the truth or was saying it to make them laugh.

4

After dinner, Ambrogio left again to go to Igino's house. He was beginning to feel a certain weariness. The day had been fairly intense, especially on the emotional level.

Igino lived less than a hundred meters away, on the same uneven cobbled road, Alessandro Manzoni Street. Stefano was already waiting in front of his door. *Just look*, Ambrogio told himself, *Moonface is already here, with all the work he had to do when I left . . . He must have eaten in five minutes.* A few steps from him, he said, "You've been here a while, eh? This is what happens to people who have nothing to do."

The other grimaced, a look of wry forbearance on his face, and informed Ambrogio that Igino was not at home.

"Ah!" Ambrogio exclaimed, taken aback.

"I sent his brother to let him know. But, if you agree, we could go to wait for him in the square."

"Yes, of course."

They went off together.

"Besides, if we go to the square," Stefano added, "we'll meet some of the others going off tomorrow. Are you interested?"

"Of course!" Ambrogio said.

They were not the only ones in the street, which, after some curves, led to the main square, to where the church and town hall stood. There was an unusual amount of activity for these hours.

"What are all these people doing in the street?" Ambrogio asked Stefano.

"It's the hour of benediction", the latter answered. "Didn't you hear the bells?"

"Oh, yes!" Ambrogio said. "We're in the month of May, that's true."

Stefano added, "Today's the last day."

Going into the square—wide, and on the two sides, to the north and the west, like a belvedere facing the amphitheater of the mountains—an unexpected and formidable clanging of bells dinned over them. They stopped and looked up to the top of the bell tower, where the bells were moving frenetically, almost turning over on themselves.

"The sacristan is in good form tonight!" Ambrogio shouted to be heard.

"What?" Stefano screamed back. Ambrogio shrugged his shoulders.

"It's already the third!" Stefano shouted again.

"Yes, the third ringing", Ambrogio repeated.

The ceremony would begin in five minutes. They had time to get to the church calmly; however, the people in the streets and square, after that explosion of sounds, accelerated their pace. The swallows, as on every afternoon, flying low over the broad cobblestoned square, immediately began crossing it like arrows, carrying out every kind of pirouette.

Almost everyone going by, mainly workers, would greet the two young men, generally with a nod.

"We all know each other here", Ambrogio suddenly observed, no longer having to scream, because the din of the bells had unexpectedly ceased. Only a kind of buzz hung in the air, like the muted growl of dogs after they have unleashed their fury.

"Always the same faces", Stefano said, moving his head disapprovingly.

"Well, for me . . ." Ambrogio did not finish the phrase. He would have liked to say that for him, especially when he was returning after a long absence, like today, these same faces were very welcome, and he realized it every time he returned. He was afraid of sounding sentimental.

He took a pack of cigarettes from his pocket and offered one to his friend. Meanwhile, people kept crossing the square. The familiar figure of Sister Candida was among them, their teacher when they went to lower school: a little humped now, accompanied by a young novice. Behind, like chicks following the brood hen, a handful of little girls trailed.

Romualdo, the town's official drunk—as he had been aptly defined once by Stefano's grandmother—was coming along from another part of the square. He was the town drunk for two quite different reasons: because he was the biggest drinker of the district and because, in a professional sense, he had a connection with the town. He watched over the small parking area for bicycles next to the town hall. Romualdo, at this moment, was walking straight, not zigzagging—a sign he was not drunk, or at least not very—and with a sad face—a sign he was going through one of his repentance phases.

Tea and Isa, cousins, both students, a little younger than the two boys, arrived hurriedly. Tea, plain looking and quick to laughter, was becoming a teacher. Isa was doing accounting in Monza: she was every inch a woman, with chestnut hair, very pretty, perhaps a trifle too massive for her age (destined to fade early, poor girl, Ambrogio predicted every time he saw her). The two girls overwhelmed the boys with exclamations and words of surprised joy, intermingled with news about the closing of their respective schools, which had also been early, and critical remarks about the two boys being there in the square like two idlers instead of in the church.

The two boys, especially Ambrogio, would have liked to answer them but had to put up with the deluge in silence, while Stefano shook his head disapprovingly. Until they suddenly took off at a run, pulling each other and saying, "Let's go, let's go, we'll be late, too." "Come along."

"What chatter!" Ambrogio commented. Stefano only showed his disapproval with one last shake of his head.

There was a group of three workers there from the Riva factory: Costante, straw blond, corpulent, with a red face; Tarcisio, tall and straight, his eyes and curly hair black (Ambrogio remembered that during the Great War, he had been brave); and Ignazio, small and a little hunchbacked, his suit always threadbare and his head that, at every step, seemed to be nodding yes. The three of them showed they had realized that Ambrogio had returned home before the usual date, but they did not stop. They exchanged greetings and continued on quickly. They went to church as if they were arriving late for work.

From Manzoni Street came Marietta "of the shuttles", also a worker from Ambrogio's father's factory: about fifty, very tiny, with twisted legs, she was the most uncouth worker in the entire factory. Her hair was thin and curly, repulsive, and she had an incredibly large and yellow face, in which lamblike eyes had somehow lodged. Her supreme aspiration was to go unnoticed: Ambrogio knew that and greeted her with the slightest nod of his head, almost without looking at her. He knew that if he had addressed a word to her, she would have answered incoherently, unintelligibly, hurriedly, and if he had insisted, she would have taken fright.

With her hand in that of Marietta "of the shuttles" came Giudittina, Ambrogio's little sister—a child of five with blue eyes and blond hair gathered into two ponytails behind her ears—and she delightedly greeted her brother, shouting, "Hi! Hi! Hi!" while walking with Marietta, who scolded her for shouting with mysterious whisperings and stammered phrases. When the two young men were behind them, Marietta, calm now, seemed to pull herself together: with little children she was in her element.

Then the elderly Mrs. Eleonora appeared, so dignified (where are you, bygone time, where are you? With words only shadows can be evoked), dressed in sequined black, in the style worn at the beginning of the century, and wearing a hat with ostrich feathers and carrying a cane for promenades. How old was the ancient lady, without a single living relative in the world, who went out of her house only to go to church? Since as long as Ambrogio and Stefano could remember (from their births), they had always seen her like this, exactly as she appeared at the present moment.

Miss Quadri Dodini, a schoolteacher at a nuns' school in Monza, also crossed the square. Middle aged, crippled, her hair cut like a man's, she also needed a cane and wore thick glasses. *She*, Ambrogio thought, *would have arrived on the last train, after having eaten any old thing for dinner.* A few young boys, thirteen or fourteen, caught up with her, walking in long strides and passed her (cruel, without realizing it) and hurriedly entered the church before her.

"Do you realize? We've seen two people with canes."

"Not two, three."

"Who's the third?"

It was Galbiati, employed at the Savings Bank and mutilated in the battle of Piave: with one leg missing, he also walked leaning on a cane. A son of Galbiati, Giordano, who was finishing law studies, was going to the Alpine officer's school: if war broke out—Ambrogio thought—Giordano, too, would suddenly find himself involved up to his neck.

A few more latecomers went by, and the last was Carlaccio. He was of an undefinable age. At one time he was the strongest person in the village: no one was able to get the better of him in his work, which was building carts. Unfortunately, he wanted to take out an enormous stone from an excavation: "Either you or me", he said, raising it for the admiration of the bystanders, and he collapsed, or rather his spine did. Since then his large back was as if pushed inward, and his arms hung slack. Carlaccio greeted the two friends with his perennial melancholic smile, which seemed to say, "You see how unfair fate has been with me?" The two boys responded sympathetically.

When he had gone by, the square was left empty. Only the swallows went on flying across.

5

Suddenly, from a street that gave onto the square a few meters from via Manzoni, came Igino's voice, alternating with that of another recruit, nicknamed Castagna. Ambrogio and Stefano went over to meet them. Igino and Castagna were coming along talking loudly, as Italians often do when they are in public, aroused as if instinctively to show off. This evening these two were aroused even more because in a way they really were protagonists. Ahead of them by a few steps was Igino's nine-year-old brother, who turned back toward them every now and then to urge them on, like the old ladies he had seen dragging their drunken husbands out of the tavern.

Before they even reached them, Ambrogio greeted them jokingly: "But what a racket, such a noise!" Castagna stopped and lifted his large head, opened his arms, and recited the verse of a recruits' song: "It's the Twenty-First on the march." Afterward, as if he had said something quite funny, he began to laugh uncontrollably. He worked on his own as a craftsman, a blond, with a pink face and puffed-out cheeks. Igino, a worker, had a sharp face and dark hair, combed straight back without a part: he smiled in a way that always seemed forced, even when, as at this moment, it was not.

"Hi", Ambrogio said when they were close enough to talk and held out his hand to them. "Where were you? In Pasqualetta's tavern?"

"Yes", they both answered.

Igino's brother explained, "I found them there. They were with the other conscripts."

"With the other conscripts?" Ambrogio said, surprised. "Then . . ."

"But not all!" Igino said. "We met four there, rather, five, by chance, but it wasn't something planned. Well, come along, too. Why don't you?"

"I've come especially for that," Castagna declared, "to bring you two back to the tavern, dead or alive." And turning toward Stefano, before he could open his mouth, he added, "You won't say no."

"Of course I'll say no!" Stefano exclaimed. "I've nothing to do with this. I'm second semester." He was really thinking that tomorrow he had to get up early for work. Castagna understood very well, so much so that he replied, "Who cares if it's this semester or that? What you really mean is that tomorrow at five you have to milk the cows! Tell the truth!"

"Yes, agreed, that's why", Stefano admitted.

"You're a beast!" Castagna insulted, again shouting, as if he had caught him out in who knows what fault, and he began to laugh at his own joke.

"I see you've been drinking", Stefano only said.

"Well?" Igino asked of Ambrogio. "Are you coming or not to Pasqualetta's?"

Even though he felt like going (it was lovely, at that age, to find themselves together again, with so many hopes and illusions in every one of them!), Ambrogio could not. It would not have been correct to leave Stefano in the lurch after having made him come to the village. "No", he answered. "I'm pretty tired, and I don't feel like making a late night of it. I only wanted to ask you one thing: What time do you have to be at headquarters tomorrow?"

Instead of answering, Igino asked him, "But how come you're back so early this year?"

Ambrogio explained.

"Well, if it's like that, then the war's going to come for sure", the other boy murmured worriedly.

"No way!" Ambrogio said. "Well, I don't want you to waste your time. Just tell me . . ."

"We've more than enough time", Igino assured him. "Come. At least we can sit down for a moment at home."

They made their way slowly.

<h1 style="text-align:center">6</h1>

There was no one at home. His mother was—it hardly needed saying since the villagers were all practicing Catholics—in church.

"It's my father's shift at the Beolco factory", Igino explained, as he turned on the light.

"Ah, so they're on shifts in Beolco?" Ambrogio asked.

"Yes, in the factory they are", Stefano answered for Igino.

"Wouldn't it also be because of the war?" Igino suddenly conjectured. Like his father, Igino also worked in the factory.

"But what war?" Castagna shouted. "They make chains and gears for bicycles in the factory there!"

"And the bicycles for the Bersaglieri? How about them, eh?" Igino observed, half serious. He turned to the other two with his forced smile and indicated with a gesture of his head at Stefano, who in his recruitment had been assigned to the Bersaglieri. "The Bersaglieri, how about them? Come, let's sit down", he concluded.

The others followed suit and seated themselves around the table, which was covered with a synthetic iridescent damask cloth, its colors wavering between red and blue. A little enameled lamp hung over the table, with a round shade and a pulley with weights to regulate its height. Igino went to the sideboard, opened its tiny crystal doors, and took out a yellow metal tray, a bottle of Braulio *amaro* and four small glasses. "You, go play outside", he said to his nine-year-old brother, who followed his activities with keener interest than the others.

Forgetting the judiciousness he had displayed up till then, he began to protest, and so Igino—making disapproving gestures—added a fifth glass to the tray and put it all on the table.

Not to appear stingy, he filled the glasses to the very top. Ambrogio noticed it, and perhaps the others did, too, but for them this kind of behavior was taken for granted: it would have seemed strange if things had happened otherwise, according to some other ritual. Besides, everything else there was also anticipated: the furniture, vaguely modern, but also somewhat shabby, bare; the two oleographs on the walls, one of the Holy Family and the other of a deer at a fountain; the wood stove—in the absence of the traditional fireplace— served for cooking as well as for heating: in short, it was a typical worker's home. Perhaps a little less usual was the presence, over the sideboard, of a tiny statue of a half-nude woman, who supported a fruit bowl on her upturned arms.

Having finished serving the *amaro* (the child with a half dose), Igino raised his glass.

"Cheers!" he toasted.

"Cheers!" the others echoed.

"Here's hoping the threat of war will go away!" Ambrogio wished with singular originality. However, it was what the others expected of him. They were thoughtful.

"And if it doesn't . . . if it doesn't . . . if it really does break out?" Stefano suddenly blurted out.

"Then who knows what there will be. No one knows how it will end", Ambrogio said. In those days, more than once he had heard that twenty-five years before, the Great War had been declared with the certainty that it would end immediately, and instead . . .

The only lively one was the child. He declared, "To tell the truth, if the war comes I'll be happy." His eyes shone.

"Go and play", Igino repeated.

Puckering up his face a little, the boy finished his half portion of *amaro* and went out to the street, inwardly surprised by the cowardliness of the adults.

But Igino did not agree with Ambrogio. "It's not like last year now, when we didn't know who was going to win. Now," he observed, "the English and French are only making a show of hitting back, and besides, they're running away on all sides. If we go in, victory is assured."

"I wonder . . .", Ambrogio said, shaking his head. "You can't be sure about these things ever", he answered, defining his own feelings more concretely.

"Eh", Stefano agreed sincerely, remembering his father's remarks.

"No", Igino insisted, with an unexpected touch of bitterness. "This time England and France have to surrender. They're about to pay their dues, my friends. They can't go on having everything their way and depriving us of the minimum of . . . of . . ."

Ambrogio looked at him, surprised.

Castagna noticed it and jokingly said, "Does he or doesn't he talk like Alfeo at the army training meetings?" He began to laugh, happy too to have thought of this comeback, which he celebrated by moving his big head.

(Alfeo, a noncommissioned officer, was one of the few people in the village who believed in fascism. To be more precise, he halfway believed in it, because he subscribed to the prevailing Nomana opinion, as well as that of Brianza, that fascism was foreign: a phenomenon with motivations, developments, and results better suited to some other place, not their region.)

Without paying attention to Castagna, Igino concentrated on the other two, especially Ambrogio, almost defying him to refute him.

27

"But Igino ... do you mean to say you're on the side of the Germans?" Ambrogio asked, almost scandalized. "The Nazis?"

"That's not what matters", Igino said. "What matters is ... well, what I've already told you!"

"So why don't they make him secretary of the local party?" Castagna went on jokingly.

"But tell me, what is it that attracts you?" Ambrogio wanted to know. "Tell me the truth: Is it the spirit of adventure? Is it that you want to prove yourself? I'm asking because I feel the same way, too, sometimes."

Igino looked at him, surprised. "No! Adventure? What in the devil do you mean by that?"

"Adventure ... The pleasure of taking a risk, in short."

"No, Ambrogio. Of course not. It's simply what I've been saying: the rich nations this time will have to give in, to cough up a little. The time has come."

"But to become allies of the Nazis ..."

"Whoever, with the devil himself if there's no other choice."

"Good heavens!" Ambrogio exclaimed, looking at the other two.

"Well, listen, it's useless to argue", Stefano said very sensibly. "No matter what we do, we can't decide anything."

Igino agreed with this. He suggested, "Another touch of *amaro*?"

Castagna raised his glass. "I'm thirsty", he said.

"Then wine is better", the host said, getting up.

"No, wait", Ambrogio objected. "It's better you go back to Pasqualetta's. The others will be waiting. We've seen each other and talked. It's fine for one evening ..."

"Yes, but we can have a glass of wine", Igino said. He went to the small sideboard and took out an opened bottle of wine and four glasses. He shut the glass door of the sideboard with his elbow. On the other side of the door was an old photograph of their school class. Nothing less than the second grade in elementary school! While returning to the table, he pointed it out to his friends with his head: "If instead of calling up only one semester they had called the whole class, we could have been arranging a farewell party for the women conscripts."

The others agreed, smiling. Ambrogio stood up and went over to the photograph, which he remembered well. He brought his eyes closer to look at it. "Look, Paolina with her curls ... Olga, Teresa Conti. And Stellina, look ... poor Stella."

"She remained a dwarf", Igino murmured.

"We didn't realize then", Ambrogio said. "She just seemed a little smaller than the rest of us. She didn't even realize."

"That's right", Stefano said. "Then she didn't grow any more. She stayed like she was then, more or less."

In the face of that, Castagna also shook his heavy head.

"She too was at the receiving end of the punches we dealt out to the girls at recess, do you remember? Just to show we were stronger", Ambrogio said. "What animals we were."

"Well," Igino replied, while he served, "they were the punches of eight-year-olds . . ."

"But for them, for the girls, we hurt them," Ambrogio insisted, "so much they sometimes cried, don't you remember?"

"Especially Iole, it's true", Igino agreed on that. "How she rebelled!"

"Where is she? I don't see her." In the dim light from the little lamp, Ambrogio looked for her in the photograph until he recognized her. "Ah, look at her, here she is."

She was a little girl with a black smock and her arms crossed like the others, but blonder, the only real golden blond, with singularly bright features, very intelligent.

"What an end she came to, poor girl", Stefano murmured.

"Is she . . . still away?" Ambrogio wanted to know.

"Yes, of course", Stefano said. "Who knows if she will ever leave the insane asylum."

"The same way her older sister ended up", Igino observed.

Ambrogio went back to the table. Igino put a full glass in front of him.

"Even without a war, there are more than enough troubles in life", Ambrogio said, taking the glass.

"To hear my father, war is still worse, no comparison", Stefano said. "It's something one can't even imagine. And if he says so," he added, "it really is."

The four friends looked at each other. Down deep they had no experience in these things. After a moment, Igino said, "Well, if we two are to go back to Pasqualetta's, we'd better decide."

They quickly emptied their glasses, stood up, and went to the door.

"If it's all right with both of you, tomorrow I'll take you to district head-quarters with the car", Ambrogio said at the last moment. "As there's room for another person, you could let Pierello know. Is he at Pasqualetta's?"

"No", Igino answered.

"It doesn't matter. I'll let him know", said Castagna, who, like Pierello, lived in Lodosa.

"OK. What time should we meet here?" Ambrogio asked.

"Do you really want to come with us?" Igino asked while opening the door.

7

The next day, in early afternoon, after getting permission from his father, Ambrogio arrived at Igino's house in the automobile. He had planned to go by the

Lodosa houses with his friend to pick up Castagna and Pierello, but it was not necessary, as they were both waiting there too.

Castagna was carrying a package tied with a string under his arm, and his rosy face bore the traces of worry. Pierello—who had left his own package on a chair for the moment—was a solid-looking boy and at the same time timid, with a round head and light brown hair and eyes. He greeted Ambrogio with his captivating smile. "If you want to take me, here I am too." He said this as if he had not been invited, and, in response to the cordial handshake, he opened his arms and raised his eyes to the sky, exactly as Ambrogio expected. Pierello had this unique habit of opening his arms for any reason, at times even without a reason, and raising his eyes to the sky, like someone yielding to his destiny.

Igino was ready also: his small cloth suitcase sitting on the floor beside the door. Too impatient to wait, he turned to his mother to say goodbye. But she protested, "But what's the hurry, Igino? Is someone chasing you? Wait a minute."

She went to the sideboard and took a little glass for Ambrogio and put it on a metal tray, which was on the table, next to the bottle of *amaro* and some glasses that had just been used.

"A little *amaro*, Ambrogio? Should I pour you some?"

"Mother, please don't make us waste time", Igino protested.

"Yes, thanks", Ambrogio answered. "What's the hurry, Igino? You're not getting married, are you?"

His mother poured the liquor, carefully filling the glass to the brim. Then she moved aside and timidly smiled at her son.

Igino had had enough. Puffing with impatience, he poured what remained of the *amaro*—two half portions—into Castagna's and Pierello's glasses, then picked up his case and went up to his mother: "Tell Father goodbye. And don't drive yourself crazy for no reason. There's still no war on. You understand? There is none, and maybe there never will be. Now goodbye."

As his mother had not resigned herself to giving him her hand, he squeezed her wrist, turned, and left the house.

The woman covered her face with her hands and began to cry silently. The others swallowed the *amaro* and took their leave, embarrassed, except for Castagna, who, in his laudable attempt to resolve the situation in a lighthearted manner, sang a verse that came into his head:

> These stones will cry, will cry
> and so will the girls on this street
> because the Twenty-First is saying goodbye . . .

It was obvious how inopportune the words were. Even Castagna realized that, and to rectify the matter, in some fashion, while leaving the house, he made a kind of pirouette, mostly making a clown of himself.

Ambrogio shook his head indulgently; Pierello, looking at the woman, brought his index finger to his head to indicate the other fellow was a bit mad, and then, with his eyes turned upward, he opened his arms as usual.

In the automobile the three recruits held their small parcels on their laps. Igino's mother followed them as far as the street and looked at them while covering her mouth. Ambrogio immediately turned on the motor and, out of emotion and lack of practice—he had only had a license for a year—took off joltingly.

They crossed through the middle of town. Thirty-five hundred inhabitants: it was not a big town. For the most part the houses were two or three floors high, fairly diverse, and had been built during various periods around and within a more ancient and uniform nucleus. This nucleus—which in some way even now characterized the whole complex—was composed of some old courtyards with porticos formed from the remains of brick columns and wooden galleries. Occupied then by workers, no longer by peasants as in the beginning, and adapted in diverse ways, they had a look of something halfway between the country and the outskirts of town, a rustic and urban mélange.

The departing young men stared at the walls, on which writing had been painted with fresh whitewash during the night saying, "Long live the Twenty-First, the iron race" or "The Twenty-First have left / so all the girls / to the convent have gone" and other similar jingles. They knew the words already and only pointed them out with a half smile.

As they went by the largest courtyard of the town, the only one that still looked rustic, Ambrogio glanced at its interior through the entrance: a flat arch bearing the date A.D. 1777. He glimpsed carts full of grass on one side, left in different positions; on the opposite side were women seated on chairs sewing and chatting; between the women and the carts a group of children were running and, almost at the same level but with greater speed, were flying a flock of swallows.

"In Sansone's courtyard," he said, pointing with his head and breaking the silence, "I don't know if you realize it, there are always swallows."

"In winter too?" Castagna asked, again being funny.

The others, who—like himself—felt an enormous weight on their hearts at having to leave their town for the first time, smiled politely.

"I meant", Ambrogio continued, turning and smiling toward Castagna, "that while in so many other places swallows don't make their nests, even if one would want them to, here, in this courtyard, a lot do."

"Well, it's because of the mosquitoes", Igino, though not much interested, looked for an explanation. "With all this manure . . ."

"In my house they sometimes make them under the eaves of the woodshed," Ambrogio continued, "but not every year, even rather seldom."

"I'm not surprised", Igino said. "Your brother ties ribbons on their feet, so . . ."

"What? Ribbons on swallows' feet?" Pierello asked with curiosity. Ambrogio nodded.

"Yes, Pino does. Once he took them, parents and babies, from their nests and marked them to find out if they would return the following year: he tied an inch or so of red ribbon on every swallow."

"And did they return or not?" Castagna asked, also interested.

"What do you mean return? In the last two years not even one has been seen in the woodshed, not those or any others."

They all smiled approvingly. By driving along Santa Caterina Street they left the town toward the south, went by *I dragoni*, the ancient villa of Signora Eleonora, the one whom, dressed always in sequined black, Ambrogio and Stefano had seen in the square the previous night. On the nineteenth-century façade, between two land lots, were eight fine-grained stone medallions, with names and profiles of illustrious Milanesi from the last century. The large door was, as usual, closed.

Ambrogio seized on that point in order to keep the talk going: "I've never seen that door open", he nodded toward it. "Never. Have you?"

"Neither have I", Igino responded. "From what I hear it's opened only once a year, for the carts with wood for the stove."

"It's true. But it wasn't that way before", Pierello said. "When I was a child my grandmother told me in the old days carriages came and went through that door because there were endless parties in *I dragoni* then. Poor woman! She told us this as if they were fairy tales."

"In those days," Igino snarled critically, "people led lives that were even more wretched than they are now. If the peasants didn't obey their masters, they could easily be beaten by them."

These words destroyed the glimmer of enchantment created by Pierello's words. Ambrogio observed Igino out of the corner of his eye as he sat next to him. As usual his face was tense, his hair slicked back stiff. *That bad humor comes from his going under the military boot*, Ambrogio thought. *But this knack of saying disagreeable things—he's always had it, since he was a boy. Whatever, it's there to stay; take it or leave it.* Ambrogio did not want to leave it. Among his old classmates Igino was the one who lived the closest to his house and perhaps the one he had played with most.

"However, these people", he went on, "were not landowners. Signora Eleonora was a singer when she was young", he said, turning toward the others. "Did you know that?"

Only Pierello did.

Ambrogio continued, "When she was once married, her husband, a Milanese like herself, didn't want her to go on singing. Because of all the admirers, you know."

"Yes," Pierello went on, "my grandmother told me that too. They must have been very much in love, if she agreed to that."

"But they must have sacrificed earning a lot of money", Igino pointed out, rubbing the thumb and index finger of his right hand together. "And why? Out of jealousy!" Once again he shook his head disapprovingly.

"Then", Ambrogio continued, "her husband died, and later her son, in the war. Her only son, poor woman."

"He was an officer, wasn't he?" Pierello asked.

"Yes," Ambrogio assented, "a cavalry lieutenant, I think. He was barely twenty when he died." He paused, not out of emotion for having remembered that death ... They would be twenty soon, but the episode was so far off ... Ambrogio was considering a question of an entirely different kind: "There's something I don't understand," he said, "and that is where does she find those incredibly strange dresses she wears? No dressmaker or any shop makes or sells dresses like those, so where does she get them?"

Meanwhile, the aristocratic villa with its military name, *I dragoni*, was being left behind. Santa Caterina Street, after a U turn, went down toward the valley. If they had looked to the left, the four young men would have been able to see the ancient garden, as if suspended, among the fields. Who knows if the old lady, whose life had been smashed twice, did not sometimes walk in that solitary garden? None of the four even contemplated the question. The four of them were very young. For them, Signora Eleonora and her story of grief constituted a part of the landscape, as if it had always existed, like the ancient houses themselves or even the mountains that shut out the horizon from the other side of Nomana.

8

The street continued downward, no longer cobbled as in the town, but tarred and smooth, so much so that merely seeing it one wanted to race along it. Ambrogio speeded up and pressed down on the accelerator even more when he came to the main highway, which went, with its ups and downs, through a landscape of well-cultivated green hills, rich in trees, especially mulberry.

Now the Millecento was going at full speed. *A pity*, Ambrogio thought confusedly, *that the goal was military headquarters. How much better would it have been just to go out, without any special place in mind, as I did last summer to learn how to drive.* Despite his desire to enter into his friends' state of mind, he could not do it. However, he inwardly argued, but without any real conviction, *the war, after all is said and done, perhaps will never take place, at least, we should hope, not during this vacation time.* Because today—it was not to be forgotten—was his first day of vacation, a vacation different from any others, at the end of which he was no longer anticipating school but university instead, a totally new experience. Other similar thoughts revolved confusedly, but he was alert to the wheel, and, when necessary, to the brakes.

Obviously, the state of mind of his three friends was quite different; theirs was dominated by a feeling of suspense or disquiet, well concealed in Igino's case, less so in Castagna's, and even less in the meek face of Pierello, who, for something to do, moved his packet of clothes, tied with a string, that he held on his lap, every so often. Oh, the military life, here we come! The three of them had heard talk about military life in disagreeable terms from the time they were children, except for some incomprehensible joke or other in which the recruits themselves were the butt. If it had to do with the war, the military life was recalled, by the old people, as something tragic. The good thing was that now there was no war, at least not yet, and that was really lucky. The fact remained, however, that within a very short time, each one of them—lowly recruits—would be at the mercy of whoever outranked them. Besides, for the first time in their lives they would be outside of their own familiar surroundings in an unknown world.

The highway, leaving Raperio from Nomana, on the right, went down a wide gorge, thickly planted with trees, along the river Lambro, and over a reinforced cement bridge with only two strong arches, and then climbed a little to get onto the plain, which extended—as the four of them well knew—for many, many miles, far beyond Monza and Milan, to the Apennines, visible from Nomana only on the clearest days, such was their distance.

One after the other, the towns of the Brianza plains—starting with Incastigo, located right after the bridge—were left behind, with their houses, new and old; their green gardens; and many factories, small and medium sized, bordered by fields, which rose in waves of grass, as if wanting to stem and cover up the injuries inflicted on the lovely landscape.

A little before Monza, at the wall of the royal park, where the automobile races took place, the highway widened and became a shaded road, flanked by two rows of enormous plane trees. The automobile continued for a couple of kilometers parallel to the park wall and then passed the great villa of Austrian viceroys. Immediately after came the city streets, with small, open buses, different from those of Milan. A little later they came again to the Lambro River, which ran clear under the large Incastigo bridge, with long emerald-green aquatic grasses bent in the direction of the current; here, however, the waters were dirty, almost leaden. They continued along the river course to the headquarters, situated on the other riverbank and joined to the street by an iron footbridge. Ambrogio stopped there and turned off the motor. The four stepped out.

On both sidewalks were boys of their age, in groups. Some of them crossed over the footbridge, and others could be seen there gathered in groups in the courtyard of the barracks. Each of them was carrying a small suitcase or package under his arm.

"What a racket!" Igino complained, already in a bad mood. Then he turned to Ambrogio, "Well, thanks and goodbye", displaying the same rush as he did in Nomana on saying goodbye to his mother.

"Wait a minute", Ambrogio said, driven by that very hurry to slow things down. "There's a bar in this street. I saw it. Since I'm not going away, it's my turn to invite you for a drink, no?"

"Forget about it", Igino said, smiling in irritation.

"Yes, it's better; forget it", Pierello agreed, also preferring not to drag things out.

Castagna would have liked to accept the offer but, confronted by the others' refusal, he did not want to give the impression that he needed a drink, so he did not protest.

"No, it's only a moment", Ambrogio insisted, despite everything. But he was interrupted by a voice, loud and grating, which suddenly called out from the footbridge. It was a corporal and, at his side, a soldier, who were crossing over to the street. The corporal began to bellow, "Come on here, you loafers! What are you doing there with your balls in your hand? Do you think we're here to waste our time? Do you think the train's going to wait for you?"

"The stinking shirker", Igino, who a little before had been complaining of the recruits' disorder, retorted in a low voice. "You guys, yes, shirkers in the barracks, have plenty of time to waste. Naturally, you've got nothing to do."

Even Ambrogio looked angrily at the wise guy. *If I become an officer*, he thought, *if anybody had the nerve to talk dirty like that, I'd get rid of him with pleasure, strip him to the bone.* Then he turned to his friends, smiling, and said, "Well, it looks like your military training's begun."

Igino shook his hand and, together with the others, went to the footbridge. Castagna laughed because a funny idea passed through his big head; before going across the footbridge he turned toward the street and shouted, "Step right up, ladies and gentlemen, the more the merrier, and the more people who enter, the more animals to see!"

The recruits around him smiled condescendingly at this joke, which was as old as the hills. The corporal looked at him with a frown, but then he smiled too, with a roguish air: a sign he could easily be satisfied, as his loose chatter had also seemed to presage. Pierello then put his two hands on Castagna's shoulders and pushed him forward on the footbridge, while the other clowned around. Turning his head to Ambrogio, Piero threw a farewell glance in his direction and lifted his eyes to the sky for an instant as a comment on his friend's silliness.

The two military men gathered all the recruits together and had them go through to the courtyard of the barracks. For one moment they wanted to drag Ambrogio along with the others, but he remained alone in the street.

9

He lit a cigarette.

What should he do? Stay there until his three friends came out, on the way to the train? He would know their destination and if they had been assigned to the same regiment or not. But perhaps he'd have to wait several hours.

The Lambro River ran leaden to the other side of the parapet of the road. *How dirty it is*, Ambrogio thought, and threw down the match he was holding between his fingers. He saw it float lightly on the surface and then suddenly reel, as it was carried on the current. *I too am doing my part to dirty the water*, he told himself. *Poor fish!* Because, even if the water was dirty, there were fish: a little farther on, in the valley, where the river turned after an artificial curve under the Nomana railway bridge, amateur fishermen (generally pensioners) could be seen, bent over their fishing poles, killing time, the little they had left. Almost every time Ambrogio went by in the train he had occasion to observe them.

He sighed, bored. What could he do?

From the barracks came voices giving orders. Then suddenly there were footsteps accompanied by a muffled metallic noise: some thirty recruits, marching in quite a well-formed row, entered onto the footbridge toward the street. Each one was carrying a blanket over his shoulders and a canteen in his hands; that was what caused the slight metallic clanging. Only one uniformed soldier followed the group.

Ambrogio waited till the head of the group reached the street and then addressed one of the first recruits, a redhead with what looked like a worker's face. "Say, where are you going?" he asked in dialect.

"Mantua, infantry", he answered without changing pace.

"Are you one of those who went into the barracks a little while ago?" he asked the young fellow. "I mean about ten minutes ago."

"No", the redhead answered and made a gesture, as if to say, *Don't I wish!* "We've been ready for two hours at least. Now we're going to the train."

"Goodbye", Ambrogio said.

The other waved back. Ambrogio stopped.

The recruits, all of them of his class and even his same semester, went off toward the train station with their small baggage, and also the uniformed soldier behind them, like a sheep dog after its flock. They were going along the sidewalk parallel to the river Lambro. He kept looking at them: in formation, so many together, those fellows finally reminded him of small and large school groups, on the way, for example, to the bus for a tennis match or football game, with their bags slung over their backs, others with them under their arms, and the prefect father, in a soutane, behind them. But these boys—and here was the big difference—were going off not to play football or tennis but to an unknown barracks where they would be met by weapons stacked in storehouses: rifles, machine guns, mortars . . .

Suddenly the young man felt as if something new, solemn, unknown to him, was beginning.

Stirred up, he threw his cigarette in the Lambro, without this time looking where it fell, crossed the street absorbed in thought, got into the Millecento, and started it up.

In a few days Italy entered the war.

It was June 10, 1940. Ever since morning the radio had been announcing—and repeating insistently over the course of the day—that the Duce would talk "to the Italians and to the world" that afternoon at six o'clock. The people were invited to gather in the squares, where loudspeakers had been set up. The Fascists from several organizations would be there; workers, too, as many as possible, should go in formation from their factories to places with loudspeakers.

In early afternoon, the Fascist secretary of Nomana—Signore Cereda, a good-natured fellow, apprehensive by nature, whose only political credential was his combat service—had telephoned Ambrogio's father, Gerardo, the textile industrialist, at his office. "Well, Sergeant Riva, you've heard the news."

"Yes, I've heard it."

"Well, I only wanted to be sure you had. The meeting place here in Nomana will be in front of the town hall." After the first words in Italian, he slipped into dialect. The shuttling of the looms could be heard clearly over the telephone.

"But what's happening, Sergeant Cereda?" Gerardo asked, also in dialect. "It wouldn't be a declaration of war . . . ?"

"I really think so", answered the worried voice of the political secretary.

He knew that Riva was not a Fascist—no one, or almost no one, as it has already been said, was a Fascist in Nomana, not even the secretary himself. As a young technician, Riva had started the first Catholic Action group there, and then the group for the popular party: he was, then, a committed Catholic, and the political secretary was afraid he would become angry and shout at him on the telephone.

But Gerardo did not get angry and only said, "Then God help us!" He said it in a tone of voice that made his words sound less like a commonplace than like a true invocation of God.

"What time were you thinking of closing the factory?" the political secretary asked after a pause.

"What time? I can close at five-thirty, as usual. A half hour is time enough to get to the square, isn't it?"

"Let's make it at five", the secretary said. "Yes, at five. I have to telephone the other factories", he added in closing.

While he hung up the receiver, Gerardo thought of Manno, his nephew, the orphan, who had grown up in his house as another son. He was at officer's school right now. What would happen to him? And his oldest son, Ambrogio, who was already of military age . . . Worried, he addressed one of his employees: "Please tell everybody we're closing at five today, when you go around today, and that everyone, men and women, on leaving here, must go in file in front of the town hall."

"And those who work overtime?" the employee asked, a scrupulous type. "Should I tell them to come back after the meeting?" Gerardo hesitated a moment. Everyone assigned such importance to the work there, in his factory, that the question did not seem out of place at all to him.

"No", he answered. "After the meeting they'll have other things to think about. There won't be any overtime today."

At five the factory siren sounded to signal the end of work, and for many that off-schedule signal seemed to sound different from usual, in a way mysterious, as an augury of misfortune.

Gerardo left his office a few minutes later, together with his few employees. From the warehouse almost three hundred workers were leaving. As it was a textile business, they were mostly women. Once outside the gate, they all walked toward the piazza, Gerardo mingling with the others and, at his side, his son Ambrogio. The predominant feeling was one of anxiety.

"There'll be a declaration of war for sure this time round", someone said.

"We've managed to stay out—up till now, and then, one thing on top of the other, and we land right in the middle of it."

Not one person seemed to approve of the irrevocable step that was about to be carried out; among the middle-aged men—a couple of them had been mutilated in the previous war—there was a kind of unease at the idea that they had to side with the Germans. How was it possible after so many of ours had died fighting them? Many of the women there had someone in their families who had fallen, and the memory was still painful. But to blame it on fascism—even if it did not exist in Nomana, at least not at any serious level—no one even gave it a thought.

Except Gerardo. *It's insane, the responsibility these Fascists are taking upon themselves: they are bringing Italy into war against everyone's will,* he was thinking while walking along. *Who can ignore the fact that no one in Nomana, in all of Italy, rich or poor, wants this war? Besides, on the side of the Nazis . . . !* He thought of the minister of foreign affairs, Ciano, in his efforts—unconditionally approved of by everybody—to keep the country out of conflict. *Among the Fascists themselves there are those who don't want war! Yet . . .* Racing through his mind, while he walked, were the thoughts of the far-off years of his political militancy in the popular party, his painful disillusionment during those days. *This is what comes of those endless fights, those filthy struggles between political parties, which in 1922 brought the nation to a standstill, in such need of order, that it only had to drop like a rotten apple into the hands of the Fascists.* Neither he nor the other militants had been able to do anything against that irresponsible squabbling at the top.

The workers were filling the street: the men modestly dressed, the women, almost all of them wearing black aprons, imperceptibly stained with hemp powder. He knew these people, one by one, their good points and their defects, and he even knew many of their secret worries, because they came in person to tell him, sometimes looking for advice, other times for economic help. What would happen to them tomorrow?

He did not order his workers to go lined up in a column, as the radio requested—what Fascist foolishness!—but simply went with them, and they appreciated it. He could see it in their looks, their gestures. *Thank God, not even the foolishness of the others, the reds—who were really the first cause of all the disorder and the consequent rise of fascism—not even their foolishness has any effect on these people.* He made it more specific: *On us. Because, how am I different from these people?* He could hardly feel different just because now he was an industrialist. Before he had been a worker, and then, for a time, a technician, and, as for studies, he had only done the primary grades, the same background as the rest. And his popular outlook—like that of almost all the other industrialists of the area—was Christian, like the rest of the population. The fact that the industrialists came from the people had allowed the Christian culture of the people to rise to the surface and assert itself in every aspect of life during the previous decades. When the landowners had been in power, it was their liberal and Masonic views that had prevailed, and the popular culture, which went back to San Carlo Borromeo, could express itself only at a subordinate level. But since the landowners had been overcome and even replaced by the industrialists of working-class origin, the culture of Brianza had become uniformly *white*. Even if Gerardo, and not only he, was not fully conscious of it.

Next to him, his son Ambrogio was turning over quite different thoughts: he was thinking about those who were in the forces at that moment, especially his cousin Manno, who was a brother to him, and his two friends Pierello and Igino. Where would they end up? Would they be flung into that furnace that would no doubt be produced on the French front? It was taken for granted that from tomorrow on, even from this evening, a terrible combat would break out on the French front, like the Austrian front in the previous war.

While the young man was thinking about this, his eyes met those of a worker, the mechanic Luca, two years older than himself and so the age of Manno, both friends from the time they had attended grade school. Ambrogio instinctively made a gesture of greeting, and worry at the same time.

The mechanic, who was walking a few steps ahead, stopped and waited for Ambrogio. Luca was a handsome fellow, wide shouldered, with a thick head of hair that fell onto his forehead. "And Manno?" he asked as soon as they met. "What the devil will happen to him now?"

"I was wondering myself", Ambrogio answered.

"I'm afraid he'll land himself in that mess immediately."

"Right now he's in the officer's course. He was to finish in August. Do you think they'll send him to the front?"

"I don't know about these things", Luca said. "He's in Pesaro, isn't he?"

"Yes. And your brothers?" Ambrogio asked.

"They're also . . . who knows?" And the mechanic opened his arms in a gesture of impotence.

"Where are they?"

"Both of them are near Bolzano."

"Alpine troops, aren't they?"

Luca nodded, then went on, "Angiolino is in the artillery in a mountain unit."

Gerardo, who was listening to them in silence, glanced at Luca sympathetically. He knew Luca was a friend of Manno. Gerardo remembered his satisfaction, some time ago, when his children—Manno, too—continued being friends, when they were already in college, with their old school pals, now workers. "This will help you keep your feet on the ground", he would tell them.

At the windows of the houses were any number of women and children looking out at everybody passing. At the door of the pharmacy was the pharmacist, Doctor Agazzino, with a white coat on. He nodded to Gerardo. The industrialist responded by courteously touching the brim of his hat. He remembered that the pharmacist, too—a native of Piacenza—had been an active popular party militant in his hometown. *For whatever good that was*, he thought.

It was not far to the piazza when Ermanno Ghezzi, the shopkeeper, who was on Gerardo's other side, decided to recount a war episode to him. "My father was a muleteer sergeant in the Great War", he began. "You know what kind of man my father was: there was no joking with him. Once, one of them bringing the mules, in order not to cross a spot battered by machine-gun fire . . .", and he started on an involved tale. Under the circumstances, they—Ambrogio included—would have preferred not being distracted from their thoughts, but they ended up listening.

II

There were already some people waiting in the piazza. Everyone was looking at the electrician, who was also the town plumber. He was busy preparing the loudspeakers, which were being set up haphazardly in the town hall.

The flood of workers—their numbers reduced noticeably because a number of mothers had gone home on the way—stopped behind the people waiting. From time to time the political secretary, Cereda, looked out from a window of the town hall. On one of these occasions he called, waving his hand, to one of the three or four men in black shirts, who were also waiting in a group to one side. The fellow called hurried to the place under the window, and the secretary told him something. The man—it was Alfeo, chief of premilitary instruction—moved quite energetically in front of the people. "Those in front have to line up in a straight row", he ordered. But the people, though they were looking directly at him, seemed unable to decide to do so. Then he started to line them up himself as if he were dealing with his pupils. "This way, this way now . . ." Then the others lined themselves up.

The secretary was watching over the fulfillment of the order he had given and approved. Behind the row arranged by Alfeo, the people stood motionless, but the secretary was not annoyed. *They're not in favor of a war*, he thought, *I'm certain. Who could be so much of a beast as to want war? But one thing is clear: the people from Brianza perhaps won't play the hero at the front, but they'll do their duty even in the most inhuman situations. Different from those ridiculous students who are going around shouting "long live the war"*. He had been in the last war and knew what he was saying. *What more could the party want of me?* he concluded. He left the window. Alfeo went back to join his little group.

Gerardo, Ambrogio, and Luca had ended up next to another group in which a disagreeable type was pontificating in dialect. They knew him only by sight. He was Mr. Pollastri, a civil servant in Incastigo. So as to make himself heard by someone of authority, like Gerardo, he raised his voice a bit. "The Germans already have victory in their pocket", he maintained. "Don't you know? Hardly a month ago, no, exactly a month, as the newspaper says, the tenth of May, they attacked Belgium and Holland, and went right through like a hot knife through butter, and the entire French front has had to surrender. And the English? The few that have been saved did it by running like rabbits."

He was referring to Dunkirk. Ambrogio knew he was telling the truth, and for that reason it was even more unbearable. Like other young men educated in the elite Catholic schools of Milan, he knew the judgment passed by Pope Pius XI, a Milanese himself, and, what is more, from Brianza, who repeated to members of his former Milan diocese, when they went to visit him, that the Nazis are the real antichrists, in the Gospel sense of the term. That the Nazis could take over now, in one stroke, all of Europe—as their present and spectacular victories made him fear—was for Ambrogio, and for his schoolmates, even if confusedly, a possibility so intolerable that they did not even want to consider it seriously.

"And this other attack of the Germans that began a few days ago?" Pollastri continued. "Haven't you read the newspaper? They've smashed the whole new French front, and they're already marching on to Paris. No one can stop them. Is that the way it is or not?"

Unfortunately, this really was the situation. *So is it for this that we, too, are going to hit out at France?* Ambrogio mentally answered him. *As the Russians did last year against Poland when it was already on its knees? How awful!* It was such an ignoble prospect that the young man finally turned his back on Pollastri. In front of him were a group of his father's workers observing with growing interest the electrician's efforts to get the two loudspeakers working: "Look at Pirovano Oreste, look at him."

"He's screwing it up."

"Not a bit."

"Oreste, watch out you don't fall off the ladder!"

"Look at him! He's hitting the loudspeaker to make it talk."

"What's the matter, Oreste, is it yes or no?"

"Harder, hit it harder."

These digs were bothering the factory electrician, Tarcisio. Tarcisio was the worker, tall, with curly hair, who had distinguished himself in the last war and whom Ambrogio and Stefano had seen cross the piazza ten days ago on the way to the benediction. He was a good friend of Pirovano Oreste. "They don't use them much," he was explaining to the people around him, "and that's why Oreste is having trouble getting them to work. When did we use them last? Maybe at the time of the economic sanctions."

"Oreste," one of the jokers screamed then, "you'd better get them to work if you don't want Alfeo to hit you with some sanctions!"

Even Luca, who was a serious fellow, broke into hearty laughter. And Tarcisio himself also had to laugh, though his head shook disapprovingly.

Meanwhile, other people were arriving in the piazza and stood behind those already present. The parish priest and his coadjutor, Don Mario, left the church, remaining on the portico, walking between the granite columns with a worried air.

Suddenly a tremendous noise was heard, which was prolonged, rising and falling, until Pirovano Oreste regulated the loudspeaker volume. Then the noise was transformed into the acclamation from the crowd in Rome awaiting the words of the Duce. The political secretary, who went to the window of the town hall to see what had happened, hurried to the piazza and stood in front of everybody. The announcer in Rome was describing with exaltation the flags, the squadrons, the "oceanic" crowd—an expression that, like the ideologically opposite but no less dehumanizing one, the "masses", made more than one person nervous—and bits of military music alternated with the descriptions. Finally, acclaimed by renewed and powerful shouts, Mussolini, who had come out to the balcony of the Venice palace, could be heard.

Once silence was obtained—no doubt with one of his resolute gestures—he began to speak. "Combatants of land, sea, and air. The black shirts of the revolution and the legions, men and women of Italy, of the empire and the kingdom of Albania, listen. An hour, signaled by destiny, strikes in the heavens of our land: the hour of irrevocable decisions." Once again fervent shouts and acclamations burst from the loudspeakers, and then again silence. "The declaration of war has been presented to the ambassadors . . .", another outburst of exultation interrupted the speech. "The ambassadors", Mussolini continued, "from Great Britain and France . . ." More jubilant shouts and acclamations interrupted the discourse, and whistles directed at those nations.

In Nomana no one joined in. Alfeo and some of his group tried, but halfheartedly, and soon gave up.

The real point was something different, and of that there was no longer any doubt: war had begun, the most terrible of collective calamities of the modern epoch. Everyone in the town remembered the invocations of their priests, which had been especially repeated during the previous weeks: "*A fame, a pesta, a bello, libera nos Domina, Libera nos . . . Libera nos.*" The Lord had not listened to their entreaty, a sign that man's sins had mounted to the point of impeding it. For a long time Don Mario had been explaining, "Watch out! It is true that God is Love, but he cannot continue treating men like irresponsible children." Who had committed those sins? Where? Yes, even in Nomana it was useless to deny it. "Look to yourselves. It is not necessary to search far afield", Don Mario said, and he was right when you thought about it. And now there was nothing to do but roll up one's sleeves and face up to the tremendous disaster they were going into, a disaster in which more than a few would die. How many of the town would be destined to die, and who in particular?

Mussolini's speech continued, "Forty-five million souls . . .", but the people were now listening out of inertia. What they really wanted to know, what interested them, they now knew: the disaster most surely had begun. Mussolini ended, "People of Italy, to battle!" ("Yes, yes!" shouted the multitude. "Do you hear those Romans?" someone murmured irritably.) "And show your toughness, your courage, your valor."

The speech over, the political secretary turned to the people. "I beg you to abide by the rules on the blackout regulations", he said with a good deal of common sense. Then he suddenly raised his arm in the Roman salute: "Comrades of Nomana, hail, Duce!"

"*Viva!*" Alfeo and some others shouted back.

"The waiting is over", the secretary said, and entered the town hall. The people began to scatter.

12

That evening in Gerardo's house the daily Rosary was recited with more than usual attention. The women, that is, the mother, Giulia, and her two grown daughters, Francesca, seventeen, and Alma, thirteen, were excited, and for that reason even Giudittina, only five years old, was forcing herself to pray with devotion. With that in mind, she opened her blue eyes wide to keep from nodding off sleepily, which was not unusual during prayers.

"Today the Rosary will be for Manno and for our country", the mother had said at the beginning. The boys, however, did not seem to be impressed. "Did you hear? We're not praying for you", Fortunato, the sixteen-year-old, the boy next down in age from Ambrogio, whispered in Ambrogio's ear jokingly. Keeping up the joke, Ambrogio opened his arms. "But you will be in a few days, when I've also picked up my rifle." Unlike Fortunato, who at sixteen showed a worldly, businesslike mentality, Ambrogio prayed with the intensity he displayed in everything he undertook. Like the other boys, Pino, fifteen, and Rodolfo, seven, Ambrogio prayed the responses of the Rosary walking about, coming and going through the room, as on every other afternoon. The women, in contrast, who normally prayed seated, had knelt on their chairs. The mother, forty-five, and already a bit faded and worn, who never had bothered much with her looks, put her whole passionate self into her prayer, all the ardor of which she was capable. A profound believer, she seemed impelled by the Holy Spirit, so much so that, like some women of the people, when she prayed one had the feeling that for her the first and truest reality was not of this earth but was transcendental. Francesca and Alma tried to follow her example. Francesca had a serene temperament, with chestnut hair that she wore gathered at the back and that contrasted with her blue eyes in her slightly long and very expressive face. Alma, also with chestnut hair, had more even features, almost perfect, but so inexpressive that even her brothers and sisters called her "the little statuette" or, more often, "the marble kitten".

The invocations of the Rosary went one after the other. In Giulia's mind, as in all of theirs, each one sounded like a knocking on the door of the beyond, according to the invitation of the Gospel: "Knock, do not tire of knocking, and it will open to you."

As for Ambrogio, he asked with faith the Mother of all men, who was left us by Christ on the Cross, to help Italy, *which today has joined so senselessly with the Nazis. But you cannot abandon a people like ours, who, above and beyond our stupidities, have always had and always will a genuine love for you.* He also asked for the personal salvation of his cousin Manno and the others he knew, mentioning them one by one. And he asked that all Italian soldiers be protected, and here it seemed that he also prayed for himself, because surely within a few days he would be a soldier.

As background for this communal prayer, the pendulum clock, on the longest piece of furniture in the sitting room, which shielded the radiator with its twisted copper strips, monotonously ticked off the seconds. It seemed like the sound of time passing on that quiet afternoon.

13

During the following days more than a few mobilization cards rained down on all sides of Nomana. Stefano also received his. Not he directly: his mother received it from the postman's hand. The postman, Chin, well known for being foolishly emotional, which made him continually go beyond limits and interfere in others' affairs, during those days outdid himself. As he knew that the delivery of one of these cards at a time of war could be the beginning of a tragedy, each time that he had to turn one over he felt obliged to do something strange. Sometimes, if the person receiving it was an interested party, he would press his biceps to express his emotion, true or pretended, by way of encouragement. On other occasions, especially if it was the end of his daily run and he felt tired or bored, he would repeatedly wave his right hand in front of the perplexed other party, thus signifying disaster ahead. If the parents were receiving the card, he would assure them that he had nothing to do with their son's enlistment, that it was not his fault. Not infrequently the outcome would be irritated insults.

Lucia, Stefano's mother, came to the door when he arrived on bicycle to the Nomanella farm. Chin, who a little before had been insulted by one of the soldiers being mobilized, handed over the pink card without speaking, with an almost lapidary gesture, so much so that the woman was slightly intimidated and so did not immediately reach out for the card but first dried her hands nervously with her apron. The arrival of the postman had surprised her while washing vegetables, and a green bit or two had remained stuck to her fingers.

She signed the receipt in silence and thanked him in a voice she was forcing to keep as calm as usual: "Thanks, Chin." He responded to her thanks by making a rapid hand gesture, like someone leaving, meaning that she should not under these circumstances thank him. He put the receipt in the thick leather bag, bulging with mail, that he carried over his shoulder and took his leave by raising the fingers of his right hand to his visor with an almost military air. It was his usual greeting. He turned his bicycle and continued on, serious. Serious, but not more than his hopeless emotionalism allowed him, and scarcely outside the farm he turned several times, twisting his neck, to see the effect of his visit.

But Lucia had already gone back into the house. She was not even aware of him, nor would it have mattered at all. She sat down on a chair next to the turned-off oven, with the pink card in her hands; she read a few words slowly and carefully. There was no doubt of it: this was the expected mobilization of Stefano. She was irritated to find herself at home alone at that moment. If Giustina or Ferrante or the grandmother, at least, were there . . . They were so used to sharing everything. In any case, being alone was beside the point, insignificant compared to this other fact, so much more important, serious, that her son, her Stefano, would have to go off to war. A mixed batch of reminiscences were roused in her: Stefano when he was a child, with his long smock and his hands outstretched to her, trying to say his first words: and, smaller still, only a few months old, soaked in sweat from that tremendous fever, on the brink of death; and then when he was about eight, strong as a little bull, running through the high grass, laughing because the wind rushed against his face; and Stefano, a few days before, young, serious, who took the bundle of wood from her hands, for it was he who wanted to be the one to chop the wood to make the fire for the polenta. "Why didn't you call me, Mother? You know I don't want you to do these heavy tasks." Her Stefano! Mingled with these recollections were the things that she had heard from Ferrante and others about the war: a dead Austrian and an Italian who had been buried together in the same grave, so the parents could never distinguish their remains . . . and . . . and . . . so many other confused, grandiose, and terrible events, which heaven knows how had really happened. And, at the same time, the names of those killing machines, especially the machine gun—and who knows how they work—and not only this, but other names like that, all hateful for a mother. And soon her son, her Stefano, would be involved in such terrible things.

He would become a *Bersagliere*, one of those soldiers who are so much at risk.

Certainly Stefano would not bluster about or search out danger on purpose, but neither—and this his mother felt most definitely—would he lag behind. *He's one of those who act, not one of those who talk*, she thought, as if she were unconsciously talking with someone, and there would be so many occasions of death . . . She was overcome with anguish; her inner emotions were so charged she felt she needed air. Her eyes sought the image of our Lady on the wall: a popular picture in which blue predominated, the color of a sky. The beloved face of the Mother of God, and even that color was powerful enough to calm her a bit. Lucia then began to move her lips, to pray, blaming herself for not having done it before. From whom would come comfort but from him who could ask us for anything and instead asks us above all for love, pity, and compassion for our fellow creatures? That he existed was shown no less by the Church than by her own experience. We are not alone: there really is someone who cares for us and our beloved, and at times, in the most decisive moments, we feel his intervention, a reality that comes to be perceived with great clarity, even if later it is difficult to explain it to others with words. But not always is there this intervention, only at times . . . She focused her attention on a postcard stuck into a corner of the picture. It showed our Lady with the dead Christ on her knees, a reproduction of a marble sculpture. The text said it was in Saint Peter's in Rome, and it was from Rome that Giustina had received the postcard, sent her by Sister Candida during a memorable pilgrimage a few years before. The image reminded the mother with terror that when the supernatural mingles with human things the outcome may be painful all the same, since they killed the adored Son of our Lady herself.

14

A couple of days later, on the afternoon of June 14, Stefano departed. Ambrogio did not drive him in his car to the barracks because now they were only using it—and then conservatively since gasoline was carefully rationed—for necessary factory business. And besides, being a student—despite the declaration of war—he would have to remain at home; to accompany Stefano would have caused some embarrassment. Stefano arrived at the Nomana station alone, and there he met a few other recruits waiting for the train. Contrary to his expectations, the mobilization was being carried out in a rather desultory manner: almost every day someone left, but there were never many at a time.

Arriving a little ahead of time, the young man decided to wait together with the others on the only platform there. He crossed his arms in the involuntarily important stance of the active man who suddenly finds himself without anything to do. At his feet was a small suitcase of an unusual trapezoidal shape, which his sister Giustina had bought with her own savings in town the previous afternoon. With the typical distrust of a country person, Stefano kept an eye on his case. It contained, apart from a change of clothing and toilet articles, something sweet, a peasant cake, which his mother had personally made for him. *Mother*, the young man thought, lowering his head, stirred. *What women don't worry about! More than anything else she wanted to make the cake.* It crossed his mind that this cake was his friend Ambrogio's favorite sweet, and he had heard him declare so more than once. *And he's right. It really is very good*, he agreed. *Ambrogio is a bit upset these days because we are going and he's staying behind at home. He doesn't understand that no matter what your lot is, even this, you have to be happy. Well, I'm happy for him.*

From a flowerbed next to the platform, a lilac bush in flower was wafting a lovely perfume all around. With nothing else to do, Stefano ended up examining the lilacs. Up close he saw that at the base of the bush a small cluster of pansies was growing, in lively and eye-catching colors. He bent down to look at them with an almost professional interest. Seeing him thus, one of the recruits a few steps from him came up and asked, "What are you looking at?"

"These flowers. We never think about growing flowers. It wouldn't require much effort though."

"Sometimes the women of the house think about them."

"Yes, but not much . . . a carnation or geranium, and usually in pots, not like this in the earth."

The other fellow changed his expression and looked at him with curiosity. "But who do you think you are, a lord of the manor? Of course, since now you'll have nothing to do, you'll be able to cultivate flowers." He then addressed a third recruit, who was nervously shifting his weight from one foot to the other and looking from one side to another as well: "Listen to this, Giovannino, you know, now that Stefano hasn't anything else to do, he's going to devote himself to becoming a gentleman. He's talking about growing flowers. I, on the other hand, wouldn't. Even if I had a few meters of earth left over, even just a meter, I'd plant onions. What do you say?"

Giovannino, the baker's apprentice, worked nights and slept days. His face was so pale it looked as if it was dusted with flour. "You bumpkins," he said, "you don't know how to think about anything except land. Here we are, not knowing how we'll end up, if we'll sleep in a bed or a haystack tonight, and you're going on about flowers and onions."

Stefano began to laugh, amused. Giovannino pointed to his case and asked, "What do you have in there, in that square suitcase? Besides dirty socks, that is."

"A homemade cake. For me and my friends."

"That's talking sense", Giovannino said. And as a baker he knew what he was talking about, especially about cakes. But then he began looking around himself nervously.

Even Stefano started looking around. The station was bordered, a little beyond the tracks, by one of those concrete fences that then protected all tracks in practically every town. Right after the fence was a small wire factory, closed on two occasions, as everyone knew, and now half abandoned, with a broken window here and there and weeds growing in the yard. The same weeds—horsetails and the like—that grew between the tracks: green things would never give up, and even if life were abandoned, they would overcome and manage to take over untrodden, and this met with the unconscious approval of the country boy. Beyond the wire factory the large green hollow began that extended to the north until it was lost from sight, that is, toward his house and toward Beolco and farther on to the amphitheater of the mountains. Stefano noticed that the mountains were very lovely at this hour, with the sun illuminating them at an angle, and their elevation and folds stood out with light and shadow. *It's the beautiful view Ambrogio talked about*, he told himself.

An electric bell began to ring insistently, then another, and the young men glanced around searchingly. They were at the front of the station, under a small metal roof, where wasps had made their nest. Irritated by the double noise, the insects fluttered angrily around the two bells. *Everybody has his own troubles*, the young man thought. A railwayman came out from a door and, without looking at them, pulled at some lever that rose from the ground. *He must have closed the level crossing. But why two? Are two trains coming?*

15

There were two: one, which the recruits were awaiting, which came from the north, from Lecco; the other, from the opposite side, from Monza: two diesel cars that crossed one another in the Nomana station.

The one from the south arrived first; bells sounded; six or seven people in all got off. They seemed excited. One of them, an old man with the look of a commercial traveler, stopped in front of the peasants waiting on the platform. "Did you hear? Do you know or not?"

"What?"

"What should we know?"

"They don't know", the old man said with satisfaction to the others who had gotten off from the train. And then to the people who were waiting, "The Germans went into Paris this morning. It was on the radio fifteen minutes ago."

"Paris? In Paris?" some of them said softly.

"Yes. And it's a big step. The war is almost over", he declared.

One of the travelers, younger and on the fat side, with an air of slight intelligence, addressed the recruits, who looked as if they were out of place with their parcels under their arms, "Where are you going? To the barracks, eh? And what are you going to have to do there now? Didn't you hear? The war is just about over."

"We're going to the barracks all the same," the recruit Giovannino of the floury face answered rapidly, and then went on to make fun of him, "but we're only going there to march off our bellies", he declared, alluding pointedly to the traveler's fatness.

At that, the ambassadors of the important news added nothing more and went toward the exit, only chattering among themselves.

One of the recruits started to get on the train through the door that had been left open. Giovannino quickly grabbed him by his flowing jacket. "What're you doing, Tito?" he shouted, as he pulled both jacket and recruit back. "What're you doing? Do you want to go to Lecco and take a boat across the lake? You're easily satisfied! What did you think? That the war was over?"

The so-called Tito looked around with a frightened air. "Isn't this our train?" he babbled. He had only gone once, at most twice, on a train. The others started laughing, and even Tito joined in.

"Tito, if you make a mistake like that when you're carrying the cross in the processions," one of them chimed in, "everyone will end up at Pasqualetta's tavern instead of the church."

They all laughed again, including Tito, even though the crossbearer of the processions was not Tito, but his brother Giacomo, at least ten years older than he. Tito and Giacomo lived in one of the houses on the outskirts of town, beyond Lodosa, and were Pierello's cousins.

Stefano was listening to the joke distractedly because his attention had been caught by Signorina Quadri Dodini, who, leaning on her cane, limped behind the other travelers toward the exit. He had seen her many times in church (including that evening on the piazza with Ambrogio waiting for Igino). *She's a very pious woman. That's why she teaches at the nuns' school in Monza*, he was thinking. *They say she's good. If I talk to her, she won't be offended.*

His glance shifted several times from Tito—who now was being funny to make up for his awkwardness—to the Signorina Dodini, who was about to leave the station. At last he decided and, picking up his case, in four long strides reached the teacher. "Pardon me, ma'am."

"What do you want?" The woman stopped and lifted her two eyes, which seemed still more idiotic because of the thick lenses of her glasses. She did not even seem to realize that the boy with the case in his hand was going off to military service: an important moment in the life of a villager.

"That news about Paris. It's the capital of France, isn't it? You know after that . . . regarding the war, I mean, do you think . . ." He stopped talking when he saw the woman was not looking at him but at some other spot, her face flushed, her eyes looking swollen.

"Signorina, what's wrong?" the boy murmured. "Are you all right?"

"It's nothing, nothing", she stammered, and then started to cry. She took a little handkerchief out of her purse quickly and pressed it to her lips, and while she clumsily walked on, her voice grief stricken and so soft that Stefano could scarcely hear her, she said, "Poor France, poor culture!"

The young man stood stock still, surprised, holding his unusual case and looking at the teacher from the nuns' school, who was going off in tears because of the Germans marching into Paris.

He turned, wondering if he should tell that strange happening to the others, but as he came closer they could hear the happy noise of iron, and there arrived the second diesel car. He hurried then with the others to the doors, and once in the compartment he no longer thought about anything but finding a good place.

Four hours later he got on a longer and heavier train, which left the Monza station toward Milan. Stefano had been named head of a dozen recruits designated for the Third Regiment of the Bersaglieri, that is, for one of the most prestigious regiments in the army. A fact he did not know and which, at that moment, could hardly have interested him, since he was concerned about something else: that eleven young men whose names were on the pass should arrive together and in good order at the Bersaglieri barracks. "Why me? What in the devil was in that officer's head when he chose me?"

16

For those who stayed in Nomana life went on almost as usual. There were, it is true, rationing cards, but with or without one, one could find everything in the country. The automobiles had their lights shaded, and in the evenings it was necessary to observe the rules on dimming lights. However, France was on its knees and England battling in a sea of disasters, and no enemy plane had bombed Milan.

Ambrogio could do nothing but continue his vacation. He spent the morning getting experience in his father's factory. He thought, *It's one thing to know, sitting in an armchair, the various tasks that your employees perform and quite another thing to know them by having done them yourself.*

For that reason, the young man had put his own system into practice, even on previous vacations. He stayed close to an employee—beginning each work operation at its most basic stage—and, under his guidance, filled in for him for as long as it took to master the work. He often got to the point of substituting for absent employees, and that suited everyone concerned.

He also began, during these wartime holidays, to accompany his father on his visits to his clients.

"This is a job it takes years to get to know well", his father warned. "With time you'll learn that the most difficult part of our work is not producing but selling."

Gerardo only tried, however, to involve his son in the business to a certain degree; he knew if he did otherwise his studies would be put to one side and left unfinished. Many children of industrialists he knew had ended up like that, and he, who had undergone privations, or nearly so, in childhood and adolescence, feared above anything else that his children might drop their studies. He would repeat to them, "Until you have your degree your real work is your education, and don't forget it." And then, "A degree, no matter what happens in life, will at least guarantee you your bread." And in saying bread he was not speaking metaphorically; he really meant everyday food. There were days when he was a child that he had seen terror in his mother's eyes, the terror of a widow facing the prospect of not being able to provide bread for her children.

His administrative and technical offices were in the same buildings in which he worked: a complex of prefabricated sections, with different-sized yards in which some linden trees grew. The pay office, where Ambrogio was currently working, had windows that gave directly onto the area in which the looms were running. The roar of the looms and the other textile machines was slightly muffled as it came through the walls and accompanied the work of the office staff during their whole day's work.

One morning, in which the songs of the factory girls were added to the usual sounds, Ambrogio lifted his head from the books and grew distracted listening. Often, as on that morning, they sang popular songs, especially those from the mountains. "That Bunch of Flowers" and others similar, but often they also sang religious songs, in Italian or Latin, in particular the litanies of the Rosary, whose rhythm seemed to suit the monotonous rhythm of the looms. *Why don't they sing the songs that are popular?* Ambrogio wondered. *Perhaps because they seem odd to them, they don't belong to their culture . . . Well, let's not get sidetracked.* Once again he became involved in his numbers, but after half an hour the songs had stopped, and he felt that something was missing.

He finished putting the accounts in order and stood up. "I'm going to have a look around the factory", he told the two girls working there.

He pushed against a small inner door, which, when it was barely cracked, let in a rush of even greater noises that spread through the office. After he went through the door, it closed quickly behind him on its spring mechanism. Before him were the looms that were the cause of all that noise, ranged in parallel rows and worked by pulleys, whose leather belts turned rapidly. Under the attentive look of the weavers, the shuttles came and went like lightning flashes, their movements alternating with that of the combs that, after every sweep of the shuttle, beat the weft with greater or lesser force, depending on the density that had to be given to the fabric.

Ambrogio began his inspection tour. At certain points in the row lined with looms there were other machines: winders, warping mills with their innumerable horizontal threads, and many others. To feed all those machines there were boys in khaki overalls pushing iron-wheeled carts along the passageway, carts loaded with skeins of thread or yarn rolled around large spools. Almost all the workers seemed concentrated and serious. Ambrogio walked slowly, and his eyes went from the fabric of one loom to that of another, or he would stop a moment to watch a work detail of greater interest or greet someone occasionally with a nod of his head, someone he had been at school with or whom he had known for other reasons.

At the back of a double row of large looms, Giustina, Stefano's sister, was working. Like all the other weavers, she had a black apron on and her hair gathered back into a net. Before reaching her place, Ambrogio went through the section of small machines, the bobbins, where Marietta of the shuttles, with her large, yellow face, always a bit frightened, was teaching from morning to night (for ever and ever, the rhythmic noise of the loom seemed to say) the recently arrived girls that basic of textile chores: preparing the shuttles. So she might not become upset, Ambrogio avoided looking at her; in fact, just seeing him, Marietta, as always, became nervous and, for no reason, started to tell her girls in whispers and gestures that they should concentrate more on their work.

Coming to Giustina, Ambrogio greeted her with a nod. Even on the rare occasions when he happened to stop to look at the material falling from her two looms, the young man avoided speaking to her. As for Giustina, she usually acted impersonal and distant, but this time she seemed embarrassed. *What's this about?* Ambrogio remembered the last time he had passed by her—a few days before—he had noticed a tinge of uneasiness about her. *Could there be some defect in the fabric?* he had wondered. *We'll move on and not stop.* Immediately afterward he had seen the mechanic Luca, the contemporary of his cousin Manno, the person he had been with in the piazza on the day of the declaration of war, on his knees examining the mechanism of one of Giustina's looms. Ambrogio had greeted Luca cordially, and Luca had answered, "Ambrogio, it looks like I have only a few more days."

"But . . . aren't your two brothers already in the war?"

"Yes, but . . .", had said Luca, his chestnut hair falling on his forehead and his face, which was as serious as ever, coming up to make himself better heard over the din of the machines. "Well, my sister-in-law, my older brother's wife, it seems, is pregnant." While he had spoken he had gestured with the screwdriver he was holding in his right hand. "We'll wait to be absolutely sure, and if it's certain, . . . I'll . . .", and he gestured, as if to say, "I'll have to go." And he then explained the situation with greater clarity: "I'll have to take my brother's place."

"My father will be very sorry," Ambrogio had pointed out, "you know."

Luca, after having agreed by opening his arms in Pierello's usual gesture, had gone back to the gears of the loom. *This is the reason Giustina feels uncomfortable,* Ambrogio had thought, as he went to another place. *It's because of the trouble with the loom.*

A few days ago . . . all right, but now? How come she seemed embarrassed now? The young man did not know what to think when he noticed Luca approaching again along another passageway. *Could it be because of Luca? But why?* At that moment Giustina—who was looking from the boss to the mechanic—noticed a broken thread in the warp of one of her looms. Suddenly, her attention drawn to her work, she stopped the machine with such a brusque movement that a box of spools fell, some rolling along the floor. Ambrogio was about to help her pick them up, but he thought Giustina might not like that and went on his way. Luca, on the other hand, leapt on the fallen spools. By this unusual gesture, since what had fallen was not heavy, and even more by the expression on his face, Ambrogio concluded that Luca loved Giustina. *That's why,* he told himself. *It's all clear now. The things that happen!* And while he continued his inspection, *How will Stefano and his mother Lucia and everyone else in Nomanella take the news?* He thought they would be happy because Luca was a good fellow, one of the best around. *If I am not being fooled, there'll be news soon. Luca will propose to Giustina. I'll have to tell Francesca to write Manno. Although . . . when would they be able to marry?* Luca had to substitute for his brother at the front, there was that. *She'll have to tell Manno about that, too. No matter what, the war isn't going to last forever.*

17

If in the morning Ambrogio went to the factory for his apprenticeship, in the afternoon he was enjoying his vacation.

He spent long hours of his free time reading in the garden. Normally he sat on a lounge chair under a fig tree that had come up spontaneously at the edge of the lawn. Around it were wildflowers, yellow ranunculuses, daisies, chicory flowers, and others whose names he did not know. During the sunniest hours there was usually no one in the garden except the two little ones, Rodolfo and

Giudittina, who entertained themselves playing on the ground with clay and molds. The two children wore white caps well pulled down to the napes of their necks, and their gestures were slow, as if drowsing. They were so bent over it seemed as if the sun, from its height, might plaster them against the earth with its intensity.

During those hours only the sound of buzzing insects, the chirping of sparrows on the roof of the house, getting louder at times and becoming a tumult and then dissolving into silence, reached Ambrogio's ears. The sparrows, men's closest neighbors among the birds, also seemed the most quarrelsome. From time to time the well-modulated trill of a blackcap, a warbling of a few notes, delicately alternating, symbolized the very voice of summer in Brianza for him. If the warbling was repeated with more insistence, the young man even interrupted his reading and listened. Then he would become lost in his thoughts, his eyes on the foliage of the fig tree overhead or even on the clouds that floated high in the sky. He thought of so many things ... For example, of the girl, still unknown to him, who would one day be his wife and who no doubt lived somewhere. And he sometimes tried to picture her; at other times he thought about what would be his country's destiny, his country dragged senselessly into this war, and which now seemed, quite truthfully, very little committed; he also thought of his personal destiny, when he would be called up to arms. Then he came back to the present and went back to his reading.

Occasionally he stood up, left his book—*Ivanhoe, Ilia and Alberto*, or *The Brothers Karamazov*—on the seat and stretched himself by walking along the garden and orchard paths. Among the trees, even on the hottest days, he felt an agreeable freshness. They were trees of different heights; a few spruces, in particular, were taller than twenty meters. Between the trees grew a variety of bushes and grasses, but not in the thick parts of the garden, where ivy covered everything mustily. And where the branches opened up a window of light, ferns could be seen among the ivy besides a rare and mysterious plant with deformed flowers of a dark color. On the slopes facing north, instead of ivy moss grew, which came up spontaneously as it did in the forests of the region, like all types of minor vegetation.

With his arms at his back, Ambrogio strolled along the paths edged with lily of the valley.

His brother Pino, who was fifteen, had gone with the others to the mountains; otherwise he would be here chasing the birds with his Flobart gun. But now Pino was away, and the birds in the branches were enjoying a truce.

Besides spending his afternoons reading, Ambrogio also went on outings, even in the van, since the automobile could no longer be used for pleasure trips. The factory van carried out transports more often than before to different places, mainly to Turin or Genoa or its outskirts, where there were new clients working the arsenals: they had begun producing for the army and navy. The young man, who did not lose sight of the worker origins of his own family, not only did not think traveling in a van beneath him but happily would have taken turns at the wheel with the driver if he could have. But Celeste, the driver, the father of a large family in the style of Gerardo, though he appreciated Ambrogio's company and conversation, refused all offers of assistance: "I'm not an old man who needs help", he would say.

"But, don't you understand? This way you're making me travel like a tourist", Ambrogio objected.

"And you're complaining?" the driver responded. He smiled with his sky blue eyes, the reason his parents had dubbed him with the name Celeste.

Ambrogio took long outings on his bicycle more frequently than in the van, to the neighboring lakes of Brianza, for example, or to Lake Como, or even to the Bergamo countryside, rustic and warm, with its houses of curious wooden galleries and balconies of wood, different from any other place.

This is the way he spent the remainder of that month of June and then July, day after day, doing such small things.

18

The month of August, by his father's express wish ("Come along, make up your mind, go and stock up on a little sun, since you don't know what the future holds in store for you." "Papa, maybe an intensive cure in Africa is what's waiting for me." "You can get rheumatism even in Africa."), Ambrogio spent at the seaside, in Cesenatico.

During the train trip he had time to reflect on his father's worries, his father, who practically imposed these vacations on him: *He who never has a vacation and doesn't even understand one. And the strange part is that everyone in the factory ends up thinking somewhat like him* ... As a result, of the three hundred workers there, only the female office staff took vacations. And on occasion when an employee, some man, decided to take a vacation, instead of going on working and being paid for it, he felt he was performing an action hardly worthy of a man. *This really is nonsense, as well as unfair*, Ambrogio concluded. *When I'm in the factory, this will have to change. It seems to me that at least the young people— Luca, for example—will think I'm right.* Nevertheless, he was not exactly sure, so much had the custom taken root in Nomana.

As Ambrogio came closer to the coast, the light in the sky became gradually clearer, more luminous, as if reflecting the enormous mirror of the waters. The landscape, too, became lighter, markedly so, and these colors and other details of the landscape evoked long-forgotten feelings in the young man's soul, feelings he had experienced in the already far-off years of childhood during the first trips to the sea. He was not, however, the sort to dwell on such things.

He let these feelings pass; they would disappear, willy-nilly, because only a fragment, here or there, could be recovered from the past, and only at times, and only during the brief period it took to come apart.

In the Cesenatico station Ambrogio hired a light horse-drawn coach, ordering the coachman to one, two, three rooming houses that he had mentally taken note of the previous year, when he was there with his school group. The last of the three, the Iris, almost new, clean, surrounded by a little sandy garden that gave directly onto the beach, seemed the most suitable: he found a room without difficulty. The ease at finding a place at the seaside and in August, as well as the presence of the military in many of the stations he had crossed through, were the only facts reminding him on that day that they were at war.

He washed and dressed quickly and went down to the dining room for dinner. A discreet murmur of voices came toward him, then suddenly became muffled and almost ceased when he appeared. The eyes of those seated at the tables, some thirty people, were focused on him.

"Good evening, everyone", he said with an ease that was slightly forced. He took a seat at an empty table.

Once he was seated, the chatter started again. Now it was his turn to look the others over; he examined them discreetly. *After all*, he thought with unconscious timidity, *this company doesn't interest me. The school group is only a stone's throw from here, and that's why I came to Cesenatico.*

The company that didn't interest Ambrogio was composed mainly of mothers with children, a few fathers, children of different ages, and three or four girls. It was on the latter that he focused his attention, as might be expected, until he felt he had observed them sufficiently. *Enough*, he told himself, *quite enough*. But even after his resolution, while swallowing the insipid vegetable soup he had been brought (and this was another thing that reminded him of the war), he darted a glance at them, despite himself. To be exact, he looked at one in particular, the prettiest, who was seated with her family at a nearby table.

She was of medium height, well proportioned, with short, golden-blond hair, gray eyes, and something special about her mouth: when she laughed her two canine teeth stood out slightly from the rest of her teeth. This gave her face a vaguely feline tinge, not at all disagreeable. *A tigress, that's what she is: a tigress*, Ambrogio decided. *But she's pretty. I have to admit she's pretty.*

The tigress quickly noticed the young man was observing her, and she in turn looked at him to see if he maintained his interest in her, something that amused Ambrogio and, at the same time, forced him to stop looking.

19

The following morning Ambrogio left through the little garden for the beach. He was wearing his bathing suit and carrying a bag with a spare suit.

The Cesenatico beach—very long and occupied by few people that year—extended toward the right until it was out of sight. Bathers did not go into that part, beyond a certain limit, and the beach was dirtied by a scrubby vegetation and the residue left by the waves. Toward the left, that is, toward the center of the city, the old port and its canal stretched two piers into the sea. In this part the colored beach umbrellas and lounge chairs were thicker, as well as wooden cabanas, which in some spots formed a continuous row. However, even here there was no lack of free space.

Ambrogio noticed there were already several clients from his hotel (including the tigress, wearing enormous dark glasses and a conical-shaped hat on her blond head) sitting on the lounge chairs and sand beside the parasols. Some of them looked up at him, and perhaps they would have liked him to sit down beside them, but—once again, adolescent as he was, shyness was the determining factor—he decided it would not be a bad idea to spend the first morning with his school group.

He went off to the right. He knew the place well, and in any case he would have found them, so unmistakable was their ecclesiastic-Ambrosian look, lively in the somewhat prosaic sense that the Milanesi understand Christian joy and, above all, practical and judicious. He recognized them, moreover, by a little blue flag with the school emblem—an almost Olympic emblem, formed by three interlaced rings, the ancient emblem of San Carlo Borromeo—which was flying gaily at the top of a pole. At that point, Ambrogio left the cool shore of the sea, on which he had walked with confidence, the walk of youth, and crossing diagonally over the dry sand he went toward the beach umbrellas. To reach where he was going he had to cross the place where some boys were playing volleyball, shouting, and with an interest and joy that until yesterday he had shared. He recognized several of them, all younger than himself, and some greeted him but were evidently more intent on their game than on his visit. Seated on lounge chairs in the shade and in the sun he met the vice rector of his old lycée and three or four professors, all of whom were pleasantly surprised by his appearance and greeted him with a show of cordiality. They were in robes or bathing suits instead of soutanes, but they were no less authoritative for that. *What is most frightfully lost,* the young man noted, *is the aesthetic.* And he repeated a resolution formulated on other occasions: *As far as you are concerned, remember that up to the age of thirty and no more, not a year more in a bathing suit.* He sat down with them and took part in their summertime conversations, very different from those of schooltime and, above all, more rambling.

Later he swam with the schoolchildren when the bathing attendant—from Romagna, with black, curly hair, whom he had also known for a long time—signaled with a whistle that it was time. All the boys, leaving everything, started to race to the sea, shouting, "Swim! swim!" Ambrogio swam along with a little group of kids who were younger than he, but no less skillful as swimmers, some even more so than he, one in particular, perhaps a future champion, who was doing a crawl, proud of showing off his ability. After the swim, he lined up with the others, behind the cabins, for a freshwater shower. Then he threw himself down on the sand to dry in the sun like all the others.

But while all this was going on—the swim, the shower, the sun, the conversations—a little figure leapt continuously to his mind, that of the tigress, just as he had seen her next to the beach umbrellas, with her conical hat on her blond head and a bathing suit with a white-and-blue-striped skirt.

Ambrogio was roused by the vice rector, who, small and black (because of his dark color the students called him "Indigenous Clergy"), came up to him stuffed into his big white robe, saying, "Riva, Riva, don't make me be your nursemaid, too." How well Ambrogio knew the inflections of that voice—he had heard it for years. "You're grown up now." The vice rector had a jar of cream against sunburn in his hand, which he handed him. "Where did you leave your common sense? Or do you want to get burned? It's only the first day."

The young man took the jar, not too convinced. "This Vaseline is good for women, children, and vice rectors", he said. "In any case, thanks."

"Fool!" the vice rector shouted. "A viper's tongue and bandit!" It was his usual way of expressing himself when he was happy. It was familiar language for Ambrogio and the other students. It was not spoken by chance but because the vice rector, like other educators of recent times, had adopted the language of the boys.

Ambrogio rubbed a little on his back and arms and returned the jar to the priest: "Thanks, Don Vaseline." The priest stumbled back toward his seat, small and black, in his big white robe, mumbling a series of interjections such as "Den of thieves, young barbarians", and others of the same type, to which "Geronte"—a graying redhead, Monsignor, Greek professor—reacted by wrinkling his lips disapprovingly. As for Ambrogio, when silence was restored, he went back to thinking about the tigress.

He saw her again at midday, at lunch, and he found her still more attractive.

Later, during the silence of the afternoon rest, with the sun blazing hot against the closed shutters of his room, he could not sleep: that girl refused to leave his mind. He finally got up and went from one side of his room to another, pacing, and carried out a brave examination of his conscience.

What was happening to him? He liked the girl, that's all. Was it shameful? No, of course it wasn't. It was simply something natural: the most natural thing in the world. So far fine, let's go on. Go on . . . where, in what direction? (While pondering these things, the youth was in no way making light of the matter: his analysis was meant to lead to something practical.) *The fact is I'm becoming obsessed. This is the crux of the matter. I saw her yesterday for the first time. I've still not spoken to her. I don't even know her name, if she's intelligent or stupid, nor do I have the slightest idea what she's like inside. But I definitely have to say I like her, not to the point of marrying her though, because she's not my type, at least not totally* . . . He mingled reason and fantasy. The fact is that since he was shaped by the moral standards of the time, apart from girls, he was giving this meeting a great importance, despite himself. As far as the prospect of an insipid love affair was concerned, it did not enter into his plans at all.

He paced the room for ten minutes or so until he decided, most naturally, that "to become acquainted with this girl was not forbidden" and that, given the situation, "as soon as he could, he would".

Later he went down to the beach and rented a small sailboat and took to the sea. He did not manage it skillfully, and, though he had decided to reach the end of the port canal, he was forced to return, humiliated, using oars. He arrived at the hotel quite late.

20

After dinner Ambrogio did not know what to do. Should he go out alone? Join the school group? The school group, no, enough for one day. He was strolling irresolutely about the vestibule of the hotel, back and forth, when he saw the tigress seated in a shaded corner. She was dressed to go out, with a white wool shawl in the form of a stole and a purse on her lap. Evidently she was waiting for one of her family to come down, her mother perhaps. Incredibly enough there was an empty seat beside her, to which the young man went with alacrity. "Good evening", he said, as he sat down.

"Good evening."

"Student?"

"Yes."

"Ah . . . then perhaps we should address each other with our first name, because I'm also a student. Where do you go to school?"

"In Rho."

"In Rho? What a small world!"

"Why do you say that?" the tigress opened her gray eyes wide. It was truly lovely to see them up close, as if striped with gold. "I've never seen you in Rho."

"You've certainly never seen me there. I must have been there only a couple of times in my life at the most. How could you have seen me?" The young man wondered if he should say something about her eyes, but he did not dare. The tigress laughed. "Then why did you say it's a small world?"

"Why? Because you're from my area, that is, from Milan. And here we're really quite far from Milan, aren't we?"

"Yes, but many of the summer guests are from Milan."

"Yes . . ."

The tigress began to laugh again. Now she, too, was watching him, trying to understand him, so cultivated apparently and evidently a solid fellow, and at the same time so awkward.

"What's your name?" Ambrogio asked.

"Patrizia."

"I'm Ambrogio. Forgive me for not having introduced myself yet." He stood up, stretched out his hand, and said his surname, "Riva."

"Malinverni", the tigress chirped, extending her hand and laughing again. "Good heavens, standing on ceremony", she commented.

"Observing the rules when it's necessary is necessary", the young man observed, who was enchanted with the sensation produced by Patrizia's hand, a sensation that he summarily judged as "aesthetic". He never would have believed that a hand—a simple hand, despite the painted nails—could be so pleasant. *Heavens*, he thought, *what a masterpiece women are!*

"Let's go on with the exam", he added. "You said you were a student: What year, and what do you study?"

Instead of answering, Patrizia, straightening up, looked beyond the young man toward the staircases. Ambrogio also turned his head. Dressed to go out, and with her hair gathered high on her head, Patrizia's mother was coming down the stairs. She was a woman between forty and fifty, quite well conserved and, at this particular moment, moving with unusual solemnity, as if everyone were staring at her, even though—Ambrogio noticed—none of the few people present was looking at her. Who knows, perhaps she was looking at herself. "Mother, I'm over here", the girl indicated, waving her hand. Her mother suddenly became more spontaneous and, after getting to the bottom of the staircase, went toward them. Ambrogio stood up and introduced himself with the necessary formality, in order to abide by his words of a little before. The woman shook his hand maternally. "Milanese? Student? I see, I see. How nice . . ." Now she was behaving exactly as he expected a lady from Rho to behave.

"Tricia and I are going to the ice cream parlor at the corner of the big piazza. Do you know where it is? My husband and little girls are waiting there for us. We're already late. Are you coming?"

"Yes, thank you, delighted." And instinctively, so as to keep an opening for an eventual exit, he added, "I was going in that direction anyway."

While they were walking on the lane of beaten down earth, adorned with maritime pines, among people whose numbers were growing little by little, Ambrogio would have liked to talk to Patrizia, that is, Tricia, as he had heard her mother address her. However, the lady who was between the two of them (it was he who had changed place in order to be correct and have her in the middle) was talking without a pause, and there was nothing he could do.

The last light of the day was shining on everything; the bright colors of the summer clothes the people were wearing could still be made out, though with difficulty, as well as the style of the women's dresses, with their long shawls of many or few colors; what stood out with the men, curiously enough, were their two-toned shoes, which were the fashion. Soon, Ambrogio thought, night would fall completely, but the people would continue strolling under the stars, which emitted a very faint light, but sufficient—as many would notice during that period in which they were obliged to dim the lights—for strolling in the dark. Perhaps under the stars—the young man fantasized—Tricia's golden head would have shone almost like a lamp . . .

Having arrived together at the ice cream parlor, he immediately realized that he did not feel like going through the ceremony of meeting the father, the doctor, as his wife called him, and he remembered a previous engagement confusedly and took leave of the two women.

"We'll see each other tomorrow, eh?" Tricia told him in charming fashion.

"Yes, tomorrow," the young man answered, "on the beach."

21

When Ambrogio left the little hotel garden the following day for the beach, Tricia was already there—dressed in red this time, but with her conical hat on her head—lying down next to the umbrella sunning herself. She greeted him cheerfully, waving her hand. The young man threw his bag of clothes under the umbrella and sat down on the sand at her side.

"Hello. I see you're a real early bird", he said.

"I've always liked getting up early."

"A responsible girl," Ambrogio said, imitating the voice of the vice rector, whom she obviously did not know, "responsible and virtuous."

Tricia smiled. "I just think it's silly to miss the morning sun. Don't you agree?"

"Yes, of course. By the way, I didn't finish my interrogation last night. Where were we? Ah! We were talking about school. What do you study?"

"At the moment, I'm in high school. I've finished my fourth year."

"Where, in Rho?"

"No, in Milan. In the Liceo Berchet."

"Ah, luckily not in Rho. So it seemed to me."

"Why?" she asked, perplexed. "Do you have something against Rho?"

"Of course," he answered, "and you ask? What well-born person wouldn't?"

Tricia laughed. They continued making light talk. Ambrogio picked up sand with his right hand and sifted it through his fingers. *We're like sand*, he thought, as if it were a presage of what was going to happen to him; actually it was not, but the girl's company made him rise above the usual commonplaces. The beach was already filling up; more umbrellas were being opened. Tricia's two little sisters of five and six arrived. After greeting Ambrogio very gravely, with a kind of pawing the ground meant to be a bow, they began to play whole-heartedly. They dug up moist sand with their spades and began to fill their bright-colored tin molds with animal and puppet shapes.

Her father and mother will arrive soon, Ambrogio was thinking, *and I must think up an excuse to leave before they arrive. What could I suggest? A ride in a rowboat or sailboat?* Until he remembered the Rubicon.

"Listen, Tricia, I have a brilliant idea."

"Yes?"

"Have you ever been to the Rubicon?"

"What . . . what do you mean?" she said, a bit surprised. "Is that a metaphor?"

"What do metaphors have to do with it?" Now it was the young man who did not understand. Then he realized: "Oh, you think I'm talking figuratively, that I'm making a metaphor? Metaphors, not at all! I'm speaking realistically, let's say in the style, more or less, of Giovanni Verga. You've studied Giovanni Verga, or are you a bit behind at the Liceo Berchet?"

Tricia shook her head, amused. Really, talking with a girl inspired Ambrogio.

"The Rubicon," he continued, "to begin with, is a river."

"Thank you, I've got that far", Tricia said. "We've also got that far at Berchet."

"Go on", Ambrogio said. "I wouldn't have imagined that. Congratulations! All right, so it's a river. So far so good." He stopped and looked hard at Tricia's eyes. "Listen, you wouldn't be pulling my leg?"

"Who should I?" she said, surprised.

"Don't you know that the Rubicon is about two steps away from here?" he indicated with his arm outstretched. "Over there, a few miles. Or did you know that?"

"A few miles? Oh, of course!" she recalled. "By Rimini, isn't it? You said over there?"

The young man felt reassured. "Good, I see you're not completely ignorant, but to know it better, it wouldn't be a bad idea to have a little review. What do you think about making an inspection? Should we?"

"Take a walk?"

"Well, let's call it a walk. The river isn't far. We can get there in an hour, more or less."

"And what is there to see?"

"In the first place, the Rubicon is a current of water that empties into the sea. Does that seem slight? In the second place, there are the dice." He remembered a school joke. "Caesar's dice. Do you understand?"

"Caesar's dice?"

"Yes, the dice he threw when he said, '*alea jacta est.*' You can see Caesar was a realist, too. He never spoke in metaphors: he really threw the dice."

"Don't tell me they're still there after two thousand years?"

"Of course they are. I'm serious. Big ones, because Caesar was big."

"Go on!"

"Do you want to bet? Listen, Tricia, if we don't find the dice in the Rubicon . . ."

"But where can the dice be now?"

"They're there, on the ground, near the Rubicon. Listen, if we don't find them I'll give you a book. If we find them, then . . ."

"What?"

Firm in his chaste principles, Ambrogio rejected the sudden temptation that came to him to say "then you'll give me a kiss". "Well, in that case, I'll only invite you for an ice cream. Come on, should we go?"

Tricia decided. "Yes, I'd like a walk." She stood up and brushed the sand from her red outfit. She looked herself over carefully, reconsidered, and said, "Wait for me. I'll be ready in a minute."

She went to the cabin and shortly returned with the white-and-blue-striped outfit Ambrogio had seen the day before instead of the red one.

Heavens, how charming! the young man thought, and, without bothering about being repetitive, he made the same commentary: *What a masterpiece women are!*

"Should we go?" he said happily to the masterpiece.

"Yes", the masterpiece answered, who was telling the two little girls, "Tell Mama I've gone for a walk." As it seemed they were not paying attention, she repeated, "I'm telling you something. Did you hear?"

The older child raised her head from the sand, "We heard you, we heard you, all right", she answered. And with an unexpectedly roguish air, she added, "Do we have to tell Mama you went walking by yourself?"

"What kind of foolishness is that?" Tricia exclaimed severely. "When have I ever asked you to tell lies?"

"Oh, naughty, naughty!" the little one insisted, even though a little insecurely now, and she waved her forefinger reproachfully. Without lifting her head the younger one also pulled a roguish face.

"Eh, you two little imps", Ambrogio intervened. "What kind of words are these? Say goodbye to me right now, like before. I'm going. Hurry up, on your feet!"

The two little girls stood up, irritated, and repeated the same kind of pawing on the ground they had greeted him with before, and immediately went back to building castles.

"Then . . . should we go by the shore of the thundering sea", Ambrogio suggested. Tricia agreed, still smiling at her little sisters' carrying on.

22

Tricia and Ambrogio set off then for the shore of the thundering sea, where the sand was cool and hard, next to one another, young people, secure in the life ahead of them.

They immediately came to the school group, marked by the little flag, almost Olympic, with its three rings, which fluttered happily on its pole. As on the day before, several boys were involved in a fierce volleyball match. This time, however—unlike the previous day—since Ambrogio was not alone but with a pretty girl, all or almost all of them, while running and screaming, stared at him, at them.

Besides the boys, from the lounge chair in which he was sunk, the graying redheaded professor of Greek saw the two young people go by together, and inwardly he was happy. *For that man leaves his father and his mother*, he quoted mentally, *and will follow his wife*. In contrast, the young vice rector of picturesque language, frowned and thought, *Just look at him, the jackass. He still hasn't left school, and he's already given himself up to dissipation. Where has all our teaching led him? When I see him, I'll give him a piece of my mind, the wretch!*

The school group was quickly behind them, and also the rest of the beach, with its people, beach umbrellas, and cabins. The two young people met up with a group or two and then isolated individuals who meandered, sunk in their thoughts. Then they met no one.

The strip of sand lapped by the Adriatic extended in front of them toward the south, virginal, until it was lost from sight; only very far off did it seem to end in a confused and scarcely visible white spot: Rimini. Even more than by the sky, this solitary landscape was created by the immensity of the sea, on that day two-colored, as Tricia pointed out to Ambrogio: a green close to the shore that was gradually transformed, farther out, into a more and more intense turquoise. The sea was calm and its sound minimal, rhythmic: a sound of water and silence, tirelessly alternating, constant, the sound of water and silence, like a game, but a giant's game.

At some moments the giant seemed to want to play with them both. "Look, Tricia, it looks as if the sea is playing with the tracks we leave behind. Do you see?" They stopped. The parallel tracks of their nude feet remained traced as far as they could see, marked out in the moist sand. At some spots the sea left them intact; in others they were scarcely touched, deformed a bit; in others they were covered by a veil of water, and then receding, the tracks were almost erased, then reduced to a bare sketch, like some old and distant memories, and at last totally erased.

They continued walking. After Tricia pointed out the color of the sea, Ambrogio let his eyes skim over the surface, and each time he received a feeling of immensity he would not have known how to transform into words. He tried. A couple of times he said, "If one looks hard, how vast the sea is", but then he gave up. Everything, including the sea, was at that moment for him only a background against which Tricia moved, walking at his side, lively and charming in her striped white and blue outfit, and with her hat perched on her golden head.

His eyes felt more attracted by her than by the sea; although he was overcome, he did not keep looking at her. *I'm a man, and I must know how to master myself.* The vice rector's teachings and, even more, those of his parents had taken root in him. (They would stay with him for the rest of his life.)

Tricia was going along in a carefree manner. She was eighteen, a year younger than Ambrogio, but at that age, being a woman, she was more of an adult than he, though equally inexperienced.

The river mouth of the Rubicon made itself apparent after almost three-quarters of an hour of walking, thanks precisely to the dice: cubic bulks of concrete, a meter on each side, set on both banks, to form an embankment. When the two young people were close enough to be able to distinguish them, Ambrogio pointed them out to Tricia: "Look, you see? There are the dice."

"The dice?"

"Caesar's dice, yes. You should learn from this moment on to believe in me blindly."

"But they're not dice . . . well, perhaps yes, but not for playing. Nobody could move them."

"Neither of us, no, Tricia, but you don't know about Caesar's strength."

Tricia laughed. "But those . . . those things must be at least that big", she indicated with her hands.

"More", Ambrogio said. "They seem like that to you because we are still far away, but they're a meter on each side. They're concrete dice of a cubic meter each. My classmates and I measured them, of course."

"Besides, you see? They're made of cement. Nobody could move them."

"Yes, Caesar", Ambrogio insisted. "Tricia, you've no idea of Caesar's strength."

Tricia smiled. "All right, you've won the bet: the dice are there. Just buy me that ice cream."

While they went on, Ambrogio peered harder. "What's that there?"

Tricia looked. "What did you see?"

"Those . . . things. Nothing special, but I don't remember them being there before."

"But what?"

"Those posts. Don't you see them?"

"I don't see anything."

"There, in front of the dice. And in the middle, or so it seems."

Those posts, when they came up closer, turned out to be supports for barbed wire that stretched along a part of the nearest embankment of the river.

They were at war, yes. Ambrogio suddenly remembered, and being with Tricia he felt a kind of shame at not being in the army but on vacation this way, like a little boy.

"Look, look," he said, overcoming the disagreeable sensation, "they must have set up a vigilance post or something like that."

Among the blocks surrounded by the wire a small roof of cement emerged, perhaps a casement, perhaps only a shelter. A short distance away, half hidden among the blocks, was a soldier, who had his elbows resting on one of the blocks, observing the sea with binoculars.

When Ambrogio discovered that, he pointed the soldier out to Tricia. "Yes, it's a lookout point", he said. "From there they can see submarines at sea, or airplanes."

The girl accepted the explanation as if it were coming from an expert in military matters, so much so that it induced the young man to think, albeit confusedly, *I've no reason to be ashamed: if I'm not a soldier now, I'll be one shortly, that's for certain.* He ended up by feeling comradeship toward the other soldier, the real one. "Tricia, there's one thing that surprises me: that he, instead of looking at the sea, doesn't look at you with those binoculars."

As if he had just heard Ambrogio, the soldier, repeating a gesture he had already made more than once, without them realizing it, focused his glasses on them. He was going to turn them toward the sea, but this time he continued looking at them. They were quite close. The soldier suddenly seemed to come to life and called someone.

"Now here we are! What did I say", Ambrogio said.

Along with the first soldier, two others appeared: although they could be seen just by looking, they wanted to peer at them, one after the other, with the binoculars, most certainly to enjoy the sight of Tricia. Ambrogio realized they were making comments among themselves, perhaps even vulgarities. One said something to the others, and by sketching some lines in the air with his thumb, there was no possibility of doubt, it was the figure of a woman's body.

"Look," Ambrogio said, with some irritation, to distract the girl, "do you see the sign over the barbed wire? And there are others farther on." The closest one was legible: "Military Zone. Entry Forbidden."

"I think it would be a good idea to go back now," the young man said, and added, "even if it's only to keep from becoming a spectacle for those wolves."

Meekly, Tricia turned her back on the Rubicon and began returning to Cesenatico. She paid no heed to the behavior of the three soldiers, which she had hardly noticed anyway. Ambrogio, on the other hand, was bothered (because "when something has happened, not even God can make it not to have happened") and irritated: when his turn came he would make sure he'd keep this kind of soldier in line.

Little by little, the Rubicon and the concrete blocks and the cheap barbed wire and the soldiers of the same quality were behind them. The vastness of the landscape seemed to absorb the two young people: the long wild beach, the unlimited expanse of the sea, which now looked churned up at moments by unexpected gusts of wind, which caused it to froth and whirl here and there. Gradually the serenity of the landscape once more flowed into Ambrogio.

23

At the end of their month's holidays, Tricia's family left. There were two more days before the feast of the Assumption on the fifteenth of August.

In the morning Tricia, along with Ambrogio, had been swimming interminably. They could not make up their minds to come out of the water, as if doing so might mean not only leaving the sea but also many other inexplicable things.

At lunch Ambrogio, who was observing the five members of the family from his table, was struck by the idea that he would never see them again. He was not considering dropping his friendship with Tricia, but the others, would he see them ever again? Beginning with the doctor: he had scarcely spoken to him. It could be said he scarcely knew him. With his pop eyes like those of certain fish, it seemed, if one looked closely (Ambrogio was realizing this for the first time), he was always a bit frightened. And her mother? The first time she had come down the stairs in that strange way, admiring herself like a fool, and then later she showed a great deal of common sense. Her only defect was her tongue, "verbal incontinence". And the little girls, those two puppets? Tanned, amusing, seated correctly, eating quietly: eventually they would be two pretty girls, like Tricia; not blond like her, but with chestnut brown hair and bangs. Who knew if he would see those people again, and who knew if he would really see Tricia herself again? They had arranged to see each other at the university when she went up to it too: not this autumn, but the following. More than a year away, and they were at war! Who knew where he would be in a year?

After lunch Ambrogio saw them off. He helped them load the suitcases and packages onto the coaches that would take them to the station. He had fallen into a rather depressed state of mind. Tricia realized it and looked at him fixedly for a few minutes, as if to probe further, but there was something that left her perplexed. There were the normal handshakes, exchanged farewells, promises not to forget one another, good wishes for a pleasant trip. At last the two coaches went off. Ambrogio entered the little garden of the Iris very much alone and sat down on a bench.

24

During the evening of the same day, at dinnertime, Ambrogio's cousin Manno telephoned him from Nomana. "I'm here, at home. I've been on leave since yesterday evening. The exams? They didn't go too badly. . . . Your father wants me to get some sun, store it up! Imagine . . ."

"But this has become a real obsession of his", Ambrogio could not help but comment.

"A real what? Obsession? Exactly", he answered his cousin, laughing. "Are there rooms vacant where you are? Yes? Then reserve one for me, because tomorrow I'll be there like a shot. What train should I take? They're all fine. What train did you take?"

Ambrogio told him. "I've already written it down. It will also do for me", Manno said. "I'll put Mother on." (Manno called Giulia that.) "She wants to say hello."

The next day, on the eve of the Assumption, Manno arrived punctually at Cesenatico. He was not wearing a uniform. He took no coach at the station. From the little garden of the Iris, Ambrogio saw him arrive on foot, dressed for summer, with his bag thrown over his shoulder, sweating, walking energetically.

He's already starting with his peculiar ways, Ambrogio thought in an impulse of sympathy. No doubt this idiosyncrasy had something to do with the random sarcasm from Gerardo on how easily today's youth gets tired. He went out to meet his cousin and shook his hand. His cousin, whose right hand was holding the suitcase over his shoulder, put out his left hand. They looked each other in the eyes happily. Taller than Ambrogio, thin, with blue eyes and fair hair (a Titian blond, the women of the family said, explaining that "his mother was from Veneto, from Vicenza"), Manno, an architecture student, did not resemble his cousin, not even in his character, which was so extroverted.

"And they say", he said, shaking his head, "that military life is uncomfortable . . ."

"Why didn't you take a cab?" Ambrogio asked him.

"Because there was a real mob in front."

"Of course, at this time of year . . ."

"I would have had to line up and wait my turn. Imagine, as if I haven't done enough standing in line for mess and everything else."

"You'll have to give me a detailed rundown of military life."

"All right. You'll see how wonderful it is."

"Give me the case."

"No, why?"

Ambrogio took it off his back, and they went into the little garden together. Manno, despite the sweat, at first glance presented a more elegant aspect than his cousin.

"How long do you plan on staying?" Ambrogio asked him.

"About two weeks. . . . Well, until you leave. I have a month's leave, and I wanted to be with all of you for the last two weeks of it because I've no idea where they'll send me. Besides, yesterday Don Mario put the idea in my head of giving classes to the children of the Oratory, and I wouldn't want to disappoint him, poor man."

Ambrogio was surprised by the un-Lombard expressions. "You're turning into a polyglot", he murmured.

25

At the end of August the two young men returned together to Nomana, where Ambrogio resumed his old life: the mornings in the factory and the afternoons in reading and bicycling.

One day he decided to visit a classmate who lived in Brianza and like himself was going to enroll in the Catholic university at Milan. His friend was Michele Tintori, from Nova, only son of an invalid from the last war. Tintori was an interesting type whom Ambrogio had known from grade school and who was set on becoming a writer, no less.

While he cycled in the late afternoon toward Nova, Ambrogio pondered the very original personality of his classmate. There was no doubt that his inclination to art came from his father, who boasted no great cultural background (a craftsman in marble, he had perhaps gone through the fifth grade of elementary school) but had sculpted some dramatic bas-reliefs, now scattered among several churches of the region. Other classmates, too, Ambrogio recalled, were intent on becoming writers or perhaps poets: some of their poems occasionally appeared in the school magazine. (*But why are they all so hermetic?*) The infamous school magazine! Ambrogio smiled. It was only *obtorto collo*, and because of a complete lack of any better magazine, that the future poets decided to publish their work right next to the rector's exhortations and the chronicles of school life. *I wouldn't bet a dime on any of them; on the other hand, Michele Tintori . . .* He was fashioned out of special stuff. It is true that he, too, had published more than one poem in the bulletin, but that was when he was in the lower school, not in junior high or high school, like the others. Ambrogio remembered it well: Tintori had started to write poetry in the third or fourth grade of the lower school. He obviously had no knowledge of meter then, and his work was not authentic verse but infantile compositions in rhyme, as Tintori himself had said later. Then, suddenly, he had had the intuition (*In the end, therein lies the power: in intuition.*) that he was not on the right path. And even though a child he resolved to stop writing poems, even those that the school paper (not so disdainful then) would have published. Ambrogio remembered the time, later on, at the beginning of the liceo, when a text of Homer was distributed to be translated. Up until then Tintori probably did not know of Homer's existence—like the other students—but he had scarcely looked at one of the pages before he became so entranced that he never stopped reading him. It was incredible how fascinated Tintori had become by that poetry. Ambrogio went on recalling those past events while he energetically cycled amid the stubble of the countryside, turned blue with the last of the cornflowers

69

between Seregno and Desio: *How often I've seen him rush through the rest of his homework in order to get to his Homer!* Young as he was, Tintori experienced that exhilarating passion with happiness painted on his face and—something unusual in their circle—would become irritated at having to leave the book when the bell rang for recess. *Later, half way into liceo, he began to write novels.* Ambrogio smiled. "The novels", as his classmates called them, were actually fantastic stories, usually situated in the epoch they were studying in history class. During these classes, while the professor spoke, Michele Tintori's fantasy took off: every episode, every fact, even the pictures that illustrated the texts, including the unusual names on the geography maps, were suggestions for his imagination: with those as points of departure he invented passionate tales. He had begun to write out these fantastic tales in tiny handwriting at the back of his notebooks. Study time was insufficient for him, and so he began to write during class time. The outcome of that was that one professor or another would catch him at it and confiscate his "novel".

As happened one day with Professor Zaròli: "Why don't you pay attention, Tintori? What are you writing? Let me see." He handed over the pages of his notebook: "Phoenicians? What do the Phoenicians have to do with anything? We're studying the Romans now! What are you saying, that a Phoenician ship in the Atlantic is attacked by . . . indigenous canoes? What foolishness is this?"

Tintori, only slightly mortified, tried to elude explanations: "Forgive me, I beg you to forgive me."

"But what are you writing here?"

"My pen ran away with me and . . ."

"And what?"

"I don't know."

The entire class, calm until then, suddenly burst out, "A historical novel!" "The math teacher took one away, too." "It's the third they've taken from him." "The first was a story of the ancient Greeks who explored the Caucasus." "Yes, with bronze weapons and a line of mules, like Xenophon's hupozughia, and . . ."

"So you're in love with mules, eh?" Professor Zaròli said sarcastically. "Answer me."

Tintori decided to avoid explanations no longer, and he said, "Yes, mules and ships and . . . everything that exists." That, more or less, was the response. What Ambrogio remembered was that the word *mules*, the word *ships*, on that occasion, in the mouth of his classmate took on a kind of strange enchantment.

After having shown his disapproval with the severest look he could muster, the teacher continued his explanation. The novelist got his novel back at the end of the course, when the pocketknives, the whistles, the table tennis balls, and other strange objects sequestered during class were returned.

How many memories it seemed to Ambrogio that he possessed already at the age of nineteen!

26

The first signs of Nova were coming into view, the green, straight streets, natural to the plains (Nova is situated on the extreme southern side of Brianza). And here the door leading to the courtyard of his friend's house; in front of the invalid's home there was a space surrounded by a wall, behind which bamboo was planted. Ambrogio knew the place well, as he had come several times; he got off his bicycle, and while he opened the door, he felt a sense of anticipation. He would talk with these people—father and son—in whose words, on other occasions, he had found important reasons for reflection, luminous points that later had served him as orientation.

He found the small courtyard partially flooded with soapy water, which meant he had to get on his bicycle again in order not to fill his shoes with mud.

"Welcome, Riva! The maid converted this into a lake", Tintori explained, noticing his friend's maneuver. He had gotten up out of a lounge chair that was in the shade of the bamboo. "She just finished throwing out the wash water. What do you expect? She's a squanderer." With a book in his hand he stepped toward his visitor. "Come along, save yourself and get on solid ground." At last he shook his hand. "Hi. I'm happy you've come to see me."

"Hello, Tintori. Could you tell me what you're doing here, so calm and collected, while, as Zaròli would say, Hannibal is at the gates?" Ambrogio responded.

The other frowned. "I am afraid that we are the Hannibals waiting at someone else's gate", he murmured. He was somewhat taller than Ambrogio, with black eyes and hair.

"Your father, how is he taking it?" Ambrogio asked. Tintori shook his head. "Try not to talk about the war in front of him", he warned in a low voice. "It's taken a lot to calm him down."

Ambrogio squeezed his friend's wrist, as if to seal an agreement. "Good you warned me."

"Should we go in the house, or would you prefer staying out here, *patulàe sub tégmine bàmbui?*" he asked.

"'*Bàmbui*'? It's the genitive of 'bamboo', isn't it?" Tintori explained.

"Then it's *bàmbui*", Ambrogio responded. "I'm happy under the *bàmbui*." They looked badly cared for, like the shabby wicker seats in the shade, and the small courtyard, like the house itself, which had an air of an aristocratic mansion transformed into a village dwelling. *Besides the poverty, you can see the lack of a woman's touch here,* Ambrogio thought, rather unoriginally. He remembered that the wife of the invalid—a modest nurse—had died giving birth to Michele. "Wait a minute. Let me put the bicycle away first."

Followed by his classmate, Ambrogio went to leave the bicycle under a small portico, as on previous occasions, where two bas-reliefs had been placed with hooks on one of the walls: the only ones left to the marble worker from the time when he could work.

This time, too—if only out of courtesy—the young man stopped a moment to study them. They were bursting with dramatic figures, in great relief, showing the struggle of Archangel Michael against Lucifer. (It was the favorite subject of this singular sculptor. The other was Christ on the road to Calvary.)

"I don't dare make any comment, but, as you know, I like them", Ambrogio said out of courtesy. "My cousin, Manno, who is in architecture, also likes them, and he understands more about them."

His friend agreed. "I remember well what Manno said when he came here. That time, unlike today, you did risk commenting on these sculptures."

"Heavens, I shouldn't have dared", Ambrogio joked. "I was too young."

But Tintori wasn't joking. "It was a couple of years ago. You classified them as *naive* sculpture, do you remember?"

"If you say so . . ."

"Manno corrected you. He said, 'Would you call the work of the medieval maestros of Como naive? No, because even if they are ingenuous, objectively they are quite different from what today is understood as naive. To my way of thinking, these sculptures derive directly from the same cultural source that produced the works of the masters of Como, because they are, like those, a spontaneous manifestation of our people, of their inner world, and without any external influences.' This", Tintori concluded, while he crossed the small courtyard, "was, for me, one of those commentaries that left a mark, and that's why I remember it almost word for word. In a certain way it opened my eyes to my father's art." (He was about to add, "And on mine", insofar as for him, as for the sculptors and architects of Como, it was normal that art should be transmitted from father to son, but he preferred letting the matter drop.)

They sat down together next to the bamboo, at whose base were lilies of the valley, small and humble, like grass. ("My mother planted them", Tintori had told Ambrogio on another occasion, and, though no one looked after them, every year they came up, tenaciously, despite their fragility, like certain loving memories that, even if we neglect them, keep popping up in our mind.)

"And where's your cousin now?" Tintori asked. "Is he still in Pesaro?"

"No, he's in Nomana these days, on leave, waiting to receive his assignment as a second lieutenant. He has to be back on the fourteenth of September. I was with him for two weeks at the seaside, in Cesenatico."

"He's a great fellow, and there aren't many like him. I'd like to hear from him about life in the army."

"Yes, he is interesting. You should have heard the vice rector's comments. Now Manno's at home. If you like you could come up one day. My brothers and sisters who have just come back from their holidays are all there, too."

Tintori had already been to Nomana more than once. He knew the whole family, more or less.

"One of these days? No, I'm going through one of my idle phases", he answered.

"In any case, the invitation stands." The two young men smiled cordially. "Tell me," Ambrogio intervened, "on the way here, I was wondering if you've written any more novels."

"What novels?"

"What do you mean 'what novels'? Like the ones you were writing at school. Don't you remember, Professor Zaròli took one away from you?"

"Ah, when we were still in school. What in the devil are you dragging those old rags out for? No", Tintori answered, and in dialect he quoted "Pumpkins and Melons in Their Time and Seasons". "I've written nothing since then."

Ambrogio looked at him quizzically.

"Do you want to know why? How can someone write, if, first of all, he has no experience of reality, of life? We're nineteen now. It's too soon to write."

This is another of Tintori's characteristics, Ambrogio was thinking. His vision of the limits of youthfulness, a vision typical of the people from Comasco, which very few boys at our school shared. Despite his arrogant impulses, he never wanted to get ahead of his age. Quite the reverse, if anything.

27

Tintori's father came out of the house in his wheelchair, pushed by a soldier from the Health Division whom Ambrogio had seen before.

Ambrogio stood up as a sign of respect. The invalid smiled and greeted him with a wave and motioned his guide over to where they were. Ambrogio again noticed how uneasily he moved his head. It was as if his body—a flaccid body—was held up on the spot where his spinal cord was broken. The son asked solicitously, "Are you going for your outing in the village, Papa?"

"Yes, but first I want to greet your friend." He was speaking in the local dialect and shook Ambrogio's hand. "I'm delighted you've come to see Michele, my Archangel Michael." He paused while observing the visitor with pleasure. "I won't ask about the results of your exams, as I know you were all promoted in May without them."

"Yes, but while it seemed an enormous piece of luck then," Ambrogio said, "now," and he suddenly lowered his voice, "since the war's started . . ." (*What a gaffe, heavens*, he thought to himself, *I've said exactly what I was not supposed to say.*)

"Well . . . it's still a piece of luck," Michele said naturally, "since last year's students had to kill themselves with exams and now they're in the same spot we're in because of the war."

Ambrogio smiled in agreement. "That's true."

"Besides, for me," Michele continued, "the most important thing is that next year I won't be a burden on him", indicating his father, "with all my school bills. Our school was very expensive, one of the most expensive in Milan. University will cost a great deal, but far less."

The soldier who accompanied the father, a good lad with glasses, timid looking, who had been seated on one of the wicker seats, half laughed, as if to show he was taking part in the conversation.

The invalid looked at him and then at his son, practically without moving his head. "It was expensive, yes, but it was also one of the most secure." He looked at Ambrogio, "Isn't that so?"

The young man agreed vaguely, uncertain what he meant by the word *secure* in dialect. "With teachers like ours, who write—at least some of them—texts that are then used in other schools (for instance, Nangeroni, whose geography text half of Italy uses as a text, and Mazza, and Consonni), so with teachers like that a school necessarily has to be expensive."

The invalid said neither yes or no.

"We've had instruction that couldn't be bettered", Ambrogio concluded.

There was a pause; the invalid remained silent.

"That's not the reason", the Tintori son then explained. "I don't know if I ever told you, but that's not why my father had me study ten years at a school that cost two-thirds of his monthly pension. It's because he considered it the most secure school from the moral point of view."

"Of course," the invalid confirmed, "exactly."

Ambrogio, as if he had just made a discovery, said, "The truth is that I'd never thought about that, but I suppose my father must have thought the same." He winked at his classmate.

The invalid saw him. "You're too young", he said condescendingly. "You joke about that because you don't realize what it means for a father to risk losing his own son. And that he may be lost to God our Lord also, because of all the mistaken ideas rampant in the world today."

"But, Papa, I'm no longer a little boy", Michele protested. "I can defend myself, can't I? You know that as far as my turn of mind is concerned, I'm more of a traditional Catholic than you."

"Now you're solid because you have had an adequate upbringing", his father said. "And I'll always thank God for that. But when you were a little boy?"

"With all those little girls around . . .", the soldier suddenly blurted out, who had more or less understood what was going on.

"Well, enough of that", Michele snorted.

There was a pause. "You are two fine young men", the invalid said, by way of conclusion. And to the soldier, "All right, Piero, let's have our stroll."

After standing up again and shaking hands, Ambrogio looked at him go over the muddy courtyard as if crucified on his wheelchair.

"You've known him this way from the time you were born, haven't you?"

Tintori nodded. "I wouldn't trade my father for any father in the world."

"In school they taught us the sense of pain, its role in the economy of salvation of all men, et cetera, but to experience it, I don't know . . .", Ambrogio said.

Tintori continued, nodding, "These explanations sanctify the experience of pain." And lowering his voice a bit, "They are not human reasons. In school they simply transmitted to us what Christ taught before he was yielded up to his torturers, who nailed him on the Cross. My father gives a hand to Christ", and unexpectedly his eyes filled with tears. "He continues the Passion of Christ, and he is conscious of it."

After having uttered these words, he calmed down and changed the subject. They continued talking for an hour, seated in the shade of the bamboo, and a little later, while planning their future university life, they went back to joking a great deal, as is only natural with two young people.

28

In the course of the two weeks that Manno spent in Nomana before going back to the army, he devoted himself—as he had promised Don Mario—on some afternoons to the children of the Oratory.

He took up his art classes again at the point he had left off. "Art, if it's authentic, brings us to God." (The reader should not be surprised at finding another young person impassioned by God immediately after meeting Michele Tintori, since we are in Brianza, after all, the Brianza of those days.) "This, as I repeated any number of times to you before I left, is the conviction that is fundamental to all our explanations; you know that."

The boys seated in front of him in the straw-bottomed chairs of the Oratory listened attentively. They knew that, unlike his cousins Ambrogio and Fortunato, Manno was not going to be an industrialist. (Besides he did not have the looks of one, at least of one from Brianza, who, as already mentioned, almost always had working-class origins: Manno was of quite a different type, more refined and self-possessed.) Still, he had to have strong reasons, the boys thought, for rejecting the opportunity life offered him.

"Carlino, let's see", the young man asked. "Why is it I say and repeat that art takes us to God? Do you remember, or don't you? Or perhaps it seems to you that I'm saying this because we're in the Oratory now?"

The one questioned, standing up, was having trouble answering Manno correctly. He said, "Because in art, it is the particular, no, no, I mean the universal. I don't remember exactly."

The other boys laughed, but in moderation. They all had the same difficulty in remembering the abstract concepts analyzed for them so patiently by Manno, the second-year architecture student.

"Art", the young man said, "is the universal in the particular. This is what you meant to say and what we've already said so many times." (On repeating this ancient definition, which guided artists for centuries when Italy was truly outstanding in art, Manno felt not the slightest attraction toward the new aesthetics, all of them, more or less, in opposition to one another, and whose examples fill textbooks and specialist magazines these days.) "But what does this mean in ordinary words, this phrase. Try to explain it in your own words."

"It means that art is . . . is a kind of . . ." Carlino Valli, seventeen years of age and an apprentice gardener, tried to remember.

"Well, I see we need to have a general review. Try to pay attention, because these things will be useful to all of you, as much to those of you who become workers, to enrich your mind, as well as to those, above all, who will have to carve wood or work iron, or those who go into industrial design, the kind of work in which we of Brianza have always distinguished ourselves. So much so that our school here in Nomana, though small and only for night classes, every year manages to win a prize in one or another provincial competition, and even in national ones, like your brother, Umberto, isn't that so, Giacinto? who three years ago was the national design winner."

"Now Umberto is in Udine, a soldier", Giacinto said, pleased.

"I know", Manno answered.

"Giacinto, don't interrupt", Don Mario intervened. "Your brother being in Udine or anywhere else has nothing to do with what we are talking about." The young priest—his hair cut short, baby faced, wearing wire-rimmed glasses—always attended the classes with the boys. "I also want to learn", he declared.

In his absence, the smaller boys, who were not permitted to attend Manno's classes, remained in the courtyard without anyone in attendance, of which they sometimes took advantage. They went out of the gate, for instance, to throw stones at the street signs or at some poor stray dog wandering the outskirts in search of food. The Italians—as this war was also going to prove—had no lack of love for their neighbor, but they took no pity on animals, and the residents of Nomana, especially the children, were no exception to the rule.

One afternoon some of the brats who were at the door of the Oratory ("Today there's a lecture for the grownups, and Don Mario won't know if we take off") discovered a stray dog. "Look, eh, look!" one of them screamed. "It's the tavernkeeper's dog, the one he doesn't want any more."

"He doesn't want it, no, because he has a new dog now."

"We can do what we want with it."

"Hey, you, Fido," one of the boys called to it as he approached, "come on here, Fido, poor dog", and taking out his handkerchief from his pocket, all bunched up, so the little animal could only see a patch of white, he held it toward him as if it were a piece of bread. "Come on, Fido, take it."

The little animal, weakened by a terrible hunger, skinny, with a paw so badly injured that it didn't put that paw to the ground when it walked, stopped and lifted its muzzle to sniff, about twelve meters from the boys.

"Come on, Fido, take it."

The dog showed its obvious fear (it was afraid of everything), even if hunger drove it to that simulacrum of bread. It was a mongrel, small, of a nondescript color. From one day to the next its owner had denied it shelter and food, hitting out at its muzzle with the door, saying, "Get out of here, I don't want to see you any more. Out." As the little animal had not strayed from the house for days, looking for a chance to get back in, the man, who did not have sufficient spirit to kill it, had beaten it hard until it took off whining. "Now", and he swore, "you'll have understood, once and for all." Despite this, the dog had not decided to go off completely. Where could it go? For countless generations animals of its kind have not learned to acquire food by themselves because of their wish to receive sustenance from man, to whom they give, in exchange, companionship, pleasure, and total devotion. Howling with hunger, especially at night, the dog would start to tremble, and one night, trembling as it was, it dragged itself onto the porch where its plate had usually been placed in former days, and the owner—alerted by the barking of the new dog—went to it furiously and kicked it, which broke one of its paws irremediably. From then on the dog wandered through Nomana and its outskirts, whining continually over the painful paw and avoiding the owner's house as if terrified. It poked through the garbage, and occasionally someone would throw it a piece of bread, but if the animal tried staying in some yard or other, it was thrown out: "Still there? Here no, not here, out! Get out, you disgusting brute!" It was nothing but skin and bones, literally, and that was its condition when the boys of the Oratory called it over pretending to give it something to eat. With its imploring eyes and tail between its legs, it let them come close to it, and they grabbed the animal.

"Now I've got you, now I've got you!" ("*El gh'è! El gh'è!*") The one who had gone toward it with the squeezed-up handkerchief in his fist screamed and grabbed it by the nape of its neck, saying, "Now I've got you."

"Careful, don't let it get away."

"Careful, yes, be careful."

The children surrounded it. "Don't get bitten."

"Do you think this ugly cur could bite?"

They were happy. "And now what should we do with it?"

"A tin can. Come, let's tie a tin can to its tail."

"Yeah, a tin can."

"Great! Come on!"

No sooner said than done. The string they needed was already in one of their pockets, and that was pulled out. The tin can had to be found, but none of the boys wanted to be out of sight of their prisoner. "Look how it's trembling."

"Disgusting piece of sh——."

"Back there are cans. Come on, Gino, you go get one."

Gino did not want to go, and they ended up all going together with the little dog, whose neck had been tied round with the string like a collar.

Sure enough, there were some rusty cans on the ground. They picked one out and tied it to the animal's tail. They let it go, pushing it away: "Get out of here. Go on, you filthy thing. Hurry up."

"Get out, hurry up."

The dog tried to go off and flee immediately, as the can bounced on the stony ground and knocked against its back legs. The poor dog turned a second to see what its new torture was. It saw the children running behind shouting, and then it also took off at a run, while the can bounced about making noise and hit against the little injured paw more and more with the cutting edge of the lid, and now it was forced to rest the paw on the ground. The little animal began to howl with pain, it ran and howled, and the boys behind were cheering: they could not have had better fun.

Along the street of the Oratory, from the opposite direction, came Aristide del Ghemio, a fifty-year-old mentally retarded man, with a flushed complexion and with face and neck characteristically deformed by his condition, which was so pronounced—especially when he was excited—that he could only talk in jerks.

He had also been the butt at times—if adults were not present—of the jokes and mockeries of the gang of boys, and he realized that they were tormenting the dog. He went instinctively to its aid by opening his arms wide to block their path. At the same time he bleated out some convulsive shouts of disapproval. The dog passed by him, and as soon as it entered the piazza its whining and the rattle of the tin can could no longer be heard.

The children stopped, looking at Aristide, first with fear and then with growing vexation. The most daring, without getting too close, began to insult him, and in a moment they were all jeering at him.

"Aristide can't catch anyone!" screamed the one who had captured the dog, and picking up a stone, aimed it and threw it.

"Whoever tries to get away is a coward!" another shouted.

Since against a wall there was some rubble, they began to pick up junk and throw it. Aristide—struck even in his face—did not dare to move. Incapable as he was of pronouncing complete words, he moaned with his blurred pronunciation and waved his arms awkwardly while the boys shouted him down. They had found new fun.

From the door of the Oratory Don Mario came out running at full speed, followed by the others. "What are you all doing? How shameful!" he shouted. The boys, it seemed, did not want to leave off from their undertaking, but the older ones who had come out with Don Mario grabbed them by the napes of their necks and let loose a slap or two. Some of the smaller boys began to whine.

"Bad boys! Shame on you!" Don Mario said. He seemed about to cry. "Take them all to the billiard room, where I'll be in a while."

The priest went up to Aristide, who, pressed to the wall, did not calm down. Don Mario took out his handkerchief and cleaned off some of the spots caused by the rubble and began to talk to Aristide with affection and pity. At last, taking first one of his hands and then his forearm, he persuaded him to let him take him to his house, which was on the same street.

Then a reprimand to the naughty boys followed in the billiard room (they were all, more or less, in tears caused by the strong ear pullings that the older boys had delivered), and after that another solemn reprimand to all the boys, without exception, of the Oratory. That afternoon the class lecture—interrupted no sooner than it had begun—did not take place. "All of you go home and try and realize what happened", Don Mario said. "If you don't, then the Oratory is useless, and so am I."

Manno decided it would be a good idea to accompany the priest to his home, as he could not calm down. "Did you see what they did? Did you see the evil of it?"

"Calm down, Don Mario", Manno said. "Calm down. They're little boys who haven't had time to be educated, molded."

"Yes. That age," said the priest pausing and looking at the young man with his childlike eyes behind his glasses, "and also the age immediately preceding this one, are perhaps the worst ages. It's when they discover sexuality and . . . so many sins, how filthy, if you only knew."

"But afterward, later on, you see it yourself, they straighten out. Try not to be too pessimistic. Is it a fact or not that the greater part of the Nomana boys, not to mention the girls, come to marriage as virgins? Does that seem a small conquest? You know how things are in other places."

"Yes, later on we manage to educate them quite well, almost all of them. But how tiring it is! How much praying must be done!"

They continued walking. The priest stopped again. "Why must it be like this? Why are they so difficult when they are young?"

"It's obvious that children aren't born 'naturally good'. This is another fact proving it."

"This is a time of life", the priest said, "in which the fate of a soul is sometimes decided."

They went back to walking. They did not speak of the dog, which they had heard about. (Should we update the facts? Thirty years later, under the secular influence of television and new ideas, the Nomana boys would no longer be that way: they would torment animals less, and they no longer tormented idiots in public, surely two advances, no doubt about it. But they would begin—something that had never occurred in the history of the town—to hate certain social groups, and also none of them, or almost none, would be virgin at marriage. So limited is human existence; it gains on the one hand and loses on the other. There seems no way out of this. In a way one is reminded of the pretty little birdhouses for the starlings set out by the tenderhearted butchers in the Auschwitz barracks.)

When they reached Don Mario's house and the priest was about to open the door, he suddenly remembered: "The parents of Aristide del Ghemio! I haven't gone to explain, to say how sorry I am. I was only thinking of scolding the boys, and . . . I must go immediately. Goodbye, Manno, we'll see each other at your next class, Tuesday."

Manno took his leave and watched Don Mario go off into the first fall of evening's darkness. He went off quickly, as if lost in his soutane, which made him seem more fragile.

"What a good person!" he murmured.

29

Later on, in the middle of September, Manno left for his new assignment, Piacenza. His cousins and uncle and aunt, who took the place of parents, accompanied him to the train.

Tall and blond, with his new second lieutenant's uniform on, his belt and boots, Manno, it has to be said, cut a handsome figure. But above all it was evident that Manno was going to be a real officer.

On the slow return home, the conversation centered on the war, while the younger ones listened attentively. To tell the truth Italian military operation during those three months had been slight. The humiliating combats against France, already brought to its knees by the Germans, had lasted only a couple of weeks, and confused voices had even circulated about this—that our troops had managed only to make further advances in small, limited sectors. The army, according to these voices, had shown itself completely unprepared. In any case, an armistice had since been declared, and there was no telling. There had been, besides, an exchange of cannon fire between our navy and the English in Punta Stilo and Capo Spada, of dubious success. Rather than battles, as described in history books, where one navy overcomes and another loses, there was something similar to a rehearsal, an initiation to battle. There had been an easy Italian advance in East Africa, that yes, but no more than skirmishes in Libya. The latest, in September, was that our troops had apparently decided suddenly to take the Suez Canal but had stopped before reaching it, and for a few days the radio and newspapers had been arrogantly insulting whoever questioned the whys and wherefores of this delay. A question of that sort—they warned—constituted a signal lack of faith in our glorious armed forces. "Which means", Gerardo pointed out, "that the official journalists themselves realize the strangeness of the situation."

"Yes. I really don't understand why even before beginning the war, our leaders hadn't at least anticipated the occupation of Malta and the Suez Canal, which, it seems, were very slightly defended," Ambrogio said, "as Tintori told me a few days ago. And heavens, if they had occupied Gibraltar, it would have borne fruit to the former Spanish effort. Do you realize it would have sufficed to throw the English out of the Mediterranean? No naval battles would have been necessary then."

"They're the questions that even the Fascists themselves pose, my friend Mazzotti from Milan told me", Fortunato said. "Not even his father, who's a Fascist leader, can explain this inertia. And we're retreating without having really used the air force we took to Belgium to bomb England."

"For me the strangest thing is that all, or almost all, the factories keep working at only just above their normal pace", Gerardo said. "I mean that industry has not been subjected to any great effort, and this signifies we've gone into war without being prepared, and we continue the same way. No civil affair would have been carried out in a similar fashion."

Talking this way, surprised by these facts, they had walked down the large promenade shaded by oaks (the only promenade of the town), which went from the station to the Nomana piazza. Once there, Giulia suggested going into the church for a moment, "To pray for our Manno, so that the Lord will protect him." Giulia had not participated in the conversation because, after her nephew's departure, she could not keep from thinking of the distant and almost blurred departures of her two brothers for the previous war, from which one of them—Uncle Francesco—had not returned.

In the darkness of the church they saw Don Mario at a bench, kneeling; he was praying, quite alone, with his head between his hands. In the large niche of the high altar the crucifix was exposed and illuminated as on solemn days, without doubt at the request of parents of some local soldier who could be in serious danger (it must be—Ambrogio explained—for Roberto Beretta, from the 1920 class, who had embarked on a submarine that hadn't returned to base). Giulia then included Roberto in her prayers.

After leaving the church and separating, Gerardo and Ambrogio took their way to the factory and the others to their home.

The war kept developing along the same lines in the following weeks. They did not see, or almost did not, its consequences. Many young men were still in civilian clothes, busy with their daily tasks, as if no war were going on. They had to dim lights at night, true enough, and all the vehicles had their headlights covered and their mud guards painted white, but enemy aircraft still did not appear.

Except for one night when an isolated airplane arrived; the radio and newspapers talked as if a serious English attempt was being made to bomb Milan. The plane dropped one bomb only in the vicinity of Monza, and the only casualty was a small villa under construction, not far from the large street bordering the Royal Park.

Ambrogio thought of going on bicycle to see it. He was surprised by the insignificance of the damage: two masons, with plaster and bricks, could repair it in an hour. Then this was the extent of the damage the air force could inflict? The young man returned home perplexed.

30

This stagnant atmosphere underwent a shock at the end of October because of such a really unexpected and almost paradoxical piece of news that at first it could not be believed: the news of our aggression toward Greece.

"Greece? Why Greece? What have we to do with Greece?"

The radio and newspapers took it upon themselves once more to channel people's minds: in the course of a few days, however, their tone changed from triumphal and enthusiastic to more cautious, and then—for those able to notice it—to almost worried.

Things on the Greek front had suddenly gone bad for us, the aggressors; those who did not back fascism were secretly happy, and some were openly saying, "Some part we've played!" "What an imbecile that Mussolini is!" "He was thinking of repeating his last year's stroll through Albania and went into battle without even the forces he needed. He's made himself ridiculous in front of the whole world. I'm overjoyed!"

It was taken for granted that the necessary forces would be immediately sent over and that the conquest, after the initial slip, would be rapid. It was out of the question that things could be any other way.

But they were: after weeks and weeks of combat it was becoming clear, irremediably so, that for us there was even the danger of losing Albania and being thrown into the sea. Despite the explanations on the radio and in the newspapers, which did not explain anything, despite their insistence on partial success, inexplicable news was filtering from the front: our troops could no longer hold out, the only ones resisting were the Alpine troops from the Julia Division, and it began to be rumored that the units that had to be sent to Albania were all the Alpine troops that were available.

Don Carlo Gnocchi, chaplain of the Tridentina Division, was on leave in Nomana during those days; he was wearing his soutane and helping out in the church. One day the Rivas saw him arrive in uniform carrying his little suitcase: "I left a little early to come by and greet you."

"But Don Carlo ... wasn't it meant to be a week from now when you had to go back to the army?"

"Yes, actually, but a telegram ordering me back immediately arrived this morning."

They had him sit down in the living room, and Francesca hurriedly called the factory for Ambrogio and her father to come home. They appeared shortly.

"What's happened, Don Carlo?"

"And how should I know?" he smiled timidly. He had a refined face with the high forehead of an intellectual.

"Are they sending you to Albania?"

"Perhaps, I don't know. If they are sending my Alpines . . ."

"But do you want to go?" Alma, the little statue, asked. They were all seated round him. The seven-year-old Rodolfo could not take his eyes off the Alpine hat, with the feather and the gilt chevrons, placed on the sofa next to the priest.

"Want to go, Almina? Go to war? But the chaplain should be where the soldiers are. Don't you think so?" Don Carlo replied.

"A fine mess those big shots have made for us", Fortunato observed. "Is it possible they're as brainless as all that?"

Don Carlo opened his hands, as if to say it was so, but in fact said nothing.

"Why do you think they've done this? I mean, why, in your opinion, do you think they've attacked Greece?" Ambrogio asked.

During peacetime Don Carlo would write for the Catholic daily newspaper; his opinions were read. Now, however, it was evident that he had no desire to verbalize them, and he did not answer.

"Why in the world do you think they've done it?" Gerardo answered instead, repeating in front of Don Carlo his own opinion, already expressed on other occasions. "Mussolini got tired of always playing second fiddle to Hitler and thought he might surprise the world by an undertaking all his own. That's all."

"Well, he's certainly taken the world by surprise", Don Carlo murmured.

Rodolfo had leaned over the Alpine hat to examine it better. The chaplain put it on him, and the boy let out a shout of satisfaction and would have gone off with it, out to the street, if his mother had not grabbed him by the arm.

"Is it true that the only forces to hold out in Albania are the Alpine troops?" Ambrogio asked. "Do you know something? Have you heard of those two companies from the Julia Division that managed, by themselves, to defend the front abandoned by an ordinary division?"

"I heard something", Don Carlo replied. "But who knows how things really happened. So many stories are rumored during wartime."

"I have the feeling that this isn't a story."

"Who knows?" the chaplain said. "In any case, it's true you can count on the Alpine troops. I know them: they're the least warlike of our soldiers, but they're not people who run away, not ever."

He was not at all eager to talk about war. In this respect he was also like his Alpine troops. He changed the subject to the time when Gerardo headed Nomana's Catholic Action group. "I was a child then, but I remember many anecdotes." Later he talked about Manno, whom he highly respected. "He's a lad who will do a lot of good. Send him my regards."

At last he stood up. "I can't stay any longer", he excused himself in front of Gerardo. "I'm really sorry to have interrupted your work in the middle of the morning."

"Don't even mention it, Don Carlo!"

The chaplain addressed Giulia last. "My mother ... I hope you'll be able to keep her company a little." He looked at her eyes. It was clear that this was what most mattered to him, the main reason for his visit.

"Rest assured", Giulia said, "and don't worry in the slightest about this. We're in this world to help one another, isn't that so? Besides, I'll be delighted to do so."

Don Carlo answered appreciatively, "Thank you."

Francesca addressed Rodolfo. "Come on, give Don Carlo back his hat."

Rodolfo paid no attention. Don Carlo took the boy by the hand. "Walk me to the gate. You'll wear it up to there."

They all accompanied him to the gate.

At the end of a week, approximately, his mother received the first letter from Albania.

The Alpine troops and other reinforcements stopped the Greek advance there. Winter came, paralyzing all action in those craggy mountains. One gets used to everything: the Italians got used to a stable front with Greece, and life continued as before.

31

In November university classes began, and Ambrogio started attending. He left from the Nomana station on the seven o'clock train, to arrive after many stops, about eight in Milan. From the Babylonian (insofar as the architectural style and movement of the people were concerned) station, it took another half hour by tram to reach the Catholic university. Every time he entered the university, he found it more lovely, situated as it was between the two large Bramante cloisters, with their elegant granite columns. When he crossed toward the Economic Science Department, he looked around with constant interest, like the provincial he was. This particular architectural complex took form in the sixteenth century as a convent. Then it became a barracks, and only in the last ten years did the Catholic Italians recover it in order to establish their university, their first university after two centuries of positivist upheavals. This undertaking was still alive in the minds of all middle-aged Catholics, also in Gerardo's mind, and he still sometimes talked about it with enthusiasm. For Ambrogio everything seemed new, even the two Renaissance cloisters, which were so distinctive that he scarcely noticed anything else, and later nothing else stayed in his mind. "Well, there's not much to say. Gemellone knew what he was doing, devil of a man", he repeated with satisfaction.

At times Ambrogio found himself personally with Gemellone (alias Father Gemelli, Franciscan friar, founder, and present rector magnificus of the Athenaeum). He really was a magnificent man, over six feet tall, with rough and ready looks. During the first weeks of the academic year the rector usually took a turn through the cloisters and corridors with an appearance of bad humor, his hands stuck in the sleeves of his habit, walking among the recent arrivals at the university. He was a professor of psychology and a famous psychologist beyond the confines of Italy and so took pride in knowing a person at first sight. For that reason he investigated among the new students, whose numbers mounted to thousands, to see if there was someone valuable for the Church or for science among them, so as to pluck him from the general run of the mill. From time to time—but not too often—he would stop and ask someone, "What's your name?" and while the other, a little nervous, would answer, he would go on, apparently taking no notice. When Ambrogio met him, thanks to the opinion his father had of this friar, he could not help but show warmth when he lifted his arm in the then obligatory Roman salute: the rector noticed the warmth and, by way of answer, deigned to show a few of his teeth.

When Ambrogio reached the corridor of his department, he did not always go straight into the classroom where his first course was to begin, attended by some two hundred to three hundred students. This was because after so many years of preuniversity school he could not believe that this freedom from total control was true, that he could, for example—without anyone saying anything—not go to class. From time to time he did not go, if only to demonstrate to himself that he could do it. In these cases, after an hour and a half traveling to reach the university, he would wander around aimlessly, up and down the corridors and cloisters, sometimes with another freshman who might have arrived late, that is, after the door of the classroom—the professor already inside—was closed.

The person who most often accompanied Ambrogio in his comings and goings (not because he habitually arrived late, but because he also liked to enjoy his recently won freedom) was his ex-schoolmate, Michele Tintori, from Nova, the future great hope for Italian literature, who had enrolled in law school.

"Why in law, I'd like to know? What in the devil got into your head?" Ambrogio asked him when Michele told him.

"Well, you see . . .", the other responded evasively, "you see . . ."

"No, I'm curious. Explain it to me. Why did you enroll in law? Wouldn't it have been more logical to have enrolled in arts and letters?"

"But arts and letters . . ." Tintori snorted. "Letters, after our classical high school education, we know a bit already, don't we? And the rest is in books, which we can 'bone up on' in the library as much as we want. Laws, rather, law, is . . . is something I don't have the vaguest idea about. Even though it's an essential component of our civilization: the contribution of Rome. Because what really did introduce man to civilization, together with Greek philosophy and art (which we've studied for years), was Roman law, even though no one or almost no one thinks about it now. Well, one of these days we'll be able to talk about it with full knowledge of the facts."

"But to study law you must have the right kind of mind. It's necessary to have a mentality . . . how is it called? Juridical, I don't know, a taste for arguments, and . . ."

"Come on, now, stop arguing yourself. Let it go", Tintori cut him short.

The fact that Tintori had enrolled in law came to mean for Ambrogio that they found themselves habitually together, since the classrooms and seminaries of the law faculty were next to those of the economic science faculty.

On their idle strolls, they often ended up wandering off, usually to the Normal School, where there were many girls.

"I don't know if Apollonio has class today or not", Tintori sometimes said when they came in. One day Ambrogio answered him, "What do you mean you don't know? I've heard you say this before. It's very easy to find out. Just glance at the bulletin board."

"Oh, of course."

"Come on, we'll go right now." Ambrogio pushed him toward the board. Professor Apollonio did not have class that day. "But he has class tomorrow, two of them, at ten and another at eleven. Try to remember."

"At ten and eleven, no?" the distracted Tintori replied. "I read an article of his on *The Man* last week. You can't imagine the insights. Perhaps there isn't another literary critic in all of Italy like him. A pity he writes in such a hermetic style. I don't like that, a pity."

"Now remember, tomorrow, at ten or at eleven. In what halls? Let me see, here it is, in Salvadori Hall, and at eleven in Sant'Agostino. Should we stay? Make a note of it."

"A note? But what will I do in his class? Well, for once . . . but only once. I'll go, if only to see him, as I never have . . ."

"You know, you're a strange duck! If he interests you . . . what else would you like to do, if not go to his class?"

"I'd like to talk to him freely. Tell him, 'There is this problem, and I see these solutions. What's your opinion?' I'd like him to teach me, but me alone. Am I explaining myself? Above all he's a writer, not just a great critic. It would be lovely to do what they did in the Middle Ages, when universities were first invented."

"The Middle Ages? But listen . . . for goodness' sake! You have a real obsession with the Middle Ages. In Nova, when I went to see you, you were talking about those master sculptors of Como and all the rest."

"Yes, of course. And why not? Do you have something against the Middle Ages? Look around you." Michele pointed through the windows. "Look at these university buildings. They were built then, more or less. Compare them

86

to the others, with what came later, with that modern one there, for example, and tell me if people knew how to build better then or now." He snorted. "There's no comparison!"

"All right, I agree with that," Ambrogio conceded, "but from medieval times to today many years have gone by."

"And what do you mean by that? Besides, all this has nothing to do with Apollonio. I only mentioned it as an example."

"You know something?" Ambrogio said. "I have the feeling that you, before going to listen to Apollonio, if you do go, what you want to do is fantasize a little in your own way, as you did with the Phoenicians in school. That's what's happening to you."

Michele paused a minute and looked at him, surprised. "Well, you may be right."

The corridors of the Education Department, the Normal School, were the domain of the girls. At that moment, however, the domain was deserted, because all of the women, without exception, were at class, behind the row of closed doors. "Taking in every word with their mouths open, like seals", Tintori suggested charitably.

These two, no. Those two men, free and unprejudiced, were not spending their time in class but were walking back and forth through the corridors, their hands in their pockets, waiting for the classroom doors to open.

At last they did when the bell rang. The female students then began to stream out in swarms, interspersed with a few pallid male students. They began to flow around the two young men who had remained motionless in the middle of the corridor like a reef and, in passing, would comment on the class just finished, arguing, approving, disapproving, sometimes gathering together, three, four, or five of them, around one of the pallid males.

"See those wretches?" Tintori said, always charitably, pointing to the pallid youths. "They've enrolled in this department because they're profoundly convinced they're poets. They would not have done it otherwise, with the prospect of a miserable salary. But how many of them really are poets? Can you imagine their bitterness when they wake up one of these years? What a disillusion. Poor fools", he concluded with a feeling of true sympathy. "And nothing can be done to open their eyes."

Ambrogio looked at Tintori out of the corner of his eye. The idea that he too might find himself in the same situation one fine day did not even cross his mind. Ambrogio began to laugh, shaking his head.

All the girls were wearing black gowns with white collars, as the rules prescribed. For the most part they were unhealthy looking from the many hours spent over their books. A few were acceptable, and only some were truly pretty. The latter seemed not to consider that aspect important and were chatting spiritedly with the ugly ones and the passable ones about semantics, romance philology, and—as Tintori added in his charitable language—

other analogous frivolities. If the two students looked at one of the girls a bit fixedly, she would then turn halfway around to observe them surreptitiously and would bring her hand to her hair, or straighten her collar or the belt of her gown. Gestures that did not go unnoticed by the two young men and which amused them.

One girl, however, had attracted their attention, and she had not stirred in the slightest. They had known her by sight for some time. She was a brunette, with a high forehead and a way of speaking proper to the people from Emilia, wearing the badge of the Women's Catholic Action on her gown. "She must be someone who attaches a high value to badges", Ambrogio had observed some days before.

Now they heard one of her girlfriends say her name, "Nilde, hey, Nilde, wait for me."

"Nilde what?" Tintori immediately asked the girlfriend. "Leonilde or, God help us, Brunilde? Or is it some other name?"

The girlfriend did not answer. Nilde turned around and hurled a look of condescension at him and, instead of answering him directly, said to her friend, "There are some people who don't just waste their own time but want to waste other people's, too."

"Eh," Ambrogio said to Tintori, "she hits out hard. Seems this Nilde knows it all."

"Nilde is a defender of good manners", Tintori answered.

His attempt at an approach was cut short after these brief phrases when a friar arrived, tall and handsome, who, unlike the other male students in arts and letters—who were all a bit reserved, even when impassioned—came out of a classroom in showy fashion. Behind him were a number of students. "Father Bertrando, Father Bertrando," they were saying, "have you written something else? Yes? Do you want to read it to us? Is it another patriotic poem?"

In their desire to catch up with the friar, the female students pushed the two outsiders up against the wall.

"Patriotic poetry?" Ambrogio asked his friend after the tumult had passed. "What do they mean? I don't suppose this friar would be writing odes to Mussolini."

"I'm afraid so", his friend answered, who now seemed to be elsewhere. "At least if it's the friar I've heard about. Father Bertrando, it must be him."

"But, a friar . . . Does he have a screw missing?"

"He likes showing off. Didn't you notice?"

He had noticed. While sweeping along the corridor the young and fatuous monk kept gesturing and looking around himself with flashing eyes, like a prophet.

"A friar writing poetry about Mussolini! I can't believe it."

"Well, see for yourself . . ."

"How stupid can he be?" Ambrogio concluded.

While they set on their way again, Tintori took a pen and paper, already with notes on it, from his pocket and scribbled something.

"What did you write? That her name is Nilde?"

"What? Nilde? No, I've written something else. Have you ever asked yourself how the problem of ugly girls, even more, ugly people, will be solved in the other world?"

"But what are you talking about?"

"Just say that we are resurrected in the other world with our own body, that's the question. Be serious, please, and help me solve this problem. I'm not joking."

Ambrogio nodded, "Well, go on."

"What is most certain is that one can't go on being ugly or, even worse, very ugly in the other world. I'm referring to someone who is saved. Because ugliness would be a reason for constant disturbance, disquiet. For all of eternity? If it were that way, paradisiacal eternity would not be joyous for him. And, if you think about it, neither would it be for those around him."

"Where is all this leading?"

"Look, when we say man is made in God's image, for me this, of course, refers not only to the spirit of man but also to his body, at least as far as the material reflects the immaterial. Do you agree?"

"What do I know about this?"

Tintori continued, "Every one of us reflects God, say, from a different perspective, each and every one from his own perspective. And so we are not all equal, and do you realize how boring that would be? It is precisely there, it seems to me, that each person's individuality is derived. I mean that each one of us is so much more himself when that special feature of God that is reflected in us is most fully restored, when we make the most progress in restoring it. Is that clear? Good. But this wasn't what I wanted to say. How can someone who is ugly here come to be handsome there and still be himself? Look, I've gone off the track. I've strayed from the subject."

"Well, no ...", Ambrogio said, who had had a small revelation while the other was talking. "May I offer my humble opinion, or do I have to listen as that brain of yours buzzes about?"

"No, no. Tell me."

"Listen, I have a cousin whom I occasionally see, and he looks very much, extraordinarily so, like his mother, even though at first sight he doesn't. If you look closely, you see they have the same eyes, the same forehead, the mouth is the same, and so on. And despite this, she is really ugly, a monster, and he, in contrast, is a handsome fellow. This verifies just what you are saying: he has succeeded in ... reproducing the same features and even perfecting that similarity, while she has not. In short, what I mean is that even having the same features it is as possible to be very good looking as it is to be very ugly."

"Ah, perhaps we've got it!" Tintori took out the paper and pen from his pocket again and wrote "Riva's cousin". "We could establish it that way", he proposed euphorically. "Here someone's looks can easily be deformed by all the miseries that get in his way right from birth, from before even, but once he gets to the other world, where these miseries no longer exist, he will reflect God without deformations: that is, he will reflect him most fully. I mean that, for example, an incorrect face here will correct itself there, according to its own model, that is, it will necessarily respond in an adequate way, while still being the same face. Yes, it seems we've got it now."

"And for those who are already handsome creatures here, how will this apply? For a beautiful actress like Alida Valli, for instance, or whoever . . . for the Apollo of Leocare? For them, for their body, I mean, not much would have to be done for perfection, I suppose, given the fact they're quite ahead of the game."

"Not much, and don't joke. Try seeing Alida as painted, for example, by Beato Angelico. She could be the model for a madonna, no? To my way of thinking she would be resurrected as in the days of her greatest beauty."

"And Nilde? In the world beyond will she have that high forehead? Or will it be reduced a bit?"

"Why? I don't think so. Her high forehead seems to be quite all right! It could be something like a kind of snapshot of God-intelligence. No, Nilde would not have to change very much, as long as she merits her little place in paradise, naturally."

32

One day—it was not long before Christmas—they both went into one of the corridors of the Department of Arts and Letters exactly at the same moment that Father Gemelli entered from the opposite side, at the back. "Here comes the Magnificent", Ambrogio warned in a soft voice.

"Yes, that's him", Tintori said. "And we're going to bump right into him."

They had time to turn around and get away, but it was not dignified, especially now that they were free citizens and not schoolboys.

"Halfway down the hall, to the left, is the library", Ambrogio suggested as a way out of the situation. "We could go in."

But even that was not dignified. "After all," Tintori said, "what does it matter to Gemellone if we waste our time or not? Besides, it could be simply because we've come late."

"It's not that", Ambrogio said. "It's because we're in the Arts and Letters area."

"And so?"

"The notice . . . Haven't you read it on the bulletin board? That about 'for reasons that do them no honor'."

"What are you talking about? 'Reasons that do them no honor'? Ah, it's true."

The notice Ambrogio was alluding to was a kind of reprimand written by the rector: "It has come to my notice that students from the Colleges of Economic Sciences and Law, for reasons that do them no honor, frequent the corridors and classrooms of the Colleges of Arts and Letters and Education . . ." They frequented these corridors and classrooms because most of the girls—as has been said—were concentrated in these colleges. From now on, the announcement proclaimed angrily, anyone caught there would be expelled from the university.

"Do you know Baget was expelled?" Ambrogio said worriedly. (He was a schoolmate, besides being the nephew of an important Church prelate.)

"Yes, I know, yesterday", Tintori answered and smilingly shook his head. "Gemellone has remained in the Middle Ages concerning these matters."

"That should make you happy."

"Why not?"

"Of course."

Meanwhile, the presence of the rector, who, with his hands tucked into the ample sleeves of his Franciscan habit, advanced with long strides over his big feet, was becoming imminent.

"Do you think he'll stop?"

"Maybe", Tintori answered, lowering his voice, in awe despite himself of that impressive presence. "On one of the first days here he asked me my name. But it seems he didn't hear me. Instead of listening to me, he turned around to shout at a poor girl who was wearing lipstick."

"Two pieces of rudeness at once", Ambrogio commented bad humoredly.

They said nothing after this, trying to go forward with an indifferent look on their faces. When they reached the rector they raised their arms in the Roman salute—which was obligatory, as we have seen.

The rector did not take his eyes off of them and looked them over from top to bottom. "Hello, Tintori", he said in a clear voice and continued forward.

They both stopped and looked at one another, surprised. "What the devil!" Tintori said softly. "What a monster he is! More than a month has gone by since I told him my name, and without paying any attention besides. How can he remember these things?"

They looked, without stirring, at the rector, who was going off with a far too jaunty air, as if conscious of having carried out one of his bravuras.

"He is a monster, yes", Ambrogio said. "But I've always liked him." He was thinking, too, and was about to say it, "If he has noticed you to this point, it well may be you're going to be someone out of the ordinary. Perhaps you'll really end up being an important writer. Who knows?" But enemy of exaggeration as he was, he instead said, "Yes, his big head's registered you, and you'll see how, sooner or later, he'll call you. You can be sure of it. To see if you are on the right path or something of that sort."

They continued walking. "It will be later", answered Michele Tintori, who truly had been very impressed by what had happened. Then, seriously, almost pensive, he added, "There's someone else whom I'd rather follow, really, like a disciple with his master, and that's . . ."

"Professor Apollonio."

"Yes."

"Have you seen him at least? Have you attended any of his classes?"

"Not yet. But soon."

The bell rang in the deserted corridor, marking the end of a class.

"Soon, you'll go soon . . . I was right."

Tintori raised no objections.

"Well, now we can take advantage of the safe conduct Gemellone has given us, and we'll finish our first term brilliantly, at least as far as our inspection of the Department of Letters is concerned."

"Finish brilliantly? Hmm. And how do you mean to do that?" Tintori asked.

"I don't know. Between the two of us, you're the one with the imagination."

"I haven't approached a girl in my life", the future great writer confessed.

The doors of the classrooms were opening one after the other. The students were beginning to come out.

"Really, I saw the great success you had that time you tried it with that girl . . . What was her name?"

"Who?"

"The one from Emilia, the girl with the high forehead who knows it all."

"Oh, Nilde. Yes. I don't know if she's Leonilde or Brunilde."

"We can ask her", Ambrogio suggested.

But Nilde was not there this time, or they did not manage to find her.

"And if we should decide to go to our classes?" the imaginative one suddenly proposed. The truth was that their senseless coming and going appealed less than usual after the greeting from the rector.

Ambrogio agreed. They both took off briskly for their respective sections. In the end they were practically running.

"Don't forget to tell me if Gemellone calls you", Ambrogio said hurriedly, at a distance from his friend, rushing into his classroom, whose door a student was about to close.

The other fellow nodded yes and began to run.

But they could not attend many more classes because immediately after Christmas holidays the GUF (that is, the organization of the university Fascists) asked for all the students of the class of '21 the "privilege" of being called to arms as ordinary soldiers. The "privilege" was granted.

PART TWO

The misty early February day on which Ambrogio was due to leave Nomana seemed to arrive before it was expected. His mother rose from the table before coffee was served, saying, "I'll pack your bag for you. Will the one with the straps be all right?"

"Sit down, Mama, take it easy. I don't leave until three."

"No, I want to, let me. The one with the straps?"

Ambrogio recalled Igino's mother and how worked up she had become just before he left. Now it was his mother's turn. His sisters, already up, stood with his mother, who looked at him as she awaited his reply, as if thinking his choice of bag would affect the success of his service in the military. Alma, the little statue, showed her usual smile, but Ambrogio knew she too was deeply moved by the moment.

He remembered the packages held together with string with which Pierello and Castagna had left, and Igino's fiber suitcase. "No, Mama, not the one with the straps. Better the small green fabric case."

"Won't it be a bit small? Well, you know best. Come on, girls."

The maid, Noemi, who had just entered with the coffee, hurriedly put the tray on the table and followed the women upstairs; at forty-five she didn't have a family of her own and tended to share in her employers' family life.

After a while Ambrogio heard light, quick movement on the stairs and watched as Noemi carried in the green case. Following her, braids bouncing on her shoulder, came Giudittina, her blue eyes flooding with tears.

"Where are you taking it?" Ambrogio continued with his coffee.

"Over there, to the saddler, to change the lock. We couldn't find the key."

"Leave it. It's not important. I won't need a key, hold it . . ."

But Noemi, with a negative motion of her head, was already through the door, followed by Giudittina.

At the usual time, the father also left the dining room to go to the factory. The room was pleasantly perfumed by a light Christmassy aroma of allspice. He was followed by Rodolfo, who said, "I'm to the woodshed to feed Pino's birds. Be back soon."

Ambrogio remained seated, the silence seemingly amplified by the continuing ticking of the grandfather clock, which seemed to impart a sense of continuity. Picking up the newspaper, he saw the usual; no definite news about the war's progress. He felt calm, perhaps slightly and agreeably excited. If it had been up to him, none of these events would have happened, and yet . . . At twenty years of age, he found that competition, even a terrible competition like this one might turn out to be, attracted him.

Not being a hypocrite, he didn't hide this from himself, nor was he at all troubled by what his mother feared above all, as she had said the night before: that in this experience he would have to mix with corrupt delinquents, both on our side and on the enemy's, something hard to avoid in war. He wondered why it should always be up to others to keep delinquents at a distance. Why did he have to leave this to someone else, perhaps not as well prepared for it as himself, or perhaps more indispensable to their families.

Having lost interest in it, he refolded the paper and went upstairs to the room he shared with Fortunato, who since early January had been at school in Domodossola. Pino, fifteen years old, was also away at school, in Milan. Methodically, as always, Ambrogio set about organizing his kit and, finding himself short of razor blades, sent Giudittina—who by this time was back—to buy a supply. Running, the young sister went off on her errand, no longer crying, even beginning to enjoy events. Back almost immediately, blades in hand and out of breath, she said, "Signore Ravasi down at the store told me to wish you luck, and to say there's no danger, as his brother-in-law is also in the war."

Everything finally ready, the green case was placed on the chair by the street door. Comfortably heated against the cold mist outside, the whole house seemed to be waiting for Ambrogio to take his leave. His older sister, Francesca, crossed the lobby, almost on tiptoe, to the telephone. "It's time to call for the car. Perhaps Celeste is at the garage; pity we forgot to advise him yesterday. Perhaps he's taken the truck out . . ."

"If Celeste isn't there, don't worry, Massimino will take me", Ambrogio smiled at her.

Giudittina piped up, "Massimino is as skinny as a rake."

"Don't talk nonsense, you." This from Alma, dispirited by the sadness of the moment.

A skidding of wheels on gravel from outside announced the arrival of the Millecento, driven by Celeste, who soon arrived at the door, wearing the peaked cap seen only on special occasions.

"Of course, Papa would have arranged for the car", Francesca said softly, as she moved away from the telephone.

Addressing them all, Ambrogio said, "Goodbye, people. Get it in your heads that I'm not going to the front and that soon, unless they send me to Bari or Palermo, I'll get a short leave, so don't worry yourselves."

He hugged his mother, then his sisters; all their eyes started tearing up. He also embraced Noemi, who had been with the family since Ambrogio was a young boy, and then lifted Giudittina up in the air, which made her all the more emotional, and she started crying out loud with apparently unstoppable tears.

"I'll have to go quickly now." With a voice broken by emotion, Ambrogio waved his arm in farewell, adding, "Goodbye to you all!" Picking up the green fabric suitcase with the new lock, he placed it on the back seat of the Millecento and sat behind the wheel. Celeste, embarrassed by the emotional goodbyes, sat in front beside him. The women of the family clustered around the door to the house, his mother forcing a smile through her tears. Finally, she placed a hand over her mouth, covering her emotion, in the same way as Igino's peasant mother had done when he left.

"Say goodbye to Rodolfo. I don't know where he's hidden himself!" shouted Ambrogio.

"He'll be with the birds. You know how he is", said Francesca, eyes starry with tears.

Alma, the lovely little statue, in control of her emotions, smiled and waved.

Ambrogio started the motor and waved, a final gesture, and the car drove off. Leaving the garden drive behind, the car crossed Nomana quickly, heading for the factory, whose main gates were open. They stopped in front of the offices, and Ambrogio stepped rapidly inside to take leave of his father.

His father was sitting at his desk, reading from a typewritten page. Other reports and documents sat in baskets or on his desktop, mixed with swatches of cloth and rolls of fabric. Standing out against all of that was an antique wooden picture frame holding a photograph of Gerardo's mother, with, at either side, her daughters-in-law, Giulia and Manno's late mother. Holding on to the long skirts of two younger women were their first children, the very young Manno, Ambrogio, and Francesca.

The thumping noise from the looms pervaded the office, making everything vibrate slightly, and in particular a picture of a crucifix that was hung on the wall, the same crucifix that was venerated at the local church in Nomana.

"Papa, I've come to say goodbye."

"Yes", said the father, glancing around at his staff. The three assistants stood, each shaking Ambrogio's hand and making some farewell remark, before leaving the room.

The father was silent, visibly affected by the occasion.

Dear Father, he's even more emotional than Mother, the young man thought.

Finally, Gerardo said, "With this step you are becoming a man. Right now you don't understand what that means, but you'll soon realize . . . also the fate of your companions can at various times depend on your behavior, your decisions; it's no laughing matter, you'll see . . ." He paused, as if to add more advice, while Ambrogio, facing him, smiled trustingly.

"Well, may God help you", said the father, blessing his son with the sign of the Cross. They shook hands, and the son said, "As soon as I can, perhaps tomorrow, I'll phone and let you know where I've been posted."

"Good, good, God bless you", added the father, as Ambrogio turned to leave.

95

While waiting, Celeste had turned the car around and opened the hood and was tinkering with the engine. Besides driving cars, Celeste was the factory's mechanic, and he loved any kind of machinery. He would look at an engine any time. Standing next to him was Luca, obviously waiting for Ambrogio, and as the youth approached the car, they closed the hood and Luca came forward and said, "I came to wish you good luck."

"Thanks." Ambrogio squeezed Luca's arm, as friends do.

"I'll be following on your heels. I'm also going. I received my notification yesterday. I have to report in at Merano on Monday. This way my brother can leave Greece and come back home."

"You're going to Merano? Oh, of course, you're *d'in somm*, you come from the heights", joked Ambrogio. He'd used the dialect to refer to the "heights", a joking way the people of Nomana had of talking about mountain people. In fact, Luca had been born and lived only three kilometers from Nomana, but just over the line into the province of Como and therefore within Alpine recruiting country.

"Alpine troops, double food rations", Celeste commented laconically.

"And also double the route marches", smiled Ambrogio.

Luca, rebellious forelock hanging over his eyes, grinned and shook Ambrogio's hand, then stepped back a couple of paces, as if to get a better view of his friend's departure.

The car went out of the gate and headed south through Nomana, passing Sansone's muddy front yard, looking cold with no flights of swallows to brighten the scene. Ambrogio thought back to what Igino, Pierello, and Castagna had said when he had accompanied them to the barracks.

On passing in front of the aristocratic villa *I dragoni*, with its front door always shut, Ambrogio did not wonder what state of mind the old Eleonora might be in at that moment; he did not even think about this woman, whose own son had left for that earlier war, just as he was leaving today, but was never to return.

He listened with interest to Celeste, who had been General Badoglio's personal driver back in '26. Earlier, when Ambrogio was little, Celeste had often recounted his experiences, even to people who didn't want to listen; but gradually he stopped talking about it. Now, his story, and certain details in particular, seemed new and interesting to Ambrogio, and Celeste couldn't get over finding him so attentive. They talked about the types of automobiles used at that time by the military staff. Also about Luca, and his brother's luck at returning from Greece, and of the size of the Alpine troops' mess tins. In this way, reminiscences flowing, they arrived at the Monza barracks.

Ambrogio got out, retrieved his case with the new lock, and, turning to Celeste, said, "Goodbye, Badoglio", turning and stepping decisively onto the footbridge over the river Lambro.

A few hours later, Ambrogio, in the company of twenty other students, again crossed the footbridge for the railroad station, on the way to Cremona and an artillery unit. He knew none of the young men in his group, but during the long wait for the train, he became acquainted with a pimply faced engineering student. They discovered that they had a mutual acquaintance, a packaging salesman from Turro who had occasionally supplied the Riva company. He was a distant relative of Ambrogio's new companion.

2

The group arrived in Cremona late at night to find the square in front of the station dotted with mounds of dirty frozen snow. Loaded with their suitcases and summarily kept in formation by a corporal, they started to pick their way between the piles of snow, all feeling far from home. On seeing the familiar sight of a still-open bar, they suggested to the corporal that they stop and have something warming. "Come on, Corporal, we'll pay the round. You're invited", several said, wanting to establish some relationship within the new military world they were about to join.

The corporal, a poorly clothed wretch who had some difficulties in speaking besides, didn't wait for a second invitation and led the group into the bar, where several of the recruits offered him drinks and cigarettes. All came from well-off families except for one boy, who was poor and looked it and who, feeling the difference between them and wanting to be part of the group, was loudest in insisting on paying the corporal's tab.

After a while the corporal, whose meager vocabulary made him difficult to understand, told them it was time to go and that they shouldn't waste their money on him as he wouldn't be with them for long and had to return to Monza the next day. Some of the customers laughed at this, while the students insisted on buying the corporal another round, as if they had not heard. Finally they finished their drinks and returned to the cold outside.

At Ambrogio's side walked the distant relative of the package manufacturer, who, although absent, had created a bond of sorts between the two recruits. In very unmilitary style, they strolled along Cremona's principal street, the via Campi, dark and deserted at that hour, until taking a turn down even darker cobbled side streets, they reached the barracks.

The corporal knocked on the gate. Inside, steps were heard, a peephole was opened; the interior looked dimly lit. The guard asked the corporal who they were, where they were from, and the corporal answered him. The guard made the corporal repeat his information twice: "Speak more clearly, damn it!" and then closed the peephole.

After a longish wait, one of the recruits asked the corporal, "Why doesn't he open?"

"Take it easy. He's gone to advise the duty officer."

Shortly, the sound of several people walking toward the gates could be heard, then the rattle of a bunch of keys, and a wicket opened, big enough to allow entry to one person. Out of this stepped the duty officer, a good-looking young man with a determined expression, wearing a blue insignia on his bandolier.

"Monza district, you said?"

"Yes, Lieutenant. Here are the orders." The corporal extended a piece of paper.

"You keep that. You have a little farther to go." The duty officer stepped out on the cobblestones, pointing. "You see that street, first on the right? Well, take that down to the end, you understand? To the end. The street ends at a large gateway. That's where you have to go."

"Ah, yes, I know, the stables", mumbled the corporal. Making him repeat what he had just said in his usual unintelligible way, the duty officer said, "Yes, I see that you know the place. That's where the stables used to be. Now, come, don't hang around here, or you'll all freeze." He acknowledged the corporal's salute, lifting a gloved hand to his cap, then turned and entered the door.

Reassembled, the group marched over the cobblestones and turned into the dark side street and up to the gateway described by the duty officer. Knocking and then banging on the door brought a reply, in the Lombard dialect, "Coming, coming, oh, good heavens, what manners!"

The doorman let them in and led them across a small yard to a large room, barely furnished. On the ground, dimly seen in the available light, were an untidy heap of mess cans, apparently unwashed, and a pile of military blankets. There he left them, saying, in dialect, that he would fetch the sergeant, "*el sergent magiur*".

3

The sergeant major, an old man with a very wrinkled face, came wearing a partially buttoned uniform. As he sat down on a stool in front of a very long table, he yawned. Holding the transfer list under the hanging lamp, he carelessly slurred the first name: "Acosio?"

"Arosio, here", replied one of the students. Wordlessly the sergeant, still yawning, signaled that the recruit pick up a mess can (one finger) and two blankets (signaled with two fingers). The student, thinking the first finger signified one action and the two fingers a second action, picked up a mess can and one blanket, always with an eye on the laconic sergeant. "Two blankets, two", mumbled the sergeant. "These recruits, oh, these recruits . . .", grumbling to himself.

Waving the recruit to one side, he ticked his name off the list and continued on down the list.

Ambrogio watched attentively, trying to assume the best, but he felt perplexed: military surroundings, at this first contact, were not making a great impression on him, but told himself not to make a hasty judgment. *I already want to judge, and I haven't seen anything yet . . . I'll only be able to draw conclusions when I've actually seen something.*

Almost immediately there entered the phlegmatic Lombard guard who had let them in, whom Ambrogio had mentally named "Good Heavens", this apparently being his preferred expression. Following behind Good Heavens came another bunch of recruits—perhaps sixty of them—who entered talking loudly. They said they were from Rome, Tuscany, Naples, Umbria, and other parts, arriving here via Piacenza.

Ambrogio, watching curiously, found it difficult to tell where they were from by their accents; he would pick up this ability during his service. The new arrivals were more confident than his own group of Lombards had been, more outgoing; only excepting a small group of youths, all seeming calm and of noble features (these were the Umbrians, although he didn't then know it). Ambrogio thought they all looked like large marble cats. This group seemed more ill at ease than the Lombards.

Finished with the Monza group, the sergeant turned to the latest arrivals and called out the name of the first on their list. The recruit, a blond youth with a pointed head, stepped forward. "I would respectfully inform you that we Tuscans haven't eaten yet this evening." And, waving at the others, "These who have come farther, haven't had a noon meal either."

Well, thought Ambrogio, surprised, *none of our group would have said something like that.* His own feeling was that it wasn't manly to complain about missing a meal; he wouldn't have done so at home. And yet one complaint might be the beginning of getting things done.

The sergeant looked at the Tuscan recruit in disbelief, then turned to Good Heavens, saying, "They're recruits. What else can you expect?"

Good Heavens started to laugh. "Didn't you see the military messes in the railway stations? They're there especially for military people to use. There are big signs. Why didn't you go in and eat?"

The blond youth with the pointed head turned to the sergeant. "It was due to the timing. When the train stopped, it wasn't a mealtime."

"So what do you want? That I should wake the cooks to prepare a meal for you?" Turning again to Good Heavens, he added, "Would you believe such dolts still existed!"

The young Tuscan looked around at the other recruits, seeking support, then launched into a series of impressive, well-practiced curses.

"Hey, you! Your name! What's your name?" in hard tones from the sergeant, who glanced down at his list, looking for the last name he had called.

The recruit, startled by the sergeant's harsh tone, stopped swearing and adopted the cringing look of a whipped cur. The upper hand having been established, the sergeant grumbled, to himself, "What crappy people they send us."

Ambrogio went through a variety of reactions to all this. First of all, he wondered why the down-at-the-heels corporal from Monza who had brought them here hadn't stopped at the Milan station to feed the group at the military mess there, as it should have been part of his duties. Probably, thought Ambrogio, the corporal had himself already eaten and didn't want to be bothered. That was why. A good punishment would persuade him to do his duty.

And then the Tuscan's blasphemy mixed with obscenities had shocked him. *How many of us here believe in God?* he had thought indignantly. *Love him as much as our father and mother? Why does this foul mouth insult him? By what right? Fine, when we're alone, if he looks like he's going to start swearing, I'll insult his mother. We'll see how he likes that.* And, threatening, *And we'll also see how it ends.* But when he saw him become a complete coward, ready to grovel, his indignation left him, replaced by disgust. *To think such an individual might become an officer!*

The sergeant major signed his pass and signaled the coward to take the mess tin and two blankets, then went on to the next recruit: the first no longer interested him. But what kind of man, Ambrogio wondered, was this sergeant major anyway? And, to begin with, what did the two ribbons mean that he was wearing on his chest? He turned to the one closest to him: "Do you know what those two ribbons mean?"

"I think one is for the African campaign in '36. I don't know about the other one."

"So, he would have been in the army since? Since '36? And maybe even earlier, since '35 or '34?"

"Maybe so, from the looks of him."

"And the other ribbon, what could it mean?" Ambrogio, intrigued, tried asking the distant relative of the manufacturer from Turro, then a lad from Monza with a crewcut who was standing next to him, but neither these nor the others knew.

"Perhaps," the distant relative said jokingly, "perhaps it means he was in the first Punic war!"

"They began to laugh. The sergeant major heard them, looked at them suspiciously, and ordered Good Heavens to hurry them up. "Take these cretins from Monza and put them to sleep in the 'grand hotel'." And as they were leaving: "You can always ask the livried waiters for soup, you pile of university incompetents!"

4

Following in Good Heavens' footsteps, the group crossed through two dark courtyards before arriving at the "grand hotel", a well-illuminated old stable, in which rows of recruits were already sleeping on clumps of straw. Despite being tired by the events and emotions of the long day, Ambrogio still felt a faint, pleasing sensation of adventurousness.

"Here, and here," said Good Heavens, pointing kindly to vacant spots on the ground, "there's a lot of straw. See the bales of it over there. There's all you want."

The twenty recruits busied themselves with separating straw from the bales for their bedding, with the exception of one, who asked, "Do all the soldiers in Cremona sleep on straw?"

"No, in the regular barracks, the soldiers use folding cots."

"Well?" asked the recruit.

"Oh, good heavens, don't you see you've arrived at a time when nobody expected you? Don't worry, in a few days you'll also have a bed."

"Oh, great, a few days."

"Listen to me, boy! At least here you have a roof over your head, and the straw is clean, not a flea in sight, and here you won't suffer from the cold."

Ambrogio arranged some straw into a thick, loose mattress, put his case and overcoat against the wall to use as a pillow, and pulled the two blankets over himself. The engineering student built a bed for himself alongside Ambrogio. After a while, both rearranged more straw to cover their cases, which were too hard to use for pillows when they covered them with their coats.

Good Heavens had gone out to fetch the other batch of recruits, and the local corporal had gone with him. *I'll bet he'll get a good bed for himself,* thought Ambrogio, trying to relax and get some sleep. He could hear several of the recruits from his group talking to each other and to the earlier arrivals. At his side, the engineering student also started talking softly about his difficulties with the course at the Milan Polytechnic Institute. To Ambrogio, it sounded as if the youth was half talking to himself, convincing himself that he could rise above the present circumstances, the same as he had with his studies.

A noise from outside heralded the arrival of sixty or so other recruits, led as usual by Good Heavens. On entering and seeing the straw, the recruits' reactions varied, with some laughing, some swearing, and others, apparently for the pure love of noise, shouting out loud to one another, ignoring the recruits who were already asleep. Some of the newly arrived Tuscans threw themselves down on the straw and in their characteristically lively voices started telling each other dirty jokes. Some tried besting each other's funny remarks, giving orders to imaginary room maids of the "grand hotel", asking for meals and other items, plus imaginative personal services, all to the accompaniment of loud laughter.

Eventually they settled down to singing a Goliardic song that Ambrogio and the other Lombards had never heard before. The song's obscenity would have been, up to that point, unimaginable for them.

Ambrogio asked himself, *Why am I grumbling about the military environment when the moral climate of civilian life can turn your stomach? How could the military be wholesome when it is made up of people like this?*

He turned to his distant relative and remarked in a harsh voice, "It doesn't surprise me that the Greeks gave us a thrashing. It seems that in many of us our brains have been replaced by our genitals."

"Good thing Italy isn't composed only of boasters like these", the young man muttered indignantly.

The recruit on Ambrogio's other side, one of the late-arriving group of sixty, added to the exchange, "I agree; they're pretty foul mouthed." He spoke with what sounded like a southern accent, not familiar to Ambrogio, who asked, "Where do you come from?"

"From the Abruzzi."

"Ah, well, I've never met someone from there before."

"Well, now you have", said the southerner coolly. "I'm only sorry that I should be the most worthy example here."

Ambrogio, taken by the man's simple dignity, raised himself onto an elbow and looked at him. The face was long, with well-defined vertical lines, giving it an angular look, and brown eyes. He nodded amiably at the southerner and once more lay back, thinking, *Where have I seen another face like that? I'm sure I've seen him before.*

The late-arriving Tuscans, meanwhile, continued to shout and sing.

How disgusting, they're really revolting, he told himself, but with half a mind on where he might have seen the youth from the Abruzzi before. Suddenly, with a half giggle, he remembered. His second-year history book in the lycée had a drawing of the head of a warrior from Capestrano, which was right in the Abruzzi; this man had the same face.

Ambrogio, with a half-suppressed laugh, turned again to the other. "Eh, you, from the Abruzzi, you'll be descended from the ancient Sammites, or from the Oscans, one of those peoples?"

"No," said the man, in his quiet, solemn way, "the Sammites are from further inland, south of the Marsicans. As I live in the Chieti province, I'm more of a *Marrucino.*

"A what?" asked Ambrogio, lifting himself once more onto his elbow to look his neighbor in the face. He couldn't make out whether the Marrucino was joking or serious; certainly he wasn't laughing.

He's either joking or I just don't understand him, the Lombard said to himself. "Look," out loud, "we'll talk about it tomorrow, eh?"

"At your convenience", courteously from the Marrucino.

"What's your name?" Ambrogio asked.

"Virgilio De Lollis."

"I'm Riva."

"My pleasure", from the Marrucino with grave courtesy.

"Well, yes. All the pleasure is mine", replied Ambrogio.

5

The next day more students arrived, and again on the following day, these latter all Sicilian. This was the last group to arrive, there now being about 240 recruits living in the former horse stables, which in more recent years had been used as a warehouse.

Right away, a training program was started. It included marching, military regulations, familiarization with equipment, and personal hygiene. Between classes and after lunch, the recruits strolled the courtyards, some finding sheltered spots in which to sit down and contemplate the first struggling shoots of greenery. Later, it became known that the long recesses between classes reflected the lack of clear planning in the initial curriculum, the officers in charge not having been advised of the future employment of these recruits.

Surrounded as they all were by the symbols of an earlier age—mangers, straw, the rusting hitching rings on the walls, dry water troughs—few of the recruits, much less Ambrogio, had enough imagination to visualize the long lines of mules, horses trotting in pairs or alone, the healthy smell of hay and oats, the orderly routines of the past. Day by day, however, Ambrogio acquired frequent additions to his store of information about military life. Without changing his opinion of the foul-mouthed ways of the Tuscans (and such an opinion of Tuscans would stay with him for life), Ambrogio changed his mind about picking a fight with the blaspheming blond Tuscan with the pointed head, principally because of the way the recruit had backed down in abject fear from the sergeant's harsh words. The swearing recruit, far from being the focal point of the Tuscan group, continued to show erratic behavior toward all around him and was nicknamed "Geppetto" by his fellow Tuscans, who regarded him as unreliable and hard to get along with. Observing his fellow recruits, Ambrogio noticed that the Tuscans didn't automatically band together, segregating themselves from the youths from other regions. Rather, there seemed to be a process of tacit rivalry similar to the behavior he had noticed in school. Later in his military service, it would be a surprise for him to observe that even within the structure of the army some boys form a group, but there are others who were already friends in civilian life, such as the mountaineers. For his part, whenever he had some free time, Ambrogio spent it with the engineering student, the distant relative of the packaging manufacturer from Turro; not because they had much in common so much as from a sort of silent obeisance to their common Lombard background.

The engineering student let it be known that he strongly objected to the word *volunteer* being applied to the student recruits. "How can they call us volunteers when we were drafted?" He also objected, as did Ambrogio, at the uncertainty of their future assignments.

"The GUF would be happy to see us sent out of here as plain soldiers", said the engineering student. "But it seems that if there's one thing there's plenty of, it's plain soldiers. There's a rumor going around that the higher echelons are thinking of training us as officers, but there seem to be enough of those around, as well. I only wish I knew why they needed to call us up."

Ambrogio replied, "Well, you know, there's the fact that Italy is at war, and everybody of our class is under arms. It wouldn't be proper to stay home just because we are students."

"But then, what about the class of '20? And the classes of '19, '18, '17, and '16? Why have we of '21 been called and not those others? Do you think that's fair?" Ambrogio, unable to answer, simply spread his arms in a sign of ignorance.

Ambrogio also spent some of his time with the Marrucino, De Lollis. He enjoyed the man's serious composure, and he had detected in him a religious faith that he kept hidden, and he wondered if this was the usual thing among people from the Abruzzi. When he asked about this, De Lollis said, "In my country we are all sincerely religious, especially the common folks. There's no doubt about it." He did not add anything on that matter.

In fact, both Ambrogio and De Lollis were by nature reserved, and both youths enjoyed walking or spending time together, without talking all the time.

At the time when it was decided to issue equipment to the two "university batteries" into which the students had been divided, they were shown two 1911 vintage 75 mm cannons. These had large wheels with iron tires, and the members of each battery were forced to spend much of their time clustered round their cannon, in groups that were too large, learning its operation.

There also started a slow, piecemeal process of giving the recruits with an odd kind of stinginess their uniforms and only the most necessary pieces of equipment, with the young soldiers being taken in groups of one dozen at a time to the supply barracks every day by an instructor. In the evenings, on liberty, they saw each other on the streets of Cremona, makeshift soldiers—the city contained several different barracks. Many of these were also fresh recruits, students in uniform with their shoes still yellow, they were so new, herded together with others in business clothes that were increasingly wrinkled. One day, the engineering student brought news for the Marrucino and Ambrogio, saying, "Have you heard? There's been a dispute about our future, and it seems the higher echelons have ordered that we receive the same training given in the officer schools. The news arrived in a circular today, which says that in forty days we will take an exam, and all who pass will be promoted to corporal."

"Corporals?" from Ambrogio.

"That's what they say. I got it from a headquarters clerk."

"In that case," calmly said the Marrucino, De Lollis, "more than the victory of the higher officers, it seems to be a compromise."

"Call it what you like, the important point is that they'll be training us as officers."

And soon after, the two batteries of corporal candidates moved from the stables to the main headquarters buildings, where they were lodged, no longer on straw, but in normal rooms with cots, complete with sheets and blankets. For Ambrogio and his colleagues there started a new life, in between that of candidate officers and that of common soldiers.

6

The other soldiers looked with jaundiced eye at the students who often heard shouted epithets directed at themselves, along the lines of "So here are the ———— who were shouting, 'hurrah for war'." "Look at them, the swine." "Now that we're at war, you're happy, right?" and "Look at the *lifers*!"

This attitude didn't go down well with the students, some of whom felt quite offended. Particularly unhappy were those, the vast majority, who had not taken part in the parades and agitation for entering the war. Others, among them the engineering student, were particularly offended when they found out the meaning of the term *lifer*, used in a derogatory way to classify those who in peacetime reenlisted for another term, largely because of the lack of a job in civilian life.

"*Lifers*! Did you hear that, Riva? Lifers! Us!" said the indignant engineering student.

"Why let a little thing like that make you mad?" from Ambrogio.

"Of course I'm mad!" And he would go to great length, alone or with some colleagues, to try to convince the soldiers of their error. But among all those boys of roughly the same age—students or not—misunderstandings could not last for long, and they were dispelled by repeated declarations that the students were just draftees. Undistracted by the dispute, Ambrogio tried to gain an understanding of how the army worked.

Headquarters consisted of several buildings, all looking alike, separated by large areas. The regiment itself was not in residence, having been sent to fight in Albania. They might as well have been on another planet. Nobody had news of their doings; nobody, not even the officers, seemed to refer to or even remember them. The general objective was the formation of another regiment, which could have been done in no time, except for the shortage of trucks, truck transporters, and other material. The shortage of material was due to the inefficient pace of delivery, with everything arriving piece by piece. Once the soldiers became aware of the lack of equipment, they used a mocking marching song as their comment on the situation:

> The motorized artillery
> paraponzi-ponzi-po
> You don't see any motors
> and you get to go on foot,
> paraponzi-ponzi-ponzi
> paraponzi-ponzi-po . . .

Upon hearing it, the student recruits adopted the song as their own. Apart from the growing new regiment, there were at headquarters some one thousand recruited troops, divided into training sections. The essential day-to-day services at the camp were mainly provided by veterans—discouraged, to hear them tell it, by the periodic drafts that had continually interrupted their civilian jobs in the preceding six to seven years. Among these were Good Heavens, the older sergeant who communicated almost solely through gestures, and a few other exhausted older men whom Ambrogio remembered from his early days of sleeping in the stables. These were also now attached to headquarters, where they seemed to spend their lives wasting time and in strolling about the base, taking care to avoid bumping into any officers.

At headquarters, crowded around the two old cannons, the students also served their "equipment apprenticeship", while in other courtyards men of the alternate regiment continuously repeated the same exercises around their weapons and while the recruits of the training batteries were busy, not with true military exercises (for which they didn't have the equipment), but with endless sports. They ran without stopping in every sense, in shirtsleeves, with sweat running down and faces on fire. They gave anyone who saw them the distinct impression of being carefree, carefree like those boys who play impetuously in the courtyards of village youth clubs and with whom, without the artillery belt, flared trousers and military gaiters, they might have been momentarily confused.

Nobody seemed to be thinking about the progress of the war, and while Ambrogio trained (always, it seemed, helping push the iron-tired cannon from one place to another, often accompanied by the song of the unmotorized artillery) he asked himself if perhaps Italy's entry as a belligerent in the war wasn't based on a huge bluff, as some maintained. Where were the means? How could the war be waged without adequate equipment? Why, when the country's leaders had for years been praising war, he wondered, did they not spend as much on preparing for war as they did on highways, bridges, and schools? And why, now that the fighting had started, was there not some serious effort to make the desperately needed materiel? Even though he was only a naive student, Ambrogio worried about one of the current sayings, which held that in confronting England, they'd be facing a people not to be taken lightly.

During those months of training, Ambrogio received postcards and military letters (prestamped and made with gray paper) from his friends who had gone ahead of him into the army. There were messages from Stefano, Igino, Pierello, from his cousin Manno, and from Michele Tintori at Nova.

Michele wrote Ambrogio that he was based in Mantua, where his basic training seemed to be similar to Ambrogio's but destined to make him an infantryman, "the best outfit there is to bring you into contact with the ordinary citizen", wrote Michele, who in a later short letter said of the infantry that, although it didn't inspire enthusiasm, it did represent the country, being a cross section of all the Italian people.

At the time appointed by the circular, Ambrogio and his fellow soldiers were promoted to corporals, and, some six months after they had been drafted, and following a tough examination, they became sergeants.

7

The Greek campaign was over in April, thanks to the sweeping German attacks, which came after they had invaded, unopposed, both Romania and Bulgaria and, after twelve days of violent combat, Yugoslavia, with some help from Italy.

On the Western front, the Germans faced England from across the Channel, limiting themselves to attempting to starve the British by laying distant siege to those islands, using their submarines.

Suddenly, and unexpectedly, still in 1941, the Germans threw a major part of their armed might against the Soviet Union, and immediately Mussolini announced the formation of an Italian Expeditionary Force to take part in this campaign. From that moment, Michele Tintori entered into a state of great excitement, saying he wanted to go to Russia at any cost. He told Ambrogio of his decision in several letters, saying that he had applied to join any infantry regiment going there, and asked Ambrogio if his father could help influence the matter.

One Sunday, Ambrogio saw Michele, who had appeared in Cremona that afternoon, intending to push his application to go to Russia.

Ambrogio was delighted to see his friend, but asked him, "What happened? Why all of a sudden have you become such a warmonger? What's it all about?"

"Warmonger?" Michele had answered, surprise on his face. "Ah, you think I . . . and with my father at home in a wheelchair since the last war? No, Riva, you're wrong, although of course, once I'm there, I'll do my best, you understand. I want to go to Russia for another reason. To see it, you understand? To see how it is."

"Just to see it?" asked Ambrogio.

"Yes, to see what they've built, the Communists, before the Germans get to change everything around, hide what has been done. You understand?"

Ambrogio didn't seem to understand. "Is it because you want to write a book about it?"

"I don't know yet. The Communists have started a unique experiment, hadn't you noticed? Or let's say they have just started a movement to save man and society without using Christ or Christianity. And to take it forward, they've isolated themselves from the rest of the world. For us Christians, it's important to know what it is all really about. They say there have been millions killed, yet others say that's not true, that it's all Fascist and capitalist propaganda. The French Catholic writer Mounier, for example, fiercely defends the Russian Communists, even though he's a Christian. You understand?"

Laughing, Ambrogio replied, "Understand? Of course I understand. It's the kind of thing I'd expect of you!"

"I want to talk to the ordinary people of Russia, with workmen, farmers, everybody. It's a unique opportunity, an extraordinary time", Michele repeated, almost to himself. "I want to see it with these eyes. It's not enough to depend on hearsay."

"That's fine, but I don't think my father can be of any use; I don't see how he could help you."

They continued to stroll up and down the via Campi, as if they were back at the university, cutting a class. Tintori had to be back in his barracks by bedtime, having left without authorization, which was why he was dressed in civilian clothes.

They didn't exchange their most recent experiences; in the short time they had found together, they talked only about how to get support for Tintori's application. As neither of them had much knowledge of how to maneuver within the military machine, they both eventually agreed to consult the retired general who taught military history at the Catholic university. Tintori decided to ask for a Sunday pass in order to visit the old general. As they strolled among the other soldiers on the via Campi, on their way to the station, Ambrogio had been saluting passing officers, and on one or two occasions Tintori nearly saluted as well, forgetting he was not in uniform.

"Is Mantua as full of soldiers in the streets?" asked Ambrogio.

"Perhaps there are more than here. The pay is so poor, the only thing to do to pass the time is to stroll around the town."

Ambrogio exclaimed, "And here I haven't offered you anything yet! What kind of host am I?"

"What are you offering?" Tintori asked.

In the end, it was only a shot of cognac at the railroad station, which had to be gulped down when his train was announced.

Despite the retired general's kind interest in his case (he had warned the youth, though, not to put too much faith in whatever effort he could make), in the end the three divisions of the Expeditionary Corps left for Russia without Corporal Tintori.

Having tried to obtain the assistance of every influential person he could think of, Tintori eventually fell back on prayer, and every morning at reveille he'd stand with his soap and towel under his arm and start a prayer, which continued while he hurried to his morning wash. He would explain patiently every day his reasons for wanting to go to Russia. Speaking directly to God, he'd say, "Lord, don't deny me this important experience, I beg of you. In my life I want to serve you, and you know much better than I the importance to a modern writer of an experience like this. Please don't play a joke on me by letting me miss an opportunity such as this one. You have said, 'Knock—and it shall be opened unto you.' And so here you have me, praying myself hoarse to be let in. I hope you are listening, Lord."

In hindsight, it can be said that God heard Tintori and had every intention of giving him his wish but, showing no sign of doing so (and probably with a Godly smile), left him to his prayers.

8

In July, both Ambrogio and Tintori were promoted to sergeant and sent to officer-training school, where they were to undertake a stiff and concentrated course lasting six months, after which they would become second lieutenants. Shortly after arriving at this OTC, Ambrogio received the news that his cousin Manno was being sent to the front in Libya. In December also came the grave news that America had entered the war, which apparently made Mussolini happy, as he announced that his prediction of a "war between continents" was becoming fact. The remark left the student officers rather perplexed. Tintori learned that the candidates with the highest marks would have the right to select their assignments and started his studies with great determination, in order to join the Russian front.

The course was extremely demanding, consisting of tightly scheduled classes, fieldwork, and tests; life during this part of their training was hard on the students. Some of the candidates said the curriculum was probably a relic of medieval barbarism, which annoyed Tintori: "A typically stupid reaction in this enlightened culture!" Compulsively, he would always come forward to defend the better quality of the Middle Ages' civilization vis-à-vis modern life. (In fact, the reason he disliked criticism of the Middle Ages was because he considered it to be the direct source of his own religiousness and that of his people in Brianza and even the source of Catholic piety in general. It was only much later that he discovered the Catholicism he knew should be attributed rather to the reform of the Church—to the authentic reform, whatever one wishes to call it—carried out much later than the Middle Ages by San Carlo Borromeo and the Council of Trent, and stubbornly maintained by innumerable people, who are in general unknown because they were as humble as apostles and disciples in Christ's time.)

Although he was not endowed with great military talents, Tintori, apart from his intelligence, had a good memory and an ability to absorb military theory and the disciplinary regulations. (As a result, he finished the course among the first ten and earned the privilege of choosing his own regiment. For this he had to fill out a form in which he was required to name his first three choices, and for these Tintori listed three infantry regiments already with orders to go to the Russian front. He got his wish when he was assigned to the 81st Turin Regiment, then in Parma.)

Ambrogio, although close, did not figure among the first ten in the class and was assigned to a detachment in Casale Monferrato. Both of the new second lieutenants were given graduation leave, their first furlough since joining. They had a month off before they were expected to report to their new outfits, in February 1942. They left OTC snappily dressed as new second lieutenants— like Manno before them—in gray-green uniforms, with elegant boots and belts.

On leaving Nova when his leave was over, Tintori tried not to think of the tremendous worry he had seen in his father's eyes—since he was kept up to date on his request for an assignment to the Russian front.

9

When Tintori reached his destination, he was to begin a long wait without any news of his transfer to Russia. The war in Russia seemed to have been stabilized after the great German advances in 1941 and the subsequent retreat from Moscow in winter. There had been one enormous but isolated battle, in which the Germans had inflicted much damage to the enemy near Kharkov. The Italian divisions hadn't taken part in this action and consequently didn't need replacements.

Tintori, who had never given up his entreaties, intensified them, if only because there were at least twenty other second lieutenants at the depot who, for reasons of patriotism or love of adventure, had also asked to be sent to the Russian front. Tintori would look at the others and ask under his breath, "Why couldn't you have asked to be sent to the Riviera, or the Côte d'Azur; why not go down there and enjoy swimming in the sea, instead of being here, making problems for me?" He knew he was being illogical, but the prospect of being left out when time for transfers came along made him nervous.

Eventually he got his wish. Perhaps the CO of the detachment, an older colonel, detached and ironical in outlook, took pity on Tintori and his determination to go east; perhaps God himself decided the case. In mid-May he, along with five other officers, were advised to be ready to go eastward.

With little time available, Tintori managed to get home to tell his father of his assignment, aware of the real possibility that he would never return. From Nova, Tintori called his only other relative, a maternal aunt who lived with her husband in Monza, and told her of his orders. He also telephoned Nomana to ask Ambrogio's family to tell him his news.

Giulia, Ambrogio's mother, came to the phone. "Ambrogio will be in Nomana next Sunday, three days from now. Will you be home then?"

"Well, I hope so. I'm due back at base this evening, but if I'm not on duty or do not have to depart early, I'm planning to be here Saturday afternoon and all day Sunday."

"Well, why don't you come to see us? You'd be able to spend some time with Ambrogio."

"Come to Nomana? What a good idea; I'll get away from here, a couple of hours, maybe ... But, as I said, I can't be certain ..."

"Well, in any case, I'll get some ice cream made; I know you like it. If you can come, we'll welcome you with open arms."

So, the next Sunday, Second Lieutenant Michele Tintori was pedaling his bike across the countryside on a mid-May day. So that he could travel in shirt sleeves, he was not wearing his uniform, and as he pedaled he daydreamed about the great trip he would be making next. As he went through several small towns, he noticed the large number of young men still in the streets. *There's hardly any difference between this and peacetime,* he said to himself on each occasion, *and elsewhere, what real signs of war were there? Few, very few. I mean to ask Ambrogio if at least the factories are stepping up production.*

They were, yes, but only a little. This is what Don Gerardo briefly explained after Ambrogio, at Michele's request, posed the question: "because that's your province, your domain, Papa."

"I don't understand", said Tintori. "Why aren't the Fascists and generally the ruling class—why don't they get involved with production?" They were sitting in a family group on the cast-iron garden chairs, under a pergola, shaded by foliage.

Gerardo pursed his lips disapprovingly. "It's been said we haven't got the raw materials to work with. In the last war we were getting our supplies from America, but this time . . ."

Tintori added, "And the army gets equipped with little and infrequently, as if they were using an eyedropper. Your son will have told you. I only hope that at least at the front things will be better."

"And it's not only a question of quantity. There's also the question of quality, newer designs. At least in the artillery—did you know . . .", said Ambrogio, who turned to include his brother Fortunato, while his mother listened attentively, "that they continue to make 1911-model cannons? The 75/27 model, from 1911! Our going to war seems to have been a pure surprise to the people directly responsible for producing our armaments, that seems to be a fact."

"Let's admit their surprise, but how do you account for production continuing at snail's pace even now that we're at war?" asked Tintori.

The younger members of the family suddenly interrupted the conversation, approaching the seated adults with shouts: "We want to be here with everybody!" They had appeared from the house, carrying between them a hand-cranked ice cream machine. It was evident that their previous efforts hadn't caused the mixture to freeze. Putting the bucket on one of the iron chairs, and after a dispute about who should do so, the cranking of the handle continued, amid much talk: "It's Pino's fault if the mixture doesn't freeze", proclaimed the nine-year-old Rodolfo, for the benefit of the adults. "He won't stop lifting the lid to see if it's frozen, and it keeps melting."

The blond-headed Pino (he was even blonder than Giudittina), seventeen years old, reacted, "Shut up, you, or I'll melt you too!"

"I think", shouted Giudittina, the seven-year-old, "that the cream won't freeze because you keep on turning that handle. It needs to rest a while, at least for a moment."

"A moment, a moment; I'll moment you. Don't talk nonsense." This from Pino, sweating from the effort with the handle.

Ambrogio offered to help. "No, today you soldiers are the guests. Today you don't have to work", Pino told him.

The eighteen-year-old Fortunato, seated with the adults, indicated the ice-cream machine with his foot. "This antique must be from the nineteenth century."

Tintori laughed. "It would go well with the material the army is getting! Eh, Ambrogio?" Ambrogio also laughed, nodding his agreement.

"Two hours trying to make two kilos of ice cream. It's ridiculous. There's no reason for it", from Fortunato.

The nine-year-old Rodolfo counterattacked, "Look at the great industrialist, making judgments on work and production." Fortunato, although young, had a propensity to judge everything in terms of production. The habit at times surprised even his father.

Tintori intervened, "I feel guilty, to be the cause of all these problems."

The family reacted to this, particularly the two older girls, who had meantime been putting out soft drinks and the plates for the ice cream. "No, don't even mention it . . . you must be joking . . ." Giulia also joined in: "Don't say that! The children are joking with each other; it's normal."

"Yes, forget it, Tintori, let it be", from Ambrogio.

Noticing that their guest's glass was already half empty, Francesca, pitcher in hand, served him more, urging him, "Is it cold enough? This week the ice came late, just last night."

The other sister, fifteen-year-old Alma, known as "the little statue", who was bringing a different drink, suddenly blurted out, "I wonder if, over there in the desert, Manno has enough to drink today. Or maybe they don't even think of drinking if they're shooting at each other."

Francesca shot her a disapproving look, as if to say, "Whatever made you say that, particularly in front of Mama?"

Ambrogio stepped in to prevent an embarrassed silence. "By the way, Tintori, we've heard from Manno. He's written from Africa. We got the letter yesterday. Nothing out of the ordinary, he says."

Gerardo added, "He writes every week."

"Where is he, exactly?" asked Tintori.

"Right now, we don't know," said Ambrogio, "but a month ago he was around Bir Hacheim, just below Tobruk. We found out from a soldier who was here on leave. Maybe he's still in the same place."

Fortunato joined in, "His letters are always interesting. He has a keen, observant eye."

"He's a good boy", said Giulia, and sighed.

Francesca said, "There's also been word from Stefano. He wrote home to Nomanella, saying he's well."

Ambrogio explained to Tintori, "Stefano is a good friend of mine from the school here. He's been in Russia since January with the Third Bersaglieri."

Pino chimed in, lifting his head from the ice machine, "Hey, maybe you can meet Stefano in Russia?"

Tintori said, "Russia is big . . .", and, switching to another thought, he turned to Ambrogio. "How come you call this Stefano by his first name and with me you use my last name?"

"Why, I don't know. I suppose it's because at college we got to calling everybody by their family name, whereas in the local school we just naturally used first names, as kids."

Tintori smiled. "The bourgeois way at college and the more familiar way here?"

Ambrogio agreed. "You're right. And maybe it's time for me to start calling you Michele. What do you think?"

"I should say so."

"Of course," from Giulia, "you should have done it long ago."

"Yes, but you also must address me in the familiar."

Giulia smiled. "Yes, agreed . . . what a nice young man." There was a perfect stillness around the pergola, and facing Tintori there was a flower bed, ablaze with an arrangement of snapdragons, petunias, forget-me-nots, lilies, and zinnias. He had been glancing over at the flowers, and Alma noticed his interest. It was part of her duties to help maintain and water the plants. She moved close to Tintori and commented, her voice lowered in order not to interrupt the others, "That bed of flowers consists of annuals. The gardener raises them in the greenhouse and then transplants them out here. When I'm not at school, I help him."

Tintori looked at her and thought he'd rarely seen such beauty. She was almost too perfect to be true. He said, "It's certainly delightful, and restful to the eye."

Alma nodded her agreement, but gave no sign of saying more. "Tell me," asked Michele, also lowering his voice, "I've always wondered. These annuals, does that mean that when winter comes, they die?"

"Yes, they just last a year, the poor plants." Although she showed no outward sign, it was clear that the mention of dying plants had affected her sensibilities.

Michele said, "Well, for them one year is enough. It's the same as with butterflies and other small creatures that only last a short time. But we mustn't be sad about that. They're not aware of how short their time is, so they don't suffer or feel sad about it."

Almina sighed. She didn't seem to agree. But her beautiful face continued to keep her feelings from showing.

And yet within, underneath that marble smile, she must be sensitive, perhaps ex-traordinarily sensitive, reflected the future author. *Otherwise, at that age, she wouldn't be worrying like this about others, and plants as well.*

In the background, meantime, the cranking of the ice-cream machine continued, with the family taking turns (excluding the two soldiers, who were not allowed to help), until Giulia, her confidence in the project gone, turned to her oldest daughter, Francesca. "Go to see Erba, the baker, and see if there are any of those peasant tarts left. Mind you go into the back of the shop. There may be none left in the window, although it was full of them when we passed on the way to Mass."

Francesca went and was back in no time, holding a magnificent tart, crusty and flaky. Ambrogio got up and went down to the cellar, soon to return with two bottles of white wine. The ice cream had been forgotten; the tart had replaced it. The tart was served; it was delicious, all agreed.

Pino said, "It used to be said that at Erba's, the only one who knew how to make these tarts was Giovannino, the boy who always had flour on his face and in his hair. Yet now Giovannino is away being a soldier, and here we are eating this great tart. I don't think I've ever eaten such a nice tart from Erba's."

II

The pie had been eaten. The ice-cream bucket had been banished to the kitchen, with a parting suggestion from Gerardo: "Try putting ice on top of the lid. Maybe that'll stop it melting."

Under the pergola, cigarettes were lit, and the conversation became more reflective. "What a great world out there . . . who knows where you'll be this time next Sunday?" Ambrogio told Michele, who replied, "Maybe still in Italy."

"In that case," said Pino, "you must come back to Nomana. You'll see, next Sunday the ice cream will freeze."

"Absolutely," said Giulia, "you have to give us a chance to serve you the ice cream I promised."

Michele smiled. "Thank you, and thank you, too, Pino, but I can't come."

Ambrogio chimed in, "Why ever not? I won't be here, but if you're in Nova, you have to come."

Pino piped up, "You won't be here? And why not? You have to be here, too."

"Well, you know I can't just come when I want. I have to ask for permission. For Michele it's different, as he's about to ship out. Also it's possible that I . . . but I'm forgetting," he turned to Michele, "tomorrow at nine I'm supposed to report to the colonel; he's called for me and three others." Giulia turned to listen to her son. "I don't have the faintest idea what he wants; last month he sent two people to Florence to bring back optical equipment. They were gone all week."

Michele said, "Perhaps you've all done something wrong, and he just wants to yell at you?"

Gerardo said hesitantly, "It won't be . . . might it be to tell you you're going to the front?"

Ambrogio looked at his father. "Where do you think they'd send us, Papa? To the Greek front? No, they sent the replacement soldiers and officers they needed in Greece already, last month, and in any case, it didn't amount to many people. And then, they wouldn't send beginners like us, when they have plenty of experienced officers on hand."

Meanwhile, the two teenagers, Pino and Alma, had wandered off and started playing a shuttlecock game. Tam tam tam, the racquets drummed. The conversation around the pergola lagged.

Ambrogio was thinking of his coming meeting with the colonel, which had not been in his thoughts since he left Casale. Michele thought about his father and his imminent departure. Gerardo would have liked to withdraw, as he always did on Sunday afternoons, to read a few pages of his favorite novel, *The Betrothed* (he hardly read any books and knew this one almost by heart). Giulia sat thinking about Manno, her nephew, whom she regarded as another son, wondering what sort of a day he was having in the North African desert. Francesca was annoyed because the ice cream had not worked ("What an embarrassment, and to think that last summer we made it twice without any problems"). Alma, the fifteen-year-old, still playing badminton with her brother, was feeling sorry that she hadn't been able to befriend their guest and entertain him. *When he's gone, we'll remember him and think about him, as we do about Manno, yet while he's here I don't know what to say to him.*

Now and then, Michele would look over at Alma and enjoy watching her freedom of movement. *How graceful she is. Why would anybody call her a statue; when she moves she looks like a young lamb, leaping out in the fields. Only fifteen, but she's an unusual person. She looks like one of those sublime women from the Middle Ages.* And then he thought that, considering his own cast of mind, he could not have paid her a higher tribute. He felt like watching her more closely, but at that moment there was a general move by the group, and he started to thank his hostess and say goodbye preparatory to returning to Nova.

The following morning, back on duty, Michele was advised of his posting; that same afternoon he was due in Bologna, which served as a gathering point for troops moving to and from the Russian front. He immediately set about rounding up the other few officers who had been posted, agreeing to a meeting time for later, said goodbye to several colleagues, and continued on to the officer's mess, where he bought some stationery. Both the paper and envelopes were headed with the regiment's emblem and its motto, *Fide ac virtute*. He then sat down and wrote a few words to his father.

Behind him, at the bar, he heard the ringing of a telephone but didn't stop writing. He heard the white-jacketed orderly who had lifted the receiver answer, saying, "From Casale Monferrato? For Second Lieutenant Tintori—yes, he's here, you're in luck. I'll call him."

Surprised, Michele had raised his hand. "They want you, sir", said the orderly, handing him the phone.

At the other end of the line was Ambrogio's voice. "I didn't expect to get you. I was going to leave a message. Tell me, how are things with you?"

"I have to be in Bologna today, to leave on the first troop train east, either tomorrow or the next day."

"Great", Ambrogio said. "When you get there, save me a place!"

"When I get where?"

"Why, Russia, of course! You want to be the only one going?" Ambrogio began to laugh. "This was the reason the colonel called me in."

"When?"

"This morning. Two hours ago. Didn't I tell you yesterday that I had to report? We talked about it at Nomana."

"Yes, in fact." Michele paused. "How are you going to tell your family?"

"That's exactly what I've been asking myself."

PART THREE

I

The main departure point for troops sent to the Russian front was Bologna. Some weeks after Michele's departure in June 1942, Ambrogio also left from Bologna. The city (pleasure loving, secular, and so not very congenial to his own nature—though he was rather insensible to this) seemed to him, the little he was able to see of it, vaguely disagreeable. The local dialect, slowly spoken, had a harsh sound. Ambrogio thought it made the speaker sound somehow insincere. He was slightly offended, also, at the Fascist salutes being given around the train station, particularly those given by three or four uniformed Fascist females. These, who looked to Ambrogio a little sickly and pale, were walking about, handing out tokens to the uniformed men. Little flags, cookies, three cigarettes tied with a tricolor ribbon, held out to servicemen who seemed a little puzzled by the offer. The women sought to lighten the atmosphere, exchanging cheerful remarks on the meanness of their Fascist secretary, which fell rather flat as most of the soldiers did not understand the local dialect they used. It became clear there was not going to be a farewell party at the station, and instead of bands and speeches, the soldiers were to be seen on their way by this small group of Fascist women. The women, in turn, feeling the need, acted toward the departing soldiers in motherly fashion. They were there primarily, because they could not get out of the duty, but there was also a genuine concern for the departing soldiers.

Leaving on the short train (it consisted of only six or seven cars) were reinforcements of various kinds. There were some sixty infantrymen, forty Bersaglieri, a group of flame-thrower engineers bearing their distinctive emblems, some drivers and other specialists, plus a contingent of junior lieutenants who hadn't been assigned to a specific unit. The whole trainload, a good representation of the country's youth, not enthusiastic but neither loath to leave. Listening to them talk among themselves, Ambrogio thought there was a certain air of expectancy, some of youth's love for adventure.

While standing by the side of the train, waiting for it to leave, Ambrogio involuntarily recalled part of one of the previous war's songs:

> The train which from Turin
> departed for Milan,
> now goes directly to Piave
> goes directly to Piave
> carrying the youth to burial . . .

and thought, *I'm glad this war isn't the same as the last one was, a war of extermination; or at least I hope it won't be, for us Italians. Just as well.*

Climbing the high steps of the car, Ambrogio went to the third-class compartment in which he had placed his shoulder bag. He sat for a while talking to the other junior officers, all destined for the eighth Pasubio artillery regiment, and after a while went to stand at the window, pouring himself a drink from a thermos bottle he'd just bought. The large Bologna station, with its many tracks empty or taken up with long, empty train cars, didn't pay much attention to the short train and its soldiers, nor to the four Fascist women, their farewell committee. On some tracks, trains waited to start a new journey. A long train arrived, packed with people. Ambrogio watched them and identified the train as coming from Rome. He leaned out of the window for a better view, and in the process, his new thermos slipped from his hands and fell on the dirty stones of the road bed, splashing hot coffee. The small accident gave Ambrogio a sudden and overwhelming presentiment of disaster, which he quickly shook off. He withdrew from the window, annoyed. *I don't have time to buy another. I'll have to do without*, and looking at the screw top in his hand, *At least this might be useful.* He drank the small quantity of coffee in the cup and put it away in his bag. Then he went back to the window.

2

The train was in the stretch between Mestre and Postumia as dusk approached. It moved slowly, sometimes at walking pace, and slowly went past the ossuary at Ridepuglia, site of the fierce fighting for Trieste in the Great War and now the resting place for over 100,000 fighting men. The Russia-bound soldiers crowded the windows to see this grim remembrance; the setting sun cast a slanting light on the whole scene, picking out every detail in the stony greenish-colored landscape.

Damn it, thought Ambrogio, *this is a warning. When did this happen—less than twenty-five years ago? Good thing this war won't have the high casualties of the last.* His three traveling companions were also looking out of the window. One said, "What a disaster!" Another added, "What a bad joke." The third youth, a goodhearted boy from Veneto, was silent, watching the passing cemetery with wrinkled brow.

What's he thinking about? Ambrogio asked himself. *Perhaps that some of us looking out the windows won't be coming back. One thing is sure, some of us are spending the last hours of our lives in Italy.* He smiled at the worried-looking young officer from Veneto and thought, *He's a nice type. I should try to make friends with him.*

After passing Monfalcone and its smoky shipyard, the train was approaching Carso when they noticed that in the bushy terrain on both sides of the road bed there were military encampments. As they moved along this stretch, the number of tents increased. All around the tents, men stood or sat, infantrymen, and when the train went by, some waved at the soldiers hanging out of the windows.

The young man from Veneto, named Bonsaver, wondered out loud, "What's this all about? Why these large numbers of tents?"

One of the others answered, "It can only mean one thing. The area must be infested with partisans, and these people are here to protect the railway."

"But we're still in Italy!"

"Well, yes, but this area probably is peopled by Slavs."

Ambrogio said, "The newspapers have said nothing about partisans in this area. It's hard to imagine."

When they reached Postumia, the train stopped for a while. They were now close to the frontier. Once in a while, shots were heard, and on looking out of the windows, the soldiers occasionally saw uniformed Fascists, a few simply wearing black shirts, all looking very alert, firearms in hand. One, Ambrogio saw, carried a Breda machine gun; he pointed it out to the others, meantime wondering what all the commotion was about.

Within the station, nobody paid attention to the noise, even though occasional machine-gun fire could be heard. Neither the civilians nor the military working in the station seemed worried; some of the sentries yawned repeatedly. As night fell, the train pulled out, without any of the four officers finding out what had been going on in the town, even though all the activity was obviously very close to the station.

In the middle of the night the train jolted to a stop, waking Ambrogio from a deep sleep. He was stretched out on the hard wooden seat, with a still-asleep Bonsaver perched up on the luggage shelf above the seat. On the other side of the compartment, the other two soldiers also slept—one up, one down. All their luggage had been put on the floor between the facing seats, and the curtains were closed, allowing very little light into the compartment. The windows were open, letting fresh air and also outside sounds enter. There were occasional snatches of music, as if coming through a door suddenly opened, and there were the sounds of footsteps.

Still half-awake, Ambrogio realized they were not the usual noises. The footsteps were all hobnailed boots, and as for the voices . . . yes, as for the voices, none of them belonged to women. The train had stopped. The young man sat up, with his feet on the seat and his back against the window. Then, turning halfway around, he pulled back a corner of one curtain. They were in a brightly lit station, and a sign said Ljubljana.

Intrigued, he had a further look around and discovered only Italian soldiers, and not many of them because of the time. One or two of the train's soldiers had stepped out and were wandering sleepily around, as if still in Italy. A bright light took his eyes to a glass door, around which stood an armed guard detachment. He couldn't tell whether this was composed of infantrymen or perhaps the Fascist militia. They weren't near enough to see, but they were armed and very disciplined. This detail he noted well.

He thought, *Over here they have to be on their toes. There are no jokes or easy duties like in Italy; here their lives are at stake.*

Looking at the station's name sign, Ambrogio remembered the family disagreements, the arguments among friends, at the time when this non-Italian city had been annexed to Italy. What nonsense! Now it wasn't a question of debates and disagreements any more. Now the people posted here had to be alert, with partisans appearing all over the place. Anyone here had to be fast and aware. They had to do their best just to save their own skin and also to prevent the local civilians from cutting each other's throats. *Better at the front than a life like that,* he thought.

3

The next morning the train crossed through the last Slovene valleys, among thick woods. The soldiers woke when the sun was already high. The landscape changed quickly (and without bureaucratic formalities), and they found themselves traveling over the plains of Hungary, immense and beautiful.

First hint of the Russian steppes, thought Ambrogio, who from the window could see the distant herds of cattle, some just dots in the distance. Now and then the train crossed swampy river areas, frightening into flight the many different species of birds feeding there. The various types of ducks, lapwings, sandpipers, and bustards would circle in the air and dive down to their places among the reeds after the train had passed.

Then once again the train reached more dry plains, occasionally going through some isolated station stuck out in the middle of the landscape between the unreachable-looking horizons. Some of the stations had bright masses of lilacs in bloom, reminding Ambrogio of the railroad station back home in Nomana.

Leaving Hungary, the train entered the mountainous gateway to Slovakia, with its silver firs and spruces, and when the soldiers next woke on the following morning, they were crossing southern Poland, going at high speed. There was, in the untiring progress of the massive convoy, something ineluctable and almost fatal; it was as if its monotonous din would never stop.

Once more at the window, Ambrogio and Bonsaver, sitting facing each other, observed the passing countryside, Poland's farmland. Less intensely cultivated than their own Po Valley, there were still similarities that made them think of home. Dirt roads flanked by spiny vegetation, and, in contrast to Italy's small crossroads country chapels, there were at some of the crossings great tall crosses, each supporting a realistic Christ in agony.

As they passed one of these large crucifixes close to the rail line, Bonsaver crossed himself in an absentminded way, afterward looking over at Ambrogio. "I haven't said my prayers yet this morning", he was not ashamed to confess. Ambrogio, also crossing himself, said, "I haven't said mine yet either."

"And yet, we had time to say them", Bonsaver smiled.

Agreeing, Ambrogio said, "I see you're also a *paolotto*, right?"

Not understanding, Bonsaver asked, "A what?"

"A *paolotto*, a practicing Catholic."

"Ah, yes, that's right, I am." He smiled, his blond hair and open, country face reminding Ambrogio of Bonsaver's origin, Veneto.

"I understand you're taking engineering?" asked Ambrogio, and when the other nodded, "I thought so. You have the look of an engineer."

Bonsaver smiled again. "And you, what are you studying?"

"Economics."

"Sounds boring."

They'd reverted for a moment to their former world, students talking idly to one another; but now they turned to watch the Polish country flashing past. Both were thinking of Poland's Catholics, and therefore their fellow Christians, living under the rule of Nazi Germany.

The train slowed and went through a level crossing at walking pace.

Country folk, men and women on their four-wheeled carts, watched silently as they went past.

Bonsaver said in dialect, "To think that, helping the Germans, we're in a way enslaving these poor people . . ."

One and then more of the Polish farmers waved to the soldiers on the train.

"Look, they've recognized us. They've seen we're Italians", exclaimed Bonsaver, putting his head and shoulders out of the window, so as to wave back.

"What marvelous people, the Poles", commented Ambrogio.

Bonsaver replied, "For them, Italy is the Pope, it's the Catholic Church, which gives them heart. For the Church they put up with much and forgive everything."

"Yes," Ambrogio agreed, "and yet we, on the other hand . . . well, it's better not to think about it." He shook his head, thinking that he wished Italy wasn't such a nation of windbags, so inadequately armed. Sadly and painfully, with the purity of youth, he wished his country were a valiant nation, using its strength to help others, and not only for its own self-interest. A gentlemanly concept of war, which sometimes comes to the surface in the Catholic.

The next afternoon, the train ran through the last of Poland, toward its old boundary with Russia. The rail line went through gently undulating country, and the train seemed to be making a great effort, cutting across it, traveling slowly. There were very few villages to be seen; those they passed looked poor, consisting of mean houses, decorated in blues, reds, bright colors, and appearing inadequate to the Italians. In the country between the few villages, nothing moved under the huge sky except occasional flocks of crows, flying from one place to another nearby, landing and wobbling, high in the trees, looking like scraps of funeral crepe, black and ragged.

They saw their last of Polish peasants in a cart, on a dirt road parallel to the line. A young boy among them wore a *budenyi* cap, the sinister pointed cap of the Bolshevik revolution. As they would systematically do from now on, the soldiers waved, and the farmers returned their greetings. One of the adults, perhaps the father, said something to the boy, who quickly tore off his cap and threw it down. Noting the soldiers' applause, he picked it up and threw it down again, finally jumping up and down on it, encouraged by the cheers and whistles coming from the train.

4

At last, they entered the Soviet Union, which greeted them with long rolls of barbed wire running off into the countryside, and, as a complement, lines of tank barriers behind.

Farther along were thick cement bunkers, with the firing ports blackened by the smoke of flamethrowers and, here and there, abandoned red-starred tanks.

The four young soldiers looked out on all this with interest, switching from the compartment window to the one in the aisle to get a better view. Some of the time they had the impression of having entered, not a world of mystery or wholesale slaughter, but one that was unbelievably backward and almost petrified. While their approach to Poland had revealed a gradually poorer country, the contrast with their present surroundings was sharp. The mean little huts had straw roofs; there were no roads or cartroads, only beaten tracks; and even the towns they passed had no paved streets.

The four soldiers were particularly struck by this. A surveyor in civilian life asked, "How is this possible? Haven't they even heard of asphalt here in Russia?" The others agreed: "It's certainly strange."

The Russians they saw looked much like the Poles they had seen, but were more poorly dressed, almost in rags. Their faces, up close, were blank, tired out, beaten. This was something Ambrogio would never forget, these, the faces of the Russians under Stalin.

Bonsaver put it into words for the others: "The way I see it, there's more than just a lack of asphalt, or poor and backward people. There is something here that doesn't work, something ugly and dirty." The rest agreed but without managing to make their own impressions more concrete.

As the train continued on its way, faster now, in the dark night, its lights dimmed. Ambrogio thought of what Michele Tintori had said about Russia. Maybe it was this "something" that Bonsaver couldn't describe. These poor people must have been through a frightful, tremendous experience, suffered inhuman pressures. He'd have to talk about it next time he saw Michele. *I want to hear what he has to say.*

The next morning, the horizon seemed to have receded more and more. The land looked larger; often there would be stretches of totally featureless scenery for hours, broken only occasionally by a sign of war. They saw abandoned tanks, looking tiny and insignificant in that immense landscape; they saw a burned-out farm tractor, and once the remains of a crashed airplane, reduced in size to look no more than something like a tree stump, hard to identify in the grass.

Toward the end of their journey, days later, in the industrial basin of the Donets, they saw more people. Ambrogio, glued to the window, wanted to see everything. He didn't want to miss any detail of this country. He saw enormous bombed-out factories, gray masses; between factories there would be the occasional large tenement house, sometimes a small suburb, miserable, depressing, alongside slag heaps, and very rarely, an isba. *Where did the laborers live? The few houses I've seen will only hold a small portion of them*, thought Ambrogio, and then his eye was drawn to a shanty town, a collection of lean-tos and shacks, one leaning on the other, a chaotic anthill. There they were, worker's areas. *Look at how they had to live, miserable wretches, and of course they had to pretend to be happy. But inside, they must be holding on to a lot of resentment, if they're anything like the working class I know. Who wouldn't harbor rebellious thoughts at having to live under these conditions?*

At intervals, as if to give the travelers' eyes a rest, between factory groupings there would reimpose itself on the landscape a stretch of Russia's eternal steppes, miles and miles of short herbage and wildflowers.

Sometimes from the train they would see a strange ant column of Russian civilians, walking, heads down, coming and going, many of them lone individuals carrying bundles on their backs, pushing wheelbarrows or pulling rudimentary carts. The soldiers wondered at what could drive these people. Only later would they discover that Russians from the cities constantly took various household items out to the country, to trade for pitifully small quantities of grain or other food, hunger having the vast land in its grip.

The train's destination turned out to be well behind the front line, at the small town of Jassinovataia, of only some tens of thousands of inhabitants.

On going through Poland, the train had picked up a German civilian car, only half full of Wehrmacht personnel, who had invited the Italians to spread out and make use of the available space. This led to Ambrogio witnessing a short but disagreeable incident between an Italian officer and a German rail-roadman as they all detrained on arrival. The German was accusing the officer of being a thief, because over his military pack was spread out, in all its splendor, a striped velvet-covered cushion, part of the German car's furnishing. The officer was putting the responsibility on his orderly, who, to help him, pretended to be dimwitted and claimed not to understand anything the German was saying.

Looking around, Ambrogio couldn't find any representative of the Eighth Artillery, either at the station or in the town itself, so eventually he and his three traveling companions decided to stay overnight with others from the train in a nearby requisitioned tenement house, where they slept in cots. During this brief stay, Ambrogio received another lesson in his military apprenticeship. When he returned to his bunk from having washed and freshened up, he found that his spare pair of shoes had been stolen by his countrymen.

5

The following morning, the four youths rejoined their regiment's command post, about twenty kilometers further east of Jassinovataia, by using the twice-weekly mail truck. On arrival they were given a fatherly welcome by the colonel in charge of the post and soon after were assigned to different groups, so that Ambrogio was separated from Bonsaver and the others. After having loaded his baggage onto an aged Millecento car that his new group commander had kindly had sent out from the line, he left the same day for the town of Kamenka.

The driver, a corporal, showed great skill in driving over the irregular dirt road while simultaneously answering Ambrogio's many questions in an attentive manner, like a tour guide. "Yes, this is the lieutenant colonel's personal vehicle, and I'm his regular driver. Yes, the Eighth has been in Kamenka since November. Air-raid shelters? No, we haven't been able to dig any, because the ground is frozen, hard as a rock. The batteries of cannons are in place within the town, whose houses are scattered, as you will see; we've been staying in the civilians' houses all through the winter, only recently we've been using tents."

"I suppose the civilians heaved a sigh of relief when you left to go to the tents, eh?" suggested Ambrogio.

The corporal glanced at him, "No. Well, maybe some, but generally they were sorry, I'd say, especially the women, certainly." He smiled, then became serious again. "Also, I'd say the remainder of the townfolk. As you'll see, the Russians love us Italians."

"Do they have food?"

"Not much. It's sad, at least here at the front. When we're being served our chow there are always a few—particularly kids and older folk—who come around with their plates and tins, to ask for soup or stew. The cooks try to keep something for them, and we ourselves usually try to give them some off our own plates, but it's an unhappy spectacle, you'll see. Back there at the rear, Jassinovataia, for example, there must have been deaths from starvation now and then." Kamenka came into sight, a mining town. Some slag heaps showed against the skyline. "Those coal mines were here before the revolution", said the driver.

"How do you know?"

"Everybody knows it. You can tell, for example, from the cemetery. It's falling apart and abandoned, just like any other Russian cemetery, with wooden crosses and the cows grazing among the graves. Russians don't make a big thing out of death. But there are also some old tombstones like ours, with names and inscriptions in French. Those are the ones of the mining technicians of earlier times."

Going through the town's streets, they passed individual artillerymen, shirtsleeved and wearing leggings. A battery of four small (100 mm) cannons, silent and covered in camouflage nets, was sited near a row of houses. Behind the battery, scattered among the houses, trucks were parked, with here and there several tents of varying size.

Ambrogio felt an emotional reaction at seeing the peculiarly Italian tents, in which the basic component was a waterproof piece of fabric, two meters square. It was like looking at a little piece of Italy. Who could forget these Italian tents after having spent nights and days in one?

Each soldier was issued one (square ones for officers and triangular ones for enlisted men), and, being multipurpose, they could be used individually as raincoats, putting them on through a hole in the middle; they could be folded in half and filled with leaves and straw as a mattress; they could be used for covering and protecting piles of ammunition or other valuable equipment, or finally—their most appropriate use—as individual tents, or, joined together, to erect larger tents.

The effect of having these colored tents dotted about any area, like here in Kamenka, was an unexpectedly ancient and harmonious design, transforming the place into a picture. Even the squalid atmosphere of Kamenka, with its black dust and the few low houses alternating with the isbas and slag heaps.

The corporal stopped the Millecento in front of an isba. "Here it is, Lieutenant. We've arrived. Here's where we have the group CP."

They went into the command post, and Ambrogio was immediately surrounded by the officers there, who welcomed him and stormed him with questions about conditions in Italy. One said, "Most of us have been here for ten months."

A lieutenant, bald and with a long skinny face, interrupted and introduced himself as the adjutant, saying, "Hold everything. First let me introduce you to the lieutenant colonel. What did you say your name was? Riva, is that right?"

One of the officers, a doctor, commented jokingly on the adjutant's businesslike manner. "You see the bank clerk? The poor man is hardly here, and already he's got him filling out forms."

"Who said anything about forms", said the adjutant, shaking his head. "Come on, Riva", and turning to the driver, "you wait here to unload the stuff you're delivering", and preceded Ambrogio to the CO's office.

Major Casasco, graying and fortyish, a man of refined manners, was seated at a camp table. He smiled at the hesitant boy who had stopped at attention before him, then got up and held out his hand in welcome. Returned to his seat, he tried to get some idea of him, questioning him about his abilities and his possible preferences.

The adjutant was also studying Ambrogio. "He's a Milanese, like you", the commander said suddenly to Ambrogio, indicating the adjutant; and he joked: "Milanese, but worse, he's a bank clerk. Isn't that awful?" The adjutant's long face produced a satisfied smile in response. Among the officers of the group, his equine face had earned him the nickname of Tired Horse.

Assigned to the Third and last battery as "artillery-line officer" Ambrogio prepared to take his leave, but the major said, "You'll go to your new battery after dinner with us here, but before that, you'll have to give us news of home."

Later, when he arrived at his new post, he received another cordial welcome from his brother officers. The battery was manned by four officers, six non-coms and 110 enlisted men. It wasn't located very far from the CP and was headed by a lean lieutenant from Marches, an engineering graduate, who gave Ambrogio a cursory familiarization with the cannons. "Just in case we have to open fire overnight . . . in the morning I'll give you more detailed instructions."

The battery's enlisted men, many in shirtsleeves, some even wearing slippers and clogs, behaved less formally than the soldiers in the barracks in Italy. They had noticed Ambrogio's arrival and surrounded him as soon as he was finished talking with the lieutenant. They also had for the most part been away from Italy for ten months and wanted to know how everything was back home. On the whole, they made a good impression on him. He sensed no enmity in them, only some reserve, which—he hoped—would cease when they knew him better. He knew it would be up to him to show them leadership, earning their respect and trust. Although a novice at soldiering, Ambrogio already knew how important mutual confidence was from his experience with the workers at his family's factory.

Some while later, back at the battery's CP in the ramshackle isba, he received further briefing on their area of the front from the lieutenant engineer. "As they'll have told you at group HQ, the front here has been stagnant for some time. The last fighting of any kind was back at Christmastime, when the Russians tried to break through the Bersaglieri, over there on the right flank."

Ambrogio thought, *Of course, the Christmas battle; it was soon after that, in January, that Stefano came out as a replacement for the people who didn't make it through that very battle. I wonder where old Moon Face is now?*

The lieutenant was saying, "I guess you're curious about our losses to date. Well, in the battery, we've had one killed—only one—since the beginning of the campaign. In the rest of the group, some four or five dead, most in the combat involved in our attempt to cross the Dnieper last fall. When things are going well and we're making advances, the artillery takes few hits, therefore no losses. For the infantry, of course, it's different; when they're in close contact with the enemy there are always some who fall.

"Over there, ahead of us, is the Seventy-Ninth Infantry, in trenches, about three kilometers away. You should see the trenches: they're dug into ground rich in coal. Out there, the coal comes to the surface, pushing aside the flowers. This country is so rich in coal, I wonder why the people who live here lead such miserable lives."

Ambrogio had earlier informed the lieutenant of the theft of his shoes, and now the latter said, "Up at the front the attitude isn't like that rabble back in the rear echelon; there's a better feeling up here, not only better than in the rear (which I got to know well in Albania) where it is always disgusting, but it's even better than stations in Italy. There's some order here and, well . . . You'll see for yourself. There's concern for each other. There's also a spirit of patience and even a hint of happiness."

"I've already noticed something of that", said Ambrogio, inwardly relieved.

He went to sleep very tired. He'd been given a place to sleep in the officer's tent, which had been augmented by adding three of the standard two-square-meter panels in order to accommodate him. From the nearby fields came the sound of quail, and this background of soft sounds accompanied a review of events running like a movie through his thoughts—the long week's journey out here, the Italian officer who tried to steal the train's cushion, those comically pathetic Fascist women at the Bologna train station, his home, his mother. In his bedroom in Nomana, as a young boy he'd lie in bed, and occasionally he'd hear the tiny chomping sound of termites. The sound was very persistent, to the point where he sometimes thought it existed only inside his head. At times he'd cover his ears with both hands to find out if the sound would stop. It was many years since he'd heard the termites, and he had nearly forgotten them, but now in his half-asleep state, the termite sound and the long incessant quail calls merged, and just before he sank into slumber, he thought of Stefano—old Moon Face—and of Michele Tintori, wondering if they also could hear the quail—and slept.

6

In early July, bulletins issued by the Germans began referring to great battles taking place in the south, involving Wehrmacht armored units, breaking the stalemate in existence since the previous fall. In Kamenka, discussion among the Italian officers brought agreement that the German intentions were to seize the large Russian oil wells. Soon after, speculation gave way to action when the Italians received orders to advance.

The whole southern front, about one hundred divisions, ground into movement toward the east, in the direction of Stalingrad and the lower reaches of the Volga River. The three Italian divisions—Pasubio, Turin, and Celere—being part of the northern flank, arranged themselves to place the Bersaglieri of the Celere division, regarded as their best, right up at the front. Under their pressure the enemy, already overcome in the south by the German tank forces, began to retreat, fighting fierce defensive actions before giving up some villages and towns.

Following on behind the Italian advance came a wave of displaced civilians, men and women, carrying their possessions in sacks on their backs, like a river of ants, foraging to survive.

Among the Bersaglieri was Stefano, the farm boy from Nomanella, whose company took part in several actions of close combat. The first of these, just four days into the general advance, took place near Ivanovka (one of several places of the same name in Russia). The battalion trucks bringing up the support troops stopped in a wooded gorge when the advance guard mounted on motorcycles ran into a line of enemy resistance. As the Bersaglieri poured out of the trucks, the sound of the motorcycle corps' machine guns could be heard, along with the deeper sound of the Russian heavy machine guns and the crackle of rifle fire. It was midmorning, and the terrain—rather wet in that region—was filled with great trees, their leaves glistening from a recent shower, interspersed by patches of meadow.

As they advanced through the tightly packed trees, many with their rifles still slung on their backs, they encountered small clearings, when they could see, off to their right, another of the battalion's companies, going forward in line with them. When there was a pause in the firing up ahead, they could hear nearby the call of a solitary turtledove. This was Stefano's first experience of being exposed to enemy fire, his previous confrontations with the enemy having been confined to sporadic back-and-forth fire from the safety of a trench. He felt very nervous. His job was as assistant shot for a machine gun, so as he ran forward he carried a heavy tripod and spare ammunition.

Suddenly, they came on a number of haphazardly parked motorcycles and halted, while one of the motorcycle troops gave their captain a quick briefing. Both the captain and the motorcycle soldier disappeared up forward to get a closer look at the still invisible line, from where the now louder sound of firing came to the halted troops.

Stefano slid his heavy tripod down to the ground to relax his back and shoulder muscles. Every now and then he would hear the *thunk!* of an enemy bullet hitting a tree trunk, but after a while neither he nor his comrades paid close attention to the sounds. Upon returning, the captain ordered them forward and led them to the edge of the woods, where he told them all to dig in and make shelters where they could.

The Russian defensive line was about three hundred meters away in a large field and consisted of pillboxes made of tree trunks, with the loopholes put at ground level. It looked as if the pillboxes were linked by trenches, but these couldn't be seen clearly.

The Italians already at the front exchanged periodic fire with the Russians, but when the newly arrived Bersaglieri took their posts, they had been strictly ordered not to shoot.

"What are we waiting for?" Stefano asked his machine gunner. Both were lying in a rudimentary foxhole scooped from the earth.

"It must be so our mortars can get ready, and probably our artillery, too."

The solitary turtledove continued to sing again in the moments between the firing. Stefano thought the bird must be seriously in love to sing under these conditions.

The second lieutenant in charge of the detachment—a man from Turin named Acciati—trotted up and down the line a couple of times, cautiously checking on the weapon placement and to see that the depth of the holes had good cover. He kept up a steady flow of talk, half seriously and half jokingly: "Come on, you men, no loafing about, give yourselves something to do, dig deeper, get under cover."

At noon they chowed down, right on the spot. Mess cans had been handed out the previous night. Soon after their lunch, an artillery second lieutenant arrived, accompanied by five or six soldiers loaded up with radios and other equipment. He stared at the Russian line from various positions, moving about and joking with Lieutenant Acciati (until recently, both had been students in their twenties) until he decided he could better direct artillery fire from the position at which he'd left his captain.

"Even though from there you see little enough at ground level." And, turning to his men, "Let's go!"

One of his men muttered, "You'll see, when we get back there the lieutenant will climb a tree for a better view, like that time in Petrikovka."

His buddy replied, "Just so long as he climbs it alone and doesn't make us go up there, too."

7

Sometime later the same afternoon Stefano heard the voice of a radio operator who was transmitting data from the artillery spotters, swiftly followed by the whistle of an artillery round passing overhead; it exploded into a patch of black smoke as big as a sheet near one of the enemy positions. When the smoke cleared, more rounds were fired, each corrected for accuracy, until one shot hit directly on target and firing ceased.

Next it was the turn of the mortars. Using heavy-duty missiles, they ranged in on their targets, each round making the ground shake, exploding with the bang of very large pots crashing down. The Russians responded with continuous bursts of heavy machine-gun fire aimed at the woods.

Soon after, the real firestorm began. Kneeling, to be able to reload his machine gun, Stefano asked God's blessing and no longer thought about enjoying the reloading mechanism of his machine gun, which like the others was firing nonstop on the Russian loopholes. From around them came the noise of the firing of their other machine guns, the dry *crack* of rifle fire, and the *whump!* sound of the cannons. Mortars and smaller handheld cannons served to increase the level of noise and metal being thrown at the Russians, until one of the enemy positions was silenced, and smoke rose from another.

When the general firing started, the Russians had picked out the Bersaglieri front and had begun to batter it with automatic weapons, but as the bombardment continued, less return fire was heard as the Italians began to make their mark on the defenders' positions. Finally, the Italian fire ceased. All the soldiers on both sides felt especially in their blood and in their heart that the moment for an assault was near. And soon, from here and there, singly and in twos and threes, the Russians started appearing from out of the ground and retreating. One or two machine guns followed these decamping troops, but a general shout went up on the Italian side: "Leave them. Isn't it better if they get away?" There was little time to think, however.

On the right, from a position near the captain, a voice shouted, "Ninth Battalion, up and at 'em!", followed by other commands and shouts, like "*Savoia! Savoia!*" The men, from then on, without exception, entered into a state of terrible tension.

Echoing the captain, Lieutenant Acciati shouted, "Let's go! Out!", and he dashed forward crying "*Savoia!*" as he ran like a fool, with almost no cover, toward the pillboxes. "*Savoia! Savoia!*" His Bersaglieri, running still faster, tried hard to catch up with him so as not to leave him exposed.

The whole battalion had left the woods; most of the men, following the captain's example, ran in a crouch toward the enemy's position. Amid the firing could be heard shouts. Over on the right, beyond the captain, one company of advancing soldiers had fixed bayonets.

Stefano and his partner went forward at a fast walk, unable to run with the weight of their gun, the tripod, and the spare ammunition. Others, similarly loaded, advanced in the same way; these included some soldiers who had been ordered to support the attack from behind. On the left flank, another company had been brought to a halt; some of the Bersaglieri were in retreat, others, wounded and calling out, sprawled on the grass. Others dived for cover and reopened fire with rifles and machine guns. Stefano, his ears roaring with blood, was unable to take it all in and kept his attention on his immediate surroundings.

The enemy defense seemed less determined, and now more Russians were retreating. In their khaki uniforms they would emerge from the earth and either run or hurry away, taking big steps; others must have been dead or wounded, or crouching in the pillboxes not firing any more, awaiting the moment to surrender.

Right, thought Stefano, *there's a group of them, already prisoners.* He hurried over with his heavy machine gun and looked at the prisoners up close. All had their heads shaved and looked terrified. They wore poor quality uniforms like no other troops in the world; they looked like cannon fodder.

Poor devils, poor people! thought Stefano, the farmer from Nomanella in him reacting to these defenders of their own land. *They also have mothers, wives at home, people who need them.* He winked at one, whose face was deeply pitted by small pox, an ugly, brutalized looking soldier. Stefano, in dialect, said, "Hey, you, ugly one. What are you afraid of?" The Russian looked at the corporal and at the machine gun he and his partner carried, his mouth open, gray faced.

"Afraid we'll shoot you with this? We're not animals; come on, cheer up!" Stefano smiled at the prisoner, getting no response.

Around the pillboxes and in the trench itself that linked them were the scattered bodies of Russians and a large quantity of firearms.

What's this? Stefano thought. *So many arms and so few prisoners . . . Many must have sneaked out, leaving their guns behind.* Among the abandoned guns were a couple of unusual submachine guns equipped with a round, horizontal magazine, one of which Lieutenant Acciati examined with curiosity. The retreating enemy's fire had become intermittent, more distant.

"OK. Let's group up and get going toward Ivanovka. We mustn't give the enemy time to get reorganized", commanded the battalion commander. The chase began, the Italians in three columns, one for each company. Many already showed their fatigue, but Ivanovka was quickly in sight. The usual untidy collection of factories and homes, railroad lines, dirt streets lined with clumps of nettle, dumped pyramids of coal waste, broken machinery; another typical town of the Donets Valley. There were the expected isbas, and one whole district of deserted tumbledown shacks, abandoned by a general evacuation.

Marching into the town, the Bersaglieri were overtaken by a motorcycle squad; in the distance, leaving the other end of town, could be seen the last of the enemy's rear guard.

8

A few days later, in the afternoon, Ambrogio's artillery group arrived at Ivanovka. He had them halt in the woods precisely where Stefano's section had initiated their attack. Battery by battery, their trucks, trailers, and cannon were parked underneath the trees, while the soldiers quickly erected the tents. Some went to look for water, found it in a ditch, and then began carrying an assortment of containers, going back and forth between the ravine and the batteries (the drivers used canvas buckets from the vehicles). One of the first to return bearing water was Ambrogio's orderly, Paccoi, a farm boy from Umbria. Sweating, and as usual with his cap crooked on his head, he carried a pail he'd managed to liberate from the civilians in Kamenka in exchange for bread. He put the water on the running board of the nearest truck and with a satisfied look announced, "The water is ready, my lieutenant."

Ambrogio, having just finished supervising the emplacement of the ammunition trailers for which he was responsible, thanked Paccoi and, stripping off his shirt and undershirt, started washing. The soldiers too started washing their hair, arms, and torsos. From the wood could be heard several singing turtledoves. Before he had finished washing, one of the artillerymen who had been fetching water came up and announced that just outside the wood, in a line of pillboxes, several enemy dead and a cache of arms had been found. "It's over there, that way", he said. "There must have been something like a battle."

A corporal nearby, about to dunk a soapy head into his washbasin, said: "I don't want to look at corpses. Not me, thanks." Others nearby agreed. A few, however, decided to go down to have a look, just to the edge of the woods, where they were still within hailing distance of their batteries (no one could, in fact, go any farther from the battery without permission), and, when they'd finished their washing, picked up their rifles and cartridge belts and sauntered over in small groups, or even alone.

Ambrogio, finishing his wash, turned to his lieutenant, who was shaving in front of a small mirror hanging from the dusty side of a truck.

"I'd like to take a look, too, if you don't mind", he said.

"Mind? Not at all. Go right ahead, relax."

Heading over toward the arms cache and enemy dead, Ambrogio followed a path; he was accompanied by two privates and Sergeant Facchi, head of the first artillery group, a stocky, easygoing crewcut man from Brescia. "I'm really curious about what happened here. I suppose it was the Bersaglieri", he said to Ambrogio with a sympathetic smile.

"I'd say so", replied Ambrogio. "At least if you can believe *radio scarpa* (the rumor mill)."

The sergeant looked at the young officer as he spoke, mouth half open. Like most artillerymen, after months of continuous campaigning and firing of artillery pieces, he'd gone a little deaf. Ambrogio raised his voice: "According to *radio scarpa*, there was a clash here, near Ivanovka." The Pasubio and Turin divisions following them up received only very vague reports of the front-line action of the Bersaglieri of the Celere Division, who were opening the way for the rest of the Italian corps.

"Couldn't it have been the Germans?" one of the privates asked. "You know how they are, and in the confusion of an attack . . . it wouldn't be the first time they exchanged shots with our crowd." The question reflected one of the then-current rumors, that in some unnamed village, and at a time not specified, the timetables for an advance had not been maintained, and the Bersaglieri and the Germans had opened fire on each other with one or two casualties on each side.

Ambrogio answered, "In any case that would have been more to our right, where our operational area touches on the German lines; certainly that sort of thing hasn't happened here."

At this edge of the woods there was a field cut across by a line of pillboxes; thanks to the rain the grass was an intense green and overgrown, deeply covered with flowers. The slanting sun gave it golden hues. While from the woods could be heard the continuous sound of the turtledoves, the open fields gave forth the chorused sounds of scattered quail.

The stocky sergeant, Facchi, looked around him and said, "In spite of everything, the world is still beautiful, even here in Russia." Ambrogio, also enjoying the scenery, nodded agreement.

All along the abandoned positions, artillerymen were already checking the area, exploring the pillboxes. Ambrogio and the other three strolled over to the nearest fortifications, constructed by the Russians out of logs, now deeply scarred by bullet and mortar fire. Scattered around, they could see abandoned ammunition and some rifles, one of which had a long, sharp bayonet fitted; inside the trench there was more abandoned equipment. "If only there were a machine gun. We could use one in the battery", Ambrogio said hopefully, but there were only regular rifles.

A shout came from one of the soldiers who had moved away along the trench: "Hey, look here!" He pointed down into the long grass with one hand and pinched his nostrils shut with the other. Sergeant Facchi went over, then said to Ambrogio, "Lieutenant, there's a dead Russian." Walking over with the other soldier, Ambrogio could see that the body, already swollen, was dressed in a khaki uniform and still had its cap on (this was the first time he had seen an enemy uniform). The already decomposing body had liquefied in parts and soaked the uniform, attracting swarms of slow-moving flies and giving forth an unbearable smell.

Looking down at the dead Russian, the Italian soldiers felt a deep sorrow, and Ambrogio thought, *This is what happens to you when things go wrong.* He realized that he was undergoing his first real contact with the meaning of war. "I won't let this get me down. You can't ever allow yourself to feel beaten, not in war or in peacetime. Let go, and you end up a toy, manipulated by people with more guts; you stop being a man; I have to be ready, even for death, even to end up like this."

The dead Russian, probably poor and illiterate, lay there in his horrible state, as if declaring by his wounds and position that he'd known his duty and had not given way under pressure. *Certainly it's not easy to be a man,* Ambrogio reflected, *but then I guess I've always known that.* Turning to the others, with him "Poor devil, what a way to go."

The others agreed, repeating, "Poor devil."

Walking away from the corpse, they followed the line of trenches. All were losing interest in the green fields and shady woods, the happy sounds of the wild birds, as well as in continuing their exploration, Ambrogio, however, like the good officer he was, decided to have a detailed look at the fortifications, to see how they were built. *Who knows? We might fall into a similar situation.* In the end, he collected a couple of Russian rifles and some packages of bullets and gave them to the soldiers who were following him.

During the walk around the trenches, Ambrogio had noticed that although most of the Russian dead had already been buried inside the trenches, there were still a few unburied bodies. At first he had done nothing about them, but when he returned to the battery, after consulting with his CO, he detailed a few men with picks, shovels, and ropes to bury them.

9

Their advance continued for several weeks. The artillery went forward in leaps, alternating their forward movement with stops, which sometimes lasted several days. The group continued following in the wake of their major's beat-up Millecento, pushing forward with their three batteries of guns, beat-up trucks, trailers, small cannon and one motorcycle. For the first few days, intermittent rain caused the roads and tracks to become deep in mud, slowing their progress. The soldiers remarked, "We're lucky we don't have to keep moving forward at all costs, like we did in the fall." It couldn't be much fun for the Bersaglieri up ahead. Once the rain stopped, there was dust—every vehicle, traveling always and only on the tracks of beaten earth, since no other route existed, raised a long plume of dust, so that the column was constantly moving into a cloud of dust. To protect themselves, the artillerymen covered their faces with handkerchiefs, up to their eyes.

Refugee civilians continued to follow their advance, like columns of ants, trying to stay alive by sweeping up anything left behind. Sometimes the group's military vehicles would advance to run alongside the infantry, marching forward at either side of the road. These soldiers, sweaty and dusty, loaded down with the "long 91" rifles, machine guns, and backpacks, often stripped down or just with their shirtsleeves rolled up, seemed not to be moving at all in the immense countryside. To keep from covering them with dust, the column of vehicles reduced its speed from time to time and even, when possible, would leave the tracks and take to the fields. But this was not always possible, and then the abuse of the foot-soldiers regularly accompanied the passing artillery.

From their trucks and trailers, the artillerymen—feeling vaguely at fault—laughed and tried to joke with the soldiers. Some responded with jokes; others were still more irritated. The dust problem, in any case, was undoubtedly worst for the artillerymen riding on the rear of each truck, who ended up completely covered with it: their caps, the handkerchiefs over their faces, their eyebrows and eyelashes all covered with it.

Ambrogio, his eyes resting momentarily on a passing infantry lieutenant leading his section, thought, *I wonder if Michele is somewhere on the road, marching like this or if he's riding about in a truck?*

But, as events turned out, Ambrogio didn't see Michele or anyone else from the Turin division during the whole period of the advance.

10

In fact, Michele was neither marching nor riding. At the end of one week of advance, in fact, he had been left with a group of men in one of the many apparently unnamed settlements on the Russian plains to guard a stockpile of supplies. The supplies, which included some explosives, were kept in a large wooden barn, thatched with straw. (Because of the serious shortage of trucks, the Italians moved their supplies up in leapfrog fashion, setting up caches of material at intervals along the rear of the fight in advance.)

Michele's infantrymen mounted a twenty-four-hour guard over the cache. The officer had no other duty but to supervise the changing shifts. A more relaxed officer might have used the opportunity to catch up on lost sleep, but Michele was unable to forget that since he had arrived in Russia, he'd not had the chance to talk to the ordinary people. He had decided to use his time in the village to make contacts.

He was fortunate in having the services of an interpreter, a young Russian of about fifteen, adopted late the previous year as kitchen helper to the company. Since then, this boy, Alexander by name, had taken over as company cook. The infantrymen took to calling him *Malenko*, the Russian word for a young fellow. He was a weird one and had hardly learned how to cook, but, on the other hand, he had learned Italian with no apparent effort.

Alexander had been equipped with military clothing but seemed unable to stay neat. His buttons always undone, his unlaced boots slopping on the ground, he went unwashed and managed to get his trousers and jacket pulled out of shape and dirty. Well fed due to his cooking job, the youth seemed to concentrate much of his interest in smoking, and albeit only fifteen years old, often looked older, adopting tough poses, cigarette in hand. He often repeated: "I'm just a *besprizorni*", with an air that was both arrogant and sad. Right at the start, Michele had asked Alexander what the word meant and was informed that it stood for "without mother nor father."

"The *besprizorni*", the boy said matter-of-factly, "are often rounded-up by the Communists and executed."

"You mean . . . the firing squad?" Michele had asked.

"Yes, *kaput!*" Alexander had replied.

"The Communists execute orphans? What are you saying? It's not possible!"

The youth only nodded his head sadly, confirming his words, and although Michele pressed for a more complete explanation, the young kitchen hand would say no more.

It was only much later that he learned more about the *besprizorni*. A special category of orphans, the Russian *besprizorni* were children of those who had been in the recurrent outbreaks of violence within the country; their parents had died in the civil war or in the various "repressions", in famines, and in the periodic deportations. Unadopted, these orphans had gradually joined together in bands, living from trickery and theft. Mainly living in the cities, these bands of *besprizorni* eventually became a nuisance, and the Communists would round them up to educate them into useful citizens. But sometimes a band of orphans had become so savage and unmanageable, and a series of mass shootings had taken place. However, Michele did not know this yet. Actually, the only thing he was aware of was that of all the disasters of the Communist period, the one that still affected the people of the Ukraine the most (at least the peasants—he had not had any contact with other social classes) was the famine that followed the collectivization of the land ten years earlier. Even given the fatalist nature of the people, he noticed they still remembered the hungry times with fright, and he determined to learn more about this famine.

He had chosen an isba at the edge of the village as his billet; from the windows he could keep an eye on the barn that held his supplies. The isba, although old and battered by time and weather, had some pleasant wooden carvings, particularly on the front door posts and windows, and it was these, as strange as it may seem, that attracted his artist's eye and determined his choice.

On the evening of his arrival, with Alexander as interpreter, he went to visit his involuntary hosts. He found the family sitting around the main kitchen table, having just finished dinner. In addition to the middle-aged husband, there were two women, a girl of about eighteen years, and several children. Through the open window came the song of quail calling, sounding to Michele like the voice of the immense Russian plain. After introducing himself and engaging in small talk with the uneasy Russian family, he offered a cigarette to the man as well as to the *malenko* and started questioning him about life in the area.

"Yes, it's true, ten years ago there was great famine here", Alexander translated, sitting next to him, legs straight out in front of him, emphasizing his badly shod feet, smoking with clear enjoyment.

"And was it as bad as they say?"

"Yes, it was a terrible thing."

"How was it—how did it happen?"

"He says that when the food ran out, they ate the dogs, and after that the . . . how do you say the skin of the trees?"

"Were there deaths from starvation in this village?"

"Yes, obviously. Absolutely, like in all the other villages", the *malenko* translated. "They say that this is something everybody knows."

"But why do they think there was a famine? What caused it to start?"

At the translation of these questions, the farm family looked uneasily at each other, fright on the faces of the adults. The interpreter added a few words of his own, perhaps trying to clarify the question, then turned to Michele and said, using the basic military language he'd picked up, "These people are sh——ing their pants. I don't think they'll answer . . ."

The young girl—graceful, with blond hair the color of corn—made a movement, as if to say something, but a commanding gesture from her father silenced her. The man turned on the *malenko* and spoke forcefully for a while. Alexander, unruffled, translated, "He says they were reasonably well-off farmers and that he was never a member of the Party."

"Well, tell him from me that it hasn't occurred to me to think he might have any responsibility; tell him I don't believe he was involved. Also tell him that I'm a student and only wish to understand how things happened." Perhaps it may have been the word the *malenko* chose to translate *student*, a term that might have been difficult for him to understand, but it was clear that the whole family was now even more afraid.

The farmer said, "I'm a working man, no more", and repeated it several times, even after Michele had asked the interpreter to reassure him, to tell him he was merely interested in past events.

"It's all right", Michele cut short the farmer's protestations, not wanting to ruin future opportunities. "Tell him that if he doesn't want to talk of the famine, it doesn't matter. Tell him I'm a friend in any case."

The family listened closely to the translation of Michele's words and seemed utterly confused. The older woman, the man's mother or mother-in-law, clearly upset, half turned toward a battered gilded wooden icon of the Holy Mother and crossed herself several times, using the Orthodox blessing, three fingers extended, the other two folded.

Michele thought, *Look at how the poor thing is frightened*, and decided to return to less upsetting subjects. Turning to the *malenko*, he said, "Ask them why so many fields are planted in millet." Alexander himself answered, "I can explain that. It is kasha. All us Russians eat kasha."

Michele cast about for something to say that would calm these people and, hearing the glorious singing of the quail coming through the open window, said, "Ask if the quail are as numerous every year as they are now."

"*Da, da*", (yes, yes) said the farmer, looking fixedly at Michele. He couldn't understand how, after the questioning about the frightening happenings, this officer could calmly switch to talking about quail. Turning to the interpreter, he asked, "Did he really say quail?"

Michele thought, *Well, I couldn't have been less successful, could I? I can really be proud of myself.* Turning to the *malenko*, he said: "Thank him for me. Tell him I don't want to disturb them any more, that I'm going to turn in."

The *malenko* translated.

"Tell him that if they want to, we could talk some more tomorrow. And, if they don't want to, it doesn't matter. I'll still be their friend, even without talking." The farm family listened to the *malenko* translating Michele's words, always with uncertain looks on their faces. Only to the girl did the words seem to be courteous, evidence of tolerance on the part of the young officer.

II

Michele had been advised that the village had a newly appointed *starosta*, a sort of village headman. He didn't know whether the Germans or the Italians had selected the new *starosta* or whether the appointment was permanent or temporary.

On the morning of his second day in the village, in order to proceed with his inquiry, he took Alexander along as interpreter for a meeting with the village's new leader. Alexander was wearing creased and dirty gray-green uniform trousers; as usual he wore a shirt without a jacket, and his boots were secured with pieces of twine. The *starosta* lived in the village center, which was made up of thatched isbas that stood quite close to each other. He proved to be a bony older man, taller than average, with a pinched face.

He seemed to live alone and received them in the kitchen, which, it appeared, he used as his office. Invited to sit, Michele gave some thought to the unsatisfactory conversation of the previous night and decided to choose his words more carefully.

"I have not sent for you to come and see me, preferring to come myself, because I thought you are probably busier than I." He smiled. "And because", he added seriously, "you are an older man, and I respect age." The *starosta* acknowledged this with a dignified nod of the head, bowing slightly.

Michele then came to the questions he had carefully prepared to make his visit seem plausible: the possibility of utilizing some stables located at the far end of the village. Were they available, or were they being used by civilians?

The village chief replied that the stables were the property of the *kolkhoz* and should be considered as being at the disposition of the occupation forces, like the one already being used by the Italians to store their materiel, "at least for the moment".

"Why do you say that? For the moment?" asked Michele.

"According to what we've heard, all the *kolkhoz* are going to be reactivated soon by the Germans."

Strangely enough, the idea seemed to annoy the *starosta*, and not a little.

"You don't think that's a good decision?" Michele asked.

The older man replied, "What I think, or rather, what all of us Russians think, appears to be unimportant."

Michele considered him, dumbfounded. Maybe he was one of those people whose land had been confiscated by the Communists. One of those who had never forgiven them. Maybe this was why he'd been appointed *starosta*.

He ventured, "Maybe the authorities don't mean to put into effect great reforms while the war is going on. After the war, I'm sure the land won't remain collectivized."

The old man listened to the translation by the *malenko* and then only commented, dryly, "Let's hope so."

Not one to give up, Michele tried again. "Here in the Ukraine, the collectivization of the land must have been a true tragedy."

The *starosta* agreed, nodding his head. Obviously the thought was painful.

"And I've heard it said it caused a great famine. Is that right?"

Another nod.

"Were there many deaths?"

"*Da, da*, a terrible number of dead", he answered with a low voice.

Michele was on the point of asking, "Would you be willing to tell me what really happened?" But bearing in mind the failure of last night's conversation, he decided against it.

Someone knocked on the door. The *starosta* stood, excused himself, and went to the door, which, as in most isbas, was located in a small vestibule off the kitchen. There he exchanged a few words with the new visitors, probably asking them to wait. But when he returned to the kitchen, he found the young officer standing. As he approached, the *malenko* interpreter also stood.

Michele said, "I see that you are needed." The old man nodded yes. "Well, I don't want to bother you any further. But I would like to talk with you about these things when there is more time. Why don't you come down to the *kolkhoz*? Later today or tomorrow, for example? We can have a brandy together."

The old man thanked him, but was evasive. "Thank you. It's not possible today or tomorrow; perhaps some other day?"

This one doesn't seem disposed to speak, either, Michele reflected.

"Yes, all right, that's fine", said Michele, putting a good face on the situation. "Whenever you wish. I don't want to press you."

The Russian was confused by so much courtesy, he seemed about to say something, but restrained himself and finally, still standing, started speaking. Slowly, phrase by phrase, the interpreter translated his words.

"When your troops arrived here, we received them at the village entrance and offered them bread and salt. They were mounted soldiers."

Michele thought, *The Savoia Cavalleria it must have been: they were in the advance alongside the Celere.*

"The commanding officer accepted our bread and salt and spoke to us with courtesy, like a real *gospodin*, a gentleman. It made the hopes we held in our hearts blossom. But now we get nothing but bad news from Voroshilovgrad, our chief town. The Germans are executing thousands of our countrymen. A great pit has been dug outside the city, and their firing squads are filling it. Didn't you know?"

The genuinely bewildered Michele looked the *starosta* in the eyes. "It's not possible", he murmured.

"It's not only in Voroshilovgrad that the Germans are killing civilians", added the *starosta*, who had noted Michele's sincerity. "And we had welcomed you with bread and salt!" He shook his head and walked ahead of them, to the door.

Taken aback by the accusations of the *starosta*, Michele said, taking the hand of the Russian before leaving, "Listen, I'll do what I can to get information about what is happening in Voroshilovgrad. I'll be expecting you in the *kolkhoz*. Do come."

The *starosta* shook Michele's hand in silence, thinking to himself, *What crap! What kind of conquerors are these? They don't seem to know that during the civil war the Reds emptied the White forces simply by distributing the land to the peasants. Instead of doing the same thing with the forces of that mangy dog Stalin, they go around shooting the ones who didn't flee, who waited here to welcome them. And just because they are fighting the Communists, I've made the mistake of believing in these pieces of sh——!*

The news of the Voroshilovgrad firing squads and others didn't seem to bother the *malenko*, but it deeply troubled Michele. He walked back through the village totally absorbed, musing on it, unaware of the chickens scratching about the front of some of the isbas, not noticing the glorious yellow of the large sunflowers in the gardens or a woman drawing water from a well at ground level through a primitive wooden pump.

What if the whole thing was based on unfounded rumors? Or originated with the enemy's propaganda mill?

But something inside him said no, that with the Nazis you had to expect such things. You couldn't go on, like a simpleton, believing the Fascists and the Nazis were on the same plane, as if National Socialism were some German version of fascism. Running through his mind were the rumors that used to circulate back at the Catholic university, the judgment of Pope Pius XI, according to which the Nazis should be considered as the real antichrist, as described in the Gospel, no less. And, after all, "By their deeds will you know them." Perhaps even now the SS were exterminating the Jews in Voroshilovgrad, that city of isbas but, he reminded himself, of the same size as Florence or Bologna, which he had passed through several days earlier. Maybe that was exactly what was happening, the Jews were being eliminated . . .

At this stage of the war, no news had emerged about the Nazi concentration camps. These camps had started to operate only a few months before. But intelligent people who thought about the fate of Jews in territories being occupied piece by piece by the Germans already felt a certain feeling of horror.

Whether it is Jews or prisoners of war in Voroshilovgrad, if I really want to get a clear idea of the fruits to which the distancing from Christianity leads today, I've got to look at what the Nazis are doing as well, not only at the Communists. Yes, I must try to find out, try to know, thought Michele, mournfully.

A call from the *malenko* brought him back to the here and now. "Look, Lieutenant, here comes Beniamino." Like most Russians, the *malenko* always referred to people by their first rather than their family names. Michele looked around and saw an infantryman coming toward them, an ill-humored look on his face, as if he resented having to chase around after officers. On approaching, he stiffened to attention and addressed Michele: "Sir, four truckloads of materiel have arrived. Where do you want them unloaded?"

Michele quickened his pace, saying, "I'm coming right away."

12

Later that same day, the heat intense, Michele was lying on his cot, trying to put his thoughts into some order when he heard the unexpected chugs of a motorcycle. He went to the window and saw that the machine had stopped by the sentry. Two soldiers with engineer badges were riding the motorcycle and were in the process of asking if this was the supply depot for the Eighty-First Infantry.

"We have a temporary depot here, but apart from myself, I think everybody is sleeping."

"Yes, well, we're with the Engineer Corps", explained the sapper seated on the back. "We're camped not far from here, in Fedorovka. You know where that is? About ten kilometers from here."

"Yes, and . . ."

"Well, we urgently need incandescent mantles for our pressure lanterns, and our captain advised us to come here to see if you have any."

The sentry turned and indicated Michele, looking out at them from his window. "You'd better speak to him, to the lieutenant."

Quickly the two soldiers turned the motorcycle around and drove over to the isba's window, where the one on the rear seat once more introduced himself and made his request: "We don't need much. We're looking for incandescent mantles for our Petromax lamps. Ours were in a truck that hit a mine, and they all burned up."

"What? They burned even though they were incandescent?" said Michele.

The sapper smiled. "Yes, even though they were incandescent mantles." In contrast to his driver, this man was perfectly dressed in uniform, with the regulation necktie and all the rest. "It sounds like an unimportant request, but we have night work at the plotting table. It's a hell of a mess."

"Right", said Michele. "I don't know if we have them. Let's go have a look."

Quickly putting on his leggings and pistol belt, in his shirtsleeves, he joined the other two outside and led them into the large barn where the supplies were stacked.

Turning to the impeccably uniformed soldier, Michele asked, "Are you a student?"

"Yes, Lieutenant, architecture."

"Where, in Milan by any chance?" Michele vaguely hoped he might be a friend of Manno's.

"No, in Rome."

"Oh, right."

The barn was simply constructed, like all the others in the *kolkhoz* and from the inside could be seen the rough uprights and roof supports to which the thatching had been fastened. There were no windows; light came from one end of the barn, where a section had been left unthatched.

"Look at the way they built this stable for the animals. It's made of planks and straw, poor things", commented the architecture student from Rome.

"Poor things who? The animals or their owners?" asked Michele, busy helping the other sapper open a crate.

"The people from around here, I meant", replied the other.

"Oh, yes! Really they are quite poor", agreed Michele.

The student looked over at Michele. "You know that they've started eating each other?"

Startled, Michele quickly raised his head and looked at him. "What?"

"Yes, Lieutenant, they've reached that point—cannibalism."

"But . . . what are you talking about?"

"I assure you. I don't know about this village, but in Fedorovka, where we are camped, ten kilometers from here . . ." He turned to the other sapper. "Isn't that right? You tell him."

The driver, who from his manners Michele took for a laborer, confirmed, "Yes, it's right. In Fedorovka all the civilians say so."

"But . . .", Michele repeated, interrupting his search and looking the other two in the eyes, "what are you saying?"

The driver spoke again. "At our village, some thirty meters from our isba HQ, there's a woman who cooked a dead child, to give it to . . . , well, in short, to her other children to eat."

Michele continued looking questioningly at the other two, gooseflesh raising the hairs on his arms and back.

"Frightful, isn't it?" said the student. "But this case wasn't recent; it's supposed to have happened during the famine ten years ago, when the land was collectivized. That's when people in Fedorovka were eating the dead. This woman's son had died of hunger, and as she had other children at death's door, she cooked his flesh and fed the others. The smell of cooking meat drifted around the village, and the people went to find out what it was, and that's how they discovered it, do you follow me?"

"That's how it was, all right", confirmed the driver.

"And what about the poor miserable woman? What is she doing now? Does she talk about it?"

"She lives near our HQ. No, she doesn't talk about it, naturally. We learned about it from the other villagers. They told us."

"At first," continued the student, "when the rumor started going around, just a few days ago, you can imagine how it was. Some of the soldiers wanted to see her, and she would weep. She'd run and hide inside her isba. Because some of the men really upset her by making stupid remarks, trying to be funny, you know how they are. When this happened, our captain gave strict orders to stop pestering her."

The driver shook his head. "And our captain is a hard guy. You don't fool with him ..."

"But you said, if I understood you correctly, that there have been other cases of cannibalism in Fedorovka?" Michele asked.

"Yes, there have been other cases, so people maintain." But the two men were not in a position to say how many, even approximately.

At length, they found the lamp mantles they had been seeking. Under different circumstances, Michele would have felt proud, somehow, that he, part of the beaten-up infantry, had been able to satisfy the requirements of the gentlemen of the Engineer Corps. But this time, he had other things on his mind. He was reminded of the chronicles of Josephus Flavius, the reproach addressed to the gods by the Romans during the siege of Jerusalem in the year 70, when the news came to them that inside the city the Jews were eating their dead. *It's as if we've gone back 2,000 years*, Michele thought, stunned, *2,000 years.*

The student had been busy writing a receipt with his fountain pen. He handed it, already stamped and signed by his captain, to Michele, who read aloud "Captain Carlo Cipolla."

The sapper said, "Yes, he's from Milan."

From Milan? thought Michele. *Perhaps I can go to see him. Surely I can get more details from him ... but when can I do that? I can't get away from here.*

Later, in the evening, sharing dinner with a group of his foot soldiers, he felt strongly impelled to tell them of the incident, to talk with them about it, if only to get it off his chest. However, the soldiers' comments were totally inadequate.

13

It took Michele a few days to absorb the engineers' story. Then he wrote to Ambrogio, asking him to gather any information about cannibalism he came across. Meanwhile, he pursued his inquiries around his village, but without result. The *starosta*, who obviously had better things to do than satisfy his curiosity, never made an appearance.

One night, he woke suddenly, his head full of thoughts of innocent people being massacred in Voroshilovgrad and of cannibalism. Annoyed at the effect all this was having on him, he thought, *Why should I, alone, torture myself with these things?* He tried to think of other matters. *My duty, right now, is to think of my responsibilities, and most important, let's see . . .* He sat up, thinking that since arriving at the village he had not carried out a single night inspection. Getting up, he got dressed, unhooked his pistol belt from the wall by the cot, pulled his flashlight from under his pillow, switched it on and went out.

The sentry—a simple soul, a peasant—was at his post, leaning back against the barn's wall, thinking of his girl back home in the south of Italy, reproaching himself for the hundredth time for his failure to propose before leaving her. The appearance of his officer brought him back to earth, and they exchanged a few words.

The deep infinity of the night sky stretched over the village and the great Russian countryside. Stars shone brightly, and there was a feeling of purity in the air they breathed, and even at this hour, they could hear the quail calling to each other out in the fields.

Michele breathed deeply, and, looking around, thought, *How beautiful is God's creation! Absolutely beautiful! How is it possible that we men regularly, in every generation, transform it into a nightmare worthy of Dante?* Absentmindedly saluting the sentry, "See you later, Califano", he turned and walked slowly back to the isba. But instead of going in, he walked up and down outside, taking deep breaths of the wonderful cool night air. He was and felt very young, reduced in importance by the immensity of the night, touched by the beauty and peace surrounding him.

The quail continued their tireless song. *They're singing of love*, he thought. *How eager they sound! What ardent feeling they put into their singing!* He felt physically aroused, and despite his strong religion-based morality, sensuous fantasies ran through his mind. He thought about the young Russian girl in the isba . . . he met her several times every day.

Just a minute, he told himself. *This girl isn't for me; she's intended for someone else. I mustn't get involved, because right there is when it starts, the damage that spreads from there to all creation, transforming it into a nightmare . . . Yes, that's right where it starts.*

There was also the question of what he owed his future wife. Who was she? Where was she at this very moment? He continued walking up and down outside the isba, trying to imagine the woman who would be his life's companion. What would she look like? She probably had to be very young. Almost certainly he had never seen her. Unless ... Suddenly, he could see in his imagination the enigmatic, smiling figure of Almina, Ambrogio's fifteen-year-old sister. *That day in Nomana, watching her playing on the grass, jumping like a young lamb. What an extraordinary creature, truly unique!* He could very well imagine her to be the one. Overtaken by ecstasy, Michele began to think it could be she, his life's companion ... *Of course! Why didn't I think of it before? She's a perfect creature!*

Thinking of Alma helped control his desires for physical satisfaction, the sudden temptation that had seized him. The natural beauty of his surroundings still kept flowing into him, but without stirring him physically any longer. Soon he was thinking of Alma in poetic terms, and he remembered two lines from an old favorite: *Lord, who willed the creation for me of this distant love* ... A strong need came over him to write down his feelings, to sing of this marvelous love that was growing in him.

He thought, *Songs for Alma*, and, being practical, *But where can I write? By flashlight?* There was no table in his room. Well, he'd think of a way ...

Going back inside the isba, he pulled out of his order box his government-issue writing pad and a pen and put them on his pillow. Then, in darkness except for the few rays of moonlight entering his large, open window, he started to pace up and down the room. The words and rhythm of his song formed in his mind, and once again a feeling of excitement fired him.

Suddenly he had the sense that someone was moving around outside. This brought him back to reality with a shock. He was in a war. Since he still had the flashlight in hand, he pointed it toward the door and switched it on: the door was opening very quietly, furtively pushed by the young Russian girl, who ended by coming in and closing it behind her. She was barefoot, dressed only in a nightdress, her wheat-colored hair gathered in a single thick braid. In the pale light of the flashlight, she looked at the young man with a mixture of impudence and shame.

Oh, God, what a trial! Michele truly feared himself too weak for such a temptation. "Masha", he murmured with difficulty, his voice low. "What are you doing here? What do you have in mind?"

The girl didn't understand his words but only pointed her finger, first at him, then at herself; again at him and then at herself. Her intention unmistakable.

Michele felt himself filled with an emotion so violent that his earlier poetic thoughts, which had seemed so strong to him, appeared trivial in comparison. Worse still, the former seemed to invade the latter, to be gathered up in it. Dizzy with emotion, he lowered the flashlight to the floor. *I can't. I don't have the right, I mustn't give in! I absolutely must not give in!* Then, in as firm a tone as he could: "Masha! No. It's not possible!" His words were as much aimed at himself as at the girl.

The girl seemed not to want to move and continued looking at Michele. Even in the dim light she appeared to Michele indescribably attractive, alluring beyond words. Never in his life had Michele—who made it his duty not to look at her—experienced so strong a temptation, anything so overwhelming.

"*No dobre*, it's not right", he said, using one of the few Russian phrases he knew; he repeated, "*No dobre!*" The girl gave a small sigh and shrugged her shoulders in disappointment, yet she still did not move.

Michele went toward the door, trying to reopen it without making any noise. Masha shook her head and sighed once more (how feminine she was as she did this!) and finally turned and left the room. Michele closed the door.

He had succeeded in turning away temptation, as morality prescribed. But the emotion of it did not leave him for all that. Trying to regain control of himself, he murmured: "It is God who commands this, this God in whom I believe and whose teaching I am resolved to follow." He even tried to formulate a mass of arguments of the rational order. "This girl Masha is probably a virgin and almost certainly will one day marry some poor devil, and I don't want to take from him the privilege of the honeymoon night. It's not for me to ruin that for him. And all this had to happen to me on the very night when . . . when my love for Alma was being born. So that, besides everything else, if I had given in, the memory of such abject inconsistency would have followed me for the rest of my life." Wise, holy words, and yet . . .

Writing pad and fountain pen forgotten, he continued his pacing, countless thoughts racing through his mind, violently disturbing him. He did not have Ambrogio's powers of concentration, his ability to detach himself from things by dint of will. Because of this, quite a few contrary arguments presented themselves to him: to begin with, the constant bragging of one of his soldiers—the envy of all—who claimed to have had relations with a woman in the village. And the stories he'd heard of colleagues and soldiers who had spent the previous winter in the isbas with the civilians, living like married men. And yet the Russian country women were not corrupt; they even had a true sense of modesty (military men insisted on holding forth on the subject in the coarsest possible way; some seemed unable to talk of anything else). But what he really had to struggle against was his own imagination, which, interposing itself between his positive and negative reasoning, like a traitor, made him glimpse the image of what would have happened if he had not refused the girl.

To escape, he had to have ardent recourse to prayer; and what came to his aid, more than anything else, was that constant practice of purity, cultivated since childhood at the price of so many struggles and appeals to the supernatural. It took him hours before he felt calm and was able to sleep.

The next few days were difficult for Michele. The girl was constantly around and, true daughter of Eve, behaved as if nothing had happened. However, she frequently looked Michele directly in the eyes, and the temptation came back to him stronger than ever. Fortunately, for him, he received unexpected marching orders.

This order was brought to him by an officer from the support section, who arrived on the scene with enough trucks to take charge of all the supplies. At the same time this officer also gave him some important news: "Soon, we'll be reinforced from Italy by three more infantry divisions—another army corps to fight alongside us. Also on the way is a corps of Alpine troops, but I think they'll be sent to more mountainous country than this; perhaps they'll go to the Caucasus. But behind the lines people are talking as if they'd already begun to arrive. When they're all here, our forces in Russia will be three times the size. We'll go from one to three army corps."

Michele asked the officer how so many people could be transported on the existing rail system. "All the railway lines, from the border right on, have been demolished, without exception. I've seen them myself in quite a few places."

"Were demolished, you mean," the officer said, "and perhaps some small sections still are, but the German corps of engineers are everywhere now, repairing the tracks."

14

The whole of the southern front was on the move. The German front line troops were reaching the Volga River at Stalingrad and advancing rapidly in the Caucasus and were already climbing it for their new objectives—the petroleum sources and the Persian border.

The artillery group to which Ambrogio belonged had long ago left the industrial Donets Basin behind. They had traveled for weeks through flat fields planted in grain and sunflowers; the country seemed to be never ending. Later, they'd gone through broken country, where cultivated areas were interspersed with grassy steppes, wild and open. There were no more groups of civilians to be seen along the roads; their truck convoys seemed to go on forever without coming across any villages; there was not sight or sound of humans except for their own presence. The endless blue sky curved off into the endless landscape; soldiers asked one another where they were, where they were going. At times, it seemed they'd reached the end of the world. Up ahead of them, the Bersaglieri occasionally made contact and fought skirmishes with a retreating enemy, but when news of these reached the column, it would be distorted by rumor. Also, they weren't taking part in these actions, so their significance and intensity would often be underrated. As a matter of fact, only at the end of their advance, when nearing the Don, did the Bersaglieri have some serious combat to handle, as the retreating Russians tried in vain, with the help of tanks, to hold on to bridge heads (one was at Serafimovic) on their side of the big river.

By this time, the Italians had left the Ukraine behind and were in ancient Cossack country. The three Italian divisions lined up elbow to elbow on the banks of the Don, facing north. From the eastern wing of their formation, Stalingrad was only 150 kilometers away.

15

A few weeks later, the first of the recently arrived Italian divisions, unexpectedly attacked by the Russians, was forced to retreat. Their position on the Don was to the right of the Pasubio, and upon giving way they left a thirty-kilometer unprotected gap in the Italian lines. With great difficulty, replacements were found to throw into the gap, and among these was the Savoia regiment of cavalry, which took part in the historic charge, the last-ever cavalry charge by Italian mounted troops. But decisive in regaining the lost ground were two battalions of Alpine troops, thrown at the enemy immediately upon their arrival by train.

For Ambrogio, these were days of continuous confusion; his group was called upon to fire not only by various observation posts on the Don but also by others hurriedly pushed into the unprotected area to the right of the Pasubio, east of the line.

Also thrown into the gap was Bonsaver's group, and the young officer participated in a frantic series of firefights, some of them at close range. Pitched into action and totally absorbed with their own immediate duties, Bonsaver, Ambrogio, and Michele Tintori, each in his own area of the line, didn't have time to ask questions about the greater battle. For example, why a complete Italian division had abandoned its sector, without apparently putting up any serious resistance, and why only two battalions of Alpine troops were enough to do in a short time what ten standard battalions hadn't found themselves fit to handle?

Such questions (if they had been made) would have made them better acquainted with the military qualities of their fellow citizens. The front line once again became reestablished and, after all the previous frantic movement, settled down to routine days of military boredom. Summer stretched on.

The four cannons in Ambrogio's battery had been emplaced three kilometers from the Don, near the mouth of a flood channel. From this place, no other signs of military preparation could be seen, since a wooded area nearby concealed the battery's command post, transportation, and kitchens. Behind and to the right of the battery was open flat country; facing it, the ground rose slightly and then dropped in softly rounded ridges down to the river. Little could be seen of the river from the battery, due to the densely treed riverbank. On the opposite bank, in plain view, could be seen the Cossack town of Veshenskaya, which looked abandoned. Standing clear in the center of all the thatched houses was the small onion-shaped tower of a church.

In the area around the four cannons there were no trees; the ground was covered with the patchy wild grass of the steppes, so that the tents of Ambrogio Riva and his some fifty artillerymen, set up close to the cannons, were fully exposed to the late August sun from morning to night.

Ambrogio was now the only officer at the battery; the other two second lieutenants had returned to Italy to take university examinations (the army allowed such luxuries), so Ambrogio couldn't go far from his post on the bank of the flood channel. The tents became very hot, and inside most of them could be detected a heavy aroma made up of the smells of crushed grass, hot metal, and human bodies. Unable to go far from their cannon, though calls from the observation posts to bring down fire became infrequent, the men sat around in the tents or in groups outside. Ambrogio got into the habit of opening one side of his tent each morning and supporting the flap on poles, to give himself shade in which to read, talk to passing soldiers, or just think about life.

On some days, generally around twilight, there would be a gathering of soldiers, sometimes three or four, sometimes up to ten, sitting on the grass outside Ambrogio's tent, and they would talk.

Nowadays, someone might think that the soldiers' attitude was influenced by the opinion that later prevailed in Italy—that victory on the Russian front could bring no direct benefit to Italy and that instead an increase in Germany's strength would be less than good for Italy. Or that they should have been affected by the guilt attaching to invading conquerors (but then it was only a short while before this that Russians themselves had entered Poland, Lithuania, Latvia, Estonia, and Finland as conquerors). In fact, there was none of this. The soldiers didn't question their being there, apart from questions of immediate comfort. At the center of their conversations were their faraway homes, their girlfriends (when they had one), health, their parents' work—in one word, family.

As for the connection between each family's future and the fate of that nation, the soldiers were uninterested, thought only vaguely about it. Insofar as the concept of "nation" was concerned, whether northerners or southerners (apart from the constant and stale parochial arguments among themselves), they saw themselves having a relationship with the state rather like their involvement with nature—one is born and then periodically suffers from storms and floods, all of which have to be faced. Some face these with more or less courage or decency, or even indecency; some, above all the Christians, with varying degrees of nobility, some with none at all. This was all there was—the battles, the war, would leave them all with memories similar to their remembrances of the storms and floods of life.

Ambrogio became ever more aware of this, and sometimes, instead of waiting for visits from them, he would go poking his head into one or other tent. "May I interrupt," he asked, "or am I disturbing you?" The soldiers showed their pleasure at his visits. "Please, Lieutenant, make yourself at home. Even if it's not exactly a palace." He'd sit among them on the palliasses, and they would talk, the usual subjects of soldiers everywhere: the faraway town or village, women, fathers, mothers, the problems of life, women again. Some shyly, some boastfully, the young soldiers, most of them barely in their twenties, seemed to feel obligated to talk about women. Some with the confidence of experience, some humorously, some timidly. There were always one or two who could recount some amorous adventure, usually the same one, known down to the last detail to their tentmates, the victims of previous recountings. Others were unable to express themselves without being pornographic and talking like "pigs", as the saying went. One twenty-year-old, Moioli, from Bergamo, gun layer on the number-one cannon, would talk of women with great confidence, sometimes ending up with, "What a wonderful thing is love!" said in his own ingenuous way. One day Ambrogio was part of a group in Moioli's tent, and after he'd said his piece, asked Moioli, "But do you know about love from your own experience?"

Moioli looked embarrassed, paused for a while, then replied truthfully, "No, my lieutenant, not really . . ." Being a good honest fellow from Bergamo, even though embarrassed before his companions, he couldn't deny the truth. (May a writer say hello to you, Moioli? You would be dead soon, like the others, and the bravery of this boy blooms again, if only for an instant, before being swallowed by time.) "That's why you talk the way you do, all this respect for women", broke in Corporal Costanzo, a tractor driver, over thirty years old. "Now I know why you doubt me whenever I say that women are all whores. Of course, it's because you don't know them."

"Well," said Ambrogio, "all whores . . . ?"

"Absolutely, Lieutenant", Costanzo replied. "We've seen it even here in Russia; last winter in Kamenka, when we were billeted in civilian houses. How many from our battery didn't form a temporary marriage? Ten, twenty percent at the most."

Sergeant Facchi, a farmer from Brescia, rough and tough, calmly explained, "Specially those guys who'd been educated by priests, who'd been to chapel schools, like me."

Costanzo came back, "And the Russian women would talk about their husbands every day, most of them off fighting at the front, and they'd cross themselves in that strange Orthodox way. Then, at night they'd come and sleep with us, without our ever asking them. That's how they are. Women are all whores." All his comrades knew that Costanzo had left a young wife at home and was furiously jealous; what nobody knew was if he had good reason for his jealousy.

There was a silence while they absorbed what Costanzo had said, but even more because the group was surprised at Moioli's declaration of virginity. Moioli now was blushing. Ambrogio, feeling responsible for causing Moioli's confession in front of the group in his own tent, said, "Well, neither have I experienced physical love yet."

Several voices reacted, "What, what did he say ... ?" and "But, Lieutenant, that's not possible ..."

"So impossible that it's the truth. And with God's help, I hope not to experience it until I marry", Ambrogio asserted.

With suppressed delight, Sergeant Facchi asked, "So in your case, it's also for religious reasons, eh?"

"Yes," answered Ambrogio and was about to add, "and because of faithfulness", with an explanation of why, but he felt this would sound like sermonizing; the plain fact was the better witness.

Campanini, ammunition passer from Liguria, totally taken aback, blurted, "But, Lieutenant, it's not possible ..." One of the many soldiers who admired, almost revered, Ambrogio, Campanini had always been impressed with the way the young officer's Milanese efficiency had been gradually imposed on the battery and was genuinely shaken by his admission of virginity.

Ambrogio looked Campanini in the eye, noted his bewilderment, and, having nothing more to say, laughed, relieving the tension in the tent. After a short silence, the group went on to talk of something else. These informal gatherings gave Ambrogio a chance to get to know his groups better; he also knew they helped them to understand him. He was aware that mutual understanding could be very important if difficult times ever arrived.

16

One afternoon, Bonsaver came to visit (after warning him by telephone, "Expect me sometime this week"). He found Ambrogio sitting under his tent flap, reading. Stopping a few steps away from his friend, he shouted in his best parade-sergeant voice, "Second Lieutenant Ambrogio Riva!"

Ambrogio, startled, jumped to his feet. "Oh, Bonsaver, it's you!" He started laughing. "Welcome. It's great to see you here." He put out his hand. "Come on in, make yourself comfortable."

"Riva, hello, how are you?" Bonsaver looked around. "You seem to be living a good war, enjoying aristocratic privacy, eh? Far from the smelly soldiery and a good distance from your leaders ..."

"Not quite. The battery CP is less than two hundred meters away, over by the flood channel, and the company command is a little beyond, over there ..."

"Yes, I saw them on the way here", replied Bonsaver.

Offering him a seat, Ambrogio told Bonsaver, "Sit here. You've no idea how happy I am to see you." As for him, he sat on the cot, which took up most of one side of the two-meter-square tent. Once seated, Bonsaver took a book he'd been carrying under one arm and held it out to Riva. "I've brought this book for you to read. Remember, I'm only lending it to you, eh? It came to me in the mail two weeks ago. It's a propaganda book, all about Communists, all that ..." And indicating its thickness, he continued, "Naturally, I've not read it all, but it seems interesting because it mentions this part of the world. It's about Veshenskaya, Jagodnoie, Meskoff, all these towns. And it's called *Quiet Flows the Don*, by Sholokov; I think you'll like it."

Ambrogio was turning the pages, "Ah, yes, look, here's Veshenskaya." And then he saw a dedication on the front flyleaf, in a definite female handwriting. "Ho, ho! What's this? Eh? 'From Cenzina to her distant hero'! Who would this distant hero be? You? Am I right? Come on ..."

"Come off it. This was sent to me by my war godmother. It's natural she'd write a few words. You have to expect it from women", said Bonsaver.

"Naturally, why not?" replied Ambrogio. "And who is this war godmother of yours? No doubt she's fat and has a mustache, am I right?"

"No, you're mistaken." Bonsaver had become serious. "It's that girl I've spoken to you about. Didn't I tell you her name is Vincenza? No? Well, it's her."

"Ah!" said Ambrogio. "This is the one ... the girl you're trying to return to the fold, like the prophet Hosea?"

"Who is this Hosea?" Bonsaver asked.

Ambrogio smiled at his friend. "This Hosea is the one from the Old Testament, who married Gomer, a lady with many men friends."

Bonsaver, a little uneasy at this turn in the conversation, only said, "I'd never heard of him before."

"I only remember this," Ambrogio said, "that he was a prophet and he'd married this easy lady, with the intention of converting her to righteous ways, I suppose. But tell me, how has Vincenza come to be your campaign godmother?"

"It was her idea. Maybe so she could send me books and goodies to eat without my being obligated ... I don't know, it was her idea ..."

Smiling again, Ambrogio said, "And all the time, you keep on writing her sermons ... now that she can't talk back to you?"

Bonsaver shook his head in pity, faced with his friend's outrageous remarks. He was about to answer Ambrogio, but before he could say anything, the phone installed on a box next to his friend's bed rang insistently, and Ambrogio hurried to answer it.

"Artillery group. Yes, right away!" Ambrogio dropped the book on the cot, grabbed a megaphone, and raced out of the tent, shouting toward the enlisted men's tents. "Gunners, man your guns!" Going back into the tent, Ambrogio, megaphone still in hand, picked up the box and the telephone in his right hand and carried the whole thing outside, shouting to Bonsaver, "It must be four days since we've fired these guns. We needed a distant hero like you to bring us a little life!"

The gun layers and ammunition passers meantime had run over to their places, pulled the camouflage nets and leather covers from their cannons, and opened the breeches and aiming sights. Almost simultaneously, all four cannons' crews were ready, and the corporals in charge of each piece held a hand up in the air, firmly gripping a small notepad and pencil, signal to Ambrogio that all were ready.

Squatting on the ground near the field phone, a signaler held a pad and pencil ready. Almost immediately, coordinates were being fed to them by the OP on the Don. "Direction 34 and 20!" repeated Ambrogio, shouting them, holding the receiver to his ear with his left hand and the megaphone to his mouth with his right. Every word repeated the coordinates to his men: "Third piece ready." "First piece ready." "Fourth piece ready . . . second piece ready." They shouted to the officer. "Lead gun, load!" ordered Ambrogio. There was movement around the third gun, led by Corporal Zanini, who finally raised his hand at Ambrogio.

Ambrogio shouted, "Lead gun, fire!"

"Fire!" ordered Zanini. The gun jerked and shot forward, producing a violent cloud of smoke, a deafening explosion, and a recoil of the barrel, which immediately slid back into position.

Bonsaver, standing next to Riva, shouted, "Goodbye!"

Ten or twelve seconds later, the battery's crew heard the explosion, muffled by distance.

"Up 24, left 2!" Ambrogio shouted, and then under his breath to Bonsaver, "Who knows what we're shooting at?"

"Didn't they tell you?" asked Bonsaver.

Ambrogio shook his head. "I'll ask them later."

The lead gun fired seven more times, with corrections being applied before each shot, the men following their almost automatic routines. Then, after the last correction, the whole battery fired six more shots: twenty-six shots in all thundered out at the common target.

Then came a "Hold your fire!" from the observers, and shortly after "Cease fire!" Ambrogio grabbed the phone and shouted into it, "Hey, Bellei, how about telling me what it is we've been shooting at?" He listened for a bit, then nodded and smiled. "Thanks, good luck."

Handing the phone back, Ambrogio turned to Bonsaver. "Someone saw movement in a small wood over the Don. They thought the Russians might be assembling a patrol to probe our lines. Nothing confirmed, but according to our infantry, intelligence from deserters says that there's some sort of company command post in there."

"So in your sector here, you also have lots of Russians deserting?" asked Bonsaver.

"Quite a few, but according to gossip, many less than last year."

The signaler took the field phone back to Ambrogio's tent and was followed by the two officers. Riva put down the megaphone and resumed his seat on the tent's single cot. Bonsaver went back to the stool under the tent flap.

17

As if there had been no interruption, the conversation came back to Bonsaver's campaign godmother. "So, my distant hero, we were talking about a certain lady, and you've not yet given me all the details."

"You're trying to make fun of me . . .", said Bonsaver, and it was becoming clear that he didn't enjoy the joking tone his friend had adopted.

Ambrogio sensed that he shouldn't continue but went ahead anyway. "I mean, after all, you might even succeed in changing her evil ways." Turning the pages of the Sholokov book, he looked again at the dedication and smiled. "The idea of saving a good-looking girl isn't all that bad . . . from the religious point of view, of course. I only hope you don't expect the Lord to award you merit points or give you praise for your excessive zeal."

Bonsaver shook his head. He would be able to talk about the girl to his friend if it weren't for the joking way Ambrogio treated the relationship. He said, "Girls are weaker creatures than us men—more fragile. If some S.O.B. takes advantage of a weak moment on her part . . . would you want to let her continue along the wrong path? But these are things that can only be talked about in a serious manner."

Ambrogio immediately knew he'd gone too far with his friend. "Please forgive me for what I've said." He patted Bonsaver's knee. "Look, there's something I've got to know."

"About girls?"

"No, I'm not talking of girls. It's clear that for some weeks you've been right in the middle of dangerous fighting."

Bonsaver looked very serious. "One heck of a row those guys in the Cicai started." (Within the Italian army, the Ukrainian word for *escape* was commonly being used when referring to the division that had retreated, leaving a gap in the Italian front.)

"You're right. What I don't understand is why it took so long to reestablish control. Do you think the Russians meant to go through the gap?"

"I don't know . . . maybe in the beginning it was just another probing attack, but when they found the way clear, they just threw themselves forward." And Bonsaver went on to explain the details of the action. Some of the facts he produced were unknown to Ambrogio, particularly the erratic behavior of some of the Italian units sent in to retake the lost ground. It became clear that Bonsaver had been deeply involved in the action. Ambrogio asked him many questions, looking for more precise details, but the other was in a position to clarify only those actions in which he had personally taken part. In any event, these were neither few nor uninteresting.

They had been talking for about a half hour when Ambrogio, looking past his friend's head, noticed some distant black dots in the sky, far away on the other side of the Don. *They must be German planes*, he thought and asked, "But how did you people in the observation post handle the retreat? Were you in phone contact, or do you use radio only nowadays?"

"As long as we were able, we used the telephone ...", and he continued relating some of what he'd seen. Alongside his head, the black dots were still there, and Ambrogio pointed them out to his friend.

"Over there, you see, there are planes, the other side of the river."

"Yes, I see them." Bonsaver shaded his eyes with a hand. "There's about a dozen of them—they must be Germans."

"Right, that's what I figured. They must be returning from a mission. We see very few Russian planes around here, and then generally at night."

Bonsaver smiled. "The old motorbike, right?"

Ambrogio, smiling, said, "Yes, practically every night he comes overhead, the bastard, but he almost never drops bombs." He paused. "These, now, they're coming toward us."

He got up and went outside the tent for a better view, and Bonsaver followed. The black dots were bigger now, could pretty nearly be identified as pursuit machines, although some looked bigger. Ambrogio commented, "They're very low. I'd say they're at 200, maybe 100 meters, not much more." Nearby, a group of artillerymen stood near their tents, also watching the planes and commenting among themselves. As they watched, the planes became identifiable; they could see that about half were twin-engine and the rest fighter escorts.

"Look at the small ones, the fighters", said Ambrogio. "What's the reason for their circling like that? I've never seen the Germans do that before."

"It must be because of speed", said Bonsaver. "Maybe the fighters are too fast for the others to keep up with, and the fighters have to maneuver to keep on station, along with the bombers."

Ambrogio thought, *What if they're Russians? What if they attack this position?* He glanced around. The four cannons of his battery were some twenty meters from each other and, although covered in camouflage netting, were easily visible, out in the open, being surrounded by defensive trenches and machine-gun emplacements, also easy to pick out from above. His cubic tent and the triangular soldiers' tents, although camouflaged, would also stand out in the grass. At either end of the small battery there would also be seen two round foxholes, deep enough to protect a couple of men, and each having one of the battery's two aerial defense machine guns on tripod mountings. Ambrogio looked over at the nearest machine gun. Bonsaver followed his look. It was about twelve paces away. The planes, engine noise increasing, had reached the area parallel to the battery, about one kilometer to their left. Flying over the food channel, and paralleling the Don, they suddenly dropped their entire bomb load. The ground trembled and vibrated under their feet, like an earthquake; the noise, louder than the engine sound overhead, drowned everything, expanding outward over the plains.

From the battery could be heard shouts of alarm, and the artillerymen were seen running from their tents to the sheltering trenches around the cannons. Ambrogio and Bonsaver ran toward the nearby machine gun, jumping and landing almost at the same time inside its circumference. The planes, meanwhile, were turning to fly back to their own lines and would reach their position in moments.

"Do you know the Fiat 35?" Ambrogio shouted the question at his friend, while feverishly tearing at the leather cover, finally arming the machine gun.

"A little!" Bonsaver shouted back.

"Feed the belt for me!" shouted Ambrogio, who felt the tumultuous beating of his heart despite an effort to stay calm, and opened fire.

"Right!" acknowledged his colleague, grabbing for the leaping belt. At a height of about 100 meters, and with a deafening, unbelievably loud buzzing noise, the attacking planes passed overhead. This close, they seemed enormous. Ambrogio, slightly panting, aimed for the cockpits, the pilots, whom he could see as they passed before him. The planes also were firing, using their machine guns on the battery, their bullets hitting the ground around the machine-gun emplacement, raising dust.

"It's like in the movies!" Bonsaver shouted excitedly.

"What? What did you say?" Ambrogio shouted back.

"Never mind, come on, keep firing!"

Ambrogio nodded. He had a twin-engine plane under fire, and as the enemy formation distanced itself toward the Don, he kept firing at it. He stopped firing when all the planes were out of range. His heart continued beating heavily; he could feel it in his throat.

"That went badly", he said. "Did you see?" He was cross. Looking into the ammunition box and at the unfired side of the belt, he realized not much had been fired, but everything had happened in seconds . . .

Bonsaver, attempting to cheer him up, said, "Your shots may have all gone home, but if you don't hit the pilot or some vital part of the motors . . ."

"I was an idiot!" said Ambrogio. "That's how I behaved, like an idiot. I shouldn't have gone from one plane to the other that way! I should have aimed for one only, stayed with the same one. My mistake. What a cretin!" Immediately, he thought, *What about the other machine gun?* He climbed out of the foxhole, going toward the other emplacement; he hadn't heard the other gun firing, and then he saw that the gun still had its leather protectors fastened; the gun hadn't been fired.

"Vassena!" he shouted. "Vassena, where are you?"

Vassena, a corporal, who was responsible for the reduced machine-gun squad, was emerging from one of the trenches.

"I'm here", he said surprised. "What's up?"

"Why didn't you fire this gun?" Ambrogio shouted at him.

"Why . . . ?" said Vassena, in a low voice. He didn't know what to say.

The planes, in the meantime, had recrossed the Don. Bonsaver, who had by now climbed out of the foxhole, joined Ambrogio in watching them fly away, until they were once more reduced to small black dots in the distance.

Then the unexpected happened. First one, then a second and a third of the planes made sudden turns and headed back. They began to grow in size as they approached; they were three of the pursuit planes.

"They're coming back!" exclaimed Bonsaver. "Look, they're coming back!"

"Right, I see them", replied Ambrogio. And turning to Corporal Vassena, "Watch out, they're coming back. Now you fire on them, or you'll be sorry."

Vassena turned and ran toward the second machine gun, followed by his helper. Ambrogio and Bonsaver jumped once more into the foxhole, while the remaining artillerymen returned to shelter in the trenches.

The three fighters were still out of range, but Ambrogio already had the machine gun's grip in his hands, thumbs on the trigger and his left eye lined up with the middle of the three fighters. He muttered, almost to himself, "They think they're coming here without any risk." He was gasping for breath, and his heart was beating rapidly again, as if out of control. "They think they're coming to machine-gun us, our guns and our stores and ammo, without running risks." His head nodded slightly.

On his right, his head no more than a handsbreadth away, mouth half open, blue eyes seemingly smiling, Bonsaver held the ammunition belt ready. The "distant hero" designate now almost too close, he winked.

"Come on", Ambrogio said to the Russian planes. "Come on, and see . . ." Then his words were lost in the roar of the machine gun as he pressed the trigger; the gun shook on its tripod, which was held firmly by the nervous Bonsaver. From the other side of the battery, Vassena also opened fire, and so did the three Russian planes, all guns blazing away. Sitting in his transparent cockpit, the pilot of the middle plane was totally visible, and it was obvious that he had spotted the foxhole occupied by Ambrogio and Bonsaver from which he was being fired upon, and he turned toward them, firing and ignoring the remaining targets in the battery area. The two in the foxhole area lowered their heads as far as they could and tried to shrink in size while keeping up their firing. The ground around the foxhole jumped as if being struck by a huge bullwhip.

"Come on, you; all that noise and not one hit!" shouted Bonsaver in the direction of the pilot.

The plane soared overhead, enormous at this close distance. Ambrogio continued firing at it as it turned and once more headed for the Don. He fired after it, even after it had gone out of range. The three planes, in formation, crossed the Don and became smaller, then smaller still, until they disappeared, without giving any sign of ever having been hit.

"Damn it!" muttered Ambrogio. "Damn it . . . it's impossible that it didn't come down. How did he manage to escape?"

Bonsaver was just as mad as his friend. "Screw the S.O.B.!" he shouted. "But if it had been me firing, the same could have happened."

"He's gone", said Ambrogio. "You know what? As far as I'm concerned, I've lost my faith in machine guns as defense against air attacks." They climbed out of the foxhole; the artillerymen were emerging once again from the trenches. "Is anybody hurt?" Ambrogio asked, but there were no casualties.

"Check the guns", Ambrogio ordered each gun chief. "Take the nets down and check each gun inch by inch."

"As if they were good-looking women!" shouted Corporal Costanzo, the eternal foul mouth.

From the other side of the battery came another contribution, by another gun layer: "In which case, where you'd have to examine real carefully is right between . . ."

But Ambrogio cut in, "Vicari, don't talk dirty." Then, turning to Bonsaver and continuing their discussion about the air attack, "It's incredible. It's totally incredible."

"Listen," replied Bonsaver, "in July, during the advance I saw a Russian plane that had been shot down. Believe me, he had some fifty or sixty holes, from previous engagements. They'd covered them with red rubber patches. Fifty or sixty holes, I tell you! If you don't hit the pilot or don't reach a vital part of the machine, you won't knock it down, you understand?"

While the gun crews were removing the camouflage nets from their pieces, the ringing of the phone from Ambrogio's tent reached them. "What do they want?" muttered Ambrogio, and ran for his tent. "They're going to ask us for fire at this point . . ."

It wasn't a request for fire, only Ambrogio's superior officer, the battery commander, asking if there had been casualties or damage.

"No casualties", answered Ambrogio, pulling a nearby footstool toward himself with one foot and sitting down. "As far as damage, I don't yet know; we're still checking. When we've finished examining the guns, in a couple more minutes, I'll call you."

"Don't bother", said the voice. "Call me only if you come up with a real problem."

"Right", agreed Ambrogio, idly toeing something, a shining object on the ground. "No bad news with you, Lieutenant? What about group HQ?"

"Looks all right", answered the lieutenant. "All the bombs seemed to end up among the infantry reinforcements, down there at the bottom of the water course. There they certainly took some casualties; don't know for sure how many. Got to go; talk to you later."

Hanging up the phone, Ambrogio bent to pick up the shining object he'd been kicking around. It was a 20 mm round from one of the fighter's machine guns, which fortunately had not exploded—it was still hot. He turned it over in his hands, examining it, then searched the canvas walls and ceiling of the tent for an entry hole, but could find none.

"What's this, an unexploded shell, on the ground? I wonder why it didn't bury itself in the ground? How can it be?" Bonsaver entered the tent, and Ambrogio showed him the projectile. "Look", he said, then pointed to the spot where he had found it and asked his friend the same questions he had asked himself. Bonsaver also examined the overhead and walls of the tent, mentally drawing trajectories between the assumed positions of the attacking planes, calculating angles.

"All right", said Ambrogio. "I know you study engineering—go to hell!"

Bonsaver decided the shell had been fired from a great distance, had hit the ground, and then toppled end over end until it came to rest inside the tent.

"Right in my tent, eh?" Ambrogio handed over the shell. "Take it, as a memento of today's adventure. You distant heroes probably have your regulation box full of unexploded bombs, rusty bayonets, and other stuff, I guess."

But after having examined the souvenir, Bonsaver handed it back, saying, "It ended up at your address, which means it was destined for you, and therefore it belongs to you." He placed the souvenir on the telephone box. "See how good it looks?"

The four gun chiefs, Sergeant Facchi and three NCOs, arrived to report there was no serious damage. "Only two hits, on the armor shield on my gun . . . eh, what did you say?" the sergeant interrupted himself. "What was that, Lieutenant?"

"I said nothing", answered Ambrogio and was about to add, "what's the matter with you?" but then remembered that they were probably deaf, or nearly deaf, after so much heavy fire. He also thought that Facchi would be particularly affected.

"Nothing, nothing, carry on", he told them. "Two shots on your armor, you say?"

"Yes, Lieutenant. Two good dents, but no damage."

"Just as well", muttered Bonsaver.

"Eh?!" said Facchi, turning to him.

"He said 'just as well', Facchi", shouted Ambrogio and shook his head, smiling.

The four gun chiefs laughed. With their leather bandoleers slanting across their chests, the effect was to give them a portly look; more solid looking than the other artillerymen, as if the weight of authority carried with it an increase in bulk.

"Professional complaint", said Bonsaver to Facchi, laughing and pointing to his ear.

"Yes, but fortunately it doesn't last", said Facchi. "So that when we don't fire, after some months it goes, so everybody says."

"That's right, that's what they say", confirmed one of the other chiefs.

"Have you carefully examined the hydraulics on the backfire and the return?" asked Ambrogio. "They shouldn't lose fluid . . ."

"Don't worry, Lieutenant", Facchi assured him. "It was the first thing we checked."

"You three also?" the young officer looked at the other three NCOs. All three nodded, smiling.

Ambrogio felt a wave of regard for these four fellows, loyal and with an honest dignity, only a few years his senior, to whom responsibility had given an early maturity. They sensed his fondness for them and returned the sentiment, smiling.

"All right", said Ambrogio.

"Can we close up our pieces and put back the nets?" asked Corporal Zanini, chief of the lead gun.

"Yes, except Facchi's gun. I want to have a look at that shield." And as the four turned to go, he said to Facchi, "Here, take this", holding out the unexploded shell. "Show it to anybody you want. It fell here, in my tent. If by chance anybody finds any more of them, tell them to show them to me."

18

Bonsaver stayed for dinner with Ambrogio. He planned to hitch a ride with the ammunition trucks, whose usual route late in the evening called first at this position and then later at his own post. Ambrogio's orderly, Paccoi, brought dinner up from the kitchen down in the water course. He carried in two mess cans in one hand and two deep plates in the other. The plates each had another plate inverted on them as a cover, with a knotted napkin tied around them, and Paccoi held these by the knotted fabric ends. Under one arm, he also brought a spare folding stool. He arranged the meal on the telephone box, having put the napkins down as tablecloths, so that the two officers could eat facing each other. Looking with satisfaction at this work, he said, "If something's worth doing, do it right."

He had been hiding a surprise. In the deep plates, apart from the usual meat ration there were servings of crispy fried potatoes. "A little treat from the kitchen corporal", said Paccoi, "for the guest lieutenant, who by luck didn't get killed in the air attack while visiting us."

"And if he had," added Ambrogio, "I'd have had to pay out of my own pocket, because the battery has no third-party liability insurance."

The valet, a country boy, stood to serve them during the meal, a little embarrassed, but trying to behave as he thought an officer's mess steward would have done. Although there was little he could do but take away first the mess cans and then the well-cleaned plates, he did so with as much style as he could.

He did all this without being ordered; he simply admired and appreciated Ambrogio, took his duties seriously, and therefore wanted to do what he could to make his chief look good to this visiting officer.

After the meal, the two lieutenants took their stools outside to enjoy the fresh air of nightfall. The sun was just going down; two sentries with shouldered carbines started their measured patrol up and down the line of guns. The off-duty soldiers sat in circles on the grass outside the tents, some talking mainly about the air attack, others listening to shrill songs played on small portable wind-up gramophones. The singing and the songs reached the ears of the two officers.

"If you like," Ambrogio said, "instead of being here, we could sit on the grass with the men. I'm sure they'll want to talk to you; you know how it is; they always see the same faces here . . ."

"You socialize with the soldiers, eh?" said Bonsaver: "You feel at ease with them . . ."

"Yes."

"I've noticed."

"I already know all the ups and downs of each man's life, and even their parents' lives. I learned from my father to take an interest in them."

"Why is that? Does your father act that way with his laborers?" Ambrogio nodded. "With him, it's natural. Didn't I tell you that before he became an industrialist he was himself a laborer?"

"I don't remember it", said Bonsaver, getting up and adding, "come on, let's join them."

But right then the telephone rang. Ambrogio quickly entered the tent and shortly after came out holding the megaphone, shouting through it toward the troops, "Gun chiefs! Calling the gun chiefs!" Then turning toward the nearest tent, and without using the megaphone, he called, "Borghi!"

"Here!" shouted Borghi from his tent.

"You come, too."

"Right away."

"Now you can see personally", said Ambrogio to Bonsaver, "how much of a pain in the neck it is when you observers sound the alarm when we're about to go to sleep." The five people who had been summoned came up at the run; none had his bandoleer on, and two wore slippers.

"You, Borghi," said Ambrogio to the battery's artificer, "go and light up the survey post. You others get ready to fire."

"Ready?" asked Corporal Zanini.

"Yes, it's not certain that we'll actually open fire straight away. So remove the nets and leather cowlings, open the sights, and everybody be ready to open fire as soon as we're advised."

They all assented, chorusing, "Yes, Lieutenant."

Before turning to leave, Facchi, in an aside to Ambrogio, said, "Colombo, the fellow who sings so nice, he's in our tent, visiting from the group HQ."

"Mmm . . ."

"Up till now he hasn't wanted to sing for us. But if you ask him, he'll sing." The sergeant half pointed to Bonsaver, meaning that it would be a nice gesture, a little singing, for the visiting officer.

Ambrogio nodded, agreeing, but added, "Afterward, when we are done with this alert." The four gun chiefs saluted and left at a run for their tents.

One hundred or so yards from the battery, a red-and-white vertical-striped post was driven into the ground, to serve as a point of reference, to aim the guns by using the theodolite; on the pole was hung a small red lantern. As soon as Borghi lit the lantern, it was a sign for all the artillerymen to be ready for action. Ambrogio couldn't leave the telephone, but looking around at the deep dark moonless night, he noticed the slowly intensifying light coming from the tightly packed stars above.

"It's a pity not to know the stars' names", said Ambrogio, "and also the names of the . . . what are they called, the groupings?"

"You mean the constellations?" asked Bonsaver.

"Yes, the constellations. In earlier times people knew these things. More than once I've thought that if we knew them, the stars could keep us company when we have a night watch."

"That's true", said Bonsaver. "That's the way it is."

"Why? You're not going to tell me you know the stars?"

"A little, yes. When I was younger, seventeen or eighteen years old, I liked studying the stars."

"Well, I never . . .", Ambrogio said with enthusiasm. "Look at how reticent our distant hero can be! Great, well, in that case, come on, start licking me into shape." He looked up at the night sky. "For example, what's that group of stars called, the one directly overhead?"

"That's Lyra. But you shouldn't try to learn the stars' names just like that, with a blind stab. You need some kind of system. Listen, you always have to use as a point of reference—always, you hear?—Polaris, the pole star. You know how to find it?"

"Well, yes, if only to get my bearings . . . don't exaggerate."

"All right. Always remember that the whole sky goes around in circles; I mean it looks to be going around, and the axis on which it turns goes from one pole to the other, passing through Polaris . . ." And as no orders came from the OP to commence firing, Bonsaver continued for a while explaining the stars to his friend. Following his indications, Ambrogio located the most important summertime constellations one after another and also the principal stars; he tried to memorize them, repeating their positions and names several times. Bonsaver indicated a group that looked like a chair, or a short ladder, that in the course of the night would half turn around Polaris. This was Cassiopeia, although who knows why the ancients gave it a princess' name. Next, going east of the pole star, there was the great square of Pegasus, the winged horse. And between Pegasus and Cassiopeia, the long shimmering horse's tail, two fine lines of stars, curiously also named for another princess, Andromeda.

Going back from the east to the sky overhead and set against the phosphorescent background of the Milky Way was Cygnus, the swan with open wings, and nearby on their own, a small group dwarfed by the bluish brightness of the largest in this Lyra group, Vega, which, Bonsaver observed, is the brightest in all the summer sky.

To the south, ten or twelve second-magnitude stars formed Aquila.

"Although to tell the truth," said Bonsaver, "I have always called this constellation Zambon, because, as you can see, it doesn't look at all like an eagle; to me it looks more like that apparatus our village plumber, Zambon (a real drunk), uses to thread the water pipes."

"In that case," said Ambrogio, "I should call it Pirovano, the name of our plumber in Nomana." Ambrogio thought back to the big meeting when war was declared, when their own "eagle", Pirovano Oreste, couldn't make the loudspeakers he'd attached to the town hall work. *All right*, he told himself, *the Pirovano constellation*. Following on toward the west from Pirovano, they could see—so low it seemed to be touching the horizon—Boötes, the oxherd, which in fact looks more like one of those kites children play with, the waving tail having at its end the big, strikingly reddish star Arcturus.

Now that he could start identifying the convoys of stars that slowly cross the immense night sky, to Ambrogio it became more tangible, easier to understand. The truth of it is—as Bonsaver kept reminding him—that these convoys are not fixed, because if some of the stars may be a few light-years away and others may be far more distant, and as each follows its own course at unimaginable speeds, the constellations will constantly be separating and others being created. The thing is, as Bonsaver described it, in the brief period of one of our civilizations, the shifts and reformations are imperceptible. And although taken lightly by some, most observers are fascinated by these movements; they let us fantasize; they move as if engaged in courting dances.

"Apart from the constellations nearest to Polaris, which you can see all year round, the others change with the seasons", Bonsaver repeated. "You have to look over there at the horizon between the east and southeast; that's where Orion emerges, the great hunter. It'll rise in the sky during the night and will fill all that part of the sky—then watch out." Bonsaver almost seemed to be giving himself the warning. "It's a sign that winter is coming." The terrible Russian winter! Just thinking about it gave Ambrogio gooseflesh, raising the hair on his arms. He growled at Bonsaver, "The heck with you. What are you telling me? When I want to know winter is coming, I don't need to look at the stars."

The phone in the tent rang. Ambrogio stood up with a jump and then started laughing. Bonsaver also laughed and said, "You wretch, you've broken the spell . . . you see how the stars can play tricks on you?" Lifting the receiver, Ambrogio agreed.

But the call wasn't to order the firing of the guns. It was the administration warrant officer, advising that the ammunition trucks had arrived. Ambrogio asked to speak to the lieutenant, and when he came on the line he reminded him that the battery was still standing by on alert. The lieutenant advised to continue on standby. Ambrogio looked at the time; since the start of the alert, an hour and a half had gone by. In other words, he had been talking stars with Bonsaver for ninety minutes.

Bonsaver, hearing the ammo trucks had arrived, got up from his stool. "It's time I went", he said. "The vacation is over." He shook Ambrogio's hand. The day's visit had without a doubt strengthened their friendship. Then, led by an artilleryman with a flashlight, he walked toward the battery CP, following a marked path with grassy edges.

19

Time hung heavy in the battery. More than one soldier went back to his tent to throw himself onto his palliasse, clothes still on, first having agreed with some comrade that he'd be called in case they got the order to fire.

Ambrogio spent another half hour sitting on his stool, and after arranging for the signaler to replace him at the phone, he went over to sit on the grass with his artillerymen. Inevitably, when he joined them, the talk turned to the earlier air attack, which now seemed to have happened days ago. Someone then asked the officer the reason for the alert and if he had any ideas what their target might be. Ambrogio replied negatively and added, "It's probably something to do with the movement of transport, trucks, for example. Maybe the OP heard motors, or they've seen headlights behind their lines, something like that. And they want us to be ready to fire in case the trucks or, I hope it's not the case, tanks pass one of the pinpointed areas, which we've got cross-referenced."

"Cross-referenced?"

"Yes. For example, if they reach a crossroads, or a place on the road at which we've already fired, then we'll have a record of the angle of fire, traverse figures, etc."

"Tanks, Lieutenant?" asked one artilleryman, a little concerned. Then, from another, "Do you believe that here in front of us there are tanks?" And from a third, "And since when?" The voices came from the darkness: "Tanks, there are tanks?" "Who says there are tanks?"

Ambrogio realized he had touched a nerve. Naturally, any advancing tanks were the job of the first line, the infantry. They should destroy the tanks. But most of the men knew—or felt—that the Italian infantry wasn't up to the job. "Tanks . . . ? What tanks?" he said. "I was giving an example, just a for instance. I didn't say there were tanks. Quite the reverse. I told you we hoped there weren't any tanks."

A poor and unconvincing answer, as he himself knew. But it served the purpose and was good enough to reduce the soldiers' concerns. After all, since they'd been in Russia they'd done nothing but go forward, so why get worked up? Particularly when it was time to go to sleep.

The conversation around the seated officer died away. One of the soldiers with a gramophone put on a song, popular a few years before; the record was very worn, and the voice low and harshly metallic to the ear. Everybody had heard the song many times, but even so they all ended up falling silent and listening:

> If I could get
> a thousand lire a month,
> I'd be sure
> —no exaggeration here—
> of finding all my happiness ... !

The song about low-budget happiness came to an end with a mechanical hiccup, and there was silence during the time it took the soldier to change the record and wind up the machine, which, with its low, scratchy sound, next reproduced the song of a gypsy violin:

> Oh sad and ardent singing gypsy,
> dreaming of your sweet Hungarian home ...
> Do you also think
> of that great love down there
> under distant skies?
> Oh gypsy violin ...
> Oh gypsy violin ...
> Oh gypsy violin ...

They all knew that at this point the record was damaged, but the soldier hadn't taken the trouble to lift the needle, to push it into the next groove away from the repeating section; finally he gave the needle a nudge. Somebody made a joking remark, and the record played to the end of the song.

Next, the popular tenor whom Facchi had wanted Bonsaver to hear, Corporal Colombo, unexpectedly started singing "O mia bèla Madunina". In the Milan dialect, he went at the song with his untrained but lively, earthy voice. The natural use of dialect made for a perfectly measured diction. Colombo sang very well. When he finished, all the soldiers, Ambrogio included, burst into enthusiastic applause. After a brief pause, he sang another song, and then a third. The men from the entire battery sitting on the grass before him no longer applauded each song; some gestured encouragingly between numbers, and all of them listened with rapt attention, enchanted with his lovely singing. In the great darkness that covered the steppes, the gun-calibrating red light shone, seemingly far away; but the two sentries had moved closer, listening attentively, standing at the back of the seated soldiers.

Why do songs affect us this way? Ambrogio asked himself. *If the lyrics were read out loud instead of being sung, they'd make us laugh, or at least smile. On the other hand, sung like this, they move us, they take on an indefinable significance; they don't make us laugh at all—it would even be stupid to laugh. I wonder what causes this transformation? I won't get to the bottom of it now, but the more often we experience some things, the less we question it.* Remembering the criticism of fashionable tunes that everyone seems to feel obliged to make, he also remembered that he too had criticized them, but now he preferred to admit the feelings such songs gave him. The songs of his youth—he was somewhat confused—were precisely these, with all their short-comings and failures. Just as his father and older people took pleasure in certain old refrains (which he'd only heard on records: "Under the eaves of the old tower/ when the almond blossom is in bud/the friendly swallow has just returned . . ."), for him they would always be part of the memories of younger years, and he'd also probably remember them better than anything else.

Meantime, Colombo had started singing "Villa Triste", just then in fashion. In the deeply dark surroundings, his enchanting voice drew pictures of a nineteenth-century romantic villa, which all present thought they had seen or glimpsed who knew where in a faraway Italy . . .

> How many things were hidden
> by the windows' shades:
> the questions, the answers,
> the color of your dresses,
> the melodies you sang,
> the lies you told . . .
> Over the myrtle hedge
> the wind sobbing goes,
> each tear a star
> which no one will gather
> Villa triste . . . sad, sad house . . .

All this distance from their country, the song melted their hearts. The singer took a breather, describing some of the songs in semiprofessional musical terms. He, as much as the audience, felt let down by the pauses between songs; he told them the next song would be his last and then launched into an old Nea-politan song, "Signorella", his best song:

> Pale young miss,
> My neighbor sweet
> there's not one night I don't dream of Napoli,
> and I've been far away these twenty years . . .
> In my town it's snowing
> the church belltower is covered in white,
> all the firewood is turned to ashes . . .

The words described somebody else's experience, not the singer's or his listeners', and yet, heard like this, sung with all the nostalgia in the singer's heart, it made Ambrogio homesick and affected each of the other soldiers.

On finishing the song, Colombo stood up and, amid general regret and unhappiness, said his goodbyes to the officer. Ambrogio, knowing it would please the singer, thanked him for the concert with a solemn air. The amateur tenor walked off in the starlight, alone, down the grass-lined path leading to the battery's storehouse.

The audience of soldiers got to their feet. Sergeant Facchi turned to Ambrogio and asked, "What will we do now?"

"We'll all go to sleep," replied the officer, "but be ready to leap into action in a hurry. And understand, we leave the nets off the guns, and the calibrating light stays lit."

"Yes, Lieutenant."

They all went to their tents, and there were no calls during the night.

20

The days of summer went by. The observation posts called for fire less frequently, and the four guns in the battery remained unfired for weeks, still under their camouflage nets.

When he had nothing to do, Ambrogio passed the hours sitting under his tent flap, reading the thick Sholokov book that Bonsaver had brought him. Often he would interrupt his reading and take his binoculars with him some hundreds of yards to the edge of the rise in front of the battery, from which he could look at the town of Veshenskaya. Some of the action in the book had been placed in Veshenskaya, but he found it impossible to locate the places he had read about, and each time he would end up gazing at the old church in which Sholokov had placed the Cossack recruits' swearing ceremony. Now its topmost dome showed some shell damage. "We caused that, unfortunately, but then it seems it shelters a Russian observation post, so . . . just as well we were using small shells."

Around him, the short grass of the steppes was covered in wildflowers of various colors. Looking at this, one day the youth thought to pick a few, which he put in an envelope and sent with a few lines of greeting to Tricia, in Rho. *These days she's probably not in Rho*, he told himself as he mailed the letter in the mailbox outside the CO's office. *Maybe she's at the beach or at the mountains, letting herself be courted by somebody else.* He asked himself, irritated, *And why shouldn't she let herself be courted by somebody else, since I have no intention of doing the same? And why should I be upset about that?* arguing with himself illogically, still the adolescent.

He didn't finish the Sholokov novel; apart from its fifteen hundred pages, it seemed to him that some sections were contradictory, and anyway, his lieutenant had asked to read it. All he had left to read was a couple of university textbooks he had brought from Italy; he looked at them without enthusiasm. How could one feel inspired to study?

Unable to go any distance from the battery, Ambrogio would sometimes pass the time observing the small colorful hawks through his binoculars. The view from his tent facing the battleline to the north was partially obscured; over to the east and southeast, however, there was an enormous open moorland, over which the hawks glided during the day, the only animal life seen moving. Slowly and tirelessly, each hawk hunted alone, its hard eyes focused on the grassy surface, looking for prey; sometimes they would hover on quivering wings, ready to dive. It was easy to see every detail through the glasses, and their skill often made him hold his breath.

Occasionally, a curious artilleryman would ask to use the binoculars, and the officer would hand them over, listening to the soldier's joking comments and adding his own.

One of the most anticipated happenings at the front is the time for mail call. Mail would arrive at the battery once or twice a week, in the truck that brought the "groceries", and by standing order of the lieutenant was distributed without delay by the quartermaster sergeant major. He tended to follow the same procedure every time, placing himself in front of the quartermaster's tent, having preceded this with one call only: "Mail! Mail!" He would then hear the echo of his call running from mouth to mouth, just the one word—"Mail! Mail!"—then the soldiers would gather around him, and he would start distributing the awaited mail. At this point, he would stride over to the battery, holding a handful of the yet undistributed letters, his sober face reflecting the serious regard he held for the task. Normally, on arriving at the battery, he would find the artillerymen in a group, already awaiting his appearance. On this September afternoon, news of his coming having preceded him, he arrived to find Ambrogio waiting among the other men. The sergeant major saluted the young officer and, paying no attention to the soldiers' witticisms, started distributing the mail: they all knew that when he was through he would allow himself to smile at their sallies.

The sergeant major was bald and bull necked and always held himself stiffly straight, which produced an impressive effect. (*Tough luck for him if the Russians get hold of the poor man!* Ambrogio thought sometimes when he saw him.) In reality the sergeant major was very mild mannered with an unreasonable fear of superior officers. He was happy with small blessings, such as receiving a ream of writing paper or a new ribbon for his typewriter. Not that the soldiers were aware of this gentle side of his nature.

"Missori, Aristide!"

"Here!"

"Sergeant Facchi."

"Here I am!"

"Giovanni Paccoi."

"Here."

"Aristide Missori."

"Another one?" quipped several soldiers. "Hey, listen, how many sweethearts did you leave in Italy, that you should get so many letters?"

"Maialetti, Vito."

After each name, the sergeant major would hand the letter to the addressee or, in his absence, to his gun crew chief.

"Sublieutenant Riva!"

Once again, "Sublieutenant Riva!" Looking over the heads of the soldiers surrounding him, he caught Ambrogio's eye and his nod in the direction of his orderly, Paccoi, standing at the front of the group, and gave the runner two letters.

"Eh, Lieutenant, you wouldn't also have several sweethearts at home, would you?" joked Costanzo, the corporal to whom all women were street walkers (but who now, anxiously awaiting a letter, seemed to contradict his philosophy).

"Costanzo, Alfredo", called the sergeant major.

The soldiers all laughed.

"Ottone, Aldo, Reginato, Valcarenghi, Giacomo, Gola, Gimondi, Moioli, Campanini, Giuseppe, Medici, Dal Cero, Paolo, Ugo Meddiolaro, Paoli Antonio, *Signor Tenente Riva* (*and three,* Ambrogio counted to himself, *today is really a letter harvest*), Corporal Giuseppini . . ."

Having distributed the mail, the quartermaster sergeant major smiled at the group of soldiers, saluted Ambrogio, and then with a nod executed a turn in which one almost heard his mental command, "Leefft . . . turn!" and went back to his office on the creek bed.

All the letter recipients went off to read their mail in privacy. "Look at you all", exclaimed a disappointed Corporal Zanini, who had received nothing. "You look just like the dog who caught the bone in his mouth and runs to eat it by himself."

"Why do you say that?" the good-natured battery corporal Facchi asked him. "Do you want us to read you our letters? What good would it do you?"

Ambrogio smiled at the exchange, although Zanini's comparison seemed not inaccurate to him. He accepted the three letters from Paccoi, who was visibly happy for his superior (never had so many letters arrived at one time for his chief), and then retired to the lean-to outside his tent to read them.

The letters were from his sister, Alma, from Michele Tintori, and from Igino. He opened Alma's letter first. In her very girlish handwriting, she told him of the latest news from the home front in Nomana, expressing herself in her usual pleasant, candid manner.

Saturday we had hailstones, which according to what we hear has caused a lot of damage to crops; maybe you've already heard?

[Ambrogio, amused, nearly chuckled.]

Sunday, after Mass, the priest and Papa were talking (I was with them), and the priest quoted an epigram, which I pass on to you: the Omnipotent on high sends us the tempest, the omnipotent on earth takes away what is left to us, and we, between the two highnesses, end up in poverty. What do you think? Always the same, our parish priest, isn't he?

Before continuing, Ambrogio looked at both sides of the envelope and the writing paper, to see if there was a censor's stamp. No, there was nothing. The censor had allowed the letter through without examining it.

I'll have to tell Alma to be more careful. Some kind of marble feline! thought Ambrogio, then amused, he started to laugh at the priest's joke.

Then he went on to the other two letters, reading Igino's first; it came from some unspecified location, perhaps in the southern Balkans.

Dear Ambrogio, I'm well and hope you're the same. I received your address from my folks, who were given it by your sister Francesca. At present I'm near to (the place name had been blotted out with a stroke of thick Indian ink by the censor) in which lousy place the people sit in front of their houses, or rather their hovels, without bothering even to wave away the flies from their faces. Only as partisans are they worth anything, but to us this is no bother.

And further on:

There are vultures here, and when an animal, say a donkey, falls into a ravine and the next day we go out to lift it out, all we find is the remaining half these scavengers have left. Or sometimes the meat is taken by the partisans. If the news on *radio scarpa* [the rumor mill] is right, and I think it is, the partisans fight more among themselves than they do against us. The Communists want to lord it over the rest, and every now and then we find dead bodies, sometimes family members of partisans, killed with great cruelty. And all this is happening in

and here there was a line of the censor's Indian ink. Where could he be writing from? Macedonia? Albania? Montenegro? Maybe these things were happening all over the Balkans. The letter ended:

What with the flies, fleas, and partisans, I miss Nomana a little but try not to brood on it. Greetings from your friend, Igino.

Michele Tintori, with whom he had exchanged two or three letters, wrote from some place on the Don, perhaps some fifty miles away from the great river, although he didn't write the place name. His letter started by saying how grateful he was that Fortunato and Pino had kindly gone to Nova to visit his father and continued,

As far as my life here, insofar as I have free time (I have little, in fact), I continue with my research into life in this part of the world before we got here. It is clear that the local chiefs, absolute bosses, without the restraints we have back in Italy, didn't expect anybody to enter their houses; in fact, they were sure that nobody would do so. Sometimes it seems to me I'm trying to explore the hidden face of the moon ... also, here near the Don what most people will never forget, over all other events, is the famine of 1933, brought about by the mandatory collectivization of the land, followed by hunger and cannibalism, about which I've already written you. Since hearing about these things, I assume you've made your own inquiries. (I'm counting on you to do that.) I've come to believe that the atrocities of past ages we learned about in history class, which impressed us with their violence, have been surpassed in horror and bestiality by these events in our own time that we are hearing about. Do you agree? But I don't want always to be talking to you only about this. Let's get on to something else: about the Cossack environment here, where I sometimes detect a behavior, perhaps a feeling, something I'd not expected beforehand. I'd like to have your opinion; have you had a chance to observe these people? The Cossacks are certainly different from the Ukrainians: well, in short, they remind me of ancient Greeks.

Sholokov didn't say this, didn't even imagine it, reflected Ambrogio, amused. *What an unusual fellow, this Michele!*

Perhaps before the arrival of communism the Cossacks and the Russians in general were successors of Greece? The reasons why I think this are not easy to set out in a short letter (I'm not good at diagrams), but you should try to observe them, and when we meet we'll exchange impressions.

What the devil is he talking about? Ambrogio asked himself. *Maybe the Russians' extravagant manner? To tell the truth, there really is, in the Cossacks described by Sholokov a ... a Dionysian quality that could be related in a way with Homer's characters. I wonder if that's what Michele is getting at?*
The letter went on:

The towns are also different from those we've seen so far, each with an impressive church (usually converted into a storehouse), and the very air one breathes, I think you'll agree, is different. After having observed these people, it doesn't surprise me that in past centuries they reached Alaska, farther, nearly to California. But this doesn't have anything to do with their classicism; I'm getting two separate themes mixed together. Well, we'll have a more ordered conversation when we see each other.

The letter ended with the hope that the meeting between the two friends could be soon, and it reiterated:

... get together and discuss our experiences of the country.

My experiences? What do I know of these people? In the first place, here at the battery we don't have an interpreter, which he has, thought Ambrogio, letter in hand. *We see the people more or less as tourists would, superficially, that's how it is for us. He, on the other hand ... what a character!* He recalled when Michele had told him that he entreated God every day to concede his wish to be sent to the Russian front and how he reveled on receiving his orders upon graduating from officer school.

What an odd person! Even at the university the rector, Gemellone, had noticed! Ambrogio smiled at the memory. *Michele is a personality who will go his own way, all the way. Yes, I'd like to see him again soon.* Not, however, to hold an intellectual conversation: this prospect did not attract him at all.

In the following week, the mail service delivered to Ambrogio a letter from his cousin Manno, on the Libyan front, or, as he said in his letter, in Egypt:

> The summery weather here in Egypt goes on and feels as if it will never end.

Manno was an artillery observer, and:

> Whether I'm at my post, observing (and if you take away the rocks and the sand, there's little to observe), or resting under the hot canvas of my suffocating den, in the quiet and long hours I have for reflection, I reflect and meditate continuously.

He didn't specify what it was he meditated on and only said:

> The meaning of certain specific parts of civilian life in Italy, which earlier I didn't understand, and now I think I do.

Manno went on to recall with exceptional nostalgia specific episodes from their times in Nomana. The letter, somewhat short, ended on a note of anxiety:

> We'll have a lot to tell each other, and I hope I can get to see you soon because the situation here in the skies seems to be going belly up.

What did Manno mean, there at the end? Did it mean the English were achieving supremacy in the air? Ambrogio reread the sentence a couple of times: it couldn't mean anything else. *An unhappy prospect,* he thought, perplexed. To tell the truth, the news even from Italy was about increasingly frequent air raids on cities. *But even so, so what? Probably Manno had written when feeling depressed,* thought Ambrogio. *Probably the RAF have made a big strike, and as he wrote he felt the weight of this.* But that phrase of Manno's, so enigmatic, kept returning to his mind over the next few days.

That same week Ambrogio received a note from Stefano, his former school colleague from Nomana. This, instead of arriving in the mail, came by hand of the driver who brought up their rations:

> Dear Ambrogio, I'm well, as I hope you are. Please forgive me for the scribbled handwriting, but I'm in a rush, as the company transport is leaving for Dubovi, where you go to draw your rations too; that is, if that is not also another rumor. Just to let you know that my battalion is at rest in Rassipnaya, and from here to Dubovi is just a short four miles. Your dear friend, Stefano Giovenzana.

Stefano, if one read between the lines, was taking a rest, was nearby, and seemed to be asking him to go and see him. Ambrogio immediately thought he ought not to let the chance go by. He went to see the battery commander, who said he would give him leave for twenty-four hours, on the condition he find a subordinate qualified to substitute for him on the battery while he was away.

The search for a substitute took some while, even though Ambrogio started looking right away. And when he found a volunteer, there was another delay because the man then became sick. It was only ten days after receiving his friend's note that Ambrogio was able to leave.

21

He climbed onto the only surviving motorcycle owned by the battery, an old Guzzi Alce that had been through the Yugoslav campaign and then in the autumn of 1941 had managed to overcome the mud of the advance through Russia. It was one of the few functioning bikes remaining to the regiment. The battery's transport chief, Sergeant Feltrin, had kept the old "Moose" going through many tough times and had brought it up to scratch in the few days prior to Ambrogio's trip.

The old engine ran well, the timing slow, producing resonant chugging noises. Leaving the battery behind, the young officer rode down into the flood channel, making his way between the vertical bare earth walls. He had seen similar canyons, clean cut, usually only a few yards deep, but generally two or three times as wide. There had been great numbers of these across the Russian plains; he had heard they were dug by the waters of the spring melt, although he didn't fully understand how this worked. The flood channel he was using ran for half a mile toward the west, parallel to the Don, before reaching the river. The surface over which he rode had scattered bushes, and parts of it were covered by the sparse grass typical of the steppes. A few minutes wiring down the smooth curves of the cutting brought him to group HQ: about ten tents, five or six trucks plus the lieutenant colonel's "recon" Millecento, all lined up beneath the trees at a point where the canyon widened out. One of the square section tents was larger than the others and had at its side a triangular section tent that had many telephone wires leading inside—these were obviously the HQ and communications tents. A little farther along was the medical tent; sitting down in front were some bored-looking artillerymen (waiting to report sick) among whom was a man from Ambrogio's own battery, who waved and then saluted his officer as he went by.

After a few hundred yards, he passed the Second Battery and its equipment park and, immediately beyond it, the first line of guns. These two batteries were lined up close together along the north wall of the canyon, which because of earlier landslides took the shape of a broken slope, overgrown with bushes. The track, formed by dirt thrown onto the grass, continued onward under open skies toward the west, where in a while it forked, the canyon dividing into two. Just before reaching the fork, the canyon became populated with trees, and both under and around these trees were infantry tents and supplies: it was here that the Russian planes some weeks back had dropped their bombs, Ambrogio knew, just before they had turned to attack his battery. There were quite a few signs of the bombing: broken tree branches, a burned-out tent, bomb craters, and other blackened debris. On approaching the canyon's divide, the young officer slowed the bike to a walking pace and looked around: the main branch curved off to the right to run on down to the Don and seemed to get deeper and wider; the left divide was a smaller flood channel draining the plains to the southwest, in which direction he headed. He found, as he had been advised by the soldiers bringing the battery's rations, that the canyon was less deep here and widened out over some distance, getting ever wider, and then became narrow again, the vertical bare earth walls only a few yards apart.

At one of the clearings where the walls widened out, he came across a Cossack encampment: the old, women, children, they all had had to abandon their riverside village and move to this spot. Without stopping, the young officer tried to look them over: they had carved shelters into the low canyon walls, covering them with branches. There were no military-age men in view; those he saw were all taller than other Russians he had seen. Many had long, pointed white beards; some of the Cossacks' beards reached their waists.

As he went past, they regarded him gravely with their blue eyes and heads erect: this reminded Ambrogio of what Michele had written to him in his last letter. *He said the Russians could be the successors to ancient Greece, and really, these Cossacks give that impression. Something classic, really unusual, it's there, they have it. But I don't think Michele was writing only about external appearances . . .*

He tried to keep them in sight while continuing on his way. *It's true they don't look like the other Russians, for example, the ones in Kamenka; they're not beaten, vexed, or frustrated . . . and yet under communism, these must have suffered more than the others, and probably now their suffering has increased since our occupation. These aren't people who would take the invasion of their land lightly. Well, we'll see what Michele has to say.*

Shortly after the Cossack encampment the canyon opened up, become level and running between enormous fields of grain, some of it already harvested, and quantities of dried-out sunflowers. Occasionally, Ambrogio saw far-off abandoned farm tractors (the great track-driven Russian vehicles, vertical smoke-stacks, old fashioned, which dotted the plains at that time; if looked at closely they would all be found to be rust corroded and falling apart). Along this stretch, there was not a soul to be seen; the old bike, impelled by its potent unstuttering motor, continued traversing the track, until it finished, running into a highway. Differing from the track only by being wider and dustier, the highway was lined with an endless series of rough telegraph poles. Following these in a southerly direction, Ambrogio reached a village with widely separated isbas, many with crooked walls and thatched roofs; here he finally came upon some people, women principally, dressed in black, their heads covered, and holding young children by the hand. In the village center, the crossroads were marked by a telegraph pole from which drooped broken wires. Also on the pole were wooden pointers indicating the directions of other villages and various military units; they had been attached haphazardly at different times, and lack of space had caused some arrows to be fixed to the pole right down to within a palm breadth of the ground. Ambrogio followed the Dubovi sign and arrived there within a half hour, covered in dust, acquired when he had passed a convoy of trucks coming down from the front line.

At Dubovi there were many military groups, all guarded by sentries or detachments of guards. Ambrogio knew that among these units would be the supply people who provided his own group with its food and ammunition. Twice a week, his battery's truck would come here to do their marketing and fetch the mail; he looked for signs indicating the supply outfit but couldn't find them. He lifted his right wrist to check his watch; it was just after ten. He continued toward the southwest.

The bike's motor continued to run true, a pleasure to hear, and presently the young officer noticed he had entered another division sector. As if to confirm this, he saw a small group of Bersaglieri, with their bright red fezzes, and soon after, files of tethered horses bivouacked in a wooded hollow. Perhaps they were a detachment of the Savoia cavalry? Of the regiment, that is, which only a month back, in August, had participated in the charge of Isbuchensky? Or perhaps they were from the Novara? *Whichever it is, I've entered a new area*, he thought happily. *I've arrived in Celere country, even though on the road there was no indication, no sign, unlike in Italy.*

At this point the town of Rassipnaya, where Stefano's battalion was camped, couldn't be much farther. *I wonder if it's really true that in a little while I'll see Moonface again?* He started to feel excited.

But he didn't see him, at least not immediately. On entering the village, he stopped the bike to speak to the first Bersaglieri he saw, to ask, nearly shouting to be heard over the engine noise, where the Ninth Battalion was. Almost jovially, the soldier told him the Ninth had returned to the front some days before. "Now it is we who are here, the Eighth, in their place."

Ambrogio felt disappointment but immediately had a practical demonstration of the Bersaglieri reputation for adaptability when the soldier added, "Do you want to go to the Ninth Battalion? Come with me, Lieutenant?"

"Where do you want to take me?"

"To my company HQ; it's nearby."

"All right, get on."

The Bersagliere climbed on the bike, then directed Ambrogio to a space between the two isbas, which looked as if about to collapse beneath the weight of disproportionately large thatching. The impression of imminent collapse was reinforced by the frames and glass in the windows, leaning and sloping away from the vertical. While the Bersagliere got off the bike, Ambrogio stopped the motor, got off himself, put the bike on its stand, and followed his guide into one of the isbas.

22

Inside the isba, the furnishings were a mixture of Russian (a few chairs, a stone-built stove with steps, candlelit icons in a corner) and Italian military: a campaign table covered in a gray-green cloth, stools, and two studded foot lockers, also gray-green in color. Sitting at the table was a bareheaded crewcut lieutenant in shirt sleeves, cleaning a disassembled pistol. The smaller components lay in a gasoline bath made from a mess-can lid. He looked up at the Bersagliere, who saluted and nodded toward Ambrogio. "This lieutenant is looking for the Ninth Battalion", he said. "He thought he'd find them still in the village."

The seated officer looked at Ambrogio. "I'm sorry", he said. "The Ninth went back to the front some days ago. Our battalion, the Eighth, is in their place."

"Yes, I'd heard that." He stepped forward and presented himself to the senior officer by coming to attention, following military courtesy. "With your permission, sir. I'm Second Lieutenant Riva of the Eighth Pasubio Artillery."

"Galimberti", replied the lieutenant, introducing himself.

"Sorry I can't shake your hand; as you can see, mine is dirty. Let's consider we've shaken hands in spirit, OK?" He smiled.

"Sure." Ambrogio smiled back.

The Bersagliere spoke up. "With your permission, I'll leave you, Lieutenant. But I'd like to mention that Della Valentina's van hasn't yet left for the front line." He made as if to leave.

"Wait", said his officer, and turning to Ambrogio said, "It's none of my business, but why are you looking for the Ninth Battalion?"

"There's a Bersagliere from my town in the Second Company: a school friend named Giovenzana." Galimberti didn't seem to recognize the name. "I just want to go and see him."

"In that case, all you need is a couple of hours . . . but with that accent, from the Ticino . . . are you a Comasco?"

"No, I'm from the province of Milan, but close to Como. From the way you talk, I'd say you're also a Milanese?"

"Exactly. Perhaps a little less obvious than you; I'm from the city itself, from around the Porta Vercellina."

"Go on with you!" exclaimed Ambrogio. Then quoting, he said, "'Protect yourself from sun and mist, and from those of the Porta Vercellina.'"

The lieutenant, smiling, shook his head negatively, and corrected the old saw: "and from those from outside the Porta Vercellina."

"Ah, yes, of course", admitted Ambrogio, who had purposely twisted the old Milanese saying.

"In other words, you're from Brianza . . . may one know from which town?" asked Galimberti.

"From Nomana."

"Ah, I've been there, a pretty place." He turned to the Bersagliere. "The van, you say?" The soldier nodded yes.

"But I don't want to bother you", said Ambrogio. "My bike is outside; if you give me directions, I'll go by myself—if you think it's possible."

"Yes, of course it is", said the lieutenant. "Why wouldn't it be? Besides, en route, they'd probably take you for one of our own artillerymen. But if you go in the van, it'll be better. You'd be there for a couple of hours, more or less, time for a visit", and turning to the soldier, "Are you sure it hasn't left yet?"

"A few minutes ago, it was parked at Battalion HQ."

"Good. You go to Della Valentina" ("the van's driver", he explained to Ambrogio) "and tell him before he leaves he's to come here. With the van, understand?"

The soldier brought his heels together, saluted, and turned to leave.

"Look," said Ambrogio, stopping him, "let me at least thank you. You've been very kind." The soldier nodded his fezzed head happily, then turned and left.

"What luck to have such smart people", Ambrogio said to his brother officer.

"We're not complaining", the other answered, then reflecting, he added, "Yes, we're not complaining. They're all good boys in the Third, workers, and smart. So, you're from Nomana, eh? Well, I've been through there two or three times."

From the room next door came the ringing of a telephone.

"Damn!" he exclaimed, getting to his feet. "They don't leave you in peace even during these few days of rest."

Meanwhile, he was searching for something to dry his hands with. Ambrogio also looked around and then picked up a piece of paper from a pile on the table, which he handed to Galimberti, who took it and then hurried into the other room, where the telephone continued ringing.

Ambrogio went over to the window and looked at his parked motorcycle. Should he leave it there for the few hours he'd be away? Wouldn't it be better to insist on taking it? It would give him more freedom. The opportunity to be with the Bersaglieri for a while was appealing. He was considering his options when the main door opened and an old Russian woman entered, black head-scarf on her head. She went across the room toward the interior door; as she passed the icons, she bowed and crossed herself.

"*Dasidània zinca*" ("Good morning, lady"), he greeted her casually, in the soldiers' poor Russian. The old lady turned and, bowing slightly, murmured, "*Dosvidània*".

Poor little old lady, thought Ambrogio when she had gone. *How unlucky are these poor country people. First the revolution, then their lands expropriated and great famines, and now the war.* He looked at the icons in the corner: there were two painted on worm-eaten wood. He thought, *Who knows how much determination and effort the old lady had needed to protect them from the semiliterate politrucki, whose so-called scientific knowledge made them treat the Christian beliefs of the older people as a laughing matter.* (This was one of the most repeated complaints of the country folk: it was so well known that even Ambrogio had heard about it.)

He didn't have much time for his musing, however, as he spotted the arrival at the isba of the Bersaglieri van, which stopped with a racing skid. At the same time, the lieutenant, phone conversation completed, came back into the room.

"The van's arrived", he said. "Let's go."

He walked out with Ambrogio and, turning to the driver, whose feather-helmeted head was out of the window, said, "All set? Ready to go?"

"Yessir!"

"Good." He turned to Ambrogio. "Sit up front if you like."

And turning again to the driver, "You'll take the lieutenant to the Second Company, Ninth Battalion. When you return, pick him up again and bring him here. Understood?"

"Yes, Lieutenant, I have that." And to Ambrogio, "Please get in, Lieutenant."

"Thank you", said Ambrogio. He hesitated, looking confused, and said, "The bike . . ."

"Don't worry yourself. I'll look after it", said the lieutenant. "Come on, don't waste the little time you have. Goodbye."

Turning to where the bike was parked, he pushed it off its stand and wheeled it toward the house. It was clear he was familiar with motorcycles, perhaps more so than Ambrogio.

Climbing into the front seat of the van, Ambrogio was quite surprised by the small dimensions of the cab. As soon as he was seated, the driver, Della Valentina, started off and headed down the packed dirt road without doing his habitual wheel-spinning racing start, either out of consideration for his guest or because his lieutenant was watching them leave from the isba.

23

Along the way, Ambrogio had a long conversation with the driver, Della Valentina. On the robust side, with black hair and mustache, the driver spoke—he evidently enjoyed talking—with an Emilia-Romagna accent. He started by informing Ambrogio that Lieutenant Galimberti wasn't the CO; he was the second in command, standing in for the company CO. He added that the lieutenant had been decorated with a Silver Medal for his part in the battle of

August at the river bend in Serafimovich. He described the fighting and told anecdotes about some of his personal experiences. He asked Ambrogio why the field artillery was so ineffective when it came to engaging enemy tanks; he had witnessed this himself on two occasions. Ambrogio explained that the standard shells weren't armor piercing and were therefore useless against tanks; they landed on tanks like bare hands, not like steel. Besides, there was also the need to save ammunition, which was in short supply, and the gunners were therefore not trained against moving targets. As usual when speaking about defense from tank attacks, they came to no conclusion. Using the Italian-issue 47 mm armor-piercing shell, it was necessary to hit a tank from close by or there was no possibility of stopping it. The Italian army didn't have grenade launchers or bazookas, which could be used from cover, as did all the other armies. Ambrogio thought, *The descendants of Leonardo da Vinci don't have even the most basic technical supplies ... really, as far as arms were concerned, the Fascist party hadn't got far, being too busy chattering about inessentials!* According to Della Valentina, you could always, like the Bersaglieri, put land mines under attacking tanks by hand; he added that the Bersaglieri in Africa had done this more than once, and when mines weren't available, they'd destroyed tanks with gasoline-filled bottles. But, Ambrogio pointed out, not everyone could expect to defend themselves against tanks that way, and one couldn't expect even the Bersaglieri to be as brave on every occasion as they'd been in Africa. Not only that, added Della Valentina, you had to distinguish between Bersaglieri: you could ask anything of the members of his regiment, whereas the Sixth, the other regiment making up the Celere Division, in comparison, was made up of 50 percent losers. Ambrogio was surprised by this and tried to find out if it represented one of those visceral shows of esprit de corps (as he thought) or if in reality the two regiments were really so unequal in efficiency. He asked his driver a few questions along these lines but couldn't reach a clear conclusion. They were approaching the Celere Division lines along the Don. The country hereabout consisted of rolling fields covered in grain, partially harvested in sections; in the hollows grew stands of large-leaved trees whose intense green distinguished the valleys and other topographic details of the country. They passed a few villages, groups of isbas, most with dumps of military supplies belonging either to the Bersaglieri or to the 120th Artillery. On the outskirts of one village they saw a battery of cannons emplaced among some vegetable gardens.

"These people", said Ambrogio, "have solved the problem of winter quarters. Instead of building quarters with pick and shovel like we do, they just move into the isbas." When nearing the Don, they followed a large, bushy runoff that took them to the area behind the riverbank, where they passed branches of the path going down to the river. Della Valentina slowed the van and started looking into the woods. "The Second should be around here", he kept repeating, stopping shortly by two Bersaglieri, walking with slung rifles.

One of them was carrying a handful of felt-covered, dripping canteens by their straps.

"Eh, please, where's the HQ of the Second Company?"

"That's our company", said one of the soldiers.

"Headquarters is right on the line, in a bunker", added the other, in Sicilian-Italian.

"Can we get right to it in the van?"

"Why not? Sure you can." The Bersagliere carrying the canteens made a gesture with his free hand signifying they should look at him, then turned and said, "You follow this path until you get to a grove of trees; go into it and continue until you find a small vehicle park, right?"

"Yes," said Della Valentina, "I remember it."

"Right. When you reach it, there's no need to stop and ask: there's a path to the right, uphill, which will take you directly to Company HQ."

"How far from the parking lot to the HQ?"

"It'll be 100 yards more or less."

The first Bersagliere interrupted, "Well, perhaps a little farther."

"I've got it, thank you very much", said Della Valentina, putting the van in motion. Ambrogio added his thanks with a friendly wave.

When they reached the parking lot they found there were very few automobiles. One or two had their hoods up, with mechanics servicing them. At this point the path divided with one fork—crossed by a smaller track—going off uphill to the right. They took this turn at speed, going by a field kitchen at a widening of the path. They assumed it must belong to the Second; it was wood fueled, and two cooks were busy rinsing out two large cooking pots. Further along the trees thinned out, and they found a rise, with the front line running along the top. It was easily identified by the blockhouses, with vegetation on their roofs, spaced out in a line about fifty yards from each other. At a widening of the path, they found a few tents and another van next to one of the blockhouses, which looked as if it could be a company HQ.

Della Valentina stopped the van next to the other and said, confidently, "Here we are."

A sergeant major, probably the company clerk, emerged from one of the tents.

"I've brought this artillery lieutenant here on orders from Lieutenant Galimberti", the driver told him. "I'll be back to pick him up in a couple of hours."

"Ah, Lieutenant Galimberti", murmured the noncom. He saluted Ambrogio as he got out of the vehicle. "Come on in, please. I'm sorry the captain isn't here."

"It doesn't matter", Ambrogio replied. "I don't need to speak with him."

"He's gone over to Third Platoon," the sergeant said, waving at the line to the right, "as tonight we need to re-lay some barbed wire."

From another tent came voices; then a Bersagliere emerged, carrying sacks full of bread rolls. He dropped them carelessly into the other van, returning to the tent, evidently to fetch another load.

Ambrogio explained to the sergeant, "I've come to see someone from my village, Bersagliere Stefano Giovenzana. As I'm short of time, I'd like to go to wherever he is, soon."

"Giovenzana? He's in First Platoon." The noncom pointed over to the left, then paused, thinking. "We're about to deliver chow to the platoons. If you'd like you could go with the kitchen orderlies."

"That seems a good idea to me."

Della Valentina had meantime turned his van around and now left, waving happily.

The Bersagliere loading the food emerged once more from the supply tent, more bread sacks in hand; behind him came another soldier carrying small metal jerrycans of wine; in comparison with the treatment given to the bread, these cans were packed into the van with care. The van was quickly loaded up after a few more trips into the tent. The sergeant led Ambrogio to the front seat; one soldier climbed in the rear, the other got behind the wheel, and they drove off. In order not to raise dust, the driver went slowly along the path paralleling the blockhouses.

Every now and then, the van would stop, usually near one of the blockhouses—which were about ten yards from the path—where generally there would be a Bersagliere waiting (if nobody was at one of his stops, the driver blew the horn, and somebody would come hurrying up), who would collect a few cans and return some empties.

"Isn't it dangerous to blow your horn here, up on the line?" asked Ambrogio.

"In fact it's not allowed," said the driver, smiling, "but you know how it is, Lieutenant; blowing the horn avoids waiting and means less fatigue."

They proceeded, stopping and starting, continuing off toward the left protected by the elevation alongside, until they arrived at the rear of the First Platoon, which was at the end of the path. Here, two Bersaglieri took the last of the van's load, and Ambrogio got out. The blockhouse to which the detachment commander had gone was a stone's throw away; the two soldiers led Ambrogio down a footpath that gradually became a trench. At the blockhouse, the trench (less than a yard wide by one and a half deep) became a T; off to the right it led to other blockhouses and the command-post blockhouse; to the left were even more blockhouses.

One of the Bersaglieri went with his load of rations off to the left. The other put his load on the ground and called out, "Chow, chow down!" Immediately, from blockhouses and elsewhere nearby came soldiers, mess cans in hand.

24

Ambrogio went into the CP. He found himself inside an area of about three yards by three, a hole dug out of the ground: the roof consisted of whole tree trunks, topped on the outside with turf. On the side facing the enemy were large loop-holes, also built out of tree trunks, and, in the central loophole, a little bigger than the others, was mounted a fully loaded Breda machine gun, ready to be fired. Next to it was an empty ammunition box on which sat a sublieutenant, binoculars trained through the loophole. On the other side of the Breda sat a corporal, the machine gunner, also looking out through the loophole. On noticing the arrival of a stranger, they both turned, and Ambrogio asked, "May I come in?"

"Of course", replied the lieutenant.

"I've come visiting, but really I feel I'm intruding, strolling around the front line like a tourist."

"Intruding?!" said the other. "Brother, don't even say that in fun. Anybody who visits an old seat in the field is performing an act of military mercy, didn't you know?" He had a long, thin, crooked face and a cheeky-sounding Piemon-tese accent; Ambrogio figured him to be the same age as himself, and also a student.

"Thank you", he said, and putting out his hand. "Riva, from the Eighth Pasubio Artillery."

"Acciati", the other introduced himself, half getting up from his seat and offering his hand. "I see you don't have the same badge as our artillery."

"We're over in front of Veshenskaya, some twenty-five miles away, over to the right."

"Ah, good. In that case, tell me, brother, what good fortune brings you here?"

If only Manno were here, thought Ambrogio, *he'd know how to reply in the same jocular tone, probably even managing some amusing classic quotation. Why not me?* he asked himself. But the mere effort of thinking up some smart reply left him speechless; accustomed as he was to being straightforward, he didn't even try and—as usual—gave up the effort of a brilliant reply, saying simply, "I've come to see someone from my hometown, the Bersagliere Stefano Giovenzana."

"Giovenzana is a friend of yours? Show me your friends, and I'll know who you are", quoted Acciati. "You have a good friend; Giovenzana is worth his own weight in gold." He paused. "His weight in gold, I tell you. Were you by any chance friends at school? You were also born in '21, eh?"

"Yes."

"Me, too. Good. I'll have someone call your friend right now. Or maybe you'd like to see the beast in his own environment?"

"Yes, in his environment."

"All right." Acciati turned to the blockhouse door and shouted, "Polito, hey, Polito!"

"Here I am, my lieutenant", answered Polito, his orderly, coming through the doorway loaded with mess cans. Some of the cans held stew, others wine, and under one arm he carried a roll of bread.

"What are you doing, loaded like a camel? Just look at him!"

"I had a brilliant idea", said Polito, who had obviously adopted his superior's manner of speaking. "I said to myself, if there are two officers, you, Polito, should bring two servings."

"That was indeed a brilliant idea, and you're right", said Acciati. "Bravo, you read my mind; that's the way!"

"No, but I can't accept", objected Ambrogio firmly. "Are you joking? After barging in and causing you problems ... in any case, look, I've already eaten."

"No", answered Acciati, slowly wagging his index finger in Ambrogio's face. "No, Mr. Artilleryman, you can't pull that one on the Bersaglieri; we're not that dumb ... how can you have eaten if you've traveled from twenty-five miles away?"

"But ... seriously, please, no."

"Yes. Now you just sit down with us poor people and get yourself a bellyful of meat and gravy. You'll experience something special." The machine gunner and Polito laughed at their chief's speech.

Ambrogio felt obliged to accept, although he felt uncomfortable about it. It would have been different if the Bersaglieri had been off the front line, with food to spare. He took the mess can Acciati offered him. "I don't need bread, thanks", he said, still trying to put up resistance; he figured that for sure the bread rolls were counted and rationed.

Acciati came right back: "Please take the bread, despite the fact that my faithful assistant here has brought them over tucked under his armpit, like a Tartar putting his steak under his saddle to tenderize it."

The machine-gun corporal laughed. Ambrogio smiled and took the two rolls from Polito, holding one out to Acciati. "I thank you, Polito", and turning to Acciati, "you're a hospitable people, you Bersaglieri."

"Sit down, Lieutenant." The corporal got up and offered his seat next to the Breda to Ambrogio. Silently, Ambrogio sat. Being near the loophole, he automatically looked out, to be confronted with the wide panorama of the front.

"Ah, look!" he exclaimed, half to himself. The long, bushy embankment of the Italian line fell almost vertically to the Don; the great river's waters washed the edge some ten yards below them. At this point the river wasn't very wide. "More or less like the Po, at Cremona", Ambrogio judged. The opposite bank, held by the enemy, was flat with trees at a lower level than their side. Farther away, beyond the trees on the enemy's side, the country toward the north consisted of endless fields, and on the horizon, bluish in the distance, were two or three villages, identifiable by the sad sight of their abandoned churches and thatched roofs.

Acciati noted the direction of Ambrogio's gaze. "That village over there in front of us is ———— and that other with the onion dome on the church is ———— and the farthest one, nearly out of sight, is ————", he explained.

"Where exactly is the Russian front?"

"Effectively it follows the other bank of the river, at least their forward elements. We can tell better at night when they're firing at us." He added, "There are also snipers on their riverbank, normally up in the trees. And we're trying to locate one in particular who is bothering us."

He put the mess can Polito had just given him on the ground, picked up the binoculars, and spent some time examining the enemy's lines. "This morning he grazed one of my Bersaglieri—nearly took off half his ear." He gave a snort, as if about to laugh. "It's no laughing matter", he said seriously. He gazed fixedly through the binoculars at the top of a tree, moved to continue observing the other side, then shook his head. He put down the binoculars and picked up his mess can. "Tonight. With luck tonight we'll have him. I've been thinking of making a puppet, put a helmet on its head, then have it move around in the trench at the right time. If the sniper fires, we'll have him."

"At the right time?"

"Yes. I guess you've never been in an observation post, right? I mean when dusk comes, it's beginning to get dark, so you start to see the lick of fire from his rifle, which by day is invisible. If he doesn't see through our trick, maybe he'll be eager to end the day with a good score; he'll shoot, we'll spot him, and ..." He put his right hand on the machine gun, much as one would pat a good hunting dog on the hindquarters. "It'll be us that'll be cutting ears."

Ambrogio said nothing.

"What a macabre conversation, if you think about it," declared Acciati, "but that's the life we lead ... well, that's enough of that. Bon appetito!" lifting his mess can as if making a toast. They went back to eating.

While they were eating, other Bersaglieri had come into the blockhouse and sat down on boxes or on the floor, leaning against the walls, to eat their rations. As they ate, Acciati spoke occasionally, out of politeness to his guest, telling about his life as a civilian. It turned out he was studying in Turin at the Faculty of Chemistry. Although no brilliant conversationalist, Ambrogio felt that he ought to contribute, so he spoke about the Cossack refugees he'd seen that morning, camped near Veshenskaya; he mentioned the Russians' enormous churches, some of which could be seen in the towns across the river from where they sat, and he also talked about Sholokov, the Communist writer (who much later would be awarded a Nobel Prize) and how he felt the writer had written about the Cossacks in contradictory terms. Over on their right, toward the east, they heard a few distant shots; a machine gun replied briefly, but the Bersaglieri present paid no attention to these sounds. Every now and then, Acciati would glance instinctively outside at the riverbank, and Ambrogio would stop talking and join him in staring outside. Neither the enemy nor any of their positions could be seen; the lead-green river flowed lazily in the midday sun. The woods concealing the opposing side's trenches were thick with leaves. The faraway plains looked darker under a heat haze. *The last heat wave of summer*, thought Ambrogio. In contrast with the Russian lines, the Italian positions could be seen clearly on both right and left, and as far as the eye could see, the blockhouses served to pick out the profile of the embankment.

When they finished eating, Ambrogio pulled out a pack of cigarettes received from home and offered them to the men around him: without exception they all took one, smoking silently for a few minutes with evident enjoyment. Finally Acciati said, "Brother, we've detained you here to enjoy your company for a while, but it's clear you didn't come here to stay. I won't delay you any longer."

Ambrogio got to his feet. "I've enjoyed your company for this short time. I'm not just being polite; I mean it. I'm beginning to know more about the Bersaglieri. But you're right, it's time I went."

The lieutenant's runner, Polito, also quietly got to his feet. "Good", Acciati said to him, nodding his head. The two officers shook hands across the machine gun. "Take care with the snipers", Acciati reminded his guest. "I'm serious; it's no joke."

Ambrogio nodded his agreement. "Before I leave I'll come back and say goodbye and properly thank you for the meal." He turned and followed Polito, who had meantime slung a rifle on his back, muzzle down.

25

They entered the left-hand trench, which was built with gentle zigzags. They walked hunched over to avoid being seen by the enemy, but still their heads and shoulders sometimes became exposed. They passed several dugouts, curtained off with tent canvas, behind which Ambrogio glimpsed blanketed bunks with canvas mattresses, backpacks, helmets, and occasionally overcoats, hanging from pegs driven into the earth walls. There were Bersaglieri lying down, enjoying a siesta, or sitting on boxes at the wider parts of the trench. One sentry watched the enemy lines standing, but with his eyes at ground level, his head camouflaged with branches of foliage; by his side were his rifle and several hand grenades. They walked on through the narrow trench and after a while ran into another rest area, Bersaglieri relaxing while a sentry watched. This sentry was posted at a loophole open to the sky, with a mounted Breda machine gun.

This can really be called a long, thin line, Ambrogio thought as he walked, *paper thin!* It was as he had heard, that the Celere covered more than thirty miles of front—it must be correct. He mentally calculated, *On this front line, there must be more or less one man every ten yards.*

Ahead of him, Polito continued hurrying along, crouched over, and soon they passed another blockhouse, more rest areas, and, at one point, a Russian machine gun (the characteristic round magazine identifying it) mounted at a covered loophole, but unmanned. A little farther on, a motionless Bersagliere sentry stared fixedly beyond the trench area. On seeing this man, Polito hesitated, then turned to Ambrogio with a knowing smile; it was then that Ambrogio also recognized the sentry—Stefano. Under the feathered helmet, the youth looked thinner than he remembered. He couldn't help thinking, *He has the same neck as his mother and Giustina.*

Stefano turned briefly to look at the two behind him, recognized Polito, and turned again to look into the distance. Polito walked on a few paces, then stopped and turned around to look at Ambrogio, who realized he should go along with the joke. Putting himself at his friend's back, he yelled, "Hey, Moonface!" and put a hand on Stefano's shoulder.

Stefano turned suddenly, quickly lifting with his right hand the rifle he'd had pointing out of the loophole. "Oh, Ambrogio, it's you!"

"How are you, Stefano?" Ambrogio greeted him with happiness and mixed emotions. His Bersagliere friend rested the rifle against the wall and held out his hand; Ambrogio shook it, then gave him a hug.

"So you've really come to look for me", said Stefano.

The young officer nodded. "You've no idea how much I've wanted to come and see you."

Stefano turned to face down the trench to one side. "Sergeant Bellazzi . . . squad leader, ho!" he called. The expression on his face reminded Ambrogio of the many times when he spoke to the factory hands in Nomana while they worked at a task that couldn't be interrupted. The sergeant came immediately. "Giovenzana, what the f—— what's going on? What's up?"

"There's no attack," Stefano reassured him, "only a visitor, come to see me."

"What is this, an army post or a college, receiving visits?" grumbled the sergeant, blondish and bristly. Then he noticed Ambrogio's rank and saluted. Ambrogio held out his hand cordially. "I've come to see my friend Giovenzana, with the authorization of Sublieutenant Acciati", he said, nodding toward Polito.

"Yes, of course", replied the sergeant. "I'll relieve Giovenzana right now." He turned toward the area from which he'd come. "Biondolillo, ho, Biondolillo . . ." He paused, then, shaking his head, added, *"Che ti venga un accidente . . . !"*

"Here I am", a voice, evidently Biondolillo, said.

"Bring your rifle and get over here."

"I'm coming."

Biondolillo came immediately. He had black hair and coal black sparkling eyes in a handsome southern face.

"Maybe you're a Lillo, but for sure you're not a 'biondo' (blond)", the sergeant said to him in a bantering tone: evidently the joke about Biondolillo's name and coloring had been used before, and Bellazzi was bringing it out once again for Ambrogio's benefit, but only Polito laughed.

"Maybe I'm not a blond, but all the women like me just the same", replied Biondolillo, in what was an equally well-used reply.

"Well, seeing as there are no women present, you just set about relieving Giovenzana here."

"Right away", Biondolillo replied, glancing through the loophole and placing himself in the sentry's niche. Turning to Stefano, he asked, "Is there a password?" Stefano shook his head, no.

Biondolillo turned again to look through the loophole. "Who wants to bet that I spot the sniper before I go off duty?"

"Oh, no," replied Polito, "we'll be settling with him ourselves tonight, with our heavy Breda." His tone indicated the matter had already been decided. Then he turned to Ambrogio and said, "Lieutenant, with your permission, I'll return to my post."

Ambrogio thanked him, dismissed him, and then followed Stefano along the trench, with Bellazzi bringing up the rear.

"Let's go farther ahead", Stefano said in dialect. "There's a widening along here where we can be comfortable." It proved to be quite comfortable; the trench at this point had been widened and deepened and covered with a roof of tree branches, and although the leaves were drying, there was still shade from the sun. "On hot days this is the best spot", said Stefano. Sergeant Bellazzi added, "It's our living room."

On three sides of the living room there ran a bench, built out of wooden ammunition boxes, and seated on this were three or four Bersaglieri, who stood when Ambrogio entered.

"Please sit down", he said to them.

Indicating his rifle, Stefano said, "I'm going to get rid of this and be right back." He took off his helmet and turned to leave.

"Where will you put it, in your bunk?" asked Ambrogio.

"Yes, it's just a few steps."

"In that case, let me see it?"

"Sure, come on, let me show you how luxurious it is."

A little distance from the "living room" were niches carved out of the walls, curtained with tent canvas, like the ones Ambrogio had seen when following Polito through the trenches.

"These were all built during the nights", said Stefano, speaking in dialect, as usual. "You've no idea how we've had to work this past month, particularly to dig the trenches. Well, now it's done." Then he added, "But now we'll have to work at winterizing everything. Bah!" He pulled aside one of the canvas curtains covering the entrance of the shelter, revealing empty straw bunks. Strewn about were backpacks, a rifle, a helmet hanging from its leather strap, a cloth bread bag, and boxes half filled with personal items. From nails driven into the wall was a photograph of the actress Alida Valli, and next to it, a picture of the

Nomana crucifix, identical to the one in Gerardo's office, but small in size, like a postcard. Stefano dropped his rifle and helmet on the bed, under the religious picture.

"I see you have our Lord of Nomana here", said Ambrogio.

His friend nodded, a serious look on his face.

"Don't the others pick on you for having it?"

"Back in the barracks they tried, but here, no."

"Yes, right", said Ambrogio. His own mother had placed a small wooden crucifix in his valise when he left home, and he had experienced more or less the same during his training. He looked around, noted the roof of the shelter made out of sheet metal, boards, and mud, and asked, "And what happens when it rains?"

"It's perfectly waterproof, believe me", said Stefano. "Maybe it doesn't look it, but we don't get one drop in here."

Ambrogio nodded. "We've also managed to work miracles with our tents."

"Oh, yes? And how are things with you?"

"The artillery isn't as close to the Russians; we feel safe, more relaxed."

"War is still war", said Stefano. "When I hear the rustling noise of their artillery going overhead," he nodded up toward the sky, "aimed at our artillery ... well, at those moments, I'm happy I'm here."

Ambrogio disagreed. "No. You're much more exposed. There's no comparison. But look, what news do you have from Nomana?"

"Giustina writes me every two weeks without fail", Stefano replied. "She keeps me advised about everything. Back on the farm they're all in good health; of course my father has a lot to do, having to do my work as well. I understand that, although Giustina doesn't mention it in her letter. All in all, we can't complain. After all, Father is still healthy, and Giustina brings in her monthly paycheck. So ..."

"Yes. I understand; so it's only you that causes problems for your family?"

Stefano smiled. "Exactly. And your family?"

"They're well also. Just now Giudittina has mumps."

"Yes, I know. Can you imagine that Giustina wouldn't have told me?" He went silent for a moment. "You knew that in Beolco last month people were worried about Luca?"

"Worried about Luca? Last month? What's it all about?"

"Yes, they were worried that he'd disappeared, because a fellow from the Fifth Alpine wrote home—mind you, he wasn't even in the same outfit as Luca. He hadn't checked his facts, and a rumor flew around rapidly. Imagine my sister, she was worried to death. But it turned out to be another fellow called Sambruna; same last name, but not our Luca."

"What an irresponsible creep, this guy from Beolco. Missing. Missing, that's the same as saying 'killed'."

"You really believe that?"

"Yes", Ambrogio said. "At least I'm afraid that's how it is. It's very tough, but that's the way it is."

"Around here, many of our people are convinced that the Russians kill all their prisoners", said Stefano. He bent down, picked up his backpack, took out some aluminum cigarette lighters, hesitated as if about to choose one, then put them in his pocket and said, "But let's not stand around in here. Let's go back to the living room. Or better yet, we could go farther along, to our lookout point. From there, we can enjoy the panorama of the front even sitting down."

"The what? The panorama?"

"Yes, that's right. Want to take a look?"

They went out, toward the lookout point. As they walked along the trench, Ambrogio observed, "The Russians, or I should say the Communists, turn everything into a political act. That's their way, and when they look at us, they see us as enemies of communism. You know, they kill their own colleagues without pity when they work against the party and kill them even when all they have is a suspicion of treason. Imagine what they'd do to us."

"Right", Stefano said. "But no one knows for sure. Sometimes I think what you say is right. It's like death; nobody has returned to tell what happens. So we can't know for sure if there are prisoners in Russian hands or not." He slowed down; they'd arrived, and Stefano swept his hand before him. "Here's the lookout point."

26

They stood at a point where the embankment ended. The land before them fell almost vertically. It was here that the tree-covered gulch down which Ambrogio had arrived in the van dived into the Don. The trench also ended at this point, having widened into rising ground terminating in a small area of beaten earth, from which there was an open vista toward the north and west. Around this area a semicircular seat had been constructed, consisting of earth and odd pieces of wood. Without giving a thought to possible snipers, the two friends sat down. In the foreground below them were the tops of the trees, which grew down to the riverbank.

"Look over there!" exclaimed Ambrogio. "Those hills remind me of the valleys near your house, over by Beolco."

"Imagine how I feel!" Stefano said, then, suddenly serious, "My home!"

Ambrogio reached in his pocket for cigarettes and matches and said, in sympathy with his friend, "La Nomanella . . ."

"Who knows if we . . . I mean I . . .", murmured Stefano, then stopped.

"Who knows . . . what?"

"If . . . I'll ever return home."

Ambrogio dug him sharply in the side. "What nonsense are you talking?"

Stefano looked at his friend, and for a moment his eyes took on a harsh, pain-filled look, something Ambrogio had never seen before; his friend's whole expression had changed.

"What is this, a hunch?" the officer asked, giving his friend another elbowing. "Come on, Moonface", he said, and Stefano relaxed again and smiled.

"What's happening with you? Do you often get gloomy like this?" asked Ambrogio.

His friend gestured, no. "Rarely. Almost never."

"In that case it looks as if I've brought gloom with me."

"It's possible . . . it was because we talked about home", said Stefano, laughing.

"Well, you just listen to me", Ambrogio said, emotion giving him an air of prophecy. "When the cherries ripen on the big cherry trees at Nomanella, we'll both pick them together again, as we've always done."

"In that case, see you next year in June", agreed Stefano. "Sure, why not?"

Ambrogio offered his friend a cigarette and took one himself. "Wait", said Stefano, reaching in his pocket and pulling out the aluminum lighters. They were handmade. He chose one and gave it to Ambrogio. "Use this. I made it myself. It's a gift."

"You made it yourself? Since when have you been doing that?" said Ambrogio, striking a light. "It even works!"

"Of course, what do you think?" Stefano replied. This time it was his turn to jab his friend in the ribs with his elbow. He lit his cigarette in the proffered flame, and Ambrogio lit his own. Ambrogio continued striking the lighter several times. "Look, it works every time! See what I mean? Your grandmother was right when she said you should have been a mechanic. Just look at it! Tell me, how did you learn to make these?"

"One of the fellows in the platoon taught me. We got the aluminum from a downed airplane; it crashed over there, on the riverbank. The flints get sent out to him from home. We make the lighters and sell them."

"What a good business! In that case, I'll pay you for this one."

"Didn't I tell you it was a gift?"

Ambrogio nodded. "All right, thank you."

They continued smoking in silence, then looked at each other and smiled, pleased they could get this short time together.

"We're a good way away from home, eh, Moonface?" Ambrogio repeated.

"Yes, and here we are sitting on a bench, just as we used to in school", Stefano replied. "If Miss Camatini could see us now . . . by the way, do you have any news of her?"

"Yes, she's well. Every now and then she sends me greetings through my sister Isadora."

"All right. Now tell me all about what Giustina has written."

Stefano started talking, telling his friend his recent news, but rambling and mixing in some older events. Ambrogio already knew about some of the news, but when something new was mentioned he would ask Stefano for more details. When Stefano couldn't recall any more news, the two exchanged surmises, imagining what could have happened since their absence. Ambrogio then told his friend about the news from his own home. They spent half an hour, just talking.

Looking at his watch, Ambrogio noted he hadn't much time left. They both got up from the seat and returned to the living room, where they sat briefly. The squad leader, Sergeant Bellazzi, was there, along with some ten other Bersaglieri, clearly waiting for the visitor's return. They all hoped to be able to speak to him, hear his news, speak to someone who was new, a different face from those always around them. Seeing the same faces, day and night, it was worth waiting to hear from someone different, with news from home, so they engaged Ambrogio in conversation. Following a remark of Ambrogio's about Italian machine guns jamming, they turned to talk about the captured Russian machine gun, which the squad had placed in their trench. They agreed that it looked clumsy because of the large magazine but that it was effective. Asked by Ambrogio how he liked it, Sergeant Bellazzi paused, considering the matter, then volunteered that it was better than the Breda 30, "because it doesn't jam so much."

Those present discussed the Breda's tendency to jam, until a corporal, whose ability with the Italian gun was recognized, said that, being a delicately engineered gun, it needed to be treated with care, in which case it didn't tend to jam. There was general disagreement from the other Bersaglieri, Stefano included; they told tales about previous experiences with the Breda. One of them referred back to the previous winter, when during a Russian attack, only one of the five Bredas in the line continued firing.

"The Breda", said Sergeant Bellazzi, "doesn't work well in the Russian winter because of the cold; in Libya it works poorly because of the sand. In other words, this is a machine gun that will work well so long as it is being fired on the Riveria." Talk turned to other weapons, particularly those of the Russians'; among these they discussed the Katyuska, which was to them a new device. Ambrogio was able to contribute to this talk with some knowledge, having seen several abandoned at Tarassovka during his march to the front with his own regiment. German tanks had destroyed some, but some others were intact, including more than one with the sixteen rockets still loaded, ready to fire. He described the Katyuska and also told them of another thing he had noticed; the trucks on which the rocket launchers were mounted weren't the usual old-fashioned-looking Russian trucks (they look like the Keystone Cops, remarked one of the group) but modern, streamlined trucks; he'd noticed they were American-made Dodges.

From talking about enemy weapons, they went on to talk about the enemy troops and of the possibility of an eventual victory.

Ambrogio and all the others were in agreement that the Russians' chances of winning were practically nonexistent, even though now the Russians didn't desert in large numbers as they had the previous year, and when the Germans and Italians advanced, they now found the enemy putting up much more of a defense. There were still many cases of desertion, and there was sabotage in the manufacture of ammunition. Frequently Russian shells didn't explode, a sign that the munitions factory workers were sending them out purposely inert. The Russians also seemed to be short of adequate numbers of rifles; when doing sentry duty, they could be seen handing rifles over to one another.

"Besides," said the sergeant, "how could they compete against us, particularly the Germans, when they are so backward?" Somebody brought up the ubiquitous thatched roofs and the fact that nobody had yet seen an asphalted road in Russia.

"As far as equipment is concerned," said one of the Bersaglieri, "they've got good weapons, even though they are rudimentary—and this could be advantageous—and they have good tanks and armor; but their trucks are inadequate. How could they succeed in advancing on Berlin using these old Keystone Cops trucks?"

Another soldier replied, "New types of trucks could be provided by the Americans."

"Do you know how many trucks that could be?" objected another. "The Americans have first to think about their own army's needs."

This seemed to be a winning argument; none of the soldiers had any idea of the extraordinary American manufacturing capacity, of which they would soon hear news from home, brought there by Italian troops returning from Tunis.

"And above anything else, in war it's a question of courage", added a sharp-faced happy-looking southerner, somewhat impetuously. "They almost always get drunk before they attack. As far as I'm concerned this says nothing in their favor." All agreed; Ambrogio noted that the usual arguments between northerners and southerners, so current in the army, didn't seem to be prevalent here. *Who knows?* he thought. *This might be because there are so many good and capable southerners in the Bersaglieri.*

The time for his meeting with Della Valentina was approaching; after looking at his watch a couple of times, Ambrogio got to his feet (followed by all the others) and said his goodbyes.

Stefano, now wearing his plumed helmet and carrying his rifle on one shoulder, accompanied his friend through the various sections of trench until they reached the area of the CP. There they learned that Acciati had the duty as deputy commander of the company. On arriving at the path, they could see, behind the CP, two parked vans; one was quickly identified as Della Valentina's. He was sitting in the driver's seat, waiting, and as they came up to him, he said to Ambrogio, "It took me less time than I thought."

"Yes, I see. Have you been waiting long for me?"

"Oh, no", answered the Bersagliere, waving a hand dismissively.

"Well, it looks to me as if you've been waiting, so come on, let's go."

Stefano took another of his aluminum lighters from his pocket. "Please accept this as a gift", he said to Della Valentina.

"Why should you do this?" the driver questioned him.

"Man, just to thank you."

"No, don't do it; it doesn't make sense."

"I make these lighters myself; they don't cost me anything. Come on, take it."

Della Valentina looked at Stefano, the look of surprise still on his face; Stefano made the lighter work.

Della Valentina smiled and took the lighter. "But why? Well, if you insist, I thank you." He lit the lighter, then said, "It does work, and how!"

"Right", said Stefano.

"It's time to go", said Ambrogio: "I'll say goodbye to Lieutenant Acciati, then I'll be ready."

In a few minutes, having seen Acciati, he emerged from the command post blockhouse, shook Stefano's hand, and got in the van. Della Valentina, after waving cordially to Stefano, headed the van toward the embankment, having first done a wheel-spinning sporty start.

Stefano, Nomana's Bersagliere, stood there, gazing after the retreating van; Ambrogio had laid eyes on him for the last time. In the long years to come he would often remember Stefano at this moment, happy, his skinny neck supporting the feathered helmet, his rifle on his shoulder.

27

They had no problems during the return journey. Arriving at Rassipnaya, Ambrogio took his leave of Lieutenant Galimberti, got on his motorcycle, and set off. Once again he rode across the huge prairie, the only vehicle crawling along the immensity of the country like a small beetle.

Riding through the dead sunflower patches with dusk approaching, Ambrogio felt an overwhelming sadness. As on his outward journey, the officer saw nobody; he stopped and switched off the motor, without dismounting. The air was calm, not a breath of air; an almost incredible silence surrounded him. Never had he experienced a silence so total.

You couldn't get this at home, he thought. *You'd only get this silence on the tallest mountaintops.* He sensed the need in himself for a noise, any noise; more than that, he felt the need of the company of fellowmen. But all around him there were only dead sunflowers, scrawny and weak looking, giving the impression of skeletons, with heavy skulls peering down at the ground; they looked as if they were leaning on each other for support before they fell down once and for all. With a strong kick he started the motor and moved off.

Reaching the encampment of the refugee Cossacks on their embankment, he saw they were eating by the light of several campfires. Each family group, Ambrogio noted, ate at strange-looking earth tables, around which had been dug a trench into which the diners' legs fit when seated. The motorcycle went slowly past the nearest family, in which the leader seemed to be an old man, bent at the shoulders (probably the great-grandfather); another man, white bearded, was a robust giant, and all around them were women and children. One of the women had placed a tureen of soup on the earthen table (perhaps it was millet soup?). The great-grandfather lifted his hand and blessed the meal with the sign of the Cross (an unexpected gesture, to Ambrogio), after which he started ladling the food for the family into unmatched bowls. The family's collective blue eyes went from their plates to the sight of the Italian officer going past on his motorcycle.

Ambrogio drove to the end of the long wooded hollow without having to turn on the headlight. The sun had not yet completely disappeared by the time he reached the battery's command post. At the sound of the motor, the lieutenant commander came out of his tent. "Don't get off", he said, holding out an arm. "Go right on to the artillery line. An order to fire is coming in."

Ambrogio immediately made a half turn on the motorcycle and traced a circle in the field. The communications sergeant, Feltrin, also emerged from the tent, to look over his old bike, apparently lamenting the extra distance the venerable Alce was being asked to cover.

Once again Ambrogio stopped the bike and gestured to Feltrin that he should mount behind. "Get on", he said with a smile. "Then you can bring the bike back straightaway." Quickly the sergeant climbed on the bike's rear seat.

28

One week later, it was Ambrogio who received a visitor: Luca, the family firm's mechanic, with whom he had attended the meeting in Nomana at which war was announced.

Behind the lines at Veshenskaya there had started an east-west movement of Alpine troops: column upon column of men, mules, and mountain equipment. The whole Tridentina Division was on the move. This division, no sooner had they arrived by train the previous August, had distinguished themselves by closing the gap that had been left open in the front line and had thereafter remained in the area. Now they were heading for what would be their winter positions: on the Don, but farther west, beyond the bend in the river, where they had been preceded by the other two Alpine divisions. From Ambrogio's battery those large moving columns could sometimes be seen, long lines of black dots, almost out of sight on the plains. Seen up close, the Alpine troops seemed bigger than the other soldiers (the current joke was to call them "our armored cars"): they marched steadily, with steps that seemed to crush the path, heavy packs on their backs, topped by a large, horizontally mounted 91 rifle. Often their hats (a medieval design, according to Michele) would be tilted back, leaving their foreheads clear to perspire. In single file they marched, exchanging few words, perhaps some comment or joke, but always with that calm attitude normal among Alpine troops. Scattered in the column of men were mules, calm and well behaved, as if influenced by the men. Now and then the columns halted, at which the men would fall into groups, putting their heavy packs on the ground and, if the day had been a long one, sitting on the earth and leaning against their packs. Although there were always those energetic or curious soldiers who, if the stop wasn't scheduled as a regular rest stop, would wander off, exploring and inspecting everything of interest in the surroundings.

Sometimes these explorers would come to the embankment: they would look at the cannons, the two machine guns, everything in the battery. The gunners would explain this or that detail, engaging them in harmless chatter; the strangers would stand leaning on one leg or the other (a habit reminiscent of the mountain villages on market day back home); rarely would they initiate a conversation.

Ambrogio also talked to a few: he tried to get them to talk about what had really happened back in August, when they had closed the gap in the front. But, like all soldiers, the Alpine troops could only talk about events in the areas they had personally been in. Now they complained about not being in the mountains. "If the Cicai Division hadn't given up," one said in his Brescia dialect, "we'd be in the Caucasian mountains by now: much better than these plains." They spoke calmly without dramatizing the situation. These soldiers had the number 6 on their hats; they belonged to the Sixth Regiment of the Tridentina Division. When they had all marched on, soldiers of the Fifth Regiment appeared. Ambrogio asked each one he could what battalion he belonged to: "Are you from the Morbegno?" "No, I'm from Edolo" "No, with the Tirano" "The Morbegno you're asking about have the white pom-pom tassels." The last group of Alpine troops to pass by did have the white pom-pom tassels: "Do you by any chance know a Corporal Sambruna, Luca, from Beolco?"

Finally one of them answered, "I know him, sure I know him. He's a machine gunner in my company: Corporal First Class Sambruna, Luca, from Beolco; that's him." He spoke in the dialect of Como, with the accent that in Nomana was referred to as "from the summit", but which is also heard in the people from the rustic villages on the slopes to the south of Lake Como.

"So, they've made him a corporal first class. Could you tell him that you met a fellow villager here?"

"Right, I can."

"You'll have to tell him Second Lieutenant Riva, from Nomana."

"Ah, so you're from Nomana? Well, look, I'm from Roncio."

Roncio was a group of small houses, populated by one hundred or possibly two hundred souls, set on a forested secondary road leading from Nomana to the lake of Pusiano, known in eighteenth-century neoclassical poetry as Eupili.

"Well, that's so close we're nearly neighbors."

"It can't be more than six miles from Roncio to Nomana", estimated the soldier in his primitive accent.

"Yes, more or less," agreed Ambrogio, "but Roncio is Alpine country."

"Well," said the soldier, wagging his head in disagreement, "it's goat country." Then he thought better. "Goats, mountain men, mountain paths, and caves." He had a solid build, freckled face, and tawny mustache; for fun, he had his hat turned around, so the insignia and brim were backward, over his neck. Ambrogio looked at the hat and felt like laughing: when he was at recruit headquarters in Cremona, there had also been a Roncio man there, a country boy with big ears, his head large and round as a cooking pot. *For one reason or another, you people from Roncio are unique*, he thought.

"In any case," continued the floppy hatted Alpine soldier, "if you want to see Luca, there'll be no problem; within an hour, he'll be here before you, I assure you", and indicated on the ground in front of Ambrogio the exact spot in which he'd find Luca.

Strange as it may seem, that is really how it turned out. No more than one hour had gone by when, accompanied by another Alpine soldier, Luca appeared. Both of them approached from the twisting track that came up from the southern plateau to the battery, striding out with big steps. They both wore beards. They stopped at the beginning of the company area to ask an artilleryman the way; Ambrogio had already seen them and went toward them. He shook hands with Luca and then with the other mountaineer, whom Luca introduced: "He's from our neighborhood, from Monticello, his name is Tremolada." Ambrogio took hold of each man by the arm and turned to lead them to his own tent.

The three sat on stools and wooden boxes under the open tent's winglike shade. The faces of Luca and Ambrogio shone with the happiness of seeing each other. On taking off his hat, a forelock tumbled down Luca's forehead: this, along with his reddish beard and the grave manner acquired by life among the mountain men, projected an impression of a solid tower of a man, even though Luca wasn't so tall. Ambrogio quickly told his friend about his recent visit to Stefano; then they talked of Nomana and Manno—Ambrogio's cousin and Luca's friend—from whom Luca had received a letter the previous week, from somewhere in Africa. Ambrogio asked about Giordano Galbiati, second lieutenant, the son of the Nomana savings bank's crippled employee. Luca advised, "I hardly see him at all, for he's not in my company, but I know he is well."

"And how about Don Carlo Gnocchi?"

"Him I see frequently; he comes down to battalion each week, even though he is chaplain to the whole regiment."

"Yes, of course, you Alpine types have a chaplain for each battalion."

"We have more chaplains than anyone else, and the biggest and best rations", said the mountain man Tremolada, in a joking tone.

Luca smiled, but shook his head in disapproval at the jest; to him this was no joking matter. "Don Carlo is a kind of saint", he said. "All of us hold him in high regard."

Of greater interest to Luca was the recent visit Ambrogio had paid to Stefano. Noticing this, Ambrogio recounted the details of the visit. "Your future brother-in-law", he said, "receives a letter from his sister Giustina every other week. And you?"

"Yes, to tell the truth, I do", replied Luca, lowering his voice reverentially. "Sometimes she runs out of things to write and tells me of the priest's last Sunday sermon."

"Look at the problems you give the poor girl!" quipped Ambrogio.

Tremolada burst out laughing, as if the remark had been an enormous joke. Being a simple, uncomplicated type, he was very happy, just from having met Ambrogio, a near neighbor.

The two mountain soldiers stayed for lunch. Ambrogio's orderly, Paccoi, who had outdone himself in discretion for the dinner visit by Bonsaver, this time paid less attention to form and more to substance. He was thus rather distressed at being unable to set a couple of bottles of wine on the table, or rather on the box that took its place. This became a more necessary task after a remark of Ambrogio's, to the effect that "these Alpine troops are serious people". This had provoked an account by the Monticello mountain man about a farewell party of serious proportions, highly liquid, which his company had celebrated the day they left Italy. Luca, quiet as usual, confirmed the anecdote: "You had to see it. Even after putting people aboard the train the party continued; you had to run after them because they would get off on the other side of the train, some of them reduced to crawling on all fours."

"Yes, on all fours!" chimed in Tremolada.

"And for those that weren't completely drunk, it was quite a job to keep the others together", Luca added.

A distraught Paccoi, squeezing one fisted hand with the other, murmured repeatedly to himself, "And we have no wine. We have no wine."

Then Ambrogio remembered that he had two bottles of brandy, recent arrivals in the mail from Italy. "Go and fetch the brandy", he told Paccoi, who hurried to do so, a look of relief on his face.

When they had finished eating, the four battery corporals and some other soldiers came up in order to meet the two Alpine soldiers: they also were offered a cognac, as was Paccoi, which caused the emptying of the two bottles in no time.

After consuming his share of the brandy, Tremolada, having mellowed somewhat, gained the attention of all present, entertaining them with tales about incredibly stubborn mules, about memorable sunny meals back home, of mountain marches when feet had to be wrapped to prevent freezing.

Ambrogio and Luca left the group to stroll up and down behind the line of cannons, talking about their distant hometown and of the people they had left behind, of the factory and the wartime problems they guessed it was experiencing.

After a while, shaking his head in friendly disapproval, Luca called to Tremolada, who got up from his stool and came toward his friend, his hat turned backward and sweat running freely down his brow. Once away from the group, Tremolada became serious and said goodbye to Ambrogio; despite all his thunder and lightning, he retained his countryman's innate good manners. And although both Alpine soldiers had taken a lot of cognac, when they turned and walked off, their pace was steady, even hurried, designed to have them reach their detachment before the end of evening parade. In the distance could be seen the outline of men and mules milling about the darker patch of the assembled Alpine troops, ready to march off, destination unknown.

29

Autumn arrived: a cold wind started blowing from the northwest of Siberia. The wind soon became so biting that the artillerymen on their own initiative dug holes inside their tents, so they could sleep out of its reach.

During this time, like the soldiers in all the other commands, the artillerymen had begun to build real winter quarters, piling earth up over these shelters, even installing glass windows "liberated" from abandoned villages along the banks of the Don. Doors were fashioned from the wood taken from ammunition boxes, and stoves made out of fuel drums cut in half; thus from each barrel two stoves were made.

From his trench high over the riverbank, Stefano could see the forest below, changing color as each day went by. Before falling to the ground, each leaf, in a sort of farewell feast, turned into different and beautiful colors: gold or red, a delicate yellow, rusty tan or dark brown, with variations, according to the type of tree. From the northwest, the origin of the cold wind, high in the sky, came flocks of ducks: flying in a V formation or simply in an oblique line ahead and honking continuously. The youth watched them pass with the frustration natural to the seasonal hunter, strict orders having been issued prohibiting the use of military weapons for potshots. The hoarse honking, coming at various times of day and night, came to represent to Stefano a kind of greeting, and a farewell: advice from the ducks fleeing the inclement weather. After all the ducks had gone, another migration started, totally unexpected, of spiders. Strung along the tops of the blockhouses, on telephone wires, on bushes and tall grass, appeared spiderwebs, their quantities increasing with each day. At first nobody noticed their arrival; a night sentry, looking up at the moon, saw a continuous parade of floating webs. Keeping his voice low, he called a couple of companions to come and take a look. Hearing their wondering exclamations, other Bersaglieri left their rest and came out to look, Stefano among them. In the air above the trench, a myriad of spiderweb strands flew horizontally, taken by a breeze; on each strand rode a tiny spider.

"I've never seen anything like it."

"Me neither."

"And me."

"How come?" one of the Bersaglieri asked, and another answered, "We have the same thing in my village during the Indian summer of Saint Martin. That's why, back home, we call the Indian summer 'the spiders' summer'."

"Oh, come on now . . ."

"No, seriously."

There was no wind, only a soft breeze, and it wasn't cold, so the Bersaglieri stayed out on the moonlit trench to watch the migrating spiders. One of them commented, "By the way, have you noticed that we no longer hear the quail calling?"

"Yes, you're right. I hadn't noticed, but you're right."

"Of course he's right! It's been weeks since we've heard quail."

"The quail, the quail—who cares?"

"The quail must have received their transfer orders," said a corporal jokingly, "just like the Pasubio Division."

"That's true, too. Have you heard about the Pasubio? What a bad joke."

"What a screw-up."

"I heard they had to move out from one day to the other and had to abandon the winter quarters they'd just finished building", said Biondolillo thoughtfully. "Let's hope the same thing doesn't happen to us."

"No, it shouldn't happen to us. Lieutenant Acciati is sure of it", said Bellazzi, the sergeant. "He told me so tonight when he did his rounds."

"Not much fun to have to start all over, eh?"

"But where are they sending the Pasubio, anyway?"

"Over there, along beyond our left, on the other side of the Turin. We'll be together again, like last winter, division alongside division."

"A good arrangement. Because after the screw-up in August, I don't trust those recent arrivals from Italy."

"The problem is that the veterans from the Pasubio and the Turin are about to be given leave. Those who have spent a winter in Russia get to return to Italy: the changeover takes place next week", said Bellazzi.

"What about us?"

"You didn't know? We'll get our orders to rotate after theirs."

"Yes, but who knows when?"

"What more do you want? Do you think it depends on me?" Bellazzi replied.

Stefano remained quiet. He knew that, having arrived in Russia in January, he would not be receiving orders to rotate.

"Well," said a soldier, "if they don't play the trick on us of moving us now that our winter quarters are ready ... at least we won't be feeling the cold."

No one was worried about the front line; after all, up to now all they had done was advance, so why be concerned about it?

In fact, the fall of 1942 had seen the point of maximum advance by German arms and consequently, in a way, of Italian expansion as well. From the Pyrenees to the North Cape and as far as Crete, practically all of Europe was in German hands. Here in the east, their enormous front line, starting from the Arctic seas, covered thousands of miles toward the south, reaching Voronezh, in the upper reaches of the Don, following the river's course eastward, toward Stalingrad. Only there, at the most forward point of the front, was there fierce fighting, as there was also at the foot of the inaccessible Caucasian mountains. Behind the protection of the Caucasians lay the source of the enemy's oil supplies. In the position occupied by Stefano (and the same for Ambrogio, Bonsaver, Luca, and Michele) details of these battles arrived as a distant echo. News of this fighting would come in old newspapers or via bulletins that someone at headquarters would copy down from radio broadcasts and circulate. Sometimes, when the news from Italy was being broadcast, a signals man might telephone one of the front-line positions and say, "News bulletin!" and then put the telephone close to the radio, radios being plentiful at headquarters. In this way, any common soldier could listen, once the signals men had raised the receiver in the air. Often, a soldier would listen to the news on the telephone more to hear a voice from home than because of the news content. It reminded many of them of home, of the family together in the evening, listening to the radio at suppertime. In war, what truly preoccupies the soldiers, what absorbs them to the point of leaving them indifferent to the news from elsewhere, is the situation of their own sector.

It was thus that the beginning of serious difficulties caught them unprepared.

PART FOUR

I

The unbelievable news that they would have to abandon their positions on the Don reached Ambrogio at the plotting table. After the veteran outfits returned to Italy, Ambrogio had left the battery assigned to the fire-control post.

Wearing the sleeved sheepskin cloak and balaclava helmet that had been issued to all the troops, and with only his eyes showing, he was as usual looking at the enemy positions through his binoculars. At this point, the enemy was at a lower level than the Italian positions; every once in a while, he would put his glasses down and beat his woolen-gloved hands together in an attempt to warm them. He frequently glanced at the telephone beside him; it had been severed in the neighborhood of the gun batteries. He wondered what had happened to the two soldiers he had sent out to repair the line. *Haven't they been able to fix it yet? How much time are they going to take?* he asked himself.

The door to the plotting room opened, and Valorzi entered. The second lieutenant in charge of that sector, Valorzi was from Venice, an intellectual-looking youth with a high forehead.

"Eh, Valorzi", Ambrogio greeted him.

"Have you received the order yet?" the other quickly asked.

"What order? About what?" Ambrogio asked, almost jovially.

"The order to retreat."

"To what?" exclaimed Ambrogio, his voice involuntarily loud; he stared at the other officer.

"I see you're not up to date. Heck, the order to beat it: we all have to leave."

"But ... but ..."

"My platoon has to abandon its position at two, on the dot", he pointed to his watch, looked at it to check the time, and pressing his lips together, frowned. "We're running short of time."

Ambrogio was still trying to catch up. "What did you say? Who told you such a ... such a dumb ..."

"I've just come from company HQ. We were called together in order to be given that order."

"Ah, I see now. I've had no communications with the group for more than an hour: my two signalers are out, trying to fix the fault."

"Well," said Valorzi, "I've advised you", and turned to leave.

"Hey, just a moment." Ambrogio tried to delay the other's departure, to find out more about the retreat order. Valorzi kept going, closing the shelter's door behind him. Ambrogio looked at the telephone again, then tried winding its handle, attempting a connection, but all he got was the white butterfly symbol in its little window, signifying an interrupted line. "Devil take it", he muttered. *What the heck can be going on?* he asked himself, beginning to feel concerned.

Today was December 19, he remembered. Three days before, along on his right, some of the division had been forced back, abandoning their positions before an enemy attack. The line had been reestablished some miles in the rear in the snow, by throwing in reserves of blackshirts and German troops. (*Poor unlucky souls, in this deathly cold.*) Afterward there had been less firing off to the right.

So, the problem now can't be coming from there. From the left, maybe? There had also been some giving way on the Pasubio front, on the left, although the line had not broken entirely. Perhaps the trouble would be coming from farther on the left, then. There had been rumors via *radio scarpa* about a break in the line in the Ravenna Division sector, at Boguciar, beyond the German 298 Division position. But afterward, hadn't they heard that these were all rumors? And yet, for days and days, from over there on the left, there had been the noise of incessant firing. Since yesterday morning there had been silence. That silence led his mind to imagine the sight of column after column of enemy troops silently advancing over the snow behind his position. He became increasingly worried. *Hey, I hope something lousy like that isn't really happening.* He got up and went outside, where the cold was much more intense than inside the observation post. Ambrogio walked along the trench to the nearest men's shelter. *It must be twelve or thirteen below zero*, he thought. There was no way to tell; the front line wasn't equipped with thermometers. Reaching the shelter, he found only the corporal he had relieved a half hour before; he was dozing on a straw mattress, covered with his cape and some blankets. The temperature inside the shelter was bearable, there being a well-stoked wood stove.

"Hey, hey you! Are you awake?" called Ambrogio.

"What do you want?" muttered the soldier. "Why don't you go and ..." Then, recognizing the voice, he said, "Oh, it's you, Lieutenant", his accent identifying him as a southerner. Looking up, he saw Ambrogio standing holding the blanket separating the sleeping area, allowing both light and a cold draft to enter.

"Hurry, return to the OP to relieve me: there's news. Quickly. I'll be back in a couple of minutes."

"News? Yessir, right away."

"If while I'm away you hear from the two linemen, Mazzoleni or Piantanida— they might call to test the wire—tell them to keep the line open and not move from where they are without first talking to me; it's important."

"Yes, right." The corporal's tone had become concerned.

"Come on, move it."

Ambrogio left the shelter and went over to another nearby, bending over to pass through the low entrance. This was an infantry shelter, allocated to about fifteen men. Inside, the infantrymen were getting ready to leave, their only illumination coming from an oil lamp fashioned from a sardine can. Most were emptying their backpacks of less necessary items, replacing them with hand grenades and rifle clips. Some were putting on all their spare underwear; one or two were spreading antifreeze jelly on their feet, massaging them for warmth. Meanwhile, they expressed their fears.

"This time we're really in for it!"

"Where are we going to go in the snow, with temperatures of twenty or thirty below zero?"

"Well, first let's avoid getting surrounded, then we'll see . . ."

"It's so cold, every time I finish a turn of duty, I don't think I can survive another ten minutes."

"Amedeo, what should I do—fill the backpack or leave it light for easy carrying? And if I fill it, what should I put in it?"

"Now you think about it! What've you been thinking about lately? Have you been thinking about Carolina?"

"Why ask me that? Don't tell me you were aware we'd need to get out of here."

"Take my advice, fill the backpack. It's better full of ammo and rations, you understand? And stick in all the woolen clothing you have."

"I'm going to be taking at least one rolled blanket. What do you think? At night, we have to sleep, right?"

"And what about rations? Will we be given rations or not?"

"They're supposed to give us rations, or else . . ."

"Where and when do you think we'll get rations?"

"Where? Why, at company HQ. You'll see, when we get there they'll give us something."

"And do you believe they actually have reserves of rations down at company HQ?"

"Sure. What do they call them? 'Untouchable stockpiles'. Didn't you know? Cookies, dried fruit, conserves; they have them saved for situations like this."

"'Untouchable', you say? In that case you can be sure they'll stay untouched. They'll leave them for the Ivans . . ."

The intellectual-looking lieutenant, Valorzi, joined Ambrogio in the shelter; he'd finished inspecting his outposts and had returned to prepare to leave.

"Look, you," said Ambrogio, "I'd like to know why . . . can you tell me, in a few words, why we have to abandon these positions? Down at company, what did they tell you?"

The other officer looked into the semidarkness, where his infantrymen had been following the exchange, then turned toward Ambrogio and shook his head. "I don't know anything. They just told me the platoons have to be there before two-fifteen, because with us or without us, the company will set off and march to battalion HQ." He looked over again at his troops, then added, "The rest of what I heard consists of rumors, and nobody knows anything more for sure."

Ambrogio would have liked to pursue the matter but contained himself, although he hadn't yet decided he should leave. The other officer started getting ready, putting a dozen grenades into a bag, along with as many rifle clips; then he checked the bag's weight, frowning. He handed it to his orderly. "Here, put in whatever you can find in woolens. And don't forget my diary. Got it? The diary."

"Right away, sir."

Valorzi turned to Ambrogio. "And you, what'll you do?"

"At the moment I'm out of touch", he replied. "I'm out of contact, no phone, and I have two men out looking for the break."

Valorzi smiled wearily. Ambrogio, getting a better look at him, noticed the distress, a look of suffering on his face; he seemed to have no illusions about what was going to happen. Meeting Ambrogio's eye, he seemed to confirm his dejection. "Well, now, I'd better go and take care of the 'heavy one' (referring to the machine gun). We have to take it with us at all costs."

A head was thrust into the refuge. "Is the artillery lieutenant here? Ah, there he is." The head pulled back and called toward the outside, "Yes, he's here!"

The observer corporal who had relieved Ambrogio entered. "The phone line is working, Lieutenant."

"I'm coming", said Ambrogio, and followed him outside.

Running, they both headed for the OP. Ambrogio went in and picked up the phone, sitting heavily. "Yes? Who's this?" he asked.

"Lieutenant Riva? Good, at last! This is the communications center at group. Please hold the line. I'll connect you with the adjutant."

The adjutant came to the line: that long-faced lieutenant, the bank clerk, who had welcomed Ambrogio on his arrival in Kamenka back in June; despite his nickname of "Tired Horse", he seemed now to radiate energy. "Is that you, Riva? Leave everything and get down here to group."

"Will I bring all our equipment?"

"Equipment? Don't you know what's going on? As far as the equipment is concerned, do as you see fit. The important point is that all of you come here immediately; within an hour you have to be here."

"Just a moment . . . look, just so I know what to take with us. The oil and gasoline stocks—you've had them picked up?"

"No."

Ambrogio felt his insides turning over; a sense of dismay came over him. "What did you say?" he got out faintly.

"These aren't things to talk about on the telephone," the other officer said, "but you've asked a question, and the answer is no. So just use that to make your own deductions." He added, "You can take it for granted that this time I'm not sending a truck to pick you all up."

"It's not the truck ... that doesn't matter", said Ambrogio.

"Evidently", agreed the adjutant; then, softening his tone, he added, "You know I was about to send a couple of men up to you? One is your orderly, what's his name?"

"Paccoi."

"Right, Paccoi. The last half hour he's been pacing up and down outside the office here. If I hadn't decided to order him out, he was going to come up personally and save you."

"Sounds like Paccoi; he's like a broody hen." Ambrogio stood up, trying to keep from getting upset. He swallowed hard. Finding out about Paccoi's loyalty under pressure made him feel better.

"Right, well done on reestablishing contact by phone", the adjutant said. "That's all from me. Hurry and leave", and hung up.

Ambrogio remained standing, holding the telephone and trying to control his feelings; then speaking into the phone, he said: "Hey, you, Piantanida, are you there?"

An answering voice said, "Yes, but I'm Mazzoleni."

"All right. Did you hear what was said?"

"Yes, sir, but not on purpose. I was told by the corporal to stay on the line, not to take my testing clips off the wire."

"Good, you've done well to keep the line open. Is Piantanida there with you?"

"Yes, sir."

"How far away are you? I mean how far away from the OP?"

"We'd be about two miles away."

"In that case, you're nearer the battery ..."

"That's right, much closer." Mazzoleni's voice took on a complaining tone. "Those signalers from group should have fixed the wire, and not us. I told Piantanida, they were much closer." From the background came Piantanida's voice. "Cheeky son of a ..."

"Forget all that and listen to what I'm telling you to do. Follow the telephone wire and leave right now for group. You're to go to group, you hear? Not back here."

"To group; right, Lieutenant."

"Right, that's all. Now I'll hand you over to the corporal; if there's anything of yours here that you need, tell him about it so he'll take it with him."

"You mean, if there's anything ...?"

"Tell Piantanida what I've said."

"Right, Lieutenant."

Ambrogio handed the phone to the corporal and went to look out of the loophole.

In no-man's land—the frozen river and both banks—there wasn't a sign of movement; all that could be seen were leafless trees plastered white with snow and frost, standing rigid and brittle as glass, and endless snow. Farther off, the horizon was concealed by a bank of frozen mist. "And this is the weather we'll have to march out in ..."

To one side of the loophole, the wall had a chalked note of the last few days' temperatures: highs and lows, as passed to them by group:

Dec.	11	−10°	−24°
	12	−4°	−16°
	13	−4°	−15°
	14	0°	−7°
	15	0°	−3°
	16	−15°	−35°
	17	−12°	−32°
	18	−14°	−27°

Today's temperature had not yet been called through. They would have to march in some very cold weather. *For how many hours, I wonder? For how many days?* Ambrogio asked himself. *Perhaps for weeks? But in that case, who could survive it?* He felt that same apprehension in his gut and thought, *I wonder what's happening to our rear? Are we still safe, or are we about to be surrounded, or perhaps we're already surrounded, in the bag.* As far as he knew, when the Germans had surrounded the enemy, not one single Russian had managed to escape. *Not even Stalin's own son, and that was during the summer.* He put aside these frightening thoughts. *Let's try to concentrate on the immediate problems.*

Turning to the corporal, he said, "Well, what do they say?"

"They want us to bring too many things, those monkeys", complained the southerner, using a northern expression. "Should I tell them to come here and get their own things?"

"No, there's no time for it. If necessary, I'll help you carry some things. All right, tell them that's all and hang up."

The corporal didn't need to be told twice; speaking into the telephone, he said, "Mazzoleni, I've been ordered to hang up, goodbye." He added, "Go stick it ...", and hung up.

"Cheer up", said Ambrogio. "Let's get ready the things we need to take with us. Then we'll destroy the theodolite, take an ax to it, and disable the telephone and anything else useful to the enemy."

"The theodolite?" asked the corporal, frightened now.

"Right. Why do you ask? We certainly don't want to leave it as a present for the Ivans."

The corporal looked at Ambrogio, a scared look in his eyes: he had just come to an understanding of what was about to happen to them.

"Thank goodness we don't also have radios here."

"Right. Come on, let's not waste time."

Soon after, Ambrogio and the corporal, after cleaning out the area and loading themselves down with clothing and packs, followed the line of laden infantrymen until they reached the company HQ, where, like everywhere else along the line, there were units lined up, ready to march. Reaching the HQ, they took their leave of the infantry and their lieutenant and headed south.

Along the way they passed a resting mortar platoon. Like all Italian troops, they wore the gray-green sheepskin-lined coats and a balaclava helmet under their caps. On the ground while they relaxed were the heavy mortars, each broken down into two parts for carrying slung from a back harness. There were also several boxes of mortar shells. *Poor wretches, having to march with all that weight!* Farther on, they came on another group of infantrymen, a mixed bag, also heading south. And although the nearness of other people was comforting to them, the loneliness produced by the endless horizon made Ambrogio and the corporal want to run, not to be left behind, feelings they both suppressed and concealed. Even though loaded down, they marched briskly ahead, reaching the line of batteries within an hour of having set out from the OP.

2

The group's three batteries were lined up more or less close to each other next to the leafless forest, now covered in ice. In the early darkness, the men's shelters could be seen behind the cannons, identified as oblong heaps in the snow, each one having a chimney on top. Here and there could be glimpsed trucks glazed with ice.

Ambrogio and the observer corporal made their way through the batteries deeper into the woods, toward group HQ. Confusion reigned all around them: several tractors had been made ready and were being used to push or pull trucks or flatbed trailers into position. A couple of tractors had already been attached to their cannons and were slowly moving them out of the clearing, with noncoms shouting orders to the soldiers clustered around their own guns. Groups of cold-looking soldiers, supervised by officers, were being given grenades and bullet clips by armorers: Ambrogio noted that they were also being issued rations. A lieutenant was busy supervising the unloading of an ice-covered truck, apparently lightening it for the retreat. A master sergeant was adapting overcoat belts into a backpack for a Fiat heavy machine gun, normally part of the battery's perimeter defense and not rigged for portability. Other soldiers were coming and going, using the ice-covered dirt ramps leading to the shelters. (Ambrogio thought, *What a lot of effort it had cost to build the shelters.* No sooner had work been started than the ground had become hard with the freeze-up, causing the speed of work to become frantic. The rock-hard ground caused pickax handles to split and shatter—even Ambrogio had taken his turn at digging—and a squad of men had to be detailed to fashion more handles, in order to keep going.) To Ambrogio and the corporal, the din of tractor and truck engines was pleasant, indicating a readiness to get along.

"Perhaps Tired Horse didn't tell me everything on the phone, or maybe the fuel had been delivered after I spoke to him . . . that's why they've been able to get all these motors going."

They were passing close to the Third Battery's position, the guns for which Ambrogio had been responsible until late in the fall. The remaining veteran runners became cheerful on seeing him, greeting him in a friendly way. "Welcome, Lieutenant! How did it go at the OP? What's happening? Lieutenant, how's this going to end?"

Ambrogio waved and replied with the expected standard phrases: "Keep your chin up, don't worry, been keeping fit, and you?" But he went on without stopping until he ran into Feltrin, who was very busy. This was the trucking sergeant who had readied the motorbike on which he had visited Stefano back in September. Waving him over, Ambrogio asked, low voiced, "How is the battery off for fuel?"

"How are we for fuel?" Feltrin said, surprised; he was looking at the packs on Ambrogio's and the corporal's backs, "You've just come from the OP, so you won't be up to date. Unfortunately, this is a disaster, a real disaster, Lieutenant." His voice dispirited, he added, "In the vehicles' tanks we have the few gallons that remained after we made our last advance in October, when you were still here. In the whole battery, that's all we have left."

"How much fuel, on average, for each vehicle?"

"I'm not sure; perhaps three or four, maybe five gallons per tank."

"Only four gallons?"

"Lieutenant, you know how they distribute fuel for moving the batteries. It's measured out according to need. Well, maybe one or two of the tractors have seven or eight gallons."

Ambrogio was silent for a minute, then said, "Didn't anybody think to consolidate the available fuel into one or two vehicles, put it all in one tank, maybe?"

"I'm glad to hear you say that, Lieutenant. That's exactly what I suggested to the new captain: he agreed, and I think he phoned HQ, but later told me to forget it. 'Leave it, Feltrin', he said to me."

Ambrogio remained silent.

"Even if the retreat lasts only a few hours," Feltrin commented, "we'll have to abandon everything." He gestured disapprovingly with the wrench he was holding. "Apart from which, only the gasoline motors will work in this cold. The diesel engines are difficult to start, and few of them will run. So we'll have to abandon a great deal of equipment."

"Not a happy thought, eh?" said Ambrogio, then, dismissing the sergeant, "Well, good luck, Feltrin."

Feltrin saluted and said, without a trace of irony, "Right you are, Lieutenant."

Ambrogio set off again, followed rather than accompanied by the corporal, who, having understood the meaning of the conversation, had now taken on the look of a whipped dog. They continued on their way through the icy trees toward the command post. "Leave all the equipment behind!" muttered Ambrogio. "Abandon everything, that's easy to say. Leave the guns, ammunition, food rations, blankets, everything. It's plain madness . . ." A shout from the corporal interrupted his thoughts; he had spotted a hometown friend coming toward them. The distraction served to reduce the nervous tension felt by Ambrogio. The hometown friend, a corporal, shouted back, using obscene words and gestures; as they got nearer to one another, their voices were raised. When they were face to face they exchanged friendly insults, using a southern dialect, incomprehensible to Ambrogio.

The exchange was liberating for Ambrogio's observer corporal, and their jabbering aroused comforting reminiscences in him. The two corporals, finally running out of insulting words, began to laugh and laugh, without knowing what they were saying.

Leaving them behind, Ambrogio entered a clearing surrounded by earth mounds. Nearby was an unpainted wooden shack, recently constructed and new to him. A little farther away between the trees, he could see the six or seven headquarters trucks, an ambulance, and the colonel's old Millecento. Ambrogio noticed that none of these vehicles had its motor running. *Of course, the Millecento is too broken down, and the ambulance and trucks are diesel driven.* Around these vehicles were their drivers and an unknown officer, presumably a transportation man. Some of the men were under the trucks, waving flaming fuel-soaked rags near the engine blocks. *Let's hope they manage to warm the motors without setting them on fire,* he thought. *Although it really doesn't matter one way or the other.* He noticed a group of soldiers being assembled in the clearing.

3

Going directly to the shelter allocated to the men of his two observer platoons, he descended the frozen ramp and opened the roughly made door with his foot. He entered sideways because of the two full packs he carried and found himself in a large hole with earthen walls, roofed over with logs and tree branches. The shelter—wonderfully warm—was almost dark; what light there was came through a truck windshield built into the roof and from the red glow of a wood stove. While he was straightening up and taking a look around, the senior man present, a sergeant recently arrived from Italy, called out, "Attenshun! On your feet." As the twenty or so soldiers stood and came to attention, the sergeant hurried forward and saluted. "First and Second Observer Platoons, present and accounted for."

"At ease, Sergeant", Ambrogio ordered.

"At ease", repeated the sergeant and approached Ambrogio to help rid him of the backpacks. His orderly, Paccoi, his face showing relief, also hurried to take the backpacks.

"Great! You've arrived at last, Lieutenant."

Some of the other men, already wearing their overcoats, came to stand around their officer, who noticed that Mazzoleni and Piantanida were already back from their excursion to repair the phone line. He pointed at one of the backpacks. "That's yours; the corporal is bringing the other one." Then, looking them all over, but addressing himself to the sergeant, he asked, "How's it going? What orders have you been given?"

"We've been told to be ready by three", the sergeant replied, and looking at his watch, "Just a few minutes to three."

"And are you all ready?"

"Yes, Lieutenant. Ready for the last half hour. And while we waited for you, I've had them doing what you call working rest, and we built up the fire to acquire heat, while we're still inside."

"Good work. What preparations have you made?"

"I got everybody to load up their packs with all the ammo and hand grenades we had here. The rest of the space, each man will fill as he likes."

Ambrogio looked up at the men around him. "What are you all taking?"

"Me, four clips and three grenades."

"Me, six clips and no grenades."

"Me, three and three, Lieutenant", responded some of his men.

"Didn't supply distribute more clips? And food rations?"

"No, Lieutenant, no rations."

"Good. I mean bad", Ambrogio corrected himself. "Let's see what we can manage to get hold of, right away. What about orders to destroy the equipment?"

"What equipment?" one voice asked.

"The radios, to start with . . ."

"We've received no such orders, sir", said the sergeant.

"Right. I'm going to see the major for further orders. Meantime, collect all the remaining ammunition boxes, radios, the Second Platoon's theodolite, telephones, and other equipment—everything valuable that should not fall into the enemy's hands—and assemble outside, ready for when I return." On hearing this, the soldiers looked at their officer with uneasy expressions on their faces; the low buzz of conversation died down.

"Well?" Ambrogio raised his voice. "What's the matter? Would you prefer to pack all this materiel out of here on your backs? Right, enough of this, get going."

As he said this, Ambrogio felt that he had never been so decisive before and realized that this was the result of having to set an example.

"Bear in mind", he added, "that there are retreats in all wars: as it's now our turn, we'll just have to bear it; that's the army for you." He turned to his orderly. "Paccoi, while I go up to see the major, please get my pack ready: take out any impractical clothing, put in the antifreeze jelly, and . . . well, whatever will be of use, but don't fill it too much. After that, go over to supply and get me a rifle and ten clips."

"A rifle?"

"And ten ammo clips."

"Right, Lieutenant." Paccoi looked disconcerted. The others also looked glum, watching their officer in silence. Who had ever heard of an artillery officer carrying a rifle, as if he were an infantryman?

Ambrogio was going to say, "We're about to lose our cannons, or haven't you noticed?" Then he thought it best to go easy on them, so he turned to Paccoi. "Hey Paccoi, I nearly forgot the most important item; get hold of a couple of pairs of long johns. When I return I'll put them on top of the pants I've got on already. Later, if they're uncomfortable, we can always use them for a windsock."

The soldiers smiled, but unlike their usual bantering style, not one of them followed up on the windsock remark. Ambrogio gestured at the sergeant. "Don't order them to stand to attention. I'll be back soon." He turned and left the shelter, followed by the sergeant.

The cold immediately surrounded them, and, like so many other times, Ambrogio felt that he could be involved entirely in combating the low temperatures, to the exclusion of any other activity. *Come on*, he told himself fiercely, *try to think of something more cheerful.* Heading for the wooden shelter across the clearing, which the sergeant indicated to him, he looked over at the vehicles in the woods. *They're in exactly the same spot as before; not one has left yet*, he thought. The same thought had also occurred to the group of soldiers gathered in the clearing, as well as to the lieutenant colonel. He was standing outside the wooden shelter with older Adjutant Tired Horse (who, like him, had not been dismissed yet) and a junior officer, a very young mapping officer (recently arrived from Italy) at his side. The two officers at the major's side nodded at Ambrogio and smiled a greeting. Ambrogio stopped before the major and saluted.

Major Casasco looked at him with a vacant expression, apparently having trouble recognizing him. "Ah, Riva," he got out, "what about the infantry?"

"By now they must have abandoned the line. When I was on my way here, an hour ago, the companies were getting assembled. I came across some detachments already on their way."

"Right", acknowledged the major, returning his gaze to the vehicles. As always, he looked distinguished and, instead of the regulation sheepskin coat, wore a lined gabardine garrison overcoat; his face was very pale.

Ambrogio turned to Tired Horse, who, as usual, bent his head down, pointing one ear toward him to hear what he had to say. "What orders are there for destroying the equipment?"

"There are no orders", replied the adjutant, looking sideways and rolling his eyes at the major, as if to say, "Be careful what you say, he doesn't want to hear about it."

"But . . . but . . ."

Both Tired Horse and the mapmaker replied by opening their arms and shrugging, as if to say, "What can we do about it?" After a moment of indecision, Ambrogio turned back to the senior officer and said, "Major, sir . . ."

The major looked at him with the same vacant stare as before.

"I'm getting together the platoons' equipment: the radios, the telephones, theodolites, etcetera. Should I have them destroyed right away?"

"No", said the major, his voice strained.

"In that case, when do we leave?" asked Ambrogio, puzzled. "And then there are also the platoons' two trucks; if there's no fuel for them, we could at least destroy the motors . . ."

"You'll do nothing of the kind", the major replied aggressively.

Ambrogio stood there, mouth fallen open in incredulity.

The major turned angrily on Tired Horse. "Are we still on this subject?" he asked, his mouth working in excitement. "Haven't I explained myself clearly on this?"

"Yes, of course, sir," said the adjutant soothingly, "and the appropriate orders have gone out to the batteries, and everybody concerned has been told not to destroy any equipment. In Riva's case, he didn't get the word as he was away from the OP."

Major Casasco turned back to Ambrogio. "If we destroy everything, what'll we find when we return? Eh? How could we defend the line then?"

Ambrogio immediately understood; the major refused to accept reality. He became worried and thought, *Probably our situation has upset his mental process . . . yes, that must be it.* He now understood the outstretched arms and shrugs with which the other two had tried to silence him. *What a time for the major to let us down!* He cast a questioning look at the adjutant, who avoided his eyes. Ambrogio felt depressed and at the same time had room in his heart for pity, like a son before the failure of a distressed parent. In the same way that he expected his men to show him respect and consideration, he naturally extended the same feelings toward his own superior officers, even when they barely deserved it.

After looking straight at Ambrogio, waiting for an answer, the major appeared to forget he was there and turned once more to contemplate the vehicles.

The transportation officer left the group around the trucks and came toward them, making clearly negative gestures. The mapmaker lieutenant was a Neapolitan; he had a straight Grecian nose that dropped from his forehead, giving him a classic profile. He turned to Tired Horse. "What shall we do? We can't wait any longer", he said, his voice low. The adjutant looked at his watch. "Major," he said, "according to the orders we have, our group should have been marching off already a few minutes ago. With your permission, I'll order the men into formation."

The major looked wordlessly at him, then turned back to watch the approaching transportation officer.

His voice firm and decisive, Tired Horse turned to Ambrogio and the mapping officer. "All right, you'll assemble your people, and I'll telephone the batteries"; then, turning to a nearby group of soldiers, "right, get in line, move it!" He turned to the major. "I'll phone the batteries and be back right away", and then went into the HQ shelter. Ambrogio set off at a run for the shelter in which he had left his platoons, went inside, and ordered his men to leave the equipment where it was and to assemble outside. Then he called to Paccoi, "Give me the extra woolen underwear", and began to take off his outer clothes in order to don the long johns.

Shortly thereafter he followed the soldiers out of the shelter, overcoat flapping open, taking the prepared rifle from Paccoi and slinging it on his shoulder.

In the clearing, some fifty of the headquarters men were getting into columns of threes, by squads, following the instructions of the mapping lieutenant. This officer, his classic young good looks marred by a frown, went about assembling the men by walking up and down the column. The group of men who had been near the trucks had now joined the column, having abandoned the vehicles.

Ambrogio went up to the adjutant, who stood, chin thrust out by the shelter door, watching the activity before him. Ambrogio paused, uncertain of how to begin. "Um", he said.

"Yes?" Tired Horse kept his voice low.

"I know I shouldn't be questioning orders, but, in order to get hold of the gasoline ... and the major not being well ... have you thought of phoning direct to the fuel dump?"

The adjutant shook his head. "In order to phone the fuel dump, I have to go through the division headquarters' switchboard, and in the last two hours I've tried several times. I've also tried regimental HQ, and I get no reply from either place. Satisfied?"

"But no reply ... for two hours?" stammered Ambrogio.

"Exactly, and don't ask me why. I don't know if division has cut the wire or what. All I know is, there's no time to lose; we're on the point of being surrounded."

Ambrogio said nothing.

"Now are you happy?" said the adjutant sharply; but then, putting on an understanding smile, "Look, I'm counting on you to help get us out of this pile of sh———, if it's possible to do so. Knock on wood." And he rubbed the door with his gloved hand. Then, going over to the major, he asked, "Sir, can I give the order to march?"

The major replied, "Yes, thanks", and then in a low voice said, "I'll march at the head."

"As you say, sir", acknowledged the adjutant; then, raising his voice, "Officers, head up your sections. Lieutenant Riva, bring up the rear. Forward ... march!"

4

The headquarters detachment moved off, led by the major, the adjutant, and three or four other officers. One of these, the medical lieutenant, thought unhappily of his surgical instruments, left behind in the abandoned ambulance truck. Behind the leading officers came the other HQ sections, each headed by a junior officer; and at the rear came the two platoons, followed by their chief, Ambrogio. All had on the short sheepskin-lined coats, and all of them had wrapped woolen blankets around the outside as further protection from the cold wind. By contrast, the major wore his gabardine overcoat.

Unimpressive and gray, the column marched through the forest. Twilight was upon them; at that time of the year daylight lasted from seven o'clock until three in the afternoon. Each of the men wondered how this strange march so poorly supplied would turn out, what would be each man's fate.

More than one let his imagination run forward to the tragic lamentations back home, if . . . if . . . Ambrogio, wanting to be alone with his thoughts, ordered Paccoi to join the platoons after the loyal orderly had at first placed himself alongside his officer.

After a while, immersed in his thoughts, Ambrogio looked up to notice that two artillerymen were walking on each side. Both wore blankets over their sheepskin coats and had their hat brims pulled down around their necks at the back, and the front brim unmilitarily bent flat.

"Eh", signed one, Mazzoleni.

"Eh", signed the other, Piantanida.

"So, what do you represent? A separate republic?"

"The observation post republic?" suggested Mazzoleni, in a conciliatory tone.

Ambrogio shook his head; for a while they walked in silence. The snow underfoot, freezing with the approach of darkness, cracked with each step.

"Well, you two have already been out in the weather some time, walking the telephone wire. How do you feel?"

"Eh", agreed Mazzoleni.

"Eh", said Piantanida. "You too, though. What an army, eh, Lieutenant?"

In the past Ambrogio had often thought of these two as loafers, goldbricks, a view of them that was shared by their comrades. Now, stuck in a situation beyond their understanding, they seemed to him to be just two anxious young boys needing to know what their future might be, and despite orders they had dropped back to be with him.

We're all in it up to our necks, thought Ambrogio.

Piantanida seemed instinctively to read his thoughts. "It's a tough life, eh, Lieutenant?" Like Mazzoleni, he was from Lombardy, and stress had emphasized his accent, which identified him as coming from Busto Arsizio, on the plains of Olona. Ambrogio nodded his agreement.

"Bad deal, what a crappy world", murmured Mazzoleni, still in dialect.

A few cannons remained behind, scattered among the empty gun emplacements. The road emerging from the forest carried a slow-moving line of guns being pulled by tractors; in the line there were also the noisy armored cars, engines belching smoke and condensation. Following behind the column of guns and tanks were three sections of soldiers on foot, who had been unable to find a ride in one of the vehicles. Reaching the line of vehicles, the major halted, bringing his headquarters staff to a stop behind him. The adjutant called for the officers to assemble, and the shout of "Officers!" was passed down the line, bringing all the officers to their major at the run. The arriving officers were identified for the major by the captain of the First Battery, the senior staff officer. But when they were all in a circle around the major, he chose not to speak, only gesturing toward the adjutant, who spoke for him. "I just want to repeat the orders that some of you already received by phone", he said. "The men on foot will march in good order behind the staff, each formation led by its senior officer. The motorized column", he tried again, "will be led by the major . . ."

"No," the major intervened with a frown, "I'll remain with the troops on foot."

"Well, good; the motorized column under the command of the First Battery's captain will precede the men on foot and will travel at walking pace." He turned to the captain. "As I told you before, if maintaining a walking pace is impossible, or if you have other problems, the motorized column will have to proceed ahead to the town of Meskoff."

"That's where the main road leading south starts", interrupted a Second Battery officer, who knew the area.

Tired Horse, annoyed by the interruption, lowered his long face and closed his eyes, remaining silent for a moment. Ambrogio thought to himself, *For a bank clerk, he doesn't do badly as a military organizer.*

Tired Horse, raising his head and looking around at them, continued. "The cannons must reach Meskoff. It's about forty miles from here—remember the name, Meskoff, Meskoff. Once there, the pieces will be placed in position at the south end of the town, I repeat, the south end of town, and will await the arrival of the rest of us on foot. Any questions?"

There were none, but the captain of the First Battalion, with unwelcome realism, added, "Only the vehicles that have enough gasoline are going to be able to get to Meskoff; in other words, very few." He paused. "Well, can we get going?"

The adjutant looked his question at the major, who nodded.

The captain called the officers to attention and received a low-voiced "You can dismiss" from the major. Dropping their arms from the hand salute, the officers trotted away to their posts. The staff group moved past the batteries to take the lead, and the foot soldiers in the vehicles followed behind.

5

The defeat of the Italian forces was not a limited retreat confined to one sector; the entire southern front was collapsing. Some twenty-five miles to the left of the Pasubio (Ambrogio's division) three days earlier the enemy had broken the Ravenna Division, near Boguciar, and had advanced in great numbers, totaling two army corps. One of these, consisting of the Russian First Corps, was an armored unit consisting of thirteen brigades, with a total of 754 tanks. The other was the Sixth Infantry Corps, counting ten ordinary divisions and four motorized brigades. This enormous force was marching southeast, behind the Italian lines, to join up with more Russian units approaching from the east, having opened a great breach in the Romanian Third Corps.

In order to avoid being surrounded, the Axis forces abandoning their positions along the Don were making for the only available major highway, the one that led to Meskoff. On the left of the front was the German 298th Division; next to them the Pasubio, then the Turin, the Bersaglieri Celere, and finally, the most easterly, the Sforzesca Division (which the Italian soldiers in Russia usually called the Cicai, the "runaways", because it was the division responsible for the sudden retreat back in August). Now, apparently, all the other divisions were also becoming Cicai.

Beyond the Sforzesca, toward Stalingrad, the remnants of the Romanian Third Corps held onto the front, desperately trying to seal the gaps, and, barely assisted by German armor, faced the massed Russian forces that were advancing westward from the surrounded Stalingrad in the direction of the Romanians' homeland. Conscious of the horror approaching Romania, the Third Corps soldiers, although poorly armed, fought tenaciously and desperately, with an extraordinary valor unrecorded by history.

The Celere, sitting on the edge of Meskoff, was in a peculiar position. Having been severely punished in the last few days by the enemy forces pressing toward the strategic highway system at Meskoff, the Celere also had to face a Russian force that had broken through at Boguciar to the west and which, after making a circling movement, was converging on them.

Although reduced in numbers and less well armed than other divisions, the Celere, based on their reputation for valor, were given over thirty-five miles of front to cover, more than the other divisions, which in any case were themselves stretched to the limit. One stretch of front was covered by three companies of the Sixth and one company of the Third (Stefano's regiment); this line was attacked on the freezing morning of December 17 by a whole Russian division, which drove into the Italians like a wedge. Preceded by smoke-screens, which forced the use of gas masks, the Russian force outnumbered the defenders (three regiments against four companies), but even with their superior forces, after three days they had not broken the Bersaglieri. The Third hung on tenaciously and had not given up even one trench. The point of the Russian wedge, made up of mere mortals, took severe punishment from Italian machine-gun fire amid the confusion and smoke, and the enormous Russian juggernaut was held back. A diminishing number of companies belonging to the Sixth Regiment had been forced to redeploy, though at a gradual pace, counterattacking all the time, and eventually the Russians had managed to advance only six miles in two days. When the general retreat began late on the nineteenth, Meskoff, although under attack, was still in Italian hands.

That afternoon, division HQ had ordered the Bersaglieri's Third to retreat when it became dark, to go backward to where the Sixth was located in and around Kalmikoff, defending the highways that from the northwest led to Meskoff. It was planned that the next day a second retreat would take place, ending with the two regiments taking defensive positions around Meskoff. Far from the action, division HQ had also ordered that reinforcements be urgently sent to Meskoff, and this consisted of an elite SS force, the Schuldt group, who were emplaced outside the town.

All the division's vehicles were assembled in Meskoff; there was no shortage of fuel. On the nineteenth, in order to make room for the additional incoming trucks, the Celere command ordered that these vehicles all relocate further to the south. Forming a column of over six hundred trucks, trailers, pickups, and specialized vehicles, they made good time down the main highway. Suddenly, during a stop near the town of Verchiakovsky, large numbers of Russian tanks launched a surprise attack from the direction of the breach at Boguciar. Moving fast, the tanks had cut the highway ahead of and behind the Italian column, with the bulk of the Russian force throwing itself at the stationary column, firing with all guns.

Gradually, the Russians overturned or crushed the Italian vehicles, which seemed to be dwarfed by the size of the attacking tanks. Here and there a tank would ferociously trample a truck under its tracks, turning alternately right and left, converting the metal into a tomb for the mangled bodies inside. The Italian drivers had only pistols and rifles with which to defend themselves, and some tried to drive their vehicles off the road to avoid certain destruction. Many ended up immobilized in the fresh snow, wheels spinning uselessly. Others left their vehicles and either tried to leave the road on foot, chased by bursts of machine-gun fire, or used their trucks as shields from which to return the enemy fire, aiming for the vision slits on the Russian tanks, until they were finally crushed. Others, remembering their reputation as Bersaglieri, ran forward toward the tanks, grenades in their hands, meeting death by machine-gun fire or in a burst from a flamethrower.

In six or seven minutes, the long column had been annihilated. Only about sixty of the six hundred vehicles were not destroyed, having been able to reach Verchiakovsky, where they sought concealment among the houses: others escaped along secondary roads. News of this defeat reached division HQ in the afternoon of the nineteenth, when bad news also arrived of another set-back; increasingly heavy Russian infantry attacks against the Sixth Regiment had proved to be overpowering, and at several points there had been big breakthroughs.

The same two pieces of bad news must also have reached the Schuldt SS group, which, after considering the implications but without advising their allies, left the Italians to hold Meskoff, marching away. It was already dark, and the retreating forces from the other divisions were approaching Meskoff when hurriedly the Celere command sent out the order to abandon the town, advising all who were still in contact about the taking of the highway by the Russian tanks. Simultaneously, they ordered the already-shattered Sixth to break off contact with the Russians and relocate toward Kaskary some forty miles south of Meskoff; the same order was addressed to the Third Regiment, but all the lines had already been cut, and the order didn't get through.

6

During the night of the nineteenth, while all the other divisions—even, late in the day, the Celere—were desperately repositioning themselves, the Third Regiment had deployed in Kalmikoff. They had arrived there late, having quietly left their trenches on the River Don. Confident of their valor, the Bersaglieri had laid down sketchy lines and snow trenches around the silent town. Deployed all along these lines were small numbers of automatic weapons, light antitank cannons, and a few mortars. Manning these weapons, out in the killing cold temperatures, were sentries sheltering in bivouacs, maintaining a lookout, as ordered. The remaining men had spread themselves out in houses and stables, crowded to the point where some were forced to try to get some sleep while packed up against the exterior walls.

In Kalmikoff alongside the Third there was a unit of the Croatian Legion, made up of nationalist Ustashi recruits dressed in Fascist uniforms. These Croatians, far from being dedicated Fascists, were motivated by love for their country and, by forming alliances with the Axis powers, hoped to maintain Croatia independent and free of the Serbs. Third HQ had assigned them one part of the town to defend; their positions were easily distinguished from the Italians' by the fires they had lit in the snow.

Half of Stefano's platoon was sheltered in an isba along with soldiers from other units; the platoon's other half was outside in the snow, manning one of the four-hour watches. Lieutenant Acciati was hunkered down on the snow among the men out in the open. In the killing cold, he didn't even try going to sleep. Lying on a spread tent canvas, he had on a balaclava helmet, so that his long face was covered and only his eyes could be seen. The collar on his over-coat turned up to overlap his helmet, his gloved hands in his pockets, Acciati felt disconnected, his thoughts wandering lazily. Up to this point, things had gone well for his company; they hadn't been directly involved in the Russian attack of two . . . no, how many days back? Yes, two . . . two days before. And even then, when the Third Regiment threw themselves into repeated attacks on the Russian right flank, finding themselves contained by an iron-hard de-fense, even then they weren't called upon, though the Russians were prevent-ing the crumbling Six from retreating. *Up to now, things haven't gone badly for us, that's clear.* Of course, who knew what the future held . . . but this wasn't the time to think about it. *In any case, there would be no use to it; I mean, when the hardships begin, we'll take care of ourselves. And for now, it's already enough that we have to deal with this beastly cold. At least I'll get to spend half the night inside the house, in shelter.* Heat, body heat! Necessary to life, vital—heat was as enjoyable as life itself. Nobody thinks about it under normal conditions. Into Acciati's head came the memory of his warm shelter on the banks of the Don, which he had abandoned some hours before. *Well, that's enough, it's pointless to go back over it. Better to think about Italy, the good times to come, in Turin.* Turin, how did the saying go? Turin—city ready for pleasure. Turin, his remembered Turin, but not Turin by night; rather Turin in summer, warm, with its tree-lined streets full of sunshine. *Turin, city of sunshine,* he thought paradoxically. And yet, com-pared to these places . . . he thought of the faculty of chemistry at the univer-sity, which he had attended for only a few months; there was always sunshine, endless sun, shining into the class windows, and outside, hotly bathing the treetops.

A few yards away, inside the isba, Stefano slept on the floor squashed by the tightly packed sleeping men. As usual, after lying down he had crossed him-self, even though he had difficulty moving his arm in the press of other bodies. Being tired, he said only a short prayer, a requiem for the recently fallen, and a brief Angele Dei for himself. The prayers had reminded him of his mother, as if there were an inseparable connection between his mother and the prayers; and in a way that was right, that was exactly how it was. Who knew what Mother would be doing now, in Nomanella, over the snows, seven days away by train. At this hour, Mama Lucia would probably be asleep. In his imagination Stefano saw her brown eyes open in the darkness of his parents' room, looking at him with sleepy warmth. "You go to sleep, Ste-fano; have you said your prayers? Well, then, sleep now; you know that in a few hours you'll have to go back outside." His mother! Putting the imagined maternal advice into practice, Stefano fell asleep, tender thoughts of his mother sending him off. Sleeping in the isba around him were Bersaglieri and a few frightened townspeople. The air was filled with their breathing, as heavy as a thick blanket spread over them all; some reddish light came from the unlatched door of a large brick oven, which occasionally emitted a tumbling sound as the coals inside crumbled.

Outside, despite the numbing cold, some of the sprawled soldiers finally fell asleep, watched over by Lieutenant Acciati on his patch of tent canvas, waiting for the hours to pass before his turn inside the isba. Every now and then he would half open his eyes, and on a couple of occasions it seemed to him he could see, far to the east, flashes of light reflected by the snow: evidently the Russians weren't asleep but were up and active. But what the devil were they up to? He listened intently for a moment but couldn't hear any sound in that dense, muffling snow. *Well, it's not my problem*, he thought. *There are people on watch, sentries and lookouts; they'll have it in hand.*

He made an effort to return his thoughts to something peaceful, relaxing, something about Turin, or sunshine, if possible. In a few minutes he had managed to do so, and his mind swam in a mixture of drowsy satisfaction, not alert or awake, but still aware of the unrelenting cold. The hours dragged on.

7

Soon he felt someone shaking his shoulder. "Eh, what?" he growled, opening his eyes and seeing his captain leaning over him.

"Acciati, get up", said the captain in a low voice.

"Yes, right." Acciati rose and shook himself into wakefulness, his ice-covered overcoat crackling, and looked at his captain. He pulled his coat around himself, moved his cold-stiff gloved fingers, and felt like stamping his feet on the ground.

"Pity you haven't spent the last few hours inside the house", the captain said.

"Well . . . my turn inside comes soon."

"No, it's a pity, but you'll have to go out on a patrol, right now."

"Ah . . ."

"Get hold of five or six of your people and follow me to regimental HQ."

"Right, sir."

The captain was a handsome, athletically built thirty-year-old. He stood with shoulders braced, a little shorter in height than his junior. He looked at Acciati: "Do you want a hand?"

"No, no, thank you."

The young lieutenant went over to the door of the isba and gave it a push, not surprised when he found it jammed: the men inside, asleep on the floor, had spread out to block the doorway. He pushed harder, using both hands, gave the door a few kicks, and called in a half shout, "Bellazzi, Sergeant Bellazzi."

Soon a voice from inside answered, "Here, Lieutenant."

"Bellazzi, before we do anything else, let's get this door open."

Bellazzi, still half awake, could be heard grumbling from the inside: "What sh——ty luck . . . is it time to change over already . . .? Yes, coming, Lieutenant."

Moments later, Acciati was inside, facing a Bellazzi with sleep-tumbled hair and sticky eyes who held a lit match, throwing light on the occupants. Those nearest the door had sat up—some complaining and blaspheming—but the remainder continued sleeping, sprawled in a tight mass on the floor; everything disappeared again as Bellazzi's match went out.

Bellazzi repeated his waking question: "Is it time for the changeover?"

"No, I think not. That's to say . . . let me see the time; light another match, please", said the lieutenant, pulling back his left sleeve to look at his watch.

"Nearly two", said Acciati, and checked the watch again. "Yes, nearly two o'clock. Still an hour to go to the changeover. Look, let the rest of the men continue to sleep, but wake five men from your squad; we have to go out on patrol. Make sure you include Giovenzana and that sharp guy with the mustache."

"Biondolillo? Right, Lieutenant."

"Let me light up this time." Acciati pulled out his lighter and illuminated the area with a yellow light that lasted some ten seconds, time enough for Bellazzi to get going and wake a couple of his men. The sergeant lit more of his own matches to help find the rest of them, then turned to his officer. "All right, Lieutenant, we're ready."

"Right, let's go." Acciati led the group toward the door. Once outside, he lined the men up; some sleeping soldiers rose from the snow and hurried inside to take the vacated places. He looked them over, checking their equipment; the men shivered in the dreadful cold. Counting the group, he found he had six men, not five. Without saying a word, his orderly, Polito, had followed them out and joined the patrol. Acciati looked at the man with what he hoped was a disapproving frown. "Polito, who asked you go get up? What are you doing here?"

"Who me, Lieutenant?" said Polito, and stood there, in his peasant dignity, shivering in the cold.

Acciati felt he was witnessing a noble act. "I hope you get first prize, Polito", he said finally.

The captain came over, looked at the group, and said, "Let's go, quickly." The patrol followed him, with Acciati at their head and Bellazzi bringing up the rear.

Regimental HQ was in an isba in the center of the village: the two officers went in, leaving the men to wait outside. The adjutant, a captain with silver-gray hair, was seated at a table, smoking pensively; in a corner, half concealed by a tent canvas suspended from a rope, someone slept on a mattress. Acciati wondered if it could be the colonel.

"Well, well, look who's here." The adjutant spoke in a half whisper; the young lieutenant and the captain came to attention, their heels coming together. "Shhh!" hissed the adjutant, gesturing with his cigarette that they should approach the table. "Come over here, and let's try not to wake up the boss; he'll need his rest to be up and at it tomorrow."

Acciati looked over at the sleeper; all he could see were gray-socked feet, and he thought, *Right enough he needs to sleep; he'll be really busy in the morning,* then, turning to the adjutant, said, "Just as well you're here, old-timer."

The colonel, unlike the adjutant, was a new arrival, having led a column of reinforcements from Italy, arriving at the front three days before. He had been retained at the front due to the wounding of his predecessor. It was said of the new colonel that he was a good leader, albeit obviously a tenderfoot, like so many of the other battalions' Bersaglieri. Acciati thought, *Thank goodness our Ninth Battalion soldiers aren't inexperienced, too.*

"Well," said the adjutant, "how's the heat wave affecting you?"

Acciati smiled. The adjutant pointed to the map on the table and in a low voice said, "Look at this; you see these two roads to the east of Kalmikoff? Kalmikoff is the name of the place we're in, you knew that?"

"Yes, right", said Acciati.

"Good", the senior officer continued. "There's been movement observed here. You see where these two roads are, to the east? One is about two and a half miles from here, and the other about three or four. Well, if there's movement, it must be the enemy."

Acciati didn't interrupt, but thought, *Those lights I saw reflected in the snow.*

The adjutant went on, "Our lookouts over here to the east have seen lights from time to time. I suppose it must be truck headlights. Whatever it is, your job is to go and check. We need you to confirm what exactly is over there: if they're trucks or something worse."

"Armor, you mean?"

The adjutant nodded his gray head, glanced over at the sleeping colonel, dragged deeply on his cigarette, and lowered his voice. "Exactly, tanks and armored cars." The smoke trickled through his lips. "We need to try to establish their numbers and strength—if there are foot soldiers and how many. You understand?"

"Yes, Captain."

"Your job is to reach the first road and, time permitting, have a look at the second. I'm not ordering you to go to the farther of the two roads, because you need to be back here by sunrise. Although you should be able to get a look at the second road from a distance. Right, I know you'll do what you can."

"Yes, Captain."

"Now, look over here, in the other direction, toward the south, see? Along the road to Meskoff, the one we'll be taking tomorrow; there's a Croatian patrol that just left to go along there. As you're going east, you shouldn't meet them, but it's as well you should know about them; they'll also be seven or eight in strength."

Acciati nodded, his likable craggy oval face now visible after he'd pulled his balaclava down around his neck.

"Your password", the captain started to say, his voice suddenly louder, which caused the other two to glance over at the sleeping colonel, "is Milano, and the counter is Corso Italia."

"Milano, Corso Italia," Acciati repeated, "our home barrack's address."

"So you'll remember it easily", said the captain.

"Do you have a compass?" asked the adjutant.

"Yes." Acciati took a compass out of his pocket and showed it to the senior officer.

"Good." The adjutant looked at his own watch. "It's two o'clock. You have two hours to get there, one to sniff around, and two more to return. You have to be back here before daylight, that is, before seven. If not, apart from the danger to your group, your news will arrive here too late to be of use, is that clear? Because the regiment won't wait for you." He gestured a farewell. "Good luck." Then he held them with another motion and turned to the company captain. "About that fire, the signal fire the colonel mentioned, it's understood you'll take care of it?"

"Right, agreed."

"Now, go ahead, *ciao*."

"Right, sir."

The two officers went out into the dreadful cold. "I'll go with you as far as the start line", said the captain. As he left the shelter of the isba, Acciati, the compass still in the palm of his hand, used the light from inside to check their direction. Once outside, he put himself at the head of his men and set out, the captain walking at his side.

Around the houses and snow-covered dry walls that separated the vegetable gardens, the vague shapes of bivouacked men could be seen; none raised his head to look at the passing patrol. Those who had not managed to sleep were too concentrated in the exhausting fight against the cold to worry about anything else.

Beyond the last isbas they reached the trenches in the snow, where several Bersaglieri lookouts were standing, stamping their feet, while others sat on ammunition boxes or in the snow itself. Yet others leaned against whatever shelter could be found, gloved hands in pockets or pushed under armpits. They all wore the Bersaglieri plumed helmet, stiff with frozen snow, and as they passed through, Stefano's patrol had to use the password several times.

"Around here somewhere, there's a big haystack; it should be over there, more or less, to the left", said the captain, leading the way through the dark shadows of soldiers, until, after going some twenty yards beyond the trenches, he pointed. "There, do you see the haystack, you see where it's located? In four hours, at six o'clock, we'll set fire to it. It'll help you, if you need help, to find your way back. Understood?"

"Yes, Captain."

"At six, don't forget. Now, into the lion's mouth, and good luck." The captain shook hands with Acciati. "Remember," he raised his voice to be heard by the men in the group, "you have to avoid getting into a fight. It's more important to us to have the information than to get rid of two or three Russians."

"Right, sir", replied Acciati, thankful that his captain should thus give him prior justification for any cautious decisions he might later make.

The captain held the handshake, as if to transmit steadfastness to his junior.

"Don't worry, Captain; we'll bring you your information", Acciati said, and saluted. He turned to his squad. "The password and countersign, as you've already heard, are Milano and Corso Italia. Understood? Milano, Corso Italia, remember. All right, let's go!" and turned to march off. Behind him, his orderly Polito repeated, as in a litany of his own, "Password and countersign—Milano, Corso Italia 56, second barracks."

"Keep that address in mind, it's a great whorehouse", joked Biondolillo, smiling beneath his mustache. Contrary to regulations, he wore the uniform belly band as a scarf around his neck.

Some of the men laughed.

At the rear, Sergeant Bellazzi growled his disapproval. Joking about the regiment's home base to him was like making fun of the flag.

The eight men passed by the forward sentries, following the snow-covered pathway that stretched out toward the east. There was some wisecracking between them, but after a while they all fell silent, and the only sound heard was the squeaking of their boots in the icy snow.

8

The ground, which formed a bowl around Kalmikoff, quickly became uneven. Their path took them through some bare woods, gloomy, the trees covered in ice. Here and there in the hollow ground were patches of mist, still and dead. At each rise in the ground, a few of the men would instinctively look back; the village was visible for a while, identified by the bonfires lit by the Croatians, which became smaller with distance and then disappeared. With no stars visible, Acciati decided to stop every fifteen minutes to check their direction with the compass. Polito was able each time to illuminate the small dial using a match cupped in his hands. To do this, he would take off his flannel-lined waterproof gloves, which hung around his neck, connected by a cord (the Bersaglieri had learned this from the Germans), and instantly felt that his hands would freeze. Each time the compass reading was done, he would thrust his hands in his pockets, holding them against his body until circulation was restored, then he would once more put on his gloves.

Stefano was a member of the patrol and, like Bellazzi, he too was shocked, although for other reasons, by Biondolillo's joke on leaving Kalmikoff: "keep that address in mind, it's a great whorehouse". He had always believed it a good practice (and particularly so when one was in danger of one's life) to speak and think unsullied thoughts, as he had been told by Father Mario, back in Nomana. Although under great tension like the others, Stefano wasn't exactly afraid. The patrol was very risky, and he was aware of the danger, but it wasn't any more of a risk than other missions that had seemed almost impossible but had been successfully completed. In addition, Stefano had confidence in Acciati, feeling for him a profound reliance, akin to faith, a feeling not unusual among men in elite units when they have a good commander. His feeling of well-being could also be attributed to the sleep he had been able to get back at the isba; he felt fit and warm, unaffected by the awful cold.

Acciati led the way, advancing at a swift pace, even though he hadn't had a rest since the previous morning; at times he even pulled ahead of his squad. His first worry was that the enemy might have sent their own patrols out in the direction of Kalmikoff and that they might accidentally stumble into each other. He peered ahead, straining his hearing, but didn't slow down, conscious that their time was limited. After forty-five minutes, he found himself at a crossroads, which had him puzzled, so he consulted the compass with great care: the main path unexpectedly swung off to the southeast, that is, roughly toward Meskoff. Another smaller path, only wide enough to pass in single file, its snow untrodden, seemed to lead to a shapeless ridge some distance away. After considering the matter, Acciati said, "I'm sorry . . . but we ought to continue straight ahead." His orderly, Polito, hands in his pockets, repeated, "We'll go straight ahead; nothing will stop us", mimicking one of Mussolini's phrases. Acciati turned to look at him. "Having fun, eh?"

"You bet", Polito replied, matching his chief's tone.

Acciati laughed. "Let's go, forward, *procedamus*", then turned and set off down the smaller path.

Thinking back to his liceo, Acciati chuckled to himself; that *procedamus* was his religion teacher's saying. He thought of the man's long, doleful face and laughed softly, as he usually did when thinking of people or matters relating to religion. He wondered why and thought that perhaps it was because he had as a child seen his father do so, and since then so many others, among the Bersaglieri as well. *But perhaps that's not a good enough reason*, he told himself, still a little confused. But, at the end of the day, was he a believer or not? He understood the serious implications of that question, the question of the beyond . . . There are people who believe and others who don't, and among them both were people accustomed to contemplation and people who hardly think at all, the educated and the unlearned.

And I . . . well, I don't really know. He was tempted to analyze the question this time around, not to leave it up in the air.

Why would I do this now; as if I didn't have enough to worry about, in this cold? That's all I need . . . He put the thought aside, as he had so often done in the past. Like many otherwise generous, right-thinking people, he never found time to explore seriously the things that most affected his destiny.

Sooner than he expected, they reached the foot of the great ridge (*as always, the darkness made me miscalculate the distance*, Acciati thought); here the narrow track curved off to the left, toward the Don.

"What the . . .", the young lieutenant muttered, coming to a stop and turning to Polito. "Light a match, but careful here not to show too much light." He pulled the compass from his pocket, examined the pointer, and then blew out Polito's match. Muttering, "We don't have a choice", he left the path and resolutely advanced through the virgin snow covering the upward slope. The group's progress slowed and became more tiring, the snow up to their knees. Before they reached the ridge line they could hear the rumble of motors and could spot fleeting reflections of light.

Acciati, hiding his concern at what this meant, accelerated the pace despite his tiredness and wondered, as did the men following him, if they would find trucks or tanks. When they reached the ridge and could see over, they halted. Their luck was holding. There were no tanks, but they were faced with the discouraging sight of an endless column of men and trucks. From their position, neither the head nor the rear of the line could be seen as it moved below them along a snow-covered major highway. As they came up to his position, Acciati signed his Bersaglieri to silence, and they quietly crouched down into the snow to observe the fine spectacle. The Russians marched in silence; the trucks among them had their headlights either switched off or masked. The sight struck them dumb, but one Bersagliere, his voice low, asked, "They couldn't be our Sixth Regiment, retreating?"

Acciati shook his head. "These aren't Bersaglieri."

"Italian infantry, maybe?"

"Sure . . . maybe!"

A sudden beam of light revealed a stretch of the column for an instant; a truck had for some reason briefly switched on its unmasked headlights. "That's what those light reflections were. It was from here", murmured Acciati. "Who would have thought . . . these Russians obviously feel safe enough."

There was no doubt they were Russians; the trucks he had seen in the brief flash of headlights were of the obsolescent design the Italian jokingly thought of as the Keystone Cops model, although the sight of them wasn't in the slightest amusing now. The marching men's profile was also unmistakable; the watchers had seen their fur hats, earflaps down, and their long overcoats.

Biondolillo, white belly band around his neck, watching tensely as the enemy moved past, reacted typically. "If those guys catch us spying on them, they'll castrate us at the very least."

If they catch us, thought Stefano, *and by some chance they don't kill us, they'll surely take our coats, balaclavas, and other gear to wear themselves and leave us here in the snow, half undressed.* Stefano felt dismay, as did all the Italian troops in danger of being captured by the Russians (and with good reason, as they later discovered). Biondolillo, with an air of resolution, said, "Well, they won't take me alive. My last grenade will be for me." He held up a grenade, safety removed, and tapped his chest with it. Obviously, that was not such a great prospect either.

Stefano, however, thought, *As it happens, we're not in their hands. We're free, we're armed—and we're Bersaglieri.* Yet the fact remained that the regiment's situation was far more critical than they had thought. How could that human tide run unhindered toward Meskoff? And how come even from its head, no sound of combat reached them?

"Try to rest just a little, men", Acciati gasped out. "We have ten minutes' rest, no charge for shivering; then we need to get going again." He added, "That's if the Ivans will let us, of course."

9

The Ivans did let them. The young lieutenant had noticed that every now and then there were gaps in the passing columns—probably the separations between different units—some of them quite large intervals. As much as the darkness allowed, he studied the terrain near the highway, and when their ten minutes' rest was over, he got up, going back down the slope a short distance to remain concealed, and, followed in silence by his patrol, circled back toward the highway. The ridge here stretched toward the main road, sloping downward and with good forest cover.

They descended between the trees and bushes, stepping carefully until they were twelve to fifteen yards from the highway, in a stretch of snow-covered bushes. They crouched down there unmoving for what seemed a very long time, hearts beating fast, with some of the men having trouble breathing due to the tension. The less steadfast among them felt torn by two almost irresistible impulses: to sink into the snow and disappear, or to get up and run, escape from there, come what might. Nerves tense, some with eyes closed, they waited for the steadier among them to take the lead. Soon another gap opened in the passing enemy column. "Move it!" said Acciati, teeth clenched as he launched himself forward, bent over, with the group of men following closely behind him. They crossed the highway at a run, the exposure making them feel the hostility and danger surrounding them. Then, still running bent over, they had covered barely a hundred yards into the flat terrain when the inexorable flow of the enemy forces resumed along the highway.

They continued walking in single file over the trackless snow, thoroughly tired. Soon they no longer thought of the danger they'd left behind, and although their hearts beat fast, they thought only of the second highway they needed to observe and of avoiding being sighted by the enemy. Soon after, Acciati ordered a halt, and they rested while he consulted the compass.

One of the men said, "Tonight it would have been good to have white coveralls."

Another answered, "Better still if we could just walk along the highway instead of floundering through the snow like this."

From the rear, Sergeant Bellazzi called, "Lieutenant!"

"Hey, don't speak so loudly", said Acciati.

"Perhaps we should take turns in leading the way?"

"Forget it", replied the lieutenant. "Leading the way is my job. To each his own."

"No, sir", argued Bellazzi, "I want to be clear about this. It's not just for your sake; you ought to rest for the sake of the group. To complete the job we have to do and also to save everyone's hide."

Agreeing with their sergeant, several muttered their approval.

"Oh, really", said Acciati. "Just look at all of you. You remind me of *The Heart* by De Amicis."

"Heart, what heart?" asked Biondolillo.

"It's a book. A book without women in it", said Acciati, setting off again.

A few paces farther on, Polito said, "To tell the truth, about books, I've only read one—*Pinocchio*."

The man behind him said, "Who cares?"

Another asked, "Did you really read it?"

"No, our teacher read it to us."

"The teacher?" queried Biondolillo.

"I should tell you she was at least sixty years old", Acciati replied, panting with tiredness.

The others laughed.

Biondolillo thought, *What do you know, anyway?*

Another of the men turned to the rookie, a solidly built youth, recently arrived from Italy. "You, from Molise, have you read *Pinocchio*?" The youth from Molise, whom Bellazzi had picked for his size, was also a man of few words and made no reply.

Bellazzi, from the rear, called out, "Lieutenant, what about it?"

"You don't give up, do you? Well, all right. We can change over every fifteen minutes, head and tail. All right?"

"That's good, Lieutenant", Bellazzi said. "If you like, we'll start now."

Acciati stopped the whole group and made the change. Then they resumed advancing, positions reversed, Bellazzi leading.

The terrain once more became uneven, with tree-covered rises and obstacles. After about one hour, Acciati estimated they had covered only about two kilometers. He thought to himself, *If we don't find something here, we'll have no luck at all.* Climbing up another fatiguing rise, they reached a dip between two mounds, led by Bellazzi. The sergeant suddenly stopped and halted the others in the squad. The snow hereabouts was strangely flattened, and large numbers of small-arms cartridges littered the snow. These bullet casings were not Italian.

Wordlessly, Bellazzi peered into the darkness, head forward. "There", he said, his voice low, and gesturing with one hand. Tensely, the others knelt and unslung their rifles. Acciati ran forward, also at a crouch, reaching the sergeant in a few strides. "What's happening, Bellazzi?"

"Look over there."

10

Down in front of them, the ground dropped to a narrow plateau on which grew a row of leafless trees, at the foot of which there was . . . something. "You men stay here quietly", Acciati half whispered. He gestured to Bellazzi to join him and cautiously went forward, to a spot from which they had a better view. Below the trees, there seemed to be a large snowdrift, behind which could be seen shadowy bodies.

"What kind of sh—— is this?" murmured Acciati, then added, "It looks like a snow trench, and if that's what it is, it'll be ours. You see the terrain, the way it slopes down and it's facing north, facing the Don?"

"Yes", agreed Bellazzi, low-voiced, and after a few moments, "Look, it's positioned in order to cut off the highway, off ahead there, see, where it rises toward the trench?"

"Is that the highway?" murmured Acciati. "It's not very clear in the dark. You can't be sure."

Bellazzi looked at his officer, sure that this was good news; even his low-voiced comment carried his hopes. "Maybe things aren't going so badly; maybe we're about to link up with a detachment from the Sixth", he said. "We can take the good news back to our people at Kalmikoff."

Acciati had continued peering at the figures in the snow.

"I'm not convinced", he whispered. "Why are they so quiet? So still?"

"What if they're sleeping?"

"Just like that? At least there'd be a sentry. Well, there's nothing else for it. Let's go and see." He turned to the sergeant. "You go ahead, Bellazzi, and take a man with you. Be very careful. If the Russians get you, there'll be little we can do for you. Remember the captain's orders? Be very careful."

"Right, Lieutenant."

They went back to their Bersaglieri, finding them still hunkered down, waiting. "Giovenzana", Bellazzi called out in a loud whisper. "Do you want to come with me?"

Stefano, totally ignorant of where it was he had to go, stepped forward silently. He listened attentively to the instructions from the sergeant and the lieutenant, to the effect that when they reached the trench they'd circle it, then followed Bellazzi. The others went forward silently, rifles at the ready, to take new positions nearer to the snow trench.

Making a deliberately wide circle and listening carefully, the two Bersaglieri reached the trench without attracting attention. Had there been sentries posted, it would have been unlikely they would have been spotted, having executed a perfect encircling maneuver, but there were no sentries. The trench held only dead bodies. The majority of the men were frozen in combat postures, kneeling and with rifles pointing out; others seemed to have died unarmed, and yet others lay sideways in the snow, but still rigidly pointing their rifles, like ice statues that had been kicked onto their sides by the attacking enemy or perhaps thrown there by a final blow from a bullet. Most of them still wore their plumed helmets, covered in frost.

"They're Bersaglieri, all are Bersaglieri", Bellazzi muttered in dismay.

He leaned over one body, brushing the frost clear of the helmet to expose the coat of arms. Stefano helped by lighting a match. "They're from the Sixth . . . what a pity, look at the holes in this helmet."

But that wasn't the only one. All the helmets had holes in them, they both noticed. There were bullet holes everywhere, in the bodies, in the trees; bullets had bent some of the rifles, shattering the stocks on others. There were half-severed tree branches hanging down; others littered the area.

"They've been turned into colanders. What a frightening slaughterhouse! How many men did it take, firing like this on these poor men?"

Stefano felt bewildered, struck silent by what he saw. Both in front of the trench and behind the snow was flattened, as if a great crowd had gone by. But now all was deserted; there were only the dead.

"Come", distress broke Bellazzi's voice. "Let's see how many dead there are. Then we'll rejoin our people."

Slowly they walked through the trench, which was about one hundred yards long. They saw a mortar, an 81, and where the trench crossed the road, a small antitank cannon, its operators dead beside it. At this point in the trench, about the middle of the bodies, weapons and everything else were even more shot up—if that were possible—by the prolonged firing.

The massacre created in Bellazzi a fury that increased as he walked stiffly through the trench, sniffing the air. He determined he would repay the enemy in their own coin as soon as he had the opportunity; he blasphemed, spat out curses in his rage. Stefano reacted differently, having been struck speechless, dumb from the horror.

Reaching the end of the trench, they retraced their steps to the antitank cannon. Near it lay the body of the captain in charge of the annihilated detachment. Around the captain's chest was the supporting strap for a map case, in whose interior they found a celluloid-covered map. They took the map with difficulty because of the frozen fastenings on the map case and its leather straps and because the body, rigid as iron, was hard to move.

"The map will help in identifying the detachment", Bellazzi said, handing the folder to Stefano, who took it and flung it across his shoulder.

After counting the bodies—there were eighty of them—they noted there were two junior officers among them, but neither carried identifying map cases. Sergeant Bellazzi kept looking around, and also at the area in the surrounding clearing, and finally said, "What about the Russian dead? Where are they? Is it possible that they've already come and taken them away?"

He leaned on the cannon and looked around the field of fire, then said, "Those two piles of wood must have been in the way. Why didn't they use them to reinforce the parapet here?"

"Wait a moment", said Stefano, going over to the two piles, his boots squeaking in the dry snow. He reached the nearest heap, and as he had suspected they weren't logs but the bodies of Russian soldiers, covered in frost, just like the Italians'. He turned to the sergeant and in a toneless voice said, "They're not tree trunks; it's them. Nobody has taken them away."

"Ah," said Bellazzi, "so they also lost some, eh?"

Stefano returned slowly to the trench, thinking, *What brutal butchery . . .* He was shocked, his mind blocked by what he had seen; although he was able to carry out the job at hand, he was unable to comprehend or grasp at a reason for what had happened. Vaguely he was aware of a memory, the sad and distressed tone in Father Mario's voice back in Nomana, also his father's pronouncements about war, "You young men can't imagine what a squalid trick war really is . . ." But he didn't want to think about it, not now.

When he rejoined Bellazzi, the sergeant pointed out more dead bodies piled by the side of the road. "Also down there, see? The damned S.O.B.s have paid dearly."

"Yes", said Stefano.

Bellazzi was silent for a long moment, then declared, "Come, let's go back", and led the way back to where their group waited.

When they made their report to Acciati, both had difficulty expressing themselves. They were overwhelmed by what they had seen. For his part, Acciati tried to overcome his horror, asking them repeatedly about the apparent importance of the highway crossing the trench and making them go over several of the specific facts they gave him. He wanted to find out if that road was the second highway at which he'd been asked to take a look.

Bellazzi didn't think so. "No, Lieutenant, it looked to me like a secondary road. One thing for sure; there have been large numbers of people through there." Stefano remained silent, tight lipped.

The lieutenant looked at his watch. "It's already past five, and we have orders to be back at seven. We'd better turn around and go back. As for crossing that road back there . . ." He made a gesture as if to say, "Who knows how long it will take us?"

They all looked one last time, distressed, back toward the trench filled with dead men, then set off.

11

Having cut a path of sorts on their outward trip, the first part of their return was less fatiguing. Each of them kept thinking of the horrendous trench full of the dead and about the need to recross the enemy-held highway. When they had it in sight, Acciati called a halt. Once again the masked headlights could be seen, seeming to crawl along, frozen, faraway lamps in the surrounding darkness.

"Obviously we can't just walk toward it without any cover. That would be too stupid", reflected Acciati, murmuring softly to keep feelings of fear far from their minds, already upset by their recent find.

"Right!" said Bellazzi.

"So, we'll leg it, going forward along here, heading south. We'll stay parallel to the highway until we find a wooded area, a watercourse, or whatever the heck gives us concealment. *Forza!*"

Walking with difficulty through untrodden snow for a fair distance, they all felt weary and exhausted. They had begun again to take turns leading every ten minutes.

"Think of the good side", one of the men said during a brief halt. "When we get back, we'll need to get marching once again, with the regiment."

"Yes, a wonderful prospect", grumbled another.

"Think about saving your rear end, not your prospects", Bellazzi said.

A few laughed. Stefano remained silent; he carried the dead captain's celluloid map folder across his shoulder. Who knew if the topographic maps and other documents would be useful; every now and then he checked with his gloved hand to ensure they hadn't been lost. Who knew which company of the Sixth, which battalion had been involved? Maybe from these papers someone would be able to shed some light on the last event lived by the dead men. Who knew what they had thought or said while awaiting the enemy, before their last watch.

Probably, he thought, *they thought and joked around just as we are doing now.* A shiver went up his spine. *It's impossible that what happened to them should also happen to us.* But a little voice in his head said, *Why impossible? Answer me, why?*

Finally they came to a breach in the ground. It was a frozen stream zigzagging off toward the highway. Walking alongside this stream, they followed it until they were able to walk along inside the frozen riverbed, passing between untidy ice-covered willows, ghostly alders, and marsh reeds burned by the cold. As they approached the highway, Acciati made them take concealment among the reeds and then went ahead with Polito, until they could carefully lift their heads from behind a tangle of briars. The highway crossed the stream over a small bridge, about two yards high, a stone's throw away. Foot soldiers were going by them. They were so close they could almost smell them. On the bridge, one man paused to urinate; there was a shouted "*Davai, davai* (forward, forward)", followed by an incomprehensible comment that raised a quickly stifled laugh.

I wonder how long this parade will go on? Acciati asked himself, panting slightly, while trying to keep count of the enemy's strength.

The Russian soldiers were all well loaded, with big backpacks, rifles, and submachine guns, carried or slung in every which way. Every now and then one would pass pulling a wheeled Maxim machine gun with a shield, looking old-fashioned, something unusual in Russian weapons. The march past them looked to be interminable. *But maybe*, Acciati thought, still panting and trying to master the oppressive anxiety that at times threatened to stop him breathing, *maybe it only appears that way to me. These few minutes drag past like hours.* He began to worry about the possibility that the enemy might call a halt. *If this column stops, someone could come down into the riverbed and . . . well, things could get ugly for us.*

As luck would have it there wasn't a halt, but there began to be interruptions in the column, and eventually there was a large gap. "Quickly, Polito," ordered Acciati, "call the others."

"Right, Lieutenant." No sooner had he left, it seemed, than the others had joined him.

"*Forza*," said the lieutenant, remaining at his lookout spot, "cross underneath the bridge. Wait for me under cover about one hundred yards beyond. Understand? Right, get going." They all complied; only Polito remained with his officer.

"*Forza*", Acciati repeated, as he watched the rearmost man disappear under the darkened arch. "Now it's our turn."

They managed to get through to the other side of the bridge without problems, and once on the other side continued rapidly over the icy river, with bushes and reeds on either side, more interested in making speed than in being cautious. They thought they heard a voice behind them; without pausing Acciati looked backward. He seemed to see someone standing near the parapet; his heartbeat increased to the point of nearly bursting.

The damned bridge (or was it a blessing?) disappeared behind them in the darkness. The Bersaglieri were waiting, hidden in the bushes. "Forward", ordered Acciati as he approached them. "Bellazzi, take the lead."

He had just finished speaking when the swift blaze and roar of a fusillade of shots came from the bridge. They also heard shouts, perhaps raising the alarm or maybe an attempt to frighten them.

"You S.O.B.", panted Polito in reply. "Your pig-bitch of a mother . . ."

The Bersaglieri picked up their pace to a run, their exhaustion forgotten. After a while, the rifle fire died out.

"Why aren't they still firing?"

"What are they up to? Are they following us, the S.O.B.s?" asked another, and the possibility made their hair stand on end.

Bellazzi ordered, "Save your breath, you."

Then a blinding white light flooded down on them; a flare had been launched.

"Be still", hissed Acciati, standing as still as a statue himself. For a moment the light showed everything as clear as daylight as it wobbled its way down; then the light slowly went out.

"At the run," Acciati ordered, "there's a wood there ahead. We have to reach it."

But they had no sooner entered the wood—or rather a tangle of willows— when a second flare shot from the bridge, pushed upward by a long trail of sparks. Reaching the summit of its trajectory, it shone with a blinding white oscillating light, lasting long seconds while the device swung as it dropped.

"Thank you," said Acciati, "but that's really enough. The rise we're heading for is over there, I've seen it." Then he ordered, "Let's move it. They can't see us in this tangle." They started out again at a fast pace. Simultaneously a machine gun started firing from the highway. They heard the whistle and zip of bullets nearby, and some hits, but none reached them.

"They're fanning their fire to see if they get lucky," said Bellazzi, "just trying, obviously."

"They must be cracked", said Acciati. "It must have been ordered by some kid fresh from officer school."

As if his comment had been heard by the enemy, the Russian fire ceased. It was good to be able to walk through the tangle of plants, even for a short distance, as their tracks were less visible.

Reaching the foot of the rise, the patrol started up, once more plowing tiredly through the undisturbed snow. On reaching the top they immediately headed down the other side, veering gradually toward the north, seeking the narrow path they had opened on their way out. Finding it at last, the Bersaglieri followed the path till they reached the permanent roadway that led to Kalmikoff. Ever since they had left the high ground, Acciati had gone back to halting exactly every ten minutes, to check their heading against the compass.

After a time, Polito said, "Lieutenant, look over there, it must be the haystack." In the distance, between the folds of the terrain, they could now see a wavering halo of reddish light.

"Yes, surely that's it", agreed Acciati and slowed the pace in order to give himself and his men a respite.

"They've set the haystack on fire; they're waiting for us."

"And keeping themselves warm, crafty S.O.B.s", said Biondolillo.

Reaching the snow trenches at Kalmikoff shortly after seven, they found two headquarters runners waiting for them, stamping their feet to keep warm. "Hurry", one said. "Are you all here? The Croatian patrol returned an hour ago. They lost a man in a brush with a Russian reconnaissance unit."

Staying close to the men of the patrol, the two runners led them toward the HQ isba. "There's a meeting of the battalion commanders", they told Acciati.

In the darkness, units were being assembled here and there in the village. From the Croat sector came the neighing of their horses, and on the main road, a solitary pickup sat warming its engine.

The eight men, their dangerous patrol over, all felt proud at having carried out such a difficult task. Outside the headquarters isba they came to a halt, and Acciati went inside to make his report.

12

He found the colonel of the Third Regiment of Bersaglieri seated at a table; around him stood the commanders of the three battalions and the Croatian legion commander. On handing the adjutant the dead captain's map case, Acciati watched as the contents were immediately given a cursory examination; nothing was found to identify members of the detachment; the papers were marked only by the Sixth Regiment's rubber stamp. The report brought by Acciati hit them all (to use the normal joking language of the Bersaglieri), like "a punch in the kidney", although it was absorbed without too much comment. The young lieutenant was asked to provide more details and was soon dismissed.

After Acciati's departure, the colonel got to his feet and walked up and down the room, meditating. "And not to have even one single radio to ask for information from division", he murmured. "It's unbelievable ..." He thought for a moment, then returned to sit at the table.

"There is a chance that our people are still in Meskoff", he said. "I don't think it's possible that they'd have left without advising us." He paused. "Or maybe, with your more experienced background here than mine, perhaps you think it possible that they have left? I'd like to have your views."

One of the battalion commanders spoke up. "Maybe the village is still in our hands; maybe the Russians haven't yet entered it, although they'd surely be concentrating for an advance into Meskoff itself. In which case it would be important to know if they have or haven't cut the road from here to Meskoff, which we should use ourselves."

"I'd say it's been cut," commented the Croatian officer (he spoke quite good Italian), "since an hour ago my patrol met a Russian recon unit on this very road."

The others nodded, and for some seconds nobody spoke.

"And what if they've already entered Meskoff?" suggested the colonel. "As you know, the major highway to the south starts out from Meskoff. This is the route chosen as the principal channel for the divisions in retreat. And all the divisions are already on the move, to rendezvous there. If by chance the Russians have already entered Meskoff, blocking access to the highway, we have somehow to find a way to dislodge them."

The others agreed. But did they have enough strength? That was the question. If the Sixth Regiment of Bersaglieri, the divisional artillery, the Schuldt group, and the other troops entrusted with the defense of Meskoff had needed to fall back, it would mean that the enemy forces were very superior. And what about that detachment of the Sixth that the patrol lieutenant had reported finding, riddled by bullets?

"In theory," suggested the colonel, "we have an alternative; we can shift ourselves over to the right and join up with the Turin Division, which as you know is the nearest to us, and then jointly march on for Meskoff."

"No", exclaimed the major commanding the Ninth Battalion (to which Stefano belonged). He was a young man, and determined. "Apart from costing us some precious time, let's not fool ourselves. Colonel, I don't know how things are going on other fronts, but I have experience of this one, and we shouldn't delude ourselves that we can achieve something with normal troops—even large numbers of them—that we aren't able to do ourselves with the Bersaglieri."

The colonel turned his head to look at the adjutant, who was standing behind him, close to the chair. "Your very words . . ." he observed. The silver-haired adjutant merely nodded.

"If that's the way things are," the colonel resumed, "we only have one move left; we need to clear the approaches to the highway at all costs."

The others nodded gravely.

"It has to be done", said the Croatian in a toneless voice. "Otherwise for us Croats there'll be no way out. My men are aware of this and have decided to kill themselves rather than be taken prisoner by the Russians."

"Even our own fate would be no picnic", muttered one of the Italian battalion commanders.

"Well, then, *forza*", the colonel concluded. "Let's not lose any time. Each of you give it all you have." He gestured them his permission to dismiss. They all came to attention.

13

It was already light enough to see when a little later the Third Regiment of Bersaglieri and the Croatian legion left Kalmikoff heading south, on the road to Meskoff.

It was December 20; the pale clouds of smoke that Acciati and his men had half seen here and there during the darkness had now extended considerably, concealing whole sectors of the horizon.

In tightly packed ranks, the Croats led the way, with a nucleus of reconnaissance men at point, ahead of them. Some Croatian detachments rode horses, and several foals, numb with the cold, followed alongside their mothers, bucking and circling unexpectedly. Their handlers couldn't decide whether this friskiness was a means of warming themselves, or because they were frightened by events, or if it was simply in their nature. The horsemen and foot soldiers following behind—generally heavy, coarse types—wore Fascist uniforms, which in Italy were usually worn by high-strung types and looked out of place on these men. And so they were: none of these Croatians were Fascists at heart.

Behind the Croats on trucks came some of the Third's headquarters staff, then the regiment's three battalions, well equipped with horse-drawn sleighs and carts loaded down with supplies, interspersed on the road with the marching men. The supplies they carried had been meant for the Third's division HQ, but unknown to the marching men, this headquarters no longer existed.

All, or nearly all, the Bersaglieri walked or drove vehicles, wearing their plumed helmets, quiet and determined looking. The eight men just back from night patrol walked silently within their own company, indistinguishable from the others.

More or less halfway between Kalmikoff and Meskoff next to a small bridge they came upon the frozen body of the Croat killed by the Russians during the night recon. His companions picked him up and loaded his body on a sleigh. But apart from some hard-to-see footprints in the snow, there was no sign of the enemy. It was surprising that there was no evidence of the Russians, if only a few mortar shots: it was really improbable that a column such as this could advance without being seen.

Hidden in the natural folds of the terrain and behind hastily built snow parapets, the Russians awaited the arrival of the enemy in front of Meskoff. Invisible in the dark, they occupied the top of a long hill that hid the village as well as the other rises that ran along both sides of the highway in the final stretch in front of the hill. They were sure the Italians would come and fall into their trap. They had, behind them in the low ground, a group of mortars at the ready, their cold round muzzles pointing upward. Three of the Russians, belonging to the 1180th Infantry Regiment, occupied a pit right at the top of the hill, from which point they could see Meskoff, laid out below and behind them. Meskoff at this end was composed of groups of houses and open stretches, in which isolated houses were separated by flat land and fields of vegetables.

The three men were Corporal Nikitenko, a laborer from Voroshilovgrad; Infantryman Sukorukov, a Caucasian farmer from Vologda on the Don; and Lieutenant Larichev, a painter (at least in former times, when he was still able to paint, not only before the war, but also before that, when he had been exiled into forced labor in the dreadful year of 1937). Stinking in their sweat-dried clothes, the three of them half dozed, slowed by the cold; they looked and felt stupefied. The lieutenant was the only one who now and then turned around to look at the village, where two hastily assembled defensive lines had been established. The first line, the nearest, stretched to left and right, from the edge of the village out to where there were no more houses, concealed by the snow-covered raised roads.

The other line of defense was farther back, along the far side of the River Tikaia, whose large, snowy banks divided the village in half. Unlike the lieutenant, neither Nikitenko nor Sukorukov was the slightest bit interested in what occurred behind them. Every now and then Sukorukov extracted a small smoked fish from a dirty cloth bag, chewing on it very slowly, bones and all. Forced to blow his nose continually because of a cold, he used only his fingers. Like most Russian farmers, he could usually blow his nose without wetting his fingers, but now with his cold . . . "Well, it doesn't matter, *nichevo*."

Even for the Russians, sitting still at fifteen, maybe twenty below freezing became an ordeal. Lieutenant Larichev's mind often dwelt on the roll calls at his labor camp, out in the open of the Siberian winter dawn, when the semi-literate guards would insist on fouling up the roll call. What nightmares he had about those days! And now he was required to be on good, even perfect be-havior, for his sentence (the notorious decade) for political crimes he had not committed. *Life is cr——!* Waiting out in the open reminded him of some companies that over the last few days had been ordered to wait on this side of the Don facing the Italian lines. They had been placed on alert up to forty-eight hours prior to the attack. When the time came to go forward, they had already effectively ceased to exist, being either dead from the cold or killed by the Italians' incessant mortar fire. *My God*, the lieutenant thought, remember-ing, *how demoralizing those mortars were even for me when I was just observing it from our position.* Practically all the Russian soldiers had lived through that mortar-ing with their usual innate fatalism, just as they had fatalistically accepted the years and years of arbitrary, unending deportations, of which the entire pop-ulation was aware. *My poor people, they're used to being mistreated and massacred since forever!* He understood, without approving, the way his people sometimes reacted to provocation with spontaneous savagery, terrifying behavior.

With the coming light he could better observe the troops at work down in Meskoff (and those on the riverbank by using his binoculars), establishing the double defensive line, most of them digging in the snow with their small field shovels. And parked among the village's more distant isbas he had also spotted some tanks; how many were there? He would have liked to know. Meanwhile, along the road from the northeast, from the Don (the road Acciati and his men had crossed during the night), other troops were arriving and were now going directly toward the farther defensive line, on the river. *Look at where they're being sent. Why not put them here, with us, as reinforcements? It's true that we are already many.*

During that period of forced inactivity (the men waiting in ambush on the hill had been expressly ordered not to move from their hiding places for any reason), Corporal Nikitenko also sat and let his thoughts wander. He watched Sukorukov at his side, chewing slowly on his smoked fish, spitting out the bony bits, scattering them over the side of the pit, making a mess. *What an animal, this Sukorukov!* thought Nikitenko. *Even when drawing rations in the company store yesterday, he got into a discussion with the server over a small piece of dried fish, an incredible discussion over a fish tail. How can we win the war with fighting men like that?* Truth to tell, until a few months ago, Nikitenko himself hadn't been interested in winning the war. He was a laborer in a country that proclaimed itself a workers' state, in theory, a privileged class. Although un-educated, he knew that someone doing his job in any Western country re-ceived much higher pay than his. This was more than theft, and not the capitalist value-added expropriation to which reference was made at the oblig-atory indoctrination sessions. Worse even than the starvation wages was the permanent state of uncertainty about one's fate, the continuous danger of being exiled by the Cheka, the institutionalizing of fear, the black beast that had accompanied each Russian for years, by day and by night. At one time, when he was still a child—he remembered—the "ex" were taken out in the street, members of the one-time oppressor class, the bourgeois, the nobles and priests (in fact, they were killed—scientifically suppressed, as explained by the propagandists—phooey!) Later, they took out the petit bourgeoisie. It wasn't quite understood what they were, but for sure there were a lot of them. At the end, some ten or twelve years ago, there took place the enor-mous deportations of kulaks, small farm owners. The greatest of all the re-pressions, with who knew how many millions killed. And among them, two of his uncles, his father's brothers, crowded into cattle trucks like animals, together with their wives and children, even the dying grandmother, whose fate nobody could later determine. They were all, he knew, poor and wretched, despite the small piece of land they owned. Even poorer than his father, who at the start had made the right move by leaving behind his small homestead—which in any case wasn't enough to keep them all fed—and moving to the city to become a laborer. Since that time, since the extermination of the kulaks, and after running down the whole herd of ex, the Communists hadn't held back from taking away and killing the common people, and sometimes even members of the Party. They took numbers beyond millions—an infinity of victims. Nikitenko reflected on the fact that there wasn't one Russian (even among these soldiers with their frostbitten faces), not even one, who hadn't at least one relative killed or deported by the Communists. The same people who in the meantime didn't stop making their pretty humanitarian speeches to enrapture the people. This was why, when the Germans invaded the country, a majority of Russians, himself among them, wanted their advance to continue, until the Communist plague was removed once and for all. But the Germans, stubborn pigs that they were, didn't understand. Having as an ally a force they couldn't have bettered even by invention—the Russian people—and from the beginning they also had dedicated themselves to the massacre of the population, to such an extent that the people on the Russian side of the front didn't want to believe the reports. Why would the Germans decide to ruin their opportunity, committing crimes that were at times worse than those carried out by the Communists? On the radio the Communists continuously denounced the German atrocities, and similar stories were in the newspapers. It had to consist of invented reports, Red propaganda. With the passing of time, though, more and more people came into contact with the front lines and talked about happenings, some more, some less, and the people had to be convinced once and for all that the radio and newspapers told the truth. Why the Germans committed their beastly atrocities, against their most basic interests, was incomprehensible to everyone, including Nikitenko. Equally incomprehensible was the fact that the Communists—without any need for it—continued the massacres and deportations of workers and others of the population, whether members of the Party or not. *What a crappy world we're compelled to live in!* If he at least could have talked about these things with Lieutenant Larichev, who with his calm approach must be one of these fine intellectuals. But Corporal Nikitenko knew that he'd never be able to talk to the lieutenant or anybody else about the subject, that in the Soviet Union these things represented highly dangerous taboos. In any case, this was now only a background. For some months he had been concerned about the damage these criminal German swine had done last summer in Voroshilovgrad, his home town. He had received the news from two separate and reliable sources. An enormous antitank trap, a huge trench dug to protect the town, had been filled with the people executed in a hail of bullets. Who were these victims? That was the question. The Jews, of course, to start with. The Jews, a people who had always had a common understanding with the Communists—or maybe they had invented communism—had their executions witnessed by the people, flocking to watch it as if to a performance of a show. But the Jews weren't enough; there were too many thousands of executed people. Who were the others? Who knew if among them—terrible thought—one of his two sons? Perhaps Andruska, the youngest? They had to erase them from the earth, sweep up these insane invaders, go personally to Voroshilovgrad to see, to find out ... to ...

"Lower your head", Lieutenant Larichev warned. "Here come the *petuki* (cockerels)."

Nikitenko came to with a jolt, as if waking. Sukorukov spat out the fish he was chewing, but then, as if unaware of doing so, put another of the smelly fish in his mouth and resumed chewing.

Down there in the background, along the road from Kalmikoff, the lieutenant's binoculars allowed him to distinguish swarming movement, rather like the agitation at the entrance to an anthill. Slowly a platoon of horsemen approached. Why on horseback? This means that they couldn't be *petuki*; Larichev knew the Bersaglieri didn't ride horses. The platoon came forward at a good pace, alone in the vanguard. Behind them, small as ants, came other advancing horsemen, with, behind them, other soldiers, and the farthest back, if his binoculars didn't lie, the *petuki*. Had to be, for no other soldiers in the world wore this incredible plumed tuft in their helmets. In that case, who were the horsemen in front? Germans, maybe? They didn't look like Germans.

14

The patrol of Croatians, being some three or four hundred yards ahead of the column, reached the hill at Meskoff and started riding up it.

At the same time, following their commanding colonel's orders, squads emerged from the three battalions of Bersaglieri and fanned out into the virgin snow on either side of the road, to take positions in the low ground of the valley, emplacing numbers of small 47 cm cannon, 81 cm mortars, and some 20 mm machine guns in the hollows, out of the direct sight of the enemy. The officers in charge of these dispersed weapons immediately started examining the hill through their binoculars. They concentrated on the edges of the track that climbed the hill, going toward the left at an angle before reaching the pass at the top. They looked particularly at some long artificial-looking mounds of snow near the pass. These were most likely trenches. But built by whom? Probably, they thought, by their own Italian and German defenders of Meskoff, days earlier.

The Croatian sublieutenant at the head of the advance patrol could also see the snow trenches with the naked eye and held a burning hope in his heart that they would find the trenches empty. Why did they appear to be empty of defenders? He asked himself if it wouldn't be wise to send a squad up ahead, but decided right away that this would be a waste of everybody's time, so he continued resolutely advancing.

The path he and his men were taking cut diagonally across one of the snow trenches, some hundreds of yards before the hilltop pass. When the leading horsemen reached the intersection, they unexpectedly found themselves between two lines of waiting Russians, who looked them up and down in silence, weapons leveled. The young lieutenant didn't have time to fire the preplanned rocket signal or even to shout out; he was struck down, as were the other leading riders. The fusillade was so brutal that he was thrown from his horse, parts of his flesh being torn off by the hail of lead. The following riders tried to turn their mounts around but were also struck in turn by the heavy rain of bullets.

In a brief ten seconds, nothing was left standing except a foal, which started off at a run back down the hill, where the main body of the legion's horses were still in motion. Then it stopped, came back, leaping and bounding in panic, to its mother, who was lying near death in the snow, and began to sniff her, muzzle to muzzle, neighing softly.

From the valley bottom the first cannon fired. With a whistle the 47 shell hit the trench where it crossed the road, exploding with a small puff of smoke. Another, a third, and then a fourth shot from the cannon also exploded in and around the trench. Then, with a distinctive rustling, came the first heavy caliber mortar shot, which blew out a piece of the defensive wall. The Russians' fire became general and rapid, coming not only from the hillside but also from each side of the rise. Fortunately for the men moving below, the fire wasn't accurate, mainly because of the distance.

We will not describe the approach to the hill, executed on the run, or the operation by which the Croatian legion and Seventh Battalion of the Bersaglieri advancing on each snow-covered side of the road, pushed their way through to reach the pass. On their right, the Eighth Battalion climbed the hill frontally right to the top. The rest of the Italians—the Ninth Battalion, to which Stefano belonged—followed at a distance behind the Seventh, since they had received strict orders not to get into the fight.

Therefore, Stefano, Acciati, Bellazzi, Biondolillo, and the others who had been on the night patrol climbed the hill without getting into combat, gritting their teeth with fatigue (how long had they been walking?), and little by little becoming excited by the successes they were witnessing. They were vaguely aware of each new assault by the leading forces because, in the middle of the din, they heard, in waves of sound, the rallying cry from the Italians, "*Savoia, Savoia!*" and from the enemy, in Turkish, "*Urra, Urra!*" (kill, kill!). They also heard an increase in hand grenade explosions and on several occasions had to halt, awaiting the clearance of the road ahead. Going by the scenes of some of the fighting, they saw many Italians and Russians dead, both inside and around the shattered snow trenches, many of the Russians still leveling their weapons in death, just like the Bersaglieri in that awful trench of the dead that Stefano and his sergeant had explored during the night (how long ago that seemed!). There were also wounded unable to walk, and these (including the enemy wounded) were being attended by stretcher bearers and medical corpsmen from the Seventh Battalion.

In the last stage of the climb, Sergeant Bellazzi received a back wound from a bullet probably fired from afar, from one of the rises off to the left. Stefano saw him take a few stumbling steps, but the noncom managed to stay upright. He opened his overcoat and felt around under his clothing, taking his hand out covered with blood. "Baptized", he said brusquely, continuing to walk nearly perfectly, "they've baptized me."

Acciati turned to him. "Where?"

"In the hip."

"Stop here and get it attended to", ordered Acciati, then, turning to another Bersagliere, a former medical orderly, "Bordegato, stay here with the sergeant." Bellazzi gestured "no" repeatedly with his bloody hand.

Once they conquered the pass, the Seventh Battalion and the Croatian legion had briefly halted; consequently the Bersaglieri of the Ninth Battalion behind them also halted, separating out on the ground by companies. Despite the losses suffered by their companion battalion, they all felt an extraordinary exhilaration at the truly superb success in breaking up the enemy ambush and a clear desire to continue pushing ahead. Each one of them seemed to feel that with companions like these, they could reach the end of the world, come out ahead in any endeavor.

15

The captain in charge of Stefano's company (he was the same thirty-year-old athletic-looking type, shoulders braced, who had woken Acciati and sent him off on the nocturnal patrol) came running to the squad to check personally on Bellazzi's condition.

He threw himself down in the snow next to Acciati. "Keep alert. In a little while we start off again; no more than a few minutes", he warned. "As soon as the Eighth Battalion reaches the crest of the hill, we'll set off. But look, what's the news on Bellazzi? Have you checked that it's nothing serious?"

Acciati didn't answer; he lay facedown at the head of his men, his head resting on a forearm. As there were still bullets flying about, whistling through the air, mostly coming from hillocks on either side, the captain became alarmed. Many of the enemy hadn't yet been cleared, and now and then a bullet buried itself in the snow. "Eh, Acciati, I'm talking to you. What's happened to you?" He grabbed the lieutenant with one hand and shook him repeatedly. Then Acciati moved his head a bit and with apparent difficulty opened his eyes. "Eh?" he snorted, and gradually seemed to take notice of his superior officer beside him.

"I fell asleep", he mumbled, shaking his helmeted head and blinking his eyes to wake up.

"I shouldn't have woken you", said the captain. "I just wanted to know how Bellazzi is."

"Ah, Bellazzi", said Acciati. "Mmm . . . he's over there", and nodded his head to indicate the sergeant's direction, about fifteen yards back. The sergeant, annoyed, lay in the snow, his coat, jacket, and trousers unbuttoned despite the tremendous cold, getting bandaged by Bordegato, the former medical orderly.

"Right, I see him", said the captain.

"So, he's let himself be bandaged, eh?" Acciati muttered.

"I'll go over and see how he is." Embarrassed, the captain paused. "I'm sorry I woke you; you need as much as you can get, since you haven't slept all night."

"No problem, Captain."

"Well, now it's done. Listen, so you'll be able to get organized. As soon as the Eighth Battalion gets to the crest—they're nearly there—the Croatians and the Seventh will leapfrog ahead again. Then we'll follow them, making sure we form a second echelon."

"We'll still be in reserve?" murmured a surprised Acciati.

"Yes, that's how I got it from the colonel. Once we're in the town, the colonel will give us an order to take over the first line, that is, our own Ninth Battalion. Then it'll be up to us to throw ourselves forward frantically and get through to the river bridge as fast as possible. There at the bridge is where the main highway starts, right at the town's center. We'll have to hold the bridge and occupy the surrounding area; that's our job."

"Can the bridge be seen from here, above?"

"From the position where the Seventh are, yes. A short while ago, I went to take a look. The bridge is about three hundred yards beyond the church; it's a big church, built on a rise. Remember it; the church can be useful as a reference point. As for the rest, it'll be all right if while we advance you keep me in sight." He nodded, "Well Acciati, *ciao*."

"Right, Captain."

The company commander stepped lively over to Bellazzi's side and leaned over him. All the men could see him talking to the sergeant while holding his shoulder with one hand. It was clear to his men that the captain held their sergeant in great esteem; finally they saw the officer take his leave and trot, bent over, back to his post.

Bellazzi—particularly now that he'd become aware that his wound wasn't serious (the bullet had entered and exited, but without touching his intestines)— was secretly pleased by the interest shown by a chief who was clearly worried about his wound. At the time he had replied to the captain with standard words, assuring him he would not leave his post within the platoon. But once his superior had left, the regiment's motto went through his mind: Only the fallen can rest along the way, and he was upset with himself that he hadn't said it. *How stupid! That's what I should have said to the captain. I should have said that, and no more. What an idiot I was!*

16

Before the Bersaglieri could begin going forward, they were unexpectedly attacked by large Russian formations emerging suddenly ("*Urra, urra, urra!*") from the folds in the terrain just the other side of the crest. Consisting of fresh troops sent to the hill as reinforcements, they had not arrived in time for the first action but had stopped their comrades' retreat and now pushed them back into the attacking enemy. Appearing in front of the Bersaglieri, the firing once more became intense, and at very close quarters. In the confusion of this attack, and the subsequent counterattack, the Bersaglieri and the Croatians— chasing the enemy down the other side of the hill—came upon the unexpected second line of Russians, waiting at the nearest edge of Meskoff. Defeating this second line, which required the unstinted use of the Ninth Battalion, cost the Bersaglieri cruel losses no less cruel than those they inflicted on the enemy, and also cost them time.

The Italians and the Croats managed to go ahead with difficulty between houses and gardens. In some sectors, however, where the houses were built solidly instead of with the usual mud and straw, the defenders had better protection, and the attackers succeeded only after repeated harrowing efforts. Gradually, the front line of attack became an interrupted, worrisome advance. At this point, the Ninth Battalion's chief decided to take personal charge of his men and launched an attack against some weaker points, heading resolutely for the capture of the bridge. Thanks to the outstanding valor of the Bersaglieri, they overwhelmed positions that normally would have required more numerous troops. He couldn't, however, take the church; with its thick walls and situated on a rise, it had been turned into a fortress by the enemy. Leaving the church to one of his three companies, the lieutenant colonel circled round on the right with his other two companies and reached the river's edge and the long wooden bridge, built last summer by the Italian engineer corps. On trying to cross over the bridge, he was held back by unbelievably intense artillery fire coming from the Russians' third line of defense, which ran along the river's opposite bank.

Logically, this was the end of their hopes for taking the bridge, but it was imperative, even against all logic, that they get across. In order to mount what looked like an impossible attack on the bridge, it was necessary to bring all the available forces to the riverbank, but to achieve this, and to ensure clear passage for their vehicles, they had to eliminate the church fortress. The colonel sent one of his men with a report to the colonel in chief to advise him that in the meantime he would try to take the church. Then, with heroic self-sacrifice, he led the company, which he had left facing the church, into attack; he was seriously wounded and didn't manage to enter the building.

The remaining hours of daylight were used to consolidate the irregular Italian wedge, particularly untidy around the area of the church, and in establishing concentrations of prisoners and wounded in places out of enemy reach. While there was still light, above all, they made repeated attacks against the bastion of the church, led alternately by companies of Italians or Croats. The building was defended with extraordinary doggedness by an enemy humiliated by recent events; a fire destroyed part of the church. The blackened walls and crypt areas underground ended up divided as strongholds, Bersaglieri in one part, Russians in another.

As night was falling and the Italian attacks were subsiding, the Russian command in turn ordered a very strong attack on the Italian right flank, using troops that had been filtered out of the high ground; they successfully reached the church.

The Italian forward group was made up of elements from the two companies of the Ninth Battalion that had gotten to the river and other smaller pockets. With the arrival of the Russians, they were cut off.

17

Stefano found himself on the river's bank, hidden behind a retaining wall. He was extremely dispirited due to tiredness, and even more because of the unbearable uncertainty, which seemed to worsen as nightfall brought colder temperatures. It was cold enough to immobilize; it even made rational thought difficult. After the fierce losses they had experienced in reaching this spot and in the unsuccessful efforts to gain the river crossing, Stefano's battalion had been subjected to a pitiless bombardment by mortars and Katyuskas, whose terrifying 130 mm rockets often arrived, one slightly after the other, shaking the earth like an earthquake and raising spectacular clouds of smoke. Then the Russian tanks joined in: three or four of them placed themselves in full view on a rise of the highway beyond the town. Once they had established that the small Italian 47 mm cannons were out of effective reach, they fired shot after shot, harassing various targets, including the embankment behind which Stefano's platoon was sheltered. The tank's extremely fast shells seemed to travel in a straight trajectory, hitting their targets like a descending bolt. Seen from one side, they gave the impression of having a completely uncontained brute force. The Russian tanks! Where the devil had they managed to get all this power, when during the summer they had seemed to be on their last legs? After this bombardment had prepared the way, an unexpected enemy attack had suddenly occurred on the battalion's right flank. Some of the exhausted platoons deployed along the river were sent hurrying off toward the right, leaving a few men and their automatic weapons behind. Ordered by Acciati to remain at their posts, Stefano and the Molisano were the only members of their squad left in position. This meant they became separated from Acciati, his orderly Polito, and all other faithful friends wherever they were, perhaps with the regiment, over beyond the enemy incursion, or maybe already corpses in the Russian-held sector. (In Biondolillo's case, he lay dead next to one of the embankment pillars, his cummerbund bloody but still wrapped around his neck; Bellazzi, wounded a second time just before noon, had been taken away on a stretcher and, since then, no more had been heard about him.)

Many of the isbas were burning and providing a dismal illumination to the massacred town, the abandoned vehicles, and the dead bodies of Italians and Russians scattered all over the area. Meanwhile, the surrounded men at the river had a breathing space and time to reflect on their fate, while continuing to watch with grim determination the space in front of them. Not far from Stefano, Laiolo, a wounded Bersagliere from another squad, kept up a continuous stream of phrases such as "disgusting Reds, sh———-faced bastards! You wait to see how the Duce will make you pay big for all these dead Bersaglieri ... Communist pigs ...", and so on. Notoriously known as a Fascist, either Laiolo felt he should speak this way, or perhaps he was delirious from loss of blood. He didn't want to be sent to a first aid post nearby and sat doubled over wearing a blanket that a friend had draped over him. The other men thought about their situation; knowing they were cut off, but still influenced by the success of their earlier advance, they were confident that some counterattack by their people would reestablish contact, then, all together ... but even together, what could they accomplish in their exhausted state? How many of them were well enough to attack? At this conclusion, the more thoughtful among them started to notice, secretly, a sense of helplessness and of the approaching end. Even if the regiment and the Croatians managed to open the road up to their position, it was very clear that then, even together, they would not be able to break the strong line before them at the river and reach the great highway that would lead them to safety. Except that, being Bersaglieri, they achieved the impossible. In their perturbed state, more than one of them thought seriously about the possibility: Hadn't they, after all, reached this point by opening the way against apparently insuperable obstacles?

The colonel's thoughts were different: in darkness, sheltering behind a wall that had become the new front line near the church, he considered their situation. On the ground near to him, two Bersaglieri manned a small assault mortar; one had his head bandaged. The Russian incursion, which had split his attacking troops, was not very wide. He would have been able to throw them back, possibly losing more men than the hundred or so Bersaglieri and Croatians who awaited rescue on the other side. And then what would he do? The enemy line across the river was much better supplied than the two Russian defensive lines they had beaten, at such cost, during the day. His own soldiers were now exhausted, drunk with tiredness; he knew as well as anybody that his own mental resistance was at its limits. Of course, if he could have assembled the major part of his men at the riverbank and ordered them to attack, the Bersaglieri would doubtless launch themselves into action once more. It was, however, almost certain they would not break the enemy line; but if theoretically they won in one sector or another, how many could then reach the other side with enough reserves of strength to fight on beyond there? And then what should they do? What was the use of having a few detachments reach the highway tomorrow, when most of it was inevitably controlled by tanks? For sure it wouldn't help protect the retreating movement by the other divisions. What about the rest of the regiment, the wounded, the trucks? My God, what a blind alley! Enough, let's make a decision. Giving up, surrendering to the enemy was unthinkable: the colonel thought of it only because it was one of the alternatives left to him. No, surrendering would simply mean the massacre of all the Croatian fighters; a bullet in the back of the neck for every one of them. A fate that probably wouldn't affect the Italians; however, once they were in the hands of enemies like these, they would die, most of them, in any case, once in jail. How many would die? Eighty percent, 90? What a tremendous prospect! For a moment, the colonel told himself that there was no objective proof on which to base speculations about massacred prisoners; all he had to go by were the suppositions of his officers. And yet, as a new arrival at the front, how could he fail to take their opinions into consideration? (Now, after the war is over, it is clear that the colonel was mistaken about the Croatians' fate, but not about the percentage of deaths in jail, but this became known only in the light of news received later.) Surrender, therefore, was unthinkable. The only solution left was to withdraw to Kalmikoff and start marching west from there at first light of the next day and then try to join the Turin division in order to find another way out together.

But what if the road to Kalmikoff was already blocked? In that case, whether or not they were exhausted, they would have to open a way by fighting through the enemy. And on the other hand, it would be better to die fighting than to have your hands tied behind you and get shot in the back of the neck . . . or maybe die of privation in a prison camp, covered with lice and suffering all manner of indignities. Or perhaps to die after near starvation forced you to turn cannibal, eating a comrade's flesh, as had happened to the Russians ten years earlier.

With deep-felt pain the colonel came to a decision. He would retreat to Kalmikoff with the Croats and the remainder of his regiment.

He left his observation post behind the wall, made his way to the nearby basement in which he had located his headquarters, and gave his adjutant the marching orders. He had no sooner given the order than he wished he could countermand it; he felt confused by events. In the faint light of a lantern hanging from a wall, he stood in the basement (there were no chairs or anything that could be used as such, and he would never allow himself to sit on the ground) and closed his eyes, thinking of his tremendous responsibility. Would he one day be accused of showing little faith in the valor of his soldiers? What, really, was he duty bound to do? He thought for an instant—after all, he'd already given his orders—of picking up a rifle and going out to charge against the enemy . . . it was an enticing thought, to do something decisive. But what about his men? Did he have the right to give them an order that he, their leader, wasn't prepared to obey?

He opened his eyes again. In the wavering light from the lantern, the adjutant was observing him, looking worried. "Have you passed on the orders to the battalion, Captain?"

"Yes, Colonel. The runners have already left."

"That's good. Now let's get ourselves ready, as well."

18

The cold wind continued to rage against the surrounded men near the river. Despite a killing exhaustion, Stefano beat his hands together every now and then and stamped his feet in the snow to prevent frostbite until at one point those around him asked him to be quiet and listen. From the direction of the main regimental force came the muffled sound of motors. The sound wasn't loud, but by listening carefully, they could hear motors. The waiting Bersaglieri looked like snowmen, and not only because of their slow, clumsy movements. They looked at one another with rising excitement. "You hear that? It's happening; they're preparing to come and get us."

Nobody said more; one man told Laiolo to be quiet, but being only semiconscious, he wasn't aware of what was happening and was nearly delirious. They all listened intently, hearing the rumble of motors with difficulty, but they were clearly audible. One or two of them got to their feet and moved a few yards nearer to hear better. The sound of motors went on for about twenty minutes; but strangely, the sound seemed to be diminishing, getting progressively weaker. "You know what's happening? They're circling, trying to keep from being heard while they prepare to attack." "Oh, right . . ." After a while the sound disappeared; there was no sound of motors. The attack by their countrymen had to be coming soon.

But time went by without any sign of an attack. The sense of desolation when they realized they had been abandoned was indescribable, their anxiety total. The enemy kept up occasional fire, using tracer bullets and flares for illumination while they cleared, house by house, the area that had held the regiment. When they had achieved control, they tried to continue advancing against the group of surrounded men, which provoked a furious defensive action by the Bersaglieri. The Russians didn't continue; with their habitual slowness, they organized a pursuit of the regiment, gathering men as they went along—man after man, force and more force—with the usual dimmed headlights on their trucks, climbing the road that went up the hill, toward Kalmikoff.

The First Battalion of the Russian 1180th Infantry Regiment, home to Corporal Nikitenko of Voroshilovgrad, Infantryman Sukorukov from the Vologda farm country, and Lieutenant Larichev from Leningrad, had not participated actively in combat, apart from firing upon the Bersaglieri of the Eighth Battalion while they climbed the hill. Right after that, while the Russian counterattack on the hillcrest went ahead, the First Battalion had received orders to prepare for action. Lieutenant Larichev had left his cramped cave, limping from poor circulation in his legs, and made the rounds of his platoon's positions. Most of his soldiers had a dumbfounded look on their faces, the poor faces of men who are asked to face death. "Get ready", he'd told them. "As soon as we get the order to advance, we'll throw ourselves against the 'cockerels.'" He had added, "See for yourselves. Even though they puff up their combs, they're nothing more than a few plucked chickens, too few to get by us. The sooner we cut their gizzards, the sooner we can go to bed." Hearing the phrase, his runner Balandin, the country boy, had given him a smile from his place in the trench, either because of the farm talk or from simple affection. On smiling, Balandin had shown, as usual, his steel teeth, like a small fence. *Look at what a condition our chiefs have reduced us to*, thought Larichev, as he had so often done, *and then they ask us to die for the system!*

As it happened, the order to go into attack hadn't come either then or after the Bersaglieri had repulsed the Russian counterattack and gone on down to occupy the town. Larichev had been surprised at the time by the courage shown by the cockerels. *And there are people who insist that Italian soldiers aren't worth much*, he had thought. *How can they say that? They are formidable soldiers, and that's the truth.*

He waited for orders to move the battalion behind the *petuki* to catch them between two fires, but this order didn't arrive either. Instead, after a long wait, they received orders to drop down into a small valley next to the hill. Here, out of the enemy's sight, there converged other battalions from up the hill; the new force remained there in untidy formations in the snow, while furious fighting continued in Meskoff. Only at noon did this group—but not Larichev's men—depart, to perform an intricate circling maneuver to reinforce the riverbank, bringing it up to a strength that would be insuperable for their exhausted adversaries.

Larichev's men were left to wait in the small valley, ordered not to light fires, although this would have been difficult, there being no wood. In silence, each man left with his own thoughts, they had handled the passing of time with fatalism, fighting the cold hour after hour; they stayed there waiting in the cold until after nightfall, until word arrived that the Italians had withdrawn (already they had noted an absence of firing). Only then had a small number of soldiers started an indifferent grumbling. "If the *petuki* have retreated, what is HQ doing? Have they forgotten us?"

Later still, news came that the Russian detachments were following one another, grouping up and going toward Kalmikoff. It was a brutal prospect, to have to march after having spent so many hours out in the open at very low temperatures. Finally, around midnight, the battalion received orders to move, but not to Kalmikoff. They were to go to Meskoff instead, to help protect the Katyuskas, which it seemed would be staying there. Larichev received this order with genuine relief, as it would enable his soldiers to spend some of the night in the warmth inside the houses—if there remained houses in which to shelter—or at least around a fire. This would in any event keep many of them from being frozen.

19

After a while, Stefano had fallen asleep in the snow in the shelter of the embankment. Next to him, sharing an overcoat they had taken from a dead man, was the recruit, the Molisano, the only companion left to Stefano from his squad. Although asleep now, the Molisano had during that tremendous day proved to be a very brave soldier. They had gone from a worried, exhausting doze into a deep sleep, appropriate to youth so cruelly tired.

The enemy hardly fired anymore. They'd stopped the tracers and flares; the far-off reflections of their dimmed headlights and the confused rumblings of their motors weren't enough to interrupt such a deep sleep. As time passed, other Bersaglieri also fell asleep here and there at their icy posts, and more than one talked or shouted while asleep. Some moaned from within nightmares; others were delirious while remaining awake. Yet others, consciously or half asleep, abandoned their posts during the night, going to look for shelter anywhere. Stefano and the Molisano didn't notice this, being joined in heavy sleep.

They were awakened just before dawn by an unknown Bersagliere who came to crouch down at their side.

"What . . . what's happening?" mumbled the Nomana farmer, opening his eyes. He needed a few moments to recognize his surroundings. Then he remembered the desperate, apparently hopeless situation he was in.

"They've called for a state of alert. Wake up!" replied the stranger.

"Alert?" Stefano and the Molisano shook off the frost-covered overcoat they'd been using as a blanket and started moving clumsily, shivering and placing themselves on their knees back in their stamped-out positions behind the yard-high embankment. Staring out toward the enemy, all they saw was a stretch of ice and frozen marsh reeds, all still in darkness except over to their left, eastward, where the sky seemed to be lightening in the gloom.

Feeling the unwelcome signs of incipient frostbite, Stefano lifted himself from his kneeling position and tried to see what he could of the Italian line. A lot had evidently happened since he had slept. To his right, the Bersaglieri didn't seem to be the same people who had been there the previous night. To the left, beyond the Molisano, instead of Bersaglieri, there were Croatians. The only surviving 47 mm cannon was near the embankment, out of its place, but sill manned by its crew.

He turned to his newly arrived companion. "Tell me, do you know why they've called an alert?"

"Because of the noise", the Bersagliere replied.

"What noise?" Stefano asked; then he turned his head, listening. He heard the distant roar of motors. "Is it our people, coming back for us?" he asked himself in a fit of unreasonable hope, but it couldn't be. The noise came from the other bank.

"The tanks are warming their motors", explained the other man. "That's what the lieutenant told me."

"The lieutenant?"

"Yes", the man nodded vaguely off to the right. "He came along the line a while ago."

Stefano noticed that his neighbor somewhat resembled Giovannino, the baker from Nomana with whom he had reported to the service two and a half years ago. Giovannino, the pale-faced baker, who gave the impression of always being covered in flour.

"Tell me, do you know why the Croats are here on the embankment now?"

"Because anybody who has decided to sell his life dearly—whether Bersagliere or Croatian—has come here to the embankment."

"Anybody? But what about the rest of the defenders in our circle? Who's taking care of . . . ?"

"There's no longer a defensive circle", replied the soldier. "There are too few of us to man the previous line. You've been asleep for some hours, I guess? You're not aware of anything that's happened?"

"I was asleep", replied Stefano.

"Lucky you!"

"My friend and I", said Stefano, pointing at the Molisano, who nodded back, "spent all last night out on patrol, without sleep."

"Oh, right, good. Well, those who are not prepared to die like rats, they've all come here to the river's edge, all in the last few hours."

"And the others?"

"They're sleeping in the basements, or at the first aid posts; their idea is that in those places, all being well, when the Russians arrive, they can use a white flag."

"Heck, what a terrible situation. My God, everything's upside down! And everything happened from one day to the next . . ."

Stefano stopped talking and, getting up, started energetically swinging his arms and stamping his feet. He felt an overpowering need to keep his circulation going, feeling the risk of oncoming frostbite.

Then they started on what turned out to be a long wait, waiting for anything that would face them, but it seemed that this anything could only be death.

Not one of those men heading for martyrdom really believed he was going to die. None could fix in his mind the thought that in a short time he would be dead, in the same way that it is impossible to grasp a red-hot iron in one's hand. They had elected to "die well", but preferred not to think about it. Truth to tell, they chose not to be miserable complainers, who in all probability would in any case die. All they had left was to die fighting, but this didn't mean an acceptance of death. Man, even when he himself rushes to death, never really thinks he will die. The minutes ticked by, unbearably slow.

Suddenly one soldier, unable to stand any more of the intolerable tension, got up and, wobbling with the stiffness of cold, left the embankment, stumbling as if drunk; shortly thereafter another followed him, and then another, in disorder. They didn't know where they were headed. They only wanted to be far away from the enemy, and death. But the enemy, and death, had them surrounded.

The single officer present didn't intervene at first; he merely watched as men left their posts. Among the Bersaglieri were some resolute souls, however, and one of these became mad and shouted, "What did they think it was going to be like here? Why did they come—to make trouble?" Reacting, two similarly minded men grabbed hold of one of the men leaving the line and shoved him back into his place behind the embankment; after that, no one tried to leave.

Stefano would never have been one to leave; apart from anything else, where could he run to, surrounded as they were? Besides, for all his modesty, he could never run away. The toughest among them had come here, to this embankment, to join in the fighting to their last breath. He would also do his part, as he had done all his life. Others—Russians, Germans, Italians, and other people—had found themselves in situations like this and had done their duty without crying or squawking. Now it was his turn. He made an effort to fight off the terrible anguish that at moments seemed about to overwhelm him and silently started praying, asking God to forgive his sins.

20

The noise of motors suddenly got louder. Soon the Bersaglieri saw a tank—perhaps a T34—creep slowly toward the opposite bank, not exactly in front of them, but slightly off to the left, near the opening to the bridge for which they had fought so hard. Each man's heart was hammering in his chest. In the darkness sounded the first shot, from the Italian cannon; the battle had started.

In the middle of the furious din, Stefano knelt, like the others, behind the embankment, and fired frugally, shot after shot, trying not to waste ammunition, like a peasant spending his money. How long would his ammunition last? How many minutes? With surprise, he saw the tank come to a halt among the reeds. The small Bersaglieri cannon fired incessantly and repeatedly scored direct hits on the tank; the much more powerful bursts of gunfire from the tank replied, and finally one of its shells scored a direct hit on the Italian piece, tearing its crew to pieces. After this, the tank began to go backward, riding badly and with difficulty, until it stopped again, between some reeds on the riverbank.

On seeing the tank apparently retreating, there were one or two foolish shouts thrown toward it: "You still haven't taken us, eh?!" and "The Third takes some killing!" and so on. But out there in the distance, both to right and left, a few shadowy hostile troops had managed to follow a number of tanks that had made it across the river and taken shelter in the houses that made up part of the encirclement. On the left, where the defenders were the Croats, the enemy was closer in than over to the right, but these brave defenders had managed to dig in to the snow and continued firing on the advancing Russians. Suddenly one of the Croatians stood, ignoring the shower of Russian bullets; then another rose to his feet, and yet another. Stefano thought they must have run out of ammunition. But the Croatians, standing out in the open, began asking one of their officers for something. The man was holding a pistol and seemed to be denying their evidently insistent requests. Then something horrible happened: the officer gave signs of agreeing, then, pointing his pistol at one militiaman's temple, fired, killing the man. Immediately others pressed around the officer, seemingly also asking to be shot dead. There was even a noncom who unholstered his own pistol to assist in the grisly task. Stefano looked away, appalled, but despite the loud sound of general firing all around could still pick out the distinctive dry crack of the two pistols with which the Croats were killing each other. He then heard shouting and looked over to see one of their junior officers trying to get the men to stop, but the men seemed to be in paroxysms, replying incoherently. It looked like the officer was offering to lead them in a retreat—they were dying anyway—but was followed by only two of the men. The others, despairing of any rescue, went back to shooting one another. Frightened and upset (*Not that . . . not like that . . . don't you realize, you unhappy wretches, that you're about to receive God's judgment? Catholics . . . you're also Catholics, aren't you?*), Stefano once again looked away from that scene of collective suicide, enjoining himself to look only toward the enemy, and managed to do so. There were too many other feelings pressing in on him. His ammunition was about to run out; he had loaded his last clip and had twelve shots left, and to judge from the muzzle flashes coming from the enemy infantry, they seemed to have started advancing again. At his side the Italian sublieutenant had thrown caution to the wind and stood firing his rifle, and suddenly he fell. Then the Molisano was also hit, falling with a cry. Stefano bent over him, frightened. The Molisano had been hit squarely in the forehead. Even his last friend from the squad was gone! The boy nearly gave way to screaming, but managed, with difficulty, to control himself. The Bersagliere at his right turned a pale face toward Stefano for a second (this was

254

the soldier who reminded him of Nomana's young baker, Giovannino), then recommenced firing with fervor; he must have had ammunition still. Forcing himself to keep down his terrible anguish, Stefano threw himself forward onto the embankment for support in order to take aim at one of the shadowy forms, the killers of his squad companion. But before he could fire, he felt a blow to his chest, as if a fist had punched him. He lost strength and couldn't even think about continuing to fire. Weakening, he let himself slowly fall back off the embankment. *They've got me in the heart*, he thought. Around him the noise of combat continued, but he no longer heeded it. Other thoughts took over his consciousness, as if the blow to the chest had driven out his present circumstance, filling his head in his last instants with images of his terror, not so much of death but of what might be beyond death; and he thought of his mother. But over everything else was this pain ... this unbearable pain in the chest: "Oh, ah ..." Giovannino of the pale, floury face turned to him, furiously angry, and said, "I've finished my ammunition", and then affixed his bayonet. Stefano didn't hear him, as he softly moaned, "Oh, ah ..."

The pale-faced soldier could see the blood-soaked gloved hand that Stefano held against his chest and heard his moaning. Stefano was half lying, crouched against the embankment. The other soldier, putting down his rifle for a moment, leaned down and lifted him into a sitting position. The pain in Stefano's chest diminished. He stopped moaning, but didn't open his eyes. His gaze was fixed on his mother, seated just over there in her usual place in the family kitchen. His mother, wide eyed, gazed intently at him. Stefano pleaded, "Speak to me, say something. With this wounded heart, I can't speak ... and there's no time, Mama, there's just no more time left." The image of the mother wavered, became indistinct. "Mama, Mama!" he shouted.

This one also, thought the pale-faced soldier. *He also. At the last moment, they all call out for their mothers.*

He leaned over Stefano again and saw that the mortally wounded man's eyes opened, looking at his own face close to his. *Giovannino, from Nomana*, Stefano thought, as if from inside a cloud. Then "No, no ...," he said, "it's the face of Death!" and making one last supreme effort, lifted his hands to push the vision away. His soul left his body. Stefano, as when he was a child in the family barnyard at Nomanella, resting his waist on the shaft of the cart and swinging over, so that his feet were in the air and his head down near the ground, looking at the world upside down; so now, he felt everything around him overturned in an enormous gyration.

21

At the same moment, back in Nomana, two thousand miles away, a tapping on the bedroom window woke Mama Lucia, who abruptly screamed, "Stefano has died! Oh, poor me, poor me, poor me."

Ferrante woke with a start. "What? What did you say?"

"Our Stefano is dead. He's died."

"Calm down, Lucia." Ferrante reached out, felt for the light, and pressed the switch. A yellowish light bathed the grieving mother's disheveled head. She had sat up in bed, fingers pressed to her mouth, pulling her face out of shape; her eyes showed her distress. Around them, the familiar humble room still looked reassuringly ordinary.

"Calm down, Lucia. You've been dreaming, surely."

"No, no, Ferrante. Not this time. This time I really feel it . . . oh . . . Stefano is dead." Poor Lucia, finding it impossible to explain herself, broke down and wept.

"Listen, if you've dreamt about Stefano dying, you must know that what you've done is lengthened his life." But Ferrante wasn't so sure. He had rarely seen his wife in such a state.

"The bedroom window", she blurted out, pointing toward it. "I heard him knocking on the window . . . perhaps . . . perhaps he's broken it?"

"Who would break the window?" Ferrante said doubtfully, then sighed and swung his legs out from under the bedcover. He put on his old worn slippers and got up. The bedroom was cold as he went uncertainly toward the window and then opened the shutters. By the weak light near the bed he examined the icy glass panes one by one (outside it was still dark, and the blinds were closed), then closed the shutters.

"All the panes are unbroken," he said, "and nobody could have tapped the glass because the wooden slats were closed. Maybe you heard ice cracking outside. Calm yourself, Lucia. You've been dreaming and . . ."

"I tell you it wasn't a dream. I wasn't dreaming about Stefano; I've done that many other times, but not tonight. It was he who woke me, going past here; his soul, you understand?" She was excited, nearly shouting.

"These aren't things to talk about now. Tomorrow . . . I mean today, when morning comes, you can talk with Father Mario, and he'll tell you the same, too. You'll see, what's happened to you is . . . what do they call it? . . . super-stition, that's it."

He looked at his wife with his gentle brown eyes and forced a smile. "A believer like you, woman, believing in superstitions! How long has this been going on?"

"Oh, no, not this", said Lucia. "No . . .", and wept again quietly.

Ferrante looked at the big alarm clock on the chest. It pointed to 7:15. Involuntarily he thought, *If Lucia's feeling was based on fact, Stefano's death must have happened five minutes earlier, at 7:10. But . . . what kind of thoughts are these?* he berated himself. *Am I going to lose my mind, too?* Then, to his wife, he said, "Do you want anything, Lucia? Shall I heat some coffee for you?"

Without stopping her crying, she shook her head no. Then "Forgive me, Ferrante", she murmured.

"Cheer up", her husband told her. "You need to be strong."

Standing there, he didn't know what he should do. He pulled and twisted at his tawny mustache. "Try to control yourself and . . . well, be strong. Look, you know what I'm going to do? I'm getting back in bed . . . and you, too. Put the covers back on you, that's right, that's good; and now you'll be warm. If you like, we can say a Rosary, asking for our son to come back safe and sound, despite your dreams."

Lucia gestured no, please no, shaking her head on the pillow. "It wasn't a dream", she whispered.

Ferrante put out the light.

On top of the snow at Meskoff, the soulless body of the young Bersagliere lay among signs of a violent and desperate fight. The sort of confused scene experienced by the souls of the damned, on the other side. Here there took place the last spark of resistance, when the enemy took the embankment. All the defenders' efforts were cut off; Meskoff was taken. The only defenders who managed to escape and join the retreating column of the Sixth Bersaglieri—after incredibly hazardous experiences—were the Croatian sublieutenant and the two legionnaires whom Stefano had observed fleeing over the snowy embankment sector. From them, and only from them, the Italians received news of the battle of Meskoff. They had no more information until three years later, when the war was over. This was when the very few survivors of the Third Bersaglieri who had lived through the battle returned home, after also surviving the dreadful prison camps.[1]

[1]Author's note. The battle of Meskoff was officially reconstructed later, using the testimony of eyewitnesses. In this book, I would have wanted to follow these sources about the battle proper, but I have had partially to differ from them so as not to omit the episode about the surrounded men at the town's river edge, whose fate was recounted later by the three escaped Croatians. I heard about this action at the end of January (a few weeks after it happened) from officers of the Sixth Bersaglieri, who had taken the Croats' statements. It seemed to represent an important part of the overall picture. It is for this reason that it was included, even though, in the thirty years since it took place and despite all efforts, I have been unable to obtain any more details about it (although there is a confirmation of it in the memoirs of Colonel Carloni of the Sixth Bersaglieri in his *Italianzy Kaputt* [Rome: CEN, 1959]). Among other things, it has been impossible to determine to which battalion the surrounded men belonged. That is why in this novel I have quoted a fictitious number for the battalions that made up Stefano's regiment.

PART FIVE

I

At the moment of Stefano's death, the column to which Ambrogio belonged was heading south, only some thirteen miles west of Meskoff.

The column was very long, made up of the Pasubio and Turin infantry divisions, the remainders of the Montebello and Tagliamento legions of Black-shirts, army corps units, and the 298th German division (incomplete): alto-gether there were twenty-five thousand Italians and about five or six thousand Germans. During the previous night (the first night of the retreat) these units had found that the enemy had closed all the roads going west out of Meskoff and had ended up converging on a single road heading south, with unit after unit joining the column. Leading the column were the Germans, wearing their quilted white uniforms; men marching on the left of the road and the dirty-white machines (trucks, tractors, cannons, and all types of trailers) on the right. Mixed into the traffic were many sleighs and farm carts, pulled by the small Russian horses, their hides plastered white with snow. Each German squad had at least one of these rustic vehicles, which carried the men's arms and ammunition, freeing them to walk unencumbered. Bulky in their very military white-camouflaged uniforms, they marched energetically, apparently impassive despite the hard cold. The flanks of the German and Italian columns were patrolled by eight or nine German tanks, which reconnoitered in quick forward dashes. These tanks were survivors, so it was told, of a useless battle a few days earlier, around Boguciar, an attempt by some twenty or thirty of German tanks to contain Russian armor numbering in the hundreds. (Years later it was found that the enemy tanks that had entered Boguciar and now followed behind the Italian column were more than 750 in number, all large tanks.) As the Italians had noticed before, during their halts, despite their present situation the Germans continued to show a very Germanic pride in the strength of their resources (even with the shortages in the face of the enormous re-quirements) and faith in themselves, while demonstrating a haughty disdain for the enemy.

The Italians who marched behind them weren't composed of a double file like the Germans; they marched in single file, with men and vehicles mingled. Instead of the German winter-white, they wore the standard gray-green, so that the much larger column of Italians looked, in the darkness, like a vast moving column of smoke, drifting between the snow banks on either side of the road.

While at the start of the march there had been many Italian trucks, tractors, and cannons, by the second night of the retreat these had dwindled to a meager handful. The rest had to be abandoned because of the lack of fuel.

While walking rapidly forward, Ambrogio turned over in his thoughts the first few hours of the retreat. Nobody could have imagined how long it would last. From the first these regular troops had reacted in a different manner from the Bersaglieri. In his mind's eye, the young officer saw the roadside back near the Don: strewn with innumerable objects—pieces of equipment, uniform parts, gas masks, ammunition cases and clips, packs, wrappings, mortar tubes and bases, even machine guns—abandoned by soldiers who had carried them on their backs for many miles. After some hours of march by the column, this untidy spectacle had given way to an even more impressive abandonment, when trucks, tractors, cannons, and other trailers began to be left behind, the numbers increasing with the distance covered. The vehicles abandoned within the last few hours belonging to the rear-echelon detachments, who had gone past around noon, could be distinguished from the more recently abandoned by the coating of crystal-clear ice that covered them completely. At the start the abandoned vehicles were empty; soon men could be seen in them. Ambrogio was horrified on seeing injured men left behind. Noticing his interest, some of these miserable souls started shouting and asking for help. Along with other officers, he transferred these wounded into vehicles that were still mobile; this was possible for a while, but as the retreat progressed, he and his brother officers had to give up. The wounded men who were no longer fit enough to move, and whose numbers were increasing, had been abandoned to their own fate and would probably be dead from exposure before the enemy reached them.

Who knows, Ambrogio asked himself, *how many of the poor soldiers abandoned yesterday will still be alive?* It was an agonizing question.

Because of the undulating terrain he could, every now and then, see the last part of the German column, like a dirty-white serpentine; also ahead of him he could see the long lines of Italians, who also stretched out of sight behind him. His orderly, the farmer Paccoi, who walked beside him, kept looking at a small spot on the left—east—horizon, where a red halo shot through with occasional flashes silently colored the lower part of the sky. These were the last moments of the battle of Meskoff, although none of them was aware of it. "What could it be?" Paccoi finally asked.

Ambrogio abandoned his thoughts and came back to the present. "What are you talking about? You mean that red glow in the sky?"

"Right."

"What do you think it is? It's a fire."

"What else could it be?" asked the mapmaker lieutenant. The twenty-year-old officer (the one with a Greek nose) had a lump of ice sticking to his balaclava, like all the others.

"It's a bonfire. And we have not seen many bonfires these last two nights, my dear Paccoi."

Ambrogio smiled and then turned to look at the soldiers behind. He now found himself, along with some headquarters officers, leading this group, which continued to be well organized. The few vehicles that were still working, if there were any, had pushed on ahead and were out of sight of the marching men.

Yesterday afternoon, during a long stop in the town of Popovka, the men had dispersed to seek food or shelter in the surrounding isbas, but now they marched in formation, battery after battery. The colonel and his own headquarters officers led the entire column.

After leaving Popovka, they walked without halting for eight hours. Major Casasco appeared to be suffering, stretched to the very limit of his physical capacity, although making a dignified attempt to hide it. *For him the memory of yesterday's disorganization must be even worse than for us younger people,* Ambrogio reflected. *Last night we managed to reorganize the various detachments by some miracle, probably helped by the strange rumor that only a few hours' march would bring us to reunite with our own lines . . . wherever they might be!* The tendency to disperse that Italian units had shown continued to disconcert him. *It's a fact that we can't issue food rations; then there's this crazy cold, which makes you feel you can't survive another instant, and the need to keep moving, even during the rest stops, in order not to freeze. But even so, how is it possible we haven't realized that this state of disorder is, above all, the most dangerous of our misfortunes? I don't understand it. The crucial point with us Italians is that we never trust others, whether they're superiors, inferiors, or the same rank. That's the real problem; we don't have faith in one another.*

Dawn approached, haltingly; the road had started to climb gradually, so that Ambrogio could better see beyond the Italians to the white German serpentine, which disappeared into the darkness. As usual with the approach of dawn, the cold became pitiless, measurable by the increased amounts of ice adhering to their balaclava helmets, around the nose. Few of them talked any more. The futile belief that the column was about to leave the enemy encirclement had been increasing rather than fading as the march progressed, and if anyone talked, it was of this. Rumors began circulating in parts of the column, rumors that changed each minute: the friendly lines were six miles away; no they weren't, they were only three and a half miles; it was just ahead of the long slope they were climbing; there, just ahead (quite possible, even if the lack of light prevented it being seen) was a crest, and, well, the new line extended along the ridge.

"What do you say about that, Lieutenant?" asked Paccoi. "With all that open country in front, the line has been well placed, don't you think?"

"The what?"

"The new line."

"Yes, of course, if there is a new line . . ."

"Why shouldn't there be one?" murmured Paccoi. "They all say there is one."

"In that case, great", concluded Ambrogio.

Paccoi was perplexed. After cheering himself with this prospect, it wasn't easy to give it up or entertain doubts. He turned toward a soldier two paces behind; it was the observer corporal who had left the OP on the Don together with Ambrogio. The corporal was explaining the situation to his neighbor in a low tone: it wasn't only one line; to be precise there were two lines facing either other, one the Russians' and the other ours.

"Eh," Paccoi asked him, "this new line you're talking about, are you sure that it really exists?"

The corporal threw him an irritated look, but answered calmly enough. "Everybody says it exists. Have you just found out about it?"

"Sorry, I just want to be sure. Who told you about it?"

This was indeed the question. The observer corporal searched his memory; above all he didn't want to appear foolish. "The news comes from the Germans", he finally said in a distant voice. "A German-speaking friend of mine from the Third Battery told me."

"Ah, yes," said a relieved Paccoi, "just as well!"

The corporal would have been happy to believe, but he couldn't. A hidden corner of his mind was burning over the thought that his friend from the Third Battery, with whom he'd talked of the front line yesterday, well, maybe he spoke German, and then again maybe he didn't. Of course, the man was a student, and therefore it was quite possible he knew German. But there remained the fact that he hadn't actually said he had talked to the Germans. *Go stick it.* He mentally rejected the problem and turned to think of less troublesome thoughts.

They went on marching.

2

The road did indeed climb to a rise, or rather to a sort of very long ridgeline. At the point where the road crossed the rise there could be seen a few thatched huts. Upon reaching these, Ambrogio saw that the huts were the start of a rather large village, the buildings well scattered, and there was a sign with a place name: Posnyakoff. Here the Germans had halted and taken positions at the village edges, as if expecting an attack from any direction. They had posted their enormous trucks in the center of the village and at the main crossroads, with their motors running.

The Italian troops continued arriving; now there were disconcerting rumors running among the soldiers: they were in no way out of the enemy's encirclement, and they were in fact in a more dangerous position than before, because the sector was infested with enemy tanks. Ambrogio heard the rumor from one soldier, then from a second, and then from the young Neapolitan mapmaker. This news had no sooner spread than another rumor came around: this one held the other view, that the friendly line was actually much closer, almost just outside the village, there, just over a couple of humps in the ground. Ambrogio couldn't understand it: Who circulated such rumors? Or, better yet, how did they get started? Based on what?

As the Germans had stopped, the head of the Italian column halted. Ambrogio's regiment, with its three following groups, the colonel walking at its head, also stopped, and they joined other Italians, standing along the road.

Behind them, along the rise up to the ridge and the village, the major portion of the Italian column—tens of thousands of men—hadn't halted; they continued climbing toward the ridge.

Meanwhile, Ambrogio took a look around him. The village, as far as he could see, was scattered over a fairly large area, with the thatched houses giving it a look of poverty. To judge by the trodden snow between the houses, many people had been past and perhaps had even stopped there. *Perhaps our rear-echelon people?* he asked himself. His eye was caught by the many marks left between the isbas by tracked vehicles. *Could they have been left by German tanks? No, there are too many tracks. Damn! How many were there? How could they be our rear-echelon crowd? Who knows how many Russian tanks passed through here? Surely they had to be coming from that direction, from Boguciar. They just had to have come from there. If not, where from? And where could they be now?*

As the dawn light increased he could see far outside Posnyakoff toward both south and west, but saw nothing except desolate expanses of snow, in some cases covered in mist, totally inhospitable and with no sign of life.

From time to time he heard shouts behind him, repeated orders, sounding like "Halt." "Hold steady." "Atten-shun!" "Halt, halt." It was evident the officers were trying to prevent groups of men from colliding with others. A couple of steps away from Ambrogio, Tired Horse, wrapped in a fur overcoat, stood talking to the major. "We can't just stand still here", he said. "These formations behind are anxious to get away from being surrounded; shortly nobody will be able to hold them back. They'll march all over us, and then we can say goodbye to any chance of maintaining order."

"In that case?" asked a gloomy major.

"We have to get off the road. For example, move to that open space over there. Perhaps other detachments will follow our lead. In any case, let them do what they wish: we have to preserve order in the group. After that, we'll see."

"Are you forgetting that now we are reincorporated in the regiment?" objected the major. "It would have to be the colonel who gives that order."

"That's true, but if he doesn't give it . . ."

A short time later, shouting came from the rear, and became louder. "There's no time to lose!" insisted Tired Horse. "Let's get off the road. Major, I'll take the responsibility, if you wish. If necessary we'll say that I gave the order on my own initiative, but let's not lose any more time."

"No. Even that would lead to disorder", said the major.

Meanwhile, the confusion in the rear increased.

"You could do this", decided the major. "Go and see the colonel and see if he agrees to our taking the whole regiment off the road."

"Me, sir? Go to ... and leave you ... ?"

"Yes, go, go!"

"Maybe there's not time for that, but I'll try", said Tired Horse. A worry, a doubt, touched his eyes. "I'll go, and be back right away. Right away", he repeated. "Understood, sir?"

Reluctantly leaving the major, he walked off with rapid steps toward the head of the column.

From behind, soldiers kept on going forward, even though slowly, but like a river overflowing its banks. Unwilling to halt on the sloping road, outside the protection of the German guns, neither did they want to stay on the wrong side of their own rumored front, if that front existed. The vanguard of the river of men reached the village; at the rear of the headquarters detachment, the energetic captain of the First Battery and his junior officers had started shouting, trying to maintain their own men in formation. Ambrogio and the mapmaker also left their places in line and tried to give orders to the headquarters artillerymen, shouting, "Hold it, stand firm, you men! Don't move! Stay in formation, in formation!" exactly the same orders as had been given by officers at the rear, without effect.

Even these orders proved futile. Many of the soldiers behaved as if they couldn't hear the orders or didn't understand them and, instead of getting in line, just stood there; some avoided meeting the officers' eyes, behaving as if they were blind. Of course, there was also the cold, in which many found it unbearable to stand still; others, on falling out, thought to find some food in one of the nearby hovels.

The part of the column made up of men from Ambrogio's group was reached and overtaken by the many arriving soldiers, breaking up and being absorbed by the crowds. Ambrogio, who up to the last moment had made efforts to maintain order, dropped his arms, dejected in the face of this collapse of order. He defiantly remained where he was; the moving soldiers for their part didn't confront him or even touch him. (Far from rebelling against the officers, the men were vaguely thankful toward those officers who showed their concern.)

Making his way through the troops, the mapmaker approached him. "What is this chaos, Riva? What can we do with soldiers like this?"

Paccoi joined them. "Here I am, Lieutenant."

Reaching the German rear formations, the press of men was obliged to come to a halt. Then it began to increase in size, until many had to move to one side or were even squeezed back in order to avoid the throng. The column kept arriving slowly up the road. More recent arrivals, bewildered, asked, "Are we already out of the encirclement? What's happening?" A little later, they also came to a halt, joining the troops already in the village, forming a great multitude, dense in parts and sparse in others, but particularly packed in the areas near the German tanks. Italian transportation also arrived. Trucks overloaded with wounded and frostbitten men, one or two tractors still pulling their cannons and covered with clusters of men, sleighs, and numbers of horse-drawn carts.

A group of five or six men halted near Ambrogio. They had two large mules, one of which was pulling a small antitank 47/32 cannon and the other a sleigh into which had been loaded the cannon's ammunition. They were, incredibly, Bersaglieri, led by a sergeant whose face bore an extraordinary resemblance to Virgilio De Lollis, the Marrucino from the recruit center in Cremona. With a voice carrying the accent of the Abruzzi, the sergeant grumbled, "What a mess! Just look at this sh——!"

One of the sergeant's men said, "Instead of being a bit more disciplined under danger . . . just look at this mess."

"Just great! To find all these people here, and not our own . . .", said another.

Ambrogio suddenly thought about that other Bersagliere, his friend Stefano. *Who knows how he's doing right now, old Moonface? Will he have been encircled also? Or maybe the Celere had time to escape up the main highway? But what are these Bersaglieri doing here with us?* He vaguely remembered that some Bersaglieri squads had been attached to his own division to operate in an antitank function. *Yes, that's right.* He returned to thinking about Stefano. *I wonder how things have gone with him? The Russians have cut the roads between us here and Meskoff . . . that's bad news . . .*

Bad news, yes, but the Bersaglieri weren't like the rest of everyday troops; they were efficient, perhaps no less than the Germans. He imagined his friend walking resolutely up the road with his companions, scarf wound around his long neck. (Ambrogio didn't know that Stefano now walked only in eternity, having broken free of earthly things.)

The Bersaglieri sergeant meanwhile continued to look around himself, spotting two German antitank pieces emplaced over beyond the crowd. He looked hard at them, then turned to his men. "Come on," he said, "we'll go and put ourselves at their side." The squad moved on and a few minutes later came to a halt next to the long white-painted German cannons. The strange, small Italian 47 looked like a toy in comparison, even though—it was generally accepted—it could be a fearsome weapon in the hands of determined soldiers like these.

The crowd continued to grow and shuffle, mixing separate units; fortunately, there was no sign of the enemy. Meanwhile the Germans did not seem inclined to move, looking on incredulously and making occasional comments about the Italians and their disorganization. Among the Italians, first small separate groups, then larger groups started to drift out of the village, looking for who knew what; others in increasing numbers followed, and once joined, the mass acquired a sort of confidence, increasing their distance and splitting into several directions. Seeing how far away they were, not a few others thought they must have discovered something and crowded after them.

"Look!" said the mapping lieutenant. "Look at what's happening."

"It's madness," Ambrogio murmured to himself, "absolutely incredible."

"They'll end up losing all contact; they'll get lost."

"Yes, you're right; they'll all get lost. But why? We can't let it happen ..." Ambrogio shook his head stubbornly. "No, no no! It's unacceptable to reach this level of disorganization." Was it possible that this was how Italians, his people, were made? It seemed that he was only now becoming aware of how they were.

Paccoi, a pained expression on his face, watched his officer. Ambrogio decided. "Let's go! Let's go look for the colonel and put ourselves at his disposal. He'll have to give us some order."

They pushed through the mass of gathered troops in the direction the column had been taking, finding some groups standing, others in movement, the general direction of movement still coming from the north. They asked directions of several groups and individual artillerymen from their regiment and even the occasional officer; none was able to tell them where to find the colonel. Mazzoleni and Piantanida, pushed this way and that by the crowd, were able to say they had seen only the adjutant, who had himself been looking for Major Casasco. "Which way did he go?" asked Ambrogio.

"That way", replied the pair, joining him and getting into step. "If we hurry maybe we'll catch him; he has to be over there, just beyond those houses."

3

Over on the other side of the group of houses, the terrain broadened out and became a level esplanade, at the entrance to which they found Tired Horse, head inclined to one side as he did when perplexed, watching a curious spectacle. Out on the esplanade a young infantry sublieutenant was endeavoring to reorganize the Italian troops. In a clear and strong voice, he shouted tirelessly, "Fall in! Fall in!" and ordered, "In lines of four. Get into fours!" Pointing to six men lined up before him, he said, "X Regiment over here; Y Regiment there; Z, over there. Come on, wake up!" His forceful voice insisted, "Let's behave like men, not sheep, not like cattle. Hey, you over there, fall in. Fall in!"

Other junior infantry or engineer officers came to his assistance, reinforcing his orders. Surprisingly, not a few soldiers came over and got in line.

Ambrogio had been watching this with open mouth. He had recognized the shouting sublieutenant to be his classmate Michele Tintori, the budding writer from Nova. "Look at him", shaking his head. "Only Tintori would get into an enterprise like this."

Tired Horse commented, "They're all so confused they'll obey orders from the first crackpot that comes along? That's obvious."

"Well," Ambrogio quickly decided, "nothing left but for us to go and help this particular crackpot. Come on, let's give him a hand."

"Give him a hand? Us?" said the distracted Tired Horse, returning immediately to his first worry. "By the way, Riva, have you seen the major?"

"No."

"I don't know where he could have gone", he muttered, and added, "I can't find him", in a tone that told Ambrogio how worried he was about his chief. No doubt he was worried that, given the major's confused mental state, he might really be lost.

Tired Horse noticed Ambrogio's reaction to what he'd said and tried to turn the whole thing into a joke. "Looks like we've reached the point where senior officers are not only revered and have us wagging our tails but even need a custodian; otherwise the poor things get lost. Well, I'm going to take a look around over there."

"I'm going to help this fellow get things in order."

"Good", said the adjutant vaguely, and went. Hesitating briefly, the map-maker turned and followed him. Mazzoleni and Piantanida, the two gold-bricks, also tried to slip away, but, "Hey, you two", Ambrogio stopped them. "Follow me." He placed them alongside Paccoi in the Eighth Artillery column. "That's right, you stay there." Ambrogio then went about sorting out soldiers into columns as they reported to him.

Very soon the six columns lengthened. Ambrogio noticed Michele looking at him and waved to him. He hadn't met him since May, the day of Michele's visit to Nomana. Recognizing Ambrogio, Michele was filled with happiness. "Ambrogio, *tu quoque*", he called out. "All well?"

Ambrogio gestured back, well, as well as could be expected. "We'll talk later about Cossacks and ancient Greeks", he shouted to his friend, "and everything else."

"Talk . . . what did you say?" asked Michele, not understanding. "Ah, yes . . . sure, agreed." He held out his hand toward Ambrogio. Ambrogio loped over to shake his hand. Michele said, "You know that during last night's march I was thinking of your house? That sunny day when we tried to eat ice cream, with all your family around us."

Ambrogio nodded yes.

"Tell me, how is your family? Well, I hope?"

"Yes, I received a letter from Alma a few days ago."

"Alma!" Michele said emotionally. (It was precisely because of Alma that he kept on remembering that visit to Nomana.) He would have liked to ask more detailed news of Alma, but shyness held him back. Turning toward the heads

266

of the six columns, he started calling again, loud and clear, "Come on, fall in, fall in!"

"Tell me, what do you intend to do?" asked Ambrogio before returning to his part of the task.

"I'm hoping that a senior officer will come", replied Michele. "Meanwhile let's get a little order here. We can't just let all these people go wandering about, don't you agree?"

"Right. Let's try not to lose sight of each other."

"Right."

Ambrogio returned to his columns and continued his task. *The senior officers,* he thought, *it should be they who get this lot organized . . . yet, maybe it's because of the cold. The older officers can't take the cold as well as their juniors; it seems the cold freezes their brain and willpower.* (He considered anyone above thirty to be old.)

They had gathered together several hundred men when Ambrogio saw the Neapolitan mapmaker with the Greek nose approaching, looking for him.

"Hey, Riva."

"Yes?"

"The adjutant sent me", he said hurriedly.

"Who, Tired Horse?"

The Neapolitan nodded. "He told me to advise you and . . . that other fellow", pointing to Tintori, who was still organizing the troop formations, "that over there to one side, you see? Just the other side of this rise, there's a general who is also organizing troops into formations."

"A general who has woken up? What's he called?"

"I don't know."

"Come." Together they walked over to Michele Tintori and told him.

"Well, at last, some good news!" he said. "But," he said to Ambrogio, "please go yourself. Go over there and check it with your own eyes, then tell me."

"Right."

"Thanks, I'll be waiting."

Ambrogio was soon back, advising Michele that in fact there indeed was a general gathering troops on the other side of the rise. He had assembled men in columns and seemed to have as many men as they had here.

"Very good", said Tintori. Then, raising his voice, "Attention, men, listen up. Over there, not far, they're assembling everybody. Now we'll go there in good order. I repeat, we'll go in good order, as we are, separated by regiment, not like sheep. Is that clear? All right. Let's start."

He went over to the column nearest the rise. "Regiment . . . atten-shun!" he ordered, and all the men stood at attention.

"Take them over there, will you?" Tintori addressed Ambrogio, giving him an invitation that was really an order.

"We'll follow behind you. Forward . . . march!" he shouted at the column.

Ambrogio immediately put himself at the head of the group, which followed his decisive steps. One after another the remaining columns added themselves to the marching group. Toward the rear, the organized column broke down into disorder again. They all managed to flow into the mass of men lining up before the general, though. The latter was a man of medium height, easily spotted from the silver insignia on his cap. For a few instants, Ambrogio caught sight of his schoolmate. The unlikely formation that Michele had organized was now in good hands. Mingling with the others—now just another junior officer—Michele went to take his place with the men of his regiment. *I'll look for you soon*, Ambrogio promised himself.

The general continuously sent officers into the village to call together the troops, but these started flowing toward the assembly area of their own volition; the general's silver insignia acted like a magnet. From his vantage point, Ambrogio could again see over to the south and west. He noticed that the crowds of soldiers who had streamed out of the village were now returning. *Just as well the Russians aren't nearby, or we'd have had a slaughter!* he thought.

An older colonel and some fifteen officers took places at the head of his regiment. Five or six of the officers belonged to his own group. However, Major Casasco, Tired Horse, and his friend Bonsaver were still missing. A few ranks back, he could see Paccoi's round face, where he had positioned himself in order to have his officer in sight. The intense cold continued; many of the men stamped their feet on the ground, beat their hands together, or swung their arms around their bodies for warmth.

Finally, the general spoke. "Listen carefully; don't believe anything you hear about friendly front lines", he said. "No one knows where they are, or even if they exist. It's more important to reestablish order among ourselves, not only to avoid being ashamed of ourselves but also to enable us to survive." He spoke well. His voice showed energy, even though it was not strong enough to reach everybody. "I repeat, you have to understand, get it well in your heads that the most important thing for us is good discipline. Your officers shouldn't tolerate any nonsense." He looked at his wristwatch. "Within an hour we'll restart our march, with our German allies in the lead. We need to cross an area infested with enemy forces, and because of this we have to be ready to fight at any moment. Remember that." He paused, not sure if he should remind them of battles they had been through and won in the past. Then, of course, there had been gasoline and, therefore, arms, ammunition, and food rations, and those most important things, discipline and good order. He left it, continuing, "We leave the village in that direction." Against the expectations of many, he pointed off to the southeast, where the last few of the village's isbas stood on folds in the terrain, cutting off their view of the horizon. "We'll form up militarily, battalion by battalion, company by company, taking what transportation we have left, so, get ready. Courage, and each officer make preparations."

4

Beyond the folds in the land that the general had indicated there was an extensive plateau that sloped away beyond, toward the southeast, reaching to a very large valley. Into this valley—although the Italians were not yet aware of it—the head of the German column had entered, looking like a thin, white serpent, dirty looking against the pure white of the snow. Farther back, the remaining German troops were leaving the village and descending toward the valley on a roadway; also going downward, using steep narrow paths, were lines of Italian soldiers that had not been part of the general assembly or even heard about it. Where their path crossed that of the Germans, the Italians had to stand and wait because the Germans, sure of their priority, wouldn't let them in to upset their files.

The formation of the Italian detachments started on the esplanade where the general had addressed them. Nearly all the soldiers—including those who had not heard the general's words—were clearly aware of the need to maintain ranks. They were also conscious that it was in the interest of all to let the Germans march in well-organized ranks, in order to follow behind them. Despite this, when those officers who were willing and able to step forward and act—not all of them by any means—tried to reorganize the detachments, few of the men cooperated. Not that the soldiers protested the order; rather, they remained stiff when they should have been moving, as if they heard or saw nothing. Sometimes this was so as not to be separated from a fellow villager or even (and this was a paradox) in order to remain as close as possible to the officer giving the orders and who therefore inspired confidence in the men. It was not that the men weren't well disposed; most were and had previously demonstrated their willingness on many occasions before this retreat. However, these men, who were prepared to follow orders, who in normal times would inspire others, creating the cohesive whole that was an army (the same people that in Italy make of the country a people), now couldn't overcome an enormous and extensive inertia, leaving them standing, as if paralyzed.

Meanwhile (although not visible from this point), more men, sleighs, carts, and trucks entered Posnyakoff coming up the hill from the north and were passing through the village like a human tide, soon to reach the plateau, adding to and increasing the sea of men.

Slowly, as if mesmerized by the sight of the moving German column, the mass of men began to swell and to fill the descending paths. Their officers quickly saw the impossibility of reorganizing the men into detachments and tried to steer them toward a road of beaten snow that dropped down into the valley, attempting to keep them together. Officers shouted, waved their arms, and cursed the men's stupidity to their faces, trying to slow the pace to keep them from falling head over heels into the valley.

Among these officers was Ambrogio. His throat hurt from his continuous shouting: "Are you men or beasts?" hoarsely, pushing at the nearest men: "Hold it, go back!" But the men would take one step back, then start pushing forward again. These weren't men from his regiment, who were obeying his orders and stayed back. "Do you want to go on, like lambs? Wretches!" At his side, Paccoi tried to help, now and then pushing a soldier in the chest. On the left, immediately behind Paccoi, five or six carabinieri—set apart from the other soldiers as much for their silent and efficient devotion to duty as by their uniform badges—linked arms and formed a barricade. Over on the right were a stalwart veteran sergeant major, some junior officers, a captain, and various other noncoms, all trying to stop the uncontrolled dispersal of the unstoppable crowd down into the valley. Down in the valley bottom, the Germans continued marching, indifferent to the surrounding disorder.

"If you really want them to defend you, at least don't throw yourselves on top of them!" Ambrogio called out. Then, "Sh——, oh what sh——!" One soldier, his face almost in Ambrogio's, gestured to him, meaning that yes, he agreed, that it was shameful, really sh——ty behavior, that they should have to depend on the Germans. . . . Just the same, the soldier wasn't making the smallest effort to cooperate with the young officer in holding back the rest and didn't even try to hold himself back.

Things were getting out of hand when there came the sound of distant rifle fire. Even despite the general shouting, including his own, Ambrogio heard the shots quite clearly. Who was firing, and where from? But there wasn't time for questions. The distant shooting resumed, and now even the whistling of passing bullets could be heard, some very close. *It's the Russians!* he thought, terrified. Soldiers around him now became aware of the firing, and more than one man replied, opening fire with rifles without taking aim, since no enemy was visible. *Wretches!* thought Ambrogio. *But where are they firing from? Where are they hidden? Now it's even more important that we should stop this uncontrolled flight.* He shouted at the soldiers, opening his arms as a barrier against an increasingly nervous mass of fleeing soldiers; his cap fell in the snow and was lost, trampled underfoot. The shots and whistling bullets continued intermittently, some of the bullets coming too close. *Maybe only a few yards away? How come nobody has been wounded? Or maybe there are wounded, but in this mess, we haven't been able to see them?*

He saw one of the carabinieri fall backward into the snow; he wanted to check the extent of his injuries, but couldn't reach him because the crowd continued pushing ahead. Then from among the crowd came shouts of pain; no doubt the firing was taking casualties. "Down!" Ambrogio shouted. "Down on the ground! Get ready to open fire!"

Nobody paid any attention. The human tide pushed him backward, breaking the attempts at containment by the sergeant major, the carabinieri, and others. The crowd, pushed by the mass of men behind, lost control and started flowing down into the valley. "At this point, they've stopped being soldiers", the young man exclaimed, turning his head (covered by now with dirt) to his attendant. He turned the arm around and discovered an entry and an exit hole in the sleeve. He told Paccoi, "I've had a bullet go through my arm, but don't feel pain. How strange!"

Standing rigid before him, his orderly looked at him with distress; now they were surrounded by the fleeing multitude, which meant that at least they were protected from further bullets. Ambrogio looked at his chest but couldn't find any holes in his coat. Nevertheless, he felt under his undershirt a moist burning on his skin.

"Paccoi", he said.

"Tell me", replied the orderly, very tense.

"Help me unsling the rifle, slowly, without jerking."

"Right."

Moving slowly and deliberately, the rifle was unslung, but some movement caused a sharp burning feeling. Paccoi took Ambrogio's rifle and slung it on his own shoulder, next to his own.

"Did you put my first aid kits in my pack?"

"Yes. One set of them in yours and one in mine. In your pack there are also field bandages and those envelopes of white powder that were in the first aid box."

"Ah, the disinfectant, great. Let's go inside one of those houses."

He paused. It would be hard on Paccoi to have to go back some hundreds of yards, while everybody else was going in the other direction. "I think maybe I've been hit also in the chest; you understand why I ask you to come back with me? I want to see what's wrong and have you give me first aid. Then you can go; you needn't then stay with me." At these words, Paccoi blushed confused, like the simple farmer he was. Perhaps the lieutenant had read his mind? But it wasn't that straightforward. He had indeed felt like rebelling at the thought of having to go back, but had immediately thought that come what may he'd not behave like a pig, abandoning his officer right at the moment when he was wounded; that he'd never do.

Ambrogio looked at him doubtfully, concealing an incipient feeling of anguish.

"Don't worry, *sor tenente*, let's go", said Paccoi, in his Roman dialect. "Don't worry, let's go back to those houses, Lieutenant."

5

They went toward the houses, the orderly holding on to Ambrogio's elbow, ready to support him if necessary. Ambrogio felt strange being helped in this way; he would have preferred to avoid it but didn't want to offend Paccoi a second time. In any case he remained unaware of the extent of his injuries. As far as walking was concerned, however, he noted he could do so without difficulty and considered this to be a great piece of luck.

The soldiers going slowly in the other direction didn't hold them up. After a couple of steps they came upon the fallen carabinieri. He looked like a few scattered rags upon the snow. They had hit him in the head, the bullet going right through. Next to his bloody head lay his cap, with its distinctive flaming insignia. *A few inches higher*, thought Ambrogio, having his own wound in mind, *and I'd also now be lying in the snow.* Next to the dead man was a comrade in arms, standing and holding his rifle at the port; he looked disoriented, almost standing guard over the dead man.

"Is he dead?" asked Ambrogio.

"Yes, Lieutenant."

The young officer and his orderly both nodded; the carabinieri said no more.

They continued on toward the houses. *And to think that in Italy they make so many jokes about the carabinieri, about their loyalty and self-denial,* thought Ambrogio. *How mistaken they are!* Meanwhile the Russian rifle fire—probably from snipers—continued. Who would they wound next?

Before they reached the isbas, they heard a voice from behind them calling out in a fake official tone, "Hey, what are you doing there? I'm talking to you, Sublieutenant Riva!" They turned, surprised, to be faced with the lively figure of Bonsaver, who had six or seven artillerymen following him in single file, push through the retreating troops. Bonsaver had a pair of binoculars around his neck and carried his rifle horizontally on his back; his men were also armed. "Ah, it's you", he exclaimed.

"Well, look here, it's the 'distant hero'", Ambrogio greeted him. "Where the devil are you going?"

"We're going along over there, on patrol", answered Bonsaver. "But not reconnoitering this time. We're going to look for these S.O.B.s who are shooting at us. Orders from the major."

He seemed to be happy at having a definitive order to obey, his country face framed by the regulation balaclava.

With a sense of relief, Ambrogio thought, *At least here's someone who has remained a soldier and retained his manhood.* Bonsaver noticed something out of the ordinary in his friend's behavior, and in Paccoi's, too. "Hey, Riva, what's the matter?" he asked.

"What's the matter is that they've just given me a 'peck'", answered Ambrogio.

"You've been hit? You've been wounded? Where?"

"In the arm and . . .", he touched his chest with his left hand, "In the arm", he repeated. "And another I want to check now."

"Some shots, these Russians, eh?"

"Right."

"Do you want me to check this other wound? We'll go into one of these houses and ..."

"No", said Ambrogio. "I have help," indicating Paccoi with his chin, "and you have to carry out your orders; you haven't got time to waste."

"All right. As you wish", Bonsaver agreed, smiling encouragingly, and then became serious. "Listen, Riva, I don't know how much time I'll need. But when I return I'll come by here, by these houses. If I find you still here, we'll take up the march together. Agreed? I'm not saying you should wait for me, understood? You decide for yourself."

"That's good. I thank you."

"In that case, *ciao*."

Ambrogio saluted him with his right hand, not lifting it but only waving with his fingers.

"Well, imagine that it had to happen to you of all people", Bonsaver commented, then, turning to the men standing in line behind him, "Let's go, you men", he said.

Followed by the men, he cut obliquely through the river of retreating soldiers, heading northeast.

His patrol maintained single file through the virgin snow, heading toward a medium-sized elevation in the terrain, where they halted. Bonsaver raised the binoculars to his eyes and started methodically to examine the surrounding country, stopping and looking carefully at any feature or irregularity in the expanse of snow: the skill of scouting had been something at which he had become proficient, more proficient than at any other work. The intermittent shots by the enemy didn't stop, and he was able to establish that they came from the east. He asked his senior man, a sharp-faced corporal, to check his observation, and he confirmed the conclusion. They agreed that to get a better look in that direction, they would need to go some hundreds of yards farther on, to another hump in the middle distance. As they went toward it, they noticed another squad emerging from the retreating mass of men, heading out, also on patrol. "Ah, somebody else has woken up. Good work, I say."

6

In the meantime Ambrogio and the orderly had gone inside the nearest isba. They found it full of soldiers but not so crowded as to prevent their task of first aid. As in all Russian country houses, where a second, immovable window was put in place in winter, they breathed a strong unpleasant smell, made worse by the presence of so many people. There was, however, plenty of heat, an indescribably pleasant heat, coming from a stone-built stove. In front of this, slightly separated from the soldiers, was an old woman with her head covered by a black shawl, a young girl at her feet; neither she nor the child moved, like two sphinxes. Ambrogio greeted the women without receiving a reply (his gesture wasn't lost on Paccoi, who was pleased that his officer hadn't forgotten his manners) and went toward a box on the ground against a wall. He took off his shoulder bag, lifting the strap over his head and putting it on the ground near the box. Then, when Paccoi had put down the two rifles, and helped by the orderly, he began to remove his clothes. He took off the belt and pistol holster, the balaclava, the sheepskin coat, his jacket, a thick gray knit sweater, elegant and very unmilitary, which he had received from home; then the gray-green shirt and wool undershirt, both bloodstained. The wounds came into sight. His right biceps had been hit in the fleshy part, the bullet going straight through and carving a furrow some twelve inches long through the flesh of his chest. The entry and exit holes on his arm were very small and had bled little, as had the bullet's entry hole on his chest. Where the bullet had emerged, however, there was a red groove in the flesh, from that had come all the blood that stained his clothing.

"Look at that", said Ambrogio, "just how it felt. But by luck it's not a deep wound."

"No," Paccoi agreed, "it's not deep." Looking more closely at the wound, Paccoi made Ambrogio turn his chest toward the light from the window, so he could examine it carefully. "At most, where the flesh is thickest, it can't be more than two or three centimeters. The bullet can't have touched any bones . . . or anything." He meant to say no vital parts.

"It looks like you're right", agreed Ambrogio. He felt his bare right arm with his left hand, tracing the bone. "Here, too, it didn't touch the bone." Then he thought, *Right next to this bone there should be a vein or perhaps an important artery, and that's not been touched, either. In spite of everything, this has been a piece of luck.* With real relief, he said, "Paccoi, this has been the work of providence."

"Yes", agreed Paccoi with conviction. Immediately, however, they both remembered the long walk that awaited them in the deadly ice and snow; they saw in their mind's eye the limitless expanse of snow, in which after walking great distances, one felt the sensation of being always at the same spot; the days and nights of walking in that polar climate, enough to strike terror even in a healthy person. Even though much in control of his feelings Ambrogio felt the sensation of relief leaving him, to be replaced by the beginnings of doubt.

Paccoi noticed the change in Ambrogio's eyes and said, "Perhaps, who knows, Lieutenant, our own front line is really close."

This inappropriate remark was enough to make Ambrogio regain control of his feelings. *Don't give in*, he told himself firmly, *Never, while there's a breath of life left.* The effort of willpower caused his face to pale. He tried not to think about providence. *Let's not mix God up in our filthy butchery*, he told himself. (However, in his love for man, God continually intervenes in the world's miseries. Later, much later on, Ambrogio was to look back on this episode, putting it into perspective and regretting his former attitude. The principal reason he survived was because this wound had removed him from the massive retreat, preventing him from taking part in battles in which—given his habit of throwing himself wholeheartedly into situations—he would almost certainly have been killed.)

The unknown soldiers sheltering in the isba occasionally looked up at the officer and his orderly without speaking. Their relief at not having been similarly wounded was clear in their faces. Only two came closer: one character who seemed to be very sure of himself and a second, whose face seemed to show continuous fear, who closely followed the other, not leaving his side for an instant.

"By good luck, Lieutenant, the wounds aren't serious", the first one said compassionately.

The second man moved his lips as if to say something similar, but didn't speak.

"No, thank God, no; they're not serious", agreed Ambrogio, his face still pale; then, turning to Paccoi, "Come, take out one of those bandages. But first, one of those envelopes with disinfectant powder."

"Right away", replied Paccoi, opening a bag and taking out what he'd been ordered.

The Russian woman got up and wordlessly opened a little door on the stove, taking out a cooking pot of which the soldiers weren't aware. Followed by the little girl, who grabbed the old woman's skirt with both hands, she went over and put it on the wooden box, near Ambrogio's clothes and first aid kits.

Ambrogio and Paccoi saw that the pan held steaming hot water. The woman gestured at the water and to Ambrogio's wounds and said something in incomprehensible words. She responded to Ambrogio's tired smile and his thanks by saying something else, then returned to her seat. She took the child in her arms, after which both returned to their sphinxlike posture.

She looked as if she had turned to wood. *Of course, this poor woman is just waiting until all these disasters pass by: first our retreat, then the war, and then maybe communism itself. Communism as practiced by the village-level propagandists, who harry and worry the older villagers, particularly Christian old women full of kindness . . . in reality, her situation is unenviable.*

"Lieutenant, shall I wash the wounds with the water?" Paccoi asked him.

"Eh?" Ambrogio snapped back to reality. "No, I don't believe it is sterile. Use the water to wash your hands; it must be two days since we've had clean hands. Then you can bandage me, but first sprinkle the powder on the open flesh . . . come, wash your hands."

Paccoi looked around, his round face clearly seeking the means to do so. The sure-of-himself soldier picked up the pan of water in both hands, pointing with his chin at a nearby bucket, and said, "Come over here." He went with Paccoi, who held out his hands over the bucket and scrubbed them together while the soldier poured hot water over them. The man's companion, the soldier with the fearful face, followed them and stood off to one side, not close enough to bother them.

Outside the isba the noise of firing seemed to be increasing considerably. *I wonder if our people have discovered the place from which the Russians were firing and are now firing on them*, Ambrogio asked himself. But it was hardly the moment to be thinking of other problems. *It's just one thing after another.*

Paccoi held his wet hands up and shook them to dry, but after seeing this would take too long, he carefully put the fingers of his right hand in his overcoat pocket, taking out a not exactly clean handkerchief on which he finished drying his hands. Ambrogio watched him in silence, and when he was finished said, "Now the powder."

Paccoi tore one corner off the envelope and generously covered the four wounds with the powder. Then he spread the powder evenly with a clean bandage taken from the field dressing packet. Then, at Ambrogio's suggestion, he covered the holes that did not bleed with sticking plaster and the bleeding chest wound with a sterile dressing, attaching it with more sticking plaster. Then he wrapped all the bandaged parts with gauze bandaging.

The firing outside, after varying in intensity, seemed to reduce in sound, then became intermittent.

"I thank you", Ambrogio said to Paccoi, and, "Right, let's get these clothes back on."

Getting dressed, even doing so cautiously, didn't take long. When Ambrogio was about to sling his pack on his shoulder, Paccoi suggested, "Perhaps it's better if you don't carry that; the strap will press on your chest wound."

"You're right", agreed Ambrogio.

Paccoi patiently transferred the more useful items from the officer's bag to his own.

"I can't carry the rifle either", said Ambrogio. "Wait a moment", he added and, going to an internal door, called to a sergeant he'd seen in the next room. The sergeant was sitting on the floor leaning against a wall, surrounded by sitting and sleeping soldiers. He got to his feet reluctantly, his face sullen; clearly he didn't want to have any problems.

"Here, take this", said Ambrogio, holding out the rifle and shoulder bag in his left hand. "They could be useful to someone who has lost his equipment. In the bag there are some hand grenades."

"Yes, right", said the sergeant dubiously, taking the rifle and bag from the officer.

Will he just throw them in a corner? Ambrogio asked himself. He momentarily felt like checking on it, but *I don't have the strength now to waste on these things*, he said to himself. He was beginning to realize the limitations the wounds would impose on him. Paccoi had put on his own pack and picked up his rifle. They were ready to leave. "Wait", said the officer. He went to the nearest window and stared out. "It's the same as before", he said. "What about if we stay here for a bit, say, ten minutes more, here in the warmth? For sure we'll only find our people when the column makes its next rest stop. On the other hand, Bonsaver could arrive, don't you think?"

He seemed to see a shadow of disapproval in the orderly's eyes.

"Are you still decided to stay on with me?" he asked. "Look, don't think you're obligated to stay on."

Paccoi stood straight and with dignity said, "That is something you don't have to repeat. Is that all right with you, Lieutenant? I know what my duty is."

"So I see", replied Ambrogio.

They sat down next to each other on the box, in silence. A small rest in the warmth, after all . . . were it not for the danger of the situation and their worry over the wounds they would probably have slept, not having rested for the past two nights.

Outside, the shooting continued intermittently. Some soldiers had left the isba; others—complete strangers—had come in, among them one who spoke excitedly about mortar fire, saying, "The worst is not being able to give return fire . . . to have just to bear up under fire and not react . . ."

Ambrogio cocked his ear to the noise outside. Maybe what he was hearing now wasn't rifle fire. Perhaps he could now hear mortars. "Enemy mortars?" After a while he looked at Paccoi. "Eh, Paccoi, perhaps we'd better check what's happening outside." Paccoi nodded, agreeing. "Right, let's go."

They went outside, into the pitiless cold that surrounded and seemed to bite at them. After having gone a few paces, the young officer remembered that he had not taken his leave of the Russian woman who had given him the water to dress his wounds. He felt bad, but *we can't go back now*, he decided.

7

The rifle fire had stopped completely; now there was fire from a Russian mortar, only one. The mortar rounds hit with a constant cadence at a point in the valley where two streams of soldiers merged. From Ambrogio's vantage point he could clearly see the blackish smoke puffs of the exploding missiles.

"What a sight!" he murmured. "But where could Bonsaver be? Maybe he's gone to look for that mortar?"

No, here was his squad coming back now. Was it really his patrol? Yes, Ambrogio recognized the leading man, the sharp-faced corporal, who didn't at first seem to recognize Paccoi and his officer; then he gestured at them with one hand. What could he want? When he realized he'd been seen and recognized, the corporal stopped and exchanged some words with his men, who gathered around him. He pointed toward a nearby isba (not the one Ambrogio and Paccoi had left), apparently indicating it as shelter for his squad. Ambrogio noticed the corporal now wore the binoculars around his neck; a growing concern took hold of him. What did it mean? And, above all, where was Bonsaver? Maybe those binoculars . . . ?

Together with Paccoi, he went toward the small group, some of whom were already shuffling through the snow to the isba; the corporal and another artilleryman came toward Ambrogio excitedly.

"Lieutenant", said the corporal from a few paces away; he looked as if he wanted to start giving important news but didn't know where to start. "Lieutenant Bonsaver . . . he was your friend, right, is that right?"

"Was, but . . . what are you saying? He died?"

"Yes, he's dead. He and Verdi are dead", said the artilleryman. Instinctively, Ambrogio's mouth opened to reply, but he didn't get one word out.

"Oh!" said Paccoi, dumbfounded.

For a moment the four of them kept silent.

"It was our own people, those f——ing pigs, rotten, disgusting . . .", said the corporal. "As soon as the mortar started to fire, that bunch of turds opened fire on us. You understand?"

Ambrogio looked at him, speechless.

"You can even see them from here", said the corporal. "Look!" He took a few paces to one side to get a line of sight and pointed, his arm extended. "You see those two objects on the snow, nearly touching each other? One, the one on the right is Lieutenant Bonsaver."

"The one on the left is Verdi", said the artilleryman (he wore light blue ski gloves with a geometric pattern and gestured, showing their strange nonmilitary color). "You remember Verdi? The one with a freckled face from Emilia?"

"The one with a freckled face? Yes", replied Ambrogio, in a low voice, and then forcing himself to speak in a more normal tone, said, "Yes, I remember him."

"He was my friend", said the soldier. "A great guy, very good."

Ambrogio thought about Bonsaver, his lively gestures of just over a half hour ago, when he found out that he, Ambrogio, had been wounded. For an instant, there came into his mind the charnel-house Redipuglia, when they'd seen it together from the train on the day they'd left Italy, and he thought of the unspoken question: Which one of us will end up like them? Well, to start with, Bonsaver. He had remained, wouldn't return to see Italy, ever again. Neither Italy, nor that girl who had sent him the Sholokov book, and . . .

The corporal was explaining how this terrible thing had happened.

"It was our people, those stupid f——ing pigs", he repeated, pointing toward the moving column. "Not necessarily these now, but the people who were here. They'll now be in the valley, all of them. At a certain moment they started shooting at us without any reason, understand?"

"I heard the shots while we were in the isba", said Ambrogio.

"Yes", added Paccoi.

"That was when the Russian mortar started", the ski-gloved artilleryman repeated. "I also noticed that, it was then."

"It was as if they'd lost their heads, you know? Suddenly", said the corporal. "Then it took time for them to come to their senses, mad, filthy carrion. And what connection could there possibly have been between a Russian mortar and our patrol?"

It became clear that what had happened was that when the first Russian mortar rounds landed (which didn't fall, as they later did, in the valley, but among the soldiers on the plateau), there had been an outbreak of panic. Running without direction here and there, many soldiers started looking around. Looking for the invisible enemy that was sending death among them, several fired blindly at the surrounding heights. Starting with these few shots there developed a fusillade, which soon became concentrated—at least partially—on the few Italian squads out on patrol. A few soldiers who to this point weren't aware of the presence of these patrols started calling attention to them, pointing them out to others within earshot. Others, aware that the patrols were Italian, but seeing them being pointed out as enemy targets, began to doubt their information, and soon the small distant silhouettes took on a suspicious look. Perhaps they were the enemy, and—surprised that they hadn't noticed their enemy, their executioners, just there, within rifle range—they started firing furiously, trying to make up for lost time. The great majority, evidently, hadn't lost their heads to this extent, and many soldiers as well as noncoms and officers attempted to stop this madness, in some cases having to push or kick the more stubborn before they stopped firing. The firing only stopped altogether after the mortar changed targets, to start bombarding the moving column down in the valley.

"Lieutenant Bonsaver and Verdi were hit almost immediately, by the first shots. If there hadn't been a sort of ditch near us in the snow, we'd have all ended up dead", explained the corporal.

"One of our men, Tenconi, even though down in the ditch, got hit by a glancing shot, in the backside. What barbaric . . . what crappy soldiers!"

"Yes," said Ambrogio, "it's the right word exactly: crappy soldiers. There you were out there to help them, and they fired on you. They couldn't even just let themselves be helped. More than crap!" He paused. "Bonsaver, dead!"

The corporal nodded repeatedly. Then, with some difficulty because of his cumbersome clothing, he put a hand inside his jacket and pulled out a billfold. "I also came over here to see you for this. It's Lieutenant Bonsaver's billfold", he said to Ambrogio. "At first I intended to take it to our own command, but afterward I thought that it would be better if his mother received it from a friend, like yourself, instead of . . . well, via the bureaucracy."

"Yes," said Ambrogio, "you've done well."

He accepted the billfold, opened it clumsily with his gloved hands, then closed it and put it in one of his pockets.

"The binoculars", the corporal said, touching them. "I'll take them back to group."

Ambrogio nodded agreement. He looked again up at the two distant bundles in the snow. My God, poor Bonsaver! A doubt entered his mind. "Are you sure they're dead? I mean, are they both definitely dead? Were you able to check, being under fire like that?"

The corporal, although a little offended, smiled. "What should we have checked? There was nothing to check. Lieutenant Bonsaver has half his head torn from his neck." He pointed to a spot at the nape of his neck. "A hole torn here you could put half your hand in. And as far as Verdi . . . and on top of that, both of them received several bullets, even after they'd died." He shook his head; the artilleryman in blue ski gloves also shook his head negatively. "Have no doubts, my lieutenant", said the corporal. "There isn't the slightest doubt about their both being dead."

"It's not that I doubt you. I just had to be sure." He paused. "Poor Bonsaver", murmured Ambrogio.

"He was always good to us", said the artilleryman. "He always treated us soldiers well."

"We'd gone out to unearth the Russians," said the corporal, "and those swine fired on us. Now, let them go looking for Russians. I'm not exposing myself any more, I assure you, for nothing in the world. I'm through."

Ambrogio asked about some other details, then asked them to repeat their names. "For Bonsaver's relatives, if by any chance they want to talk to someone who witnessed his death."

Finally the two soldiers, who seemed in a hurry to join their comrades inside the isba ("They've gone there so they can bandage poor Tenconi, the one shot in the ass"), took their leave and went. Throwing one more look at the two bundles up in the snow (Could it be possible that when spring arrived Bonsaver's body would remain there, rotting in the grass?), Ambrogio and Paccoi joined the walking men (there were no longer many vehicles in the column), who flowed downward, from the village to the valley floor.

8

Other streams of men, both ahead of them and behind, continued emerging from Posnyakoff, joining up when they reached the main flow of retreating soldiers down in the valley bottom.

The Russian mortar continued dropping missiles into one of the points of confluence. It maintained a regular cadence of about one shot every half minute. Ambrogio bitterly thought, *Really, why should they hurry and fire more frequently?*

They can fire like this, without overheating the tube. The dry snapping noise of the launch, although weak, could be heard, then the whistle of the mortar round and the explosion, which lifted a black cloud of smoke among the walking men. For the men on the receiving end it must have been terrifying. The mortar was probably an 80 mm caliber, which meant a killing reach of shrapnel for three or four yards around the point of impact. There were many men lying on the beaten earth of the track; many more had to continue walking after being wounded, slivers of metal buried in their flesh, and some still managed to keep walking although suffering from serious lacerations. Despite this, the column didn't even pause on reaching the bombed area. Due to the slow cadence of the explosions, it was possible, soon after the last shell landed, to pass unhurt. Those coming along behind would accelerate their pace, and those even farther behind, instead of detouring off to the snowy sides of the path, would hesitate or wait nervously, some of them holding back and others running forward; thus there were always new targets of men on the spot when the next round landed. Ambrogio and Paccoi went down the hill with this continuing tragic sight before them. They stayed on the track like all the others, while Ambrogio repeated to himself, *We'll be better off leaving the track; to stay on it would be madness.* Meanwhile, they continued approaching the impact zone. The young second lieutenant kept glancing sideways at the bordering snow. It was fairly deep, coming to just over a walker's knee. Walking in the snow would have been fatiguing, and with his wounds to handicap his movement, he couldn't decide to get off the track. Fortunately, some of the people ahead of Ambrogio decidedly set out to leave the track. They were some sixty or seventy yards away from the area of impact, and they intended to circle around the right of it. Bit by bit some of the column followed them, then others moved, including Ambrogio and Paccoi. They left the path to follow the irregular detour, the going made difficult by the powdery snow underfoot. Looking back, the young lieutenant was able to see the entire column, including the few vehicles, abandoning the path to enter the detour. What would the mortar crew do now? Many of the marching men asked themselves the question as they watched the mortars continue striking the same spot on or near the track where the dead men lay, adding to the dirty holes dug in the snow by previous bursts. All around, the wounded were trying to scramble or crawl away, some dragging themselves, others continually getting up and falling back down in the bloodied snow. One poor man stumbled toward the river of men in the detour, his arm held out entreatingly, and he was saying unintelligible phrases. Nobody went to help him; they all thought only of themselves, wanting to flee the area of explosions as quickly as possible, wondering if the mortar would be recalibrated before they got past the new detour. The wounded man eventually fell to his knees in the snow a few yards from the marching men and stayed there, one hand on the ground to support himself and the other held out toward his fleeing comrades. Having passed the impact zone, the column swerved back on to the principal path. A small number of men still were using the part of the road under bombardment, and some minutes later the mortar was adjusted to strike the path some hundred yards behind. Ambrogio and Paccoi for a long time continued hearing the mortar explosions, but these faded away to be drowned out by the other, louder strikes, but no one in the column had an explanation regarding these. Perhaps the Russians were attacking the village? Was a new battle starting? But between what forces? Could there still be people among the Italian units ready to enter combat? Eventually, after going around the curved walls of the valley while still descending to its floor, no other sound reached Ambrogio and Paccoi except the incessant squeaky noise of boots in the snow.

9

Slowly the column stretched out, with the strong going on ahead and the weak, the wounded, the frozen losing ground and steadily falling behind. Among these were Ambrogio and Paccoi, who continued walking together. Many, individuals and groups, would pass them by without a word, walking vigorously. Every now and then a truck would go by, overloaded with men. From the back of one of these trucks a junior officer shouted, "Back there in Posnyakoff, the Russians are attacking with tanks and infantry! It's a slaughter!"

After they emerged from the valley, the road continued climbing and dropping. It passed through some miserable villages and then emerged onto a flat deserted prairie that looked endless. As much as they walked, they felt that they were marking time in the same spot. The prairie stretched out indefinitely on both sides of the road, dotted here and there by abandoned agricultural vehicles. In the distance, part of the horizon was concealed by banks of mist. The white snow was glacial, blinding, relieved only occasionally by a patch of dried-out crops, sometimes by sunflower stalks bent and crumpled by the snow, rattling with a sound of dry bones in sudden gusts of Arctic winds.

The hours began to accumulate. Ambrogio's thoughts were fixed: *Will the tanks also come to attack us? And how much time can I bear this anyway?* Walking like this, without making abrupt movements, his wounds didn't bother him too much; there was only a continuous burning from his chest. But for how long would this go on? Nobody spoke any more about friendly front lines, whether nearby or far away. Finally the landscape changed again. The terrain started to show humps, the road going up and then down in smooth undulations, tiring and time consuming to climb, and the nature of the countryside continued to change as they went forward. Just after noon one day, Ambrogio and Paccoi, walking slowly but not stopping, noticed an occasional Italian truck, abandoned along the way; they had come this far, loaded with wounded and frostbitten men. Many of these soldiers, having tried to continue on foot, lay here and there on the road, looking on with desperation as their still-healthy countrymen went by. Paccoi wondered if there were still wounded left in the trucks. To check on this, he hoisted himself up into the rear of a Fiat 626 and looked around inside. There were wounded men lying there, and they started to call to him, entreating him not to leave them there. One of the wounded men, lying among those nearest him, was silent. Dumbly, he just looked at Paccoi, the look in his eyes despairing, showing an indescribable hopelessness.

He jumped back down and said, "It's . . . it's appalling. Inside there it's like . . . a tomb, but in which the people haven't yet died. What a sight, my God! I couldn't look anymore."

Ambrogio felt his flesh creep. It was evident that anyone not able to walk was destined to suffer a sure and horrible end. *My God, it's savage!* he thought.

A very long upward slope, and some sleighs couldn't continue. The horses and mules, unfed and pulling for days, couldn't go one step farther, floundering in the snow. Breathing painfully, their bony ice-covered flanks pumping in and out, they stamped their hooves fitfully, without making any forward movement. The dying mules in their agony appeared to be defending themselves from the men's blows and their impossible demands, and reacted by attempting a weak kicking that served only to make them lose their balance. The horses, in contrast, showed a willingness and dedication that were hard to comprehend. Even though falling repeatedly, they continued in a noble effort to go on pulling ahead, as if understanding the meaning of their drivers' anguished voices, the importance of the wretched and mute cargo of wounded men. The farmer in Paccoi led him to observe the animals' behavior, which he watched with a sort of professional interest. *My God, what great-hearted creatures these horses are!* he thought. Ambrogio then tried to pull Paccoi away. It was as if he felt shamed at the condition these poor animals had been reduced to by man.

In the slow uphill effort, they started overtaking some isolated squads of slow-walking Germans. *These people are part of the detachments that suffered the most back on the Don,* thought Ambrogio. *Perhaps they were the ones defending our right flank in those final days in the snow. Who knows what they have suffered?*

Paccoi, on the other hand, uttered such phrases as "Tiredness for one is the same as tiredness for all, eh, Lieutenant?" almost with a kind of satisfaction, but not with any malice. It was just that this semblance of reshuffling suited him, nothing more.

Many of the unwounded Italians began to slow down, too, reducing the rhythm of march and gradually causing a crowding on the road. As they continued walking, they saw completely exhausted men falling into the snow, sitting or kneeling.

Nightfall came with an air of menace. The road continued to climb and entered a great forest of icy, skeletal trees. Soon after, Italian soldiers in various parts of the column began firing into the trees (without bothering to take aim, as there was nobody to aim at), despite shouts and orders from the few officers and noncoms still interested enough to bother. Among them was Ambrogio, who muttered to Paccoi, "It was behavior like this that killed Bonsaver. Damn the bastards!"

Right behind Ambrogio, a lone German officer walking among the Italians began shouting disdainfully, "*Schweine! Schweine!*" then in French, "*Porcs! Porcs!*" He turned to Ambrogio, who gave signs of understanding French, and said, "In the forest there is nobody, absolutely not a person. Why are they shooting, then? Do you call these soldiers . . . ?"

Ambrogio made no reply; what could one say?

"Do you want to attract the enemy?" the German continued berating them. "Or perhaps you're firing because you have too much ammunition? Eh? A surplus, right?"

To Ambrogio it was hard to have to recognize that the German was right. He felt like saying, "Instead of shouting now, you should have provided us with gasoline when we needed it." But the shortage of fuel wasn't justification for that nonsensical shooting. No, it was easy to enter into polemics, a spineless solution; there was unfortunately no justification for this shooting. He continued walking, in silence. *Was this the way his countrymen really were?* he thought. How much work, how much effort, to teach discipline to the men, to build an army. Even he had contributed, had done his part, however small. *And all it took was three days, no, two days of retreating to reduce them to this state. How defeatist our people can be!*

The German now walked alongside Ambrogio and continued his harangue, even gesturing pedantically, professorially. He had crooked teeth, a bit of a paunch. His pear-shaped body separated him from the usual militarily upright Germans. Ambrogio thought he might be a captain. *He must be a schoolteacher; he has all the mannerisms.* Mentally addressing the man, he thought, *Well, don't you think you've said enough? No? Well, continue, get it out of your system.* Then he thought again and considered that the German might even be showing a certain regard for the Italians. He at least thought them important enough to merit some shouted advice. *While other Germans, by not talking, probably are showing their absolute disdain for us, probably think us to be irreparably inferior. And the sad truth is that by this shooting, and our inability to reestablish a minimum of discipline, we prove to them that they're right . . . but how did we get to this state, my God?*

Once the firing died out, the German stopped his litany; he walked in silence, bad tempered, like a teacher after scolding a pupil. In the silence, Ambrogio reflected again on the nature of his people, distracted only minimally by the continuous burning feeling from the wound in his chest. *The fact is that we're even undisciplined in civil life, that's the thing . . .* He recalled the increasing noise and disorder in the streets and everywhere, the hubbub and uproar just to get on a train, the confusion generated by the simple buying of a movie ticket. Added to this, the joy with which Italians flout old forms of authority (except maybe, to tell the truth, family discipline, which nobody argues with), and the satisfaction, almost a point of honor, in cheating the government revenue service out of taxes. *You can't expect the mere fact of putting on a uniform to convert a people like that into disciplined beings. Just look at this, now . . .* Beginning to feel discouraged, he thought, *And what would happen if for any reason things began to go truly wrong in civilian life? Maybe everyday life could fall apart into a chaotic situation, like this one right here.*

It wasn't the best time for profound reflections about life, so he tried to raise his spirits by thinking about Nomana. There, after all, people weren't undisciplined, they really weren't (*I wonder if that's why we didn't feel the need for fascism?*), and there was a community feeling—and how! It was not for nothing that it marked the beginning of Alpine country, where our best troops come from. Unexpectedly, one of the soldiers walking ahead of Ambrogio (he couldn't have understood one word of the German's harangue) unslung his rifle, pointed it into the forest, and fired.

The German shouted out, "*Schwein!*" and once more launched into a stream of criticism.

"Wretch!" shouted Ambrogio. "Hey, I'm talking to you, you wretch! Why did you fire?" He ran up to the man, followed by Paccoi. "Ah, that burns", he moaned to himself at the chest pain. The soldier, having prepared his rifle to fire again, turned to the advancing Ambrogio, mouth open. About ten paces to the rear another soldier also fired off a shot, then another farther to the rear; the shots provoked a renewal of panicked firing.

Reaching the soldier's side, Ambrogio shouted, "What have you done, wretch? Why did you fire?"

The soldier's lips moved, but he didn't speak. "Why did you fire?" Ambrogio asked again with growing anger. "Come on, explain yourself. Why did you shoot?"

"The Russians", murmured the man.

"Where, what Russians? Are they in the woods?"

The soldier didn't answer.

"Where did you see Russians, in the trees? Answer me!"

"No", murmured the soldier, quickly slinging his rifle on his shoulder. He increased his pace, soon getting lost among the men ahead. Ambrogio couldn't follow.

10

As time passed, the number of men who couldn't go on increased. More frequently, men would fall, collapsing in the snow, to be seen vaguely in the darkness, evidently unable to take another step. Few spoke. Sometimes one would ask his companions for help in a weakened voice. Ambrogio had become feverish; he felt hot and cold shivers and though eating quantities of snow couldn't get rid of his thirst. What was worse was that he himself noticed a numbness, a sort of muddling, as if losing his reason.

He felt a pulling at his overcoat. One of the men, falling to one side, had in stumbling grabbed Ambrogio's coat pocket. The young officer didn't have the heart to shake him off; he leaned over the man, joined by Paccoi, who had been holding him by the arm.

"Why are you all leaving me?" whispered the fallen man. "Give me a hand. Don't leave me here to die."

"We can't help", answered Ambrogio with pity and shame, "because I've been wounded."

"And what about my mother?" he murmured weakly. "Don't you have a mother yourself?"

Paccoi released his grip on Ambrogio's arm and bent over the man. Without a word he helped the man to his feet, putting the soldier's arm around his neck and holding him around the waist. The man hung suspended, trying to walk, but he couldn't make use of his legs. "He's already lost any sensation in his feet. They're frozen", they noted with horror. Paccoi dragged the man some twenty yards, laboring with great effort. Ambrogio, following silently behind, saw his orderly stumble more than once. Finally Paccoi stopped and lowered the man to the snow bordering the road; he straightened up, panting for breath.

"Why are you leaving me?" the man said, weakly. "The friendly lines are very close. I beg of you."

"Right," said Paccoi, panting, "they're close. So listen, as soon as we get there, I'll get hold of a sleigh, a cart, or something and come back to fetch you. You understand?"

"The lines are close. It just needs a little more effort!" pleaded the soldier.

"Come on", Ambrogio told Paccoi and, in a low tone, "We can do nothing for him. Let's go."

With his usual bemused expression, the farmer-turned-artilleryman obeyed.

As night advanced the cold attacked them pitilessly. On their balaclavas the ice built up, and the air they breathed into their lungs was so cold it burned. Increasingly tired legs made everyone crave a rest, even a brief one. In contradiction the brain (itself confused by the cold) advised that to stop meant giving up the battle to the cold. Even for those who thought they knew the limits of their endurance (and few did: the strength and resources of the human body are surprisingly deep), the prospect was frightening. It was better not to think, not reflect; just to keep going, to the end: that was important.

From the distant head of the column came the muffled sound of firing. At first these were the sounds of rifles and machine guns, but later cannon fire could be heard. *What a moment to start a battle*, thought a half-conscious Ambrogio. The men around him listened carefully. The shooting seemed on the point of dying out, but revived, then dropped off and stopped, only to start again and become continuous. The use of cannons made everyone realize that this was a skirmish that had been thought out and not senseless firing, as before. The column gradually slowed down, with the men from behind continuing to press forward, causing the column to overflow the road on both sides. The cold seemed to get worse, attacking savagely. Each man tried to pull his head down, shrinking down to maintain body heat. The column stopped and started; men collided with each other. It was impossible to tell how long this interrupted progress continued, and eventually the terrain changed, and besides ravines and alleys, there were isbas . . . a village maybe? The shooting continued.

Over there, to one side, tracers split the darkness. Other incendiary ammunition crisscrossed the sky: Germans and Russians, for sure, as Italians hadn't been issued this nighttime ammunition. A great German tank was parked at the roadside, and ahead of it another, which fired its cannon. The muzzle flame, about ten yards long, lightened up the smoke and made dots of light dance in the eyes of those who were facing it.

Another interminable holdup. Rumors flew; they would have to cross a village occupied by the Russians, who occupied the surrounding heights. The Russians were many; no, they were few, and it would be possible to go through their line; they couldn't go back—back to where? They had to go forward or accept that this was the end.

The column was stopped. Ambrogio saw German detachments, formed up, off the road. A bit farther ahead, also off the road, were Italian soldiers belonging to the M battalions, which like the Germans gave signs of preparing for combat.

What shame for us in the army, who have always been contemptuous of the M battalions and made jokes about them, now to see them doing our fighting for us. Of course, these troops weren't just any blackshirts; if they'd been selected and trained for the M battalions they were special. But the feeling of failure persisted . . . what was it that persisted? Ah, yes, the humiliation . . . what humiliation? Yes, the . . . let me see . . . Ambrogio's thought processes were now confused; every now and then his mind refused to retain clarity of thought, couldn't remember things. The column remained immobile. So were the men out on either side, where the engorged column had pushed them. Halted also were the ordered detachments. Would there be fighting or not? Ambrogio tried to think of nothing, occasionally stamping his feet on the road's compacted snow to prevent frostbite. Paccoi stationed himself purposely at his right side to prevent anyone colliding with his chief's wounded arm; even he kept his head down against the cold. Some yards away, a voice from within the crowd repeatedly said, "The soup, the hot soup, the soup . . .", and asked, "Give me some hot soup."

"What soup? Armando, stop talking nonsense", another voice would say, doubtless a friend.

"The hot soup . . ."

Coming out of his reverie, Ambrogio noticed that Paccoi was pushing him toward a burning isba. "There, Lieutenant, there; let's get near the heat, there are fewer people."

Other isbas were also on fire. The column seemed now to have lost any organized shape, having dissolved into clusters of unmoving soldiers. Some wandered among the hovels of this unidentified village. The two of them reached the burning house, even finding a seat on a tree trunk projecting from the snow.

Heat! At last! What a marvelous sensation, heat. More necessary than any other condition. The smoke from the houses carried a familiar smell (the nearest peacetime equivalent was the smell of burning rags). *I wonder where the peasants of this village went?* Ambrogio asked himself, warming himself in the reflected heat. *The poor wretches who lived in this isba, for example? The women, the children . . . who knows if they escaped in good time or only at the last minute? Where to?*

The flames warmed them, but also scorched. It was essential they keep turning around, for the flames warmed one side of their bodies, while the other side remained icy. It was like a new torture. Many of the men had gathered around the heat thrown out by the house; they formed a ring, each one of them trying to warm himself, sitting if possible, but the majority standing, without talking. Only the flames broke the silence, popping and crackling, then a dull thud as a beam fell down inside, throwing out a cloud of sparks rising in the hot air. Suddenly, a stone's throw away, a machine gun opened up, firing wildly. Was it ours or theirs? Nobody seemed to want to know. Soon it stopped.

Weary from the enormous tiredness and fever, Ambrogio had his eyes closed. As time passed he entered a kind of unconscious state that gave him some sort of rest; sitting at his side Paccoi fell into a deep sleep. Neither noticed a man who approached the various groups of men, asking them questions. Every now and then he would lift his voice in a shout. "Major Casasco! . . . Major Casasco . . . Casasco, answer me!" It was their artillery adjutant, Tired Horse, who came to their group in front of the burning house and asked about his major, but nobody answered. He went on to another group of soldiers, farther away; occasionally he called out his major's name. Neither Ambrogio nor Paccoi saw or heard him: they would never see him again.

11

The two woke at first light. They were no longer near the fire—the house had burned out hours ago—and found themselves under a lean-to roofed with reeds, lying among a group of strangers. Soon Ambrogio became aware of the serious situation they were in: trapped, his wounds, the collapse of their army

. . . The young officer suddenly remembered the death of his friend Bonsaver and felt a bitter pain. He couldn't remember coming to this spot from the ashes of the isba. He could remember wandering in the dark and intense cold, leaning on Paccoi's ever-ready arm, and how they had had to halt periodically to stamp their feet in the snow.

They knew that if they remained under the lean-to unmoving they would run the risk of freezing, so they stood and started walking. Although there was little light, they realized that they were in a country village with well-separated isbas and soon found out its name: Arbusov (Watermelon). The village was set in a shallow round valley, with a main road running through it. This was covered in compacted snow, and they assumed it was the road by which they had arrived. Lines and small groups of soldiers continued to arrive on the road.

But where was the enemy? Soon the Russians were spotted; they occupied the heights of the valley to the east, south, and west, surrounding the village, and perhaps they even held a part of the village over to the east. As soon as there was enough light the Russians started firing on the halted column, which was concentrated in and around Arbusov. They were using handheld firearms, inefficient at that distance, but also used mortar fire and occasionally a cannon shot, frightening in destructive power. The Germans, who had reestablished a vestige of a defensive line to the south and the east, answered the Russians' fire with cannon shells, but these were unaimed, because all the enemy's heavy guns were down over the brow of the valley rim and couldn't be located. Clearly the situation was untenable; they had to move, but why were they waiting to leave?

The rumors started flying, as usual: a German armored column was expected; no, they were waiting for planes to drop supplies of gasoline (which would in any case be dropped for the Germans, not for the Italians); no, perhaps they were waiting for the upper echelon to advise by radio of an escape route empty of enemy forces. Meantime, there was hardly a shot from the Russian heavy guns that didn't claim casualties. When an incoming cannon or mortar shell was heard whistling, the area soldiers all would throw themselves on the ground, picking themselves up later to flee, leaving dead comrades lying in the snow next to smoldering black craters.

"It's a lucky thing", explained Ambrogio to Paccoi, after having attentively observed the action, "that the Russians, at least right now, aren't here in strength and don't have many heavy guns in place. I think it's time we started to look for our group."

There was also the fact that remaining still was awful in the terrible cold. Ambrogio and Paccoi started walking in circles one alongside each other, covering the spaces between the houses and the beaten snow surrounding them, sometimes walking through still groups of men or alongside individuals wandering vaguely, looking for who knew what. "I have to get the squad together again, whatever I do", said Ambrogio.

"Yes, right, but we need to find something to eat", Paccoi suggested, and in order to keep the talk light despite everything, he repeated a benevolent saying in dialect from Umbria that Ambrogio had already heard from him before: "May the Lord lead us to where people are eating well."

They wandered in desultory fashion for hours and more than once tried to enter into an isba, but they were all crowded with Germans, who stopped the Italians from going in, shouting at them (that they were doing all the fighting and therefore needed to get rest under comfortable conditions, it was only right). But for the Italians there was no other option but to be part of a shapeless disorderly multitude. As the enemy bombardment continued taking lives, the two decided to join some other men who were going to leave the village and took shelter with them in some shallow folds in the ground, intending to sit in the snow and rest. Some of these hollows were sought out by several Italian trucks loaded with wounded and frostbitten men, but Russian shells started falling nearby, and the trucks left, being in danger of getting stuck in the deep snow as they departed. Paccoi commented, "If these people keep this up, they'll use up the little fuel that's left."

"And the trouble is, our drivers and chief cannoneers have forgotten what to do", murmured Ambrogio.

As time passed, the situation became more serious. Ambrogio felt an increasing need to rest, which was not possible out in the open air at ten degrees below freezing. However, he also persisted in wanting to reunite his artillery group. He met some officers and soldiers who had been left without resources and learned from them that the artillery group had fallen apart like so many other detachments. Around noon, they found two members of Ambrogio's patrol, Mazzoleni and Piantanida, who joined them willingly, but even though they wandered about together looking for others of the battery, they couldn't find any. Before it became dark, the enemy bombardment became heavier as they received reinforcements of heavy artillery. The great part of the Italians—at least twenty thousand men—was concentrated in the small area of the village and its environs, and all of them, in the expectation of leaving, did nothing to defend themselves. The Russian cannon and mortar shots now fell with increasing frequency among this multitude, cutting them down as if, rather than men, they were reeds or grass.

Ambrogio and his small group were forced to throw themselves on the ground when the bursts fell nearby. On two occasions they found themselves within the compass of shellbursts, but were able to get up unhurt while around them others lay still or threw themselves on the ground like madmen, wounded and crying out for help.

After one of these close calls, Ambrogio and Paccoi once more found themselves alone, without Mazzoleni or Piantanida. Ambrogio decided to stop looking for his men. He didn't feel physically fit, and the wound-induced fear had worsened after he was caught by the blast of the explosions. To Paccoi's increasing concern, Ambrogio was more and more exhausted, to the point where the orderly asked himself, *If he can't walk any farther, what will I do?* and looked at the men around him, deciding fearfully that not one of them would come to his help.

He recalled a trapdoor he had seen that morning, near a burned-out isba on the edge of the village. Like many soldiers, he was aware that many civilians hid in these shelters when war came their way. Who knew if the trapdoor he'd seen led to one of these refuges? Other Italian soldiers hadn't concerned themselves with these shelters, probably because they were difficult to find; or because they were afraid that if they found one and went inside they'd become separated from the column. He, in contrast, asked himself if in case of real necessity he couldn't leave his officer safe in a shelter for a few hours.

Time went by, and the column showed no sign of returning to movement. As Ambrogio's condition worsened, Paccoi's thoughts returned to that trapdoor as to a magnet until he set off with his officer, doubting his earlier belief that there would be a shelter, but finding it again, a few yards from the isba. The area seemed deserted; after looking around to see if he was being watched, Paccoi used his foot to scrape snow off the trapdoor and lifted it up. Taking out a layer of straw, he then removed some boards underneath, revealing the top rung of a ladder; he put a foot on the ladder and started down. An unbearable small of packed humanity surrounded him as he went downward, and he found himself in a hot dark cellar space, which held several sheltering Russian civilians. As soon as he was standing in the space, the Russians, who so far had remained silent, all began complaining at the same time. Someone lit a candle, and the farmer-artilleryman was able to see other farmers, one old man, some women, some children seated or lying on rugs spread on the ground. The space was very small, barely holding the civilians, but if not here, where was he going to find shelter for Ambrogio? He tried to explain with gestures and a few words what he wanted and went back outside, returning with his officer, at which the Russians renewed their protests with real anger. Their complaining died away when they realized that the soldier, after making his officer lie down, intended to go back outside. One of the women even placed a small woolen pillow under Ambrogio's head, though the young officer, feverish eyes staring around him, didn't seem fully conscious.

"To eat", said Paccoi to the Russians, pointing to his officer. "Eat", miming the filling of his mouth with fingers and thumb joined, then shrugged his shoulders.

"Lieutenant," said Paccoi, "I'll be outside, on guard, to make sure the column doesn't leave without us. Meanwhile, you try to sleep, despite the stench. Do you understand?"

Ambrogio gestured yes. "Thank you, Paccoi", he said in a low voice. The orderly returned up the steps.

12

It was already dark, and the attack on Arbusov by cannon fire and mortar shells had been augmented by the Katyuskas, when Paccoi saw Michele Tintori, the second lieutenant from Nova, who, tired out and thoughtful, was wandering along the icy ground, head down, far from the crowds and the falling explosives.

The previous day Michele had fought hard in Posnyakoff; he'd never had to fight like that before and was lucky to be alive. As he walked he thought (who would have believed it?) of General Cadorna. He had always had a sort of personal dislike for the dead general; he blamed the general's style of archaic rigidly planned mass frontal attacks in the previous war (and his implacable decimation of the detachments that had been found to give up ground) for the high number of Italian dead and for being responsible for sending his own father back home reduced to a living ruin. Now, however, he asked himself if perhaps Cadorna hadn't been a master in his understanding of the Italian soldier. Of course, it's sometimes necessary to do whatever is possible to avoid war; however, when one is forced to go to war, and with soldiers like these over here . . . look at that! Some of them had even thrown away their rifles!

Looking around him with a pained expression, his black intelligent eyes were what made Paccoi recognize him. There he was, the lieutenant ("When was it? Only yesterday morning!") who had tried to get all the regiments organized. He knew the officer to be a friend of Ambrogio's, because his chief had himself told him while they marched. He instinctively went toward Michele, waving him to stop. "Lieutenant, pardon me. I'm Second Lieutenant Ambrogio Riva's orderly. He is your friend, isn't he?"

"Of course he's my friend. Where is Riva?"

"He has been wounded."

He explained the why and wherefore and all the details; Tintori then asked him to lead the way to the cellar. Before opening the trapdoor and following Paccoi, he looked all around, in case someone saw them and decided to follow. They found Ambrogio deep in sleep. *Look at him*, Michele told himself, emotionally, *my companion at school, brother to Alma; gravely wounded and his life in danger*. For a moment as he came down the steps he had imagined that having managed to save his life, he'd have been deserving of Alma's eternal gratitude. *What a great event!* But now, seeing his friend in that state in the middle of that stink, his usual serious expression still on his face (as if even in sleep he intended to take on any obstacle), he regretted his fatuous imaginings.

"Leave him be, don't wake him", he told Paccoi.

The old Russian, explaining himself with his hands, told them that they'd made Ambrogio eat something: "*Castòsca . . . c'scet . . . cstòsca!*"

"They've given him potatoes to eat", Michele said to Paccoi. He signed approbation at the old man, then took his hand and shook it. "*Spassiba*, thank you", he said repeating it twice. And to Paccoi, he said (he was really talking to himself), "What incredible characters, these Russians!"

They stayed in the cellar only a few minutes more; Michele looked around in the wavering candlelight, while the women and children looked at him, at the pistol holstered on his belt. "They're squeezed in like sardines", he said to Paccoi. "They barely fit, hardly have enough space to lie down. Let's go. Let's not bother them any further."

As he climbed the steps he told himself, *What strange and unusual people, these Russians. They've used starvation to kill each other, millions of their countrymen have died under incredibly cruel conditions, and look, here they give food to a wounded enemy.*

Once outside in the atrocious cold he asked Paccoi if he had scouted out a place to sleep. "No," Paccoi answered, "but it mustn't be far from here."

"I'm thinking of going over there, where there's a haystack on that elevation above the village", he pointed. "You see it? There's also a first aid post there. If you want to come as well . . . Sleeping in the open air is tough anywhere, but over there one can at least sleep under some straw." The prospect of sleeping under straw tempted Paccoi. However, he didn't want to be far from Ambrogio and told Tintori so.

"Are you joking? If the column starts up, the first thing we'll do is to come back here for your lieutenant. How can you think otherwise?" said Michele, impressed by the man's rare loyalty. "Although I don't think they'll get the column going tonight."

While Paccoi accompanied him to the hayrick, he told him, "Lieutenant Riva has been my companion at school for many years, did he tell you? And now we're at university together, and he's nearly from the same town as I. You don't think I'd leave him behind! Tomorrow, we'll think about what we should do." And after a few more steps, "We need to find him room in a sleigh, at all costs. That's what we'll do first thing. Then we'll follow that sleigh wherever it goes."

Reaching the hayrick (the building was eighty yards long), they found hundreds of wounded men in parallel lines, sitting or lying on a thick layer of straw. They were all on one side of the rick, the other side being exposed to the terribly cold open air. The wind had been blowing from the north for some hours, and up here on the high ground it blew colder than down in the village. Apart from the wounded there were many other soldiers who had gone there to sleep: some of these had climbed up the haystack and were throwing down armfuls of straw for themselves and their friends. It was only possible to take it from the sheltered side, the other side being frozen still with drifted snow. On seeing this, Michele also climbed up the rick—with slow movements caused by his enormous tiredness—and threw down enough straw for Paccoi and himself. Having curled up under the straw, Michele prayed briefly and with fervor; unlike Ambrogio he tended to bring God into all his efforts. More than that, he understood all history (down to all his doings and those of friends and neighbors) as sacred history.

13

Seen from the Russians' positions, the surrounded Italians didn't appear to be disorganized, which was quite evident when seen from up close.

At the eastern flank of the valley, Lieutenant Larichev (who two days before had been in Meskoff) was observing them closely through binoculars, kneeling behind a rudimentary wall of snow. Night was falling; a few paces away from Larichev were crouched some of his platoon, among whom were his second-in-command, a gigantic sergeant wearing a worn overcoat, and at his side the orderly Balandin, known to all as Bannister. In a dip behind them was the battalion, which had followed a battery of Katyuskas from Meskoff and now awaited complete darkness, under cover of which they would take the main valley.

Down in the valley—a worried Larichev continued examining them—the Italians were much more numerous than they'd been in Meskoff, while the Russians here, at least from what he'd heard, weren't many. He would know the exact number of Russians soon, when the major in charge of the battalion returned from sector HQ, to which he had gone for instructions. Whatever the number, the enemy's was greater. Having had recent experience of the Bersaglieri in Meskoff, Larichev was very concerned. *How come headquarters haven't sent all our Meskoff troops here?* he wondered. *Above all, the tanks. Where else, devil take it, could they be more useful than right here?*

The enemy looked to be gathered in great dark masses in and around the village, each conglomeration made up of maybe tens of thousands of men. They were all concentrated on Arbusov; the rest of the valley looked deserted. The really strange fact was that very few machines could be seen among the enemy, the amount of large equipment was decidedly out of proportion to the number of men.

What does this mean? Maybe they're getting ready to attack? Larichev asked himself, while worriedly looking through his binoculars. *But if they've been positioned since earlier this evening, or so I'm told . . . where could they have hidden their vehicles? It's a mystery!* He could see some concentrations of lined-up detachments, which led him to suppose that all the enemy troops were at the ready and that only the dim light stopped him from seeing them. In all, at least at first sight, they didn't give the menacing impression of efficiency that he'd seen among the *petuki*, the Bersaglieri, in Meskoff.

It's no great consolation, reflected Larichev. *Besides which, there are the Germans, there they are, over there with the white uniforms and also with tanks. The tanks! And here we are, with not one tank. Bad business.*

Suddenly from behind him in the dip one of the four Katyuskas escorted there by the battalion fired its first burst of rockets. Larichev heard them whistling overhead and looked avidly at the enemy mass to see what effect they had. The sixteen 130 mm rockets exploded one after the other among the enemy, creating brilliant flaming colors and tremendous explosions. At first individual bursts could be heard; then the noise seemed to build up into one huge turmoil.

"Good. Stick it to them . . . another, great!" he heard the muttered comments from the soldiers beside him. Although sharing his men's jubilation, Larichev just the same now looked behind and round about, instinctively seeking a direction in which to retreat. *Because now, these people are going to come after us, looking to silence the Katyuskas. They won't just sit there waiting to be killed.* He was even more concerned about the danger that the enemy might roll over them and take the highway, where they'd discover their countrymen massacred, each one shot in the back of the neck. His battalion had taken one stretch of this highway, about one mile back, and found on the side of the road many dead Italian prisoners—several hundred—all with bullet wounds in the nape of the neck. What insensitive butchery! "Why would they have killed them in this way? Probably so they wouldn't have to assign men to escort them", the Russian soldiers had said among themselves.

A second, a third, and then a fourth burst from the Katyuskas rained down, like the first, on the unmoving men down in the snow.

"But . . . what's happening?" Larichev saw that there was movement among the enemy; where rockets had fallen they separated, only to reform nearby. The more tightly packed conglomerations received repeated salvos. "But what are they doing? Why don't they react? Not that I care. Just as well", decided the lieutenant, "that the Katyuskas take a while to be reloaded, otherwise . . ." And, in fact, he could see where rockets had burst. They had left what looked like small dark roses, in groups of three or four dead men; they were undoubtedly corpses, those stains in the snow, although he could barely distinguish them through his glass in the fading light.

"What butchery", Larichev mumbled to himself, disconcerted. "What butchery. But how come these Italians are so different from the ones in Meskoff?"

A German battery replied to the Katyuska fire, but from a long distance, evidently unsupported by observers to spot their accuracy, their shells fell uselessly on the steep violet-blue walls of the valley behind them. The Italians remained there, being killed by the enemy fire, apparently unable to do anything to defend themselves. Soon the darkness hid the sight from the Russians' view.

Night fell, and the temperature dropped. Down in the dip the men of the 1180th Infantry regiment, dismounted from the cold trucks they'd been in all day, now waited, occasionally turning their cold-mottled faces to their officer, but fatalistically not expecting much; they knew the officers were waiting for the major to return. As the waiting lengthened, Larichev's superior, an elephantine captain, gave orders for the issuing of cold food rations and climbed, puffing, to have a look from the improvised OP.

"What do you see from here?" he asked as he arrived.

"Now, nothing", answered Larichev. "Only those tracer bursts down there—Do you see them, Semion Grigorievich? Those are Germans. Facing them, there, you see the machine-gun fire from our people? You see them, they're easy to pick out."

"But here, right in front here, in these spread out isbas, are there any enemy?"

"I've not seen any. They're all piled on one another down in the area around the village. But there are many, really a lot of them."

"That doesn't mean there aren't any in the isbas", the captain observed. "While you've been up here, I've spoken with one of our lieutenants who has been observing them since yesterday. Our lot have taken many prisoners, and with little effort, because there are great numbers of disbanded troops, lost from their units; I'm talking about Italians, of course, not Germans. Every one, from first to last, has said the same: their units are scattered, broken up."

"Ah," Larichev said, "now I understand ... before, when I was checking their positions, there was something that wasn't quite right. But why have they become disorganized?"

"They must have abandoned the Don in a great hurry, without waiting to refuel. That's what the prisoners have told us."

"They must have been really in a hurry, eh, Semion Grigorievich?"

The fat captain smiled. "The fear that they might be surrounded ..." He added, "And as they are motorized troops, when their gasoline got used up they had to abandon all their weapons, everything."

"In other words, they have no gas. That's why they have hardly any trucks, as I observed."

"Yes, right. As it is, the Italians go behind the Germans like sheep, to go forward when the Germans have cleared the way for them. Because the Germans do have gas, and when they get low their planes bring more with parachute drops; there was a resupply today. As far as the Germans are concerned we should not fool ourselves." He thought, nodding, "So you've seen it too, eh, that the Italians have no transportation? Well, that confirms it. Good."

He continued there in the darkness studying the terrain for a few minutes. Behind him, a couple of steps away, Infantryman Sukorukov, his smoked fish all finished, noticed that cold rations were being distributed to the company and began to feel uneasy. "Cold rations ...", he said, looking at his sergeant. "Feodor Cusmic, down there in the company they're handing out cold rations." The sergeant didn't even look at him.

From the darkness the Katyuskas launched a few more salvos, then ceased in order to save ammunition. The Russian bombardment went on for a while, with the mortars hidden in the hollows to the south continuing to fire for a time. In contrast to the brilliant golden fire of the rockets, which flashed and illuminated, bursting with spectacular lights, like a dress covered in sequins, the mortar rounds landed like little writhing dust devils.

"Well, I'm going back down", said the captain. "You carry on with your vigil. But as soon as you see the battalion on the move, join us with your four slaves." He looked over at Sukorukov, at Bannister and the others crouched elbow to elbow in the snow.

"Right, Semion Grigorievich", replied the lieutenant with a half smile.

"Here's what I think. I'm convinced that we'll all end up like sardines in those isbas down there." He paused. "I don't see any other solution: a night in the open like this would reduce the battalion's efficiency. Besides, disorganized as they are, the Italians probably won't bother us. In the meantime, if you can, find out if they've reorganized, and where, and if they've built a line here in front. If they've not done anything to improve their position, you'll be able to tell by watching their light-arms fire."

"Right."

"Well, I'm going", and he went.

Larichev watched as the captain walked heavy footed down the slope; he was a particularly graceless man, coarse, his head under his cap like a pumpkin. He was neither good nor bad; he was, in fact, totally indifferent toward other people's suffering, thought Larichev; in sight of other people's pain he felt neither pleasure nor pain.

That, at least, thought the lieutenant, remembering certain incidents he'd witnessed back in the political prison, *is a good thing, if he doesn't feel pleasure at other people's suffering.*

14

It wasn't long before he himself experienced the captain's indifference. Finally the battalion had advanced into the main valley's silence, predictably reaching the outermost, eastern isbas in Arbusov, in which the soldiers had taken shelter, filling them. But not Larichev and his men. "Not you", the captain had said. "You should take your platoon and get yourself in one of those isbas over there, ahead of us, and don't let the enemy see you. You'll be observing, with one quarter of the men at a time on watch. That's an order. You and your men will be there to raise the alarm in case of attack. Take more men if you like, but not less than you have now."

"Right, comrade Captain."

"Your orders, whatever happens, are not to move without being ordered to do so. The major wants it that way."

Larichev nodded and thought, *That way, in case there's an attack, we'll finish up between the enemy's fire and the battalion's. A magnificent prospect.*

At this point, Sukorukov, who being behind the lieutenant had heard everything, turned to the sergeant. "Feodor Cusmic, you heard? We have to go. What about our food rations? Our rations?"

"I've already drawn them for us", replied the sergeant.

"And the vodka, Feodor Cusmic, have they distributed the vodka this time?" The sergeant made no reply.

"I've chosen your platoon", the captain said to Larichev, "because from the heights you've become familiar with the enemy positions."

"Yes, comrade Captain."

"Good. You already know very well what your task is: if you see, for example, preparations for an attack, if they start assembling or some other nonsense, you let me know immediately by sending a runner to me here. Better yet, send me two, all right? Two. Well, I think we've said it all. Now get on with it." The corpulent captain once more turned to go.

"One moment." Larichev's face, normally reflecting a patient approach to life, seemed to show bitterness. "Supposing we end up having to defend ourselves in this OP, and to send you two runners . . . this would mean seriously weakening the platoon."

"And so? What do you want me to do?"

"What I meant to say, if you could give me two, better yet four of the company's runners . . . it's a reasonable request, it seems to me, Semion Grigorievich."

The captain seemed annoyed, then thought again and smiled ambiguously (in the darkness, Larichev didn't notice). "All right, two. You'll get two." He turned to a passing noncom and said, "Macarov and Calatov, get them sent here right away. Have them come here."

Larichev bit his lip. "Curse it! How come I didn't think . . . ? The two spies . . ." But there was already no way to change the order. The two politicals were found by the platoon sergeant, not the passing noncom, who had no interest in getting involved. This took some time, as the two men were sheltering in different isbas. Without blaspheming or complaining—which normal soldiers would have done—the two spies took up position in the platoon's leading squad, putting themselves behind Corporal Nikitenko, the farmer Sukorukov, and the orderly Balandin, Bannister.

Heading for two adjoining isbas some two hundred yards out in front, the platoon went cautiously down the valley-bottom path, taking some time to reach them and go inside. The first watch was taken by the lead squad. Larichev had ruled that watches should be for one hour, but the prospect of being in the intense cold with the resulting suffering (when they had at their backs two sheltering isbas) made him judge it necessary to put himself on the watch list with them.

The Russian watchers were divided in two groups outside the isbas; three were posted with their officer near the edge of the road, behind a snow-covered pile of rocks; four more were hidden in a chicken coop. The enemy was totally invisible, but close by, for occasionally smothered voices would be heard, sounding like the complaining of wounded men.

From time to time tracer fire could be seen from different sites on the edge of the village, German fire, which sometimes crossed with Russian tracers; in the southern sector an isba burned for a time, probably set off by one of the last tracer bullets. *What an incredible amount of suffering; even here in this lost village with the stupid name, Arbusov (Watermelon)*, thought the former painter Larichev. Immediately, he tried to drop the thought. He shouldn't be thinking of the "big picture", which he well knew would only end up exhausting his brain. The fact of being an artist inevitably made him sensitive, receptive. He shook his head. *Artist? I'm finished with art. Besides, what could I paint? Busts of Stalin? Or commissioned paintings of kolkhozes or laborers with happy, stupid faces?* What an irreconcilable environment his own great Mother Russia had become as far as art was concerned. *Of course the hack writers, daubers, and ass lickers prosper nowadays. After the regime's big shots they're the group that now get the fat grants and fees. But how many real authentic artists are left? All the really great ones have been killed by the Communists or have committed suicide.* His thoughts ran over a number of personages and names: Gorki, Mayakovsky, Esenin, Babel, Pilniak, Gumilev, Mandelstam; others, some totally unknown whose lives he'd seen extinguished in the prison camp, unable to resist the harsh life there. And what a pile of hypocrisy, if you thought about it, the versions invented around those deaths (the deaths of important people, of course people known abroad, not the secondary characters). Hypocrisies like the Communists' killing of Gorki and then the naming of a city after him. Where on earth could one see hypocrisy such as that? But why? Why?

A total and permanent silence had fallen on the names of the smaller artists; one would never hear of them again. He remembered two in particular: the deaths of those two companions in misery in the *lager* had been a cruel loss for him. He always—particularly after being deported—had felt a desire to meet other artists: the discussions, criticisms, consensus, dissent, the interchange of ideas with them. That's the way he was, and there was no remedy . . . but enough! Larichev breathed deeply of the stinging air: he was overtired and shouldn't (shouldn't, he repeated to himself) wear himself out with these thoughts. *Leave it be; it's not the moment to think.*

Sitting on a log at his side, the farmer Sukorukov periodically pulled pieces of ration-issue herring from his pocket, putting them in his mouth and chewing slowly, afterward spitting out the bony residue onto the snow, where it created stained patterns. Sukorukov's cold was worse than ever, and he frequently cleared the frozen snot from his nose using his fingers. On Larichev's other side was Bannister, who always when he was under tension clicked his steel teeth. *It's a shame*, thought his officer, *that they don't manufacture dentures for the ordinary people, instead of only for the . . . but that's really enough, stop, I don't want to think of these things any more. I should simply wait for the watch to be over. Then I'll have three hours—three consecutive hours—in the warm isba, able to sleep.*

But it's easy to say "don't think of it"; one has to be able to do it. And the ex-painter Larichev was not able. Now, for example, all his troubles, his sentence to ten years of hard labor, which had shortened his life, all returned to his mind. *If there's one thing I shouldn't think about, it's that.* But his mind refused: espionage for France, Article 98, him! They'd accused him of spying, him! Could you imagine anything more absurd? Even though he was aware that most of the prisoners in the *lager* were innocent, Larichev couldn't, even today, swallow his indignation at his treatment. The only proof brought forward against him were request cards in his own handwriting to a library specializing in books in French. *And what did that prove? Am I not a painter? The requests were for textbooks on art, painting. What did they expect me to ask for at a library? Manuals on coal mining, maybe?* So, without any proof or valid reason, they'd given him ten years. Ten years! He still had six to complete, with the additional risk—worse than any other alternative—of ending up at one of those camps like Kolima, from which almost nobody returned. Of course, there was now the hope that, if he behaved well in the war ... But he still felt offended and humiliated. When eventually, at the end of a long hour, Larichev's squad left the snow and ice to go inside the nearest isba, the lieutenant still hadn't managed to stop thinking about the wretched life he had suffered.

He ate avidly of the same dry rations as his men, drinking the hot tea he'd sent Bannister to make ten minutes before the watch change, and then lay down to sleep on the beaten earth floor, in the space vacated by the squad going out on watch.

15

Three hours later the gigantic platoon sergeant was there to wake him up for the next shift of guard duty. "It's time, your turn comrade ... Lieutenant.

"Mine ... already?"

Larichev sat up listlessly and rubbed his eyes. Bannister and Nikitenko were doing the same thing beside him, on the floor. The sergeant was holding a flashlight that shone faintly.

"Any news?" the officer asked him.

"Yes, we killed an Italian."

"A ... a what?"

"An Italian. About a half hour ago. I came to tell you immediately, but since you hadn't wakened with the shots, I thought ... well, I thought it was better to let you sleep."

"But what in the devil happened? Was he alone? Who killed him?"

"Corporal Calatov shot him."

Ah, the spy, Larichev thought, standing up.

"The Italian came by himself, walking along the highway, talking out loud. I wasn't posted on the edge of the highway. I was in the other part, at the hen-house. But we could see everything from there, because as I said, he was talking out loud. He was also gesturing. I think, how do you call it? He was delirious. Or maybe he had gone mad, I don't know. In any case, there was no trouble getting him—I couldn't believe it—because we saw he wasn't armed. Just like that."

"Not armed, Feodor Cusmic?"

"Right, not armed. That beast Calatov, without a word, let him have it with a round from his parabellum. Got rid of him."

"Beast is right", the lieutenant agreed in a low voice. "Would have been better for us if he'd taken him alive."

"That's what I said, too, We might have made him talk. I called Calatov a beast, but he turned on me, as if I wanted to protect a Fascist, you know what I mean? That's how he put it."

"The imbecile", Larichev said. "And where's the dead man now? Did you leave him on the road?"

"No, we brought him back behind the house. In case others should turn up, you know?"

"You did the right thing."

"Here's his wallet."

The sergeant—who took it from his pocket—handed the officer a thin, worn wallet made of imitation leather.

Larichev took it. The soldiers for the new shift—already standing and ready to go—were coming up to have a look, curious.

The officer checked his watch. "You go on ahead", he ordered. "Tell the others outside to come in. I'll be right there."

They left glumly. The other men entered the isba immediately afterward. Calatov had a short fur-lined overcoat stained with blood, no doubt the dead man's blood, slung over his shoulder booty style. Larichev was watching them as they exchanged a few words about what had happened, while they settled down on the floor to sleep; with rough and ready satisfaction, Calatov threw his bloodstained coat over himself as a blanket.

The officer opened the wallet. "Feodor Cusmic, bring the light closer", he told the sergeant.

There was a little money in the wallet, Italian lire and German occupation rubles, a sacred image, which Larichev examined carefully and then put back in its place, some crumpled, written-on pages, a few photographs, and only one document. Larichev said, "His identity paper". He translated it easily for the sergeant because of the similarity between Italian and French, though it was the first time he had personally checked that out. "It's a kind of internal passport", he explained.

"A lot smaller than ours, it seems."

"Yes. They don't fill in all the dates like they do in ours. There's something here below, let's see. For instance, his profession." He read it out: "*Fa-le-gna-me* [i.e., carpenter]." He repeated the word. "That isn't like the French. Who knows what it means?"

He also read out the name of the place he was from: "Misilmeri", not know-ing what that was about. A bit below there was another word, which he rec-ognized: Palermo. "Palermo", he repeated and explained, "He was from the city, perhaps the province, of Palermo. Sicily, then. Do you know where it is?"

The sergeant shook his head. "He's a small-framed boy, with dark skin and hair. Looks Armenian", he said.

"It's as hot in Sicily as it is in Armenia," the lieutenant said absentmindedly, "maybe more so. If I have it right, it never snows there, and the temperature never goes below zero. Who knows, this poor wretch, out there in the cold, may just have lost his mind."

"He shouldn't have come here to fight a war with us", the sergeant observed.

Having been accused shortly before of having protected an enemy, he was now wondering if the lieutenant wasn't, by chance, testing him. Like the oth-ers, he did not know the officer had come from a forced labor camp, but even if he had known . . . it wasn't so unusual for the NKVD to pick their spies from the camps.

Larichev read the sergeant's thoughts. "Yes, of course", he said sadly.

He put the identification document back and took out the photographs. The dead man could be identified because he was present in all of them, wear-ing civilian clothes. In one square format he appeared with his hair slicked back, wearing a jacket and an open shirt. He hardly seemed more than a boy, with the look of someone who had gone through some trials and tribulations. In another—a small snapshot—he was part of a group of extraordinarily dig-nified people, all of them dressed in black with flashy ties on. Most certainly they were his Sicilian relatives. In a third, he was shown with people who could have been the same, except for one circumstance: they were all seated in shirt-sleeves around a table covered with bottles and glasses. The boy, with an exaggerated and playful gesture, was holding his glass up to the camera. In the last photograph he was serious, at the side of a girl with hair as dark as his, and as insignificant: they seemed to be absorbed with one another. On the back of the photograph were scrawled words and a great many exclamation points. Ardent declarations of love from him, which she would never read: Rocchina my love!!!! My lovely!!! My life!!! Larichev, after having tried in vain to deci-pher the words, put the photographs back in the wallet in one of his overcoat pockets. "Feodor Cusmic, let's go have a look at the dead man", he said to the sergeant. The latter led the way, concealing the light under one of his long overcoat skirts.

The dead boy was stretched out on the snow behind the isba. Without a tunic, and not even a balaclava, he seemed even more slight that Larichev had imagined. He still had a very human look, though. He was not like the messy oblong of leftovers that the dead of a few hours resembled. The sergeant, after having looked around to check for any enemy movement, lifted his long thread-bare overcoat and lit up the dead boy's face better. It seemed twisted into one tragic gesture, which made Larichev wonder if it was the same individual as in the photographs.

"All right, let's go", the officer said at last.

Having dismissed the sergeant, he stepped a moment at the guard post by the henhouse, where he notified the soldiers that if by chance another straggler should show up, they should not shoot him but take him alive instead. Then he took up his post on the roadside. He also informed the guard there not to shoot unless he had to. Of course, it was highly unlikely that another stranded enemy would show up, even more—as Nikitenko took the liberty to point out—it was most improbable that such a strange case would be repeated.

Almost, but not entirely impossible, as it turned out. Hardly a half hour had gone by when another enemy was there. This time it was no less than Michele Tintori from Nova.

16

Second Lieutenant Tintori had awakened after a couple of hours of sleep in the hayloft. His teeth were chattering as they never had done before in his life, in a way he had never thought possible, almost like a caricature. He immediately realized that the straw that was covering him had been taken off. Someone had robbed him of it. Someone, but who? Leaning on one arm, he sat up to have an angry look around. Paccoi was still sleeping there beside him, also without any straw to cover him. The others—a blurry extension of shadows—were stretched out in the same way, wrapped in sleep. The officer had no other recourse than to get up and go above again, with the greatest effort, to the icy hayloft and take more straw, which—on his way back to sleep—he threw onto Paccoi and himself. Waking up again, shortly afterward, he realized he had again been stripped of straw. He was overcome by anger and stood up in a rage. This time Paccoi heard him. "What's happening, Lieutenant?" he mumbled.

"Nothing. They've gone off with our straw! I'm going to find out who's doing this."

"But what are you going to find, Lieutenant?" Paccoi murmured, but Michele was already on his way to . . . to check out the prone figures. There were, as we know, hundreds, and others were still coming helter skelter from Arbusov, hoping to find shelter here in this big hayloft, some relief from the icy air that had martyred them in the open ground between the village isbas. Some of those sleeping there were covered with straw, others not, and among those without any straw, some kept so still that their blankets and coats had gone white with frost, as if they were dead. *Frozen to death*, the officer thought, upset. *Frozen!* Something that could have happened to him, too, transforming him in his sleep from a young and living man into a yellowish block of frozen flesh. Because of these pigs . . . just to avoid going up to the haystack, they had . . . He inspected row after row of sleeping bodies, still in a rage, stopping to examine the cover of straw of a fresher appearance. He was perfectly aware he was being absurd, senseless, but overcome with unceasing rage, he was unnerving himself in this futile effort, looking for some sign among these abject creatures, who, apart from having taken away his straw, were now compelling him to carry out this exhausting activity. At moments he thought he was ranting, but that lasted only instants. Then he would come to. *If someone realizes he's ranting, it means he's not ranting at all,* he thought mistakenly.

The man stretched out at the end of the second row, completely hidden under his blanket, lifted up one end and uncovered his head. "I'm waiting for you", he said in a strange intonation. "I've been watching you. You're looking for me, aren't you?"

Michele observed in silence. He could not see his insignia or his rank. He noticed that his face was ashen, decomposed looking.

"No, you don't have any straw. I'm not looking for you", he answered.

The other fellow ignored his answer. "I'm dying", he said in a low voice. "I know it. My guts are all out." He paused, then stretched out his arm to hand him something. "Here's the water flask."

Michele looked at him without understanding what he meant about the water flask. At last he took it. "But . . . what do you want?" he asked.

"The worst thing is the thirst", he answered, exhausted. "I hope you'll never have to suffer thirst like this. I've finished all the snow. But it wasn't enough . . . I need water, real water."

The second lieutenant noticed there was no snow around the wounded man, none as far as his hands could reach.

"Since night came no one has gone to get water", the man said. "It's something terrible . . . you're reduced to desperation . . . then I invoked Christ on the Cross. Don't let me die desperate, I've told him. I'm at peace with you. Grant me to bear this patiently, Christ our Lord."

Repeating his prayer, the injured man raised his voice. No one around them, in any case, looked at him. Maybe no one heard. *He's wandering in his head, for sure,* Michele thought. *He can't be conscious of what he's saying. But he's behaving very strangely, all the same.*

"From the Cross Christ answered me that he would send someone", the wounded man said. "And then you came."

"Listen," Michele decided, after remaining silent a while, "for the love of Christ, I'll go for water. But are you really wounded in your belly?"

"Yes", he answered with a voice suddenly struck with horror. "My guts are . . . oh . . .", His eyes rolled back. "How awful", he murmured, or something similar, with such a low voice the officer could not catch the word exactly.

"I'm going for water for you," he repeated, "but it will take a while. Do you understand?"

"Yes, go, please go, don't make me wait any longer, I beg of you."

"It will take me time", Michele said. "But you wait. Don't worry, I'll be back. All right?"

"Yes, go."

Michele took the flask by its fiber handle, and with the rifle he had fought with the day before in Posnyakoff against the enemy slung over his right shoulder he left. It was because of this battle he was now feeling so tired. After having spent hours stopping the enemy, he'd come to this village with the last of the men, with the few in the division still willing to resist, despite the general disarray. Heavens, if they'd not been there to protect the column . . . then they had to go miles and miles at an accelerated pace, pursued at first by enemy bullets, even helping along some of the injured to keep them going. Even after reaching the end of the column—he remembered now—what a job it was dragging the injured! That was why he was having so much trouble walking now, why he felt so tired, so blasted exhausted. To tell the truth, instead of dwelling on his own tiredness, he would have rather been thinking about the strange business he was going through now, but it was because of that, because he was too tired he couldn't think about it. Who knows, maybe God had made him go off on that absurd tangent (now he didn't doubt it) to look for straw, so he would be taken to the dying man to help him. Michele confusedly was inclined to think so.

While going along the heavily trod-on snow toward Arbusov, he noticed that on three sides of the town—the north, west, and especially the south—the German machine gunners were exchanging occasional gunfire with the Russians. He could see the crisscrossing tracery—luminous and swift—fading into the darkness. Toward his left, the east, no one was firing.

Suddenly he was wondering: Was that really the east, and was he really walking toward Arbusov? He could scarcely recognize any of the places. His own thoughts were fluctuating, as if swimming between scrolls of hideously cold darkness, through which his body floated. He at last lost all orientation, but that did not keep him from continuing on.

After a while, he came to himself, came back completely, and remembered what he was doing. Then he stopped and had a look around, alertly, and remembered some detail of the town. *Why, I've ended up going the wrong way*, he realized. *What tricks tiredness plays on you!* He had practically walked the entire town. *So much walking for nothing.* He turned back and moved between large groups of sleeping figures spread out on the snow around the isbas. How would Ambrogio Riva be right now, over there in that hole with the Russian civilians? *Maybe he's thirsty, too, being wounded, like that fellow. But we'll think about him tomorrow.*

He finally reached the well. He glimpsed the rough lever made out of a tree trunk, and he could see someone working the lever, bringing up water, in the dark. *Just as well I won't have to break through the ice to get water.* He let the other fellow—he looked like a chaplain—pour water into his bucket made out of a kind of canvas, of the type that belongs to truck supplies. Then he worked the lever, drank out of the metal cup, filling it with as much water as he could (really icy, comforting), then he filled the flask, and made his way back to the hayloft.

Good God, how tired he was, how exhausted! What an effort getting up this snowy hill. When he reached the hayloft, he tried to get his bearings to find the wounded man. His mind was about to cloud over again. Then he prayed, mentally placing himself in God's hands: "Lord, help me, I beg you to help me fulfill this mission." The Lord did. His mind cleared, to the point of being— once again—a little surprised at having begun to faint. Once in the right direction, he reached the wounded man, concealed under his blanket. He bent over to scrutinize the big blanket, fearful of finding only a dead body. "Eh", he called softly. "You there!" The other one lifted an edge of the blanket. "Ah, you've come back, at last", he said in a voice even weaker then before, practically fading. Trembling, he stuck out an arm.

"Take it", Michele told him, placing his hand securely onto the flask.

"The water," he murmured, "the water!" He brought the receptacle to his mouth with great difficulty and sucked hard from the aluminum mouthpiece, only stopping from time to time to breathe. "The water", he repeated.

The officer watched him in the dark. Finally he said, "Now I'm going to sleep, too, because I can hardly stay on my feet. Tomorrow morning, as soon as it's light, I'll come back to have a look at you. Did you hear? Tomorrow morning."

"There won't be any tomorrow morning for me", the wounded man said. "I'm dying."

"Come, come, what do you mean?" Michele countered, feeling the skin on his arms bristling with goosebumps. Paying no attention to Michele, the other man continued, "As for you, God will save you tonight."

"Save me?" Michele asked, surprised. "How?"

"Remember I told you that", the dying man repeated feebly. "God will save you tonight."

Well, well! the officer thought, shaking his head perplexedly. Like all the others he was unaware, at that time, of the fact that on this tragic front the dying sometimes acquired the gift of prophecy. (The inexplicable phenomenon frequently established by the Italians was authenticated on an incomparably larger scale by the Russians, especially among the soldiers who died in the besieged Leningrad.)

The wounded man again brought the icy mouthpiece of the flask to his lips, again drank from it at length. Then, shuddering, he pulled the blanket over his head and remained like that.

"Listen, wait", Michele would have liked to say then. "Tell me at least your name and your division, so tomorrow morning ..." But he said nothing and only stood there a few minutes looking on dubiously at the tragic, blanketed figure before him. Then he thought that he must go, he had had enough, absolutely enough. Now he had to find a way of sleeping. *If I don't go, I'll keel over worse than before.* He shifted his rifle from one shoulder to the other because it was less bothersome and reached the hayloft.

17

Where was that opening, that passage into the straw that he had climbed twice? Where in the devil was it? He could not find it. He went back and forth on the north side of the hayloft a couple of times, exposed to the mortally cold air. The south side was blocked by all the many stretched-out figures. He tried to pull some straw from the side of the pile, but it was so stuck together and iced over that only bits of it came off onto his cloth gloves. He felt he was really going under. *I have to get some rest*, he decided. *I must rest at least . . . at least ten minutes, and then . . .* Then what? Again he was unable to get his thoughts straight. He sat down on the snow, with his back against the loft. This icy air, almost like waves, like a strange vortex that was swallowing him up, incessant . . .

Maybe that air was coming from some door left open on the outside . . . who would have been such an idiot as to leave a door open, letting in this terrible draft? In the hallway of this mountain inn! The air was surely coming down from the outside, from the mountain, gusting in through the open door of the inn. "Shut it, damn you all. Shut it!" Quite easy to tell them to shut it. There was no one in the hallway; no one heard him . . . He'd try sleeping on the floor, leaning against the wall . . . but it was so cold on the floor, like ice. *The door, damn it all, the door.* Michele ended up asleep, seated against the loft on the ice and dirty snow, on the side open to the wind, where no one was. He slept a half hour perhaps, and his nightmares further weakened his brain.

Once awake, he stood up, not recognizing the place. He wondered how he had gotten there. Neither did it matter either. What did matter was to find his schoolmate Ambrogio Riva. He was certain he'd seen him there in the town of the first afternoon. Of course, in this mountain lodge they'd come to with the school to ski . . . but what lodge? Where was it? And what school? What was he saying? There was no lodge here, no schoolmates either. And as for skiing . . . well, maybe yes and maybe no: things weren't too clear regarding this.

"Nothing at all!" he screamed. Ambrogio, yes, he was the one he had to see, but how did he get into this muddled situation? Michele did not really understand how he did get into it, but he most definitely had to see him.

"Ambrogio!" he tried calling out loud. He repeated the name. Then he started screaming, "Ambrogio Riva!"

No one answered; no one appeared. But how cold it was, the cold of death and dying, horrifying. Michele moved off, began walking. In the alley houses in the snow could be glimpsed. The village was there, below the lodge ... it must be Madesimo.

Maybe it was Madesimo, maybe not. In any case, Ambrogio must certainly be there, in one of those houses. (*He's hidden in the heat, clever of him, the rogue.*)

Step by step down the incline, the officer reached the icy road that ran to the bottom of the valley. There wasn't a soul there either. After looking around, he went east on the road toward the Russians. He was armed only with a pistol, the rifle having been left against the hayloft. At the first house he reached he tried calling again, "Ambroogioo ... Ambrooogiooo!" He wasn't there, it seemed, neither Ambrogio nor anyone else ... no one. "What's happened to you?" the ex-schoolmate murmured in that direction and went on walking.

Of course it was strange, it just didn't fit, the fact that the Madesimo house had a thatched roof. But he had no time or desire to think about it. The houses, he noticed, in that area were scattered. Some far from the road there, in front of him, were too close to the road and to each other. And there Michele was pretty sure—or almost—he'd find his old schoolmate Ambrogio. He walked forward, looking at the two houses with bright eyes, blinking, and, as he came closer, he started calling, "Ambroogioo, Ambrooogiooo, answer me!"

18

With their weapons aimed and their hearts in their mouths, Lieutenant Larichev and the other Russian guards followed every one of his movements. "Alive", the officer muttered between his teeth. "We want this one alive." He looked out of the corner of his eye at Corporal Nikitenko, hunched up at his side behind a pile of stones. "Vitia, get over to the other four", pointing to the henhouse with his chin, "and tell them again they must not shoot. Tell them that we'll take him. That they must be ready to intervene only if others come after him. Go and come back immediately."

The corporal left and in a few seconds was back again behind the pile of stones covered with snow, panting. They could hear the Italian coming closer now, his voice, also the sound of his boots on the snow. When he was at the post, Nikitenko, Bannister, and Sukorukov all leapt on him at once, while Lieutenant Larichev, coming out with them from their hiding place, pointed his pistol against him. "Quiet. Quiet", he told him in Russian, in a strained voice. Michele did not understand: he instinctively reacted by pulling himself back and trying to escape, but he was gripped firmly. "What kind of joke is this? You devils!" he protested, not understanding a thing, his mind totally confused.

Sukorukov, who had seized him with all his might, twisted his left arm and caused great pain. "Devil, that you are!" Michele screamed. "Dev ..." He tried hitting him with his head, but Corporal Nikitenko grabbed his chin and mouth with one hand. The trapped lieutenant bellowed and struggled as much as he could.

"Quiet", Larichev again ordered in Russian. "Keep quiet." While the other two held him, Corporal Nikitenko, with his free hand, put his muffler on his mouth and gagged him.

"All right, let's take him to the house", Larichev ordered, lowering his weapon. The prisoner, who was following, twisting with fury as he went, was dragged to the isba. A lamp was lit there that lit up the men spread about on the floor. Larichev kicked a few with his foot to make them move over to have a little room around a small table against the wall. They took the belt with the pistol in it off of the prisoner, and he was taken to the table. The muffler was removed from his mouth, and his arms too were freed. On both sides were Bannister and Sukorukov, ready to grab him again.

19

He looked around him, terrified. The violent trauma had at last brought him back to reality: he had fallen into the hands of the Russians. All at once, his brain was filled with the comments of other soldiers and colleagues about the cruelty of the enemy and also those strange words of the dying man: "God will save you tonight." Instead he had fallen into the hands of these beasts! And, the worst thing, the information he had gathered on the extermination of civilian Russians by the Communists. *It's the end. It's all over for me.* He felt as if he were going mad. In the face of death his entire being rebelled convulsively.

The Russians who had captured him, with their big overcoats and fur hats on their heads, for the moment were silent. Most of those spread out on the floor continued sleeping, snoring heavily. Only the few the officer had awakened, seated now on the floor, were looking at him; one of them broke wind.

Most certainly they'd question him now, and to make him talk, they'd beat him, perhaps torture him. *Better to die and get it over with.* But die how? In the face of death, however, not only his mind but also every cell in his body rebelled.

This inner tumult did not show at all on his outer being. The young man—illuminated now by the lamp that had been put on the table—only panted lightly, but that could have been attributed to his recent struggle and the gag that had just been taken off him.

"An officer, at that", Corporal Nikitenko remarked with satisfaction as he showed the others the pistol belt he was holding in his hands.

"It went well", Lieutenant Larichev said.

"Yes, it did", Bannister agreed, the only one among the Russians who showed any emotion.

Again there was silence. Sukorukov said nothing. For him friends or enemies, poor or gentry (and this one was certainly gentry) were all the same: for good or bad, they didn't do anything, one or the other, but break his . . . He then squeezed his nose with his fingers and freed it of snot, which—because of the cold—in part fell to the floor while the rest dribbled on his chin.

"Now go out", Larichev ordered the corporal. "Call one of the men in the henhouse and set up a watch point on the highway." And to the other two: "You stay here for the moment and keep guard on the prisoner."

Corporal Nikitenko rolled the pistol taken from the enemy into the belt and put it on the inner ledge of a window. Then, after glancing at his two comrades who were staying behind in the warm house, he made his way, disgruntled, to the door and left.

Larichev took out a stool from under the table and sat down, removed his fur cap from his head and put it on the table; his forehead was pale and pronounced. "Well, let's get down to business", he said in Russian to the prisoner, who immediately tensed up.

"Let's begin with the rank and unit you belong to."

Tintori did not understand Russian, and he stood there stiffly, his mouth half open.

"This fellow", Larichev said to his men, "doesn't understand a single word of Russian. Let's try French." He repeated his question in French.

This time he did understand perfectly, and he looked at his interrogator in surprise, who, at that moment and in this place, was using a language linked in his memory to quite different states of mind, quite different times.

"I'm a second lieutenant from Regiment 81 Infantry", he declared softly.

"The Eighty-First?" the Russian repeated, as if to engrave it in his memory (he had no paper to write it on).

Michele nodded.

"How many Italians are here with you?"

"I don't know", the prisoner answered. He was beginning to get some control over himself and began to torment himself with the idea of having committed an error in admitting to a knowledge of French.

The Russian modified his own question. "How many Italian regiments are here in front of us?"

Second Lieutenant Tintori did not answer.

Larichev repeated the question, in Russian and in French, without obtaining an answer. Michele, meanwhile, was trying to think. *Perhaps I'm making a mistake, because if these people are convinced they can't get anything out of me, they'll kill me straight off?*

"You'll have to tell me how many Italians and Germans are out there and what they've planned for tomorrow."

The prisoner continued to be silent.

Larichev looked at Sukorukov. "He seems to be set on not talking", as if thinking out loud.

"Should I twist his arm?" he asked. "If between the two of us we twist his arm, even break it, you'll see how he talks."

"No," the officer murmured, "it could possibly stop him talking completely." Indifferent and cold, Sukorukov again blew his nose with his fingers.

Larichev addressed the prisoner with a new question: "What battalion are you in?"

This seemed to Michele a question acceptable to international conventions (he was up on these rules and regulations, though Russia did not adhere to those conventions). "You want to know what my battalion is?"

"Yes."

"The First Battalion of the Eighty-First Infantry."

The French word *battalion* repeated brought him back nostalgically to heaven knows what corner of memory, to a poem by Victor Hugo he had studied at school, a verse that referred to the battle of Waterloo, which was appropriate to the present situation. So appropriate that Michele did something without thinking and the absurdity of which he only noticed while in the process of doing it (in other words, he did one of those things that are done at decisive moments in one's life simply because *someone* makes us do it): he recited the verse in question, softly: "*La pale mort*", he murmured, "*mêlait les sombres batallions.*"

As was only natural, Larichev was struck dumb and remained silent for a while. Then, to the genuine bewilderment of the prisoner, he completed the quotation: "*Waterloo, morne plaine . . . dans ton cirque de bois, de coteaux, de vallons, la pale mort mêlait les sombres . . .*" He recited without going as far as the rhyme, fearing the reaction of his soldiers. "Victor Hugo, isn't it? Do you like Hugo?"

Michele did not answer, and the Russian also fell silent.

The two young men scrutinized each other. They were not, as far as appearance goes, anything but two soldiers at opposite poles from each other, but first of all they were both artists, each with a different and great tradition behind him. The fact of being an artist did not make the Italian different from the rest of his people, who were, in a certain sense, all artists (too much so, as we know). However, it did make the Russian different, profoundly so, as a man marked off by destiny from his fellow countrymen. While the Italian felt no more than the occasional need to communicate with other artists, the isolation of the Russian made him, in contrast, always on the *qui vive* to capture the presence of someone with whom he could communicate. *This fellow, who comes out with Victor Hugo at a moment like this, has to be sensitive to poetry.* He was already beginning to detect the artist in the other fellow, a situation he imagined as solitary and heart rending as his own.

"What is your profession?" he asked, forcing himself back into the impersonal tone.

Michele did not answer. What could he do with a question like that? Maybe classify him as for or against the proletariat?

Larichev was not taken aback by his silence. "Are you . . . are you, by any chance, an artist?" he asked him slowly, almost spelling it out.

Michele turned to stone. *What? Do I have it written on my face? This fellow's guessed it, like Gemellone at the university . . . better to admit it,* he decided and once more did something that, if he had been free not to do it, he certainly would not have. "At the moment I'm only a student," he answered, "but, as you say, I am, I want to be a writer."

A kind of reverberation passed across the intelligent face of the Russian. The prisoner noticed it, and he became fearful. *A beast, what a beast I've been! If these people are not used to keeping their prisoners alive, so much less for someone who will one day relate their savagery . . . I've committed the worst possible thing among all the possibilities open to me.*

Once again he became agitated. What had he done? His fate was decided: it was the end, the end. He could not concentrate, and he was no longer interested in analyzing the personality or at least the face of his interrogator. If he could have got hold of himself, he would have found that the face in front of him, pale, slim, as if marked by a kind of singular goodness (exactly that), deserved analysis. That face would have made him think not of a colleague in art but of a saint instead. And he was on the point of thinking that for a second, under the influence of those sorrowful eyes, but, *A saint? Is my mind wandering again?* he suddenly wondered. *Am I slipping back into that delirious state again?*

Conscious of being momentarily incapable of adopting any kind of strategy to save himself, he shut his mouth and lowered his head. He would not say another word.

The Russian officer was aware of the change he had experienced even though he did not know to what to attribute it. He would have liked to explain that he had asked that question because he, too, was an artist. But it was a dangerous subject, even more with an unknown prisoner, who could have told about it.

He let a certain time slip by, and then he said, "In your interest, *c'est-à-dire*, in the interest of your life, listen well to what I'm going to ask you now." For the benefit of the other Russians, he assumed a more inquisitorial tone. "You're going to have to spill the beans with me. Do you understand?" he exclaimed in Russian. Then he formulated his questions in French, sometimes repeating them in Russian. "How many Italians, more or less, are rounded up out there in Arbusov? How many Germans? What heavy arms do you have? More specifically: How many armored tanks? And what's planned for tomorrow? What are you thinking of doing tomorrow?" After each question, he stopped, silent, as if expecting an answer.

The prisoner remained mute, staring down at the earthen floor.

"Remember this well: I've asked you these questions", the Russian officer concluded. "You've understood?" Then he turned to the two guards. "He doesn't want to talk."

"But he's said something", Bannister observed, really only to please him, and he smiled, showing the peculiar metallic plate in his mouth.

"Yes, he did say something, interesting, too", Larichev agreed.

This wretch realizes how slim is his chance to escape, he thought meanwhile. The sight of the dead bodies a few miles before Arbusov, on the side of the road, crossed his mind, all those split necks with the brain on the outside.

You're not wrong, you poor unlucky artist, . . . but I'm going to do my best to save you. He still did not know how.

He said, as if thinking to himself, but talking to the guards, "If we send him to company headquarters half fainting like he is now, as soon as he hits the air outside, he might begin to scream and rave like a lunatic. We'll have to try to revive him first."

He looked at his watch and said to Bannister, "Come on now, the men from our shift are about to come back. Make tea for everyone."

"And him? Do we leave him?" the soldier asked about the prisoner.

Larichev said they would leave him, touching the holder of his own pistol, as if to signify that he would be keeping guard of the prisoner.

At that gesture, Michele shuddered.

Bannister went to the stove.

"Listen to me, writer", the Russian lieutenant said, after having looked at the prisoner again. "I'm going to make it possible for you to save your life. In these interrogations, you'll tell no one, absolutely no one, ever, that you're a writer. Do you understand?"

Without looking him straight in the face, Michele gestured his agreement.

"That's right. Meanwhile, I'll try to think up something. The essential thing for you is to get back alive to the rear guard. You know that, don't you? I'll say that you have, or it seems you have, information about . . . about . . . well, we'll see. I'm doing it to help you. You know that, don't you?"

More than ever dubious, Michele nodded a second time, without looking at him.

"That's it (*voilà*)", Larichev said.

20

One of the guards came into the isba to awake the next people on guard duty. As soon as these fellows got up, they found the prisoner, surrounded him, examined his jacket enviously, his boots. "*Sciassi*? (a watch)", one asked. But as Tintori did not answer, the Russian grabbed him with one hand by the hair and ear and began to shake him hard. "Wake up, you slime", he said. Larichev intervened, and with a few words the man desisted. "He has important information for us", he said. "Don't touch him." The eyes of the other soldiers turned toward him, astonished. "We've been lucky", the officer said, and this he uttered most sincerely.

The change of guard took place. The men who had been relieved came into the isba, commenting on the capture. Larichev ordered them not to approach the prisoner. He had Bannister give him a half cup of tea and a piece of black bread. Michele, who had not eaten for days, started to eat slowly (who knows when he'd eat again . . .) and forced himself not to show his hunger. The Russian officer ordered him in a severe tone of voice to get down on the floor against the wall.

"He's going to be delirious every so often", he explained to his men. "We can't send him to the company like this. He might try escaping through the snow, and it would mean our having to . . . and we want him alive."

He turned to the prisoner. "You're going to have to tell everything, you know that, don't you? Everything you know about the Germans coming to Millerovo, everything." He repeated these words in French. "You've told me about the German reinforcements arriving at Millerovo. You understand that? The Germans at Millerovo. Don't forget it."

Michele did not answer. Afterward all the Russians, the officer included (except one of the squadron who was to guard Tintori and had sat down on the stool), stretched out, and Michele tried to figure out what was happening to him. *What has come over that fellow? Was he serious, or was he pretending? But why would he have to pretend? Yes, but why would he have to be serious? It was certainly strange, inexplicable . . . what kind of mess have I got into?* He had gone through Millerovo the summer before, when they were advancing: those enormous factories scattered among thatched huts . . . But what did Millerovo have to do with it now? In any case, his enemies were leaving him alone now. No one was bothering him. He could (for how long?) enjoy this heat that was reviving him. *The first step is to take in as much heat as I can, relax my nerves, rest my mind. Especially that. Afterward, not now, but when I've come to a bit—I'll study the situation. I'll have to do a good job with that, because it's my own skin at stake this time.*

The stove, replenished shortly before, was gently crackling. The sound reminded him of the old wood stove in his house at Nova. Nova, his father. No, no, he couldn't think about his father now . . . It would be goodbye to any kind of repose. His house, yes, he could think about his house, the yard, the bamboo, so green in the sun. The noises from outside, even the occasional shot, sounded muffled, as if coming from a long distance, far away. *Yes, very far away, very far,* the prisoner repeated mentally, in a kind of unconscious counterpoint to the crackling of the stove. Suddenly he reacted. *Dear Lord, in what a terrible situation I'm in . . . my guardian angel, help me. I have never had greater need of you since I've been in this world. And you, too, Saint Michael, chief of the loyal angels, whose name I bear. It wasn't by chance that my father dubbed me with your name, you know that. But how shall I enjoin the battle of the faithful if now I should . . . die? When that poor man gave me your name . . .* His father! He must not think about his father, no. He must try to relax.

Relax, the most important thing was to relax, relax the mind, the nerves. The few external noises were still coming from far off, very far, very . . . He was stretched out in the heat, after three days and three nights of an exhausting march through fierce ice. Without realizing it, he fell into a deep sleep.

He was awakened by Lieutenant Larichev when the next change of guard duty took place. He had him tied up, this time without so much ceremony, his hands at his back, and he sent him off to company headquarters accompanied by a sibylline note that singled him out as "probably a source of important information regarding the Millerovo sector". A good enough reason for the pachyderm of a captain, after having removed his watch and addressed a number of questions in Russian to him, and then—through a totally inadequate interpreter—in German, he freed himself of the prisoner and sent him on to the major, who, without wasting any time, sent him even farther away. And always with the warning to keep the prisoner alive as a probable source of important information relative to the other sector of the front. Which, in the end, meant Tintori's salvation.

21

A few hours later, a little before it was time to become light (at that time of year there were sixteen hours of darkness during the day), Lieutenant Larichev was awakened by the sergeant, who had come into the isba urgently. "Come, immediately, Comrade Lieutenant. Something's wrong. It looks as if the Italians are getting ready to slink off."

Larichev leapt up and quickly put on his overcoat—draped over him like a blanket—grabbed his pistol and binoculars, and ran outside, along with the sergeant.

In the violet, scarcely incipient light, the enemy, indeed, could be seen gathering over in Arbusov, not in a very orderly fashion, it might be added. Perhaps not to set off at a march, because it did not seem they were forming into columns, but into large groups instead. Larichev observed them carefully with the binoculars in the sketchy light, as a growing vertigo permeated his guts.

"Feodor Cusmic, sound the alarm, wake everyone, and get the platoon in formation", he ordered, "and tell Macarov and Calatov . . ." He interrupted himself. "They're in the isba, aren't they?"

"Yes, they are."

"Call them first and tell them to get here in a hurry."

The sergeant moved off, voluminous in his long overcoat, hurrying to fulfill his orders. The two spies came out of the isba immediately. Calatov had the jacket of the dead Italian over one of his shoulders.

"You two, get to the captain at a gallop. As fast as possible, and don't let the enemy see you, of course", Larichev ordered. "Tell him, first, that the Italians are massing their troops and that, in my opinion, they're planning to attack. Second, you'll have to ask him what the orders for our troops are, and third, get back here immediately with the orders. I mean immediately!"

They both seemed a bit too impatient to be on their way. "One minute", Larichev stopped them. "You realize the fate of the entire platoon, everyone's life, depends on you?"

"Of course, Comrade Lieutenant", Corporal Macarov answered.

The officer would have preferred sending a couple of men he trusted, but it was all the same, he couldn't do otherwise. *As messengers, the captain assigned me these two pigs, and who knows if they'll come back?* "I'm giving you ten minutes to get there and back", he said. "Is that clear? In ten minutes you have to be back here, no matter what. Get going."

Calatov was all set to go. "One moment", Macarov objected. "Ten minutes if the captain gives us an immediate answer. But if not?"

Look here, just trying to find an alibi not to come back, Larichev thought. "I'm counting on you", he said. "I know you'll be back as soon as possible. But in case of an unjustifiable delay, you'll have to deal with me, rather, with all of us. You know I'm not joking. Go on. Don't waste any more time."

They did not wait for the order to be repeated. They were off running, one after the other, toward headquarters.

The officer went back to observing the enemy; meanwhile, the platoon was hurriedly getting in formation, within and without the two isbas. The only machine gun was set up in a window.

The men stationed with Larichev beside the highway turned from time to time to look at Macarov and Calatov, and once they disappeared from sight, they looked at the company isbas. Especially Bannister, who said to himself, *Let's hope the captain sends us the order to return in time. If not, we'll be stuck between two fires here.* Larichev guessed what Bannister was thinking, also the others, their fixed idea, and he answered mentally, *The order to station us here came from the major and was transmitted to us by the captain. To get us out of this mess, the order would have to be modified by the captain, and he won't do it.*

While he was mulling over these thoughts, the Russian heavy arms emplaced in the margins of the valley were beginning to fire, picking up at the point where the interrupted massacre had been left the night before. Then the Katyuskas came into operation. One rocket after another went off among the enemy masses. They blew men to pieces and forced the Italians to throw themselves frenetically to the ground, later to flee to some other spot.

"That's it, that's it", the soldiers from the platoon approved. "Very good, very good. Just so those S.O.B.s stop wanting to come here and make war."

Nevertheless, the Italian formations that had just gathered were beginning to move out in circles over the snow. It looked as if they had decided to become masters of the entire valley, no doubt to get away from that target shooting, in which almost any shot killed.

Larichev noticed that not all the Italians present in the town were attacking, perhaps not even the majority, at least for the moment, though there were many on the move. Toward the south they were already carrying out a great deal of fire fighting, reaching the first Russian positions in the snow. They were on the run, screaming and attacking with bayonets. In the general din the echo of their strange war cry resounded: "*Savoia! Savoia!*" *What a disaster*, Larichev kept saying to himself, more and more disturbed. *What a disaster! It'll be our turn next.* Here and there, mingling with the Italian troops, he could make out small nuclei of white-uniformed Germans, along with their weapons, machine guns or mortars. *Look how they back up the Italians*, he was thinking. *Where killing is concerned there'll be no lack of Germans.* And meanwhile no order from headquarters was forthcoming.

He could no longer watch the outcome of the battle. He had to concentrate all his attention on his limited sector, because the Italians were swarming up in great numbers from the bottom of the valley. Their bullets—not many now, as if testing—whistled through the air. Some hit the two isbas, sounding like a lashing of whips, breaking an occasional window. Suddenly the platoon machine gun opened fire noisily, and the soldiers began to fire from their rifles. Almost at the same time, two hundred yards farther back, the company weapons opened fire, then those of the battalion. Quite a few bullets were now hitting against the back part of the isbas. Two, three, four German mortar shells landed around them, too, deafening everyone posted there. The Italians, out in front, started to run. Some fell—many, he hoped—but others went on forward, screaming and shooting. The platoon defenses covered with snow—actually more an appearance of defenses than the real thing—were soon riddled with bullets, many men hit. The machine gun from the isba had gone silent, their operators no doubt killed. A step away from the officer, Bannister let out a scream. Larichev heard it despite the deafening clamor of a machine gun from the other side and turned his head. He saw his orderly wrapped around some stones, his forehead bleeding. Inside the second isba the gigantic sergeant with the threadbare overcoat was shot, and the men who had been with him rushed outside the building and set off at a dash like madmen toward company headquarters but were simultaneously run aground by enemy fire, as well as that of the company.

Quite a few of them who were still alive inside and outside the isbas, crouching on the ground, decided to be taken prisoner. The Italians were only a few yards away, vehemently shouting their war cry: "*Savoia! Savoia!*" In a few seconds they would be into the platoon defenses. On the highway post, Corporal Nikitenko, along with Larichev, was now the only survivor. He suddenly pulled a machine gun from the hands of a dead man and screamed, "Lieutenant, comrade, get out, get out!" He hurled himself toward the company. Totally stupefied, terrorized, unable to control himself, the officer followed him.

"Here!" Nikitenko screamed in the whirlwind of gunfire. "Here!" After a few big leaps on the road, he threw himself behind the closer isba, followed by the lieutenant. For an instant they saw some of the enemy at their backs, with bayonets aimed, going into their posts, shouting.

One of the enemies, the first, who preceded the others by a step or so, was not shouting but laughing. Larichev saw him only for a fraction of a second, but he was sure, so impressed by his face—rosy, young, without a trace of a beard, blue eyed, literally the face of a girl—that he was not shouting but laughing, seeming to be enjoying himself. Of slender build, the smiling enemy— but this Larichev had no time to notice—had the gold insignia of a noncommissioned officer on the sleeves of his jacket.

22

The two Russians did not remain in the shelter of the isba for more than a few seconds. They jumped over the corpse of the Sicilian carpenter, now covered with frost. (Larichev fleetingly remembered the photographs they had found, those very dignified looking people. When had he looked at those photos? How long ago was it? It had been during this same night, incredible! The dead man's wallet was still in his pocket.) They both took off toward the company. They made their way between lifeless bodies of comrades who had tried fleeing before them, trying to avoid bullets. Nikitenko was zigzagging furiously, and Larichev forced himself to follow suit, and, "Ugh!" the corporal suddenly grunted, and, "Ugh!" he grunted again, harder, after a few steps. A few yards from them, and perhaps thirty from the isba, there was a ditch in the shape of a funnel in the snowy terrain. Rather than entering it, Nikitenko threw himself into it. He had been carrying the machine gun but now left it, with obvious difficulty, on the snow, then hunched up. "It's all over for me", he murmured.

"What do you mean?" Larichev exclaimed panting.

"They got me here, and . . ." Nikitenko whispered, and he looked as if he was going to vomit. From his mouth came a little blood. After a pause, "I'm not going to make it to Voroshilovgrad", he whispered.

Larichev was beside himself with terror. "No! No!" he started to scream. "Vitia, it's not true. You're not wounded, nooooooo!" He stood up to go on, but it did not matter where, and the whistling of the bullets around him continued, and he had to throw himself into the ditch. Nikitenko had his forehead against the snow. A thread of blood coming from the corner of his mouth was the only movement in him. Larichev threw himself down at his side, his face and the front of his fur hat against the snow.

He had always, day after day, done his duty as a soldier, despite his unjust deportation, despite everything. But now . . . he was too sensitive . . . *I'm not fit for war. I know how to master myself for a certain time, but then . . . no, I can't go on, I simply can't. I've had enough, enough.*

He was breathing hard. And to have to, above all, give one's life to defend an abominable Communist dictatorship!

No, not communism. I'm defending Russia, not communism, but Russia. Just imagine, if in the past, everybody who disagreed with the leaders had refused to defend Russia. This thought was on his mind. He had thought about it so many times, and he was convinced of its evidence, and now that evidence was uppermost. *Of course, this went for the others, too, the Germans, the Italians . . . those poor wretches, too!*

He had been granted a moment of truce now, and this, more than what he was mulling over in his head, allowed him to muster his forces again.

Why have they stopped? he wondered.

"Vitia!" he called him again. "Vitia." The blood from Nikitenko's mouth was dripping now. But the corporal, like so many during those days, innumerable men, had undertaken the big journey, had left behind these atrocious miseries forever. Perhaps, Larichev thought—he believed in survival beyond the immediate—Nikitenko wanted to go to Voroshilovgrad to find out if his son had been shot; now he would go with him in spirit. Or perhaps now the things of this world were no longer important to him, not even the fate of his son, so far is this life from eternity.

Next to the dead man was the machine gun. Larichev cautiously stretched out his arm, took hold of the weapon, and placed it in front of him, on the edge of the hole. The enemy must all be lying crowded together on the ground by the isbas. *They must surely be getting ready for an attack on the battalion.* He knew there were hundreds, even though now he could only see—by raising his head—just a bit of helmet or jacket here and there, the outline of a back.

He tried the bolt of the weapon: it worked. Then he aimed at where he saw enemy helmets and let out a short round of fire. The helmets disappeared among clouds of snow. Larichev also had to duck rapidly back into the snow when it was his turn to be shot at.

23

At the round fired off by Larichev, Reano, the sergeant with the baby-girl face, stopped smiling. He was squatting with others in the shelter of a stone wall topped with snow. "This is what happens when you stop", he was muttering with vexation, and, "You never should stop during an attack", he insisted. He had made a mental note of it to the unknown captain who had ordered the stop. "Are we supposed to reorganize? Meanwhile, look what happens: so many dead, and the damn machine gun aiming at us from above!"

He turned around to look for the captain. He must have been some six or seven yards to the left; farther back, far off, the bulk of the others who had stayed in the town could be seen. *Completely worthless*, Reano thought. These people, though, who had joined this attack without anyone making them practically, well, they, after all . . . but even these, if it had been delayed a bit, only a bit, who could guarantee they wouldn't have turned back, they wouldn't have been overcome with fear, panic? He couldn't understand his compatriots since the beginning of the retreat. Until now he had thought they were the best soldiers in the world, and now . . . *The worst, that's what they are, the very worst!*

Ah, if his comrades in the exploratory platoon at Abrossimovo had been here . . . they were real men! He could see them now, one by one, people with guts, beginning with Mangiacavalli, the best of the lot. *Mangiacavalli!* Reano thought. He had been killed before the retreat during the action with the observer from artillery, Second Lieutenant Corte or Curti (if we want to be exact it was Corti, the future author, incidentally, of this novel). The second lieutenant had saved himself, he, who led the action, had saved himself, while Mangiacavalli had been left behind. As for the other scouts, almost all of them had died on the sixteenth, the first day of the big offensive, when the Russians managed to advance up to Abrossimovo and overwhelm them. Well, if his comrades were no longer about, it was his turn now, that of Sergeant Reano, the nineteen-year-old volunteer, instead of twiddling his thumbs, to do something in the old style, for instance, to cut off that damn machine gun, situated over there in front of them. The moment had come for him to use his "bomb".

He turned to those nearest, squatting a few steps from him. "Hey, you, can you hear me?"

"Yes", one voice answered.

"Is the captain there?"

"Yes, he's here behind the corner of the house."

"Tell him that I'm going to hurl myself on the machine gun. Did you hear me?"

"Yes, but . . . just a moment."

"Tell him to be all ready, as soon as that machine gun's cleared out, then everybody out."

"Wait 'til I tell him."

"Well, hurry up then."

Ten seconds went by. Reano—who was beginning to enjoy himself again and to smile—heard the voice of the officer giving the order to be ready. "Everybody ready for the attack." Then, again, the voice of the soldier at his back. "Eh, you."

"Yes? My name's Reano."

"Reano? The captain says all right, we're ready."

"I'm off then."

He took a heavy Russian hand bomb with a handle from his belt, far more effective than those Italian toys. (He had kept it for weeks, since Abrossimovo: Mangiacavalli and Lieutenant Corti laughed about it then.) He gripped it with his right hand and with his left hand took his automatic machine gun, breathed deeply, then leapt out and began to run like someone possessed toward the machine gun. After ten or twelve yards of running, he threw the bomb hard. "*Savoia!*" he screamed, and, while he ran, he yelled, "Come on, out, out, all of you out! *Savoia!*"

"*Savoia!*" the others yelled, leaping to their feet and running forward like madmen.

It was a question of seconds. While the bomb spun around in the air, the enemy machine gun opened fire against Reano: one, two, three shots. The bomb fell behind the machine gun and exploded. The machine gunner, Lieutenant Larichev, had his head blown off. His weapon fell forward and was left like a broomstick, while the little sergeant Reano, with the automatic in his left hand, fell face down, smiling.

The others followed at a run, together with another big formation that came forward from about a hundred yards to the left. They hurled themselves forward, firing and shouting toward the isbas occupied by the battalion, from which the Russians began to flee in disarray, and, still falling back, they continued to fire. Many of those attacking fell under that retaliating gunfire. Most of them, however, continued forward.

No one, at that moment, had eyes for the Italian Sergeant Reano or the Russian Lieutenant Larichev. No one would have been able to help: both their deaths were instantaneous. No one could have repeated Reano's name later, because the soldier Reano had told his name to, after having repeated it several times to himself with admiration, had forgotten it. And as for Larichev, the only one of his men who was still alive was Sukorukov, from the region of Vologda, who pretended to be dead under the bodies of two dead comrades at the henhouse. (Those made prisoners by the Italians were no sooner taken to the town than kidnapped and killed by the Germans.) He did not make a move until nighttime, swearing in his heart about war, the enemies, the friends, the cold, and communism, which had deprived him of his little patch of land, as well as the cold in his nose, which required constant blowing. Already dark, he stood up cautiously. In their bayonet attack the Italians had managed to occupy all the crests of the Arbusov Valley, which they took custody of with the few who had survived the battle. There were not many, because the others in the town had not gone to their aid, not even when the combat was over. So it was not difficult for Sukorukov, walking silently over the snow, to get by the enemy posts—not even realizing they were that—until he left the valley. He was lucky enough to meet up with a bivouac of Russian tanks farther up on the road and was led back to his company, where the first thing he asked about was his food ration. Concerning Lieutenant Larichev he could only say that he had probably been killed in combat.

24

The column remained three whole days in that atrocious Arbusov Valley, which later, in the conversations of the survivors, was dubbed "the valley of death". Actually, when a count was made of the bodies of the dead Italians, scattered over the length and breadth of the snow, there turned out to be thousands, perhaps more than in any one of the big battles of the war—for instance, the '41 Christmas battle on the same Russian front or the battle of El Alamein in Africa. Here, however, the great majority did not fall in combat; they were vainly fleeing here and there under enemy fire.

After the Russians were pushed farther back beyond the high edges of the valley, the firing was intensified, as new mortar and artillery units were added. But they had lost some efficiency because they were deprived of observation and, too, the space in which the Italians were surrounded had grown.

The usual young men of goodwill had sustained the weight of the attacks to push the enemy farther back out of the valley: always the same young men, those who even before the retreat had been the backbone and cement of the detachments. Among these, a certain number had died in recent combats over the Don; others—like Bonsaver—in the encounters at the beginning of the retreat, and all or nearly all the others were to die in those attacks. Those gone, detachments were no longer detachments, and nothing remained—as Ambrogio declared many times—but an atomized mass of terrified individuals, intent only on saving their lives, yet incapable for that reason to exercise the most minimal initiative or discipline. During the terrible marches that followed the halt at Arbusov, leaning heavily on Paccoi's arm, the officer often remembered the words he had been saying at the moment he was wounded: "These are no longer soldiers", and he bitterly had to admit their validity.

After three nights and two days of almost continuous marching, with night temperatures truly polar, and after repeated combats to open the way, now carried out only by the lead Germans, the column—very reduced—reached the city of Cercovo. There a small Italian contingent, made up of clerks, warehousemen, and rearguard staff that a Bersagliere lieutenant colonel had brought to the front line, held out, isolated in the dead white of the plains.

Cercovo is situated next to a train line running to the north and to the south, a kind of extension—between Voronez and the Azov Sea—of the immense eastern German front, which then still connected the glacial Arctic sea to Voronez intact. The tragic column received orders to entrench themselves in the small city, while other retreating Italian and German forces were being sent by convoys to protect other areas on the same railway line. Fresh German troops were expected from France meanwhile.

The Russians had the city completely surrounded, the start of the apocalyptic days of the Cercovo siege, which we will not go into here, as the reader may find this tragic story described in another place. Suffice it to say that Ambrogio lived through those days in a state of semiconsciousness, because the very morning of their arrival he was injured a second time by an insidious mortar shrapnel that became lodged in his back near his kidneys.

With his chest wound suppurating, burning with fever, tormented by lice, he spent the first part of the siege in a makeshift "infirmary" that was soon transformed into a living hell where the newly wounded were continually being carried and from which new cadavers were being removed every morning to be buried in huge holes dug out at the side of the door. The surviving officers of his group (Major Casasco was not among them, nor was Cavallo Sanco, his aide, or the young Neapolitan topographer) took him from there to their isba. His assistant Paccoi followed him everywhere, doing what he could for him. Toward the middle of January, during a Russian bombardment that left not a single building in the little town intact, Paccoi was also wounded: a splinter from a red-hot grenade went through his left wrist, miraculously missing the veins. (There would have been no hope for him otherwise.)

Meanwhile, since the enemy push continued toward the west, gradually beating back the random German troops that were trying to contain it, the reestablishment of the front along the railway line was deemed impossible. Those who were besieged received orders to march out—those who could—and to join the precarious Germans lines before they withdrew.

The column left Cercovo and reached them on the night of January 17 in Bielovosc. Of the twenty-five thousand Italians surrounded over the Don on the night of December 19, scarcely four thousand, a good part of them frostbitten or wounded, remained. The majority of the others had ended up in the hands of the enemy.

That fifty-mile walk from Cercovo to Bielovosc was carried out slowly by Ambrogio and Paccoi, hanging on to each other's arms. ("And then, Lieutenant, there will be those who say we weren't lucky. What more would we want? Haven't we still got one good arm left?") Little by little they lost ground, becoming separated from the column. They at last found themselves in the paralyzing immensity of the plain, moving like two ants, stopping every so often because of Ambrogio's fatigue. A few times he ordered Paccoi to go ahead, at least to save himself. ("I'm in charge here, you understand? I'm giving the orders.") Paccoi shook his head with the patience of a peasant, let Ambrogio talk, and then asked, "Well, are you finished with your complaint, Lieutenant?" and they went back to linking their arms. They reached the column only thanks to its extended stops, provoked by the combats that the

Germans and the remainder of Battalion M were forced to carry out in order to open their way.

Once in Bielovosc, their strength depleted, both of them running a fever, they entered an isba and stayed there several days, unable to start walking again, now indifferent to the idea of falling prisoner. The other Italians were taken by trucks to Starobelsk, thirty more miles to the west. The Germans on the mobile front who were preventing enemy entrance into Bielovosc picked up the two wounded men—a Russian woman had pointed out where they were—and at the last moment took them from the city. In Starobelsk, where the train was still miraculously functioning, they were put on a "train turned into a hospital" (composed of goods carriages equipped with cots and stoves), which left them in Leopoli, Poland, after a week of painful travel.

25

Ambrogio and Paccoi stayed in the Italian hospital at Leopoli for several weeks, enjoying a bed with clean sheets. Under treatment, they were able to recover. Paccoi responded faster, and both of them were on the same floor, but in different wards. After only two or three days of convalescence Paccoi began to visit the officer. He had his injured wrist wrapped in the whitest bandages—a pleasure just to look at them—and his arm in a sling, which was also sparkling clean.

The hospital was well organized and was surrounded by a garden, spacious and almost new. "Lieutenant, do you know what the orderlies in my detachment say? That this was the madhouse in the city, and the Germans killed all the inmates, poor things, and transformed it into a hospital for their own men. Then, when we came into the war with Russia, they assigned it as a 'hospital in transit' to us."

"What, they killed all the inmates?"

"Yes", Paccoi answered. "They killed them all. Poor people, don't you think?"

In the bed to the left of Ambrogio (on the other side was a window that gave onto the garden) was a captain who had been there for a month, his face drained of blood, his two legs amputated. He confirmed Paccoi's statement. "Yes, they killed all the mental patients. That's how it was."

"But ... excuse me, where did you hear this? May I ask who told you?"

"I was told by the orderlies. But down below, in the basement area, there are still Polish sisters who worked in the madhouse laundry and who occasionally come up to help our men even if it is forbidden. I asked them straight out. At the beginning they did not wish to answer, but then they confirmed it." The captain was speaking with the most obvious pain. Ambrogio was not sure if it was out of physical suffering from his destroyed body or because of the words he was speaking. If you think about it, what an immense amount of pain there is in the world! Only now, here among those suffering, did he begin to be really aware of it.

With his aide and other men there on the mend, the young man would converse, mostly about Italy, where they would be returning shortly. And they brought up—it was inevitable—the events of the terrible retreat, which became better and better expounded. Names of friends and acquaintances came up, whose fate was unknown to them. Who knows if those who had ended up in the hands of the Russians, as they fell back in the marches or were cut off (according to the most widespread opinion—as we have already said—the majority must have been missing) were still alive?

People in the hospital in Leopoli did not know what to think. Many stories of massacres committed by the Russians circulated. One of them—not so new, in fact—was brought by Paccoi one day to Ambrogio. "Lieutenant, I've heard still another story, even worse than the one about killing the mad people, but done by the Russians, not the Germans."

"What's that?"

"Well, when they left Leopoli, the Russians killed all the middle-class Poles who were in prison. All together several thousands: the men, many women, too, and the priests. Since they couldn't take them with them, they killed them all, shooting them down in the head, here behind, at the nape of the neck."

This episode was also confirmed by the captain in the next bed. "It happened at the beginning of the war, but, from what the orderlies say, the people in the town are still talking about it a lot. It was the Communist policemen—here they call them the 'blue caps'—who carried out the slaughter."

"Exactly, the blue caps, that's what I heard", Paccoi said.

"Good God, what an awful world we live in! The poor Poles", Ambrogio murmured. "But Giovanni" (he now called his aide by his given name), "why are you bringing me these stories?"

Paccoi looked at him, confused. "So you'll know. You always want to know everything."

Ambrogio had to admit he was right. Lying back in bed, his face looked grievous. "This is one of the stories Michele would have been interested in", he murmured.

"You mean Lieutenant Tintori, don't you? I still don't know how he could have disappeared that night in the 'valley of the dead'. Who knows if he even made it?" Paccoi said. "During the night he had stretched out next to me in the hayloft, and then I heard him get up. Then, in the morning, he wasn't there. Where could he have gone?" He thought a moment. "Who knows if he's still alive? In Cercovo, you know, none of the infantry officers from his battalion said they'd seen him dead."

"Yes, but if this story you brought me now is really true ..." Ambrogio murmured, interrupted himself, and did not continue.

"If it's really ... ?" Paccoi asked, inviting him to go on.

"If he was taken prisoner by the Russians, what hope would there be for him, and for all the others?"

A little ways from them the Red Cross ward nurse was working, Sister Glicerie, an old pale woman, as pale as those convalescing, but very active. After having glanced over at them, she came up to his bed. "Lieutenant, you know you shouldn't be tiring yourself."

"I'm not", Ambrogio answered, half smiling.

"A little patience", the sister said. "It's a matter of days, given the fact that your organism, as the professor said, is recuperating." She turned to Paccoi. "Now you, young man, I'm not telling you not to come to see him, but don't get him talking. Is that understood? You shouldn't."

Paccoi gestured a yes, confused as usual.

"Thank you, sister", Ambrogio murmured.

"That's it. You're fine boys."

The woman went back to what she was doing, arranging a night table for one of the patients who had lost almost all of his fingers through frostbite. She had the manners of a genuine lady, and she did not mind doing the most humble tasks.

Ambrogio and Paccoi looked at each other with the smile of schoolboys. Thanks, above all, to the sisters from the Red Cross, what a difference between this clean hospital and the infirmary at Cercovo, where smoke permeated the rooms from the ceiling to almost a yard from the floor, where lice swarmed on all sides, where there was a stench because the corridor had been made into a water closet, and where, hardly outside the door, pits were filled with frozen corpses.

At the end of a week Ambrogio had also recovered quite a bit and was able, in his turn, to visit Paccoi. They then began exchanging visits. In Paccoi's ward—much larger than Ambrogio's—was another soldier from the patrols being treated for frostbite on one foot: Mazzoleni, Piantanida's friend. The latter had remained behind in Cercovo forever, buried under a little straw and snow; thus, of the two friends, one had been taken and the other remained. Also in this big ward was Sergeant Feltrin, in charge of the automobiles in the Third Battery, who, on the evening of the beginning of the retreat, had informed Ambrogio of a lack of fuel. Now Feltrin had a strange nervous disease: he was unable to sleep, and his eyes had sunk incredibly. He was hoping to get better, though, and so he clung to Ambrogio's assurance. "Once back in Italy, you'll see, there are specialists for these nervous disorders, and you'll get well, I'm certain of it."

"Really?"

"Yes."

"When you can, Lieutenant, come see me. You cheer me up."

In the same ward—there were more than forty patients—there was also one of the Alpine troops from the Tridentina Division, who sat the entire day with his back against the headboard of his bed. A redhead, with a red beard, as skinny as a toothpick; there was no chance he would survive, and he knew it. During an operation to remove a piece of shrapnel, they had discovered—despite his youthful age—an already advanced tumor. Ambrogio went to see him more than once and found out that he vaguely knew the chaplain Gnocchi, but not Luca or Lieutenant Galbiati. The only thing he knew about the Tridentina Division was that these days they were shut into a dead-end passage together with the entire Alpine army. A situation—he kept repeating—he would gladly change with his own: better the evil outside—he affirmed—no matter how tremendous, facing it all together with the Alpine troops, than this silent and atrocious evil inside, for which there was no remedy.

The sum total of pain in the world is unlimited.

26

One night, Ambrogio was awakened by a persistent shouting that penetrated his world through the closed door. What could be happening? He had the impression it was coming from Paccoi's big ward, situated at the back of the corridor.

The lieutenant tried to get back to sleep but could not. He realized the captain in the next bed was also awake. "What could it be?" Ambrogio asked in a low voice. "All this uproar?"

"It seems they're asking for the bedpan, or they want to be turned over in the bed", he answered, also in a low voice. "Probably all the orderlies have fallen asleep."

"Ah."

"After the latest wounded come in, the nursing staff don't get around to everybody. You know they've given up their day off, but they want to sleep at night."

"I see."

"It happened last month, too", the captain said. "They let them shout for hours."

"How long has this shouting been going on? I just woke up now."

"Well, about an hour."

Ambrogio tried going back to sleep, but the voices from the other side of the door seemed to be growing more intense, and sleep was impossible. He decided. "I'm going to see if there is something I can do", he murmured.

Trying to avoid any brusque movements (he still had the shrapnel in him, near his kidneys), he put his feet outside the bed, stepped into his hospital slippers, and stood up.

In the corridor the shouting became even more noisy. The young man opened the door of the big ward and, walking slowly, went inside, guided by the light of the bluish night lamps. He noticed the redheaded Alpine man seated, as usual, against the headboard of the bed. He waved to him, and the other nodded back. He seemed very tense. Feltrin was also awake, his eyes open in the darkness. Some of them that needed help noticed his presence and began calling, almost yelling.

The officer—in his pajamas, not recognizable for what he was—came up to one of them with a bandaged head. "Calm down", he said. "What do you need?"

"The bedpan. I can't hold it anymore. Please, the bedpan", the other man grumbled.

"All right, I'll bring it. Where are they kept?"

"How do I know? The bedpan, I need it", the wounded man said in a fury.

"A little patience. First I have to find it."

Seeing him going between the beds, others began to call him, some swearing. *Where in the devil are the bedpans?* the lieutenant was wondering. *No doubt in the ward bathrooms. They must be there, or else there . . . one of those two doors; perhaps the one at the corner, we'll see.* The tumult was growing.

Before he reached the door at the corner—which gave on to the service staircase—it opened, and two nuns came into the large room. *They must be the Polish nuns from the laundry,* Ambrogio immediately decided.

He went up to meet them. "Would you happen to know, please, where the bedpans are kept?" he asked.

The first nun nodded.

"It's for . . . them", the lieutenant said, pointing to the bed.

The nun made another sign of agreement and went quickly toward the locker. The nun beside her went into action quickly, too. The officer would have liked to help, but he let things be immediately, since the two women knew better than he what to do. They went from one bed to another, carrying bedpans and then bringing them back. Where help was needed to turn over one of the injured men, they acted jointly. When he saw them having trouble turning over a soldier of some weight, the officer helped, but he stopped when he remembered that this kind of effort was forbidden him because of the shrapnel in his own body. He ended up watching—in the bluish light of the night lights—the Polish sisters, who were performing a duty discreetly and silently, intervening without confusion at all places they were needed. *After all they have suffered and go on suffering, all because of us,* the young man reflected, moved, *they only think of doing good, and do just that despite orders to the contrary . . . have ever better people been seen living . . . physically living the Gospels?* In a short while, his emotion was transformed into a kind of irrepressible joy, because, just look, creatures like this do exist on earth! *This is a way to answer the evil there is in the world. Just look, it's right in front of my eyes!*

He remained in this joyous state until—the entire ward now calmed down—the two sisters were about to leave. Then, he thought, it was time to thank them, time to show them that he had understood them. But how if he didn't know their language? He could, at least, shake their hands ... he did that in a kind of embarrassed solemnity, but he did not know how to do anything else.

It was the redheaded Alpine soldier—he was also moved—who resolved the situation. When it became silent once again, he began to sing this sad Alpine song, in a restrained voice:

> Sister dear, sister dear, I beg of you,
> give a flower to my mother,
> for tomorrow I won't be back,
> tomorrow, I won't be back tomorrow.

The two sisters came and stood listening in silence. They understood the word *sister*, they also understood the word *mother*, and no doubt they made the connection. Ambrogio saw them nod a few times. They left when the soldier finished his song.

27

The following morning the aide Paccoi, as awake as his temperament allowed, came in to see Ambrogio. Paccoi had slept the night through, unaware of anything that had happened. "Lieutenant, do you know who's here among the latest of the wounded? Tremola."

"Oh, yes, Tremolada you mean, from Monticello."

"The very one."

"What floor is he on? He's hurt?"

"Yes, he's wounded, but not too seriously. He's on the floor below us. It's his arm. Maybe he'll lose his elbow, he said, but maybe it can be saved."

"Did he say anything about Luca, my countryman, Corporal Luca Sambruna?"

"No. He said the Alpine troops are now stuck in a cul-de-sac."

"We already know that. Well, take me to him."

Tremolada was delighted to see them. His right arm was out stiff and wrapped in snow-white bandages. A bullet, he explained, had gone through the length of his forearm, from his wrist to his elbow. "It happened on the thirteenth, almost two weeks ago, in a fortified position over the Don. It wasn't any real big thing, a little nothing of a patrol. Luca was letting off the 'heavy gun', and I was loading it, when a spray of gunfire—but few shots ..." As usual, he spoke in dialect: "The thirteenth, Lieutenant, and then some say the thirteenth is lucky!"

"Well, you've avoided getting caught in the cul-de-sac, perhaps."

"Oh, perhaps that", Tremolada agreed, not entirely convinced.

"Of course, only by the skin of your teeth. If you'd had to carry on, injured that way, you'd have been lost from the start, you know that?"

"No, why? If it had been necessary, I'd have gone on a sled", the Alpiner said faithfully. "In the Morbegno Battalion they don't abandon the wounded, surely. The town where the hospital was, Podgornoie—that's the name—well, on the fourteenth, the trucks that had brought the ammunition were filled with the men with light wounds, and also not so light. Maybe they felt the approaching storm."

"Did you see Don Carlo Gnocchi?"

"Yes, of course. He came to the hospital while we were being loaded. 'What are you doing here?' he asked. 'And only because you wanted leave to go to Monticello, was that it?' 'Wouldn't I like that!' I answered. Then he told me to give my regards to Monticello, that as a kid he always went there with his mother for the feast day of Saint Agatha. He even recited those verses, do you know them? 'Monticello / pretty and little / if it were on the plain / it would seem part of Milan.' But it happens to be in the mountains, and looks like the bottom of a basket, I answered like a child. Oh, Lieutenant", Tremolada went on. "Don Carlo even made me drink a sip out of a flat-bottomed flask. How good it was: it was as if the Lord had swum in it."

Ambrogio and Paccoi spent more than a half hour talking to him. They could not, obviously, get anything clear regarding Luca's situation or that of Lieutenant Galbiati from Nomana. The Alpine man seemed full of confidence—without any boasting, however—about the success of the terrible situation in which the Alpine troops were then involved.

Because he doesn't really know what it is to be in a cul-de-sac, he has no idea what happens when you're surrounded like that, Ambrogio told himself later, full of pessimism. And he could imagine Luca marching over the endless stretches of snow, his face drawn with fatigue, stupefied with cold.

At night—every night—he relived the events of his own route, and Luca repeatedly became intermingled in it. On occasion, Luca appeared in his dreams with his Alpine uniform on, his reddish beard, like the way he looked when he came to visit the artillery line over the Don, and other times he was dressed in his mechanic's outfit, without a beard, the way he looked when he was working in the factory in Nomana, during peacetime.

PART SIX

I

Actually, Luca was spending that night (the ninth day of the retreat of the Alpine forces) at Nikitovca, a big town situated about 130 miles walking from the old front over the Don. The young Alpine corporal was worn out, which hardly needs mentioning, terribly tired, not so much from the marching and continuous combats, but from having carried the machine gun on his shoulders, even if he did it alternating with mates from his squadron.

The previous night, when he had unloaded in front of the isba, where he was now sleeping, he felt so light it seemed he could levitate into the air. And that impression had not disappeared even when he was later seated on the dirt floor of the isba, avidly devouring his survival kit mess (honey mixed with wax), or even later when he, along with the other Alpine men, joined in the responses to the Rosary recited by a corporal from the mortar unit in a very inexact Latin. The young man then stretched out on the ground to sleep, squeezed between the rest of the men in his squadron. Though the isbas of Nikitovca had been divided up by the Tridentina staff among the Alpine units and the stragglers, following in their tracks, it is most certain they could hardly hold all of them; and this despite their having ordered the bulk of the column vanguard to go ahead toward Arnautovo, a tiny village situated some miles ahead toward the west.

Luca's isba was situated on the western end of the town, therefore toward Arnautovo. A little before midnight noises and light from gunfire began reaching them from there. But, as they were all sleeping under the weight of a fierce tiredness inside the isba, none of them took any notice of it. Even if they had been aware of the noise and gunfire, they would not have worried themselves about it, because the Tridentina command functioned smoothly, and therefore, had it been necessary, they would have intervened. General Reverberi was in charge, and all the Alpine troops from the division trustfully referred to him as "our father". (In their simple minds a more appropriate term to express the concept of authority did not exist, in spite of—if we may be allowed to give our opinion—all the foolishness, even scholarly, that in following decades was proclaimed against "paternalism".)

It was warm in the isba, and apart from the muffled sounds coming from outside, nothing could be heard but the breathing and snoring of the sleeping Alpine troops and the cozy crackling of the fire, which was reminiscent of mountain shelters. As in the shelters, the cracks in the stove spread a tenuous light over everything. During the night no one awoke except one or another of the mule drivers (it was normal for them to awaken periodically—tired or not), who, careful not to step on the sleeping bodies, would go out to have a look at the mules. The air that filled one's lung outside was so icy after the warmth within the isba, it felt like melted lead. And the mules in front of the isba all had their heads lowered and their tails between their legs, standing still in the merciless cold. The mules and sleds beside the other isbas could also be seen in the darkness. After having a look around to see if there was anyone or anything suspicious (it would happen, in fact, that an occasional straggler would steal an animal for food), the mule driver would go up to his mules, check the frozen blanket, even caress their necks a while, as well as their frost-covered muzzles, uttering a rude word or two in its ear, by way of comfort. They were excellent animals and completely fulfilled their roles as helpers to the Alpine troops. Then the driver would go back in the isba, throw another log in the stove if necessary, and return to his place to sleep.

2

One of these mule drivers accidentally stepped on Luca, waking him up with a start. It was around three in the morning. After a brief exchange of insults and embarrassed excuses, as the young corporal was going back to sleep, he felt drawn by the sound of the firing, which was then coming through with particular intensity. Even the glass in the small window blinked with the lights of the distant battle. *Seems they're really going at it*, the young man told himself tiredly. *Let's hope the battalions that went on ahead yesterday evening won't end up like the Morbegno did . . .* It was not something he could do anything about, of course, but he could not help but think about the totally unexpected tragic outcome of the Morbegno, his battalion, which finally made his blood boil until he was completely awake. He still couldn't believe it . . . the disaster had been so unexpected! Only by a miracle were he and his squadron now still in the Alpine column and not dead or taken prisoner like the other men in the battalion. That is, if there were any prisoners . . . but was it possible that all of them, really all of them, all those men in the battalion had died? It didn't seem possible. Luca changed his posture, rather difficult, squeezed as he was against the others. Giordano Galbiati must be dead by now, because on the evening the Morbegno took the wrong road, he was already fading away on one of the ambulance sleds. It had gone bad for him a few hours before, during the battle against Seliakino. Lieutenant Galbiati was one of the few who had had the guts to get close to an armored car with a bottle of gasoline in one hand and a Breda bomb in the other. When the distance was just right he hurled the bottle against the tank and then threw the bomb on the gasoline. But he could not make it in Seliakino. What a problem—Luca thought now—to have to tell his father and mother back in Nomana. He sighed. Nomana, his family, Giustina . . . he had the last of Giustina's fortnightly letters in his pocket, from his Giustina . . . what a pretty face, so honest, and when she laughed those two dimples, her delicate neck, and her chestnut hair gathered at the nape of her neck . . . she wrote punctually to him one week and to Stefano, her brother, the next. Stefano! Stefano! God knows if he was still alive now, after the Bersaglieri had been swallowed up by the Russian advance. And Ambrogio Riva? Where would he be now? As for Giordano Galbiati, he, yes, he was undoubtedly dead. If, at least, on that filthy evening when the Morbegno took the wrong road, he, Luca, had checked to see how his compatriot was, if only he had picked up one of his last words to take back to his family. And to think the sled Giordano was stretched out on at the end of his life went by him only a few yards away! Luca was aware of every detail: the ambulance sleds came by as usual at the end of the battalion, accompanied by a chaplain, Don Caneva. He, Luca, was with his squadron on foot at the wooden bridge, with the order to protect the passage of the stragglers from a possible return offensive by a group of partisans that had been put to flight by his company. When Don Caneva went by with the wounded men, Luca had left the machine gun momentarily and had gone up to him. "Is Lieutenant Galbiati still alive?" he had asked. Without stopping the chaplain signaled he was. "Are you from his town?" he asked him.

"Yes, that's why I'm asking."

"Tell his family he's confessed like a good Christian."

"Why? Won't he make it?"

Don Caneva gestured negatively with his hand. Luca, bowed down at that moment, did not know how to do anything else but return to his machine gun. *I should have insisted on seeing him! But how was I to know then that those were the last hours of the battalion, to imagine that in the course of the night the Morbegno would be wiped out?* He and his squadron were saved only by the act of being left behind at the bridge, a kind of miracle. Luca turned over again; outside, toward Arnautovo, the shooting continued.

And how many other terrible cases in the course of that retreat! The young man remembered the tough battle in Malacaievo, where long lines of the dead were left on the snow: dead men like weeds . . . mainly Russians, that's true, but a lot of Alpine men, too. And in that other town, what was its name?— when the combat went on in the middle of a furious storm, and they were all fighting like blind men? And in . . . Livigno? That long village, so long, with a single row of isbas constructed along the length of the street. Some of the men, when they saw it from far off, had said, "It really looks like Livigno, our Alpine town," and it seemed to be a good augury for all of them. But, there too, it was tough going. He also remembered when that strange column appeared from the right, and they didn't know who they were. A mountain cannon was shot once, but they didn't react, only waved their arms and signaled, poor wretches, and they turned out to be Hungarians—several thousand Hungarians—who had been left without ammunition and had managed to escape, who knows how, the Russians. They then joined up with the Tridentina, along with other stragglers. And the shots from the partisans in that town with windmills? And the big to-do among the disbanded stragglers in Opit, maybe on the second day of the retreat, when . . .

We cannot go on this way, heaping up the memories in Luca's mind. To give the reader an idea of what the situation was at that moment it is necessary to relate with a minimum of order with the events of the retreat, so different from that of the Bersaglieri and the ordinary troops. We shall do it as briefly as possible.

3

In the second part of December the enemy had penetrated up to Boguciar and beaten back the other two bodies of the Italian army situated over the Don. On the northern front, the bulk of the Alpine army remained on the right flank, exposed. As we know, it was along the river, just a bit before the big loop, so looking to the east. The Alpines had only been able to pull out the Julia Division from the middle of their formation and employ it over the snow toward the right, where there was a great gap. Somehow, to cover this gap to the south of the Julia, the Twenty-Fourth German Armored Division had appeared, the only reserves ready (despite the name it scarcely added up to thirty armored tanks, apart from the two already very depleted German infantry divisions). Against the Julia Division, as well as this corps, the new enemy attack was rapidly developing, no longer led—as was believed—by the forces that had entered Boguciar but by huge fresh forces composed of two armored tank corps (about 350 tanks), an infantry division, and also a cavalry division. During one entire terrible month the Julia—stationed in the open, on the snow— had resisted the Russian infantry attack without retreating. The attacks went on almost without respite. In front of some companies—such as the Fifty-Ninth from the Vicenza Battalion, the so-called company of the friars—more than four hundred dead were counted in one single day. At no point did that famous division yield even an inch of the line, which was only a few yards wide and some thirteen miles long, which made up its new front. The Abruzzi from the Aquila Battalion, though persistently attacked, had not given up either, even after having lost three-quarters of their men. From time to time, as far as the most distant Alpine fortifications over the Don—where an uneasy calm prevailed—news would come of the incomparable bravery of the mountaineers from the Abruzzi who went on resisting imperturbably.

The German Twenty-Fourth, in contrast, had not been able to contain the enemy armor, far superior, and within a few weeks had all but been annihilated. Their chief, General Wandel, had fallen in battle. His successor, General

Jarr, when the armored tank division was left without any more tanks, committed suicide, and his successor, General Eibl, had retreated with the slaughtered remains of his troops behind the Julia bastion. There were only very few weapons of any efficiency left: four mobile armored cannons, or *panzer jager*, which are memorable because they proved extraordinarily useful once they were integrated into the Alpine formations, and six thousand or seven thousand exhausted men who were—quite unusual for the Germans—almost unarmed.

Meanwhile, in the course of that month, on the other flank of the Alpine positions, that is, toward the north, the enemy had thrown in still more impressive forces than those operating in the south, to be precise, the Fortieth Army and the Eighteenth Armored Division, destroying a long stretch of the front line held by the tough Hungarian Division. The two Russian blocks, in the north and in the south, had through converging maneuvers, joined each other at the back of the Alpine army. So when, on the seventeenth of January, the high command of the Italian army transmitted by radio the order to the Alpine troops to retreat, they had also warned them that the Russians had already arrived within a hundred miles behind them and were continuing their westward march.

Luca had left his base over the Don on the night of the seventeenth of January (the same day that, more to the south, Ambrogio left his besieged area), along with his battalion, the Morbegno, which, like all the rest of the Tridentina Division, was performing with perfect efficiency. There were a large number of mules in the Alpine ranks, almost all of them in good condition, which carried ammunition and other materials on sleds, except for what was needed for immediate use, which was carried by the men themselves, on their shoulders. Luca had the 20 kg machine gun on his shoulders, for instance.

During that atrociously cold night and the following day, the eighteenth of January, the formidable battalions of the Tridentina Battalion gathered in Podgornoie, a large rearguard town. Here Luca met up with an unexpected and incredible concentration, not only of Alpine troops and sleds and beasts of burden, but also of rearguard motorized units as well as an enormous number of disbanded stragglers, said to be around forty thousand men, made up of Italians from other divisions, Hungarians, Romanians, Germans in white uniforms. Some supply deposits were burning; others were about to be savagely pillaged. Nevertheless, there were still some of the non-Alpine units carrying out their duties. Among them was the antiair artillery unit, which brought down an enemy reconnaissance plane (one of those evil airplanes that in the next days would have the column under its control, periodically flying over it at a great height). While he remained in Podgornoie, the young man had a spectacle in front of him not different from the one offered by the rearguard of ordinary troops at the moment of abandoning the front. He was most impressed by the chaos and the material goods scattered everywhere on the snow. The Alpines kept clear of the disorder contagion. After calmly awaiting the arrival of their platoons that had stayed behind in the trenches to provide cover for others, toward evening they began to proceed out of the city, each battalion alternating with a mountain artillery group, thus beginning the great march to the west, leaving the disorder behind them.

Mountaineer Alpine and artillery troops were different even in appearance from the Bersaglieri and ordinary troops. Physically solid because of the tough mountain life they had led from the time they were children and completely alien to assuming heroic attitudes, they gave the impression of strength—rough and calm at the same time—to anyone observing them. Although not inclined to being aggressive (in Greece this at first had created serious problems for the high command), neither were they ready to yield in the face of the strength of an opponent, because to a man, even the most modest, to yield is not dignified. Their celebrated esprit de corps—quite evident—was a natural outcome of the spirit of their village and valley, in which they all felt themselves to be, down deep, members of one big family. Added to this was the secure confidence that every Alpine man had in his own comrades (and this undoubtedly was their greatest strength), something that, no matter what the circumstance, kept them united. If, by chance, the vicissitudes of combat did separate one of them, that individual would do his utmost to reunite with his own men.

People of simple hearts, the Alpiners were quite bereft of cunning. If only other Italians were a little more like them, at least in this respect. As a rule, each mountaineer looked after his own modest tools with great care (also his own weapon) and was ready to sacrifice himself not to lose them, and yet they did not have that kind of cult of the machine that characterizes the Germans, for example, though they are undoubtedly brave soldiers. A minimum of weapons were enough for the Alpine troops, the indispensable individual ones and those of the squadron, hardly more. For that reason, even when they were deprived of their most potent means, in difficult situations, they did not become discouraged. We do not want to idealize them, but it seems to us that in the present world and civilization of material goods and machines, these people, without realizing it, supported themselves on their spiritual strength, and that in itself was very exceptional. Even when they were conquered, in their heart of hearts (because they had done their duty) they did not feel vanquished. However, to conquer them was quite difficult.

On the night of the eighteenth of January, the Tridentina (the Lombard Mountaineers) left their gathering point in Podgornoie. A little farther to the south, and on a parallel route were the Cuneense (the Piedmont Mountaineers), while still farther to the south was the other division of the Alpine army, the Julia (the Veneto Mountaineers and the few Abruzzi survivors), all of them already quite exhausted. The vicissitudes of these last two divisions do not concern us in this history. We shall only say that they, too, like those of the Tridentina—in temperatures oscillating between 25 and 44 degrees below zero (January is even colder than December)—had to enter into innumerable combats against the enemy to open a way through.

But let us restrict ourselves to the Tridentina column in which Luca was marching. Already on the day after the departure from Podgornoie, the nineteenth of January, the column met up with masses of enemies on the roads, so crowded that the Fifth Regiment had to open the way by battling in Scororib, and the Sixth in Repieva. At this last spot the Russians—many of them, and supported by armored tanks—with a dangerous maneuver on one flank tried to bring down the column at the rear of the attacking battalions. The engineer corps of the battalion left the column to face the Russians and after a terrible fight routed them, losing, however, 60 percent of their active men. At the end of this action the injured Alpine engineers were taken off on sleds (who could possibly describe the suffering of those days, loaded onto jolting sleds, with no rest, amid a glacial climate?), and those still fit gathered into a single company and took up their march. This was the first breakthrough in the front.

At dawn on the following day, the twentieth of January, while they converged over Postoiali, the vanguard of the two regiments met up with a large organized concentration of Russian artillery. The battalions that went into the attack underwent a difficult battle, very tough, against more numerous enemies. At midday, however, the way was open, and this was the second breakthrough in the front. Simultaneously, an enemy attack at the rear against the enormous masses of stragglers—at that moment concentrated in and around the city of Opit—was repelled by a single Alpine company that the division command had prudently deployed in the rearguard.

From Postoiali onward the Tridentina and the disbanded who were following went in a single column. In the evening they planned to stop in Novo Carcovca. The command had made a point of giving the fighting troops and the stragglers when possible a rest every twenty-four hours in the warmth of isbas for at least a few hours, and until now that plan had been adhered to. In Novo Carcovca, however, when they arrived it was already dark, and two Russian battalions were there buttressed by numerous armored tanks—and this was the greatest obstacle. The battle went on until midnight, in an infernal racket of tanks jousting in the darkness, against the small Italian antitank cannons and the four German mobile cannons—which were now always out front at the head of the troops—firing off from a horizontal emplacement. In full battle, a new Russian column, perhaps attracted by the shooting, arrived from the north. Before joining up with their own men they met up with an Alpine battalion, which stopped them and pushed them back. At midnight the city was occupied: the third breakthrough in the front.

The troops were granted only two hours of sleep in the Novo Carcovca isbas. They left at 2:00 on the twenty-first of January. After a few hours a storm broke out: the jackets, knapsacks, and helmets of the marching men turned to ice; the wind pierced the crust of ice and clothing and stung the flesh. Frequent snow flurries lashed down on their eyes like a whip. No one in that threatening darkness could see more than a few steps in front. The wounded, under blankets stiff as metal plate, lost consciousness and froze; the mules, completely covered with a layer of ice, kept pulling with the same desperate effort as the men themselves.

Limarevca became visible in the first glimmering of light and flash of lightning. It was a town with isbas scattered on the back of a big hill. It was crammed with enemies, but they were not lying in wait for the column, and luckily there were no armored tanks there. Gritting their teeth, the exhausted Alpine mortar company took up combat formation and in a series of successive encounters, almost blindly, crushed the enemy and moved into the village in their place. There, the majority of the men had to stay outside in the open air, in the torment that kept raging, lasting the entire day.

On leaving, as soon as night fell, there were no longer either trucks or vans. The first had been abandoned the day before on the orders of the high command, their fuel transferred to the vans. The vans, their gas tanks now empty, were left here. The wounded who had not died out of exhaustion and the ammunition were now being carried on sleds.

On the twenty-second of January, a little before dawn, Seliakino appeared, a big village situated in a valley: in a soup bowl was Luca's thought when he saw it. His regiment was the Fifth. (The Morbegno, the Tirano, and the Edolo Battalions were marching at the vanguard. The enemy was posed, waiting for them, behind long parapets of snow, along with numerous tanks.) In the column they were beginning to realize that in every place connected to a major road from the north or the south they had to expect an enemy barrage. The battle—with many maneuvers—lasted the entire day. And it had been settled by the battalion (with the green pompoms) after an exhausting and perfect encirclement maneuver to the left. This was the fourth breakthrough in the front. The town, which the column crossed through at nightfall, seemed strewn with dead enemy soldiers and with the abandoned Russian artillery: a pity, the Alpine troops were thinking, that they could not take at least some of the antitank guns with them.

Before it became completely dark, they could make out a small column isolated on the snow. Were they enemies, perhaps? No, look, mules . . . a group of survivors from the Julia Division, which immediately communicated the terrible news: the brave Julia Division, of great renown, no longer existed. On the nineteenth, their column, made up of men already worn out by a month of incessant combat in the snow, had been overcome by an infantry concentration, as well as Russian tanks, in Novo Postialovca. The battalions, and then the rest of the battalions, supported by firing from the short and small mountain cannons, followed one another in a furious attempt to make a breakthrough in the front. The battle lasted thirty hours with the help of forces sent by the Cuneense, and at the end of the thirty hours the Julia no longer existed: its Alpine troops left on the snow, the small mountain cannons crushed by enemy tanks, together with the brave artillery men and their faithful mules. Only a few units and small surviving groups managed to get away to the north, intending to reach the Cuneense or the Tridentina. There were not many survivors. Soon there would be great mourning in the little homes of the Veneto, Friuli, and the lovely Abruzzi.

The Tridentina Alpine troops—the heart-rending news immediately began to spread among them—continued the march, heavy at heart, in the direction of Landomirovca, where they planned to rest.

That day the Morbegno Battalion (with white pompoms, Luca's battalion), after taking a gallant part in the Seliakino battle, marched as a second echelon, a bit separated from the detachment that preceded it. At a crossing they took the wrong road, along the right, toward Varvarovka. A large Russian formation was concentrated at that spot, along with many armored tanks, probably sent by the enemy high command to cut the Tridentina in two. The Morbegno Battalion, though stupefied by weariness, was still effective and deployed its companies in combat formation in order to push forward. Surrounded at the rear and crisscrossed by enemy tanks, it continued to attack, wedged itself into the adversary's formation, fought hard on four fronts, finally conquering at the cost of a terrible loss of yard after yard of terrain, and under a more and more brutal concentration of fire. At last, establishing the impossibility of getting through, the battalion tried to open a way at the rear. However, they were unsuccessful because there, too, the enemies were in greater numbers, and despite their unspeakable efforts not one single man got through. Thus, also for the Alpine troops with the white pompoms, their march to the west— toward life, as they in their simplicity called it—came to an end. There would no longer be any white pompoms in the great retreating column, and in the little homes of the western Valtellina and the mountains around Como there would soon be more great mourning. The large enemy formations, although victorious, had received a stunning blow, such a blow that it remained in its place without attacking the Tridentina column.

As we said, Luca, at the moment of the attack, was with his squadron on the road and so was saved only by chance. He first reached the tail of the long column, his machine gun still over his shoulder, and the following day the other battalion of the Valtellina, the Tirano (with red pompoms), to a detachment of which his squadron was assigned.

The night between January 22 and 23 the Tridentina—they had also repelled a tank attack coming from the left (perhaps the southern arm of the pincer maneuver that was meant to cut it in two?)—rested only for three hours in Landomirovca, without even taking the wounded from the sleds. They left before dawn on January 23, as a high wind began to blow from the north that glazed the right sides of the men, the mules, and the sleds with powdered ice. Forward, forward! In Covalev the road was crowded with infantry tanks, and in the middle of this storm word was passed from mouth to mouth, a "human telephone": weapons to the fore! The small forty-seven cannons were rushed in, as were the mountain ones with their curved shot, immediately opening fire: a tank was hit, another, and still another. They were obviously not hit through, but they left ... Then it was the turn of the battalion companies deployed alternatively over the snow. The struggle was tough but brief. The Russians ran toward their vehicles and abandoned Covalev. It began to snow, and then a truly authentic storm broke out, the second one during the retreat. The plan was to reach Nicolaievca and stop there (which later, in Alpine legend, would be called "Nicolaievca the Little" to distinguish it from the other one, where they would do battle three days later). They arrived an hour before it would turn dark; the little Nicolaievca lay in a gray shell crowned by trees as bare as skeletons. Between the isbas two windmills stood like custodians of the skeletons, and the area was filled to the brim with enemy soldiers, who— warned by aerial observation—were awaiting the Tridentina. A battle broke out there that was so tough it was enough "to put you to sleep", as the Alpine troops put it, and a new breakthrough in the front took place, the seventh. And that night they slept under shelter. (That day, without anyone in the column knowing it, war bulletin number 973 from the Supreme Italian Command had announced the loss of Tripoli. Things in Africa were going no better than they were in Russia.)

The twenty-fourth of January. They left little Nicolaievca just before dawn, and the cold on that morning was beyond belief, as they kept walking toward the west. Once more enemy reconnaissance planes flew high over the column. At 10:00 they made out the village of Malacaievo. The Russians were also waiting there for them, and behind their infantry troops was an artillery formation, which immediately opened fire. To the right, in a large forest area, was an array of armored tanks. The Sixth Regiment was marching at the head of the Alpine column. Quite rapidly the Vestone and Val Chiese Companies (the Veronica, the other company of the Sixth, was now half destroyed) fell into combat formation and advanced. The small antitank guns, the 47/32, and the small cannons were set up at the edge of the road and were firing on the tanks and Russian cannons. The three surviving German mobile weapons, surrounded by the Alpine troops, who watched over them as they would the pupil in their eyes, because they alone were capable of piercing the armor of the tanks without any problem, advanced firing. One of them was hit straight on by an enemy shot and burned, much to the Alpine troops' dismay. The others continued forward. Several Russian tanks were also on fire. The Malacaievo combat was very tough, and many Alpine men fell or were left wounded. In the village six hundred enemy cadavers were counted, together with twelve artillery weapons and dozens of machine guns and abandoned mortars. The Alpine men gathered up only the parabellum and ammunition, which, in the last days of breakthroughs, had proved to be one of the most useful weapons for them. In the village there were barrels full of gasoline, a real blessing for the German chain vehicles.

They went forward immediately to Romancovo. The temperature was still lower, 40 degrees below zero; a new storm was brewing. They reached the village at nighttime; the place had just been abandoned by the enemy, who in their hurry had left plenty of victuals. There was also real forage for the mules, which so far had had to subsist on the weeds that came through the snow (collected for them by the mule drivers) and with the straw from the roofs of the isbas. The mule drivers enthusiastically gave their thanks to Saint Anthony, their patron saint (the pig, as well as the mule) and begged forgiveness for the innumerable blasphemies that they had until now addressed to him. In Romancovo the fighting units were able to rest in warm houses and also most of the disbanded stragglers.

On January 25 they left Romancovo in broad daylight toward Nikitovca. The sun was shining, and they crossed through a zone supplied with provisions, especially honey, because these were villages specializing in beekeeping. Before Nikitovca they underwent another combat of the "to put you to sleep" variety, and they entered the village, still partially infested with enemies, just before nightfall. It was here we left Luca. As we said before, the Tridentina command had given orders that the vanguard (the Vestone and Val Chiese Battalions, the two remaining German mobile cannons, and the thirty-second and thirty-third Batteries from the Bergamo Group) should continue on toward Arnautovo, a village situated some miles ahead.

So we have returned to the night of January 26, to the isba where Luca slept.

After turning over the various episodes of the retreat in his mind, the young man suddenly decided to cut his thoughts short. *Thinking about all this doesn't help at all. Besides, it's not doing me any good because I'm staying awake, and I have to sleep if I want to get to Nomana, my mother and Giustina . . . they wake us at six, then we'll have to go through that town, where—according to what the command is saying on the radio—we'll meet up with our last concentration of Russians. Who knows if it's true about it being the last . . . one thing, however, is certain: there'll be a big uproar. The firing we hear now is probably a sign of things to come . . . so, no matter what, I must get rest; I must sleep.*

And he finally did fall asleep.

4

But he was awakened hardly an hour later by screams from outside the isba. One of the Alpine company command was banging noisily against the door with the butt end of his rifle. Someone opened the door, and he came in, screaming, "Wake up, all of you, get moving, we're leaving! Everybody out! The Tirano on their feet!"

Still half asleep, the Alpines, cursing, hurried to get their boots on, collect their weapons, the ammunition, and a few other things: they began leaving. Around the nearby isbas activity could also be seen, the usual movement that preceded every departure: loading the injured on sleds, hitching up the mules, getting the platoons into formation. The rest of the village seemed still to be encompassed in sleep.

"What's happening? How come the others are still sleeping?"

"What time is it?"

"Four, just four." The red pompom Alpines were all chattering in the Valtellina dialect, very similar to the dialect of Nomana and, therefore, like the Milanese.

"But weren't we meant to leave at six?"

"Is the Tirano the only one going? Why? What's happening?"

"Sh——, where are we going?"

A few officers were waiting on the road, scarcely intervening, while the detachments lined up in column on their own; others were running back to the isbas to make sure no one had been left behind asleep. Someone asked and received the explanation, which immediately spread through the ranks: "The Thirty-Third Battery of the Bergamo, a few miles from us, in Arnautovo, is surrounded on three sides and can no longer hold out. We have to go and help."

So it was: from the west, in Arnautovo, came a steady crackling of gunfire, and the flashing in the darkness was continuous.

"Ah, the Thirty-Third."

"But aren't the Vestone and the Val Chiese with the Thirty-Third?"

"Guess not."

"Where've they gone?"

"I don't know."

Still in a bad mood—tired as they were—from having been awakened out of their sleep before the others, the Alpines, basically, were of one mind; they could not let the Thirty-Third Artillery down. At the end of ten minutes or a bit more, the command, the two companies, and the antitank unit of cannons were on the march. The company that had stayed behind, sheltered in the middle of the village, was informed, and they, too, got ready to march as soon as possible. And, it was said, a mountain battery also would join them.

The road to Arnautovo, with a slight upward climb, crossed through great orchards, the bare trees covered with frost, faintly lit up by the full moon. Luca still had the machine gun on his back, and his aide, the tripod, with the other ten or eleven men of his squadron (the only white pompoms among the red ones from the Tirano Battalion, though no one was looking at pompoms now) following closely behind, each of them deep into his own thoughts.

After the climb came a long descent, then another long climb, at the height of which was undoubtedly the Thirty-Third Battery of the Bergamo Group they had come to help, because all around there was a storm: in the dark, on that summit, the Russian tracking fire could be seen to be converging from three sides, but especially from the left. At that point, the mountain artillery men responded energetically. From time to time the flame from one of their cannons filled the darkness with light, and the din was incredible. By order of the commanding officer of the battalion, Major Maccagno—a man of few words—the back of the column, which was at the foot of the upward climb, went immediately into the snow toward the left, taking on an alternating formation. Luca heard his commanding officer, Captain Briolini, give the order: "Forward, Forty-Ninth, company of God!" The detachment command in which Luca's squadron had been incorporated, the antitank weapons of the Forty-Seventh, and the other company, led by Captain Grandi, a modest but resolute officer, continued cautiously along the road, hoping to reach the enemy battery undetected.

At the top of the climb were a handful of isbas—was this all of Arnautovo?—among which were strewn sleds and mules and any number of dead, frozen men, some with a leg pointing upward or their white teeth expressing a tragic grimace. The four cannons were set up before the tiny village, around which lay the many corpses; the mountain artillery survivors, tremendously tense, were posted here and there on three sides in the snow. They were taking over the defense with their rifles and automatic arms and the only working cannon that remained. An artillery man was stretched out prone over one of the non-functioning cannons. An enemy shot, after having gone through him, had left a strange red flower made of the wool from his jacket on his back.

"At last you've got here", said one of the operators of the weapon to the first Alpine men arriving there. "We've held out best we could since midnight." He was talking in the dialect of Bergamo.

"Well, now the Tirano is here to lend a hand."

"About time, too."

"The hen's laid an egg", a pachyderm of a corporal from artillery commented in dialect from his post in the snow, hardly turning his head.

While Major Maccagno and Captain Grandi deliberated together with the battery officer, who came up immediately (he was the only one uninjured), Luca was putting down his weapon and having a word with a stretcher bearer seated against the wall of the isba.

343

"If you'd got here any later, you wouldn't have found anyone alive", he later told him. The dead strewn on the snow around them testified tragically to the truth of his words.

"But weren't the Vestone and Val Chiese with you?" Luca asked, crouching on his heels next to him.

"They didn't stop here yesterday evening, except for the last Val Chiese squadrons, luckily. All the others went ahead because there was no place to sleep here."

"Ah, now I understand. Well, you'll see that as soon as the Tirano comes forward the Russians will give up."

"Let's hope so, but it's not easy, because there are so many of them."

By way of emphasizing his words, a salvo of mortar shot landed between the isbas. It was a real miracle that none of the recent arrivals—all of them motionless, waiting—was wounded.

"Where's your captain?"

"Lieutenant Capriata, you mean? He's the one who's been in command of the battery since yesterday midday. Well, he was in command, because now he's over there in the infirmary isba. Unfortunately he was injured."

"Ah."

"He was the one who ordered those two skiers to go back and call you."

"Two skiers? I didn't see them. And the other officers?"

"All of them injured, except Bughi. We've only one gun left. Can you imagine?"

The stretcher bearer pointed to it. It had just fired at that moment, leaving a blinding flash. It was immediately loaded again by the operators on their knees in the snow, holding on to the buckler. *Say, they look like a picture*, Luca thought for a second, a painting colored red from the reverberation of a burning isba. In answer, from the enemy line came tracking shot, shard, and even more.

"I have the feeling they are going to attack again soon", the stretcher bearer said.

The major, after rapidly sizing up the situation, gave Captain Grandi orders for the action of his company, who were leaving the village without wasting a moment, getting into combat formation in great silence. Luca was displeased to see Captain Grandi going. He only knew him by sight, but without him he somehow felt impoverished, so much confidence did that unknown man inspire in him: a real father in the Alpine sense. Meanwhile, they were setting up the Tirano mortars and small cannons, and the platoons of the command detachment were taking up positions around the isbas on the same line as the mountain artillery. Luca placed his own weapon in front of the tiny village, protected by a snowy fold in the ground. From here, raising his head a bit, he could see the terrain that went down in front of him irregularly, strewn here and there, under the moon, with enemy corpses wrapped in big overcoats. But

344

the company (the young man remembered his young captain calling it "the company of God") was already going down to the left and making contact with the enemy. Shortly afterward the company that had gone out with Captain Grandi did, too. The enemies responded with an incredible volume of fire. They were—obvious from there—considerably greater in numbers than those attacking. That is how the Arnautovo battle started.

5

Surprised by the Alpine attack, which was made impetuously all of a sudden, the Russians were at first pushed back, especially in the flanks, but then they held their ground. The terrain beyond Arnautovo went downward for a stretch, then upward, forming a wide passage crossed along the whole watershed by a kind of shallow ravine. It was quite irregular, partially uncultivated and wooded, and partially barren, with an occasional hayloft.

To lend support to the action, the commanding major sent to Captain Grandi two of the command detachment platoons, keeping only one at the level of the isbas. He sent a messenger to Nikitovca to solicit his Forty-Eighth Company urgently and to ask for the intervention of at least one whole artillery group. He tried in every way not to waste any of his men, who believed in him as they would a father, but at the same time he realized that this time too many of them, in their attempt to open a way for themselves and for the others, would die with their boots on. He still did not know that around Arnautovo there were as many as three Russian battalions. He realized, however, that the enemies' numbers were very high. He tried not to be overcome with anguish. He knew that in the great Tridentina column, along with its stragglers at the back, there were four still efficient battalions: two of them—the Vestone and the Val Chiese—had already gone ahead, beyond this enemy concentration. (Heavens, let them not be left on their own. Who knows what their fate might be . . . ?) To the rear of the Tirano there was only one, the Edolo, doing rearguard duty.

The strenuous battle fought by the Alpine troops in the snow at about 30 degrees below zero resulted in terrible losses and was truly painful. At moments it seemed desperate, above all because of the volume of enemy fire. Notwithstanding, the battalion did not let go its hold. With perspicacity and firm determination each squadron, every single man, exerted himself to destroy the centers of adversary fire and continue on. And, in fact, the front had started to advance again, though at a tremendously slow pace. The Forty-Eighth Company arrived and immediately joined the battle. Its participation was vital. A little later the splendid Val Camonica Group arrived too. Full of fury with their eight 105 cannons at the area of Arnautovo, they opened fire vigorously, and their participation also made a difference. Despite everything, the battle, which had already been going on for two hours, was not over.

The enemy forces—worn out with combat (which for them had been going on since midnight, in that temperature)—had been pushed back, practically all of them, by the Alpine troops, into the valley, at the level of the watershed. At that point they finally all gathered, as in a trench. It turned out to be quite difficult to rout them from there by attacking frontally, and in an hour, at seven, there would be light, which would render the attack even more difficult.

The Alpines from the command detachment that had remained in the isbas, and who now had recovered some breath, were perhaps still more worried than the ones in the trench below. It was absolutely necessary to do something. Carlo Gnocchi, the chaplain of the regiment, was also worried. He had arrived from Nikitovca on his own initiative (chaplains had great authority and freedom among the Alpine men) to comfort the wounded and confess the dying, like the Tirano chaplain, Don Crosara. (Once informed of Don Carlo's arrival, Luca found a substitute for a few seconds at his machine gun and ran looking for him among the isbas. He wanted to greet him and ask for his blessing. He found him bending over the wounded in the isba infirmary and did not dare bother him. Luckily, Don Carlo was aware of his presence. On his pleasant face with eyes strangely sunken was an expression of surprise, as if to say, "Well, well, my countryman, you're still with us!" He raised his hand and traced the sign of the Cross over him. That was enough for Luca to return to his post comforted.) Now Don Carlo—the same as those wounded who were still conscious and asking how the battle was going—was worried that so much sacrifice might not come to anything. They all felt that something had to be done, but what?

The lieutenant of the platoon that had remained in Arnautovo suddenly left his own parapet in the snow and joined a gigantic sergeant, stationed not far from the machine gun. Seated on his heels he started talking to him. Luca, who was with his own men about twenty steps away (they were still at the same place in front of the isbas, half frozen from standing still), heard him talking in dialect, but without understanding him. It seemed to him that both of them were glancing over at him. Then he saw the lieutenant run back to the isba, where presumably the major was. The officer came out shortly, waved to the gigantic sergeant to follow him, and unexpectedly called Luca over, too: "You, corporal from the Morbegno, come here."

The sergeant and Luca—the latter rather nervous—stood up and hurried to join him. Without saying a word, the officer preceded them into the isba, where he said, "Let's go." Then he explained to Luca his plan, which the sergeant already knew and which the major had approved. The idea was to make a partial encirclement of the enemy huddled in the channel and to take it in enfilade under fire of at least a machine gun. "It won't be easy taking a weapon up there, but if we carry it off, they'll have to get out of there." The

346

officer expressed himself in dialect, in a very hoarse voice that was hard to hear in the continual racket of battle. "Your two squadrons will try together on the right, while I'll go in on the left with the other machine gun. Whoever gets there first begins to shoot. You, from the Morbegno . . . by the way, what's your name?"

"Sambruna. Corporal Luca Sambruna."

"Good. I see you're a cool fellow. Did you understand everything?"

Luca nodded his head that he did.

"All right. Now, get going, because there's hardly another hour of darkness left. The major will take charge of letting the companies know when to advance at the exact moment."

"Agreed", Luca said.

Without adding anything, the other officer went off to get ready, too, to leave.

"First, we'll get our men together here, behind this house", the sergeant told Luca. Standing up he looked even more gigantic. "I'm going for my men."

Luca again motioned agreement. To establish something of human contact between them, the other added, "My name's Pedrana. In my squadron we're almost all of us from Bormio."

Luca nodded, smiling. "I know. Mine are mostly from Tartano."

"Ah!" Pedrana gestured a sign of appreciation, then turned and went toward his position.

He was back in a few minutes with his weapon on his shoulder, followed by his aide with the tripod, and the other Alpine men from his squadron, eight or nine, with a box of ammunition. Luca and his men arrived at the same time.

"Let's go", Pedrana said.

Before setting off, the Alpine troops from the two squadrons all made the sign of the Cross.

They turned back between the isbas of the village as far as the Val Camonica formations and then went down, in single file, the incline on the right. In front were those from Bormio with their red pompoms; behind, Luca's squadron with white pompoms. The terrain along this side was quite wooded, and luckily the moon was on the wane. At this half turn the patrol managed to conceal itself behind undergrowth, trees, any irregularity in the terrain. However, they did not have much time, and enemy fire came whizzing by more than once. "God, how much shooting!" one of the Bormio men murmured.

"Come on, let's get them this time. Then we'll only have to open the way in that town farther on, because beyond that the Ivans haven't got. You know that", the sergeant said.

Let's hope so. If not, goodbye, Giustina, Luca thought, having already decided to give his all for all.

The encircling maneuver did not turn out to be easy. First there was one encounter and then another with small pockets of enemy soldiers, perhaps stragglers. One of Luca's group was killed, and two of Pedrana's seriously wounded and left on the snow under some undergrowth, with the idea of returning for them after the combat was over. To tell the story of that march of hardly three-quarters of an hour adequately would require many pages and make our narrative too long.

When, running with sweat despite the 30 degrees below zero, emotionally and physically exhausted, the Alpine troops appeared on the other side of the channel and through a tongue of woods could reach a position in some way dominant, they were presented with a spectacle that took their breath away. The enemy was all together in the channel, their weapons on an incline behind, covered with hedges and piles of straw. It was beginning to get light, and it was possible to see. The Alpine men quickly set up their machine guns, while Sergeant Pedrana studied the situation in silence. "Stay here", he told Luca at last. "We're going over there." He indicated a slightly higher point, perhaps forty yards away. "But first, check the carriage for the weapons. See that it's not iced over. Come on."

"But we'll have to dismount ours again . . .", his aide objected.

"Who told you that?" Pedrana asked him and got to his knees to arm the machine gun. Despite all the shooting during the course of the night, the arm carriage was blocked by ice.

"I figured that", Pedrana muttered, as always in dialect. "Come on, we'll pee on it." The little amount of urine the Alpine troops had in their bodies was not enough, however. It was necessary to rub it down hard with a woolen blanket. (Here the reader must not think this is some sort of literary expedient to increase the tension. This was, point by point, what happened, as it was reported by one of the protagonists.) Finally, the weapon was ready; Luca's, too.

"Wait 'til I begin", Pedrana told Luca. "Look at me. As soon as I begin, shoot. You have to keep shooting into the channel, understood? Always there, not stopping. I'll take care of those farther back. Besides, you'll see that as soon as we begin, our other men will arrive."

This said, the outsized sergeant took hold of his machine gun (between the weapon and the tripod 40 kilograms of weight) and, clutching it against his chest like a baby, walked along the snow with enormous strides—his squadron behind—toward the established point. No doubt more than one of the enemy saw him, but they must have thought they were Russians.

"You and you," Luca said, placing himself behind his own weapon, with two men behind, "don't forget to keep the tripod completely steady." Afterward, while glancing back and forth from the channel full of enemies to Pedrana's squadron, he mentally began to say a prayer. This time it wouldn't be easy to have things go smoothly. Certainly the enemy would have to move out of the channel, but how would it end up for them?

He saw Pedrana and his men crouching on the snow, shortly after he heard the ta-ta from his weapon, and he immediately opened fire, too. *Now and in the hour of our death*, he was mentally saying at that moment and continued saying it while shooting away, *now and in the hour of our death, now and in the hour of our death, now and* ... He saw, under the unexpected enfilade of fire, how the enemy soldiers were moving like grass and were beginning to mingle one with the other. It seemed some were firing in his direction. The firing was being centered on him and then went elsewhere. Always firing into the channel, he went up and down several times, while his aide kept loading one cartridge after another. *Now and in the hour of our death, now and in the hour of our death, now and* ...

The enemy soldiers were abandoning the channel, leaving at a run, obliquely, to get away from the terrible double sickle thrust of the two machine guns. Luca then turned his fire on the mass in flight over the snow. Only some wounded remained in the channel. From where he was there did not seem to be many. *Just as well!* Just as well because Luca did not like this horrible game at all, but there were people he had to save: the two wounded men they had left under the thickets above all, and then the men from the sleds and the tens of thousands of the disbanded who were waiting for them to open the road, and his mother at home, and Giustina. There was no other way out. *Now and in the hour of our death, now and* ... It came to him that now he was saying that prayer for the wretches there on the snow running from his firing.

The first Alpine squadrons appeared at the channel, while, from Arnautovo, the eight Val Camonica weapons, too, began firing on the enemy in flight. Luca suspended fire; shortly afterward Pedrana did, too. Not one man from their squadrons had been wounded.

6

The battle over, the massacred companies of the Tirano Battalion convoyed on the road out of Arnautovo and began to get the column into formation. It was almost nine in the morning. The wounded were quickly gathered up and loaded onto sleds. On some they had to be piled up: there were sleds with ten or more wounded on them. The battalion chaplain, Don Crosara, moved among them. However, Don Carlo Gnocchi was not to be seen. As Luca was to find out, he had gone to the channel with two volunteers to try somehow to look after the Russian wounded, to see if there was a truck coming for them. (Two days before he had attended General Eibl, the German commander of the destroyed Twenty-Fourth Tank Corps, as he lay in extremis.) As they lined up in formation, the companies took the painful count: three hundred men were missing at roll call, which meant more than half of the red pompoms, and the greater part of those brave officers who had led their Alpine men, above all, by example. All three company commanders had fallen (Briolini: "*Avanti, forty-ninth, company of God*"; Grandi, who inspired Luca with so much confidence; and Piatti of the forty-eighth, the company that had gone into that furnace a little after the others). The price it had cost to open the way had been tremendous. Meanwhile, the enormous number of disbanded—who had been waiting hours already, with their injured and frozen men shouting out from time to time their desperation from the sleds—were pushing more and more at the rear. The artillery men from the mountain unit had already closed the way in the village, and some of the stragglers went off on a secondary path. The mass followed them: they made the turn at Arnautovo and the battle zone, leaving them to the left.

At last the Tirano men set off, too, in good order as usual, only now the column was half as long. At the head was Major Maccagno with the remainder of the command detachment, at the end of which was Luca's squadron. Once more the young man was carrying the machine gun over his shoulders, but the straps were already cutting his armpits like knives, and the march had just begun. Behind the command detachment came the company that had been Captain Grandi's, and then the others, two others. Unlike the other company commanders, Grandi—with his belly torn away by a bullet shot—was not dead, but on the verge of death. At the moment of lining up, the Alpines had, without talking, put him on a sled at the head of the company so that he, while still alive, was in front of them as he always had been. Luca and his men—at the end of the command detachment—came just before that sled, and every so often one or another of them would turn to have a look at him. The captain was wearing a hat with the feather covered with frost and was deadly pale; he must have lost consciousness. Behind his sled, the Alpine troops, more numerous there than in the rest of the column, marched in silence. Some were crying.

The cold was always overwhelming, but there was a little sun, which made it possible to see ahead to the desolate horizon; little by little their pace became brisk. The battalion, followed by the Val Camonica Group, which dragged the eight 105 weapons and the only surviving Thirty-Third Battery arm, reached the point in which, after having made the turn at Arnautovo, the disbanded were able to converge onto the main road. Before its armed formation, which meant security for everyone, the disbanded (at this point Germans, in some way more orderly than the others) stopped for the necessary time to enter the column in an orderly fashion. The march then continued in silence; only the accelerated step of boots on snow and the squeaking of the sleds could be heard. As time went by the entire surroundings seemed to become one huge set of lines: even when the march was quickly moving along, at moments it seemed they were stopped in that immensity.

After a sudden jolting of the sled, the captain with the torn-away belly opened his eyes. He slowly recovered the consciousness of his own situation and looked around him. He met with the look of an Alpine walking at his side. "How did the battle go?" he asked. "Is it over?"

"Yes, it's over."

"We made it, didn't we?"

"Yes, we've opened the way."

The only officer left in the company rushed up to him and bent over the wounded man. "We made it, Captain. We've opened the way."

"Just as well."

"How do you feel, Captain?"

"I? Little time left."

The officer did not contradict him. Instead he said, "There were three battalions of them. And now we know it for certain. The Tirano has been reduced by half, but", he repeated, "the way is open for the column."

"If you get back, tell my mother that."

"Yes, I promise to tell her."

"Tell her I've done my duty, and that's why I'll die in peace with the men and with God."

From both sides his Alpine men came up and looked at him with anguished faces. The man leading him walked with the mule's reins slung over his shoulder and every so often turned to look at him. There were tears in his eyes.

"What do all these long faces mean?" the captain suddenly exclaimed. "Sing with me!" And trying to pitch his voice, which would have been ridiculous at a less tragic moment, he started the powerful Alpine song about the captain who is dying and making his will:

> The captain he is wounded,
> wounded and about to die.

Immediately those around him joined in. Some of the men made signs to those following also to join in, and soon the entire company was singing together, terribly sad. In the song, the dying man directs his body to be divided into five pieces:

> The first piece to the mountain,
> which will cover it in roses, in flowers.

What a torture, the grief of remembering their native mountains amidst the vast and limitless plains . . .

> The second piece to the king of Italy.
> May he never forget his soldier.

And the third to the regiment.

In the long column of ants marching steadily along yet seemingly immobile in that immensity of ice, there was that small section singing.

And the mother enters into the song, also the beloved wife:

The fourth piece to my mother,
may she never forget her son,
and the fifth for my beloved,
may she never forget her first love.

Goodbye to you, my first love, goodbye forever, our dreams will never be
. . . goodbye, my mountains, my native land, my regiment, goodbye, dear mother
and my first love, and so they sang. They sang and they cried, those brave
Alpine men, and in their patient song there was the torment of our human
impotence. They were still singing when the captain had already stopped, accompanying them only with his eyes. They only stopped singing when they
realized that Captain Grandi had died.

7

At six that same morning, the vanguard, which had spent the night in the first
village beyond Arnautovo, started to march again according to the orders they
had received. It was composed of the Vestone and Val Chiese Battalions, the
remainder of the Verona, the two surviving German mobile weapons, and the
Thirty-Second Battery of the Bergamo Group. All these men were totally unaware of the attempt of the enemy to cut off the column at the rear. Indeed,
they had heard incessant gunfire, but "each to his own". Likewise, all their
thoughts were projected on Nicolaievca, where, in a short while—according
to the Tridentina command—they would break through the last enemy barrier. They could make the city out at about 9:00. It rose upward over a small
isolated mountain at the center of a wide, scooped-out basin. In front of it ran
the railway embankment, and it most certainly would serve for a defensive
position. It was also literally filled with enemy soldiers lying in wait for the
column. While the Alpine cannons and mortars and the one German Katyuska set up on the edge of the basin opened fire, the two formidable battalions
from Brescia came down in combat formation—under a cloud of enemy fire—
along the bare incline, then overcame a stretch of the embankment with an
explosive assault and penetrated into the city. Here their initial impetus ran
aground because of the overwhelming number of enemies. The massacred companies could not make it forward.

The big column and the Tridentina command arrived a few hours later, in
time to watch from the edge of the basin a Russian counterattack, which,
despite the superior numbers of the assailants, was beaten back by the furious
Alpine resistance. Toward midday the Tirano Division arrived (the half that
remained), also the Val Camonica artillery with the eight small 105 mountain
cannons, still working, a real marvel, and the Vicenza Group with other armed
detachments. Under enemy fire they ran down to the area to join up with the

Alpine troops from the Vestone and Val Chiese Divisions, who had barricaded themselves between the isbas. The remainder of the Julia men, again armed, descended the incline with them, too. With these reinforcements the Alpine penetration was once more resumed, and though there was some advance, it was in no way definitive. Meanwhile, the mass of disbanded—perhaps thirty thousand to the few thousand actually fighting—watched the fierce spectacle from above with growing anxiety. Enemy cannon fire exploded frequently among this mass of men, and some Russian airplanes came down to grazing level and machine-gunned them three times. But down below the battle was not decided. One night in the open air, 30 degrees below zero, exposed to the enemy fire, might well have been the end for everybody. There would be no departure the next day or any other day. Each and every one in his heart saw himself, with irresistible revulsion, as a corpse on the snow, the same as so many other corpses there already, miserable piles of frozen flesh and rags. Here and there from the wounded men's sleds, especially from those men most weakened by hunger, came mass screaming, as if in an attack of madness.

The Edolo! The Edolo was needed, the last stronghold. Summoned by a messenger from the division command, the Edolo Battalion, with green pompoms, was at the rearguard. It was not easy making their way without being separated, considering the crowded condition of the road. Scarcely out of that disorder the downward march began. When General Reverberi, the Tridentina commander, saw the Edolo next to the embankment, he got in a German chain vehicle, shot his pistol into the air repeatedly to call everyone to attention, and hurled this famous shout: "Tridentina, forward! Everybody forward! Everybody forward!" Many of those around him, armed or unarmed, repeated the shout and threw themselves forward together with him; they passed him. The enormous mass began to launch themselves down the hill, despite the enemy lead against them, a vast mingling of Italians, Hungarians, Germans, all running tumultuously downward, toward Nicolaievca. On the front line rushed the panting chief of the general staff of the Alpine army, General Martinat, the clever and tenacious strategist who had directed the most difficult battles. He was among the first to fall.

Under the sledgehammer blow of the Edolo and before the avalanche of men falling upon them, the Russians began to abandon their positions—not all of them though, because the bravest held out and had to be driven out by the Alpine troops. The others who abandoned their positions rushed to their trucks and, pursued by the cannon fire, got away to the roads beyond the city. It was almost three in the afternoon; it was already getting dark.

Luca was drunk with tiredness, and besides he was wounded; a bullet had gone through the calf of his left leg while he was going down along the embankment. (An embankment composed of earth or dead men? At the point he went over it there was a layer of corpses with the blue pompoms of the Vestone.)

Luckily, it was not a serious wound, but he wondered how he would be able to carry the machine gun the next day. Two men from his squadron—two cousins from Tartano—had been killed battling between the houses (the second while trying to help the first). Others had been injured. Crouched behind a little wall, the survivors had continued firing with determination and thrift, until the green pompoms of the Edolo reached them. Luca then helped the new arrivals destroy a nest of enemy fire inside one of the isbas. (Next to him, one of the Edolo men— standing against an angle of a building—had fired off his machine gun from the shoulder of a comrade.) When they at last went forward, Luca sat down heavily on the low wall. His ideas were all jumbled. His few mates, totally exhausted, sat down around him in the snow.

"Corporal, we'll have to get something to eat", one of them grumbled.

Luca agreed.

"Will it really be the last breakthrough?" another asked, also in dialect. (That would be breakthrough number eleven—as it was later verified—since the retreat had started nine days before about two hundred miles from where they were.)

Luca lifted his chin a little, as if to say, "Who knows?"

"Dear God, if that's true I'll have a Mass said in Val di Sacco when I get back", a third man murmured.

From a nearby isba a Russian soldier unexpectedly came out. He was armed only with a dagger and did not appear to have any intention to do battle. He sat down in the snow against the isba wall and stuck his hands in his pockets. Perhaps he considered himself a prisoner, worn out as he was.

The first disbanded men arrived, Hungarians in long overcoats. They were talking with one another, probably looking for something to eat. They went off without stopping.

The Tirano chaplain, Don Crosara, a Franciscan, also came by. "Are there any wounded in your squadron?" he asked.

"Eh", Luca nodded.

"Anyone seriously wounded, who might want to confess?"

"Serious, no", Luca answered. "Thanks. But tomorrow room in the sleds will have to be found."

The chaplain suddenly noticed the Russian soldier and looked at him with surprise. Then the Russian took his hands from his pockets and with his right one removed the dagger from its sheath, while with his left hand he lowered the collar of his overcoat to stab himself in the throat.

"No!" the chaplain yelled. "What are you doing? No, no!" He raised his crucifix on high and ran to him. "No, no, don't do that!"

The Russian looked at him in dismay, confused. The chaplain grabbed his hand with the dagger and waved the crucifix with the other in front of his face. "Why do you want to kill yourself, why, why?" he kept shouting.

At last the Russian's gaze turned to the crucifix. He clutched the priest's hand holding it and pressed the Christ figure to his lips. The Alpine men were watching the scene in silence. The Russian handed the priest the dagger, which he hurled as far as possible. "The Mother of God loves you", Don Crosara panted out. "Dearly loves you, you understand? God is not like us men."

The Russian, without understanding the words, wearily made a sign that he did.

The breakthrough of the front at Nicolaievca, the eleventh since the beginning of the march, was indeed the last carried out by the Tridentina. The Russian vanguards, in fact, had gone some ten miles more to the west, so although the Tridentina command, in anticipation of still another need for a breakthrough, had gathered up whatever troops were still functioning into two formation battalions—only two, there were no more left—there was no need to use them. That night they tried to skirt around the village of Novi Oscol, occupied by the enemy, and the maneuver was successful, maybe because the enemy preferred to close their eyes. (It had experienced how difficult it was to stop the Alpine men.) To reach the new German mobile front protecting Kharkov, the column needed five more days of marching after leaving Nicolaievca, some of which Luca did on foot, limping, and partly on a sled from the detachment of the Tirano command, on which they had loaded his machine gun. The red pompom Alpines already considered him a brother.

Now that the road back home seemed assured, he and the other men were wondering what the outcome of the other large Alpine column would be, the Cuneense Division. Where might they be at this moment? Had the Piedmont Alpine men managed to get here?

We know they did manage to. After continuous combat and unspeakable vicissitudes they also reached the meridian of Nicolaievca, about thirty miles more to the south, where the enemy had prepared, in Valuiki, a concentration analogous to that of Nicolaievca. Here, on January 27 (the day after the Nicolaievca battle), the Piedmont Battalion had concentrated all their efforts for a breakthrough. But they did not make it. At the end of that fatal day the commanding general of the Cuneense had accepted a surrender for his detachments, exhausted and in large part overwhelmed. The Mondovi, which arrived at the same place the following day because it was in rearguard, did not accept surrender and tried to break through the front alone. It was totally sacrificed in the impossible attempt.

Acknowledgment of Alpine bravery is endless. It suffices to remember what one judge, qualified as few others, gave by way of testimony about the Alpine troops, at the end of the war. In the words of General Guderian, chief of German General Staff: "The Italian Alpine infantry brigade are the only infantry formations in the world that truly bring enthusiasm to a military man."

Meanwhile the Russian advance was not over. Stalingrad fell on February 3; Kharkov—abandoned shortly before by the Tridentina—on February 16. This last city would be conquered yet again by the German divisions coming from France, which, thanks mainly to the new Tigre tanks, managed to reestablish the front in the month of March.

BOOK TWO

THE PALE HORSE

PART ONE

The departure of Ambrogio and Paccoi from Leopoli took place on a hazy morning at the end of February.

Unwilling to be taken to the station on a stretcher, the officer put on his worn gray-green uniform, which, after having been oven disinfected, was now unbelievably wrinkled. As he put on the belt, made of imitation leather, it came apart. He tested its holding power by stretching it, and it fell to pieces totally, so long had it been cooked. He could do nothing but throw it away. What was there to replace it? The young man decided on a length of string, which he passed through the loops of his trousers and then tied in front.

While he was carrying out this maneuver, Sister Glicerie watched him silently. She suddenly covered her pale face with her hands. "Italy's officers!" she exclaimed, grief stricken. "Mercy, what a state Italy's officers are in!"

Ambrogio instinctively concealed the string by pulling down his jacket flaps. Then he smiled at the Red Cross nurse and all the while shook his head. "Calm down, Sister. We must control ourselves, you know that? It's also part of our duty."

The old lady removed her hands from her face and straightened up. Ambrogio was still smiling. "You see, this non–army issue belt means I'm still alive, and if I get back to the Sixth Division, I'll still be of some use, won't I?"

Even he was surprised by the maturity of his words. *After all is said and done, it's clear the war is making me grow up,* he thought. He added, "The Russians here in the east also had to use belts like this, and they didn't give up."

"Forgive me, Lieutenant", Sister Glicerie murmured softly, upset by her own weakness.

Ambrogio dismissed the matter in a friendly fashion and went on dressing with an air as if to say, "Don't give it another thought." The old lady, after hurriedly spreading the blankets, left the dormitory.

Poor soul, the lieutenant thought. *She looks every inch an aristocrat. Outward appearances must mean a lot for her. Perhaps a slip in appearances is the same as a slip in substance for her. On the other hand,* he reflected, *after what I've seen, maybe the traditionalists of the old school are right after all.*

In the military bus carrying the men to the train station, Ambrogio sat down next to Paccoi. As they had arrived at night, they had not been able to see the city: the streets, houses, palaces, and gardens were remarkably like the ones in

Italy. "It almost seems we're in Italy. It's incredible, Giovanni, truly incredible", Ambrogio repeated over and over. On any number of the palace façades were large bronze crucifixes: just as along the Polish country roads, the Cross was a constant reminder. "The Poles are more openly Christian than we are in this respect." The crosses suddenly reminded him of the wretched madmen assassinated by the rational blond beasts, and the wretched bourgeois and priests assassinated by the rational red beasts. Who knows where they were buried? According to the hospital orderlies, the victims of the reds were buried in the same place they were executed, which meant on the edge of the eastbound highways. A nebulous worry stirred in him. *And if the Germans don't manage to win out? And the Bolsheviks in the end do? Who'll prevent these* blue berets *from coming back here? And get as far as Italy even?* The gray February sky seemed to weigh even more heavily on him. At that time no one thought of America as a possible defense against communism.

Under the large iron arcades in the station a good Italian hospital train was waiting: a real hospital train, not made up of open merchandise cars, but with compartment cars, on whose doors figured the enigmatic monogram SMOM, under a small white cross on a red background.

"SMOM", Ambrogio muttered. "What would that be?" One of the soldiers in the health corps explained, "It means the Sovereign Military Order of Malta."

"Of course", the lieutenant replied in agreement.

"What is it?" Paccoi wanted to know.

"It's an order that's been in existence since the Middle Ages. You should know more about those things than I do, seeing you're from Umbria."

Paccoi looked at him with his honest face, a little embarrassed. "Don't tell anyone," Ambrogio then confessed, "but neither do I know any more than that."

Again the soldier from the health corps came to his rescue. "It's a hospitallers order, the most ancient in existence. It's called Malta because it prevented the Turks from landing in Malta."

"The Turks? When was that?" Paccoi asked.

"Some time in the 1500s."

"And it's been going on since then?" the aide exclaimed, surprised.

"From way before", the soldier answered, totally serious.

"And how come you know all this?"

"Because I work on the train. They teach us these things." Once he had started, he produced still another fact from his storehouse of knowledge. "It's an order of monks who even before the year 1000, that is, before the Crusades, worked as nurses for the pilgrims to the Holy Land, and later they attended the Crusaders, and when it was necessary, they also fought side by side with them. That's why they were both monks and cavaliers at the same time." Then he added, "In a certain way they anticipated today's Red Cross by a thousand years, even if their cross wasn't red", and he pointed to the door of the cars. "But white instead on a red background. Not much difference, after all."

360

"That's so", Ambrogio agreed, while thinking, *How Michele would have liked this explanation! So mad about the Middle Ages as he is.* Smiling to himself, he promised, *Well, I'll tell him about it.* The smile froze on his face. *If he ever gets back home.*

The explanation at an end, the soldier left with a friendly wave. "You know those monks then", Paccoi concluded, "were what orderlies were meant to be, not like those rotten ones now, who didn't even bring bedpans some nights, so the nuns have to do it." (One detail in fact annoyed him in that episode. He had slept like a log through the whole procedure, completely unaware.)

2

On the train they did not find, as they expected, hospitaller monks. They found out from the chaplain that the order supplied the Italian army only with a certain number of trains like this one, but not any personnel. In any case, it was a perfectly prepared convoy train, with stretchers that made up into beds, arranged on two levels along the walls, and brilliantly clean sheets.

After some hours traveling, Ambrogio's fever rose, even to the point of delirium. And though his head was at the height of the window, he was only partially cognizant of the places the train passed through. Only some images of huge factories in the dirty snow of Silesia and of Bohemia that were working full blast, given the huge black clouds of smoke rising from their chimneys. He was not aware of the convoy's entrance into Italy either, in the still dark early morning.

A few hours later he regained consciousness, but it took him a while to realize he was in a hospital train. Turning to one side, he met with the unmistakable round face of Paccoi. "You're awake, Lieutenant? Thank God! We're in Italy, Lieutenant, Italy!"

He recounted that when they had stopped at Brenner Pass, some of the men had gotten off to kiss the ground, "Mazzoleni among them, and who would have imagined that scoundrel!" He also told him that an hour before, they had taken off forty injured men in Bolzano and put them in ambulances. At that point he was afraid they'd be separated, "Without even being able to say goodbye."

"But you got off at Brenner to kiss the ground, didn't you?" Ambrogio asked in a strained voice, trying to joke despite everything.

"Me, Lieutenant? That all seems quite silly to me, but they did it in all seriousness, you know, so serious they almost made you cry."

A medical officer went by and stopped, saying, "At last!" He wanted to take a look at the fellow who had regained consciousness. He asked a question or two and ended by saying, "Sorry not to have been able to get you off at Bolzano. Those fellows were taken to the Grand Hotel Emma in Merano, a first-rate hospital and first-rate head doctor there, too. "Well," he decided, "we'll get you off in Verona in a little while. What do you think? Happy?"

"As far as I'm concerned . . .", Ambrogio answered, as if to say that one place is the same as the other. Then he nodded toward Paccoi. "How about him?"

"Fine, it'll be Verona for him, too", the doctor agreed, and added, "He's been your nursemaid for this whole trip as if he had nothing wrong with him. A great guy!" and he went away.

Many of the injured were taken off in Verona. The station appeared to have been damaged seriously by aerial attacks. Sheets of roofing and iron supports were lying about here and there, and the walls were cracked and full of holes, and there was the dust of the ruins swirling about on the sidewalks.

Even though carried on a stretcher, Ambrogio tried to get a view of every-thing, but glancing from side to side he could not see much. He did notice, however, that the injured were being dealt with in a rapid and orderly fashion, and the soldiers of the health corps were being meticulous. Still affected by the nightmare of the Russian blockade, the behavior of the Italians seemed almost amazing. But he had no time to dwell on this as he was stretcher borne, along with other injured soldiers, into an ambulance. They crossed the city—or so it seemed—and were then going through the country, no noises outside and no jolting. *So the hospital is outside the city*, he thought, becoming more and more blurred with so many emotions. "Are we very far from the hospital?" he asked the orderly in white, seated at the head of the narrow passage between the stretchers, his back resting against the driver's compartment.

"Fifty miles or so", he answered.

"Fifty? But . . . how come?"

"Yes, in Schio. We're not going to the military hospital in Verona but to the civilian one in Schio. Much smaller, but very well organized, a good place. You'll see."

"We're going to Schio?" the wounded man above Ambrogio interrupted. He had also been in the Dantesque infirmary at Cercovo. "I was there once as a civilian. It's a pretty city, surrounded by mountains and a lot of factories."

And Paccoi? Ambrogio was wondering. *Was he one of them destined for Schio?* He wouldn't know until he got there. And if he weren't? "Why didn't they tell me before I got in the ambulance?" he asked the soldier in white, vaguely recriminatory.

The other fellow shrugged as if to say it wasn't his affair. He was wearing the cap with the complicated health emblem on his head, Ambrogio noticed. The same emblem as that worn by the Leopoli hospital staff, the wounded man recalled, despite his growing dimness: a confusion of many elements, none of which could ever be singled out. Where a number was in the central circle in other regiments, in the health corps there was a thread of a red cross, so thin that if the cap was a bit awry, as it usually was, it couldn't even be seen. *Why did all of them in that regiment wear their caps pulled so far down that way?* he was wondering. *They hardly seemed to be caps, but more like the cloth caps of the male nurse, though they weren't white . . . one second, why weren't they white? Why? But they were white. Yes, looking at this fellow's cap, isn't it white? It's almost luminous . . .* Ambrogio was staring at him hard, but not aware that his eyes were closed, trying to see better . . . inside the whiteness, tenuously luminous, to see what was expanding within his head, growing so large he was about to become submerged in it.

"Hey, Riva, I saw the signs on the highway", the wounded man above him enthusiastically announced. "Vicenza, I don't know how many miles. I didn't have time to read it. Listen, we're on the highway, the highway! You realize that? If we'd been told we'd be here when were in the Cerkovo infirmary, eh? What about it, Riva!"

Ambrogio did not answer. The medical orderly rose from his seat and, bracing himself from one side to the other between the stretcher, reached Ambrogio's side and, leaning over him to have a look, replied, "He can't answer. The lieutenant's unconscious."

Ambrogio moved his lips, muttered barely perceptible words, and the orderly put his ear to his mouth. "There are tracer bullets . . . they're coming, yes, careful, careful, they'll be here . . ." He had sunk back into the Russian blockade.

3

Ambrogio regained consciousness in the hospital, asked immediately after Paccoi and was told he was not among those hospitalized in Schio. The health corps people figured they had put him in the military hospital at Verona. "The majority of the wounded who got off the train were taken there. It's a big hospital, almost too big, full of people. You're better off here."

Ambrogio needed the rest of the day to convince himself that they had separated him from the peasant artilleryman who, through so many vicissitudes, had saved his life. *Well,* he finally decided, *when I get out of the hospital I'll look for him. And we'll be friends from then on, like I am with Stefano.* Stefano! He hadn't thought of him much these last days. *Would he have managed to get out of there?* Despite his searching through the dormitories in Leopoli, he had been unable to locate a single Bersagliere from the Third Division. He would have to telephone Nomana as soon as possible to let his parents know he was back (*What would they be saying about the disastrous Russian front?*) and also to find out if they had any news of Stefano in the town. (*Not likely, but one never knows.*) He had to telephone Bonsaver's parents, too, who didn't live far from here, to come for the dead fellow's wallet. Some business to look forward to! God help us! Well, one thing after another.

The next morning he awoke feeling quite a bit better. He took advantage of the momentary absence of the section's nursing sister to put on his ruined uniform to go to the hall, where there was a telephone. He asked for Nomana and sat down on an armchair and waited for the call.

At the end of a half hour his sister Francesca answered. He recognized her voice the second she said, "Hello, the Riva residence."

"Francesca, is that you?"

"Yes, but who is this?"

"Ambrogio. I'm in Italy."

"What? Ambrogio? Don't tell me! No, how can it be?" She became quite excited and could not speak. "It's not possible!" she exclaimed.

"Listen, Francesca, I'm in Schio and ..."

"Fortunato! Fortunato!" Francesca began to scream. "Hurry! Ambrogio's on the phone!"

Fortunato was right there. Ambrogio could hear him tell his sister, "What are you saying? Ambrogio? Give me the phone. You're an idiot! Hello, hello . . ."

"Fortunato, it's me, Ambrogio. I'm in the Schio hospital. I arrived in Italy yesterday."

"Ambrogio! In the hospital? Are you wounded?"

"Yes, but nothing much. It's not serious. Is Mama at home?"

"No, she's in Milan with Papa." (Meanwhile Francesca could be heard screaming, "Almina, Noemi, hurry! Ambrogio's on the phone!")

After a brief accounting of his news, Ambrogio asked if they had news of Stefano in Nomanella. "No, his last letter came at Christmas, about the same time as yours."

Ambrogio wanted to talk to Francesca again, then Alma. "And how are your friends? And Michele?" the little marble statue asked happily.

"I'll tell you when I see you", Ambrogio answered.

"But Michele, how is he? Is he wounded, too?"

"I don't know", Ambrogio said. "We've not been in touch these last weeks."

Alma realized that something not too pleasant must have happened, and she stood speechless at the telephone. "Listen, Alma", Ambrogio went on. "You'll have to come and see me one of these days, too. I'm looking forward to it, and I'd like to try one of your famous cakes you've been writing me about in your letters. Agreed?" Then he said goodbye and hung up, since Noemi was too excited to talk to him.

The following day his father and mother were in Schio. His mother stayed a few weeks, until he began to recuperate from the surgery to remove shrapnel from his back. His older brothers and sisters took turns coming to see him and keeping him company. Bonsaver's parents also came, broken up and practically unable to speak, two humble people—the following night Ambrogio did not sleep a wink. The Cederle family, relatives of Manno's mother from Vicenza,

364

also came more than once. Other acquaintances visited, too, and a professor from his school, a native of Schio. The professor informed him that news of some of his classmates in North Africa was no longer arriving. Our troops and the German ones were retreating now and being pursued by far superior forces. (They had been reduced to seven or eight to one on that front, but that was not known in Italy.)

4

In April, after a two-month stay in Schio, Ambrogio was transferred to Riccione, to a Fascist seaside camp for boys that had been transformed into a convalescent home. His back injury had healed, as well as his arm and chest wounds.

The building, spacious and spalike, boasted large windows that looked out onto the beach toward on the outskirts of the city, on the seaside highway going to Rimini. The bed, the night table, the dishes, and, in general, the other objects of daily use were proper to a summer residence rather than to a hospital, which made it quite pleasant for the inmates. The large windows looking onto the beach and sea were especially delightful.

Ambrogio adopted the habit of spending hours in front of one of those windows. Behind him, the usual military hospital conversation quietly flowed: the improvements and relapses of lacerated tissue, the outlook of the war, war, first and foremost. The young man could look down to the wide grounds of the settlement that was divided into playing fields by metallic netting painted in bright colors, some reaching the base of a row of tamarinds with dry bark, suited to that sandy soil but in stark contrast with their vivid green and their lacy branches, so delicate they seemed like vaporous clouds. The beach was farther on, in a state of neglect—it seemed to be returning to the original contours of dunes. And beyond, the sea, always true to itself, although now, so abandoned, it breathed a sensation of overwhelming solitude. All of which fit in well with the young man's thoughts. He imagined himself walking "along the shore of the thundering sea" with Tricia in her blue-and-white-striped outfit and her conical hat. Where would Tricia be now, her blond locks, where would they be, her thoughts, her life? *Luckily, Rho is too stupid a place to be bombed,* Ambrogio sometimes told himself, mentally going on with those joking conversations, sometimes even laughing out loud to himself. (The other residents would look at him then.) Of course, wherever she was, she would not be thinking about him, and if she did occasionally remember him, the most she would feel would be a passing wave of good feeling, as was made evident by the few postcards he had received these last three years, including the last tiny letter—so pedestrian—in which she thanked him for the flowers he had sent from the Don. (*Three years away! How they've gone by . . . incredible!*)

Besides, he had only felt a vague liking for the girl, and yet now he was continually searching for her in his thoughts, and not just because of this place and this sea, which reminded him of her all the time, but because he felt the compelling need, after all the inhuman things he had gone through, things he continued to relive every night in dreams that were more like nightmares. A woman—that is, the inexpressibly vital perspective of love—was, after all, the most natural and spontaneous objective for him, after having just escaped from the fetid depths of death.

He ended up wondering seriously if he was not falling in love with Tricia now, perhaps, after not seeing her for so long. So one day he decided to write her. April was almost over, and he now could go out for short walks. He took an army postcard (one already prepared without stamps, gray, that folded over with its three edges glued and its stamped slogan, "We shall overcome!" which has brought families from all fronts an endless, bewildering rush of thoughts, facts, boredom, cowardice, and heroism), and on it he summed up his most recent experiences. It seemed to him he was writing an almost free and easy letter, joking, in his old style. However, it turned out to be something between reflective and dramatic, but on reading it, he was only vaguely aware of that.

He dressed in his uniform (the only one left to him: a twill fabric, elegant), and like any young fellow sending off a love letter, he went personally into Riccione to mail it. Despite all the expected inconvenience, because it was no short distance, he was inwardly pleased. *Worthwhile things must be paid for,* he thought. On the fact that he was attaching so much importance to this postcard he did not dwell.

5

A few days later, a Sunday morning about ten, already washed and shaved, Ambrogio was lounging, half dressed on his bed, waiting for Sunday Mass, when a message was sent up that he had a visitor to see him.

He put on his jacket, belt, and gloves and was still dressing as he went down the stairs, wondering who it could be. He had spoken only a few days before with his family, and none of them had mentioned a visit. Other relatives, perhaps? An acquaintance or soldier pal? Or perhaps, perhaps . . . would it be possible? Maybe Tricia, instead of writing, had had the opportunity to come in this direction . . . *But what opportunity? I'm not talking rot. Well, maybe looking for a place to spend their next vacation* . . . Of course it wouldn't be Tricia, but still he had to keep from running down the stairs.

In the hall he found his father and mother waiting for him, standing side by side, intimidated by the hospital environment. A flush of disappointment went through him when he saw it was not Tricia! But it was his mother, who lit up with happiness at the sight of her son. Her still-pretty face had not been marked by pain, as would have happened had he not returned. It was her, *thanks be to God*, her usual self, the same as when she came to visit at school. Ambrogio was almost feeling guilty for having hoped it would be Tricia. He hugged both parents, and then he felt a wave of shyness. "Terrific! I'm so glad you've come, and such a surprise! What's on the program?"

"To be together until five", Gerardo smiled.

"Have you been to Mass, Ambrogio?"

"Not yet, Mama."

"Then we'll do that first."

"Yes, of course. Do you want to go now? Have you noticed, I'm wearing gloves?"

His elegant uniform of the early days made him look younger. Only now he was wearing a ribbon of distinction in his buttonhole, a German one used in the Italian army, too, called the "ice badge", which bore witness to the fact that he had fought on the Russian front during the winter.

His mother did not take her eyes off her son. "But how are you really? Are the wounds still bothering you?"

"No, not any more."

The young man took their arms familiarly and guided them to the door.

"One minute", his father exclaimed. "I want to say goodbye to that nice young man." He went back and amiably shook the hand of one of the hall orderlies, most notorious for his laziness. While waiting for his son, Gerardo had talked to the orderly, asking him, "Are you also one of the brave soldiers busy with the wounded?" In the face of that flattery, the idler could do no less than posture modestly and take credit for great merits. Now, with one eye on the other orderlies and another on Ambrogio, the known idler responded with smug satisfaction to Gerardo's courteous greeting. Knowing his father, the young lieutenant could imagine the scene that had transpired before his arrival, but he said nothing.

They heard Mass in an all but empty church. ("Of course, we're *in partibus infidelium*", Ambrogio remembered.) Later they strolled along Riccione's main street, which was crowded with convalescents since it was a feastday. There were Italians and Germans on the streets and along the sea; the seaside resort had been transformed into a city of convalescents. Any number of them were using one and even two canes ("You see, Papa? They're the ones the ice got to.") or crutches, and they looked out of eyes glowing with astonishment, not so much because they were still alive, but because—after all that had happened and they had seen—everything continued as before in the world. Every so often a German would salute Ambrogio, straightening himself and clicking his heels in a gesture of respect for the decoration Ambrogio wore in his lapel.

After having walked for quite a while, talking of many things, especially about Manno, who was in Tunis; about Don Carlo Gnocchi, the priest who had returned from the front unharmed physically, but very spiritually affected;

about the disturbing bombings of Italian cities; also about the atmosphere of Schio, a city that had been industrialized in the last century and that was deeply Catholic, like Nomana. *Who says an industrial civilization could not be reconciled with Christianity? The truth is exactly the opposite: it is more Christianized than that of agricultural society.* They went to a restaurant, where they were able to eat quite well, thanks to the ration coupons Giulia had brought with her.

They then resumed their walk until Giulia feared her son might be overdoing it. She conveyed her worry to Gerardo discreetly, and he immediately picked out a table at a bar. The conversation touched on Manno frequently. After a long retreat from El Alamein, full of reversals, he was now fighting in Tunis, with the sea at his back. Things were going quite poorly for the Italians and Germans there, although the radio and newspapers did not really tell what the situation was.

"I told you I received a postcard two days ago from him," Ambrogio reminded them, "and I sent it on to Nomana immediately in a sealed envelope. It was dated April 30, less than a week ago."

"We've had nothing for three weeks now," Gerardo said, "and that's why we're worried."

"In his card, you'll see for yourselves, he says he hasn't a moment to take a breath. That's why he's not writing. Besides, in a war like this the constant movement doesn't allow for pauses. You're not left a minute's peace."

"Maybe he's been wounded, too?" Giulia questioned. "And not for the first time, or sick? Like that friend of yours from Lodosa, the blond fellow?"

"You mean Castagna?"

"Yes. You know he came back from Libya with a stomach infection? Imagine how many privations Manno must also have suffered since he's been in Africa—more than a year and a half now, so many we can hardly imagine them."

"Yes, but in his postcard he's joking as usual, you'll see", Ambrogio said. "He can't be in a hospital because the card is normal, has stamps on it, and it's passed muster with his outfit. Come on, Mama, try to look at the bright side. Manno hasn't had time because they're retreating in the desert with those seventy-five guns."

"Poor boy, what he must be living through", Giulia murmured.

"In any case, listen to me." Ambrogio wanted to make one thing clear, to comfort them. "He isn't confronting the Bolsheviks but the English and Americans instead. Say he's taken prisoner. These people don't kill prisoners or let them starve to death. And if he were to be wounded, they'll take care of him in their hospitals, just as we've always done with their wounded."

"The English and Americans are civilized, yes," Gerardo agreed, "but . . ." He put his hand on the table in the shape of a shower, indicating a precipitation of bombs. Of course, there was no answer to that.

Leaving that bar, Gerardo, with the excuse of taking them to a more comfortable bar, made them sit down again. As it was nearing 5:00—their departure time—he ordered a horse-drawn carriage from the waiter: "Because," he said, "it's been years since I've been in one of those, and seeing them there outside, I suddenly feel like being in one."

It was obvious that it was simply an excuse to keep his son from having to walk back to the clinic on the outskirts of Riccione. When they reached the clinic, he had the carriage wait to take them to the train station.

They took their leave on the street in front of the hospital. "We expect you'll soon be coming home", the father said to his son. "I'm sure that the air of Nomana will be better than any medicine."

"If Manno should happen to write you from Africa", his mother said, turning halfway in the carriage, "telephone immediately and read me what he writes word by word."

"All right", Ambrogio promised, stepping back a little to let them leave.

His mother then touched her mouth and lifted her finger upward. "What?" the young man asked, smiling, though he had understood, and again coming up to her, he brought his face close to hers.

"You pray, too, for your cousin", his mother said softly.

"Of course, Mama."

The driver, from Romagna (and he had already shown himself to be of an extravagant nature), seated behind his horse, twisted around to look at the mother and her son in his elegant officer's uniform who were talking about praying. At last Gerardo told the driver to leave, and with a pull on the reins the carriage moved off, at an angle behind the bony horse.

This is the reason I was saved, Ambrogio thought, while watching the vehicle go off. *This is the reason I'm here today and not under the grass in Posnyakoff, or in one of those pits in front of the infirmary of Cerkovo. The Gospels say, 'Knock, and it will be opened to you', but with Mama it's not just a knock, she opens the door with tooth and nail.*

Slowly he returned to the clinic, flanked by a cloudy row of tamarinds. *Manno*, he was thinking, *how his ears must have been burning today! We've done nothing but talk about him all day.*

6

Without noticing any burning in his ears, Manno at that moment was on a small cove of Le Kram on the outskirts of Tunis, together with some military men and a civilian beside a boat. It was midday on May 6, 1943. In Italy it was still not known, but on that day the last two Italian-German units in Tunis (those that had protected Tunis and Bizerta) had put down their arms. The next day the two cities would be occupied by the Americans and English.

On that small cove next to the sea, surrounded by ruined constructions used as secondary deposits for the army, there was no noise of war at the moment, only the quiet lapping of the tide on the beach.

Manno (who had become a lieutenant a few months before and was wearing his almost new stripes on the sleeves of his safari jacket) and the others
beside him were focusing their attention on the engine of a boat: a car engine,
which was quite incongruous for the Arab craft, but which had somehow
been fit in.

"I don't understand how you've installed it", he commented. (He was very
tired—so tired he did not realize his ears were burning—but he was trying to
keep it from being noticed.) "What are those beams down there for?"

"We didn't have a navy carpenter", a warrant officer from the automobile
center answered with a smile. "To be exact, we didn't even have a real carpenter. We only had him, Vernazza," and he pointed, "who let us think he was
a carpenter but is really a woodcutter. Only when he began the work did he
confess."

"A woodcutter who chops down trees in the woods, you understand?" added
an infantryman in the communications unit, a friendly, long-faced fellow.

"Who, Vernazza? Of course, he was a woodcutter from very early on", Manno's aide, the artilleryman Battistessa testified. "Isn't that so, Vernazza?"

The fellow questioned nodded, smiling. He was a driver from the automobile unit. (Except for Manno and his aide, everyone there belonged to the
communications unit.) He was short, with a slight belly, light hair, a florid
face. He looked more of a shopkeeper than he did a woodcutter. "Yes, but the
way I put that motor in, not even cannon fire will move it", he declared softly
in a Piedmont dialect.

"Ah," Manno said, amused, "now I understand."

"It was Sergeant Vestidello," the chief from the motorized unit explained,
"the mechanic from the aviation field over here, the one I told you about:
someone who knows his job like an angel. He directed the mechanical side of
it, and the adjustment for sailing was done by Zustovic, the lieutenant from
Trieste, in the aeronautical unit, who knows about boats. They were to come
with us, both of them—as I said—because they were, in a way, the backbone
of the undertaking, and this morning, I don't know how, but they found a way
of leaving in a plane."

Providence, Manno thought, *providence has made it happen this way, this chance
for me and my aide to get back home.*

"Of course, they were in luck", the man with the broad face commented.
"They'll be safe and sound back in Italy now."

"Sure, if the English planes haven't gotten in their way", one of them with
a Brianza inflection pointed out. Besides Manno, there were two others from
Brianza in the little group: two brothers, Ulisse and Felice Vigano, from Merate. They were both small creatures with big heads and vulturelike features.
Sons of a highway worker, they had been in Africa in communications, also
working on highways. Their skin was the color of leather, burned by the sun
and tar.

370

With this reflection they were all, more or less, in serious agreement. The danger of the enemy aircraft—especially the fighter planes, day or night—also affected small boats, and inwardly they were more worried about them than any other danger, even more than the mines, which were serious enough.

"Well, there's the boat", the chief said to Manno in a conclusive tone of voice.

"Yes. And it looks as if it will work well. Once again, it's a great pleasure to be going with you." He turned to his aide. "Isn't that so, Battistessa?"

"Of course, Lieutenant", he answered assuredly.

"I'm glad", the chief of the motorized unit answered. "Because without Lieutenant Zustovic . . . the lack of a mechanic doesn't worry me. I know about motors, too. It's my job. But without the lieutenant . . . I'm from the motor unit center, I don't belong to a combat detachment. Of course, all these boys come voluntarily, and each one is responsible for himself, but one never knows. It could happen that making some decision or other would mean putting someone else's life out on the limb. Well, I . . . in short, now I'm happier."

"Naturally, I understand, but what I don't understand is where your officers are. Don't you have any to invite?"

The chief mechanic shook his head, a tinge of irony in his eyes. "They knew we were getting the boat ready", he explained. "For more than two weeks we worked there, in that shack," pointing to one of the dilapidated buildings that bordered the cove, "and when they came to the shed, they saw it, but none of them ever proposed coming along in it. The planes, you understand? Too many out there. They never stop striking the airport and the port—you can see it's nothing but a ruin now—and the sea, there."

The sea stretched before them peacefully at this moment, without airplanes, bordered in the distance, toward the right, by the mountainous peninsula that culminated in Cape Bon. It seemed huge, not easy to cross with a makeshift craft like this one. *But,* Manno thought vaguely, *if the men at the front had an opportunity like this . . . !*

"There are no planes now", the chief mechanic said, waving toward the sky, which was beginning to glow with the colors of twilight. "It's odd because you see them the whole blessed day fine combing the gulf. You can't imagine."

"Oh, yes, we can", Manno said, glancing toward his aide. "From morning to night, they also fly over every highway and inland road and even gun down isolated men. Well and good, but I must tell you one thing: I don't know anything about sailing—I know how to use a compass, a topographical or nautical map, which basically are not too different, but that's all."

"Go on. Lieutenant Riva is completely competent, let me tell you", his aide Battistessa interjected. He addressed the chief mechanic. "He'll be of use for what you first said: to make decisions. He knows how to get people out of any situation. You should have seen him after El Alamein. That's why they sent him and no one else to take the post to the airfield—because they wanted the post to go out, no matter what. Yes, that's how it is."

Manno, smiling, shook his head. Actually, for him to lead men in time of trouble, and in general take over leadership at the front, came more naturally than it did to his cousin Ambrogio or to Michele Tintori.

"Good, good", the man with the long broad face exclaimed, who was quick to enthusiasm. "It looks as if we'll make it to Italy, and we won't end up as fish food." He turned to his friend the woodcutter. "What do you think, Vernazza?"

The other fellow agreed, but not as enthusiastically. His only comment was, "If I come along it's because I'm also sure we won't end up in the belly of a fish."

Then Manno turned to the only civilian there, who was listening, a pack slung over his back. "Come on over. Here are the keys for the motorbike", he said.

They both went off a ways from the others. Manno took a small key from his pocket and gave it to the civilian. "I'll show you how to start it."

"Yes."

"It's a Matchless 350, spoils of war, booty. As I already told you, it's not army property, it's mine, if that's of any interest to you. I found it intact during our last advance, when the English took flight. Because", he said with a voice that suddenly changed, "at one time, two thousand miles from here, we were advancing . . ." He fell quiet for a moment, as if thinking.

"I know, Lieutenant. Things change in life. There are ups and downs." He tried to comfort him in his strong Sicilian accent.

"Yes. Careful the English don't see it. In any case, it's your problem."

The civilian handed over the pack. "I'll take care they don't take it away from me", he assured him. Then, referring to the contents of the pack, "There are twenty boxes, forty packs of biscuits, and two new mess tins. Check it out, please."

"I trust you", Manno said. (It was all military booty. What else could it be? At least it meant, in their present situation, a guarantee of health.)

The civilian, before going off, offered to help push the boat into the sea.

Manno referred the offer to the chief mechanic, who seemed dubious, looked at his watch, and said, "Yes, perhaps that would be better. Thanks. At 8:30 then. Still three hours to go, but it's better to be ready . . . never know . . ."

Nobody objected. There were eleven of them with the civilian. They arranged for five on one side and six on the other side of the boat, which was pointed toward the sea. First they lifted the prow and placed a drum under it and in one move pushed the boat all together with all their might. The boat made it out a good stretch. They placed a second drum under the prow, got ready a third a little farther up, and pushed again. After recovering the first drum, they put it farther upon the sand. The two Vigano brothers turned out to be particularly handy at these maneuvers. They were used to handling weights.

At last, with all the pushing and shoving, the prow of the boat dipped into the water.

"And now?" the two brothers asked, practically in unison. Ulisse, the older one, held a drum in his hands that he had just taken from the dirty sea surface.

The chief mechanic addressed Manno in an uncertain tone. "Lieutenant Zustovic decided to leave at 8:30, when it would be totally dark. But if you think . . ."

"I don't quite understand. Is there something in particular worrying you? That your higher ups might change their minds, perhaps?" Manno asked.

"No, I wasn't thinking of them. Really about the others. I'm not sure, the ones scattered about, the Germans, one never knows. More than a few are aware of our boat, and that's why we've all been here since the morning, armed."

A dull roar of motors at sea could be heard.

"The Spitfires!" Battistessa exclaimed.

They all looked out to sea. In the distance they could see three or four thin shapes, like sharks, on the horizon, carrying out a high-speed inspection run.

"The bastards!" Vernazza muttered. "They never stop combing the sea. They never get enough."

Manno looked at the chief mechanic. "I don't think Zustovic was wrong. Better wait until dark to put the boat into the sea."

"Well, then," the civilian said, "I guess I'll be off." He shook hands with the chief and with Manno, and then one of the soldiers, and finally all of them. He seemed a bit emotional now. "Greetings to my Sicily", he said.

"Life isn't easy for you Italian civilians here in Tunis, it seems", the older of the Vigano brothers said and added, "I have a sister, a nun, in Somalia." He looked at his brother, who nodded agreement, and they said no more.

The civilian waved a final farewell in a circular movement, then, step by step, went up to the cove, to a passage between the buildings. What could he live on, Manno was wondering, with a war on, probably unemployed, and no prospects? And no doubt he had a family to feed.

7

After a quick camouflaging of the boat, some of the men went back to the buildings. The others—Manno among them—sat down on the sand to wait. He could feel the cold at this hour through his desert trousers. He was slightly dizzy: everything was happening with such speed. Just a few hours before (How many? Three? Four?) he had left the weapon site in that little cork-tree woods to bring the last post to the airfield. The chance of leaving Africa had not figured in his plans in any way.

It was Battistessa—armed with a machine gun, acting as a bodyguard, riding pillion on the motorcycle—who suggested visiting a fellow countryman of his

("He's only a little way from the airfield . . . if I haven't the directions wrong."), who was busy with some others putting a motor in a boat. "I told you about the boat a few days ago, do you remember?" Battistessa reminded him.

"A few days ago? Oh!" Manno remembered. That morning in the observatory, with the American tanks coming and going from the line of fire behind the hills . . . an appropriate place for talking about boats. "Yes, of course, but you didn't explain", he had answered.

So, while the motorcycle sped along the highway, Battistessa had explained. Now there was time to talk about boats, because their unit, out of arms, had no choice but to surrender to the enemy: the cannons had been destroyed by hammer blows. Neither of them was in any hurry to return to a unit in that state. *After all*, the officer was thinking while Battistessa was filling him in on that boat, *this boat thing could be an excuse for hanging around with the communications people.* Even if not an aspiring writer like Michele Tintori, the future architect, Manno Riva, tried as much as possible to look carefully at what was going on around him. And so he answered, "All right, Battistessa, as soon as we deliver the post, we'll go look for your boat friend. What did you say his name was?"

"Vernazza."

"Almost Vernaccia, like the dry white wine. Wonderful!" and he began to laugh happily, speeding up the motorcycle in whose tank only a few inches of gasoline splashed.

At the airport, quite ruined, the post had been not only accepted but also loaded, before their very eyes, into a plane, which then took off with such an uproar of metal it brought the mechanics on duty out, thinking there was a seriously damaged plane arriving. The carefree courage of the Italian pilots appealed to Manno, who knew that the takeoff of that piece of junk had been decided only in order to save a handful of terrorized French "collaborationists", who, if they had fallen prisoner, would no doubt have been shot down by the De Gaulle faction.

Afterward everything unfolded in record time. Vernazza, whom they found easily, suggested leaving in the boat. Used to the indecisiveness of communications people, he did not expect the two of them to accept immediately. When they did so on the spot, he took them to meet the chief mechanic, the warrant officer. There was a kind of examination carried out by the latter and the Vigano brothers. (The fact that Manno was from Brianza provoked almost hysterical enthusiasm from them.) Then there was a private conversation among the warrant officer and the two brothers. Manno guessed the reason for their hesitation. They were wondering that if by accepting him, they were not imposing a master over themselves, depriving themselves of freedom. The idea of a trip like that, an adventure, was greatly appealing. His imagination had already taken off: he would relive the adventure of a young navy officer from his region, Daboni from Lecco, the son of family friends, who, along with a few others, two years before had, from just off Tobruk, reached Sicily in a motor-boat, thus escaping prison. It was true, though, that Daboni then died at sea, after having signed onto a warship that went down.

Manno, to wipe out any objections, told the boat owners that he was will-ing to go—until they reached the Italian coast—as a paying guest. And, if the money he had with him—two months' pay—three thousand lire—was not enough, he would give them his word that they would have the rest once in Italy.

More than the material offer, it had been the spirit of this declaration that had decided the three men, who had gone into conference and decided they would be satisfied to take him and his aide. The money offer was turned down (by the Vigano brothers, with a polite refusal that had rather sharply reminded the young man of the distant world of Brianza), but they immediately sent for a civilian active in the black market in Carancha, so the lieutenant could pro-vide them with some victuals.

The little time left was taken up with final details, most especially various trips to bring fuel from a secret hiding spot to the boat. To camouflage it better, the extremely precious liquid had been transferred to tanks usually used for drinking water.

Now, lying on the cold sand waiting for the departure, Manno recalled all these things, mingling them in his imagination. He already saw himself in the boat, which would move tirelessly over the sea, humble but free, with an al-ways even rippling of water, with a lost gull following them in slow flight, measuring—like the boat—a measureless sea. Given his fatigue, he finally slept. He did not hear the explosions of an aerial bombing that came from the air-port zone or the distant shooting of a machine-gunning at sea. He dreamed of his brothers in arms, with whom he had lived through so many tough expe-riences, who had remained behind in the cork grove with their useless arms. "I can't take you with me, you understand. You understand, don't you?" Some nodded, happy that at least he was escaping a prisoner's fate; others shook their heads, disapprovingly, because he was abandoning them.

8

At the hour agreed upon, the boat was pushed out to sea. There was no trou-ble starting up the engine; its regular sound—which to the ears of those leav-ing seemed quite loud—was actually quite muffled by an ingenious rudimentary silencer that the diligent Sergeant Vestidello had installed. They began to sail immediately to the northeast in the dark. At the helm was the only one of the ten men who had any real experience with boats and the sea, and precisely of that sea, which was why he had been carefully selected by Lieutenant Zustovic during his time: the soldier Patane, who as a civilian was a fisherman in Mazara

375

del Vallo, Sicily. On the bench to his right were Manno and the chief mechanic; Manno had set up a compass on the seat beside him, with the axis parallel to the boat. It was a pocket compass the Viganos had managed to procure for him. On his knees he had a celluloid reconnaissance map (similar to the one recovered by Stefano, the Bersagliere, five months before, in the trench of the dead), and over that, open, a map of Tunis with a protractor to measure angles, instruments left by Lieutenant Zustovic. The chief mechanic was lighting up the map, protractor, and compass with a small electric flashlight. "You see?" Manno pointed out to him. "The coast as far as Cape Bon has this contour. So we should keep in the direction of 65 degrees eastward."

"Yes", the chief agreed, "yes." The others were looking back to the shore they had just left, where, along its length, were outlined one village after another in the dark, Le Kram, Kefredine, and Le Goulette, a continuous strip of Arab houses mirrored in the sea. No one spoke.

"At this very moment," the chief mechanic suddenly announced, and then interrupted himself, consulted his watch with pedantic meticulosity, after switching off the flashlight, "it's 8:35: at this moment my friend the warrant officer Saltamerenda is telephoning the coast guard warning them not to fire on us, should we be spotted at sea. I told you already about that."

"We hope it all goes well", the younger of the Vigano, Felice, muttered worriedly.

His brother, Ulisse, who was seated on the bridge of the prow, said nothing. He was very rigid, clutching a big electric flashlight in his right hand, ready to light it if necessary, meanwhile scrutinizing the sea ahead of them, which, under the systematic power of the motor, cut the swarthy surface without so much as a bubble of spume. The others, too—distributed carefully for the sake of balance on the two lateral benches along the two sides of the boat—were glancing at the water. Manno, too, though no coward, felt a kind of faintness every time he looked at the water. The sea, under these circumstances and at this hour, with something impenetrable and repellent about it, was unrecognizable.

There was no moon, and so it was not possible to see the distant profile of the coast to the right, parallel to where they were sailing, but Patane, at the helm, seemed to take no notice of the coast. Small, dark skinned, with an aquiline nose and a black mustache, and wearing a most dilapidated uniform, he looked Arab. *To him this native caique must seem more or less normal*, Manno thought. He could see him search out the polar star every so often and then straighten his course ever so slightly by turning the helm. At the beginning he asked the officer a few times if the corrected course was right, and each time Manno checked it with the compass, confirming or correcting the direction a bit. Patane, at last, felt quite secure and no longer asked to be checked.

In each of them there was an inner core of secret tension, fed largely by the distant, small flashes of rockets hurled from invisible enemy planes onto the sea, but the boat continued purring the even rhythm of its motor, not coming across lines or detaining nets or any other obstacles. They were beginning, however, to feel the cold and dampness, disagreeable and unexpectedly harsh, and one of the men pulled out his blanket from the bottom of the boat and wrapped himself in it. The others followed suit. The older of the Viganos, Ulisse, left his place momentarily at the prow and, walking awkwardly the length of the boat, went for his blanket under the poop bench.

"Did you see anything out there?" the chief mechanic asked when he passed.

"No, only darkness", he answered. "The sea and air are one color, like ink."

"Then you can stop watching, if it's that way."

Vigano, after groping about for his blanket under Patane's seat, on his way back said, "No, one never knows", to the chief. "In a while I could get used to the dark, and I do have this." He lifted the switched-off flashlight.

"Besides," Manno commented, "if you're here or there, it's all the same."

"If we happen to stumble on a mine," Ulisse Vigano said, gloomily, without wanting to be, "I'll no doubt have the chance of being finished off in one blow, with a clear course ahead. I know what I'm saying," he added, "and I prefer it that way. My father was blinded ten years ago by a mine bursting." He went off walking a little crookedly, toward the prow, where he sat down with the blanket over his shoulders.

The first hour went by without anything untoward happening. Then the second hour. The flashing of light from enemy planes seemed to occur at ever-lengthening intervals, and the tension and anxiety began to subside in all of them, but not entirely, insofar as they were all aware that until the last moment of sailing any mortal surprise was possible.

Manno thought of Daboni, the navy man from Lecco, a friend from the Milan Polytechnical College days, and not so much—as he had done at noon before leaving—of Daboni's lucky trip in a boat from Tobruk to Sicily, but rather of his later tragic end in the ship that sunk, which he had been assigned to, a corvette. What state would his body be in now, if there was anything left of it, in its metal tomb at the bottom of the sea? How long would bodies last without decomposing, buried in the inside of a sunken ship? Of course, if this turned out badly, there wouldn't even be that kind of tomb.

Being imaginative, he conjured up images of himself and his comrades as a variety of human forms at the bottom of the sea, *perhaps surrounded by fish, tearing us to shreds with their revolting mouths.* But for him the really worrisome part was not this physical death. More disturbing for him (and for so many others today, as it was one or two thousand years ago) was what would happen after the death, not of the body, but of the spirit, the fate of the soul in the Great Beyond. Once again the big problem: What would our fate be in the Great Beyond? Would all of us be saved? In the Gospels, some words of Jesus— that is, God made man for our salvation—lead us to think that, others not at all. That is why the self-satisfied confidence of some, especially among the young priests, for instance, in the salvation of all seemed arbitrary to Manno. *What was their confidence based on? They forced themselves to be optimistic, if only out of charity, pity . . . To begin with, doesn't hell already exist here on earth? Of course it does, and how!* Certain moments in El Alamein came back to him and those stories of life in the trenches in the last war (of the very recent events in Russia he was still not aware). He also pondered the Jews—men, women, and children—fallen into the clutches of the Nazis. (*Luckily the Italian Fascists won't let them be touched.*) *So, if there is a hell here, why should we deny the possibility of one also on the other side? The fundamental difference being that there human beings will be outside of time, they'll be in eternity, and so, also the eternity of hell . . .*

With his eyes shut, wrapped in a blanket given him by the chief mechanic, a little bent forward, Manno persisted in his thoughts. He felt the moist night air on his face, and added to his thoughts came the tireless sound of the engine and the lapping of the water against the keel. *What amazing resistance, if you think about it, there is in the metal that engines are made of.*

"But God is love, you know?" the very confident priests would insist. (So did his regimental chaplain, with whom he had discussed this on a bivouac beside a road in Sirte one night when they were faint with fatigue.)

"Would you, imperfect as you are, send someone to hell, to torment for all of eternity?" the chaplain objected. "And do you want God to do so? He, who orders, above all else, that we love one another and avoid making each other suffer."

But, Manno told himself, that was precisely the point: it was not God who was sending them there. Just as God does not shove men into the hell on earth. They do it to themselves, by entering into wars, for instance, by inventing racism, and so much else, all because of their terrible freedom. And they go against God, his will, his Commandments . . . *And then later, perhaps, the more rash decide that God doesn't exist, given the fact there is so much evil on earth!*

Besides, there was the mention here and there in the sacred texts of the eternal fire. Because of this not a few believers concluded only a metaphorical meaning to the word *hell*. *And many nonbelievers, because of those references, are confirmed in their opinion that the sacred texts are an unreliable mixture of myths, legends, historical tales, diverse precepts, put together by a seminomadic people.* For him, in contrast, these references to fire made the prospects of hell something awful—and even at this moment—and still more plausible. *Because if man is really to be one with God, like the vine shoots and tendrils with the vine, the idea of being definitively separated from him (this, and this alone, is hell) would imply—for the immortal human—a kind of permanent disintegration . . . And what other thing on earth could give a better idea of disintegration than fire?* The fact that those seminomadic people, only partially conscious of what they were writing and certainly unaware of the relationship between the vine shoots and vine, should have used the word *fire* would indicate, he thought, that they had written under a higher inspiration. Enough thinking about all this, these great problems, enough for tonight . . .

At his side the chief mechanic moved about from time to time. Finally, he lit his flashlight carefully and looked at his watch. "Eleven", he announced, breaking the general silence. "If Lieutenant Zustovic's estimate of the speed—about five miles per hour—is not off, we should have gone about twelve miles."

"The engine's good", Manno said. "An engine that runs as it's supposed to, no doubt about it."

Vernazza, who had installed the engine in the boat, smiled contentedly, as if he had been personally complimented. "I had to set it in quite high," he mentioned once again, "so the screw would also be up high. Since Vestidello was sure that the mines were all about three or four yards down . . ."

"Do you think we've gone over a mine or two?" the broad-faced fellow asked.

"More than one, for sure," the chief answered, "because there are different minefields in the gulf, but we do not even reach a yard's depth."

"What I'm happiest about", the younger of the Viganos said, "is that the engine works as well in the water as it did in the tests in the hangar. There's not an engine that Vestidello can't get the better of."

The helmsman Patane, who knew about boats, nodded agreement. "If every engine only worked as well as this", he said, and went on nodding in the dark.

"Who knows how much time that one has spent on boats", Manno reflected, and then asked him, "Do you want me to take over for a while?"

But the other quickly replied, "No, Lieutenant", with a tone of southern self-assurance. "I'm good for all night", he added.

After a few more words, the even purring of the engine and the lapping of the water on the keel were all that could be heard. Another hour went by, and still another. The airplanes, headed toward Tunis, were still sending out flashes of light over the sea.

Manno again began thinking about Daboni from Lecco. At the Polytechnical College, where Daboni had studied engineering and Manno architecture, they had known one another, and even before, because Daboni came from a Catholic industrial family, like Manno's uncle Gerardo, who had maintained a business and friendly relationship with them over many years. The young man was part of a family of eleven children, ten girls and one boy. And it was precisely he, the only male, who had died. How would the Daboni family manage in the future? Who would take care of the business later? It was an important metal construction business with many workers. They had built one of the biggest iron bridges in Italy, for example, the bridge for the Piacenza railway over the Po. When the train slowed down close to the nearby stations, the company's name, Daboni-Lecco, could be seen in relief letters on the main crossings. *Worthwhile people these Dabonis. They did not stand still in peace or in war. But how would the old man go on alone? Perhaps one of the girls will be able to help, to carry on the work in some way. Adriana, perhaps, the one who's in school with Francesca, at the same nuns' school. If one day the old man should pass away, I wonder which of the ten girls would assume the responsibility of carrying on the business.* (We now know: it was Francesca's schoolmate, who—even though she had every intention of becoming a nun—was the most gifted for engineering among the ten girls and did in fact become an engineer. She carried on the family business for several years while still very young, and, when some of the brothers-in-law were ready to substitute for her, she entered a Carmelite monastery.)

So many things, memories, thoughts . . . crossing not only Manno's mind, but also the others', because no one, given the tension, managed to fall asleep. The noise of the engine and the water continued incessantly, until it began to deafen all of them. Over their boat, and over any other, over the warships moored in the harbors or en route across the sea, and over submarines hidden below, and over the mines and long rows of torpedoes practically on the water's surface, a vast starry sky stretched. Manno mused lazily. A pity not to know the constellations. The summer before his cousin Ambrogio had written him from Russia, enthusiastically, about the stars. His friend Bonsaver had awakened this interest in him, and he had told him that he had asked Alma to buy an astronomy manual for the two of them, Ambrogio and Manno. Manno liked this initiative in Ambrogio, but neither Alma nor Francesca had found the right type of manuals. In the Milan bookstores the two girls had found only thick scientific tomes replete with numbers and diagrams, which had not seemed the right ones to send them. And so he had remained ignorant of stars . . . what an expression—ignorant of stars!

As time passed, though, as when he was on observation duty, Manno tried to apply the few names he did remember—Lyre, Scorpion, the Bull, Berenice's Mane—to the constellations whose shapes seemed to correspond to those names. He was wrong about all of them, and though he was unaware of that, he was still dissatisfied.

9

An hour, more or less, before dawn (despite the nervous tension, a few of the men had slept), the chief was directing the boat toward the right, to that side of the coast, culminating probably near Cape Bon, which they had not seen but only guessed at during the night. According to the plan, as soon as it was light they would have to get the boat on land, to a deserted place. They did it with no trouble, tying up on a small beach surrounded by bare hills, covered with reeds and cane burned by the sun. Using them as camouflage material, it took them no time at all to hide the boat. ("From our enemies, and from our friends as well", the chief commented.) Then they all got into a sandy grotto, not too far off. Battistessa, Manno's aide, sat at the entrance to take the first turn at guard duty, his machine gun on his knees. The others stretched out on their blankets over the sandy ground. It took them no time to fall asleep.

Manno awoke toward midday, leaned up on his elbow, and looked at the time. The others went on sleeping. Heat flowed in from the grotto entrance, together with a yellowish reverberation of sun and a strident chirping of cicadas. He sat up. At his side the chief was asleep. From time to time he grimaced slightly. He had kicked off the blanket, and now it was wrapped around his legs, and next to his head, on the sand, were his binoculars. The officer picked them up and also his own portfolio of maps, stood up as quietly as possible, and went to the entrance of the grotto, where the broad-faced man was now doing guard duty. They smiled, and Manno told him softly that he was going to one of the hills to have a look around. While adjusting his belt with the pistol attached (he had not removed it for sleeping), he asked, "Have you seen anyone up until now?"

The guard shook his head. "No one", he murmured.

"Good. I'll be gone about twenty minutes."

He went from the darkness to the dazzling sunlight. With one hand over his eyes horizontally, he looked around for the most suitable height for his purpose. He decided on one not too high up but half surrounded by the sea and headed toward it. In a matter of minutes he was atop it. He stretched out on the ground between two thorny thickets and began to scan the sea systematically.

The sea was of an intense turquoise and totally deserted. He turned the binoculars toward two yellowish islands. From his vantage point, though only modestly high, he could make them both out perfectly. He observed them attentively, then pulled out his nautical map and examined it closely. *Could be those little islands we see from here. If I'm not mistaken, farther on from the islands there ought to be this other isolated thing . . .*

He checked the sea in front of the coast with binoculars. "The other thing"— a very rocky island—was there indeed, though he did not see it very well for the distance.

Just as well I took the chief's binoculars. Now I'd better get a measurement of the islands. On the map, here it's . . . more or less three millimeters, which will make it so many meters. Yes, we must be here. The measurements corresponded. He continued his surveillance calmly; there was time. He came to the conclusion that the boat had moored *right here, at this very spot on the coast.* He penciled in a mark on his map.

They were, then, close to the end of the peninsula that extends seaward from Tunis to Sicily, and they were not too far from Cape Bon.

The young man finished his surveillance, stood up between the thickets, and looked around carefully at the land area around him, which was quite reduced because of the surrounding dunes. It looked like a desert, without a trace of human life.

He began to feel a great sensation of adventure, as if he were living who knows what kind of legendary experience. If the lotus eaters had shown up at that moment he would not have been surprised. Even though he looked all around, he saw no sign of those mythological creatures. Instead, he discovered some strange birds that came and went from holes excavated on the vertical side of a hill. He watched them sharply with the binoculars. Certainly there were no birds like these in Italy. He took one last sweeping glance around the surrounding landscape, went slowly down the hill, and returned to the grotto.

The others were still asleep. He sat down then next to the sentinel at the entrance, his back against the sandy wall. The sentinel momentarily took his eyes off the pile of reeds covering the boat and followed every gesture of the officer seated there.

"I found out where we are", he said softly.

The guard nodded, smiling.

Later they had chow—each one for himself—and stretched their legs, then another short nap in the afternoon, and the second feed. Several times during the course of the day enemy planes appeared over the sea. A couple of times they fired against invisible targets at high sea, repeating the process several times.

Toward evening a series of black points were outlined on the horizon, which grew bigger in volume until it could be seen they were ships: a naval formation apparently heading toward Tunis.

"Are those ships ours or those of the enemy?" the fugitives wondered. "Perhaps the navy has finally decided to come and rescue the army?"

"Don't be ridiculous; if the navy could have done something, they'd have done it before now, when it's too late."

"Must be the English or the Americans."

"Perhaps both."

"Would they be on their way to bomb? Or maybe the city's already theirs?"

10

A little before it got dark they pushed the boat out again to sea. With the even ta-ta-ta of its engine they started up again, at first going along the coast. The fading light was enough for the people in the boat to see some not very distant Arabic huts along the shore, and also a small military settlement, from which some Italian soldiers in short trousers were looking out, curious and perplexed by the boat. They figured, no doubt, it had to do with some fleeing fellow-countrymen, and they did not bother to set off the alarm, although neither did they wave a salute.

When it was totally dark the boat was once again in open sea. Its route, however, was kept parallel to the coast, east-northeast, until it went beyond—

according to Manno's calculations and those of the chief mechanic—Cape Bon. No matter how hard the ten men strained their sight, they could not see the cape. But the breeze had increased noticeably; also the waves—though still not high—were more forceful.

"I've the feeling we're in open sea, that we've left the Gulf of Tunis", Manno said. "What do you think?" He asked the helmsman, "What's your opinion, Patane?"

"Can't tell", he answered curtly. "I don't know."

The chief mechanic turned in the darkness to the officer. "What do you think, Lieutenant?"

"I'd say, to be on the safe side, that we continue on another half hour this way, and then we could safely turn the prow to the southeast."

"From here to Pantelleria we have fifty-six long miles."

"Yes, and it's no joke, but the idea of making a second stop on the Tunisian coast was discarded even before our departure. So . . ."

"And it remains discarded", the chief said.

"That's it for Africa", the two Viganos proclaimed, too, almost in unison.

"Courage, then", Manno concluded. "When the boat makes the turn two of us will stand guard. I'll start right now. Who will come with me?"

"I will", his aide Battistessa offered, standing up.

"Come on, then, we'll get ready."

They both went along the boat to the prow deck, on which they placed themselves, Manno with the Viganos' flashlight.

The boat kept going without changing direction for half an hour, and then, at a word from the officer, Patane moved the wheel, and the boat veered toward the right at a 90-degree angle. An hour later the two Vigano brothers came to relieve Manno and Battistessa. The lieutenant went back to his place next to the chief.

"Now we can be sure", he said sitting down, "that the cape and the Tunisian coast are behind us."

"Yes", the chief agreed. "If not, we'd have met up with it by now."

They turned once again to the coast, to try to see it. There was only darkness. Like the night before, however, in this direction the stars did not come down to the level of the sea, but remained a bit higher up, the ones lower down being hidden behind the invisible mountainous peninsula.

The chief suddenly murmured softly, "Goodbye, Africa."

Manno looked at him, surprised. The darkness prevented his seeing the other man's face.

A soldier at his side—the youngest of the small brigade, almost a recruit—who had heard the phrase despite the noise of the motor, in his enthusiasm took it up and repeated it several times out loud, "Goodbye, goodbye, goodbye, Africa! No more bombs, heat, thirst, danger! No more stench, no more putrefying death. Isn't that right? The end of it!" The others, some more, some less, agreed, stirring a bit with some commentary or other. For all of them it was a feeling of great release, and yet . . .

"Quiet", the older of the Viganos warned. "The danger isn't over yet for us. What do you think?"

The enthusiasm died down immediately.

After a few minutes, Manno asked, "How many years did you spend in Africa, Chief?" His neighbor did not answer. The officer realized then that he was crying.

Who knows what he must be feeling, the young man thought. *So many memories . . .* Perhaps, an old man (about forty, but old for someone Manno's age), he had spent an important part of his life in Africa. *His best years spent there, and no way of continuing them . . . suddenly for him it must seem an awful experience. Poor man.*

"Yes, there are people who can never go back, and for them it's even worse", the young man said after a while, speaking softly.

The chief did not answer him this time either. Actually, he did not feel at all old. If Manno and the other young fellows could have penetrated his mind, they would have been astonished at how young he felt. That was not the point. Nor was he worried, at least not now, about his future money problems, as he was used to poverty, always at hand (despite an occasional turn in the other direction), given the life he had chosen. What he could not manage to accept was the sinking, the death of a dream of his. If he had been told, not even he would have believed it, and yet that is how it was: the sinking of the dream he had always secretly harbored from the time of his youth, the dream of participating in an extraordinary experience, an undertaking out of the ordinary, not exactly clear in his mind, perhaps, but a real one, something truly living, even if only in communications. Coming from a very poverty-stricken background, he did not join the forces to become a hero—and the fact was he had not gone into a combat division—but once in the military . . . he did not limit his horizons to the small and steady pay. He felt the need to believe in the meaning of his activity, which struck him as a way of greater glorifying his country. And in spite of the clichés, he truly had believed in "the luminous destinies" of his country. More than money and the possible material benefits of life, even the warrant officers of the motorized division—rough and ready fellows—obviously felt the need of an ideal in order to live. Now he was experiencing, most unequivocally, the disintegration of his country, a tremendous root. And what was even more painful, without leaving so much as a trace of a memorable feat, in the style of the detestable Germans. Here in Africa, as in Greece and in Russia, some of our divisions had surrendered with inexplicable ease. (One, it was said, had crumbled during the course of a single night. The soldiers recounted this episode as they would a joke.)

"Should we look at the map?" Manno suggested, in order to get the warrant officer thinking of something else. Putting the portfolio on his knees, he took out the map and lit it up with the flashlight. Then he placed on it the double decimeter. "Let's see. I haven't forgotten . . . so many centimeters to so many kilometers. That's it, isn't it? I'm not wrong, am I?"

"It's fine", the chief answered at last, becoming absorbed by the problem.

"At this speed we should be in Pantelleria about ten, more or less, which means there'll be five or six hours of sailing in daylight."

"God help us!" the chief replied jokingly, though not in a totally steady voice.

"He has helped us up until now, and he will until the end. You'll see", Manno answered confidently, while his inner self prayed a few seconds to the Lord to help them in this undertaking and especially to perk up the old motor chief, to let him overcome the grief he was clearly suffering.

"The most important thing is that we don't get the direction wrong", he continued. "The angle as regards the north, if we measure it with the compass, is . . ."

11

About four in the morning it began to get light. A deep green glow was beginning to gather in the darkness of the east, which a little later defined a segment of the horizon, a trace of separation between the sky and sea, both still black. The stars became more tenuous as the light fanned out, and the deep green spread gradually changed into red, gold, into more and more colors. A single star, a tremulous drop of light, the first evening star and the last to fade in the morning, hung in the sky over the vast expanse of sea: Hesperus. At last the marvelously luminous point emerging from the flatness of the sea grew into the circle of the sun.

The ten men wrapped in their damp blankets were watching the spectacle quietly, while the boat sped along, driven by its most unesthetic engine.

As day broke they washed up—face, arms, torso—in the few buckets and basins available. Some of them, obviously embarrassed, also emptied their bowels.

While performing their ablutions the first airplanes appeared: three of them, unmistakably American, double fuselage, the "Lightnings", swiftly streaking across the sky. Luckily they were not close.

"Starting early, aren't they?" the chief commented. "We'll camouflage ourselves as best we can."

The camouflage consisted of an old fishing net (more a memory of a net than a net), which was draped very visibly over the boat, and two or three nonmilitary shirts, white, which some of the soldiers wore instead of the usual khaki ones. Most of them—Manno included—were in their undershirts even though the air was still cool, and some had knotted their handkerchiefs around their heads. Patane did not change. His uniform was so ragged he could easily pass for any other fisherman.

Battistessa checked a few times to make sure his tommy gun was well placed under his seat, so that he could grab it quickly. If the boat were attacked, he was thinking, he would fire a shower of ammunition at the exact moment when the enemy were very close. Manno was watching his aide's preparations, and he nodded his approval: neither of them was aware of Ambrogio's experience of having uselessly fired against enemy aircraft not with a simple tommy gun but with a machine gun.

Another enemy formation also appeared in about a half hour. Consisting of about a dozen four-motored aircraft, it was imposing and still distant, headed north, toward Sicily.

Still very far off, three German planes, transport planes it seemed, flew over afterward in the opposite direction, not to the right but to the left of the boat. They did not either see the boat or bother with it.

At last two Italian pursuit planes of the latest model, the C205, good to look at and technically up to par (about time, too!), arrived to offer some competition. Veering from their course, they dipped toward the boat, their motors roaring, and flew over at about twenty yards, the Fascist emblem plainly visible under the wings. The ten occupants of the boat waved their arms, shouting joyfully by way of greeting.

"They came from Pantelleria for sure", the recruit said. Meanwhile, the broad-faced fellow shouted in excitement, "Did you see? One of the pilots waved back!"

The airplanes immediately regained altitude. Like racehorses rearing and devouring space, they disappeared toward Tunis.

For nearly an hour the sky was empty, and their spirits slowly expanded. The unlimited calm of the sea's surface surrounding them became theirs. Manno, his eyes focused on the horizon off the prow, began mentally to say his morning prayers. He became distracted occasionally, and his thoughts drifted. To begin with, he thought again of his incredible luck in not being taken prisoner. It was not chance; he felt it keenly at that moment. For years he had been experiencing, at difficult moments, the feeling that providence had set aside an unknown task for him, and for a while, he thought it was to be a missionary. Now this unexpected turn seemed ever more related to the unknown task. He was also thinking about his comrades-in-arms—this one and that one—and the many war experiences that linked them, left behind along with the useless arms in the cork grove. What would they have said when he did not come back? What conclusions would they draw? They might very well all be prisoners by now. He prayed for them, prayed that they would not be corrupted in prison, that their hearts would remain pure as in the days of danger. Farewell, old pals. Again Daboni from Lecco came to mind, he whose brilliant escape was terminated by death on his return to the homeland, leaving his family in mourning. What weeping from his sisters—something similar to Greek tragedy! But also something natural to his native background, the industrial ambiance of the country north of Milan and Como, in short, Brianza. His native place, Nomana. In a few days—God willing—he would be there! But wasn't he saying his morning prayers? So why was he becoming distracted? Time was going by.

There in front of the boat a tiny shadow could be made out, an indefinite little spot. In front of the boat? An island visible in that direction? It had to be Pantelleria.

"Look over there, Chief", Manno said to his neighbor, pointing.

"What?"

"There on the horizon, that little spot you can barely see. It has to be Pantelleria."

"Where? I don't see anything."

But the others did and confirmed it. "Yes, yes, over there. Look! Is it possible? Already?"

They all looked in the direction the officer's hand was pointing to, a little right of the prow. The chief took his binoculars out from under the bench and focused them. "Yes", he said. "It's an island, like a flattened mountain, as if it had been pruned or lopped off", he clarified.

Manno smiled at that unusual and expressive image.

Patane stood up to see better and, with his right leg on the helm, declared, "So that's Pantelleria. A lopped-off mountain? Exactly. And what color is it? Black or yellow?" he asked.

"Well . . . looks black."

"Then it's Pantelleria."

"You saw it first", the warrant officer said to Manno. "Obviously you're an artillery observer."

Manno laughed. Then he looked at the time. "I don't understand marine distances, and so I wouldn't be sure by eye, but we ought to be about thirteen miles away. What do you think, Patane?"

The helmsman looked toward the island again, then a spell at the sea, trying to evaluate the consistency of the surrounding haze, and once more at the island, "I figure about ten nautical miles", he said and sat down, putting his forearm back on the helm again.

"Ten nautical miles are how many land miles?"

"I don't know", Patane said and mumbled, "Who cares? We're at sea, not on land."

The warrant officer had the answer. "A nautical mile is about 350 yards."

"Then if we continue like this we'll get there in two hours or a little more", Vernazza calculated.

Someone else was also calculating.

"We'll be going into a hot zone, maybe very much so", the warrant officer warned. "Let's hope these two hours also go by without any trouble."

And that is how it was. Trouble, in any case, was on the island, which— when they could see it better—was under an enemy air attack, completely invisible from the boat. The explosions were echoed gloomily at sea, reaching the fugitives, who noticed with relief, however, the antiair defense was not like the most recent in Tunis. There was not a second's respite in artillery fire.

In a half hour there was another bombing, and that lasted a shorter time than the previous one, only a few minutes, but sufficient to worry the sailors. Would it go on like that all morning? And if the planes showed up again while they were mooring?

But the enemy aircraft did not reappear. The boat reached the island, the coastal city of the same name, situated on the extreme west. There it stopped, a bit in front of floats and buoys. The motor was switched off, and the boat, turned crosswise for better visibility, bobbled gently on the water.

This, too, entered in the plan anticipated by Lieutenant Zustovic and the chief. "Well studied", Manno said. "No doubt we've gone over several mine obstacles before Tunis and even Cape Bon, but now we must not take useless risks. In some way or other you had been informed there, but who is to say there won't be mines here, too, on disembarking? They are most surely observing us from land. They have to lead us across the mines."

12

The waiting period began in the bobbing boat and became more and more worrisome as time went on. The men, hoping against hope that enemy planes would not arrive, put their uniforms back on, while the warrant officer and then Manno and a few others picked up the telescope to see what they could of the town and the little port in front of it.

The island was not the yellowish color of Tunis, but blackish and densely covered with vines, even in the upper parts. The port and almost all the walls in sight from the sea were built of black rock (some bomb damaged), as was a curious building that dominated all others: a kind of somber castle that culminated in a tower painted bright red.

"I wonder what the red tower is", the warrant officer muttered.

"It's the Barbacane castle", Patane explained, but could add no more.

"Do you know what period it's from? I mean, is it old?" Manno asked, showing himself to be the architecture student he was.

"Yes, of course. All great things are old", the helmsman answered, convinced.

"I see." (*Here, maybe,* the young man mentally continued. *The name Barbacane seems to fit the building,* Manno was thinking, amused.)

Meanwhile the woodcutter-carpenter, Vernazza, and the two Vigano brothers were filling the motor.

"Let's put in as much as possible, because once on land, I'm not sure these Barbacanes won't relieve us of our full tanks", the older Vigano mumbled.

"If it was up to me, I wouldn't set foot on land", his brother added, and repeated it.

"So you'll stay here, eh?" the first brother teased him to calm himself down. "Until the planes come and wipe us out?"

"The airplanes . . . wipe us out . . .", the younger one grumbled. They were talking in the Lombard dialect, with overtones that reminded Manno of the common people of Brianza.

Finally, when they were really beginning to get into a state of nerves, a motorboat came from the port. At first it came slowly, following a definite course that Manno and Patane, each on his own, tried to observe attentively, then—once past the mined barrier—it picked up speed and finally stopped perfectly parallel to the boat.

Some white-uniformed sailors were in it, and also an artillery lieutenant in a more or less unwrinkled khaki uniform, with the insignia of frontier guard on it. Manno and Battistessa recognized them immediately. That insignia reminded them of the depressing batteries of old cannons (some still with the rigid gun carriages, models already obsolete in the 1915 war, and how much more so now) situated mostly along the coast and Alpine frontier.

"Part of the GAF, do you see, Lieutenant?" Battistessa whispered to Manno.

"Yes", he answered in a still quieter voice. "Just right for the Barbacane castle."

"Where are you coming from?" the lieutenant asked.

"From Tunis, the city", Manno answered. "We left the evening of the day before yesterday."

"From Tunis?"

Suddenly Battistessa burst into noisy laughter. The idea of the GAF officer in conjunction with the Barbacane castle seemed—even though it was a delayed reaction—so amusing that he could not contain himself.

The GAF lieutenant looked at him, bewildered. They all looked at him. "What are you laughing about, Battistessa?" Manno felt obliged to ask. The artilleryman stopped then, bowed his head, and said in a conscience-stricken voice, "Nothing. Forgive me."

"A touch of nerves", Manno said, aware that he was only saying part of the truth and, addressing himself to the other officer, "We're a little tense because of the situation, you know. Please excuse us."

"What's your regiment?" he asked, still looking unconvinced at Battistessa.

"We're from different corps and specialties: the mobile unit, the commissariat, infantry, artillery."

"So?"

"This boat is what brought us together, that is, what kept us from becoming prisoners. That's how the motor came to be installed."

"You say you left Tunis the day before yesterday?"

"Yes, at 8:30 in the evening."

"Before or after the Allies entered the city?"

"Did they enter? We didn't know. We're hearing it now for the first time. In any case, the day before yesterday, we Italians and also the Germans laid down our arms. For instance, in my unit we didn't even have a bullet left."

"Do you have documentation?"

Manno and the warrant officer nodded. "Here's ours." They took out the portfolios—the others followed suit—with the identity cards and military papers. The lieutenant did not bring his motorboat close to take them. Things were not advancing. "I suppose you'll be continuing on to Sicily."

"Yes", he replied, and Manno added, "But not by day. Tonight, if possible, as soon as it's dark."

"That's all right. Headquarters will grant your staying here, but only on the condition you make no contact with anyone. Is that understood? You talk to no one. Understood?"

There was a moment's silence.

"Excuse me, but why?" the older Vigano wanted to know. "Why is that, Lieutenant?"

"They don't want their people to learn from us about getting away", Manno explained.

"But we left Tunis when there was nothing left for us to do, when it meant becoming prisoners, no more."

"But, look here . . ." Others in the boat seemed offended.

"Let it be", Manno recommended. "Do you want to get into an argument? Our conscience is clear, and that's enough. And they have their problems here on the island. It will soon be very hot here."

"Well put", the GAF lieutenant said gloomily.

"We'll do what you've suggested", Manno promised.

"Not I, headquarters", the other man corrected. "Keep close to our motorboat. We've been out too long. Pay attention. It isn't difficult. You have to go by grazing the eight orange buoys, always on the right. Don't worry about the other colors. Is it clear? The eight orange buoys are those indicating the passage between the surface mines." He repeated the instructions, addressing the helmsman directly. Then he looked at the sky. "Hurry up, dammit", he said. "They haven't stopped bombing for eight days."

The warrant officer and Vernazza turned the motor on, and their boat followed the motorboat. The crossing of the mine obstacle presented no complicated maneuvers. Once the mouth of the port was reached, the lieutenant had the motorboat stopped and gave further instructions. "You don't have to go into port. You go on your own now to the left to that little cove, where there are those boats on land. See them? Yes, those. You can take the boat out of the water if you like, whatever you choose. You'll see trenches on the beach. They'll be useful during aerial attack. That's all. And, I repeat, no contact ... even with civilians. Don't force us to use sentries. It would be disagreeable."

"Nothing to worry about", Manno told him. "Rather it will be us doing the sentry duty. All right? I beg you to convey the message that we'll be leaving as soon as it gets dark. Goodbye and forgive us, especially since you had to come out here and for the risks you've had to run."

"Don't mention it. Well, good luck ...", the GAF lieutenant said, and for the first time he smiled and then waved. His few sailors did the same and started up the motorboat and entered the port, trailing a stream of light crystalline spume in its wake.

Their boat, awkward in comparison, left slowly for the small cove. They did not pull the boat onto the sand. The occupants decided to leave the keel in the water, judging that they would be less exposed to possible damage that way.

Meanwhile, they all circled the boat and moored it to the shore and then camouflaged it as best they could, and the younger of the Vigano brothers, Felice, went into the little cove for the relief of his physical needs. In a few steps he was beside a trench, where he stopped and satisfied his two needs at once: he began to urinate inside and inspect it in hawklike fashion.

At that moment the antiaerial artillery opened fire, as the roar of motors was beginning to be heard in the distance. An enemy formation high in the sky was coming from the west, from Tunisia; one of the ten or more planes was reflecting the sun like a mirror.

"Come over here to the trenches!" the younger Vigano brother shouted, as he went on urinating, but not into the trench.

The others left the boat. Two started to run, and the rest went slowly. Manno came last and meanwhile looked up at the planes. "Four-motored, it seems", he said to Battistessa, who was next to him.

And they were. They carried out their first attack on the coast, hardly outside the town. The new arrivals witnessed the spectacle halfway out of the trench. They could see the bombs falling through the air quite clearly, oscillating or turning over on themselves. When they were quite high up it seemed as if they were going to land on them, so close that a few squatted low in the trench. At every explosion or group of them, the earth trembled like a sheet of metal being struck hard. The planes took a spin over the sea and then carried out a second attack on the coast but farther out, more to the north. Then they went off.

It was the first of five bombings the little island suffered during the boat's stay. An occasional bomb fell on the land near the port, others in the water of the cove, but the ten men and their boat were not damaged. They witnessed one plane falling into the sea that had been hit by the navy antiaircraft guns, and they saw another leave the formation trailing a tail full of smoke.

13

The last of the five bombings took place at twilight. Immediately afterward the ten men took off to sea. The boat reversed its path slowly, along the course indicated by the buoys and, once in open water, set out in a northeasterly direction. Patane was at the steering, as usual, his uniform in an even worse state of repair, black from the earth of the trench now. The warrant officer increased the RPMs, and the third stage of their trip to the Sicilian coast was under way.

The sun, quite low over the sea, turned Pantelleria blood red, and the black rocks of the island covered with vines were turned that color, and in the distance, from the boat, it looked like a smoking brazier slowly disappearing. Then the sun turned into an orange circle that could be stared at now without squinting, and it began to sink into the sea, as the island became totally black.

Several dolphins popped up at the right of the boat and performed a few turns. Patane watched them excitedly, his eyes glowing, mouthing incomprehensible Sicilian words. For the others they were like friends that, in a world wracked with violence, took an interest in them. They entertained with their simple frolics—the extent of their talents—and then night fell and swallowed them up in the darkness.

The next day Sicily was in front of them, clear in the dawning light, a long line of irregular mountains, slung low against the horizon. Patane could immediately make out the location of Mazara del Vallo, to the left, his native city, and so set his prow in that direction; with only minor corrections, he was on course. The occupants were in for a surprise. Before the white houses of the town appeared at sea, there were two, three, then ten, twenty sailboats, and even a motorized fishing boat or two. "Look, look, look!" the excited Patane shouted. "They're still fishing! Imagine! They went out last night to fish. How wonderful! God bless them!" He recognized some of the boats and rattled off their names. "That's *Niculicchia*, and the other one there is *Santa Rosalia*, and gosh, there's *Ntonio Regale* . . . and the *Veneranda*, too. I'll be damned, that's it! Fellows, I used to fish on that boat when I was little."

"Well, we made it!" the warrant officer exclaimed, absorbed in his own thoughts. "You realize, folks? We've really and truly made it. We did it", he repeated, looking from one to the other.

"And how. And now we can get ready", Manno agreed happily. The two Viganos were also in agreement. "Those boats will help us enter the harbor without any trouble. It'll be quite enough to get in front of the town and follow the first one in."

They looked at the boats, each other. They laughed. They looked at the vast and endless sea, now a friend and helpmate in daylight, then they looked at the boats again, emotional and exhilarated.

14

In no time, they moored the boat quite far up in the long port canal. Patane, in conversation with some of his noisy friends from a fishing boat (in dialect, of course, and the others did not understand a word), was told of the existence of an indicated path of buoys, which could be crossed at that time of day. Two other boats had arrived the day before from Tunis, he was told, both carrying dead and injured. They had been gunned down by the airplanes.

The boat, which had fulfilled its mission so well, was moored at the head of a row. It stood out from the others not so much for its shape but by its anomalous motor set onto the poop. The men—each of them grabbing their knapsacks or bags—climbed onto the pier. Some of them, including Manno, glanced back a few times with a look of thanks at the faithful boat.

At the other end of the pier was a lively neighborhood made up of almost Arabic-looking houses, quite similar to those in Tunis. Though these neighborhoods are normally overcrowded—which is what no doubt makes life difficult there—at this hour there was not much activity. There was almost no one on the pier.

The moment for farewells was at hand. Their ways were different, one from the other. Two or three of the ten men were in an enormous hurry to leave because they thought they might be caught up in the navy roundup, which would mean reporting immediately to military headquarters. They were trying, instead, to get home for a day or so and then would show up at their respective outfits, as if they had come directly from Tunisia. It was an irregular and dangerous procedure (the risk of desertion loomed) and not easy, in uniform, with a long train voyage ahead. Manno shook their hands most graciously, in any case. "Don't lose the slip of paper with my address I gave you this morning. If necessary, I can vouch for you. Good! Thanks for your company . . . and lots of luck."

He turned to the others and announced, "Battistessa and I are going to military headquarters at midday. If anyone else wants to join us, we'll meet in the station in front of headquarters at twelve sharp."

The warrant officer and the two Viganos said they would be there, but first they wanted to work out the problem of the boat. It belonged to the three of them, apart from Lieutenant Zustovic and Vestidello, and Patane had agreed, entrusting it to a close friend, to get it sold. He wanted, however, to put all the papers in order, as well as to have a written authorization from the three owners present to sell it, but also authentication from the authorities (not even he knew what authorities he was referring to). The subject had been thoroughly talked over that morning, and the four of them had decided to go to the harbormaster's office. At the last moment, Manno offered to go with them. "Maybe Patane would like to go home first. Would be only fair."

Patane shook his head. He seemed still smaller on land. Swarthy, with a thin black mustache, he really looked an Arab.

"Are you far from your house?" the warrant officer asked.

"No, it's close."

"Do you want us to go by for a second? Just time to tell the family you've arrived safe and sound?"

"No", Patane said. "My house is not . . . not for you."

He meant—and the others understood—that it was not presentable, too poor.

A swarm of little children had gathered around the military men meanwhile. Suddenly Patane called one of them by his name: "Alessio!" (Imagine, they know one another, Manno noticed, and neither one of them show it.) Then Patane proceeded to ask him something in dialect. The boy went off at full speed, waving his arms upward triumphantly, because the solider had sent him home to tell his family he had arrived. A few other children, also barefoot and with clothes in tatters, followed him with leaps and bounds. "Let's go", Patane said, "and try to get things done quickly. I sent word home I'd be there in an hour's time."

But the reality of the situation was not so simple at the harbormaster's office. The five of them returned to the pier and the boat after two hours, accompanied by the harbormaster himself, very well disposed to help, he assured them repeatedly, his colleague in the mobile division. But they were in Italy's deep south, legalistic, formal, and nitpicking, and so every initiative was frustrated.

On the pier two women were waiting: Patane's mother (to all appearances an old woman with a black handkerchief tied around her head, visibly moved, dramatic), who ran to meet him. Even more than embracing him, she fell on him screaming, "My son, my son!" and broke into tears amidst a string of incomprehensible phrases in dialect; and a sister, younger than he. She was mute and so communicated with hand and finger gestures and with her face. Weeping and glowing at the same time because of her brother's return, she panted a bit, emitting erratic noises.

In his ragged uniform, Patane displayed a manly distance from these effusive outpourings. "Why did you come here, Mother? You were told to wait for me at home. Why didn't you?" Still, inwardly he was more moved than ever before in his life.

The person who most impressed Manno was the mute sister. Her futile attempts to speak, express herself with words out of sheer emotion, disturbed him. *We ask soldiers to serve, to sacrifice. Do we ever think they may have families like this one, who depend on only one man for support? How complex and tragic life is for some people so often!*

At the military headquarters, they were well received. With the exception of the first three, who had gone off on their own, and Patane, for whom Manno got a forty-eight-hour pass, they all left on the first train to Palermo, each to his own destination. Manno and Battistessa, the latter still armed with a tommy gun, were heading for Piacenza.

394

15

A few days later, in Riccione, Ambrogio was again lounging half dressed on his bed (inwardly he blamed himself for laziness, as on the morning with his parents), when, exactly as on that other morning, a visitor was announced.

He stood up and took his jacket and belt from the hanger—this time calmly—and put them on, wondering who his visitor could be. Certainly not his parents, *and let's not start thinking about Tricia,* he told himself, recalling her little figure, which was already coming to mind most decidedly. If not his parents or Tricia, who would it be? Perhaps one of the three or four men from his regiment convalescing in other settlements in Riccione, but not Paccoi, unfortunately, or maybe convalescents from other corps he had met during those days in the city. *Well, I'll know in a matter of minutes. What is this, feminine curiosity?*

The last person he expected to find waiting for him in the hall was his cousin Manno, who was there, with his forehead practically pressed to the big windows, his gaze focused on the gray-green foliage of the tamarinds. His back to him, tall, thin, and blond, he was wearing a desert jacket, indecently wrinkled.

"Manno!" he called out softly. "Is it really you?"

His cousin turned quickly, and his very bronzed face brightened with a smile. In his tanned face his eyes seemed even more blue. "Ambrogio!" He went to meet him with his arms outstretched. "Vacationing", he said. "Are you staying on here for the Red Cross nurses to flatter you? How shameful!"

"But how come . . . how come you're here? What in the devil did you do to . . . and how in the world did you cross the sea?"

"I'll tell you everything right now. Can we go out, or are there disciplinary measures, or doctor's visits, things like that?"

"Nothing at all. Let's go." They left the hospital and walked to Riccione. "Tell me how you got out of that mess. Go on."

"If you want the truth, I left like a sportsman, by boat."

"By boat?"

"Yes, and it happened exactly on the last day, the day before the English entered Tunis . . . let me count. It was last Sunday. Hardly a week, and it seems—who knows how long? Well, on the day before the English were to arrive, my aide and I came across, you could say by chance, a boat with a motor on the point of shoving off. It had been outfitted by some of the communications people, the mobile unit and other groups, and a fellow countryman of my aide was among them. Well, they had two places free . . . incredible. And when we arrived, these two spots had been free only a couple of hours."

"And you immediately thought providence had provided them to measure for the two of you? Tell the truth."

"Yes, I did," Manno recognized, "and to be absolutely sincere, I still do."

"Still the same, aren't you?" Ambrogio commented. "Lieutenant and all, and by the way, congratulations on the promotion."

"Thank you."

"Your turn to buy the drinks, don't you agree?"

"All right, at the next bar. To put it in a nutshell, the boat trip was no problem."

"When things go smoothly in wartime, that's how it seems", Ambrogio observed. "But only afterward does it seem so, when it's all come out well."

"That's true", Manno agreed. "You're right."

"So, you and Daboni from Lecco did the same thing", Ambrogio said. "I was thinking about him this morning, actually, and you, too, and I was wondering how you'd get by the barbed wire . . . because I thought you'd become a prisoner, and you, on the other hand, were repeating Daboni's adventure."

"I also thought of him endlessly those last few days."

"But, listen, have you been in Nomana already?"

"No, not yet. I'm on my way from Piacenza on ten days' leave. I telephoned Nomana as soon as I arrived yesterday morning. I told them not to let you know because I wanted to surprise you. I thought about being at home for supper." He paused. "At home for supper!" he repeated to himself. "It doesn't seem real."

"Yes", Ambrogio agreed. "If we think about all of them . . . well, go on, you were talking about the boat."

"We must have gone over mined areas, but we never realized it because it was a local boat and drew very little water. As for the planes, we saw enough of them, but what can I say? Maybe they felt sorry for us or thought us beneath notice. I don't know. The fact is, they flew right over us. We were in luck, because some other boats didn't make it." He laughed boyishly.

They were walking side by side on the street: Manno, taller than Ambrogio, elegant despite the wrinkled khaki desert outfit and the floppy, worn boots, beside his cousin, not as good looking or noble in feature, pale, too, but more robust, more solid, in his smart uniform and unscuffed boots intact. The sea road to Riccione was not then totally flanked by buildings, and the view to the left frequently looked on to the sand beach and sea.

"The sea here", Manno observed, "isn't as brilliant, full of color as . . . how to put it? It's different from Africa. This is more homey, inspires completely different feelings. What do you think?"

"What it inspires is up to you, not my field. I'm in economics, not architecture."

"What I mean is that this sea, its color, the beach too, everything . . . reminds me of vacations during peacetime, more than anything else."

"Listen . . ." Manno was smiling again. "What was that girl's name, the one at Cesenatico, the one you liked so much? I never even saw her. When I arrived she had already left, but you in your desperate grief, carried on . . . remember?"

Ambrogio nodded yes, he remembered, but did not want to follow that line of conversation. Only then did his cousin seem to take notice of his ashen color. "Look here, are you sure you feel well enough to be out walking like this?"

"Yes, why?"

"Did you have breakfast?"

"Of course, more than an hour ago."

"You don't look well. You're pale."

Ambrogio shrugged his shoulders. "You know what they say", and he recited the old song: " 'the air of Ortigara has changed my color'."

"You must have been worse off than me", Manno said. "Yes, much worse. And that's not taking into account being wounded. I've heard a bit about what happened in Russia, but I still haven't got it clear. Now it's your turn to talk, not mine."

"Let it go. Go on. You've been more than a year and a half in Africa, haven't you?"

But how pale Ambrogio was! Instead of talking, Manno looked around for a bar. "It's farther up, at the second crossing, to the right", his cousin said.

"The what?"

"The bar where we can sit down."

Manno began to laugh. "What a character! You realized that I . . ."

"I know you."

They spent three hours together talking of their experiences and personal adventures, their friends still away (Stefano, Michele) and those who had returned (Luca, Don Carlo). They talked about Russia and the situation on that front, the air power of the Allies, the loss of Africa, the war in general and that perhaps they had come to the point of no return. ("Though it's not certain the Americans, Russians, English, and partisans of half of Europe will manage to overcome those Germans . . . but have you ever seen such spectacular soldiers? I'd never have believed they were that spectacular." "It's true, has to be admitted.") Manno also recounted his train trip across Italy briefly. "You see remains of bombings everywhere. In Catania, for instance, for miles there's not a house standing. The same in Naples. You've no idea what's happened there. No need to mention the shipping on the Straits of Messina. Disastrous! The very air in Italy has changed since I left, and the strange thing is that everyone acts as if nothing has happened. Everything goes on in the good old way, without any direction. Or am I wrong?"

"I think not. You're not wrong," Ambrogio replied, "at least from the little I can gather in the hospital."

Ambrogio ended up arriving late for his dinner. Manno, who had boarded the train without eating, stopped at the bar at the station in Bologna and bought a bag of caramels and other assorted candy, happy to be able to make up for missing the midday mess in one way or another.

16

Close to Nomana, as the train sped across the slopes thick with acacias between the hamlet of Raperio and the town, Manno gazed out, even when the train stopped.

It was the hour when evening began to fall, the hour when—as he well knew—the workmen were leaving the factory and farm people were beginning evening chores in the stables. The lilac bush was again in bloom in the station garden (as it had been three years before when Stefano left, along with Giovannino of the flour-white face and the others of '21). A new and spontaneous generation of pansies was blooming at the base of the bush, as if to express in vivid colors their joy to be alive. Springtime in his town, as it always had been . . . and how he remembered it! Instead of looking to see if someone was waiting for him on the platform, the young man moved quickly to the opposite window and looked out in that direction. The scrubby weeds were still there between the tracks, which beyond the station wooden fence grew and grew and stretched far into the distance, alternating with fields of grain, beyond Nomanella, beyond Beolco, as far as the huge arc of mountains. Everything was exactly as he remembered it except for one thing, the wire-drawing mill. He saw that the windowpanes of the small factory bordering the station (it had closed twice, he recalled) were not broken, but new and in one piece, and its little yard weeded, and a warehouse was being built as an extension.

The young man left the window, picked up from the luggage rack his new suitcase, bought in Messina a few days before and which held only his shaving gear and a few other toilet articles, and went to the door. He was the last person off at Nomana. He saw five family members waiting for him, the only ones in Nomana that day: his Uncle Gerardo, the *mater familias,* Aunt Giulia, his ten-year-old cousin, Rodolfo, on tiptoe trying to see inside the train, and his cousins Francesca and Giudittina. Francesca was still wearing her long blond braids. They all noticed his surprise and began to laugh. *No doubt they saw me going back and forth at the windows,* he thought. *They know me . . .* He got off the train, which was ready to go off again quickly, and hurried to hug them one by one.

"Welcome!"

"How are you?"

"You're a lieutenant now!"

"Congratulations!"

"My darling Manno."

"I'm so happy . . ." The usual words of people who love us.

"Welcome!" Giudittina shouted. "How wonderful, how wonderful!"

"Manno, tell us how you came from Africa in a boat", Rodolfo excitedly suggested, as he took the suitcase forcibly from his hand. "But it doesn't weigh anything . . .", he commented.

"That's because it's empty", Manno told him smilingly.

"On a little boat", Aunt Giulia protested. "It must have been a . . . a . . .", and her hands drew a massive shape in the air. "Wasn't it, Manno?"

"No, Aunt Giulia", he replied happily. "Rodolfo's right. It really was a boat, hardly as long as from here to there. I'll tell you later."

Meanwhile, they were all going to the exit. "What were you looking at from the train?" Francesca, now twenty, asked smilingly.

"You didn't expect us here at the station, did you?" his Uncle Gerardo said. "But you telephoned yesterday yourself saying you'd arrive, you remember?"

"Yes, of course. But I said I wasn't sure I'd be able to make this train because I wanted to see Ambrogio first. And yes, he sends greetings to all of you. He's fine. I left him only a few hours ago."

"Ah, those two calls from Riccione at midday . . .", Aunt Giulia said. And then to Manno, "But we didn't manage to talk. If you knew what a mess it is with the telephone some days. I'm sure it was Ambrogio who wanted to let us know you were arriving."

"Yes, probably", Gerardo agreed.

"Manno, don't you want to tell me what you were looking at from the window?" Francesca asked again.

Everyone wanted to talk at once to him, ask questions.

"I was looking at the factory", Manno answered. "What's happening there? It's cleaned up, no broken windows, not a one, and besides it looks as if it's being expanded."

"A company from Milan bought it, a glassworks. It was Papa who closed the deal for the Milan people", Rodolfo said. "As they had to move some of their staff . . ."

"A glassworks?"

"Yes, to make textile fibers out of glass. It's work for Nomana", Gerardo said with a smile. Manno looked at him agreeing. He remembered that his uncle had a definite idea of creating new jobs, considered that as one of his main duties. Manno, too, had witnessed how painful it was to say no to people, often to the head of families—who even came to the house asking for work.

His uncle was observing his nephew, who, despite his battered uniform, always had an air of personal distinction. "It's twenty months you've been away from Nomana, isn't it?"

"Yes, almost twenty months of Africa, a good treatment", Manno joked.

"Now you're back," Giudittina interrupted, "you won't leave."

The soldier patted her head and smiled. His blue eyes were shining in his tanned face.

"If only that were so", Aunt Giulia sighed.

"Meanwhile, we'll be together for ten days. I've got ten days' leave. That's a lot."

"The other news in the town besides the new factory", Francesca said, "is that there are evacuees."

"Evacuees?"

"Yes, because of the bombings. Didn't you notice those people getting off the train? Look over there, for instance."

"Yes, I did notice."

Far more people than usual got off the train in Nomana and were still gathered together in a small group in front of the revolving door of the station.

"That group is nothing", Francesca went on. "You should see the afternoon train, or the early morning one, when they leave for work in Milan or in Sesto. Almost a crowd. They've had to add freight trains. You know people even travel in freight trains now."

They reached the exit, and they had to go out one by one. The officer stopped to let the others out first. Giudittina took his hand. "You know there are evacuees at home?" she informed him. "Three of them. But not really. They're relatives: Uncle Ettore from Milan and two aunts from Monza."

"Why do you say they're not really evacuees?" her mother asked. "What do you mean, Giudittina?"

"They're our relatives, aren't they? We knew them before, so they're not really evacuees."

"But look at her", Rodolfo said, and imitating what he had seen Manno do a little while before, besides patting her head, he pulled one of her braids with his free hand. The little girl responded with a kick, but it only landed in the air.

"Giudittina! Children!" their father called them to attention.

A paved and wide street went from the little station square to the church. It was Dante Alighieri Street, the main thoroughfare of the town. On both sides were solid earth walks, planted with water oaks. It was also known as memory lane: on each trunk was an iron pole with a sign attached giving the name of a victim in the First World War. The street was of recent construction, so new that on either side were agricultural plots.

The small party went to the righthand walk, under the branches of new foliage, whose leaves were clearly notched, typical of oaks. Manno's eyes were scanning the names of the dead from the preceding war, each one with a date and place of the man's sacrifice: Podgora, Gorizia, Monte Santo, Col di Lana. How many times as a child had he spelled out those names coming and going from grammar school! *Now*, he thought, *they'll have to add other placards*. (Little did he know that in the future there would be no public remembrance for the victims because of their defeat.)

"Well, are you going to tell us about the boat or not?" Giudittina asked. "What was it like? Did it have oars?"

The others burst into laughter.

"It had a motor", Manno told them. "A soldier had installed a car motor in it." And talking directly to his uncle, he said, "Underneath and all around it, to keep it well secured, it was entirely propped by beams, which were really laughable." And then to Giudittina, he said, "Because, you see, that soldier was not a carpenter but really a woodcutter."

His uncle laughed, shaking his head.

"Poor boys", Aunt Giulia lamented, and her eyes expressed the fear she felt for them.

"But it was a motor all right, that much has to be said, which ran as it was supposed to," Manno continued, and he began his tale.

Once at the square, they would have crossed over it without interrupting the fascinating story if Aunt Giulia had not stopped. "We have to step into the church, if only for a minute," she said, "to thank the Lord. He let you return, Manno." And suddenly her son's presence was also vivid to her. "He brought back both of them alive and uninjured, which is no small thing."

The soldier prayed intensely for some minutes in the church, his forehead pressed onto his right hand. When he finished he found himself beside Don Mario, the assistant pastor, a trifle flushed with emotion, his eyes shining behind his glasses. The priest, who until yesterday had believed Manno to have been taken prisoner, was filled with joy, delighted with his return, but talking in a soft voice since they were in church. (*His familiarity with sacred things has not diminished his veneration for them*, Manno noticed, as on other occasions, pleased.) "Welcome", Don Mario repeated softly. Later, worriedly, he added, "You must tell me everything, promise? You have to tell me what's happening."

"I'll be happy to, everything I know, though it's not much."

"It seems things aren't going too well for us, isn't that so?"

"That's how it is", Manno said. "Pretty bad. I'll come and see you tomorrow. We'll have a quiet talk. I'm falling apart this afternoon. Besides, I'm just coming from visiting Ambrogio today."

"Ambrogio!" the priest exclaimed. "And how is he? Pretty well now, I've heard."

"Yes, he'll be able to leave the hospital soon", Manno confirmed.

"Good, Manno", Don Mario exclaimed, happy as a child. "I'm happy you're back. We need you here. Your absence is felt."

"But what do you mean?" the young man exclaimed, despite being pleased, and he laughed.

"No, that's true, very much so. You're cultured, you know how to explain things, argue, and . . . the evacuees, you know about them? Poor folk, so much misfortune, they must be pitied. But about some things they're a little . . . it's not going well, no. It must be said. And the boys—even ours in the Oratory—and the town's girls, seeing them and imitating them." Don Mario's face clouded over. He let go of the young man's hand and bowed his head. Manno recalled his sorrow over the mean treatment of Aristide del Ghemio during his leave some years back. (He's not changed—your zeal consumes me—he mentally quoted.) "You're still the same, Don Mario," the young man told him, "and this makes me very happy. Well, I must be off. 'Til tomorrow."

Once outside the church, while the little party went on to the house, he had to take up the narration of his adventure again: not just the boat episode, but events farther back, from the time we were advancing, as Rodolfo expressed it. (Would that time ever come back?)

17

At the table he had to talk, too, begged by one guest as much as another to do so, despite Aunt Giulia's repeated attempts to stop the interrogation. "Enough questions. Let him eat in peace ... think how long it's been since he's eaten with even a trace of comfort. And, moreover, he hasn't eaten today and he's tired. Don't you realize that?"

"No, Aunt Giulia", he protested. "Don't worry."

After those admonishments the others did leave him alone for a while, but then he finished by asking questions. "It seems as far as food goes, things are about the same as twenty months ago. I have the feeling you still have everything. Or am I mistaken? Or maybe tonight you made something better than usual for me ... because of me? Noemi, is that so?"

Noemi smiled and acted mysterious, not answering, going back and forth bringing things, waiting on him no less than on his relatives.

If it had not been for the bread (mealy and greenish, hard to be replaced with homemade cakes) the meal really could not be distinguished from those before the war.

"In the country here," Francesca explained, "we have almost everything, though the evacuees are causing the prices to go up a little."

"It's not that way in the cities", Uncle Gerardo pointed out. "To get something not in the rationing book in the city—and even in industrial outskirts like Sesto or Cinisello—is a real problem."

"But here in Nomana," the young man inquired, "how are the workers doing?"

"They all cultivate a little, you know, or they have relatives with a plot or two", his uncle answered. "They're all right for the moment. For the moment", he emphasized.

"Yes", Aunt Giulia added. "The ones who are worst off are the poorest, those who, even in peacetime, have their troubles. Serious help is needed now, especially for those people with children. Without help they'd die of hunger." (Serious help ... One of Giulia's favorite maxims was "We are in the world to help one another". And Manno knew it was not her custom to limit herself to words.)

"The workers are making out in many ways", Francesca said. "Celeste, for instance, with all his children, kills three or four rabbits a week, and so they have meat. He's rented another bit of land, and there he's growing greens and cabbages for the rabbits."

"And they're great animals, you should see", Rodolfo made clear. "And I've exchanged some with him. They're all the huge rabbits from Belgium or crosses of the local ones with the huge ones."

"No, he has the others, too", Giudittina interrupted. "The reddish ones, what are they called?"

"Oh, yes, I know", Manno told her.

"The what?" Rodolfo asked roguishly. "The reds from Burgundy?"

"Yes, that's it", Giudittina answered.

"Well, it isn't. See how dumb you are? It's at least four months since he's had those."

"Well, never mind", Manno said to pacify them.

But it was mainly Uncle Gerardo (who hardly ever, when he had the chance, neglected to inform himself: that was the way he had acquired the culture he possessed) who put more questions to his nephew, asking for details. His nephew likewise questioned in return, about the work situation or the bombings, for example.

Their dinner over, the evacuated relatives came from their rooms to join the others for coffee (a substitute, in fact). After the greetings and usual questions they sat around the table, practically huddled around Manno. While drinking his coffee substitute, the young man had to start the adventure of the boat crossing from the beginning. None of them, when the table was cleared, got up. Everyone wanted to continue listening, even Uncle Ettore from Milan, an engineer with a nineteenth-century air, who wore pince-nez spectacles and added a slightly strange note to the ambiance. The two old aunts from Monza—great-aunts, really—did not pose questions, though they occasionally burst into exclamations such as "Oh, those poor boys!" or "Poor children!" accompanied by gestures of surprise. They were, along with Noemi, the most emotional there. Beyond the solid facts, what stirred them in unspeakable fashion was the fact of hearing everything told, what had been lived through, and so they, too, participated in some way, they whose lives that had always been uneventful.

It was an evening in May, fragrant with hay and pierced by the shrieking of swallows. They were also—Francesca remembered—back from Africa. They nested on the jutting roof edges, in cracks under the eaves, and before gathering together every night, they flew around the house in a flock, shrieking, in furious pursuit, gliding, rising, capering joyously in the air.

By the time Manno went to his room, the shrieking had already stopped, and now, in silence, he heard the nightingale in the garden. Without switching on the light, the young man opened the window and looked out. The song, as always, came from the yew trees, solitary, facing the northeast, toward Beolco and the mountains.

On his bed were his pajamas, ready to put on, left there by his Aunt Giulia with maternal care. While he took off his old desert uniform, Manno thought that perhaps he would never again put it on. While on leave he would be dressed in civilian clothes, and later, back with his regiment, he would put on one of the gray-greens. He remembered the old warrant officer's tears on the boat. He realized, even if confusedly, that during those days the history of his country had reached a decisive point. What was going to happen next?

"My God", he murmured, as he rubbed his forehead.

18

The following day he had to repeat the adventure of his escape in a boat several times: the first time as he went into the garden at dawn, on meeting the gardener-porter, and the last time at twilight in the church, to acquaintances who had approached him while arriving for the Benediction.

As it was the month of May, the church bells rang out, gathering the town to the religious rite, sounding shrill, impetuous, and then suddenly becoming a thick buzzing, the same as the May of three years earlier, when Ambrogio had returned for the last time from school. Now Ambrogio was no longer a schoolboy but a soldier, a veteran at that, in a hospital letting his wounds heal. And Stefano, who had been with him under the campanile three years before, equally deafened by the sound of the bells, was dead and buried in a place whose existence then was not even imagined—Meskoff, in a common grave, without crosses.

Meanwhile, life went on: the procession that Ambrogio and Stefano had witnessed on the square was repeated for Manno with only slight variations. Costante, Tarcisio, and Ignazio went by, as did other workmen, then Oreste Pirovano, plumber and electrician, followed by Sister Candida and another sister from the asylum with their chirping brood and, at last, Marietta of the shuttles among a small group of women workers, only a bit to one side, with her long yellow face and hideous hair, with eyes of a decapitated lamb. She had a little freckled-nose niece of hers now by the hand instead of Giudittina. Neither was Romualdo, the local drunk, missing, staggering, unfortunately, the expression on his face sad rather than conscience stricken, a sign that he was in the stage not of remorse but of desperation. Nevertheless, he was going to church all the same. Carlaccio went by, also Chin the postman, and four of the seven children of Celeste, the company chauffeur. They ranged in height like a series of steps, and some had the same extraordinarily blue eyes of their father, including the oldest, a boy of Rodolfo's age, very bright looking. Then the old Signora Eleonora, dressed in her usual black-sequined outfit, a hat decked out in ostrich feathers and carrying her cane reserved for walks. That afternoon she was not alone, as she usually was. On her arm was a young girl dressed in white, who moved slowly for the sake of the old lady's pace, stiff as ever. *Who could that be? A relative who was evacuated?* Manno wondered, without staring too hard.

When he was about to go into church, the schoolteacher at the Monza nuns' school, Quadri Dodini, arrived, she who had wept at the news of the Nazis in Paris. Years before she had given Manno review classes in French and enjoyed intellectual conversations, and now she greeted him warmly and asked not only about the war but also, as if by chance, if he had seen some particularly interesting types of Arabian construction in Africa, on which he perhaps could write a good article: "Like the one you published three years ago in the *Cittadino*." (*Il Cittadino* was—and is—the Catholic publication of Monza.)

"I wasn't really thinking about writing", the young man answered. "But," he added, not to appear discourteous, "I think I'm maturing, and that, after all is said and done, will be of use to me in the future as far as writing goes, too."

"Very well, Manno. I like that", she replied in her professorial tone.

"Signorina, we're all living through an experience that will furnish us with something to reflect on for a long time, and for me, perhaps all my life."

The old teacher—without committing herself—indicated agreement with a flicker of her eyes, which shone behind her thick glasses. At last she squeezed the elbow of the future architect hard, to show the confidence she had in him, and then took her leave. Manno went into church after her.

He went to the right, the men's section. As usual, the church was full: to the right, in front of the men—old and young—were the boys, restless as ever. Don Mario went back and forth the length of their crowded benches, monitoring them. To the left, in front of the women, were the little girls and young ladies, calm and calmly monitored by the nuns. There were not many of the evacuees, who did not come at ten. They stood out, too, from the local townspeople because couples did not separate; they sat together whether women or men.

I guess they don't like our ways, Manno thought. *Let them do what seems right to them.* He was tolerant by nature, even more so in church. He recalled the division in Libya that disintegrated in one single night, and he shook his head. *If they don't subject themselves to discipline in civilian life, they won't be worth much in military life. Just think of the towns of Alpine recruiting instead . . .* In connection with this, he still had no clear idea of what the Alpine troops had done in Russia. From whom could he get firsthand information? His friend Luca, who, after having been home on convalescent leave—a leg wound—had written to Manno in Africa, still under the impression he had come through something exceptional, had gone back to the army. *Maybe one of these days I could take a walk with Don Carlo Gnocchi in Nomana . . .* But today Don Carlo was not in town, or he would have been in church. In church! Manno suddenly remembered he was in church. He reproached himself for his distraction and tried to pay attention to the ceremony.

The ancient parish priest was officiating, a priest who recalled the shepherds in the mountains with his jungle of white curls on the nape of his neck. (*He really does come from a mountain village—an Alpine recruiting center,* Manno thought, in line with his preceding thoughts.) Quite in keeping with the pastoral aspect of the priest, there was a fresco with two rows of sheep on the apse of the church. (*By race, Bergamasque, like the nomadic flocks that stop over in Brianza during the winter.*) The sheep from the left and those from the right converged docilely at a central symbolic fountain. Four altar boys in white surplices, their sandals and shoes down at the heel, were in attendance for the ceremony on feast days and, at that moment, torn between the restlessness natural to their age and the reverence of being next to the Sacrament. Observer that he was, Manno could not help but notice it. However, *Think about the Benediction!* he once more insisted to himself.

Benediction is a minor rite, simply a sacramental, that is, one of the means that the Church looks to not only for spiritual well-being but also for material, physical benefits from the giver of all grace, God.

The women's contribution in the ceremony consisted in singing the very ancient Latin hymns, those that were sometimes sung even during working hours in the factories and brought comfort, rising above the din of the looms— the *Veni Creator Spiritus,* the *O sacrum convivium,* and the *O salutaris hostia.* Here in the serenity of the church, with the last rays of sun shining softly through the stained-glass windows, these hymns carried one back in time, not to the far-off medieval fathers who composed them (totally unknown to the person singing) but to the generations long gone of grandparents and other venerable figures, from whose voices these hymns had been learned during the first years of life. They were truly enduring chants, that never go out of fashion, and the last our people had. Along with an avalanche of memories, tangled and stormy, they filled the heart of each and every one with a sense of the time that passes and that of eternity.

It brought back the memory of his mother for Manno, dead when he was four years old: Mama, with that fresh fragrance of hers (one of the few things he remembered about her) when once, in church, they had been squeezed close to one another. It was especially that and a few other little things, along with the fresh fragrance that emanated from her, that Manno remembered about her. More complex reminiscences had to be formed from successive reconstructions, transpositions perhaps of Aunt Giulia's gesture, she who had taken the place of his mother. Like the image he had of himself as a child, who, on the lap of his mother, lifted his eyes to look at her, and then her light hand, caressing and directing his face to the altar—to Jesus . . .

Once more he looked toward the altar, after having opened and shut his eyes repeatedly to overcome this melancholy distraction.

But another one awaited him. The girl dressed in white, who had arrived at the church with the old lady Eleonora on her arm (probably an evacuee and so included on the list of people that a little before he had rigorously classified of slight worth and interest) was in view, a bit beyond the central nave, and in looking at the altar he could not avoid seeing part of her silhouette.

And this partial silhouette consisted of a head, that reminded him—at least in this three-quarter view, or perhaps it was the hairdo—of the heads of Greek statues in art books. And this partial silhouette consisted besides of a neck *clearly more spiritual than the ones on Greek statues, should the adjective spiritual be applied to a neck,* something the young man quite properly doubted. And, finally, of a slim waist, virginal, which attracted his glance. Again Manno admonished himself, *Am I in church, or where am I? Then . . . !* He felt a kind of contempt for himself. *This is an afternoon of distractions, and I should have had instead an afternoon of concentration, of filial thanks to God for having come back home safe and sound.* He begged heartfelt forgiveness of God and still once more focused on the religious act, which was now reaching its culminating moment, in which the celebrant raised the Host in the monstrance and traced on those present a large sign of the Cross, the sign of regeneration. Manno crossed himself devoutly, youthfully, inwardly thankful to our Lord Jesus Christ, who had sacrificed himself for him, for the others of Nomana and of the entire world, including the evacuee dressed in white, who constituted at that moment an element of very obvious trouble for him.

He followed the last ritual chant, the *Tantum ergo,* whose musical form tangibly heralded the end of the proceedings. The feeling of having received spiritual grace, which always occurred to the faithful during Benediction, permeated the people attending.

The evacuee, who at the sign of the Cross had been—like the older woman—on her knees devoutly in the family pew, stood up at the same time as everyone else. *In no time*—Manno thought instinctively—*she'll be off, and perhaps I shall not see her again.* In the face of that possibility, he felt a kind of uneasiness. *This was inadmissible; it should not happen.*

And why shouldn't it? What am I thinking about? Why inadmissible? he wondered. *Look how idiotic I've become. To have been away from Italy and from women these last months, all it takes is seeing one female a little prettier than others, and I'm practically having palpitations, and, to top it off, I'm in church. Let's just say it: I'm disgusting.*

19

That established, he left his bench, genuflected until his knee touched the floor, turned, and left. *Prettier than the others?* he thought. *Well, maybe yes, maybe no. Probably not. Why didn't she seem pretty when she went into the church? Must be one of those that when you look them in the face they fade. I really am an idiot: all this over a girl who isn't even pretty.* He left the church and stopped in the atrium, his back against one of the shiny granite columns. He'd just stay there and have a good look at her face, and that would prove how mistaken he was and, finally, to wind it up, his own stupidity.

The girl and Eleonora appeared shortly afterward, still arm in arm. They were constantly overtaken and blocked by children, who—when Don Mario gave them permission—left the church in flocks. The two women were strolling quietly—the older one rigid as usual; the younger one natural, pleasant, and obviously amused by the racing youngsters, and flying among them were the long braids of Celeste's daughters.

Now, Manno told himself a little before time. *Now, look.* And immediately after, almost without missing a beat, *Were you saying she wasn't pretty? Of course she is! She's . . . she's . . .* He did not manage to find the right adjective. *But how come I didn't realize it before, when she went into church?*

The evacuee passed by a few yards from him. She was tall and slim, very young. (*She can't be more than eighteen.*) She went down the few steps of the portico watching the steps of her companion affectionately, and then, her arm still linked to that of the older woman, they began to disappear among the people on the cobbled plaza.

And what am I to do? Do I let them go? the young man wondered. *I can visit her at the villa, with any old excuse. But letting them go off like that . . .*

Meanwhile acquaintances approached, and he left the church with Don Mario. (The young man had been waiting to accompany him to his house.) The questions began, on this and that subject, and he answered them with his usual elegance and also, as was his style, with brio, but his mind was elsewhere. *Who knows what he must have seen of the war?* Don Mario was thinking, and also, *Perhaps those terrible things are going through his head right now.*

20

On the afternoon of the following day, at five o'clock—teatime—after having walked through the town, Manno showed up at *I dragoni*, the nineteenth-century villa belonging to Signora Eleonora, with its façade adorned by stone medallions of the most illustrious Milanese of the past century. The young man had awaited this hour with secret impatience, and now—setting the bells to ringing repeatedly—he pushed open the wicket of the large portal, and he felt his heart turn over. *Almost like at the front before an attack,* he reflected and told himself, *Come on, don't make me laugh.*

On the other side of the door was a small vestibule paved with granite ground for carriages—the lovely and erratic granite of Brianza—which extended through the whole of the villa as far as the inner courtyard. Only two doors gave onto this vestibule: one to the left, in which the main core of the building was located, with hermetically sealed doors and wooden door knockers; the other, smaller, to the right. This one had windows with curtains that made it look like the door of a worker's home. It must have been the entrance to the porter's quarters, because the old porter looked out.

"Good afternoon", Manno greeted him first.

"Good afternoon", the porter answered in dialect, slightly surprised, coming out into the vestibule all the way. "Should I tell the signora you are here?"

"Yes, please."

"Follow me, then."

Manno started to follow. He immediately and clearly realized that, after having looked at the hermetically shut door, the old fellow did not really know where to take him. So many years had gone by without there having been visitors at the villa that he did not know how to deal with them.

"I'd prefer waiting here", the young man decided.

"That's all right. I'll be back right away", the other replied, and he went along the courtyard, leaving Manno alone.

The young man began to pace back and forth along the vestibule, until suddenly a swallow swooped like an arrow to its high nest, constructed almost against the roof. It rapidly fed its young and then left again like an arrow to the sun and air. Manno stood under the nest and examined it carefully. He could see the granite paving stones were stained with swallow droppings. The rustic savor of the place was enhanced by a decrepit vine with an enormous trunk that stretched its green branches horizontally toward the exit of the vestibule. The young man went under them, thus entering the courtyard. The villa—not big, with a U-shaped base—was composed, on the right, of rustic quarters, including the porter's rooms and stables; the middle section and left side were manorial. A stone fountain jutted out from the wall of the rustic side, on which there was a wheel pump from the beginning of the century, which was, most surely, the trough of the stables. At that moment, Graziosa, the spinster daughter of the porter, was working the wheel to bring up water. Even the hairstyle of the woman—no longer young—smacked of something that recalled past days.

Seeing the visitor, Graziosa greeted him by bowing her head slightly, with spontaneous good breeding, and without stopping the wheel working. (People said that even though Graziosa was a spinster, she was not tormented by the fact. Her heart was tranquil.) "Good afternoon", Manno greeted her politely.

"Good afternoon", she answered.

But from the main section of the villa the porter was coming out to the courtyard, and with him—none other than the evacuee. She was dressed in white again today, though not the same dress as on the previous day. Manno, who wanted—no matter what—to see her as a Greek figure, decided that the dress was similar to a Greek tunic. *She knows how to choose dresses that suit her*, he told himself.

The porter and the Greek figure came toward him together. He went to meet them with a smiling bow toward the girl. After pointing out the visitor with great directness ("Here you have him"), the porter left and went back to his quarters.

"Riva", Manno introduced himself, stretching his right hand out to the girl. While she shook his hand, the girl murmured her own name, which he did not catch. "My aunt would like you to come in", she said.

"Either I'm mistaken, or you are, by the way you speak, not from here. Not from Milan either?" the young man asked.

"I'm from Novara", the girl answered. Her eyes were gray-blue, deep set, and unusual, and her head truly did recall those out of art books.

"Ah, Piedmontese then", he said, and in his enthusiasm he found even this surprising. "Are you a student?"

Again the girl said yes, that she was. "I'm in second year at the lycée. But follow me, please."

They went toward the main entrance of the villa, bathed in the pleasant sunlight of the courtyard.

"Then," he was trying not to waste time, "since I'm a student, too, we ought to use the familiar form of address."

"I guess we ought to", the girl repeated, half smiling.

"And besides your name . . . I mean, your surname, your first name is . . .?"

"Me? Colomba."

"Colomba!" the young man exclaimed, stopping a second. He was about to say, "You know your name suits you perfectly", but instead he said, "My name's Manno."

"Manno. Then, short for Ermanno."

"No, only Manno. It's a medieval name, seldom used, so seldom no one is named that. It means man, that's all."

"It sounds like an important name", Colomba said.

"It's not the name, it's I who am important", Manno clarified pleasantly.

The girl smiled, amused now.

"But listen, vacation must have begun early this year", the boy went on.

"Vacation? I'm not here on vacation. It's only for a few . . . four more days. I had a stubborn cold, and Papa, who's a doctor . . . but before the end of the week, Friday, I have to be back in class."

"Ah!"

Colomba really was a pretty girl, though perhaps not as much as he had imagined, after having thought about her and idealized her in his imagination the previous afternoon. And especially, since she was so tall and adolescent, her limbs were very undeveloped. This detail did not bother the young man, who was looking at her with eyes, as they used to say, that were platonic, without any wicked intention.

"Come. My aunt's on the veranda", Colomba said, and crossing a small hall she opened an inner door.

They went onto the veranda, closed against the courtyard with glass and wrought iron doors, nineteenth-century style, with a granite paving and wicker furniture. Signora Eleonora was seated on a small divan; beside her, on a flower-patterned cushion, was a piece of embroidery with the needle stuck through it and her glasses on top.

The young man bowed deeply, then shook the bony hand that the old woman—observing him with her strikingly light eyes—stretched out to him. He wondered if it would not have been better to have kissed her hand. However—coming from a working-class industrial family—he had never kissed anyone's hand in his life.

"Riva", he announced.

"From the textile people?"

"Yes."

The old lady nodded. She continued gazing at him with her blue eyes, lighter than his own. Then she said, "I know you."

"In these small towns everyone knows each other, isn't that so?"

"I don't know you that way", Eleonora clarified. "I didn't intend to say that. I was at an art exhibition of yours, and I remember it well."

At this, Manno felt a bit disconcerted. "At an art exhibit?"

The old woman smiled. "That was a long time ago, a kindergarten event", she explained. "You drew a doll with chalk on the board, then you commented in rhyme about what you had drawn. You were about that tall, wearing the boys' blue-and-white-checked smock."

"Ah, yes!" Manno exclaimed. "I remember." He turned to Colomba, who was following the conversation with curiosity. "The blue-and-white smock suited me fine: my first uniform." He added, nodding his head, "What times those were, great . . ."

But the woman had again assumed a serious note. "I also saw you in your military uniform", she declared, keeping her eye fixed on him. She still did not know the reason for his visit.

"What? You're in the service?" Colomba ventured.

The young man nodded.

"An officer?"

"Yes, on leave, as of two days ago." And, then, addressing Eleonora, "I've come exactly for . . . well, more or less about this."

"More or less about what?" the woman asked, perplexed.

"Well, I've just come from the Tunisian front," he began to recite the lesson he had prepared, "and though I'm not attached to the cavalry unit . . ." The old lady, at these words (her son had been with the cavalry), was startled, and her eyes widened.

Only then did Manno realize the measure of rashness, not to say cruelty, involved in his plan. The old lady looked at him fixedly, her eyes wide open.

For the first time in his life Manno became aware that the grief of his ancient countrywoman was not mere invention, not just one more element in the landscape, but a cutting knife. It was something that destroyed, something like the repugnant feeling of disintegration so frequently experienced on the battlefield after combat.

He tried to think rapidly, gather all his wits together. "My dear Signora, I realize that I must seem like the elephant in the china shop at this moment." He interrupted himself, thought it over, even forgetting the presence of Colomba.

"I told myself that if I, just back from the front, don't go to see the mother of a second lieutenant fallen in the other war, who will then?" He tried putting it a bit better. "Who more appropriate could I go see?"

The wide-opened eyes of the old Eleonora began to fill with tears. Her rigid head nodded repeatedly; she approved.

Who will go to see her . . .? To think I've said that! Manno thought. *I am disgusting, really disgusting!* He felt boundless shame for not having realized in time—and he a soldier—the sorrow of this mother. But still, even if his intention was not wicked, to have decided to use a situation like this to . . . to get next to a girl!

But now, he decided inwardly, *now that I've put my foot in it, I'll help this old woman. I'll come to see her for her sake alone and because she is alone, independently of her niece. And, in the future, when there is peace, I . . .*

"Well," he said out loud, "that's why I'm here."

"But you're standing. Sit down, Lieutenant", the lady whispered, as she tried to wipe the tears with a little handkerchief. She pointed to one of the wicker seats.

Manno sat down. To lessen the tension he immediately began recounting, once more, the crossing of the Mediterranean in a boat. (It seemed a made-to-order subject.) Then, more seriously, he related some of the details of the El Alamein battle, the culminating experience of his life. "It was truly an unequal struggle, four or five men against one . . ." Then he spoke of more recent events in Tunis. Would Signora Eleonora like to hear an entertaining episode? There are some mountains there that rise suddenly out of the desert plains; they're called *gebels*. Well, since a regular mountain artillery unit was nonexistent, a certain Colonel Giaccone, head of the general staff of the centaur, solved the problem Italian style. What did he do? He rented ("For a price, of course but not too high") three hundred camels with their Arab camel drivers, loaded them ("the camels, not the drivers") with arms and munitions, and sent them to the *gebels* of Berda and Orbata. So, when a powerful American armored division, led by a certain General Patton, appeared between those two *gebels* or mountains on its way to El Guettar to cut the Italian army in two, our men could stop it and even keep it blocked for eighteen days, shooting from positions impossible for the American tanks to reach. Manno's story had become amusing, almost. "I was there, too, on the *gebel* Orbata, as an observer for the transport troops on camels, provisionally so. Well, in the middle of all that carrying on, it was a sight to see the worry of the Arab camel drivers for their own camels, their own property. I assure you it was quite another thing from the worry of our horse drivers for those horses of ours that belong to the government." The story of the young gentleman—inspired and permeated with an elegant sense of adventure—turned out to be fascinating.

Especially for Colomba, who now was surprised to have found a young man like this in such a "sleepy backwater". Manno, above all, had taken great care always to emphasize—as was general among soldiers on leave—the nontragic aspects of the adventures he related.

Eleonora did not interrupt. For her, war was quite different from what it was to this twenty-four-year-old boy. But she did not dwell on this, but on the fact that through these light and careless tales unexpectedly came the memory of other stories, different, and yet in some way similar, heard in the far-off days from her son on his leaves from the front, which she had gone over and over so many times in her memory. The old woman began to feel genuine gratitude to Manno and, at the same time, a sorrowful maternal compassion.

The young man, completely at ease now, thought that at a given moment it would be a good idea also to talk about the cavalry—of which he knew very little—and he tried to explain the difference between what would have been its deployment in the previous war and this one. "In Russia, however, in Isbuchensky—have you heard of it, no?—well, our cavalry fought there in the old-fashioned way, as in the old days. My cousin Ambrogio was there with his artillery unit. He's in the hospital convalescing, but he'll be back home soon. One day I'll bring him here."

An hour went by rapidly, at least for the two young people. During a pause in Manno's talk, the signora, attending to her duties of hostess, requested her niece (who turned out to be a grand-niece, not too closely related) to prepare the tea and bring it in. "It's my only weakness, Lieutenant", she explained to Manno. "I still have a few unopened tins, real tea, the best, you'll see." Meanwhile, she kept on nodding and occasionally glanced at him with her light and steady eyes.

After the small tea ceremony, Eleonora changed the course of the visit. "I'm almost eighty," she explained, "and I no longer am too . . . mentally alert. You've told us really interesting things, but now I need time to assimilate them because I don't want to forget them. You understand?"

The young man stood up regretfully, ready to take his leave. "No", the woman stopped him. "I don't want you to go. On the contrary, I'd be displeased. This is your first visit to *I dragoni*, isn't it? My niece, then, will be your . . . guide. I notice you are already using the familiar form of address."

"Because we're both students", Manno explained warmly.

"Well, blessed are the young. Colomba, then, if it's all right with you, will be your guide."

413

"Of course, Signora, your villa interests me."

The woman addressed her niece. "You could show him the weapons room to begin with. Being an officer, I imagine he'd appreciate these things. Then the stables, and the garden."

"Yes, Aunt."

"Yes", Manno chimed in.

The woman extended her bony hand, covered with blue veins. "If you come to see us again soon sometime, it will be a real pleasure. If you're not bored, of course . . ." Suddenly, she became sad. "I know that just a day, even an hour's leave, is important for a soldier, very important."

"But I'm not bored. How can I be? What are you saying?" the young man exclaimed. "I'm delighted to come, and, if I'm allowed, I'll come again tomorrow to . . . to continue our conversation." Hardly did he utter those words when he wondered if his state of mind wasn't too obvious. But it seemed not. *Perhaps because of her diminished mental alertness, which she mentioned before.*

21

The weapons room—the door panels framed with adornments painted in gold and pale blue—consisted of two small intercommunicating rooms, with panoplies of slightly rusted arms and foils, and fencing masks on the walls. Between the panoplies there were colored engravings on the walls, old ones, each one picturing a game bird or beast hung by its feet or paws. There were hares, pheasants, wood cocks, partridges with their pretty breast markings: the drawing was strangely hard, in a style not too much in vogue.

Almost by way of continuation of these images, in the other room, piled in a corner on the floor, were the necessary tools for fowling with an owl: notched branches spread with birdlime, kept in reed sheaths with iron-tipped points, little cages for the decoys, larger bell-shaped cages, the leather arm for carrying the bird of prey . . .

"My poor Uncle Hermes used these things," explained Colomba, who was not too sure how seriously she should take her role as guide, "or at least that's what I've been told."

"Of course. I realize he died before you were born."

"Now the porter uses them, but not in this season, in autumn, when the birds migrate."

"Ah, no, not at this time. I understand." Manno pulled an exaggeratedly serious face, nodding as if he were a caricature, even uttering, "Humph, humph . . ." as an old man might grunt in a museum listening to the explanation of the official guide.

"Stop that now", Colomba burst into laughter. "Or I won't go on with my explanations", she threatened.

The young man approached the only window in the room, with ancient glass that slightly distorted the images, the panes linked by strips of lead. He opened it, and almost below the window sill, he could practically touch them, were the branches of the vine that shaded the entranceway of the vestibule.

"From here, when it is the season (the same one when the birds migrate), it would be easy to pick the grapes", he said.

Colomba looked out at this side. "My, it looks like a green carpet", she exclaimed.

Under the green carpet, but visible through some open patches, the swallow that Manno had already seen on his arrival flew by.

"Did you see it?" Colomba asked. "It's the swallow that has its nest in the vestibule. It has four fledglings, you know?"

Manno nodded, this time not joking. "I saw it, yes."

"The day before yesterday," Colomba said, "I put a little dish of bread and milk out on a bracket next to the nest, hardly this far away. But the swallows paid no attention to it. They were totally indifferent to it. I finally took it away."

Manno laughed, shaking his head. "Not all newborn animals feed on milk. Each one to its own nourishment", he said. Then he went on laughing harder, his physiognomy changing imperceptibly, his eyes sparking another joke. "Of course, if instead of swallows, they'd have been Alpine swifts, then your dish would have been suitable."

"Why? Do swifts drink milk?"

"No, they drink *eau de vie*."

"What? But . . . what do you mean?"

"That if you set out a dish of *eau de vie* near them, even better in their beak, Alpine swifts, even a few days old, will swallow it all, you can be sure of that."

Colomba did not understand. She knew nothing of Alpine men and their drinking bouts.

Manno had to explain. *How naive she is*, he thought tenderly. For a second the thought of the Alpine troops crossed his mind. *Don Carlo* . . . he remembered. *I must find him, talk to him* . . ., but he forgot him immediately.

Once out of the weapons rooms, they went through a corridor, passing a console with photographs of a young Eleonora when she was still singing—perhaps at La Scala, perhaps the Carignano theatre in Turin. The visitor pretended not to see them in order not to have to comment or flatter. After going down a staircase, Colomba led him across the court to the stables, which opened by working a chain, with no need of a key. Scarcely inside, the young man knew why. Inside, next to the door, was a bucket with laundry soaking in it. "It's Graziosa's laundry", Colomba explained.

That humble laundry was the only contemporary touch in there. The place was divided into six stalls for horses: three to the right and three to the left with a central cobbled aisle, at the back of which—on the wall in front of the entranceway—was the vertical shaft for dropping the hay from the hayloft above. The stalls had wooden walls, worn smooth by use, and in each one a crib of iron, of an almost elegant design. Over the cribs were some rectangular stains, like those left after taking down a painting that had been hanging in the place a long time. They had been left by the name plates of the horses, and only one remained, with the name in block capitals, adorned.

"Nestore", Manno read aloud.

"Yes", Colomba said. "It was my Uncle Giulio's horse, Giulio, my aunt Eleonora's son who died in the war."

Manno thought back about that time, not so far off—the epoch of carriages—when gentlemen must have gone through the streets of Nomana on horseback. It seemed incredible today, in this town of laborers. *How everything disappears*, he thought.

"Come, now you must see the carriages", Colomba announced, feeling more than a little uncomfortable among these dead things, so much so that her eyes glanced back to the bucket of laundry, as if to focus on something to anchor her, even if only prosaically, to the present, to life.

The carriages, two elegant four-wheeled traveling carriages covered with dust, were in a coachhouse attached to the stable, in which there were also some leather harnesses, protected by cloth no less dusty, hanging from wooden pegs jutting from the wall.

After leaving the coachhouse, the two young people walked to the garden. They could see—through the glass of the veranda—the silhouette of the old lady, still seated on her small and solitary wicker divan, but they had no time to think of her.

Between the courtyard, enclosed on three sides by the bulk of the villa and the garden, there was an incline of several yards, and so that side of the courtyard was protected by an iron banister that was interrupted halfway to give access to a short two-branched staircase made of granite. The banisters of the staircase, which were in the same seventeenth-century style as the courtyard, were covered with blossoming jasmine and passionflower. The two young people went down the staircase amid their perfume and came to the garden, oriented to the south, separated from the surrounding countryside by a decrepit wall. (It was the same garden Pierello, Igino, and Castagna had talked about three years before, on leaving for military headquarters.) It was not very big and was centered around an oval meadowy section around which trees grew in homogeneous groups and at the lowest part mingling into a small wooded area; beyond the wooded area there was a small orchard. Among the trees, there were some shiny-leafed magnolias, whose flowers wafted a penetrating perfume, and many laurels, which also gave off their fragrance, and then a very distinct scent from the fir trees, which grew to great heights, an Alpine scent. As in Manno's and Ambrogio's garden, here, too, there were tiny paths bordered by beds of lilies of the valley.

416

"I know where there's a nest", Colomba exclaimed. "The porter showed it to me. Do you want to see it? Or maybe you think you're above that sort of thing?"

"I think I'm above, yes, but not to that point", Manno replied. "Come, let's go see it."

Colomba entered a tiny path that bordered the meadowy area. "It's in the orchard," she explained," and it's quite far down. We don't have to climb up. It's this high", and she showed him with her hand.

"Then it'll be a blackcap."

"No."

"Then what is it?"

"I know, the porter told me. I want to see if you, so keen on birds and their brood, can figure it out."

"I'll take the bet", the young man said with assurance. "Now we'll see." Meanwhile, he could not stop looking at his very nice companion.

How pretty she was! Her lovely adolescent head with its blond-chestnut hair, her eyes slightly deep set, the feminine line of her neck, her whole figure. He did not focus his eyes on her more "concrete" parts—her breasts or legs, for example—as that would have seemed a sacrilege, a profanation.

The girl, with her hairdo that reminded him more than ever of someone in his art books, and her nose, which if one really looked prolonged the line of her forehead. (Perhaps it wasn't exactly that way, but why did Manno want to see her that way? Colomba was pretty as she was.) She most definitely had a Greek air. *She has a Greek look, figure, absolutely. Another Andromache in the world* . . . They were going by the laurel, with its distinct, ordered, and consistent foliage, its outlines well delineated. The boy stopped; so did Colomba. She looked at him questioningly.

"Do you want to know what tree looks most like you among all of them here?" he asked her.

"Among all these trees? What one looks like me? What do you mean?"

"The laurel. The laurel is most like you. Trees also have their style, a way of being themselves. Don't you think so, Colomba? Like people."

"You make me laugh", the girl murmured. But she didn't laugh. Quite the contrary, she looked upset. She had suddenly noticed his strong emotion, and she began to think that perhaps this good-looking young man had come to the villa just to see her.

"I mean you are a woman . . ." He hesitated, unlike his usual manner, to express his own thoughts, "that is, classical." He nodded at this.

"But what are you saying?" Colomba continued to look at him attentively. For the first time her femininity, her being a woman, was catching the attention of others, arousing strong feeling. An entirely new experience for her and as pleasant as it was unbearable, almost.

Though he was new at these things, intelligent as Manno was, he registered her state of mind. "Come, let's go see the nest we have the bet on."

They started to walk again and reached the orchard and found the porter there, with a straw hat on his head, busy gathering produce. The nest—very rough, made of tiny sticks and roots clumsily entwined—was between the two main branches of a small willow. It held five, no, six fledglings, with stiff plumage, gray, that took no notice of them. They were only interested in the worms and other chopped-up insects the mother bird would soon bring. Any other form or presence that was not food held no interest for them, as if nothing else existed.

"They're shrikes, a nest of them", Manno declared, after a quick examination.

"No, you're wrong", Colomba said. "The porter didn't say shrikes. He said something else, very strange-sounding." She looked over at the porter as if she wanted to get proof.

"Perhaps *sgalzetòn?*" Manno asked.

"Yes. Oh, you do know! It's almost unpronounceable, isn't it?"

"That's how we say it in the local dialect."

"Shri . . . what is it again?"

"Shrikes."

"Well, shrikes."

Manno slowly let go of the long and flexible willow branches he had spread to look at the nest. "They're very common birds, almost ordinary, like their name." He liked the idea, and he went on to emphasize his point. "You see? Even species of birds have their own style, their way of being, like trees."

They reached the porter, who greeted them by putting his right index finger on the brim of his straw hat.

"I hear you hunt birds in the autumn", Manno said in dialect. "I saw the birdlime."

"Well, I don't do it that way any more", he replied, also in dialect. "We did it that way before, a long time ago, when poor Signor Hermes was living. But now . . . too few mountain birds come by for that. It's not worth the time it takes."

"I'd say this garden would be a good place, suitable."

"Ah!" the porter shook his head. "It was before. But now there are too many hunters about, more than there are birds."

"So now you no longer set traps?"

"I still do, yes. I still like it too much, you know, but I don't use the owl any more. Now I trap the goldfinches with the decoys. They don't have to be watched over. I keep an eye on them while I work."

"Oh, I see. And where do you put the birdlime?"

"Over there, on the other side of those trees, at the edge of the meadow, that part."

"It seems a good place", Manno judged.

"Yes, but we don't get many; two or three, the most four or five a day."

Manno nodded, and after making a gesture of resignation with his arms, he took his leave. He wanted to go on strolling with Colomba. The visit to the garden—which, as we said, was not very big—could not, out of decency, last too long.

They started walking again. Colomba now asked him questions about the war, as if she were now seeing it with new eyes after his words, and was newly aware of it. They did not, however, reach the heights of emotion of moments before, when he had bizarrely compared her to a laurel.

They found themselves, at last, at the double-ramped staircase covered with passionflowers, walked up it, and crossed the courtyard. The girl accompanied him to the little door that gave on to the street.

While they shook hands, he said, "Then, I'll come back tomorrow."

"Yes", she replied simply.

"Later you'll have to come and see my garden. Not as pretty as yours perhaps, but in any case . . . I'd like you to meet my family: my cousin Francesca, for instance, who's like a sister to me. You two could be friends when . . ." He waved his hand in a rotating gesture, as if to indicate things that happen one after another. He meant to say, "When I go back, return to duty."

"But I won't be here in Nomana for many more days", Colomba reminded him. "I told you I was at the lycée, and I have to be in class in Novara on Friday morning."

"Yes, but then you'll come back to Nomana, won't you? For vacation, for instance."

"Well, I'd like to, but now I must say goodbye, Manno."

"Goodbye, Colomba", Manno said.

22

Out in the street, he found himself under the stone medallions with their profiles of illustrious Milanese. When he was a child, he had thought the name of the villa, the dragons, had derived from the eight gentlemen on the façade. No doubt the children of the town now harbored the same thought. He looked up as he walked to see their profiles better, and he read the names: Pietro Verri, Gian Domenico Romagnosi (*Do you two think you're so very illustrious?*), Alessandro Manzoni. Manzoni a dragon! The very idea made him laugh. "Well, so long, dragons", and he waved to all of them at once.

Crossing through the streets of the town, he looked at everything, the well-known details of his familiar world, and now, after the meeting with Colomba had, as it were, restored him, everything, even the most trivial, seemed a discovery, evoked intense joy in him. He stopped a moment in church *to thank God for having spared me from danger*, but the prayer that spontaneously came to his lips was the Gloria. He said it once, and once again, and still once more in an almost solemn, crashing crescendo, like an organ, in the darkness of the empty church. He was not grateful to God for having saved him from the war, the sea, but for having created Colomba, for having made her as she was, for having put a creature like that in the world. He prayed, as if transported, to the Mother of God, blessed among women, asking her to look after Colomba, to help her remain as pure and as charming as she was now, for all time.

Once through the gates of Uncle Gerardo's villa (which, as we know—unlike that of *I dragoni*—had been a factory before and still bore traces of that, even if disguised), he went into the garden with the idea of reflecting, pondering what had happened.

The sun, already low in the sky, discouraged him from sitting under the trees, where the air was already too cool. There was a little path at the edge of the orchard that led to the balcony on the north, flanked on one side by hedge of hornbeam and on the other by beds of wild chamomile, with its good dry scent. The young man began to pace the length of the path, back and forth, his hands crossed behind his back, going over everything in his mind with emotion, occasionally kicking a little stone with his foot. *She's an absolutely classical creature*, he told himself. *I can't describe her any other way; a classical woman. In this day and age it's something incredible! Objectively speaking, she could be a sister to Andromache, and, why not? a sister to Beatrice, as much for her beauty, let's say her exterior image, as for her inner world* . . . (It did not occur to him that he knew nothing of Colomba's inner world. He was idealizing her as he had done in the morning and the day before, but we should not smile at that. Maybe things went like that, more or less, for Andromache and Beatrice, too. And are for that reason their figures less admirable, both having probably been constructed with one part reality and one part fantasy? A new and exalted creature was taking form in the young man's mind, one who nevertheless could not have been born without the flesh-and-blood Colomba—that enchanting, attractive, girl—who lived at *I dragoni*. Manno instinctively, without making problems for himself, was becoming enraptured creating this synthesis of reality and dream, as many other greater artists had done before him.)

But in the path where he was walking he did not go by, as his classical thoughts would have had it, an ancient laurel tree but instead a yew tree, isolated, in the northeast of the garden where a nightingale sang nightly. The nightingale was even there at that moment, and having its nest on the ground in the hedge of hornbeam, it anxiously spied the comings and goings of the man so close to it. Each time Manno became more distant, the little bird—which Manno did not see—relaxed and moved with relief and gaiety, and even out of audacity, a posteriori, lifted the plumage of its head like a little cock, to return, however, in a trice to lower its head and to concentrate on its anxious observation of the intruder who—stolid as a pendulum—had reversed his direction and neared the defenseless fledglings, fragile living treasures, enclosed in the small shell of leaves.

Finally the nerve of the little bird cracked. It could stand no more. Then it left the shelter of the yew shrieking and flew to the top of the thick and compact hornbeam hedge and chased Manno, quite closely, not desisting for an instant, in a shriek that came from its entire body.

This maneuver was not new to the young man. He had seen other nightingales do the same when they confronted a prowling cat, and from the time he was little, he had intervened more than once by hurling stones and shouts at the intruder.

"Now I understand", he said to the excited creature as he stopped. "I understand. You don't want me here so close. It's all right, I'm going." He turned and went toward the house. After a few steps he turned. He saw the nightingale perched stiffly on a branch of the hedge, looking at him victoriously, its crest raised, chirping boastfully. He began to laugh. *Irresponsible creature*, he screamed at it mentally. *Don't you know the poetic thoughts you've interrupted? You, a singer like you?* The little bird, seeing the man had stopped, went back to making signs of nervousness, shrieking. "That's enough, I'm going, I'm going," Manno said and continued on his way to the house without stopping.

23

While opening the door, he heard the telephone ringing. Francesca, who was setting the table at that moment, ran to answer.

"From Genoa", she told Manno. "They're asking for you." And she handed him the receiver. "Be careful, it's the mother of someone you were with in Africa. She called this afternoon. I told her to call back at suppertime."

"Do you remember the name?"

"No. She said something like Lieutenant Massone or Marrone, something that ended in 'o-n-e'."

"From Genoa? Wait . . . Mussone perhaps?" With the telephone in his hand, waiting to talk, Manno looked questioningly at his cousin.

"Can be. Yes, I think so."

"All right. She's a widow."

"Widow?"

"Mmm . . ." Manno nodded and put the receiver to his ear. (He had heard her quite extroverted son say so more than once; when things weren't going well, Mussone would sometimes leap up and say, "I'm an only son of a widow. What am I doing here? I'm going to turn in my papers and go back to Italy." Manno smiled. These words were also frequent after Mussone let off a barrage of insults to anyone who would listen, anyone not enjoying his privileged situation. "I'll leave you all here. You're all a gang of undesirables, miserable wretches without a document to your name, who won't get repatriated. A bunch of mindless brutes." Mussone was a comedian on occasion. In any case, he never turned in his papers.)

"Hello, hello! Lieutenant Riva? Ermanno Riva? (*Wait a minute*, Manno replied mentally. *My name is Manno, not Ermanno* . . . , but he said nothing.) "Are you the one who just returned from Tunisia?" The mother of his colleague was asking in excited tones.

"Yes, ma'am, I am."

"My son is not writing. I'm not receiving any letters. He wrote before, every day you could say, even if only a postcard. It can't be, God help us, that something happened . . . ? Ay, Lieutenant, I'm going crazy, crazy!"

Strangely, the young man thought of Eleonora, the anxiety she must have suffered during those days when she lost her son. "Try to calm down, Signora", he managed to say. "I . . ."

But she did not let him talk. "How come you're back and my son's not? The adjutant major at headquarters was so nice. He gave me your telephone number. What's happened to my son . . . ?" Her voice broke with emotion. "My . . . my . . . treasure . . ." She could no longer speak, and he heard her crying.

Manno made an effort to calm her down. "Signora, I left your son on May 6, a Sunday, and he was fine, totally well", and he repeated it. He explained that the English and North Americans did not treat prisoners badly. "They're like us. We don't treat them badly when we take them, and they know that perfectly well. So you have no reason to get worked up."

For moments, the woman seemed to be swallowing his words, and at other times, she seemed not to be listening, despairing.

"But why are you crying this way? You shouldn't, Signora Mussone."

"If you only knew how I've cried in my life . . .", she murmured.

When he hung up, Manno was left meditating. Colomba was not the only one in this world. (*That dear white Colombina*, he thought, *what luck such a dove exists, along with all the other winged creatures that have surrounded her today—the swallows, the barbarous shrikes, and just a while ago, the nightingale . . .*) But it wasn't only she who existed, or the joy that emanated from her. He must not forget that.

In the days that followed he received some other calls and also a letter or two asking for news. He answered the best he could to relieve the anguish of those who called or wrote. He was forced to admit that the war—even though for him momentarily interrupted—was in no way over.

He felt a kind of determination, very strongly, to see Colomba while circumstances permitted. (But were they really circumstances, mere chance, that had brought about their meeting—he asked himself that at times—or maybe providence, a deliberate choice? And, in any case, he remembered "that not one single bird falls without God's consent". Wasn't this meeting with Colomba perhaps a bit more important than the fall of a bird? So, Colomba became, along with the swallows, the *sgalzetòn*, the nightingale, at one with the sparrow of the Gospels.)

24

The young man did not let a single afternoon go by without visiting *I dragoni*, and each time, coming and going, he went by the medallions of the eight illustrious Milanesi; a kind of familiarity with them developed, corresponding to the exuberance of the occasion, and he often took to joking with them. "Hi, there, Don Alessandro", he would address Manzoni, who among them all was much the most familiar to him. "You, too, put your foot in it in your way, no?" He observed the effigy with joyous eyes. "For instance, do you remember how you fought passionately against classicism and defended romanticism, not realizing your own work was classic? So much so that for us now you are, without a shadow of a doubt, the greatest classic of your epoch. What do you say to that? Or perhaps up there in heaven—where you surely are—these things no longer interest you?"

Those days were of extraordinary fullness for the young man, a fullness he had not experienced until then. The old woman and the young woman took to him with ever-increasing warmth, and they gave clear indication of enjoying his presence. Unfortunately those days flew by like a breeze—Colomba had to leave very soon.

Manno did not stop visiting the old woman regularly after that, but, in the absence of the girl, his conversation lacked the sparkle of the previous days. "Manzoni? But what are you saying, Lieutenant? How dare you speak of him in a mocking tone, that great, great man?" Eleonora would protest, repeating the title of a book that Manno had seen in his Uncle Gerardo's hands. (As we know, his only reading matter was *I Promessi Sposi*, and if he were given a book, it would inevitably turn out to be a new edition of the same novel, or a study on it or on the author.) And once, when the young man attacked another of her favorite medallion figures, Porta ("But who is Porta? Nothing but a vernacular poet known only for his vulgarity."), Eleonora went so far as to dress him down lightly. "You shouldn't talk like that when it comes to poets. Poetry, together with music, gives the greatest comfort in life."

Age, Manno thought, brings about this rhetorical sentimentality. Rhetorical or not, the old woman, her house, her garden, all reminded him of Colomba, and for that reason Manno kept up his pilgrimages, as he called them, in a state of exaltation.

Ten days' leave go by quickly, however. The hours and minutes fly by like sand sifting between one's fingers. The time for him to leave also came.

25

The twenty-fourth of May—a fatal date, at least in the memory of those who had fought in the preceding war—Manno left Nomana to return to his regiment in Piacenza. He was wearing his new gray-green uniform, not the colonial one, bought in Milan at the Unione Militare in Monte Napoleone (Montenapo, the elegant snob street even then, despite the wars and the symptoms of disintegration).

At a small station before Monza, where the train stopped to hitch up with another, he looked out the window to see if his cousin Ambrogio, whom they were expecting from one minute to the next in Nomana, might be on it.

Ambrogio was not on it; at least he was not looking out from this section. However, Pierello was on it, he who was a fellow conscript with Ambrogio, a timid, round-faced boy, who would open his arms, raise his eyes to the skies as a sign that he would abandon himself to destiny. He was wearing an old uniform with the infantry badge. He recognized Manno, and as he was the first fellow countryman he had met, he greeted him happily, waving to him, and then, once he had attracted his attention, he gave him the military salute: "Manno, Manno . . . my lieutenant", half familiarly and half out of respect for the rules. "Ten days", and he made it clearer by raising the fingers of his two hands. "Ten days' leave, and no one will take that away from me. Great, eh?" he glowed.

"Where are you coming from? Slovenia, aren't you?"

"No, Croatia . . ."

"Well, Slovenia, Croatia . . ."

"It's all the same sh—— . . .", Pierello admitted. "Ten days' leave, wow!"

"You'll see how fast ten days go", Manno felt like saying, but instead he said, "I'm glad."

"Yes, I'm glad, too", and he kept nodding, and finally he opened his arms, as Manno expected he would, and lifted his eyes to the heavens, in conformity with the destiny that had granted him this marvelous leave.

"Wonderful, Pierello!" Manno said. "I'm delighted!" His train seemed about to move. "Listen, have you seen Ambrogio in your train by any chance?"

Pierello did not hear him, and he nodded. "Ten days", he repeated.

"Fine, but I wanted to know if you saw Ambrogio in your train."

"What? Ambrogio?" Pierello turned to look in his compartment.

The convoy Manno was on was picking up speed, and it was impossible to go on talking. "Bye, Pierello!" the officer shouted. Pierello looked out again and responded by waving and then saluting in military fashion.

26

Ambrogio arrived in Nomana a few days later. He also noticed the new works and expansion at the factory as the train entered the station. *Imagine, at times like this there are people who think of building,* he said to himself, a trifle surprised. *Better this way.* And then, *Let's hope this goes better than the ones before and there'll not be a third flop. But who on earth feels like building today? I'll ask Papa.*

Francesco and Rodolfo were waiting for him on the platform. His parents and Giudittina, who had come twice already to meet earlier trains (that he most obviously wasn't on), had not come this time.

He got off the train exactly in front of the lilac bush, flowering now and, as usual, surrounded by the small multicolored cluster of pansies, but he did not take notice of it. In the niche of the station's façade, one of the two bells was ringing insistently, announcing in its usual way the arrival of another train. *All those poor men are dead*, the young man thought, *and here it's as if nothing had happened.*

The three of them left the station together, without lingering, and strolled under the new leaves of the water oaks, down Avenue Dante Alighieri. They walked quickly, though this was not easy for the veteran, who really wanted to take turns with Rodolfo in carrying the suitcase. It was futile for his brother to ask him to share some war event, as Manno had done twelve days earlier. At the boy's insistence, Ambrogio would smile and slap him on the back, but without answering his questions. He seemed to be in a big hurry to get home. Francesca—a bit concerned—was trying to give his arrival an air of normalcy, quietly talking about what would most interest her brother, while also striding along with big steps. ("Did you know Pierello's on leave now? Did you know that Manno was paying court to a girl?")

When they reached the square, Ambrogio—like Manno twelve days earlier—went into the church, followed by the others. The church was empty this time. The big niche on the high altar was open, and the crucifix, swathed in a tenuous halo of light, could be seen. *Look, they've exposed the Lord. I'm sure it's for some soldier in serious danger. Who could it be?* The tiny reproduction of this crucifix nailed to the wall in Stefano's shelter came to mind, the shelter in the Bersaglieri trench on the Don, on the same earthen wall where there was a photograph of an actress . . . the young man moved his head imperceptibly. Francesca, who was observing him without his being aware of it, told him she was going to say some prayers for the war dead. Ambrogio responded docilely to the prayer, while the war dead mounted in his mind, those poor wretches on the road beside Posnyakoff, on the morning he was wounded the first time, and those scattered in the hideous valley of Arbusov, and those others in the pits in front of the infirmary in Cerkovo—even outside the pits were bodies piled up . . . and so many others, in this place and that, here, there, farther beyond. And the distant stain that was the body of his friend Bonsaver . . . with spring, would the peasants of the *koljos* have buried the body, or would it stay there until it decomposed in the weeds? Or would they have ploughed his remains under, perhaps?

"As you wish", Bonsaver had greeted him a little before he died, and then to his soldiers his words, "Let's go, let's go", last words Ambrogio had heard from his lips. Ambrogio moved his lips a bit. "Let's go . . . let's go where? Didn't you realize?" But he pulled himself together. He was a soldier, an officer, and whining, crying was not permitted. He breathed deeply: enough, and he cut off all his feelings, as if crushing them with his foot. He had to control himself; it was his duty now. He managed; he controlled himself. After blocking his feelings, he felt empty, a little stupefied, but ready to face up to "any eventuality". He signaled to Francesca to finish. Following her example, he crossed himself and genuflected deeply. Rodolfo imitated him. They then left the church and went toward home.

They passed by the bell tower and then in front of Igino's door in Manzoni Street. The soldier looked through the windows to see if there were anyone in, but the curtains cut off any view of the inside. "Better return tomorrow", he decided.

"Igino's still in Yugoslavia", Francesca informed him.

Ambrogio nodded. "Tomorrow I'll go to see his family." After a few steps, he added, "But I'll go to Nomanella first, tomorrow." A few steps later, he concluded, "And one of these days I'll have to go to Nova to see Michele Tintori's father." *The three friends from the same draft calling,* he thought. *We left for the Russian front, and I'm the only one back.*

"Giustina's a wreck", Francesca said. "How sad . . . when you see her. And her mother, Lucia! It's terrible!"

Ambrogio nodded without commentary. "The priest", Francesca continued, "told them they'd have to wait until the end of the war, that they shouldn't lose hope until then. Stefano could have been taken prisoner."

"Yes," Ambrogio concurred, "that's true."

"But if he's a prisoner, why doesn't he write? Why is it that none of those missing in Russia write home?" Francesca asked.

"The war in Tunisia ended a few weeks ago now", Rodolfo chimed in. "And some have already written from prison."

"That's true", Ambrogio agreed.

"Yesterday one of them wrote from Raperio", Francesca added. "On the other hand, from Russia . . . how long is it . . . maybe five months and still no one, not one person has written. Why is that?"

Perhaps because there's not one of them alive able to write, her brother responded mentally, *and maybe they've killed all the prisoners.* That eventuality was ever present for him during the war, in good times and bad, and the present and absolute silence seemed to confirm his most sinister fears more and more. "They've ended up in the hands of cruel people", he said at last, "who aren't worrying about their families."

"Poor Stefano", Francesca murmured, "and poor Michele."

"Yes", Ambrogio said.

They came to the garden gate.

You're home, the veteran said to himself. *You see, you're at home. You've arrived. You worried so much when you were out there in the snow, and now you're here, you're back.* He felt no joy. To come back when others didn't was no joy. *Come on, let's get on with it,* he told himself weakly.

Noemi saw them enter the garden from a window she was cleaning, and, getting excited, she gave the alarm, repeating, "Ambrogio's come. Ambrogio! Signora, Ambrogio's here."

"And she's not even a sentry", the soldier said, half smiling.

At Noemi's words, his mother came running from the house, followed by Giudittina, her braids flying. The two evacuee aunts from Monza also came quickly from their rooms into the garden, and Uncle Ettore from Milan, with his pince-nez glasses that gave him a slightly artificial air, came directly into the garden from Gerardo's office, where he was working. "Just look at him", he murmured, "look at him." From the orchard, carrying a leaky sprinkler, which it seems he hadn't had time to put down, came the gardener-porter, too, at a quick pace, a small person, middle aged, with a tobacco-colored horizontal mustache.

Giudittina raced out and got ahead of everyone, leapt at her brother, and hung on his neck. "Wonderful! You're here. Wonderful!" she screamed happily.

During dinner, to avoid the gaps of silence they were in danger of falling into, Francesca talked about Colomba. "You know, Ambrogio, we've still not given you the details about Manno courting a girl."

"So, that pillar of the Church has taken to courting. Well, well. But is he serious, or . . . ?"

"Of course he is, and how!"

"Well, don't exaggerate", Giulia put in. "Let's say they kept each other company." Even she let slip a smile.

"Yes, kept company every single day. Imagine Ambrogio, he went every afternoon to *I dragoni* while she was in Nomana."

"After all, he's at an age . . .", Gerardo pointed out indulgently.

Francesca addressed her brother. "He even brought her here, home, and he even wanted me to become friends, imagine. He almost ordered me to make friends. And then I could cheer her up, poor thing, when he was away. Do you understand? Manno has fallen head over heels in love, I tell you."

"Don't exaggerate", her mother repeated. "Come, come, don't exaggerate."

"Listen here, you're getting me interested, really", Ambrogio said. "Who is this girl? What's she like?"

"We told you. She's the Signora Eleonora's niece. But now she's gone back home to Novara."

"Well, well, Manno!"

"Her name's Colomba", Rodolfo piped up. "It's a pretty name . . . isn't it?" he said quietly, strangely timid.

"I bet she's pretty, too", Ambrogio said with a smile.

"Yes, I should say", Rodolfo answered, still timid, and then he suddenly blushed to the roots of his hair.

Ambrogio thought, *Listen, it's Manno who's in love, not you*, but he said nothing and left him in peace.

The scent of hay and the happy shrieks of the swallows circling the house before retiring for the night were carried in from outdoors. Life in Nomana went on. All those boys had died, but life went on.

The young man turned in shortly after dinner. He went to his room readily, taking an invitation from his mother: "You're convalescing, remember that. You shouldn't stay up late, especially now, at first."

"You're right, Mama. Besides, I am a bit tired."

Besides his own bed, there was Rodolfo's, but his mother explained, "Your brother is going to sleep in Manno's room, at least for a few days. Otherwise, he'll keep you awake wanting to hear war stories until God knows what time."

"Yes." Ambrogio raised no objection to this either—he felt empty. From outside, apart from the good odor of hay, came the nightingale's song. The young man took off his uniform and put on his pajamas, turned off the light, and opened the window wide.

The song came from the northeast. *It always sings in the yew tree.* He listened for a spell, unaware of the litigation between the tiny beast and Manno that had transpired a few days before. In the pauses of the song, he could hear another nightingale singing farther off, toward Nomanella, like an echo.

He lifted his eyes to the starry sky. Above him was the group of stars Lyra, next to the great cross of the swan, and a little farther off stretched that badly outlined, as if twisted, constellation of the eagle, alias Oreste Pirovano. He felt like laughing. Here he was in Nomana, and the plumber Pirovano was two steps away, with his little shop full of washbowls and faucets hanging from the walls. He could laugh. The constellation Pirovano! For months in Russia he had called it that, from that afternoon Bonsaver taught him how to recognize it. He said he gave it the name of his village plumber—a Veneto name—because the outline of the stars of the eagle looked, not any bird, but like some hydraulic mechanism. Bonsaver! Bonsaver and all the others. . . . Ambrogio closed the shutters. His smile was turning into a grimace. The song of the nightingales continued outside.

27

The following morning, Sunday, the young man went to see the family at Nomanella after Mass.

Luca was already there talking with his girlfriend, Giustina, the two of them standing in front of the door, facing one another, dressed in their Sunday best.

428

Luca still had his reddish beard and also, even in civilian clothes, his Alpine look. He had a blue badge, a decoration for bravery, in his lapel. Giustina, almost as tall as he, was very thin. Absorbed as they were in their own emotions, they did not notice Ambrogio's arrival.

I didn't know Luca was still on leave, he thought. *Look at the two of them. It's a pleasure to see them! But what an uncomfortable place to talk!* He knew they were behaving that way in order to abide by the local custom that prescribed that the girl, when with her boyfriend, be within her mother's line of vision. (The two of them were "talking at each other". "Talking at each other" is the exact expression the Lombard dialect used to designate the period of courtship.)

They saw Ambrogio when he was only a few steps away.

"Look at the two lovebirds, just look", he said in dialect and went up to Luca to shake his hand, quite emotionally, and then embraced him.

"Luca! You've also been through the mill, eh?" He meant, "You've gone through the horrors of the retreat, the wounds."

"Yes, but mine's been a minor thing", he replied, referring to his own wound, pointing to his left leg. "Besides, it happened in Nicolaievca, when we were about to pull out altogether."

"Come, come, I know what happened in Nicolaievca. And I also know what you did before. I see they've given you the silver medal . . . I heard. My sincerest congratulations. Giustina, do you know what that decoration means? That your boyfriend's a brave fellow." He nodded, as if to emphasize his own words. Then he went back to talking to Luca. "But I didn't know you were still on sick leave."

"Oh, no, that ended some time ago. I'm already back now. What happened is that yesterday we went to Milan on truck duty and they let me go home for a few hours."

There was a pause.

"Well, the two of us managed to get out of that mess."

"We can thank the heavens above", Luca said, becoming serious, and he really meant our Lord.

At these words Giustina's pretty smiling face contracted into a frown. *Stefano didn't manage to get out,* Ambrogio thought. *I've struck a false note.* He turned to the girl then and shook her hand with great warmth. "And our Giustina, how are you?"

"Welcome home", she said softly, a trifle embarrassed.

"Soldiers' letters!" Ambrogio exclaimed. "This fellow," he pointed to Luca, "as well as your brother, have really been work for you, haven't they?"

"Yes!" Giustina admitted.

"When we saw each other in Russia they told me that you wrote every week dutifully: one week to one of them and the next week to the other."

Giustina went on nodding, saying, "Yes", and smiled shyly. Then he saw she wanted to switch to the serious topic but did not know how to broach, it, until she finally uttered, "Ambrogio, do you think my brother, that he ..." She stopped, as if she had repented. "Mother's in the kitchen. I'm going to call her."

"No, don't", Ambrogio said. "I've come especially for her—for her and your father. Don't call them, I'm going", and he went into the kitchen, the other two following.

Lucia was seated in the kitchen with one hand on the table and the other on her lap. She had heard Ambrogio's voice before and had gone to the door, but then she had gone back in and had sat down. The prospect of having to hear, no matter what it was, another confirmation of her son's tragic situation paralyzed her.

"Mama Lucia", Ambrogio exclaimed on entering. "My dear Mama Lucia!" He took the right hand of the peasant woman into his own, shook it, and kissed it. "My dear Mama Lucia!" he repeated.

The woman, who had stood up, looked him over from head to toe, her brown eyes brimming with tears.

Ambrogio made her sit down again and, pulling up a chair, sat down in front of her, on the same side of the table, which was covered by an oilcloth with a faded pattern, which he remembered very well. Lucia took her handkerchief out of her apron pocket and meanwhile wiped her docile eyes. "Yesterday evening his father and I wanted to go and see you", she said, "as soon as we heard you had come back to Nomana. But then we thought you'd be tired ..." She paused. "They wounded you, poor Ambrogio."

"I would have liked to come yesterday evening, too, but I didn't. I was exhausted. Being in the hospital so long has made me become lazy."

Lucia shook her head to say that was not so.

"Unfortunately, I have no news of Stefano for you", he said, his voice as steady as he could make it. "You know that already, Mama Lucia. The little I did know—all I knew—I've written already."

"Yes, you wrote twice from the hospital, poor Ambrogio. I am very grateful." She burst into uncontrollable sobbing. "It's all useless", she said haltingly. "Pointless, because Stefano is dead."

"You can't say that", Ambrogio protested. "No one has seen him dead, and so it can't be said he is."

"That's true", Giustina added. Luca reinforced her words, too, by nodding his head.

"There's no news of him or of his regiment", Ambrogio said. "As I wrote, no one knows what happened with the Third Bersaglieri." Behind the woman, next to the railing, he could see the tin bucket for lifting water from the well, with its ladle hanging on the rim. How out of place were all these recollections of death in this peaceful atmosphere. "Mama Lucia," he began, "God knows how much I'd like to bring good news. But I have none. It's incredible, but no one knows anything about the Third."

Luca intervened. "I've explained it, too. I tried to get information in the hospital, but the Bersaglieri there were all from the Sixth. It seems impossible, but none of them knew a thing about the Third."

"That's because the Third had to go through a village called Meskoff at the beginning of the retreat." Ambrogio traced some useless lines on the oilcloth of the table in his desire to make everything clearer for Mama Lucia. "But in Meskoff, the Russians arrived before the Bersaglieri, and there may have been a lot of Russians. That's why the Bersaglieri did not get through."

"Oh, heavens, heavens," Lucia murmured, "heavens", and as she tried to imagine what happened, unable to do so, she began to move her head back and forth, torturing herself. "There were many? Many! God knows what happened."

"But the fact there were many", he tried to pick up the pieces, "could be . . . perhaps . . . could mean that all went well. Even if I don't know, of course," he added, because he really did not believe in what he was saying, "and no one knows, but because of the disproportion in numbers, the Bersaglieri might have had to surrender. If that's what they did, perhaps many of them are now in prison."

"But if he's a prisoner, why doesn't he write? I'm sure Stefano would go to any lengths to write. He'd find a way, because he knows that any other way that we here . . . that I . . . in this condition would die."

They all knew this wasn't just talk. It was as true, atrociously true, of her as of any number of mothers in that condition. *How is it possible,* Ambrogio thought, *that no one writes from prison? Perhaps they've killed them all . . .!*

As if she guessed what was going through his mind, the woman burst into a fit of tears.

"Calm down, Mama Lucia", the young man exclaimed, an unexpected knot in his throat. "Calm down. You mustn't despair because . . . God is all seeing and caring . . ." Neither did he know what to say.

"We must keep faith, Mother", Giustina said. "Recite the Rosary. Recite it over and over until our Lord grants grace." Her chin was trembling as she said this. Her boyfriend looked away from her.

"But if he's dead, it's all useless, don't you understand?" Lucia rebelled. She turned to Ambrogio. "If he's a prisoner, why doesn't he write?" she repeated. "Tell me why. It was all over in Africa a few days ago, and yet some of those who were taken prisoner have already written home: one from Raperio, for instance, and here in Nomana, Carletto Astori, the fellow who does whitewashing." She lowered her voice. "I'll tell you why: only the dead don't write."

Ambrogio shook his head. He did not feel up to answering again, to bring up reasons he did not believe.

"Mother, you can't think that everyone missing throughout Russia has died", Luca intervened softly. "There're some hundred thousand of them, you know?" He looked at Ambrogio. "Isn't that so?"

"Yes, a hundred thousand missing, that's what they say," he confirmed, "and not a one of them has written home as yet."

"And if they're all dead?"

"A hundred thousand people? How can you think that, Mother?" Giustina asked with consternation.

"I don't think so", Luca calmly declared. "I don't think so because six or seven from my battalion, after a week of being held prisoners, we freed them in Nicolaievca. I saw them with my own eyes. I told you. They hadn't killed them. Quite the contrary. The Russians fed them."

"You're a good boy, Luca," Lucia said, "and you did tell me about that, and I've thought a lot about it."

"Yes," he insisted, "it happened exactly that way."

"I think about it continually," Lucia affirmed, "but six or seven among so many . . . what are six or seven?"

"It's all we know," Luca made it clear, "but even if it's not much, it's something that raises one's hopes."

Lucia reflected. Something almost imperceptible began to take over the features of her face. Ambrogio had the impression she was going from desperation to hopefulness. *Good God*, he thought, *how many times—maybe daily—will she go through these ups and downs!* Lucia looked him straight in the face. She wanted his opinion; he realized it was impossible to avoid giving it.

"Listen, Mama Lucia, something happened like what Luca told you at our outpost. The Russians took away a driver for their army, making him drive a truck, because they were in great need of specialists. They had told him that when the war was over they'd send him home. Instead of that, in a matter of a few days the truck collapsed at a crossroads in front of us. There were a few shots; he was saved and returned to our column." He hesitated briefly. He thought of the soldier from Varese, from the thirteenth Artillery, who repeated he had been in the hands of Russians, too. He claimed to be the only survivor from a column of Italian prisoners massacred by Russian gunfire, in the outskirts of Arbusov. Perhaps, who knows, he fantasized, or he might have been completely mad. "So," Ambrogio concluded, "there are people alive, even if they can't write now. To know if there are many or few, we need to wait until the end of the war."

He was silent, and Lucia looked at him in dismay: the end of the war. How much time, how many years would she have to wait? "The priest told me that, too", she murmured. She looked over at Giustina, who nodded.

After a brief silence, Ambrogio asked, "How is Ferrante? And the grandmother? And aren't the little ones here?"

"Grandmother took the youngsters to Mass at Monticello," Lucia replied, "because there's a feast today, and there'll be stalls full of treats in the square. Ferrante, however . . . poor man . . ." Her grief kept her from going on.

"Papa's in the stables."

"I'm going to look for him. I'd like to say hello", Ambrogio said as he got up. "Then I'll be back."

Indeed, Ferrante was in the stables, but he was not working. Like Lucia, he also was aware of Ambrogio's arrival, but he had not yet had the heart to go out and meet him. The young man found him busy pretending to put things in order, raking the cow's straw, which was already in order and in no need of raking.

"Thanks for having come to see us", Ferrante said.

"I would have liked to come bearing good news", Ambrogio replied.

"Certainly . . . !" Ferrante said, and looked as if he were concentrating only on his work.

"The last time I saw him was in September." From its stall the little chestnut horse lifted its ears and looked at the visitor. It, too, seemed attentive.

"Yes," Ferrante assented, "he wrote us. He said your unexpected visit cheered him up a lot. We still have the letter in the drawer."

"He was happy, yes, and so was I."

"Of course." Ferrante went on raking, without looking at Ambrogio.

"Did he tell you how I shared the Bersaglieri mess with his platoon? All of them, from the first to the last, were great fellows and very united. I'm certain that in any case of need they'd have helped one another. No doubt of it, and they'd do the same now in prison."

"Yes, yes . . ." Ferrante approved generally.

There was a long pause. The picture of Saint Anthony with the pig was still there, hanging where it always did. It should have radiated peace, but it did not manage it then. Tears were brimming in the peasant's eyes, but he managed to hold them back.

Ambrogio was feeling ill at ease; he would have liked to leave, to slip away, and he was ashamed. *Losing a son to war*, he said to himself, *has no poetry about it, nothing. It's about the same as letting bodies decompose in among the weeds, after the battles are over . . .* The same kind of thoughts that had come over Manno, too, during his first visit to Eleonora.

The young man passed the time in the stable without saying much more. As if to test the silence, the mouse next to the Saint Anthony's picture stuck its head out from the hole. Could it be the same one as that other year? Seeing it, Ambrogio felt a tremendous wave of anguish. He waited a bit more and then decided to go back to the others. "When I reached Stefano at the front," he said, by way of leaving, "he was posted as an observer. You've been to war, too, and you know what that is, a line and a trench." Ferrante nodded, interested, despite himself. "One of these days," Ambrogio continued, "I'll come back, a little more calmly, and I'll tell you how Stefano lived there, above the Don, in detail. So you'll know."

"Yes", Ferrante approved. "Yes and thank you."

Ambrogio grasped the peasant's hairy arm at about the elbow and squeezed it. Then he want back to the kitchen to see Lucia and stayed with her and the sweethearts for another half hour. Lucia joined in the conversation when it touched on a subject not related to Stefano or his fate. Finally, the visitor shook the bony hand of the peasant woman, took leave of the sweethearts, and left.

28

His spirits dampened, Ambrogio walked along the grassy path; two parallel tracks were furrowed in it from the tread of wheels, and it was sometimes flanked by hedges—high ones, low ones—of hawthorn or mulberry. At his back, to the north, the horizon was shut off by the great pre-Alpine arch, illuminated by the sun at this moment. (The mountains ... the young man remembered what Stefano had said regarding those mountains three years before: "It's as if they didn't exist for me", and he was about to raise objections, as he had then, but his friend was no longer there.) At either side of the road were lovely fields of green grain, in full flourish, and alternating with them were recently mowed fields, with their rows of mulberries and vines.

They've already cut back the hay and the alfalfa. Could Ferrante have cut back his without help now? It seemed so. The field with the row of mulberries, where he'd first met Stefano and their little chestnut horse, was carefully cut back. Ambrogio remembered that day. *Exactly three years ago: it was May then, too, when we were just two boys ...*

How many memories! And other memories, also far off, like the one, very far off, and reduced to pale images, of the time when, escorted by Marietta of the shuttles, he had gone to Nomanella with his cousin Manno, to visit his then kindergarten playmate Stefano. Ambrogio—not as interested in Marietta's stories as Manno—ran along the road, and suddenly from the opposite direction came a horse without harnessing, its chest covered with foam (he still remembered that detail). It was bearing down at a gallop as it approached, and he, paralyzed with fear, felt unable to get off the path. The horse was already almost on top of him. It was going to run over him, and suddenly at the last moment he leapt away, and, like a huge dark spot, it went over him without touching him ... "The guardian angel, it was the guardian angel!" Marietta and Manno had shouted in unison. It must have happened at that point, where the hedges on either side were a little taller. *Death didn't carry me off, it left me ... then, and now this winter at the front ... why?*

Before the end of the walk, the road wound around the wall of his garden, surmounted by a high myrtle hedge, except for the middle part, where there was a balcony with a view toward the mountains. *For sure there's no one on the balcony at this hour,* the young man thought, and he looked up. But Giudittina was there, quietly, quietly watching him with her devilish eyes. Their eyes meeting, she shouted, "I've found you, I've found you! Coming back ... at last." Francesca, at her side, her braid encircling her beautiful head, looked out, smiled, too.

Ambrogio waved to his two sisters. *They're not there by chance*, he thought. *Francesca must be worried about me.*

His sister seemed to have guessed his thoughts in some way because she came forward with an excuse. "Ambrogio, you must have forgotten that today we're eating with our aunts and uncle, the evacuees. Tell the truth."

"But you see," the youth stopped a second, "I'm on time." He waved again to the two girls. At the angle of the garden he saw the niche with the fresco of our Lady of the Rosary. The young man read the long inscription on the arch over the figures: *Regina sacratissimi rosarii, ora pro nobis.* He bowed his head as a greeting, and, without stopping, he repeated the prayer several times, replacing the *ora pro nobis* with *ora pro eo, pro eo, pro eo.*

29

At the table was Uncle Ettore, an engineer, who as a young man had studied in Germany for two years. Completely unaware of his nephew's state of mind, he insisted from the start on asking about the strategic situation that had been created on the Russian front.

"After you left, the Russians finally took Stalingrad, didn't they?"

"Yes, in February."

"And then they made big advances."

These conversations also had to take place. Ambrogio would have liked to point out that any news he had—what everyone else had—had been culled from the newspapers and radio, but he did not want to appear rude to his uncle. He summed up the strategic situation, and even though he was speaking directly, as if he knew from experience, he had the feeling of being a bit deceitful.

The Russians, then, had not only "finally taken" Stalingrad, but on the southern front had really advanced a great deal, building up a great salient around Kharkov. The Germans, however, with fresh divisions poured in from France, had—with their usual violence and, one could say, this time with ease—cancelled out that salient, taking Kharkov again and reestablishing the front in a roughly straight line from Cape North to Rostov on the Black Sea, more or less as it had been at the end of the first winter of the war. The two enormous armies—with hundreds of divisions each—were about to face one another, preparing to hurl themselves against each other.

"It's a dangerous situation", Uncle Ettore commented, looking at his nephew out of his light eyes, somewhat blank looking behind the lenses of his pince-nez. "If the Russian army should get the upper hand, what will happen?

Theoretically, it wouldn't have to stop after occupying Germany and could even get to the Atlantic."

"How things are going to end we cannot guess", Ambrogio answered, trying to take such a prospect into consideration. "But the Germans, one by one, or if you prefer, unit by unit, are far more efficient than the Russians. It's true that the numerical disproportion is great, and if you consider that the Germans also have other enemies ahead, then the disproportion really becomes something to be reckoned with."

"You mean the Americans, don't you?" Rodolfo piped up.

"Yes, and the English, and the partisans coming together on all sides. To put it one way, they already have half the world against them. In any case, if the Russians break through the front and advance—something I'm not too sure of—every bit of progress will be paid for by a high price."

"You mean they'd reach Germany exhausted, decimated?"

"Yes, I think so."

"Yet they might not stop because of that, once they haven't any real opponents."

"They might not, no", Ambrogio admitted taciturnly.

"Or maybe Stalin and the other top dogs could at some point start worrying if their people were being bled to death? Communism is born of humanitarianism, let us not forget that", Uncle Ettore announced. He, whose background was secular, was the only one among the diners ready to credit that openly atheistic ideology.

"Uncle, no. What do you mean? Humanitarian? No, you're wrong about that!"

"I'm saying they were at the beginning, when they started, at least as a program."

"At the beginning, I don't know, perhaps they were. But today!"

Ambrogio related something of the massacres, really true hecatombs, they had made to force the peasants to go into the collective farms. Then he told of his own direct experiences of the inhuman way the Soviet leaders treated their men.

"You saw that!" the interested Uncle Ettore muttered from time to time. "You saw that! Not even General Cadorna in the other war abused his soldiers that way."

"The poor people", Gerardo, who really did come from the people and was genuinely sensitive to their sufferings, observed. "All in all, they're boys like our own, or fathers like ourselves . . . poor people."

"And this fact alone, that now they don't let the prisoners write home?" Ambrogio pointed out to his uncle. "Isn't that a fair enough indication of their level of humanitarianism?"

Giulia chimed in. "Can you imagine?" she reproached her brother-in-law. "Godless people being humanitarian? Can't you see it's a contradiction?"

The two ancient aunts nodded their heads approvingly. Uncle Ettore—being of a secular persuasion—began to smile behind his Trotskylike glasses. (Perhaps others, too, will laugh at Giulia's words, without realizing that the facts, the invincible facts, bore out her good Christian sense, very much so.)

Noemi, meanwhile, was coming and going between the kitchen and the dining room with platters of food; from time to time Francesca and even Giulia would get up to help out. Even Giudittina tried to get up to help, but her mother had her sit down each time. "No, no, you stay there. No need for you to help today", she explained. And Rodolfo added, "You help? Help what? Upset everything?"

Giudittina replied by sticking out her tongue and letting loose an insult or two. One or another of the aunts from Monza would intervene. "To your little brother? What manners! Behave yourself . . .", and would smile benevolently, inviting the two children to make it up. As for the rest, the two aunts—inwardly horrified by the prospect of merciless violence—took no part in the conversation unless asked direct questions by Francesca and Giulia. They preferred listening, not missing a single word said by the others, especially Ambrogio, they claimed. It was their way of participating in the great events taking place in the world, these events that recently had lent their drab and predictable lives some emotion. (Their uneventful lives! It was a kind of endless waiting, but for what? Once, already many years ago, when they were two young girls, they had waited for love to complete their lives. But there was no love for them, and they had gone on waiting and would not stop until the day they died. Maybe they did not realize this, but if they did, they said nothing so as not to pain the others, not to disturb—their constant worry—the others.)

The conversation went back to the Germans because Gerardo wanted to be informed better about their efficiency. The subject interested him, as he had had business dealings with them in the past, in exporting, and he expected, reasonably enough, once the war was over, he would deal with them again.

"I don't understand", Gerardo observed. "If there is that disproportion of strength you're talking about, between the Germans and the Russians, how come things went the way they did in Stalingrad?"

"I can't explain it either", Ambrogio admitted. "I must say I didn't expect that surrender. Of course, it was one army against five or six in Stalingrad, and helped by the air force, or half helped, but even with experience, I was convinced that the Germans, once they realized they couldn't hold the city, would have broken through the encirclement and left. As they did in Cercovo, as we know. If they had, the Russian lines would have given way, of this I'm convinced. Why then didn't they move? I don't understand."

He did not know that it had been Hitler himself who stubbornly prevented the Sixth Army from retreating, against the better judgment of the military men. He did not know—and would not know until the end of the war—of the insistent demands of the surrounded German commanding officer, in

December, to be allowed to leave the city and get to the two hundred armored cars of General Hoth, who from the south, after having opened a way, destroying one thousand armored cars in a row of the Russians, had arrived about thirty miles from Stalingrad.

"The fact remains that even if they are enormous eaters, they are tremendously efficient soldiers," Ambrogio said, "and not only their organization, which is perfect, but also one by one, they're brave in the best sense of the word. I mean that no soldier is as well disposed to giving his life in battle as they are."

They were all listening without making any commentary.

"This must be recognized", the young man continued. "To each his own. As it must be mentioned that the Germans are incredibly blind about certain things."

"What things?" Uncle Ettore wanted to know.

"Well, it's enough to point out that they could have taken Russia with far fewer divisions than they brought with them."

"But . . . how's that?"

"Yes, because at the beginning there were few among the Russians who seriously opposed them. Don't you know that? This is not propaganda, but fact. The Russians were hoping the Germans would free them from communism. Going into many villages—I'm talking about the beginning of the war— the people would come up to the troops, to the Italians, too, with bread and salt, and there were no partisans. The Germans had more trouble from the vast spaces and the lack of roads, perhaps, than they did from the Russian army, which, however, at the beginning was armed to the hilt. That's why they reached Moscow in a few months, and had they not been stopped by the mud, they probably would have taken it in the autumn of '41. But how did they respond to the expectations of the Russians? They considered these poor wretches less than dirt, treated them any old way, continually threatening them and killing enormous numbers. This is something they've not a clue about in Italy. And the deserters? There were a lot of them at first, but because the Russian command infiltrated a few partisans, the Germans treated all of them as possible partisans, that is, savagely. The outcome was that the Russians began to fight them with all their might, and in occupied zones they took to the woods. You understand, Uncle? That's what the Germans managed to do with their blindness."

Ambrogio fell silent for an instant, nodding as if there would still be too many more things to add.

"It's incredible!" his father uttered. "Incredible!"

"It's their . . . how do you say it?" Uncle Ettore was dead set on explaining that he knew about Germany to Gerardo and the others. "Their . . . schematization, the German mental schematization . . . that's what I mean."

"Well, enough of this", Giulia put in, worried that her son might become tired. "You know you shouldn't tire yourself out. Let the others talk a little now." Ambrogio tried to defend himself, but then he passively followed the maternal advice. The conversation that followed, to which he contributed only an odd sentence or two, ended up interesting him less and less. Instead, the thought of Lucia, Stefano's mother, came back to him painfully, how he had seen her just hours before in Nomanella. His own mother could have been in this state of mind now ... and suffering like Lucia were the large majority of mothers of Italian soldiers he had met and seen in the course of the winter on the Russian front.

Every so often the young man poured himself wine, without realizing it and almost automatically, from a crystal clear carafe he had in front of him. He finally finished it. Then Noemi took it away and brought it back full, and again Ambrogio went back to serving himself more drink. He got up from the table a little bewildered.

30

He lingered in the parlor with the others—before going out to the garden—standing, drinking a coffee substitute. He was about to ask to be excused to go to his room. (*My wounds will excuse this stupor brought on by the wine*, he thought, *but that would be turning it into something noble. When shall I truly be ashamed of myself?*) However, the porter buzzed through the "intercom" to say that Pierello from the Lodosa housing estate was there, with someone called Savina, the mother of a soldier missing in Russia.

"Tell them to come in", Ambrogio told Francesca, who had answered, and went out into the garden to receive them.

They were already coming toward the house, accompanied by the porter-gardener. The mother of the missing soldier was—to look at her was enough—a working woman. She was in her Sunday best and was carrying a photograph in her hands, and not knowing the place, she looked around shyly as she walked. Pierello, on seeing Ambrogio, stopped and spread his arms out wide. Ambrogio greeted him by waving his hand wildly. Then they ran to each other and shook hands effusively.

"I knew you were on leave, Piero", Ambrogio said in dialect.

"Well, here I am. You're ... you're rather pale. You look as if you've gone through the other world, don't you?"

"Yes", Ambrogio admitted. "But listen, how long has it been since we saw each other last?"

The other fellow sank his head between his shoulders as if he were facing up to eternity. "Well, since that day you took me to headquarters. Remember?"

"Oh, yes, yes."

"So much to tell!" Piero said. "Enough of that." He introduced the woman, who seemed to have taken the show of friendship for a good augury. "This is Savina, the mother of Dino, Dino Rigamonti from Lodosa. As she lives near me, I thought of bringing her. All in all, just a short walk, and maybe Ambrogio can give her some news, I thought."

Ambrogio shook the woman's hand compassionately. "He hasn't written since Christmas, isn't that it?"

"Yes", the poor woman answered, looking at him out of eyes suddenly fearful.

She's like Mama Lucia, the young man thought. *She wants news more than anything else in the world, and at the same time she's afraid.* "In what regiment was your son?" he asked aloud in dialect.

"His name is Rigamonti Davide. Here he is." The woman showed the photograph she was carrying in her left hand.

It showed a young village boy dressed as a soldier, a half-bust photograph.

"I remember him", Ambrogio said. "Yes, I know him by sight. From Lodosa, of course." He turned to Pierello. "He's a little older than we are, isn't he? So, he was in Russia, too. Do you know in what division, regiment?"

Pierello shook his head. "I couldn't answer even if you killed me. I only know he's in the infantry. But Mama Savina, you must have all the details."

"He went in with the class of '18", the woman answered, glancing from one to the other.

"The class of '18, all right. But what regiment?" Ambrogio asked again.

"The last time he wrote was the fourteenth of December—one of those postcards."

"Do you have it here?"

"No", Mama Savina replied. "My husband should have come with me. Maybe he knows, but then at the last moment he did not feel up to it."

At these words, the porter, who had followed the conversation attentively, gestured negatively with his head, letting it be understood that in his opinion it was not a question of low spirits on the husband's part. Then he moved away and went back to the porter's lodge.

Ambrogio glanced at the back of the photograph. "Ah, look, the division is here", he read out. "Rigamonti Davide, class of 1918, 37th Infantry, 2nd Battalion, 2nd Company. Military address 53. That was ... I mean that is the Ravenna Division."

"Rav ...", the woman murmured. "Then you know something! You've seen him? You met him?"

Ambrogio shook his head. "I'm sorry, but I haven't seen him or met him. I saw no one in Russia from this division. We were not close. I'm sorry not to be able to give you any news."

"Oh!" the woman murmured. "Oh, oh, poor me, poor Savina!" Tears began to well up in her eyes, but she did not let them fall, trying to hold them back.

440

"Come", Ambrogio said to the two visitors. "Let's not stand out here. Let's go in the house."

"No, no, it's useless", the woman answered. "I've already bothered you too much. If you know nothing of my Dino, it's useless."

"Come in the house, Mama Savina", Ambrogio insisted, taking her arm. "We'll see if we can find a way to get news. Come in."

"Oh, if you only knew, sir," the poor mother lamented, as she yielded to his amiable insistence, "how many places his sister and I have been to. In Milan, at the central station when the trains arrived in March ... with the photo, holding it up high for the soldiers to see, but nothing, it all came to nothing. And if you had seen how many women were there with photos! The poor things! My daughter also went to the hospital in Baggio, and other places, but always ..." She shook her head. "So many places that now she doesn't want to go anywhere. She says, 'It's enough, enough. It's doing no good, Mama, can't you see? Nobody knows anything.' Her spirit's gone, understand? And to think she was so strong at first, and in the beginning it was she who perked me up."

Ambrogio had them come in the study and made them sit down. Then he sat down with a pad of paper and a pen in his hand. But the only plan that took shape in his mind was to go to the depot of the Thirtieth Infantry to ask about survivors from the front. It was no good, though, as the sister of the missing soldier had already been to the depot in Alessandria twice.

"But she did talk personally with your son's comrades? I mean with the ones in his company, who were with him when they retreated."

"Yes, the chaplain called her. Yes, she talked, but no one knew anything concrete to say to her. Unless ... unless they're all, especially my daughter, keeping the truth from me."

"But no, Mama Savina. What are you saying? Why would they do that?" Piero objected.

"Why would they do that? Here I am with all this uncertainty, and I'm going mad. Mad, and she—my daughter—knows it. Anything is better for a mother than this uncertainty. How can I have a moment's peace with this torture in my heart? I can't stop wondering if he's alive or dead. For me it's a ... it's like ... I mean ... I can't explain."

Ambrogio looked at her with a knot in his throat. Pierello also fell silent, only nodding his head.

"Anything would be better than this uncertainty, even knowing my Dino is ... is ... no, no, that no. I shouldn't say it, I shouldn't think it, otherwise our Lord will punish me, and I'll lose him forever."

She looked at the two young men, frightened for having dared to think those thoughts to release herself from the torture.

"Why would the Lord want to punish you?" Ambrogio said. "Punish you? But you're as crucified as the Lord himself. Like him, without any fault of your own, the very same way."

"Yes, yes, that's how it is ... how well you've put it! I'm crucified, most surely."

Francesca came in with a bottle and two little glasses on a tray. Seeing the woman in that state upset her, and she did not know if she should interrupt. She put the tray down on the writing desk, and while she poured the liquid into the glasses, she looked at the woman out of the corner of her eye.

"No, don't trouble yourself, Signorina", the woman said sobbing. "Besides, I never drink liquor. I'm not used to it. Oh, how shameful. I'm causing so much trouble."

Pierello, pained, followed every word, shaking his head.

"Don't talk about troubling us", Francesca said sweetly. "You shouldn't talk that way."

"Listen, Mama Savina, suppose it was I who hadn't returned—stayed behind," Ambrogio gave as an example, "and today my mother had gone to your house for news. Would you have called that a bother, trouble? I'm sure you wouldn't. There are times when these things don't even cross your mind. Isn't that so?"

The woman nodded her sad agreement.

"Well, then don't think you're being a bother."

"But I can't drink liquor ... I'm not used to it."

"That's all right", Ambrogio said. "A coffee instead. Yes, that's better. But I warn you," and he tried smiling to relax the tension, "it's only a substitute coffee. We just had some ourselves."

"No", said Francesca, who was handing the little glass to Pierello. "No, you don't know, but we have a little real coffee. I'm going to make it now."

"Good", Ambrogio agreed.

Seeing herself the object of so much attention, the poor woman again began to weep.

Ambrogio, who had lifted his glass to make a toast with Pierello, waited until Savina calmed down a bit, and then he repeated, trying to be convincing, the hopeful arguments that together with Luca, he had given Lucia a few hours before, that one hundred thousand were missing ("I repeat, a hundred thousand men ..."), and they couldn't have just disappeared into thin air. Many of them must necessarily have been taken prisoner, and when the war was over the prisoners would be sent home. But why, if it's like that, the woman asked, don't they write? The usual and repeated question: Why have they written from Africa, and there's even been news from America, while there's been nothing from Russia from anyone?

Ambrogio hinted at the carelessness of the Soviet regime in their treatment of people, but he did not dwell on it too much, in order not to scare her on that score.

Francesca returned with two tiny cups of good and fragrant coffee. She offered one to the woman, and the other one she began to sip gracefully, quietly, trying to distract the woman with pleasant talk. Afterward, along with her brother, she accompanied the woman to the street.

Pierello stayed with Ambrogio for a while, but he was so upset—and contrary to what his friend expected—he did not open his arms once with that gesture of his of accepting his destiny. He left with an excuse, promising to return the following day "when we'll both be in better spirits".

Ambrogio went to his room, his spirits at rock bottom. He had made Mama Savina promise to send through her daughter all the available information on the following day to see what he could do. But he knew already it would be impossible to get at anything concrete. *It really is incredible,* he thought. *There's not even the slightest news from all those boys. What could have happened to the poor boy? And Stefano? And all the others? Michele Tintori? What would Michele's father say . . . ? I don't know what I'd give right now to find out if there were any prisoners alive in Russia.*

PART TWO

I

"Est locus extremis Scythiae glacialis in oris, triste solum . . . Frigus iners illic habitant Pallorque Tremorque et jejuna Fames." (There's a place in the remote and barren lands of icy Russia, a sad place . . . there dwell inert cold and pallidness and fear and starving hunger.)
—The Seat of Hunger, Ovid, *Metamorphosis* VIII

Though frighteningly few, there were actually some alive, and among them was Michele Tintori, because in the winter of 1942–43 the Russians had not killed all the Italians who had fallen into their hands. At that period they were systematically killing only the Germans, carefully routing them out, even among the gray rows of Italian prisoners. If they picked one out (*"Niemiez! Niemiez!"*), they would kick him and slap him out of the group, kill him with a stream of machine-gun fire or put a bullet through his head. Among the Italians (as among the Romanians and Hungarians) the standard was to eliminate only the injured incapable of walking, sometimes firing at them instantly (in the battalion of Val Cismon of the Julia Division, they killed four hundred in a few minutes after their surrender). In other cases they would regroup them in ruined buildings or even in the open air and would leave them—guarded or not—without feeding them or attending to them in any way, which, in these temperatures, would result in all of them, or almost all those injured, dying in the course of a few days.

The others, those who were well or the wounded who were able to walk, were taken on foot to gathering places beyond the Don. These had been the terrible *davai* marches, accompanied to the shout *"davai, davai"* (forward, forward), that the guards used to spur on the exhausted men, stupefied with hunger, fatigue, and cold, to continue. Not even these prisoners were issued food, except by a squad leader more human than the others. As a rule, the guards even prohibited the women peasants from the village—still Christian and pious— from crossing the lines to hand a crust of bread or cooked potato to the prisoners, something they would try to do from time to time. He who did not hold out and fell in his tracks had a bullet through his head (more rarely, the dying man was left to the white death of freezing). And these shots, which rang out frequently along the lines of the columns, acted as an even greater spur than the incessant shout *"davai, davai."*

These hideous marches lasted anywhere from a few days to weeks, depending on the distance that separated the point of capture from that of the gath-

444

ering places on the other side of the Don, and at these places they had often to be on bivouac for days and days in the open air—always or almost always without being fed—waiting for trains to transport the prisoners to camps. During the *davai* marches and the waiting for trains in the open air, around 40 percent of the Italians died, according to the accounts later made by the prisoners themselves.

Michele had the great luck of not participating in these marches, thanks to the enigmatic note written by the Russian lieutenant who captured him in Arbusov, in which he was singled out as a probable source of information regarding the German defense of Millerovo. The army police had not had time really to look into the matter, and, after some inconclusive interrogations, he had simply been moved to their own positions. Even after the Russians took Millerovo, they continued taking him with them as a matter of routine, allowing him to eat fairly regularly and—a fact of prime importance for him—sheltering him under the same roof as that of the police themselves, within their isbas, together with the arrested Russians, both military and civilian. In that way the lieutenant was able to recuperate quite rapidly and even to recover a portion of his strength.

During the second half of February—two months after being captured—he was taken before an Italian political commissar—an exiled Communist—with whom he immediately realized it would be impossible to pull any tricks. In any case, he in no way wanted to. He had seen, with his own eyes, the terror the police inspired in the arrested Russians, and he was quite worried regarding the outcome of his own strange adventure. Besides, he had heard repeatedly from the arrested Russians—much to his relief—that prisoner-of-war camps did exist; concerning this, no one seemed to be in doubt. And there he hoped to go.

For that reason, he had expressed his surprise to the Italian commissar regarding the whole story of Millerovo, which he could not manage to explain. "In the interrogations," he recounted, "the Russians went on asking if I had been in Millerovo, and I always answered yes, because in fact, I had gone through there in the month of July, when my regiment came into the vicinity of the Don. How they then got it into their heads that I had information about the German forces in the city, I simply do not know. I was in Millerovo a couple of hours this summer, while crossing through, and no more."

The commissar—black haired, with the accent of the Emilia country, seated at a table next to a Russian policeman, was wearing—despite the heat coming from the nearby stove—woolen gloves, and on the back of his chair hung a large black leather jacket. Michele heard, at last, after two months, his first words in Italian. However, the instinctive relief he felt did not last long, given the unpleasant way the other fellow was questioning him.

"What was your assignment in the regiment?" he asked.

"I commanded a platoon."

"What kind? Did it form part of a regiment command?"

"No, it was a normal company platoon, fusileers. The second in the First Battalion."

"What is your profession in civilian life?"

"I'm in law school, a student."

"In what city?"

"In Milan."

"Father's profession?"

"Marble worker, now a pensioner."

"Where do you study in Milan? The state university or the Catholic?"

"The Catholic."

The commissar paused and looked at him. He exchanged a few words in Russian with the policeman.

"So, you're a student?"

"Yes."

"Of Fascist persuasion? One of those who shouted 'long live the war', I suppose?"

"No", Michele answered sincerely. "I've never subscribed to fascism."

"But Catholic, yes?"

At this question, the young man had an instinctive reaction of fear, but he was not ready to yield when it came to his beliefs. "Yes, Catholic I am", he answered softly but firmly. "It's my religion, and I believe in it."

Quite unexpectedly, the commissar began to laugh in his unpleasant way. "You talk like an idiot!" he commented.

The prisoner kept quiet.

"You think you're brave, don't you?" the other provoked. "Well, you're not, forget it. You're not risking anything with that declaration. We don't kill anyone, neither the priests nor the half priests, like you. You're nothing but . . ." He suddenly fell into the dialect of Emilia. "You're one of those losers who follow in the steps of that crook Pacelli. He can be damned and his mother, too."

Michele kept quiet. What was there to say?

The commissar did not persevere in his insults. He took a folded paper from his pocket, opened it with his gloved hand, and read it, then—after having exchanged a few more words with the Russian policeman—he went back to the subject of Millerovo. Without attacking him, he put several questions to him—he obviously knew all about interrogations—and behaved, all in all, almost correctly, modestly. As he knew and felt himself to be the absolute power between life and death for the prisoner, that is, the man in front of him, he was placated and so inclined to be modest. Such composure after the outburst of fury shortly before confused Michele. *What a worm*, he told himself as he continued answering his questions attentively. *He must have left Italy because he despised fascism, great. But once in Russia, after finding out that communism is incomparably*

446

worse—if only because it's endlessly more bloody than the clownishness of fascism—instead of getting out, which would have made sense, look at him, he's preferred to lower himself to being the inquisitor of his countrymen for the Communists. It did not so much as occur to him that the commissar—notwithstanding the bloody aspects of communism—could still be a convinced Communist, and considering himself such, as acting out of his ideals. Given these considerations, Michele's behavior became—without his realizing it—infused with something of disdain, a kind of self-sufficiency.

Self-sufficiency that the other immediately grasped. *How disgusting these sh——ty bourgeois are to me, no ideals and bursting with presumption,* he thought. He looked at his gloves, which covered his hands. *If he even knew, this little Lord Fauntleroy, that my comrades pulled out all my fingernails, and with all their unfair accusations and torture, they've made me half crazy. And, yet, I'm still here* (and he was proud of it), *still here struggling for the realization of communism, and I'll struggle until my last breath, my dying day. This animal will never be able to understand the strength one gets out of scientifically based humanitarian ideals like ours* . . . So, accustomed to think schematically, he did not grasp the personality of his prisoner, which without a doubt played in Michele's favor. The commissar—and consequently the Russian policeman (a professional terrorist, little interested in prisoners of war, and so outside the range of his specialty)—ended up by deciding there had been a mistake made on the front. "They must have fallen into their usual confusion on the front. This lieutenant is just one more idiot, and as for Millerovo, he knows nothing", the commissar decided. "Listen, I'm in this zone, as you know, because I've the job of inspecting the war prisoner camp at Crinovaya." At that moment an icy sheen glittered in his eyes. "If it's all the same to you, I'll take him there."

With the same indifference they had shown in taking him along for two months, the Russian police got rid of the Italian prisoner of war Michele Tintori.

2

The automobile provided by the military police for the commissary (a very modern American model with a van) reached the camp well into the night.

On the commissar's request, the prisoner was immediately assigned a detachment. "You don't happen to have a squadron commanded by a priest?" the commissar asked mockingly, first in Italian and then in Russian, of the commanding colonel. "Send this fellow there. It'll give him great pleasure."

It seemed there really was a squadron commanded by a priest because the Russian officer responded with "*Da, da*" (yes, yes).

Clearly tipsy and disquieted by the unexpected visit of the Moscow envoy, he passed on the necessary instruction in a few words to one of the soldiers of the guardroom.

Walking ill naturedly ahead of Michele, they went through a spacious dark yard of well-trodden snow and ice, which was incredibly dirty. The prisoner looked around almost eagerly; getting out of the van in front of the door of headquarters, he had been able to see little until now about his destined whereabouts. He had the impression of being in a courtyard of an enormous stable, perhaps, who knows, from czarist times ... whatever the situation, within a short time, he would be among his fellow countrymen, which moved him emotionally ... a matter of minutes. To avoid stumbling, the guard lit up the passage from time to time with an electric flashlight, whose cone of light suddenly illuminated the head of a naked corpse, the mouth agape.

Before that vision, Michele opened his eyes, closed them, opened them again. There was no mistake. "What is this?" he exclaimed, horrified, and stopped.

The guard half turned, said a few incomprehensible words, and so as not to come to a standstill, he screamed, "*Davai, davai!*"

The young man started walking again, and every so often turned to look in the direction of the body. His spirits were in a turmoil. What kind of place had he landed in? He tried looking around to see if there were more corpses, but it was dark, and the filthy snow, bereft of reflections, prevented his getting an answer. Crossing through the entire courtyard, they headed toward a door that also had the look of a stable. The guard lit it up for him and, a little way from it was a heap of strange, whitish objects, irregularly shaped, which turned out to be corpses. He said something, moving the cone of light back and forth over these contorted shapes, which had been young human bodies until some days before.

"My God!" Michele exclaimed, unable to help but invoke God mentally, looking with dismay at that terrifying human entanglement.

Two Italian soldiers suddenly surged from behind the heap of dead, wearing their unmistakable fur-lined coats. They rose from the ground—where they had undoubtedly been squatting—and fled tumultuously over the frozen snow. The guard let out a yell, and pointing them out with his flashlight said some excited words to the lieutenant, the prisoner, then calmed down, shrugged his shoulders and ended up saying, "*Nichevo*" (it doesn't matter). Reaching the door, he kicked it open, and lighting up the interior, he ordered the prisoner, "*Davai.*"

He entered. There was no way he could explain the strange appearance and flight of the two soldiers. *What in the devil could they have been doing hiding behind the dead?* But he did not dwell on this question; instead he gathered up all the courage he could. *After all,* he told himself, *even in this place the worst that can happen to me is to die. I've faced death so many times that ... well, let's get on with it.*

Inside he could clearly see that the place, indeed, was a stable, old and in a very bad state of repair. In many places the ceiling had fallen in, broken, the windows—all shaped in half moons—were without panes, and on the walls a patina of ice glistened here and there. The horse boxes were there and were filled up, but also scattered among the passageways—conjectured rather than seen—were innumerable human bodies, from which snoring, confused and heavy, emerged, mixed with an occasional broken voice and moans. The air was reeking with the disgusting stink of human excrement.

The guard pointed his flashlight over one of the boxes close by, oscillating the light over it. "*Pop,*" he said, and then repeated, "*pop.*"

The lieutenant went up to the box, closed like the others with a wooden railing; inside on the ground he glimpsed a layer of stretched-out bodies. "Here?" he asked the guard.

"*Da, da*", he responded and, taking the cone of light off the box, made a half turn and took off.

Michele was once again in the most complete darkness. He remained motionless for a while. Then he groped slowly with his hands on the wooden railing and his feet on the floor. Then, overcoming his disgust (those dead bodies outside gave him reason to think that he had fallen into a place infected with some sort of epidemic), he bent his knees slowly and sat down on the ground, his back against the railing.

Then the body sitting directly on the other side of the barrier moved.

"Who are you?" he heard himself being asked softly.

"Lieutenant Tintori, from the Eighty-First Turin Division. And you?"

"Don Turla, chaplain from the Saluzzo Battalion."

"You're the pop squadron leader?"

"Yes, the *nacialnik.* That's me. Why?"

"They assigned me to your squadron." He paused. "You said Battalion Saluzzo? Any Alpine troops here?"

"Of course, masses."

"From the way you talk, you seem to be from Bergamo or Brescia."

"Bergamo."

"I'm from the Milan province."

"And what did you say your name was?"

"Tintori. Michele Tintori. Is there anyone from the Eighty-First Infantry Division here inside?"

"I don't think so. Perhaps the soldiers' stables. Here we're all officers."

All officers, Tintori said to himself. *How many must they have taken? Were the Alpine troops surrounded like us, too?* He was about to ask, but the other man asked him instead. "You're not from this camp, are you? Where are you from?"

"They just brought me."

"They've just taken you prisoner?"

"No. They took me in Arbusov, a little before Christmas. Have you heard of Arbusov?"

449

"No."

"Terrible place, that."

"As far as terrible places go, in war there's no picking or choosing", Don Turla from Bergamo affirmed sensibly. Then, "You said before Christmas?"

"Yes. The Russians took me prisoner and got it in their heads that I had I don't know what military information. A complicated story. I'll tell you. Only today did the police let me go. I mean, I was brought here."

"Before Christmas? You were two months with the police?"

"Yes, but . . . what do you mean? With the police, as a prisoner. What were you thinking?"

The chaplain, on the other side of the barrier, seemed perplexed.

"But what were you thinking?" the lieutenant repeated. "Think what you want now. Later you'll know me and you'll believe me." He paused. "What's the name of this camp?"

"Crinovaya. The prison camp of Crinovaya."

"Tell me something. I saw a heap of dead bodies outside there. What does it mean? Is there an epidemic of some sort? Typhus perhaps?"

"No epidemic", Don Turla said. "We're covered with lice up to our ears, but there's no epidemic now. Thank God."

"And that heap of dead people?"

"They're dead of hunger. There's not just one pile in the courtyard but many. You'll see tomorrow. You really know nothing? We're dying of hunger here: that's the situation."

This time it was Michele who turned silent. He felt as if a kind of anxiety was overcoming him, keeping him from breathing properly. Dying of hunger was a horrendous death, locked up in a prison. It took him some interminable seconds to recover himself.

"A happy ending", he said as well as he could, with a hard voice trying to sound fearless.

Suddenly, the story of Count Ugolino crossed his mind. He remembered the horror—a truly extraordinary horror that lasted a long time—that he felt as a child on reading that tragedy from so many centuries before for the first time. Thinking of that, he was about to be overwhelmed a second time by dismay. And for the second time he overcame it with difficulty.

"Then that's why there are no prisoners from the Turin, that is, prisoners from before Christmas. Could it be they're all dead?" he asked.

"I see you're not very well informed", the chaplain answered. "This is a clearing-station camp close to the old front, even though they haven't sent anyone or almost anyone from here to their destination. But who knows how many other clearing-station camps and prisons there are?"

The lieutenant no longer spoke.

"We keep hoping these beasts without a conscience might finally feed us. God help us! We've been promised so often . . ."

"Ah, so they've promised! . . . " At that news, Michele felt irrationally happy, almost exalted within himself. "So, they don't make prisoners die of hunger as a matter of policy, a tactic."

"I can't tell you", the chaplain responded. "You've no idea of the suppositions we've made. But we'll talk about that later. You said they assigned you to my squadron?"

"Yes."

"Then it's better you come into the box."

"In all that darkness? Is there any room inside?"

"When we arrived, two weeks ago, twenty-seven of us were piled up in here. Now there are fifteen, fourteen, so you'll find room."

"But . . . perhaps I didn't see it well, but it seemed only space for a horse."

"That's right, it's four meters by four."

"And you were twenty-seven?"

"Yes. I'll light it up now, so we'll see and make room for you", the chaplain said.

"Wait", the lieutenant replied. "Tonight, no. Tomorrow." And he added bad humoredly, "When you realize I'm not a spy."

"I already know you're not", the chaplain murmured. "Listen, if I've offended you, forgive me. Here no one trusts anything or anybody, you realize that? Poor thing, what an inferno you must think you've fallen into! And I . . ."

"Let's not speak about it any more", Michele said.

"In the name of Christ, I beg your forgiveness."

"Thank you", Michele exclaimed, moved. "You've no idea how wonderful it is to hear the name of Christ in a place like this."

There was a pause. "I'm going to light it up a bit", the chaplain repeated. And he called out softly, "Ghiglione, eh, Ghiglione. Do you hear me?"

"No, wait", the lieutenant still objected. "Let it go. Tonight I'll sleep out here. The only difference is that inside there'll be a bit of straw."

"It isn't the only difference", Don Turla said. "The difference is dysentery, and not everyone manages to make it outside. Before tomorrow morning, the corridor where you are will be a sewer of bloody diarrhea."

"But . . . there are others who sleep in the corridor."

"No", Don Turla answered. "You're wrong. They don't sleep. Listen, let me do it." He had got on his knees, stretched over his neighbor, and moved to the officer who was farther on, "Eh, Ghiglione."

"What do you want?" the Alpine officer Ghiglione grumbled at last, raising himself onto one arm. "What's happening?"

"There's a new arrival. Give us some light, please."

"Someone new. Good."

The officer maneuvered about a while and at last lit a match and brought it to a rag he had in his hand, which began to burn with a feeble bluish flame.

"Come on, get in", Don Turla then said. Still on his knees, he looked around at the others stretched out. "There", he pointed out to the new arrival. "Over there, between Ghiglione and the other fellow. Come on, you two, make space where Don Caneva was."

There was a show of movement among the men stretched out. More than one head was raised. In that sepulchral light, Michele was beginning to see, after more than two months, Italian faces again, faces that were sunken, covered with grubby hair, with febrile eyes, but unmistakably Italian, similar to the ones he had beside him during the long nights on watch at the front. He felt an absurd sensation of having gone back home.

"Coming from the front?" Ghiglione asked him.

"Yes", Michele answered, as he settled into the place between him and his neighbor. "But they captured me before Christmas. I'm from the Turin Division."

"Do you know how things are going at the front?"

"No."

"Do you know if the Tridentina managed to get out of the blockade?" the man at his other side asked. "If they at least did get through?"

"The Tridentina blockaded? I know nothing. How long have you been here?"

"We're from the Cuneense, and we've been here two weeks. They had us march here from Valuiki, practically without food."

"Have you heard of Valuiki?" Ghiglione asked.

"No."

"It's at least 120 miles from the Don. That's as far as our column got."

"Listen, where you were before," another asked, "was there anyone from the Second Alpine Division?"

"Someone", asked another voice, "from Val Varaita?"

"And Val Maira?" another voice piped up. Everyone seemed to be talking in an extraordinarily slow fashion.

"No."

"No one from Cuneense, then."

"No. Are you all Alpine troops here?"

"The majority of us in this box, yes, from the Cuneense."

Another voice asked, "Did they feed you in your camp?"

"I wasn't in one. They had me isolated until today. That's why I know nothing about the others or the front. I'll explain tomorrow."

"But did they feed you?"

"Yes."

"Enough?"

"On some days, yes."

"Listen to that!"

"Incredible."

452

"It's, it's . . . mad."

"What did they give you to eat, you happy creature?"

Michele, meanwhile had settled onto the little straw covering the floor of the box, incredibly stubbly and filthy straw. The flame had finally consumed the rag Ghiglione had held up in the air until the last moment, and once it went out, they were again in the dark.

"Listen," he asked in a softer voice of Ghiglione, "the chaplain, the one . . . the one who had this spot where I am now . . ."

"Don Caneva, also one of the Alpine troops."

"What did he die of?"

"He didn't die. Yesterday they moved him to the box where the ones from Morbegno are, prisoners with him at Varvarovca. Since there was more free space there . . ."

"Ah."

"Listen," Don Turla intervened, already stretched out, "you'll talk tomorrow. Let's sleep now."

But Michele could not sleep the entire night. Squeezed between the bodies of his two neighbors, he chatted at first with them, then with the others, all stupefied with hunger. He learned that to get here from Valuiki these boys had had to walk for seventeen days: seventeen days, practically without eating. Of the three thousand already caved in with fatigue, which constituted the column at the beginning of the march, just over five hundred arrived, and the others died on the way. He began to realize the terrible fate the prisoners on this front had, and he grasped the vital importance, for him, of the unusual paper written by the strange Russian lieutenant at Arbusov, with his saint's face. At dawn, he was still awake, terribly tense and nervous.

3

When he went out in the morning, he was brought up to date on the situation in the camp, and the problem of food became for him, as the others, an obsession. The Russians up until then had distributed, every two or three days, a hundred-gram ration of bread per person among the officers. They also issued daily—but not at fixed hours, sometimes even at night—a pot of boiled, salty water, without any fat, containing potato peels and a few grains of millet floating in suspension. The soldiers were treated decidedly worse than the officers. In the course of two weeks the Russians had only twice distributed fifty grams of bread per person, and the broth was not given to the soldiers every day. As a result of this treatment, the soldiers (like the officers, not all of them Italian, but also Hungarian and Romanian, who had arrived at the camp exhausted by the terrible marches) would have all, without exception, been dead by now of hunger if they had not decided to eat human flesh. In general—a lieutenant

453

explained to Michele—they ate the liver and the heart of the dead men, less frequently the brains or one of the fleshier parts of the body. Thus, the episode of the first night could be explained: those two soldiers that fled from the heap of corpses were two cannibals who had come to collect food from the corpses of the officers, perhaps deeming them less undernourished.

In the face of such a situation, what could Michele do? Pull his hair out, hurl screams into space, wallow in the snow at the horror of it all? Of what possible use would that be? "I've come to a great place", he would repeat, like an automaton, walking with his hands sunk in his pockets, back and forth across the vast yard, yellow with urine and covered with human excrement and nude cadavers. "Truly, a great place!"

He walked for a long time, bowed down with anguish. At last he calmed down a little and decided to visit the soldiers' area, too—while he was still able to control himself—in order to explore all he could of this horrendous reality. He went toward it with slow strides. From the yard of the stables reserved for the officers, he entered the soldiers' zone, where they were lodged in big stables constructed as a continuation of the first ones, as well as in a group of half-ruined barracks, which in other times had been destined for horses. Surrounding the camp buildings stretched an immense forest, white with frost.

In the courtyards of the soldiers' area, the dead were even more numerous. Hundreds could be seen, all without clothes, isolated or piled up here and there between filth and excrement. The traces of cannibalism were even more evident. Many of the bruised and skeletal bodies were opened, gutted, over the ice; spread about were viscera and even an occasional decapitated body.

Michele could not avoid visualizing the soldiers—in groups of two or three—carrying off a head and then in secret breaking it open with a stone and taking out the brain. Struck by the horror, he closed his eyes and imagined his own head carried off in this way; he could even see it crushed by the blows from the stone, until it opened and the brain poured out. He was overcome by a wave of nausea and a desire to go back, to flee and snuggle into his refuge among still-living creatures. But even among the barracks he was walking toward there were still-living human beings; perhaps there were among them some of the soldiers with whom he had shared his life at the front. *Such times these are, such times, dear God!* Did he want to flee them? No, he had to go on, continue forward. He managed to do so, while slowly muttering some prayers for those wretched dead, as if to fortify himself.

In the area around the barracks, behind the stables, a few soldiers could be seen outside, a Hungarian or two with their long, ruined pepper-colored overcoats, Romanians with caps made of horsehair on their heads, and Italians in their short fur-lined tunics.

One of them—short, slightly hunched, with a dark mustache and a shaggy beard on his cheeks—was coming toward Michele along the same path, holding his hands behind his back. When he was in front of him, he stopped and looked at his face; the lieutenant noticed his slightly twisted nose, his mild expression.

"I think they'll be giving out the broth in a little while, don't you, Lieutenant?" the small soldier remarked. He seemed to be hoping for some sort of confirmation. For an instant his looks took on something of the supplicant. His hair, under the cap with the insignia of his outfit on it, was black and curly.

"We can't be sure," the officer replied compassionately, "but I think so, too."

"That's why", the soldier began (he stuttered a bit), "that's why I've come out with this." He brought his hands to his chest. He had a metal can in his right one.

There was a pause, Michele smiled feelingly. "Things are pretty grim here, aren't they?"

"Grim!" the soldier sighed, as his eyes suddenly reddened.

"Where are you from?" the officer asked affably.

The other fellow rubbed his hand across his face slowly, then shook his head and mentioned a place "in the Pavia district. I'm a day worker at home." And then, after a brief pause, "In the sappers corps, here, and at home, a sapper without any corps." It must have been some kind of joke, and heaven knows how many times it was repeated on different days. "And you, where are you from?" he wanted to know.

"I'm from Nova, in the Monza district."

"Then we're practically fellow countrymen, from Lombardy."

"Yes," the officer agreed, "almost."

There was another pause.

"I wonder what could be happening now at home, don't you, Lieutenant?"

"We really should be worrying about what's happening here", Michele answered in dialect, looking around without any special reason.

The soldier looked in the direction in which the officer's hand, covered in a cloth glove, had stopped for a second: there, a few yards from the two of them, was—most hideous vision—a naked corpse, his body opened from his throat to his navel.

"I've only done it twice", the soldier exclaimed, also in dialect. "I swear it, on my child's head. I've only done it twice, when I was mad with hunger. If I hadn't, I'd have been dead by now", he stammered.

"But what are you talking about? I wasn't referring to . . . to that", Michele murmured, embarrassed.

"If only they gave us a little to eat", the soldier moaned. "You can't live without eating, impossible. But, Lieutenant," stammering now more than he had before, "I've never done it to someone living, about to die, that is, like some of them, because it's too much trouble to open frozen flesh with a penknife. I never did it to someone living, or to those recently dead either. Fresh blood I've never drunk, never!" he almost screamed.

455

"Calm down", the lieutenant told him. "Try to calm down. I wasn't talking about that, and I'm not blaming you. What right would I have to? Come on, calm down."

But the small soldier, with his tin in his right hand, rubbed his hands on his forehead and, altogether hunched up, went on screaming, prey to an uncontrollable agitation.

Michele no longer knew what to say or do to calm him; some confused screams made him turn around. Some trucks escorted by armed guards were about to enter the barracks zone, carrying metal containers from which a heavy vapor rose.

"Ah, it's the broth", he pointed out to the soldier. "Come along, perk up, the broth."

He lifted his head as if electrified.

"You see? You said it, and you were right", Michele said, going back to Italian. "Soup's on!"

The other fellow did not so much as hear him. He turned his reddened eyes fixedly on the trucks, then the barracks, from which other prisoners were coming out from one minute to the next. Then he raised his tin can toward the sky, took a few hurried steps to the trucks, stopped, turned back, stopped again to look at the metal receptacles coming in, an expression of mad anxiety on his face, then, almost running, he headed toward his own barracks from where other soldiers were beginning to come out, their voices raised. Then he stopped once more at a certain distance from the barracks, turned toward the trucks, his tin can again raised. The others rushed to line up behind him; they were mainly Italians, but also Romanians and Hungarians, equally filthy.

Other disordered rows began to line up in front of other barracks or groups of barracks. Hearing the shout "the soup, the soup", the prisoners who had been lying inert and listless on the straw and filth woke from their lethargy. Opening their eyes, and with canteens, a variety of tins, canteen lids, they abandoned their shelters and rushed outside to the food. A small part—not Hungarians, but Romanians and Italians especially—instead of lining up ran straight to the trucks, from where they were thrown out by the armed guards, who pointed their long and fearfully sharp bayonets fixed in their guns at their chests. Meanwhile, prisoners kept coming out of their refuges, some dragging themselves on all fours over the snow. If they were already incapable of walking, they got to the lines helped by a fellow comrade, who carried their tins for them; cases like these—though rare enough—showed that some vestiges of ancient solidarity had not disappeared. Quite the contrary, it had become more heroic.

Michele—after having checked, with egotistical vexation, that no truck had gone to the officers' stables—decided to take advantage of the occasion to have a close look at the soldiers. They were very skinny, some like specters. They had all lost dozens of pounds of weight. The canteens with their lids they held in their hands were in general blacked by fire because their horrendous meals had been cooked in them. (Michele remembered having seen other canteens, just as black, in the officers' refuges, too.) The rows went on forming, more and more like traffic jams than rows, especially after the metal receptacles (gasoline drums cut in two) were taken from the trucks, one at the head of each row. The cooks and prisoner helpmates were shouting for them to get into order, hitting out at those who came too close, using their heavy iron ladles. They pushed them against their chests and also against their faces to keep them back.

The lieutenant stopped near the row with the small soldier from Pavia, who, his tin still in his right hand, his heels dug into the snow, braced himself to keep back the others pushing against him. A small group of those who had been turned back from the trucks tried to force themselves into the row a little behind him: the entire row shouted, vociferously, pushed, until something terrible happened. Michele clearly saw the small soldier fall, after being given an unusually big shove, into the receptacle, head first into the boiling soup. His shouts, confused with the others, could not be distinguished. Then he saw his legs wave in the air for a few instants and finally fall flabbily over.

He rushed toward him and, together with those closest, pulled him out by his legs and tunic. The soldier remained in his arms, his head reclining, and his tin on the ground between the overturned boiling soup, both soup and vapor reeking from his clothes and his black hair, pulled slack, no longer curly. "You scum!" the lieutenant screamed at those around him. "You damn wild beasts!" he screamed again, as if crazed, at the Romanian cooks. And they were yelling back, "Out! Out!" as they made signs with their ladles. They were there to dish out the food. In fact, only the first ones in line had really known what had happened and were struck dumb, while the others kept on pushing and screaming. The officer got control of himself as he held the small soldier, his head reclining, and stepped back a few paces.

"Who will help me take him back to the barracks?" he asked in a changed voice. "Well, who'll help?"

"I'll do it", someone behind him responded.

Michele turned: it was a bearded chaplain wearing an Alpine hat. He looked exhausted and must have just come from the barracks, along with the last soldiers.

"You think you can?"

"Yes."

"Well, let's go, then", Michele said. "Take him by his feet."

"Yes", the other sighed.

They carried the unconscious man into the barracks. He did not weigh much, and his clothes continued to drip soup.

"Here", the fatigued chaplain said, pointing to a spot with his chin. "This place must be his. He's from Pavia, isn't he?"

457

"Yes, from the province of Pavia."

After having arranged the man between rags, "I never saw you before", the chaplain panted.

"I arrived last night. What's your name?"

"Father Norberto Fiora, a Capuchin monk."

He was skin and bones and as worn out as the others. His face was flushed by this latest effort.

Michele told him his name and, pointing to the unconscious soldier, said, "Do you think he'll come out of this?"

"No", the chaplain answered, closing his eyes for an instant. "No, he's too scalded."

"You know about these things?"

The other gestured that he did. "I was with the medical division of the Julia."

"Then what can we do?"

"What can we do?" the chaplain repeated. "I'll wait until he comes to in order to absolve him. Of course, when he awakes he'll scream with all his might out of pain. I've seen people burned with flame throwers. Some morphine would be of use, but . . ."

He sat down on the rags and junk next to the unconscious man, took off his Alpine hat and put it on his knees. Then he looked at the lieutenant, perhaps hoping he would also sit down to wait.

But he did not feel up to this. "Don't think I'm a coward", he said. "I'm going back to the officers' barracks. I arrived last night and . . ." He shook his head and said no more.

The chaplain assented. "Yes, of course, you have to get used to this. Later, strong as you are, you'll see how much you'll be able to help."

"Me? Who knows. Well, bless me, Father", the young man said. "Even better, absolve me, too." He got on his knees and took off his cap.

Without rising from his place on the rags, the Capuchin monk raised his right hand, murmured in Latin, and made the sign of the Cross. Michele then noticed his thin neck, short hair, sparse beard, and light, childlike eyes. He was reminded of the Capuchins who nursed the plague-stricken victims in Manzoni's novel.

"Say, you know you look like Saint Francis", he observed after getting to his feet. "What did you say your name was?"

"Father Fiora."

"Goodbye, Father Fiora." He put on his cap and saluted him militarily, then turned and went out of the barracks.

Outside, the horror went on in front of the stockpot. There were even individuals on the ground, stretched between other people's feet, who were sucking up the soup that had fallen into the mud. Without stopping, the lieutenant went to his own quarters.

458

He saw from a distance, inside the courtyard of the stables, the Italian commissar who had accompanied him to this hideous place. *He must have finished his marvelous meal* ... Wearing a black leather jacket, the commissar was walking—a severe air about him—with two Russian officers, to whom he was pointing out something with his gloved hand. *Just look at him, he who's saved civilization from fascism. Who knows what on earth he could be talking about with those other champions.*

4

Once inside his stable he decided to put off the idea—which had been smoldering within him since morning—of exploring the long inner corridor scattered with cadavers and feces, and he got into the box in his squadron, where all the others, so as not to waste their energy, were stretched out on bits and pieces of straw.

He got into his place between the lieutenants Ghiglione and Dal Toso and answered some questions in an effort to join in the conversation, slow and fragmentary as it was. But after a short time he could no longer manage to speak. The things he had seen were churning up inside him, hurling shrieks inside, until he could hardly follow what the others were saying.

"Are there any medical officers in the camp?" he suddenly asked, anguished by the thought of the small scalded soldier. (*By now, maybe he's regained consciousness, and he's screaming with pain. Day worker, sapper corps, sapper without corps at home ... my lieutenant? Oh, you poor little man!*)

"Of course, there are medical officers in camp," Ghiglione answered, "and some are kept quite busy. For example here, two boxes down from us, is Giannetto from Messina. But you see the situation yourself."

"The doctors have figured out that if things go the way they've been going, we in the Cuneense have, on the average, fifteen days to live", Dal Toso said. "They say some of the less undernourished may last a month."

"How many prisoners in all are there in the camp?"

"No one knows. Some say twenty, others thirty thousand, but no one knows. New people arrive from time to time, now almost only Hungarians."

"There are five hundred dead daily, that we know, because up until three days ago, we carried them out every morning with a sledge and carts from the camp and dumped them into a big water pit."

"Without burying them?"

"Of course. How would you be able to dig up frozen earth? Just dumping them in the pit is already terribly tiring. You'd have to see the place. It's filled to the top with bodies. Who knows how many thousands there are?"

"We no longer have the strength to carry them in the carts. The Russian command insisted at first. Then they let it go. Besides, they don't care."

"But if we don't take them out," Michele remarked, horrified, "this camp will become a tomb for the living and the dead mixed together. Something frightful!"

"Isn't it already?"

"Listen here", the lieutenant said, sitting down, so excited he could no longer manage to control the movements of his mouth. "Why, since there's no way out, don't we ask that they shoot us all?"

"Who told you we haven't asked already? If you want to know, we have. Together we delegated Colonel Scrimin, who is the Second Alpine Unit Commander, to make the request. The Russian commander—also a colonel—received him, and do you know what the answer was? Simply that he was not authorized to shoot us. Scrimin then asked them to let us harvest the potatoes from the fields on the other side of the pit of the dead. The peasants over there, because of the disorder in Russia or perhaps because of the closeness of the front, I don't know, haven't harvested them yet, and with the thaw they'll all be of no use. You know what the Russian commander did? He burst into laughter, told Scrimin that this would constitute individual initiative in Russia and so was inconceivable, more or less like that. Then he told him not to get himself involved in these messes, that supplies would be arriving."

"Yes, the Russians always say that", someone sighed. "And yet they let us die, not because they are sadists, but rather not to give other Russians the impression that they're in cahoots with the enemy."

"It's not only that. By nature they pretend not to know anything, and they're also slothful."

"And besides, the fact is their own life is so miserable, they place no importance on it. So you can see how much regard they're going to have for ours."

Their gloomy conversation was interrupted by the return of the *nacialniki*, or squadron leader, Don Turla, who had been called away to give the last religious rites in another box to someone dying. "Come on", he announced at the door. "It's time to remove the dead and clean up the corridor." He looked at Michele. "You'll be of great help to us, strong as you are." Then he turned to the other three. "Massobrio, Francescone, Torsegno, today it's your turn. Come along."

The first ones called got into a sitting position and then onto their knees and finally onto their feet; they were in a deplorable state.

"Cheer up", Don Turla said. "Take the belts."

He went himself to take some trouser belts from a hook (Who would they have belonged to?) and left the box with the four of them. They started their thankless tasks; then they slipped the belts around the ankles of the cadavers (most of them had been taken out of the box and into the corridor, but some were still inside), and, with two to three men per body, they slowly dragged them along the ground covered with feces, urine, and bloody diarrhea to the outdoors. Seeing their example, another squadron or two—not many—and a few isolated individuals came out from some of the other boxes and got down to work.

In the afternoon they were made to feel the beneficial effect of the visit from the Italian commissar: not for the purpose of distributing food, that no, but to gather together the *nacialniki* to make them immediately form anticannibalism squadrons, which would be headed, as coordinator, by the energetic Captain Fortunato Amico of the Cuneense Division.

The squadrons—it was explained—would have to take turns watching and would be armed with iron bars and clubs. "Because only some good swift blows, dealt out unmercifully, would put an end to cannibalism", the commissar explained. He seemed well up on the subject. Don Turla, who was listening to him with the other *nacialniki*, became distressed. What did this mean? Were these horrors occurring in other camps, too? He tried to quiet himself by telling himself it wasn't that way; it wasn't possible. Perhaps the commissar had participated in the struggle to get the peasants into collectivization. Everyone knew that in those circumstances—ten years before—hunger had provoked cases of cannibalism in Ukrainian villages.

"Cannibals caught red handed", the Russian commanding colonel interposed, "will be handed over to the guardhouse and shot immediately." Heavy, well fed, he spoke of shooting men down with aplomb. He did not figure that soon, very soon—given Communist practice at that time—his turn to be shot down would come.

The squadron chief proposed and obtained permission to finish carrying out the evacuation of the dead from the camp, something that would be done by the recently arrived men, still not completely worn to a frazzle by hunger. The occupation took the entire day, using the same carts employed for transporting the metal soup receptacles.

5

On the second day after his arrival, Michele—worn out (after having helped the colleagues from his box in carrying out bodies, he had taken over the cleaning by himself and even accompanied and held some of the weakest while they defecated)—lay as still as the others on the straw, his eyes closed. He had been given only one hundred grams of black bread during those two days. No one spoke. Despite the continuing terrible cold, Don Turla had taken off his tunic and rolled up his jacket sleeves and was slowly rubbing one arm, which had become frostbitten, with a woolen rag.

Suddenly the door of the stable was opened wide, and, like a madman, one of the Alpine troops burst into the corridor. "Father! Where's Father Turla?" he shouted.

"I'm here", the chaplain answered. "Over here."

The soldier rushed to the box and grasped the bar. He looked very emaciated and yelled, "Father, come, come immediately. They want to eat my cousin."

The chaplain looked at him for an instant in silence, then put his clothes back on and said, "I'm coming."

"I'll go with you", Michele told the priest, also getting up.

They followed the Alpine trooper quickly. "The sight of blood made them lose their heads. They've gone mad", he recounted in the dialect of Brescia. "A guard shot my cousin, damn it all", he related in bits and pieces. "While coming back from moving the bodies he saw some junk on the other side of the street. 'Potatoes, pieces of potatoes', he said . . . For days he's been seeing potatoes on all sides. I didn't have time to hold him back, and hardly out of line, a guard shot him, the swine, practically destroying one of his legs. We put him on a cart. But with all that blood . . . Oh, Father!"

"Where is he now?"

"He's shut into the stable. Two countrymen from Val Camonica are guarding him."

"And how many are there who want . . . who want to eat him?"

"Four, four of them."

They entered the nearest stable, not subdivided into boxes but into enclosed stables. A streak of freshly flowing blood led them to the wounded man. Against the battered door were four soldiers pushing away insistently. They were trying to open it with a tree trunk directed against it.

"There they are, you see?" the Alpine trooper said.

They did not so much as look at who was coming, as if they did not exist. They seemed not to see, hear, or think about more than one thing: the red blood, the meat, the fresh viscera ready and waiting behind the door.

Running toward them, the lieutenant shouted, "You, over there, what are you doing? Have you all gone mad? Stop it, stop it!"

"Stop it!" Don Turla also repeated, running up.

The two men on the other side of the door were pressing hard to prevent the others opening it up, and, they too, from the sound of their voices, seemed to have gone a bit mad.

"Boys, boys, listen to me!" the priest said, addressing the four outside with great seriousness. "Do you realize what you're doing? Do you want to kill a man, a miserable creature, like yourselves, to drink his blood? It's monstrous. Try to think."

"And if I should kill one of you, how about that?" the Alpine trooper screamed. "And I swear if you . . . I'll . . ." The priest stopped him with a gesture. "Calm down", he told him.

"Yes, do", Michele repeated.

The emaciated fellow lowered his hands that had been raised like claws.

Nothing seemed to influence those four infuriated men. They continued dead set in their project, like men obsessed. "Push", they were telling one another, snorting. "Push hard, with the point . . . get the trunk here, here I say—come on, push."

Don Turla, crouching down, got in between the four attacking the door and stood up facing them, his back against the door. Michele put his right hand on the trunk they were maneuvering, ready to hold it back. At least he would not let them use it as a weapon. "Try to reason a bit", the chaplain told them in a voice trying hard to be calm.

The four of them stopped at this point. One of them had his face practically against that of the priest's. "Ah, what do you want?" he said confusedly, looking at him with murky eyes.

"I want to speak to you", Don Turla replied. "I'm a chaplain, and I've come here to talk to you."

"A chaplain?" He opened and closed his eyes several times. "A what . . . oh?" He seemed not to understand as he swayed perceptibly, weakened by hunger.

"Yes, a chaplain", Father Turla repeated. "Don't you want to talk to the chaplain, boys?"

They did not answer him, but the four of them now looked at him out of queer eyes.

"Your home in Italy", the priest said. "Your mother. Don't you think about that?" He turned to the one who was face to face with him. "Your mother. Where would your mother be right now? What would she be doing? Tell me. Your mother. Your mother."

The other fellow kept looking at him, his snout raised, backed away a bit, opened and closed his eyes repeatedly, began to breathe hard. "My mother . . .", he snorted.

It seemed that slowly, very slowly, a tiny flame of reflection was beginning to illuminate them.

The others on the opposite side of the door were keeping it blocked, and every so often, they pushed against it still, continuing their furious talk, not understanding what was happening on the other side.

The chaplain looked from one to the other of the four outside, wondering if they were really coming to their senses. He had the four of them in front of him, but they were no longer behaving so aggressively.

He went back to talking, speaking directly to one or the other; he talked about their villages, their far-off homes, their mothers. Then he began to talk of God, of impiety, of what—in the face of God—they, driven by their hideous hunger, had been on the point of doing. He was feeling exhausted (from being famished, from the rheumatic pain in his arm, and now, from all this emotional upset). One of the four, perhaps the least rough among them, came to some realization, suddenly took the priest's right hand, knelt, and kissed it.

The chaplain leaned over to embrace him, as the other three stepped back a bit. "Stand up", the priest told the kneeling man. "Stand up", and he stroked his face, which was bathed in tears.

At this point the Alpine trooper beat against the door hard, calling out the names of those on the other side. "Open up, open up, the chaplain's here", he said in the dialect of Val Camonica. It was hard to make them understand.

Finally the door was opened. Preceded by the Alpine trooper, Father Turla and Michele were able to enter. The other four remained outside, stupefied and still half stunned, at the edge of the door.

There were about twenty soldiers in the stable, and only two of them were standing next to the door, quite excited. The others seemed apathetic. Exhausted, depleted, they were stretched out on the ground, and inside the manger in the shadowy coldness, they were reminiscent of a group of ghosts who, prostrate and inert, were ruminating on their own personal anguish, untranslatable into words.

The wounded man—to whom his cousin immediately went—was conscious; he had followed, one could imagine with terror, the efforts of his two countrymen in keeping out the blood drinkers. Don Turla bent over him and tried to comfort him, repeating that there was no longer any danger now. The other fellow asked to be confessed. He was very weak, and most surely not more than a few hours of life remained to him. The cousin moved away, and the priest confessed and absolved the dying man.

Then, standing up, he turned to the others and, in a sad voice, reproached them for their past indifference. The ghosts looked at him, stunned. With words perhaps a bit improper—suited to his mountain background—but also with the highest authority of being the mouthpiece of God, Don Turla recalled them of their destiny as men, their incomparable dignity. Then he invited them to recite the act of contrition together: he would absolve them, he said, collectively, with the absolution *in articulo mortis*, which is given on the battlefield. Some of the specters got to their knees at Don Turla's invitation, and also the four wretches who were still at the door came in and, bumping into one another in the little space there was, knelt on the ground. Uncertain voices accompanied the chaplain's voice, word by word, in the prayer of repentance.

6

Several days later, Michele, overcoming his own revulsion with an immense effort, decided to go on with the exploration of the camp. He left the officers' zone and, in a pensive state, went to the sector in which, according to what he was told by the colleagues in his box, the Russians had never, or almost never, handed out food rations. "And there are people there who arrived ten or fifteen days before us." If things were really that way, the lieutenant wondered, how could those poor wretches still be alive?

By chance he entered one of the stables of that sector, externally the same as the others. The inside, semiobscure, was not subdivided as he expected into

464

boxes or smaller stables but instead formed one very long single hall. And in it, to his amazement, the prisoners (there were from three hundred to five hundred, according to his rough guess made on the spot) were all seated on the floor, in almost orderly files. A first row was seated against one of the larger walls; in front of them a second row was seated that in some way rested against the first; then there were more, each one supported by the one behind it. Between the seated soldiers—all Italian—and the wall in front was a passageway that the lieutenant entered, crossing through a stench of putrefaction that was positively maddening.

From his first steps he had the feeling that, in the relative silence of the place, all or almost all the soldiers he was walking by were looking at him. While he proceeded, step after uncertain step, he began to scrutinize the rows of worn faces, to see if there was not someone there known to him; and many of those young men, as if magnetized, accompanied his steps with a slow movement of their heads. Who knows if they weren't raving mad! But not all of them—he realized—were really looking at him. Even if their eyes were open, more than a few were dead. There were also dead men with their eyes closed, and some with their mouths open. How many dead were there? After a glance around him, the officer judged that—perhaps a third of the men seated on the ground were already corpses. He stopped. He would have liked to speak, but his tongue had become paralyzed, it seemed.

One of them, without a cap, against the free wall, pulled himself up with difficulty, from his knees to his feet, and came toward him in slow strides. He was wearing the insignia of a sergeant. His eyes were closed, but he opened them imperceptibly now and then. "The bread's about to arrive, isn't it?" he said when he was in front of the officer.

"The ... the what?" Michele stammered out.

"The bread. We're waiting for it because we know it has to come."

Instead of answering him, the officer looked at him squarely for an instant. "You ... who are you?" he asked, speaking laboriously.

"Sergeant B., from the Fifth Alpine Division. Barrack room chief."

"How come in this barracks you're all in rows, this way?"

"It's a question of order. The Italian commissar was here yesterday, and he told us if we stopped being cannibals and were quiet, the Russians would feed us. And I convinced all of them, you see? We got all the dead out, and the ...", and his two hands gestured as if he were opening his chest, "we've made them disappear."

"Disappear?"

The other fellow assented, winking wisely, and nodded upward, his eyes closed, to a slit in the ceiling, from where four stiff legs hung out.

"You hid them up there ... open?"

The sergeant nodded affirmation. "So now they'll have to feed us."

"The Italian commissar was not here yesterday. It was three days ago", the officer murmured, puzzled.

465

"What?" the other fellow asked, not having understood.

The officer did not repeat the phrase, suddenly realizing that it would plunge these poor wretches into a state of despair.

"Were they all alive when you made them sit down like this?"

The sergeant, his eyes half closed, gestured positively.

So, in hardly three days, a third have died, the lieutenant estimated. He felt permeated with a welling up of terror. *Here no one will be saved . . . we'll all die,* he told himself. *There's no other way. Each and every one! All of us!* He could think of nothing else. He made a gesture to the sergeant that was meant to be a salute, and without trying to utter a single word more, he turned to the door. As he walked through the stench that took his breath away, the mute looks of the soldiers seated on the floor followed his footsteps.

Once again outside, the officer ran breathlessly back to his quarters and curled up in silence in the box between the others in his squadron.

From that day on, he did not go out exploring and decided to devote his day to resting, to avoid expending energy, to surviving. He was ashamed of that decision and his capacity for incredibly merciless egotism, which he was discovering in himself, but the terror of seeing himself reduced to a subhuman state, of dying of hunger like some of those he had talked to the night of his arrival, was too much for his sense of duty and dignity.

He stayed in Crinovaya a few days more, during which time he received, like the other officers, one hundred grams of blackish bread. He ate it very, very slowly, keeping his mind off those soldiers in the large hall, who most surely were there, alive and dead, seated all together waiting for their bread.

7

On the fourth of March 1943, the Italian survivors were taken by train from Crinovaya to camps in the interior: the ordinary soldiers to Siberia, and the officers—numbering 438—to the Volga zone.

In the course of the trip, which lasted eight days (eight terrible days to cover less than six hundred miles), the officers were given daily a thin bread roll and also some dried fish, but most of the time they were not provided with drinking water, and in some of the cars not even once.

"At the stations there is water", they went on telling each other, and every one told himself, *Why do they give us bread, even fish, and no water?* It was the same old story: the train guards (they were not the same ones from the camp) wanted to show the many spies scattered among them that they were not being soft with the enemies of communism. For each and every Russian guard, this was a necessity, which they carried out all the more willingly since it took less effort. The guards even exchanged jokes of this type: "They eat our dried fish; let them at least pay a little for it in thirst."

The torture of thirst is still more tormenting than that of hunger; the prisoners began to lick the frost that formed on the inner walls of the trains, in particular the iron screws. During the interminably long stops they screamed and screamed all together for hours to be allowed out to gather up some snow, but always without any effect. They were dying in still greater numbers: in the morning when the bread and fish were passed out they would open the cars, the bodies piled up next to the doors to be thrown out, but not a living soul was allowed out.

Curled up among the others, Michele became more and more terrorized. The experience of those days of siege had seemed unmatchable in its atrocity. Then there was the incomparably more atrocious experience of Crinovaya, and now this, death by thirst, locked in freezing trains. How many centuries had it been, he wondered, since the Italians had suffered such barbarous treatment? To find something like it, one would have to go very far back, perhaps to the time of the Turks, and perhaps that was not far enough. Back to the wars against non-Christians, in any event. But wasn't it he who had looked for this experience in an un-Christian country? Had he not done everything possible to come here, not caring about anything else, not even the suffering that this would cause his father? Now he was here, all right, living out this experience.

Every car had, in a corner, a hole, filthy with sticky manure, which served as a toilet. Through that opening the prisoners managed to force some tins to get snow from the track bed, and, more and more filthy, they did, as it turned out, get a little. In Michele's car, it was the only drink available during the entire trip, which lasted eight days.

On the twelfth of March at the station where they arrived, their prison keepers counted them; out of 438, only 195 were alive, so more than half had died. They were lined up in columns and made to go on foot—not an easy project for people so enervated—to camp 74 at Oranchi, five miles from the station, in which there were already a few hundred Italian officers. The camp—Michele noticed on entering—was a former convent for monks. Like the clarist stables at Crinovaya, this convent, before being used as a prisoner-of-war camp, had functioned as a place of reclusion for deported Russian civilians.

At the end of April the medical lieutenant De Ponti and the Russian interpreter Sergeant Malerbi arrived from Crinovaya. They both reported that with the thaw, the pit in which the dead had been heaped up (about twenty-seven thousand according to the Russian high command's estimate) was spreading a stench that permeated the air for miles around, making it unbreathable for the civilian population of Crinovaya. At the beginning, the Russians, using military trucks, transported earth to the pit, but to no avail. Then they abandoned the camp slaughterhouse and enclosed it with barbed wire, especially at the

467

points of access and at the spot that led to the pit of the twenty-seven thousand cadavers, where they had placed sentries to keep anyone from entering.

8

Much later, after having spoken with prisoners who had gone through the most diverse experiences, Michele and others were in a position—as has already been said—of estimating the losses suffered by their fellow countrymen during the terrible *davai* marches, subsequent to capture; on the average, the figure came to four out of ten. About four out of ten of the survivors had died, too (approximately, then, 25 percent of those captured), in the trains taking them to the camps. Of those who finally arrived at the camps, it was also about four out of ten (15 percent of those captured) who died during the month of April, not only from hunger or fatigue but from an exanthematous typhus epidemic that spread everywhere. At the end of April 1943, only 20 percent of the captured Italians were alive, and even the possibility of survival for them was minimal, because—despite their having stopped the epidemics (thanks to the efforts of the prisoner doctors)—mortality was high due to the always inadequate diet.

That is how things stood at the end of April when an unexpected event occurred: an order from the NKVD—the omnipotent political police on which camps of every type depended—had ordered, from one day to the next, that the prisoners of war be sufficiently fed. Mortality figures declined suddenly; gradually the men, practically all of them reduced to human shadows, began to revive.

There was a great deal of conjecturing in the Oranchi camp about this miraculous order. Stalin *pricàs* (an order from Stalin), as it was called. According to some it was due to an imaginary threat from Hitler to let, by way of a reply, all the Russian, English, and American prisoners in his hands die of hunger. This conjecture was easily overturned by anyone who had observed that Hitler did not care a whit about his own soldiers taken prisoner. Rather he denied the existence of prisoners. As for Stalin, much the same, his own Russian soldiers taken prisoner meant nothing to him. They all still remembered that those employed by us during the war working on fortifications had great fear of being liberated by the Red army because—just for having been taken prisoner—they were regarded and judged deserters. (And so, after the war, the repatriated Russian prisoners—even if they had fought with the partisans against the Nazis—were deported by the NKVD.)

(*Author's note:* On this date—the end of April 1943—the Italian prisoners of war in the Soviet camps came to about 10,500 [as could be reconstructed later from the number of those repatriated, which came to 10,030]. It can be deduced from these facts that the Italians captured by the Russians [not counting

468

the injured, unable to walk, the dead, or those left to die in the snow at the time of being taken] must have totaled between fifty thousand and sixty thousand, and not more than one hundred thousand as was generally thought at the time in the camps and in Italy, based on the triumphant news then being broadcast by Radio Moscow. The approximated number of fifty-five thousand captured [of whom 10,030 were repatriated and forty-five thousand died in prison] agrees with the overall figure published several years later by the Ministry of Defense [74,800 total dead in battle and in prison].)

It must have been something else that caused the Stalin *pricàs*, but what? Only a few prisoners guessed the true cause as being the necessity of Communist propaganda, and they were right. In the spring of '43—they argued—the Bolsheviks were presented with the possibility of winning the war, and so their old project of extending communism all over Europe was brought up to date, revived. And if no prisoners returned from the war, it would have represented a strong deterrent in their propaganda program.

The greater number of survivors, however, continued believing it impossible that the Russians—so backward in everything—could win the war. As for the extension of communism, after having experienced Russian barbarity, they refused to take it into consideration. The discussions went on for months, kept alive by the news discreetly communicated by a Hungarian commissar to his prisoner compatriots, that the Russian commander at the Crinovaya camp had been duly executed for his negligence regarding orders about cannibalism.

Michele also joined in those discussions, after having gone through a bout of typhus, at the point of dying, but now slowly recuperating.

As food, still scarce, was kept within the necessary limits for subsistence, in May he began to harbor timid hopes—like the others—of surviving. So much more when their food was enhanced by a small bit of protein every day—of incalculable value, as the prisoner doctors explained—derived from the soybeans sent to Russia by the Americans for war prisoners.

This particular detail of soybeans struck Michele as extraordinarily comforting. *So the Americans are thinking about us*, he would tell himself at times, stunned with emotion. He would try to explain to himself why. How was it possible that these foreigners, especially enemies, could be interested in mere leftovers of men, like himself and his comrades, if they weren't civilized and humanitarian? *So, at least the Americans have managed to remain human*, he argued. *They at least have conserved the civilization that Christianity has built up over centuries: they've not lost it as other countries, in the vanguard of modernity today, have done, such as Germany and Russia. They should be blessed a thousand times over!* (It should come as no surprise that the young man was interpreting his present extraordinary experiences on the basis of a time-honored reasoning: after what he had lived through in the Nazi and Communist world, his Christian vision of history had been strongly confirmed, and it appeared to him even better founded and convincing than before.

469

With the arrival of good weather the lieutenant had still other experiences. The Communist commissars got busy with the unfortunate prisoners—incapable of reacting because of their state of starvation—and set to work trying to influence and change their thinking. In Michele's view—as he had not the slightest fear of being converted—it was something of an aberration and, at the same time, an interesting experience, which he made no attempt to escape, intending to take advantage of it—if perhaps he ever returned home—to help his countrymen defend themselves from communism. On the other hand, the large majority tried to avoid it; they were physically compelled to be present at the so-called lessons in antifascism but refused to listen or pay any attention whatsoever, even accidently.

The prisoners, however, not only had to withstand the systematic hammering of propaganda, they also had to go out daily in squadrons to work in the fields, thereby discovering—in a wave of emotion—that in the vast forest region of Oranchi there was not just their camp 74 for prisoners of war but dozens more, full of deported Russian civilians. Several times Michele's squadron had to pass by these camps, especially those close by, entirely reserved (so they were told) for intellectuals: professors, schoolteachers, journalists, artists, writers, and specialized workers. Despite strict prohibitions, the Italian military people managed to exchange some words with them. They were Michele's first encounters with the universe of Communist totalitarianism, whose immense extension he did not clearly realize at that time. Beyond the spontaneous feeling of compassion he felt for those filthy and famished deportees (suffering is truly beyond any limits among the Russian people), the young man noticed, no matter how confusedly, that this reality had to be correlated with Communist ideology, the same that the instructors were trying to force into the prisoners' heads. This fact, little by little, further increased his desire to grasp the true, the terrible mechanism of that ideology.

Meanwhile, the months went by, and he was still alive. The war went on, and he was not dead.

And as Ambrogio from time to time thought of him, so he—especially at the end of his long useless days, stretched out on his cot—occasionally thought of Ambrogio. Would he have managed to get out of Arbusov and then later the siege, injured that way? And what would he be doing now? What would be happening in Nomana, where that strange and attractive creature lived, the silent Almina? For a long time now, from among all the girls Michele had met in his life (not many, really), Almina, Ambrogio's second sister, had been coming to his mind more frequently than any other. He saw her in his imagination, which had again begun to light up, the slim figure, that pretty face—for all appearances, indifferent—with its clear eyes, her chestnut hair, and gestures that seemed merely tentative (*even the last time at Nomana, while running in her games . . .*). Between Almina and the surrounding reality there seemed to be a kind of rupture, a caesura. What did her brothers call her? Little marble statue.

470

She really is that. What an interesting creature . . . but that's how Almina was when I left, he occasionally reminded himself, turning over on his hard plank bed. *But today?* When he saw her last, Alma had been fifteen; perhaps she was no longer the same, maybe completely changed.

And as for the rest, how many other things would have changed in Italy? His mutilated father, how would he be? His father! Already crucified in another war, with his spine broken . . . Michele often thought about him. How would he have withstood the complete lack of news from his son, the one good thing and only interest left to him?

PART THREE

I

At that time in Piacenza, Manno found himself without much to do. In the afternoons, forcing himself not to think only and always about Colomba, he strolled along the streets in which, before leaving for Libya, he had thought of so many things, had gone through so many new sensations, had put so many questions to himself. The streets looked the same as then, and the movement of the soldiers during their free time was more or less the same. The young man knew, however, that the military situation had radically changed.

East Africa and Libya were lost, the Italian army destroyed in Russia, with no hope of being replaced, the occupation zones in the Balkans were infested with ever more numerous guerrillas ("It's all the same sh——", Pierello had said about the situation), the aerial bombings on Italian cities were more numerous and almost unopposed. It was necessary to reflect. Such a reality carried large implications that he would have liked to delve into and analyze. But the streets of Piacenza—and especially that of Faxal, the tree-lined street that goes along the ancient southern bastion of the city, walked along so many times with soldiers and colleagues now prisoners in Africa—regularly finished by distracting him from the subject, carrying him off to very different thoughts. He stopped on the sidewalk of Faxal in view of a square of shorn grass on which so many times he had done exercises with weapons along with his old pals. (Headquarters was not far away and could be seen from the other part of the bastion.) Here, exactly next to this plane tree, he had given an awful reprimand to poor Sciulli, the little corporal from Abruzzi, who later in El Alamein had died next to him in the observatory, with an arm and his entire shoulder carried away by shrapnel: through that horrible wound he had for a moment seen Sciulli's heart and lungs still functioning. After that Manno had not thought any more about that bawling out (provoked by the corporal's habit of screaming "goniometer ready" before having leveled it off), but now it came back to him. He could see the corporal's contrite face clearly, and he could see himself, tough with him, his voice loud with fury. What a lot of nerve he had had, bawling Sciulli out like that, a real sh—— rather, because the poor fellow, being his inferior, could not answer him back! Besides, that type of anger was not his style. The corporal had not been upset about it and had forgotten it immediately, and during the war he was always at the ready, in his nice way, typical of the people from Abruzzi, loyal, modest. And because of all this he had kept him at his side during those atrocious days in El Alamein in the observatory, on the stone lookout. Dear God, it was sad . . .

472

All the others came to mind, his "old brothers", the way they were always joking before they left for Africa, as when they would carry the cannons by hand to the field. ("The motorized artillery, that's us / though there's not a motor to be seen / so it's off we go, on foot, of course": the usual joke, then the motors did arrive.) Even in battle they continually joked. Would they be joking now behind barbed wire? Probably they would be. If they were still together at least ... Here in Piacenza the target for their jokes was often the artillery man Corneo, whose intelligence was not below average but who was a bit slower than the others to get the gist of things, and whose body was already bent over despite his being young, and his mouth always slightly agape, a peasant. Sometimes, to give himself airs, too, Corneo would come out with something foul mouthed. *He even offended God for no reason,* Manno thought, disapprovingly. *How will he be doing now in prison? Won't the guards be on top of him more than the others? If I had stayed with them, instead of leaving them there, maybe today I could* ... Of course not. The officers were most surely separated from the soldiers, and he would not have been able to do anything. Absolutely nothing. Besides, there were other officers there, and for more than one he felt deep respect. The image came back (in very imprecise fashion, as it does in one's imagination) of the features and always discreet gestures of one of them, the cautious, at times a bit apprehesive manner of another, who, though he really was apprehensive, reacted very well at the moment of truth. The image of Mussone's footloose and fancy-free style came back to him, Mussone, whose mother had telephoned him in Nomana. Dear old pals, comrades in arms! Boys between twenty and twenty-five, forced to grow up prematurely by tremendous responsibility and experiences, which a man sometimes does not have to go through in his entire life. The tough necessity to make decisions—quick, without backtracking— which could make the difference between life and death ... and the obligation to be at all times the perfect example for the soldiers. (If not—Manno knew by experience—goodbye discipline, and, for many, the same as saying goodbye life.) If it were not for the constant vision of Colomba's little head, the young man would have found it hard, being in Piacenza where everything had a memory, to keep his mind off his old comrades in arms.

Twenty days after his arrival, he suddenly had a new and more urgent reason for reflection. He was informed that he had been included in a group of re-placements scheduled for Greece. He had to be ready to leave within a week.

He was taken by surprise at the assignment. For the most part the junior officers, about sixty of them, had never been in the operational zone and were there idling away uselessly. Why, then, were they sending him to Greece, hav-ing just returned from the front? The adjutant major, whom he asked about it in joking fashion at the table, answered him quite seriously that he inspired confidence precisely because he had experience. And for the same reason, he said, the veteran lieutenant, Pigliapoco, who had also come from Tunisia, had been selected, too.

This fellow—a kind of mule, scrupulous as to duty, repatriated some months before because of injury—explained the situation to Manno philosophically. "Believe me," he said, "here you don't need to think about recommendations or influences or anything like that. It's quite simply that in war it's always the same ones, but really always the same ones, who slog away. After all is said and done, it's a matter of fate, nothing else."

After giving the question some thought for a few days, going through different moods, Manno ended by telling himself that this, too, would be a useful experience, probably a new step forward in preparation for the unknown role he felt predestined by providence to play. He hurriedly made up his baggage, as his spirits became more serene. So much so that one night at the table Pigliapoco spluttered out, "What's going on with you? You not only pulled out of a depression, but you seem downright happy. What do you have to be happy about, I'd like to know?"

"Franciscan joy", another officer piped up, a fellow who liked Manno for his total disregard for what others thought when it came to his beliefs. Every time he sat down at the table he made the sign of the Cross.

"No," Pigliapoco grumbled, "it's a case of juvenile recklessness."

The departure for Greece (which, by Manno's request, did not include his aide Battistessa) was delayed several times. Summer went on full of uncertainty and idleness. In Piacenza, as in Nomana, as in all of Italy, everyone's spirits— military as well as civilian and even those of people who seemed only involved in their own everyday affairs—were hanging fire. What next?

Not even the events going on were enough to modify that sense of expectancy—for example, the fall of Pantelleria, which could be taken for granted after the loss of Tunisia. (At the table the diners closest to Manno were amused by his description of the Barbacane castle and the GAF officer, who was its guardian, nothing more.) Not even the landing of the Anglo-Americans in Sicily on the tenth of July—which was a very relevant event— rid people of their sense of expectancy. A few days before the newspapers had published a speech made by Mussolini in which he said that the landing had been, some way or other, foretold, but at the same time he predicted its failure, and so people were simply waiting to see. Mussolini himself, it seemed, was as inert as everyone else; as the supreme commander, he had not prepared and was not preparing to move the fresh troops still available to Sicily.

2

In Nomana, Ambrogio discussed the situation with his father and Uncle Ettore from time to time. "What a disaster! What will happen here is that the war will spread over the entire peninsula. All our resources will be routed, not to mention the loss of human lives ... and we, meanwhile, looking at it straight in the face. Why doesn't Mussolini organize the defense of Sicily?"

"Because it's obvious he doesn't have the forces to stop them", Uncle Ettore said.

"That's not so. You heard Don Carlo: at least three of the Alpine divisions have been reformed, and with them they could give anyone a good fight. And what a fight! Why doesn't he use them?"

(Don Carlo Gnocchi—recently named chief chaplain of the Tridentina— had been to visit the Riva family during those days. From his measured voice Ambrogio did not get the usual fragmentary reports but a complete rundown of the retreat of the Alpine troops in Russia. From Don Carlo the Rivas found out that the Alpine divisions, hurriedly reformed with new conscriptions of mountaineers, were now again ready for action in the Alps headquarters.)

"Is it of some significance that they have their best divisions near Germany?" Gerardo wanted to know. "I wonder, if by chance, at the meeting the other day of Mussolini and Hitler at Feltre ... I mean, if it's Mussolini's intention now to break away from Germany."

"Quite the contrary. Perhaps he asked Hitler for more help in Sicily, especially arms."

"It's strange that we don't manufacture sufficient arms for our few divisions, while Germany produces more than enough."

"In peacetime the relation between Italian industrial production and German production could be—who knows?—one to three, one to four, maximum one to five: but now it looks as if it's become one to one hundred."

In the course of these slightly unreal days, Ambrogio repeatedly tried to apply himself to work in his father's business, but with his state of malaise he accomplished little. "I'm not managing to do a thing", he declared. "It's as if I haven't the strength. Something odd." No more than at work did he manage to concentrate on anything for very long. He immediately felt tired. *Air, air, movement* ... an inner voice prompted, until he would finally get up and leave the office puffing for the factory yard. "To get a breath of air", he would say.

His father was observing him without his seeing it. He had the feeling that his son was not recuperating and that his health, in fact, was worsening. One afternoon (the last week in July, and already very hot), "Why don't you go to the seaside?" he proposed. "Isn't it tomorrow that you have to go for a checkup at the military hospital at Baggio? Look here, I had it in mind to tell you that as soon as that visit's over—day after tomorrow, for example—you could go to Cesenatico."

At the idea that his weakness was so evident, Ambrogio blushed and looked at his father, who was pretending not to take any notice of his look. "You've had a lot of cold this winter", Gerardo vaguely observed. "It seems logical to me you should go to the seaside for a few days."

"My comrades" (meaning Stefano, Michele, and all the others—if they were still alive . . .) "are not going to the seaside", Ambrogio retorted, almost aggressively. "So you think they'd criticize you, disapprove if you went? I don't think so." "In fact, no", Ambrogio agreed. "They wouldn't disapprove. It's I who would, and I'm not thinking of going."

"All right, as you wish", his father concluded.

That afternoon he focused all his attention on his work, but even then not doing it better than on the previous days. In the afternoon, he got up from his desk at the office, very nervous; he had noticed the old employee seated at the desk in front of him was looking at him every so often with a worried expression. Before leaving he addressed her with a "keep your spirits up, Miss Tilde!" talking to himself as much as to her.

Fortunately supper was waiting for him at home, which was even more quiet since his brothers and sisters were all at the seaside (the boys at school in Cesenatico).

He ate with his father and mother in the usual room, which, given the absence of so many of them, seemed empty. His mother was serving, since Noemi was also at the seaside with Francesca, Alma, and Giuditta, for a rest. From time to time Giulia's thoughts floated off to her distant children. "What would they be talking about now? What would they be doing?" she kept repeating.

"Doing? What do you think they'll be doing?" Gerardo remarked. "They'll be eating, just like us."

"Yes, of course. I imagine so."

"Mama feels sad not having all her little chickens here under her wing", Ambrogio said, smiling. And addressing her, "The three at school will be up to one of their silly jokes they always play at the seaside. Especially Pino, you bet."

"Oh, my Pinetto!"

There were spells of silence at the table. The song of the nightingale did not come through the windows now as it did in springtime. What did come through, quite noticeably, was the sudden shriek of the swallows, whose fledglings were flying, swooping through the sky with the adult birds, no longer distinguishable from them.

Ambrogio listened hard to these constant shrieks, and suddenly he asked, "What day is it today? Not the twenty-fifth of July, is it? The last day of the swallows." He explained, "You hear how many must be outside there? Well, tomorrow there won't be a single one."

"What do you mean?" his father asked.

"The swallows migrate every year on the twenty-fifth of July, absolutely on the dot, as if they had a calendar. Pity Manno isn't here. He understands more about this than I do. He found the date in a book on ornithology. We checked it together twice, and that's exactly how it happened. You'll see tomorrow."

"And if it's a leap year? How do the swallows manage to find out?" Gerardo joked.

"Papa, you can believe me or not, but it's the way I say it is. We checked that at least from Nomana they do, indeed, leave on the twenty-fifth of July, no mistaking. Other species of birds aren't quite as methodical, or anywhere close to it. Besides, the others don't leave all at once like the swallows, or at least I don't think so. In any case, tomorrow we'll check that out." Now the army of swallows fell silent, not swooping over the windows. Only the old pendulum clock on top of the radiator cover ticked out the time imperturbably, which went by not only for the swallows, but for everyone, also for men and their history.

"Was it our Manno really who told you these things?" his mother asked. "Poor boy! And to think that after twenty months of war in Africa, and so much danger, he's now to go off to Greece."

Silence fell once again, and once again only the tick of the pendulum clock was to be heard, quietly ticking off the time.

"And the migration of birds, what you were talking about, is also a sign that summer is finishing", the father said, feeling his way, but firm in what he once started. "No more than a few weeks of real heat are in store for us." He turned to his wife (but Ambrogio realized it was a maneuver involving him as an object). "Giulia, why don't you make up your mind once and for all to join your daughters at the seaside? Or perhaps go with him, how about it?" indicating the young man.

He could not keep from laughing. "Papa, may I say you're persistent?"

"Of course, it would be a good idea if Ambrogio went to the seaside for a few days", Giulia agreed. "I've already told him, and I've also repeated it. As for me, you know I can't. Who'll be here to take care of you? And Manno, who's about to leave . . . and besides, if Milan's bombed again like last October, and if I were far away . . . so it's no. I must stay here."

"To do what? To prepare antiaerial defense for Milan?" her son asked.

"Oh, don't joke", Giulia pleaded.

Gerardo continued, "It's hard to say who's more . . .", and he knocked his knuckles against the table, to indicate the harder head, and finished, "Mother or son."

Ambrogio had it on the tip of his tongue to ask, "Why leave yourself out, Father?" But he thought all of this was more to be taken as a joke. There the three of them were, each one trying strategically to do some good for the other one.

3

When they had finished supper and drunk their substitute coffee, father and son stayed at the table to read the newspaper (a page each) while Giulia cleared up in the kitchen. Every so often, she would return to the room to put something on the buffet, such as the clean and shiny dishes. Then she would express her thoughts out loud, interrupting the reading of the other two for a moment.

"It's been three days since Manno has telephoned. Would they have put the departure day off again? He promised to spend a day at home before going, you know."

"Who knows? It's possible they may not even send him to Greece", Gerardo said. "Can you imagine . . . with the Americans and English in Sicily . . ."

"And soon in Calabria, if all continues the way it has", Ambrogio added.

"Of course, that's why."

"But are the Americans occupying all of Sicily?" Giulia wanted to know.

"Yes", Ambrogio replied, lifting his eyes from the newspaper. "It's sad, but that's how it is. We can no longer throw them in the sea." He looked at his father. "Once I thought that in a case like this, even wounded, I would rush out there to fight on my own. And now . . . if I'd go, I'd be laughed at. Some situation we've gotten ourselves into. My God!"

Gerardo tightened his lips. Giulia left the dining room with a sigh. "I'd like to know if at least our people are putting up any serious resistance or not," Ambrogio said, "or if the only ones fighting are the Germans."

"Of course . . . I was also hoping that the Sicilians and Calabrians especially, even if only to defend their homes and women . . . but you heard what Manno said: in Piacenza there are people who have deserted to go back home, to flee from the war."

"Well, there may be some who'll fight. But how many? What a situation!"

After Giulia had finished clearing up, they said the Rosary, as they did every night. When it was over, Gerardo glanced at the clock, only a short time before the news would come on. He stood up and with his usual gesture turned on the radio. As a program of no interest was on, father and son went back to reading the newspaper. When the news began, neither one of them even realized it. It was Giulia who called to them in an astonished voice: "Gerardo, Ambrogio, are you listening? Do you hear what they're saying?"

The radio was announcing that his majesty the king had accepted the resignation of the chief of state *cavaliere* Benito Mussolini and that he had put in his place Italy's commander-in-chief, Field Marshall Pietro Badoglio.

"Mussolini's fallen . . . the end of fascism", Ambrogio observed. "Do you realize?"

His father signaled him not to talk. He had his ear to the radio not to miss a single word. However, no more was said on this subject, and then, most surprisingly, a program of music was switched on, undoubtedly as a filler.

"Fascism has fallen, yés", Gerardo then said gravely, looking at the faces of the other two. "About time!" While Giulia's thoughts were rushing toward Manno (perhaps, thanks to this, he'd not go to Greece), the two men's thoughts dwelled on the Germans. What would their reaction be?

They agreed that now they did not have to worry about the Fascists. They had brought Italy to military failure, had shown themselves incapable of any serious attempt to avoid it. It was now no longer they who could cause con-

478

cern but the Germans. "And they", Ambrogio observed, "never joke around. We'll see how they react."

Gerardo agreed. The lighthearted music on the radio continued. The three of them waited a long time still, impatiently, to see if other details concerning the news would be broadcast. At last Gerardo stood up, went to the radio, and turned it off. "*Sic transit gloria mundi*", he said, almost solemnly, he, who did not know Latin. Then, in a fashion more in accord with his modest beginnings, he expressed the same idea with a popular proverb: "You saw? The proud went out in carriages and came back on foot."

Ambrogio was about to smile at this, but he stopped himself. He remembered that his father, as a young man, still not an industrialist, had founded in Nomana the Catholic Action group, as well as the Popular party. He was not a man to express himself in words but in actions.

"Now that fascism no longer exists", the young man asked, standing up, "and apart from what the Germans do, how do you think we'll get ourselves organized?" He recalled with perplexity some of the episodes from the pre-Fascist epoch, which he had often heard: certain phrases bandied about by town chieftains in the squares before he was born, so demagogic and idiotic that people still laughed at them even after so long a time and, worse still, not in Brianza, but in the rest of Italy, cases where power had been abused by the reds, who equalled the blackshirts in arrogance: priest baiting, officer insults, disorders, trains stopped only because a priest was riding on it.

"As soon as possible the different parties will reorganize, without a doubt", Gerardo answered him. "We'll get ourselves organized again democratically, you'll see." He seemed confident of a return to a normal political situation, and so did Giulia. Neither one or the other imagined the uneasiness that troubled the mind of the young man.

Whatever the outcome, he concluded to himself, *the political mess for the moment is nothing in comparison to the danger the Germans present.*

After some other commentaries (this was truly big news), father, mother, and son went up pensively to their rooms. They reached the first floor, said goodnight, and separated, the father and mother going off to the double bedroom and the son to his own room.

Before going to bed, he set the alarm for six o'clock. The following morning, he had to go to Milan for his medical checkup, his first since he had been on leave.

4

The following day he put on his uniform, and in the bracing cool of the morning he walked to the station at a good clip. Along the Avenue of Memories he had to slow down, as he felt dizzy. *What the devil's happening to me? I'm worse now than when I came . . .*

479

People were talking about the great event on the train, all commenting in dialect. "Who knows where Mussolini is now? The radio didn't say. What do you expect, he'll be quietly at home?"

"No, that's not possible."

"Why not possible?"

"That he could be at home, yes, but quiet, no, after dragging us into this war, having all these dead people on his conscience."

"Besides, how's he going to be quiet after having lost all his power so suddenly? Him, with his arrogance?"

"Wow . . . the rage he must be feeling now . . ."

"Yes, what rage."

"Arrogant is arrogant, but did you see how he let himself be ousted like a lamb? At least as far as we know."

"Sure, that's what we know. But what really happened we don't know."

The diesel car had few partitions inside, so many of the people were able to see each other and talk together.

"In my opinion, the real fault of the Duce", an old man asserted, "was having taken Italy into a war against everybody's wishes."

"Not exactly everybody's. Remember the students?" a woman intervened. " 'Long live war. We want war.' Who didn't see the demonstrations in Milan?"

"Students don't count", the old man said. "They have no way of judging things. One day it's black and the next white. All that matters to them is to make a ruckus, like geese gone mad."

"Whatever the case, they cause trouble", the woman pressed.

"Yes, of course they do," the old man agreed, "but when I say the Duce's brought Italy into war against everyone's will, I'm not talking about young riffraff. I'm talking about others, people with some sense. Even some of the Fascists—and this has to be said—didn't want war. You remember? Yes or no?"

"It was also because of the Germans." Someone at least came to his aid partially. "We were always against them, even in the 1914–18 war, and there are dead in practically every family." He turned to the man beside him. "You, too, Guglielmo, isn't that so? Two in your family . . ."

The aforementioned Guglielmo, who was hunched up with his hands in his pockets, nodded but did not intervene. He never so much as wasted a word on what he called the idiocy of politics.

"So, now we have a big problem", another, who looked like a clerk, joined in. "They've got rid of Mussolini, but what about the war? How are they going to get out of that, and with the Germans", at this point he involuntarily lowered his voice, "on our doorstep? If God doesn't lend us a hand, I don't see how it'll be done."

There was a pause. Practically speaking, everyone present—except for Guglielmo—agreed that this was the big problem now.

"That loser?" someone exclaimed. "When he got us in this war, he thought we'd win it in a matter of months, effortlessly."

"The bastard, a——hole!" another man, rather young (about thirty), who up until now had not spoken, let loose passionately. "A stinking piece of garbage if there ever was one."

The others were taken by surprise by this new possibility of publicly insulting a man who, until yesterday, was only exalted publicly. But they were not all entirely in agreement, so no one carried on the line of insults sparked by the thirty-year-old.

A boy sitting beside him asked, "Do you have someone who died in the war?"

"Me? No, why?"

"Then . . ."

"We all have war dead", the thirty-year-old answered vaguely. In any event he realized that his way of talking with these people—his people—did not fit. He snorted and did not say another word. But his attitude from then on made it clear that he promised himself to be revenged when he reached Milan, in a place not filled with stubborn heads (he really thought them ignoramuses) like these people. *Look at them*, he told himself, *these stunned faces of Brianza. Before none of them were Fascists, and now, just look, they look as if they're sorry!* One of his acquaintances tried to help him out. "I'd like to see the higher-ups", he blurted out, "when they get themselves kicked in the pants, and they'll have to get rid of everything they've eaten, the bastards."

"But if they've eaten and digested everything," an older workman interjected, his face the white of the devout, a not too unusual type in Brianza, "what do you think they'll have to get rid of?" It was obvious that the insults and this type of bullying—anti-Fascist bullying—were irritating the majority of the passengers, even Ambrogio, who, because he was in uniform, had decided not to get involved in any case.

The conversation ended with all of them talking about the war, which—as the radio had said—would go on. All those present, always excluding Guglielmo, were of the opinion that the newly responsible parties—the king and Badoglio— were studying a way to get out of it. But what in the devil could they come up with? It was indeed difficult.

"And while the others go on bombing, what will happen? Will the bombing continue or not?"

What incredible power they'd demonstrated.

"And that wretch, when he got into the war, didn't think about America's power. He didn't even consider it."

At the Villasanta station, just before Monza, a fellow of about forty got on the train wearing his "bug" (in reality the national party Fascist badge, very common until the day before) in his lapel. Some of them were aware of it and smiled. Evidently this fellow had not heard the big news. The fellow sat almost in front of Ambrogio, next to the woman who had brought up the prowar student demonstrations. He stuck his two hands in his jacket pockets, leaned his head back, and closed his eyes. The woman glanced at the others, by way of consultation to see if they agreed to let him know. Having decided not to intervene, by way of a response, Ambrogio looked through the window. The others also acted as if they were unaware of anything. As the woman wanted to do something, she decided to talk to another woman she knew about the news on the radio of Mussolini's resignation. "Cavaliere Benito Mussolini", she repeated more than once. The fellow with the badge made no sign of having understood. *But he must have heard me. I'm certain of it,* the women thought. *So now he knows . . . well, let him do what he wants. But if he shows that badge around . . .* She looked again at the people nearby. A few finally smiled, a shade embarrassed. Then she made up her mind and tapped the fellow's arm with the tips of her fingers, and he opened his eyes.

"That badge", the woman said softly. The fellow looked at his badge, twisting his neck a little, and then looked at the woman. "The king has replaced Mussolini. Did you know? It was on the radio last night. Well, I know it's not my business, but I'm telling you for your own sake, because if some hothead sees that badge . . ." She said no more.

The man looked at her once more and then closed his eyes again.

The woman raised her chin and tightened her lips, as if to say, "I've done what had to be done. Now it's his affair."

They reached Monza, and at the Lambro River, slimy and green, not clear as in Brianza, the train moved practically at a walking pace over an iron bridge that arched obliquely over the river. Ambrogio looked outside to see if even after the big news of the fall of fascism the same old fishermen were still at their usual places. Yes, they were there, though few, as it was so early; of course, shortly there would be more, as usual.

After stopping at Monza, the train continued on its way to Milan. The woman looked at the man with the closed eyes from time to time. *He must be one of those thick-skinned Fascists, one of those that won't give in for anything,* she told herself. *God knows what he has in mind now . . .*

In that man's head was an incredible muddle. *Just look what's happening to me,* he thought. *Mussolini sacked by the king . . . incredible. The thing doesn't mean a thing to me, that's understood; I had to join the party or else, to be able to work, even if these people don't know it. How was I going to sell my stationery to the town hall? And to private parties, since to have the party's membership card is . . . was obligatory. Just as well we're all in this together, in the same boat. But that's not the point. Mussolini has fallen . . . naturally, that can't be a joke. No one would risk joking about that. But now what worries me is something else. It's this fool with her fiddling. . . . What role do I play now if . . . of course, they're all waiting for me to take off this badge (damn*

482

thing) to laugh at me. But I'm not going to give them the satisfaction. What happens happens. I won't take it off in front of them for anything in the world. When I get to Milan, when no one sees me, then . . .

With these and other similar considerations and ideas the ten- or twelve-minute trip from Monza to Milan went by. The conversations—at least the ones out loud—about Mussolini's fall were at an end. The iron wheels of the train resounded more and more as they went over the changes in the tracks, which were increasing, four, five, six pairs, many more, then a complete set of tracks, and here and there the service sentry boxes, then a building with levers and other apparatus in and out, cars from stopped trains, locomotives, the occasional railwaymen moving about. . . . The Milan central station was close. In the last bit the tracks extended over an enormous platform, which on both sides—separated by streets deep as canals that could hardly be seen from the train—was a long line of houses and deformed tenements, crowned by filthy billboards for neon advertising that had not been functioning for a long time. The train was slowing down, finally to a walking pace, under the huge iron arcades of the station, unusually dark because of the bombings. Many of the panes of glass that let in light from the top had been replaced with fiber and cement slabs. The train finally made its last stop, and the passengers all rushed to the doors.

5

Ambrogio had the feeling that there were more people than usual on the platforms. And in the station there seemed to be still more. From time to time far off an unexpected clamor could be heard. *What in the world can that be?* the young man wondered.

What can be happening? What are they doing? some of the other recently arrived passengers walking toward the exit were also wondering.

Groups of people were going by talking animatedly. People did not seem to be acting their usual selves. Many seemed to be excited. Suddenly, as one of the groups held up the flow of passengers coming from the train, someone shouted, "Look, there's one!" and many voices, boy's, men's, then a whole group, surrounded someone not far from Ambrogio. Look, they had discovered the fellow with the bug whom Ambrogio had forgotten about completely.

"A Fascist!"

"Wearing the badge, look, still wearing the badge, the pig!" a big young man yelled.

"The stinker!"

Many were coming from a distance, shouting and even laughing.

Ambrogio tried, since he was in uniform, to go ahead, but the crowd of people prevented him. He saw a shirtless fellow holding onto the lapels of the

483

man's jacket, on which the bug was still pinned, the same person, his face ashen, who had got off the train from Nomana.

"Leave me alone", he was protesting. "Leave me alone. I'm as much a Fascist as you all are, neither more nor less."

"Call us Fascists? Us? You wretch!"

"What a sh——!"

"Pig, son of a whore!"

The fellow was pulling harder and harder at the lapels and finally pulled them off, after which—to the acclamations of the others—he raised them in the air as a trophy, satisfied.

"The police!" a woman's voice screamed out at that moment. "The police are coming!"

The alarm created a certain effect. They all looked around. The group of people surrounding the fellow dispersed a little, but the police were not in sight.

The person with the lapels in his hand went up to Ambrogio. "It's not the police!" he screamed. "It's the army." He lifted the bits of material up again. "Long live the army!" he screamed. "Long live the army, they've gotten rid of the sh——s . . ." After not getting a fair response from the army, he went off, followed by the others. The fellow with the torn jacket stood stock still. "They can't do that, they can't", he repeated.

Ambrogio went up to him. The people who had arrived in the train were going off among a plethora of comments. "Come on", Ambrogio said to the man. "Come on, before they get it in their heads to come back."

Behind them, the woman who had suggested to the man he take off the bug in the train was walking with several others. "He was told", she repeated excitedly, "I told him so." Ambrogio glanced back at her. Then she lowered her voice a little but continued the refrain: "In the train I told him, I told him."

He saw a police patrol standing next to the ramp of the central staircase and another one farther on.

"If you like, you can go to the police", Ambrogio said to the fellow.

"The police? Yes, of course", the other answered, still shaken.

"More than anything else, in case those others decide to come back looking for you", Ambrogio said, and left him.

At the exit of the station there were some individuals with hammers and ladders all set on demolishing Fascist symbols on the walls. Surrounding them were groups of people applauding, but mostly laughing.

6

Without stopping, Ambrogio took the trolley to Baggio, a rather long ride, which crossed through a good part of the city. From time to time he could see groups and crowds of people, also police patrols and, more often, army people, quiet or walking. "Long live the army!" people were screaming here and there, applauding the soldiers.

How long will this applause for the soldiers last? the lieutenant wondered sceptically. Despite the disagreeable adventure of the fellow with the bug, however, he had the impression that the demonstrations in general were not violent. There would probably be no bloodshed.

The trolley left him at the end of the line, at a large unfinished square on the western periphery of the city, between headquarters buildings and military hospitals. "Baggio", the conductor had called out.

The young man, after asking instructions from one of the passengers, got off with him, started down a wide semideserted street, its sidewalks sprouting weeds here and there. He was walking rather slowly, finding it inexplicably difficult to walk. In front of him was someone walking even slower. At last Ambrogio caught up with him and passed in front of him. He was an old Fascist militiaman, with the regulation fasces on his crooked cap. He was really old, and by the looks of him he seemed to be suffering, poorly dressed, with a nonregulation muffler around his neck and a decoration on one sleeve that showed he had been wounded in war. They looked at each other. Ambrogio made a little gesture of encouragement. The other did not respond, nor did he salute as he should have. He was carrying in one hand, the hand that should have been raised in the Roman salute, a threadbare fiber suitcase.

In the big hospital, in the section indicated on the postcard he had received in Nomana, the lieutenant found his place immediately. In a short while he was seen by the head doctor and two assistants, all dressed in white gowns and without rank. From the deference shown to the head doctor, Ambrogio had the impression that he must have been some luminary in the field of medical science, perhaps a university professor. He knew that from the beginning of the war any number of famous doctors were on duty, though they were not obliged to be so, in military hospitals.

"Well, well, and how's everything?" the head doctor asked with a distant professional pleasantness, then not paying any, or hardly any, attention to his answers.

"Seven months have gone by since I was wounded", Ambrogio explained. "Now I must be better. And since . . ." His voice faded, as if he feared sounding a braggart, "I've been home those months . . . well, it seems to me it's time for me to get back to the army."

The head doctor stopped, looked at him. "You're dreaming, my boy," he told him, "dreaming."

"But . . ."

"I'm afraid I won't even be able to send you back home. Most certainly not."

"But what do you mean? Stay here, in the hospital, I can't. I can't because . . . I . . ."

485

"Calm down", the doctor said. "Calm down. The visit's over now. Later we'll do the tests, then . . . then we'll decide. All right?"

"Yes, sir."

Afterward he was put through the prescribed tests. Waiting for the results, he did not want to eat in the hospital restaurant; he preferred going out, as if having a meal in the hospital restaurant would constitute a precedent.

He went into a modest restaurant on the square at the end of the trolley line station. His mother in the morning ("Take it with you, one never knows, and careful you don't lose it") had put his rationing card in his pocket, which now, it turned out, was useful. The waiter asked for it. It was no more than so many faded pieces of paper, subdivided into small squares covered with stamps. The waiter cut out some of the squares with stamps, using scissors and in exchange brought him a bowl of vegetable soup ("This is not ration-book soup"), a miserable grayish bread roll, a plate with three transparent slices of salami, a spoonful of puree, and an unappetizing apple.

What could the head doctor have found? "Kidneys . . . there are some renal complications here", he had said. Perhaps that was the cause of his dizziness and his listlessness. *Well, I'll know in a few hours. I'd better not get into a state of nerves like some young girl.* He then switched his own increasing bad humor onto the food. *I'd have been better off not eating,* he told himself as he wolfed down the meal voraciously. (The constant voraciousness he had had since returning home, it was as if, even after months, he was unable to compensate for the hunger he had suffered during that siege.) *I would have done better not to take this meal away from a civilian. What is it for a soldier to skip a meal? Nothing at all, really.* His thoughts turned to his comrades in arms who had not been able to get out of that siege. *God knows the suffering they're going through, that is, if they're still alive.* To think about them, however, didn't help at all really.

He returned to the hospital to wait. In the afternoon he was called into an office by one of the two assistants, who was no longer in a gown but instead wearing the uniform of a medical lieutenant. "Listen here, it's not a matter of the greatest urgency, but it's necessary for you to be hospitalized", he said immediately. "I'm sorry."

"But . . ."

"No. This is not a joking matter. You can't fool with kidneys." He put the whole clinical picture to him, without digressing.

Then he handed him a paper. "Your leave is extended for two weeks. The professor is trying to make things easier for you, as you can see."

"But . . . I wasn't asking for my leave to be prolonged." He stopped. He thought of Manno. This additional leave would at least allow him to see his cousin.

"Well," the young doctor said, "it's already done." And he added, "What's absolutely clear is that you'll not be able to return to your regiment."

486

Then he gave him two more papers. "The prescription for the medicines you must begin to take immediately—immediately, understood?—with the diet. And this is the paper for your hospitalization, at the end of these two weeks, directly in the Isola Bella military hospital on Lake Maggiore. Do you know those little islands in front of Stresa? A lovely place, you'll see. And above all (and this is very important for you) there's a director there, Braga, who's a saint when it comes to kidneys. That's why we're sending you there."

"Besides, it's not very far from my home", Ambrogio murmured.

"Great, and anyway, the situation we're in here ... and if the bombings begin again, I don't think the planes would drop bombs right on these little islands in the middle of a lake."

"Not likely."

"Don't forget what I told you", the doctor concluded icily. "There's no reason to be alarmed, but you must take care. You'll really get back in shape only if you begin to look after yourself seriously. Listen to me and don't waste time."

7

But he did waste time. And it was Manno, quite inadvertently, who made him do it. Manno's telephoning from Piacenza to say he would arrive in Nomana on the twelfth of August made Ambrogio—who was due to arrive in Stresa on the tenth—decide to wait for him. On the twelfth Manno still had not arrived, and once again he telephoned. The departure from Greece was once more postponed for a few days, and so he would not get to Nomana until the fifteenth or sixteenth. Despite his father's and, even more, his mother's opinion, Ambrogio decided to wait for him. He felt an odd premonition that after this meeting he would not see his cousin for a long time, a very long time.

They were trying days in the Nomana household, given Ambrogio's state of health and the situation in general.

The popular demonstrations soon stopped, and without any special violence. A tense climate of expectancy remained. Would the new government be able to pull the nation out of war? Everyone now knew that Mussolini had been not only arrested but also deposed. Nonetheless, the Fascists were not reacting in any way. ("They are also fed up", the people were saying.) The Fascist militia had agreed, without rebelling, to replace their own insignias—the fasces of combat—with the army stars.

"But will the king and Badoglio manage to pull Italy out of war?" everyone kept asking. "How?" No one who posed the problem objectively was able to see a way out.

The Germans, in their detachments, here and there put on a gloomy appearance, but they did not react for the moment.

The newspapers began to publish revelations about the past regime, especially about the way in which it fell. It became known that the Fascist leaders themselves, at their last meeting of the Council, had been the ones to put an end to fascism, in the hope that the Italians would align themselves with the king and unanimously oppose a foreign invasion. The Fascist leaders had actually put something else (national interest) ahead of party and ideology, thus showing themselves not to be truly totalitarian, as were the Nazis and Communists, who never would have committed self-liquidation in the interest of Germany or Russia. (In the years to come other Fascist leaders would do the same—for example, Salazar, the Greek colonels, Franco—as the Italian Fascists.) But the attention of the people was focused not on this unexpected phenomenon but on the fact that the Duce had a steady lover, something that came as a surprise to the large majority. The lover's brother, the newspapers were saying—indulging themselves—he was a no-good, an opportunist. There had also been opportunists of this sort among the higher echelons of the Fascist party. However, this came as no surprise, since people had always thought this phenomenon was much more important than what it now seemed to be. The new government, in any event, had put forth a law to strip the guilty of what had been illegally garnered.

Yes, but what would the Germans do if this precarious situation continued? It was rumored that their troops were arriving through the Brenner Pass and France, perhaps even through the Balkans. News was brought to Ambrogio by Luca, now at Val d'Adige. He arrived at the Riva home one afternoon on bicycle, boasting his new rank of sergeant. After Ambrogio congratulated him on his promotion, Luca said, "We came to Milan with two trucks to take back supplies, and I have to be back with the truck before five."

"But what's happening? You're turning into one of the truckers."

"Yes, as long as it lasts." (As usual, he was talking in dialect.) "When my battalion has to furnish a truck for some job outside our area, I'm usually made chief of the vehicles, as I'm not bad as a mechanic . . . and it didn't seem right going to Nomana without stopping to see you." Despite his being all in a sweat—even his reddish beard was damp—he maintained his usual calm appearance. This time it was he who was wearing the Alpine hat quite far back, showing his forehead. "The situation in upper Adige? What can I tell you? Thank God I'm not there down in the valley, because German columns are going over the Brenner Pass, and it's real chaos. At Bolzano there's a Bersaglieri post over the Isarco bridge, with two machine guns in place. They have orders to let the Germans through from the divisions already in Italy, but not the others. And what can they do? They can't tell them that we're not going to shoot you, but you others, yes. So they let all of them go by, real chaos, I tell you. In my battalion the alarm's gone off twice, too. It seemed we were to take up positions in the valley. Then, after a bit, they canceled the order. Nobody knows a thing. You know what I think? That they won't take us, the Alpine troops, to the valley because if they do we'll start fighting with the Germans even without orders. Everything that happens there in the valley is infuriating. The people from the villages follow and applaud the Germans. They're all in favor of the Germans in those villages, you know. And are many divisions going through? I'm afraid there are, and all of them motorized. They have the trucks camouflaged in yellow, not like in Russia; rather as in Africa, it seems."

He accepted a glass of wine, in which Ambrogio joined him.

"It's good. Let's have another. We'll finish the bottle", Ambrogio proposed.

"The bottle, no. Only another glass, enough, because I told you, I have to be in Milan before five."

Had he been to Nomanella? Of course, he arrived right in time for the midday break. "So I saw Giustina. And Lucia and Ferrante. Imagine, they wanted me to stay and eat with them, and we drank a bottle of wine, a bit of a party, even if they have their son always on their minds. Well, now I have to go." Suddenly he remembered something. "Oh, one second, greetings from the chaplain for you and Manno, you know, Don Carlo Gnocchi. I forgot to tell you."

"Thanks. Do you see Don Carlo often?"

"Yes, he's stationed at Merano, but he's always around. On Sunday he came to say Mass for the battalion, and we talked. He's now obsessed with the idea, and says it, too, that when soldiers are on the front they're like Christ on the Cross."

"Yes, I know. He's right."

"Of course he's right."

"Well, when you see him, return our heartfelt greetings. And tell him Manno is about to go to Greece."

"They told me about that in Nomanella. What a mess for him, isn't it? In any case, I'll tell him."

8

When Luca left, Ambrogio went out to the garden and stretched out listlessly in the deck chair under the fig tree. He was no longer going to the office. *All in all, I'm not getting a thing done.* He tried studying for the university, but he did not persevere, as he could not concentrate.

He put his hands behind his head and stretched out his legs. It was a very hot day. Every so often a blackcap in the foliage of the trees trilled out a song, a cascade of notes that in Brianza is the very voice of summertime. Up above, beyond the slim branches of the fig tree, the pale blue sky was streaked with patches of clouds. He followed their passage with his eyes. How come he didn't see the black crosses of the swallows? Of course, they had already gone . . . they left without either him or anyone else checking the day of their departure.

Suddenly a faint echo of shots could be heard; they came from the south, from the Milan side. *It wouldn't be the antiaerial guns, by chance?* he asked himself. *And Luca on his way to the city.* From where he was it was impossible, in any case, to see out toward the south. The shots, far off and faint, scarcely audible, kept on going; then an uncertain and muffled crash of explosions began to mingle with the shots. *This could be a bombing . . . but what's happening? It seems they're bombing Milan . . .* He stood up and went into the house. He hurriedly took his father's binoculars out of a dining room drawer, old and worn-out excursion binoculars that could not be compared to the military ones he was used to.

His mother was in the dining room at the moment darning, seated in a corner, her glasses on, and beside her was a chair with a pile of boy's socks. She had not realized anything. "What's happening?" she asked him, seeing he had the binoculars. "Where are you going, Ambrogio?"

"It seems they're bombing Milan", he answered.

"What?"

"I think they're bombing Milan now. I want to check if I can see anything from Ronchetto."

"Heavens!" Giulia said. "Bombing Milan, you said? Those poor people. Oh, those poor people."

"I'm not sure, Mama. I want to check."

"You can hear it." The mother left her work, got up, and went to the door of the house, followed by her son, who, trying to give the impression of a combatant, did not want to appear emotional. The distant noise of the shots and explosions continued.

"Jesus and Mary," Giulia said with agitation, "help those poor people, take pity on them."

Drowning out her words came the mechanical whistling of a siren in the air, which was immediately joined by one more and then another: three sirens from the Nomana factories were sounding the alarm. "Do they always do it like that when there's an alarm in Milan?" the son asked.

The mother nodded without speaking, as her lips moved intensely in prayer.

When the sirens stopped, the sound of the far-off, faint echoes of explosions could be heard. Giulia was still silent, praying.

"Did you hear it?" Ambrogio asked. "That's more or less the noise you hear on the front when there's combat going on in a sector that's not yours. It sounds more or less like this."

"Jesus, Mary," his mother repeated, "help them, take pity on them. How many people are dying right now!"

"Yes, I fear so", Ambrogio agreed. "God help them. It seems like a fairly big bombing. Did you hear it so strong last October, or stronger?"

"This seems stronger", his mother answered uncertainly. "Those poor people."

"Well, I'm going to have a look, or try to", her son concluded.

But when he was on top of Ronchetto (a small grassy hill with a few fruit trees, situated not far from his house and where, as far as the eye could reach, all the rooftops of Nomana were in sight, and beyond to the left, the plain of Milan), he saw it was all a haze from what seemed—though he could not be sure—to be rising smoke. *It could be smoke from the fires,* he thought. His father's binoculars, which he repeatedly held to his eyes, were of no great help, and so he stopped using them.

He remembered the ineffectiveness of the first bombs dropped in 1940, at the beginning of the war. He had gone on his bicycle to examine the damage of a bomb that had exploded near Monza, which turned out to be insignificant. Bombing techniques had advanced a good deal since then, he reflected. There were cities in England and in Germany that had been reduced to ashes.

There was not a living soul on the hill; he had stopped at the very top, near a tiny rustic hut, one of those small constructions used to store things in the country. In front of it pecking away in the grass was a brood of young chicks of various colors; far off the bombing continued. Ambrogio approached the little animals. One was drinking from a stone trough in the scant shade of a grapevine; the others were pecking at the clover. It was such a peaceful sight that it was stirring. *When will this war be over once and for all?* the young man wondered, as he contemplated that peaceful picture. *God knows when.*

The shooting did not stop; he suddenly seemed to hear a sound of motors. *Airplanes? Are they returning? And if they fly over here?*

The sound was clearer and increased rapidly until the sky was filled with its din. *They're bombers, no doubt of it.* The first one, four motors, was flying incredibly low . . . *Could it be a flying fortress? But what is happening? Look, they've hit it, they've hit it, it's on fire.* One of the propellers had stopped, and clouds of smoke were clearly puffing from one side. Its insignia was easy to see, the concentric circles of the English.

So, those ancient wrecks of antiaerial defense are managing to get something! Ambrogio told himself excitedly. *At least they got this one out of the air.*

The airplane went close by him, with its vast roar (it reminded him of the roar of planes he had twice shot at, in vain, on the Don front the year before), and then flew off to the north. No more went by. *Perhaps their pilots,* he thought feverishly, *were trying to reach Switzerland before parachuting down. But will they manage to get altitude before jumping? They're too low* . . . Right now they must be between the devil and the deep blue sea, poor fellows, just as he had felt at times at the front. He felt divided between the instinctive sense of participation in the life struggle of those boys and a deep satisfaction because those who had come to destroy homes and people had got what they deserved. *In any case, the antiaerial defense of Milan is insufficient; everyone says so. Too few weapons, and they're short of . . . of everything; they can't do much.*

Finally, about an hour later, no further explosions could be heard. At last the three sirens in Nomana sounded the end of the alarm. The workers had gone from the factories to the surrounding countryside; now they would go back to work. *How long will all this go on?*

9

The airplanes—all of them English—came back in greater numbers during the course of the night and, orienting themselves by the fires started in the afternoon, carried out terrible destruction. The next day—the fourteenth of August—the city was given respite; but during two successive nights the winged formations returned, even more numerous, and carried out destruction that had not until then been seen in any Italian city. Later, when the census was taken, it turned out that of the 930,000 residential sites that made up Milan, about 560,000 had been destroyed or damaged.

Innumerable houses had caved in—covering the streets already broken by cracks and holes. Many streets, naturally, were rendered impassable, which made it difficult to get help to people trapped in shelters and cellars. A dense cloud of smoke hung over the city, and fires lasted several days.

The trains carrying the evacuees out of Milan (they were refugees now) could not leave from any of the city's stations—all destroyed. They started out from the different lines beyond the first stops. Luckily, the residents by that time had largely left the city, and those still working in the city systematically left it every evening. (It has to be said that at least in this respect the spirit of initiative of the Milanese showed itself fully.) Thus, the number of dead came to a little more than one thousand, incredibly few, given the scope of the destruction. One dead to every five hundred and some residences destroyed or damaged. It took a long time for people to believe it; many still do not, having heard stories of people who had left with only what they had on their backs (women especially, who got off at one or another station in the province—some had got as far as Nomana), stories that put God knows what disasters in mind.

On the sixteenth of August, at the height of the bombings, the sad news that Michele Tintori's father, the sculptor, had died reached Nomana. According to the doctor, death had been caused by heart failure.

A relative of the Tintoris living in Monza had given the news to the Rivas by telephone, telling them that the funeral would take place on the following day. Gerardo—who had received the call personally—purposely communicated the news to Ambrogio one day later to avoid his attending.

Heart failure means probably that he died of a broken heart for lack of news from his son, the young man thought, *and I, during my entire leave, went to see him only once, at the beginning . . .* When Michele returned he would not find any of his family waiting for him; maybe he would not even find his house standing. These thoughts weighed on Ambrogio for days, affecting him as deeply as the bombings did.

Meanwhile, with the telephone lines in bad repair, communications with Piacenza had become difficult. Manno managed at last to let them know that his departure was going to be postponed once more. Ambrogio then allowed himself to be talked into going to the hospital. His father and the driver Celeste accompanied him. (Celeste had been driver to Badoglio, now the new chief of state. "And that makes you", Ambrogio told Celeste during the trip, "at least five inches taller, doesn't it? Just like that.")

10

Manno made the long-awaited visit to Nomana about a week later, on the twenty-third of August.

His train—coming from Rome—could not reach the central station in Milan and had to stop on the outskirts of the city in the shunting station in Lambrate.

"The trains have only been getting this far since yesterday", a railway man told him. "Until the day before yesterday they had to stop some miles back, where there are those holes the workers are busy in."

"Workers and holes, true enough. I've seen them in several spots."

"Where there are more workers, at that strange hole, with the track raised high up."

"Oh, yes, I remember."

The young man got off at the Lambrate station, also in bad repair, its roof strewn with holes, jutting pieces of the walls torn out, and large cracks in the concrete staircase that went down from the level of the station to the city. He had never had to stop at this station in the outskirts, through which, however, he had gone many times, and so he was looking at it with curiosity, and, as happens in such cases, he found it more complex than what he had imagined.

Reaching a small square in front, he noticed that the streets were, without exception, covered with rubble and debris, so littered it seemed to him at first glance they were impassable.

Some place I've landed, he thought and began to worry. Besides seeing his relatives in Nomana, he hoped to see Colomba again, and he did not have that many hours to call his own.

Stopped in front of the station were two dump trucks in very bad repair and a motorcar of Unpa, the antiaerial protection service. The driver of the motorcar, a young fellow in a coffee-colored uniform, perhaps part of the fire brigade, noticed his perplexity. "Lieutenant", he called out, without getting out of the vehicle.

Manno went up to him. "I don't know where you're going," the driver said, "but I'm waiting for the boss to go back to town. We just finished loading some picks and shovels, so if you want to get a ride . . . only a matter of minutes."

"Great", Manno answered. "Thanks."

After a short time the boss emerged from the underground area of the station, a chief in surveying, carrying a briefcase under his arm. He shook hands with the officer and sat him down next to the driver, while he sat down to the left. "We're a bit tight, aren't we?" he commented laughingly, but his mind was elsewhere, on his difficult job.

The few travelers who had got off with Manno and who were still in the little square—two or three—on seeing the truck leaving came up. After having announced they were going to town, the surveyor let them get into the back of the car.

They took the widest street. Reaching the first heap of rubble, which from the little square seemed to obstruct traffic, they ventured down it at a walking pace, the car jolting and leaning over to one side, the side farther down, which had been leveled in summary fashion.

The same maneuver was repeated throughout the successive rubble heaps, a continual series of ups and downs.

Milan, the officer realized, had been harder hit and more damaged than the news from the radio had broadcast and led one to believe. He had the impression that not even a single house had been left standing. Many, more even, many more, had been razed to the ground into heaps of debris, and still more were those partially demolished. On the inside of the damaged walls, the buildings that had disappeared were sketched out in squares of different colors. On some there was still a picture or a bouquet of artificial flowers hanging askew. Sections of flooring could also be seen that still held up, as if they were brackets, a piece of furniture, a chair for example, a coat rack, or even an iron bed half hanging in the air.

The streets—even those few that had already been in a certain way cleaned up— were all without exception covered with minute fragments of glass, because it seemed that not a single window had remained intact. In the occasional window frame where the glass had partly stayed in place, strips of paper had been pasted on, as had been suggested by knowledgeable authorities. *Our way of running a war,* the young man thought bitterly, *our answer to four-motored planes.* He reflected, with justice, that in the cities from which the English planes had taken off there would also be broken windows with neat strips of paper pasted on . . . he felt no animosity toward the enemy. *That's how the Anglo-Saxons, the English and Americans, make war.* He had known them in Africa. *They'd never beat the Germans on a battlefield, but they have incomparably more machines, especially planes, which they can use to destroy cities and the enemy rearguard, and they destroy them. Any other way they couldn't win, and in the end they would be beaten.*

But leveling the Italian cities while the new government was making an effort in every way to get out of the war . . .

It's obvious they don't trust the new government; they don't believe in it. So they don't trust us, the Italians, just as the Germans don't—and they're right. All in all, poor Italy.

494

Street after street always the same sights of desolation, where many squadrons of laborers were working. The motorcar reached the center of town. They stopped on the La Scala piazza, covered with dust, where other similar vehicles had been parked and a certain number of trucks.

"You see the situation here, too?" the surveyor said to the lieutenant after they had stepped out, pointing to the surroundings.

The dome of the great theater, the pride of the city, no longer existed; it had sunk, disappeared. Of the sixteenth-century Marino Palace, seat of the town hall, which faced the theater, only the blackened walls remained. The interior had fallen in, devoured by fire. As for the Galleria (the salon of Milan, the young man remembered), which joins the square of La Scala to that of the Duomo, it was totally obstructed by its huge iron-and-glass arcades, which had fallen or were hanging to the ground.

"Some business", the young man murmured, in the language soldiers used when faced with an unavoidable tempest, be it water or fire.

"Ah", the old man sighed. Then he seemed to collect himself. "If you want to get a train to Monza, I advise you to go to the driver of those vehicles back there. One of them is surely going to Sesto, or nearby . . ." He shook the young man's hand, and Manno thanked him.

So it was. One of the vehicles most probably would be leaving for Sesto within an hour. It was a recently commandeered three-wheeler, though more in a state of ruin than the previous one. The mark of its ex-owner, who worked with tin, could still be seen under the hurried coat of paint.

Divine providence, the young man suddenly thought. *If it isn't providence coming to meet me.* He could not but wonder if, in such an enormous disaster as this, one could think of providence worrying about an insignificant mortal like himself, and his not very vital problem, that of going on leave for a day. He remembered the phrase from the Gospels: even the hairs of your head are counted, and he answered with the conviction that providence was, neither more nor less, concerned with an insignificant mortal like himself. But the problems of the others, then, those who had died crushed or choked to death in cellars, or still others who had lost their homes and goods . . . what about them?

While he waited for the vehicle finally to leave, the young man began to walk back and forth along the pavement of the La Scala square, in front of the imposing Banca Commerciale. Yes, but what about the others? A second phrase from the Gospels came to him: What importance is a sparrow? And still, not even a sparrow falls without God's leave. Did he then have to answer as regards the others that providence—now looking after his leave—had consented, with indifference, that they be killed? *Let's see, we'll try to understand.*

It was necessary to take the matter a little farther back to overcome an obstacle like this. There was a providence (a conservative and God-generated action)—of that he was convinced—that presided over the course of the stars

495

and the galaxies (what was that mote of dust we call our planet Earth, if we confront it with the billions and billions of stars in the universe?) and also presided over Earth, over the growth of every blade of grass and its evolution over millennia. Only a creature deprived of intellect could believe that it was the product of chaos and not the work of an Intelligence. And what an Intelligence! And applying all this to men . . .

Before going any farther, the officer wondered if it was necessary to ponder so many existential reflections in the middle of a catastrophe like this. He decided it was. *Is it when the event we are living through is bigger than the usual, or particularly tragic, that we should renounce reflection?*

Then he thought of men, who are unique among all created beings, who have it in their power to go against the order established by God in creation. Men, indeed, are the only creatures truly free, precisely because they are free before God. This very disorder, this enormous disaster in front of his eyes, was proof of it. Because certainly God had not wanted this evil. It was quite sufficient to think of the words of Christ or even only those of the Pope against violence and war. God had to tolerate, that is, he had to allow this evil, and all the other badness and rottenness of man's creation, not to go against man's freedom. The big problem of evil in the world . . . In order not to impede man's freedom (which would be equivalent to, most surely, denaturing man), God is obliged to tolerate evil.

Once again, there was providence, that is, a conservative and God-generated action, in which he delights and lovingly participates, even in the case of the tiniest creatures (the case of the blade of grass and the case of Manno's leave, for example, as the young man so well noted). And there was this human freedom that—alone—can work against the divine order. Things being what they are, it is a blessing that evil is connected to suffering, which in some way stops men from the destruction they can wreak on creation and themselves.

The fact remained that in Milan and in other places more than a few completely innocent creatures had perished. Suddenly God had stopped protecting them, helping them. He could no longer do so . . . in order not to stand in opposition to men's freedom. All that God had been able to do was to die—in Christ—for them, innocent, along with the innocents, and so uniting his own sacrifice to theirs by sublimating the latter. Christ and all the innocents with him compensated for the evil carried out by other free beings, most particularly, those not wanting to change . . .

The hour of sacrifice can come to every one of us, but those innocents will have not died in vain, that is the point, and this made sense of things.

The young officer decided—if one day he was called to sacrifice—from now on, he would answer, "Present!" He could not have imagined that such a day was approaching with tragic rapidity.

After a few hours, at midafternoon, he was on the train to Nomana.

In his compartment the people talked of nothing but the bombings, and this time, too, the conversation included everybody or almost everybody present, many who did not know each other.

"I got off at Milan this morning to search among the debris of my house," one of the evacuees was recounting, "but it would have been better to have saved myself the trip and avoided the disappointment."

"You can't imagine", another evacuee said, "how painful it is to find yourself without anything, with only the clothes on your back. It's a horrible sensation. It almost seems as if the earth is opening up under your feet."

"Oh, I'm sure."

"What a disaster! What a disaster! We're only now beginning to realize."

"That's true. Never has such a disaster as this been seen. Never."

"The way I see it, the worst damage was caused by the fire bombs. The fire."

"Yes," said the woman who had gone to rummage among the ruins of her house, "the fire. Someone from Unpa said the same thing. He said the worst damage was caused by fire."

"Fire or bombs, the fact is—we're going to have to face it—that Milan no longer exists. I have been to three places, all to do with my company, and you want to know something? I found all three destroyed. In one, an office on the ground floor, I went in and found myself staring out at the sky. In another, where a whole row of houses had caved in, I didn't even manage to know where the place was. On my word of honor, I couldn't find it." He added, "Milan is already a heap of ruins, and the houses still standing but hit are worse off than the others, and they'll have to be demolished, and that will take some work and effort."

A middle-aged man, with a very serious look about him, agreed quite gravely, "It's true. Even more, do you know what I say?" He repeated that phrase several times, until he had everybody's attention. "Do you know what I say? That it's no use reconstructing Milan where it was. Better to go to a clean place and make it all new. I'm not joking." (One could see that indeed he was not.) "I'm trying to be sensible. That way the work of demolishing and transporting rubble, which could be immense, could be avoided. It's for madmen."

The others looked at each other, stunned. "Yes", one person agreed. "What's left intact? Practically nothing. It would be better to reconstruct the city in a new place perhaps."

There were a few seconds of silence. What surprised Manno was that even he, at such a mad proposal, found it perfectly sensible. *Of course it makes no sense. It can't be. In any event, I have to remember these words for later on because it gives an idea of the state to which Milan has been reduced.*

The plains were behind them, and the first undulations of the hills and then the hills themselves came into sight.

To the complex emotions aroused in him by the Milan disaster, still another was cropping up in the young man's mind, an emotion very familiar to him: the emotion of going back to his town, which he experienced every time he returned after a prolonged absence, and this time—how curious—a touch of palpitations, a little like when he returned from school on vacation. And besides, he would see Colomba again this time in Nomana. Despite the war and the bombings and his imminent departure for Greece, and any other big thing, within a short time he would see the girl. The thought of this marvelous encounter was little by little surmounting anything else in him. "Colomba, Colomba", the train wheels and the green hills began to repeat. "Colombina, Colombina". From the time she had left for Novara three months before, he had not properly written to the girl, except for two or three lighthearted postcards. He had tried writing her in a serious vein but never managed to do so, because phrases came out that he judged excessive.

After crossing the Lambro, the railway line began to climb between acacia woods, cultivated terrace fields, the plains, his native landscape. *We're already in the Monte di Brianza,* the youth told himself in high spirits. *But what mountain? Where is it? This is a heap of hills, not a real mountain. What were they thinking?* Manno even began to laugh, less and less inclined to take into account the presence of his neighbors.

A few miles before Nomana, the bell tower of Raperio with its little granite terrace came into view and, next to the train tracks, the little cemetery. They had built it a little away from the other much more ancient one, now almost overgrown with chestnut trees, where only the old vagabonds who died in the hospital were buried. Nearby, between the acacias and chestnuts, the huge and erratic mass of Raperio could be seen, with the dimensions of a small house, carried there by quaternary glaciers. Immediately after were the first signs of his town.

Neither Ambrogio nor Colomba was in Nomana. His Aunt Giulia, looking tense, gave him the news as soon as he set foot in the house.

"But ... didn't you tell me, only a week ago, that Colomba was expected from one minute to the next at *I dragoni?*"

"Yes, that's how it ... it was. But then she didn't come. Maybe because of the bombings."

"And Ambrogio?"

"He's been in the military hospital near Lago Maggiore for the last five days. He's not too well, you know?" And Giulia's eyes began to brim with tears.

How disappointing! But to his aunt, "Come, let's not worry this way. Ambrogio's been released from that inferno. How important can a . . . can a relapse be?"

"Yes, my dear Manno, yes."

Uncle Gerardo, informed by telephone, left his office immediately and came home. "How many hours do you have?"

"I have to be back at base tomorrow at four because our train leaves at 6:30."

"Listen, spend the afternoon with us. Then in the morning perhaps you'll want to take a ride to Stresa . . . or would you rather spend those few hours here in the house quietly?"

"No, Uncle. Would you let me have . . . have the car?"

"Yes. I was thinking of that. Officially, I'll send you to one of our clients in Omegna, in case, you understand, someone stops you on the road. Of course, you don't have to reach Omegna really."

"Terrific!" Manno said. "Wonderful." He reflected, "On my way back, perhaps I could go by Novara?"

His uncle understood. "Of course. Give me a minute to think." He considered the matter a few seconds. "All right, let me arrange it. I'm going back to the office now and . . . it will be better that it all be arranged immediately."

He returned home in a while with two envelopes: one addressed to the client in Omegna, and the other from the office of the Argati factory in Beolco for the military arsenal at Piacenza. "Commander Argati is a good friend, you know, a charming person, and is on the hospital board, like me. Well, it's he who's ordering—pro forma, it's understood—you to make this visit to Piacenza. That way you can go by car, and Novara is on the same road between Omegna and Piacenza." He took a letter out of the envelope, and read, "Doctor Manno Riva, hereby presented, has been ordered by us to make a visit connected with the arsenal, with regard to our provisions of . . ." He interrupted himself and said jokingly, "He calls you doctor, did you realize that?"

"Well, that's only fair", Aunt Giulia said. "Doctor, because you'll graduate soon."

"Me? I've hardly done the exams for half of the courses", Manno laughed. "Besides, what does this doctor have to do with a degree in architecture? I'll never be a doctor."

"That's something else", his aunt insisted. "It means a graduate here."

"I bet", Manno said, laughing.

His uncle finished reading the letter. "Well," he said, "it's not absolutely necessary you go to the arsenal. These are, let's say, mere safe conduct papers. You'll return them with Celeste when you reach Piacenza. I'll explain to Celeste what he has to say if they happen to stop you." He concluded, "This way you'll have a few hours more. If not, with the railway tracks up . . ."

Manno looked his uncle straight in the eye. Despite the light tone of his words, it had not been easy for him to resort to this kind of subterfuge. How well he knew that. "You're helping me as my father would have if he had lived", he said.

"Yes, that's how it is," Gerardo answered, stirred up by these words, "as much as I can."

Manno put the two envelopes in his pocket. So, besides seeing Ambrogio, he would see Colomba. *Providence again*, he thought, *at the ready*. And despite the endless ruins he had witnessed, he would have liked to break into a song of joy.

12

The following morning he saw his cousin on the promenade that stretched along the Stresa. Notified by telephone, Ambrogio wanted to go to meet him. He waited for him seated at a table in front of a bar, under a lopped-off linden tree. He was in uniform, and at his side was seated a young woman from the Red Cross. He did not stand up, but received him saying, "I'm so glad you've come to see me. I've really wanted to see you, too." Then, after a strong handshake, "I'd like you to meet Sister Mayer."

The introductions over, Manno and the driver, Celeste, sat down at the table.

"Tell me", Ambrogio suddenly said. "I'm really curious. Did you find Colomba in Nomana?"

Manno noticed that his cousin was looking quite bad, as he had never seen him before, worse even then when he was convalescing in Riccione. "Colomba?" he answered. "Would you mind telling me how you came to know about all this? Ah, I do know, Francesca . . . God knows what that silly thing told you."

"Come on, Manno, answer", Ambrogio insisted. "Don't digress."

"Well, if you really want to know, I haven't seen her yet because she's not in Nomana, but in Novara."

"In Novara? You mean to say Novara? Oh, I'm really sorry." And he really was. "But then," he exclaimed, "what are you doing here, so calm and collected? Get going, leave, get to Novara."

"Just listen to what he's saying", Manno said to the Red Cross worker and to Celeste. "Here I make an uncomfortable trip to see my poor sick cousin, and look how he receives me. He sends me on my way."

The girl from the Red Cross burst into laughter. Her manners were quite natural, not formal as Manno would have imagined all Red Cross girls to be. The young man was watching her without her noticing it. She was incredibly young and graceful, with eyes of an agreeably strange light color.

Ambrogio noticed his interest. "You know who she is?" Ambrogio asked without further ado.

Manno lifted his head a bit and tried to put himself on guard, not being able to tell where his cousin was going to stop. "I didn't hear her name well when you introduced us. Sister Jucker, I think you said . . ."

"Mayer", she corrected. "Epifania Mayer."

"Did you hear? Epifania. It's mad, unbelievable!" Ambrogio continued. "Did you ever hear of a name like that?" Even though he was exhausted, he couldn't keep from joking, in the presence of a girl.

"Pay no attention, Sister", Manno said, shaking his head with obvious disapproval. (Celeste also joined in and likewise shook his head.) "He's like that, but not really a bad fellow, even if it seems so."

For the second time the girl from the Red Cross burst into joyous laughter. "It seems so. Yes, that's true", she agreed.

"Sister Epifania, when she's seen in the street, is called Fanny, and in the Catholic university, in the economics department, we called her Fanny GE, which means Green Eyes", Ambrogio continued.

"Ah, so you're friends from the university. Terrific!"

"Yes, I'm in the economics department, too," Fanny GE said.

"Perhaps you heard me mention her."

"Oh, of course", Manno said. "Now I remember." He really did remember, but only vaguely. Ambrogio had spoken of Green Eyes during a leave, yes: one of the few decent schoolfriends in his course, he had said, or something similar. "Just imagine!" he commented. And addressing Fanny, who really did have green eyes, "So, Sister, you have to put up with his unbearable presence not only in class, but also in war."

"Oh, my," she joined in, "poor, poor me!"

"If I were in your shoes, I'd ask to be transferred", Manno advised.

"That's what she's thinking", Ambrogio explained. "Exactly that, but it isn't convenient. She has her home here in Pallanza, and it suits her quite well to be in service here in Stresa. Actually, for her it's like doing military service in a summer resort."

During the entire visit—a good hour—they did not move away from the little table under the tree with its top lopped off. Along the road by the lake— the national Sempione highway—there was not much traffic, and everything had the usual air, but the gravity of the situation was in the air and the faces of the people. It was reflected in them, too, despite their trying not to show it.

In addition to all the rest, Manno felt secretly worried about his cousin's health. In all his life—he repeated to himself—he had never seen him looking so bad off. Ambrogio finally realized this, and to Manno, looking out of the corner of his eye, he said, "Don't worry about me. You see," he motioned toward the Red Cross sister with his chin, "I get every possible care." Then he let escape, "In any case, it's the others we have to think about, the ones who've been taken prisoner in conditions worse than mine." He looked out for an instant on the peaceful extension of the lake. "If there are any prisoners", he murmured.

The others looked at him in silence. "Why don't you think there are prisoners?" Celeste questioned, horrified.

"I didn't say that. I don't know. No one can say."

"Listen, why don't we talk about something happier?" Manno suggested, and he tried to lead the conversation toward pleasanter subjects.

While he watched him joke again, making Fanny laugh more often, Ambrogio felt, as he had already days before in Nomana, the unexpected premonition that he would not see his cousin for a long time, a very long time. *For all the time left in my life, perhaps?* he wondered mockingly, almost as if making fun of himself. *Maybe so,* an inner voice answered him. *Probably so. But all this is foolishness I'm inventing because I'm worried, not well,* in an attempt to do away with the problem.

"In Greece," he said, picking up on a joke of Manno's, "don't make yourself out too much of a smart guy just to be able to tell Colomba all about it when you get back. I know you."

"Smart guy?" the other fellow exclaimed, his eyes still laughing. "Can you imagine what kind of smart guy you can be at a time when everyone's getting ready to push off?" At that moment he guessed his cousin's secret worry. "Listen here, I have the feeling that the two of us are playing the game of seeing who can worry more about the other one, like two nursemaids. Doesn't it make you laugh?" He laughed, and Fanny and Celeste smiled.

Ambrogio shook his head disapprovingly, but made no objections.

"Come, come, Ambrogio", Manno then said. "You know how I see things, don't you? If providence decides I go to Greece, it means that it's good for me to go to Greece, that it serves the end for which our Lord has prepared me, whatever it is." He gestured with his hand, as if he held a covered plate. "And until then, until my entire role is fulfilled, nothing can happen to me. Am I making myself clear? Even if I am thrown into fire, nothing will happen to me."

"Do you hear him? He sounds like he has a direct line to God", Ambrogio addressed the other two. And to Fanny, "You won't believe me, but as far as predestination is concerned, he's not joking at all. He's already said all this in total seriousness many times."

Fanny opened her GE, smiling.

13

An hour after having left Stresa, Manno was in Novara in front of Colomba's house, on one of those boulevards—wide, silent streets shaded by rows of thick-foliaged chestnut trees—that surround the most ancient part of the city.

On ringing the bell he felt the same palpitation he had when he appeared for the first time at *I dragoni* in Nomana. *And I'm not even going into combat,* again he thought, and again this time he had to feel silly. *Please, don't make me laugh.*

Colomba in person came to answer the door. "Oh, Manno!" she shouted with pleasure. "Manno, it's you! What a surprise, how wonderful!"

Instead of speaking, the young man contemplated her for a few seconds. "How pretty you are, Colomba", he said emotionally. "You're charming."

Colomba would have liked to answer lightheartedly, but she felt so upset she could not manage to utter a word.

"How are you, Colombina?" he asked her, with a voice that had come down to earth. "How are you?"

"Manno, you remembered me", Colomba murmured.

"Of course. What did you think? But what's happening? Aren't you going to invite me in?"

Very emotionally the young girl made room for him to enter. She regained her speech only when, in the vestibule, he stopped, waiting for directions. "Mama, Mama!" she shouted. "Come, Manno's here. Come."

An old white-haired servant stuck her head out from an inner door. "Cleofe, call Mama, please. He's . . . he's here . . . call her, please."

The introductions then followed (her father, they explained, was out working), and also the first formal and awkward words in the salon. "Manno is an officer, you know?"

"Yes, Colomba, you've told me."

"Why didn't you come in uniform, Manno?"

Manno—handsome as he was in plain clothes—explained why he was not in uniform and recounted the pretext assignment. "So, it's as if I were carrying out a professional errand, as a technician, or traveling salesman. Not even I know exactly."

Colomba laughed, shaking her young head, as she regained control over herself. "Now I'll change. What do you think, Manno? I won't be a minute."

She returned shortly wearing the dress that he had already seen more than once in *I dragoni*, which Manno thought similar to a Greek peplos. As for her hair, she had gathered it into a chignon with rapid impatience in front of the mirror in her small room: a hairdo tried out once and again secretly in order to look more womanly and probably more Greek and, in any case, less of a little girl.

"For the love of God!" her mother said, seeing her, but added nothing else.

And as for Manno, he was not thinking of becoming surprised or of laughing. Once more his mouth was agape. He was at the point where if she had showed up disguised as a clown, he would have admired her all the same. *What a lovely creature. Thank you, dear Lord, thank you!* he thought.

Noticing her mother's perturbation and fearing some intervention or correction, Colomba immediately suggested to Manno, "Should we take a walk? What do you think?"

503

"Yes, of course." He accepted the invitation on the fly.

Her mother ventured, "Go out like that", and was about to add, "with your hair that way?" but changed that statement to, "like that at this time of day?"

"Yes, Mama, why not?"

"Why not?" Manno echoed.

"As you wish, children."

The two young people left and strolled under the chestnut trees of the boulevard, chatting more and more spontaneously. At a certain point Colomba, with the volubility of her eighteen years, let herself inwardly be influenced by her mother's reasons and took out the hairpins that held her chignon in place. Her hair fell loose, but without returning to its normal style. And so the girl's hairdo seemed somewhat strange, bizarre. "To wear a chignon, I think my hair's too short, don't you think so?" she justified herself.

"No. Why?" Manno replied. "That hairstyle suits you very well," and in a softer voice he added, "almost Greek."

Colomba shook her head that it was not so and then burst into laughter.

"Well, no matter", Manno said. "This style looks good, too. You're pretty any way, too; you're always pretty."

The entire time Manno was able to spend with her—almost two hours— they walked up and back the length of that avenue and the surrounding area. They spoke of so many things, but they might very well have spoken of nothing at all. They were two young people living through a new experience, the birth of their love, that astonishing gift of God.

Finally—faithful to his instructions—Celeste arrived in the Millecento. Seeing them, he went to park next to the pavement a little way off, and, without getting out of the car, he took a newspaper out of his pocket and unfolded it, rather ostentatiously.

His presence, in any case, indicated that the moment had arrived for farewells. Colomba became uneasy. "You're going off to war", she suddenly exclaimed, interrupting the conversation they were having.

"Well, that's one way of putting it", Manno replied, smiling. "I'm going to Greece, to an occupation zone. There's been no war there for a while. But we already talked about that."

"The war's everywhere", Colomba said.

"Yes, if you want to look at it that way. Then I, too, should do my part. Am I not an officer, more or less for that reason?"

Colomba clearly realized that the young man who was speaking to her was not one to shrink from duty. "Don't laugh!" she exclaimed, frightened. "There's no joking about war. It's a hideous and horrifying thing." She added, "Now I understand it, too."

She was no longer a child speaking, but a woman, and at that moment more adult than he. Manno realized it with surprise. "Oh, Manno, Manno", Colomba lamented.

"Colombina, what's wrong? Come, come, cheer up." The young man laughed again in careless fashion to reassure her. Meanwhile he gazed at her with his blue eyes, the blue eyes of a young gentleman who wanted to be devil may care. "Listen, Colomba, I came back in a boat from Africa. If it's necessary, I'll come back swimming from Greece to see you again. All right? I promise it." Colomba did not laugh. "It's atrocious!" she said, following her own line of anxiety.

"But what can I do? You wouldn't want me to leave the others 'in the soup' and I stand aside. What kind of man would I be? You'd scorn me yourself."

"Yes, but . . . oh, such things, what things happen in life," Colomba exclaimed, "and our life is beginning now." She put a hand on his shoulder. Her eyes—Manno realized—were full of tears.

What pleasure to have the contact of her hand! The young man took it delicately and kissed it, deeply moved. "Don't worry. You'll see. I'll be back. In fact, do you want to know something? I *must*", and he stressed the word, "I *must* come back. I'm not joking. To explain it all now seriously is not possible in a few words. My cousin Ambrogio knows it. I spoke with him this morning. When it's convenient, he'll explain it to you, all right?"

"Ambrogio? Explain?"

"Yes, Colombina: explain how and why I'll come back."

The girl looked at him with her young gray-blue eyes full of tears. Would Manno go on joking?

It seemed not. "That's it, Colombina. That's exactly how it is. Well, now I'll walk you home."

14

Manno and Celeste had lunch at the Roma Restaurant in Piacenza. It was after three in the afternoon, but the owners knew the officer and put together something without any trouble. Then Manno had Celeste take him to his lodging in a little house in the outskirts, where he put on his uniform and, on coming out, gave Celeste a case in which his civilian clothes and a few other things were packed to take back home. He also gave him his industrial "credentials". "Take these papers, Badoglio. If someone stops you, you know what to do. A pack of lies, eh?"

"Lies of this type are not lies", Celeste responded loyally. "I've also been a soldier and know what it means to have a few hours' leave."

"Thanks." Manno paused. He felt the need of lowering the dramatic temperature of the situation a little. "Are you still carrying the chestnut against rheumatism in your pocket?"

That was a source of old jokes. Celeste turned red. "Yes, of course. You can all laugh, but it's true. I've put it to the test."

"Look after yourself . . . with seven children at home," Manno said, becoming serious, "and greetings to everyone, my uncle and aunt, my cousins, Don Mario, the oratory people . . . to one and all."

"Yes, of course." The driver took on a more serious air. "I know you, you and Ambrogio, since the day you were born. Manno, be careful. These are bad times. Try to keep out of danger. I tell you . . . from my heart."

"Yes, yes, of course."

"The two of you, you and Ambrogio, will be needed in Nomana in a few years. I mean, to make more work, when the children of today grow up."

In any case, it's up to providence, Manno thought as he shook hands warmly. "It's all right. I mean I'll watch out in Greece. Goodbye, Celestino. And so many thanks for having taken me this far."

"Goodbye and good luck, Manno." Celeste lightly doffed his cap.

It was Manno's farewell from his world.

PART FOUR

I

The groups of reinforcements left for Greece without further delays that same afternoon, by train. However, in Brindisi there was a layover for several days to wait for one particular ship to Albania. By that time the Americans and English had completed the occupation of Sicily and were on their way to Calabria. "Perhaps," the soldiers were saying, "we won't even go to Greece. Maybe they'll send us to Calabria."

"We're only a reinforcement group, on our own, and our weapons are with the Greek regiment, so what makes you think they'll send us to Calabria?" Lieutenant Pigliapoco, the group's commander, objected, though he was also somewhat uncertain.

On the evening of the fourth of September the group, together with other groups, were shipped out at night to Albania. They disembarked the following morning with their knapsacks on their backs, at the port of Santi Quaranta, christened Porto Edda in honor of the Duce's daughter.

No one was there to meet them because the vehicles sent over from the respective regiments were waiting in Valona. They arrived at Porto Edda that day, but unfortunately for Pigliapoco's group there was only one truck, insufficient to transport all of them. "A fuel shortage", the chief mechanic explained. "Just think, more than a month's gone by waiting to move the regiment from the Peloponnese to the area around Athens, but it can't be done for lack of fuel."

Lieutenant Pigliapoco, after inveighing harshly against headquarters and their logic, as well as the army in its entirety, decided to leave with as many as he could transport in the truck. He left Manno and twenty artillerymen in Porto Edda, where by disposition of local headquarters, they were incorporated for mess with an antiaerial battery to defend the port.

It was a twenty-millimeter machine-gun battery situated on a small height at the side of the sea. His commanding officer, Lieutenant Cioffi—middle aged and incredibly slovenly—indicated a spot to Manno among the olive trees where his men could pitch their tents. "If you like, you can come and sleep with us in our royal quarters", he said. "We're only three, not four, because the adjutant commander is in the hospital with malaria, so there is room in the tent for the officers. But if you prefer sleeping in town . . ."

"No, it's better I stay here with my men."

"As you like. You fellows, given the few days you'll be here, can consider yourselves on vacation. A great vacation, you'll see! Great!"

The newly arrived Manno was puzzled.

In the face of such bewilderment, Cioffi burst into laughter. "It's all right", he said. "Take one of your men, or two or three, and make up a bed in the officer's tent."

"I have my cot."

"Well, fine. Then let them make it up."

Manno gave his artillerymen orders to set up the tents and watched over the operation personally. Moreover, he made them dig a supplementary latrine in a dusty cane thicket. "We'll have to try to bother the battery as little as possible, as they already seem to be quite bothered on their own." At evening mess he and his men had a cold meal—as they had already had at midday. "From tomorrow on the battery will take charge of the food for us, too, so we'll be eating normally."

The old soldiers at the post, even more slovenly than their commander, lazy, too, continued poking fun at the labors of the newly arrived. After mess the old fellows and the new ones mingled, some of them on leave to town, the others seated in circles under the olive and carob trees. Even toward twilight the sound of crickets did not stop for an instant, it was very hot, and there were a lot of flies and dust. However, the place—for anyone who bothered to look at it—was very pretty, with the blue sea not far off and the mountainous, green island of Corfu, which emerged in front of them.

Manno went to the tent, where the three officers of the battery were seated around a rustic table on old benches. Cioffi had unloosed his belt and was striking himself occasionally on his belly with the longer end. They had just finished their mess. On the table, along with the crumbs, was a half-empty bottle of wine and some glasses. They made the newly arrived Manno sit down, exchanged a few conventional phrases, and then asked him about his boat trip (Had he seen any submarines? No? How strange!) and about Italy, how the people were taking the situation, and so on. But they did not seem to pay much attention to his answers, as if it had to do with something that, everything considered, had little to do with them.

From time to time, Manno glanced at the eight small machine guns of the battery, set up a short way off among the thickets.

"You're looking at our toys?" the commanding lieutenant asked. "Since we've been here—it's been two years already, two years, maybe it doesn't seem long, but . . . well, we've still not had any occasion to fire a single shot."

"Not even one?"

"Not one. No one comes to bomb this port. Why should they? Our ships seldom use this port: only when they come across some English submarine near Valona. Something like that must have happened last night."

"So you end up a little bored, don't you?"

"A little?" Cioffi said and turned to his two officers. "Did you hear that? A little ..."

The other two smiled drearily. One of them, quite young, with a good-hearted face, said, "I came after the others, six months after. I've only been here a year and a half. At first, on hearing that no one came here to bomb us, I was quite enthusiastic, and I thought, 'This is the ideal spot to spend the rest of the war', as I had been on small boats between Puglia and Albania and ... well, that was quite bad. All in all, this spot seemed ideal to me at first. For months I thought this, and so did the soldiers who arrived here with me, but then ..."

"Yes, then", Cioffi said with a touch of melancholy.

This is really a detachment of bums, Manno was finding out. *In Libya, in some of the interior posts, the soldiers were also like this before the war came along to kick them in the behind* ... "I understand", he said out loud. "But now, given the situation we're in, all this is about to change. We'll get into action."

"Action?" Cioffi questioned without much conviction, shaking his head. "Mmm", was his only response, and then again, "mmm."

"It goes without saying", Manno said. It seemed obvious to him, and he tried to tell them why. "I imagine the first to come here will be the partisans, who ..."

"What partisans?" Cioffi exclaimed. "There aren't any partisans in Porto Edda. They're back there in the mountains." He pointed vaguely with his hand. "And from what we hear, they are, fortunately, busy fighting among themselves. Because in Albania there are three classes of partisans. Are you aware of that?"

"Three?"

"Yes, Nationalists, Communists, and the Ballisti. And all of them each other's sworn enemies." He yawned.

Manno was wondering if the other fellow might be pulling his leg or if he had not understood. "What did you say?" he asked, disconcerted. "Nationalist and Communist partisans and ... ?"

Cioffi noticed his amazement and started to laugh. "Ballisti. Exactly. To tell the truth, you had to come to Albania to find out there were Ballisti."

"And what political beliefs do they hold?"

"Do you know? Nobody does. I've only heard they're the fastest goat thieves when it comes to robbing the peasants, among other things. And we don't know much else."

Manno also began laughing. "In any case," he insisted, "these are crucial days, and ..."

"But who told you?" For a moment Cioffi felt vaguely hopeful, despite himself. Then he gestured negatively. "But no, this time I won't be fooled", he said. "I won't be taken in, like after July 25. These are simply boring days, like all the others."

"But don't you have a radio here?" Manno asked. "Don't you get the news?"

"No," Cioffi answered, "we don't have a radio. We had one I brought from Italy, but my aide let it fall. When was that? Oh, yes, about six or seven months ago. May it rest in peace. I mean the radio. It broke." Then he added, "Maybe it's all for the best."

"Besides," the sublieutenant with the good-natured face joined in, "we know all about the wonderful things happening in the world from the army paper that gets here every two weeks. And we also get some other papers."

"Every two weeks?" Manno repeated.

"Come on", Cioffi said, no longer hitting his stomach with the belt. "Why don't you have something to drink?" And he thrust his chin toward the bottle. "No label on it, but it's Greek wine and not at all bad. You don't have a glass, do you?" He was about to stand up, but he thought it was better in front of an outsider to show more organization. He turned toward the troop tents. "Carapelle!" he yelled, and then again, "Carapelle!"

His aide appeared. One could not exactly tell if he was dressed in shorts or in undershorts, his feet stuck into two sabots of his own fabrication, uncombed, and looking around with a questioning air. "Bring a glass", Cioffi ordered.

Carapelle checked the number of glasses on the table with a glance. "The only thing left is the mess tin."

He went into the officer's tent, searched around a while, and came back with a small aluminum tin. Right in front of the guest's eyes he calmly wiped the edge of the tin to remove any possible dirt. Manno noticed it. *Don't worry*, he said to himself. *I've just had all my vaccinations.* Then he began to drink. "It's good", he had to admit. "Wow, but it's strong!"

"Oh, at last there's something you like", Cioffi said. He turned to Carapelle. "Come on, open another bottle."

Carapelle obeyed. Twilight was approaching, and along a narrow and stony lane came the peasants, back from the fields, many on donkeys, with the women—their faces covered, their trousers tied at the ankle, wearing old knit Turkish slippers—following on foot, close to the camp.

"They're all Moslem here, aren't they?" Manno inquired.

"Not all, but the majority are."

"I saw a small minaret in the town."

"Don't talk to me about that minaret. Please, just don't talk about it!" Cioffi exclaimed.

"Why? What do you mean?"

"I know very well what I mean."

"It's because of something that happened this summer", explained the good-natured lieutenant. "The soldiers had taken to gathering every evening under the minaret to imitate the *muezzin*. Among the artillerymen who were down below and the one up above, they tried to see who could shout the loudest. Imagine the uproar! But in a while it didn't seem quite enough, and one afternoon two or three wretches began to fire into the air with their rifles, not to hit the *muezzin*, it goes without saying, but just to add to the uproar."

"Those f——head solders!" the other lieutenant exclaimed. "But do you realize it? This is our imperial mentality." He looked straight at Manno. "Do you realize that?" It was the first time he had joined in the conversation, his first words since being introduced. Manno nodded. He could not make out if he was a Fascist or an anti-Fascist. He was balding, and he had the face of an embittered intellectual.

"The fact is that the *muezzin* was scared out of his wits by the shots," the good-natured fellow concluded, "and he came down like lightning, fled from the minaret, and for days he wouldn't even contemplate going back up. And so the Moslems of the town were in a state of turmoil."

Cioffi every so often nodded. "Yes," he snorted, "it was a royal pain in the neck because then those sh——s at garrison headquarters took it out on me, you understand?"

When this subject was exhausted, the conversation returned to present-day topics. Manno tried to get the others to participate in the sensation of expectation that prevailed in Italy, but once more with little success. It seemed as if they instinctively refused to expose themselves to a state of mind that could perturb their vegetative life. As for the lieutenant with the face of an intellectual, he receded into the shell of his own silence.

I hope only for one thing, Manno finally concluded to himself, *and that is that things won't be like this in the regiment we're being sent to.*

2

The following day also passed for him and his men in the same way: without anything for them to do. But at dawn of the next day, immediately after coffee—a substitute—was passed around, he presented himself to Commander Cioffi. "We'll stay here for quite a few days. I'd like to know, in the case of an attack, what our job will be."

"Your job?"

"Yes. It'll be necessary to get ready."

"For an enemy attack?"

"Yes."

"What kind, an air attack or a naval one?"

"I beg you not to joke", Manno said. "We're here under your orders, and . . ."

"Only for mess", Cioffi clarified.

"I'd like to be put in the picture in case something should happen."

"Something happen? Ah, but this is a real obsession with you."

"Suppose the Allies show up here off shore and try to land."

Cioffi looked at him as if bewildered. "The Allies show up here?" He paused. "Well, above all touch wood", he continued, putting one hand on a tree and keeping it that way for a good spell. "Then, he who among us is alive after the naval artillery fire will defend himself any way he can."

"Fine", Manno said, seeing he would not be able to get any more from him. "Agreed, then. I'll get my men ready for that eventuality."

"Terrific", the other answered, happy to have put an end to Manno's annoying questions.

The last thing he would have expected was that the young man would call his men together immediately, divide them into two squadrons under the command of the two noncoms, and put into action a real antilanding practice. *If it's of no other use*, Manno thought, *at least I won't let them get bogged down here. What else can we do? Sit all day in front of the tents and stare at our navels?*

They continued their taking-of-position exercises until it was time for mess, returned to their tents, then took new and better organized positions behind some rocks situated toward the sea. In the afternoon he kept them busy the whole time digging between the rocks, preparing a system of defense that way. The following day—the eighth of September—new positions were established, and a zigzag trench was dug next to the tents. This, as experience had taught him, would be very useful should they have an unexpected air attack.

His soldiers—occasionally smiling at the incredulous faces of the others—fulfilled their duties without any discussion. The best of them were secretly delighted to be led by an officer who was showing himself to have initiative. They realized that this would be quite important in case of necessity. Only a few whined on the sly. Imagine, they'd fallen into the hands of a fanatic who'd not had his fill with the war in Africa and had come back to Italy in a boat just to break their balls. "But why didn't the damn boat just go down?" they grumbled softly to each other. "Why?"

On the evening of that day, the eighth of September, Manno—as on the previous evening—after mess took a walk around the town. There was not much to see besides the minaret of the famous *muezzin*, with the mosque next to it, the miserable shacks of the Albanians, and the scrupulously whitewashed ones of the few equally poor Greek inhabitants. He ended, as on the previous day, by going along the coast road, this time toward the north. Meanwhile, he reflected on the difficult situation of his country and dreamed about Colomba. When this damn war was over, the two of them would marry (of course, he had to finish his studies first . . . a few more years!), and they'd come back here together to the island of Corfu, which emerged, not far off, so beautifully from the turquoise waters of the sea. There were hotels . . . but first it was necessary to pull out of the present tragic situation. Nothing could be planned if they didn't come out of this.

The coast road was rising more and more. Step after step the young man was getting farther away from the town, and, immersed in his daydreams, he reached a small and singularly solitary cove. A sign spelled out its name: Porto Limione. From the road—at this point high over the sea—his gaze stretched far over the Ionic sea toward the west, toward his homeland. There was a vast silence, emphasized by the irregular hum of the cicadas and a pungent odor of aromatic herbs.

Suddenly he heard the sound of a motor, and he immediately realized he was alone and carrying only a pistol. What was this about? Heaven forbid, could it be a car full of partisans? Cioffi had told him they had never seen any in Porto Edda. The young man knew, however—having better informed himself—that they were not far away and that they frequently attacked neighboring detachments, like the one at Delvino, about nine miles toward the interior as the crow flies.

Fortunately the vehicle that arrived did not belong to partisans. It was a motorcycle from the Italian forces, with two soldiers in it. When they reached his spot, they stopped. The driver, a sergeant, seemed very excited. He raised his goggles to his forehead. "Lieutenant," he said, "do you know yet at Porto Edda the big news? That there's an armistice?"

"What? What are you saying?"

"An armistice. Italy's signed an armistice with the Americans and English. Radio Roma is repeating it endlessly. We heard it a half hour ago in Porto Palermo. Just in time to get here." The sergeant turned to his comrade. "It's true, isn't it? Tell him."

"Yes, it's true", the other fellow, a corporal, confirmed. "The war's over, Badoglio's order."

"Well, we have to be on our way", the sergeant said, and without giving Manno a chance to ask any questions, he took his leave and left, almost tearing off.

3

Manno turned immediately and went back to the town, taking big strides. Now he was excited, so much so that it would not have taken him much to start talking to himself and discussing the big event. He felt an intense need to know more details. He made and rejected conjectures and occasionally got annoyed at the two fellows on the motorcycle. *What apes. At least they could have told me everything they'd heard on the radio, everything they know. If the Germans, for instance, are in agreement (and that's not possible!) If . . .* More and more questions came to mind, one more worrying than the other. *Will the navy get the army out of the Balkans? At least the troops close to the coast? Will they even try?* He did not know that some hours before the navy had received orders to move to Malta and give themselves up and that already the ships (the big and powerfully armed ships, which in the days to come could have been so necessary here) were all on their way south. And still more: the Germans, up until hours before their own allies—men, after all is said and done, of flesh and blood, like any others—how were they going to manage in the Balkans alone, after the Italians defected? *In the middle of this swarming mass of partisans, what will they do? After all, they came here because of us. As for them, without Mussolini's stupid brainstorms, they wouldn't have come.*

Very soon he reached Porto Edda, where he met the soldiers from the detachment command, the ones from the hospital, and a certain number from the antiaerial battery in groups. They were going back and forth to gather information, shouting from time to time, and overwhelmed with emotion.

He hurried to get to the machine-gun emplacements. Lieutenant Cioffi had sent his two sublieutenants to the garrison headquarters. "They have a radio there. I want to know if there's any truth in this tale."

"Why? Do you think it's a joke?" Manno asked.

"I don't know. I don't know. Maybe you were right when you said that these are days . . . how did you put it? Decisive days? Well, now we'll see."

"Yes," Manno agreed, "we'll see."

The two lieutenants returned in about a half hour, the one with the intellectual face carrying a paper in his hand and discussing its contents with the other as they walked along. Back at the officer's tent he handed the paper to the commanding lieutenant, while the soldiers of the battery crowded around, happy. "Here it is written, more or less, the words of the armistice proclamation", the sublieutenant said. "There's no other news on the radio. Every so often the proclamation is repeated, and then there's just music."

"So there is an armistice! An armistice!" the soldiers yelled. "It's true! Peace at last!" A few began to scream enthusiastically. "Home again, home again! Everybody home! Viva! It's over, it's over!"

Cioffi read the paper attentively and then ordered silence. "Quiet already! It sounds like a whorehouse here!" He reread the paper to all of them out loud, and before he finished the soldiers started clamoring again, applauding, slapping each other on the back, jumping with joy. "The war's over, it's over, home again! We'll all get home again!"

The officer tightened his lips, perplexed. Then he turned and went in the tent with the other officers. "What do you say?" he asked, looking at Manno questioningly.

"It's this phrase," he observed, "that we must no longer defend ourselves from the Americans and English, but from all others who attack us."

"You're thinking of the Germans, aren't you?"

"Yes, exactly. But the partisans, too. To go no farther, they'd like to get hold of our weapons."

"And so? We can give them to the partisans. At least they'll do some good", the intellectual exclaimed aggressively. "The Germans, never. Never", he repeated.

Manno looked him straight in the face. "When you deliver over your farm to the partisans, you'll be emptyhanded", he said toughly. "And then how will you defend yourself from the Germans? Or do you want them really to screw you?"

"But ...", the good-natured officer added, quite surprised. "Weren't you until a little while ago ... haven't you always been a Fascist? So now what are you saying?"

The intellectual did not answer. There was a moment of silence.

Cioffi rolled his eyes up to the sky. "This place will be some hell of a whorehouse for a while", he mumbled.

"It's possible a number of battalions will be moving here to the coast from the interior", Manno suggested, paying no attention to the intellectual.

"Yes," the good-natured fellow agreed, "very possible."

"But we're already here", Cioffi exclaimed, as if he wanted to make the right precedence quite clear. "We've been here for two years, so as soon as a ship arrives it should be us who embark."

His lieutenants and the intellectual, too, agreed most fervently with this. It seemed, however, they weren't concealing from themselves the difficulties involved in this.

"Let me read the proclamation again", Manno said. "Let me examine it carefully."

The commander handed him the paper. The four of them would read it over and over during the course of the days to come, to keep searching out some sort of illumination, a more precise directive, which it did not contain.

Outside, the soldiers went on shouting, even those who inwardly were beginning to share the same worry as the officers. But they did not intend to renounce the party atmosphere, and after all, in life it was one thing at a time.

4

The whorehouse they feared did not immediately materialize. It took more time for that to happen than the men involved had expected.

The next day and the following ones only small detachments and a few groups of dispersed soldiers (these, too, in general, with their weapons, except for a few who had been robbed by the partisans) arrived from the interior, and they camped out on the port dock, waiting for the ships.

The ninth, tenth, eleventh of September, and not a sign of ships from Italy.

Instead, a few local service launches came from Corfu, which loaded up and took off to the island (considered more secure because it was an island, defended by an intact infantry regiment) the small detachments and dispersed soldiers, as well as a part of the Porto Edda detachment. The launches would return to carry off more of the dispersed in the next days.

The twelfth, the thirteenth of September. More troops came from the interior. At midday on the thirteenth, an armored car and two German trucks going toward Valona went along the coast road. The soldiers of the battery manned their machine guns and watched them, very tensely, from a distance. The Germans watched the Italians in the same way and continued on their way, not stopping.

The fourteenth, the fifteenth, the sixteenth of September: launches again came from Corfu to move the troops coming from the interior and from a few close-by coastal positions.

New soldiers kept arriving, now often detached singly.

Two infantrymen who arrived by chance at the antiaerial unit told them that the nearest infantry battalion, which was in Delvino, had started marching a few days before, but instead of going to the coast, it had taken the road to Argirocastro, where the rest of the regiment was.

"And why didn't you follow it?" Manno asked.

"We lost contact. It was nighttime."

"They weren't coming here to the sea. They were going in the opposite direction. You understand?" the other fellow clarified.

"Ah, now I understand."

"Lieutenant Colonel Cirino is in command of the battalion, and he doesn't joke around."

"You can say that again! He made the men bring all their weapons and ammo. They were loaded down worse than beasts because there's no fuel."

"And how is it you didn't follow the others?" Manno asked once more.

"Us? But Lieutenant, we were lost. It was night. I already told you."

"We were a little behind, and then we found the road cut by the partisans."

"Yes, cut by the partisans."

"So why weren't you taken prisoners?"

"We're not so stupid as to let ourselves be caught, no."

"But, Lieutenant, I assure you it was no easy matter. It took us five days to get here, walking only at night, with our hearts in our mouth."

They stole away as soon as they could, to mingle with the other dispersed soldiers in the port.

The seventeenth, the eighteenth, the nineteenth of September. A German reconnaissance plane, which apparently was controlling the coast, passed over Porto Edda every day now.

"Just look, a target for your little toys, isn't it?" Manno commented to Cioffi. Cioffi spread his arms out. The armistice proclamation instructed them to shoot only when attacked. In any event, he had visibly livened up. In imitation of Manno he had made his men carry out positions with their machine guns, along the coast road, as well as an antilanding emplacement toward the sea.

On the nineteenth, a small group of ten men arrived at the antiaerial post, who announced they were bearers of serious news and so were led to the officer's tent.

"We're from Argirocastro."

"We were prisoners of the Communists. They released us precisely for us to come here to report to you."

"There's been a battle in Argirocastro. It happened on the fourteenth", the highest ranking of them related, a sergeant, his face covered with bruises. "On the mountains surrounding the Italian camp was gathered an enormous group of partisans, at least thirty thousand, divided into two opposite bands: the Ballisti on one side and the Communists on the other. Every so often they'd fire at each other. And they continually sent, one as much as the other, delegations asking for our weapons, especially cannons, because they knew we had no gasoline. On the fourteenth, all at once the Ballisti came down en masse from their mountains, completely into the open. At first, our men yelled for them to go back, but then when they were only a few yards away, they opened fire. It was a massacre. They killed endless men. I had been taken prisoner by the Communists the day before. Until then they had done nothing but slap us around and kick us, but then they took us off in a great hurry, the prisoners, that is, to see the battle, or rather the rest of the battle, from a kind of nearby observatory. We saw all the dead and injured strewn on the ground, and our men continued advancing to rout the Ballisti from where they had hidden in the Drino backwaters, forcing them out with hand grenades. Then the Communists released the ten of us to come here and spread the news. They were as happy as larks because the others had been destroyed. 'Go over to your men on the coast', they told us and repeated, 'and tell them what's happened: nothing else. Explain to them that it was your men who killed them, and that they didn't give over their weapons. Tell them the Italians, none of them, should give weapons to the Ballisti.' This they kept saying."

Manno, very concerned after having listened with Cioffi and the other officers to this account, accompanied the ten men to headquarters. What a situation, he thought, especially since it was not just the soldiers involved in this difficult situation. What would happen with civilians, divided, one against the other? While walking, he asked question after question of the soldiers, who— the majority were in bad shape with wounds, their clothes in shreds, hungry, in a state that could only arouse pity. They could not answer the questions because they did not know the subsequent developments in Argirocastro.

What had really happened was that the day after the battle, the fifteenth of September, the Communist partisans sent a delegation to propose that the Italians turn over 75 percent of their heavy arms. "We ask only that. Since there's no gasoline you won't be able to take them with you, especially the cannons. Later, if you like, we'll escort you ourselves to the sea."

The Italian commander in Argirocastro was a general. He parleyed, asked questions, and then withdrew to consider his men's difficult situation. By now the Germans were against them, and their sworn enemies were also the Ballisti. The partisans, the Communists, were offering a kind of truce that perhaps might allow them to reach the sea without battling between those terribly craggy mountains. After having reflected on the matter for several hours, the general decided to accept the Communist proposal. Their envoys left the camp radiant with joy.

But as soon as the commanders of the battalion were informed of the agreement, they firmly rejected it and immediately sent a message to the Communists to let them know the agreement had been canceled. They stood their ground firmly, especially Lieutenant Colonel Cirino, who knew that if the partisans could avail themselves of the cannons they would be able to block their exit to the sea, and any other way, too. It was not necessary to put themselves in their hands like this, or in anybody else's. The general at first argued back but at last recognized that his battalion leaders were right.

The soldiers in the camp—between infantrymen and artillerymen, they came to nearly ten thousand—had been waiting from the day of the armistice (a week by now) to set off to the coast. They knew something about the agreement and something about it being canceled, and they wanted to know more. Realizing that the decision did not depend on one person alone, they decided, on their own, to form up in columns, and they did it all together without waiting for orders, getting ready to march off toward Porto Edda.

Abandoning Argirocastro would have meant the loss of many weapons and tons of munitions: a sizable reduction in firepower. The commanders, having been in radio contact with the Italian headquarters in Brindisi, would have preferred not to move until there were ships on the coast to load the troops. In the face of the danger of total chaos, however, they decided to leave as soon as darkness fell. After that decision, the soldiers once again submitted to discipline, dissolved the columns they had been forming, and went back to their combat positions.

Once Brindisi was notified of their decision to set off, the commanders ordered the destruction of all radio apparatus, weapons, and ammo that was not transportable, and anything else that could not be carried was burned. Later, the command with the infantry battalions and a complete artillery group, as well as service units and all the detached troops, flocked to the camp. They reformed and left the spot in perfect order. It was three o'clock in the morning. Little by little gunner sections were sent over the mountains to the sides of the columns—in line with security norms—and also squadrons of machine gunners were sent ahead to occupy strategic points.

The Communist partisans (probably led by Enver Hoxha, the future and merciless dictator of Albania, a native of Argirocastro) did not dare to attack that strong formation. They limited themselves to following en masse, harassing

518

with skirmishes, while to maintain security measures the Italian formation was forced to proceed intermittently. The third day the Communists even sent over a supply of victuals—bread, actually—to the column, making it known that in the end the weapons must be delivered to them and not to other partisans.

On the twenty-first of September, they rested in Delvino (the locality previously occupied by Lieutenant Colonel Cirino's battalion—how many memories!), when two Italian airplanes, very low flying, sent from Brindisi, hurled a message saying two transport ships (completely insufficient, but more could not be obtained) were going from Brindisi to Porto Edda.

The afternoon of the following day, Manno and the others from Porto Edda saw the arrival of the column.

The battalions situated themselves immediately around the town. The artillerymen—led by Major Costadura—took middle positions over some heights, positioning themselves in a way that made it possible for them to open fire toward the interior, against the partisans, or to the coast road over the sea, against possible German attacks. Not far from the olive grove, where the anti-aerial battery was set up, Cirino's battalion began to dig trenches.

5

Without losing any time, Manno went to introduce himself to Cirino. He found him busy organizing the line; he had to wait a half hour before he could speak to him. At last Cirino received him. He was standing on a path, and he had—the lieutenant noticed—a face that was no longer young but very decided, covered with dust and sweat.

Here's a man who has not let himself go stale—and never will, he immediately noticed.

"Who are you, and what do you want?" Cirino asked Manno decisively.

Manno stood to attention and explained his own situation. He had arrived from Italy a few days before the armistice with twenty artillerymen and was temporarily in the territorial command of Porta Edda because of the question of feeding his men, and for that reason only. His men were disciplined, and he knew them well. "If you agree, we can form one more section under your orders", he said. "What we'd like is to be doing something, not just being a burden for those really working."

Instead of answering him, Cirino inquired about the present situation in Porto Edda and effective forces of the place, displaying surprise at their slight numbers. He asked, too, how many were ill in the hospital, how many disbanded soldiers had come from the interior (there were already hundreds). He pondered a while, and at last he seemed to make a judgment about Manno. "Leave your artillerymen where they are, since at least there, if nothing else, they'll have something to eat. Then we'll see. As for you, if it suits you, you can transfer over here with me. You could be useful as a link between the battalion and the local garrison. And, by way of beginning, go at once and let the commander of the garrison know that along with us a general has arrived. Tell him, if he has not already done so, to present himself immediately to him and to give an account of how things are here in Porto Edda. It would be useful to be brought up to date before we gather for the report. Go now." He turned and went back to take care of arranging the line.

Manno carried out the order, and it took some time. He also notified Cioffi, who now was displeased at separating from him, and then returned rapidly to Cirino. "You can come with me to the meeting", he told him quickly. "You'll act as my aide, since it's better my adjutant major stays here during my absence."

The lieutenant followed him to the town with pleasure, where once again he had occasion to notice that after the arrival of the column many of the missing and a good many of the service units, of no particular use to a defense, had arrived.

The report given by the higher echelon officers had scarcely begun at the territorial region quarters when two ships appeared far off at sea. Manno and the other aides, gathered in the vestibule, were made aware of them by the shouts of joy launched all over the town. "The ships! The boats! They've arrived!" At first they feared they might be German ships, but from the room where they were holding their meeting a battalion commander came out and addressed his own aide: "Please get to the port and make sure they've the flag hoisted." They were the ships they had been waiting for.

It was beginning to get dark. The disbanded and many of the servicemen ran from all sides toward the dock of the port. Hearing their racing to the dock, Manno stepped out to have a look at them. They were dressed in a jumble of clothing, much of it torn, their beards grown long, filthy, without any baggage. Many of them were screaming excitedly, but others, quite the contrary, walked the narrow streets grim faced and uncommunicative, their eyes strangely fixed. The young man realized that no power in the world would be able to stop them. To climb onto the boats they would commit crimes. Even more, they would climb over the body of someone they loved, even of those same relatives with whom they intended to reunite, at any price. Never, not even in Africa, had he been witness to such a state of mind. *It's an obsession, a kind of collective madness*, he told himself. He noticed the lieutenant with the intellectual face from the battery among the disbanded, some of the artillerymen, too, but he pretended not to see them.

In a little while, another of the officers in the hallway, a captain with a monocle in his eye, was sent to the port with orders to accompany the officers from the boats as soon as they had moored. He returned in about an hour followed by two navy officers and an infantry lieutenant in his shirtsleeves, whom he did not know. They were led into the meeting place immediately.

As soon as the door was shut behind them, the other aides surrounded the captain with the monocle, who appeared to be worried. "Things are going badly", he told them. "The Germans have taken over Scutari, Valona, and all the other Albanian ports except Porto Palermo, that tiny port close by here. It seems that our troops are not really holding out anywhere in the Balkans, except in Cefalonia, where they've really fought seriously, but . . .", and he shook his head.

"On the island of Cefalonia? What happened? Are things bad?" one of them asked.

The captain looked around to make sure there were no soldiers about to leak the news. "Yes, very bad", he said, nervously fixing his monocle. "A real disaster, a massacre."

"But . . . what's happened?"

"As you all know, the Acqui division is in Cefalonia. They disarmed the German garrisons on the island, but then they couldn't keep other Germans from landing. There was a pitched battle that lasted seven days. Yesterday it was over."

"Seven days of fighting?"

"Yes. In some sectors, as in Argostoli, the second city of the island, our men captured more than five hundred Germans, but it was of no use, because they were finally beaten."

The captain screwed up the eye with the monocle in it and lowered his voice. "They've executed all the Italian officers, one and all. Every single officer of the Acqui division, and thousands of soldiers, those in the sectors where the fighting was most bloody. They're probably still shooting them down while we're standing here talking."

"How did the navy find out about all these things?" Manno asked.

"They know all this, first, because the Brindisi headquarters have kept radio contact with the Acqui division, in fact—even though this might seem strange—up to yesterday evening, when the battle was over and these two ships left the port. And in the second place, because the boats came across a German motorboat taken over by our men, in high sea, coming from Cefalonia. Did you see the infantryman who came in with me? The one inside there now giving information? Well, he was the one driving the motorboat, along with a few others from his platoon. They took it in full daylight, a surprise attack, not firing a shot, using bayonets like daggers—a desperate attack—and left Cefalonia without the Germans even knowing it. They had five prisoners with them tied like sausages, who are now in one of the ships here in port. Among them is an Austrian lieutenant who has corroborated the executions; he said it was an order from Hitler and that he considered it fair."

"Then," one of them said, "now that pig will consider it fair if we execute him."

"We execute? But when have we ever done that?" another piped up. "Imagine."

"Well," the captain said, "in the meantime that's the order given to the Germans."

"To shoot all officers?"

The captain nodded. "Every single last one, any garrison officer who puts up resistance, and also the soldiers, but, it seems, for them it's up to each German commander to make his own decision."

An unpleasant silence ensued.

"A great outlook", another fellow commented at last.

"And all those idiots! Imagine them saying the war was over for us."

A lamp on the table lit up the small meeting of men, who, in different ways, had already given and suffered so much and now found themselves unexpectedly plunged into this new and menacing situation.

"Well, I've told you everything I know", the captain with the monocle concluded.

The only consoling news they were able to obtain from him was that the island of Corfu—facing them out there at sea, in front of Porto Edda—was still in Italian hands. According to the navy officers, their radio had been keeping contact constantly between Cefalonia and Brindisi.

After about an hour the meeting ended. The navy officers came out of the room, as well as the daring infantry officer, and went off toward the port. The higher echelon officers and their respective aides went quickly back to their own battalions. But as Lieutenant Colonel Cirino tarried, Manno looked into the meeting place. He saw the general seated at the table. He looked a sedentary, good-natured fellow, but at that moment he seemed distressed. In front of him were Cirino and an artillery major with a decisive air. No doubt, the young man was thinking, it was Major Costadura, the commander of the group on the heights over the town.

"It's you", Cirino said when he saw him and went up to him, leading him out to the hallway. "Get over to the antiaerial commander. These are his orders. He should load the machine guns and the staff personnel to go with them and all the ammunition available onto the two boats: four guns on each one. He must—without waiting for further orders—get them on the deck to reinforce the antiaerial operation that's already on the boats. Am I making myself clear?"

"Yes, Colonel."

"As for the rifle ammunition in the battery, and anything else useful for the remaining battalions—but above all the rifle ammunition—tell them to carry it down to the wharf, next to the ammunition they are unloading from the ships. Is all that clear?"

"Yes, Colonel."

"Fine, that's all. Go and do what I've told you, please."

Manno hesitated a moment. "Colonel . . ."

"What is it?" Cirino asked him. "Ah, your people. They'll go along with the antiaerial battery, naturally, just like you. You're free from now on. The decision's been taken that everyone who was in Porto Edda when we arrived should embark. Thank your lucky stars." He started to turn away.

"Colonel", Manno repeated.

"Well, what is it?"

"I'm going to ready your orders immediately and make sure everything is carried out. But I'm staying with you. You named me your aide, and I don't intend . . ." He wanted to add something more definite, to make his decision clearer, but he felt that would be wasting too much time.

"You know about Cefalonia?" Cirino asked.

"Yes, Colonel."

"And despite . . ." He paused and smiled. "Good. If you really want to stay with me, then there's more reason for you to get ready to leave. I'm also going to Brindisi."

"You're joking", Manno could not contain himself.

The lieutenant colonel burst into laughter. "No, I'm not joking. You'll find out. I'm going to Brindisi. Well, that's not your business. Go and do what I told you, and then wait for me in . . . on the bigger of the two boats."

He turned; the conversation was over.

6

Manno left the headquarters quite bewildered (not a single civilian was to be seen in the surrounding area: they were all shut up in their shacks in God knows what state of mind), and he hurriedly went off to the antiaerial posts. Cioffi and the greater part of his soldiers and the good-natured lieutenant were waiting on pins and needles for their instructions. They were expecting them to be brought by the intellectual lieutenant who had gone over to town several hours before.

Manno transmitted Cirino's orders in the presence of the soldiers, who started to shout joyfully. He ended by saying, on his own initiative, "I am in charge of personally carrying out the moving of the ammunition, the carbines, and all the other materiel of the battery, except the rifles and the ammunition for them. If something is missing, the one responsible for the missing piece stays here, doesn't leave. I warn you, I'm quite serious."

The soldiers fell silent. In the darkness, brightened by the first stars and some faint reflection from lanterns hanging in the tents, they listened attentively.

"You must dismantle the tents, the storage area, the kitchen, in a word, everything, and take it all—in as many trips as are necessary—to the port. When the machine guns are loaded on, each one of them must be working perfectly, so, naturally, complete with its gunners. If not, the weaponry chief remains on land."

Some of the weaponry chiefs began to shout. "That S.O.B. Mancini beat it!" "And that swine Liberatore hasn't come back from his trip for water. Is that our fault?"

"All right!" Manno yelled with such impetus that they all shut up in a flash. "They couldn't have got too far away. Now Lieutenant Cioffi will give you his orders about moving everything to the port in orderly fashion. I'll be there to receive the things. Before getting on the ships with your weapons, look for your deserters, the missing, each squadron its own. You'll deliver them the kick in the ass they deserve, also for the work you'll have to do now instead of them, and then bring them back in formation. It goes without saying that, once in Italy, they'll be tried for deserting." This said, he turned the floor over to Cioffi.

"Line up in squadrons immediately", he ordered bad humoredly, obviously put out by the evident downgrading of category, but at the same time with a display of decisiveness. "First of all, we'll take out the list of everyone missing."

It turned out twenty men were missing among a few more than one hundred. Among the group Manno had brought from Italy some were also missing. The intellectual-faced officer also remained missing.

The soldiers set to work diligently dismounting the tents, while others immediately began moving the materiel to the port, a job that was tiring, especially in the dark, and which kept them busy for hours. It does not bear describing. It is enough to say that while they were at it, more than a few of the deserters made contact with the squadrons, lining up in secret. Even some unknown deserters joined up, too, who only went away after having found out that a number of officers, with the help of the carabinieri, were organizing the entire lot of deserters into company formations for an ordered embarkation.

Loaded down with the hospital patients, the antiaerial men and their weapons, the mass of deserters, and all the other men present in Porto Edda before the arrival of the big column, not counting the minor detachments, the two ships—filled to the brim with men (to the point of disbelief)—weighed anchor. Dawn was about to break.

7

After making sure Cirino was aboard, Manno embarked on the larger boat. No sooner was the ship out of the port than he started—moving with great difficulty in that crowd—looking for the lieutenant colonel. The boat picked up speed little by little over the dark sea. Its motor pulsed promisingly, making the entire structure vibrate. Suddenly the idea of going home, going to Colomba, filled the young man with a vast feeling of freedom. An overflowing joy took hold of him, canceling out any dark thoughts.

The thought of those who stayed behind on land, of the battalions spread out in the black of night around Porto Edda, evoked in him, indeed, a kind of malaise, almost rebellion: as if those patient men, who instead of deserting had made a virtue out of necessity, came to him now as an obstacle, a hateful stumbling block. He interrupted his search for the colonel and looked out over the side. The water below ran very black and hardly visible along the ship's side. *What's all that have to do with me?* he argued. *The problems, and they weren't small, I've already gone through in Africa. I got here at the last minute by pure chance. I don't owe a thing to them.* A phrase of Ambrogio's went through his head. *Do try, once you're in Greece, not to play the smart guy. I know you.* How right Ambrogio was! So, with his obsession for helping out Cirino—unasked for—he was playing the smart guy. Luckily, nothing had yet been lost. If he did not report now to the lieutenant colonel, the latter would surely never search him out, and in the end no one would know anything about this whole story, and even less would it be known by the infantrymen lined up out there in the darkness of Porto Edda. It was this last consideration that made him come to his senses. Even those, who asked nothing of him, and from whom he now wanted to separate his own destiny, each one of them had his own family, and who knows how many had his Colomba to whom he desired with all his soul to return . . . He reacted, *What kind of officer would I be if . . .* He closed his eyes, and, as was his wont at crucial moments, he began to pray. He ended up imagining Jesus in the garden of olives; he, too, had wanted to shun the bitter chalice. This memory comforted him. After all, he was not a reptile if, for one minute, he had yielded to temptation . . . the important thing was not to let it overcome you.

He found Cirino readying a mattress that had been brought to him from the ship's commander, in a corner of the captain's bridge. He stood at attention. "I carried out your order to the best of my ability", he communicated.

"Yes, I saw the antiaerial emplacements on deck."

"Do you have any other orders to give me?"

"That you sleep as much as possible. There'll be plenty to be done in Brindisi."

"I'll try to sleep", the young man answered, smiling, happy, and at the same time anxious again—the tail end of temptation—because the colonel had not dismissed him definitively.

"Come with me, Lieutenant", the ship's commander invited him kindly. "I'll find a place to sleep for you."

He not only found a place; he also had a blanket brought. Stretched out on the place he had indicated, Manno made the sign of the Cross and slept almost immediately, determined already to carry out what his conscience told him was his "unrenounceable duty".

He slept long and deep. When he awoke, what most bothered him was his thirst. The motor of the ship kept up its deep and promising throb, causing the whole metallic frame to vibrate. The young man straightened his hair with his hands and went up on deck. It seemed to be midday, and Brindisi lay only two hours in the distance. Far off, the coast of Puglia could be seen, and the soldiers were narrowing their eyes to look at it, occasionally pointing it out. The anti-aircraft gunners, wearing helmets, their weapons piled around them, greeted him with gratitude as if this happy repatriation had depended on him, on his energy.

Commander Cioffi was also there, wearing his helmet. He stretched out his hand delightedly. "Where have you been 'til now?"

"Sleeping. I just woke up."

"You can see it in your face."

"As soon as we land, I'll have to act as Cirino's aide. He has a mission in Brindisi."

"Oh."

"I don't have any antiaircraft weapons, so I want to be as useful as possible."

Cioffi smiled. The bad humor of the previous evening had completely disappeared. "It was the navy, you know, that called us on the ship's deck against possible German Stuka attacks."

Manno nodded, interested.

"Your twenty men are in the hold," the other fellow continued, "squeezed in like sardines but happy as larks . . . I went down a while ago to have a look."

"I forgot about them totally last night", Manno said.

"Well, we're already here, aren't we?"

"You'll have to worry about their mess in Brindisi, too."

"I'll take care of it. Did they ever go without food?" Cioffi was happy, feeling useful. He took a jug from the closest machine-gun seat, a jug covered with damp felt, at which Manno had glanced several times. Cioffi gave it to him. "I imagine you're thirsty."

"Yes, of course, very."

Manno took some very long sips. The water was good and quite cool, without any naphtha taste.

"Well, now it will be better if I go down to my men", he said as he returned the jug. He took a last glance around, to where the eye took in the great stretch of peaceful and indolent sea. The other ship followed not far behind. Manno noticed that farther out there were three or four specks, ships. "They're English", Cioffi explained. "We came across a lot last night."

To everyone's satisfaction the tragic Balkan world was far behind them. No one gave a thought about the civilians—men, women, and children—and the atrocious situation into which they had been led by the whimsical Italian occupation.

8

The port of Brindisi turned out to be quite different from how Manno had left it fifteen days earlier. It was now crossed over by silver captive balloons, quite a bit more crowded with boats and incomparably more jammed with traffic on the wharves. On all sides could be seen heaps of light-colored khaki material, which Manno knew very well from having seen it in Africa: the color of the Allies.

The lieutenant was one of the first to land, along with Cirino; he then realized that he was also followed by another aide, a mature man, a noncom. "I think he told me to follow in order to leave me here," the other man said, "perhaps because I've five children at home. I can't find any other explanation but that." The man appeared to be puzzled. "It's not easy to leave the colonel", he asserted. "He's a commander . . . way out of the ordinary."

Of the many headquarters to which Manno expected to accompany Cirino, the number was reduced to only one: navy headquarters, a complex of ancient buildings situated in a dominant position over the port, which in those days also housed the Supreme Command of the Italian Armed Forces or, in other words, the chief general of the General Staff and a few other high-echelon officers who had fled from Rome, in the wake of the king and the government.

Cirino and his aides were taken there in a navy car. It seemed to them to be the only vehicle (the one they were in) of Italian make circulating in Brindisi, so enormous was the gap between the scarce Italian traffic and that of the Allies. They stopped in front of the building reserved for the Supreme Command, whose doorway was attended by two carabinieri in field uniform, wearing the gray-green hats of their outfit. While Cirino was immediately received by the staff general and then accompanied to a floor above, Manno and the other aide were made comfortable in a corridor on the ground floor, transformed—by means of some clumsy and oversized sofas and chairs of the same style—into an improvised waiting room.

Every so often, between the sofas and chairs of the corridor, an office worker or officer would go by. After an hour or so an officer wearing an artillery insignia came by whom Manno seemed to know. Where on earth had he seen him? The other fellow—a small fellow, a lieutenant with a serious face, carrying a handful of typed pages—also seemed to be wondering, so much so that he stopped and turned around. "Haven't we seen each other before by chance?"

Hearing his voice, Manno recognized him. He stood up, smiling, and gave him his hand. "Yes, in Alamein, in the Twenty-First Artillery. Remember? You didn't stay very long with us. You were wounded shortly after your arrival, the first or second day of combat."

"Yes, of course, in Alamein. You're Riva, aren't you?" the other fellow asked as he shook hands.

"Yes," Manno answered, "and you're Gambacorta, if I have the name correctly."

"It's Gambacurta."

The two of them stood there shaking hands. "The twenty-first", Gambacurta repeated, nodding. "Those were the days." He was wearing a decoration on his sleeve for having been wounded. "But how come you're here? Where are you coming from?"

"From Albania. I landed about an hour ago."

"An hour ago? It can't be. Sit down; tell me about it."

He made him sit down again on the small sofa and sat down beside him. "How did you manage to get out of Albania with everything that's going on there?"

Manno told him in a few words. The other listened attentively, interested. His eyes were brown, and his hair was thinning, despite his youth. He gave the impression of a gentle nature, but at the same time strong, with the manners of a cultivated person. In fact, Manno remembered, he was above average (as far as cultivation was concerned).

"But you must also tell me about yourself", he told him at the end of his own brief tale. "And not only about you. I'd like to know what's been happening here in Italy since the signing of the armistice. Because I must tell you I haven't a clue as to how things have developed. Up 'til now, I've only had bits and pieces, today especially, on the boat, from the navy people. So what is happening now? Tell me."

"Things have gone from bad to worse", he answered, as if grief stricken. "On the eighth of September, two weeks ago, after announcing the armistice, the king, the prince, and Badoglio, along with some ministers, and the chief of state, Ambrogio," he pointed with his right hand to the upper floors, "left Rome and, by way of Pescara, arrived here by sea. Did you know that?"

"Yes."

"It was practically a rout. But now this means that we have this side of the lines—outside of the territory controlled by the Germans—the king, and the government, that is, the legitimate authorities. This, after all is said and done, is something."

"How come they came to Brindisi?"

"Because when the armistice took place, the Allies carried out two simultaneous landings, one in Salerno and the other in Taranto. Did you know that?"

"Not about Taranto, no."

"Well, that's it. From Taranto they went through Puglia, from which the Germans—only a handful—beat a quick retreat, without waiting for them. Only later did the Germans form a continuous front, which is now cutting Italy in two, from Salerno to Foggia. The Allies are trying to push them toward the north, but they go so slowly, they still haven't taken Naples. Well, here in Brindisi, the few Germans who were here left, and the Italian army stayed, and most especially—still rather strong—the navy. That's the reason the king and government landed here."

"And the rest of Italy? What's been happening?"

"Chaos is what has happened. None of the commanders knew what to do. The body of soldiers thought of only one thing: go back home. Practically speaking, after a few days the army fell apart, or rather disintegrated. Some troops are fighting, in Rome, for instance, but a mere nothing. A real disaster, I tell you, really awful." The little lieutenant shook his head from time to time.

"You can imagine," he went on, "seeing the war was lost, no one wanted to hear about dying. And besides, why sacrifice yourself against one enemy, when it's been made clear that it had been useless to sacrifice yourself against another?" He repeated, "Everyone thought only about getting back home. Even before all this, the war made very little sense, you know that. So, it was enough for a few Germans to show up demanding a surrender. In our regiments it was more of a disintegration than it was a surrender." Gambacurta nodded once again with his balding head. "I've spoken with people coming from the north, as well as from the center and Rome: on all sides the same spectacle. During those days there wasn't a road in Italy that wasn't full of deserters—in uniform, out of uniform, half and half, a disaster. Some of them must still be on the road."

"And the Germans let them go off?"

"In Italy, normally yes, at least in the center and here in the south. But they took many officers prisoner. I wouldn't be able to tell you how many thousands. Beyond the frontier, that is, in the Balkans, where the troops in general didn't go to pieces because they were away from home, well, you know better than I that they've taken all the officers and soldiers and are shipping them to Germany. God knows what their fate will be, especially the officers. I'm afraid that ... there's no forgiving us, as far as the Germans are concerned."

"No, they won't."

"Some detachments on the coast, here in front of Puglia," the little lieutenant gestured with his hand, "fight on, with the hope that we'll be over to get them. Some have taken to the hills, where the partisans sometimes take them in, or sometimes they kill them, but you know about all this better than I. You should hear the messages we get over the radio. They make you want to cry."

"But you people from the command have taken in a lot, haven't you?"

"No, not many, a few thousand. We bend over backward, that's the truth, but we don't have the means. We have no boats. That's our major obstacle."

There was a pause, a hesitation.

"A lovely outlook for us, everything considered", Manno at last commented, feeling himself more and more overcome with anguish.

"Especially for those who've stayed there, isn't it so?" Gambacurta made more exact.

"Yes, and for me, too", Manno said. "I'm about to return to Albania with Colonel Cirino."

"But ...", Gambacurta started to say, "but ..."

From the moment they had begun to talk about the troops that had stayed behind in the Balkans, the aide had followed the conversation, moving his head worriedly, but did not interrupt.

"The Allies, however", Manno observed. "They've got plenty of boats and ..."

"Forget it", Gambacurta said. "We should expect nothing from them. The soldiers—especially the Americans, from what I've heard—fraternize quite a bit with our men, even though they don't understand why we should be so friendly. Headquarters, on the other hand ... no, nothing", he went on. "For the moment at least, we really can't expect anything from them."

An orderly came down from an upper floor and into the corridor waiting room. "The artillery lieutenant who arrived with Colonel Cirino?"

"Here I am", Manno answered, as he stood up. *Cirino still doesn't remember my name*, he thought.

"Lieutenant, the colonel wants you. I'll accompany you."

"Well, see you soon", Manno said to Gambacurta.

"See you", he answered, also standing up, still holding the typed pages in his left hand.

"You'll wait for me here", Manno suggested to the other aide and followed the orderly.

9

On the floor above, Cirino, looking out briefly from a door, issued a rather extravagant order. He wanted two sheets of paper and two envelopes. "The most presentable you can find. I mean, at least the glue should really stick. If you can't find them here, please go out and buy them for me."

It was Gambacurta, waiting for him down below, who got them. Manno took them to the colonel.

"Good", he said, cut and dry as ever. "Thanks. Is the warrant officer still there?"

"Yes, Colonel."

"Tell him I'll be busy for a while still. Both of you wait downstairs for me."

He was actually busy for several hours. It was already evening when he came down below, accompanied by a high-ranking officer.

He came up to the two men waiting for him. "I'm going back to the port", he let them know. "I don't need you from now on. You're free to go."

"Oh, no", Manno said.

The lieutenant colonel looked at him, then extended his hand to the aide. "You'll join up with the regimental services that have reached Brindisi with us today. Tell them that ... yes, that we've organized things well here, and in a few days I plan to join all of them, too." He paused. "In any event, I appreciate your long, very long assistance. Only we know the moments we've gone through together, isn't that so?"

The other officer gestured a yes. He would have liked to respond fittingly, but his emotions and inner clash of feelings prevented him from speaking. He at least tried to wish him luck, which seemed important, but the words would not come except in stammered syllables.

"Thank you", Cirino answered.

He extended his right hand to Manno, who, instead of shaking it, exclaimed with aggressive emotion, "You're mistaken, Colonel." He did not even know what he was saying. "I'm not staying here. I'm going with you, and you can't stop me because . . . you promised."

"Promised? When was that?" Cirino asked. He turned to the high-ranking officer, smiling. "I knew this one would protest." Then he went back to Manno. "So you don't want to give me your hand?"

"Well, you practically promised me", he insisted. "It was . . . more or less implied."

"You won't give me your hand?" The colonel withdrew his hand.

Manno gritted his teeth. "I'm not married. I don't have either a father or a mother", he said. "Colonel, I'm more suitable than any other person to go back there."

This time Cirino was moved, but he did not show it. "One moment", he said. "I really do have a favor still to ask of you."

He took the two envelopes the young man had brought him out of his jacket pocket. They were stamped and addressed. "This is serious. These I entrust to you. They're for my family. You'll see by the address that it's on the other side of the front, in the area now occupied by the Germans. If I return, you'll find a way of returning them to me, but in case . . . if not, you'll send them off in the post at the right time, so they arrive safely." He gave him the letters. "And now?"

Manno took them. And he suddenly blushed, red with shame at his feeling of relief, of release, which in spite of his will to leave was screaming violently inside him. He would have liked to spit in his own face, give himself a right smack.

"You're a real officer", Cirino told him. "I'm happy to have met you. Your hand", he repeated.

The young man extended his hand, while gesturing negatively with his head.

"Remember what I've told you", Cirino added, after having shook his hand. "This free zone isn't a bed of roses either. Just the opposite. Real soldiers are also needed here. You could be more useful here than in Albania, if you wanted."

Then he turned to the other high-ranking officer. "Let's go."

Manno and the aide followed them to the street, where an automobile was waiting for them and where, on the other side of the street, Gambacurta was strolling. The navy driver opened one of the car doors, the aide hurried to open the other, and the two officers settled inside. As the automobile went off, Cirino waved his hand at the back window to the two who had remained behind. Manno would have occasion to remember that farewell many times, as the colonel went off to his death.

For the time being, both he and the aide were left stunned, not even bringing up the question of what to do next. Gambacurta caught up with them immediately. "What's going on?" he asked.

"He didn't want me with him", Manno murmured, ashamed. He could almost feel his chin tremble, like a child.

Gambacurta took him by the arm. "God knows how many hours it's been since you two have eaten", he said. "Come, come along with me."

And he took them off, inviting them by the expression on his face and in his restrained voice to realize what they had avoided. "An hour ago, hardly before I went up, a radio message arrived from Corfu. The Germans have started landing there. If they take over the island, none of our ships can get within the haven of Porto Edda."

10

The evening after, on the twenty-fourth of September, however, the convoy with Colonel Cirino aboard entered into the roadstead: three cargo ships escorted by two smaller battleships. A third smaller battleship—the torpedo boat *Stocco*—had some hours before left the convoy, after being directed by radio to divert to the southeast.

On landing, the lieutenant colonel discovered that the Italian military had greatly increased in numbers because of the massive arrivals of deserters from the interior, and they were very worried about the German air action on Corfu that they had witnessed throughout the day. They were unaware of the fact that the enemy had also landed on the island.

The three ships left during the night, overloaded with soldiers. Once again precedence was given to the sick and the men put out of action. During the crossing the convoy was attacked by German dive bombers. Despite the response from the smaller battleships, one ship was seriously damaged and sunk, luckily within sight of Otranto, which meant many of the shipwrecked could be saved.

On the twenty-fifth, the battle on Corfu reached its culminating point. Our men, who on the thirteenth and fourteenth of September had disarmed the German garrison of the island in hard combat, in which two hundred Germans had died and 450 had been sent back to Brindisi as prisoners by means of the usual launches, were convinced their fate would be the same as the defenders of Cefalonia, should they be beaten. They battled away with all their might for that reason.

To cope with the German air power, the few Italian airplanes in the Puglia airports were put into action. The pilots could see the infantrymen's distress on land and so exposed themselves with great daring. Many of them were brought down, but several German planes were also brought down, since some of our fighter bombers were the very recent Re 2002 model, in condition at last to compete with the enemy's models.

The navy participated as well as it could in the battle with its small units. The torpedo boat *Stocco*, diverted to Corfu from the convoy carrying Cirino, was sighted by a formation of twelve Stukas as it arrived in open sea and was literally blown to pieces. Very few of its sailors were saved.

On the night of the twenty-fifth, the Germans were already masters of the island. Against all expectations, they confined themselves to executing the Italian commanding colonel and only sixteen of his officers.

On the twenty-sixth of September, the Germans attempted to go from Corfu to Porto Edda, but their motor craft were easily thrust back by Major Costadura's battery. Some of their men, who at the beginning had landed in big boats with white flags, were attacked and wiped out on the beach by Cirino's battalion.

In the evening one of the few Italian planes still flying flew low over the city and threw down a message with the information that Corfu was in the hands of the Germans, and so the only Albanian port accessible for Italian ships was Porto Palermo, about twenty-five miles to the north.

The general called a meeting of the high-ranking officers. They decided to move to Porto Palermo.

A column was formed that could not, however, set off. The Communist partisans, already as numerous as flies, had swarmed the coast road and the steep heights that dominated it and impeded passage. They began to negotiate. The Communists wanted arms, all of them. They rejected a pact proposed by the general according to which arms would be handed over in Porto Palermo when the troops embarked. They proposed, instead, that, in exchange for the arms, they would take charge of defending the Italians against the Germans until they carried out the embarkation. Among the Italian commanders some thought they should engage the Communist partisans in battle; others, in view of the many dead and, even more, the loss of time—perhaps some days—which that hard combat between the coastal mountains would entail, were undecided. The troops were impatient to leave, and rumors were abroad. The hours of the night were ticking by. Finally the general decided to deliver over the arms.

The totally disarmed column, but still in battle formation, was in sight of Porto Palermo the following evening. The waterways were deserted, although at the beginning a rock emerging from the sea seemed to many of them a ship, and, in a kind of strange phenomenon of collective self-delusion, it was greeted with clamorous shouting.

Some days went by. The battalions—abandoned by the partisans the moment the arms were delivered (and that in itself was a piece of luck)—tried to

533

hide in the woods, away from German air reconnaissance. They kept together in a group in order to defend themselves at least with cudgels from isolated partisans and common thieves, who stripped the soldiers if they found them alone or in small groups. But meanwhile, no ship arrived. At last the Germans did.

They sent all who turned themselves in as prisoners to Porto Edda, where they separated the officers from the soldiers and executed the officers in small groups. They chose for the massacre the curve of the coast road over the solitary cove of Porto Limione, the place where Manno, twenty days previous, had received the news of the armistice. The bodies of the dead—more than 120, including the general—were thrown into the sea, and the sea for days and weeks carried them to and fro, finally scattering them along the coast. Then they were washed away and scattered again, until they were finally carried off.

Cirino with his battalion, Costadura and his group, and a few other units had not turned themselves over to the Germans. They set off marching to the interior, pursued by them. They searched anxiously for weapons, and they partially managed to get them. On the fifth of October, finding the road shut off by an overhanging rock, they tried to open the path from behind, shooting at the Germans who pursued them, until they ran out of ammunition and then attacking with bayonets. One by one they were captured, eight hundred of them. Here also the officers were separated from the soldiers and executed. Before killing them, the Germans sadistically forced Cirino and another high-ranking officer to go up a high hill running. They were made to run until they lost consciousness, and once they regained consciousness, they were forced to run again. At last they were killed.

Costadura, who along with his artillerymen had been separated for some days from the infantrymen, died a little later, executed by the nationalist partisans of Memo Meto, to whom he had gone to offer his services.

II

Some weeks after these events took place, Manno received news of the 120 officers in Porto Limione. Gambacurta communicated the news, erroneously affirming that it had to do with the officers, every last one, who had remained in Porto Edda, beginning with the commanding general.

For that reason Manno thought Cirino was among them. He was overcome with heavy melancholy. He had the two letters the lieutenant colonel had entrusted to him before leaving for Albania. He decided not to post them but instead, as soon as he was able, to deliver them personally to his family.

He was now in a village in Puglia, Murgiano, in a school of reserve officers to which he had been assigned on Gambacurta's initiative. ("You'll be better off there than any other place", the little lieutenant had told him, his eyes wistful. "If nothing else, at least you'll be with boys with some education." He thought that the others shared his own preferences and did not suspect that Manno would have preferred to deal with ordinary soldiers, peasants and workmen, instead of students. In any case, Manno raised no objections.)

Later, however, he had occasion to appreciate Gambacurta's concern. On going to a "reclassification camp" to visit the twenty artillerymen repatriated with him from Albania, he found them in far worse condition than his own. In that camp—installed in the Brindisi and Lecce provinces, usually in requisitioned school buildings—they were bunched together, not only the soldiers who had poured in from the Balkans, but also those who had been gathered into the squadrons by the carabinieri in the streets and the railway stations, as they came from the north, after having crossed German and Allied lines trying to get back to their homes. Discipline was lax, and desertions occurred daily. In the camp Manno visited the sentries, lacking uniforms, were dressed as civilians, with their bandoleers slung across their jackets. His artillerymen had especially complained about the scarcity of food. "Lieutenant, there are days when we're only given two biscuits: one dry, which serves as bread, and the other boiled in water, as it if were soup." ·

The camps' officers had explained, "We've run out of supplies in the warehouses. If the Allies don't make up their minds about reprovisioning us, in no time we won't even be able to keep up this parody of a detachment."

The Allies, however, just as they had not lent a hand in Albania—where it would have been enough for a few ships and some decisive air intervention to have resolved important situations—did not help in this case either.

In the "kingdom of the south", besides the soldiers gathered into "reclassification centers", six or seven regular divisions were vegetating, the majority destined for Sardinia. The Allies were distrustful of them, too. As Gambacurta explained, they mainly preferred not to have the leftovers from the Italian army in their hair and were hoping they would just simply disappear into thin air.

Colonel Cirino's words came to Manno's mind frequently. *It's not a bed of roses here either . . . if you wanted, you could be more useful here than in Albania.* But how? In what way could he, a mere lieutenant, be useful in the midst of this disintegration?

Murgiano was a village like so many others in Puglia, with Arabic-looking houses with terraced roofs or domes. The officer's training center was lodged—as it had been since before the armistice—in the elementary school buildings, the largest of the town. Here it was that Manno took over, as a substitute for a sick officer, the job of teaching—provisionally—"combat training", a field in which he had an excellent personal background. He devoted himself to the teaching with great diligence. His pupils (who at first, as occurs in situations where everything is already settled, known, had viewed his arrival with an evil eye)

535

eventually, after a few days, adopted an attitude of curiosity. Some of them—especially the engineering students (better prepared than he himself was, who had studied architecture)—tried to embarrass him with theoretical questions, trigonometry, for instance. He confessed his own limitations in the terrain of theory with dignity, but at the same time he promised to try to surmount them. He went to Brindisi to see Gambacurta and insisted so much that the little lieutenant managed to find, in the course of an afternoon, the texts of combat training that were studied in the military academy before the armistice. Back in Murgiano, the young man spent several evenings trying to become familiar with the scientific fundamentals of which, in his own training, he had only learned in practical application. Then he held a special class to answer the embarrassing questions that had been formulated. The pupils were left quite impressed by his open goodwill at a moment of general listlessness.

From then on he prepared every lesson, studying it the evening before, and sometimes also at night. He did, however, emphasize the importance—especially in a subject such as this—of the practical over the theoretical, and he exemplified it using his own direct experience, undergone in his own flesh and blood, his own life.

As the other officers in the school had not, in general, participated in the big war campaigns, more than a few of the pupils began to seek out his company as a mentor even outside of normal class hours. It seemed to revive in him—as little as this seemed appropriate—the Nomana oratory experience. He spoke to them continually (in a way that was meant to be funny, but which was more often melancholic) of duty, of the soldiers who had died—as he said—paying for all the rest, even for their comrades who thought only about saving their own skin. He talked about Cirino, who, in order not to evade his duty, at the peak moment of the army's disintegration, had returned to die in Albania. He often repeated his words, "even in the territory free of the Germans there is a need for real soldiers", quoting them as reference for all of them.

"You all see what a state Italy is in today", he insisted. "Try to imagine what the future will be like if we go on the way we have been. If each one of us, one by one, does not make up his mind to pull himself out of this morass."

"But at the end of this course," one of the students objected with bitterness, "we don't even know if we'll receive our lieutenant's stripes. There are too many officers already in the south, and more keep arriving from the other side of the lines. Lieutenant, at times we wonder if studying for us isn't plain useless."

"No", Manno answered. "If only because, by stopping your studies, you'll aid and abet, as far as you're concerned, this tremendous chaos that we're in and that keeps getting deeper and deeper. There are moments, sometimes a few months, in which the fate of a people is decided for a long time to come. And we are in one of those moments now. Don't you realize that?"

During the few evening hours that he reserved for himself, the young man strolled through the dusty streets of Murgiano, immersed in reflections and meditations. Other times he would shut himself in his room to write letters, which for the moment he could not send. He sometimes wrote to Colomba, at times to Ambrogio, who had remained his best friend. For him those letters were more than a consolation; rather they gave him courage. It was not possible—he ended by telling himself—that a people, a nation that produced creatures like Colomba (who, he was convinced, had no equal on God's earth), could be destined for degradation.

One after another, he left those letters in the same box in which the two of Cirino were stored.

12

On the twentieth of October—forty days after the armistice—the legitimate Italian government declared war on Germany.

Meanwhile, the Allied front had established itself in Campania and the Abruzzi, and only on its western margin—where the Americans were—was it still moving, but quite slowly, toward Cassino. The hope for a rapid reunification of Italy was fading. It was already clear that the Allies were not intending to exercise their principal forces in the Mediterranean (to the Italian chief of staff it was already obvious that they were sending forces somewhere else). It was at this point that the Americans decided to accept—on trial—the participation of an Italian military contingent, and they fixed the figure at five thousand men.

Manno had the news from Gambacurta, who specified that the contingent would be made up partially of volunteers. "Because the troops at present in Puglia", Gambacurta said, "have become very lazy, and we're not sure they'll react all right."

After receiving that news, the officer went back to Murgiano with his head in a tumult. Cirino's last words were going through his mind like an obsession. *There you are, you see. At last you have the chance to be useful!* He thought of Colomba. (*At last I'll be able to do something worthy of her!*) Besides, there was Celeste and his words of farewell in Piacenza; he thought of the workers in Nomana, of Mazara, of the humble working people living everywhere. *If everything goes so badly in Italy, we'll end up worse off than Arabs, worse than other wretched nations, among whom, without a doubt, are people of goodwill. I realized that in Libya, in Tunis. They'd also work and do the best they could, but they simply can't . . . their only fate is to vegetate miserably.* It was necessary, no matter what, to do something for those who were humble folk, working people.

In Murgiano, the young man, on fire, presented himself to the commander of the school, who, after a brief period of reflection, at last consented to his proposal of forming a body of volunteers. The following days and weeks a series of initiatives took place in the small town.

On the seventh of December, the Italian First Motorized Division entered the lines of the American Fifth Army sector. Manno and some other instructors of the school along with about fifty student officer volunteers, incorporated in a battalion of Bersaglieri, also formed part of the sector. The Italian unit went ahead to Montelungo, one of the advance posts of Montecassino. It was a narrow rocky mountain that, rising from the plain of the Cassino Valley, divided it for a certain stretch into two parallel valleys. Its irregular watershed culminated in three successive points: elevation 343, a "numberless" point, and elevation 351.

On the dawning of the day of the eighth, after some hard blind bombing by the American artillery, the Italian soldiers went in to attack two points: one directly up the watershed to 343, the other to a point on the other side, the left. Simultaneously, an American infantry regiment carried out an attack on the opposite watershed of the valley, against another mountain.

The ample valley and, up to a certain height, the slopes of all those mountains were covered in mist. Within the mist, the battalion, in which Manno and his men belonged, ran smack into the first German positions.

An enemy shot resounded, then the usual shouts of alarm. The Bersaglieri and student officers hastened up the climb with their hearts in their mouths once again! The German Spandau, or MG34, began to fire in front of them and even among them, with a speed that doubled that of any other automatic weapon. Dragging themselves up and protected by the mist, the Bersaglieri and the student officers stationed themselves under the enemy position. Someone was hit and began to scream; someone else, stretched out in the shelter of a crag or a rock, reacted to the Spandau fire with the infuriated fire of his own machine gun. The battle broke out suddenly into many episodes, as always, and the usual repugnant performance began once again.

The assailants were all crack troops, but the Germans were always crack troops, and they were concealed among the rocks. To overcome these first few pockets of defense required time and a loss of human life. Then the advance continued upward to a second and perhaps more regular line of positions, from which the enemy continued its tightly packed concentration of fire. There were not many of these positions either, and the battalion gradually managed to wedge itself in. Meanwhile, as the sun climbed higher in the sky, the sea of mist began, in its higher stratifications, to waver, to thin out. The area around the attackers began to lighten. Everything began to take on uncertain profiles. Manno, who, at the head of his own section, had at a difficult point grasped a rock edge to scale, was suddenly deafened by a crashing noise of some device or other—perhaps a German hand grenade—that had exploded on the other side of the edge. He suddenly lost his grip on the bit of rock he was hanging onto and fell back. He looked at his fingers, amazed. They were covered with minute wounds, dripping blood. More than pain, he felt as if he had been burned. "They've hit me!" he murmured.

"Here, take this, Lieutenant", said one of the students at his left (a Milanese, thus a countryman of his), and squatting behind the rock he quickly took a first aid kit from his pocket and handed it to him. He realized the officer could not take it from him. "Wait, I'll do it." He tore off the wrapping and began to bandage the right hand, which was the one bleeding more profusely.

"Bandage it very tightly around the wrist", Manno, who felt dizzy, told him calmly.

"Very tight, yes."

The students closest by had also stopped, while the others of the platoon continued dragging themselves forward.

"And you", the Milanese said to the student on the other side of the officer. "What's keeping you? Take care of the other hand."

"Me? You mean me?"

"Yes."

But this fellow was quite clumsy and very nervous. So the first student, after having bandaged the right hand, took over the bandaging of the left one, apparently less injured. He had hardly finished when a second explosion sounded on the other side of the rocky pinnacle. They all threw themselves down on the ground.

"We can't stay here", the nervous student, who had not been able to finish the bandaging, said uneasily, half turning his helmet-covered head. "Come on, let's get out of here. We have to change our place."

"Yes", the other student agreed. "Yes." And to Manno, "Lieutenant, you go back now. With your hands you won't . . ."

"No!" the nervous student exclaimed. "What'll we do without him?"

"But don't you see his hands?" the Milanese answered him.

"No, no, no", the other one insisted.

Little by little, Manno was coming back to life. "Are you joking?" he said at last. "What's the matter with you? Go back?" He was talking and at the same time was hearing himself talk, as if echoing himself. His whole being had converged into his hands. Would he lose them? But reason and a sense of duty did not abandon him. He was still in control.

He lifted his helmet-covered head a little and looked around, searching in the cloudy mist for a way of taking in the situation. "Wait", he said to the few students who had stopped at his side. "Everybody at a run with me, first to the left and then forward."

He leapt to his feet and took off, bent forward, and with swift steps, he began the climb again, the others following.

The rest of the platoon had stopped a little farther on and were waiting. They were running the risk of losing contact with the company. Not far off to the right they heard some Bersaglieri, invisible to them, scream out in the middle of the onslaught of gunshot: "*Savoia! Savoia!*" They were undoubtedly entering some enemy positions, because from the other side came vehement German shouts.

"Forward!" Manno ordered his men, and he was at the lead. The platoon again began to climb, swarming him, but quite soon they were forced to stop again because of the insistent shower of enemy fire.

All together, the advance on the upper margins of the mist demanded time, enormous effort, and losses. Finally the zone of German positions, in that direction at least, was surmounted.

14

But there was another line a little farther up, and while those attacking continued advancing, the mist faded away, exposing them in full sunlight. Luckily, the slope was heavily covered with rocks and undergrowth, which provided them with some shelter. In any case, they could go no farther.

Guided by the radio of an observer officer, the Italian artillerymen opened fire from the bottom of the valley, thereby neutralizing the enemy positions. They were joined, as at the beginning of the attack, by the American artillery, which, however, did not have observer positions there. Their grenades— continuous as they were—all exploded too far from the mark, farther from the neighboring point 343, toward the "numberless" one and also toward 351.

Manno was squatting in a hollow of a rock with a couple of his men; he did not look at the irregular mountain crests that emerged around them like elongated islands from the sea of mist. To the left was Mount Maggiore, and to the right Mount Sammucro, on whose slope the American attack was going on; behind, at his back, was Mount Cesima. All three mountains were lit up with the yellow December sun. In front, perhaps some nine miles away, at the top of another mountain, which blocked the main valley, was a strange square building: the Montecassino Abbey. While the waiting was prolonged and the fire from portable arms, as well as the hissing and explosions of artillery mortars, went on, the young man had, for better or worse, a moment to reflect. What was happening to him? How had they wounded him like this? Injured, he, who until now had felt invulnerable, because he was fated by God to that unknown reckoning . . . how would he be able to fulfill his duty without his hands? Indeed . . . but what was really happening to him? He could not understand.

The news that he had been injured spread among the student officers whom he had brought this far with his example and impassioned words. "We have to pull Italy out of this morass" and all those speeches. He had convinced them, and now the ones closest by looked at him apprehensively. The officer was aware of it. *I won't abandon you. What's there to be afraid of?* occurred to him momentarily as a response. For nothing in the world would he have abandoned them in the still more difficult circumstances ahead of them. "If we die, we die all together", he had said and repeated then, and that's how it would be. That's how it would be, beyond any temptation to run away from this savage reality.

Suddenly, his faraway world came to mind: his family, his friends, Luca and the others, the boys in the oratory ("Art is the universal in the particular"), the workers, for whom it was necessary to make life go on in dignified fashion. Seen from this perspective, family, friends, and workers formed a kind of complete whole. But not Colomba. She was apart from them all. "For the love of God!" her mother had said in Novara, seeing her hair combed that way. A trace of a smile lit up his face. God knows what Colomba might be doing at this moment. Perhaps she had just got up and was thinking about him. He wondered who would tell Colomba and the others if it were to turn out that he . . .

No doubt it would be Luca, his friend from Nomana, a sergeant with the Alpine troops, whom he had met by chance in a small station in Puglia a few weeks before. What a pleasure it was! Luca had recognized him first. "Lieutenant . . . rather Manno, is it really you? Manno! You see, I'm here, too. Incredible!" Then he went on to explain, "On the eighth of September I was in Brindisi with a shipment of parts for the Taurinense Division, which is, I mean was, in Montenegro. But what a coincidence! Just imagine the two of us meeting this way!" Luca was ready to go with him to the "combat detachment" that second, but Manno had told him, "No, better you don't. Forget it." Why had he told him that? God knows why. It was one of those sudden instinctive reactions, irrational. *Well, it'll be Luca who will have the job of telling the others in case I . . . Enough of these thoughts, I can't run the risk of going soft.*

The Italian artillery continued beating its way to the line of German positions until the order to be ready to go forward again came at last, transmitted from man to man. The student officer who transmitted it to him (the boy from Milan, who from the moment the officer had been wounded had not left his side) ended, sighing and saying quite conventionally, "Let's hope that this time it's definitive."

"Come on, fellow", Manno said encouragingly and, turning to the others who could hear his voice, "We can't leave things half done. We must show we've made up our minds to go ahead, to pull ourselves out of this morass. Don't forget that!"

At these words, the student, stirred up, murmured something.

"What did you say?" Manno asked him.

"I said", the other answered, "that for us you're like a flag."

"Go on", Manno said.

The order "Go forward!" could be heard. The lieutenant repeated it loud and strong and rushed ahead, his bandaged hands stuck out like those of a boxer, all of them behind, while around and among them chaos broke out once again.

They set off at a run up the rocky climb like madmen, as if possessed. Where were those damned German positions? Where were they? One, two boys fell. Others, even though unharmed, threw themselves to the ground, terrorized. The teeth of one of them were actually chattering with fear. "Forward! What're you doing there? Come on, on your feet. Forward! Forward!" The student officers were firing in disorderly fashion as they ran and screaming, "*Savoia! Savoia!*" Manno ran among the first, his bandaged hands held forward. "Italy!" he screamed with every last breath of voice in his body. "Italy! Italy!" He fell forward suddenly and hit the front of his helmet against the rocky ground. Those nearest him distinctly heard the noise of the metal but did not stop in that inferno.

He had lost consciousness but shortly after regained it. He felt a great pain between his neck and collarbone, in his belly, and especially in his pelvis. His backbone could not support him, incredibly enough, and so, despite all his attempts, he could not get up. He went on bleeding rapidly. He felt it throughout his body. *A shower of gunfire*, he realized. *That's what it was, God Almighty!* It was all over for him, no way out ... how awful, inadmissible! But where were his men now? Tremendous gunfire continued. It seemed the sound of shouting was a little farther ahead ... but what did that matter now? For him, the moment to die had come, yes, to die! Here, with his face against the rock, there was nothing else left for him, nothing left for him to do on earth but die. As it came clearly home to him he felt an inexpressible sense of rebellion. No! No! No! It took a lot of strength to control himself, to overcome such futile resistance. He panted, *goodbye life, goodbye Colomba, goodbye to everything ... no! No! No, this can't be happening to me! Not me! No!* But it was happening, exactly that. So many, so very many other soldiers had died, and now his turn had come. But how would he be able now to carry out his task? What task? Despite the agitation of the moment he suddenly had a flash of insight, even if at first very confused. Providence had perhaps kept this in store for him, this ... this what? Had he been destined to ... to participate in this initial step of pulling Italy out of the morass? No, no, noooo ... and, yet ... if that's the way it was, there was no other choice but to seal his work of beginner with the sacrifice of his youthful life. Thank God it came to him suddenly, clearly, perfectly. This, then, was why that boat had been there for him in Africa, and why he had been sent to Albania, and ... but then for some time now, God was getting ready for the recovery of Italy! How much trouble God went to for him! "Thanks, dear God!" Manno murmured with his last breath. "Thanks."

He felt, not with his flesh-and-blood ears but with his spirit, a rustle of something, as if from far off came to his memory the words of the student officer: "The flag." His spirit's eyes opened to see it, but it was not the flag waving, it was angel wings. He saw the face for the first time, and he smiled, while around him the great transformation was taking place.

That day the Italians did not manage to achieve the goals they had set. In the evening they went back to their starting positions. There were forty-seven dead and 102 wounded. Eight days later, on the sixteenth of December, the attack was repeated, successfully this time. The Montelungo action was, in effect, the beginning of Italy's recovery, of its pulling itself out of the morass. After Montelungo, in fact, the Allies consented to the amplification of the small "motorized unit", and in the end two divisions were formed, which came to be known as the "Italian Liberation Corps". At the end of the war there were six regular Italian divisions in action against the Germans.

PART FIVE

I

Meanwhile, in the military hospital on Lago Maggiore, Ambrogio had been fighting for his life for some time. The young woman from the Red Cross, Epifania Mayer, known as Fanny, worried by his worsening condition, nursed him with unwonted devotion and abnegation, though little could be done for him. When his condition became worse, his mother also moved to Stresa, to a little hotel, from where she went every afternoon to nurse him, her heart heavy with anguish.

She would cross over almost immediately after eating, by boat—almost always the same one—on the stretch of water between the city and the island where the hospital was located. And she prayed. She had no eyes for the splendid landscape around her or for the lake, which during those first cold days of winter was bright, or for the surrounding high mountains, or the nineteenth-century gardens—greener even than those of Brianza—which lined the shores. She prayed and imagined the weary face of her son, which in a while would greet her smilingly, encouragingly, but immediately after would become serious. The war! The repugnant reality, inadmissible. And she—she was well aware of it—with all her grief was only one among the many mothers suffering, as many as there were boys in arms, more even, because there were also the mothers of boys already dead (and they were in so many countries, millions by now) who had been left on earth to cry and tear their souls to pieces . . . and the mothers of the missing? Poor Lucia, there in Nomana! But she, too, Giulia, in a certain way, since her Manno . . . *Manno, no, no.* He was not missing. Even Ambrogio said so. Manno was simply late in sending news. *Dear Virgin, with your Son in your lap, make it be true.*

At the end of the brief crossing the old boatman disembarked and extended his right hand, his wrist bent downward in a professional gesture savoring of the nineteenth century, for her to balance herself as she stopped off. Giulia would then hurry, crossing the ancient garden with hedges and terraces bordered with myrtle, toward the entrance of the hotel converted into a hospital. Here she suddenly found herself enmeshed in a military atmosphere, for which she felt a growing sense of repulsion and, at the same time, a bewildering familiarity. Repulsion because the orderlies in uniform (sloppy, with swords in their lapels instead of stars) who were seated on the porters' chairs of another time, personified, in her eyes, the hard reality of war; familiarity because in that world—like it or not—her son also belonged.

The orderlies no longer accompanied her to Ambrogio's room on the first floor. She went upstairs alone, each time a bit intimidated by the more and more perceptible odor of medications. She went across a stretch of corridor and entered her son's room, which he shared with another wounded fellow.

After the initial greetings and an exchange of a few words, and after a brief look at her son, Giulia felt—as she always did in her life—the need to do something. She set about arranging things, even though she actually did not have to, thanks to Fanny. She shook out the pillows, adjusted the window shutters better, took off or put on another blanket. At other times she would fill a vase with flowers she had brought purposely from the town to combat the odor of medicines. Often taking out a bag of candy from her pocket, she would put it, smilingly, on the night table of the other wounded officer—not on Ambrogio's, however, as he could not eat sweets now.

"No, but why are you doing this?" the other officer would ask them. "But why, Signora? You shouldn't. Why are you going to this trouble?" along with other similar phrases. The officer—a lieutenant, no longer young, called Decio, originally from central Italy, with very distinguished manners (more so than the manners of Ambrogio and his mother, who felt slightly provincial next to him)—was continually worried by a secret dilemma: Was it morally licit to be taken care of in the Fascist republic, while in his heart he had determined, once better, to cross the lines and go into the regular army of the south?

Giulia would at last sit down on a chair and would relate, with her own quiet vivacity, many tiny things about Nomana, the hotel, the town of Stresa, the Mass she had heard in the morning, just to keep a conversation going with the two injured men, though there were occasional interruptions, lone ones on occasion.

Both of the men (Ambrogio, too, despite his health) wanted to be abreast of what was happening in Italy and in the world. For that reason the woman, so as to be able to say something, had got into the habit of buying a newspaper in the morning and, with a certain effort on her part, reading it before coming to the hospital, where, on Fanny's advice, she did not bring it. News was never definitive. The German-Allied front was quiet between Naples and Rome, before Casino; in the Fascist republic—created because the Germans wanted it on this side of the lines—aerial bombings continued, but only on warheads, not over the cities, as before the armistice. The enormous German front in the east was still in the process of a slow retreat and was nearing central Europe. This last fact worried Ambrogio secretly, so much so that Giulia, when she realized it, did not talk about it unless he asked.

"How will they be stopped?" the young man sometimes asked, referring to the Bolsheviks.

"Don't worry yourself. The Americans are here", his mother would answer.

"Of course", Decio bolstered her. "We're in a zone of American influence. What are you worried about?" The knowledge of the American potential was then being realized in Italy. Ambrogio, however, given his experience in the east, felt not at all certain.

He asked about the people, what they were saying, how the ordinary people were living, what the Fascists were doing. "Talk freely", he would say to his mother, pointing to Decio. "He thinks the same as us, you know."

Decio, at these words, would smile with the vague air of an accomplice.

To his mother, at that time, the Fascists inspired only grief. "I don't know if in other places—in Rome or in other big cities, for example—things are different, but around Milan and also here in Stresa, only because the Fascists are forced to are they showing themselves again. They prefer staying at home. They realize perfectly that the war is lost, imagine." She would quote some example (told by her husband or else by some acquaintance in the hotel; her limited sources of information) of Fascists who, in order not to be found, had taken shelter in all kinds of ways.

"Yes, the Fascist rulers and even Mussolini", Lieutenant Decio confirmed, "have got themselves back into the limelight begrudgingly, only because the Germans made them. I have the same impression."

"About Mussolini?" Ambrogio asked.

"Neither he nor the others have got back into the limelight willingly. Except for the usual extremists, you know, the Farinacci and company, but how many of them are there?"

"I'm sorry for them", the mother said. "I'm sorry for all of them, the important ones and the little ones alike. Those who agreed to join the republic call on the others and tell them, 'When things were going well, you joined up, you were a Fascist. Now that things aren't going well, would you like to hide out?' I even have the impression that the ones who are making an effort are more honest. Surely, not the opportunists."

"That was true, especially at the beginning", Decio observed. "That's what happened at the beginning. But since then, in November, those bands have come out calling men to arms, the same ones who've made so many young men take to the hills. Things have gone sour for them. They've started an unending series of vendettas between Fascists and partisans; that's the problem. I don't really know what will happen in the future if the Allies don't hurry up the advance."

"Have there been any vendettas in Nomana?" Ambrogio wanted to know from his mother.

"Nomana, no, heavens! Who, after all? That minor officer who once gave premilitary instruction to you, what was his name?—Alfeo, took off to his house, on the signing of the armistice, just like all the others, and from then on he's been there, stewing in his own juice."

"Poor fellow. He must have thought the world was coming down on top of him with the armistice."

"I think so, really. You know something? He told Papa himself. While he was on the train on his way home, he heard that in Bologna, at the station, the

Germans captured all the Italian soldiers. And you know who he asked to find out if it was really true? A German officer who was on the same train."

"Poor Alfeo", Ambrogio murmured, shaking his head. "And how did it all turn out?"

"Maybe the officer took pity on him", Giulia said. "I don't know. He told him that danger truly did exist, and he advised him to get off at the station before Bologna and go around the city on foot."

"He couldn't have been an SS officer", Decio observed, laughing.

Sometimes the partisans were the topic of conversation. They also had to be in the hills over Lago Maggiore. At least that's what Giulia had heard in the hotel. "But I don't know if I believe it. Some say they're simply ordinary delinquents, thieves, nothing else. Others say the opposite, that they're Badoglio's men, under the command of real officers, that is, normal people who have no need to rob, because anything they might need is parachuted to them by the Americans. Tell me what I should believe."

"You can't parachute everything that's needed to a band of partisans", Ambrogio had explained on several occasions. "Whether one likes it or not, they would have to have recourse to local supplies."

Decio was interested in finding out who had told her about the partisans being Badoglio's people. "Signora, were the people who told you that trustworthy?"

Despite her faith in Decio, Giulia feared for her main source of information, the elderly and garrulous hotel porter. "No", she ended by answering. "Or rather I don't really know. I heard it from people I don't know."

Decio guessed the reason for her reluctance and did not press the point.

Fanny came in to take the temperature of the wounded men and to perform other routine tasks. She greeted the visitor warmly, and—charmingly young—she smiled brightly with her strange green eyes. The young woman marveled at the simplicity and modesty of the older woman. She did not use rouge or lipstick or powder or eye makeup or nail polish (even though her nails were absolutely perfect), and she admitted she had never played cards in her life. Compared with her own mother, who had her hair tinted blue, brandished a dress cane, no longer than two handspans ("the boss' cane", her father called it), the contrast between the two mothers was amusing.

In the hours in which neither the mother nor the Red Cross nurse was in attendance, and especially if Decio had left the room to go to the floor below with the other convalescents, Ambrogio—who did not get much sleep during the day—fell into a state of wakeful daydreaming because of his fever.

His aide Paccoi often came to mind, Paccoi to whom he owed his life. He knew that he had gone back home to Umbria since the armistice. Who knows how he was now, what with the new army call-ups and the rest? His father, Gerardo, some two months after his repatriation, had, without telling his son, sent the aide a beautiful gold watch, accompanied by a card saying, "This is not by way of payment, because that would be impossible. It is only a token of our affection and appreciation." When Ambrogio learned of it, he protested weakly, "Papa, you don't understand. It could irritate him. What he did by risking his life is of another category." But Paccoi, simple soul that he was, thanked him contentedly. "I see you've remembered the undersigned artillery man Giovanni Paccoi . . ."

In the wake of Paccoi, others sometimes slipped in to take up Ambrogio's thoughts, especially Stefano and Michele from Nova, whose crippled father had not been up to the terrible lack of news, and the poor Major Casasco, who came to his end a few days from the retreat, and Tired Horse, and those two bums Mazzoleni and Piantanida (Piantanida, poor chap, had been left under a pile of straw and snow in Cercovo), and Corporal Colombo, who sang in the evening on the grass (he, luckily, had been repatriated in November), and Feltrin, who could not get to sleep in Leopoli—what had become of him? And this one and the other . . . God knows what the fate of the prisoners had been, especially the ones who had been wounded? But even the others, those in one piece, would they still be alive? If so, how would they face another winter? With their last year's worn uniforms still on, which no doubt, they had worn even to sleep? And would the Russians have left them their fur jackets? For weeks the temperature there must have gone below zero. The previous year the icing over had suddenly begun at the beginning of November. In a few days the branches of the trees along the Don had been completely covered with frost; he could see it all still in his mind's eye. At this moment the landscape in Russia would also be the same . . . but would there be any prisoners alive or not? The eternal question. Not a single one, up until now, had written home. To think about them proved to be, for Ambrogio, like thinking about souls in the next world; there was not even a faint voice, a sign, nothing, that reached him. Besides, who was thinking of them now after all that had happened in Italy? Only their families, heartbroken, and their friends: exactly the same as they thought of the dead.

2

The frost, indeed, had turned the woods white around Lager 74 in Oranchi, in which Michele, Father Turla, and the others were still locked up. Totally cut off from Italy and what was happening there, far away, they felt as if they were on the other side of the moon.

For a good part of the summer Michele had worked in a cave digging out lime: tough work for people so run down as he and his comrades, because their only tool was a pick. Every day, to get to the cave—located within the woods—

and to return, the squadrons of prisoners had to go by an extraordinarily extended *lager*, made up of innumerable log cabins and guarded by sentries armed with machine guns posted on high towers. This camp—perhaps the largest of the many scattered in the forest region of Oranchi—contained only women, an incalculable number of Russian women.

They were all in rags, many with emaciated children in their arms or beside them, a pitiful sight. In contrast to the male deportees, they did not seem anxious to talk, and they did not move about much; perfectly still behind the barbed wire, they looked out in silence at the foreign prisoners going by. It was obvious their lives had been broken. For Michele, when he saw them at a distance, they did not look like women so much as whimsical puppets in rags, whose strings the puppeteer had let go slack.

"They're practically all wives of the male deportees. After their husbands are deported, then they go, because that's the custom in Russia", the prisoners said.

"You know all the guards, even those from our *lager*, would like to work here?"

"Yes, I've heard that."

"Because here they can scr—— day and night, whenever they feel like it. They choose the best looking at bathtime. Even if one of them wants to be good, faithful to her incarcerated husband, she has to be 'done', or she'll be killed with work in no time."

"The damn beasts", the *nachialnich* observed disdainfully, who was no longer Father Turla but a captain from the territorial division of Vicenza. And he added, "Just to think about it, how unfortunate the Russians are. We at least harbor the hope that one day we'll be released and be free men once again. But them?"

The limitless suffering of the Russian people! Once more Michele was up against it. *How many* lagers *would there be in Russia?* he wondered. Some had it that there were thousands perhaps, scattered all over. But was that true? *This is something I must talk to the deportees about. When the opportunity comes up, I must not let it slip by, and an opportunity will have to arise.*

Meanwhile, the spectacle of the women (the *cucle*, rag dolls, as the prisoners came to call them) grieved the Italians a great deal. More than one kept his own scant ration of bread, or else a potato, without letting the guards know and would throw something to those poor creatures. On receiving a gift that way, they would seem to wake up a bit. They would gather it up, famished, and would thank the soldiers with repeated bows. Sometimes, before the first bite, they would cross themselves sadly, with their fingertips together in the Russian Orthodox fashion.

They must be even more hungry than we are. For them there can't have been any Stalin pricàs, Michele thought, *which would regularize their rations. Since they don't serve for Communist propaganda in the West . . .*

Unexpectedly an opportunity arose for him to talk to the *cucle* because of a big landslide in the lime cave. Immediately after, his squadron and another one were ordered to load and transport a quantity of tree trunks for repair from the woods.

To cut and saw the trunks was the job of the women (their usual work). The Italian prisoners were meant only to load the carts by hand and transport them back to the cave. There was no regular surveillance of this work. The few guards usually watched over the comings and goings of the carts, while the prisoners who carried the trunks to the cart temporarily remained under the eye of the women's guards. The women were all filthy, the majority of them dressed in men's clothing, torn and threadbare (all of them "humiliated and violated" alike, Michele thought, who now really understood the meaning of those words). But they were not all equal to standing up to their work. Some of them were so exhausted that they raised their axes with difficulty, losing their balance as they hit the wood, sometimes not even striking the indicated cut. How long would these poor creatures last?

The young man, anguished, took advantage of a moment when there were no guards about to question one of the prisoners, different from the rest, who was a few steps away from him and who every so often observed him. He went up to her because she was different, less fatalistic looking than the other Russian women. The woman, resting her ax on the ground, listened to him with her hands and stomach against the end of the handle. After trying, with little success, to express himself in Russian, the lieutenant asked her in French, "Who are those women? Those two over there working on that log. Why are they so weak?"

"Because they're on half rations", the prisoner answered in French. "Because days ago they didn't meet the 'quota', so that's why they're on half rations." This said, she twisted her mouth and lifted her eyes showing their whites. She continued, "They don't eat enough, you understand? There's nothing for those two but to die, *kaput*."

"*Kaput*?" he repeated like an echo.

The strange prisoner nodded. "Yes," she said, "and it's for the best. Because they're both Communist dogs, both wives of big shots. *C'est bien*, it's all right", she repeated with hatred. And then, swallowing, "There are other Communists in this camp", she explained. "An Italian, yes, the wife of a Communist, who came with him from Italy. They shot him in '37. *Très bien*."

Michele had a good look at her. The skin on her face was similar to a thick sock, and her hair was cut in the style of the feminists of twenty years before, but most impressive were her teeth, with their dark roots jutting from the sockets of the teeth, in such a way that her whole physiognomy seemed to be putrefied when she opened her mouth.

Her workmates of the prisoner group left off working, one after the other. They did not seem to understand the conversation, and so all they could do was stare in silence at the officer.

"You, if I've understood you right, are no Communist", he said.

"No, *bien sûr*, no, I'm a leftist social revolutionary", she explained, still in French, with a weary air, but one that seemed to defy the entire world, and once again twisted her mouth and rolled her eyes upward.

Michele knew—thanks to the political library in the camp—the history of this extremist party. He knew that after they had enthusiastically helped the Communists in the revolution, they had rebelled and the party was destroyed.

"I know the history of your party", he said.

"You do?" the woman said, visibly flattered.

"I know it", the young man repeated, nodding. But he changed the subject to something he was more interested in. "Are you sure of what you're saying about those women having nothing left but to die?"

The woman looked at him in amazement. "*Bien sûr.*" (As if to say, by the expression in her eyes, "What planet are you on?") "To save themselves," she explained, "they'll have to become lovers with the cook or a guard. But how can they in their condition?"

"And don't any of you help them?"

"Not I, certainly not", the prisoner answered, hard as nails. "I'd like to see all those Communist dogs blown up." Seeing the lieutenant's bewilderment, she paused and moved her head, as if to say, you can't understand. Then she indicated a woman's squadron some thirty yards away. "They sometimes help them", she said. There were a few women there working methodically without getting distracted. Michele had noticed them already because of their strangely composed manner. They seemed even older than the others. (But it was difficult to hazard an age for women in these conditions. Some were bald and others gray haired women who were perhaps very young.) "They", the deportee said, changing the inflection of her voice, as if she were speaking of downtrodden idiots, "sometimes, when their group meets the 'quota', they help others that can't."

"Are they Communists?" Michele inquired.

"Communists? Nooooo", the deportee exclaimed. "They're sisters. Sisters, you understand?" and she laughed scornfully, revealing her horrible teeth.

"Sisters?" Michele murmured emotionally. "Nuns, you mean?"

"Yes", she said. "That's right. They've been in the camp longer than anyone else. They hold out only because they're peasants. The other deportee sisters who came with them a long time ago", she swore without realizing it, "have met their God under the earth." Once more she looked up and showed the whites of her eyes. "Do you see that one to the right? That's Natasha, *c'est-à-dire Natalie*. She's been here more than twenty years, deported. Incredible, isn't it? And to think so many don't even last a year, die immediately. The average length of time here is six or seven years, you know. She, however . . ."

"More than twenty years!" the officer murmured.

"Of course, the fact she worked for long periods in infirmaries carrying out sh—— has helped her", the woman laughed.

"And you?" he became interested, overcoming his own disgust.

"*Eh bien*" (at moments there was an attempt at nonchalance in her French), "I'm a veteran, too. I've done fourteen years here, too, you understand? Fourteen years! Not all at once, not like Natasha."

"Not all continuously? Fourteen years?" the young man repeated. Then, gesturing toward the nun, "Do you happen to know if she speaks French?"

"I'm sure she doesn't", the social revolutionary answered. "Do you think she's the Natasha out of Tolstoy?" she laughed. "She's a peasant from way back. I told you before. She was cutting wood before the Communists ever screwed her up."

"What do you mean?" Michele asked, wondering if the woman was speaking metaphorically or . . .

Suddenly, belatedly, she was gripped by suspicion. "I made the revolution", she declared with a pride that the officer found incomprehensible. "You're not a Fascist, by any chance?"

"No, not at all."

The social revolutionist nodded her approval. "Socialist then?"

"No, I'm a Christian."

"Christian. What do you mean?"

Two guards walking among the trees were quickly approaching. Realizing this, the other women spread the word and started working again. The social revolutionary also stopped talking and, raising her ax, began to bring it down. This did not prevent one of the guards from landing practically on top of her and delivering a severe reprimand, in which Michele several times caught the word "whore".

The woman showed not a trace of reaction. She continued working, her horrible mouth half open with the effort.

Fourteen years, the officer told himself, anguished. *Fourteen years feeding on hatred. What a life!*

The two guards—in their usual khaki uniform, their usual cap with the red star, their usual rifles over their arms, insufferably well nourished in comparison to the prisoners—kept to their post. The officer related to some of his squadron comrades in a soft voice—they had asked about his conversation, also in a soft voice—what he had learned from the woman. But he did not answer all their questions, nor did he pay attention to their comments. Every so often he glanced over in the direction of the few nuns, without their noticing it, wondering what he could do for them, what gesture, or what word of solidarity he could add to the gesture, in his inadequate Russian.

The hours went by without him deciding anything. In the afternoon he could see the sisters, their own quota of work completed (prescribed quantity of wood), interrupt their work and bow their foreheads. They were probably praying, perhaps having thanked God for having been able to finish that day's work. Then they exchanged a gesture and went over to the two exhausted

Communists, who were at this point really worn out. They could no longer go on. They raised their axes almost without being able to direct them. One of them was crying because a guard, after having yelled at her, had dealt her some blows repeatedly with the butt of the gun on her back until she screamed with pain. As if that were not enough, her squadron comrades, out of fear of suffering the consequences, looked at them scornfully. The sisters approached then, trudging over like woodsmen to the Communists, and began to help in silence. Sister Natalia, deported more than twenty years before, set to work wearily to help someone who—if she had her own way—would have deliberately destroyed her. A spectacle, Manno thought warmly, at which Christ, at this moment, would have looked down from heaven with tears in his eyes.

3

It was getting dark, and the air wafted a pleasant fragrance of cut wood. The lowering sun over the woods seemed to be greeting men, exhorting them to have a little peace, at least at the end of a day's work. A column of female deportees was coming down a long track. They were arriving slowly, watched over by a few guards, some with dogs on leashes; they stopped among the cut and hewn trunks and waited for the women woodchoppers to line up, too. But these guards—who were temporarily in charge of the prisoners of war—went up to their comrades as soon as they arrived to explain the problem; they began to talk.

Given the fact they had gone off at quite a distance, the social revolutionary took advantage of the situation to remark to Michele in French, "Pay attention. The Italian, your countrywoman, is at the head of the column. See her? In the second row, black hair. Do you see her? Do you?"

The young man looked around, but there were many with black hair. He told her, "*Il y en a plusieures avec les cheveux noirs . . .*"

"The one in the second row", the woman insisted. "The wife of the Italian Communist they shot. She's a Communist, too."

"But why did they shoot him? What had he done?" Michele could not stop asking, still trying—without success—to see the Italian woman.

"What did he do? Are you crazy? Nothing. Don't you know these wolves eat each other up?"

Among the Italian prisoners—gathering together to get back to the *lager*—some understood what the woman was saying, others not, and they asked Michele what it was about. He explained in a few words.

"An Italian? An Italian woman? The one at the head of the column?" they began to comment. "Wife of an executed Communist? And she's a Communist? Had been one . . ."

"No," Michele explained, "she says she's still a Communist."

"Bosh, how could she go on being a Communist? Not possible."

"Fellows," one of them suggested, "we have to call her. She should give us her name and address."

"Yes," another added, "a good idea."

"Where is she? You said at the head of the line?"

A heavy-set swarthy officer, with a beard hard as wire, turned his head toward the column, which was perhaps thirty steps away, and making a megaphone of his hands, "Hey!" he shouted in a deep voice. "Is there an Italian over there? An Italian woman? If there is, give us her name and address in Italy. When we're back there we'll be in touch with her family. Understand? Do you understand?"

No one from the column responded. The social revolutionary had quickly separated and mingled among the women of her own squadron. The Russian guards—who had not understood a single word—looked over at the Italian soldiers in amazement.

"If there's an Italian deportee over there," the officer repeated in a deep voice, "shout out your name and address, and we'll let them know in Italy." And he added in almost a whisper for the benefit of his own comrades, "If we ever get back to Italy." He fell silent after this because a guard had set off at a run, pulling out his parabellum at the same time. Instinctively the other prisoners bustled around the lieutenant. The commanding captain of the squadron went up to the guard, trying to divert his attention. "Nachialnik", he introduced himself, "Nachialnik." The guard then began to bawl him out, pointing his arm furiously at the Italian soldiers.

That's it, you pig, that's how it is. All right, you pig, the captain answered mentally.

In any event, the woman had not revealed herself. She had not answered. "I have the feeling she's still a Communist", Michele speculated. "Well, if it makes her happy . . ."

Once the captain was fully reprimanded, the guards turned to the women, still scattered in the woods, and signaled them to gather together. Loading their tools on their backs, they wearily went over to the meeting point—all of them; the poor sisters forgotten by the world of Christianity, the revolutionary nourishing herself on hatred, the two wretches about to die, all of them. They were grouped into a short column of rag dolls, and, after another order was issued, they joined the main column. It seemed some of the guards would stay behind to watch over the prisoners of war who would remain. The sun setting over the woods seemed again to greet them, urge them to a bit of peace, and the air wafted the fragrant odor of chopped wood.

Suddenly from the top of the woman's column a shout went up. "Bologna! . . . I'm from Bologna, Bologna . . ."

Some dogs began to bark, others to howl and pull at the leash. "Bologna, Bologna!" The war prisoners tried to make out the woman screaming, ridiculously standing on tiptoe, but they could not localize her; they could not figure out which of the rag dolls had shouted. In the quickly generalized howling of the dogs, the woman's words could not be distinguished, only "Bologna" and "Togliatti, Togliatti" and blaspheming from time to time.

A guard ran to the head of the column, seized a branch from the woods with which he began to beat one of the deportees savagely and so all of them could then localize her. The woman did not move from her place; bent over with the blows, she went on screaming and swearing.

"If this isn't a hell", Michele murmured, very tense. The dogs had turned into demons. The guards struggled to hold them back. The prisoners of war were also becoming agitated. "A woman. One of ours", they were saying. But the *nachialnik* captain, excited too, reminded them, "She came here because she wanted to. Calm down." The few guards assigned to the Italians were brandishing their rifles and machine guns. One suddenly shot off a shower of ammunition up into the air. The woman fell silent at the sound of the firing. She remained immobile, in place, squatting; the guard stopped striking her; the column reformed.

"*Davai!*" the order resounded, repeated here and there. "*Davai, davai.*" The column moved off slowly ... only the occasional growl from a dog, a snarl, their ferocity contained.

4

For months Michele had no other chance to speak to the Russian deportees. But in September—in the same year, 1943, more or less a week after the armistice in Italy—he once again had the opportunity when his squadron was busy bringing in the harvest, which in Russia, where agriculture has been collectivized, is chronically late. Their working area was far from the camp, and so the prisoners stayed there at night in a rustic house, a *koljos*. Within nearby rustic houses a company of Russian deportees were also billeted, deportees who had come from the "intellectual's *lager*" referred to previously. In theory the separation of the two groups of working prisoners should have been rigorous, but in practice the Italian squadrons and the Russians frequently were working side by side, especially when they were mowing an immense field of grain.

The men were mowing manually, at a slow pace in segmented, irregular groups, because the grain—which should have been cut months before—had turned to a dirty gray because of the inclement weather and was mixed with weeds, and in many places it had fallen to the ground.

Michele managed to get himself next to a squadron of Russians. A few steps to his right an older man with a narrow, bony face was working. His short cut hair and eyes were the color of hazelnuts, and he was wearing an old jacket with ridiculously short sleeves. (But the uniforms of the Italians were hardly presentable either.) Even knowing that not all of the deportees were to be trusted (there were no doubt informers mixed among the prisoners of war), Michele, as soon as he felt concealed from the guards, addressed his neighbor in more or less an approximation of Russian. The older man, after having looked around with circumspection, answered him without stopping his work. At first he said something in German. Then, seeing the young man did not understand, he switched to French, a language he did not seem to know as well. He was a qualified schoolteacher, he told Michele in dignified fashion. "And you, *quelle est votre profession?*"

"A law student from Milan. *Monsieur le professeur,* may I ask you where you are from?"

"Rostov, over the Don. I taught there."

This time Michele was determined to get immediately to what most interested him: the dimensions and characteristics of the concentration camp phenomenon. "May I ask you, *monsieur le professeur,* why you were deported?"

"Article 58. Do you know what it is? No? Counterrevolutionary propaganda. Like almost all the others arrested between '36 and '39. Naturally, I'm innocent, just as all the others are. Do the Italians know about these things?"

"No. Before we became prisoners we hardly knew that these camps existed."

"I understand."

"Even now it's very difficult for us to talk to the civilian deportees. I'd like you, if you would, to give me an idea of the situation in the camps."

The professor again looked around to see if any *secsoti* (spies) or any guards were about. "It's exactly what I'd like to do", he answered. "Listen carefully, and the things that I tell you I'd like you also to tell your comrades, the ones you can trust. Then, when you go back to Italy, you must let everybody know, as much as possible, of our situation."

Michele promised, restraining his emotions. He wondered if this man had not looked for a way, just as he had, to get to the side of a foreigner in order to communicate with someone. He asked, "Are all those deported innocent, as you said? Would you clarify this for me, please?"

The man scarcely nodded. "Do you see my comrades?" he said, his voice soft, not looking at Michele. "I know many of them. There are all kinds, good people and rotters (*des vaches*), but there's not a guilty one among them; not one, I mean, that has committed the crime he's been condemned for. Do you understand? Not one. And the same goes for the millions who have been deported."

Michele was struck dumb. "Did you say millions? Millions?"

"Exactly. I said millions. And all of them are innocent. In Russia everybody knows the deportees are innocent: the judges, the guards, every single person knows it. But they all pretend (*font semblant*) as if they didn't. Even more, they pretend not even to know that there are millions of their fellow citizens locked up in these camps. Because they're all afraid, if they speak out, they'll end up the same way. You understand?"

Michele was feeling more and more stirred up. He had the sensation of having at last found someone who would give him the information he had been in search of, his reason for having come to Russia. "But how can you—forgive me, *monsieur le professeur*—speak of millions? How do you know that?"

"We know it from . . . from many sources. In Russia there are camps everywhere, and the '*zek*'—*cest-à-dire les déportés*—are continually being moved from one to another. That's how they make their calculations. And also to give you an example, in March two people who worked in the central office of statistics arrived at our camp, both condemned for ten years, the 'decade', like me. Well, according to them there must be around nine million deportees. You've understood? Around nine million." With a handful of grain in his left hand and the sickle in his right, the professor stopped working an instant and pressed his lips together, as if to underscore the enormity of it all.

"It's . . . it's . . . hard to understand", the young man murmured.

"Yes. It's hard for us to understand, too, I assure you. But this is how things are." He straightened up again and looked around—without letting it be seen—at the closest deportees. The long, bony head reminded Michele of an insect, a grasshopper. Heaven knows how many troubles that poor head must have suffered. And it wasn't over yet! He saw the man bend over again to the grain and begin to cut it back rather clumsily. *Poor fellow*, he thought.

"What I've told you," the professor continued, "you prisoners must repeat in Italy. Everyone should be made to know. Even though . . . I really don't know what benefit that will mean for us." Suddenly he said in a changed voice, "The Communists are winning the war, and no one will be able to help us. Why", he asked, "have you all been so blind?" Now, although he went on working in this way, he occasionally looked directly at Michele. "Didn't you see at the beginning that our people weren't fighting, or just barely, that the people in the villages welcomed you as liberators? Why did you commit so many *horreurs*? Why were you all so mad?"

The same words uttered by the starosta in that Ukraine village! Michele thought. "Listen to me, please", he answered. "It was the Germans, not the Italians, who did that. The Nazis are the ones who did that, and they're out of their minds, *justement* like the Communists, even if they go about it differently."

But the other went on. (It was a topic, obviously, that was close to his heart. Who knows how long he had dreamed of pouring all this out to a prisoner of war?) "How is it you didn't know or understand that, hardly had the war begun, and Stalin had given it up for lost? He neglected everything, didn't issue orders for the defense, didn't even talk on the radio, nothing . . . ah, *mon Dieu!* Stalin understood that a nation in which the Communists have murdered so many millions, and where there are nine million deportees—which means so many more millions of families broken up, do you realize?—wouldn't fight to defend communism. And in fact that's how it was. No one or almost no one in this country would have wanted to defend it. You were the ones . . ."

"Not us, not the Italians", he repeated. "The Germans, yes, better the Nazis."

"What's the difference? All right, the Nazis forced our people to defend communism. You forced the Russians to come together with the Communist organization. It was the only one there was."

From far off a guard screamed something at both of them, who were talking more and more openly. And as Michele, already high pitched emotionally, did not seem to understand, the guard started to shout furiously.

"Careful", the professor whispered then. "I would like to be able to go on with this conversation with you. We must take it up again. I'm going to move off now." He took two baskets and put them under his arm and deposited them a little farther back on top of a stack. When he went back to the row of the mowers he took an empty space between two Russian deportees instead of returning to Michele's side.

Michele mentally absorbed, quite emotionally, what the man had told him, to rivet it in his memory, along with every detail, as he continued to harvest slowly and unskillfully—it was evident—as well as tiredly. Once more he was struck by the incredible suffering that had overwhelmed the Russian people for so many years, and perhaps in a certain way for centuries. What he did not understand, however, was why the Communists, who had been in power for a quarter of a century, continued killing and deporting people by the millions. It came naturally to him to think that the Fascists, the so-called Fascist revolution—even including all the victims of the disorders that had preceded it and the punitive expeditions that had followed—had meant only a few hundred dead, and as far as the confined (the Italian version of the Russian deportees) were concerned, there must not have been many more. That would indicate that to keep power no more were necessary. Why then did the Communists continue killing and deporting (to the point of deporting their own comrades) in such unbelievable numbers? What ends did it serve?

How unfortunate these Russians! On the one hand communism, and on the other an army as strong as that of the Germans—even though they were now retreating—which made them pay for every step forward with such a terribly high death toll. It is true that the Russians seemed to accept it all, in its entirety, with a fatalistic attitude. The peasants were especially adept at putting up with absolutely every incredible thing. (The nun Natalia came to mind.) But they were, after all, creatures of flesh and blood, human beings. The totality of their suffering was such that the young man found it scarcely possible even to imagine.

Now, to his right—where the professor had been before—was a heavyset man, with a big head in which two eyes, clear as water almost, were set in. He, too, like the professor and Michele, worked the scythe with an obvious lack of skill. The young man—he did not know when he would have another chance to talk to the deportees—in order to establish contact with him pointed this out. After having made a point of his own lack of skill, he gestured with his chin toward the Russian's scythe, which was being handled equally badly. The man—who before, while the professor was talking in French, had not moved a muscle—sneaked a glance toward the guard and saw that he was not watching. He also glanced toward his nearest comrades, then showed his own scythe to Michele for a second. "This, along with the hammer, is the symbol of communism," he said in a French that was halting and scarcely intelligible, "and even this field, which we're mowing by hand, months late, is a symbol of Communism. And I, too, am a symbol of Communism: a mechanical engineer being used to mow grain by hand. Remember to mention this, too, when you get back to Italy." He had nothing else to say. After he looked at the guard again with his incredibly light eyes, he continued, heavyset as he was, clumsily cutting back the stalks of grain.

5

That evening after mess, Michele, quite unexpectedly, was able to talk, and for some time, stretched out on the field under a sky clotted with stars, with the professor of the grasshopperlike head, the clear-eyed engineer, as well as a young deportee, who immediately revealed himself to be a person of some culture. At a certain point Father Turla joined the little group. Provided they did not speak very loudly, the guards during this shift—to such a degree was the Russians' behavior inconsistent—paid not the slightest attention to them. The deportees, the professor in particular, answered the questions of the two Italians, giving every possible piece of information on Soviet life, which turned out to be a tragedy of boundless proportions. Michele and Father Turla also answered the Russians' questions, which—especially those of the young man— were of an extraordinarily avid nature, anxious as they were to get to know up-to-date events concerning life in the Western world.

Meetings like these were repeated for several successive evenings, until there was a changing of the guards. As Michele let it be known, cautiously, to the professor that he wished to write about all this if he returned to his country, the professor—after making him repeat and clearly understand the points of greatest interest for him—put him in contact, separately, with a couple of deportees competent in these fields.

Those meetings were of great importance for Michele, the results of which, he realized, would benefit him all his life. Little by little, putting together what he was learning with what he had studied, he finally came to grasp the why and wherefore of the Communist slaughters, which from the 1917 Revolution had gone on almost uninterruptedly. He realized that the goal was not that of conserving the power of the Communists. (It was not necessary, as neither had it been for the Fascists.) These slaughters were part and parcel—together with the increase in material production—of the mechanism that according to Marx and Lenin was to produce a "society of new men". Such a mechanism presupposed, among other things, "violence as the midwife of the new society", by means of the "repression" of the ex-privileged classes, in theory more to transform them and rehabilitate them than to keep them in subjection. In practice—the middle class and lower middle class having been crushed for years now and without the new society having materialized—Stalin now made every class of Soviet society undergo, one after the other, repression, even the Communists themselves, high and low. The aim was to strip every member of society of the corruption that prevented the prophesied terrestrial paradise and so, in practice, to change the conscience and nature of every single person. Without in the least taking into account the objective results obtained, which consisted only in mountain after mountain of corpses, the Communists persisted along this path because stopping would have meant giving up the utopian new society—free of the evils of all preceding societies—to which they had already contributed such an endless number of dead. How many? Certainly a great many millions.

When, at the end of those moving and tragic words on the threshing floor, the officer retired to the barracks of his squadron to sleep, his own prayers came back to him from the time he was a recruit in Mantua and later during his officer's training course, that God should not deprive him of living the experience of the Communist world, of this enormous, isolated laboratory into which the Germans had forcefully entered. *I wasn't mistaken asking for it,* he told himself now. *I did the right thing.* Of course he had to go through the front line, Crinovaya, and all the rest. *What kind of writer would I be if I had known only by hearsay about this, which is the incomparably greatest experience of our time, even more, the culminating experience of several centuries of history?*

There was something more besides: the knowledge—clearer all the time—of the enormous Communist development provided him little by little with the knowledge of its relationship to the other two historical undertakings that had developed along the same lines: fascism and nazism. And to distinguish clearly, at last, between those two: the simple reaction that the first represented and the concurrence with communism of the second. But he would still need documentation regarding this.

All this took place in autumn. With the onset of the bad season the prisoners of war were brought back to the Oranchi camp, where the tough life of before was recommenced, which consisted of working and indoctrination from morning until night. Michele's squadron had been transferred from mining lime to chopping wood in the forests. They would leave the camp in the morning darkness and would reach their working area among snowy trees three or four miles distant, no longer passing the heartbreaking camp of rag dolls.

As Christmas approached, Father Turla was planning to make "right in front of the guards and the NKVDs" a Christmas *crèche*, chatting about it with Michele and his other friends.

6

Some days before Christmas—Ambrogio's health having taken a turn for the better—Giulia temporarily left Stresa for Nomana. Pino, her third son, came to take her place. Pino, who had matriculated in medical school shortly before, was considered more ideally cast for the job of looking after his brother than the second son, Fortunato. (Fortunato, who was of an age for military service, had been exempted on the grounds that he was "indispensable" for the business, his father's, where he was working, and so could not leave Nomana.)

As he grew older, Pino looked less and less like his brother Ambrogio. (Although all of Giulia's and Gerardo's children had something in common in their looks and behavior: the "trademark", according to their father.) Pino's features were irregular—especially his nose, slightly twisted—and his bones light and angular, his cranium flattened at the back and his blond hair a pale shade, not the golden blond of Giudittina. He was less and less like Ambrogio, not only physically but in his character, not at all strong, but tending more to excessive sensitivity; yet unlike his cousin Manno's sensitivity, which was all of a piece, Pino's was more unsteady. Of all Gerardo's children, he was the only one who did not get good grades in school, and he was led occasionally to eccentricities. (He had been the one, years before, who had made the experiment of tying ribbons onto the swallows to test their return to the nest.) He was also likely to take up with the most disparate company, without prejudices but also without any ability to discern. He was the only one, too, among the other children—and here he was also at odds with the character of Nomana, where boys from any sort of background normally entered marriage virgins—who at the age of eighteen had already had carnal knowledge. The consequent repentance, crises, and relapses were known only to his confessor, Don Mario.

He brought a breath of fresh air to the hospital, consisting mainly of bits and pieces of news: "Mama had to go back by train because we no longer get gasoline. And besides, the wheels of our Millecento are already as bald as a billiard ball. And the bad part is that this is not all that's missing: there's nothing left. Do you remember the railings they took away from the gardens and the bells from the towers to melt down? Well, now they've used up everything. Papa says soon it'll be impossible to find work."

Fanny, who enjoyed talking with them, too, when she was able, confirmed this. "You boys should see my mother arguing with the shopkeepers. It's really getting terrific."

"And why?" Decio asked, amused.

"Because the little there is they want to sell under the counter at a higher price. At least that's what she says."

Pino, after having given the attitude of Fanny's mother the stamp of approval, continued. "You know how many boys of military age we have inscribed in the factory as workers now, all certified? Well, I don't even know the exact number, but there's heaps of them. Practically all who ask for it, that way Papa conceals them. He says that while it's possible it's our duty to keep them from ending up in Germany."

"What wouldn't our father consider a duty?" Ambrogio commented softly.

"But Fortunato", Pino continued. (Here he opened a parenthesis for Fanny's and Decio's benefit. "Fortunato", he explained, "is our brother, the second, after Ambrogio, and the one before me", and he took up the thread of what he was saying.) "Well, that fellow in the factory is showing he's really worth something, especially in the commercial end of it." He concluded, "Well, Fortunato's not a dummy like me." (The phrase "not a dummy like me" came up frequently in Pino's conversations.)

And he went on, "Nobody in Nomana wants to hear talk about fascism. Everyone thinks more or less as we do at home. You know, Ambrogio, even Cereda, the political secretary, has sent in his resignation? And then everybody, beginning with the rector of the parish, insisted he withdraw his resignation. 'You stay on, Signor Cereda, because if you don't, they'll send us someone undesirable. Keep your place, and when the war's over, we'll all testify in your behalf. We'll say you did it because the people wanted it.' And he ended up withdrawing his resignation. We hope that then, when the war is over, they do manage to justify, really and truly, his position. Poor Cereda."

"Well," Fanny said, "not for anything in the world would I like to be in his shoes."

Ambrogio nodded seriously. Then he asked Pino, "Has anyone in Nomana had serious problems with the Fascist republic? Or nobody up 'til now?"

"In Nomana, no. But in Incastigo, yes."

"Brrr! . . .", Fanny exclaimed, already anticipating what was to come. "Brrr! What place did you say?"

"Incastigo, a village a few miles from Nomana, near Monza."

"What a strange name."

"It's a short form for *Signor-in-castigo*. Just think of it. It was the ancient name of the village. Because—at least that's what they say—in antiquity the tabernacle of the church was not in the honored position but relegated instead to one side."

"How odd", Decio commented.

"Well," Pino continued, "something really terrible happened there. The Fascists took the administrator Mambretti off—the director of Banca Artigiana." Turning to Ambrogio, "You remember him, don't you?"

Ambrogio raised his head. "You said Mambretti? Of course I remember him; we worked with Banca Artigiana. But what happened? Where did they take him?"

"To Germany. They deported him to Germany."

"Mambretti?"

"That's what happened." (Pino was happy to have found a topic that so caught his brother's interest.) "You remember that fellow, also from Incastigo, an employee of the Agrarian Consortium, no, of an insurance company, well, something like that, part of GIL? Someone called Praga, or Braga . . . ?"

"That knucklehead, Praga, yes. He's not one of ours."

"Exactly. He was the one who had Mambretti deported."

"The bas . . . but how did he do that? He was a nothing! But if you think about it, yes, he was always a social climber. Only the others in the party kept him in line." He explained to Decio, "No one in our town really felt any inclination toward fascism, and so the official jobs were filled by people who were Fascists only in name, since someone had to fill them anyway."

Pino corrected him. "Before. It was like that before. But now no one wants these jobs. Everyone gets out of them if he can. Signor Cereda, too, as I said. True, he stayed on as the political secretary, but he also had presented his resignation."

"I see. Now the moment's come for the Pragas. But how did he, a minor officer of GIL, manage to get Mambretti deported? Did he denounce him?"

"No. The only thing we know is that Praga went one night to Mambretti's house with another Fascist, someone they call Panzone, a fellow skinny as a rail—must be halfway to an idiot, I don't know. Do you know him? Since then, from what we hear, this Panzone spends his time drunk, crying in public sometimes out of fear of what he's done."

"Panzone?"

"Yes, do you know him?"

"It seems to me . . . the fellow with a belly that looks sunken . . . I think I do."

"Well, no one knows how those two tricked Mambretti. They passed themselves off as having been sent by I don't know whom. The thing is that he, knowing both of them well, fell into their trap, and we don't know what he said or what proofs he let slip about having given money to the partisans through his bank. Because, most definitely, that was the accusation."

"Mambretti giving money to the partisans?" Ambrogio thought it over. "Yes, that he could have done, after all. But with small children . . . poor devil. Mambretti is, that is, was the head of the Incastigo Catholic Action, so it will be a problem for them, too."

"Yes", Pino said. "I've heard something. Well, all in all, these two took him and carried him off immediately, the same night. Praga told him to come with them, and they led him away in plain view of his wife and children, you know? Imagine such scum!" There was a pause.

"Oh, boys, what this does to me", Fanny murmured. "It reminds me of something that happened in Pallanza."

"And of course Mambretti is no idiot", Ambrogio considered. "He was a captain in the Alpine troops, I think, in his day. I don't understand how they could have tricked him. Besides, he's a bank director, so ..." He shook his head. "We Brianza people leave a lot to be desired when it comes to politics."

"That's not the point", Fanny said. "In Pallanza, too, I didn't want to tell you for fear of upsetting you, but two of the guards—the blackshirts—took a lawyer off last week because he helped the partisans. He's from Milan, and his villa is not far from ours: as smart as can be, from what they say, and yet, they got him."

She opened her green eyes and nodded to herself. After some discreet questioning from Ambrogio and Decio, she went into the details. "What an age we live in, what an age!" she concluded.

The conversation, as soon as Pino could divert it, returned to Nomana. He went on with the news. "Before you were asking about the people going hungry in the town. No. There's no real hunger, but belts have to be pulled in a notch or two, and of course there's a shortage of everything. However, the shipment of packages to prisoners in Germany goes on as always. Papa's organized it, and it's pretty well done, obviously. What, you didn't know? You don't know that every soldier from Nomana who's a prisoner in Germany— there are seventy—is sent a package of food every two weeks? And without fail, of course. The whole town pitches in. Some give money, some things, and others do the work of preparing the packages, and Ghezzi, from our warehouse, does the wrapping and last details. Francesca and Alma always go over to lend a hand. Where do we get the things to go in there? On the black market, no helping it. If not, where?" Pino paused and shook his blond head slightly, with its flattened cranium. "The only one we can't send anything to is Manno, poor fellow, because we have no address for him. Heaven knows where the Germans have dragged him off to. Some say to the rearguard of the Russian front. Who knows?"

"Wouldn't it be possible he'd be in the south with the regular army?" Lieutenant Decio asked, who was acquainted with Manno's adventures. "Maybe he's gone over to Puglia or Calabria from Greece. It's possible, isn't it?"

"We think so, too, sometimes, but ... it strikes me as difficult."

"He went from Tunis to Sicily, didn't he?" Decio observed, who was even abreast of this. "And that was without a doubt a more difficult undertaking."

"Well, we'll see ..."

Pino was full of admiration for Decio's aristocratic manners. Sometimes he peered at him hard. "You have great style, very lordly, which reminds me of my cousin Manno", he told him on one occasion. "I'd like to have manners like yours." But he did not get to know the officer very well because, once Decio was convalescent, he was released from the hospital to spend Christmas at home.

With his gabardine coat already on, he took leave of Ambrogio, who was seated on a lounge chair next to the window. From his pocket Ambrogio took out a piece of paper and gave it to Decio. A bit surprised, Decio read it. On it was only the last military address for Manno, written in block letters. The lieutenant looked at Ambrogio interrogatively.

"Who knows. Since you live in the center of Italy, I thought you'd maybe be on the other side of the lines one of these days", Ambrogio explained. "If it happened like that, and wouldn't be too much of a bother, you could look for him and, if you find him, let us know."

Decio agreed. So Ambrogio had realized his intention of crossing the lines. "All right, Riva, I promise", he said.

"And try, between the two of you, to let us have news from you. Any way you can."

"Yes", Decio replied.

Pino wanted to accompany him and carry his suitcase to the station.

7

Decio's place was taken in a few days by a lieutenant from the "national republican guards" named Tittoni, wounded in a confrontation with the partisans not far from Stresa.

This Tittoni was a young athlete, with a pale, angular face. He spoke little. Once, however—while Pino was out—he started to speak of the military situation of the province to Ambrogio. (He said exactly that: the military situation of the province.) "The partisans are everywhere in the mountain, worse than weeds. If we don't rout them out in time, it'll end badly. They'll kill us all like rats."

Ambrogio saw him close his eyes for a few instants. "But routing them out from there isn't easy. Don't believe what they're saying in the papers and on the radio. We're badly equipped, and our organization is even worse. You know we pay 300 lire to anyone who shows up with a blanket? And if someone comes with a forage cap, twenty. But the worst is that we can't trust either the command or the soldiers, only a few. Or the people, who don't want to believe in the secret weapons Germany is preparing, which will change the outcome of the war."

Ambrogio went on looking at him without speaking. "You don't believe it either", Tittoni said.

Ambrogio made no objection.

"It doesn't matter", the other answered bad humoredly. "The reds wounded you on the Eastern front, and for months you've been between life and death", he paused, at length. "I have to talk to someone", he murmured.

"Talk freely if it helps you", Ambrogio told him then. "I'm not a bastard; I know how to respect other people's opinions."

Tittoni, who already realized this, agreed. He started to talk again. "My mother does nothing but cry. But for me honor comes before anything else, you understand? My country, my country, cannot act the whore. It can't betray its allies from one day to another to go over to the enemies, who've beaten, bombed, and burned us. To go over to the enemy like a whore and to thank them for it, to shoot your allies of yesterday in the back. No. As far as I'm concerned, this shouldn't happen. I mean, not in the small space around me." He drew a circle on his blanket with his index finger.

Ambrogio, though recognizing the nobility inherent in the other's argument, felt more than a few objections rising to his mouth. "The nation, the people, were pushed to that alliance against their will, by a government that was imposed on them. Besides, they were dragged into a war for which they were totally unprepared. In any case, the war is lost now. What's the point then of getting yourself killed or letting cities and goods be destroyed? What purpose does it serve now? That's why people hate you: they see you like a corpse hanging on to their necks to drag them off to the tomb with it. It's logical for them to look for a way of releasing themselves from that embrace, don't you understand?" These were even more valid reasons than those of the other fellow. Ambrogio noticed, however, the torment of his neighbor in the other bed. "Of course, if you think about it a while . . . poor Italy and poor us, what a pass we've come to!"

"If you want to know," Tittoni went on, "I don't even believe in the secret weapons. And I know that we, who are fighting for honor, will all end up dead, and that will be the last of it. But we won't die like lambs. Blood has to flow first . . . the blood of those who shoot us in the back and also those in our ranks who are ready to take flight, those leaders who want to have it both ways and so don't bother to organize things like they should." He had pulled himself up to a sitting position in the bed, very pale, beating each phrase out with his index finger on the white blanket.

Pino came into the room exactly at that moment. "Oh, Ambrogio!" he exclaimed. "I found out from an orderly that there's a place here on the island, around Pallanza, where the fish . . ." Realizing there was something special prevailing in the room's atmosphere, he interrupted himself. "Perhaps I shouldn't be talking?" he asked.

Tittoni, his face drawn, did not look at him.

"Don't worry", Ambrogio answered. "But now it's better you go back to the hotel in Stresa. I know you have to study."

"I can't go back to Stresa", Pino said. "I promised the analyst I'd help him today. So . . ."

"Good, then go help him. Thanks."

"All right, then. Goodbye for now."

"Bye."

Pino turned to Tittoni to take his leave, but then he did not say a word. He went toward the door stepping carefully, soundlessly, to signify he did not intend to make a nuisance of himself, but moving like a caricature of himself.

"He's only a boy", his brother said by way of justification.

Tittoni said nothing. Neither did he say anything further. He shut himself up again in his silence.

Fanny was afraid of him, so much so that one day, taking advantage of a moment when he was asleep, Ambrogio scolded her a bit. "You should pity him instead. He's a Fascist, agreed, but he's a human being first, a poor fellow convinced there's no other alternative than death."

"That's why I feel the way I do, don't you understand?"

Ambrogio shook his head no.

"Don't be so quick to judge me", Fanny whispered. "You're a kind of warrior, too, but not in a way to frighten me. Quite the opposite. I feel comfortable with you." Her face became roguish. "You know, I feel protected when I'm with you?"

"A kind of warrior, eh?" Ambrogio joked. "We're really fine and dandy, then, in that case."

"Of course", Fanny insisted, looking him in the eyes. Then she smiled at him and suddenly caressed his face lightly. It was the first time she had done that. "You're my warrior", she said in a soft voice, putting her face closer to his. Her voice was almost quivering, and Ambrogio also felt overcome by strong emotion.

The two young people looked at each other in silence.

Fanny caressed Ambrogio a second time. "I'm on leave this afternoon, you know, so I can caress you. And please don't give me one of your puritanical speeches."

Ambrogio took the girl's hand, which seemed small and fragile to him (there was nothing original about his sentiments), and brought it to his lips in silence. He realized he was taking part in something quite important, drawn by instinct, without reflecting, and yet he felt resolute about this involvement.

Someone knocked at the door in a professional way. A female voice asked, "May I?"

She was the usual nurse with the injection. "Yes", Fanny exclaimed withdrawing and fixing her cap, although there was no need of it. Tittoni sighed in his sleep. The enchantment had lasted less than a minute.

The girl left, indeed, for her time off the same evening. She could have had her days off weeks before, but then Ambrogio was in danger, and she did not want to leave him, so without saying anything, she had changed her shift with one of her colleagues.

8

Pino never did get along with Tittoni. His infantile jokes irritated the lieutenant, who took him into consideration only on one occasion, when he asked him brusquely how it was he did not join up voluntarily, since he was already

eighteen. At his insincere answer ("I'll join up when I'm called up") the lieutenant snorted as if at something unbearable. Pino ended up detesting him,
much more so because, being in the same room, he was unable to talk freely
with his brother. It came to be a continual bother and eventually irritating.

One evening, out of revenge, the boy amused himself by talking about the
partisans with the hotel porter. The porter, who did not know how to spend
his long evenings, was delighted at last to have such a ready listener. After
having affirmed and repeated—vaguely—that there were partisans all over the
surrounding mountains, he did insinuate that perhaps some of them should
not be counted because "they were chicken thieves more than anything else".
But at least two bands, or, "if we want to be exact", three bands, were quite
serious, foes to be reckoned with for the republic. "Here, in the mountains, on
this part of the lake, is Captain Beltrami's band, a rich man from Milan with his
villa in Omegna. These are serious partisans, led by real officers. They wear
blue neckerchiefs, the ones who most surely are royalists or, let's say, in favor of
the king."

"How do you know that for sure?"

"Well, if you don't mind, it isn't a question one asks during such dangerous
times. But I insist, I know. Beltrami's partisans are for the king. In the mountains, on the other side of the lake, there is, on the other hand, a band led by
two brothers, the Di Dios. According to some people, they're still part of Beltrami's men, which is not really clear. They say they wear green neckerchiefs,
not blue, that's the question. Perhaps", the porter daydreamed on, "the Di Dio
brothers were Alpine officers and keep to the color green for that reason. But,
of course, to be honest, whether they were Alpine officers or not, I can't be
sure. I say so only because it's logical, or if you like, I just guess so. Well, then
there's another important band, the ones from Valsesia. They're Communists,
with red neckerchiefs. People who," here he exaggerated a trifle, "no matter
where they go, see to it that blood flows like water. And those", he concluded,
"are the three bands that really count."

"And are they in agreement with each other, or are there shoot-ups between them, say, between the royalists and the Communists?"

"I think . . . but . . . I don't know. It's a matter of diplomacy, so naturally
difficult to know. But as all of them are partisans, I think there's a generalized
agreement."

"It seems to me it would be hard for them to agree", Pino objected. "In any
case, there's a Fascist officer, a certain Tittoni, in the hospital who was wounded
in Anzola. He occasionally talks about Anzola, even if he is a close-mouthed type.
Do you know who were the partisans there who could have wounded him?"

"Anzola? Beltrami's, without a doubt. There's a permanent control point
there of Beltrami's men. Besides, all important actions against the Fascists from
this part of the lake are carried out by them, Beltrami's brigade. That you can
be sure of."

"A permanent control point, you said? In Anzola? What does that mean?"

"Mean? It's clear, isn't it? It's on a small road that leads to the town, not on the main highway."

"But are the partisans the ones who run this control point . . . permanently?"

"Of course, the partisans."

Pino was taken aback. "How far is Anzola from here?" he asked.

"It'll be, let's say, about sixteen miles. If you take the main highway from Sempione to Ornavasso, and right after Ornavasso, the smaller one that runs at the foot of the mountain on the left side of the valley, you come to Anzola, willy-nilly. There's no mistaking it. Besides, there are signs."

The boy thought it all over for quite a while, and in the following days he questioned the porter again for more details, and the porter would have been more than happy to give them to him if he had not already given him more than he really possessed. Pino would also have liked to talk about the partisan control point with his brother Ambrogio, who by then was beginning to leave his room for short spells to go down to the ground floor, but, for fear that his brother might ask him peremptorily not to get mixed up in these things, he ended up saying nothing.

One fine morning in the middle of January, Pino made up his mind. He rented a bicycle from a tiny cyclist shop (he had inquired about it days before) and set out for Anzola.

He went up along the shore of the lake—luminous and sunny amid such cold—as far as Baveno. Going along the main—the national—highway, he entered the Ossola Valley, lying between walls cut out of the mountain, practically overhanging. The valley—at the first stretch quite narrow—is uniformly flat. Then, after having passed Ornavasso, where all the houses have roofs of gray stone, he took to the left, to the secondary road that ran along the foot of the mountain. At one bend he came to a control point of the military Fascists, which he crossed without anybody saying anything. After a few miles he saw a road sign with the name of Anzola on it. The village was hardly much farther on, consisting of a few houses and orchard gardens, clinging to the foot of the mountain.

A horizontal bar, like those at a railway crossing but in rough wood, blocked the road. Seated at one end, with a machine gun between his legs and binoculars slung around his neck, was a partisan. He was wearing an olive green windbreaker, and on his head he had a skier's cap with colored round stripes. On his feet were skier's boots. Without moving, he let Pino approach.

The boy stopped his bicycle a few steps from him and put his foot down on the ground. "Hello", he said.

"Hello", the partisan answered. He was, Pino noticed, about his own age. He did not look like a student.

"So it's true. There is a control point here in Anzola."

"Well . . ." The partisan nodded.

"I see", Pino said.

"Where are you coming from?" he asked Pino in dialect. He was talking not in the local Piedmontese dialect but that of Lombardy.

"From Stresa", Pino replied.

"And what are you coming here for?"

"To see you, meet you." He had also gone into dialect. The partisan looked at him dubiously. At the doorway of a nearby shack a second, older partisan looked out, perhaps the boss of the point. Unlike the first, he seemed to be a little more suspicious. He had an old Alpine hat on and, over his shoulders, an old German raincoat. "Who're you talking to?" he asked the control point guard in the Piedmont dialect.

"Listen, Tom," he answered, "here's someone who's come here as a tourist to see us."

"What?" the chief asked. "Have you asked for documentation?"

"No, not yet."

"What are you waiting for?"

"Do you want to see my identity card?" Pino asked. "It's right here." He took his wallet from his pocket, handed him the card and, as if that were not enough, a second document. "This is my university ID from medical school."

The control point chief, who had come up, took both documents and examined them. "Well?" he said, still in dialect. Then he switched to Italian. "Just what do you want?" He was not a student either.

"Nothing", Pino answered. "They were talking about you in Stresa, and I wanted to see you."

"You hear that?" the chief said.

And the guard started to laugh noisily. Not for a minute had it occurred to Pino that he might have got into something over his head, that his curiosity would in any way arouse suspicion.

The chief observed him. "You said you were a student, didn't you?"

"Yes, you have my ID in your hand."

The other fellow, after having looked at it again, returned the two cards. "Well, now you've seen us. You can go back to Stresa happy."

"Already?" Pino said. "But I've come sixteen miles in this cold to be here . . ."

"So what? What do you want? You want us to take you to visit our barracks, the headquarters, and have our men", he added, "do a little carbine practice for you?"

The guard started to laugh again.

The chief of the control point was serious, however.

"I'm sure you must know that if someone's not known or has no pass, he can't get in this village."

"A pass? Well . . . I should have brought a bottle of wine, at least", the boy said. "We could have drunk it together."

"You can next time", the guard said, laughing.

The chief was still serious. He had a lean, rather tired face, though young. The old Alpine hat, a noncom's, which probably was not his, suited him well. "In short, the idea of war amuses you, doesn't it? Like a party or something similar. Well, it isn't. War is one big pigsty. There's no sh—— worse than war sh——."

"I know. I'm in Stresa to look after my brother, who came back wounded from the Russian front", Pino said. "So you can guess what kind of fun that is. He's on the island hospital."

"The Russian front . . .", the chief murmured, interested despite himself. "In what division?"

"In Pasubio."

"Not with the Alpine troops, then."

"No, he was with artillery."

"But not Alpine artillery?"

"No. Why are you asking? Were you on the Russian front?" The chief shook his head.

"He, no, his brother", the other guard explained, "and a cousin, too. They were in the Cuneense. They're missing. Both have been given up as missing."

There was a pause.

"Does your brother in the hospital know you're here?" the chief asked.

"No, I didn't tell him."

The other one looked at him again. "I believe you", he said.

"Listen, couldn't you at least let me see the . . . the . . . what's it called? The control point?" Pino suggested.

"Go to . . .", the chief said. "All right, go on in. You'll see how nice the view is."

Pino did not let him say it again. With a couple of pedal strokes, he reached the shack from which the chief had come, put his bicycle against the wall, and entered.

There were two rooms inside. In the first was a fireplace with a fire lit in it, and, hung on a chain, a pot of water was boiling, and on the table was a wooden bowl full of bright yellow corn. A few rifles and machine guns as well as some loaded cartridge boxes were hanging on the wall. There were also a couple of blue neckerchiefs, rather dirty, and three pairs of mountain boots on the floor next to the chimney. The second room, tiny, was almost totally filled with mattresses spread out on the floor. On three of them other partisans were asleep, or simply resting, under woolen blankets. All together, it looked more like a shepherd's shack than like something military.

The boy also noticed two little pictures of saints nailed to the wall above the head of two of the mattresses, the way pictures of saints hung over the beds of peasants. The weapons, hung in no particular order or formality on the walls of the first room, reminded him of hunting arms, blackened like them, too, which excited the boy's imagination, as he dreamed of woods and fields and long treks, adventures with dogs and wild animals.

"Well," he said as he came out, "this is really very nice."

"God blast you, boy!" the chief of the control point, who was behind him, said. "I'd like to know what you find so nice!"

"Nice, well I'm not exactly sure," Pino admitted, "but I like it."

"So you probably think we've come here to play, don't you? Or almost."

"No, I know your life's no game. Still . . ."

The idea of becoming a soldier like Ambrogio or Manno never had any attraction for him; the discipline, being obliged to be in control of a situation and to set an example, was a prospect he had never cared for. He had always considered that a "dummy like himself" would never manage to reach those heights . . . However, a war carried out this way, simply, among boys. "Listen," not entirely realizing what he was saying, "and if I should ask to join up with you?"

"Ah," the partisan answered, looking him in the eyes, "that's why you wanted to have a look, wasn't it? Your requests come in by installments, don't they?"

"As a combatant I don't think I'm worth much," Pino said, "but as a medical student . . ." (He did not tell exactly what year he was in, nor did he mention the fact that he had not opened his textbooks up 'til now except to see how they were made.) He went on, "I could be useful. I could look after the wounded and . . . and other things like that."

"Mmmm", the chief pondered. "Do you have a letter of introduction?"

"A . . . what? No. A letter of introduction from whom?"

"Doesn't matter . . . we'll see. A medical student . . . yes, you could be of use to us. Can you mountain climb?"

"That, yes, of course."

"We'll see", the chief repeated. "What town are you from?"

"Nomana, Milan province, in Brianza. It's on the ID."

"We'll do this. I'll make a note of it: Nomana, your name, and all the rest. Give me your card a minute. It will take us ten days to have our information . . . because just looking at your face I know you're no Fascist, but still we must take precautions. Then, in ten days or better, twelve, if you still feel the same way as you do today, you can come back here, to the control point." He looked at his shoes. "With mountain boots, it goes without saying, and some sort of coat or jacket, and a change of clothes. That will do."

The boy's eyes glistened.

"Careful with the Fascists if you really decide to return. In the last stretch of the road especially. They'd cut your neck off like a chicken, and you wouldn't be the first."

9

As he pedaled energetically back to Stresa, Pino felt all worked up. An array of thoughts piled up in his head: he'd get into the war, and he—poor chap that he was—would do his part, too, and—this was taken for granted—in no undignified way. And one day the others, especially the girls, Fanny, for example, looking at him would think, *That fellow, even if he doesn't look it, is someone who doesn't joke around. He's been a partisan. Been involved in this action and that one, and that other one, too.* And in fact, he could see himself in action, with his elegant blue neckerchief tied around his neck. He was on a sloping green field, whipped by enemy gunfire, the showers of bullets raising the grass and earth, striating the ground as in a movie, a real inferno, but he was going through it all unharmed, and he reached a wounded man. "Thank God, Pino, you've come!"

"Don't talk, put your arm around my neck, like that . . ." He lifted him up and carried him to a . . . a something, saving him. (But would he really be able to lift someone who couldn't move?) *Forget about that, don't be so fussy, that's not the question . . .* After having saved the first one, he immediately saved the next one.

"Yes, sir", the other partisans were saying, approving. "Yes, Pino knows what he's doing. He really knows what he's doing."

His father and older brothers, too—not now, not immediately, it would be a disaster now, he would be shouted down—later on, when the war was over, would be so proud of him. In any case, the problem would be Mama. The prospect of her anxiety during his absence, with one son already hospitalized, and Manno, from whom they'd heard nothing . . . *Yes, the problem for me would be Mama,* Pino told himself, as if he were talking to the chief at the control point, Tom. And he immediately answered himself, instead of Tom. *Not only for you.* It seemed to be the exact right answer for a real partisan, as he already was considering himself.

When he approached the Fascist checkpoint, however, his heart began to palpitate, and he felt it almost leaping out of his chest. And if they stopped him now? It seemed they'd be able to see his plan of becoming a partisan written on his face. *I'll say I've been out for a ride, for exercise, as I'd have answered if they'd asked me on my way there. What's different about me, besides, from before? The new and big decision you've made,* he answered himself. But had he really made that decision? In what way? He hadn't thought it over in the slightest. *Is it the way, maybe, that important decisions are made, without thinking?* Certainly not. He did not suspect that often, very often, that's the way it is, that he should have answered affirmatively.

Twelve days later, on the first of February, his mother returned to Stresa to relieve him. She was not thinking of staying long because Ambrogio, as the doctors said, was luckily out of danger and was—even if only slowly—on the mend.

That day, after taking his leave of her and his brother, Pino, instead of taking the Milan-bound train, went on bicycle to Anzola. He had left—imprudently—a note on his mother's night table in her room. In it he made his "irrevocable decision" known, his decision to join the partisans with Beltrami's brigade. "I beg you not to look for me," he warned, "which would be of no purpose besides." And he promised, "You'll have more news of me during the second half of February."

10

Just beyond Anzola, at the foot of the mountain, there is a place called Megolo. There were a few houses there then and a church at the beginning of a steep mule track. The greatest ornament of the village was a stone fountain, to which the cows came twice a day to drink; as they left their warm sheds, their steaming hides could be seen in the wintry air.

Partisan headquarters were situated in a small lodging. Here Commander Beltrami received Pino with lordly affability on the same day as his arrival. This Beltrami was nearly six feet tall, from Milan, an architect by profession, with the rank of captain in the army. (And everyone called him that: captain.) There had been a hundred-thousand-lire reward being offered for his capture since November.

Most of the partisans—about eighty—were billeted not in the village but in shacks some hundred yards up in the mountains. Pino was amazed that during the first days of his arrival no one bothered with services, training, or anything else. He was consigned a rifle, which he cleaned over and over and oiled from top to bottom with the same meticulous care and quiet excitement with which, at home, he cleaned his hunting rifle on the eve before the hunting season began.

"You'd have had to get in line to have a rifle like that before", Tom, the squadron chief with the Alpine hat, told him. Two weeks before he had been at the Anzola control point. He went on, "Now we have more arms than we need."

"Why more than you need? There are never enough arms", Pino claimed. They were seated in his squadron shack. Pino, at the side of a wooden manger worn by age, was talking as he rubbed his rifle with a rag.

"Why?"

"Yes, tell me why."

"Because a few days ago more than a few left, moved off. That's why we now have arms available."

"Oh. How many left?"

"Drop it."

"No, tell me, how many?"

"Around fifty."

"Goodness", Pino persisted. "But I don't really understand. Where did they go to? What do you mean?"

"Those pigs went back home. They said goodbye to the partisan life."

"And you, the captain and . . . you let them go? They know all about you, that is, us: our numbers, positions, weapons, everything, in short."

"Yes, that's true. If they'd been with the Communists they would not have gotten away so easily. But the captain is a gentleman, and when he saw they were grumbling he told them, 'Anyone who does not want to stay with us can leave.' Do you understand? He even tried to help them save face: 'Whoever has decided he has not the necessary physical qualifications should be off.' That's what he said." Tom shook his head disapprovingly, "But naturally, it's also a satisfaction to have a commanding officer like that, someone who's not scum—just the opposite. Only someone like myself who's been in the military can realize . . . without going on about his courage, and . . . well, you'll see for yourself."

"But how is it . . . I mean why did they—fifty of them—go?"

"The winter. Because of the winter, having to be half shut up for weeks, putrefying in the shacks, while the war goes on and on. Of course fifty . . . if you think of it, it's not bad, no question about it."

Tom was seated on a low milking stool, and while he talked, he was rocking back and forth, forcing the stool on two feet. About a yard from him was a stove, sputtering quietly, which had been brought there by the partisans.

At that moment only two of them were in the shack, because the other men from the squadron had gone down to the town to have a drink at Mariuccia's Inn. ("Paying, you understand," one of them had explained to Pino, "because we're not like chicken thieves. The captain doesn't fool around about this." Pino had not gone with them. He did not like wine, and from the time he was a child it made him a bit sick.)

"But," he concluded, "what a situation!"

"What's the matter? Are you feeling like leaving, too?" Tom asked him.

"No, it's never entered my head. But listen, tell me something, is it all a pipe dream what they say in Stresa, that there are ten thousand partisans, at least, in these mountains?"

"Exactly, one big pipe dream. Our brigade is the strongest. Here at Megolo, to give you some idea, are only half of them. The others—you've probably heard—are in the interior of the Ossola Valley divided into groups, to give the impression there are a lot of us."

"But how did you manage with so few to get a control point? And, above all, to keep it?"

"Ah, well, we had a right to it."

"A right? We have rights? What do you mean by that?"

"It was the captain's idea. He . . . let me figure it out. About the first part of December, we made an agreement with the Communists in Valsesia to occupy Omegna together for a few hours, and it's a big place, a city. But as we arrived first, we did it practically alone. The Communists came later. We shared out the booty. (More than twenty tons, can you believe it? Arms, ammunition, victuals, fuel, blankets, a gift from God: we needed two trucks and three tows to carry it all.) The prisoners we had taken remained, and among them was the brother of the commander of the Fascist action squadrons of Novara, Zurlo, who had the bad luck to have arrived at that moment on the trolley from Verbania. What were we to do? If it's at all possible we don't kill prisoners. We let them go. But this time, with the Communists there, it didn't at all suit us to let them go off, especially a big Fascist commander like Zurlo, who in fact was not the commander himself, only the brother of the commander. Well, in short, the captain brought them here to Megolo with the idea of releasing them later. But when we arrived back, he thought, *Why can't we exchange them for something?* No sooner said than done. He telephoned from the inn to Novara, to the Fascist town commander Dongo, negotiated with him, or rather arranged the exchange of the prisoners for a neutral zone, a 'no man's land', if you like, between us and the Fascists, from Gravellona to Cesara. Even the German SS in the province, more powerful as a military force than the Fascists, respect it. Enough anyway. So you see why we have the control point in Anzola?"

"But how many were there then? How many men were in the brigade when you carried out that surprise action?"

"Let's say three hundred."

"And now, if I have it straight, we must be fewer than two hundred, quite a loss."

"Yes, that's so. Even more so if you consider that Di Dio's brigade, which acted on their own then, they're now with us. You know, once by mistake, in Buccione, we fired against each other? They joined us only later, about Christmastime."

"At Christmas?"

"Yes, in the winter. To make a common front against the doldrums of winter. But then Alfredo Di Dio, the leader, was shortly afterward picked up by the Fascists while on a mission in Milan. This has been the biggest cause of demoralization. He had become our second in command, a real lion! You should have seen him."

Tom stood up, half sighed. "In any case," he concluded, "the important thing is that the people left don't get demoralized. Because there should be good times ahead, and then you'll see how everything starts to work."

II

In the evening of the same day—it was the third since Pino's arrival—they received bad news brought by a woman on a bicycle. The Fascists had taken a personal friend of the captain's in Druogno, one Ferraris, a lawyer, who had acted as the intermediary between the brigade and the CLN (Committee for National Liberation) of Turin; they had taken him to jail in Domodossola.

It was almost dark, but the leaders met immediately in counsel, and they decided to act on the spot, because the next day would be too late. They took out of their hideouts between the shacks an automobile and two trucks. In the first were the captain and some officers, and in the trucks about forty men, including Pino's squadron. (Tom had offered Pino the chance not to participate: "If you've never used this kind of rifle." "What's the difference? I know how to use a hunting rifle, so . . .") The three vehicles went slowly to Anzola, their lights switched off the whole time, and there reached the main Sempione highway. Once on it, they switched on the camouflage lights and began to speed.

Pino was seated in the first of the trucks, resting his back against one of the lateral walls, his rifle between his knees and a sack of medications slung over his back, between two partisans on either side. It was raining and cold. The canvas at the back—purposely pulled loose so that the men might jump to the ground in case of need—was floating about constantly. They could see, in the light of the truck's lamps behind them, an occasional wet tree trunk at the edge of the highway or a piece of rustic wall, and crossing through villages, and with quick glances, closed-up houses, their windows shut out of fear. As the curfew was in effect, not a single soul was in sight.

"What's happening? Do the Fascists leave their control points at night?" Pino asked one of his neighbors.

"Depends. Sometimes yes, sometimes no", he answered.

"Sometimes they're there but act as if they don't see", another one said.

"Besides, the captain's ahead", the first man said, with the quiet irresponsibility of a soldier who has total faith in his own commander. "He thinks about these things. We don't have to worry about that."

"I know, but . . ." It was the boy's first sally into the world of weapons. He felt divided between keen enthusiasm for action—going boldly through enemy territory—and the fear of some unexpected obstacle, which could irremediably and suddenly jam everything up. The majority of the others, though not new to these experiences, were in a similar state of mind to his. Only a few were on the euphoric side of the adventure, and even if they did not say anything, they were wishing this nocturnal ride would never end.

But it ended in a half hour. The three vehicles stopped on a tree-lined street at the entrance to Domodossola, where it was so dark that the surrounding mountains, so close by, could not be seen. They all got out in silence, and in line with their orders they grouped into three squads, of which two started off immediately. Pino was especially impressed by the men—two to a squad—who were carrying the machine gun horizontally over their shoulders.

The squad that remained was led by Lieutenant Antonio Di Dio, brother to Alfredo. "I warn you that they'll start firing in no time", he told his men.

"They'll pretend to attack the Fascist garrison of Calvario to draw attention over there. The real action, however, will be up to us. Is that clear? All right, forward and follow the captain."

The captain, in a windbreaker and a skier's cap, was walking toward the center of the city, where the jail was. They all followed. Because of the curfew all the lights on the highway were switched off. It was almost total darkness. An insistent and bothersome light rain kept falling. In a small passage flanked by walls without windows the captain stopped; the others joined him, stopping at his back without uttering a word. The two groups carrying the machine guns put the weapons down on the ground vertically, holding them by their flash guards. From the Calvario section at last came the first sounds of shots, which shortly changed into a hailstorm of fire, and the fire from the Bredas began to be distinguished, different from the semiautomatic machine guns, a sign, too, that the enemy was firing.

The captain waited a little longer, then, "It's time", he said calmly. "Let's go." The small column began to move.

How many Fascists and Germans would there be in Domodossola? Pino wondered. *What would they be doing now?* He was overcome by a troublesome pounding in his heart, annoying, too. Just as well that the captain was there to think about everything.

As they went by a large door (a carabinieri post, though Pino did not know that), the captain stopped for an instant, and, after exchanging a few words with Lieutenant Antonio, he then—followed by the others—turned to the doorway, put his hand on the knocker, looked in the dark to see if the others had their own weapons in hand, and knocked.

A peephole opened in the door, from which a little light and a voice came out. "Who is it?"

"Captain Beltrami, open up."

"Yes, Captain", the voice responded. With a clinking of keys and chains the door was opened. They all rushed in rapidly, Lieutenant Antonio the last, and he closed the door behind him.

The carabiniere who had opened stood now at attention, very pale, in front of the captain, who was holding his own pistol. "Is the warrant officer here?" he asked.

"Yes, Captain", the carabiniere answered. "He's here."

Pino—not less stirred—realized that one of the carabiniere's knees, standing at attention, was trembling.

"Call him without moving from here."

Just at that moment the commanding officer from the detachment looked out from an inner staircase. He had heard the shooting outside, the opening of the door, voices, and noise, and he wanted to check who had arrived. Of course he was not expecting the partisans, and seeing them, he instinctively stepped back, as if to avoid a shot. However, he did not run off. He pulled back quickly and went down the stairs. "Captain." He had recognized Beltrami.

"I see it's really you", the captain said. "I'm well informed, you see."

"Yes, Captain."

The warrant officer, when he came down the stairs, stood at attention. "At your orders, Captain."

"At ease", Beltrami ordered and put his pistol in its sheath. Then he turned to the carabiniere, too. "At ease." He turned once again to the other officer, who was no longer at attention, and looked into his eyes severely. (There was a touch of melancholy in his eyes, he could see: these veteran servants of the state, who had seen their world come tumbling down around them ... heaven knows what a muddle was going on in his head.) "We've already seen one another in Omegna. A few months before you commanded that detachment."

"Yes, Captain."

"I was under the impression then that you inwardly had remained loyal to your oath to his majesty the king."

"Yes, Captain. That's true, and I'm not saying it because now I'm ... no, it's that ... loyal."

"Yes", Beltrami said seriously. "Remember, once the war's over, your fate will be decided by this."

A couple of the partisans moved their machine guns meaningfully. The police inspector looked at them out of the corner of his eye.

"Well," Beltrami said, "I need some information, and in a hurry, if you can give it to me. Where's the lawyer Ferraris?"

"He's no longer in Domodossola", the inspector answered. "I'm abreast of that. The national guard took him first to jail in the center and interrogated him, and then they took him and hid him in one of their houses, a soldier's, because they feared a surprise attack. But they didn't keep him there. Two hours ago they bundled him off in a car and took him out again, I'm sure to Novara. More or less two hours ago. I'm sure of what I'm saying."

At the captain's questioning, he explained why he was sure, giving details. Beltrami was convinced he was telling the truth. "You give me your word of honor? If you're lying, remember, sooner or later, you'll hear about it. You'll be taken to a tribunal, and you'll pay with your life."

"I'm not lying. I give my word of honor."

"All right, I believe you." He turned to his own men. "We're not staying here any longer. Back home."

The carabiniere who had opened up the headquarters (meanwhile another two had appeared) stepped forward. "One minute, listen ... I'm going with you."

"Hurry up", Lieutenant Antonio told him. "Take your machine gun and coat. Hurry up."

The other fellow went off quickly and returned with two machine guns and his coat as well as a sack he had stuffed his own things into.

They addressed the inspector again. "Do you want us to fire against the façade of the headquarters a little? Unhinge the door, perhaps?"

"No", the inspector answered quietly. "I'll arrange things. Let it be."

The group, with the "caramba" (the name the partisans used for the carabinieri) in tow, went out onto the street. Firing from afar was still going on and even seemed to be increasing.

"The red rocket", the captain said to Lieutenant Antonio. "Fire it off."

The lieutenant took a clumsy rock pistol, a Very, from a small sheath stuck in his belt, pointed his arm skyward, and shot. The flash opened rapidly upward, leaving a long hail of luminous red sparks in its wake.

"Let's go", the captain sighed. The patrol started to run back along the street to the trucks.

Inwardly, Pino was happy with the way things had turned out. There had been no combat yet. They had gone into the center of Domodossola, had brought in a new recruit, and had got away without losses, a lovely story to tell. He was not thinking about the lawyer Ferraris. He did not know him, he had never heard his name, and besides, there were so many Fascist prisoners.

On the other hand, the others were thinking about Ferraris, especially the captain, who was repeating, with bitterness in his heart, "He won't get out of this. If they have him watched this way it means they have proof against him. He won't get out of this. They beat us by a couple of hours. What fools we've been . . . only two hours! He's already a dead man, poor Paolo . . ." He did not know how right he was when he said this. Even though the lawyer Ferraris—taken from prison to prison, from Novara to Fossoli, to Mauthausen, to Gusen, these last two places as horrifying as Crinovaya and Oranchi—would be dead only by the end of a year, much later than he, Captain Beltrami, who at that moment was commiserating his friend Ferraris.

The shooting around the Calvario was already stopping. The partisans, having seen the red rocket, had started their retreat. They reached the vehicles twenty minutes after the captain and his group.

The return trip, like the trip out, presented no difficulties. Toward midnight the partisans and the "caramba" entered their shelters over Megolo.

12

During the following days Beltrami carried out other surprise attacks. In general the squadrons left from Anzola in a truck at the first sign of darkness, reached the main highway, and attacked some Fascist control post by surprise or a small garrison or a supply depot. This did not, however, do much to raise the morale, which, after the desertion of fifty partisans—even if it had been authorized—and the failed attempt at freeing Ferraris, continued declining. Pino, however—having no point of comparison—was not really aware of it.

One morning, while drinking a soda pop at Mariuccia's Inn (they did not sell orange juice), the boy did get a forceful surprise: through one of the windows he saw a German jeep stop on the small village road. A massive officer, along with a few other Germans and some partisans, were in it. Thinking some surprise attack had succeeded, he rushed outside, but it was not a matter of prisoners. They were—someone explained—the captain of the Omegna SS, Simon, no less, and his interpreter, who had come to negotiate with Captain Beltrami, after first having duly left their weapons at the Anzola post.

Under Pino's very eyes the two captains, Lieutenant Antonio, and the other partisan leaders and the German interpreter went into the Megolo nursery school, where the nuns had prepared a little room for them.

Partisans and villagers began to gather outside. "Did you see that beast Simon?" a squadron member said to Pino. "He's well over six feet, and for sure he weighs a hundred kilos."

"Yes, he's even taller than our captain", the boy agreed.

"But Beltrami, even in civilian clothes, looks better. There's no comparison", a partisan from another squadron asserted.

"Yes, did you notice? He's wearing pressed clothes with no stains. Who could have done that?"

(The nuns from the orphanage had done that the previous afternoon. When the partisans went the day before to ask for the little room for the meeting, the nuns had not only immediately lent them their services but had also made sure the Italian captain showed himself at an advantage. They had suggested he send his clothes to them, and they cleaned them from top to bottom and also cleaned the little room and four stuffed canaries under a bell jar that were the room's main ornament. But no one was aware of all this, however.)

"Captain Simon? The SS commander? The perfect hostage for an exchange for Alfredo Di Dio . . . we shouldn't let him leave."

"What are you saying?" Tom said angrily. "He's come here, so it means Beltrami's given his word. And," he added in dialect, "even if you tear him into bits and pieces, he means to keep his word."

While the talk took place, Lieutenant Antonio Di Dio came out of the nursery school and invited those present to move off, which they did unwillingly.

Later, once the Germans had left, the captain gathered the partisans together and informed them, point by point, of what they had discussed. The enemy, aware of the recent partisan desertions, had come here to try to see if a dissolution of the brigade was not possible, or if at least a truce would be made. In the first case, they offered an escort for the partisans—free and armed—to the Swiss border. If they accepted, they would escape, thus he put it, an immense offensive with which the German command were intending to clean out the valley once and for all.

Beltrami informed them that he had rejected their proposal of dissolution and also the truce, which would have enabled the enemies to use all their forces to attack in other areas. At the end of the discussion, the German stood up. "I knew I had to be dealing with gentlemen," he asserted, "but now I'm absolutely certain of it." With this in mind, Beltrami had asked him to release some relatives of partisans they had been kept as hostages in Omegna and in Val Strona. The German captain promised he would.

"Who knows if he'll keep his word?" someone commented after the meeting. "Perhaps it's all talk. It's not possible for an SS man to behave like a gentleman."

Before nightfall a telephone message announced the release of all the hostages.

This was good news. But in successive days there was bad news. They found that there had been deserters in the brigade's groups that were in the interior of the Ossola Valley and that some of these groups were already dissolved. One night two partisans unexpectedly deserted from Megolo, too. The captain then ordered by post that all detachments come together in Megolo, aware, too, that soon he would have to go into combat. It was necessary to do battle and win, to raise the morale of the brigade: it was coming to be his *idée fixe*.

Pino witnessed the arrival of the groups with curiosity. He was most impressed by the men of his almost fellow countryman Lieutenant Bettini, some fifty of them, heavily armed and displaying great solidarity. They really looked like a true Alpine detachment, and indeed, almost all of them were ex-Alpine troops. The other detachments were incomparably slighter, and one commander arrived without even a single man.

One afternoon the boy was called to headquarters. Quite excited, he went down to the village lodging, wondering what it was the captain wanted, what he might have done wrong.

The air in the pine-paneled headquarters was heavy with stale tobacco smoke. Pino stood at attention, with his blond hair tossed against the back of his head, making it look flatter than usual.

"You summoned me, my captain?"

Beltrami, seated at the only table, smiled at him. Then, stretching out one hand, he pushed a book that was on the table toward him. "Take this and study it."

Pino picked the book up and examined it. It was a university text on pathological surgery. "Ah," he said, "it's a medical text."

"Precisely. I have it on loan from a doctor, and it must be returned. You've only matriculated, haven't you?"

"Yes, sir."

"I don't suppose, then, you know much about treating wounds."

"I've worked some in the hospital in my hometown, but not too much", Pino admitted. "I'm not so great in that either . . . but I'm very fond of medicine and . . ."

"Study up on treating wounds as fast as you can and also as well as you can. I'm sure you'll soon be able to do your part."

"Yes, sir."

"After you've done your part, your duty, you won't have to worry about not being so great. Keep it in mind."

"Yes, my captain", Pino said, pulling himself up straight, which surprised him, always having been irritated by formalities.

"Well, be on your way and don't waste time. And remember what I've told you."

Pino left headquarters quite surprised. So, then, the captain knew what was going on inside, guessed his deficiencies and worries. And to think that until then he hadn't seemed the least bit interested in him. *Maybe he does this with the other partisans, too. He's a leader for sure, a real one.*

13

The first action to be scheduled was an attack on an armored train that escorted other trains along the Sempione line. It passed by Megolo several times a day, only a couple of miles off. Their job was to attack it and capture the escort, wiping it out in case it did not consent to surrender. A quick retaliation from the Nazi-Fascists against Megolo would then be expected. The partisans set to work to improve their defensive positions dug out some time back around the little village, higher up above the mountain but below the shacks.

These tasks were in no way finished when the German SS on the dawn of the thirteenth of February surprised the Anzola checkpoint and continued forward without firing a shot. They were hardly caught sight of in time by the men on guard at Megolo. Hearing the screams of alarm raised by the latter, the partisans rushed out of their houses and huts and dashed to their positions, each squadron to its own spot. To Bettini and his Alpine troops had been reserved the defense of the right side of the formation, which, for several reasons, turned out to be quite difficult.

The first shots resounded. The partisans could have still gotten away and clambered up the mountain at their backs, which was part of the most inaccessible Rosa ridge, among the highest in the Alps, but their officers did not want that. They were of the opinion that dispersing themselves at that moment would mean the dissolution of the brigade.

Pino, with his medicine kit over his shoulders, his rifle in his left hand, and his heart pounding in an indescribable fashion, ran to the first aid post that the captain had decided on: a hut at the back of the formation sheltered by a rising in the terrain. Here, not knowing what to do, he sat on the ground with his back against the wall, opened his manual, read a few lines, and closed it. He listened attentively. He had heard the partisan weapons get into action, including the machine guns. They were being answered by automatic weapons and mortar fire and a few small assault cannons. The boy could not put up with that state of inertia for very long. Perhaps some twenty yards below him, hardly below the rise in the terrain that sheltered the hut, was a trench from which—apart from the shots—fragments of voices talking in dialect reached him. He at last left the hut and with a few big leaps landed in the trench, whose defense did not belong to his squadron.

From this vantage point Pino tried to localize the enemy, but all he could see, a little farther below, was another partisan position dug out at the side of the mule track that climbed up from Megolo, and farther below that, on the left margin of the village, bits and pieces of a trench, also defended by partisans. He could also see smoke here and there. The air was heavy with shots and explosions, and his heart was pounding as if it were going to break.

After a long ten minutes he heard his name being called, "Pino, Pino!" from the defenders of the post farther down. "Is the medical student with you?"

"What do you want?" he screamed, answering them.

"There's a wounded man. Come on here."

"Get going", the squadron leader told him.

The boy leaped on to the mule track and, without bothering to take shelter, rushed down to the position. The wounded man was not one of their men. He was someone brought on a stretcher, unconscious, from the village. The carriers were still panting with the effort, squatting with their heads down next to him. "The captain ordered us to bring him up here. All the wounded who can't walk we'll have to bring up to you", he said.

"Let's go. Come on, we'll carry him to the hut", Pino said, getting hold of the stretcher's bars. They started to walk. The wounded man was frightfully heavy, and fortunately the mule track was flanked by not entirely bare trees and thickets. Unused to this type of effort, Pino reached the hut breathless. "What's happened down there?" he asked, as the two carriers set the stretcher down on the ground. The stretcher bearer who had gone up without the weight of the injured man answered. "Everything's all right in the middle, where the captain is. To the right it seems the Germans are maneuvering somehow to get up here where Bettini's positions are. Well, when they get here they'll see what's in store for them."

"We have to get back", the other carrier urged. "Bye, Pino."

"Bye." They went off, one of them with the empty stretcher under his arm.

The wounded man—seriously injured in his neck and chest—had been placed on a straw mattress. With trembling hands Pino began to expose the wounds. Then, using the contents of the medical kit, he began to clean and disinfect them.

The patient—the first patient entirely entrusted to his care, a boy from the valley, about twenty years old—regained consciousness and looked at him, deadly scared. "Don't leave me", he said. "Don't leave me!" and he started to scream.

"Leave you? Don't even think that", Pino replied, with a smile that expressed both happiness and fear, forcing himself to inspire confidence. "This is my work. Calm down. Come on, stop screaming."

He felt an indescribable pity for the physical and mental suffering of the other fellow, the same pity that had decided him to take up the medical profession: for that alone, to alleviate human suffering, he had chosen to become a doctor and not an industrialist like the others in his family.

Dressing the wound took a certain amount of time. He even took out the medical book from his pocket, as the patient again lost consciousness, and reread some lines he had read days before and that he thought could be of some use to him. Having finished the bandaging, he sat down on the ground and kept the injured man company, who, after coming to, had taken his hand and did not let it go.

Outside, the little combat—which to the two of them seemed tremendous—went on. *Who knows*, he asked himself every so often, *how things are going now?*

He was finally informed by one of the two stretcher bearers, who had come up again with another wounded man, not seriously wounded, so minor an injury that he had walked the last stretch of the path with a bit of help. "You know, Pino? Things are going all right for us. All right. Bettini's men, on the right, have beaten the Germans back down the valley. What fellows those Alpine troops are! But down in the village, too, in front of us, the Germans and the Fascists—because there are also some Fascists there—are taking to their heels. They've gone back to where they started, so much so the captain's decided to counterattack. You understand? Now, while I'm talking to you, our men are all going down with their heavy weapons and all the rest. Understand?" he repeated enthusiastically. "Well, I have to go down, too. I have to rejoin Nando, who's back on the path with the stretcher."

"Go ahead, go ahead. Thank God!" Pino exclaimed. "But what were those louder shots we've heard for a while now?"

"The armored train shooting from the track. Can't be seen because it's in the woods on the other side of the river. But it doesn't mean a thing to us, because they can't shoot against Megolo. They have to shoot higher up. Here, close by, where the shots hit, a tree or two has caught fire."

"Be careful", Pino said. "Listen, this is what I mean." A clear hissing sound whizzed through the air and ended in some almost simultaneous loud explosions. "This is what I was talking about."

"Yes, that's from the armored train. All the shots are exploding in the woods on top of Megolo."

Before the stretcher bearer went off, he glanced at the seriously injured man, who now was lying on the mattress with his eyes shut, and then he looked at Pino questioningly. He pressed his lips together hard and lifted his eyes up sadly to the sky. "Well, I'm going", he said to Pino hurriedly and left the stone-roofed hut.

The treatment for the second wounded man did not take much time. Then Pino went back to look after the more seriously wounded man. He told him how well the fighting was going, but the combat meant nothing to him. He spoke of his mother more than anything else. He was upset because of her. To judge by his clothes, he must have been very poor. Heaven knows what kind of situation his mother must be in, perhaps living in some rundown hut in the valley.

Time went by. The din of automatic weapons, which had seemed to be diminishing, had now gradually increased. Pino paid no attention, secure in the good news he had received from the stretcher bearer. He felt, more than anything, a growing desire to observe with his own eyes the way the battle was unfolding. *If it's over this afternoon, I'll have to ask the others without having seen anything.*

He made up his mind. "I'll be right back", he told the man with the slight injuries. "I'm going to have a look at how it's going, and I'll be back."

"Good", he said. "But watch out. I think one of our machine guns is firing just here below us."

Pino waved carelessly, as if to say, "What are you worried about?" and went outside.

14

He ran to the nearby trench and leaped inside. It was empty, something he had expected. From the trench he put his head out cautiously and looked toward the valley. At first he did not understand. In the positions at the side of the mule track, a little below him, there were only two men with machine guns, who were firing a rain of ammunition incessantly, furiously, down below. A bit higher up, but still below him, there were other partisans squatting behind a rock, as if glued to the terrain. He had not a clue as to what they were doing.

There below Pino glimpsed, in the woods at the side of the almost vertical climb, some camouflaged uniforms, Germans for sure. The SS! Farther below, in the fields around Megolo, there were corpses of partisans. The boy's heart began to pound furiously. There was no doubt of it. The enemy was getting the upper hand.

How was it possible? What had happened? Why had the battle turned around like this? The most urgent problem—more than anything else—was what would happen now?

Watching attentively with his mouth agape, Pino realized that the partisans clinging to the rock wanted to reach the trench where he was, but fire from an enemy automatic weapon prevented it. As soon as one of them started to leave his shelter, the enemy fire opened on the mule track beside the shelter, splattering stones and splinters of stones into the air. *Dear Lord, what a situation, what a hideous situation!*

All of a sudden the partisan machine gunner who kept firing downward shouted, "I've got them! I've got them! Out! Out!" The squatting men behind the rock leaped forward then and hurled themselves onto the mule track toward the trench above, where Pino was, and in which ten of them landed. One was carrying a machine gun, which he nervously set up. "There," someone who seemed to be the commander indicated, "and quickly, over there." The gunner opened fire on the two indicated points and began to go from one to the other, back and forth.

"Come on!" the commander now shouted to the two men who had stayed behind with the machine gun in the lower position. "Get on the path while we cover you!" In a few minutes the two of them were also in the trench. (One—Pino only realized it then—was the "caramba" who had joined up with the partisans during the surprise attack in Domodossola.) They both again set up their weapon. "Ammo", one of them said to the commander. "There's not much left. We need some."

"And where am I going to get some?" the commander replied.

Pino looked at him, scared. It was Tide, the lieutenant with the angular face, whom Beltrami used most especially for supply maintenance. The boy went up beside him. "Where's the captain?" he asked.

Tide looked at him without answering. "Where did you come from?" he asked, and then he recognized him. "Oh, yes, you're the medical student."

"Yes, where's the captain?" Pino asked again.

Tide's angular face contracted into a kind of grimace. "The captain's dead," he said, "and so is Lieutenant Antonio."

Pino's mouth fell open.

"How many wounded do you have?" the officer asked him.

"What? I? Two."

"Can they walk?"

"One, yes, if he's helped."

"Go help him. We have to leave. You come with us."

"The other's dying", Pino said.

But Tide was no longer listening. The boy knew that the other wounded man would be left behind, as he could not walk (just as Beltrami—he later learned—had been abandoned).

"Attention!" Tide called all of them to attention. The gunners stopped firing and looked at him, with their blue neckerchiefs tied around their necks, in a sweat. "The path up there is well enough hidden with thickets, concealed from view for a stretch or two. While you move off, we'll stay here, just Giuse and myself, with the machine gun. Then in four or five minutes we'll move off, too. You wait for us up there, by the rock with the cross. Understand? The rock with the cross. We'll be there about five minutes after you. Get going."

The men leaped out of the trench. The machine gunner started firing downward. "How about me?" Pino asked Tide. "And the wounded man? How are we going to keep up with the others?"

"Are you still here? Get going!" the officer shouted.

The boy rushed off to the medical station hut, went in, came out immediately afterward with his rifle and medical kit on his shoulders and the least seriously wounded man, who, terrified, was walking beside Pino with his arm linked over his neck. Two of the partisans who went before stopped, waited for them, and let them go by, following in their footsteps without saying a word. Pino and the injured man understood that they would help them in case of need. Comradeship was again working. Pino felt a gratitude toward them that he had very seldom experienced in his life.

Up above, before reaching the mountain peak through the Sola pass, at whose foothills lay Megolo, the fleeing patrol met up with Bettini's Alpine troops, who were retreating along another path, ordered into single file through the snow, carrying their arms. They had suffered two casualties—two dead.

"Now you're the commander", Tide said to Bettini, after having told him about the death of the captain and Antonio.

While they were both talking Pino—even though panting, with his blond head in a sweat, despite the cold—began to treat one of Bettini's men, who had an arm wound. All the others, standing in the snow, were looking at the SS men down below, tiny as ants in the distance, who were burning the partisans' huts with flame throwers.

More than half the men in the brigade were missing. The food provisions and the ammunition reserves had been totally lost. Bettini and the few surviving officers decided, therefore, that anyone who felt like going "on leave" could. The others who stayed would meet, after a few days walking across the mountain, the Valsesia, and would ask for hospitality from Moscatelli's Communist partisans. "We took them in once when they had been decimated as we are today", Tide remembered. "Now it's their turn to help us."

For Pino the prospect of being taken in, even for a little while, by the Communists held no appeal, even if his innate curiosity attracted him toward them. But the fact that they had as their ultimate goal to get rid of people—probably killing them—like his father was enough—for now, anyway—to hold him back. As far as that went, he could return home better than anyone, since his absence from Nomana had probably gone unnoticed. He opted to go "on leave". Lieutenant Bettini granted it, verbally, of course, after making a note of his address and with the agreement that he would be requested back by a simple greeting card signed Margherita when the brigade was ready to go into action again.

Thus Pino arrived back in Nomana at the end of a few days, the seventeenth of February, unexpected. All in all he had been away two weeks. The news he had promised to send his mother in the second half of February he delivered personally.

15

Received by his parents, who delivered him the expected dressing down—a good one indeed—Pino planned to use his leave to advance his university studies a bit. But anything that was not action bored him, studies in particular, even studying the surgical manual he had brought from the mountain.

Since he felt a bit like a partisan on a mission in his own world, he thought of making a visit to Incastigo one day to get in on the latest activities of Praga, the Fascist who in his day had deported the administrator Mambretti, the director of the local Banca Artigiana. He found out that Praga no longer lived there, that he now was in Milan with the police and, according to certain sources of information, was heading a torture squadron specializing in making partisans confess. On this point he exhausted—with no luck—his two and only sources of information: one an ex-schoolmate and the other an ex-employee of his father's. Then he uselessly asked people he did not know at the local inn. But this news was confirmed in a brief conversation with a young seminary student, as rash as himself, in the atrium of the Oratory, where the seminary student—who defined himself as "seminarian on the run"—received him with his face flushed, panting, and the skirts of his soutane raised and tucked into the waist of his trousers because he had been playing football with the boys.

"In any case," he reminded him with the typical seminary student scruples, "bear in mind that rumors of this nature are easily spread about nowadays. What we do know for sure is that it was more than a month ago that Praga went to live in Milan."

"This conversation", Pino at last said, struck by a last-minute scruple, "must be considered as having been made as a confession. All right?"

"All right", the candidate priest answered, pledging himself with a handshake.

"One moment." Pino wanted to settle another point. "And Panzone? Did he go with him, too?" (They were referring to the little local Fascist—called Panzone, Big Belly, as a joke, since he did not really have a belly and was actually quite thin—who in his day was a friend of Praga's and involved in snaring the administrator Mambretti.)

"No," the seminarian replied, "he's still around here, but he's no longer a Fascist. He's nothing. Everyone simply feels sorry for him. He stays drunk all the time out of remorse."

Pino nodded gravely, somehow feeling also obliged to be sorry for those left behind.

The candidate priest thanked him with a smile and, without more ado, went into the courtyard to return to his football game with the boys.

Back home, Pino met his father head on at the gate. He scrutinized Pino carefully, suspecting some sort of foolishness, and asked him where he had been.

"In Incastigo."

"Doing what?"

"Well . . . service."

"What for?"

"Well, to get some information."

"About whom?"

"Oh, about someone you don't know."

Then, seeing his father irritated by his reticence, he explained who this "someone" was and also explained point by point all that he had done, without leaving out the conversation at the inn.

Gerardo was quite upset. They were still in the garden, in front of the door. He made Pino go in, silently pointing out to his son the entrance to the study, and he followed him in. In the few steps from the garden to the study, Gerardo's anger mounted. "Do you realize you've got mixed up with a dangerous character, even more, a very dangerous criminal?" he began. "You couldn't have behaved in a more reckless fashion, even more, let me tell you, a more stupid fashion, you know?" And he followed this up, irritated and furious, by pointing out the possible consequences of his behavior, which could have affected others at home. "Perhaps your mother and sisters. Do you realize this, you stupid boy?"

As for Pino, it seemed part of his duties as a partisan on leave not to be undermined by fears of this type, even though out of respect for his father he tried not to make this obvious. Nevertheless his attitude left much to be desired, which inspired still further discourse from his father.

To put an end to the situation the boy proposed, "I'm sorry, Papa. I'll leave home, and that way there won't be any reprisals against the family. I'm still not of military age, so no one can say anything if I go."

"You're staying here", Gerardo said, even more worried. "You're staying right here at home. Where do you want to go? And besides, what would you do? Maybe you'll think up another piece of foolishness? What's most important now is that you avoid any other partisan involvement." He had an inspiration. "Pino, try to think. Do you think your officers and comrades act like partisans when they are at home?"

Pino did have to recognize that they probably did not, and, even though he did not say so, this put an end to the question.

When he left his father's study, however (since we always want to be a little in the right), he repeated to himself that most decidedly his father had been too impressionable. Perhaps this Praga, about whom his father worried so, was no more than another Panzone, a complete idiot.

The boy was very much mistaken about this. If he had known the man he was so much trying to spy on, he would have been terrified.

16

At that very moment, Praga was seated in his own office in Milan and was in the process also of summing things up.

The chance of leaving Incastigo had been given him by a circular letter from the Fascist party that invited people to join the police force. (Everyone was trying to leave in those days.) Thinking it over, he realized that his new life would not be exempt from troubles. To guard prisoners (that seemed implicit to him) and "make them sing" would involve great risks, but by enlisting himself he would escape the oppressing authority of the local Fascist heads as well as the Brianza atmosphere, which had always been hateful to him. Besides, he would have totally helpless creatures in his hands. It was this last factor especially that made the prospect fascinating. And like a person who takes a decision with the idea of doing good, regardless of the benefit he will derive from it, and then feels at peace in his own conscience, so he felt himself approved not by his own conscience but by some indefinable presence—a kind of counterconscience—which, in general, mocking and scornful, was lurking inside him.

Once enlisted and transferred to Milan, he realized that things were not going at all as he supposed and that the ordinary police force was still fulfilling its function, which was to respect the law, even in the treatment of prisoners. What a blunder he realized he had made.

Luckily, while he was being eaten up with disappointment, he heard another discontented colleague sing the praises of a unit or police group (one of the many semi-independent organizations that swarmed in those anarchic days) in which the policemen were "like gods" and not "poor fools like us". He immediately made contact with that unit, lodged in an old boarding house in the center of the city, and he found it breathed a more congenial air for him. So he moved there without further ado, leaving his new bosses the job of straightening out his situation. (This, too, going from one group to another on one's own initiative, was common during those times, among the Fascist armed forces and among the partisans.)

In the former boarding house—situated on a street off Via Broletto and furnished with several basement floors silent as tombs—the work quickly turned out to be interesting. Besides, the place was well protected, as he discovered when an agent, a colleague of his, was followed all the way inside by two partisans, who were quickly stopped by the guards.

These two careless partisans—whom the commander of the detachment entrusted to his inexperienced attention—were then his "debut" in this new situation. From some tiny details he had detected their belonging to the repugnant scum of "sacristy frequenters", that is—according to Mussolini's trenchant definition—to the rabble of "vile Guelphs", of whom he had more than enough experience in Brianza. Knowing their clerical mentality, he told himself, quite rightly, that both of them (and one in particular, a shortish, pimply youth, full of good intentions but half dead with fear even before the torture began) must have got involved in this desperate business, not to kill the agent or for any other negative goal, but with a positive end in mind. What was it? That was the question. They wanted to take the agent alive, that yes, but not as an exchange. It would have been far more convenient and easier for them to have taken any Fascist chief. Why, then, had they decided on following that agent, who did not even have a rank?

Thanks to a separate "treatment" of both of them (carried out under his very eyes by habitual torturers, in decidedly rough fashion, that is, by means of slaps and cigarette burns), Praga managed to reconstruct the motive behind the action. The agent who had been pursued had, some time before, got rid of a priest who was creating problems. His two pursuers were not the usual partisans. They were simply boys who frequented the oratory of that priest, and to get news of him—about whom the authorities declared they knew nothing—they attempted to capture the agent. Hardly an episode to interest the police, banal even, except that Praga, before considering the matter closed, wanted to know for sure if the responsibility of that particular agent was known outside the section. He believed it was not, that there was no reason it should be. The two boys were questioned separately at all times about who had told them that. The weaker of the two (the one who had received help from the missing priest and who was looking for him because he needed him), after some adequate additional "treatment", completely bloodied up, his features unrecognizable because of the bruises, weepingly confessed. The other boy's confession had been more difficult but had in the end confirmed everything. The special police thus finally managed to put their hands on the responsible party, one of their own men who, for a small sum, had talked.

After this first and still recent inquiry, Praga was entrusted with others, even though in this first one there was a detail that was not clear to his bosses and colleagues: the two boys, once the investigation was over, had been found killed in the basement of the prison in a most improbable "attempt to escape". No later inquiries were carried out, of course, but Praga could not help but know the risk he had run and even now, seated at the rickety desk in the office he had been lately assigned (a little room in the boarding house with a picture of a boat still hanging on the wall), was giving the matter some thought. *So, that's it, I still have to learn,* he ended up telling himself. *I'm sorry, but I still must learn.* After all, what had he done before this? What had been his great jobs? The unmasking and deporting of the administrator Mambretti to Germany (*to Auschwitz, a camp from which, with any luck, he will not return*) and later the deportation of another citizen of Incastigo, a minor Fascist leader who had tenaciously opposed his measures. A courageous bastard, as he recalled. While the other Fascists, even the important ones, were beginning to fear Praga and were wishing he would go now that discipline had eased up, that bastard had dared to say "no" at a Fascist meeting (he found out about it later): "No, we shouldn't let him go: we should have him watched here, to keep him from carrying out his dirty business." The bastard! Well, then, later he had fixed him, and while with Mambretti—it came to him now with vexation—he had acted the idiot, with this one he had been astute enough not to expose himself. That was all he had done, in any case, because the tasks to come were only just started. That was all, really very little! Unless one wanted to add something . . . no, how did that fit in? But as he started thinking about all this, his wife's inconsistent accusations two years before came to mind. (Where would she be now, that scum? *Far from here, I suppose, and if not, it would be a good time to settle the score with her.*) And that scum had practically accused him publicly of being responsible for the death of their only daughter. Imagine, simply because he amused himself frightening her occasionally at night. The girl was amazingly afraid of the dark, and he would say, "Be good, Alida. Go down and fetch me my slippers." And he'd go down behind her without her noticing it. She'd get down below, and the fool was incapable—so afraid was she of the dark—of finding the light switch. Then he'd make noises in a deep, hollow voice, and she'd begin to scream and scream. It really was incredible how worked up she'd become, until her teeth began to chatter, and she'd go on like that for a while even after the light was switched on. Even though the girl scrupulously obeyed his orders not to say anything about this, his wife one evening came home early from work and had caught him at it and stood up to him, despite her usual fear of him. That time she had really showed her claws, the disgusting bitch! Just remembering it, Praga's mouth even now twisted with fury, like then. She used the girl's poor health as a pretext (in fact, she was suffering from leukemia, but that had nothing to do with the scary frights), and then the miserable bitch took her off to her village, and he was forced to let them go because she had threatened him if he didn't to tell everything to his Fascist comrades. "Even if you kill me later, you devil." In any case, the girl died a little while later, and that was the end of it.

Well, was there any use going over all that again? Yes there was. There was— Praga muttered vaguely—moving his buttocks in his chair. He was a thick-set person, with a round head like a ball and cloudy yellowish eyes: these thoughts began taking hold of him. Actually, what came to him most was his daughter's quivering mouth, the little face that seemed to go to pieces with terror. Go to pieces, yes, go to pieces, that was what most attracted him, more than anything else in the world: that which brought him to the indefinable presence, that other *I* inside him, which seemed to create his total self. Not being able to destroy individuals on a large scale—he was only a minor official—he at least would have liked to destroy each and every one of the few in his power. With the two "vile Guelphs" this desire had got the upper hand in far too open a way. Incredible but . . . it seemed impossible that even here, in the bowels of a jail where torture was inflicted, there should be limits, rules that had to be respected! All in all, he would have to be more careful and not act as he had done with those two, whom after his brilliant success he felt he should be given as a prize. Consequently, he had tried out a complex system of torture on them that he had been brooding over in his fantasy for a long time. For how long? Well, to tell the truth, he had felt attracted by these things—at least implicitly—for many years. That enduring temptation, already as a boy, to burn tiny animals alive in a slow fire, and how seldom had he been able to satisfy that desire! Well, even if imperfect (*Of course, I'm still a beginner in these things!*), his dream system of torture had shown itself to be objectively efficient, perhaps more efficient than traditional ways. The convulsive agitation of the two prisoners, tied, gagged, their spasmodic bellowing, like madmen, had shown him he was on the right path. For him it had been orgiastic pleasure. Even so, everything considered, it had not lasted long enough. It is true that now, at least, the memory of those two trembling, their gagged mouths—like his daughter's a bit as she became breathless—was still pleasurable. But those two had been left so badly off that since they could not be returned to the cell, he had to kill them with a pistol shot, from this good pistol that was now lying in front of him on his desk. (The weapon was a delight, too, even if not a machine gun, which multiplied death prodigiously . . . still this fulfilled its role of killing, and how it killed! *Sinking flesh, bones, and . . .*)

This was the man (Can he be called a man? No doubt of it. We cannot call him otherwise, because wild beasts are not at all like that.) whom the boy Pino wanted to watch, spy on. These were his thoughts on that particular day.

17

The postcard from the partisans signed Margherita arrived in Nomana several weeks after Easter, during the second half of April 1944. Leaving a short note of explanation for his parents on his night table in his own bedroom, Pino went off on a bicycle toward Megolo, but this time he was not alone. His schoolmate and contemporary, Sèp—short for Giuseppe—accompanied him.

They arrived at the small Megolo square—after having cycled about seventy miles without anyone bothering them—and, to their surprise, realized there was not a trace of the partisans in the village.

"This is really wonderful", Pino murmured. "Really great. I'd like to know what we're going to do now."

Sèp watched him trustfully, with the unconscious trust of his eighteen years.

Meanwhile, finding himself in the theater of his previous deeds slightly stirred Pino up. With one foot on the pedal and the other on the ground, he searched out the trench at the top of the village, from which he had seen the SS men, clambering upward, striking terror, and the partisan huts, of which only the charred remains could be seen. And higher up still—high above the highest mountain ridge—the saddle through which he and the others had passed into safety. Close by, practically within hand's reach, were the small hotel where Beltrami once had his headquarters and the inn belonging to Mariuccia and, on the other side, the fountain where the cows came to water, no doubt still, with their meditative step: the modest stone fountain that comprised the major ornament of the village.

What days they were! The boy reflected emotionally. What days . . . we'll never see days like those again! He felt like a veteran returning to the sites of great battles. "Sèp, you can't imagine how many died defending these four houses", he said.

The other boy nodded obligingly.

"Well," the veteran sighed, shaking his head repeatedly, "it's time we find out what's happening."

To figure out what they should do, and also to rest a bit, they entered Mariuccia's Inn. They had hardly sat down when someone from the valley came up to them. (Pino recognized him. He was the older brother, not a partisan, of a very young partisan in the brigade.) "You received the postcard, didn't you?" he said softly in dialect.

"Yes, of course. And now I don't know where to go", Pino replied.

"I'll tell you . . . Tide's orders."

"Ah, just as well."

"You have to go to Ornavasso, to this street and number . . ."

"But we just went through Ornavasso."

"Of course."

"All right", Pino said. "The street and number you mentioned?"

"That's right, memorize it."

"Naturally," Pino said, "and thanks."

The man smiled by way of an answer.

"And your brother?" the boy inquired.

The other gestured to the mountains.

"So he, too, got away safely on the day of the combat."

The villager nodded, and smiled again.

"Do you know how many died?"

"On the day of the combat?"

"Yes."

"Ten. We picked up ten."

"Only ten?"

The other looked at him a bit surprised. "How many did you think there were?"

Pino did not answer. "Is that including the captain and the Lieutenant Antonio?" he asked.

The man nodded. "And two other officers."

Such a ratio of losses of officers to troops was in itself significant, but none of the three realized that. "The Germans gave the bodies of the captain and Antonio to the families", he said. "They allowed them to have funerals. Did you know?"

Pino shook his head. Then he asked, "And now who's in command of the brigade? Bettini?"

The other shook his head negatively and started to walk away. There were beginning to be too many questions.

"One moment. Who is in charge? Tell me", Pino insisted.

"They'll tell you in Ornavasso."

"No. Come on, you know me."

"Alfredo is the commander", the other whispered and waved goodbye as he left.

"Well, well," Pino said, "think of that. So Alfredo is no longer in jail?"

Once the other fellow left, Mariuccia came up to the table to see what they wanted. She greeted Pino with an almost imperceptible movement of her head, indicating she recognized him. Then she acted as if she did not know him at all. The boy could not tell if his presence was welcome or not and—given as he was at that moment to remembering the good old times—felt more than a little distressed. He realized the partisan actions had not been a matter of fun for the civilian population.

He drank a soda pop as usual (there were still no orange drinks), while his friend had a glass of wine. The decoration—paneled walls halfway up, angular chairs, a stuffed squirrel over the entranceway, an unframed mirror advertising Ferro China Bisleri)—was exactly the same as before, as in the days of glory. Only the arrangement of the tables was different now. They were more spread out because there were no longer partisan clients, who usually sat together in groups. Pino kept looking around, from time to time moving his blond, flat-naped head. He was overcome by emotion.

18

It was not difficult to find the place where he had to go in Ornavasso. Two young fellows who had arrived before them were already there, hidden in a haystack. Another one came in the evening. They were new arrivals, unknown to them, and they clearly felt out of place. During the night a peasant from the place led all of them—a climb lasting several hours—to a vanguard partisan post in the mountains. Pino discovered, delighted, that Tom was in charge. He was still wearing his brother's Alpine hat on his head, with its eagle insignia totally worn out. "Pino, it's you. But how's this . . . it's becoming a habit: I'm always the one to be receiving you", Tom said, as he welcomed him and shook his hand warmly. "So you're back. Good."

"You bet I'm back!" Pino said in short, as suits a man of action, but he felt as happy as a baby inside: happy to have met up with his comrade, happy because the words, too, qualified him as a veteran in the eyes of the new recruits who had arrived with him.

"You know the 'vets' are almost all back?" Tom said. "And there's a lot of new fellows, you'll see, so many I don't know if we'll have enough weapons."

"Listen, I heard the new chief is now Alfredo Di Dio."

"Marco, we call him Marco, remember. Yes, he's the commander now."

"Well, in our days he was in prison. How did he get out? Did he escape, or was he freed by you?"

"No. The Fascists let him out, just imagine. And there's Bettini, Tide, and . . . you'll see for yourself."

He accompanied the new arrivals to a small stable with rough stone walls, fixed up as a shelter. "It's best you sleep now," he said, "because as soon as it gets light we'll have a long march ahead of us."

"Where are they sending us?" Pino asked.

"To Pan Perdu, a sheepfold in Monte Massone. There are too many of us here in the Ornavasso area. You'll meet up with some of the old fellows, you'll see."

He kept the flashlight lit, which cast a pale light here and there onto the hay, until everyone found his place. Then he took his leave with a "Good night, at least for what's left of it", and, switching off the light, went off.

The march to Pan Perdu took almost the entire day. And that was not the only march. During the following days the partisan recruits, the old fellows, too, were subjected to a tough series of training marches, which were interspersed with frequent exercises of the "school on elbows" (infantry training), classes on materials and rifle and machine-gun practice. The scenery around them—sometimes they would sing songs from Beltrami's time. "March, march / it's good for your heart . . ."—was incomparable: a colorful view of hilltops and mountain peaks, which rose out of Alpine vegetation dominated by the Rosa peak, which, at 4,600 meters, is the second highest of the Alps.

The commanding officer of the camp—the "old" second lieutenant Tide—was very demanding, and he personally took charge of every one of the men, regarding their preparation, especially with weapons. But systematic carrying out of his programs was hindered by the continual influx of new recruits, who climbed up the mountains pushed on by the conscriptions of the Fascist republic.

Several times Commander Marco made a visit, Marco alias Alfredo Di Dio, who spoke to the men, trying to instill in them a proper sense of their common tasks and duties. He had less authority (if only because he was younger, only twenty-four) than the unforgettable Beltrami, but an inner fire could be detected in him that Beltrami—who was more detached—did not have. Marco spoke passionately of their country, their civilization, their God. He talked continuously of God, his passionate interest. The task of all of them was not only the liberation of their country from German oppression but also the restoration of their people to their authentic civilization, which was Christian. He reminded them that Italy had been great only when it was truly Christian.

For Pino, it seemed as if he were listening to Tintori, from Nova, and, for other reasons, to his cousin Manno—and who knew where they were right now, if they were even alive? It seemed to him that Marco was cut from the same cloth, even if his bearing was more decidedly military. "I'm beginning to wonder if our commander is a soldier or a mystic", an older partisan who had arrived a short time before said to Pino at the end of one of Marco's speeches, just as the boy was thinking the same thing.

"And if he was both at one and the same time?" Pino suggested.

"Yes, maybe that's how it is. Did you realize? The Nazis killed his brother, and yet he never talks about vengeance; that's not even part of his mentality."

Perhaps precisely for that reason, some thought, the Fascists in one lucid moment had let him get away. In times in which more than a few partisans attacked their enemies in the streets and in houses and killed them even if unarmed, a commander like this could have meant a kind of guarantee (at least for the women and children, who lived in terror of what would happen at the end of the war, already clearly lost). A civilized man like him would most certainly oppose a generalized massacre, maybe even with force.

From the military point of view, already in the following weeks, Marco, who was really an army officer, began to show himself quite capable. His formation attacks—never at random and never disjointed—led to a radical change in the balance of forces in the area. One began to have the feeling that the initiative could very well pass to the hands of the partisans now.

The influx of recruits during the months of May, June, July, and the following ones was practically unlimited. Already the Fascist government's drafts, instead of providing men for the republic, increased the ranks of the guerrillas of all colors and ideologies. "Rather than Germany, hell itself", the recruits declared when they showed up at the partisan vanguard posts.

Marco could not take in more than a certain number. His brigades had already multiplied, and to keep them armed and efficient meant an enormous logistic effort, and to sustain this the help of a new commander was needed, a young and efficient officer like himself, one Eugenio Cefis, who had taken the battle name of Alberto. More and more he showed himself to be a first-class organizer. He managed to procure means from everywhere, even money through collection centers instituted in Milan and weapons from the Allies, who now occasionally dropped material from their planes on the so-called hermitage house, where a radio station was also working to communicate with the government in the south.

The Germans and the Fascists, exasperated by the continual surprise attacks, reacted as they could, with round-ups, but never with much result because Marco—having learned from the fight in Megolo—refused to do battle in the field. In the second half of June, Germans and Fascists—with the help of impressive reinforcements brought over from other provinces—made an attempt to mop up the whole zone. Val d'Ossola and its affluent valleys of Vigezzo, Grande, and Cannobina were cleaned up as far as the Swiss border by strong-armed columns; artillery fire and mortars hammered away from below the forests, provoking fires everywhere. Detachments were dispatched up to every spot. Shelters were burned, but they only managed here and there to engage the partisans. The latter responded only with incursions to slow down the enemy advance or with different skirmishes to divert the enemy along their flanks, continually moving the bulk of their forces from one place to another. All together, it is true, they lost several hundred men among dead, injured, and missing—more than had been lost from Beltrami's brigade in the course of its history—but these losses were not such as to weaken any of the principal formations.

Pino, too, marched frenetically with the others, his medical kit always slung over his shoulder, and he could see the distant fires in some of the woods, but above all he could hear the explosions that went on day and night. Many times he saw from up above the road by the lake—so peaceful in other days—packed with armed columns.

A minor partisan formation—not incorporated into Marco's brigade—was surprised in Intra and completely captured. The prisoners, forty-two men and a woman, were taken to Fondotoce and made to walk in formation through the streets of the village with a placard labeling them "bandits". (The woman walked at the head of the line, frightened, with flat-heeled shoes on her feet, a handbag over her arm.) In the end they were all executed.

Then the partisans shot their prisoners and others, taken in the course of repeated ambushes, including the head of the *Feldgendarmerie* of the province, captured by Marco's men as he was returning from the massacre at Fondotoce.

The Germans, by way of reprisal, took twenty-one civilians from Baveno, mainly old men, and shot them on the walking path around the lake in the town.

The partisans responded with other executions. Not only Marco's men but also other nonextremist formations in which there was a respect for human life—in times past they had constituted hideouts called "concentration camps", in which their prisoners were gathered for exchange. But during these days fewer prisoners were taken to the camps, because a new element, a degrading spirit of vengeance, had insinuated itself into many of their hearts. Marco—he, too, not to be surpassed, had accepted and even ordered some executions—clearly recognized this as an evil. To face up to it in some fashion, he requested and obtained two chaplains from the bishop of Novara to work on the hardened spirits, to instill in them some heroic Christian charity.

Meanwhile, he rigorously insisted that the military training of his groups go on. The enemy troops that had arrived from other parts for the big mopping up had already gone back to their bases. The Nazi-Fascist control of the area was again circumscribed to the towns and villages and the larger communication lines. The surprise attacks of the partisans—in which both Pino and Sèp participated more than once—were on the rise. Nevertheless, training was carried out without respite. Marco had it in his head to bring about a large undertaking, something exemplary, which would eventually stir up and awaken public opinion in all of Italy, and to accomplish that, he needed an adequate instrument of war.

19

At the beginning of September, news reached the mountain that hundreds of Fascist soldiers (Marco figured about three hundred) had been taken from their valley detachments and brought to other provinces where plans were afoot for partisan offensives. A deserter—showing up at a control post in Pino's and Sèp's company—told them, in detail, that fifty Italians and thirty Germans were still in the Piedimulera garrison, in a village about five or six miles from Megolo, on the same side of the valley. The deserter made it clear that the men were demoralized.

The company—in Pino's absence: he had gone to the hermitage house to pick up medical supplies—was ordered to go down to the valley that night, according to a plan worked out personally by Marco. The idea was to attack at dawn, a surprise attack against that detachment in conjunction with another partisan brigade, that of Valdossola del Maggiore Superti (the green neckerchiefs), which operated in that area. Not to go into details, it suffices to say there was no surprise, and the attack was driven back.

A blue partisan, seriously wounded, fell prisoner, and with the ferocity born out of desperation, the men of the Fascist militia (those of the "black brigade" of Carrara), after having tied him by his feet to a cart, dragged him through the dust, along the streets of the village until his wretched body was finished off. The partisans were immediately informed of the deed by the civilians, and, highly indignant, they renewed their attack and once again were driven back.

The Piedimulera attack seemed doomed when, quite unexpectedly, the German unit abandoned the village in several trucks and went toward Domodossola at high speed.

The green partisans then left their own positions and situated themselves farther back, on a bridge over the Domodossola road, covering all of it with their machine guns and preventing passage. "We shut the stable door after the horse has been stolen", some of them mumbled. It really did seem incredible that the Fascists would try to leave now that they could not do it by surprise. However, a couple of hours later, the Piedimulera Fascist unit suddenly showed up on the highway, the whole unit aboard four vehicles. The partisan gunners were waiting to have them well within striking range. Then they opened fire and attacked the four vehicles, which, after repeated hits, stopped. The soldiers leaped to the ground, as their wounded screamed, and using the vehicles as parapets, or thrown onto the vegetation at the side of the road, they desperately tried to defend themselves. However great the disproportion of the forces was, their exposed position was even worse.

The din of the fire reached the blues, who immediately frenetically ran to the spot. Realizing what was happening, they took up positions—without being seen—in the fields at both sides of the highway, set up their weapons, and opened fire. The Fascists tried to stand up to these other enemies, too, but a crossfire of machine-gun fire, automatic and otherwise, rained down on them from three sides. The vehicles were riddled and mowed down with fire, and the Fascists responded ever more feebly, until all activity around the trucks ceased. A woman, an auxiliary, appeared with a white rag from a cabin. Then the partisans were everywhere, their weapons in hand, overcome with indescribable enthusiasm, Sèp, together with the others. He realized there were not fifty Fascists but far fewer, perhaps about thirty. They were stretched out face down on the vehicles, on the highway, on the fields around the road. Some were still alive, and the partisans—including the Christian partisans of Marco's unit—finished them off with a shot on the nape of the neck. The woman was doubled over in the cabin of one of the trucks, a stream of blood running from her mouth. She raised her bent-down ashen face wearily toward the enemies. "Please," she said in a faint voice, "shoot me in the head." And one of Marco's Christians did so.

The victors, after having counted cadavers, lined them up in a field, but quickly left them. They were beginning to feel sick and remorseful at what they had done. The two groups rapidly divided the weapons of the losers and left the spot.

The news of this fierce massacre provoked terror in the ever-reduced Fascist and German groups still stationed in the valleys, knowing they were already numerically inferior to the partisans. Besides, the ignorance regarding the real number of the enemies further multiplied the disproportion of forces in the mind of each and every one.

The German-Fascist command in the area requested—through the intervention of the high priest of Domodossola—an urgent meeting with the partisan command. Marco suddenly glimpsed the possibility of carrying out his much-coveted program. To the request for a truce he asked in exchange—in accord with Major Superti—that they clear out the entire zone, from the lake to the Swiss border (in effect, half the province of Novara). The Germans would be able to leave with their weapons, the Fascists only with their officers' personal weapons. The petition was—much to the surprise of the partisan leaders—accepted unconditionally, and the specified area was cleared out in a few hours. Marco had to act quickly and send the few trucks and men he had available to Domodossola to collect the weapons and materiel abandoned.

All this happened on the night of September 9. On the morning of the tenth, at dawn, three hundred men from the partisan brigades of Valtoce, Marco's unit (blue neckerchiefs), and Valdossola, Superti's men (green neckerchiefs), marched in close ranks into the town.

20

This time Pino was present. He entered proudly, marching in formation with his company, his rifle over his shoulder and his medical kit over his back. On orders from Marco, who set the pace, the company of partisans marched in rhythmical step, proud of their great success. Suddenly they burst into song: "March, march / It makes your heart beat strong . . ." Most were wearing khaki or gray-green shorts, many with long hair, out of necessity or coquetry. Some had beards in imitation of the Alpine troops—no longer many—which were all marching in rows and which (here as in other places, as in all big Italian partisan formations) constituted the backbone of the army. They were mostly very young and so had learned to march not in the army but in Fascist youth organizations instead.

A noisy crowd had gathered around them, quite imposing, even if it was seven in the morning. Women, men, children, thousands of people, all of Domodossola had turned out, as none had wanted to stay at home at that moment. They were all shouting, clapping, some even beating their feet. Flowers hurriedly gathered from little gardens and fields were being thrown at them. Bells from a church suddenly began to ring out the Piave march.

It's an apotheosis, Pino told himself, trying to keep step (something he was not too good at). *An apotheosis, a triumph. Thank you, my dear people, thank you* . . . There were moments when he thought they were all cheering him personally.

When they reached the main square, Marco gave the order to halt. All around them and in the surrounding streets the crowd that had followed the partisans en masse was pressing. Here Marco spoke. He named Italy repeatedly, always with a new emotion—he talked about his country as about a young girl with whom he was in love—and he reminded them of the example of patriotism and civilization that the partisans had to give to the people, and from here, at this moment, to the whole Italian people. If the savagery of war, he said, had sometimes got the upper hand (he did not name it, but it was understood he was alluding to the savage massacre at Piedimulera), now they would have to overcome it, control themselves, and once more give an example of being civilized. He also spoke insistently of God. Hours later there was a solemn Mass, which the crowd and the partisans attended together, mingling with each other, exultant, a Mass that was meant to be the culminating ceremony of that day. Such was the commander's intention.

The liberated area—half the province, as was mentioned, with sixty towns and perhaps some eighty thousand inhabitants—was more or less triangular in shape. The two sides toward the north bordered Switzerland. Only the southern side bordered the Fascist republic. This last border, about fifty miles long, comprised the impenetrable mountain chain that culminated in the Rosa, and the other half ran along the northern shore of Lago Maggiore, also quite impervious. Only at the meeting point between the chain of mountains of the Rosa and the mountains of the lake was there a small, flat stretch: the opening from the Val d'Ossola, hardly a few miles in width. Through that ran the only highway and the only train tracks that went into the liberated territory. Thus it was here, at this point—where the town of Ornavasso was—that the future attack from the enemy was to be expected. At least that would be the main target, because in the lake area there was also a minor entrance—the Cannobio Valley—traversed by a small road that went up meandering from the pleasant coast village of Cannobio. And at Cannobio the same day of the clearing out, the Fascists from Decima Mas hastened to place a bridge head, not easy to supply, however, through the lake's flat extension.

Pino spent a few days at Domodossola, where he participated, whenever duty allowed, in the spontaneous ebullience of the festivities that followed the liberation. He went about in desultory fashion through the town's cobbled streets at all hours, normally with Sèp. He kept saying vaguely that he would have to visit the school where his brother Fortunato and his cousin Manno had studied, but he never managed to do so.

There was no end of the people's cheers for the partisans, constant handshakes when they met, hearty slaps on the back, thanks all around. On the walls of the town, the threatening proclamations of the Fascist republic were covered over with a short message from the commanders Marco and Superti, announcing the takeover of power. Posters were also stuck up on the walls with the exultant words and the unavoidable rhetoric of the new local government, installed by the partisans: "By virtue alone of the noble Italian hearts ... the oriflamme of the redemption of our nation will wave over the peaks and valleys of Ossola." Partisans from other bands began to come down from the mountains, people of all colors and persuasions, Communists, royalists, Socialists, but most especially people without any party, in general young boys of the area who had gone into the partisan struggle simply to avoid being recruited into the Fascist military forces. They were dressed in the most outlandish fashion, some even as Germans, and—except for the Communists—were manifestly less disciplined than the not-too-disciplined men of Marco's unit.

Pino and Sèp questioned some of them to find out what they were thinking, but the partisans almost only answered with jokes, at which Sèp invariably laughed, amused. All in all, they did not seem to have very clear-cut plans for the future. That is, with the exception of the Communists (the "Garibaldi men", as they called themselves). They, without revealing their plans, repeated that they were determined to respect the present alliance with the other partisans, and to Pino they seemed sincere. But they mainly insisted on talking about their success in the Formazza Valley (one of the valleys that go up from the main valley to the Swiss border), from which, they asserted, they had driven away the Fascists, too, in the last few days. They displayed a most visible envy for the greater success achieved by Marco.

After a few days, the Fascist supplies that had been given them came to an end, and many of the newly arrived partisans began to hunt out "Fascist spies", which actually meant hunting out anyone they did not like. They were quickly dissuaded by Marco's fury. On the other hand, the government council, which was competent for purgings, was quite reasonable, being put together from elements of all parties. (There were recriminations at first from some of them who had wanted to have greater representation for their own factions; then—on being warned of the provisional nature of that adventure—the wish to get on with things as best they could took over in each and every one.)

From Switzerland came an influx of political refugees and military people out of concentration camps and—even more welcome—Swiss civil servants from neighboring administrative cantons, with the intention of finding ways to be helpful. The mountain population on the other side of the border was very much interested in the fate of the people of Ossola, in so many ways similar to themselves, and they wished to lend their support.

The Communists, meanwhile, went on sizing up the propaganda success of the Christian partisans (the press and the radio all over the world spoke of the Republic of Ossola) and though apparently happy, like the others, bore with it less and less. They finally decided to carry out a surprise attack and bring in their own success. They all went off to the entrance of the Ossola Valley, beyond the Ornavasso-Mergozzo line, established by Marco and Superti in the truce agreements of September 13. Together with other Communist forces that were brought in, they rushed to occupy Gravellona. If the attack had been successful they would have become the vanguard army of the partisan republic. But the Germans were in Gravellona, and they not only drove them back with serious losses but also counterattacked. In order to free themselves and withdraw beyond the line of the truce, the Communists were compelled to call on

Marco for help. He gave the help quite unwillingly, but then—fearing the Germans might also advance toward Ossola—he set about hurriedly fortifying the opening of the valley between Ornavasso and Mergozzo.

The company to which Pino and Sèp belonged was used for this work, which meant they had to leave off resting in Domodossola to go to Ornavasso.

21

The company was led by Second Lieutenant Tide, a man of few words, whom Pino had followed in his escape from the Nazis in Megolo. Tide had the habit of working together with his own men: many big trees along the national highway were cut down. Pino worked along with the others—more or less clumsily, acting very much the buffoon—using the ax and, with the others, pulling the ropes tied to the tops of the trees to direct their fall so that they would land crossways over the highway, thus shutting off passage. And also like the others, he shouted his salute as the gigantic green trees fell, with the crashing din of their branches breaking as they fell heavily to the ground. The end of each tree had something similar to the end of the world about it, and those little men became exalted by the repeated demonstrations of their power. Then, always along with Tide, who personally joined in the work with the pickax, the partisans placed charges of explosives in the pavement of a few bridges and blew them up. This, too, the destruction of human works, filled the men with joy, as one more manifestation of their own power over things. They then went on to dig a long trench throughout the entire valley, reinforcing it here and there with a buried blockhouse. They were involved in the work for several days without the Germans showing any sign of life. The work once finished, they at last began taking regular turns doing guard duty, monotonous and boring after so much activity.

Many youths from Ossola asked to join up with the partisans, so many that Marco was obliged to reorganize his troops, their numbers on the rise. He divided them into two divisions, with three brigades in each one.

"Two divisions, no less! We've become two divisions", some of them would remark ironically during guard duty.

Tide, opposed to any kind of rhetoric, finally became irritated. "If you look at the requests for enlistment, it's not out of place to use the word *division*, do you think?"

"Of course not. I'm more than convinced of that. Out of place? Who's talking about out of place? Why are you saying that?"

"Because as arms and weapons go, we should be pitied—divisions nothing. And as to training, efficiency, it's even worse. The fact is there's no way of doing any serious training."

"Tide is obsessed about training," one of them commented, "same as Marco. Some obsession!"

"Unfortunately," Tide would say, "without training, what is an army? It simply isn't an army. It's nothing. Do you know what's meant by the word *army*? It means exercised, trained. Look at the Germans. They have America, Russia, England, the partisans of the entire world against them. They're outnumbered ten to one, and besides they've got every known difficulty; but they go on, they fight back, because they're organized and seriously trained."

"But besides it's because they're . . . how would you put it . . . brave. Or not?"

"Yes", Tide answered. "They're brave. That's true, too."

"But it isn't true we're without weapons", one of the recent arrivals observed. "Apart from what the Americans have parachuted down to us, we have what the Fascists have left behind."

"That's how it is", Sèp chimed in, and he began enumerating. "Three cannons, two 81 mortars, and then machine guns, semiautomatics, and rifles."

"And that's the weaponry of two divisions?"

"We also have an armored train in the Domodossola station."

"An armored train?" Tide murmured. "Without arms, it's nothing but a milk train." He shook his head and said nothing else.

One day went into another. They were the lovely days of the beginning of autumn, warm, with a sun—not scorching as in summer—that revived the grassy meadows at the bottom of the valley, covered with wildflowers. In the middle of the valley the river Toce flowed by murmuring, shaded by trees whose trunks were swathed in lichens. Parallel to the river the Sempione railway stretched, which, without any train running on it, seemed slowly to lose its artificial aspect, to become part of the surrounding nature, with grass growing between the tracks. At the two sides of the valley the mountains surged almost on a straight line, high mountain walls, one atop the other, with a few trees, chestnuts, between the cracks here and there, and much farther up some firs, straight and black against the sky.

During his turn at guard duty, Pino, seated in the trench with his blue neckerchief around his neck, sometimes lifted his eyes from the book on pathological surgery that had been given him by Captain Beltrami to gaze at the sky ("Just look how that miserable so-and-so does guard duty!" Tide had shouted at him a couple of times, uselessly.) and fantasized. *I wonder if in Nomana they realize I'm here, talking part in this big adventure . . .* They could hardly have imagined he was on watch duty on the border of that piece of liberated Italy. "Watch duty", he repeated the phrase, which he had heard in some conversation or other, and he became ecstatic. "Watch duty." Poetry, even rhetoric, can do that at moments, even in spirits as unpoetical as his own.

Every few days Marco or Alberto the organizer, lately named second in command, would come to have a look at the line of defense. And a few miles behind, a second line was being readied, and still farther behind a third.

Rest periods were established by units; Tide's company—Pino and Sèp naturally included—could go back to Domodossola.

22

The enthusiasm of the first days of Domodossola had still not died down.

This time Pino decided to visit the college where his brothers had gone, even more decided when he learned that one of the science teachers formed part, as the commissioner for instruction, of the government council. He could not speak with the commissioner, but with others from the school, yes, among them a prefect—a cleric somewhat older than himself, with a face covered with pimples—who had been a schoolmate in Fortunato's class. "Your brother", the cleric declared, after the first conventional greetings, "without a doubt will become a real industrialist. Fortunato Riva! He's endowed with a business sense the likes of which I've never seen in anyone."

"That's true, but what deals could he manage while he was here at school?"

"Nothing here, naturally. That goes without saying. But I'm talking about his *forma mentis*, you understand? Want me to tell you something? When I talk about Milanese industrialists, I don't think, say, of Pirelli or Donegani, not at all. I think of your brother Fortunato."

"Yes", Pino agreed modestly. Then he went on to explain, "His business sense comes from our father's side."

"Manno Riva, on the other hand, was something else", the prefect continued somewhat pedantically. "And you, too, by the way you talk."

"Oh, certainly not me", Pino said. But this time he did not go on to say I'm not a great fellow. He had not said that since the time Captain Beltrami had handed him the medical manual and then said, "After you do your part, you won't have to worry about not being so great. Keep it in mind." He thought of Beltrami at that moment. *How you've helped me, poor Captain. How much good you've done me*, he thought in silent gratitude.

Pino spent a long while chatting with the prefect. Later he went back to see him again and even went out for a walk with him through the streets of Domodossola. "Whoever sees you with me", the cleric observed, alluding to his soutane, "will think they're right calling you a 'religious charity'."

"A religious charity? Oh, yes, I've heard that."

"The other partisans call you that out of envy, because you fellows with the blue neckerchiefs are the best and the real liberators of Ossola. But now even the people are beginning to call you that, because you're not embarrassed about being Christians, I think."

"Christians? If only we were! If you only knew what happened in . . ." (He was thinking of Piedimulera.) "Well, let's leave it at that." Pino changed the subject. "By the way, tell me something. What are the people thinking now, the people in general? I've heard they're forced to tighten their belts more now than under the Fascist rule."

"Yes, but they're not complaining. They all expect help from Switzerland, and, in fact, some has arrived, mainly potatoes. No matter what, better go hungry but free. Practically everyone I know thinks that way, everyone. The government commissars are the biggest trouble, for that matter . . ."

"True enough. Say . . . what exactly is happening? You must be well informed, with your professor in the government board . . ."

"Oh, if it depended on him . . ." The cleric shook his head. "He never criticizes anyone else on the board. We get nothing out of him. He, too, pulls a long face, though, when the others exaggerate."

"What others? All the others?"

"No, not all of them. Are you mad? We'd really be in great shape then. What happens is this. Some of the commissars are concerned about solving problems, especially that of food, and then transport—you know they're getting the Sempione line ready to receive Swiss help. They're also building an air field for the Americans to land . . ." He interrupted himself. "Who knows if the Americans will really land here."

"That's what we hope."

"Well, in short," the prefect continued, "some of the commissars go hard about their business, without sparing themselves. But others . . . it's like this. In general they're the ones who came later, the ones who've taken the place of the others already installed. Now they want to do what doesn't concern them, promulgating strange laws, but mainly fighting among themselves like murderers, and the end result is that they wind up driving everybody mad who's doing the work. They're not from here, they're all from outside, and they even seem to be people of some importance. I don't know . . . to tell the truth, I can't figure out what kind of people they are."

Actually they were intellectual utopians—not all of them commissars really—who thought they had the key for solving all the problems of the nation, indeed, all human problems. They had landed in Ossola (and they were still coming, like flies to honey) from Switzerland, where they had sought refuge during the armistice, as well as from Milan and Turin across the mountains. Some of them, with the support of comrades of their political creed on the board, had managed to replace some other more modest commissars already in office, and now they were preparing, all together—commissar or not—to replace the others. Meanwhile, during endless meetings together, especially at the Hotel Terminus, they discussed the renovation of culture and human nature and tried to issue decrees to further their ideas. The serious working commissars at first had regarded these utopians as a kind of joke, but now they were beginning to worry because the confusion was becoming bothersome.

"There's not time to have elections. That's the point. I'm telling you, when we can have elections, regular ones," the optimistic young prefect affirmed, "you'll see that these people won't have any followers. It will be the way to get rid of them."

"Yes, perhaps. But how strange, on the one hand there are those who quietly do their work, and on the other . . . well, it seems to me we should all try to pitch in and help the people working. All together, within the limits of our abilities, we should lend a hand. Me, for example, you know what I think? What would you think if I turned up at the hospital? If I offered to work gratis during my free time. Do you think they'd take me on?" Pino elaborated.

"If you don't charge, I'm sure they'll take you on", the prefect replied. He thought it over a bit. "Of course . . . after all, there is work in the hospital that I'd be able to do, too, especially now that they're converting one wing of the school into a hospital. To become a partisan, at the risk of killing someone, no, but hospital work . . . You know, that doesn't seem a bad idea to me."

"Then what should we do?" Pino asked. "I could talk to my commanding officer today."

Tide, however, did not grant permission. "We're returning to the line. Forget it. Besides, you wouldn't even have time to start."

And so the cleric with the pimply face went to the hospital by himself and was accepted and had no more time to waste with Pino.

A few days later, however, he met his friend by chance. He was going through the town with his company in formation, on the way to Ornavasso. The truck Pino was in had stopped at a crossing, and the cleric rushed up joyously. "I was accepted, in the hospital", he announced. "I've already begun working. You had a marvelous idea."

"Great!" Pino shouted from inside, approving. "I'm delighted."

"You know what I tell you?" the other shouted back. "You can see you're Fortunato's brother. You're an organizer, too. These Milan industrialists!"

Pino, since the motor was running faster, could not hear the last words. "What did you say?" he shouted leaning out.

"I said those Milan industrialists!" the cleric screamed back, taking his leave happily, waving his hand as the truck—quite battered, with a blanket in front somehow to take the place of the missing windshield—moved off with the promising Milan industrialist on board, his friend Sèp, Second Lieutenant Tide, and the other partisans.

23

They once again started the days of waiting at the opening of the valley, in the trench dug out by the company. Their food supplies, and every so often some military supplies, came in by truck from Domodossola. Also an issue of the division's newspaper, the *Valtoce* (hardly more than a circular, but printed), whose editorial on this occasion discussed the name *religious charity* with which

Marco's unit had come to be designated. "If by 'religious charity' these gentlemen mean to refer to the morality of our command, or to the constant protection and interest we have always displayed toward the civilian population, then we wish to answer by saying that we are indeed proud of being a 'religious charity'."

The partisans of the squadrons, gathered for mess, commented on the piece, both amused and vexed. "They're now even publishing the fact that we're a 'religious charity' in the newspaper."

"If only the others were as good as we are at making the machine guns sing."

"It's the Communists who've started calling us that, but did you see, they've asked for one of our chaplains, and how well they look after him. Communists ... the very ones, who hear Mass like us every Sunday. Isn't it laughable?"

"It sure is."

"Well, at last we've taught them something."

Pino was pleased. Not so Sèp; their nickname—Pino knew this—bothered him greatly. "Come on. Don't look like that about such a little thing", he said.

"We ought to punch in the face of anyone who calls us that", Sèp replied angrily. "Then you'd see how they'd stop doing it." The blue neckerchief around his neck was as crumpled up as the neckerchiefs the peasants in Nomana wore around their necks.

"When you go back home nobody will know they called us a 'religious charity' here", Pino told him. But Sèp went on looking annoyed.

There were more serious problems, however. There were many signs that an enemy attack was imminent. Twice a German reconnaissance plane flew slowly over the three defensive lines at the opening of the valley. Written or oral information (generally conveyed by women or post boys) about the growing regrouping of troops was continually arriving from the neighboring occupied zone. The commanding officers Marco and Superti consequently arrayed their ready combat forces on the first of the three lines, which, at the decisive moment, turned out to be inexplicably few: hardly two hundred men with blue neckerchiefs to the right of Toce River and another so many of the green neckerchiefs on the left side. The other partisans, of various colors and ideological stances—regrouped into three formations—were defending the shores of the lake, most particularly the second narrow entrance into the Ossola Valley, through the Cannobina Valley. Along this position Marco, who had scant faith in these allies, placed another one hundred blues as reserve forces. As a "mass for maneuvers" only the company under his own command remained, which he had kept together with him in Domodossola. There were not even one hundred men, but they were the best available to him.

On the dawn of the eleventh of October, the Fascists, supported by some German units, made their advance: a month had gone by since they had taken flight, and they attacked simultaneously in the Toce Valley and in the Cannobina Valley.

610

An unexpected firing from mortars warned Pino and the others that the ball was beginning. The partisans, crouching in the first trench and in the odd redoubt, returned with machine-gun fire. The enemy also began to fire with automatic weapons. Strangely enough, out in front, they did not give the impression of being anything but a patrol. There were, from one and another side, some long showers of machine gunning, which are like voices of the dead. Pino, on his knees in the trench, was firing his rifle absolutely at random into the green, wasting one bullet after another. At his side Sèp was shooting with an even greater intensity. "Enough of that!" an older partisan shouted at them. "Do you want to waste all the ammo for nothing?"

Pino and Sèp, mortified, left off shooting. The other blues also moderated their firing almost at the same time. A pity Second Lieutenant Tide wasn't here! He had gone off at the first glimmerings of light when a truck had become available to go back to Domodossola for more supplies. In his absence, some of the boldest partisans—after a certain period of not-too-intense firing—decided to leave the trench and get closer to the enemy to have a look at them, as they put it. The result was that the others, to avoid hitting them, stopped almost all their firing.

However, the fire from the enemies seemed to increase, but without getting very heavy. Then in the air—something completely new—little clouds of red smoke were opening with hard bursts. "The German 88s." "It's the German artillery firing 'on time'." Some of the new arrivals, quite shaken, threw themselves down to the bottom of the trench, and when the enemy shots burst in the air vertically over the trench, they plastered themselves down against the ground as if they wanted to bury themselves. "What are you doing? Deep-sea divers?" one of the old timers yelled.

"That's a good one," another commented, "divers."

The joke was liked, repeated, but the deep-sea divers had turned a deaf ear. Suddenly one, two, three of them left the trench and ran to the rear, and others imitated them. To be stockstill in the trench in the middle of all that confusion did not appeal to them at all. Ideas were beginning to run rampant in their heads. The movement to the rear was against all rules, just as the advance had been. Overcome with anger by so much disorder and cowardice, some of the tougher soldiers left the trench and moved forward as a demonstration. Those remaining in the trench felt useless and one after another began to get out, some going forward and others going to the rear. *Besides*, these last thought, proceeding with their weapons and knapsacks on their backs, *there are two other lines that can offer resistance.*

After reaching the town of Ornavasso (doors and windows barred, the civilians all shut up in their stone-roofed houses), they ran into Second Lieutenant Tide, who was just arriving back, and he laid into them like a wild beast. "Miserable wretches, animals! Why are you retreating? Who gave you orders? So you're supposed to be fighters?" They stopped in their tracks, frightened.

"Come on, right about turn, everyone back to the trench with me!"

They all turned around and went back, mortified, to the line. There, in a short while, one of those who had gone forward, rather than to the rear, returned. "The Fascists are at the station house", he announced breathlessly. "We got them out of there at first with hand grenades, but then they came back with more men and took it over again. We need reinforcements."

"I'll give you reinforcements!" Tide yelled. "I'll give you a kick in the pants, that's what I'll give you. Who ordered you out of the trench? How can we shoot from here if you're out there in front of us?"

The partisan—a lively, brave boy—looked contrite. "Come on!" Tide shouted. "Go back and tell the others to get back to the trench and make it fast. Fast, you understand? All of them. It's an order!"

The boy obeyed. The other reckless ones returned, swearing about the cowardice of the command (which was actually reduced to Tide himself), and the line was reestablished.

It was reestablished in this sector but not in those on the sides, neither the one more to the right, at the foothills of the mountain, nor to the left at the riverbank, where similar disorder had taken place. More to the left, beyond the river, the machine guns of the greens belonging to Superti could be heard, firing one blast after another. Who could tell what was happening over there? There were no lines.

In the face of such a confused retreat of the lateral positions, the man in charge of the blue formation in the Toce zone, a captain, ordered no one to retreat beyond Ornavasso and, as a warning, ordered the men from his squadrons to open fire in the direction of those who did not stop at the town. It meant that all the stray men stopped and threw themselves onto the ground, which, in fact, constituted an exposed line, on the fields at both sides of the town. Conscious of the fact that at the least attack this line would go to pieces, the captain, after thinking the situation over, and without consulting Tide or any other officer, ordered these men to be released and to confront the enemy whatever way they wished. "It's the only way partisans know how to fight. It's useless with men like these to try to carry out field combat. Better a disorganized struggle, with surprise attacks, skirmishes, than no struggle at all."

His decision showed him a realist. Thanks to a series of small individual attacks, many tiny and isolated combats broke out, which, practically speaking, turned out to stop the enemy, at least for the time being.

24

In the blue command at Domodossola the news from the front at Toce—which Marco received by motorized messengers that ran the course almost continuously between the front and the city—was the least of the worries. It was already clear that the enemy's main attack was in the Cannobina Valley, where the partisans of several colors had been routed after a brief advance. Several hours after the beginning of the offensive, the Fascists and the Germans going partway up the valley came into contact with the partisan second line, defended by Marco's men. Thanks mainly to the favorable terrain, they were stopped for the moment. However, it was clear they could not be stopped for long.

The members of the local government came continually to headquarters for news, and they appeared to be worried. The utopians among them seemed, more than worried, offended and impatient, because their pretty game was coming to an end. And what then? And all because of vulgar, practical reasons. Incredible! They were inwardly indignant that these inept units proved to be incapable of stopping a few battalions of Nazi-Fascists. And they, the utopians, had so often shown—often in the Hotel Terminus, with absolutely irrefutable arguments—that the Fascists and the Nazis were not worth anything, even from the military point of view.

Summoned by the other civilian leaders—the serious ones—Marco did not oppose organizing railway convoys to transfer anyone fearing reprisals to Switzerland. But he repeatedly warned that the partisans—his at least—would resist and would not flee to the mountains. Meanwhile, the depressing rumble of the cannon began to reach the city, and people went about the streets discouraged. Before night that rumble started—from the east—to become appreciably stronger, and then civilian refugees began to arrive, and the news spread like wildfire. The enemy had got up all of the Cannobina Valley and was looking over the Vigezzo Valley. Only a few squadrons of blues were fighting back. In the Domodossola railway station a first convoy was formed, with the same carriages that a few days before had transported hundreds of hungry children from Ossola to Switzerland. People rushed in from all sides loaded with suitcases, packages, knapsacks, bags. There were thousands of people, all those who had worked for the partisans or were in some way involved with them. Even those who were not involved and intended to stay were dismayed, sincerely pained by how things were going.

On the night of that first day Marco visited the Toce front, which was now on the second line of defense, and talked with his officers. He was told that he was making the same mistake as Captain Beltrami, that the partisans were not up to field battle. He laid out his reasons with passion and authority: we must show that spirit and courage belong not to the Fascists but to ourselves. If they give proof of knowing how to fight a war that is hopeless, the more reason for us to be obliged to know how to fight. Every Italian has his eyes on us, and it is our duty to give them back their faith in themselves, to awaken them. And we must also fight for the mountain people of Ossola, who have to realize they have not been mistaken in placing their faith in us, that we are not clowns, but men whom they can trust, which is just as they regard us. Who loses his life here will not have done it in vain. It will have been well spent.

That said, the other partisan commanders—Tide included, Tide, the enemy of all rhetoric—felt deeply determined to resist, to try the impossible after Marco's words. Despite his youth, Marco showed himself to be a true leader.

He left quickly, informing them that during the night, with his company from headquarters, he would reach the Vigezzo Valley, where the defense line would be reestablished at Finero. The men from his company—he reminded them—were mostly Alpine troops, and no matter how short in numbers they were, no one, not even the fearful marines from Decima Mas, would find it easy to break their line in the mountains. "Here on the plains the enemy is using a lesser force. At least while we hold on, you'll also be expected to hold on. That is your duty, and these are my instructions and orders."

Back in Domodossola he conferred for the last time in the town hall with the commissars from the government board, with those—it goes without saying—who had always worked and who now were also actively preparing to make a smooth job of transporting the civilians at risk. He then went back to his headquarters, where, next to the chaplain and the other officers who would leave with him in the course of the night, he slept a couple of hours on blankets spread out on the floor.

25

The following day the partisans of the Toce defended their second line in the same disordered fashion in which they had defended the first line. Tide went on complaining, "The lack of training. Here's what comes of not training enough! This is no battle, it's a brothel . . ." In any event the front was maintained, thanks to the improvised and brave surprise attacks, which fortunately rebuffed enemy infiltrations. The Fascists in front of them out there, however, were clearly gaining in confidence, certain of breaking through the partisan front.

In the Vigezzo Valley the command company had reestablished a front, to such an extent that the board in Domodossola had the following proclamation put up on the walls:

The Provisional Government Board
Citizens:
There is no cause for alarm. Panic broke out yesterday as a result of inexact news. The partisan forces are fighting, resisting, and holding their own on all sides. Remain calm, resume your work. Remain calm and confident as always.
Domodossola 12 October 1944

Alberto, the next in command of the blue formation, which was now located permanently in Marco's office, was however worried, almost desperate. He had received news that Marco, who had taken off by car beyond the new line to study a change of position farther from the front, had not returned. Meanwhile the enemy had made more advances. By nighttime Commander Marco still had not returned, and it was necessary to consider him missing.

The next day, the third day of the battle, the events on the Toce front were about the same as those of the two previous days. The enemy was advancing inexorably along another stretch of the way, while the partisans were beginning to run out of ammunition. The three lines of defense had been abandoned, the third at great speed, under fire of an Italian SS patrol, which had managed to get through the impervious mountain. The squadrons sent to stop them with the usual system of surprise attacks had all scattered, and it was almost only the commanders who had gone down into the valley.

During the night Alberto ordered a column consisting of a few trucks to the line and ordered a retreat in groups of all the Toce troops, blues as well as greens, toward Domodossola.

Railway convoys were now leaving continuously from the city for Switzerland. They unloaded the refugees at the first station on the other side of the Sempione tunnel and returned to take on more. Entire families were going now, those whose sons had joined up with the partisans. The departures went smoothly, since Alberto's headquarters and the government board continued to work. It could even be said that it had never worked better because the utopians—whether members of the government or not—were no longer in the way. They were all in Switzerland, woefully explaining to whoever would listen the how and why of the failure and especially what should have been done not to fail.

Pino and Sèp retraced the Domodossola highway in the same battered truck that had brought them to the line. It had been raining since morning, and the blanket that replaced the wind screen did not prevent the driver and Tide, who were seated in the cabin, from getting drenched, the same as the others, squeezed together in the open area of the back. Seeing his own commanding officer in such a state, Pino with a touch of impropriety thought, *Look at him. He's been reduced to Saint Quentin at the battle of Rocroi!* and he shook his head. On the national highway the motorized column continually passed by groups of civilian refugees, men and women, and alternating or mixed with them were partisans of every color, coming from the shore of the lake. They were all going on foot toward the town, to the railway station. The partisan trucks allowed them on the running boards and fenders, as many as could fit. *It's a miracle they don't break the springs*, Pino was thinking, his medical kit still slung over his shoulders. He had used it many times in the course of combat, and he was beginning to have a bit of faith in himself as a medic. At his side Sèp was chatting with three red partisans who had climbed into the truck with the blues. They were busy explaining their case. "They have been freer than we have to do whatever seemed best to them", he would tell Pino from time to time. "Their officers didn't bore them to tears like Tide."

"Great, but after all, what did they do?" Pino at last responded, annoyed. "Everybody knows who did the real fighting."

"That's because you people of the 'religious charity' were better armed than we were", one of the red, stung to the quick, hammered back. "More of you and better armed. There's no comparison. You even had an armored train in Domodossola."

"A train, yes, sure, but ammo?" Pino was tempted to counter back, but snorted scornfully instead. Better not to wind them up. What for?

"And besides, they had a freer hand against the Fascists and traitors", Sèp insisted. "Not like us. We couldn't touch anyone."

"Listen, Sèp, let it go already", Pino said.

While the trucks continued on in the thickening darkness, in the light of their screened headlights they could see the wet tree trunks at the sides of the road and an occasional patch of country wall beaten down by the rain. Exactly as it had been when Pino went along this same road in February, during his first partisan raid, the night when Beltrami and Antonio Di Dio had tried in vain to get the lawyer Ferraris released. How many things had changed since then. Beltrami and Antonio had died, nothing had been heard about Ferraris, and the "caramba" who had enlisted with the partisans in Domodossola, and then in Megolo, had operated the machine gun, and he was not in the units any more. What could have happened to him? Already far-off events . . . the situation was totally different then . . . yes, but what would it be now? Pino was also thinking of the injured he had treated in those days: six or seven (dead and wounded had been few, luckily, and an ambulance had taken all of them from the front to the hospital in Domodossola). What would their fate be? Would the command take steps—if they had not done so already—to move them to Switzerland? Yes, he had to trust Alberto, in his ability to organize things. If Marco was cut from the same cloth as Manno and Michele Tintori, Alberto was made of the same stuff as his brothers, Ambrogio and Fortunato, even more capable than they were at organizing things. Ambrogio, Fortunato, home . . . heaven knew what they were thinking now in Nomana if they were aware of this disaster.

While he turned these things over, the trucks reached the first houses in Domodossola. They stopped at the entrance of the road from Sempione, in front of a portico.

Waiting for them there was a second lieutenant of headquarters, who came forward in the scant light of the headlamps sifted with threads of rain. He was wearing a ski cap on his head, in the style of Captain Beltrami. "Orders from Alberto: all of you wait here, our units in formation. Buses and trucks will be arriving soon, which will be taking you . . . taking you to your new destination."

The blues got off the trucks—which immediately returned to the Toce zone—and regrouped under the portico. The others with them, dispersed civilians and partisans, went toward the station or the city center, under the rain.

26

The blues who lived in Domodossola asked permission to go to their homes to say goodbye to their families and to pick up a few changes of linen. After some hesitation, the commanders gave them a half hour. "Tell your parents", Tide unexpectedly notified them in a loud voice, "the war isn't over yet, and those who are shouting victory now will not be the victors. Tell them that he who laughs last laughs best."

After this phrase the officer with the cap, who to get a little light after the trucks had left had lit a flashlight, now switched it off. "I have no batteries left after this", he explained. Everybody once again sank into the dark and cold; they were all drenched to their bones, their heads lowered, meditating on the misery of war, this war that seemed never to come to an end, never, never.

And yet with the Allies in Rimini, Pino was thinking. (They had reached the plains in the Po Valley.) *But is it possible with their armored masses they're not in a position to spread themselves far and wide through the plains? They disembarked in France hardly four months ago, in June, and yet France is totally occupied. And what are they waiting for in Italy? And the Germans themselves, after all, with the Allies already at the Rhine, and the Russians on Germany's eastern front, why do they keep letting themselves get killed for no reason? Is there some logic in all this?* The usual thoughts during those days, the persistent whys, but the reality, meanwhile, was what he and his soaked comrades were living through: death, setbacks, weariness, and disconsolate hearts.

He turned, looking for Sèp to say a few words, but Sèp was not at his side. He called him a few times in vain. Then Commander Tide called him in a loud voice, but there was no answer. They realized that Sèp was not under the portico. Where had he gone? With whom?

"Perhaps with Albino, or Morandi, or with some of the others who have gone home", one of them ventured. "If that's the case, he'll be back soon."

Pino, however, was not convinced. "The reds . . . those partisans . . . you want to bet that bastard, that stupid ass went off with them?"

And, as it happened, Albino and Morandi and the others who had gone to take leave of their families returned one after the other, but Sèp was not among them.

The expected column of vehicles came from the west for their second transfer. There were even some buses among the vehicles, but Pino and his squadron once again had to board an open truck. The rain was still falling, and once again they were drenched. Luckily the column left immediately. First they went along the Sempione train tracks, on which the partisans saw a convoy go by with their windows partly unscreened, overloaded with people going to Switzerland. "How many, in all, from Ossola would be crossing over the border?" one of them asked. (No one was equipped to answer that question then. It turned out to be more than twelve thousand.)

"What's important is that at a moment like this, Alberto and the board continue with their job", one of the others observed. The statement was of real comfort to them.

After a while, at a crossroads, the vehicles went toward the north. Anyone knowing the area realized then they were going to the Formazza Valley, that is, the most northerly angle of the great Ossola triangle.

At Crodo, about ten miles from Domodossola, the column was stopped by an officer of the command who was waving a flashlight horizontally in the middle of the road in front of a large restaurant. "Everyone off! We're going to eat. Everyone off!" he shouted almost exultantly. This was a great surprise. The restaurant had been requisitioned by the partisan commissariat, which had prepared a mess. No one could believe it. "You have to admit as far as organization goes, Alberto is like our Lord himself", Tide murmured.

The mess—served on small restaurant tables with civilian-style tablecloths and napkins (which intimidated some of the poorer fellows a bit, who had never been in a restaurant in their lives)—was plentiful, and also quite plentiful was the distribution of wine. When they went back on board the truck, the men were slightly drunk. One of them, a young worker from Busto Arsizio, sat next to Pino in the place that had been occupied by Sèp. "And now?" he asked him in a loud voice in dialect. "Are you feeling low because your friend took off?"

Pino shook his flattish head, his hair straight up. "I think he went with those three reds. Did you see them?"

"Those chicken thieves? Of course I saw them. So?" the other said, almost screaming. "Do you mean he's a chicken thief, too? So?" Then he started to laugh loudly and, after opening his mouth a couple of times as if to test it, started to sing:

> I remember the good old days
> when I went thieving for chickens and hens,
> chickens and hens, chickens and hens,
> for my old grandmaman . . .

"For whom?" Pino asked, not having understood the last word.

"For Grandmaman", the other answered and started to sing again.

No one, however—no matter how much wine taken—felt like joining in on the chorus, under the rain that kept falling.

The worker interrupted his song. "Why aren't you singing?" he asked Pino. "Are you that crazy?"

"Crazy nothing. It's the wine", he replied. "I'm not used to it, and ..." In fact, his head was spinning, and he was beginning to feel sick.

"Listen to him!" the other one shouted. "Listen to him. Wine doesn't agree with him. But isn't wine a medicine? Is it true or isn't it, patriots, that wine's a medicine?"

"Of course!" one of them agreed.

"Come on, can it", someone else chimed in.

"No", the drunken worker insisted. "I won't because it's true. Wine is a medicine." He went back to pestering Pino. "Say so. You're halfway to being a doctor."

Pino did not answer.

"Well? Is it true or not?"

"Leave me in peace", Pino said.

"A peach? What do you want with a peach? Didn't you get enough to eat in the restaurant?" and he began to laugh at his own pun. Then, quite satisfied with himself, he slapped Pino's knee and started to laugh again, as if inviting him to join in the fun.

At last, with the effect of the nonstop rain dripping down the back of his neck, he too fell silent and put his head between his shoulders like the others.

27

The party was not over yet. The next day the blues took their positions as planned, blocking the Formazza Valley, to which they had been transported. The walls rose with indentations and jutting projections, covered with forests and surging to the sky. Their mission was to hold out for as long as it was necessary for the government board to clear out and get the wounded of Domodossola as well as the many civilians in flight.

The Fascists (who had entered the town a little before dawn while Commander Alberto was escaping with the last of his men) arrived almost immediately and attacked, forcing the new front to retreat; but they met up with them again a little farther up, and then again, even farther up.

The last encounter took place at the end of a few days, in the highest part of the valley, where the partisans had established themselves over a craggy, steep slope along the road, which at this height was continually cut through with rock trenches and the land all around already covered with snow.

The position had much to recommend itself as far as a defensive emplacement was concerned, but the attackers—in this case the parachutists from Folgore, soldiers no less formidable than the Germans themselves—did not seem overly worried. They were advancing their own way, rather carelessly, practically out of formation. They were thinking it would not be too hard to beat back the partisan recruits once again. But they were wrong about one thing. Not all the partisans were recruits; among them were still a certain number of Alpine troops, the last. And they, from their positions seeing the parachutists coming up so arrogantly, felt deeply outraged in their old esprit de corps. They exchanged a few looks and briefly talked things over, and then one of them went over to Commander Alberto. He laid out their plan in a few words, which was accepted by the commander. In conclusion, after having let the enemy vanguard advance, the partisans' automatic weapons and mortars opened fire suddenly on the terrain at their backs, preventing their retreat. Then the Alpine troops came out from their positions and with their usual expertise took over some deep hollows in the rock and moved to the right and to the left of the vanguard without their being aware of it.

Without going into detail about their performance, we shall only say that after a while they returned to their positions pushing twenty-four prisoners in front of them, including an auxiliary, a pretty blond girl. So as not to hit their own people, the enemy meanwhile had suspended their fire.

Pino was at the spot where the group entered back into the lines with the prisoners. The road here was cut through the rock, leaving a long crest several yards high toward the valley. Within that tunnel-type gorge the partisan command was situated, together with the two mortars and the first aid station. The parachutists were lined up by the Alpine troops—almost all of them wearing their hats turned back to front roguishly—against the wall within the long crest. It was evident they were not in fear of being executed, as one of the Alpine troops started to search them. Outside, enemy fire meanwhile had started again with great intensity.

One of the parachutists who was having a hard time staying on his feet leaned back against the rock wall and slowly slid to the ground, his gray-green beret twisted behind the nape of his neck like a halo put on crooked. His comrades looked at him, looked at the partisans, uncertain whether to help him or not. Seeing him, Pino went over rapidly with his medical kit over his shoulder, knelt, put his kit on the ground, and began to open the wounded man's jacket, stained with blood, in a markedly professional manner. He would not have confessed it to anyone, not even to himself, but what most counted for him in such a tragic moment was that of cutting a good figure—the figure of a competent doctor—in the eyes of the pretty girl prisoner.

Alberto said something to Tide, who went forward, and standing in front of the parachutists asked if they had taken part on the twelfth (the day of Marco's death) in the battles in the Cannobina Valley. An older noncommissioned officer, with strong manly features, answered for all of them. They had entered Ossola through the Cannobina Valley, he said, but had not participated in any of the combat.

Tide and Alberto exchanged glances, and then Tide went on to ask some questions about the consistency of the Fascist detachments in the valley. The noncommissioned officer answered that those detachments were not Fascists but

Italians, and as for their consistency, it was not the style of the parachutists—he made it clear—to give information that could damage their comrades. He spoke without haughtiness, but with courage. From his manner of expressing himself it could be surmised that, although uneducated, he was a brave man.

His behavior exasperated a partisan student attached to the mortar unit, who interrupted bitterly. "How dare you call yourselves Italians, you Fascist scum!" he exploded. "You're no more than German slaves, that's what you are! The people are against you, you know that perfectly well, so much so that to stay in power, you have to execute and massacre and deport."

"We are not slaves to the Germans," the parachutist answered, "and neither I nor many of these people", he indicated the others with him, "are even Fascists. Italy went into war with the Germans. We are merely continuing to battle alongside them, even if the war is lost now."

"Ah, so you know, too, the war is lost?" the student screamed rancorously, without bothering to take into account Tide's signs to stop.

"Of course", the parachutist answered. "We're not blind." He stopped. "But that does not seem good reason for going over to the victors to join their service."

"We're not in the service of anyone!" the student yelled. "We're the only truly free Italians, we, and we are here fighting for Italy's freedom."

"Stop it now", Second Lieutenant Tide told him. But then he added, "What he has said is so true", he observed to the parachutist, believing to end the dispute with that, "that the majority of the Folgore, at the time of the armistice, chose to remain with the king. Those parachutists are now on the front against the Germans and against you. You know that perfectly well."

"Yes," the man answered, "we know that. I also took part in the discussions in Sardinia the day after the armistice. Unfortunately, they decided to respect the oath made by the king, even though the king did not respect his own oaths."

Tide considered it inopportune to continue the debate.

"Then the honor is not all on your side", the student burst out again. "To keep his oath is a soldier's first duty. Otherwise he becomes a bandit. That I know even if I haven't fought at El Alamein, as perhaps you have."

"No perhaps about it", the blond auxiliary said calmly at that moment. "He did fight in El Alamein."

"And so what?" another partisan interjected. "You think perhaps we haven't fought? One of us . . . that one, for example, was in Nicolaievca. Just listen to that dame!"

"Enough of this", Tide cut him short. "All this talk is beside the point." He addressed the noncommissioned officer again. (Outside the fire between Italians and Italians continued furiously.) "You refuse to give us information on the forces we are facing. That is all." He added, "I warn you that your fate will depend on the fate of ours who have been taken. If ours are executed, so will you be." He looked once more at Alberto, who shrugged his shoulders. "Well, there's nothing else to say."

He turned to the Alpine man who had carried out the prisoners' search. He showed him two hand grenades and a gold ring. "This is all I've found on them", he said.

Tide took the ring. "Who did you take this off of?"

The Alpine pointed at the auxiliary. "It's hers."

The officer went up to the girl. "Take your ring", he said, giving it to her.

"Keep it as a souvenir", the girl answered. "We'll end up executed, even if you're now pretending to treat our injured. Every time you see that ring, you'll remember you executed me."

"Take your ring."

"Keep it as a souvenir."

Tide put the ring in a pocket of the girl's jacket. "We're not like you", he exclaimed. "No, we . . ." He was about to say we don't execute women, but he remembered that other auxiliary suddenly shot dead with a bullet in her head in Piedimulera. *Heavens, poor Italy! What a pass we've all come to, what a pass!* he thought.

The girl looked at him, exalted, with an air of defiance.

"Could you tell me why you've come here to make war, to risk your neck stupidly?" the officer could not keep from asking. "Who forced you?"

"It's noble to fight for a lost cause", the girl replied. "That's why I'm here."

How fanatic can you get? Tide thought. And yet she was young, so pretty, with a perfect face, blond curls!

"So instead of coming here you could have stayed home knitting . . .", the officer murmured.

Then he went back. The interrogation was over.

But they had almost finished the mortar ammunition and also that of the machine guns. That line could not be held either.

28

The narrow road going up to the San Giacomo Pass and to Switzerland was covered with snow and partially blocked with avalanches. The last partisan and Fascist wounded had to be expatriated on sledges. The few heavy arms had been buried. Several partisans, among whom was Second Lieutenant Tide, had set off marching during the night to get back toward the area of their first actions over Megolo, crossing through the mountains, a long march, so as to have a nucleus of the blues in Ossola, on which future formations could be rebuilt.

Pino and the others walked toward the border single file. Although it was over a mile, the air was not raw. There was a vast silence. The valley walls were moderately high now. Pino was no longer thinking of the pretty girl. He was thinking of Commander Marco, who was dead. The news was verified. Alberto had brought it when he had rejoined his men. Marco had bled to death (*Also like Beltrami!*) in a no man's land. The preceding day, Sunday, many of the partisans had left their positions next to a little village for a half hour and stood in front of the church to hear the Mass. They did it on their own initiative. No one told them to, because they remembered the importance Marco ascribed to the Mass. It was a way of honoring his memory. What a difference, however, from the solemn Mass of a month ago in Domodossola, at the height of their success!

Pino sighed. God knows how useful a man like Marco would have been for Italy after the war. Instead he was dead!

From time to time the thought of Sèp, who had deserted, came to mind. Where would he be now, and what foolish thing would that imbecile be up to? And if he had ended up in the hands of the Fascists? If, in the end, he had been killed? How would he, Pino, dare to answer Sèp's parents' anxious questions when he returned home? *They'll never forgive me as long as they live for having taken him away from Nomana. Really and truly, if it hadn't been for me, he'd never have left the town.*

Once again he sighed and shook his flat head no, no, no, no . . . Sèp should not have deserted the way he did. "He should not have done it", Pino murmured.

"Who are you talking about?" the partisan walking behind him asked. "Who shouldn't have done what?"

"Nothing. I was thinking to myself", Pino said softly, without explaining. The other fellow did not insist.

A little farther back the young worker from Busto Arsizio was walking, excited about going to a foreign country. (During a break he had taken from his knapsack a new blue neckerchief and was putting it around his neck instead of the old worn-out one. "Just to go into Switzerland looking less like a vagabond", he explained.) "I'll tell you what Pino's thinking about", he proclaimed loudly. "He's still thinking about his friend Sèp, who went off with the chicken thieves. Right or wrong, Pino? Tell the truth."

"Drop it", Pino said.

"Yes, drop it", the other partisan said.

The worker, on the other hand, began to sing:

> I remember the good old days
> when I went thieving for chickens and hens,
> chickens and hens, chickens and hens,
> for my old grandmaman . . .

Three or four of them in a row laughed, and Pino, too, shaking his head, smiled.

"Don't you worry", the worker told him. "Your friend will come back to your town with a new job. You'll see. He'll be a professional chicken thief."

He joked a bit more and then at last stopped.

The slow march continued on in silence. It was a sad day for them, the end of the Ossola saga, which, for all its limitations, would remain the most famous of the partisan undertakings in Italy. Not the most important: as far as objective usefulness was concerned, it was surpassed greatly by that other one—far less known even today—in which the Alpine "greens" from the Osoppo brigades, which for a long time back had been bloodily involved in the Goriziano—the Yugoslavian border—with three different enemies: the Nazis, Tito's Yugoslavians, and, from time to time, the local Italian Communist partisans, who were militarily dependent on the Tito forces. At the end of the war, the irregular line maintained by the "greens" from the Osoppo brigades would constitute Italy's eastern border.

PART SIX

I

The day Pino became an expatriate was a very busy day for Praga in Milan: the civil war had spread to the cities, too. But the romantic side, which in some way existed in the mountains, was lacking in the cities. In the city it came down to a series of savage assassinations and counterassassinations. On the one hand there were ambushes of Fascists and Germans, or their collaborators or their presumed collaborators, who were often shot dead on the streets. These assassinations were answered, especially by the Germans, with executions, no less atrocious, of prisoners and hostages. That was exactly what the authors of the ambushes wished to achieve, that the German and Fascist killers should become more and more hateful to the population. The torture inflicted by the "special police"—which the more responsible Fascists, it must be said, and the minister of justice from Salo in particular did not want—became part and parcel of this vicious context, and they were a further justification of the partisans' behavior.

Praga's section was still billeted in the silent building in the center of the city and kept its autonomy after a failed attempt to become part of Koch's tragically famous special police. The latter—even if not numerous—had ended up in Milan after fleeing from Rome and were occupying a villa in Paolo Uccello Street, in the then-outlying neighborhood of San Siro. The attempts to unite the two groups came to no positive outcome because of a sudden reaction from the Cardinal of Milan, who, as news of torture spread, drove the authorities mad with his protests. He defined it in his letters as "such horrors that will degrade our entire century", and he threatened to hurl excommunications from the pulpit, to such a point—incredible for Praga—that during the second half of September, at the orders of the prefect of Milan, the ordinary police surrounded the "sad villa" on Paolo Uccello Street, and Koch and the components of his gang, fifty-three people in all, were arrested. The formation located in the center, in contrast, considered of less importance and almost unknown, was not touched.

During the conversations that took place to unite the two outfits, Praga had the opportunity to visit Koch's secret places and to sit in on the tortures they practiced there (four of the interrogators who did the beating were called the "four saints"), and he was surprised at the coarseness of the performance and lack of professionalism. In the "sad villa" they whipped, yes, they broke bones, of course, and that was enough for any number of prisoners to confess. But these orgies of beating and whipping carried out by men who were drugged, often in a fury of screams, highly excited by the sight of blood, had nothing in common with Praga's real and proper torture. What a difference between these and those of the German Gestapo! How abysmal!

On the basis of his already numerous experiences, he was accustomed now, in contrast to their torturers, to affirm—and he had discussed it academically with one of the "four saints"—that no prisoner can resist more than a certain amount of well-applied torture. The problem was knowing how to measure it out. "For some, to make them sing, it's not necessary to touch them because it's enough for them to see the irons. Others, on the other hand, resist the treatment in an incredible fashion. In this we are in agreement. But they resist until death only if you are stupid enough to give them death. This is the question: you have to know how to stop in time, and then begin again at just the right moment (I mean neither too early nor too late), stopping in time as often as necessary. You'll find out", Praga argued professionally. "One can hold out a long time, but suddenly no more. This", he concluded, "is as clear as water." (Basically his discovery was not that great. Soldiers, too, who have confronted death a sufficient number of times end up no longer being able to hold out. At one determined moment even the strongest spiritually do not manage to hold out even one more time—they can stand no more.) No matter what, this discovery, in some sense theoretical, contributed to Praga's fame in the inner sanctum of his section. That fame, even though debatable (some held that he talked that way only to be able to go on torturing his prisoners even when there was no longer any necessity to do so), however, meant that now, more and more frequently, the difficult cases became his charges. It must be said that his personal efforts had not diminished with time. Quite the contrary. After days of a forced standstill—real suffering for him—following the closing of the "sad villa" he shortly afterward had of his own initiative prolonged his own work schedule to such a point that now he could scarcely carry it out. Nevertheless, if it had been possible he would have prolonged it still more, because the war was in its last stages, and soon he would be banned from the unspeakable pleasure of undoing the enemy (which was to say, a man, since all men were enemies of his, just as they were of that strange entity that dwelled in the depths of his being).

The day the Ossola battle was over, Praga had "worked" uninterruptedly on ordinary cases. At the end of the day—literally exhausted—when he was at the point of going off, he was brought, without having been notified beforehand, a prisoner who really was not ordinary: a Communist partisan suspected of having tortured who knows how many Fascists, or presumed Fascists, and with such barbarity he had made them "sing". He was a man with a high forehead, dry temples pulled tight, from whom—as the guards pointed out—nothing could be obtained after two days in jail using normal interrogations.

Despite his weariness, Praga studied him and was extraordinarily impressed: a murderer like this in the partisan torture chambers must have counted for at least all "four saints" together. The other fellow immediately realized that his new examiner was not just a nobody, and even though he was the prisoner there, he was trying to study him, too. They had mutually sniffed one another out, like two dogs before showing their fangs. (We use this comparison, even if improperly, because dogs, hyenas, or other fierce beasts never do the evil things that men do.) At the end of the examination, Praga decided to devote the night to him.

Now he was relaxing at the buffet waiting for his supper, a little drowsy. This prisoner must mean a great deal to the Communists. What success if he made him talk! And what a blow for the reds ... "because, they, the reds, are not a bunch of gutless fellows like our Fascist bureaucrats. They don't demand diplomas or titles to get up in the world. If someone's worth something, they promote him to whatever job." This fellow must really be quite important, without a doubt.

The buffet corridor—in the basement of the "special section"—was a squalid place, furnished with odd pieces of furniture. The chairs were mostly from offices; the counter, scratched up, came from a bombed-out shop. There were some terrace bar tables painted in bright colors and a few other things, among them an espresso coffee machine, the result of an arbitrary requisition. In a corner there were four big armchairs, wide and threadbare, next to a radio playing music at low volume. In one of the armchairs Praga had sat down. The others had been taken by two of his colleagues, also junior officers, dressed as he was in civilian clothes, and a third in uniform. The four of them were smoking, practically without speaking, letting their ashes fall from time to time into an inadequate ashtray with the words "Grand Hotel et de Milan" on it, placed on the floor in the middle of the armchairs.

"Still going on with that music", one of the four of them suddenly said, indicating the radio with his chin. He was small, no longer young, blondish, with a pale face and hands unusually pale, too.

"Why?" the person seated next to him to the right asked, a bear of a man with short, thick, hairy fingers, his face darkened by the hairs of his beard and with one earlobe missing. "Are you still obsessed with the latest news?"

"Why not?" the pale face replied. "With the outcome in Ossola—the weapons captured, the number of prisoners, and who knows what ... I've been waiting since yesterday for a special broadcast. They'd be idiots if there weren't one."

"You think so? So they'll bring those prisoners here to you?" Lopear asked sarcastically and, laughing in a sinister fashion, looked at Praga, as if awaiting approval.

However, Praga said nothing.

"Of course they won't be brought here!" the fourth person of the group exclaimed, without understanding the point of the joke at all. He was the one in uniform, an ordinary-looking individual, his hair plastered with brilliantine, and with a strong southern accent. "That's all we need! With all the work we already have ..." Of the four, the southerner was the only one without a sullen look about him. He had become part of the "special section" only a few days before, with the simple mission of taking custody of the prisoners. He winked jokingly, waiting for general approval.

But the others went on smoking in silence.

"Did I say something wrong, Chief?" the southerner asked doubtfully, addressing himself to the highest ranking among them, who was Praga.

The others looked out of the corner of their eyes at Praga, expecting one of his heavy-handed remarks or a blasphemy, but Assistant Chief Praga did not so much as move a muscle, as if he had heard nothing.

"So, you'd also like to decrease our work?" Lopear ironically remarked.

"Of course, why not?" the southerner answered. "Doesn't it seem we've too many people detained here inside, I mean, in relation to the few of us? Where I was before ..."

"You hear that? Too many detained!" Lopear joked. "This fellow, too, talks like that guy, that ministry inspector."

At these words Praga glared at him for an instant.

No, this sh—— is not trying to offend me, he decided, and turned his eyes away.

"I don't understand", the southerner murmured. "What ministry are you talking about?"

Lopear had not wanted to waste his breath with this idiot. "The Ministry of the Interior", he explained unwillingly. "A week ago an inspector, a damn fool, came here ..." Again Praga looked at Lopear, and the latter then remembered suddenly the mortification for Praga of that inspection and tried, almost in fear, to change the subject.

"Well, this is all beside the point. What don't you understand, you stupid cracker? If we had to put all these S.O.B.s in the hands of the ordinary police, it would be too easy for them, don't you think?"

"Too easy?"

"Ugh, what a chicken brain", Lopear snorted, angry.

"But ...", the southerner protested.

The other fellow clearly did not want to give him too much leeway. "Listen," he said, in order to put an end to the matter, "Assistant Chief Praga had proposed a plan to resolve the situation. But since our directors think with their ass instead of their head ... is that clear?" He concluded with a vulgar mouth gesture, a sign of spite for the department that had not understood the utility of that plan.

They were all silent.

"That certainly was a good plan", the paleface could not help commenting after a while.

"Do you realize? We would have been free to maneuver in our little spot like the Gestapo and the NKVD, and instead ..."

Again they were silent, and for some drawn-out seconds only the sound of music on the radio could be heard, the same meaningless music as always, the padding out of our age. It was absurd that such music should even be part and parcel of the atrocities that were occurring during those days.

Praga's plan, to which the two of them were referring, was centered on the proposal of transforming the lowest corridor of the "special section" into the elimination area. That corridor (already equipped with a big cargo elevator, which seemed to have been made precisely for carrying corpses away) was three floors below street level. From there the sound of gunshots could not be heard from without.

"Pardon me", the southerner went back foolishly to the subject in an attempt to clear up all those allusive and continually truncated phrases. "How did you pronounce . . . enek . . . what was it?"

The paleface looked at him for an instant in silence. "Ene-K-V-D", he spelled it out, as if talking to a child, "the Russian police."

"Ah!"

"This summer two Russian ex-agents, now working with the Gestapo, were here in Milan", the paleface went on. "And we," indicating Praga to be exact, "he and I had the opportunity to talk with them."

"And what did they tell you?"

"Well," the paleface said, "too long to explain. Just to get an idea that we're not talking lightly about the NKVD", he noted with a kind of sinister arrogance. "One of the two agents had worked in Katyn especially. Do I make myself clear?"

"Where?"

"Katyn."

"And what's that?"

"You don't even know what that is? The place where the Russian security services did away with the Polish officers taken prisoner. Was in the newspapers."

"Ay, yes, I do remember: all of them with . . . a shot at the back of the head."

"Exactly, very good: serious work. It was the very agent we talked with who led the Germans to the spot after, of course, they took him into the Gestapo. The other one in the Cheka, on the other hand, higher ranking . . . what rank did the other one have in the NKVD?" the paleface asked Praga.

He did not answer this time either.

"Before the war the other one did service in Butirca, which is the very best—according to him—of the Moscow prisons. A few years ago, in '37, for instance, they executed about a thousand prisoners a day there. You understand? They took the dead out from the subterranean area in truckloads, and sometimes the trucks couldn't even hold them all. And that was before the war had begun . . ."

Saying this, the paleface nodded to himself satisfied, as if he were enthralled by the vision. "Our agency, on the other hand, goes on rejecting people for 'special treatment' only because we lack space . . . and you, you southern jack-ass," he concluded, "you'd like to get rid of the few still left here."

"I only said that . . . jokingly", the southerner murmured. *What a mess*, he was thinking meanwhile. *What a mess, what a place I've landed in! I knew there was corruption, but to what an extent! And why did I ask to be transferred here? Only for that miserable bit of extra salary!* He began to rub one of his sleeves on which ash had fallen, nervously, almost as if he were cleaning it.

The paleface noticed his discomfort and smiled.

Once again there was silence, and only the sound of the banal music could be heard. Now Praga could not get the thought of the ministry inspector out of his head. The fact remained that the talk from these beasts had opened the wound again. The head of the special section, without accepting his plan, had responded to it with every sign of consideration, knowing who was there before him. The ministry inspector, however, who had got wind of the proposed plan by chance, had become furious and wanted to speak with him, the author of the project. Immediately, with his first words, he had begun to yell. "We're not barbarians! We're not like them!" he declared in an altered voice. (He was referring, the swine, not only to the Russians but to German comrades too.) "Don't you understand? These arbitrary actions have to stop, and torture has to be reduced to the indispensable minimum, nothing more. Because torture is not part of our Fascist style, is that clear?" That was what he had said, more or less. In short, he had been called a barbarian; he had been humiliated. It had been quite a while since Praga had been humiliated. The wound smarted . . . at that moment he would have liked to have wrung his neck. What stopped him was only the idea that if he had done so it would have meant forever renouncing what he was doing. He repeated it to himself once more: whatever humiliation, whatever affront, anything but renouncing . . . renouncing *that*. But if he had that bastard in his hands right now, he'd take him apart limb by limb . . . and not only him, but the head of the section, who left his projects around any old place, and . . . all of them, for that matter. Yes, to be able to destroy all of them, heaps of them, en masse, those filthy beasts who are always ready to get in your way: people. Every last one of them.

The conversation of the others (the southerner would now have liked to leave the group, but he did not dare) was becoming more and more desultory, with long pauses. Praga, at one particular moment, realized that the others were asking him a question, but he listened only vaguely, only enough to defend himself, if necessary, from them.

At last they, too, stopped talking, stopped "puking sh——t", as Praga put it. Now they only smoked one cigarette after another. From time to time the assistant chief looked at the paleface's deadly pale hands. Now, by some kind of strange association, the words of the ex-Chekista came to mind, those trucks loaded with dead bodies that came out of Butirca, the ones that could hardly carry the corpses, that enormous, modern work. *The Bolsheviks were serious people, like the Nazis. They weren't like these Fascist clowns, who allowed any flunky to abuse our security services; we, who have to suspend our work in consideration for the cardinals who . . . (an unrepeatable expression) their criticism from the pulpit. They had filled their cardinals' skulls with lead . . . yes, they were serious people, and that's why they were winning the war now.*

Suppertime came, and the radio still had not broadcast any special news.

2

After eating, Praga went into the room in which his new prisoner, tied tightly to a metallic chair, awaited him.

The light from a floodlight shone on the man's face ruthlessly, and though he shut his eyes as much as possible, it did little good. A guard was pacing back and forth in the little room, keeping well out of the path of that blinding light. Praga motioned with his chin for him to go. "He's hardly moved", the guard told him, and after a short salute he left, happy to do so.

The hangman picked up a stool and put it in front of his victim and, stretching his arm out professionally, turned the reflector lamp a little so that his face would be out of the light. The prisoner opened his momentarily blinded eyes at him.

"You're in my hands", the hangman informed him. "You're not stupid, and so you know there's no way out. Absolutely no way out."

The prisoner tried to take his unseeing eyes off him.

Blind him with a red-hot iron, Praga told himself. *Before killing him, remember to blind him.* But before all that he would have to get him to sing, and this was not going to be an easy job. *Someone like him could find a way of making me look an idiot, to die in my hands without having talked,* the hangman reflected with a touch of anxiety. With that prospect in mind, a wave of hatred for his victim began to form within him. *Watch it, try to control yourself,* he commanded himself.

At the same time the other fellow, despite the pain in his eyes and head, realized how things were going for him. (He had indeed tortured many people, and now it was his turn. His body was to suffer the evil treatment that he had inflicted sadistically on other bodies.) He would have to struggle to the point of agony in order not to let himself be overcome with panic.

When he had been put in this room he had grasped its character, that very "private" thing, and in his state of gloomy impotence, an uncertain and vague sense of possibility, despite everything, had seeped into him. *If I have to deal with only one of them, I could perhaps manage to corrupt him . . . yes, maybe . . .* After Praga had left and until his whole being was taken up entirely in struggling against the shock of the light on his face, he had given himself over to working out a plan. *I must count on the fact that they know they're at the end of their tether. In exchange for my life, I can offer him his, as well as impunity. (If he's not a beast, it's impossible for him not to think of the future.) But will I make it sound believable? That's the point. And I mustn't forget the money, a pile of money: these bourgeois swine want money. A first installment, and a lot of it, and get it to him immediately, as a guarantee. The most important thing though is the exchange: my life against his, and impunity.* But as he became more and more disturbed by the light, he could not draw up a real plan. He had to do it now, without wasting time.

"I warn you once and for all," Praga told him slowly, "as soon as you decide to talk, the torture will stop. Not only that, we'll get rid of all the pain immediately with morphine. If not . . ." He wanted to be certain the other fellow had understood. "Have you understood what I told you?"

For an instant the prisoner did not think of his own plan. He turned his half-blinded eyes on him again. "I know you'll torture me all the same, that you won't stop as long as there's a trickle of life in me."

The hangman started to laugh. "I understand. In other words, that's what you'd do, isn't it?" (He realized he was not wrong.) "But I? Of course, I could do the same, but" (and here he lied and enjoyed doing so immensely, lying, that is—the lovely game had begun), "I won't do it. I swear that if you start talking the torture will stop, and I repeat it and swear to it that I'll stop the pain immediately with morphine." He paused and laughed again. "You have no choice. You realize that? You're forced to run the risk of believing me."

The prisoner did not answer. He realized that he had to concentrate all his resources on finding a way out, without wasting a second.

"Now to us", the hangman went on. "There is the risk that once you're being tortured, you won't understand anything, and you'll think death is very near. Don't deceive yourself. With someone like you I'll measure out the treatment not over days but over weeks. Have you understood? Weeks of treatment. Have you got that straight? And every minute will be an eternity for you. I'll take you apart limb by limb." This said, he became silent, avidly seeking for possible reactions of anguish in his victim.

"There's one thing," the prisoner then replied in a changed voice, "and that's that my people will know. There are some inside here—more than one—who will let it be known. And there's little left for you, a few months at the most, and then it will be your turn."

"Oh, yes? Very well. Then listen: in the first place I . . ."

The reader will be spared the minute reckoning or description of the evil torment that Praga was planning to use on his victim. A trickle of saliva began to slaver from his mouth. His speech was progressing rapidly from slow to urgent. In spite of his weariness, he longed to start the "treatment". He could less and less stand the waiting.

The other fellow realized that, having gone through similar states of mind in his day. Therefore he had to carry out his intention as soon as possible. *Because it is already at the point of being too late.* But how should he get into it effectively, without making a mistake?

He was directed, almost by the demonic presence that lurked in him, just as it did in Praga. He let it explode in a string of extraordinarily vulgar swear words. After that he shut up, as if exhausted.

"What's going on with you?" Praga asked. "Don't tell me you're already beginning to whine."

"I?"

"Well, then?"

"I can't understand how . . ." (and here he horribly swore) "you're on the wrong side."

"Go on." (*The tongue: remember to cut out his tongue.*)

"It seems to me your place isn't with these swine, who are all done for, but with us", and he looked at him hard in the face. Now he was beginning to see.

"You disappoint me", Praga whispered with mocking eyes. "Don't tell me you're trying to convert me."

I can't stop now. I must go on, the prisoner decided, compelled, even though his efforts seemed to him vain, laughable. The "other" presence within him did not consent to his interrupting himself. It kept pushing him on. "I'm proposing an exchange . . . my bosses value me a great deal. You know that, don't you?"

"Yes", Praga answered with conviction. He was really curious to see where he would end up, with his idea of saving himself, how far the prisoner would go.

"If someone took me to them, whatever he might have done before . . . even if he were the chief of police . . . his situation would be fixed up."

"What do you mean? That you'd give me money?"

"If that's what you want . . . depends on you." Suddenly the prisoner had a brilliant thought. "They could give you a job with our police . . . and if perhaps you have some scores to settle with someone, you'd then be on the winning side." He added, as if talking to himself, "You don't have the faintest idea of the possibilities we in the Communist police have."

Who says I have no ideas? Praga thought, and suddenly he recalled the conversations with the two ex-Chekas about the Katyn massacre and the systematic executions in Moscow that occurred even in peacetime. Even in peacetime! *Perhaps I know more than you about it.* "Go on", was all he said, feigning an air of amusement, disbelief.

"Try to see things from our point of view. If a partisan of any color gets rid of another one, no matter which one, everyone says thanks, and that's it. And afterward, once the war is over and won, all of them will thank you a lot more still, even the non-Communists, for what you've done. You know that?"

It's too late for me, Praga thought at that point with a tinge of real bitterness. He did not feel himself to be a Fascist. For him fascism had never been anything but a means (precisely like, neither more nor less, the nebulous Communist theories had been for his Communist prisoner). But he had shared his life for so many years with the Fascists. The director of the Banca Artigiana of Incastigo came to mind: everybody in the town knew he had been the one to deport him to Germany.

"I'm not trying to deceive you to save myself", the other one continued, as he began to have a vague sense of being on familiar ground. "We've no need to deceive you because someone like you would be objectively useful to us, and that's all that interests us." He spoke with sincerity. Many of his Communist comrades—he knew it—did not want an individual like him in their ranks. Nevertheless, they were obliged by their doctrine to accept him and even to leave him an open field. For the Communist creed, in fact, a criminal is not a criminal but a hero if he works (or commits criminal acts) for the revolution. He must not scale the heights of abstract talk, however. "Listen, to show I'm not talking just to talk right now, I want to give you some proof. Tell me where you'd like me to deposit a sum of money for you. All you need to do is tell me and give me forty-eight hours' time. Name the price."

"A proof? And you", Praga answered without knowing if he was joking or not, "will deliver the goods in forty-eight hours?"

"Yes", the other fellow answered more and more attentively, despite the pain in his head, which seemed at the point of bursting. "Look," he added, "I'll expose myself completely. All you have to do is have me watched over meanwhile in the same cell by the same guards who have watched over me until now."

Praga, getting up from his stool, made several turns back and forth across the small room, forcing himself to reflect. "As proof, I don't want money", he suddenly said. "Something else instead. You must do someone in, someone I'll tell you. And not in forty-eight hours but by tomorrow evening."

"One of ours or one of yours?"

"Mine, a Fascist. Can you?"

"Yes, I think so."

"It can't be difficult. It's a functionary in the Ministry of the Interior", Praga said. "You realize I'm also exposing myself? I'll give you the details about his habits so you won't waste time." *We'll start by getting rid of that bastard*, he decided to himself. *This could be a one and only chance.* But afterward, of course, he had no intention of going over to the partisans. He was not even thinking of it, at least for the moment.

The agents on duty were not surprised when, a little later, Praga ordered them to return the prisoner to his cell. "Because I'm really worn out this evening." And in an aggressive tone, he added, "All right? I wouldn't want to make a wrong start with an important job like this."

They were surprised, indeed, however, and frightened, and there was a tremendous ruckus the following night, when it was established that the assistant chief Praga had disappeared together with the important prisoner.

In Nomana the news of Pino's emigration to Switzerland reached them some weeks later, in November.

It was not the crazy Chin, the postman, who delivered the news to the family, but the post office official Benfatti in person. Benfatti, a native of Cremona, with a gray pointed beard and a black tie à la Lavallière, and oversleeves, was one of the few declared anticleric lay figures of the town, and besides—despite his holding public office—a socialist, or better, a social democrat. As he was aware of the family's worry concerning the boy's fate, on noticing an ambiguous postcard from Switzerland (addressed to Francesca and signed from "your girlfriend Pina" but with a male handwriting), he put it in his pocket and hurriedly left the post office to go to the villa. "I don't know, and I don't want to know," he declared contentedly, "but I thought it would be better to bring this postcard over to you directly without letting it go through the hands of our local postman."

Ambrogio was there to receive it. He had been in Nomana for some months already. He was spending his not very easy convalescence for the most part seated next to the radiator in the study, forcing himself to prepare for his university examinations. The postcard—written by Pino with his usual imprudence—said, "Dear Francesca, I've been in this new place since the eighteenth of October, and I'm well, no longer in danger."

After having scanned it in a glance, he said, "We're very grateful, Mr. Benfatti", and he nodded meaningfully. Without speaking of the missive, he had the post office official sit down and served him a little glass of liqueur. Controlling his own impatience, he talked about the situation in general as well as the difficulties in sending packages to prisoners in Germany. Once Benfatti had gone, Ambrogio rushed up the steps and handed his mother the card as she was making up the beds with Noemi. "That wretch Pino is safe and sound in Switzerland", he said. "Look, it's his writing. But even if he had used a typewriter, from the recklessness you would know it was him all the same."

"In Switzerland? Pino? Let the Lord be praised!" his mother exclaimed excitedly, and as she read those few lines, she could not hold back her tears. "You must let Papa know immediately. Ambrogio, telephone him, please." Noemi was also crying.

Papa's in Milan, Ambrogio remembered, and, after relating the little he knew about the situation of those interned in Switzerland, he returned to sit down next to the radiator in the study.

It was drizzling outside, wintry weather, gloomy. The radiator gave off only a little heat because they had to use wood instead of coal. That small amount of heat sufficed, however, to arouse a certain remorse in the young man. He thought of the workers in his father's plant; also his brothers and sisters in the unheated school during this fifth winter of war. But neither the workers nor the students were those who most suffered. Far more did the soldiers in trenches on the various fronts have to bear, and still more the millions deported, and those being prevented from moving, the Jews, for example. The Jews! What would be in store for Italian Jews now that, unlike before, the Fascists found themselves forced to let the Nazis take them away? Just thinking of it all made you shudder. And the other prisoners? In Russia, in Germany, in the Balkans . . . that is, if there were any prisoners left in Russia and the Balkans. Stefano, Michele, all the soldiers and colleagues who had stayed behind in the retreat . . . and Manno? Poor Manno! He had learned definitely from some officers who had joined the Republican Fascists and had been repatriated from Germany that Manno had never reached the regiment in Greece. What could have happened to him? There were six hundred thousand Italian military men— about seventy thousand from Nomana—who were now prisoners in Germany after refusing to join up with the Salo Republic. *Why am I, on the other hand,* he asked himself, *here loafing about next to the radiator? Ah, to be able to be in the army—the legitimate one, of course, the little that remained of it*—he would now be with the Allies on the gothic line, according to the news from Radio London and Radio Bari.

Radio Bari, which he listened to almost every evening, often spoke of the army. Radio Roma, however, almost never spoke of the Italian army. Why? What was really happening on the other side of the line that separated northern Italy from central and southern Italy? The chief of the legitimate government was no longer Marshall Badoglio but an unknown politician, one Bonomi: a good man to judge by his speeches, but certainly no eagle. On the basis of what kind of compromises had he been put into office . . . but why was Radio Roma so remiss about talking about the army? It talked constantly about the partisans and still more often about the new political parties: their meetings, their confrontations, litigations, clashes, quarrels, ruthless and reciprocal, presenting them as manifestations of democracy. Perhaps—Ambrogio thought— they were democratic, but how depressing to carry on that way.

At Christmas vacation the young people came home. They told of the cold they had to endure, how they had to study with their overcoats on, and a blanket over their legs was fine for their legs, they explained, but did nothing for their feet.

Celeste, the driver, had brought them back to Nomana in the Millecento, which now ran on a gas generator. On the railway there was a constant danger of strafing from the air. The Allied air power had stopped bombing on a large scale and was now tenaciously pursuing minor objectives with machine guns, and among the objectives was the destruction of rail locomotives; two of the four diesels in service on the Nomana line had been rendered useless. Almost by way of compensation, a discreet number of civilian automobiles had begun to run using a gas generator, which is to say, a device that used charcoal and even wood. Several different ingenious artisans—copying one another—constructed these clever and necessary machines (in general, cylindrical, vaguely similar to water heaters), which, when attached to the back of the vehicles, allowed for a modest speed. The armed forces of the republic were also using them on automobiles and trucks, and even the Germans, who—even though very inferior in war materiel compared to the Allies—appeared still to have sufficient fuel at their disposal.

During the Christmas holidays the Germans launched an unexpected counterattack in the Ardennes, between France and Belgium, using impressive armored tanks, which broke through and put the American-English-French front into a critical position. This recovery, no doubt serious, seemed inexplicable to Ambrogio and his father, and they spoke of it more than once. "How had they been able to put together all those armored tanks?"

"And why are they using them in the west and not in the east, where the situation gives them much more to worry about?"

"Perhaps they want to prevent the Ruhr from being occupied? Maybe they really are preparing new weapons with which they can change the outcome of the war?"

They were perplexed.

4

Christmas dinner that year, 1944—which the evacuee relatives also attended—was really quite modest. It seemed festive only because of the holly branches that Francesca and Alma had brought in from the garden and put on the tablecloth. "Who's put these obstacles here?" Fortunato asked, putting a couple to one side after sitting down at the table.

"It's Christmas, and you have to remember that", Alma explained.

"Viva!" Giudittina shouted, applauding by herself.

When they were all in their places, Giulia recited the usual prayer. "Bless, O Lord, this food, and make it serve thy glory and for our health and salvation."

As it was Christmas, Giulia wanted to add something more. "We beseech you, Lord, for ourselves and for our children, Manno and Pino, who are apart from us now, that they may, on this holy day, they may ..." She had been smiling until that moment, but at that point she burst into tears. "Oh, Manno, Manno!" she exclaimed, standing up and leaving the dining room.

Francesca also stood up, also with tears in her eyes; but Gerardo stood up too and made a sign to Francesca to sit down, and he went after his wife. The couple returned shortly to the room, Giulia forcing herself painfully to smile.

The others then started to talk about Pino, who was safe and out of danger in Switzerland. "Of course he's safe", the two older boys emphasized, making sure their mother heard them. As far as he was concerned she could be quite at ease. And the Monza aunts reminded the younger children, "Remember never to say a word about Pino being in Switzerland, and if you spread it around . . ." But no one dared speak about Manno because this was the second Christmas without news from him. Instead of talking about him, Ambrogio spoke of Colomba, who a few days before had called to wish them a happy Christmas. "She said she'd be coming to Nomana this summer." The others already knew that, but all the same they acted interested, going on with the conversation until the tension dissipated, and the conversation could go back to normal.

The men ended up talking about the incredible productive capacity of German industry, of which they spoke in almost professional fashion. "They're producing enough to feed the war on all fronts," Gerardo commented, "so much so that now they're lacking men rather than weapons and materials. And besides, Germany is being bombed day and night. How do they manage to produce that way in spite of everything?"

"Of course," Uncle Ettore said, with his slightly artificial air created by his pince-nez spectacles, "it can't only be due to a question of willpower or force of character. There has to be something different, in the method, who knows what, something we can't put a finger on."

"Maybe it's because they've put their factories into the bunkers, underground, so to speak?" Fortunato suggested. "But no," he answered himself immediately, "no matter how ample they may be, bunkers can't cover more than a small part of a factory. The Germans can't have resolved the problem of bombardments by armor-coating the industries."

"Naturally not," his father agreed, "and I also don't believe it's a question of prolonging their work schedule or of a greater number of hand operators, for example, prisoners or women. For years their factories have worked both day and night shifts."

"Then how do they manage it?"

"Here in Milan," Uncle Ettore reminded them, "everything seemed destroyed. You know that. And yet, after a few months, everything was back to working order, and now the city is producing."

"Agreed", Ambrogio said. "But in Milan they mainly destroyed houses, not factories. The really industrial areas, like Sesto, were practically untouched. That's why the city's come back to life. In Germany, in contrast, they're bombing industry as well as houses."

"Not only that", Fortunato observed—despite his being only twenty, he was stringently realistic. "You must remember also that if Milan after August of last year had been bombed many more times that way, I'm sure it wouldn't be producing anything now."

"And then? Factories are destroyed every single day, that goes without saying, so it must be that Germans not only reconstruct systematically but, with the ones functioning, they've found a way of producing more, more than the others. Is that possible?"

638

It was possible, and it had been proved. Thanks to the system of "auto-responsibility of industry" introduced by Albert Speer, the minister of war, together with an extremely specialized production, each factory was required to produce only one single weapon, or even better, one part of a weapon, but at the greatest quantity possible. To exceed that quota continually, they were left free, each industry, to do what they believed best. There was no problem in placing their goods—that's the essential point—because the ministry took the entire production. Keeping to these standards, German war production had—despite the immense destruction—tripled in three years without having to increase hand labor. But that would be known, however, only after the war was over.

(Several speculations could be made on the system introduced by Albert Speer. A racist would see a confirmation of German superiority in this. However, Speer himself later explained that the system had been figured out, although it could not be put into practice, by Walther Rathenau, a Jew who directed the German war economy during World War I, and a "philo-Semite" could derive confirmation of Jewish intellectual superiority out of all this. On a decidedly more practical level, the four Lombard industrialists gathered around the Christmas dinner table would have been able to find in this a proof of their deep-rooted conviction that if a capable industrialist were faced with no commercial obstacles—with only the means at his disposal and without the need of any others—he could multiply his own production. As far as we are concerned, if we are allowed our opinion, we only make mention that thanks to such a system the war could, notwithstanding the vast destruction it caused, continue feeding itself. That is, it could go on, and, along with the war, the sufferings could also continue. In other words, the genial discovery of Speer-Rathenau stands out in our eyes, above all, as an unthinkable, endlessly efficient instrument of man's self-punishment in that period.)

From the subject of Germany's inexplicable production capacity, the conversation came down to earth: the sending of food packages to Nomana soldiers who were prisoners of war in Germany, which went forward despite the great difficulties involved.

"By the way, is Pierello still not writing?" Ambrogio asked his sisters. (Pierello was the conscript who customarily opened his arms wide and raised his eyes to the sky. Perhaps the reader still remembers him. After his leave he had gone to Croatia, and it was he who had brought that woman, that poor mother, Savina, to Ambrogio. After the armistice he had been deported by the Germans and was now in one of the most dangerous zones, in the northeastern sector of Germany, close to the old Polish border.)

"No, he still hasn't written", Francesca answered. "This morning, after Mass, Alma and I spoke with his mother. She hasn't had a word since October. She's extremely worried, the poor woman."

"In that family," Almina recalled, "they already have someone missing in Russia, a cousin who lives in Casaretto: Tito, the brother of Giacomo who carries the Cross in the processions. Do you remember?"

"Giacomo? Of course", Gerardo said.

"In any event, none of the packages we've sent Pierello has been returned. Isn't that so?" Ambrogio asked. "Maybe that's a good sign. Did you tell that to his mother? What's her name again, the poor woman, Ermelinda?"

"Yes", Francesca replied. "I told her that. But, believe me, it's not something very reassuring for her."

"Naturally."

The figure of Pierello's anguished mother was engraved on Ambrogio's mind and was linked with another even more painful image, that of Lucia, Stefano's mother who—for two years now—had been nailed on the same terrible cross.

5

After the meal the young man announced that he would take a walk to Nomanella. After first having put on—under Giulia's vigilant eyes—his over-coat, muffler, and cap, he left the house.

He found Stefano's parents—Ferrante and Lucia—bowed down by another calamity. Their daughter Giustina had suddenly been taken ill, and they had taken her to the Nomana hospital that very morning.

"What a Christmas you've had!" the young man commented.

"It's her worry over Stefano and Luca", Lucia said in tears, "that's making her ill."

They went into the kitchen, and Lucia placed herself at the side of the lit stove. The others, Ambrogio included, sat around the table on straw-seated chairs. The two children were there, too, Pio and Isadora, sitting quietly on their chairs.

"Giustina has no reason to worry about Luca", Ferrante argued. "They saw him in the south of Italy. You know that. So, even if he doesn't write, he's all right."

"Of course", Ambrogio agreed.

"But why, if he's alive, doesn't he write?" the woman asked. "If they're so many writing from America? Only the ones who are dead don't write."

Ferrante shook his head, distressed. Lucia could not manage to understand these things.

"But Giustina," Ambrogio asked, "do you know what's wrong with her?"

"She's not well, she's not well", the mother affirmed sorrowfully. "For months she's been ill and hasn't said anything, not even to me, and I'm her mother. She came home from work with her face as white as a sheet, and I asked her, 'What's the matter?' 'Nothing, Mama.' In the last few weeks she couldn't stand it any longer and went to see a health service doctor. She went twice, but he didn't want to say she was sick, and the last time, last week, he shouted at her as if at a dog, the poor girl. She couldn't keep on her feet the whole day, you know? So, yesterday, while she was fixing the chestnuts to cheer us up a little, she vomited blood. And this morning, when she got up, again."

"Giustina vomited blood?"

The mother covered her cheeks with her hands and motioned that it was so.

"But why didn't she say anything? If she had said she wasn't feeling well at the factory . . . it was wrong of her not to say something. Heavens, she's no longer a child."

"You know how Giustina is", the father explained. "She's never complained about anything; quite the opposite, even if she looks so delicate. Besides, since she's the only one bringing in a salary every month these days . . . you understand?"

"It was wrong of her. And you took her to the hospital this morning?"

"Yes, to Nomana, right after she got up."

"Some Christmas for you!" the young man repeated.

"Dr. Cazzaniga says they have to run some tests on her because of all the blood she lost from her mouth."

"Yes. Poor Giustina!" Ambrogio murmured.

Lucia looked at him, frightened. So did little Isadora (who was already learning what it was to suffer).

"No, I meant," Ambrogio tried to correct himself, "about the blood . . . until they do the analyses, they don't know anything."

"Yes, that's exactly what Dr. Cazzaniga said", the mother sighed, but continued looking at him intently.

The young man went back home overcome with sadness. While he walked home on the frozen road, his inner thoughts of some years before, before the war, when it seemed that death had nothing, but nothing to do with him at his age, came to mind. And to think how many had passed away already! And perhaps Stefano . . . enough of that. And now Giustina. Vomiting blood twice . . . if it happened to be . . . as it probably was . . . tuberculosis, the situation was disturbing. And that poor Luca! Cut off from home, with the prospect always at the back of his mind of returning to his girl, and instead he might not see her!

From a field covered with snow, a few steps away from him, a beautiful bird with a wintry rusty color took flight, a bustard, and then, after a few resolute wing flutterings, perched on top of a hawthorn tree that flanked the road. From its bare perch the bird—craning its neck—observed the young man coming closer and once again took flight. This time it did not stop. It went on flying toward the twilight until it disappeared into the haze. Ambrogio stopped at the hawthorn tree. It was exactly at this point he had met Giustina before the war on the afternoon when he had said to her, "Are you afraid I'll eat you?" and she had blushed and answered, "No. I know you, and I know you're clean, not only outside, but inside, too."

Luckily, I'm not superstitious, he said to himself, walking again. *If not, who knows what meaning I'd attach to that bird, which right from here went off until it disappeared into the haze.* He thought of his cousin Manno. *If he were here, he'd surely see some meaning in this, convinced as he is that everything, including things, are part and parcel of the fate of human beings.* Then he blamed himself for letting himself be carried away this way. After all, what is it about a bird's flight? *As if it weren't normal to see a bustard in winter.*

6

On the following day, the feast day of Saint Stephen, Giulia and Francesca went to visit Giustina in the hospital.

The Nomana hospital was a nineteenth-century villa that was given by bequest for the sick of the town; it had been renovated and enlarged several times and completely painted inside with a washable pale yellow paint. From the preceding morning, Giustina had been in one of the women's wards, very frightened, in her bed. She had never slept away from home for one single night until now, and this all seemed quite strange to her. But even stranger was the unknown illness that sapped her from within and had made her vomit blood. *Could my lungs be punctured with holes?* she has wondered many times. *What could be happening to me? Oh, poor me.*

On the afternoon of Christmas Day, Don Mario—the hospital was like home for him—had comforted her a little. He had devoted the entire afternoon to the sick, either one by one or in groups, and with the less seriously ill he joked. Arriving at her side, "You? What are you doing here?" he asked her, surprised. And moving closer to her, after she delivered her tearful explanations, he assured her, "You don't have to worry like that", in his convincing voice. He explained to her that tuberculosis could be cured (assuming she had that). "Don't you know how many people have had it and have been cured? Who knows how many you must have seen on the street, with whom you've talked, and you didn't even realize they once had it. Cheer up. You don't have to be worried."

How comforting were his good words, his kindly authority! But once he was gone, as night fell sadly, fear had again overcome Giustina. What did she have to do with all those strange things surrounding her? Those two odd, patched-up columns in the middle of the room holding up the ceiling; the white enameled aseptic beds; and even the other sick people, almost all of them older, some satisfied—like the woman to her right—that their old bones were there inside, sheltered from the cold. But what she most disliked was the shiny yellow color of the walls, applied especially—she understood that—so they could be washed continuously and freed from the germs that all sick people may give off. She tried to pray, with her Rosary under the sheets, but it was quite difficult. She was so accustomed to saying the Rosary for her two soldiers—her brother and Luca—that their images, their faces, became more than ever mingled in her prayer, reminding her that still another misfortune, her illness, had befallen them. Especially Luca, who expected to find her well on his return, and instead he would find her ill with consumption: his consumptive sweetheart! Oh, poor Luca! How could they marry now, she asked herself, exaggerating as often happens in these cases. She seemed to see him, with his dear, warm face, which always made her heart beat faster, and his wild hair that fell onto his forehead. He would tell her, "Be brave, Giustina, be brave. I love you no matter what! I love you the same, for my wife, and I'll love you always."

"But I", Giustina answered him, and she started to weep disconsolately, "but now I am the one who can no longer marry you. Don't you understand?"

During the night she slept very little, a very light sleep, continually interrupted. Even the sister on night duty (of the same order as that of the nursery school but in white instead of black—against the microbes, of course) eventually seemed to her a stranger. She had approached her more than once and tried to console her in a soft voice. "Don't be afraid. You don't even know if it's tuberculosis. Maybe it isn't. Maybe it's some nothing thing. Besides, even if it is, look at me. I also had it ten years ago. Well, what do you think? A few months in a sanitarium" (Here she was not telling the whole truth; it was not a matter of a few months' treatment in those days.) "and you'll be all well. Now I can do any work, including heavy work." (And that was the truth.) "And if you knew how many others I've seen get well . . . that's why we have sanitariums, isn't it?" Giustina did not answer. She tormented herself inwardly without answering. The night sister felt pity for that face bathed in tears. "Should we pray together to the Holy Mother?"

They prayed a little while facing the niche in the wall—covered with a pristine, shiny glass—in which a child Mary was enclosed, decorated in a fantastic manner by the sisters: a doll with a little white face and red cheeks and a crown of gold on its head. Until Giustina whispered, "Oh those walls, those painted walls . . . even the Holy Mother will be smothered by the paint."

"What paint?" the sister murmured, realizing the girl was delirious. She stopped praying with her and went on by herself, keeping an eye on the sick girl until she was sure she was asleep.

The following morning when Giulia and Francesca came through the ward, Giustina had still another shock. Was it so serious that these ladies bothered to come to see her? She watched them come up to the bed with her wide-open eyes—big brown eyes, like Stefano's—and her long, beautiful neck, rigid, as if paralyzed. Giulia hurried to break the uncomfortable tension by kissing her on her cheeks, as she would have kissed one of her daughters.

She's not afraid of germs, the sick girl thought with unspeakable relief. *She's not afraid of my illness! Then maybe I'm not too seriously sick.*

The two women stayed with her for more than an hour, seated close to the bed, and little by little they got her to talk. Above all Francesca, with her gentle way of talking that brought back days and hours that were wonderfully different. Giustina relaxed, even though the serenity of the days Francesca evoked, compared to the present sorrow, was still another reason for suffering. Mother and daughter left after having made her promise that, while waiting for the results of the analyses, Giustina would make sure to eat—necessary even without an appetite—and that she would rest as much as possible.

"Look, you've promised. Don't forget you've promised", Francesca admonished on leaving. "I'll make you something delicious every day, and either Mama or I or Alma will come to see you and will bring it. But you must eat."

"And rest. That's also important", Giulia reminded her. "You must clear your mind of all your thoughts and force yourself to rest as much as possible."

The visitors, however, were not able to go to see her often, because the results of the analyses were disastrous. "Galloping consumption," Dr. Cazzaniga called it, the hospital's director, when he talked to Gerardo, who was the hospital president, "and in a very advanced state. I fear we might not be able to save her." They decided immediately to petition entrance for the girl in a sanitarium. "To be thoroughly scrupulous," the doctor specified, "only that. Not because I harbor any hope of saving her. I wish I were mistaken, of course, but ...", and he shook his head.

He was a young doctor, lucid, very competent. Gerardo knew he was not often wrong in his diagnoses. To his ears it sounded like a death sentence.

The day after Epiphany, Giustina was taken on a stretcher to the hospital ambulance and moved to the sanitarium. The ambulance (a Millecento, boxed in wood with two red crosses painted on either side, its windows of frosted glass) had no regular driver. It was driven by either Celeste or Massimino, that is, the two drivers from the president of the hospital's factory. It was Celeste's turn to take Giustina away from Nomana forever.

7

During this same month of January, the post office returned a package from Germany to the aid-to-prisoners committee. It was returned because "recipient dead through war action" (in German, obviously). At the place where the packages were prepared, this gave rise to a variety of commentary.

"Poor Giovannino, so he's dead too. Such a smart fellow!"

"Wonder how it happened?"

"And his family doesn't even suspect it."

"But who is this Giovannino?" asked Ermanno Ghezzi, the warehouse man from Gerardo's firm, in charge of getting the packages wrapped out. "Maybe it's that boy from Lodosa, Ermelinda's son, who hasn't written for months?"

"No, Mr. Ghezzi, his name's not Giovanni. It's Piero."

"Oh, yes, of course, Pierello. Nothing to do with this one."

Another interrupted. "Let me see the package. 'Giovanni Morganti'. Yes, this was the Erbas' errand boy. Don't you remember, Mr. Ghezzi?"

"Oh, that boy from the bakery. Yes, now I remember."

The other began to comment. "His face always looked as if it were powdered with flour, poor Giovannino."

"Right! 'Giovannino Flourface', that's him. That's how they called him. They still don't know about it in his home."

"Yes, I remember him, too. He always went around in an undershirt."

"He was in the class of '21, the same one as Pierello Valli and Ambrogio Riva, and that peasant from Nomanella missing in Russia. What's his name, Stefano?"

"Stefano Giovenzana."

None of those present knew that Stefano, before dying, had thought he saw in the face of the unknown Bersagliere bending over him the face of that soldier, Giovannino Flourface. Nobody would ever know.

"And now? How do we let his family know?"

"That's not our job."

"Whose is it?" one of the girls asked.

"How do I know?"

"Not mine", the crazy postman Chin interrupted, who after having brought the package had stayed to hear the comments. "Not me, that's certain. Not my job."

"And who said it was?" ex-Sergeant Mario Alfieri replied, annoyed. He had left half a foot in Albania.

"Not me or my post office", Chin insisted, expanding, already beginning to defend his superiors even.

"Your post office? What are you saying?" Isa, one of the students, mocked. "Who told you the post office was yours or anyone else's?"

They all shook their heads condescendingly.

"It's my boss."

"Forget it already, Chin", Mr. Ghezzi scolded. "Let it go."

"But who's going to let the family know?" asked the girl who had already asked the question.

"This is what we'll do. I'll remove the address and this German label," Mr. Ghezzi said, "and I'll take it to the mayor. Let him decide."

Several days went by, and Pierello still had not written. After Sunday Mass, Francesca and Alma waited at the church for his mother to get information

645

and to speak a few words of comfort. On the last Sunday of January, the answer from the poor woman had also been negative. Not only had her son not written, but a letter asking for information sent by the mayor to one of the offices of prisoners continued to have gone unanswered.

Francesca and Alma had kept the woman company for a while—going toward the Lodosa hamlet where she lived—she, hunched in her black shawl and trembling from the cold and her inner distress. But she would have trembled even more if she had known her son's real situation.

8

At that moment, in fact, Pierello was in a trench with German soldiers, in the midst of terrifying combat, with what remained of the two Wehrmacht armies, in charge of the defense of eastern Prussia. They were trying to hold back the Soviet Russian advance, but in vain. The battle—begun along the Prussian frontier on the twelfth of January—was unequal. The relation between the forces was perhaps one to ten in favor of the Russians. From the first day the German front, attacked by an artillery bombardment carried out with an unbelievable number of guns (one to every yard: more than in the preceding world war in the famous Battle of the Somme), had been literally destroyed. After the bombardment, the tanks and after them, en masse, the infantry continued inexorably to advance, despite the terrible losses inflicted on them by the surviving German soldiers, who—it is only fair to say so—continued fighting without giving way to panic, with their usual bravery. What remained of the German army, the soldiers still in condition to fight, were now retreating as slowly as possible across the plains covered with snow and mist, and at each city and each village they renewed battle, utilizing the trenches dug on all sides in the previous months by the Nazis. Added to the army, most dramatically loyal to their instructions, were the sixty-year-olds of the Volkssturm and the thirteen- to sixteen-year-old boys of the Hitlerjugend, poorly armed and poorly equipped, not all of them even in uniform. At the rearguard of this destroyed front, the entire population of the region fled, spurred on by terror, even though they were Prussians, tough people, not easily given to fear.

Pierello, who was now wearing his worn-out Italian uniform over a Wehrmacht jacket—at first glance he could have been taken for a German soldier—was withdrawing on his own decision with a company from the Fourth Army, or actually, to put it better, with what remained of it. That Sunday morning (he was unaware, however, that it was Sunday, since he had lost track of time) he found himself in a tiny village with a few houses not far from Bartenstein, as a helper to a Spandau machine gunner. At his side the silent German commander, with his helmet smudged with white, scrutinized the terrain in front of the trench while waiting for the enemies.

As time slowly went by, Piero reflected. Some mess he'd got himself into! *But what else could I have done?* During the summer things had gone well for him ... he had spent five months on an estate called Hufenbach, about forty miles from here, five healthy months, as a farm worker, and he, an ironmonger. Working on the estate, too, was the Polish prisoner Tadeusz Klocek (who was also in the trench at this moment: *Just look there at Tadeusz, that good devil of a fellow, with his outrageous vandal name*) with whom he had struck up a friendship. The widow Hufenbach—Piero reminisced, in a mood for reminiscing— was a severe but fair woman, and she was not as hard on "her" prisoners as other Prussian proprietors were. As their rations were scant, she had let them know from the beginning they could partake of whatever they wanted of the fruits available on the estate. He did so to such an extent that he, in the five months there, had been restored from the long hunger he had endured in the *lager*. How many potatoes he had eaten, and how much good milk he had drunk at the Hufenbach estate! If his Nomana friends had seen him then, how they would have kidded him, especially Giovannino Flourface: "Ey, look at Pierello drinking milk instead of wine. Like the babies! Say, Pierello, should we give you a nursing bottle?" But meanwhile that magnificent milk and those potatoes, not to mention the packages received from Nomana, had restored his life forces. Besides, there was Joachim, twelve years old, the older of the widow's two sons (the other one, ten years old, was too German, as if made of wood, and did not keep them much company). Joachim, unlike his brother, had a good character. He followed him around in the fields as he worked as if he were a shadow and would make him explain this and that. He had learned a few words in Italian and even some in Nomana dialect, as well as Pierello's habitual gesture of opening his arms wide as if yielding himself up to destiny, and occasionally did it, until Pierello, seeing himself imitated this way, finally stopped doing it. He felt like laughing when he thought about it! Yes, Joachim was a nice boy, and Pierello liked him.

What a pity they had to leave the farm in September! They had finished the farm tasks in September, and the two prisoners—he and Tadeusz—had been taken by the party organization and brought to Goldap to dig trenches. In that area there were already civilians, especially women, and many French prisoners, also engaged in digging trenches. He—still reminiscing—had tried to fraternize with the French, who compared to the Germans had manners and even looked more like the Italians, but they kept their distance, and one of them had even called him a *sale italien*, a dirty Italian, a couple of times, because at the beginning of the war Italy had turned its back suddenly on France. As if it had been he, Piero Valli from Nomana, from the hamlet of Lodosa, who had done it.

Luckily Tadeusz was still there, and he understood enough German and sometimes acted as interpreter for him. At that time the front extended the entire length of the older border with Poland, and the German civilians were convinced, without exception, that the Russians would never, but never, get that far. Their own propaganda guaranteed it, and they believed it blindly. They were so very sure of it, not only the women and children, but the men, too. Pierello, at first bewildered, had also ended up believing it. *But then why are they making us dig rearguard trenches? What for?* No one among the civilians seemed to ask questions. On the other hand, the older people, and even some of the not too old, could remember very well the Russians who had invaded that land in 1914: uncouth, they said, and ignorant, but not fierce, not assassins. That memory somehow had stuck, as if to calm everyone down a bit.

At the end of October the Russians—the new ones, not those of the czar—had unexpectedly attacked and had advanced so far that there was scarcely time to withdraw the prisoners from the war. The Russians had invaded the zone of excavations and had occupied the city of Goldap, where they were stopped by German reinforcements, who poured in with furious speed. After a couple of weeks of strenuous fighting, they had recaptured Goldap and carried forward the front to where it had been before, that is, the length of the old border. When the squadrons of prisoners had returned to the spot to bury the dead and repair the destruction, Pierello had seen things he would never forget as long as he lived. Even now, just thinking of it made him shudder. There were civilians killed everywhere, people burned alive in their homes, old people bearing marks of having been tortured to death. All the women who had remained, from little girls to old women, had been raped endless times, some dozens and dozens of times by soldiers, one after the other. In the locality of Nemmerdorf—where his squadron had stopped for a week—many women had been nailed alive to the door of their cottages. "Just because they wouldn't do it ...", some Polish women workers had explained, crying, to Tadeusz, "just because they refused to have sex."

"And how did they refuse?"

"With their hands, their nails. How else?" Was that, then, the fate awaiting all of Germany if the Bolsheviks advanced?

Why, the boy wondered even now, thinking about it for the millionth time, did the Russians behave that way? Seeing them as prisoners, they seemed to be like men, like everyone else. Why, then, when they were in the army did they act this way, like killers? There was no way he could explain it to himself. He had only a vague idea of the number of horrendous crimes perpetrated by the Germans in Russia (the Germans were not the same as those under the Kaiser either), and he was unaware besides, completely so, of the battering propaganda of hatred that had been inculcated into every single Russian head, day after day. They were a sorrowful piece of humanity that had always been under the yoke of hunger and poverty. In the last decades they had been beaten down and massacred by their Communist masters and recently even more toughly massacred by their Nazi invaders. And now they could not only vent their bitterness, but were purposely stimulated to do just that on the enemy population. Thus, normal people and even good people, such as the majority of Russians were, could not restrain these possessed minorities.

(Possessed by the devil, that was it, because it is in situations like these that the enemy of man—the one lurking inside him—is more than ever free to act. The fact was simply that there were human beings unprotected by the law, undefended people, who could be assassinated or tortured for pleasure, available to them. We tend to forget it, but by this single fact, that of being undefended, the indigenous populations of three continents have almost been exterminated by our demon-possessed minorities. By this we do not mean that only the possessed commit murder. Unfortunately there are many others. But those who kill when they have an opportunity to do so, and those who do not stop killing, exterminating, are the ones possessed by the devil who kill for the pleasure of doing so—perhaps not so much them as their inner devil. And they are present in any and all people, and to give them a free hand . . .)

In Nemmerdorf Pierello's squadron had to bury about forty French prisoners who had not retreated in time and had been killed one after the other at their shelter. More than anything else this slaughter had struck the young man. After he had learned—from Tadeusz—how it had happened, and having learned that the Russians, all of them drunk, had not taken into account the declarations of those soldiers, that by being French they were therefore enemies of Germany, he had decided most resolutely that he would never let himself be "liberated" by the Bolsheviks. It occurred to him then to think about his cousin Tito with more sadness than before: if by chance he were still alive how he would be in the hands of such wretches.

The disaster over, the German civilians who had survived had ended up convincing themselves that the enemy would not manage to advance again. "But for us, the prisoners, the party suddenly put us back to digging trenches . . ."

In any event, this was all past history. With the big attack on the twelfth of January (the one at mid-October must have been a kind of test) the Bolsheviks advanced again and were spreading without a halt over all of Prussia.

What is absolutely certain, Pierello concluded in his lucubrations, sighing, his back against the wall of the trench, *is that I, no matter what, I am not ready to fall into their hands. I don't want to end up like those French in Nemmerdorf. Better even to die in battle!* What a wearying situation, after so much time in prison, to have come back to run the daily risk of dying in battle!

9

On the only road out in front, coming from the southeast, that is, from the part where they awaited the enemy, some tiny specks suddenly appeared, which grew in number to the point of forming a fragmented line. The binoculars of the German military were focused on it. "Refugees", one of them quietly announced. "They're refugees." Others confirmed it.

Pierello, who had not understood very well, made a worried interrogative sign to Tadeusz, who left his place and came up to him. "They're civilians, German civilians", he explained in a kind of broken Italian.

"Still more. Poor folk", Pierello said.

"Yes, poor people", Tadeusz agreed. Not too tall, middle aged, with a face rather concave in shape because of a flattening at the root of his nose that affected his entire physiognomy: he smiled at his friend in his usual kindly way.

The refugees took a while getting up the road to the trenches. At last the first of them crossed the formations and without stopping went through the tiny village at the back and went on toward the northwest. The majority of them were traveling in four-wheel farm carts, of a type used in other latitudes, too, by the Polish and Russian peasants. Pierello had used these carts and found them very apt for work in the field, though not as sturdy as the two-wheeled ones of Lombardy, which were so familiar to him. A pair of horses dragged each of the wagons, driven usually by a woman or an older man, sometimes a prisoner, perhaps Russian, with a long overcoat. For the most part the wagons were reinforced and covered by an awning. A few of them were uncovered, and on these their occupants could be seen better: children with their little faces chapped red with the cold, and women, old people, the sick, perhaps a dead body or two. And then there were their belongings: bundles made up hurriedly, bales of hay, clothes piled up, cooking utensils, and an occasional piece of furniture. On passing the refugees looked with inward relief at the division of soldiers that were there between them and the feared enemy, but— what disconcerted Pierello a bit—outwardly they hardly gave any sign of this.

One of them driving, a gray-haired man, stopped his wagon at the top of a trench and asked, "Do you know how far away the Russians are?" addressing a corporal stationed next to the road.

The corporal replied with a gesture that he did not and said something that Tadeusz did not grasp.

"Do you know if the 'ice bridges' on the Königsberg lagoon are still functioning?"

"Yes", the corporal answered. "Yes, they are."

"We're going to the bridges", the man said and departed, not to block the wagons coming behind his.

One of the last of these wagons was being driven by a boy of about fourteen, partially dressed in military uniform, who had beside him on the straw two big Panzerfaust rockets.

Seeing him, the commander of a small Volkssturm division lined up with the soldiers—an old man with a sunken chest, wearing thick glasses—came out of the trench and went to the road, signaling the boy to stop. The boy's eyes turned fearful as he pulled up the reins and stopped the cart. The Volkssturm man questioned him, but the others could hear no more than part of the dialogue.

"Were you in the Volkssturm?"

"Yes, sir."

"Why have you left your post and gone off? Don't you know your duty is to fight till death?"

"The defense where I was . . . well, it no longer exists. Only a few of us are still alive."

"And so you went back home?"

"I returned home, but only after the Russian Panzers had left and our line was wiped out. My house was nearby."

A voice was heard from within the wagon. "The boy didn't run away. He managed to recover two Panzerfaust, and we're counting on him to protect us if our wagons are attacked."

The Volkssturm commander advanced a few steps and, bending over, looked inside the wagon. A man with a swollen face had spoken. He was lying on the straw with his arms folded in an unnatural way. Next to him a woman was stretched out, most certainly his wife, who was asleep, perhaps in a swoon.

"Are you his father?"

"Yes, sir."

"Why are you not driving the cart?"

"My arms are broken." There was a pause. The man—it was obvious—did not feel like proffering any more explanations.

"What happened?" the Volkssturm asked softly.

The man did not answer.

"I'm sorry," the commander then said to the boy, "but you get down and stay with us here." He pulled himself up stiffly. "Come on, get someone else to take over the reins."

The boy did not move. Meanwhile, the woman driving the cart behind came up, an old woman. Like all of the women there she was wearing a scarf around her head, and her figure thickened by a coat covered with snow. "Sir," she said, "I'll explain." And lowering her voice, trying to get the commander a little bit apart, "The Bolsheviks forced Mr. Lensens to hold the lamp while they raped his wife. There was an endless stream of them inside, as well as outside the house. After a while, he refused to hold the lamp, and they broke his arm. Then they tried to make him hold it with the other hand. He couldn't for the pain, and they broke the other arm. That's what happened."

While the woman spoke, the boy on the driver's seat looked fixedly in front of him. Every so often his lips trembled, and his blue eyes began to shed tears.

The commanding officer of the company, a veteran with a lean face, had meanwhile gone to the roadside, up to the wagon. He had everything told to him in a few words, and then said, "Go on your way", to the boy.

"But Lieutenant ...", the Volkssturm man protested. "According to the rules, he's under my jurisdiction."

"Here I have the ultimate responsibility," the lieutenant answered and added, "unfortunately." Then he told the boy again, "Hurry up. Get going! Don't hold up the others in the rear."

The boy looked at him with tear-filled eyes. "These two rockets", he stammered out childishly, with irrepressible emotion, "I swear won't be wasted. Those animals will pay for it." He took the reins in hand, and the wagon squeakily departed over the ice, with its load of misery within.

The account of what had happened spread among the men, and Pierello heard it from Tadeusz. "Some situation!" he commented and, "I hope especially that the widow Hufenbach and the children, and the workers, too, managed to get away in time. What do you think?"

"Well, they have two pairs of good enough horses," he considered in his less than correct Italian, "and the widow and her workers Birgitte and Edvige are all able to hitch up the wagon and drive it." (Edvige was a deported Polish woman, therefore a compatriot of Tadeusz.)

"Yes. The only danger is that the widow might have believed the foolishness on the radio," Piero said, "that the Russians couldn't advance, and God help us" (he switched to dialect) "if they decided not to leave on time. Of course I don't understand the Germans. They swallow all the propaganda told them. They accept it with their eyes closed."

"Yes, that's true."

"They've been retreating from the Russians for two years, and now, who knows why, they were positive they wouldn't retreat anymore. It's incredible!"

"You know what our priests say? That God blinds those whom he wants to ruin", he remarked, quite appropriately.

10

Perhaps an hour had gone by from the time the refugees had passed when from the northwest, from the zone they were actually in, there came the sudden din of cannon fire and, much more faint, of automatic weapons: the usual tragic music of battle, which the Germans had so much liked before. In the silence of the trench—which had become total because they were all listening—that desolate sound came to them in waves and floated farther beyond, becoming lost over the snowy plain.

Maybe a division of Russian tanks had met up with the train of refugees. Pierello looked toward the lieutenant commander, in case he should decide to go out to help them, but the officer—the only one left in the company—was now sitting at the back edge of the trench, and he made no sign of moving. He even, as if responding to his glance, turned the binoculars in the opposite direction, toward the southeast, from where they awaited the enemy.

Not that the officer was indifferent to what was happening. He knew that between a million and a half to two million civilians, mainly women and children, were at that moment behind him on their way to Frisches Haff, the Königsberg lagoon, to cross over its precarious "ice bridges" and so put the lagoon between them and the enemy. The mission of this armed detachment and of the others was, in this area, to maintain a trace of a line, even if broken, to protect the lagoon, if not from all, at least from the bulk of the enemies. Given the forces available, nothing else could be done.

With his binoculars he suddenly made out, from afar, where a row of bare trees cut across the road, something that was moving. *Maybe that's it*, the officer thought, and without removing the instrument from his eyes, he asked someone else beside him to confirm what he saw coming. Several binoculars turned in that direction. It turned out that what they were looking at were not enemies but more refugees, who actually did arrive after a while in a long row.

Still another column came later.

The enemy appeared in midafternoon, announced in advance by sinister columns of smoke that rose one after the other in some of the villages on the plain, beyond the trees. A little before their arrival more refugees, who would be the last, came. They were no longer in carts but on foot, in an agitated flight; there were old people, still upright, plodding along with the help of canes, children, panting women, who were even dragging a little child, sometimes falling or sliding on the ice, at their sides.

Pierello moved instinctively to run and help one of these women, but a curt order from one of the officers stopped him. He had to wait in the trench, crouching again with the others, invisible to the enemies.

Tadeusz, who had gone back to his place, was sadly thinking, *Look: the innocent always pay the same as the guilty, the usual story!* That frantic flight stirred up a question in him that had been anguishing him a great deal during those days. What had happened, and what was happening in his country, in Poland? Among the prisoners contradictory rumors were circulating. According to some there were enormous masses of Polish civilians fleeing toward Germany.

The Russian vanguard were following not far behind the refugees in small groups on foot and on a half dozen sleds—gray-brown patches on the snow. They were allowed to advance, unaware of what awaited them, as far as the foot of the trench, and only at the right moment, at an order from the commander, did the German company open fire.

We shall spare the reader the description of the massacre carried out, most especially by the Spandau, the machine guns. Not only men, but also horses and sleds—absolutely everything was riddled.

After they had precipitously retreated, the survivors waited for their comrades who were following them more closely and then launched the attack, which was turned back. They carried out another under cover of the darkness, which allowed them to reach the foot of the trench despite the bengals hurled by the Germans.

This time the Germans were forced into a difficult man-to-man fight, which meant considerable losses. In pursuit of the enemy, they reached the sleds stopped during the first encounter and discovered five or six half-naked, tied-up German women in them, lying dead next to the enemies, as a result of the Spandau fire. Then some of the soldiers threw themselves like madmen on the few prisoners they had taken, threw them forcefully onto the ground, and, while the others were screaming in terror, took off their clothes to castrate them. The lieutenant commander intervened just in time, but one Russian was already mutilated and twisted himself moaning onto the grayish snow, splashing it with blood. His body would remain there to rekindle the hatred of the oncoming enemy to white heat, into a more and more terrifying spiral, which was already impossible to shatter.

Some hours later the company, by means of a courier who came on a sidecar, received the order to clear the spot in order to move a few miles farther back to defend another village. The Volkssturm, with their few old soldiers and poorly armed young boys, stayed where they were, under the command of the stubborn old man with the thick glasses. While the company truck motors were slowly warming up, he complained to the lieutenant commander, "I just heard the radio a few minutes ago."

"So did I", the officer answered, speaking slowly, as if chewing each word, out of tension, due to the previous combat. (But when weren't German soldiers tense during those days?)

"Then you'll know, Lieutenant, that the order not to yield so much as an inch of terrain is for everybody."

"Yes, in fact, it's an order I know quite well. I've been hearing it from the time I was in sight of Moscow."

The old man beat his foot angrily on the snow. "You've no right to go! You're obliged, like anyone else, to carry out your orders."

"Exactly. I'm following orders from my headquarters. You saw what the courier brought me." The officer added meditatively, still nervously chewing nothing, "But I'll tell you one thing: before long this position will be indefensible, and even without an order I'd have left it. Do you want to know what the enemy is doing at this moment? No one is more predictable than Ivan. You haven't an idea. At this moment he's encircling us on two sides to squeeze the village into his vise. Tomorrow, at the first glimmerings of light, everything will be in his hands, and no one will get out of here alive."

The old man raised his voice. "Even so your duty is to stay."

"My duty is to defend our people, most specifically women and children, while I can," the officer answered bitterly, "and to give them a way of getting safely to the other side of the lagoon first, then the Vistula, then the Oder,

654

then . . ." He interrupted himself. "I don't know if I should pity you or envy you," he said, "but within a few hours this brutal story will be over for you."

Thus the company—what remained of it—departed, and a little beyond the outskirts of the village it was greeted, to the right, by some distant flashes of parabellum, by way of demonstration that the predictions of their commander were already being fulfilled.

In the new area of formation, about four miles farther back, supplies and ammunition reached them from the rearguard—despite the decay into which the entire region had fallen. The men were able to sleep the night here, in shifts but in houses, mostly abandoned by their inhabitants. More than anything else, the soldiers needed to rest.

The following morning, from behind, that is, from the north, a formation of German armored cars arrived, accompanied by a great racket of noise. The commands—based on their already reduced aerial observation—predicted a Russian tank attack at this spot, which in fact did occur. They came fast over the plain, leaving in their wake short trails of pulverized snow. To their great relief, the German tank drivers found that their number was only twice the number of their own tanks. Therefore, they could get out to face them and turn them back without excessive losses.

After this the German tanks were urgently moved elsewhere, and the company remained alone to defend the place. It was occupied by the infantry and some tanks, and at the end of a few days they had to clear out of there, too.

Again they established themselves along a frozen stream, some miles farther back. There they received, apart from ammunition and provisions, about twenty reserves, who were what remained of another company of the regiment to which they belonged. A massive encounter took place in this position, after which they had to retreat, after suffering considerable losses.

Among the new people assigned to the company there was a Catholic priest, not a chaplain but a simple soldier. Before leaving the position, the lieutenant commander ordered him, with Pierello's help, to gather up the identification tags of those who had fallen, their wallets and documents also.

The two of them meticulously (the priest was still a German) removed the identification tags, in the shape of a medal, from each of the dead men's necks and emptied their pockets. This was done with a measure of revulsion, because at times they were splashed with blood and occasionally bowel scraps. They took—apart from the humble objects of a soldier's life, like pocketknives, pipes, lighters, twine—pornographic photographs out of some pockets and Rosaries out of others.

The priest handed every object, one by one, with a mechanical gesture to Pierello, who put it into a sack. The pornographic photographs were disconcerting to the young man (who was not accustomed to them), yet he was surprised even by the relative number of Rosary beads. He realized, better than

655

on other occasions, the deep differences existing in the inner world of the German soldiers, who were outwardly the same. At a certain point the pornographic photographs (those discourses of Don Mario in Nomana . . .) began to seem somehow united, like cause and effect, to the scraps of intestines, and so, instead of putting them into the sack, he began to throw them away. The priest, after a moment's astonishment, nodded his head with approval and, without saying a word, did not hand him any more. His behavior seemed to suggest, in any case, that after all was said and done, beyond the small decisions one could make, death was already the fate of everyone in Germany. God had taken his eyes off men. There was nothing but death left.

II

In a few days Pierello and Tadeusz, aboard a caterpillar tractor, had occasion, quite unexpectedly, to pay a brief visit behind the front lines, both of them in the service of a resolute warrant officer who had been ordered to requisition fuel at any cost.

The choice of a caterpillar tractor turned out to be opportune, because the farther they got away from the front, the more the roads became crowded with refugees. They were traveling in wagons or on foot, and the latter with knapsacks, suitcases, sacks slung over their backs or with fragile carry carts with two wheels that they normally would have used for shopping. Others pushed baby buggies in which, apart from the babies, were packed foodstuffs and other objects. Many were pulling sleds, and some a simple table, which jolted noisily on the ice with its small load on top of it. Vehicles, horses, and people were spilling over in the streets, and the tractor could go forward freely only because of the tracks, which allowed them to travel off the roads.

From his vantage point Pierello could observe everything. He noticed that in various places they were feverishly digging trenches. In other places the Volkssturm units, composed of old men and boys, with armbands and fragmentary uniforms, were watching over both old and new trenches. *This way,* he told himself, *not only the soldiers will all end up dead, but the boys and old men, too. And the women trying to get away, how many of them will survive if their flight lasts long?* Every so often he could see a corpse at the side of the road. It could not have been there long, because the Germans—with their obsession with order, very much in evidence for him, an Italian, in circumstances like this— without a doubt were continually removing them.

At the entrance of the city of Braunsberg (the fuel deposits were a little outside the city, toward the shore of the frozen lagoon) he was filled with horror at the sight of three soldiers from the Wehrmacht hanging from lampposts, one after the other, each one with a sign pinned on him with a brief message, which Tadeusz deciphered. They were deserters, he said, individuals who had abandoned their unit. "Look over there, see who got kaput?" he pointed out to Piero. The young man then noticed a group of "guard dogs", which he knew the army soldiers feared greatly. They were military police agents, with metallic plaques held over their chest with chains, which together with the look of tough mastiffs that each and every one of those men had well explained their nickname. Farther on, first one, then another of the squadrons—which moved compactly like a single man—stopped the tractor and asked imperiously to see their "travel permit". Pierello did not miss the concern that the warrant officer showed each time, even though he happened to be a seasoned veteran capable of slipping out of any difficult spot. It was exactly for that reason he had been chosen by the company commander for that mission. His anxiety proved to be well founded when, a little farther, on a roundabout, the tractor drove between two rows of German soldiers hanging, like lugubrious scarecrows, from trees flanking the sides of the road.

"But they'll end up killing everyone!" the boy repeated to himself, and the leaden sky under which—without voices or curses and in ever-renewed order—the immeasurable tragedy unfolded seemed still more distant from men.

He thought it really was time to reexamine his own situation. Not to fall into the hands of the Russians was well and good, but also not to end up killed in battle, or worse still to die as ignobly as those hanged men. He was filled with a keen sense of rebellion. What did he have to do with this war of extermination among peoples without charity, without God? One and the other had rejected God—as Don Mario would put it in Nomana—and those were the results: right there, yes, under his very eyes. He had to decide, once and for all, to finish with these people, the one and the other, and to get out of these places, too. There seemed to be, both for the Germans vanquished and for the Russians the vanquishers, nothing but death here: a death that was constantly regrouping its forces with diabolical efficiency. The young man drew his own conclusions. He must absolutely, without wasting time, find a way of getting away. Yes, but how? That was the point.

"Did you see if there were prisoners like ourselves among those hanged?" he asked Tadeusz softly.

"No, no I didn't", he answered him in the same way. "But maybe on other Strassen there are. Why?"

"We'll talk about it later", he said, still keeping his voice pitched low.

The German warrant officer was not worried about them. Rather it was Piero who was observing him out of the corner of his eye. He could see the man was absorbed by a pressing concern. The motor of the tractor, after having begun to miss before Braunsberg, was once again sputtering, causing the vehicle to proceed joltingly as well. At one point the tractor driver turned off the engine, jumped out, opened the hood, did something inside it, and then climbed in it again and once more started it up, jumped out again, climbed in again. The two prisoners heard him speaking to the officer. There was something wrong in the wiring. He had to change a part that had worn out, too old. He thought he heard them say it had to do with the generator brushes.

Since their objective was close by, the two Germans decided to carry on. The vehicle managed to arrive wearily and shakily. There seemed to be more refugees in this part of town. There were not two but three rows of wagons, not to mention the people on foot on the street where they were driving the tractor. There, in the background, livid under the desolate sky, the Frisches Haff, the frozen lagoon, stretched out, until it became lost in obscurity.

At the warehouses in which the fuel dispensing took place some army trucks had stopped. Empty receptacles were being unloaded, and squadrons of French and Russian prisoners were reloading the vehicles with full ones. Here and there were carcasses of burned automobiles, no doubt the work of Russian air power, but the dispensing of fuel functioned regularly. The warrant officer went into the office first to telephone another outfit with spare parts, situated, from what he could understand, not too far away. He came out in about an hour, while the tractor was being loaded with fuel. He made it known that the needed part could not be found in the nearby deposit but in another, at the opposite part of town. Taking advantage of some trucks leaving—he said—he would go first to police headquarters for authorization, and then he would continue on, as well as he could, to the deposit, and would be back as soon as possible with the spare part. He was hoping to be back by nightfall. In any case his traveling companions would have to wait for him without leaving the tractor.

The waiting began. Under his big German overcoat, his hands in his pockets, Pierello stood a bit apart to watch the stream of refugees who were going quite slowly along the road, which was not far off, on the other side of a row of bare trees. He again wondered if the widow Hufenbach, Joachim, and the workers from the farm might not also be on the road.

His thoughts were interrupted by the thunderous arrival of three low-flying, twin-engine airplanes, their bright colors contrasting against the leaden sky. After attacking the trucks and warehouses with a spray of ammunition, they flew off firing incessantly against the streams of refugees headed toward the dark lagoon, over which, already out of sight, several times they dropped their loads of bombs. The echo of the explosions aroused in Piero—who was getting up from the ground on which he had thrown himself, brushing the snow off his coat—images of chasms opened in the ice, and wretched women and children and horses drowning like water rats in the icy water. It came to him like a wave of nausea.

But everything passes. The nausea also passed, and several long hours passed. It was becoming dark. The column of refugees, after stopping several times, halted completely: a sign, according to Tadeusz, that the "ice bridges" had been blocked.

Being out in the air, the cold was making itself more and more felt, and for that reason the German tractor driver—who tended to regard his two comrades more as volunteers than as prisoners—suggested they take shifts. While one of the three stayed with the loaded tractor, the other two would rest inside one of the buildings. They began without delay.

The refugees meanwhile began to ebb back from the lagoon. Most of them returned to the city, but many camped out under the first shelter they could find. The old noncommissioned German officer in charge of the deposit had two empty warehouses opened for them, and they moved in and filled them up rapidly in an incredible fashion, while quite a few camped outside in their wagons. Any number of them gathered up dry branches and bits of wood and made fires, on which they began to cook, arranging things so the children could warm up around it.

What a situation, Pierello thought, observing them from the tractor, *they have been reduced to, people as brave as they* . . . but the Germans had sought out this punishment, no doubt of it. Why people, in many ways as brave and efficient as anyone, should have chosen to be the bully boy and blackguard was something that he—no matter how much he thought about it—could not manage to explain.

(We find his perplexity not unfounded. If it is true that neither superior nor inferior peoples exist in relation to other people, it is also true that every people has its moment of particular efficiency, in which it is summoned to build on a grand scale not only for themselves but for everyone. Quite logically, our century should have been that of the Germans. We saw them at the height of their possibilities for realizing themselves, as it must have been for the Greeks in their happiest epoch, when they endowed civilization with their incomparable contribution, like the Romans some centuries later, and the Italians in the Middle Ages, and the Spaniards in the sixteenth century, when they were capable of stopping the threat of Islam in the Old World and at the same time colonizing the New World. Like the French in the eighteenth century, the English in the nineteenth, when with machines and modern industry they created new and unheard-of possibilities of life for all of humanity. Unfortunately, the Germans squandered their glorious moment in the wake of false masters, in an undertaking most decidedly against God, thus excluding themselves from any possibility of creating something. And if that were not enough, the abuse of their immense energies—of which the last sparks would fly man to the moon some twenty years later—and the loss of such a frightful number of their men, men endowed with a determination that is not found anywhere else today, would in the years to follow represent an almost irreparable impoverishment for all of humanity.)

Finishing his guard-duty shift, Pierello was replaced by the tractor driver. Tadeusz took his friend to one side and with a cautious gesture (though there was no necessity for it) told him he had made a sensational discovery. In one of the warehouses who should be there but Edvige, the Polish deportee from the Hufenbach farm. Tadeusz had learned that the women and children had left the property in time—but just barely—and had covered a good deal of distance in two wagons, and by now they would surely have been on the other side of the lake if two days before someone had not stolen the wagons and horses. It seemed the widow Hufenbach had followed the thieves obstinately, while uselessly appealing for help from other refugees, until she had her legs beaten by the thieves so badly she was no longer able to walk. After that, her servants and children had moved her with great difficulty almost as far as the lagoon on Joachim's small sled. Now, if he had understood, she was not far from here.

While Tadeusz was relating all this, Pierello took heart and started to ask for details. Without wasting any time, his friend accompanied him to the Polish servant.

She was seated on the warehouse floor, next to three German women older than herself and no less bundled up. The four of them were seated around a bluish fire frying bacon in a pan. The place was full of smoke, and the people were pressed together, but not noisily, and the smell of bacon and fat cooking was in a way comforting.

"Hello, Edvige, hello. How are you?" Pierello greeted her gaily.

The woman answered him with a half smile. She had taken the scarf off her head, and her hair was gathered into one blondish braid, which hung down on one side. She seemed very tired, enervated. Scarcely smiling, she shook the hand the young man was resolutely holding out to her.

"If you two had been there, they never would have stolen the horses," she murmured, "and we'd have been on the other side of the lagoon by now." Tadeusz translated.

"But tell me, how did it happen?" Pierello asked. "Tell me", but then corrected himself, "I don't want to tire you, but I only wanted to know why the widow Hufenbach and the boys aren't here too."

The woman looked at him almost fearfully. "It's not my fault", she said. "The sled was small, but too heavy for us, and Birgitte, Joachim, and I dragged it for almost two days with the widow and the bacon on it . . . then, we couldn't go on, we really couldn't."

Tadeusz, after first trying to calm her down, translated for Pierello.

"Birgitte was the first to leave. She wanted the widow to stay here in Braunsberg. 'They give out food to the refugees in the city', she kept repeating to her. 'Stay here. Many others are. Stay at least long enough until you can walk and then start up again.' 'No', the widow would say. 'No. I have to get the boys to the other side of the lagoon. There you may leave me, even on the street, it doesn't matter, but out of danger.' This afternoon, after the aerial attack," Edvige went on, "Birgitte couldn't stand it any more. When she got up from the ground, she no longer took hold of the sled ropes, you understand? She went off on her own. What could I do? I've my children at home, too, and I don't want these animals to screw me."

"I understand", Pierello told her compassionately. "Don't think I'm blaming you. How could I . . . I, as far as I can remember, I've never taken anyone to task in my life. I only wanted to know . . . well, to see if we could do something now. Do you have any idea where the widow and her boys are now?"

To his surprise, the woman said she did. "Joachim and I pulled the sled to a tiny fir grove at the side of the road. 'Sheltered from the planes', I told them, but actually it was so that they would have a shelter for the night. Then I told her, 'I'm going for help.' The boys were crying. They knew I wouldn't return. So did the widow. 'Take a little bacon, Edvige', she told me. 'You're the one who got it out of the wagon. Take a little. If you don't, you'll die of hunger.'" On repeating these words, Edvige started to cry.

"Don't cry", Tadeusz told her. "You did everything you could. We didn't choose this war."

"Don't cry", Pierello repeated, once he knew what had happened. "But what fir grove? Which one is it?"

"A little wood with spruce or pines. I don't know", Edvige replied, swallowing her tears. "The only trees still green, the only green wood on the side of the road."

"How many miles from here?"

"About three, or four, or five, I wouldn't know, on the right of the road going toward the lagoon."

"Good", Pierello concluded, and without a second's hesitation he added, "I feel like going to get them." (Tadeusz first looked at him disconcerted, then thought for a few minutes, and translated to his Polish compatriot, "We're going to get her.") "You," Pierello asked, looking at Edvige, "what are you thinking of doing?" He looked at the three German women seated around the fire, vainly trying to follow the conversation in Italian and Polish being carried on by the two men in fragmentary German uniforms. "Are you going with them now?"

"Yes", Edvige answered. "They called me. They have a wagon, but only one, that one, knows how to drive it, and she's worn out. Now I'm with them. It's the Virgin of Czestochowa who made me meet them, so I may go back to my children." She looked at the youngest of the three women and smiled at her. The other responded with a shy smile, nodding. "As soon as we finish eating, the two of us are going to hitch up the wagon," Edvige said tiredly, "and let's hope this one isn't stolen."

Tadeusz put his hand in his pocket and pulled it out full of paper money. "The Germans just paid me," he said, "but I don't need it. It will be more useful to you." This said, he struggled to put the money into the coat pockets of his compatriot, who tried to stop him. "No, and you? What about you?"

Pierello, even without knowing Polish, had understood and took the woman's right hand and shook it warmly. "Don't worry about him", he said. "Don't worry. I'll split my pay with Tadeusz. Goodbye, Edvige, goodbye."

The two left the warehouse.

Stretched out in the half-warm room, a bit apart from several soldiers sleeping on blankets spread out on the floor, they began to outline their plan.

"Are you also ready to come?" Pierello asked Tadeusz in a low voice.

"Now you're asking me? After you've already decided everything, you ask me?"

"You're free", Pierello answered, still softly. "You can escape with me, or you can stay, whatever you want. You're free to choose."

"Free, me free, or a prisoner? Come on, Piero, don't talk foolishness", Tadeusz observed in the Nomana dialect. "Come on, instead let us talk about what's to be done." Actually he did not seem unhappy at the decision the other man had taken for him.

"Enough of this risking our necks", Pierello observed. "If we keep on the German front, we'll end up dead, like it or not. It's a miracle things have gone this well up to now."

"Ja", Tadeusz agreed. "Ja. I've thought the same all along. Well, Piero, let's talk about what we have to do."

They were in agreement that going immediately would not be the best decision. How would they find the widow in the dark? It would be best to wait for the tractor driver's next shift (the shifts lasted three hours each). Meanwhile they could get a little sleep in the warmth. They had a lot of sleep to catch up on.

But to sleep was not easy after such a serious and unexpected decision, one that had scarcely been thought out. Tadeusz did fall asleep, but not Pierello, whose mind was turning the matter over endlessly, going from one thing to another without a stop, from plan to plan, and if an occasional calm thought relaxed him, almost to the point of sleep, another worrying idea would immediately awaken him, excite him. The young man then kept tossing and turning.

By certain gestures, he realized after a while that neither did one of the unknown Germans stretched out there—almost all of them drivers of vehicles or their helpers—manage to get to sleep. He could hear him move every so often and let out a kind of suppressed sigh. Wary because of the decision they had taken, Piero asked himself several times if this meant some sort of obstacle for him and Tadeusz. As the hours went by, he also became curious about why the other man could not sleep. He would have liked to talk with him, but how—the language block was insurmountable.

The tractor driver came in and flashed his electric torch. Pierello sat up and stretched out a hand to awaken Tadeusz, whose turn it was, but the Germans made signs for him not to do so. Coming up closer he let him know, more with gestures than words, that it was not necessary, that the vigilance of the tractor had been taken over by others now, perhaps the sentries at the deposit, with whom he had probably spoken. He smiled, expecting some gesture of gratitude from Pierello, which he managed only halfheartedly to give. Then, after having a look around with his flashlight, he went to lie down near the stove.

This change of affairs put Pierello into a new state of anxiety, though little by little he calmed down. The tractor driver suspected nothing. Tired as he was (all the German soldiers were in a state of constant tension: we can never stress that enough), he would surely get to sleep. Therefore it was not necessary to modify the plan. Thus, more or less at the moment planned—about an hour before the first light—he and Tadeusz would leave as they had agreed, except now he would have to take care and not fall asleep. In a short while he heard the tractor driver snoring, and soon his thoughts turned back to where they had been before, but he had to repeat to himself constantly that he had to be alert, very alert not to sleep. The hours slipped by.

When the tractor driver entered, the unknown German had pretended to be asleep, but in fact he had remained awake. Pierello was aware of it, and again he would have liked to know why. Which one among the many causes for anguish was tormenting him, poor wretch?

From far off, probably from the east, came an unexpected rumble, like thunder, which became steady and went on unceasing; every so often the windows of the room began to shake a little. "The Russian artillery", the young man realized. "So, they're getting ready for an attack. As soon as dawn comes they'll attack." He thought of the soldiers in the trenches under that fire: tough, brave veterans, but human beings all the same, and boys with tense, drawn faces, and old fellows from the Volkssturm. Would this damned war ever finish? He was suddenly struck with a doubt: Had the hours he surmised really gone by? The Russians always attack at dawn. Could it be near dawn? He opened his eyes. It was completely dark in the room, and outside, behind the windows, it was still dark. He closed his eyes again.

The far-off grumbling noise continued without letup.

13

The noise was still going on, always the same, when Pierello, and a few minutes later Tadeusz, left the place pretending, though no one looked at them, a physical necessity. They moved, as agreed, to the side of the warehouse so as to avoid the sentry of the depot, even though at this moment he was not in sight. In the dark—there were still no signs of light in the sky—they saw a jagged row of wagons. They approached cautiously.

On top of the wagons and even below on the ground there were people stretched out. A few children were crying softly. The horses, all of them standing as if cut out of cardboard, looked like suffering statues.

It was vital for the two of them to reach the road leading to the lagoon without raising the alarm. In some way the road was indicated, in the dirty reflection on the snow, by the row of bare trees flanking it. While they walked in that direction, they tried to hide behind the wagons among which they were moving. They had both covered their backs and heads with their own blankets, hoping to be confused with civilians.

In any event, no one looked at them. Only from under one wagon, a little dog came out and, after sniffing their heels, followed Pierello.

"What do you want?" he whispered after a few steps. "Don't you see this caravan's big enough? Go away", and he threatened it with his foot. The little animal stopped, then started to follow him again, cautious, keeping a little distance away.

They reached the highway and took it, going by many standing wagons. Now the problem was to find the little pine or fir grove that Edvige had talked about. She had said it was on the right, maybe three or four miles away, a rather vague direction. The woman's words, however, made Pierello think they would find it, and not only that, but in the grove they would also find the widow and her sons. Hadn't Edvige said that it had been the Holy Mother who had brought her to the new wagon in which she would be saved? In his simple heart Pierello was totally convinced. The Holy Mother—he reflected now—could not, however, be fond of "a bad action", that is, the death through neglect of the sick widow and her children. Therefore, she not only had led Edvige to the new wagon but also had made it possible for her to meet Tadeusz, and now the two of them would find those poor unfortunate creatures.

More than plain reasoning, it had to do with an intuition, a perception. In short, Pierello realized that it had to do with one of those interventions of the Transcendent, which were sometimes confirmed in the concerns of men when their ultimate destiny is at stake. (Even in Germany, then, they were still being confirmed!) A sense of comfort came to him that helped him, among other things—in a situation as obscure as this one—to control his impatience and tension.

And impatience and tension were not lacking, so much so that a couple of times the young man wanted to vent his feelings on the troublesome dog. "Go away! What are you doing here? Go to your master; we've got nothing to eat here!" The little animal would stop a moment, but then would start to follow behind again, as if it too were taken with the obsession of going forward.

664

The far-off rumble, like thunder, of the Russian artillery meanwhile continued, and on the eastern horizon incessant flashes could be seen.

After perhaps a half hour on the road, the eastern sky began slowly to lighten. Where was that pine grove? Perhaps Edvige had not measured the distance right? Perhaps it was closer to the deposit, and they had not seen it in the dark . . . every so often now they noticed signs of wakefulness among the wagons stopped along the edge of the road. Here a woman, her hair tousled, was lighting a fire; there a French prisoner, his coat torn, was cleaning hoar frost from a horse with a bunch of straw. Farther on, some of the wagons were starting to leave; others were arriving at the road from small bivouacs in the fields at either side. They were still far from filling the road, but the two fugitives were walking between wagons at the front and at the back.

Finally they saw, in a rather shallow depth, the grove of conifers: not green at this early hour, but all covered with the white of frozen mist. They noticed on approaching that it was crammed with refugees, some still asleep, some already on the move. An occasional wagon left and, after going up a short incline, was out on the road. Pierello and Tadeusz held themselves back from breaking into a run. They found the snow in the wood heavily trod upon and covered with refuse that the little dog was sniffing out, and there were remains of fires among the wagons, objects thrown out, horse manure, and human excrement. Tadeusz immediately began to ask at his right and his left—in his terrible German—if someone had seen a woman with two boys like this or that. Some did not so much as look at him or did not understand him; some answered that they had not; others seemed dubious. A Polish prisoner who was feeding fir twigs to two skeletons of horses said he had, that he had seen a woman and two boys with a little sled, nestled together asleep under a tree almost at the other end of the wood. But even though they were both running, they found no one. Could the Hufenbachs have left alone? Or perhaps someone had taken them along? And would it be them or someone else? They were about to retrace their steps when Pierello finally saw them, still on a lesser trail that, leaving from the wood, climbed obliquely up the incline to the road.

"There they are!" Pierello said excitedly. "Look at them, Tadeusz. There they are!"

"Yes", Tadeusz answered. "Yes."

"It's the Holy Mother", Pierello exclaimed, "who's made it possible for us to find them." He hurried together with Tadeusz to the little group, as exultant as if he had seen someone from his own home. The little dog followed, also excited.

Before the two prisoners a wagon was advancing on the narrow trail. It overtook the little sled, veering just enough not to hit them. The widow was seated on the sled, very bundled up, and in front—pulling a rope—were Joachim and his little ten-year-old brother. Joachim stretched out his free hand with a supplicating gesture to the people in the wagon, futilely invoking their help. It was evident the two boys could not climb the incline.

When the two prisoners were close by, Joachim, without recognizing them, stretched his supplicating hand to them, too. "*Soldaten, diese ist meine Mutter, soldaten . . .*", he implored in a tearful voice.

"Joachim!" Pierello then shouted, leaped toward him, and held his hands around the boy's face. "Don't you recognize me, Joachim?"

The boy let out a scream, and the other boy let the rope fall and started to shout.

"So, it's you!" Pierello said excitedly in the dialect of Nomana. "And so we've found you!"

Joachim hugged him, pressed himself convulsively against him. The little boy kept stretching an arm toward the two soldiers without speaking. Tadeusz bent over him, put his right hand on his fur cap, pushing it back and forth several times, mussing up the fur. "Be brave", he went on repeating in his terrible German. "Be brave. Now we're here. You're not alone now."

Without leaving Joachim, Pierello went up to the widow, who was looking at them, sitting stiffly incredulous. "The Holy Mother sent us," he declared, forgetting she was Protestant, "the Holy Mother".

The old lady nodded. Tears began to run down her face, over her worn, aged features, poorly covered up in a dark shawl. "*Die Gottesmutter sie gebolt* (our thanks to the Mother of God)", she said at last.

It took a little while for the five of them to calm down. Then the questions, the inquiries, the reciprocal explanations began. Afterward Pierello and Tadeusz examined the sled, little more than a yard long, and found it too small and fragile. It was really no more than a toy, and so they decided that as soon as they could, they would get a more suitable vehicle. "But not now. The first thing now is to cross the lagoon and to think of nothing else. Then we'll see."

"Yes," the three Germans approved, "the lagoon. First we'll cross the lagoon." That was obviously their obsession, like all the other fugitives.

The two prisoners were ready to grasp the piece of wood attached to the cord of the sled when the widow Hufenbach pointed out that with those military coats they would have problems at the roadblocks. They both realized that and secretly were afraid of that difficulty, but what was there for them to do? The problem was solved for Pierello with an overcoat of the late Mr. Hufenbach, quite crumpled, on which the widow was seated. It was also solved for Tadeusz—after some hesitation (he, being a fatalist, was ready to risk it)—by temporarily changing his own coat for a woolen, tobacco-colored blanket, in which they cut a hole in the middle for him to put his head through. Then he tightened the waist with a string. Both the Wehrmacht coats were properly folded, as well as the two army blankets, and put on the sled. Nothing of the German uniforms of the two prisoners remained except the gray visor cap.

After this the small caravan moved off with the little dog still in the rear-guard. Pierello's brief German army service was over. It had lasted a few weeks, during which he had run more mortal risks perhaps than during his Italian service of several years.

14

They had to wait several hours on the banks of the lagoon among many other refugees. Without letting it be seen, the two prisoners—most especially Pierello—looked around every so often, inwardly worried someone might come looking for them. A small but efficient service crew of soldiers did not allow the wagons to go down the small incline in any fashion whatever, but instead made them descend one by one, in order to keep some ten yards between them on the "ice bridge". At least this was the order for the first stretch, where there were pools of water and mud, on which rough-hewn boards had been joined, more than half of their thickness sunk in the greenish ice.

From the shore, on which more and more wagons and refugees on foot were gathered, could be seen a very long moving row, which got lost in the distance over the treacherous lagoon. The sky was lowering with clouds mixed with mist. A more desolate landscape was unimaginable. Some of the pairs of horses refused to descend down to the "ice bridge", snorting and pointing their hooves. Then the driver (often a woman) on one side and a soldier on the other side would force them to move. As soon as they got over the boards, these horses would hurry up their pace, perhaps frightened, and the driver and the soldier would have to hold them back strenuously until they got into step, after which the soldier returned to repeat the operation.

The turn came for our refugees, who did not realize they had meanwhile lost the dog, who had so absorbed the impatience of the men over the delay that it had furtively left to follow one of the wagons leaving before them.

It was difficult to drag the sled over the boards. Every so often Pierello and Tadeusz would turn to glance back, fearing it would come apart. At last the boards came to an end, and the track continued over the ice itself. There was less danger of the vehicle coming apart here, and it was also easier for the men to pull it. The two prisoners kept up the same pace as the rest of the column, careful to keep the distances. Luckily it did not mean a quick step, since the pace was set by the large number of almost exhausted horses, some hardly able to move. *The pace suits us*, Pierello thought, as his secret anxiety began to vanish, the worry that had preyed on him until now: that someone might come for them.

A little later, the shore at their backs began to fade into the mist and then disappear. Now the fugitives could see nothing but the moving column in front and in back of them. They knew they had about six miles of traveling ahead of them. Despite the cold Pierello began to sweat. In spite of everything the march was becoming fatiguing, and he was already tired from the fatigue of the front that had set and stratified into his bones. Besides, he had much sleep to make up for—the night before he had not slept for a single second . . . The column, which moved in silence and seemed not to have a beginning or an end, was beginning to wreak a strange sense of unreality on him. After some time the question struck him as to where they were going, all lined up that way, looking half dead, in those unreal surroundings, as if not of this world. And what was that distant and incessant accompaniment, like thunder, that had entered his brain, never stopping, never?

He tried to make a joke of it to himself and began to argue about it with himself. Without realizing it, he was finally talking out loud. He was drawn out of this state by Joachim, who had grabbed his hand, pulling it, proposing to take over. "No, no, Joachim", Pierello exclaimed in dialect. "What's come over you? Take over? That's all we need." He took in a couple of deep breaths and smiled with silent understanding at the boy. Good God, what a relief to see a child's face! It reminded him of home, the peaceful days . . . Pierello, a little embarrassed by what had happened, decided "to take himself in hand" (using the German expression to control himself) more energetically. He pulled a rabbit's face to make Joachim laugh and every few steps repeated it with snorts and nose twitchings, until the boy, calmed down, began to imitate him, not thinking of anything else.

There were the signs of the bombardment from the day before. No, no, it could not have been from the day before, because the ice in the gashes was already too frozen. The truck swerved and went along, zigzagging among wooden poles and arrows that indicated the course. From the newly formed ice came out the sides and shafts of carts, clothes, and, look there, half a horse's head. Oh, what a hideous sight! Just as well the clouds were low today. Perhaps the airplanes would not attack. Perhaps. On the ice, at the side of the track were objects and packages, no doubt thrown from the wagons to lighten their load. Look again, one, two, several wagons abandoned, some with broken wheels, others with their shafts raised and half absorbed by the ice. At one stretch of the track they had laid down boards on the path, just like at the beginning of the "bridge", and the wheels of the wagons went over them joltingly.

And there, after about another mile of track, was the place that had been bombed yesterday, rather an extensive area. Soldiers—not many—were stationed there on the ice, keeping the column of wagons away from the dangerous spots and indicating the track, which occasionally went between cracks in the ice that were very close together.

"Where are the party people?" the widow asked suddenly. (And she meant "those who put us in this situation?") "The soldiers have to do everything."

In the puddles of dirty water, hardly covered with a film of ice, not only objects, wagons, and horses came to the surface but human bodies, too. "Poor people", Pierello murmured, and then to Joachim, who was still walking beside him, "Don't look, Joachim. Look the other way."

However, he and Tadeusz looked, and in one of those tragic pits Tadeusz discovered something that could be useful to them. He pointed it out to Pierello. They exchanged a few words and then, by common consent, pushed the little sled off the track and stopped.

"Wait for me here", Pierello told the others. "I'm going to have a look." And while the Pole was explaining to the widow why they had stopped, he went up to look cautiously into the hole. In the last few yards he was helped by the fact that on the edge of the crack there was a big slab over the paving of ice, doubling its thickness. In the brownish water a little wagon was overturned, about two yards in length, with the wheels apparently in a good state of repair.

A German sentry soldier shouted something from not too far off, then, seeing that the prisoner did not withdraw, came up angrily to him. But it was with his help and that of a hook (which the soldier, somewhat older, went to fetch from his outpost, but not without first lecturing Pierello) that Pierello and Tadeusz were able to drag the little wagon from the water. It turned out to be the kind for carrying hay, light, with hayrick sides and hand-operated shafts, and indeed, all four wheels in good condition. The moving of the widow (she suffered greatly when she was put on her feet) and their few things to the little wagon did not take much time. Pierello, now slightly embarrassed by the weakness he had shown before, set the little boy between the arms of the woman.

After another hour on the track, and three altogether across the lagoon, the little group, completed by Joachim, who, quite on his own, was pulling the empty sled behind him, finally reached the opposite shore. Only here did Joachim decide to leave the sled. He carefully left it well in sight, should someone happen to need it. But despite all appearances the little German boy, so serious and resolute that he made Pierello smile, was actually exhausted, ready to collapse with tiredness.

The five of them found themselves on solid ground for only a short time before violent explosions sounded at their backs, mixed with machine-gun fire and the noise of motors. Immediately afterward enemy aviation arrived, four planes, flying very low and menacingly. Their bright colors stood out in contrast with the gray sky. At the shore they turned with a deafening din and flew off over solid land, firing incessantly with their machine guns and suddenly disappearing to the west.

"We've been lucky this time, too", Pierello commented, getting up, smiling sadly, from the snow on which he had immediately thrown himself. It had gone well for them, yes, but the others, especially those following on the ice? And how had it gone for the lecturing soldier who had helped them recover the cart? But better not to think of all that. It was impossible to take in everybody's miseries.

15

The Frische Nehrung, the slight strip of sand about fifty miles long that separated the Königsberg lagoon from the cold waters of the Baltic Sea, was boiling over with refugees and wagons, all moving westward. It emerged about ten yards from the water (the inland waters, which were iced over, as it has been mentioned, while the sea was rough and dotted with dirty white spume) and seemed to go on forever in both directions.

The artillery bombardment, over to the east, had suddenly stopped. Perhaps it was only a pause, or perhaps the enemy they feared was in the process of attacking. They could imagine them coming closer, shouting, preceded by a shower of lead, drunk on alcohol; the poor, wretched, fierce, slaughterhouse flesh that they were, too ... here, in any case, over the Nehrung, there was a tangible silence, made more striking by the humble creaking of cart wheels, the squeaking of the metal from some sled or other, and, at intervals, the whistling of the icy wind coming from the sea.

How many people were there trying to save themselves on the modest isthmus road, which had been used only by fishermen before? Pierello—resting with the others to recharge his strength and to eat a little—thought that beyond the "ice bridges" there certainly would be a real transport system toward Königsberg, if the refugees on foot looking like city folk were so numerous. He noticed with surprise that besides the refugees there was an occasional soldier, too: German soldiers without weapons, alone or in small groups ... he even saw two very young SS men, hardly more than boys, with a stupefied expression. He felt sorry for them. It was improbable there would not be "guard dogs" ahead of them, and then what would be the fate of these poor wretches?

After a short rest and a bite to eat the small group set out again walking, but a little later it was necessary to leave the highway to let a convoy of military trucks go by in the opposite direction, straight to the east. It was a convoy to be feared, like all German convoys, but to Pierello it seemed in some way raggle-taggle, perhaps even badly armed. In any case, he told himself, it was a force that was going to place itself between them and the enemy. Joachim greeted the soldiers by waving his hand. Other refugees shouted questions: "The Second Army? Is the road to Danzig still open?" The soldiers answered that it was open. A few even tried to calm the people down with gestures. However, Pierello and Tadeusz began to see one thing clearly: that even having crossed the lagoon did not yet mean salvation, that danger and uncertainty were still ahead of them.

After a few hours they had to clear the way to let other trucks with trailers pass—coming from the opposite direction to that of the first group—which were loaded with wounded soldiers and sailors, some badly bandaged up with strips of toilet paper. A refugee with elegant manners, who at that moment was next to the little cart, explained, without their asking, that an order had been given to transform Königsberg and the port of Pillau, as well as all cities of any importance in the invaded territory, into "fortresses" and to resist to the last man, even if besieged, using every house as if it were a bunker. That is why—the distinguished refugee explained—the command wanted to clear out the more seriously wounded, useless for defense, in time.

The march over the narrow sandy strip of the Nehrung lasted some days. The refugees during the last stretch were so numerous they could hardly continue, and many of the wagons found themselves forced to get on the ice of the lagoon next to the shore, others, still more fatiguing, onto the seashore where the waves were breaking. Later, it was calculated that more than two million people had escaped from the enemy on that road. The rest periods for the wagons and the pedestrians were of necessity becoming more frequent. There was a lack of everything, but especially drinking water, and a scarcity of wood for fires and for melting the snow. More than a few horses ended up drinking the brackish lagoon water and then came down with violent colic, in no condition to go on. Meanwhile the temperature was dropping, reaching ten and fifteen degrees below zero. People and horses were beginning to die.

The little cart that Pierello and Tadeusz were pulling by hand reached the Vistula on the second or third of February. The movement of the barges over the dark river, which had seen the horrendous massacre of Polish partisan insurgents in the course of the summer, was continuous, incessant. Farther on, in Danzig-Oliva, there was finally an impressive and well-organized service to provide assistance to the refugees. The little group was able to rest a few days. It was ascertained that the two feet of the widow and an arm and the nose of the younger boy had become frozen.

Notwithstanding, like the other refugees, they still had to continue on foot to Pomerania. Simultaneous with the Russian offensive, and in support of it, another offensive was beginning using thousands and thousands of Anglo-American airplanes to blow the German railway network systematically to pieces.

PART SEVEN

I

No news reached Nomana about Pierello in the entire month of February. However, there was frequent news, even in the press and on Fascist radio, about the great Russian offensive. The people there, as in the rest of Italy, nevertheless were more interested in the Allies' air offensive, which had received a great deal of propaganda from Radio London, yet there were really no clear ideas about it. The people did not realize, among other things, what really had happened in Dresden, on the occasion of the great February 14 bombing. Perhaps the Allies themselves, who carried it out, did not realize what it was about at first. The city, which was the greatest clearing center toward the eastern front, no longer had antiair defense at its disposal, its batteries having all been moved to the front as antitank weaponry, and it was congested with military convoys and an incalculable number of refugees. On the night of February 14 it was attacked by such a quantity of English bombs that it was immediately transformed into an immense furnace. Oxygen was needed to fan the flames, and—as in a well-constructed furnace—violent air currents formed in the tunnels of the streets that lifted objects and human bodies and carried them away toward the center of the city, more than a hundred yards off, and then tossed them vehemently up into the air. The morning after, following this slaughter in flames, a storm of bombs from four-engine American planes was let loose. Fifty thousand dead were counted in the days to follow, but it was not an exact figure, since in some neighborhoods the calculation was based on the number of carbonized human heads that could be found. (After the war the figure rose gradually until the number came to be 135,000 dead!)

Notwithstanding, the German soldiers succeeded in stopping the Russians on the Oder River. The latter closed ranks over their own immense masses and threw themselves forward again. Thus began the second large offensive on German land, which culminated in the battle of withdrawal in the western Neisse. Once again blocked, the Russians closed ranks again and literally destroying everything with weapons and explosives (the photographs testifying to this are impressive), they sparked off the last great offensive, which took them to Berlin.

From the west, meanwhile, the American and English Army, the French, too, were going forward, meeting up with less and less resistance, because the German military command—at odds with the frantic orders from Hitler—were moving as many forces as they could to the east to defend the population from violence and extermination. The number of German divisions on the eastern front went from 135 to 193 between January and April, but often they were divisions in name only, some reduced to a single battalion or less. But they continued fighting with unchanging tenacity, as much on the frontline as in the several surrounded cities left behind, those called "fortresses". Side by side the soldiers, old people, and children from the Volkssturm, and even those who had been declared unfit for military service and had made up the "worker's organization", resisted with dramatic zeal (these last armed sometimes only with Panzerfaust). Königsberg, for example—against whose defense Pierello had heard the Russian artillery fire in January at the time of his flight—fell only on the tenth of April, after some of its defending survivors, taken with a kind of desperate madness, even fired on their own representatives, who, with the white flag, were going by order of the commanding general to ask for surrender.

Just then—that is, during the first half of April—the Apennine front came to life in Italy, after having stayed quiet for some months at the "Gothic line". Then the idea began to spread that the war was really at the point of coming to an end.

Ambrogio also was aware of it in Nomana. Unfortunately, at the change of season the consequences of his illness again flared up, and on certain days they kept him from doing anything. He would spend the evenings then with his father talking over the situation. "We're getting to the end of it this time. So many other times we thought so, and we were let down, but this time we won't be. The Germans are at the end of their tether. They no longer have a place to stand on."

"Yes, I think it's over this time, too."

"So, in a while we'll finally be able to find out if Manno and the others, Stefano and Michele and Luca, and my soldiers who were surrounded, are still alive. Do you realize? This damned uncertainty will be over once and for all."

"And we'll be able to get back to some constructive work and do something not for the war, not for destruction, and it's high time. You perhaps don't really realize this, but it's urgent, absolutely necessary. We've been busy destroying for years, and now most people have almost nothing to live on. It's time to do something positive."

"Yes, I understand."

"What worries me", and it was not the first time Gerardo had expressed this fear of his, "is that for us the war might end with a tremendous massacre, a great bloodbath of these wretches." He was referring to the Fascists. "Naturally, they've been thoroughgoing rascals, and it's only fair that those really responsible pay the price, that they be punished. But that they all end up executed ... that, no. It's something that doesn't seem just to me."

"Do you think Italy will lower itself to the level of the Russians and Germans, too? We're not like that."

"But if the Communist partisans were given a free hand, even if only for a few weeks before the arrival of the Americans, what would happen?"

"There are other partisans besides, and on this legitimate government, for better or worse—at least in theory—all the partisans depend. And why should the Americans delay? From the Apennines to the Alps is no big distance."

"Well, we'll see."

Concern over the fate of the Fascists was not, however, so widespread among others. To the unbearable anguish that in those days was torturing the Fascists and their families (hundreds and hundreds of thousands of human beings were involved), not even Gerardo and Ambrogio gave much thought. As far as the people were concerned, including those in Nomana, they simplified things as usual. The Fascists were guilty. Therefore they would have to pay. And even though wholesale slaughter was not, of course, being recommended, if that turned out to be the case, so much the worse for them.

News of the Allied attack on the Apennine front was becoming more and more frequent on the radio and in the newspapers, which talked of the particular violence of the fights in the valleys of Senio and Santerno, close to Bologna. Even though no details were given, it was known that the ones attacking there were regular Italian divisions, which numbered six, armed and equipped by the English. They had gained status in the complex of Allied forces in Italy.

The Germans fought back the Allied attack energetically, even after it had spread along the entire front, until suddenly, because of the enormous disproportion of forces, they were compelled to retreat toward the Po. From on high a terribly potent air force attacked them, and all around were swarms of partisans: those who had been around a long time and the more recent ones— more numerous still—who formed and reformed and were everywhere.

2

In Nomana a partisan group had also been formed after the arrival in the town of a thirty-year-old outsider, a refugee it was said, who had found work in an artisan workshop.

Given the fact that everything was known about everything and everybody in the town, it became immediately known that this fellow was making contact with the young people in the town who were known to be independent or "more secularly inclined" (perhaps for having been to the Oratory infrequently), or who were idle or, better still, dubious characters. To those he secretly suggested coming into a Communist squadron of partisans, which, he claimed, he had received the job of forming in Nomana.

No one, not even the Fascist secretary, thought of denouncing him to "the national republican guard", established some months before in the garrison, which previously was that of the carabinieri. It was clear, of course, to everyone that—while awaiting the return of the braver youths from prisons—it would be necessary to organize something to oppose him, anything that might keep the town from being at the mercy of the Communists in the difficult days to come during the transfer of powers.

It was the golden moment for the pharmacist Dr. Agazzino, who—getting wind of the contacts Ambrogio was beginning to make—went to see him one night, with great secrecy, and in conspiratorial fashion begged him "not to damage the community by getting in his way and setting up something that would amount to uselessly duplicated efforts". Wouldn't it be better to come to an agreement and to divide up the duties? Ambrogio was quite happy to leave the field open to him. He noticed a poorly hidden satisfaction in the other's eyes. They agreed, however, that Ambrogio would be available for consultation on "military matters".

Small of stature, red faced, bald, suffering from asthma, Dr. Agazzino had lived up until then with secret political ambitions as well as frustration, cloistered in his pharmacy, which looked out on a cobbled area not far from the church. He was behind the counter the entire day, with shelves of ceramic bottles adorned with arabesques and Latin names of medicines at his back, breathing the sharp odor of pharmacies in those days. He was not originally from Nomana, but from Piacenza, where in his youth he had been part of the Catholic left party of Miglioli, in that fabulous time in which Fascists dealt blows with their canes and prescribed castor oil to the members of the "white leagues". Two glasses of that oil, swallowed by him under threat, comprised the culminating point of his political past. These two glasses had given him the right to congratulate himself secretly (and a few, rare times in front of others) for twenty years for his civic superiority over these poor natives of Nomana, who had never really known fascism, or social struggles, or had ever formed white—or any other color—leagues.

In life, it must be admitted, tragedy, comedy, and farce continually mingle. It was particularly true during those days. And so Agazzino, having sensed the generalized worry (not only among those of great authority but also, and no less, among many heads of working class families), felt it was his moment to act. He hurried off to Milan to seek out his old friends from the white leagues, and through one of them he was given, in no time at all, the presidency of the CLN (Committee for National Liberation) of Nomana. Together with that he was given the job of making immediate contact with the Communist outsider, and the Socialist, Liberal, and (Catholic) Action parties. It was understood that the person provisionally in charge would be himself, Agazzino. The heads of the Socialist, Liberal, and Action parties in Nomana, however, did not exist. Thus the pharmacist, despite himself, was forced to create them. That turned out to be quite an easy undertaking for the Socialist party (given the presence in town of the post office official, Benfatti, who, as already mentioned, was known to everyone as an old Socialist). It was not that easy regarding the Liberal and Action parties. Finally, concerning the Liberals, after much anger on the part of the pharmacist, an evacuee friend of his agreed to represent them. He was an extempore poet, the author of epigrams and poetry in dialect, who although at one time vaguely pro-Fascist had also been—because of his inveterate habit of telling jokes about the Fascist hierarchy while on the train—in jail for two days. Thus the Nomana CLN considered him a brave victim of the regime. For the Action party—no one quite knew what that was—it was necessary to take old Mr. Pollastri, a clerk by profession, always ready to show himself in public. In fact, he had asked Agazzino to be made the Social party representative and, on finding out that this post was not available, had asked at least to represent the Royalist party. Realizing that there was no monarchic party in the CLN, he had to make do with the Action party.

Dr. Agazzino was no fool at all, and he realized how paradoxical all this was, even if he was far from imagining the problems that would be caused for the country in the future by a similar, almost self-imposed political system. He had hardly read a few clandestine sheets and consequently was unaware of almost anything that was going on in Italy. In particular, he did not grasp the basic idea, which was that Italy was a kind of "puppet", previously at the mercy of fascism and afterward of antifascism. He had not so much as heard of the famous "debate of the five letters", by which during the previous November the five parties of the CLN—knowing their moment to take over power was near at hand, notwithstanding the obstacle constituted by the odious legitimate government in Rome—had tried for a stable union, which would then allow them to follow "CLN politics" indefinitely even in time of peace. In November it was Agazzino's party, that is, the Christian Democrats, that had opposed a monopoly of power like that in the name of democracy. But this party too had not been able to prevent the systematic establishment of the CLN in every town hall, as soon as it found itself on this side of the Allies.

In any case, the pharmacist was, above all, a practical man, and he adapted to whatever the reality was. "I haven't created this situation", he would say sometimes, as an excuse, to some friend or other. "If I hadn't taken the job in Nomana, someone else would have been chosen surely, so it's all the same." Obviously, he was not about to explain that he had taken the job out of personal ambition and to some extent from a spirit of adventure, despite his asthma.

Besides the representatives of the parties, he also had to seek out a few young people to arm. Since he was not going to depend on Ambrogio for this (public opinion, he thought, would end up giving him all the credit), he went to the parish church, requesting the names of the ablest boys in the Oratory. For that he had to explain the CLN organization in great detail to the priest, and likewise he had to listen to the indignant response from the priest that the Oratory

676

was "something too serious to have it mixed up in matters like that". He protested, he insisted, and tried to assert his own reasons. "You, rather we Catholics, we prefer to be in peace in the shadow of the Church. I know that. But, no. At the present time we can no longer permit ourselves . . ." The old and austere priest, with curly hair that made him look like a shepherd from the mountains, had to agree, but he still would not proffer one name. "Our boys could end up shooting it out with those madmen wearing black shirts at the garrison and even killing someone. And you want me to put them in the situation of perhaps killing their neighbor?"

The pharmacist was obliged then to provide himself, some way or other, with boys he knew personally or whose families he knew. Generally they were not yet of military age and, being younger, accepted "becoming partisans" with all the more enthusiasm. He managed to gather together a dozen: a few less than those (also generally younger than twenty) gathered by the Communist stranger. So, on the evening of the twenty-fifth of April when the news—brought by commuters and evacuees—arrived that Milan was in the process of "a kind of uprising", then Nomana, too, could make use of its own insurgent forces.

3

The news of the still uncertain happenings in Milan was received by Agazzino on the evening of April 25 from Matteo, a worker and neighbor of his who worked in the city and who appeared at his home no sooner than he got off the train. This fellow—without the pharmacist suspecting it—was well aware of the business the pharmacist was involved in, and, considering it a defense of religion and the Church, he inwardly approved.

"Doctor, do you know what's happening in Milan?" he asked in dialect, going into the pharmacy.

"In Milan? What's happening?" the other responded, also in dialect, surprised and a little bit ill at ease.

"I see they're not up on the news here in the town", Matteo said, turning over in his hands the old imitation leather cap, which he had worn for years going to work. "That's how it seemed to me."

"But what are you talking about? What is happening?"

"They're staging a rebellion, or . . . just about", Matteo said.

"A what . . . what . . . ?" the pharmacist said, and even though only the two of them were inside, he signaled the worker to follow him to the back of the shop.

Would it be possible, he was thinking meanwhile, *that the CLN people wouldn't have let me know, those S.O.B.s? And with the few armed forces (well, not even armed, but they soon will be) they've made me put together! It's . . . dangerous! And how do I figure in all this now? What lousy sh——s.* Once in the back of the shop, he asked Matteo softly, "Well? Tell me what's happening."

"A real uprising, although no shooting. At least I didn't hear any," the worker said, "yet almost none of the factories of Milan is working today. Even on the train they were saying so. In certain places they started work in the morning, but during the day they all shut down."

"And the trolleys, were they working or not?" The pharmacist had not asked that question unintentionally. His party comrades had told him time and again, "It will all start when the means of public transport stop working."

"The trolleys were working this morning when I got to Milan. But they weren't by afternoon, and when we left the factory they weren't running, so I had to make my way on foot to the station. All by foot, you know, and where I work, at the Formenti, is far away."

"And what did you all do in the factory all day, if it was on strike?"

"We had to listen to the partisans, because the partisans all came out—some from the factory, others not—and they started to talk. 'You see how the Fascists do nothing against you?' they said. 'You're on strike, and they do nothing. Do you see that? It's no longer like it was in the old days when it meant watch out if you went on strike. That's all over now. The Fascists are not strong enough to do anything.' And in fact that's how it was."

"Why? Were there Fascists in the factory, too?"

"Inside no. They were outside, in the streets. There were fewer than usual perhaps, but a few were around. We could see them from the windows. They were walking around with their machine guns, but they didn't know what to do. They weren't shooting at the strikers or at anyone else."

"Well, there was also a halfhearted strike a few days ago in Milan, and the Fascists didn't get involved."

"Yes, but today . . . they all said it was different today. There was no argument about it, no comparison, I tell you. The Fascists didn't even dare go into the factories. They were in the streets, but I didn't hear a shot the whole day. The Germans were also in the streets, but mainly on their trucks. They are really breaking away, it seems to me."

"But, yes or no, was there or wasn't there an uprising today?"

"Well, I'd say there was", the worker declared. "Besides, later on others came to the factory, the party representatives, to tell us the Fascists were through. Doctor, the Communists and the Socialists came, but luckily our people came too, I mean the Christians, the Christian Democrats, in short, our people. People from Catholic Action, you understand? You could see them a mile off." He nodded gravely and repeated, "Luckily."

"But are you sure there are still Fascists going around armed?"

"Certainly. For example, in front of the central station a little over an hour ago, there were." And Matteo concluded, "The little I had to say, I've said. Now you do whatever there's to be done. I've got to eat supper."

He shook the hand the pharmacist graciously stretched out to him ("Thank you, Matteo, it's obvious you're a . . . you're a democrat."), then put on his old imitation leather visor cap, and, going through the pharmacy, reached the street. Behind him the glass doors of the pharmacy, adorned with emery glass designs of rampant serpents around a goblet, shut with a triple ring that all of Nomana recognized.

By himself, the pharmacist—quite worried—gave himself over to some deep thought. What was really happening? Leaving him in the dark, he, the president of the CLN! What orders was he to give to his partisans? And if someone came now—one of the town's elders maybe—to ask him the news? What a mess! And then—still worse, worse than anything—if this strange kind of insurrection should fail, maybe after he'd wasted words right and left, or taken some sort of initiative?

"Ah, no! No, not that! You can't leave me like that!" he murmured like a caged animal walking back and forth between the counter and the shelves on which the row of ceramic jars were lined up with arabesques and Latin names on them, all handmade. "You have to talk, you have to tell me what's happening . . ." Quite suddenly he went to the telephone, and although his friend from the white league most decidedly insisted that he never call him like that, he asked the switchboard to be connected with him. At last the woman at the switchboard told him the number he was asking for was not answering. Agazzino then asked for the number of someone else he knew in Milan who he knew was involved in politics, but that number did not answer either. He became so excited that he finally ended up asking the switchboard operator if she by any chance knew what was happening in Milan. The operator (who was not in Milan but in Brianza, in the town of Seregno) had heard some confused talk and was thinking about it, but she was afraid she might be talking to a *provocateur*, and so she answered as impersonally as possible, which seemed very strange to the pharmacist. Even she was acting mysteriously! What was happening around him, without his even realizing it? Reality, what mattered, was passing him by quite closely like a train he could not see and on which he could not get aboard. He was about to lose his mind. At that point he thought of Ambrogio, how the young man had told him he would be at his disposal in case he needed him. *He's someone who won't miss the train easily*, he reflected, and went once more to the telephone, but he had second thoughts and, instead of calling, rushed to the door, opened it with its familiar ring, dashed some ten yards down the street, and looked in at the door of a house in which a family was seated at a table dining.

"Pardon me, pardon me", he said to all of them, and addressing himself to a boy of sixteen or seventeen who was part of his organization, he said, "Giacomino, hurry, go to the Rivas. Tell Ambrogio—you know who he is, the officer on leave—to come, rather, could he please come immediately, I must talk to him. Hurry, it's urgent, so run."

The Giacomino in question smelled war, so he was off like a shot, as if hurling into a hurricane.

"At least take your napkin off from around your neck!" his mother yelled at him. He yanked the napkin off with a gesture that was meant to be deprecatory regarding such a prosaic object, and, while he ran toward the door, he threw it back on his empty chair.

"What's happening?" the head of the family asked the pharmacist after the first moments of reciprocal embarrassment. "What's happening? Is there anything new?" The pharmacist raised his hands high, waved them repeatedly with a vague gesture that could have signified, "It's better not to talk about this", or also, "I've too much to do now. I can't stay . . ." Then, with a "Well, goodnight everyone", he turned around and returned quickly to his pharmacy.

4

Ambrogio arrived there a little later, followed by Giacomino.

"You go back home", the pharmacist told the boy, who seemed disappointed. "But be on the alert. Don't move from your house. I want you to be ready. All right?"

"Yes, of course", the boy answered, impressed and satisfied with the phrase "I want you to be ready", which had, it seemed to him, something of a military ring.

"What's happening, Doctor?" Ambrogio asked the pharmacist once he was alone with him. He noticed the man's state of agitation. "Is it about the news from Milan?"

"Yes, exactly", the other answered. "Do you know anything concrete?"

"Concrete, not really", Ambrogio said.

"Come, come", Agazzino said, and taking him by an arm he led him to the back of the shop. "Sit down", he said, and he sat down in front of him. While the young man was talking, the pharmacist—shorter than Ambrogio—was watching him nervously, smiling, his face turning redder and redder. Even his bald head went red. Ambrogio's news coincided with that of the pharmacist. It had also come from an employee who had arrived on the same train as Matteo, the worker.

"And now?" the pharmacist said, standing up, agitated. "Was there or wasn't there an uprising? Damn it all!" he exclaimed, opening his arms angrily. "This really is something. To think we can't find out." He started to walk around, despite the limited space.

Ambrogio smiled. "There was one, without a doubt. It did happen", he assured him. He enumerated the reasons in support of it while the pharmacist sat down again in front of him: first of all, the news given in the latest editions of the newspapers themselves and on the radio under Fascist control in relation to the Italian front. "Yesterday the *Corriere* carried the German bulletin of two days ago, with the news that Bologna had been abandoned, didn't it? Today, also in the *Corriere*, there's talk of fighting around Modena. It was in big headlines. Did you see it? Did you read it?"

"Yes, I read it, of course."

"So it means the Allies are advancing full speed ahead in the Po plains. What I'm wondering—I say this parenthetically—is what part we're playing in this advance, I mean, the divisions from our army?"

"Do you believe?" the pharmacist said distractedly. "Yes, in fact, from time to time, Radio London . . ."

Ambrogio nodded. "Fifteen days ago, when the front on the Apennines began to wake up, the radio and the *Corriere* went on talking about the valleys of Senio and Santerno, remember? Well, Radio London has made it clear that there are—or better, there were—the Folgore and the Legnano divisions, and it was our troops that were attacking. Once it even talked about the Friuli, and I wondered whether . . . well, let's leave it at that. It doesn't matter how. So, the situation in Italy is this. The Allies are advancing along the plain toward Milan, and who knows where they've got to now. That's just one thing." Ambrogio made his idea visual by clenching the fist of his left hand and raising his thumb. "In the second place", and he lifted his index finger. "In Germany? We're used to hearing talk about the retreating Germans, so much so that it seems they're going to go on forever. Actually, now, just because of the retreat, not a piece of ground remains for the Germans to stand on. You must have read in the *Corriere* of two days, no, three days ago that the Americans are fighting in the Sudeten. The mountains of the Sudeten are in Czechoslovakia. The Americans are in Czechoslovakia. Do you realize what that means? And then— thirdly—all that news about Berlin: that it's enclosed by arms and fire, that the German women are fighting side by side with their men against the Red army (poor creatures!), et cetera. The radio and the newspapers have been repeating it for three days. What uprising must we then expect?" he concluded. "What can the Fascists and Germans, poor devils, hold onto?"

"Poor devils, yes, but they brought it on themselves", the pharmacist exclaimed with a voice that was becoming exultant. (He had not considered it ever from a military point of view, as Ambrogio was now doing.) "Poor devils, yes, but it's what they asked for."

"True, they looked for it, and they deserved it. Of course, but that doesn't keep me from feeling sorry for them."

"All right", the pharmacist said, as if to sum things up. (The picture Ambrogio had given seemed more and more convincing, beyond discussion.) "All right, but what should we in Nomana do? Because there are still Fascists and Germans around, that's the question." He stood up again. "And if we should wait till tomorrow to make a decision? Wait to see what happens in Milan first?"

"Do what you think. But in the meantime the danger is that the Communists might make a move," Ambrogio paused, "and you haven't received any weapons here yet, have you?"

"No, not yet."

"And the Communists?"

"They haven't either, I guess."

"So, the only weapons in town are those of the black guards. Are we going to run the risk of the Communists taking them over?" He reflected, "There's another thing that depends on how you handle it, Doctor, and that's the lives of those poor militiamen, who basically have never really made trouble in the town."

"Except on two occasions when they took to the streets drunk and started shooting up and . . . the first time you were still in the hospital, but . . ."

"Well, after all is said and done, they killed no one. Wait, I'm thinking . . . and if we got Don Mario to act? He could explain to the militia what's happening in Milan, should they not know it already, and persuade them to move off right away while there's time. After having handed over their weapons, let's say, in exchange for civilian clothes. Why not? And even an old bicycle or two?"

"It's a great idea!" the pharmacist exclaimed, becoming a bit exalted. "It's an idea that's really . . . how to put it—like killing two birds with one stone. I'd, too, rather see nothing happening to the militia. It's only logical. They're only boys who have mothers and fathers, too." He was sorry that idea had not occurred to him; he was tempted to appropriate it. "You know, I was also thinking along those lines. Only I didn't know, and still don't" (at this point he was on the brink of another about face), "if it's still the right moment to act or not."

"Well, something has to be risked", Ambrogio said, smiling and standing up. "Listen, Doctor, I'm going to dine now because I was already seated at the table when I was called from the house. Then I'm going to see Don Mario, and I'll ask him if he wouldn't mind—when you tell him—talking to the militiamen, and I'll come back with his answer. Let's say within a half hour or, at most, forty minutes, I'll be back here. Meanwhile, you'll have time to decide on whether or not you want to deal with the militia. Maybe in the meantime you could telephone Milan again. And perhaps (I don't know, it's up to you, these are simply ideas that just come to me and then have to be thought over) you might be able to meet with the CLN people, to decide together whether to act or not."

"What are you saying? So that the whole town will start gossiping? What are you talking about? And then we'll have to meet with the Communists, too."

"That's true."

"No, I'm the one to decide. It's my responsibility. Well, go on, go eat. What a mess we've got into!"

"Well, Doctor, you've opted for action, haven't you? You've chosen the risk, and so . . ." Smiling, Ambrogio stretched out his hand to his host and left to the sound of the usual bells.

Once left alone, Dr. Agazzino was more befuddled than ever. Of course, the situation would clear up by itself—Ambrogio had expressed that well—with Germany now almost totally occupied and the Italian front on the move. Perhaps the Allies were only a few miles from Milan . . . but that was precisely why something had to be done. Ambrogio's suggestion was not bad either. Only Don Mario would be exposing himself . . . but he hoped the militiamen would hardly cause him problems, given the fact he would speak to them for their own good. Because there was no doubt that Don Mario would go and not think twice of it. It wouldn't be otherwise! The idea of being able to avoid a bloodletting . . . he'd go as if it were to a wedding. Who would be able to stop him? In fact (and this really did create a new perspective), no sooner aware of the situation, Don Mario would act on his own initiative, without waiting for permission from the CLN. Yes, that is what would happen. And then what role would he play? He, the president of the CLN, the National Liberation Committee? (Words that really did make a certain impression.) Well, perhaps it was better like that, after all. Then, if things took another turn (if the insurrection did not succeed and the next day there'd be a backlash), no one would be able to impute it to him, to Agazzino, and to his people, the whole thing having been accomplished by Don Mario. So, after all, better that way . . . better or worse? For whom would be that bit of glory? For whom? And for what would all his work up to then have been for? Those conspiratorial trips to Milan, the dangerous contacts (even though there had been few) with the exalted world of rebellion, the confabulations and the thankless local dealings, all those . . . the dangers he had run? To what end? All that work of preparation would go completely up in smoke, and a great occasion like this one would never present itself again. In his life there should be nothing more heroic than that far-off memory of the two glasses of castor oil . . . oh, no, that, no! That could not be after having mentally savored the taste of a very different—and less ambiguous, especially—kind of glory.

He suddenly made up his mind. He put his beret onto his bald head, opened the bell-ringing door, locked it with a key, and put that into his pocket.

5

Not far off, waiting against the doorjamb of his house, was the aspiring partisan Giacomino. The pharmacist signaled him with his hand. He moved away silently from the doorjamb and joined him.

"Come with me", Dr. Agazzino whispered to him as they walked along.

Darkness was falling. Everybody was at home partaking of their modest fare around the table. It was the suitable time for relaxation, for thoughts of peace. *And I, on the other hand . . . but who's forcing me to do this . . . after all?* the pharmacist thought, crossing one street after another, with Giacomino trailing after him. They finally entered into the "Street of Remembrance" that led down to the station. In the gathering darkness, the oak branches overhead, with their finely serrated new leaves once more seemed to suggest something inexpressible, out of reach, which seemed to suspend time. But *no matter what,* Agazzino decided, *I can no longer go back. On the other hand, it's not only a question of . . . glory or something like that. It's a useful undertaking for the community I've got involved in, and that's the whole point. If something should happen to me—God forbid it!—I'd still not turn back.*

They reached the little square at the station, deserted, which was once the carabinieri garrison and now that of the "republican national guard". It was not too big a building, painted red, surrounded by a little garden with hedges of royal laurels and a little cement fountain in the place of honor. No light could be seen inside. The two of them stopped.

"Now, you stay here," the pharmacist said, panting a bit, to the boy, "at that corner, and make sure you're not seen. I'll go in. You be on the lookout, and if you see or hear anything strange, or if after fifteen minutes, better twenty, I . . ."

"I don't have a watch", Giacomino whispered.

"It doesn't matter. Just figure it out. You're a smart boy. So, if I don't come out in fifteen or twenty minutes, or if you see or hear something strange before that, you go like a shot to Ambrogio Riva and let him know. Is that clear?"

"Yes," the boy murmured, "but if you don't mind telling me, what are you going to do inside there?"

"I'm going to have them turn over their weapons to me", he said, panting again, and he felt both fear and a keen sense of pride as his face flushed red.

He left and went up to the garden gate and pressed the bell. He distinctly heard the bell sound inside the headquarters. He remained there waiting, his head lowered, and his heart pounding. *Oh, this asthma of mine, this asthma . . .* Several seconds went by. How come no one was answering? Perhaps after the events in Milan the militia was distrustful of any visitor and would not answer except with weapons? Perhaps, God forbid, there were machine guns pointed at him on the other side of the dark shutters at that moment? Or maybe, quite simply, the militia had just gone? He rang the bell a second time, longer. He could hear his own heartbeat in his ears and at the same time the sound of the bell inside the headquarters. No one answered this time either. After a little while he rang again, and then once more. He realized at last that the place had been abandoned.

Abandoned and shut up, as he could verify by moving the handle of the gate. Giacomino, who came immediately, jumped over the gate at his order

684

and checked to see if the door of the building was also shut. It was. He tried knocking then, repeatedly, but in vain.

"Hurry up", the pharmacist told him. "Come back . . . but first get out of there." Giacomino leaped back over the gate again, clearing it well, and landed outside.

"Now," the pharmacist told him, "while I stay here to keep guard—I won't move—you go to Farirö" (which means Little Smith) "and tell him to come immediately, but immediately, with the necessary tools to force these two locks. Tell him that I'm sending you, the president of CLN."

"Of . . . what?"

"CLN. The National . . . it doesn't matter. Just say the pharmacist. Go on. Hurry up. And after letting Farirö know, let all our partisans know, one by one. But, careful, only ours, not the Communists. Is that understood? And make sure no one in town sees you, not even the families of our partisans, only them. Tell them to get here immediately."

"And Ambrogio Riva?" Giacomino asked.

"Yes, he, too. No, not him. It's not necessary now. We'll call him later, afterward. Get going, hurry up."

Giacomino was off like a shot.

But he was so nervous that—together with the excitement of his running—he did not manage to perform with the necessary discretion. No sooner had the smith and the first two or three Christian Democrat partisans arrived than there also came the Communist, wearing a very angry face. He was wearing for the occasion a new fur cap with ear flaps and a red star in the front fold, in true Bolshevik style.

"Why didn't you let me know?" he asked the pharmacist rudely and swore.

"And why should I have called you?" he answered.

"What do you mean why?" and he swore again. "For distributing the weapons. Didn't we agree to share the weapons?"

"Of course, but first we'll have to see if there are or aren't any weapons."

"There have to be."

"We'll find out now."

"Half and half. Half for my people, and half for yours."

"All right, half and half."

This, the pharmacist reflected, meant scoring a point. It was not clear until then if the weapons were to be divided between the Communist and Christian Democrat partisans in halves or rather in proportion to their respective numbers. If that were the case it would have meant a few more for the Communists.

The Communist for an instant grasped what was going through the pharmacist's mind and was on the point of going back on the agreement, but instead only swore again. Then he thought that if it had come to him to take over the weapons, agreement or not, he would certainly not have shared them with the Christian Democrats, and they knew that. With that thought, he calmed down a bit.

Meanwhile, Farirö had little by little cut the padlock and opened the gate. Then he worked on the lock of the door. "I'm not cutting", he explained. "Here we'll have to try to open it without breaking it down, because it would be a shame to ruin the door."

Other partisans were arriving, all Christian Democrats. The Communist became nervous. "Look out!" he shouted at the small smith. "Move on. If not I'll see to the door." And taking a small military pistol from his pocket, he pointed it at the lock. It was clearly a gesture of intimidation for the benefit of everybody present.

But the smith did not let himself be intimidated: small of stature and bent over as he was (no longer young, with some gray hair, his face wrinkled, an aquiline nose, and drawn skin, he was also lacking some teeth), he did not allow himself to be intimidated. "Go ahead", he said, withdrawing. "Go on, try it. Just try it with that piece of junk. Shoot and you'll see if the door opens."

The Communist snorted and put the pistol back in his pocket. "Well, get going", he said.

"Remember, I could be your father", the little smith let him know severely and then went back to his meticulous work. It took him a while to open the lock without breaking it. At last the group of people there, about a dozen, were able to enter behind him in the headquarters.

The smith clicked the light switch uselessly, then lit—one after another, striking them, as he was used to doing, on the back of his trousers—two or three matches, found the main switch, and turned it on. The headquarters were lit.

Those present rushed about to inspect the various rooms. "The weapons. Come on, here they are!" someone called. In a wall cabinet there were some rifles, two Bredas, and a machine gun. The CLN president immediately shared out the weapons between the Christian Democrat boys and the Communist stranger. He did the same with the ammunition. He had scarcely finished his job when Don Mario arrived, all out of breath.

6

The following morning, the twenty-sixth of April, Nomana awoke to the rousing sound of the two machine guns, apart from the fire of other weapons, which the neopartisans were trying out in a nearby field of the town.

In the exaltation of the moment, the shooting of Christian Democrats and Communists (the latter wearing the red neckerchief, while the other had no special badges) was mingled. Besides, the boys, who had first attended the nuns' school together, then the elementary school, and later at least a year or so at the Oratory, still did not feel divided among themselves. Their instructor was the son of the midwife, Carletto Mangiagalli, apolitical, also with the reputation of a libertine (though still too young really to be one), who had deserted the Bersaglieri some months before.

What fun, stretched out on the grass, shooting away at the slope of a small hill without taking their fingers off the trigger, the weapon leaping as if it had been bitten by a tarantula, and the gun barrel going violet with overheating.

"Great stuff, isn't it?" Carletto Mangiagalli would say, interrupting himself every so often and taking his cheek off the gunstock for an instant. The others—younger than he—approved enthusiastically and kept shooting from their other submachine gun and tommy gun ("Just look at the spread of bullets!") and the rifles, all of them against the side of the hill.

Until, to put an end to it, Dr. Agazzino came on the scene and took away the ammunition that was left. "If not, you brainless kids will waste everything."

After that the partisans, with their weapons pointed or horizontally slung over their shoulders (a pity there were so few to go around), set off to make a few turns around the town all together and from time to time broke into song with "Bandiera Rossa", which was the only anti-Fascist song they knew (even though they did not know it all). The Christian Democrats all sang it too, with the idea of being amusing. People were looking at them with a mixture of familiarity, also relief (since this festivity meant the war was over), but also with fear that they might get too carried away.

Meanwhile, in the houses Radio Free Milan—occupied by the partisans during the night—frenetically emitted proclamations, news, announcements. More than one citizen of Nomana listened to it as if spellbound, unable to tear themselves away. Among others, the pharmacist, for a while, who could not make telephonic communication with his CLN correspondent in Milan until midmorning. He was informed that the uprising had taken place without a shadow of a doubt. He communicated the news in a no less triumphant voice than that of the radio.

"But there was no firing until last night!" the pharmacist objected.

"Until last night, exactly", the other fellow agreed. "But yesterday morning the bulk of the Fascists left Milan together with Mussolini. And those who remained were completely demoralized, so much so that we, once it was dark, leaped on them. Damn right there was shooting last night in Milan! You had to be here to witness it! And even more this morning at dawn. Did you know we've seized the prefecture and the radio? And the central police headquarters and police stations, in a word, everything? And no one's reacted, and now we're going for them, house to house, where they've hidden out like rats."

The pharmacist did not like the comparison, as he was, after all, a person of some refinement. "But they, I mean if they don't resist . . . what are you going to do with them when you've got them?"

"To hear them now, you'd think they were all innocent." The other fellow eluded the question. "No one's a Fascist now."

"But I'd like to know if . . ." The pharmacist shook his head and changed the subject. "Well, you won't be needing weapons now. There'll be more than enough."

"Yes," the other answered in an icier tone, "obviously."

"Then, when can I go to get mine, the ones you promised me?"

The Milanese became quite vague. "Well, then . . . whenever you want, in any case."

"Then today?"

"Whenever you want", the other fellow repeated evasively.

After that the pharmacist lost no time. He telephoned Ambrogio asking for the loan of the factory's Millecento, the one working on a gas generator, and in the afternoon of that same April 26 he went to Milan. Celeste drove, and at his side sat Dr. Agazzino, and in the back inside the van section was the Communist with a couple of partisans.

They returned to Nomana at night without a single weapon. They encountered the same festive atmosphere that they had left. The partisans were still strutting about like boastful soldiers in the streets.

7

Comedy and tragedy really do intermingle and alternate continuously in life.

At dawn of the following day, the twenty-seventh of April, a truck decked out in red with a big metal hammer-and-sickle emblem over the radiator entered the little plaza of Raperio, a hamlet in the Nomana district. Ten or twelve partisans, clearly not the latest ones, came out determined and quick and, under orders from Praga, surrounded and invaded a two-story house with a draper's shop below on the ground floor.

The townspeople, who were gathering to go to Mass, stopped and looked, both frightened and perplexed. Someone suggested that surely it was nothing to worry about, some mistake or misunderstanding at best, because the people who lived there—everyone knew them well—had never been involved in politics.

The parish priest (thin, with gray hair cut short) came out onto the church square. After a few instants of confusion he sent a young man to telephone Dr. Agazzino urgently to come immediately, not lose a second. Then he went up to the little shop surrounded by partisans.

One of them, the closest, pointed his weapon against him. "Back off", he ordered, and added quite gratuitously, "back off, you bag of sh———." The priest's mouth fell open, and he looked at the other partisans. They were hard, cold, joyless. They seemed to be—and this was strange—involved in a kind of routine work; all of them dressed in red shirts under an array of different civilian jackets and armed with English Sten guns, little rudimentary automatic weapons, dreadful in their hands. They really bore no resemblance to the improvised Nomana partisans, who had also come here the day before for the people to admire them.

"But," the priest protested with a certain slowness, "but . . ."

"I said back off", the partisan repeated, and then when the priest did not move, he poked him in the stomach with the butt of the gun, forcing him to back away. "That's it, that way, just like that", and he swore.

"Praise be to God", the priest murmured, almost automatically, by way of reparation.

Some of the parishioners approached, quite anxiously. The partisan noticed the solidarity of that gesture and mumbled some words, which the townspeople did not understand; the other partisans laughed.

From inside the little house, screams and groans suddenly could be heard, then a din that ended in noisy steps coming down the stairs, and the partisans who had entered, including Praga, burst out. In the midst of them, being roughly pushed, was a woman. "It's Fanto's woman from Incastigo", "Fanto's wife", some townspeople murmured. "But . . . how come she's here?"

The poor woman, about forty, dressed in a dark flowered apron, her hair undone and a stocking hanging, was struck with terror. She seemed to see only her pursuers, and perhaps not even them. She saw only death pursuing her implacably. "Mmmm", she hummed from her closed mouth, as if vibrating, "Mmm, mmm . . ."

"Let's go", Praga ordered, taking her by the back of the neck and pushing her toward the truck. Then he stopped for a few instants, a bit away from her, but without letting go of her. "The pig!" he said addressing the others, "look at her", and he laughed ominously. Along her legs, slightly parted, was sliding a stream of urine. It formed a little puddle on the ground under her.

"Are you finished?" Praga asked, giving her a push. "Get going then", and still holding her by the nape of the neck, he pushed her, followed by the others, to the truck and threw her into the vehicle rather than letting her get in normally. After her the partisans went in, clenching their little Sten guns, shiny and fierce. Praga got in the front, in the cabin: the truck with its rough hammer-and-sickle emblem took off.

"But isn't that Praga?"—"It is Praga, yes it is . . . Praga from Incastigo", the people were saying, shocked. "Then it's true, he's become a partisan." "And we didn't believe it!"

8

The truck left the square, reached the provincial highway, and went off into the distance. From the little shop, which remained open, someone was crying loudly, desperately. It was the shopkeeper. The priest and a couple of others entered, while the rest stayed outside, close to the door.

Seated on a chair, the woman, her face between her hands, was overcome with anguish. Her husband, at her side, was trying to calm her down. "Her sister", he explained to the priest, "is the one they took away." The priest nodded.

"They'll kill her!" the woman was screaming, covering her face with her hands, almost unable to breathe. "They'll kill her for sure. That Praga's a murderer, a hangman . . . oh . . . oh . . ."

"Last night in Incastigo they took away her husband", the man told the priest. "Fanto. Do you know him? Fanto from Incastigo, the thin fellow they call Fat Belly? He was working for Praga when a year ago together they took away the bank director Mambretti, who ended up in Germany. Do you remember? More than a year ago. Now Praga wants to get rid of all the witnesses. That's what's happening."

"But his wife? What does Fanto's wife have to do with it?" the priest ventured.

"Because she knows everything, everything, nothing more than that", the man said. "Especially because she knows—and she spread it everywhere—that her husband went with Praga to Mambretti, but without knowing anything, not an idea how things would turn out. It was Praga who did the whole thing. My brother-in-law, Fanto, also told me that a thousand times. And he was desperate—I don't know if you're aware of it—and got drunk almost every day. And he wasn't a Fascist any more, not for a long time. He was no longer anything."

"Yes, I heard that", the priest murmured.

"Last night they tortured the poor man, most certainly", the wife said, her face half covered by her hands. "If they hadn't, they wouldn't have come here. Because only he knew that my sister, in case of danger, would come to hide here at our house."

"Eh, one moment . . . we have to let Mrs. Mambretti know", the husband suddenly exclaimed. "Yes, of course, the widow . . . the wife of the bank administrator, because she also knows what happened. She must be warned immediately to get away. Otherwise that barbarian, I'll bet anything, will grab her, too."

"Luckily she no longer lives in Incastigo", the priest said.

The small crowd next to the door had grown meanwhile. Still frightened, the people were perplexed, unable to draw any conclusions. What could Fanto's wife have done against the partisans? But if she had done nothing, if she was innocent, why had she come to hide here in Raperio with her sister? Enough. And to think that a little before, on waking up, they had all felt a great sense of relief at the idea that the war and all its horrors were over.

9

The time for Mass to begin went by without the priest coming out of the draper's shop, whose door had been closed. One of its glass windows had been broken. The priest looked out only when—in an automobile run by a gas generator with a big tricolor flag (even though many felt the comedy had turned into tragedy)—Dr. Agazzino arrived with three of his partisans. After a few words had been exchanged with the priest, the president of the CLN entered the shop, whose door was again closed. The three partisans remained outside, not knowing what attitude to adopt. They were wearing new tricolor neckerchiefs and smiling cautiously at those present. Some of the others began to berate them for what had happened. They reproached them for not being able to protect the population, and one of the crowd downright insulted them. Still, there was a kind of tentative, undecided attitude among them. Ten minutes later another automobile arrived, with the red flag, which stopped next to the one that had come before. The Communist outsider and his four Communist boys came out. Agazzino—quickly informed—looked out from the draper's shop and, although surprised by this visit, signaled to the outsider to come in. He did just that, crossing the little square with slow, measured steps, on his head a fur cap with the red star and around his waist a belt with a pistol in its holder. The people could not help connecting him and his red cohorts with the other that had dragged off the woman, and they fell silent. Those who had shouted against the partisans with the tricolor neckerchief did not scream at these fellows, who also remained on the square waiting, but they stared at them hard. The newly arrived boys noticed the hostility of the crowd. They knew those people, they had always felt close to them, and now they were beginning to realize that there was something dividing them in a quite definite fashion. Hardly a word was spoken until the president of the CLN, followed by the outsider, with his dismal Bolshevik cap, and the parish priest left the shop. The president and the Communist outsider made signs for their own partisans to follow, and they reached their own cars in silence.

Only after the cars had left did the priest explain to the crowd. "They're going to Incastigo to try to get that poor woman back. If they don't find her there, they'll go to Milan, to CLN, the headquarters, and if necessary they'll even go to the jail. May God help them!"

This he repeated more or less at the altar, adorned with sacred ornaments. "Today's Mass we offer up for our sister, who at this moment is in danger of death. We must all pray for her, to try to wrest this grace from God."

The two cars, sent from one place to another, went about futilely for hours. They returned to Nomana in the early afternoon.

The partisans got out of the cars, more or less demoralized. To save face the Communist outsider took on a polemical air in front of the president of the

CLN, who, as he repeated to his own boys, "pretended to know everything". The boys with the tricolor were literally shocked, not only by the affair of the woman but also by the evidence—particularly obvious in front of the San Vittore prison—that the "liberation" was not a holiday, not at all, but rather a hideous unleashing of violence on whoever—guilty or not—was not able to defend himself. Dr. Agazzino was very upset by his own and his party's impotence. In the Communist zone of Milan—from what he had been able to learn—a carnage was going on in Nova, for example, toward the north of the zone. New corpses kept running aground against the bridge over the Villoresi canal. (They were collected and buried, more than 120, by the town administration.) *Let's hope the Americans get here soon*, the pharmacist most urgently wished. *Let's hope they don't delay.* As for the boys with the red neckerchiefs, Agazzino's disapproval as well as that of the boys with the tricolor proved irritating. They realized that the partisans in other places—the older ones as well as the new ones—were the unquestioned masters of everything. Why wasn't it that way in Nomana? Why these long faces?

There was no news about the woman for months, until it was known in Incastigo, and from there it spread to Raperio and to Nomana, that the poor woman, after she had been picked up, had been taken to a factory in Sesto, where her husband already was, and before midday "nothing was left" of either of them. So, nothing was left of them. The rumor was not specific. But by the time the news was spread, everybody knew that in Sesto, during the days of the liberation, many human bodies had been thrown into blast furnaces.

BOOK THREE

THE TREE OF LIFE

.

PART ONE

Back to Nomana, too, they started to return. Pino and Sèp—both of whom had found refuge in Switzerland—met by chance in customs at Ponte Chiasso as they were being repatriated. They had been in different camps and hadn't had news of one another since the night Sèp had deserted from the Blues to go off and join the Garibaldini. Soon after recognizing one another, they almost came close to blows—as they had often done at elementary school as children—when Pino criticized Sèp's conduct and received abuse in return. But they were no longer children. They noticed this in the intransigent tone of their exchange. "You wanted to exploit me even as a partisan, eh, you and your officers?" Sèp said, a mean look in his eye, and repeated the charge, "Just like your father takes advantage of folks in Nomana, eh?"

"Puke on yourself instead of puking on others!" Pino spat out. "Just look at him! You're just sh—— from head to foot!" They continued the exchange, insulting one another with similar phrases. Even though his lips trembled with anger at the contempt shown him, Pino decided—given his own accommodating nature—not to make a clear break with Sèp. "And when you think that we left our hometown together . . .", he said at last. "In any case, you do what you like. You can go to hell."

Along with others returning to their homeland, they walked along the green highway leading up to Olimpino, Sèp walking about thirty paces behind Pino. They had crested the rise and had started down the slope into Como (from time to time they saw the blue of the lake between the trees) when a large ivory-colored van coming from the frontier pulled up beside Pino. "Are you Riva? Are you the Riva from Nomana?" shouted a voice from the front seat. "Come on then, get in." The owner of the voice was one of the younger members of the Marsavi family, who were industrialists in Visate, a few miles from Nomana; Pino had seen the youth more than once while in Switzerland. Evidently this Marsavi had advised his family of his arrival, and, practical people that they were, they'd sent off this great van, on whose side was written "*Salumificio Marsavi S.p.a.*" (pork butcher and sausage maker), and underneath the motto, which Pino remembered from before the war, "*Labor non clamor*" (work—not confusion), and the firm's emblem, a drawing of a worker bee.

"Well, are you going to get in or not?" repeated Andrea Marsavi, leaping to the ground. "Come on, I'll open it up for you." He went toward the rear of the van; he was dressed in the faded uniform of a sublieutenant in the Corps of Engineers.

"Thank you, many thanks," Pino said, "but . . . look, there's another one from Nomana."

"Which one?" Andrea asked. "Have him get in, quick. Let's not waste time."

The rear of the van already held several passengers, sitting on the floor with backs braced on the side walls. Pino turned to Sèp, who had halted along with some others a few steps away and was observing the exchange. "Do you want to get in?"

Sèp also knew and had recognized the Marsavi meat company's truck. The lettering and the ivory-colored vehicle reminded him of home. He nodded yes, came forward, and climbed aboard, with Pino following. Other travelers halted nearby also wanting a ride.

"Where are you going? To Brianza?" asked Marsavi, holding onto the door handle. "If not, there's no point in getting in."

He took on two men from around Lecco, even though it would call for a detour from Visate, where he was headed, then closed the door behind them.

During the whole of the journey (about an hour, in semidarkness), neither Sèp nor Pino talked to each other. When the truck reached the Visate crossroad on the Lecco to Monza provincial highway, Marsavi again came around to the rear to open the door in his discolored uniform. No doubt—thought Pino—this practical way of handling things is something he'd learned at home. It was known that this boy's grandfather, father, and uncle, even though having five or six hundred workers in the family plant, were accustomed to stroll around the factory dressed in white coats and didn't mind, if the occasion called for it, giving a hand wherever necessary. Pino and Sèp jumped down. Pino thanked Andrea Marsavi, who silently gave him a pat on the arm. Now that they were close to home, he seemed to be in a greater hurry. His sharp nose (a Marsavi family pointer) wrinkled courteously as he said, "*Ciao*, partisan. I hope we'll see each other soon." Slamming the van's rear door, he returned to his seat, and they drove off. Pino and Sèp found themselves alone on the asphalt highway under the enormous sun. To the north the horizon was hidden by the familiar wall of mountains; Resegone, the two Grigne, and San Primo, higher than the rest. Before them the highway sloped downward, overlooking the roofs of Nomana, located in the fertile and flowered fields. Below, on the right, they could identify the square barns of Nomanella, yellowish among the growing green, with the three big cherry trees in front and the smaller bent fig tree.

Pino looked at Sèp. "I remember the day we left", he murmured. Sèp made no reply.

"I wonder who's got hold of our bicycles now?" said Pino, starting to walk.

"Who knows?" said Sèp, following Pino's example.

During their walk toward town they didn't speak; they were both moved emotionally by the homecoming. Although feeling this excitement, Sèp was resolved not to show it. Indeed, he hoped that remaining expressionless would better suit his purpose, to further offend Pino. (This pig, who just as likely would refer to him in Nomana as a deserter for having left the Blues and Captain Marco . . . Of course, Pino wasn't the type to go around criticizing the next man; but *i signori*—the masters—as he'd been told repeatedly by the expatriate commissar in Switzerland, are always like swine toward the workers. Even though they don't want to be, try not to be, they simply are, it's a scientific fact.) Pino was aware of his former friend's hostility and vaguely wanted to dispel it, return to the harmonious good times of the past, but couldn't figure out how to do so. He started humming a martial air, popular with Marco's partisans. ("March, march—march to the beat of our hearts . . .") The nailed boots they both wore seemed to pick up the tempo, as if wishing to bring them into harmony with their cadence, to make them agree; but the two boys did not indulge them.

They reached the first few houses. Pino wore a waterproof windbreaker; around his neck were his first aid kit bag (in which he now carried a change of underwear) and a faded blue neckerchief, from the heroic days in the past; of his partisan apparel Sèp wore only the heavy mountain boots, worn-out clothes, and a swaggering air. The first people they met greeted them in welcome, but also—they both noticed it—with a sort of reserve. As the two were unaware of the incident of a few days before in Raperio, they were not a little surprised at this more-or-less cool reception, but didn't comment on it. At the first crossroads, after grudgingly waving farewell, they went their separate ways, Pino toward the right, to his home.

After a couple of days a column of Allied vehicles came to Nomana. There were jeeps, trucks, tractors pulling cannons, and a complement of some 150 men. They erected their tents in someone's garden.

In a few hours these soldiers started wandering idly through the town, visiting taverns. As a uniform they wore light khaki shirts and trousers, and their manner was reserved. The people of Nomana referred to them as "*gli americani*", but they were South Africans from the English Eighth Army, and—at least as far as their uniform was concerned—they didn't look at all like Americans. Their vaguely humiliating presence was accepted by the Nomanese as a minor harm. They also considered their being there a guarantee against the danger of more incidents like the one in Raperio. The Communist partisans, in contrast, looked disapprovingly on the presence of the *Americani*. "They don't watch over Incastigo, a bigger and more important town," they said, "and they have to come precisely to Nomana to bother us?" It was becoming clear, however, that the Reds in Nomana were a minority. Now the older militants, who regarded themselves as Socialists and Communists of the old guard, started gathering in a local bar with the partisans. Sèp, whom they had first received with indifference, was quickly adopted as the pride and glory of the town.

2

Almost at the same time as the few refugees arrived from Switzerland, soldiers began to arrive who had up to then been held within southern Italy by the armistice. The first to arrive were those soldiers who had participated in the battles of the gothic line. They were deposited in front of their homes. Then, hours or at the most a day later, they were collected in trucks belonging to their detachments (trucks identical to those of the South Africans, built in England to a very antiquated design, but with good motors and heavy wheels). Then the soldiers, little by little by whatever means of transportation they could find, arrived from the noncombat units. Generally they had come from the harbor cities in the south, where they'd been employed doing stevedoring or other work for the Allies. Only a few of these arrivals wore the English army uniform issued in general to others; some, however, still wore the old monarchist army uniform, reduced to tatters, or a strange prisoners' uniform made from coarse coffee-colored cloth. They had been given several days' leave, although there were some who had come home without ordered leave.

Luca arrived among the combat veterans, although not a resident of Nomana (he came from neighboring Beolco). The Riva family learned of his arrival from a young cousin sent by Luca himself, who sent word to Ambrogio that he'd be over to see him sometime during the day to talk. The young messenger, who looked like Luca, was taken to see Ambrogio in his office.

On hearing that Luca was back, Ambrogio stood up, then sat down again to hear the brief message. He looked at his watch—it was 11:00. "Tell me, where is Luca at this moment?" he asked the boy. "At home?"

"Yes, at home."

"When did he arrive?"

"This morning before 8:00, when I was getting up. He arrived on foot because the army truck had dropped them in the town square, him and an Alpine soldier from Brugarolo township."

"Has he been told about Giustina?"

"Yes", the child's lively face showed sorrow briefly. "It was because Luca himself insisted on being told everything right away. He looked to be going crazy, but we had to tell him."

"Poor Luca", Ambrogio commented. "Poor devil!"

Into the office came the muffled sound of the looms, always the same and making everything vibrate slightly. Ambrogio was still. "Poor fellow ...", he added.

He looked once again mechanically at his watch. "He'll have to leave again soon, right? Do you know when?"

"This afternoon. He agreed to meet the soldier from Brugarolo over there in the square at 6:00."

"Luca didn't say anything about Manno, my cousin Manno?" Ambrogio couldn't stop himself asking.

The boy said no, but seemed unsure.

"Are you sure?" Ambrogio asked, looking fixedly at the boy.

"I'm only a kid. They don't tell me anything."

Ambrogio looked at him silently.

"This morning Luca was going first to Nomanella", added the boy voluntarily. "From there he'd thought to come here to you. He'd left word to that effect at the house, but then he came back because he was so upset."

Ambrogio nodded; it pained him to bother Luca at a time like this, while he was suffering grief due to his sweetheart's death, but he couldn't postpone it. He got to his feet. "Come", he said to the boy. They went outside to the cobblestoned factory yard, where the dark trunks of the limes—pruned every few years—bore bright new shoots. The noise of the looms wasn't as loud out here as in the office. "Listen," Ambrogio said to the boy, "I thank you for bringing me the message. Tell Luca you've talked to me and told me everything. If by chance I don't meet him first, I'll be waiting for him here this afternoon. Also tell him that I'm going right now to see him in Beolco, at his house."

"Luca's house is also my house", explained the boy.

"Good. If we don't meet, let's leave it that I'll wait here for him this afternoon at the time you said. Is that understood? You got that?"

"Yes."

"Bravo. Here, take this, it's for you for the trouble you've taken." He put some coins into the boy's top jacket pocket.

The boy thanked him with a happy nod, then went to get his bicycle, which he'd left leaning on one of the lime trees. Getting on the seat, he pedaled out of the factory gate.

Ambrogio went to his father's office and told him about Luca's return and said that he was going to Beolco right now to see him. Father and son looked into each other's eyes; if Manno had managed to get from Albania to southern Italy, they knew that now they ought to have news.

"If Luca hasn't sent word by the boy, the news can't be good", the father observed.

Ambrogio nodded, but trying to look on the bright side said, "Right now Luca has had a heavy blow, hearing about Giustina's death", he reasoned in a low voice. "He's known about it for only a few hours. In those circumstances one can't think of anything else."

"Go", his father told him. "Go quickly."

As the boiler on the Millecento's gas generator wasn't up to pressure, Ambrogio went home quickly and fetched the bicycle from his school days (the sporty blue bike, on which five years ago, back from college, he'd gone to see Stefano). Getting on it, he rode off.

"Where are you going?" shouted Almina, wearing a cloth over her hair and shaking a rug out of a window.

"I'll be right back", Ambrogio eluded the question.

He pedaled down the gravel path and out the gate, continuing parallel to the garden until the turn for Nomanella, where he bowed his head to the image of our Lady of the Rosary and followed along the downhill highway toward Beolco. For a moment he begged our Lady: if only his cousin had not died, if only he were alive, and that this long nightmare were finally over. Who knew, perhaps Luca had indeed met Manno and would be surprised that no news of him had yet reached Nomana. Perhaps . . .

From a bend in the road Ambrogio noticed, over to the left—alongside the railroad station—the newly built glass factory. Nearer to him the green of the meadows in the bottom of the valley was divided into large squares running parallel to long lines of gray-green willows and alders, with their nearly round leaves. The young man had difficulty in removing his gaze from the sight.

A little farther ahead, on the other side of the highway, was the path that led to the little chapel of the "privileged dead of Crea" where—in an urn buried in a wall—were the remains of the victims of a plague of several centuries before. (The plague of Manzoni's great novel, the people called it, but who knew if it was this plague or another? In the chapel there were no dates, only an inscription on a wall consisting of an invitation to win a "privileged" indulgence for these souls, granted in the distant past by an already forgotten archbishop of Milan.)

Farther on, on the same side of the road, there was a little valley lined with trees, fresh and green, which led to the Soldier's Fountain; no one knew which soldier or its date. Ambrogio remembered that Manno, as a child—imaginative as he was—maintained that the soldier was a Landskrecht, a German indentured soldier of the Renaissance. He felt this was supported by the presence nearby of the bodies of the plague dead. When Stefano was a young boy he would put lures with birdlime around the fountain in summer to catch the birds that landed there to drink.

At the end of the verdant valley, Beolco could be seen, an airy town split by one main street and a piazza, in which the army truck had dropped the two Alpine soldiers. Going through the town and passing the Argati industrial workshops and some old gardens, the road began to climb toward Catafame, the farmhouse in which Luca lived with his parents, uncles, and aunts.

Catafame was of an unusual construction, half fortress and half house. A crude square, it had two stories, walls a meter thick, few windows, and high, projecting eaves topped by heavy tiles. On the side facing Beolco—which jutted out from the rest, giving the impression of a castle keep—lines of holes could be seen in the walls under the eaves, looking like small loopholes, which, Ambrogio knew, gave entry to a bird loft. It was in that loft where the friendship between Manno and Luca had begun, when they were attending elementary school. Luca had invited Manno to take part in the bird trapping, a once-yearly event. Ambrogio stayed on his bike while riding through a dank passage into the meager inner courtyard of the house and recalled those early days. In the courtyard he found some relatives of Luca's; one or two others were on the wooden balcony that ran along three sides of the second floor. There was an air of animation due to Luca's return after being away so long.

Ambrogio got off his bike and leaned it against the wall. "Where's Luca?" he asked in as cheerful a voice as he could manage, as if trying to frighten off ill omens.

They answered him in a too-hurried way, which worried him; meanwhile, they all stared at him. "He's here", called the young messenger boy, emerging from a door on the ground floor: "Come, Signor Ambrogio." Holding the door open while he went inside, the boy closed it behind Ambrogio without following him in.

Luca—his eyes reddened—was sitting on a small couch. As always he wore his unusual beard, and incongruously on his light khaki English uniform were the Alpine insignia and a blue medal ribbon. As soon as his visitor entered, he got up and went to meet him, arms wide in welcome.

Having embraced Ambrogio, Luca, head lowered, remained silent for a while, very moved by the moment. "Poor Luca", Ambrogio said. "What a homecoming you've had, what a welcome!"

Anguished, Luca shook his head repeatedly, as if to say there was no justice in such a homecoming. Then, having difficulty talking, he asked hesitantly, in dialect, "You've had no news of Manno?"

"No", replied Ambrogio, feeling a shiver run up his back. "We know nothing about him, haven't heard since the armistice, since September of '43." He pulled back to look at his friend. "What do you know?"

Luca looked him in the eye without answering.

"What do you know? Do you know anything?" Ambrogio asked again.

His friend nodded yes.

"Why don't you speak up?"

"About Montelungo, about the battle there, you know nothing?"

"No", whispered Ambrogio and without saying more looked tensely at Luca.

Luca avoided his eyes. "He died in Montelungo at the beginning, in December of '43", he said in a toneless voice. He looked as if about to cry, Ambrogio noted, but he managed to continue. "In the first clash there with the Germans. Manno was a volunteer; they gave him the Medal of Gold."

"So he's dead!" Ambrogio murmured. He felt as if his legs might give way. They were shaking more than he'd ever experienced before. He stretched out a hand and, gripping a chair, sat down on it.

"He's dead", he repeated.

Luca looked at him, nodding silently.

In the room—which was a simple working man's kitchen—were also Luca's parents and a female relative of indeterminate age, probably an aunt. The two women exchanged a look of dismay, while the father, who clearly wanted to help in some way, at least to say something. "The . . . the medal", he managed to say with an effort. "Poor Signor Manno!"

Ambrogio had for a moment a vision of the anguish that his cousin must have suffered during those momentous days of disintegration following the armistice, the desperate energy with which he must have thrown himself into an effort to ascend from the abyss.

"We'd have preferred to have him here with us, and not the medal, eh?" Luca said to Ambrogio, and sighed. Then into the dejected silence he continued, "Manno and I were friends since childhood, you know, intimate friends, like you and Stefano, or Igino . . ." He stopped. "And also Stefano *por fio!*— poor boy!" Once again grief prevented him from speaking.

Then the father and also the mother tried to say something, to contribute some word of consolation for their visitor, but could only repeat the usual trite phrases.

Trying to maintain his self-control, Luca returned to his seat on the couch and told all he knew. He spoke to Ambrogio about his encounter with Manno at the little railroad station in Puglia ("It was the last time I saw him") and how soon after he had received a postcard from him, giving the address of a Lieutenant Gambacurta, in case he wanted to write back. He retold what he'd heard said about the Montelungo battle, about Manno leading his soldiers and his death. He hadn't failed to inform himself about Manno's grave and had immediately written to Gambacurta to advise him of the place, but the lieutenant already knew about all this and in his reply to Luca told him that he had some letters written by Manno addressed to his family. "Then, when they put together the CIL, the Italian Liberation Corps, Lieutenant Gambacurta and I both were enlisted. He was ordered to a staff job, and I was sent to the Alpine battalion. But I only saw him yesterday morning when I went to Verona on purpose, to Legnano Divisional HQ, to ask him to give me the letters; I went there on a pass. But he didn't want to let go of them and will come in person to bring them when he can, because he made a sort of promise to Manno."

"And when do you think this 'when he can' will be?" Ambrogio asked, still feeling dazed. "Do you have any idea?"

"No. And neither has he. You know how things work in the military."

Ambrogio made note of Gambacurta's name and address, then asked Luca some questions about events in order better to be informed. He hadn't forgotten the suffering—which he could judge from his own pain at the loss of his cousin—that Luca would be experiencing at the death of his sweetheart. He didn't stay any longer; getting to his feet, he shook his friend by the hand. "You'll be going back this afternoon, eh? You're not going alone. I hear there are two of you."

"Yes, going along with me is a fellow from Brugarolo, a certain Picozzi."

"Do you know where they'll send you now?"

Luca shook his head no. "At the moment we're camped alongside Villafranca."

"Well, I'll leave you with your family," said Ambrogio, "since it's been so long since you've seen each other." Then he added, "I'm glad you're well, after so much time."

"Yes."

The two youths shook hands again, and Ambrogio went out. Crossing the farmyard, he noticed that the people hanging around outside were already aware of Manno's death. Luca evidently had told them about it before he arrived. He got on his bicycle and, going through the damp passage, once more rode toward Beolco, slowly. Going around a bend in the road, he turned to look at Catafame, with its unusual profile. His eyes went to the line of the entry holes to the bird loft. *Sparrows*, he thought. From now on, the sight of Catafame would remind him of something very different.

3

Manno's friend, Lieutenant Gambacurta, whose visit Luca had talked about, arrived within the week in a jeep. The porter—on finding out that it was an officer bringing news of Manno—opened the gate at once, and the strange vehicle, unaesthetic and different from all other cars, came to a stop at the front door. Alerted by the porter's call on the internal telephone, Francesca and Alma came to the door together, anxiety showing on Francesca's lovely face. The statuelike lines in Alma's face remained calm, but her heart beat nearly to bursting. They invited Gambacurta to sit in the small parlor. Alas, he wasn't wearing the attractive gray-green Italian uniform. Instead—like Luca—he wore the conquerors' khaki-colored gear; the only indication that he was in the Italian army was a small tricolor flag sewn on one sleeve.

Having sat down, Gambacurta asked if the two young ladies were indeed Lieutenant Manno Riva's relatives, and on being assured that this was so, he took a bundle of addressed envelopes from his briefcase. "These are letters written by Manno," he announced, "by my friend Manno", and, looking at the top envelope, read the addressee's name. "Ambrogio Riva. This is where he lives, am I right?"

"Yes, he's our brother. At the moment he's at the office."

"Could I speak to him? I want to hand him the letters personally."

"Yes, of course", Francesca answered, and turning to Alma, "Please call Ambrogio right now and ask Papa to come also. Meanwhile I'll go and tell Mama." Both girls got to their feet.

"One moment", the little lieutenant detained the two girls and read the name on another letter. "Colomba Alberti, Lamarmora Citadel, number 14, Novara. By any chance would she be in Nomana? I know that she comes here occasionally."

"Right now she's probably at home in Novara", said Francesca. "At least I think so. Why? Are there letters for her, too?"

Gambacurta nodded and separated the letters into two bundles, holding up the thickest. "Most of the letters are for her."

Suddenly Francesca's eyes filled with tears. "Poor Manno", she murmured, "and poor Colomba!"

"I'll go and call Ambrogio", Almina decided, and went to the telephone in the hall. Shortly her pleasant voice could be heard, apparently imperturbable like her appearance. She told Ambrogio that Gambacurta had come, bringing Manno's letters. Hearing what Alma was telling her son, Giulia, who had been cleaning upstairs with Noemi, came headlong down the stairs, followed by the maid. Giulia went directly into the small parlor. The maid remained outside, keeping an ear ready for whatever was said.

Gambacurta got hastily to his feet, ceremoniously kissed the hand of the lady of the house, and waited to be invited to resume his seat. "Many thanks, Lieutenant. We were expecting you, did you know?" said Giulia, gesturing the guest back into his seat. "We were advised of your impending visit by a young man from here, a friend of my son's who is in the army like yourself." She sat down.

Gambacurta nodded. "Yes, that's right. Sergeant Sambruna."

"Yes, Luca Sambruna."

The guest nodded again. "But," he explained, "this is not an official visit. I'm here strictly as a friend of Manno's."

"You were friends, then? . . .", said Giulia. Her eyes, like Francesca's, now held tears.

"Yes. We were in the same regiment in Libya, although we weren't together long. Later we met again in Brindisi, on the day when Manno was repatriated from Albania."

"What day was that?" Francesca, her eyes still full of tears, couldn't help interjecting. "Here at home we would always ask ourselves where Manno could be."

"Let's see, it was soon after the armistice on September 8", Gambacurta said, letting his kind brown eyes rest for a moment on the girl's lovely face. "A few weeks after the armistice. Just a moment while I think about it . . . it was precisely on the day the Germans disembarked at Corfu, in which case it was around the twentieth to the twenty-fifth of September, of 1943, of course." Turning to talk mainly with Giulia, he went on. "After that, Manno and I kept in touch. We got to be really good friends." He brightened. "He was an out-of-the-ordinary fellow. Not only brilliant, he was a leader, a real leader, he . . ." He stopped and, changing his tone of voice, said, "It may seem only normal, my praising him now that he's dead, but . . ." He shook his head, indicating his words should not be interpreted that way. The three women noticed that his eyes were also reddening.

"You really liked him", murmured Almina.

Gambacurta nodded yes. "That's why I've come from Verona to talk about him to you", he said, paused, and blinked his eyes several times. Then, recovering control of his voice, he continued deliberately, "Just before going off to the front, Manno came to see me in Brindisi, which was when he entrusted these letters to me." (He held up the two bundles.) "He had written them in the evenings, night after night, after going off duty. At that time he was stationed in Murgiano, a small place in Puglia; there are three addressed to Ambrogio and eight for Colomba." He added, "Along with these letters he gave me two others, not written by him, but from a lieutenant colonel who had been executed by a German firing squad in Albania. This colonel had given them to Manno for delivery to his family; he was called Cirino. His family lives in Rome. It was a great comfort to them to receive his letters from me and to be able to read details of the last few hours he had spent in Italy. This is why I've come here personally." He looked around at them and tried to explain himself better. "It was after the armistice when Cirino came from Albania to Supreme Command in Brindisi, where I was stationed, to ask for boats with which to repatriate his troops. Manno accompanied him as his orderly officer, even though they weren't from the same regiment. He'd put himself at the colonel's disposal in order to be useful, given the seriousness of the situation. But I believe it was also because he felt an affinity for the colonel, I mean, because they were both exceptional individuals, brave men, both of them, you understand?"

"Oh, yes, and how!" said Giulia.

"On the same day he arrived in Italy, this colonel returned to Albania. Manno wanted at all costs to follow him—you should have seen him—but Cirino wouldn't allow it. This is something I'd like to tell you about later, more calmly and if there's time. It will make you understand more clearly what a good fellow Manno was, what a big heart he had. It's not by accident that he was awarded the Medal of Gold. You knew about the gold medal?"

"Yes", said Giulia. "Luca told us, the Alpine soldier."

"Well, good. I've brought along the commendation." The little officer took a document out of his briefcase. "Manno's worth, his valor wasn't just military, but also, how can one put it, civil also; he was a good citizen. At a time of great crisis Manno was a true leader, I restate it, but at some other time I'll be able to relate it better." He held the document out to Giulia, who took it in trembling hands and started to read the text. She read it out loud, but imperfectly, trying to load every word with the proper sentiment, never having read a Medal of Gold commendation. After a while she stopped and looked at her daughters. Francesca couldn't read for crying, and so she held the paper out to Almina. "You read it, Alma."

Even now Alma didn't give outward signs of her inner emotion (she never displayed her feelings, and because of this the others, including Manno when he was alive, referred to her as the "little marble statue") as she read the few lines of military prose without expression in her voice. In this way the inevitable rhetoric wasn't emphasized, leaving the written facts, stark and crude, about the death of the good soldier Manno had been. Ambrogio and Gerardo arrived, followed by an agitated Pino, his short blond hair flattened at the back. All three went directly into the parlor, followed as far as the doorway by Noemi, peering into the room to see the visitor who had brought the bad news, confirming Manno's death. Gerardo, visibly upset himself, noticed Noemi's particularly agitated state and invited her to enter. "Come in, you too, come on. You loved him as much as his family did. Go on, come in." But at this clear invitation she became even more emotional, and, making gestures to say no with both hands, she escaped to the kitchen.

After the introductions Gambacurta delivered the three letters to Ambrogio. He noticed that the youth—obviously still suffering the effects of his past misadventures—took the letters with a sort of deep sadness. This impressed the visiting lieutenant and seemed to trigger some deep mechanism in him that showed itself as a hurry to leave. He asked how far away Novara was; he had, he said, also personally to deliver the other letters. "And I have to do so today, because I don't know when I'll next have the jeep to use. Bear in mind I have to be back in Verona tonight."

It was early afternoon. Gambacurta's words let the family down; the females were almost dismayed. Gerardo, as always practical, suggested they telephone straight away to Novara. If Colomba was home, the lieutenant could go there immediately in order to be back in Nomana in time for dinner. "Also, to take a little rest, and also the soldier who is driving you, the one I saw outside. Novara", explained Gerardo, "is some forty miles from here. It's not far."

"You make good time so long as you have a set of reliable tires that won't cause unnecessary hold-ups", said Pino.

Gambacurta, after an initial hesitation, went along with the plan. He appreciated that his coming here to Manno's house to bring details of his death was very different from the arrival of a safely returned, live Manno, and this thought soon made him feel unbearably sad. On the other hand, he realized that his visit couldn't come to an end in headlong flight. He was also attracted, as any young soldier would be, by the presence of two lovely girls like the twenty-two-year-old Francesca and Alma, eighteen. He particularly liked the company of Francesca.

After going over some of the details of what he had already told the ladies for the benefit of Gerardo and Ambrogio, and having given a brief report on the battle of Montelungo and described for them Manno's burial and grave site, Gambacurta studied a map of the route to Novara with Ambrogio. On hearing by telephone the news that Colomba was indeed at home and awaiting his arrival, he got to his feet and said his farewells, being especially courtly with the ladies, as was his way.

He went outside, followed by the family, and got into the jeep. "Let's go", he said to the soldier driver. "We have to be back here as soon as possible." The driver, who had been sitting at the wheel waiting, made the jeep jerk backward and then drove forward, out of the gate.

The family didn't go straight back to their individual pursuits. They stayed in the house, divided between the parlor and the main living room, reading and rereading Manno's three letters, which were very moving (they felt they could almost hear his voice), and examining the stark wording of the gold medal document. They also talked about Manno, but were careful not to indulge in sentiments that might make them cry. However, to varying degrees, they all had swollen red eyes.

4

Gambacurta did return in time for dinner. He told them about his meeting with Colomba. "You hadn't told me", he complained, "that she wasn't yet totally convinced of Manno's death." He saw that this surprised the family. "Perhaps you weren't aware of it, but the news she was given by telephone some days ago—which was of course passed on to her with delicacy and tact so as not to upset her overly—didn't convince her entirely."

When Colomba was confronted with the hard truth, "it was a bitter pill for her to swallow." Using these words, the cultivated and discreet lieutenant went on to say that when he gave her the letters, she ran off and closed herself in her bedroom, and he didn't see her again. "She is really a beautiful creature," he said thoughtfully, "worthy of Manno's love." The girl's parents were quite upset; the father would have preferred not to have the letters delivered to his daughter so soon. "She's still almost a child. She's not even twenty, you understand?" he'd said. Gambacurta understood and sympathized with the wish, but asked himself in what way he could have done a better job.

"There's no way", Giulia acknowledged with much simplicity, and, in a maternal way, added, "For you, this labor of mercy you're carrying out must be painful—may God reward you."

"If our positions had been reversed, Manno would have done the same for me", Gambacurta acknowledged gratefully.

They invited him to the table; he enjoyed the food and thanked them. But he also talked to them, told all he remembered about Manno. He reconstructed—aided by Ambrogio, who asked him several questions—the atmosphere that reigned in the south after the armistice, the widespread frustration, the fears for Italy's destiny; in other words, the general ambiance in which Manno had made his decision to put his life at risk or practically offer himself for sacrifice. He touched on the positive reaction to Italy's having become a co-belligerent on the Allied side (helped by their first action at Montelungo) and the beneficial effect this would have on Italy's destiny.

"One thing that occurs to me", Ambrogio suddenly said, "is the obsession that Manno had about being destined by God for a specific task. Do you remember?" and turning to Gambacurta, who was at his side, nodding assent, "Manno was convinced that he was predestined, held in reserve, for a mission of providence, even though he didn't know what, exactly."

"It's true", Giulia confirmed. "That's how it was. So much so that at one time he thought of becoming a missionary, you remember? He used to ask himself if this was the road the Lord was calling him to follow. Later he saw that this wasn't the way. And in fact ... my poor boy!"

"The last time I saw him, when he came to look for me at Stresa—the day he left for Albania—he talked about this mission for which God had him in reserve. Fanny and Celeste can confirm this, having been there to witness it."

"He talked to me about the same thing, and more than once", Gambacurta said.

"Well, now we can see that it was a true intuition", Ambrogio observed. "You yourself said that the battle at Montelungo was advantageous to Italy."

"Yes, very advantageous, no doubt about it."

The entire group sitting around the table—the guest Gambacurta, Gerardo, Giulia and her six children (only Fortunato was missing), the two elderly aunts from Monza—all of them felt held, deeply touched by the unusual events discussed.

But for all that, life went on inexorably, even during the brief duration of an evening meal. At noon that day the radio had carried news about the discovery of German extermination camps, news that wasn't generally known in northern Italy, and Pino had referred to this during the evening. Gambacurta, who had been traveling, hadn't heard the radio news and now returned to the subject, asking Pino to tell him more. Some of the diners gave details that didn't always fit together; the lieutenant listened to everything attentively and asked for elaboration on some points. Then in his turn, on being asked, he told what he knew. In general, this was first-hand information disseminated by the Allies at the very time when the concentration camps were being found during the conqueror's advance through Germany. This was enormously momentous news, deserving of total attention; not to consider these events seriously would have been unpardonable. Also it was a subject other than Manno's life, which his own relatives were already forgoing to talk of something else.

The conversation went on (Gambacurta increasingly had trouble hiding his fatigue) until after midnight, and only now and then did they return to speak about Manno. In the breakfast room the soldier driver had gone to sleep at the table where he'd been given dinner. From time to time, to the amusement of the younger children, his snoring reached them through the dining room door; life also went on in these small things.

During pauses in their conversation, the sound of a nightingale could be heard singing excitably from its customary poplar in the garden. Perhaps it was the same bird that two years earlier had carried on the comic dispute with Manno. In any case, none of the people around the table knew about that trivial incident, and nobody ever would.

5

The prisoners began returning from Germany. At first there were a scattered few, transported in U.S. Army trucks, which, because rail lines were cut, came down from Austria via the Brenner Pass road. The American trucks were joined shortly after by civilian Italian trucks, organized by the Pontifical Assistance Commission.

"I've heard that the Marsavi in Visate have made two trucks available to move the prisoners", Ambrogio said one night at dinner. "They sent them to Verona yesterday morning. From there they'll go—by now they'll have left—for Germany. Papa, our truck doesn't have much work to do these days. What do you say if we . . . eh?"

Gerardo considered, then nodded. "Yes, we can do that," he said and repeated, "we can. Do you know whom we need to contact? Have you already made inquiries?"

Pino interrupted. "I can perfectly well go to Germany. Why do we have to contact anybody? I'll know what to do. It'll be more or less like being in the German part of Switzerland. Also I could occasionally spell the driver."

"I suppose you'd go with your damned medicine kit slung around your neck, eh?" joked Fortunato, who was also at the dinner table. They all laughed.

"The backing by the Pontifical Commission is essential", Pino's father said to him. "For documentation, for border passes, to get gasoline and food. It's essential for everything."

"Well, then, I could go along . . .", suggested Pino.

"We'll see", said Gerardo. He turned back to Ambrogio, who hadn't answered his question.

"I don't know whom to contact," his son replied, "but it'll be enough to telephone the curial office in Milan. Do you want me to take care of it?"

"Why the curia in Milan?" Pino objected. "It'll be much faster if we call the Marsavi, Andrea Marsavi, who was in Switzerland with me. Better still, you know what? I'll call him myself right now." And with no one stopping him, he went out to the lobby to make the call. "The Pontifical Commission?" asked Giulia, clearly pleased at this further sign of the Church's beneficent works.

"Yes. It's the same organization that delivered messages from the prisoners of war", explained Ambrogio. "Those preprinted lettergrams. You remember those two we got from the south, which brought news of Luca? I showed them to you."

"Yes, I remember."

"Now the commission is distributing food and all kinds of assistance in the country's devastated areas: everything that is received from Catholics in America. It's doing and has done great work."

"Yes", admitted Fortunato, almost despite himself; good at business, he was the least religious of Gerardo's children. "If it weren't for the priests, you tell me what we'd be able to organize in Italy. They're the only people who know how to cope with any situation. Including now. Look how they've organized the coming and going of trucks between here and Germany. If one thinks about it, it's incredible."

"Who else would you want to hand your own truck to if not them?" his brother Ambrogio asked. "To the folk in the CLN, maybe?"

"For heaven's sake!" said Fortunato.

The connection with Visate took only a few minutes, surprising because although Visate was only a couple of miles away, it was located within the province of Como, and normally required a long wait.

Through Pino, Andrea Marsavi advised the Rivas to do nothing, and that he would come tomorrow at noon to organize everything.

"At noon, eh?" commented Pino when he told the others.

"That one is coming during the lunch break; he can't bear the thought of stealing half an hour of work time; to him, it would be sacrilege."

As usual the ironical reference to work—a subject not normally discussed at the house—found disapproval in the eyes of Gerardo, the father, who instead of being amused put on a serious look. "Instead of making jokes, maybe you could learn something from him", he said to Pino in measured tones.

The next day Andrea Marsavi arrived on a motorcycle at 12:15. ("A quarter of an hour, you noticed? Just the time to reach here by motorbike from Visate after stopping work for the lunch hour", pointed out Pino—ever the loafer—to the women in the house.) Pino watched from the sitting room window as the sharp-nosed youth got off his bike—not without showing a certain childish pleasure with his powerful machine—and hoisted it onto its stand. That done, he went toward the front door, and Pino went out to meet him.

Neither Gerardo, Ambrogio, nor Fortunato had yet returned from the plant, so Pino and Marsavi went to sit and wait in a corner of the sitting room, where—mainly for the benefit of Francesca and Alma, who were setting the table—they recounted their fabulous meeting in Switzerland during a distribution of fresh extra underwear, which Andrea had helped organize. They also talked about that other happy occasion, when Pino returned to Nomana in the dark interior of the delicatessen van. While they talked—joking in a friendly way—Marsavi let his eyes rest more and more frequently on Francesca, who as always looked lovely but today seemed especially so, he thought, like an almond branch in bloom. Her brown hair in a thick braid wound around her head, she came and went between dining room and kitchen, bringing plates and cutlery; she moved easily on her long legs, turning her blue eyes from time to time on their guest and smiling. The same eyes as Gerardo, Pino, Giudittina, and, when he was alive, Manno; but Andrea didn't notice the resemblance, and if someone had drawn it to his attention, he would have been upset. *What unique eyes*, he thought instead. *Look at the light in them . . . But how come a girl like this lives here, and I haven't even noticed?*

It began to bother him to appear in the role of a former Swiss internee before this extraordinary girl, who had a brother wounded in the war and a cousin fallen in the war and with a Medal of Gold as well. He searched his memory for other episodes in his life prior to his time in Switzerland, but never having been at the front, he realized in annoyance that the only "glorious" item he could talk about were a couple of skirmishes with Germans around the time of the armistice. However, he didn't get to talk about even this, because while waiting for Pino to give him an opportunity to speak, Gerardo and his two older sons arrived, all three heavy bodied, like laborers. At their arrival he calmed himself; besides, what was it he was seeking? Since when had he thought that the worth of a man could be measured by military valor? *After all, were we born to make war?* Signor Gerardo himself probably had never been in the military service. And if this marvelous girl was intelligent (*She is!* in the enthusiasm of the moment a voice inside his head said. *She is, without any doubt!*), she would know how to appreciate other values as well: hard work, for instance, and civic self-denial. As far as these qualities were concerned, in all modesty, he felt himself qualified.

Gerardo shook his hand with great cordiality. "How goes the business in Visate?" he asked the youth and asked also after the health of Andrea's father and uncles, whom, he added, he held in esteem, in very high regard. (On occasion, not often, Gerardo would allow himself a bit of an exaggeration, for emphasis.) He let the youth precede him as they made their way to his office, followed by Ambrogio and Pino. The discussion about the Riva truck didn't take long. Andrea had come to Nomana to ask if they would allow him to volunteer the truck on their behalf by telephoning the transportation division of the Como Pontifical Commission. "Because", he explained, "I promised a certain priest from Como . . . Don Curioni. Pino, you remember him, right? Well, Signor Riva, he was one of the Church people who concerned himself about us when we were in Switzerland, and last Sunday he pressured me literally to promise that without fail I'd find him another truck besides the two from my company." While the youth spoke, Gerardo nodded sympathetically. The truck was without delay put at Andrea's disposal, and he made note of the license number, capacity, and other details.

Then they discussed Pino's desire (he brought it up again now) to go along as relief driver. "Do you have a truck driver's permit? No? In that case I'm afraid there's nothing that can be done", declared Marsavi right away. "I'm sorry you'll be disappointed. In things like that, the Pontifical Commission won't be budged."

"And with good reason", said the father approvingly. "Suppose a truck loaded with people ends up in a ditch or whatever . . ."

"Just when it's me who's driving?" said Pino.

The others shook their heads, smiling.

"Listen, we can do this", proposed Andrea. "Our truck drivers return this Friday. I'll find out the facts, and in the afternoon I'll come here and tell you how things are, whether you have the possibility of going. Agreed?"

"Yes, but you've no need to bother yourself. I'll go to Visate myself", Pino answered.

"No", Andrea replied. "What for? I'll be delighted to come."

He was really nice. The other attributed his kindness to the fact of his having been Pino's internment companion; they didn't think about Francesca.

"Good", he said in his curt way, looking at his wristwatch. "It's nearly one, and your food will be getting cold. It's time I went. So we'll see each other on Friday."

He returned on Friday and—riding his powerful motorcycle and cleaving the air with his sharp profile—on Sunday too, and several other days.

6

During the following months prisoners of war (six hundred thousand) and political deportees (some thirty thousand) returned from Germany, several thousand each day. As the rail line through the Brenner Pass remained cut, they were still being transported in truck convoys. Not only the Americans' uniform columns of identical military trucks (the famous deuces, fast and perfectly spaced, driven generally by black soldiers who in civilian life were truckers on the great highways out west), but also the civilian Italian trucks, all different makes and sizes, alike only in flying the little yellow-and-white Pontifical Assistance Commission flags. Gradually the Italian trucks came to outnumber the Americans.

Meanwhile, the prisoners of war taken by the Allies came back by ship. They came from the Bitter Lake area in Egypt, from India, England, from distant America. Those returning from America were without question the best equipped; they were dressed in elegant U.S. Army summer uniforms and carried large shoulder bags filled with all God's blessings; not a few of them also seemed to have acquired the American soldiers' happy unconventional joking manner.

They all found a terribly devastated Italy, with the major cities damaged or razed to the ground. The country bisected at Cassino and at the gothic line—where the fighting front had been stalled during the last two winters—two wide strips of land sown with explosives, with not one wall left standing and still profusely mined. Some rail lines remained cut, while in one-third of the country between Cassino and the gothic line the road bridges, without exception, were reduced to ruins. On some highways—but not everywhere—the military had erected Bailey bridges, which allowed for an alternating flow of vehicles. Certain mountain passes (for example, the pass at Bracco, on national highway number one, the Aurelia) were impassable because they were solidly controlled by bandits.

More than ever short of raw materials, factories worked at a reduced pace. This fact—among others—most worried the returned soldiers, particularly those from the industrial areas; not even the countryside—without fertilizer for years—looked as fertile as they would have liked to see. Food rationing continued at hunger level, just as during wartime. Declining respect for the law increased the size of the black market, with its consequent rise in corruption and lowering of morals.

Yet the countryside was still there, and so were the factories; and in the soldiers and in many others, young and old, there was a great will not to give way to dissolution; to work, to pull out of the enormous ruin and head toward a secure future. Wasn't it possible, pulling together, to achieve a return to the past, a move to recuperate and reconstruct? The authorities—or what should have been the people in charge—found themselves paralyzed at the time by an incredible tangle of disputes between political parties, who, while they governed under a coalition, continued arguing openly among themselves. "Yet still and all, we have to live", the people everywhere said.

One afternoon Igino arrived from Germany. Ambrogio met him by accident as he walked alone up the road from the station to the piazza. He wore an old gray-green uniform that was too loose on him, and as baggage he carried in one hand a parcel tied with twine. In his excitement Ambrogio embraced him and, forgetting his errand, turned around and walked beside him.

His usually pale face even paler than usual and his hair in a brush cut, Igino—after answering his friend's questions abut his trip with terse details—asked Ambrogio about the work possibilities: more precisely if in the Beolco factory (where he had worked before the war) they were reemploying returned soldiers or not.

His companion answered that, insofar as he knew, they'd rehired some. "Nowadays there's little work," he cautioned, "but you don't have to worry; the factories are going to keep their laborers on, including those they had before the war. Because work must resume, in spite of everything."

On hearing confirmation that there was little work, Igino grimaced. Ambrogio felt affected by his anguish. *Papa has all the reason in the world*, he thought, *when he maintains there's a fundamental duty constantly to be creating new jobs. This is really our task, the employers' mission.* "Listen," he said to Igino, "if by chance in Beolco they make trouble for you, don't worry. Just let me know, and I'll find you a place, one way or another. Agreed?"

Igino smiled halfheartedly and nodded his thanks without speaking. Ambrogio felt there was something that he wasn't saying inside Igino. *Although deep down Igino has always been like that*, thought Ambrogio, *always a little disagreeable.*

He told him some of the news: that Manno had died and that also dead were Giovannino Flourface and another fellow draftee, and that there was still no news of Stefano.

When they reached the glassed door at the soldier's house, Ambrogio paused, as moved as he was. Igino put one hand on the door handle and paused for a moment. Then he turned the handle suddenly and went in, his brush-cut head bent over. He was greeted with a shout. The mother, seated at the table with the family, got to her feet and stood with her arms open; the father (a laborer, in rolled-up shirtsleeves and wearing a vest) and the fourteen-year-old brother ran toward him. The brother grabbed him around the neck, while the father held his hand in both of his and started wordlessly shaking it, being prevented from embracing his returning son by the action of the other son.

Ambrogio put his head in the doorway. "I'll leave him with you", he said, without entering. And to Igino, "We'll see each other tomorrow, *ciao*", and closed the door.

In an irrepressible feeling of wanting everyone to share her happiness, the mother cried, "You've brought him to us! Thank you, thank you!"

The four members of the laborer's family were reunited. As soon as he was free of his brother's embrace, Igino went to his mother, who hugged him, weeping; she didn't want to let him go and held him tightly.

"What are you doing? But do you see? She's crying", said the father with difficulty, shaking his head. "He's back, and she cries!"

After a bit the mother noticed her son's slight embarrassment with her embrace and released him, drying her eyes with her hands, and asked him to sit down. "Come over here, sit down. How good, Igino! You see? You've come back in time for dinner. Sit down, that's right, good. My Igino! Maybe you're hungry?"

"Hunger never fails me, for sure", he said. "After the killing hunger we've been made to suffer." And he gave his father an understanding smile, evidently thinking he was better qualified to understand such things.

The father nodded, as if to say, "Right. There's no need for you to explain."

"And about work?" Igino quickly asked his father.

"Don't worry; I've talked with the people at the factory; they'll take you immediately. Although there's little work. The owner, however, is out all around all day, looking for it: that one, in order to find work, is capable of going and asking the devil himself, you know. For sure he'll end up bringing a paycheck home."

"But why isn't there work?" asked Igino. "I don't understand. If everything has to be rebuilt, reconstructed . . ."

"And yet!" the father opened his hands. "I don't know why. But everyone says it's only a question of time, that soon there'll be work."

"It's the people who have been making money while we were away", Igino spat out harshly. "Now they don't want to risk that money in order to put the people to work."

"I don't know!" the father repeated, opening his hands again. "I don't know. In any case you have a job. Down at the factory they'll take you on again, I told you. Therefore . . ."

Igino nodded, but didn't look appeased.

"Don't think about that", said the mother, who hadn't stopped looking at him. "Think that now you're in your home, that at last you are with us."

"Yes", he agreed.

"You have to tell me everything", his brother told him. "You hear me, Igino? Everything."

"Everything what?"

"About war, the fighting, the dead . . . in other words, everything."

"Talking about the dead . . ." Igino turned to the mother. "You wrote me in one letter that Aunt Agatha died. How was it?"

"It was two months ago", the mother answered, her face darkening. "It's almost certain she had a tumor, that's what the doctor said. She'd lost weight; it was pitiful. There was nothing could be done. She put herself to bed, and in a few weeks she went."

"A tumor? Poor woman!"

"Now will you tell me or not?" insisted the brother.

"But he just got here", protested the mother. "Don't bother him. Come on, leave him in peace, tonight at least."

"Eh, tell you!" Igino turned to the boy. "What do you want me to tell you? What can be said using only words?" He meant that there wasn't any way to translate the experience he'd lived into words. He thought again and came to the conclusion that he really could never do so. He noticed at the same time the disappointment on the boy's face. "Right, tomorrow", he promised. "Tomorrow I'll tell you."

"That's right, now leave him in peace", interceded the father.

"You're home . . .", murmured the mother, still ecstatic.

"I'm home", said Igino, nodding. "It doesn't seem true. When I think of what I've been through sometimes in order to eat just a potato skin . . ."

"Eh, the war!" murmured the father.

"Right over there I have a nice piece of salt pork", said the mother enticingly, "and a string of salami, kept for you."

"What?" exclaimed Igino, surprised. "You mean this still exists in Italy?"

"We got it off Ferrante", explained the mother. "This winter he slaughtered the pig, and at a good price, without coupons or fuss. If you'll wait a moment while your father and brother finish eating, I'll make you a vegetable soup with salt pork and a whole plate of salami. Eh? That appeal to you?"

"It must be nearly two years since I ate salami", said Igino.

"Don't believe that here it's been easy either. It's been hard," said the father, "although living in the country always helps."

"The bosses won't even have noticed the shortages, eh? The ones full of money, I mean."

"Eh . . .", his father half agreed. "The worst is always the fate of us poor people."

"The Rivas, for example, won't even have noticed?" the son wanted to know.

The father didn't answer; there was a pause.

"Well, the Rivas also had a son killed", remembered the mother. "And in addition they organized that sending of packages to you prisoners. In the town everybody lent a hand, but it was they who kept things going. Talking of which, did you always get your stuff all right? Was the food good?"

"Yes, I'd already written to you", answered Igino. He thought a bit, then asked, "The news of Manno's death was told to me just a while ago by Ambrogio, but I didn't understand clearly; who was responsible, the English or the Germans?"

"The Germans."

"They awarded him the gold medal, did you know?" said the brother.

"The gold medal, eh?" repeated Igino and was about to say, "Sure, only the officers are given medals of gold", but held back. The fact was that Manno wouldn't return, wouldn't ever experience the homecoming he was enjoying right now; the tragedy of it suddenly struck him. "But poor Manno!" he murmured.

"The rich and the poor", said the mother. "The war has been brutal for everybody."

716

7

Pierello arrived a few days later, getting a ride on a truck that had finished a run for the Pontifical Commission between Verona and Austria and was returning to its base at Incastigo.

He was wearing a jumble of unmatched clothing, part civilian and part military, topped by a Tyrolean hat, and was riding in the uncovered bed of the truck. At his side, his back also supported on the truck cabin, was an Incastigo sergeant Pierello had found in Prague, Czechoslovakia, some weeks before; then he had lost sight of him, only to meet him casually again in Verona, where he had arranged the ride on the truck for Pierello.

During the journey they had several times talked about the more recent events in Prague, particularly about the uprising against the Germans, which they had both witnessed, although separately.

"They seemed so calm, such peaceful people, the Czechs ...", observed Pierello, "and yet, have you seen such things? When they broke loose they turned into wild animals."

"You say 'they seemed'. They really are good natured, the Czechs", objected the sergeant. "Let me tell you, because I've been with them over a year. It was the Germans who brought the calamity down upon themselves. Did you know how it started?"

"When do you mean?"

"I'm talking about the fifth or sixth of May, this month, when the word in the street was that the Americans were about to arrive. You were still in Prague, you said."

"Yes, right."

"Then you also saw, in that case, how the people gathered on both sides of the street. 'The Americans are coming, the Americans are coming! They've already taken the airport!' everybody was saying, leaving the center of the road free so the Americans could go by, so that even I expected to see them arrive at any moment."

"Yes, I saw that. Who ever could have started that rumor?"

"And up to that point, in any case, they had done nothing against the Germans. What's more, they were telling them, 'Go home, the war's over!' I heard them. And also, 'Things have gone well for you, too; instead of the Russians it is the Americans who are arriving.'"

"Yes, at the start I saw that it was as you say; I was referring to later", objected Pierello, and with his forearms resting on his knees, he spread his hands to show his consternation.

"The Germans were to blame, shooting at the people to clear the streets", said the sergeant. "That's what provoked the uprising. What's more, on top of that, there was the realization that it wasn't the Americans who were about to arrive in Prague, but the Russians. The people went crazy, because apart from the poor run-down Communists with the Red flags, the Czechs don't like the Russians. The Czechs find them disgusting. You knew that, no?"

"Yes, I saw that."

"They said, 'What a calamity for us. Through the Germans' fault now we'll end up God knows how many years under Russian rule. For you prisoners of war, things are almost over, but for us everything is only beginning.' You understand why they pitted themselves against the Germans to the point of killing?"

"Yes, but to stone people to death, even women and children, to chase them down the streets with showers of rocks, even to crushing them to death underfoot . . . people who do those things can't be good people."

"I know the Czechs well", the sergeant repeated. "They're good people—they are. Put yourself in their place. Go on, think about it."

"If you think of all the sickening things we've seen!" Pierello said. "Were you still there when those regiments of Russians arrived, with the strange cross on their flag? Those Russians who'd gone over to the Germans, wearing German uniforms?"

"Ah, yes. You mean the Cossacks with the Saint Andrew's cross. No, I only heard about them," answered the sergeant, "because as soon as we were left unguarded, we escaped from Prague."

"Poor wretches. You should have seen them", said Piero. "They didn't know what to do. Some started firing on the SS, who were still resisting; some others shot at the Communist partisans. What chaos. My God!"

"Yes, what chaos", said the sergeant, nodding.

"Nevertheless, if I'm here now, I owe it to them, those Cossacks", declared Pierello. "Because when they started marching to go and meet the Americans (they knew where they were), a fellow named Tadeusz and I, a Pole who'd been with me for more than a year, we followed them closely. We didn't stay and wait for the Russians. It was by following the Cossacks that we managed finally to cross the American line at Sukomast."

Sukomast: the sergeant hadn't even heard of it.

Poor Tadeusz, thought Pierello. *What'll be happening to him right now? Perhaps with luck he too made it to his home . . .*

From time to time during the trip they also talked of other things: the situation in Italy, for example, based on what they'd seen in Verona, and what they could see from the truck along the road. They also returned to talk of the horrendous events they had each witnessed in Prague, which, because of the sole fact of being together, they could not keep from remembering.

Then—having passed the Adda over the bridge at Brivio—they entered Brianza. Toward the north the amphitheater of mountains began to become the picture that Pierello knew so well. In the trip's final stages approaching Nomana he saw familiar villages and places he knew. Over there, after the Visate crossroads, was the square Nomanella farmhouse, in front of which as always, the three cherry trees and small fig tree were lined up. Who knows, perhaps inside at that moment would be that nice quiet girl named Giustina. And would they have had news of Stefano or not? Poor Ferrante, and Lucia . . . At the northern edge of Nomana, the trees in the Riva garden could be seen. Manno . . . would Manno be back?

In Verona the driver had promised Pierello he would take him directly to his hamlet, la Lodosa; therefore they went through Nomana without stopping. Sitting in the truck's bed with his back against the driver's cab, Tyrolean hat on his head and feeling emotional, Pierello looked avidly at the passing scene. He recognized one after another of the people in the street and greeted many of them by waving and calling to them. Among these was Carlaccio, with sad eyes and hanging arms; he continued, war or no war, forever to carry his large body on his twisted spinal column. The same as the others, Carlaccio didn't at first recognize Pierello and answered his wave when he was already out of hearing range. Only Chin, the crazy mailman, riding his bicycle with the big leather bag on the handlebars, recognized him instantly and shouted, "Piero, Piero!" happily. "Good for Piero!" and then he too fell behind. The bridge over the rail line seemed to Pierello improbably small. Then, having passed the town sportsfields and some groups of locust trees, he finally came to the field that sloped down toward his own Lodosa. The field was partially sown in grain, already showing ears of an attractive green color; part of the field was in pasture and here and there lines of mulberries. Down below, along the watering place, the willows and poplars had grown thicker, to the point where the small clear stream was difficult to see. How many times as a child had he caught gudgeon in his handkerchief, the little fish looking almost like insects? He'd go fishing with Castagna and other kids his own age. To highlight the importance of his catch, Castagna used to say, "I only need to eat eight or ten gudgeon to feel full." Would Castagna be home?

Here was Lodosa. No more than a dozen houses or small dwellings, three roads at right angles to each other, with an ancient farmhouse with a courtyard, by whose name the locality was known. He knew every nook and cranny of each house. Standing up and holding onto the truck's side, his heart beating hard, he searched each detail with his eyes, to see if there had been any changes; and no, there weren't any, only that everything seemed to be smaller than he remembered.

It was late afternoon, that serene time in the country during which the last of the day's chores were done. The truck was moving slowly, and the driver's assistant stuck his smiling face out of the window and looked back. "Where's your house?"

"It's over there at the bottom. It's one of the last ones. But stop here. You've done enough. Please stop."

"Which house?"

"You can't see it. It's over there, behind that building."

"OK", said the assistant pulling his head back into the cab. Passing the intervening building, they saw the cottage. The truck stopped in front of the street—more like a lane—forming crossroads with the main road, which cut through the grain-sown fields. Backing into the lane to turn around, the truck maneuvered until it faced the direction of Nomana again. They didn't stop the engine. The driver and his assistant didn't get out of the cab.

The sergeant said, "Piero, you've arrived."

"Yes," said Pierello, "yes." Now he was a little scared. Grabbing the bag that served him as a suitcase, he adjusted the Tyrolean hat and jumped over the truck's side to the ground; this required a bit of effort, as his legs were cramped and numb.

His home was some ten yards away, parallel to the lane. A small, rather shabby place (he noticed now), with a metal-tubing handrail running around the porch; on the ground floor a small opening as a front entrance. There was nobody in sight.

Pierello went to the truck's cab, sack in hand. "Why don't you get down and have a drink?" he invited the two drivers.

From inside the cab both men smiled and made negative gestures, indicating they were in a hurry. Then, still using their hands, they said goodbye, and the truck moved off. "Hey . . . thanks, thanks a lot!" shouted Pierello.

"Goodbye, Piero!" shouted the sergeant from the back of the truck.

"Goodbye", Pierello replied. Life in the army was over for him, over forever. He went toward the house, his legs still stiff from the ride.

8

To one side of the front of the small house, carved into the surrounding grain, there was a little square of beaten earth surrounded by a privet hedge, and Piero remembered it had never grown well, probably because his mother, without thinking, would throw out the soapy washtub water there after washing the clothes.

Piero went past the square to the porch, no larger than a bedroom. High on one wall was a painting of a Madonna, which he greeted respectfully by nodding his head. Then he thumbed the latch, trying to open the door, but it wouldn't move. He checked it: it was locked.

A little concerned, the youth went to the only window between the porch and the kitchen and, putting his hands on the sill, looked through the glass as much as the lace curtains would let him. He saw, lying in its usual place on a chair, the cat, which lifted one lazy eye to look at him. (*Look at that; the black cat is still here*, he told himself happily.) On the stove was a slowly cooking pot; between the pot and lid a trace of steam escaped. Turning his head and pressing closer to the glass, the youth could also see the birdcage hanging on a wall.

On noting his interest, the canary started moving and singing. "Everything is in its place. Here's the canary. There are no problems", whispered Piero. "For sure, Mama has gone out with Martina on some errand; they can't be long if she's left the pot on the fire. And also my father, soon we'll see, he'll be returning from doing the chores. Nothing to worry about." But the most reassuring thing he saw was the old rectangular brass alarm clock, lying on its side. Pierello smiled because he remembered that the ancient mechanism worked only in this position. "Everything's in its place. Thank God!" he murmured with profound relief, pulling back from the window. "Good", he concluded. "I can wait."

He really was lucky—he thought, looking around him—to find the house the same as when he had left. Into his head came memories of German cities reduced to rubble jungles and the unending columns of refugees, fleeing after having left everything behind, their impressive silence while they walked and walked without stopping through the gloomy mist. What could have become of the widow Hufenbach, of Joachim and the other boy? "Poor people!" he murmured. And those miserable Russians wearing German uniforms, the Cossacks, whom a few days ago he'd followed to Sukomast. What incredible passivity they'd all exhibited when the Americans told them to surrender their weapons! "We're finished. We're dead men", they'd said to one another fatalistically. "They'll hand us over to Stalin. There's no hope." (They spoke in Russian, but Tadeusz translated for him.) But who really knew how it went for them . . . was it possible the Americans really handed them over into Stalin's hands? No. Coldheartedly hand over thousands, more, tens of thousands of men to die, the Americans? He thought it impossible. And even Tadeusz also thought so. Tadeusz! How would it have gone with him? "Poor Tadeusz! I have not had a friend in my life who was more a friend than he", Piero said to himself, not for the first time. What a dirty business, when one couldn't live in peace, even with the war over! It was only the Nazis and the Communists who had this sickening compulsion of not leaving people in peace, even interfering with their home life. What damned evil people! "But why didn't they behave like these others, the Americans and the English, whose presence in Italy was hardly noticed?" And from what he'd heard in Verona, they even helped people who had problems. While Piero was absorbed in these reflections, the song of the canary, excited now more and more, the giddy thing, came from inside the house, where it had begun singing really loudly.

Meantime, no one came along the road. Piero asked himself if he shouldn't go to one of the neighboring houses—to the Castagnas, for example—to ask for news, but decided that he'd be detained by them and would have trouble getting away from them.

He went over in front of the painting of our Lady; even this appeared to have become smaller. It was a yard high and a little more in width and had an inscription in printed irregular letters that said, "Holy Virgin of Caravaggio".

The Lady was shown standing with a halo. Before her was a kneeling woman, arms open in wonder at the miracle of her appearance. Between them a watery canal ran in the direction of the viewer. The canal had been painted with such a lack of knowledge of the rules of perspective that anyone looking at it—despite its exaggerated blue color—had difficulty grasping that it was meant to be a canal, which was why Pierello as a boy had used a nail to scratch in the outline of some fishes, not swimming along but in profile, across the canal. They could still be seen. *Look, they're still visible. While I was over there pulling the cart with Frische Nehrung these fish were here, and now I find them again.* Since the time his grandfather had hired a house painter to make the painting to please the grandmother (the same grandmother who used to tell Piero as a child all the stories of the old times, of the grand ladies and gentlemen who came and went through the portals of *I dragoni*) its figures had been touched up and repainted several times. The dirty paint had faded, and after each retouching the bright red border around the figures had been expanded a bit and now appeared decidedly too large. How many prayers of every kind before this sacred image? Here, every afternoon, even after the grandmother's death, was where the family would say their Rosaries and their devotions. The mother would lead, while the children's voices—Pierello remembered it well—would get slower as sleep overtook them. He saw again the suppliant face of this mother ("How many prayers have you said, poor Mother?") and suddenly recognized that this return today was connected to this constant praying, that it had in some way determined his coming back. "Thank you, Lady", he murmured with simple emotion, bowing his head. "I thank you and entreat you on behalf of Tadeusz that he also may reach his own home and that they leave him in peace, poor devil."

Cheep-cheep-cheep, the insistent canary's song came from inside, giving him its own kind of welcome. What peace there was here! This was how real peace was . . . the feeling of thankfulness to our Lady and to God for having let him return was united in Piero with this peace, making it perfect. The insistent canary continued to cheep, making Pierello smile.

All of a sudden he turned, sensing that someone was looking at him. It was Martina, his six-year-old sister, visibly flustered; one finger in her mouth, she looked at him from the little courtyard, not daring to enter the porch. She had—even though in miniature—the same round face of her brother, the same brown eyes and hair, the same humble air. She also had snot running from her nose.

"Martina," exclaimed the youth, "what are you doing? Aren't you going to greet me?" He approached the child very emotionally. "But what is this? You see me here, I'm back, and you don't even say hello?" he repeated. "Where's Mama?"

The little girl now looked fixedly at his hat. "She's gone to feed the rabbits", she finally said. Pierello placed his hands in the child's armpits and lifted her so that their faces were close, "And now? Right now will you greet me?"

"*Ciao*", Martina said softly, and stretched out a finger toward his Tyrolean hat.

"Ah, you're interested in my hat?" The youth squeezed her, laughing, and kissed his little sister. Then, putting her back down, he said, "Come, keep me company right now while I go where Mother is. Where does she have the rabbits?"

"In the Terenghis' shed", replied the girl, pointing with a finger. And now, with confidence, she put her hand in her brother's and went with him.

So one by one those who had remained alive began coming back from various places, except from Russia. In Nomana the arrivals took place over a period of months, one after the other—sometimes two or three in one day—and at other times less frequently, one a week or less.

Many found shortages of everything when they got home. Some didn't even have decent clothes to wear—so that—encouraged by his father, Gerardo—Ambrogio proposed to the board of directors of the old Veterans' Association that they start collecting funds with the objective of giving suit cloth to every returning prisoner of war. He devoted himself to the task personally, going with the association's president, an officer in the previous war, to see all the possible contributors in Nomana and the surrounding townships. Quite rapidly—although not easily—they got the required sum together, and in midsummer they could already go ahead with the distribution of the suit lengths, which took place in the Oratory, decked with tricolor flags. The handing out of the suiting was done by the town's young ladies, and thanks to their heartfelt happiness, the ceremony was genuine and pleasant.

9

Remote from all the events in Italy and the outside world, as if he was on the other side of the moon, Michele remained in Russia, living the monotonous routine of a prisoner of war. For some time past his living conditions should have been improved, because the Soviet authorities—not signatories of the Geneva Convention—had suddenly decided, for propaganda reasons, to treat prisoners of war according to this agreement, without, however, conforming to some of the important rights under the convention, among them the exchange of mail. In practice things were more or less as they had been before, with the exception of work, which for the enlisted men was not as hard and for the officers was optional.

From Oranchi—where he was last heard of—in late 1943 the young officer had been transferred, along with the other Italian officers who had survived imprisonment in the various *lagers*, to Susdal, one of the Orthodox Church's saintly places, between Moscow and the Volga. The town had several convents, all of which had been turned into *lagers*, and some fifty churches, not one of them open for worship. In the largest convent, surrounded by a seventeenth-century ruined wall, the *lager* for prisoners of war had been established. On the crumbling bastions Bolshevik guards had their sentry boxes, from which, armed with machine guns, they watched over the crowds of tattered military men—not only Italians, but also Germans, Romanians, and Hungarians.

On the inside walls of the buildings they were watched over by lines of ancient saints painted in Byzantine style: all had their eyes wide open, faces pale and stern, limbs and clothes stiff, rigid. "*Religio depopulata*", Michele would say to himself in his discouragement on meeting those mute looks, and each time—so that the images fulfilled after all the purpose for which they had been painted—he would mentally recite a prayer. He asked himself what could have happened to Susdal's monks. Who knew if some of them still subsisted somewhere in limitless Russia, like that poor Sister Natalia and the few other rural sisters imprisoned in the women's *lager* at Oranchi? While he was at work, he tried to ask some civilians about this and received confirmation that in all the holy city's convents there had been waves of civilian deportations, a practice that still continued, and that an incalculable number of them had died. About the monks who had once lived here, however, nobody was able to give him news.

The officers in charge of the *lager* and the Italian refugee commissars themselves (much more wide awake than the Russians) didn't really understand his behavior. They saw him as friendly toward individuals who had reputations for stubbornness, for their infallible and tenacious opposition to the servile initiatives by several anti-Fascists who tried to push the majority into being amiable with the guards. They also noted besides that he had absolutely no connections with the anti-Fascists, yet on the other hand they saw that nobody occupied themselves as much as he in studying texts by Marxists, Leninists, and Stalinists, both theoretical and historical, slowly absorbing one thick volume after another, to the point where he mastered the subject better than the instructors and lecturers. This ability ended up provoking feelings of reserve toward him on the part of many prisoners.

More than one instructor asked him directly if the material he was studying convinced him. He always replied that he hadn't so far studied enough and that before he made any pronouncements he needed to continue his studies.

"Well, he'll end up convincing himself", they would affirm, with a narrowness of mind that Michele thought proper to stupid mulish people. It seemed inconceivable to them, even in that authentic hell, that one could be in contact with the radiant Marxist doctrine of the future paradise on earth without being conquered by it.

In the second half of 1944, with Russian troops already in Poland, news started coming to light of the first discoveries of the German extermination camps.

The newspapers and radio in Russia had been discreet at the beginning, giving certain details and concealing others. They showed an obvious reluctance to call general attention to these human death camps, even though they were the enemy's. This reluctance didn't extend to the Italian refugee commissars, who considered they had the definitive argument to convince the mass of the POWs. In their unenlightened heads anti-Nazi (or anti-Fascist, as they would tend to say, being purposely confusing) was the same as pro-Communist.

After the disclosure of finding the camp at Maidanek, near Lublin, Paolo Robotti—brother-in-law of Togliatti, secretary of the Italian Communist party—had come personally to Susdal and in his dissertation had gravely listed the discoveries: gas chambers; crematorium ovens; nearly a million shoes, men's, women's, and wretched children's; hundreds of kilos of women's hair separated by colors, part in bales, the rest loose. "Investigations have determined", he said, again and again, "that around six hundred thousand human bodies were incinerated in the ovens." At the end of his sepulchral lecture, grave and gloomy, he passed around a number of Russian newspapers that carried the news; he stayed on for a number of days to comment upon it, strolling through the courtyards with small groups of officers.

"He was beaming with happiness. Did you see him? He's happy at the enormity of the facts, just because it becomes part of his game", some of them commented, torn between anger and dismay.

Others said, "To him this looks as if it redeemed the Communists' crimes."

Michele, meanwhile, commented to his few friends, "How stupid. Did you notice? He didn't even question why such atrocities are being committed today at the same time as the Communists', when for centuries civilized humanity thought it had left such horrors behind forever." In studying the supposedly sacred Communist texts, he'd already pinpointed some fundamental truths: in the first place that the most important ideas incorporated in them came from the same anti-Christian sources that formed the basis of Nazi ethics. In short, these ideas and behavior carried the seal of German idealism and went back in time to the Enlightenment of the seventeenth and eighteenth centuries, farther back to the Lutheran schism, and even to Renaissance anthropological centrism. They originated in streams of anti-Christian thought based on the same sources, for example in Darwinism, converted into atheist philosophy. Michele took note that both Marxism and nazism had an extraordinarily high number of ancestors in common, came of the same blood. And in fact both—in a nearly perfect antithesis of Christianity, which is love—were defined through similar mechanisms of hate, only while in Marxism there was a redeeming class (the proletariat) called to overturn and repress the other classes, in nazism there was a chosen race called upon to dominate and enslave the other races. In truth, nazism—more modern—went a step farther than Marxism in that it didn't foresee any theoretical salvation for the overturned and repressed in its new society (due to last a thousand years, like the Communists') and, once freed of the lay humanitarian utopias of the 1800s (still present in Marxist belief), simply proclaimed that it wanted to dominate, to rule, and nothing else. To offset this, however, and being—if looked at closely—more exactly a destruction of Judaism rather than of Christianity, nazism ended up being much less universal than Marxism and in the end—Michele thought—less dangerous for humanity.

The news of the discoveries at Maidanek produced perturbation in the POW camp, not only among the Italian prisoners but also among prisoners of other nationalities, especially the Germans, who found themselves particularly affected. Not a few—particularly officers and enlisted men of units from the front—refused to believe the reports. It seemed impossible to them that their generosity and spirit of sacrifice had been betrayed by their leaders in this way. One thing was harshness and even brutality while conducting the war—both historically inborn qualities in their peoples—and quite another was their massive elimination of unarmed, defenseless people, which even for Germany was a terrible innovation.

"In any case, and without doubt, this is something quite in line with Nazi fanaticism", the Italians would say to them.

The general reaction of the Italians wasn't in any case what Robotti expected. Except for the few proclaimed anti-Fascists, the prisoners didn't show any inclination to accept communism, which was "beating the Nazi wild beast". Once the commissar had left (after advising them he would return after visiting other POW camps where there were Italians), they were left to ponder the harrowing news. It wasn't enough, then, the unspeakable horrors and unmentionable bestiality undertaken by the Reds. When comparing accounts, it became clear the Nazis had committed similar or even worse atrocities (although it would be hard to think of anything worse than Crinovaya, particularly for those who had been there).

"How could the Germans also have lost their heads to such an extent?" many prisoners asked, dismayed.

"At least you now realize that this behavior isn't based on being a backward people", Michele observed to Father Turla and to his squad comrades. "That it was a mistake to associate these actions with Russian underdevelopment? If not, shouldn't we have to talk about German underdevelopment, too?"

Father Turla, sick again and down to 110 pounds, hadn't been for some time the squad's *nachiàlnik*. He spent much of his time in the POW camp convent in his cell, which he shared with Michele and eight others, sitting on his bunk under a heart-rending Byzantine crucifix, showing an emaciated Christ, surrounded by Roman soldiers, wearing long cloaks down to their feet, longer even than the modern Russian soldiers' overcoats.

"These events", said Michele one day, finally tackling the subject head-on, "have to be interpreted if we are able to use the intelligence we've been given. We have to know how to determine the reason for this incredible step backward by humanity toward the barbarian past, to the cavemen. And to decide whether we can stop it or not."

"I see. It's your old fixed idea, a general de-Christianization, right?" Father Turla said, turning his gaunt face to Michele.

"Yes. Let's just take the argument put forward by that wretch of a commissar who gave us a lecture last month . . ."

"Which wretch? There's no shortage of wretches who come here to lecture us."

"The one from Moscow University."

"Ah, the professor . . . but what are you trying to say? I didn't even listen to his trash."

Seated on their folded palliasses, the other cellmates shook their heads. It was the usual abstract argument from Tintori, his continual obsession.

"Well, if you, if all of you had listened to the lecture as I suggested, if instead of snorting now you had followed then, you'd have at least noted that without the developments in the Protestant universities and cultures, and particularly without Hegel and Feuerbach, the theories espoused by Marx and Lenin couldn't have come to light. They'd be simply inconceivable today. The same as the propositions of Nietzsche about 'the supermen' and the 'will to power'. Remember, without these, Hitler's existence today would also be inconceivable."

The others shrugged their shoulders and said nothing; even Father Turla was too tired to make a rejoinder. Michele finished, as at other times, meditating alone. It was something he was accustomed to doing. Seated on his palliasse, he reflected silently. His ideas were not pointless, uncalled-for abstractions. It wasn't a game he played. It consisted of an objective "why?" about one of history's greatest massacres. The Protestant heresy . . . here were its fruits! He recalled the era, more accurately the terror that heresy produced in the Middle Ages—in *his* Middle Ages. The heretics were then considered as harmful as a plague . . . and here was the result derived from the affirmation of heresy: the tens of millions of deaths caused by communism and nazism.

And there is nobody to say that it has finished. If the forward march of these events cannot be stopped, perhaps we're no farther ahead than at the beginning. God knows what the future holds for us! Contemplating this perspective, stirred by emotion as he was, he almost felt ready to justify the Inquisition. In the prison's library there were French versions of Llorente's books, and he had read them conscientiously. In the climactic moment of Torquemada's work the Inquisition's victims were said to be 10,220. One got the impression that this number had been exaggerated. In any case, it was evident that in all its secular history, the Inquisition had had fewer victims than Stalin and Hitler had had in a single year. *After all, if with these few thousand dead it had really been possible to avoid all the millions of today, almost, almost . . .* His eyes settled on the crucifix: Christ's tortured face—he noticed—was here to suffer painfully, even for this reasoning with which he was trying to justify, in his loving name, the fact that so many men had been murdered, burned alive . . .

Eh, Michele, what's going on? How can you accept killing your neighbor in Christ's name? Are you also losing your reason? The youth shook his head and sighed. He concluded with certainty that the Inquisition was certainly to be condemned, but with one precise condition: that the condemnation came from Christians, not others.

10

Before Robotti, the commissar, returned to Susdal, a tiny group of Italian soldiers arrived from Kazan, on the Volga.

A second lieutenant from Michele's squad—a nervous type, always on the lookout for news—after having spoken with some of the new arrivals went to his cell, pale faced, and going to his bunk lay down and without a word pulled a blanket over himself, completely covering himself.

"What's the matter with you? What's happened?" asked his surprised neighboring bunkmate.

There was no reply.

"Look", the man insisted. He was sitting leaning on the wall next to the blanketed form, a mess can and wooden spoon in his hands. (It was time to eat, and food was fetched in a variety of containers.) "What's happening with you? Come on, get it out of your system."

Still not getting an answer, he put the spoon in the can and with his free hand lifted the blanket to look at the prostrated man's face. "I asked you what's happened to you?"

"What's happened is that I've realized this sh—— will never end." And he covered his head again.

There was silence. All the men in the small cell looked at the blanketed profile.

"What's happened to you? Will you tell us?" Father Turla broke the silence. "Don't keep us in suspense, please."

The second lieutenant gave no reply.

"Well?"

Finally he lifted the blanket, evidently upset.

"Couldn't you leave me in peace?"

None of them spoke; with their eating bowls in hand, they awaited an explanation.

"Go and talk to the new arrivals from Kazan", the second lieutenant said. "I spoke to a couple of men from the Fifty-Second Artillery who . . . leave it . . .", he interrupted himself.

"What do you mean 'leave it'?" Don Turla said worriedly. Then, turning to the blanketed man, "Will you go on?"

"Every day trains arrive at Kazan from Romania", he finally said. "And . . ." Again he interrupted himself.

One of the others said, "The Russians are now *liberating* Romania, or so Robotti said. Well, what was in the trains? Women, children?"

"Yes, of course", replied the second lieutenant. "Civilians and military, all piled into the wagons as always, but that's not it . . ."

He appeared to change the subject. "There'll be a day when trains like that will come from Italy also. Now we can do nothing to prevent it. There's nothing that can be done."

"Will you please continue?" asked an impatient Father Turla.

"The trains arrive full of corpses. They travel at such slow speed that in some cars there's not one alive. And the dead are almost all opened up, with the liver missing or . . . or . . . well, you know. One train after another, all the same. In some cars there are people still alive, poor things, but already reduced to madness, or . . ."

They were all silent, shattered by the horrible news.

"The two people from the Fifty-Second, from whom did they hear it?" asked an older lieutenant, who when talking tended to cover his mouth with one hand, having lost many of his teeth.

"They were in the Kazan hospital, but almost every day they were taken from their beds and driven to the station to help the German work squads, who were unable to move all the bodies unassisted."

"But . . . what about Stalin's *pricàs*? Doesn't it apply to the Romanians too?" one of them asked, dismayed, looking the others in the face.

"In Romania the Communists don't have to make propaganda", Michele said in a hard tone. "They're the ones in charge."

"Are you all happy now?" the blanketed officer asked angrily and gasped out, "Go to hell, all of you!" He pulled the blanket over his head again, this time decisively.

There was silence.

"And your God allows these things?" the toothless officer asked the chaplain bitterly.

"Don't you blaspheme", Father Turla murmured. He silently lifted his eyes to the painted image over his head. From his position he could see it only at an angle, but it seemed to him that the unmoving eyes of Christ looked at him with pain. God had made men free. That was the point. All the evil stemmed from this. Now, he couldn't go against that freedom, couldn't prevent men from doing what they wanted. He had no other choice of action but to die together with all the murdered people, crucified with them . . . Father Turla didn't say a word.

11

"The Fifty-Second Artillery. He said they were soldiers from the Fifty-Second", Michele repeated to himself several times during the following hours, dedicated to indoctrination. "I have to find them and talk to them myself."

The next day he managed to find one, a southerner who confirmed the events related by the second lieutenant and—prompted by his questions—unwillingly gave details. The people who had arrived with him from Kazan—he said—were now in the *lager* infirmary. "Because at Kazan we were in the hospital. At any rate, I'm happy they transferred us here, where there are officers like yourself, because where there are Italian officers, the guards beat us soldiers less."

Michele nodded. He knew it was true. He also knew that this was due, not to the anti-Fascists, but to the so-called inflexibles, who for some time had opposed the bullying of the guards by attacking them in *jalobi*—written protests—containing incessant calls for compliance with international agreements, sent to the highest Soviet authorities. Obviously, none of these *jalobi* was forwarded, but just reading the addressees' names must have caused heart fluttering in the prison authorities.

"Is it true", asked the soldier, "that there's a chaplain here from Julia who kicked one of the police chiefs in the chest during interrogation?"

"Yes", Michele smiled. "Father Brevi. But he hasn't been here for some months. He was transferred to a punishment *lager*, along with other inflexibles, like Boletti, Italo Stagno, Captains Iovino and Magnani, together with some others."

"Exactly," replied the soldier, "Captain Iovino. Do you know him? He's from Resina, nearly a fellow countryman of mine. I'm from Pompei, which forms a single town with Resina. I've heard about him, yes. Iovino, he's an exceptional man, isn't that right? He's a near neighbor of mine."

"He's a very valorous type", said Michele convincingly.

The soldier looked at him sympathetically. "Are you Milanese?" he asked.

Michele nodded. "Well, from the same province."

"From the province of Milan? From which town? We have a certain Valli, Tito, in the Fifty-Second. He was with me in Kazan, and before that in *lager* 171. He's also from Milan province."

"By any chance do you know where from?"

"I don't remember. Well, let's see, what did he say . . .? From Brianza. That's it, he's from Brianza."

"Brianza isn't a town. It's a region, the same as for you Campania would be or, I don't know, Irpinia, for example . . .", Michele explained, very interested. "My town, Nova—have you heard of Nova by any chance? It is in Brianza. And this Valli, where's he from? Try to remember."

"Nova, you said? No. I haven't ever heard of Nova. Never. His town has another name . . . I just can't remember. Well, now he's in the infirmary, but as soon as he comes out, I'll tell him you're here. What's your name?"

"Tintori. Please remember, Tintori."

"Very well, Second Lieutenant Tintori. Tito will be pleased."

"Did you say his name was Valli—Tito Valli?"

"Yes, class of 1921, in the Fifty-Second Artillery."

"Do you know what his illness is?"

"Tuberculosis."

"Ah . . ."

"A serious thing, right."

12

Some twelve days later, while voluntarily working outside Susdal at a *kolkhoz* called "the Spanish colony", Michele met the soldier from Resina once again. It was the soldier—who with his squad was repairing a damaged highway— who recognized him. "Lieutenant!" he called over, making signs that he should wait. (Michele was on the road, following a farm wagon.) "Your countryman is here, Tito, Tito Valli." He pointed to another soldier, standing still and bent over a shovel, his head lowered.

"What do you say?"

"Tito Valli, your countryman, he's here."

"Ah!" Michele gestured to his companions to keep on going and approached the two soldiers.

Tito Valli, unjustifiably taken from the *lager*'s infirmary, had a very poor appearance. Not only did he weigh less than 110 pounds; he also had swelling to his face and body and was a sickly yellow color. For him, unlike the treatment given to officers, work was obligatory, and it must have been hard for him.

"I'm from Nova", Michele said, offering his hand; he spoke cordially on seeing the state the man was in. "I hear you're also from Brianza. Is that right?"

"Yes, I'm from Nomana, in Monza district."

"From Nomana?" the young lieutenant said with emotion. "But . . . what do you say? From Nomana, for sure?"

The other man nodded. "Yes, why?"

This Tito, cousin of Pierello, was the inexperienced recruit who, confused on the day all the other recruits were leaving, had climbed onto the wrong train and had been rescued by Giovannino Flourface.

"If you're from Nomana, you'd have to know Ambrogio Riva, Second Lieutenant Ambrogio Riva, year of 1921."

"Yes, he was a fellow recruit, although I've never talked to him. I know him only by sight."

"What? You've never talked to him? Did you know he was also in Russia, with the Eighth Pasubio Artillery?"

"Yes, I knew that."

"And do you know if he's still alive or . . .?"

"No, I was in the Turin."

"My division."

The soldier looked at the officer's worn insignia. "Yes", he said, and switching to dialect, "They caught me on the second day of the withdrawal, in that village where they attacked us with tanks."

"In Posnyakoff?"

"Yes, there. I don't know how it went with him, though."

From the first moment of conversation, Michele's thoughts had been running to Alma. "Tell me," he asked, also going over to using dialect, "and how about the rest of the Riva family. Do you know them?"

"Only by name. I know they're industrialists. Good people. They're very highly regarded back there."

The soldiers' guard, a Mongol with his machine pistol hanging across his chest, didn't seem to be concerned about the unauthorized conversation, and they continued talking. "The thing is", explained Tito, now a little emotional due to meeting a countryman, "that I don't live in the town. I'm from the village of Lodosa, from an out-of-the-way farmhouse called Casaretto. The people from our village don't go to school in Nomana but to an out-of-town school. That's why I don't know the people from Nomana very well."

"I understand."

"My cousin, Piero Valli, on the other hand—he was also born in 1921— used to go to school in Nomana and is a good friend of Ambrogio Riva."

"Understood", said a highly disappointed Michele. And he thought, *Great! It would have been really great! Pity, just the same, being from Nomana and not to know the Rivas. We would have had things to talk about!*

They found things to talk about just the same. And they took advantage of the meal break some hours later to do just that. Tito—concerned about contagion— had gone to sit away from his squad on a grassy bank between the *kolkhoz's* spread-out buildings. Michele drew near and, after asking about his health (*Poor fellow, look at the state he's in! Who knows if he'll manage to make it home?*), spent some time reminiscing with him—talking in dialect—about specific details of Brianza: the piazza in Nomana, the local diesel train, the bridge of Incastigo, the circle of Alpine foothills, including the Resegone, the two Grigne, and San Primo—all things that seemed unattainable forever. Afterward he couldn't stop himself asking Valli about the Kazan rail station and the frightful trains arriving daily from Romania.

"What sights! Oh, what sights!" the soldier interspersed his account with this lament. He hadn't lost his sensitivity, and on speaking about the atrocious events he'd seen, he was troubled and dismayed. At times he looked his fellow Italian in the eyes, as if seeking something there: a support, an anchor to hold onto in the middle of such horror.

"Enough", Michele said, deciding to avoid asking more questions. "For now that's enough. Look, I've got something here that I pinched from Stalin." He reached into one of his full-looking jacket pockets and pulled out a handful of wheat grains. "This'll do you, Tito, eh?"

The soldier continued looking at him silently. He looked as if his mind was still on Kazan.

"You can eat it uncooked", Michele explained unnecessarily. "Just put a little at a time in your mouth."

"Yes, I know", said the soldier. He held out his cupped hands, and Michele gave him a handful of the grain. It was clean, golden, and inviting.

"You know what we'll do?" Michele said. "Come, hold your pocket open, and I'll fill it." They were both sitting on the grassy slope near the Spanish colony (two hovels surrounded by a wire fence). Michele knelt and started putting more grain in the soldier's pocket, which Tito held open for him wordlessly.

"Besides, the guard looking after your squad" (he nodded at the only guard in sight) "doesn't much care", Michele observed. "This Mongol with his big yellow face ... you know that in the beginning he was one of the cruelest people in the *lager*, and yet now he's turned into a little lamb." (He didn't know why, didn't know that the guard's entire Crimean village, every living Tartar, had recently—men, women, children, the healthy and the sick— been banished to Siberia by the Communists. In recent weeks the last few deportation trains had been moving along Russia's rail system. The prison guard couldn't stop asking himself, day and night, what fate had befallen his family in these terrible slow trains. He'd have liked to have been able to help them, but at the same time he lived in fear of being deported himself.)

"Let's pretend we're going to a wedding in Nomana, eh?" the young lieutenant said, "and that this is the candy and rice we're going to throw."

Tito smiled. "What a lot of candy ...", he murmured.

"Pocketsful, like the fine stuff we throw over the newlyweds", said Michele.

"Nomana ...", murmured Tito. How far off it seemed to them both!

"Señor", the voice came from behind them.

They both turned their heads. A little boy had come up to the other side of the wire fence, a few yards away, and had been watching them. Michele knew that the whole colony was composed of boys between twelve and fifteen years old. There were fifty or sixty Spanish boys; he'd met them several times during the work hours. "What do you want?" he asked amiably.

733

"Candy, the candy, Señor", murmured the boy. The officer started to laugh. "This isn't candy", he said in badly improvised Spanish, showing the wheat in his hand, and continued with the task of filling Tito's pocket.

"Candy, Señor, candy!" the boy said again, louder.

Michele wagged his head smiling, telling the boy no; a few other boys had emerged from their huts and were coming toward the fence. They were dressed in rags, and most had dark, thick hair and eyebrows, sharply drawn faces, and lively eyes. They were obviously not Russians. "Candy, candy!" these others joined in. Their pronunciation was poor. They were probably rediscovering the word after who knew how much time.

"Who are these kids?" asked Tito.

"They're the Spaniards. Haven't you heard about them?"

"Not at all. But they're children . . . how come they're prisoners?"

"They're children the Reds took out of Spain when they had to leave. It happened at the end of the Civil War, in 1938 or 1939. You'll have heard about these children in Italy, surely?"

"Ah, yes, I'd heard something . . ."

"Many of them don't remember their mothers, or Spain. You can't even say they speak good Spanish. They use a mixture, part Russian. The Russians' idea was to bring them to an appreciation of communism so that later they could use them in propaganda work in Spain. And perhaps one day they will, but up to now they've just brought them up in rags, teaching them practically nothing. I found them at work in the *kolkhoz* and have talked with them."

"But", said Tito, "I don't understand. Are they the Reds' orphans or sons of others? I mean, were they kidnapped?"

"That's what I asked them myself, but these children don't know. The way they're holding them, you'd think they were the offspring of anti-Communists, but there are also probably orphans of Communists. Who knows?"

"What a shame!" murmured Tito Valli tiredly and repeated, "What a shame!"

"Yes, poor kids", Michele agreed.

"Candy!" the first boy shouted, louder now, seeing that the two Italians, instead of heeding him, continued to talk to each other. Then the other boys also started shouting, "Candy, candy!"

"Eh, you kids," said Michele, getting up and facing the children a little worriedly, "don't shout like that. *Ticho, ticho*" (in Russian, "Don't make a racket").

He walked over to the fence. "You see? This isn't candy." He reverted to Russian. "It's *zerno* (wheat). It was stolen from the *kolkhoz*; *zabral* (stolen)." He made a gesture with one hand. "In the *kolkhoz*, I suppose you also *zabral* when you can. Isn't that so?"

The children, grouped together on the opposite side of the fence, kept quiet and gazed at him with their dark disillusioned eyes. Michele felt an ache in his heart. He had nothing, nothing to offer them. "This isn't candy", he repeated with a crooked smile, running some wheat from one hand to the other.

"No, it's not candy, for sure", admitted one of the children, and then, shaking his head, "There isn't any candy in Russia."

Michele nodded. "That's right."

The boy, tattered as a beggar, had a handsome, proud face. He exclaimed, "This is a country of sh——."

Then he pushed away from the fence and, together with the others, headed toward the huts. Michele went back to Tito, who by turning his yellowed, swollen sick face had been following everything with attention. "Kidnapped children", he said. "You know, when they said it on the radio in Italy, I didn't believe it."

13

Michele's squad returned to their *lager* after a few days, just in time for the reappearance of Commissar Robotti, who didn't appear satisfied with the way the Italian prisoners in the other *lagers* had received the news about the Nazi extermination camps. In fact, and in the same way as the officers, the soldiers didn't believe in any propaganda. (Even before, though, many Italians hadn't believed much of it.) Intuitive people that they were, they realized—unlike many Germans—that the mass murders must really have taken place, but even so—apart from a few—they wouldn't allow themselves to be taken in by the mirage of communism, whose concrete results they could see and experience.

Robotti couldn't understand this widespread refusal to believe. He went back to talking with the prisoners, especially the officers, visiting them in their barracks and meeting groups of them in the courtyards.

On one of the occasions when Michele participated in such a group, he had the opportunity to examine Robotti up close: thin and blond, with hair thinning into widow's peaks, he had clear cold eyes (although one could detect signs of hidden fire). He regularly wore the black leather overcoat of a Soviet commissar, which made him seem even paler. Michele thought, *Look at him. He seems to be one of those characters out of a history book, perhaps one of those lay apostles of the nineteenth century. He doesn't look like the slow-witted guards we have to put up with each day, whose only capacity is for violence.*

Robotti would frequently say that he would like to hear the opinions of the participants in his lectures, but in practice, as is often the case in individuals whose mind is made up and closed, he didn't feel the need for others' ideas and usually ended up by being the only one to talk. Michele noted some of his slogans: "the righteous war before this one against the Fascist Finns . . . maybe some of you think that the civilian deportees are innocent, but have you noticed that among them are priests? In other words . . . this is the system of the workers and the farmers . . ."

"What farmers?" burst out one officer, a Tuscan second lieutenant, tall and skinny, his ragged uniform giving him the appearance of a stork. "Of all the ones we've talked to, not one can freely leave his village without getting a pass from the police."

Clearly impatient, Robotti briefly discussed this small detail and then went on to another subject without giving it any importance, although he, like all present, had witnessed the absence of freedom of movement many times and in order to avoid such trifling arguments didn't return to the subject of farmers again. But soon he was to have trouble on the score of the workers, when the skinny officer, pretending indifference, said, "I've heard the workers say that the unions here in Russia serve to force the workers to carry out the orders of their bosses. All the Russian workers to whom I've talked confirm this."

"These are people who don't understand anything", Robotti declared. However, he did explain, in a tone of cold apostolic patience, that for the unions, in a country where all the workers are "the proprietors of the factories", this would be the only logical behavior. After saying this—and managing to put aside all these marginal objections—he brought back the subject uppermost in importance to him, the Nazi war crimes, "which the USSR has revealed to the whole world, and is doing so in order that these crimes should never happen again. Isn't this one of the merits of communism?"

The crimes committed by communism didn't occur to him. (Years later it was revealed that he didn't really even think about them. A reading of his Marxist memoirs and those of the other expatriates who later rebelled against their ideology showed that they continued to consider the Nazis as criminals and murderers but didn't think of equally condemning their former Communist comrades.)

The POWs couldn't decide if he was sincere or not. "But as long as we're talking of crimes," an Italian captain intervened, "how do you explain certain ... happenings, which can even be confirmed right here?"

"What? What happenings?"

"Well, for example, the cannibalism."

"What cannibalism?" exclaimed Robotti, looking surprised. "Where? But what are you talking about? Have you gone mad?"

"No, but for example, in Crinovaya ... "

"What Crinovaya? Where's that? There's no place in Russia called Crinovaya. I've never heard of the name."

Apart from the Fascists, who looked indifferent or as if they hadn't understood, the prisoners looked at one another. They couldn't believe what they were hearing.

"But ... Commissar, I was in the *lager* at Crinovaya. I was there", the captain couldn't help saying. "It's in one of the bends of the Don, not far from Buturlinovka, which in itself is a pretty big town. It's not many miles from ..."

"No, it's not possible", Robotti interrupted him. "No Italian POW has ever been in a place with that name. Are you telling me I don't know? Me?"

The captain was dumbfounded. "But . . . perhaps you know the place I'm talking about by another name, but . . ."

"No", said Robotti, patiently but decidedly. "We don't give it another name. These are fantasizings, the same as the idea of cannibalism, fantasies."

The captain didn't dare reply again and only looked at him. The skinny ragged officer intervened. "Look here, Commissar, we all know that the Russian commandant at Crinovaya later went before a firing squad. But that doesn't mean that what happened didn't happen. That's how I see it."

"But no, absolutely not, no cannibalism", insisted Robotti, less threateningly than with a sad look. "Don't start getting notions or fantasies like that in your head, please. And I tell you that in Russia there doesn't exist any place called Crinovaya." He carried on walking, accompanied by the surprised group of prisoners. He walked with his back bent; everybody in the *lager* knew he had a spine problem.

Maybe the real reason for his way of rationalizing these things in his head is right here, a perplexed Michele told himself, walking now to one side of the group and thus no longer hearing clearly the commissar's words. *As the Fascists have ruined his back with beatings, he illogically now assigns them a monopoly of blame for all atrocities . . . maybe that's it?*

He was mistaken. To start with, he was unaware of the identity of the people who had broken Robotti's bones (and his teeth). It wasn't the Fascists but his own Bolshevik companions, during two tragic years of jail and torture, years that—unusual in Russia—came to a close with rehabilitation for Robotti, when his brother-in-law Togliatti was finally confirmed in the management of the Italian Communist party. (For the majority of the other three hundred Italian Communist refugees in Russia, events were different. Between 1937 and 1939, around two hundred of them were tried in various ways, and it was to Robotti that fell the task of making a list of their names for the party's files.) All these horrible experiences, however, added to the other atrocities that he witnessed daily, didn't in the slightest affect his enthusiasm for the promises—note the word—made by communism. And as objective real facts flew in the face of these promises, the facts began each day to be less important to him. In his innermost self there was room only for this messianic hope in the new society, saved forever from evil, which Marxist science promised and guaranteed. Nothing else interested him at all. This obsession had eventually in a strange way reversed his relationship—and that of many others—with reality. If history—reality—didn't follow the party's line, they could change history. In a way they believed they had already done so, rewriting their postrevolutionary history in a paradoxical way several times. As if a confirmed fact was no longer so—and in its place something different was confirmed—only because again and again they read it in their textbooks. Maybe, possibly, the previous year it had been

Robotti himself, or one of his close collaborators, who, when informed of the cannibalism that had flared up in Crinovaya, had intervened with the appropriate Soviet authorities, which in turn had sought to solve the situation by executing the *lager*'s commandant and changing the name of the town after which the camp was named. After which the horrible occurrences that had happened there were, for them, considered as not having happened ...

Michele, having again drawn closer to the commissar, continued walking through the courtyards with the other prisoners in the group, all of them listening unbelievingly to the praises that Robotti continued to weave around Soviet society. Even the less insightful among them began to notice the extraordinary inversion in thinking that was a necessary part of being a Communist. Many of these POWs would never forget this impression.

14

The following winter—1944–45—had seen the unstoppable advances by Russian and Anglo-American troops inside Germany. In May the end of the fighting brought to Susdal—organized by the anti-Fascists and the camp guards—ceremonies to celebrate victory, following the pattern of similar events in Moscow. The POWs had naturally started to talk about repatriation, but it didn't go beyond words. Always trapped by the monotony of day following day, nothing happened, not even the slightest move that pointed toward hope, something, anything to which they could attach their aspirations. The facts seemed to be going against the stream of events, because the end of the war brought an increase in the deportations to Russia and Siberia from the unfortunate countries of Eastern Europe. All the rail lines in the immensity of Russia were like the flowing of a great river, and even Susdal received some of the stream. The Italian solders were able to see, when out at work, some groups of women from Baltic countries, Germany, and Poland looking ill and humiliated, some with children clinging to them. (But what could these poor wretched women feed them?) There were also men of various ages, many with white hair, submissive as sheep, both in and around the rail station. "Look, these must be the people that semiliterate idiot lecturer yesterday described as scientifically repressible strata ..."

"Poor Europe! Once more in the hands of beasts!"

"We're told there are no trains available to send us home. But there are plenty to use in deporting these people."

"Poor people!"

The only people who watched the deportees with complete indifference were the civilian citizens of Susdal. Michele asked himself if maybe the Russians' biggest character defect—which had turned them into fratricides, and after winning the war possibly might make them fatal to the entire world—

wasn't visible just there: in their unbelievable readiness to be enslaved, manifest in every way.

With the coming of summer, a train arrived from the east bringing Japanese prisoners of war. They brought with them the news of the extraordinary new weapon, the atomic bomb, which the Americans had used first on Hiroshima and soon after on Nagasaki. The short soldiers from the land of the rising sun, still neat and orderly, maintained that the new bomb was the real reason for the surrender of Japan. The Russian newspapers hadn't given much importance to the new atomic weapon, but the political commissars—immediately questioned on the subject by the Italian POWs—found themselves forced to acknowledge its importance, an admission made by more than one of them in the process of deciding what to do about it.

That they were mortified not to possess the new bomb themselves was evident. The POWs' comments ended up zeroing in on their mortification and on the (to them) new realization of America's evident military power. For practical purposes, that was the end of it.

But not for Michele, who on weighing the surprising news found himself deeply moved. *If the general de-Christianization continues, here is the means that can be used in future massive massacres,* he said to himself. The situation in the pre-Christian era came to his mind. The violent reality of pagan times, as exemplified, for example, in some of the pages of Caesar's *De Bello Gallico. In Gaul the Romans, in a few years, eliminated two million people, more than half the population of the country.... And if they hadn't done so, it would have been done by the Germans, who were nearly ready to do so. A few centuries before the Gauls themselves had got rid of the previous inhabitants in the same way.* Not even in the East were things done differently, according to the Bible. *This is the condition to which the world will revert if we continue with these ways. Now that there are infinitely more people, there's a need for new ways to achieve extermination, and here it is.*

In his always fervid imagination, he felt at times he could see the mushroom clouds of atomic explosions rampaging from one to another area of the world "sweeping like fiery brooms". Father Turla, to whom he confided his worries, looked at him with tired eyes. "Wait till we get home," he muttered, "and you'll see that, at least in Italy, there'll be no talk of de-Christianization, not for a minute."

"Yes, that's what we have to dedicate ourselves to", a tired Michele asserted. "That'll be our new task."

During the following weeks he was able to ascertain how man—including his fellow prisoners, who possessed an extraordinary experience of suffering—was disposed to accept the atomic weapon into his world. Was it or was it not a means of slowing communism? And yes, of course, for a certain time it would prevent the Red armies from launching themselves upon the free world. In which case, it was welcome.

15

In Milan university classes started in November. Gerardo's three eldest sons traveled to the city by train each morning. In the rail station's large square the trio would leave the train. In different streetcars the three would go to their classes: Pino to the faculty of medicine in the city center; Fortunato to the Polytechnic, east of town, and Ambrogio to the Catholic University in the western area of the city.

All over the city, and in the college precincts, signs of bomb damage were visible, even at the Cattolica, where the wings of some buildings had been demolished by the bombing. But reconstruction was going ahead actively, under the watchful eyes of Father Gemelli, the rector, going from one point to another in his wheelchair—his spinal column shattered by a car accident—gnashing his teeth in impatience.

Each time he saw him, Ambrogio wondered, *Probably, with il Gemellone's supermemory, he can still recall that blustering greeting he directed at Michele when we were freshmen. 'Hello, Tintori' ... yes, he probably remembers, because he's one of those types who doesn't forget anything, ever. And what if I advised him that Michele is missing in action?* But he didn't do it, as he wouldn't let himself speak to the rector.

Around this time—the fall of 1945—Ambrogio should have graduated, but he still hadn't completed half of his courses; and as for Michele, if and when he returned home, he would have many more to take. Sometimes Ambrogio would think that if he didn't return, within a few years his name would be put on the memorial in the main cloister, next to the names of all the other youth under the superscription of Pro Patria Mortui. No doubt the faculty of architecture would have Manno's name carved, perhaps with the initials MO for the Medal of Gold (*medaglia d'oro*). At the University of Padua they'd put Bonsaver's name on their memorial, "the distant hero". (Now the name that he'd used so often while joking with his friend wasn't so inappropriate after all.) Ambrogio remembered that Bonsaver—over there, by the Don near Veshenskaya—had taught him the names of the constellations. Would he still be thinking about the stars? The nights and the silent star groups continued crossing the skies as always, but now who watched them? My God, what a melancholy thought! But he shouldn't be thinking about the dead. He had—now that he was well again—to concentrate on his studies and get all these exams behind him in order to dedicate himself to work, as an adult, and not by fits and starts, as he had done up to now. It was shameful that Luca, Igino, Pierello, and his other friends of the same age back home should be working hard, while he still went around like a schoolboy, with books under his arm. In times like these, when to restore things work was so necessary! If only his father had let him ... Ambrogio had more than once approached the problem with his father, in his usual serious way. "Papa, as far as going to the university and the pending exams, I've been thinking ... I'll have time for it later. Now my place is in the factory by your side."

His father didn't even let him finish. "No. If you interrupt your studies now, later you'll never graduate."

"Well, after all, a degree isn't that important ..."

"It is important. The degree is important. How much time before you finish— one year, a year and a half? Well, I don't want you even to go to the factory for a year and a half. Don't even think about the family firm, not you or your brother Fortunato. You're both good sons. All I ask is that you obey me in this."

"As you wish, Papa."

In the hallways at the faculty of economics he would sometimes meet Fanny (and if he didn't bump into her, he'd even go looking for her), who had fewer exams to go than he before she received her degree. Now she was no longer the young lady in the starched white Red Cross uniform and, like all the other girls at the university, wore the student's black gown. "Oh, look, my patient!" she'd greet him happily. (She no longer said "my warrior", as she'd done that day in Stresa; strangely they had not referred again to that single moment of tenderness they had shared.) "*Ciao*, Sister DOV", he'd regularly reply. "Always in good shape, eh?"

If any of the younger students noticed, none of them understood the gentle private joke. "Dov? Are you a foreigner?" one or two asked her.

"My forefathers certainly were. My name's Mayer."

"Dov Mayer?"

"Yes", Ambrogio would interrupt. "Exactly, Dov Mayer."

There remained very few of the old classmates who used to call her DOV (*Dagli Occhi Verdi*—Green Eyes). Some were in other activities, some had left the university, and others had died.

Sometimes after class Ambrogio and Fanny would go together to the Piazza sant'Ambrogio. She would wear casual skirts, looking elegant despite the circumstances, and with her pageboy hairstyle giving her a young look; unconsciously Ambrogio felt attracted.

"It looks great on you. You don't mind me saying so?" he said one noontime.

"What does?" she asked, so surprised that she stopped walking. He pointed with his chin at the plaid skirt. "I'm talking about the skirt."

"Oh, the skirt. Thank you." Then, walking once more and amused, she said, "Don't go overboard now!" In her circle, which she referred to as being very middle class and urban, she was accustomed to receiving more daring compliments. Because of this, the rare comments made by her shy down-to-earth walking companion made her very pleased.

"Listen, Ambrogio," she asked, "what are your plans today?"

"Well, to start with, let me buy you a coffee. Let's go to the bar on the corner of Corso Magenta."

"To start with, that's fine. And then . . .?"

"And then I'll even get you some pastries."

"I didn't mean that. I'm not greedy. I want to know what you mean to do after that?"

"I could take you home. You live on the via Boccaccio, don't you?" (He remembered the street address perfectly well. She had told him in Stresa. She'd also explained that she was taking her degree at the Catholic University instead of the state university for pure convenience, because she lived very close to the former. Ambrogio had been critical about her motives. "Anybody with a brain", he'd more or less said, "would choose to go to la Cattolica for reasons other than convenience.") "It is Boccaccio, isn't it?"

Fanny first nodded affirmatively to say that, yes, she lived on Boccaccio, then shook her head negatively, to say no, I see you don't understand. "What I want to know is, what plans you have for today. Are you planning to catch the train back to your own little town right afterward?"

"No, I just have to fetch a book from downtown."

"Ah, at last! Well, I'll go along with you if you want."

"Of course I want", Ambrogio replied. "Do you really have to ask?"

Looking into his eyes for a brief moment, Fanny mentally asked, *Well, in that case, why don't you ever ask me?*

16

Going into the bar on the Corso Magenta, Ambrogio ordered coffee and pastries, then commented, "And if you don't want them, not being greedy, no problem. I'll eat them myself."

"Well, if you're so keen to buy me pastries, rather than coffee, you should get me tea."

"Yes? Well, all right", said Ambrogio and changed the order.

Happy with each other's company, they sat at their table waiting for what they'd ordered when, outside on the sidewalk, a short dark-complexioned priest approached. Ambrogio immediately recognized him as the vice rector at the college, the so-called Father Indigenous Clergy (encountered earlier on the beach at Cesenatico). The student automatically waved at the passerby.

The small priest saw a hand waving on the inside of the bar window and stopped to identify its owner. On recognizing Ambrogio, he hurried to the bar's entrance, where Ambrogio met him and happily shook his hand. "Instead of being at work back at school, here you are, strolling in the street, eh?" Ambrogio said, using the cheeky traditional greeting. Seeing the vice rector was like going back in time to the good old days of irresponsibility.

"Quiet, you big goldbrick", Indigenous Clergy replied, adapting the same tone, which was his usual way of speaking. Before turning to Fanny, he cautiously asked Ambrogio, "Well, tell me, you lazy lout, are you well now? Recuperated totally? I remember how you looked when I saw you in Stresa that day; you didn't look well at all, you know that? I didn't like the way you looked." He was referring to the last time they'd met, two years previously, when he had gone to visit Ambrogio in the hospital. "But now you look well. Am I right?"

"Yes, you're not mistaken at all." He introduced the smiling Fanny, who had been patiently following the exchange. "If I'm better, I owe it to Fanny", he said. "You remember her? Don't be rude and say no; you've already met this young lady."

The vice rector didn't remember the Red Cross nurse from Stresa, not having paid her much attention during his visit there. He rummaged around in his memory to a more distant occasion and remembered the other girl, also a blond, whom he had met strolling with Ambrogio along the sea's edge at Cesenatico. Perhaps in Cesenatico she had looked more blond than now, but he thought also that women's hair color isn't something to be relied upon.

"Of course I remember. I should think so! I don't need reminding." He gave Ambrogio a slap on the back in mock punishment, then offered the same hand to Fanny. "Good morning, my daughter." He used a honeyed tone, caricaturing himself jokingly. "Very pleased to meet you again. So, it appears you believe in this ... let's call him 'fellow', eh?"

Amused, Fanny smiled, although not entirely following the direction of the priest's remarks. "So, I shouldn't believe in him, Father, is that right?" she said, playing along.

"No, miss, never; not for a moment, not even an instant", said the priest. "Be careful of this wretch when he takes you out for a walk, the way he did at Cesenatico by the sea. You could find yourself in deep water."

Fanny didn't understand. Ambrogio, however, guessed his mistake.

"Not by the sea. You mean by the lake, in Stresa. Fanny was with the Red Cross nurse at my detachment, apart from being a university colleague. It was in Stresa that you saw her. The girl in Cesenatico was someone else; her name was Tricia." He started to laugh, shaking his head. "What a blunder! You really did it this time, a real good one!"

The vice rector blushed and didn't at first join in the laughter. "In other words, they are two different girls?!" he exclaimed.

"Right, exactly!"

"You rascal!" He again slapped Ambrogio on the back, hard. "And to think that you looked like one of the few serious people in your class. Just look at you, you ... adventurer!"

Ambrogio continued laughing, joined by Fanny.

"I'm sorry, miss. I should have recognized you straight away."

"It doesn't matter. It's only a little quid pro quo, Father. Think nothing of it."

"And to think I consider myself good at remembering faces ...", Indigenous Clergy muttered.

"It's true", agreed Ambrogio. "You're not one to be trusted."

"Quiet, you polygamist." (Despite her socially easy manner, even Fanny's eyes widened a little.) "Oh, poor me, I'm getting old! It was because of the Red Cross uniform and the coif on your head and ... and at the time, given the circumstances, on that day I was very worried for this wretch, who doesn't deserve anything, and ..."

"Of course!" Fanny said, remembering. "While you were there visiting, I was only in the room for a few moments, but I did notice that you were worried. So much so that at first I thought you were a relative."

"They're all family to us, these boys", said the vice rector. "They're our sons, these miserable types." He sighed, not wanting to appear sentimental. "What a gaffe, though", he concluded. Then he turned to Ambrogio. "In that army of yours, the man who is mistaken buys the round, isn't that so?" He used the present tense, as if Ambrogio were still in the army.

"Yes", the youth replied. "Even if he's a chaplain, he's required to pay like the rest, no more and no less." Afterward, when the check came, he vainly tried to pay, but the priest wouldn't let him do so.

The paying of the bill was accompanied by an exchange of friendly insults between the two men, much to the amusement of the lady at the cash desk. (At the time there were no other clients in the bar.) The small priest sighed exaggeratedly but clearly was more amused than ashamed about his gaffe as he said goodbye.

"I've never met a priest like him", said a still-smiling Fanny to Ambrogio. "Does he always behave that way?"

"Yes, more or less. I think his motive, at least at the start, was to become 'young with the young', because of his apostolic dedication, you understand? Who was it who used that phrase? Was it Saint Paul? Little by little this manner of his has become second nature to him."

"Yes, I'd noticed, but in any case he's very nice."

"Yes, that's true."

"Now he'll think of you as an unrepentant Don Juan."

"No, he knows me too well."

"And maybe just because he does know you he'll think it?" Fanny insinuated.

"You really think so?" said Ambrogio, going along with the joke and assuming a fake-prophetic air. But he immediately became serious and shook his head, dismissing the idea. However, from then onward a shadow of doubt seemed to stay with Fanny. Ambrogio noted that incredibly her suspicion didn't displease her and even apparently increased his importance in her eyes.

744

17

From that day on they left the university more often together, normally on Fanny's initiative. Once she said, "If one wants to have something, it's not at all obligatory to go into the first bar that comes up, out of sheer passivity. There are places and there are places; for example, here on the Corso Magenta, there's the Marchesi *boiserie*, one of the most chic places in Milan."

"The . . . the what?"

"*Boiserie.* Call it a cafe. At least you'll have heard of it, I hope."

"No." Ambrogio shook his head. He'd been at school on the Corso Magenta for seven years, and yet he'd never heard mention of Marchesi's *boiserie*.

"Oh, Ambrogio, you're exasperating!" said Fanny, who felt a sort of maternal tenderness toward him.

During one of those peaceful walks, one day they found the street closed by protesters who had come up the Corso Magenta and had then entered the much narrower Via Meravigli. The parade was headed for the Piazza del Duomo, and individual participants were shouting slogans. The people going about their business in the street—like Ambrogio and Fanny—were forced to squeeze over to the side walls, with some having to shelter in doorways.

"I wonder what these people want?" Fanny asked, as she and Ambrogio joined other passersby in a doorway.

"Create a disturbance", Ambrogio answered. "Stop other people from going ahead with reconstruction, with working toward reducing other people's misery. That's what they want. Not each and every one of them, but certainly the people who manipulate them. They excite them with grand ideals, but the straightforward bare truth is the need to make a disturbance."

Fanny, more open to the protest than Ambrogio, watched the demonstrators with some interest and, turning to one of the more youthful marchers, asked, "What are you demonstrating about?"

He replied by shouting a slogan. "Down with the king!"

Another older man behind him added, "We want the queen to show us her ———", using a crude word for female genitalia. He seemed to feel that, as he was talking to a woman and was certain of impunity, he could indulge in such boorish behavior.

"Swine!" shouted Ambrogio at the man and then, looking him directly in the face, repeated clearly, "Swine."

"Fascist!" the other man replied, stuttering in his excitement. He stopped walking and indicated Ambrogio to those around him.

Fanny felt her blood run cold. Ambrogio, although touched by fear, continued looking the protester in the eye. Fortunately both the man and those around him who seemed inclined to stop were all pushed on past by those behind them.

After a few moments Fanny asked, "Whatever did you say that for? What possessed you . . . my legs are shaking so much that . . . good heavens! I thought you'd be lynched!"

"I couldn't let him talk to you that way", said Ambrogio.

"But to me what he said isn't important. It meant nothing. Don't imagine that I'm impressed by just a word."

Ambrogio realized once again how different the girl was from his sisters and his mother.

"You may not be, but other women think differently. And maybe from now on that pig will think before turning his foul mouth on other women. Especially before some small-town ladies who—I assure you—would be offended by that sort of talk, even though sometimes they may have to put up with it."

"Well, you were very brave!" The exclamation came from an older man who had also sheltered in their doorway and who had heard the exchange. "Well done, youngster!"

"Oh, Ambrogio, my Ambrogio", Fanny said, touched by Ambrogio's attitude, which to her seemed very quixotic, and taking hold of his arm she looked into his eyes while shaking her head tenderly. "Someone like you needs to be looked after."

Ambrogio didn't answer, only shaking his head in disagreement. Then he said, "Well, the street is clear again. Let's go."

They walked arm in arm. "When I think that right now you could have been down on the ground, having been . . .", said Fanny, then wiped the thought from her mind. "You've no idea what I witnessed on liberation day and on the next few days . . . One man was killed by being thrown from a window. His wife and children, screaming, had to watch it happen. I saw that, with these very eyes, and as soon as the partisans had gone, I tried to help the man, but he'd already died."

Ambrogio shook his head. He wanted to say, "And after seeing that, you still feel free to talk to excited Reds in the street?" But he stayed silent.

"Look," she continued, "nowadays they don't kill the Fascists that way. Now they process them legally, right?"

"And how many of the poor wretched people who were lynched were really Fascists?" Ambrogio said, thinking about Raperio's woman. "Those mad days were like the time of the plague in Milan in the seventeenth century, when people went out chasing witches. It was the same, no more and no less, even though things have changed now, at least here in Lombardy, where the police and the carabinieri have gone back to work. On the other hand, every day one can read in the newspapers what is happening in Emilia, especially in the death triangle."

"What awful times!" agreed Fanny.

"Just as well there's a government that has reorganized the carabinieri and the police, because if it had been left to the Allies, with their scruples about meddling in domestic matters ... Sometimes I think that Manno must have had a foreboding about all this. He sacrificed himself for this, to retain our option of survival, to allow us to leave the quagmire."

"I still remember your cousin, Manno, with those blue eyes ... what a magnificent young man he was."

"Yes, you were also in Stresa the last time I saw him."

Fanny agreed. "And so was that driver, also with blue eyes. What was his name?"

"Celeste. Well, he's still there, working at the factory."

"What a nice man. He seemed to be very close to you all."

"In Nomana that's usual", explained Ambrogio. Then, with a half sigh, "Just as well there are places like Nomana."

"Your own little town", Fanny said.

18

In Nomana too the Reds had started holding meetings and public demonstrations. There were not very many of them—a few dozen, consisting of Communists and Socialists, not yet distinguishable one from the other—who were joined at their demonstrations by a few who were undecided and quite a lot who were curious, so that at times they gave the impression of having more support than was the case. The resulting crowd excited the activists, making them noisier and even arrogant at times.

Soon after the incident in the Via Meravigli, on a Sunday morning, Nomana witnessed one of these public meetings. It started soon after the second Mass, the one attended by most people. The organizers had placed a small table on a platform in the piazza in front of the bell tower. The table had a Red flag tied to one of its legs, and a microphone sat on the table ready for use. When the first people emerged from the church, one of the speakers, recently arrived from Milan, started to harangue them over the loudspeakers. "Attention, attention, you working people. Come closer. We're about to start a meeting of the workers' party, the Communist party. Come closer and listen." Besides the man calling to the crowd, the local Red bosses had also climbed on the platform. These included Foresto (who had dressed himself as a partisan for the occasion), Sèp, and a long-haired evacuee called Millanta, a retired Milanese typographer who spent all his time preaching the Socialist-Libertarian creed in a local bar in Pasqualetta. Also up on the platform was an unknown man with very showy silver teeth, who was assumed to be the main speaker.

"Attention, working men, attention. Shortly we'll hear from Comrade So-and-So, spokesman for the resistance in Lomellina", the loudspeakers crackled.

The local Reds and other people came closer slowly, along with young children, who put themselves right in front, craning their necks to see. Most of the people leaving the church looked over to the meeting and continued on their way without stopping; one or two shouted disparaging remarks over at the speaker. Ambrogio, who had gone to Mass accompanied by his sisters Francesca and Alma and his twelve-year-old brother Rodolfo, was walking home, but paused opposite the platform.

"I wonder who the main speaker will be?" asked the "little statue", Ambrogio's sister Alma.

"I imagine it will be that one, with the teeth."

"What a beastly face, brrr . . .", murmured Francesca, with a shiver.

The older brother started laughing. "Come on, you three. Go on ahead home, and I'll follow in five minutes."

"I'm going to look for my friend Saulo", Rodolfo announced.

His friend Saulo was the driver Celeste's oldest son.

"Right", said Ambrogio, and the other three went off.

The spokesman for the resistance in Lomellina (who looked annoyed at the way that so many of Nomana's citizens kept going about their business, evidencing disinterest in the doctrines he had come to explain "like a lot of sheep", he muttered to the others on the platform) decided suddenly to start his speech. "Communist comrades, Socialist comrades, workers of Nomana", he started. "I bring you greetings from the Milan Federation of Communists. The first thing I want to bring to your attention is the outrageous wretchedness in which all of us workers find ourselves living nowadays." At this point, Foresto nodded gravely. "As far as food is concerned, for example," the comrade continued, "perhaps we're worse off than during the war, and the Americans . . . the Americans", he repeated, pointing toward a jeep going past on the other side of the piazza, driven by a couple of unaware South African soldiers, "don't help us poor townspeople. They're too busy helping—who?—why, his majesty the king."

From the crowd there came a couple of guffaws.

"Yes," the speaker spoke louder, "they help the king, and they help the priests. To them they give a mountain of stuff so as to help them make propaganda. And what's their motive in bringing in all this powdered milk and such, which they give to the kindergartens and the old folk's homes? Only to make propaganda with the nuns and priests. You follow me?" He seemed to expect some sort of approval from his audience. He certainly had their attention, and there were no more guffaws.

"And the loans they plan to make to the industrialists," he continued, "although they haven't done so yet, but have you read in the newspapers about the Marshall Plan? They'll be certain to give them money, you can be sure. To the industrialists!" he repeated, shouting, at which the Reds in the audience sensed they should make themselves heard, and some applauded, although not many as yet. "So, as you can see, it is to the Fascists' supporters that the Americans give help."

Sèp began applauding enthusiastically, followed shortly after by almost the whole crowd. "Fascist industrialists!" shouted a young fellow near Ambrogio without looking at him. Some of those around Ambrogio eyed him furtively to see if he'd react, but the young industrialist's son didn't bat an eyelash. "So that those responsible for the people's hunger can carry on being bosses, because the Americans give them help," shouted the speaker, "but the Americans won't always be here. They'll have to go back home, and in preparation for that day we should be making ourselves ready, getting organized. Because when that time comes, comrades, the power will be with us, we who have fought against the Fascists."

At this the crowd began cheering. Later, they gave him prolonged cheers when, after mentioning the name of Comrade Togliatti, he spoke of "our great comrade, Stalin", and then of "partisan justice" (a clear contradiction in terms). The crowd began to warm up. Undeniably the feeling of hysterical hate—Ambrogio noted—hadn't passed Nomana by. *I wonder how many applaud without reserve?* Ambrogio asked himself. *Forty, fifty? Yet they're enough to make a noise.* He thought he'd been there long enough and headed for home; some of the people there followed his example.

"Comrades," the sound from the loudspeakers followed him for a while down the street, "in order to achieve our goal, we should go forward step by step. Now the most important step is to get the king out of the way . . ."

So this one is going after the king, just like the ones in Milan the other day. And to think that they're part of the king's government . . . a government stitched together to include the CLN factions, with the partisan, Parri, as president of the cabinet? So, how come?

When the meeting was over, the more excited Reds—among whom were some whose faces were red as well—grabbed the red flag and toured the town's streets, shouting, "Death to the king!" "Down with the monarchy!" "Power to the working classes!" "Long live Togliatti!" "Long live Stalin!" "Death to the exploiters!"

Rodolfo, back home at lunchtime, indignant and a little frightened, told of having seen demonstrators stop in front of the rectory to shout, "Down with the Pope!" and "Put the Pope to work!" He added, "The most hotheaded of them all was that fellow who's always preaching down at that bar in Pasqualetta, what's his name, Millanta? You should have seen his face. I've never seen a face like his."

"What?! You mean this Millanta shouted 'down with the Pope'?" asked the ten-year-old Giudittina, impressed.

"Leave it", her father interposed. "You don't have to worry about these things. Rather pay attention to your risotto."

"No, I'm also interested in knowing things", she protested.

"Yes, but now you go and wash your hands before sitting down at the table; we'll all be eating soon."

The girl went off, pouting. *Papa is very right*, thought Ambrogio, *but how many little girls were killed by the Bolsheviks in Russia? And how many girls' lives have been shattered by them? How many hundreds of thousands?*

Gerardo turned to Rodolfo and admonished him, "Try not to frighten your sister."

"Yes, Papa", the boy answered.

"Come on, you too, go and wash your hands."

Gerardo and Ambrogio were left in the hall. Only Fortunato had remained with them, and he attempted to treat the subject jestingly. "I'd like to see the parish priest's face about now", he said.

Gerardo replied, "I imagine his face is like mine would be if they were outside our fence here, shouting 'down with!' or 'death to!'"

"It seems to me", Ambrogio said, "that we have to decide to get involved seriously in politics, do something serious. It's already time."

Gerardo nodded. "It's what a lot of our workers are saying, particularly those who helped me put together the Popular party when I was a young man." Behind his words there was a clear message: "Now it's your turn, you youngsters, to do something." He was immediately understood by his sons.

"Papa, I'm not suited for politics. You know that", said Fortunato. "But if I was required to choose, I'd choose to be a Liberal. Imagine how many supporters I'd have here in Nomana." He turned to Ambrogio and half-jokingly asked, "You, on the other hand, are a Christian Democrat, right? You're a card-carrying member, aren't you?"

Ambrogio nodded. "Yes. I was talked into it by Agazzino, but . . ." He shook his head; in fact, politics were distasteful to him also. "If only Manno were here . . .", he observed. "He believed in these things and had a leaning toward politics. You remember how he worked for the Oratorio? He was like you, Papa, in these things. He was your heir."

Gerardo nodded. "That's what Don Mario told me."

"Of course, if Manno were here, he'd act without having to be pushed into it", agreed Fortunato.

"But don't forget he's already played his part", underlined Gerardo. "If today we have a government, good or bad, and an army and police, we owe it to people who dedicated themselves at the beginning, like him."

"That's true", said Ambrogio, recognizing the fact.

In the background Noemi's voice was heard, announcing, "Time to sit down. Lunch is ready", and right after, the voice of their mother, calling, "Where are you? Come and sit down. It's getting cold."

As they headed for the table, Fortunato proposed, "What if we talked about it to Pino?"

"Pino?" Gerardo considered for a moment, then, pressing his lips together, shook his head no.

They went into the dining room without having come to a decision.

19

The following Sunday after vespers, Luca approached Ambrogio in the church square on the way out.

After leaving the army, Luca had resumed work at his old job in the factory. He no longer wore his reddish beard, but retained the brown forelock and the typical Alpine man's air of calm.

"Ambrogio, I need to talk to you."

"Gladly, Luca."

"Should I go to your house?"

"As you wish. But if you want to, we can talk right here ..."

"Yes, right." He spoke, as always, in dialect.

"What's the good word, tell me?"

"Good words are few and far between", said Luca and went directly to the point. "It's about Doctor Agazzino. We're worried that sooner or later he won't be able to take any more. Within the CLN they're making his life difficult, mainly some 'young hawks'. He carries on and he even shows some courage, it has to be admitted, but you know he's not entirely well. He suffers from asthma."

"So it's true what I've heard about you! You've working for the Christian Democrats. Good for you!"

Luca nodded, then shook his head. "It's not a lot of fun, but somebody has to do it."

"Have you been given any responsibility?"

He nodded again. "Yes, unfortunately. I'm the branch secretary now."

"Well ... it's the most important job."

"They gave me the job because I fought against the Germans, you understand?" He paused. "Naturally, after the war in Russia, then in Italy, and after all that's happened in my life ..." (he was referring to Giustina's death) "you can imagine that I don't have much interest in getting involved with these things. But we can't just hand it all over to these scoundrels. You've seen them, right? You too have been in Russia. You know what I'm talking about."

"Yes, right, of course I know."

"Well, there it is."

"Now, tell me, what can I do for Agazzino?"

"We've received a circular from CLN headquarters directing that the branch should now be represented by two delegates. And, as you're already a member, some of us thought you'd be the right man to give the pharmacist a hand. What do you say?"

"Well, my brother Pino is also a member", Ambrogio suggested, trying instinctively to have the cup removed from him. "Besides, he was also a partisan. Don't you think that, if he'll agree, he'd be better than I?"

"No", Luca answered, shaking his head. It was clear that this alternative had been examined and rejected. "No, he's still too young, a young boy. Whereas in the CLN, the way things are going, we need a man."

"This is not an easy thing. You do realize that?"

Luca nodded, and in a low tone said, "Think of Manno."

Ambrogio thought about Manno, but also thought about Luca himself and about the townspeople, most of whom saw things more or less from the same viewpoint as Luca. He decided that he couldn't properly avoid the job.

"All right", he said decidedly. "I'll do what you ask. But just a moment . . . is Agazzino agreed?"

"Yes, naturally."

"Because there was a time there, back around the time of the liberation, when it seemed to me that he was close to being annoyed with me. Did you know?"

"At that time it could have been the case, when the CLN was . . . well, still a bit of a plaything, a game. But not now. Now there's a lot to do, and he'll need help." He thought for a moment. "Look, I'll tell him to come and see you tonight, agreed?"

"Tonight, after dinner? All right. Just a moment, though. Tell him I'll come and see him at his place. He's the president, after all . . ."

They both smiled.

20

That evening, when Ambrogio rang at the door, Agazzino came downstairs into the pharmacy and opened the door, putting his hand up to the doorbells to stop them from making the usual tinkling sound. He tried to look cheerful, but wasn't able to conceal his somewhat depressed state. He sat facing the younger man, right there in the shop, with the shelves loaded with the labeled and decorated jars and the sharp smell of medicines all around them.

"The secretary has advised me you'll accept. I'm grateful."

"The . . . secretary?"

"The branch secretary. Sambruna, Luca Sambruna."

"Ah, Luca, of course. Well, the CLN has turned out to be a fairly large job, eh?"

"And quite hard." He paused. "There's one thing that specially bothers me, and I'll tell you right now. This Foresto, as he's called, the Communist, doesn't let one meeting go by without finding a way to pull out his pistol and wave it around. Did Luca mention it?"

"No", Ambrogio answered. "His pistol? What for? Does he use it to be threatening?"

"No, not exactly. It's used to . . . to remind me of something, a sort of warning, which he makes in his own way."

"I don't understand."

"Well, listen . . ." Agazzino pulled his chair closer to the younger man's seat and lowering his already soft tone. "You should know . . ." He paused, thinking. "Now you are a part of the CLN, and therefore it's good that you should know everything. Of course, I'm supposing that you recognize your obligation to keep this to yourself."

"I agree. You have my word. What's it all about?"

"Back in May, or maybe in early June, at the time when the Red partisans were still killing people. I don't know if you were aware that around then. L (he named one of the leading Communists in the resistance) toured around various nearby towns, towns around Milan, establishing contact with local Communist chiefs. Do you remember that?"

"To tell the truth, no."

"Well, L drove around to the major towns, and wherever he went he collected information about the numbers of Fascists who had been brought to trial. (I heard this later on in Milan.) Wherever he went, he commented, 'Too few', and right there on the spot he'd decide the number of people who should be tried in each town. Here in Brianza, where nobody had yet been condemned, he ordered that at least one Fascist in each town should be killed. 'One, but you have to try him first, to set an example.'"

"To set an example?"

"He obviously meant something else. He wanted . . . they wanted to create . . . establish an atmosphere of . . . well, yes, of terror." Agazzino was clearly uncomfortable at having to talk of these events.

"I remember when the shootings started up again in the new developments, the Red neighborhoods", said Ambrogio, "and also farther up, in the Red periphery between us, here and them. Yes, I remember. Even here in Brianza they killed a few. It was something I didn't understand at the time. You're right, it was in May."

"Well, in Nomana, too, L ordered that one man should be killed. Once he left, this Foresto, without thinking twice, went loyally ahead with plans to execute the chosen victim. It's not that Foresto is an outlaw, now that I know him, and I also now realize that under some circumstances he can even be generous."

"Can that be possible?"

"You'll see for yourself. But he lacks judgment, and as he'd received an order from his chief . . . well, I wasn't aware of it, but the Reds went to Tavelli's house and then took him down to the carabinieri barracks. Do you remember that?"

"The Tavelli case, yes."

"Well, there you are! Tavelli, he was the chosen victim in Nomana."

"But . . . that can't be so! Tavelli? The Fascist? Even if they'd picked his wife, maybe, who used to train the juvenile wing of the Fascists, the *balilla* . . . but no, not even her. She had to instruct them anyway. She was the teacher."

"Be that as it may, they picked him."

"Poor wretch. He'd be in serious trouble."

"The plan was to put him in a car under the pretext of taking him to Monza for questioning, and once there . . . you know where the cave is, along there on the highway to Incastigo? Well, they planned to let him out there on the highway, force him to run, to escape, and then shoot him in the back, kill him right there on the highway. Luckily the car's driver—one of the few partisans who can drive—wasn't a Communist. It was Carletto Mangiagalli, the midwife's son."

"Ah, yes, he was a bersagliere at liberation time, I remember, and celebrated it by continually shooting his machine gun up in the air."

"Right, him. And as he's a smart young fellow, he smelled mischief, and although he was looking forward to an outing driving the car (you know how these young fellows are), he came running to tell me what was going on. I was able to intervene, but just in time. I was almost too late. I went straight around to Foresto's house and . . ." Agazzino's face darkened. "It was a most unpleasant meeting, really a very unpleasant exchange. I didn't know if I would be successful. I wasn't sure of myself. When I put Foresto in the position where he was between the sword and the wall, he became very excited and didn't hesitate to quote me the order he'd received from his party's representative. He shoved it in my face, telling me that he had to obey orders and that this was an order that came from a higher authority. He was shouting, telling me he had to obey orders. He clearly intended to go out momentarily to do so. He had on that damned beret with the red star. I threatened him, telling him I'd file a complaint about him to the judiciary, to the Americans, to everybody, but he wasn't convinced. It's hard to imagine, but I had to give him my own written order, scribbled on a note pad, telling him to kill nobody. A written order by the president of the CLN, you understand, not to do any killing. It was crazy and sounds unbelievable now."

"Right, it does."

"I wouldn't have convinced him if I hadn't suddenly been inspired, in a way, to tell him that from my point of view he was at risk of showing himself to be an accomplice of Praga's, an accomplice of the turncoat Fascists. That got to him. He became fearful and . . . it's incredible how an unfounded suggestion like that actually worked." (Around that time, after having committed various new crimes, Praga had been finally disavowed by the Communist party and was being actively sought by the carabinieri.)

"What a ridiculous situation!" Ambrogio said, laughing in his exasperation.

"Yes, really", said Agazzino.

754

"Now I understand why you talked Tavelli into a change of scenery. You made him run away."

"That's right. And his wife immediately told the whole world that I'd advised him to flee. She's a very cunning woman. But that's not the point, which is that since then Foresto feels badly toward me, thinking that I fooled him, you understand? Just imagine the man! And now, at meetings, when there's a lack of agreement over something, he always ends up drawing his pistol to remind me of that ... pending item."

"Yes, I understand. But what does he do, exactly, with the pistol? I assume he doesn't point it at you?"

"No, but he twirls it, toys with it. Or else he'll slam it down flat on the table and shout out loud, as if he wants to cause me harm. In other words, it's very out of order."

"I see." Ambrogio could imagine the Communist chief leaning over the CLN president, shouting, both of them red faced. For Agazzino it was not an amusing situation.

The pharmacist tried a joking comment. "I'd have to say that his contributions to our discussions could be defined as paramilitary ... that's why having an ex-military man like you in the CLN would be useful."

"What a dumbbell, this Foresto", murmured Ambrogio. "All right. I'll happily give you a hand. He'll have to understand that he's not the only man familiar with guns. But perhaps we can tone him down just with sarcasm."

"Yes, but be careful."

"Right. And the others, the people from the other parties, do they also behave more or less like him?"

"Oh, no, but the others also, they're just like a musical comedy. Sometimes I run out of patience."

21

The first meeting of the augmented CLN took place soon afterward, one evening after dinnertime. Ambrogio had first gone to the pharmacy to pick up the president, and when they arrived at the door of the town hall, the other members of the committee were also arriving, one after the other. They all entered a room that had formerly been the mayor's; a name plate on the door was pasted over with a piece of paper on which "Comitato di Liberazione Nazionale" was written by hand. At Agazzino's invitation they sat around a long and narrow Renaissance-style table on straight-backed chairs, whose hard leather padding was decorated with faint designs. The two end seats (one was taken by Sèp, chosen by the Communists and also new to the committee, like Ambrogio) were particularly uncomfortable backless Savonarola seats.

Agazzino briefly welcomed the new members and then reminded them all that the communal coffers were "distressingly empty". After this he introduced the first item on the agenda for debate: the increase, caused by galloping inflation, to the dues paid by the citizens into the communal health insurance system. The health plan—Ambrogio knew—was a very useful local institution, which had been in existence since before the introduction of the government-run national security insurance. He had in any case decided not to speak. *Tonight I'll try and learn*, he told himself. But he soon noticed with some surprise that nobody talked directly about the agenda item. The various parties' representatives simply used the opportunity to make each other's life difficult. After a half hour of heated discussion, in which Foresto repeatedly accused the Christian Democrats and the Liberals of wanting, "by this means as well" to take money from the people's pockets, Ambrogio continued to listen in a detached way to the debating (*If Manno himself were here instead of me, what useful conclusion could he draw from this nonsense?*), when, out of the blue, Pollastri, the Action party representative, blurted out, "What about all these heaps of gravel?" Although he had lifted his hand several times, he had not yet been recognized to speak. There was silence for a few moments following his outburst, and Ambrogio wasn't alone in looking at Pollastri in surprise. Each of them was asking himself if he had heard correctly.

"I'm talking about the gravel in the streets, all those piles of it", he repeated, in dialect.

"We're talking here about health insurance. What has gravel to do with it?" Agazzino said.

"Well, I feel like talking about gravel," Pollastri replied, looking bad-temperedly at the president, "so I'm going to do just that. Or do you want to continue ignoring me? You want to be the only one to speak, eh?"

Pollastri represented the Action party by default. When Agazzino had asked him to sit on the committee, he would have preferred to represent the Socialists; alternatively, as this wasn't available, he wanted to represent the Monarchists. As he had at first sensed, his representation of the Action party (which had—crazily—developed into a party of intellectuals) ended up being for him an unsatisfactory activity, for despite all his persistent efforts, he couldn't find in all Nomana one single soul ("not even a dog", he used to say bitterly to his family) prepared to join this party. "You want to know what'll happen to me. It'll be just like when the Fascists were in power", he used to predict, becoming more and more distressed. "You'll see. Once again I'll not get an opportunity to make my mark. And what have all these others got that I haven't?" This secret gnawing feeling, joined to the fact that he was no longer young, had ended in changing his character. Just as he had strutted uselessly through the Fascist era, so now he seemed intractable and obstinate, and nobody wanted to waste time contradicting him.

"All right", Agazzino said. "Seeing it interests you so much, go ahead, speak. But please remember that we have people waiting in the lobby who have come here about health insurance."

"Have you noticed these piles of gravel?" Pollastri went ahead, still in dialect. "They are all over the streets of Raperio and Lodosa." He looked as if he would continue, but instead he stopped and looked at the others around the table.

"So?" asked the Liberal representative.

"What do you mean 'so'? Doesn't that tell you anything?"

The Liberal was an evacuee from Monza, vaguely Fascist, who because of making jokes about Duce during his train trips had spent two days in jail. "What should it tell us", he asked, also in dialect, "this business of the piles of gravel being in one place instead of another? Come on, explain."

"Where do you think the two municipal road workers live?" Pollastri exclaimed, as if revealing a great truth. "Haven't you asked yourselves? Well, one lives in Raperio, and the other in Lodosa. That's where they live."

"And so . . .?" said the playful Liberal, sensing the chance of having a little fun.

"And so what it means", explained Pollastri, disgusted that the group couldn't follow his perspicacity, "is that the reason these road repairers have unloaded the piles of gravel in their own towns is that these are the streets they intend to repair and not the main roads that lead here, to the county seat. And so this winter we'll have holes in the roads."

"Oh, come on now", said the Liberal jestingly. "Holes! Where we're likely to have more holes is in our belts, because this gravel unfortunately isn't polenta. I wish it were."

"Yes, I also wish it were", agreed the Socialist, a pensioner, completely bald, and a good sort.

"Look," Agazzino said to Pollastri, while laughter ran around the table, "those piles of gravel have been there at least since March. They were ordered there by Signor Paolo." (He was referring to the former mayor.) "We aren't responsible for their being where they are."

"Signor Paolo? Well, good, but we can move them to other sites."

"We can send the commune's secretary to go and have a look", said Agazzino, trying to close the discussion.

"No," the Liberal objected, "Signor Paolo is a man who knows what he's doing. If he had the gravel put where it is, he would have had a reason for doing so. We can't have people laughing at us."

On hearing this, Foresto pounded angrily on the table. "I won't have it! That here, at a CLN meeting, that someone should speak well of the Fascists", he leaned over toward the Liberal, his voice risen to a shout.

"Let's try not to get off track", intervened Agazzino, the president. "Above all, if possible, let's not waste time. I've said that the commune secretary will go to take a look. In my opinion that's enough." And turning to the Liberal, "The people won't even notice." He concluded, "That's enough. The subject is closed."

"No, it's not closed!" shouted the Communist, half in dialect and half in Italian. "Here we again have people showing enormous goodwill toward the old regime, and that's something the people aren't prepared to take! Understood?"

"Please try not to shout, as you usually do . . .", Agazzino told him.

"Signor Paolo", observed the Liberal, "is not the old regime. He's just a man with his head screwed on straight, and about this there's nothing we of the CLN can do."

"Enough! The subject is closed", repeated Agazzino, trying not to waste more time. "Let's go back to the item on the agenda—health insurance dues."

"Oh, no! Oh, no!" shouted Pollastri, who, seeing he was getting support from the Communist, exploded suddenly. "The people are tired of the stinking behavior of the Liberals and Christian Democrats. The people are up to here" (he used a more graphic description to indicate up to where the people were), "the people . . ."

Even though he had told himself he wouldn't be intervening, Ambrogio suddenly interrupted the speaker. "One moment!" he said, looking the man straight in the eyes with a hard expression. "You should withdraw the word 'stinking', and you should do it right now."

Pollastri looked at Ambrogio, surprised and somewhat impressed. "So, have we reached the time for impositions now?"

"No," Ambrogio replied calmly, "we've reached the time for good manners, time to observe the most elementary rules of politeness."

Foresto, surprised and momentarily lost for words, opened his arms wide. "It's easily seen that you haven't taken part in political meetings before", he said, openly frank toward Ambrogio. "If you remain in the CLN, you'll have to listen to much worse than this. You'll see."

But Pollastri wasn't disposed to being cut off. "The people", he said ill humoredly, "the people, and especially my party, have had enough troublemaking by the Christian Democrats. In the name of the people, I demand . . ."

"But tell me", Agazzino interrupted. He also was very annoyed at the insult gratuitously thrown at his party, particularly after Ambrogio had drawn attention to it. He was getting red in the face, like a turkey cock. "Tell me, where are these 'people' you represent?"

They all looked at him in surprise. He'd never before spoken so directly. They all knew that the Action party didn't have a single member in Nomana, so that Pollastri was the only one in the CLN who had no deputy.

"You know what you represent here?" the president continued. "You represent a rubber stamp. The Action party in Nomana consists of you and the rubber stamp you had made, and which you use every now and then to back yourself up."

758

On hearing this, all the men around the table burst into helpless laughter, effectively showing they agreed with their president.

"And now," said the irate Agazzino, having regained control, "enough about gravel and other subjects not on the agenda. Let's go ahead with the first agenda item: health insurance dues."

Pollastri, although beaten and in retreat, lifted one finger. "I protest, and I want my objection written into the minutes."

The secretary, a municipal employee, still laughing, asked, "What is it that I have to write?"

"Write that the president's behavior is against the people's will", said the furious Pollastri.

At this the mild-mannered postal service official (somewhat uncomfortably out of place in the Socialist camp) intervened, with a hurt air. "No gentlemen", he said. "No, please!"

He was a naive idealist who during the twenty years of fascism had significantly worn a black bowtie and a goatee. A native of Mantua, in repudiation of Catholicism he believed in socialism. (Of course, he believed in a democratic socialism and not the current populist socialism, allied to communism.) Because of his well-known belief, he'd ended up heading the Socialist representation on the committee. "I ask that nothing be written down; unpleasant things like this shouldn't be on the record."

Pollastri looked at him and thought, *Unpleasant things . . . but just listen to him! It's not the first time that this poor dullard has cut the grass from under my feet.* Although angry, he realized the situation wasn't favorable to him, so he kept silent, although this didn't stop him from huffing and puffing.

"We shouldn't make these people wait any longer. Let's have the two people in the lobby waiting about health insurance come in here", the president ordered.

22

The secretary got up and went to the door, where he called out, somewhat emphatically, "The public may come in."

A woman of thirty or thirty-five came in; she had darkish blond hair pulled back into a chignon (this was Angioletta, a worker from the Riva textile factory), followed by a tall thin man in his fifties, clearly annoyed at the long wait. Ambrogio didn't know the man but noticed he wore a red handkerchief in his jacket pocket, rather like an emblem.

"Oh, look, the undertaker from Raperio", murmured the second Socialist deputy, an aged man who was sitting next to Ambrogio.

Angioletta gracefully greeted the gathering and at the president's invitation began explaining the reason for her appearance there. She had read the typewritten notice on the bulletin board outside, which carried an invitation to anyone who wished to speak about health insurance to come and talk freely. "Now I'm the head of the family, as I'm a widow."

"Widowed in the war?" the Socialist deputy asked, calmly and somewhat superfluously. He had transferred his attention to her from the gravedigger.

"No, not the war; in peace."

"Ah, yes." The deputy nodded his bald head gravely, approvingly.

"The thing is", continued Angioletta, "this summer I was asked a question by the communal insurance people." She pulled two folded sheets of paper from her pocket. "It's about my oldest son. Because according to him, that is to say, according to the man at the insurance, a sickness of this kind isn't a real sickness, because since it wasn't possible to send him to the seashore in July, they gave him sun lamp treatment here in Nomana, and that is not covered. On the other hand, in my opinion it should be covered because . . ."

The president intervened politely to say that the subject should be put not to the committee but to the new councilmen responsible for the mutual insurance fund, who would shortly be elected. The woman, judging the present gathering to be more of an authority, tried to explain her reasoning in a very rapidly spoken dialect, covering her essential points several times, as one does who is not confident of being in the presence of people who readily understand these matters.

But soon, at the president's new objections, she understood that in a manner of speaking she had gone there to waste her time. So that her appearance there wouldn't be totally pointless, she came forward and held out the now-refolded papers to Ambrogio, the participant in whom she had most confidence.

"No, no, what's this? You keep the papers", Agazzino advised her.

Ambrogio took the papers from her and got up, gesturing to the others that he would take care of the matter, and accompanied the woman from the room into the lobby. There, calmly and in dialect, he explained the way of things and returned her documents.

"I know these are difficult times for someone bringing up three children, like you", he said.

The woman nodded and sighed.

"But you've always done your part and well. Your interest in your son's treatment is proof of that. It's a time to bear up with courage. You'll see how soon things will improve."

The woman thanked him, satisfied with the few attentive words. She belonged to a family of honest laborers, serious about life, and proud to have people recognize it.

On reentering the room, Ambrogio saw that the gravedigger from Raperio had launched into an explanation of his problem and noticed also that more than one of the committeemen had started to laugh.

"My assigned doctor under the health plan", the man was saying, "is Doctor So-and-So." He named one of the town's two doctors, well known to all of them. "As a doctor, he's good. I won't deny it." He paused, nodding repeatedly, then, holding out his hand toward the men at the table, came to the point he wanted to make. "But he has a fault," he paused again, "and that is, whenever he comes into the house, the first thing he does is to peer up at the ceiling."

The assembled men burst into laughter. In the village houses, the ceilings were where the family salami was hung to cure.

"What the devil?" he commented in his deliberate way. "What does he do? He comes in and looks up. The first thing he does, eh? He looks up!"

"Well, why not hang your salami in the wine cellar. Then he won't be able to see them", suggested the Liberal.

"But how can I do that? I've got none left!" exclaimed the frustrated petitioner. "This year we had very few, and we've already finished them all."

"In that case, the problem has solved itself", concluded the Liberal. The group of men were splitting their sides with laughter.

Ambrogio thought, *Just look! After tragedy comes the farce! It's truly incredible that our people are forced to put up with such leaders.*

A little disconcerted, the gravedigger waited until the laughter died down, then continued. "At the moment, I'm the undertaker in Raperio."

"A useful craft", said Sèp, who despite the discomfort of sitting in one of the Savonarola scissor seats had tears in his eyes from so much laughing.

"But maybe next year I'll not do it."

"Maybe, maybe", chorused two or three, still laughing.

Agazzino, the president, intervened. "Cut it out", he said, addressing the committee and, to the petitioner, "After all that, what is it you've come here to say? Are you saying that the doctor isn't happy with what he's being paid by the health insurance and wants something else?"

"No, I didn't mean to say that, but . . ."

"What I mean is: If you don't give him a salami, for example, doesn't the doctor do his job?"

"Of course he does. That would be a good one!"

"So, after all, what brought you here? Try at least to come to the point and explain."

The fellow fixed his gaze on Foresto, titular representative of the Communists. "Now what do I do?" he asked. "Why do you go around telling people to come here to complain, to make a fuss, and then when one comes, you don't even speak up?" He pointed at Sèp with his chin, the deputy representative for the Communists, hunched over in his scissor seat. "And this one, he even laughs, the wretch!"

Being called upon directly, Foresto felt himself forced to intervene, but caught by surprise and still laughing, he was unable to do more than make a small speech full of unoriginal commonplace phrases, railing against the "doctors and other gentlemen, greedy as leeches, sucking the blood of the people".

It was clear that nobody was impressed. "Come on, try not to talk like the *L'Unita* newspaper. Try to reason with your brain, if you have one", said the Liberal. "You know the two doctors in Nomana better than that."

But the stubborn Foresto repeated what he had said.

Agazzino let him finish, looking at him silently, then observed, "In other words, if I understand what was said, you're now going around telling people to come to our meetings in order to disrupt the CLN?"

"I go around saying what I please and telling the people what I want!" Foresto was now shouting and even put one hand in his pocket. (*Now we've reached the point when he'll pull out his pistol*, thought both Agazzino and Ambrogio.) However, perhaps because he guessed their thoughts or because the committee was now a more numerous body, he didn't take out the pistol. "The people are fed up ... the people this ... the people that ..."

The Socialist, Signor Benfatti, fearing above all that, as a pharmacist, the president, Agazzino, might consider himself to have been insulted, along with the doctors, once again decided to speak. This he did with his usual neutral tone of voice, one hand lifted, like a lay preacher. "We Socialists", he said, looking at the Communist, "are also concerned about the good of the people. Therefore—as Turati would have said—we should spare no effort to educate the people and not to take advantage of their dishonorable tendencies. I will go farther. Sometimes, for the good of the people, it can even be necessary to go against the people."

Foresto had at first intended to come back at him rudely, but said nothing. He sat there puffing and left it. This didn't please the gravedigger, who, pointing a finger at the Socialist, suddenly shouted, this time in Italian, "*Fucilato! Fucilato! Fucilato!*" (He meant that the man should be taken before a firing squad.)

At this the committeemen once more burst into laughter. Depressed, Agazzino instructed the secretary to record in the minutes that a decision on the health insurance contributions had been postponed until the next meeting, by which time "the parties' representatives would have better informed themselves". Therefore, the first item of the agenda was considered to have been covered. They went on to the next item, which didn't take much time. It concerned the repair (for the umpteenth time, as Agazzino reminded them) of one of the aqueduct's pumps. "If the maker doesn't go back to production of spare parts, we'll end up without water from one day to the next."

They went on to the third item, the temporary replacement of one of the town's employees, presently sick; then they passed on to the fourth item, aimed at discussing the redesign of the public lighting in Nomana's main piazza. Once they started talking about this, a new rumpus broke out, caused by the Socialist deputy representative's suggestion that of the six ancient metal lampposts in the piazza, three should stay there, two should be taken to the little piazza at Raperio (the proposer's hometown) as it didn't have any lampposts at all, and another should be taken and placed at the Lodosa highway crossroads. The whole affair was described as distributive justice.

When the fuss over this suggestion died down, they went on to the fifth (and last) item on the agenda, of particular interest to the left-wing members of the CLN (which made it unattractive to the others): the purges in Nomana, or rather to take up once again the dispute over the purges in Nomana. It took more time to deal with this item than the previous four put together.

While the others debated and demonstrated their verbal skills to each other, Pollastri sat there, thinking. The remark made by the president to the effect that he represented nobody but the Action party rubber stamp hadn't sat well with him at all, precisely because it was the truth. Still hurt by the sniggering he'd had to take, he made an effort to think of a way to get himself out of this thorny situation. Some way or another, perhaps there was a way. (*Perhaps . . . but it's a big perhaps. I'll first have to be sure . . .*) He examined the impossible position taken by Benfatti, with that crazy phrase of his. Without being noticed, Pollastri had made a note: "For the good of the people, it can even be necessary to go against the people." How could such a reactionary individual (he should have said one so without demagogy) continue to represent the Socialists? Particularly as the Socialists here in Nomana, their thoughts shaped and formed by the libertarian speeches made by the pensioner from Milan, Millanta, were practically indistinguishable from the Communists. If in fact, deep down, they weren't prepared to fill the streets with revolutionary blood, as were the Communists, they were certainly not left behind in terms of the violence of their words.

How is it possible, Pollastri asked himself, *for hardened people like these to be represented on the CLN by this idiotic individual with his goatee? Besides, there isn't a Socialist any more, starting with Nenni, who has kept his goatee. A man who'll come along and say* (he glanced at his notes out of the corner of his eye), "For the good of the people, it can even be necessary to go against the people." *I'm going to have to start going into the Socialists' bar, I, who as an employee don't go into bars. Then, at the right time, I'll refer to this statement, word for word and . . . or perhaps not, perhaps it'll be better for me to take the people aside and persuade them one at a time, because when they're all together, being an ignorant bunch, they might misunderstand. Well, it's something I'll have to think about. Then, when I've managed to convince somebody, I'll hang on to them. I'll make some excuse (there's always a reason to be found) and turn in this damned Action party's membership card . . . no, even better, I'll tear it up. I'll wait till the party disagrees on some matter with the Socialists, and I'll make a gesture by tearing it up. Then, based on this, I'll ask for acceptance as a member of the Socialists. After that, if things go my way, I'll be able to cut this damned Benfatti's grass.*

He asked himself how each member of the CLN would react. *That one, I think, would be happy to see me occupy Benfatti's position; that one also, and also that other, maybe. There's certainly a chance, yes, certainly . . . a chance.* He began to cheer up. *If I manage to take Benfatti's place, I'll immediately make an ally of Foresto. I'll make an agreement with him, cost what it may. The pharmacist is afraid of him, so the two of us together, that's to say, the Communist party and the Socialist party, we'll make him go cross-eyed trying to keep up with us, this wretched pharmacist, with his talk of rubber stamps . . . although now he's brought the Riva boy into the CLN . . .* He continued mentally to insult Agazzino, whose only mistake had been to give Pollastri a chance to take an active part in politics.

23

The meeting broke up at midnight. Ambrogio went out through the gateway of the municipal building between Agazzino and the wise-cracking Liberal.

"Have you ever seen such a pack of hounds, eh? What did you think of it?" asked the friendly Liberal, in dialect; then without waiting for an answer, "The only important thing here is that we manage to hold normal elections. As the Americans and the English are here in Italy, I'm convinced we'll get there. Then you'll see the end of all these uncouth people."

"As long as the elections go well . . . how can anyone be sure of that, nowadays?"

"Well, listen, nobody can possibly be sure of anything," he replied, "but I'm convinced. More than anything because Italy has so many farming people, and, as they say, 'the peasant is the Christian Democrat'. Besides . . ."

He had to pause while Ambrogio laughed at the sally.

"Besides, there are the Americans. After the enormous war they fought, they'll not be so stupid as to . . . well, there are all sorts of reasons. At the end the winners will be the priests. You'll see."

"And . . . what about the Reds? If they lose, won't they cause a revolution? Worse, won't they have a revolution even before the elections?"

"Not while the Americans are here."

"Look at Greece. The Americans are also in Greece, yet look what's happening there."

It was late, and clearly they couldn't cover any point exhaustively; after exchanging a few words the Liberal bade them a friendly goodnight and went home.

The light from the six ancient lampposts in the piazza, so recently the subject of disagreement, shone with a soft glow, enough for them to recognize familiar cherished objects: the cobblestoned ground over which swooped the swallows in summer, the church with its beautiful granite columns, the bell tower . . . while walking past the bell tower, Ambrogio only half followed what Agazzino said. He was remembering the evening war was declared, when the bells, now no longer up there, had deafened Stefano and his other friends . . . where would Stefano be, if still alive . . . and Michele Tintori, all the others . . .

no prisoners had yet returned from Russia, although there had been some messages, not enough, from the *lager* over there, delivered via the Turkish Red Crescent. Ambrogio himself had held such a message in his hands, destined for a family in Incastigo. What was more, he'd heard that Radio Moscow had recently broadcast a list of names of Italian POWs. In which case, who knew; maybe . . .

24

Pierello had gone back to his old job at the San Giovanni ironworks in Sesto. After so many violent adventures, his days had become suddenly monotonous, although at least at the moment this didn't displease him. He'd leave each morning before dawn with his lunch bag under his arm and would walk quickly to the Nomana rail station. Once he had reached the top of a certain slope out in the fields, he would always turn around to look for the house—at that time of day hardly visible in the darkness—where Luisina lived. A strange thing was happening to him. Luisina, one year younger than he, whom he'd known since school days, before even, since her birth, and about whom he'd never given a second thought (*What a strange thing, eh?!*), he recently couldn't get her out of his thoughts. At the station, he'd get on the 6:15 train, always full of laborers and almost always in the same compartment. If there was room he'd sit in the same place, between the same people, practically: workers like himself, from Nomana, or perhaps from farther up the line, from the neighboring province of Como. Some, like him, had been held prisoner in Germany, but for some time past they hadn't talked about that. Hands in pockets and coat collars turned up, they preferred to doze. Pierello would think about Luisina: her wide forehead, her brown hair pulled back into a chignon, but more than anything he thought about how agreeable she was, which was the reason he'd begun to be interested in her. Since that Sunday when—to save his mother the inconvenience—he'd gone out to buy some bread and had met her in the little shop's doorway, also carrying a net shopping bag. "Oh, Piero, somebody told me you'd returned. Are you well?" She'd spoken so gracefully.

"Yes, well", he'd answered, and then jokingly, in the manner usual to a young man meeting a young woman, "You should know by now that it's the weeds that grow strongest."

But he was impressed by her, not only by her face but also by her whole appearance. (*How come while I was away she changed so much?*) He felt like making some complimentary remark to suit the moment, but, being inexperienced in those things, he ended up saying, "Well, look, Luisina, you've certainly changed from the time you'd come to school with a runny nose, eh?"

Instead of giving him a "proper" answer, rudely, which he deserved, she put things in place by saying, "You too, Piero. You've changed a lot." And after a pause, "Goodness knows what you had to go through in Germany!" She had said this in a way, in a certain way, that told him, in those few words, that she really did have some extraordinary understanding of all the tremendous experiences through which he'd lived. It was difficult to believe that one girl's good manners could give so much pleasure; really, it was almost unbelievable!

How well she behaved. She had such an elegance of movement! thought Pierello. *She has inborn good manners. Not even a high-born lady, or very few, could match her gracefulness. And me! What an idiot, to talk about her snotty nose! And in any case, there was no truth in it; she never had a runny nose when she went to school! But she immediately understood that I was trying to make a joke . . . that I only said it because . . .* He tried against the clackety-clack noise of the train to put his thoughts into words.

On the Sunday after that first meeting, he didn't, as usual, go to the second morning Mass, going instead to the third, purposely hoping to meet Luisina. However, the Nomana church was full, so, secretly disappointed, he had slowly to go forward, to the first few pews, where he sat with two of his comrades from the military: Severino, who'd been a Bersagliere in Africa and who was, like himself, from Lodosa and Damiano, from Nomana, who had returned recently from his POW camp in Yugoslavia and who still wasn't at all fit. (*What a thrashing our class of '21 went through!*) All during the Mass he couldn't look at Luisina except briefly, by turning around. At the end of the service he left hurriedly through the side door without properly bidding his companions a farewell and placed himself near the vestibule. Having decided that, if he couldn't walk the girl home, he could at least spend a short time with her, talking and entertaining her better than on the last Sunday, and not, of course, talking about snotty noses, but about something better. Yes, but what? Let's see, what could they both talk about? As the girl and her mother left the church and went slowly down the steps, he realized that he not only couldn't think of an appropriate subject, he couldn't even think of one word to say, not one. When the two women passed by, he could only mumble a dull reply to their affable greeting.

Oh, Piero, what a novice, what a thorough novice you looked like! Just as well you got a helping hand from Saint Michael the Archangel, otherwise . . .

The helping hand from Saint Michael came to him when he was casting about desperately for something to say, and his eye fell on a blue poster on the church door, which announced the program of the festival for Beolco's patron saint, the feast of Saint Michael. Luisina had already gone past, but by good fortune his fellow conscript Severino came up toward him among the other people. Piero immediately called out, "Hey, Severino, did I tell you that this afternoon I'll be going to the festival over at Beolco? What about you? Are you coming?"

"What? What do you say . . . going to Beolco?" the African veteran Bersagliere called back.

"Yes, today is Saint Michael's Day, a feast day, so I'm going this afternoon", Piero called back, his voice still raised.

Severino came closer, the better to talk to him, but meantime—as Piero had intended—Luisina had certainly heard and knew that later he'd be at Beolco.

Immediately Piero became really anxious. *What if she didn't hear properly? And even if she did hear, what'll she do? I wonder if she'll go there also? But why should she have to go?*

He was still worried some hours later when, accompanied by his African friend Severino, he set out on the road to Beolco; so that when they neared the Casaretto farmhouse and Severino suggested, "What do you say we go and visit your cousin Tito's parents? He's still listed as missing . . .", he had replied, "Sure, but later. We'll stop off later, on our way back, not now."

At last, when they arrived at a festive Beolco, Piero saw Luisina, quietly standing with some friends over by the carousel. God in heaven, she's really come. Look at her, she's come! He felt his heart turn over on seeing her. True, he also soon noticed that there were other girls, and also a group of young fellows from his own neighborhood, younger than he and Luisina. All of these people certainly hadn't come because of his shouted hints to Severino that morning in the piazza. Also, it was possible that Luisina and her friends, well . . . in any case, he couldn't continue his musings, being interrupted by, "Hey, Piero, look who's here!" from Severino, who without pausing headed over to where the girls were standing, greeting them with an aggressive, "What are you up to, girls?" and afterward going on to try various witticisms on them.

Pierello joined the conversation. Then they all climbed onto the carousel, sitting on the wooden horses, some supported on iron chains, others carved like children's rocking horses. They were as usual decorated with glitter and with mirrors, with strange pictures of veiled women, scarcely visible beneath the many coats of varnish curling and lifting.

Pierello reassured the girls about the safety of the supporting iron chains, telling them there was no need to worry: "Because after all, iron is always iron, and stronger than any varnish", speaking in his shy but serious tone.

They enjoyed the ride on the carousel horses. The more boisterous Severino occasionally grabbed or nudged the girl ahead of him, pushing at her and making her scream with fright until she was hoarse.

Now, with the train's clackety-clack in the background, Piero thought about that afternoon, because his subsequent meetings with Luisina had all been brief. The feast day at Beolco felt to him as if it had been specially made for the two of them: the streets decorated as they used to be before the war, with red and white garlands stretched from wall to wall overhead, and all down the streets there were little trees made of bamboo decorated with paper flowers, very lovely. Or maybe the word wasn't *lovely*—Piero reflected; he'd now traveled the world and understood—but in any case, it was well done, that's for sure, because it gave the impression that there had never been a war. That was it: it made memories of the war recede.

Luisina and he, and also Severino and the other two girls, had spent the afternoon strolling among the crowds, the garland decorations above them, and when they reached the small ancient church of Saint Michael, they had bought some nougat. This was where they had run into Luca—whose hometown was Beolco—buying cotton candy for two little nephews playing at his feet.

"Look, Piero, what a coincidence! I wanted to talk to you. You know what about . . ."

Of course he knew. It was about the Democrats. He wanted him to join the party. He'd already received a couple of messages that Luca had sent him. But he hoped Luca wouldn't start talking about politics now, when he had company.

"We'll talk, but not just now", he answered, blushing a deep red, unaccustomed to being in the company of a woman, at which Luca took his eyes off the cotton candy machine and looked at Piero, then at Luisina, and, having understood, made a gesture of agreement, smiling widely in approval, the big lunk . . .

Luisina had a very pleasing figure, set off that day by a nice dress. Thinking about that, it didn't seem surprising to Piero that a girl like her could be simple, modest, and chaste: all hearth and church, he knew. Then there was the nuns' Oratory in Nomana, and her job at the Briosco weaving mills where, when the women sang, they chanted the Christian litanies. He remembered the frightful promiscuity in Germany, the behavior of the deportees and the local women, the way they shoved sex in your face. Here, though, even if one were a modest workman, one could be sure about the girl who was to become his wife. This, he knew, didn't happen by chance. It came from conscious decision and example, set by generation after generation, from the praying of Rosaries each evening, from the patient teachings of Sister Candida and Father Mario, the work of other pious priests like Father Pietro in Briosco. *God bless these guardians of a poor man's most valuable treasure.*

Luisina wasn't just serious and modest. She was also simple and natural enough, and knew, for example—with the countrywoman's grace that Pierello so liked—how to liven up a conversation when, as sometimes happened, he ran out of words. (Luisina, for her part, felt moved that Piero liked her. Above all she was attracted by his disarming yet sturdy mildness, which—it was not only her opinion, but others' also—was his most likable feature, in evidence before the war, during it—she was sure—and certainly now.)

That afternoon Piero intended to ask if she had gone to the Beolco festival because of his shouted hint after Mass or whether she had gone by pure coincidence, but when he noticed that Luisina, in any case, seemed to enjoy his company, he decided not to.

768

I'm sure I don't know what good she sees in me; I don't know and don't understand, he would conclude each time he thought about it.

Enough. But he couldn't help thinking about the girl repeatedly while, half asleep, collar up, hands in pockets, he rattled to work in the train.

Not that he spent the entire hour or so of the journey thinking only of Luisina. Sometimes, when his seat companions were quiet, he would hear comments made by people sitting farther away: normally banal discussions in which the subject was usually of interest only to the speaker, who often would repeat himself endlessly. Now and then he would hear something relevant, referring, for example, to the hiring of workers in some particular factory. Then Pierello would lend an attentive ear. "The work situation is looking up, eh?" He would even exchange a word with his silent seatmates. "And about time, isn't it?"

"What?"

"That the work situation is looking up."

"Oh, right, yes, I believe so."

"Yes, I'd say that myself", put in another one. "With all the shortages, it's still necessary to rebuild."

"You said it, all right."

"Trains, houses, furniture, everything."

"Mmm."

But why did jobs take so long to come available? The question worried all workers a little, and they didn't quite understand why.

If a Red propagandist were present, he would soon pull out his explanation. "Believe me, the fault is in the hands of those who have the money but won't part with it so that the poor people can obtain work. These are the people responsible."

The eternal argument. But as these agitators seemed to enjoy the scarcity of jobs, the majority of workers in Brianza didn't go along with the argument. In any case, it was rare for anybody to argue on the train, as they would have done in town. Aware of the atrocities that took place in Sesto during the period of the liberation, the workers preferred to maintain silence, impenetrably shut inside themselves, in order to live life peacefully.

If there were anyone in the train compartment who was not of the working class, one or another worker might make some remark for their benefit. One time Pierello was pulled back from his own thoughts by someone saying, "What we workers ought to do is not work but continue to be paid for it."

He recognized the voice as belonging to a simple worker from Nomana employed at the Marelli factory. He was certainly not a subversive type. Marelli was going through a delicate stage of expansion into peacetime production. It was pretty certain that he himself was actually working these days. Why would he say something like that?

Pierello pretended to stretch himself in order to turn around and look behind him. Sitting there, among them, was the old teacher Quadri Dodini (the lady who had cried when the Germans entered Paris; she would be thought a "signora" by comparison with the laborers), who was on her way to work in Monza at the nuns'convent where she taught. Piero realized that the man's remark was aimed at her as being the only person there who might be upset by it. The remark had been caused by the petty spirit of the man, who wanted to be annoying simply for the sake of it. Pierello was reminded of the Germans, although even they weren't as mean. Yes, but instead of making swinish remarks like this, they did even worse things. Why did men always have to behave like pigs?

So, amid reflections and drowsing, without much conversation, he would reach the Sesto station, where he'd get off the train at 7:30, which gave him time to reach the steelworks without hurrying.

25

On reaching the factory, he would punch the time clock and go to the locker room to put on a pair of coveralls, then wait calmly with the other workers (there were about one hundred in that one changing room) for the sound of the starting siren. During the brief wait they'd exchange jokes, rather like soldiers preparing to march at dawn. Here, however, there was more indifference, less emotion. The siren would send them all to their work stations. Pierello would hurry to his place on a row of three rolling mills fed by three ovens, where the iron ingots were heated to a fiery orange color. Taken out of the oven with large pincers, the ingots were drawn some ten yards along the iron floor (this was one of Piero's jobs) and lifted onto the rollers, where they were pushed into a giant mangle of two steel cylindrical rollers, which squeezed the material, flattening it. Then the partially shaped ingot would be sent through the rolling presses several times more (as many as fifteen times) to be transformed into sheets of steel. After being cut and trimmed, the sheets would rattle off to be stacked.

Counting the oven men, the men who lifted out the ingots, the rolling mill men, and the trimmers, there were seven men on each line. There was little talk except for the occasionally necessary shouted warnings. In the shed the noise was deafening from the endless roar of the fans forcing air into the ovens, the cadence of the cutting press, and the much louder banging when the top roller cylinder crashed down on the lower as the still-hot material left the mill's jaws. There was always dust hanging in the air, so the workmen covered their heads with their own choice of headgear (safety helmets hadn't yet been introduced), whether hat or beret or, in the case of the younger workers, knitted ski caps. The old men wore hats with brims. Pierello used the Tyrolean hat with which he'd returned from the POW camp. If only Luisina could see him, in his jaunty hat dragging sixty-pound ingots along to the presses, joining with the millwright to swing them accurately up onto the rollers. However, while at work, he had no time to think about Luisina. He would have had a chance to do so when every hour and a half or two hours they took a break while the ovens were being refilled with cold ingots, but thinking about Luisina never became an obsession. During these rest periods he preferred to relax with the others and exchange a few words.

Between noon and one they stopped for lunch. Normally this consisted of soup, meat, vegetables, and wine, prepared in the factory kitchen, to which each man added what he had brought from home. Piero usually ate at the same table with his workmates. The younger men would talk about sports; the others would be silent or talk about wages. Occasionally they'd talk about crime (around this time there were many holdups by bandits), often mentioned on the early morning radio; sometimes they'd talk about politics, but cautiously and without taking such discussions to a logical end. Simply because he came from Brianza, Pierello was regarded as a practicing Catholic, but wasn't challenged by the other workers for this. Rather, the workers respected each other, which was decidedly a grace. At 1:00 work would resume, to be ended at 5:00 by another sounding of the siren. Then, without dawdling, the workers would head for the locker rooms, where they would clean up at large washing founts, each with six to eight faucets, where they'd scrub black faces and necks with soap before going to their individual lockers to dress and leave the factory.

The streets of Sesto—Lombardy's largest industrial center—were no more inviting then than they are today. To these men, however, they were pleasant because the air was less polluted there than it was inside the factory (there were very few vehicles then), and because there were green trees and shrubs here and there.

The men would hurry through the streets—some would run—to the streetcar stops and railroad station. Once in the station, Pierello would check the tracks to see if his train had already arrived, and if not he'd go into the bar and enjoy a spuma. When the train arrived, he'd leave the bar with the others and an hour and a quarter later arrive in Nomana.

26

Leaving the train, he'd walk home between the autumnal farm fields, his lunch bag under his arm. Even though he felt a bit numb with fatigue, there was something marked, something peacefully resolute about his movements, as if he were sure of himself. Naturally he hadn't studied economics like Ambrogio and knew nothing about the gross national product or incremental percentiles. He certainly would have not thought that he, like the other workers, if they continued laboring, would one day, before growing old, own a car and an apartment. Had someone told him this he would not have believed it. He did have, however, the strongly held belief that with his work he was vitally useful to his family—his present relatives and, when the time came, the family he would make. Would it be with Luisina? Yes, probably with Luisina. Walking alone, Pierello, as usual, was silent. In fact, it wasn't that he didn't have opportunities to talk, particularly on the train; but like many others, he didn't like to make and repeat trite and useless remarks, which were good only for wasting your breath. Also, for a villager like himself, without any higher education, it was difficult to talk about unusual or little-known subjects, such as his wartime and POW experiences. He'd tried to talk about them several times but came to the conclusion that these things could be talked about satisfactorily only with someone else who had lived through similar experiences. Other people don't understand, can't participate in one's perception when recounting these events. And not only on the train or at the factory, but everywhere, even in the village, including the family. His mother—even though the poor woman showed concern—would end up feeling a great pity for you and the others who had lived through this. And so the enormous experiences he'd lived through and often thought about (the way the German farmers lived, the frightening march and flight of the Prussians—an entire people uprooted from their own land—the unspeakable barbarity of the fighting between people who no longer feared God—*poor cousin Tito, still in their hands!*)—all of this he kept to himself. Perhaps these experiences would little by little fade away and be lost to memory. But no, he was starting to have hopes that, thanks to Luisina (that was it!), who gave every sign of understanding things, even seemed to understand him before he spoke about it ... With her—when she was his wife—he'd talk, and perhaps then he himself would better understand. Perhaps, who knew, he had stored up some wisdom to pass on to his children, just like other people who hadn't studied and who nevertheless were wiser than many graduates and professors.

In the autumnal fields, the grass, soon to be burned by frost, was green and waterlogged. The corn, having lost its exotic ripe color, was turning a rusty gray, the color of the migrating birds. The lines of mulberry trees were becoming bare, their fallen leaves blown into clumps, like stains on the plowed earth around their roots. There, over there, was Lodosa, where among the other houses was Luisina's house. At this time, back from the mill, she would surely be helping her mother prepare supper.

Finally here was his own little house, with the small porch where—even though it wasn't yet dark—a light shone out. Crossing the porch, Piero always bowed his head to the Caravaggio Virgin before entering the house, stopping for a moment to look through the window to see his mother in the kitchen bustling around the stove and often his father at the table reading the newspaper. His young sister Martina would be quiet, sitting in the chair; the black cat, tail upright, passing by the child; and lying on the sideboard, the old brass alarm clock, which if stood on its feet would stop working.

One afternoon, as soon as he opened the door, his mother said, "Did you know, Piero? Have they told you? Your cousin Tito is back from being a POW."

"What? Tito is back from Russia?!"

His mother nodded. "But he's so wasted away, I don't know if he even weighs eighty pounds, poor child."

"And where is he now?"

"At home, in Casaretto."

27

Tito stayed in Casaretto for only a few days. He resolutely didn't want to go to a military hospital to recover ("No, enough, take me home, to my own home"), but soon Doctor Cazzaniga, who was called in by the family and visited Tito another couple of times, tried to reason with him.

"So do you want to die now that you're in Italy? Now that you have a chance of getting better?" To the family the doctor insisted, "We need to have him in the hospital for a few weeks, as long as it takes for him to recover his strength. We'll start looking for a place for him in the sanitarium so that we can help him to save himself."

Doctor Cazzaniga, a pale-faced man with an air of deliberation, generally had a cold manner, but the boy's case touched him. Even if curing the young soldier took ten or twenty years of treatment—he told himself—he would give unstintingly of himself to that end.

So Tito left the poorly heated bedroom in the farmhouse (but also left behind his mother's incomparable care) and found himself in the Nomana hospital, the same place to which, two years earlier, poor Giustina had come, suffering, like Tito, from consumption. The room he was in was painted a shiny yellow, but that didn't bother him, coming recently from a world of rags and putrefaction. Quite the reverse, he felt a comforting sense of cleanliness. However, reduced in health and weight, and exhausted—he was down to seventy-five pounds—as he was, he took little interest in his surroundings. Rather than being alive, he was more in a state of vegetation, to the point where he was unable to think much about anything.

His parents and school and army friends had been to see him, both at home and later in the hospital. Ambrogio also came to see him, even though they were not acquainted, when through his cousin Pierello Tito had sent a message that amazed Ambrogio, to the effect that Second Lieutenant Michele Tintori from Nova was not only still alive but also sent his kind regards from the POW *lager* at Susdal. Ambrogio was very moved by the news, which was confirmed to him in person by Tito. "He hasn't been repatriated yet because in the first batch they chose to send only people who were near death like me and the POWs who had converted to communism. There aren't many, and among these there are several who only pretended to go along, you understand?"

Ambrogio was filled with questions and had already asked him something, when he stopped himself on seeing the effort it cost Tito to reply. In any case, Tito had to repeat the good news about Michele the next day when Ambrogio returned, bringing with him Michele's aunt and uncle, an older couple whom he had gone to fetch in Monza when they asked him to do so.

Soon, day after day, more and more people came to the hospital to ask for news about relatives missing in action. The traffic started becoming intense, because neither the hospital porter nor the nursing sisters felt able to turn people away, particularly not the missing soldiers' mothers, whose frightened eyes told of their feelings now that—after being torn by doubts for years—they thought themselves about to hear their sons' fates. Answering so many people's questions visibly tired Tito to the point where Dr. Cazzaniga personally intervened, giving the porter and everybody else strict orders not to disturb his patient. He also had a printed sign hung on Tito's door: "Isolation—entrance strictly forbidden."

After that, the days for Tito started becoming silent and long, although he spent most of his time half asleep. The sister and the two nurses who worked in his area took very attentive care of him. From the basement kitchen also, Sister Agape, the cook, would send him something additional to the daily menu, such as real American chocolate or early tangerines or oranges. Taking turns, his mother and father would visit him every afternoon, along with his brother Giacomo, the one who bore the Cross in religious processions. They all tried not to excite him, letting him sleep as much as possible. With a slowness worrying to Dr. Cazzaniga, Tito began to gain weight.

Every morning he was visited by Father Mario. His presence pleased Tito. With his baby face, glasses, and untidy crewcut, the priest would talk about the definitive chance to salvage their souls that God had given man through Christ.

"Here we don't realize it. We'll understand when we're in the beyond, saved after having seen so much evil, so much of the evil forces, as you have seen."

"The power of evil. Yes, it's true", Tito would say sometimes, agreeing. "That's right! If only you had seen what I have!"

He had described for Father Mario his experience in Kazan, those trains loaded down with the dead—men, women, children—eviscerated and mutilated by cannibalism. "What evil, Don Mario! And who knows if it's not still happening now, while we're here talking. Oh, what sights!" His suffering-filled eyes would hold the priest's eyes, looking into them for sympathy, help.

"Now, while you're here to get better, you should try not to think about these things", Don Mario would advise him. "Now you have to rest and think of one thing only: regaining your strength." Yet while he spoke this and other

774

phrases of advice, he was himself unable to remove those awful visions from his mind's eye.

On one occasion, remembering his lectures at the seminary, he said, "The saintly curate of Ars used to say that if you remove the priest from a community, it will turn into a collection of wild beasts. And he was right, completely right."

Tito always regarded him with his pained look. "It's true, yes, that's how it is."

"But you should now stop thinking about that. Now you should think only about getting better."

"Yes, Father."

A growing weight had been accumulating in the priest's heart, and this became almost unbearable. Sometimes when he held Tito's hand in the morning and tried to force himself to smile, he succeeded only—if one looked at his features—in making the same grimace a child makes when it is about to cry. Fortunately for Tito, he had no chance to devote lingering thoughts to the matter, as he would soon feel drowsy and go to sleep.

On one occasion Father Mario, with a kind of rebellion, said, "But in Russia you must also have come across some good, some glimmer of kindness. These have always been people who worshipped our Lady; just think about all those icons. So it's not possible that in only a few decades . . ."

He noticed Tito's eyes regarding him fixedly, surprised.

"I mean to say, you must have run into some display of kindness. Like the farm women—so I've been told—who, without being asked, would massage our men's feet when they couldn't walk during the retreat due to frostbite."

"I myself never saw that happen," Tito stated, "but an example of kindness . . . well, yes, you're right. In the hospital where the guards would pull us from our sickbeds to go and unload trains at the station. In this hospital there was a Ukrainian lady doctor who took to me like a mother and made me eat many healthy things. Well, at that time I was already very sick, so sick that if it hadn't been for her, I'd now be dead." He paused. "Whenever Sister Agape sends me good things from the kitchen, I always remember that Ukrainian doctor, *Sistrà Evghenia*—always. Who knows how things are going now in that hospital in Kazan . . ."

For Father Mario, that faraway episode of the Ukrainian doctor ended up being reason for comfort.

28

One day, when Tito was alone in his room, he had a visit from Sèp, the former partisan, who was a distant relative on his mother's side.

"How are you, cousin?" he greeted Tito, in dialect. "I'm very glad you're back."

Smiling, Tito said, "The important thing is to be alive."

"That's right." Sèp held out his left hand to shake, having his right hand bandaged and in a sling. Then, still using his left hand, he patted Tito on the shoulder. He hadn't expected the way the young man's bones protruded from the skin under the touch of his hand.

"They operated on my hand yesterday", he said, holding up the bandaged right hand, a bit embarrassed. "You knew that, right? That Dr. Cazzaniga of ours, if you let him, he'd operate even on the statue of our Lady in the monastery."

Tito smiled. "I'd heard you'd been operated on."

Sèp guessed that Tito would also be abreast of his adventures in the Partigiani and of his present activity in the Communist party.

"Well", he said exaggeratedly, shrugging his shoulders to show he couldn't care less about the operation to his hand or the reservations of other people, or even perhaps those of Tito.

But in this he wasn't totally honest. He cared for his cousin and showed it by his exaggerated gestures, even using the bandaged hand. He made fun of the sign on the door—"Isolation—entrance strictly forbidden"—eliciting a knowing, conspiratorial smile from Tito. Looking at Sèp, Tito noticed that his face— even though he was only twenty—had begun to acquire wrinkles around the nose and forehead, but wrinkled faces—Tito remembered—were characteristic of Sèp's family.

"Won't you sit down for a while?" he invited.

The ex-partisan sat on the only chair, used regularly by Father Mario and Giacomo, and crossed his long legs, another family characteristic.

Tito asked for news of mutual family members, and Sèp answered at length. He talked about the difficult times people were going through, keeping to generalities, so that Tito, relieved, thought they could avoid an argument. This made him happy, as he wasn't at all interested in getting into a discussion.

However, one of Sèp's standard phrases proved to be a stumbling block, having been thrown into the conversation without apparent thought.

"Pity Stalin didn't come as far as here, because he'd have straightened things out."

Tito paled, but replied calmly enough, "No. He would only have thrown a lot of working people into jail, and then killed them, without solving anything."

At this reply Sèp paused. His posture showed the unease of the dogmatist being contradicted, and on his face could be seen the beginning of his concern, his worry that perhaps his cousin would confirm certain rumors that he'd heard circulating in the hospital. These disconcerting rumors had in fact been the real reason for his visit.

"Listen, Tito, you wouldn't by chance be on the side of the Fascists, would you, eh?" he exclaimed.

"And why would I be? Since when? You want to associate me with them now that they've lost the war?"

"Well, look, let's not argue", said Sèp, but it was only a manner of speaking. The last thing he wanted was to have to bring the conversation to an end.

"Very well, let's not argue", Tito said tonelessly. "More than anything because I haven't the strength for it."

Sèp became anxious, strained. "You know I was a partisan?" he said. "A Communist partisan? And that now I've got myself into local politics?"

"Yes, I know that . . . so what? Is that a reason why I shouldn't tell you the truth? But wait a minute, you've just said we shouldn't argue, so I've said enough."

"But, Tito, you can't put yourself on the side of the *signori*. When all is said and done you're just a poor man like me." Sèp said this almost aggressively.

"Even poorer perhaps, certainly in terms of health."

"Right. And for that reason you're wrong to go against the people, if I may say so. You ought not to go around spreading stories that have been put in your mouth by . . . I don't know whom. It must have been the officers, who after all are the *signori*, the people responsible for the miserable conditions all over. You know that, eh?"

"Put in my mouth, you say?" Tito let out a deep breath. "Look, you're talking about poor people, about misery." He turned his reddening face on its skinny neck to look Sèp right in the eye. He spoke slowly. "Did you know that in Russia there's more, much more misery than here?"

"Impossible."

"Much more. Without comparison. And as far as the people responsible, there the people responsible are your Communists, because they're the owners of everything. And they treat the poor people in ways that the bosses here have never done. That's how things are there."

On hearing this kind of talk by someone who had been in Russia, a trace of fear crossed Sèp's face. "You couldn't have seen much", he exclaimed. "You were locked away all the time. You won't have seen much."

"Look here, kid, I was there for over three years", said Tito. He looked as if he would go on, but shrugged his shoulders and wriggled into a more comfortable position. "All right. So you're telling me that when I want to know how things are going in Russia I should ask you? Now let's change the subject." He looked at Sèp, who was silent. Clearly Sèp didn't want his visit to end on this note. "I see that those who say you Communists are real sheep are right. That's what it is. It seems impossible. Sheep. Even you", Tito added.

At this Sèp opened his mouth to reply, but remained silent. Tito waited for his cousin to insult him; it was clear that his remark about sheep must be particularly annoying to Sèp, who after all had rebelled against the dictatorship to the point of taking up arms against it. The young soldier became sad. Sèp, in contrast, managed to control himself, didn't let himself get mad, and only said, "Tito, you're wrong, and you do harm in . . . in setting yourself against the hopes of the poor people."

"Leave it, Sèp, leave it. What hopes do you mean? The hopes about communism aren't hopes. They are only an illusion."

Sèp got to his feet and looked again at Tito, who had shown such stubbornness. "Cousin, today I didn't want to argue with you", he said. "I didn't want to tire you or annoy you. And yet I've upset you. I'm sorry. Now I'd better go, but I want to return. Because it's not true that I'm a sheep."

"Forget it", said Tito tiredly. "I didn't want to insult you."

"No, not at all", said Sèp. "You have to tell me about everything you saw over there."

"There have only been horrible things", murmured Tito.

"That's all right. You'll tell me about these things. I'll be back tomorrow. But get it into your head that I haven't become a sheep."

Sèp was thinking of returning the following day. But later that same day Dr. Cazzaniga declared him fit and discharged him from the hospital.

PART TWO

I

The Red year 1945 also went by, drowned in the confusion of years past, taking with it its load of hopes, killings, efforts, and the half shouts hanging in midair. The small individual political efforts of Luca and Ambrogio, along with the work of innumerable others like them throughout Italy, began to show their effect when in the spring of 1946 the first local elections were held here and there, representing a sort of rehearsal. The party with a Christian orientation showed itself able to hold its own with the Marxists: more, it was the only one able to do so, all the others having shown themselves to be inconsistent.

In Nomana, as in other places, the radio and newspapers broadcast the results after each local election.

"You see? We weren't mistaken", the male voices commented at the Oratorio meeting. "Now what we need to do is persevere and not rest on our laurels."

"We need to redouble our effort. Because it's not enough to win elections here in our own constituencies. We need to pull all the available votes together to confront the votes in the Red areas", Luca said insistently.

Ambrogio was reminded of the army and of how here in civil life too it was the willing volunteers who bore the brunt, who made things go forward for everybody.

He became even more dedicated when, after consulting with the Allies, the legitimate government picked June 2 for the first ballot: to decide between a republican and a monarchical system and to elect deputies to a constituent assembly. The young man could see with his own eyes that in Milan, as elsewhere, the Christian party was almost entirely volunteer in character, or, as it was called, spontaneous. He had begun, once or twice a week on the way back from the university, to go by the provincial office of the Christian Democrats, which occupied an old palazzo near the town center, right by La Scala. He would pick up promotional material destined for Nomana (fliers, brochures, and the first posters) and receive occasional instructions. The atmosphere, the style, were the same as those he knew from Catholic Action: he noticed that the party, both in Milan and in Nomana, was definitely a direct affiliate of the Azione Cattolica.

As the election approached, the numbers of volunteers in the Milan party office increased, and the electioneering material being collected became larger. More than once Ambrogio had to go down to Milan by car instead of on the train in order to pick all of it up. In Nomana groups of youngsters from the

Oratorio organized themselves to go out and paste up the posters, a job they did with enthusiasm, shouting and laughing, making use of a couple of shaky old stepladders. One of these groups was led by Saulo, the chauffeur Celeste's oldest boy. None of them would have thought that this skinny volunteer would one day follow in Gerardo's footsteps to create his own millionaire manufacturing business and would himself serve as mayor of Nomana.

The Communist and Socialist activists in town also kept busy, as they did in the suburbs. The news that they received from the Red zones out in the plains, where their majority was complete, led them to believe they could win the elections nationally, although they were also aware that the people of Nomana, or rather the people of all Brianza in general, if given the choice between their own beliefs and those of others, would tend to choose the Christian Democrats. As to the laboring classes, the leftists claimed to be their representatives if only because they called themselves the workers' parties, but only a proportion—at least in Brianza—and not a majority was effectively behind them.

One afternoon an activist from the Incastigo Camera del Lavoro climbed on a table outside Gerardo's factory and urged the workers not to vote for the bosses' party. In good faith (he was, after all, a Marxist) he assured them that the interests of these bosses and those of the workers were incompatible. He was irritated to note that the workers thought the exact opposite. He finished his speech with shouts of "down with the bosses!" "the bosses to Loreto Square!" and other incitements. One workman in a pair of coveralls asked to speak and also climbed up on to the table. "I also have to say something about the bosses", he said, using dialect. He was an active young fellow, recently returned from a POW prison in Germany. Luca, watching him, became uneasy. Was it possible that the fellow had fallen for the Red propaganda?

"I just want to say one thing." The workman raised his voice. "When I was in Germany, and my family here was having a hard time, it wasn't the unions who helped them. It was the boss. If we're to be men, we have to remember these things," he shouted. "We shouldn't forget!" He looked around as if expecting someone to contradict his statement, then jumped down from the table. Many of those present nodded, agreeing, and there was some applause.

"Why do you come here to shout about Loreto Square?" an older worker came forward, addressing the union representative. "Why should we need to execute the boss, or anyone else, for that matter? Why do you always talk of killing? What do you think, that we've become wild beasts?"

When later Gerardo heard about the incident, he was very impressed. In the following days his children heard him say more than once, "We have workmen who are better people than we", and, "For this kind of people, we have to find a way to do more."

The political meetings and rallies run by the Reds in Nomana didn't produce the result expected by their organizers. Not even the takeover by Pollastri of Benfatti's job did any good. At one rally outside the entrance to the glass factory (where a new pavilion was under construction) a quarrel broke out between one of the factory managers and Foresto, who had allowed himself to treat the people of Nomana as if they were "asleep". The manager grabbed Foresto by his lapels, shouting, "Where's that poor woman from Raperio? What did you do to her?" and then, "What is it that you claim to teach us, you who are murderers!"

The bricklayers had separated them and ushered Foresto out, away from the building. "Go, leave, come back some other time; but for now you let it go", they told him.

At the Christian party meetings (in the modest meeting room at the Oratory), more and more members of the voting public attended. The last of these meetings took place two nights before election day. The police, there to maintain the peace, had already arrived. (In practice they were to be there to guard the ballot boxes.) They were youths, all ex-partisans, recently recruited, and therefore wearing brand-new uniforms. Some of them decided to attend the meeting in the Oratorio and decided they didn't like the atmosphere of political moderation, so instead of keeping the peace, they seriously broke it, shouting. One of them even became hysterical. At the end three or four of these youths followed Luca and Ambrogio into the piazza outside, insulting and shouting at the main speaker, whom the two recently discharged soldiers were escorting.

Even this event must have helped to achieve positive results. The Christian party won 56 percent of the constituent assembly votes, versus the 44 percent achieved by the remaining parties in aggregate. There was little change from this result in the neighboring municipalities of the Milanese Brianza. In the Como area—Visate, for example—the Christian party achieved an even higher percentage.

In the vote for the form of government, the pro-monarchy generally prevailed, but this was more as a counterreaction to the Red propaganda than as a vote of confidence for an institution whose representatives led lives that were uninspiring or even dissipated.

2

In August, accompanied by her mother and father, Colomba arrived in Nomana, with the intention of selling *I dragoni*, the villa that had been inherited from old Eleonora. Gerardo, Giulia, Ambrogio, and Francesca went to visit them. (The rest of the family was at the mountains.) They hadn't seen Colomba for two years, since the day they had gone to old Eleonora's funeral. They felt great compassion for the girl, particularly Francesca, who, now that she was Andrea Marsavi's fiancée, could imagine the suffering through which the other had gone after the death of her fiancé. She remembered that Manno had spoken about Colomba (although the former jokes no longer seemed appropriate) and felt a need to become like a sister to the girl. She had shown her tender compassion and had insisted she come to visit.

"Come and see us, every day if you can. We'll keep you company. Otherwise you'll be ... bored." (She meant, of course, that the girl, alone, would be sad.)

Once the visitors had gone, Colomba asked her mother, "What shall I do? Shall I go there? Would it be good manners to go there?"

"Don't think about conventions. If you want to go, go. And, apart from everything else, why not? Francesca is a very nice girl."

So Colomba went to visit Francesca. She crossed town, going down Nomana's cobblestoned central streets, dusty from summer's heat. She remembered going through these same streets at a more stately pace, accompanying Eleonora to and from Mass. On passing the strange buttressed arch on Sansone's courtyard, she glanced inside. The usual old ladies sat knitting in the shade of the mulberry trees; carts loaded with hay stood in front of the cattle stalls. Swallows came and went, flying almost at ground level, just as they always did, happy to be alive.

Colomba remembered Manno's interest in the swallow's nest in the entrance lobby of *I dragoni* (which this year wasn't there). He'd made fun of her because of the little bowl of bread and milk she'd put out for the swallow's brood. "You should give them grappa, not milk", he'd said, or something like it, making a play on words she knew were used by soldiers, the humor of which still escaped her. *In those times, besides, I was only eighteen.*

Now, at twenty-one, she was even prettier. She was aware of it by the looks given her by the people she met, who seemed to be saying, "My, you're pretty." In the piazza there were also many swallows, as before, and as she crossed it walking rapidly, the birds flew close, as if complimenting her looks. "You're pretty, did you know? You're pretty!" they seemed to be saying as they flew by. The tapping of her heels seemed to beat an accompaniment on the piazza's stone surface. "You're pretty, Colomba, you're pretty."

"Eh, well ...", she muttered defensively, half sad and half pleased. She walked by the bell tower, with its new shining bells, and went by Igino's house, although she didn't know him. Then, past the Rivas' fence (still made of wood), through which she could see the clearing and the old house, which had been the original mill, surrounded by dark green trees. As she entered, she received a friendly greeting (even here, how pretty you are!) from one of the maids.

She stayed with Francesca and Giulia all afternoon. She was filled with curiosity about the place in which Manno had lived, the things around him when he was young. She had known him for such a short time that to see this or that detail of his life, unknown up to now, gave her a strange feeling, as if in reality she hadn't known him well.

Francesca and Giulia didn't talk only about Manno. They tried to entertain her by talking about current happenings, their vacations, making her feel at home. In her turn she spoke of her experiences at the university. "I'm taking biology at Pavia. Did you know?"

No, they hadn't known. "But why in Pavia and not in Milan?" asked Francesca.

"In Milan they don't offer a course in biology."

"Well, how about that? And for my part, I graduated as a teacher, but didn't continue on to use it. I'm not sure if I did the right thing", Francesca said.

"And Alma? Is she going on?" asked Colomba.

"She's not sure. She got her teacher's certificate last month. Did you know?" "Yes."

"But she hasn't decided yet whether to continue or not."

"Our Almina . . .", the mother said tenderly.

"Our little statue!" Francesca joked.

"Tomorrow I'll see her at the mountain, both she and Giuditta", said the mother, and then, in dialect, "those two imps . . ."

"Goodness knows what they're getting up to, those two," said Francesca, "but go on, tell us about Pavia."

Colomba continued about her studies, and her hostesses, particularly Francesca, showed interest in what she had to say.

Colomba felt gratified at the interest and was happy to accept an invitation to return the following morning.

Giulia having gone to the mountains, Colomba returned not only on the next day but on the following days, too. She would bring her work in a bag and would knit as she talked.

"Here at your house I'm very happy", she'd sometimes say to Francesca. "Being with you is to have good company. My mother? Well, yes, but I'm with her all year round."

"But not when you're in Pavia."

"Not when I'm in Pavia, no."

As time passed they spoke less about Manno.

3

Ambrogio, who had given up going on vacation in order to study, often met Colomba at the house. Like the others who met her, he, particularly, noticed how pretty she was. During those summer days he'd gone back to studying in the shade of the fig tree, sitting on the garden chair, just as he'd done when a youngster before the war. He'd prepare himself for the exams, sometimes three at a time. His books piled on the grass beside him, he would alternate subjects in order to avoid boredom, pushing it away as long as possible before taking a break. While he studied he sometimes heard the quarreling of the sparrows in the trees and, more infrequently, the cascading song of a blackcap, summer's voice in Brianza. "The work of the receiver, apart from being concerned with the necessary operations of management, should concentrate particularly on the twin tasks of liquidating the assets and liabilities."

Sometimes he'd also hear the chatter between the two girls, particularly when they strolled in the garden or went to the kitchen garden to fetch vegetables. Colomba happily helped Francesca with some of the household chores. "The liquidation of assets is preceded—or accompanied—by the reconstruction of the assets' value: the restoration to the current account or estate of those items that have been allowed to trickle away ... trickle away ..." What? Items trickled away? Well, yes, that's clear; to continue ...

It was very difficult not to allow oneself to become distracted. Often around 5:00 in the afternoon the two girls would bring him a cup of tea.

"You, business brain, come on. Make an effort and let yourself relax for a moment." And although totally concentrated on the textbooks, he'd get up and offer his seat, although usually the two girls preferred to sit down on the grass, lowering themselves carefully while balancing their own cups and saucers. They would talk awhile about this and that.

More than once Ambrogio, unable to ignore Colomba's beauty, would say to himself, *Look at what Manno lost. What a jewel!* or *She's prettier than Fanny, there's no doubt. But ...* , he'd continue vaguely, *beauty isn't the only thing in the world.*

Then Francesca would say, "Now we'd better go and not prolong this wasting of your study time."

"You can't imagine how much I hate not being able to enjoy your company", Ambrogio would say sincerely.

"I believe you!" Francesca would say.

"Of course, I'm not talking to you ..."

Colomba would smile at him in thanks, and as they got to their feet they would pick up the few dishes they'd brought and leave him.

"With reference to the contracting parties ..." *What's he trying to tell me? The persons involved in the contract? Ah, yes ...* "The fundamental requirement is that the contract be mutually enforceable under Articles 1321 and 1372, first chapter ..."

I hope nobody thinks I'm behaving like a lout. After all, good manners require that I should be with her, even if only now and then ...

And then, when he again heard the girls' voices—perhaps from the other side of the flower beds, talking gardening lore with the yard man—it was really difficult to maintain his concentration on hereditary rights or the laws of contract from Professor Fanfani's texts.

784

At last one day he got up and went over to the girls to spend some time with them. Francesca was surprised when he began to talk about flowers. His remarks were so commonplace that even he himself noticed and remarked, "Manno should have been here. He was the one who knew all about flowers and plants; the same with animals, particularly birds."

"Yes", Francesca said. "Manno knew all about beautiful things."

"That's true," agreed Colomba; then turning to Ambrogio, "but what you say is interesting, too."

"Well . . ."

"No, I'm serious."

And she was serious. Had she been better able to analyze her feelings, she would have noticed that Ambrogio's manner of speaking, solid and practical, was more congenial to her than that of Manno had been.

One day, just after noon, he went farther. He offered to accompany the two girls on a bicycle ride.

"Well, what do you think? As it's August, I'll take some vacation time for myself, too."

"Oh, at last! I almost can't believe what I'm hearing", Francesca commented. "We may even see rain while the sun is out."

They loaned Alma's bicycle to Colomba, and in under an hour they reached and circumnavigated—as Ambrogio termed it—the small lake at Pusiano, described by the eighteenth-century poet Parini as the Eupili.

When they had finished their ride around the lake, they recalled some verse from their schooldays. Colomba had asked which was the Brianza slope named by the poet Foscolo.

"A slope?" Ambrogio, who hadn't the slightest idea, said happily, "Slopes, around here, as you can see, there are plenty. There's almost nothing else to see around here except slopes."

"I was referring to the one on which the woman of Brianza danced, the one loved by Foscolo."

"Ah, you'd have to explain it to me. I thought the Brianza slope was a quotation from Parini."

"No, it's from the concluding episode of *Le Grazie*", said Colomba. "Wait a moment. Let me try to remember, see if I can still quote from it: 'Vaga e felice i balli e le fanciulle . . . happy and beautiful, the dances and maidens' . . . Yes, that's it, yes . . . 'with peerless braided tresses and full breasts—on the easy slope of Brianza one day, going toward it . . .'"

"Great!" Ambrogio exclaimed. "And you call me the studious one? Are you sure the lady danced around here?"

"Yes, sure, because it also describes the lake. At one point 'she forgets her bright gown under the moon' . . . etc. . . . . 'the blue and sparkling Eupili's waves . . . weeps with the nightingale.'"

"Oh, poor thing! And why does she weep?"

"Ah, the grief of love, I believe. In any case, I don't remember it exactly."

The three of them laughed happily. That ancient Brianza of the eighteenth century, a little pagan, was infinitely far away from them. It belonged to another culture, now gone, of nobles and landed gentry, gone like the unknown woman of Brianza in Foscolo's song. Nowadays, following the culture of popular piety, the typical Brianza woman would in any case be like a Lucia, out of Manzoni's *I Promessi Sposi*, a type that could be found alive and well among the people. On the other hand, somebody like that distant neoclassical dancer wasn't as interesting.

In the meantime Ambrogio ended up being slightly ashamed of himself for riding out on his bicycle, without cares, among the woods, lakes, and slopes, in company with the two girls in their brightly colored dresses. *Just like a little kid!*

To justify his behavior he gave an uncharacteristically convoluted explanation to himself. *Deep down the fault is Father's, by forcing me, at twenty-five years of age, to continue studying like a sophomore.*

Whether or not it was his father's fault, a few days later, without the two girls having suggested it, he proposed another ride. When Francesca reminded him that in the Marsavis' garden at Visate there was a tennis court, he immediately agreed to go with them to play a couple of sets. Colomba played well, certainly better than the two Rivas, and obviously enjoyed herself hugely. For this reason, in the ensuing few days, accompanied by Francesca, Ambrogio went out there with Colomba several times.

Andrea Marsavi also greatly enjoyed these tennis outings with his fiancée (Francesca's parents would never have allowed her to visit Visate alone), so much so that he took time off work (unprecedented, given his industrious character) to join in the games.

"Well, you know," he explained to one of his eight brothers when for the first time he left to play tennis, "it's not possible for three to play. And after all, we are in August."

"Right. Nobody is criticizing you."

"Well, you don't have to look at me as if I were debauched", he exclaimed, unaccountably irritated. "In any case I'm going, right?"

"But nobody is looking at you. Who's looking at you?" the brother added with a broad grin.

At the Marsavis' the sausage factory, the home, and the garden were all close to one another, so that from the tennis court a loud squealing could occasionally be heard as the poor pigs were being herded toward the slaughter and the production line.

Andrea played strongly; for the difficult shots he would wrinkle his thin nose in concentration. He played alongside his Francesca, and although he was a very courteous person, he hardly noticed the two on the other side of the net. His happiness shone out of his youthful face.

Francesca felt vibrant, her heavy brown plait wound around her head. The game wasn't important to her except as an occasion—she was in any case not very good at tennis, and this didn't worry her—to enjoy the peaceful feeling of being close to the young man sent to her by a kind providence.

Andrea, for his part, thought, *She's not a woman, she's the woman,* and felt excitement. *She's the eternal woman.* During this time of falling in love, he even became poetic.

Colomba played tennis for the pleasure it gave her, and tried to play well. Her pretty face would glow and perspire, and her smiling blue-gray eyes would shine. When she won a point, she would exclaim happily.

Ambrogio couldn't stop himself from looking at her. Of course, every now and then he would exchange a remark with her or with the others, but above all he reflected and—something new to him—fantasized. This girl didn't look like one of the ancient Greeks, as Manno had maintained. *Well, perhaps there is something in her face, something classical, maybe, perhaps the set of her head. Although the nose, by good fortune, if one looks carefully at her nose, it isn't a Greek nose, doesn't drop in a straight line from her brow. And as far as her temperament, for sure she's not a Greek.* And then, *What a lot of foolish thoughts I'm having. How would I know how Greek women look? Even less about their temperament.* He realized he hadn't the faintest idea. *Well, one thing for sure, they couldn't possibly have a modern character like Colomba's!* And on another occasion, having looked at her—without her noticing—and looked again, *Ancient women nothing. She's a girl for today, she's a splendid girl, that's what she is.*

A girl whose nearness, with each day that passed, intoxicated him.

4

He finally realized the truth of this. He conscientiously reserved the mornings for studying (and to avoid distracting encounters he now avoided working under the fig tree, using his father's study instead), but he felt an extraordinary growing impatience until the arrival of the afternoon, and with it the moment to see Colomba once more. Fanny—he realized—had never exerted such a strong attraction on him.

Hey, hey! he admonished himself. *Remember that this is Manno's girl!* But he didn't consider it necessary to overdramatize the situation. *How could I ever forget it? Why do I worry about it? Come, don't start encouraging pointless fancies.*

As for Colomba, she also increasingly enjoyed the presence of Ambrogio, but she didn't worry about it. For her part she was determined, as a matter of principle, to remain faithful to Manno's memory and not lose her head over his cousin. *As if, after all, there weren't another family in the world apart from this one.* The mere fact that such thoughts came to her should have made her cautious, but she was too honest and vulnerable to notice.

Meanwhile, the more she saw of Ambrogio the more she liked him. Of course, he wasn't brilliant like Manno, whose strong personality had dazzled her. Ambrogio showed a practical spirit in the face of all circumstances, and although a Christian believer he would never have talked of predestination (like Manno) or ever have compared her to a little tree—he seemed, at bottom, to be rather closer to her.

I have to admit he always makes me feel at ease. He has his feet on the ground. I feel good when I'm with him. For the same reason she felt happy when visiting Visate, where the sounds and sometimes the smells of working life reached even the tennis court. And so, with both of them showing little caution, it was natural that their mutual attraction should grow.

The physical union of a couple of young people is one of nature's goals. Ambrogio, who consciously avoided sensuality—it was a firm part of his upbringing—was the first to notice a change. It happened by chance and was such a small occurrence that it almost went by unnoticed. While playing a match he was watching Colomba reach for a shot. She was concentrating on reaching with her racket, ran forward, and jumped for the shot. This made her skirt swirl up, showing her thighs up to her panties. Although normally she tried to hold her skirt down with her free hand when jumping for shots, this wasn't the first time this had happened. But this time it had an effect on Ambrogio. He felt a strong emotional reaction, more profound than anything he had ever felt before.

Hey, now! he told himself, acknowledging his reaction. *Some shock! Well, don't forget what else you've seen; you've seen so much death up close, for example.* Yes, but this was a totally different emotion, not something you could just file away by a rational effort. *But what a beast I am! Here she is, innocently playing tennis, and I'm staring at her legs . . . not on purpose, for sure, but for all that, I'm not a blind man.*

Colomba didn't notice his reaction, and neither did the other two. Although Ambrogio became distracted and thoughtful, both the others also happened to be thinking of other things.

On their bicycles on the way back, going downhill, they had the great stretch of the Alpine foothills on their right, and below them in the foreground the township of Nomanella. (This was the same road Pino and Sèp had traveled the previous year on their return from Switzerland.) Colomba rode her bicycle alongside Ambrogio's. Unaware of the still-flickering emotional storm in him, she said, "Rarely have I enjoyed a game so much. To play with you all, to play with you, Ambrogio, is really tremendous."

The young man nodded seriously, more somberly than his usual way, but didn't answer. Noting a slight reserve, Colomba asked herself if she'd said anything out of place.

In a way I suppose so, she thought. *I've paid him a compliment, and it's not my place to do that, as in any case it is he who should be making compliments.*

She looked sideways at him and smiled; he was silent.

Francesca rode a little behind, thinking about her Andrea; all that could be heard was the whispering sound of the bikes' wheels on the asphalt.

What a fine person Ambrogio is, he's really a fine person! They rode on, side by side. *Well, just look . . . we look just like sweethearts. Look . . .* She nearly spoke out loud in order to laugh with him at the thought, but immediately had second thoughts because—she realized—she really did like Ambrogio. She seemed to realize it only now. She put on the bicycle's brakes lightly. "It's . . . risky to ride close to one another like this", she murmured to herself, placing her bike behind Ambrogio's. *Of course I like him!* she concluded, and addressing him in the silence of her thoughts, *Yes, I like you to pieces, don't you know?*

They reached the first few houses on the outskirts of Nomana; Francesca had pulled alongside. As they rode through the town both Ambrogio and Francesca waved to friends as they rode past. They arrived at the piazza. "Look, do you mind if I leave you here and go straight home?" Colomba asked, braking to a stop.

The others stopped with her.

"I remember I promised my mother that I'd be home earlier. I just remembered . . ."

"Of course", Ambrogio replied. "If you promised her you'd better do so."

Francesca said, "We'll see you tomorrow, right?"

"Of course", Colomba said. There was a trace of uncertainty in her voice, not noticed by either of the other two.

"Well, goodbye, Francesca, goodbye Ambrogio, and . . . thanks."

"What? Don't even mention it; thank you, *cara, ciao,* Colombina."

"Goodbye, Colombina."

Colomba thought, Ciao, *Colombina* . . . Manno had called her that often. But how nice to hear the diminutive coming from Ambrogio. It was like being caressed by this young man, alive, speaking to her in his manly voice . . . it gave her a strange feeling of being protected.

Pedaling slowly homeward, Colomba daydreamed. She pushed open the front gate of *I dragoni* with her front wheel. She was so distracted that when she dismounted in the granite courtyard, she was unsure where to leave her bike. After having leaned it against a wall, she returned to it and moved it again a few yards away. She felt befuddled by the intrusion of practical things and people, even the presence of Graciosa, the porter's elderly daughter, who had greeted her pleasantly and would happily have indulged in a little gossip with her. She even thought to avoid her mother, but as she crossed the courtyard she told herself to stop. She shouldn't give too much importance to this infatuation, shouldn't let it bother her. Adopting a change of attitude, therefore, she called out, "Mama, Mama, I'm home."

Her mother was sitting on the veranda (the same place where old Eleonora used to pass her endless hours of solitude); she looked up from her sewing and smiled at her daughter through the windows.

After dinner Colomba asked herself if she should go to the Riva house less often, but couldn't make up her mind. She went to bed determined, "to start with", to go there only in the afternoons. (*After all, he spends the morning closeted away in the office*, she thought as she fell asleep.)

5

However, the next day she was already paying no heed to that nonsensical decision.

She was attracted by Ambrogio to the point where, despite her decision to do otherwise, she went to see him, as if prankishly, during the period he reserved for study. She would find some excuse to go to the office and interrupt him with some witticism. "Listen, O fount of knowledge, Francesca asked me ... this afternoon's plan, according to Francesca is ... so, what do you think? All right, all right, I'm going right now. Don't let such a little interruption upset you ..."

One morning she showed up using the same approach. "Hey, fount of knowledge, can I have a moment of your precious time? Francesca is preparing some radishes, although she says you don't like them. I don't want to get mixed up in this preparation of hers, so what vegetable do you want me to pick from the kitchen garden?"

"Vegetable! Vegetable?" he exclaimed, shaking his head in pretended annoyance. "Radishes!" He banged a hand on the table. "Out! Let me get on with my studying ... irrational females!"

Colomba, smiling, didn't move. "Come on, tell me, what vegetable should I go for?"

Delightful creature! She was wearing a white dress evocative of the times Manno used to compare her to Andromache, pretty beyond words. Pretending to be angry, Ambrogio looked at her. Unable to remain sitting, he got to his feet. "Now I'll give you radishes", he threatened and rushed at her mock threateningly.

Instead of running away, faking fear as he expected, Colomba fell into a defensive stance, holding up her arms as if to protect herself. Something within her, some sweet emotion, kept her there. Ambrogio grabbed her hands and gave them a playful shake. "The vegetables, eh? Radishes indeed! What makes you think . . ." He noticed that he was stuttering. "Colomba, you come here to . . ." He felt an irresistible desire to embrace her, to put his face close to hers. She seemed to be waiting, her lips half opened. *To the devil with everything else!* an urgent inner voice shouted. *Now, yes, now, he'd . . . now what? Beast! Manno's dead, and this is his girl. He can't do anything, can't stop you. Come on, go ahead, you ravening beast!*

He let go of Colomba's hands. "I'm sorry", he said to her in an altered voice. "I nearly lost my head. Forgive me."

Colomba shook her head no. He shouldn't take it so hard. Nothing had happened. They were just joking around. Let's continue, why not?

"Right, well, goodbye", Ambrogio said, turning around and going back to his desk. Colomba stayed where she was for a little while, then went, closing the door.

Ambrogio didn't sit down. After the door closed he started pacing up and down. *Quiet! Take it easy, cool down! But . . . what happened? Well, if at my age I've felt a physical desire for a woman, that's natural. Yes, it's natural, just as it's natural to dream about these things while asleep, to feel physical needs. Nothing wrong with that, that's nature; the important thing is to keep a grip on the beast within, not to allow it to take over. That's right. And as far as Colomba is concerned . . .*

The mere fact of thinking about her brought back the feelings of desire. What an attractive woman! My God! Was it possible that such an attractive girl existed anywhere else in the world? *Keep cool,* he told himself, trying to view things from a rational viewpoint. *After all, even though she is—was—Manno's girl, now that he's not here, nobody can reproach me if I get closer to her in an honorable way. On the contrary, the people who are versed in ethics—Father Mario, Father Carlo Gnocchi—would tell me that life can't be detained. One ought not to worship the past, that a living being (in this case, two) shouldn't be sacrificed for the departed who . . . yes, they say such things, and doubtless they're right, very right. But above all, despite all that, I'd never be sly enough to take Manno's girl, period. And I've no reason to feel badly; everything depends on being able to be resolute, to hold back while there's time. It's all dependent on that.*

He continued pacing back and forth. *But now I seem to lack this minimum strength of character; I don't seem to have it at all. My God, what sadness!*

6

The next few days were hard for Ambrogio. If it hadn't been nearly the end of August, if Colomba had been staying longer in Nomana, perhaps his will-power wouldn't have been enough, in which case their future lives would have been different. But August was nearly over, and then one night after dinner Colomba and her parents came to say goodbye.

Colomba's father, a doctor, took the opportunity to suggest that Gerardo buy *I dragoni*. "With all the children you have . . . and soon the older ones will need homes of their own, right?" Totally unaware of anything between his daughter and Ambrogio, he continued, "Your Ambrogio, for example, who is about to graduate. And on the other hand, the older ones . . ." It was evident he wanted to be rid of the villa, which was too much for him to retain.

To his children's surprise, Gerardo said that to tell the truth, he'd been thinking about it. He continued, "However, the item isn't budgeted on the program we're developing, aimed at expanding the mill. Because, Doctor, we have to think about the workers' children also, and if we don't busy ourselves in finding them some work, who will?"

Colomba's father couldn't decide if Gerardo was trying to be diplomatically negative (*Perhaps to keep the price of the villa down?*) or what. Ambrogio was listening attentively. *Here's Father planning on expanding, and he's said nothing about it to us!*

"Well," the doctor said, "look, if you like . . . if you want to give it more thought and later decide to go ahead, you can telephone me."

"Right. Because I think you're right. Soon my children will want to start their own families." Gerardo, adopting a rhetorical tone (a common fault among the self-taught), added, "And what is one to expect? That's life; the children go forward, pushing us to one side a little . . ."

The next morning Colomba, sweet Colombina, departed, left Nomana, left it for good. Soon after, under pressure from Fortunato (and having given it some thought), Gerardo went along with his son's reasoning ("This is the time to buy, buy on faith. With inflation the way it is, if later you need cash you'll be able to sell for double or even triple the buying price") and ended up buying *I dragoni*.

As a result Colomba didn't have any reason to return to the town. Her graceful figure, her striking young face, the varicolored skirts that delighted the eye of all who met her ("How pretty . . . how pretty . . .")—all of these were no longer to be seen in Nomana. The swallows no longer swooped around her in cheeky gallantry on the bright piazza. Colomba simply disappeared, just as so many pretty girls before her, whether poor or well to do, flashy or unaffected; just as Giustina had gone, with her dark eyes and very tall, slim figure, wearing clogs; and others before as well, years and years ago, women of whom all memory had been lost.

7

The next Sunday, leaving church with his father after Mass, Ambrogio looked around at the people coming out of the church, instinctively searching for Colomba, but didn't see her. Then he remembered and once again felt desolate.

Gerardo paused a while in the church square, as was his custom. The crowd consisted of the usual people. (*Colomba has gone away, and yet here everything continues as before. How is it possible?*) And in fact everything did continue as before. There was the postman Chin, who as usual on holidays had pressed his hair flat with brilliantine. He looked citified and somewhat strange. Giuliaccio, with his arms hanging toward the back and unusual manner of walking because of a damaged spinal column.

A few paces away from Ambrogio and Gerardo were the quiet figure of Pierello's mother (Ambrogio had greeted her cordially enough, saying only "good morning". "Good morning", she had replied, not feeling much like talking); the two cousins Tea and Isa, former students, the former small and homely and the latter a bit horsy; and the teacher Quadri Dodini, who worked at the Monza convent. Nowadays she was more crippled, although it was little noticed, and she descended the church steps unusually slowly, leaning on her cane.

One of Father Mario's young choirboys—they had all started emerging from the church door at a run—accidentally jostled the teacher, and although he was some distance away, Gerardo instinctively made a gesture as if to support her, but she was in fact aided by the town drunk, Romualdo, who at that moment was sober. He grabbed her by the arm in time to prevent her falling. She blushed and thanked him, then descended the few remaining steps in as much of a hurry as she could manage. Meanwhile Romualdo, having for once been able to assist someone else and as a means of prolonging his good deed, shouted after the running boy's companions—not the guilty jostler himself, who had immediately disappeared—who continued to exit the church on the run, glancing at him without understanding why he was shouting.

"These children! Did you see? They came close to . . .", exclaimed Gerardo, shaking his head.

"Yes, you know how children are", Ambrogio answered distractedly.

"All children are the same", said Pierello's mother, who was standing nearby. "They have empty heads."

Gerardo, turning to her, smiled. Ambrogio, nodding agreement, asked in dialect, "Ermelinda, how is your Piero?"

"I thank God, right now he's fine", she replied. "After all that has happened to him, poor boy."

Gerardo, stretching out the conversation, asked, "He's not here, right?"

"No, he tends to go to the second Mass with my husband. We can't all leave the house together as it's so isolated."

"Yes", said Ambrogio, as if meaning "I know."

"Now that the weather is good, I bring Martina with me," continued Piero's mother, "my youngest. I'm waiting for her now. She doesn't want to be with me in church. She sits up at the front pews with her school friends. You know how children are." She sighed, a little conventionally, out of habit. "Ah, the children . . ."

Over a hundred children had come out of the church and were milling about, chasing each other among the crowd. Most had begun to wind down or had distanced themselves in little groups; some remained, talking among the adults.

How many there are, crossed Gerardo's mind. *How many! And in order to live, all will need jobs in the future. And yet there are only so many jobs. How can we set about solving that problem?*

None of the nearby children looked worried, nor had they a thought about the future. Many of them—mimicking the adults—had their hands in their pockets, in carefree Sunday attitudes. They didn't worry; nether did they question life or become rebellious. These were children of families that in their majority had voted for the Christian party. *Trusting in what? Providence, that's right, perhaps, but also in us, those of us who'll have to plan and provide. And how do I respond, how do I do my part?* He turned to his son. "We'll have to decide. We need to do something, get busy."

Although he had his thoughts elsewhere, Ambrogio understood his father's line of thought. "Yes, Father. I agree, as you know."

"Here she is at last, my Martina", exclaimed Ermelinda. "You see, she's the last to arrive." She called out, "Martina, hey, Martina."

Hearing her mother's voice, the girl looked around and spotted her. Her face lit up and she came toward her.

"Come here, little mouse", the mother said, taking the child by the hand. "Come on, say hello to these gentlemen."

"Good morning." The young girl shyly lowered her eyes.

"Hello there, Pork Chop", Ambrogio replied, in dialect.

Pork Chop—her older brother Piero sometimes called her that. Martina raised her eyes to Ambrogio and smiled.

"You answer to that, Pork Chop, eh? Piero also calls you that, right?"

"Yes."

"And what else does he call you, your brother Piero?"

"Chocolate Eater."

"That's good", Gerardo observed, bending to pat the girl's head. He felt a tenderness for the child, as when he caressed his own youngest daughter. "What a pretty girl!"

"Say hello to Piero for me", Ambrogio said to Ermelinda. "Tell him to show up here, some Sunday at least."

"Thank you, I'll tell him", the woman answered.

They all turned, heading for home.

"The devaluation of the lire can help us, you understand?" Gerardo resumed his previous topic. He hadn't stopped thinking about the factory expansion. "We can sell the surplus stock we have stored away, and at current prices it's real cash. We can buy looms. One can find them, even if they're not new. The real problem is to acquire land. And this, this is the problem we should concentrate on, you understand?"

"Yes, Father."

Gerardo gestured toward the crowd with his chin. "We need to do something."

"Yes, agreed." *And here I was thinking about girls. Well, not about girls in general. I was thinking about Colomba. That's different. Well, in any case . . .* "Look, Father, if you agree, I could leave the books for a few months. That'll free me to . . ."

"No. You'll not leave the books. Don't even think about it."

"Right."

8

In September of that year—1946, nearly a year and a half after the war's end—Michele finally was repatriated. He arrived at the Milan railway station as midnight struck on a working day. Like all his POW companions—about a hundred, in two cars added to the rear of a regular train—he was emotionally affected, but above all he was tired. On his first day in Italy, at the border, he'd sent his uncle and aunt in Monza a telegram advising them of his arrival. He was already aware of his father's death from an exchange of a year's sparse correspondence between Italy and the POW camp. He had received two letters, one from the uncle and aunt and the other from Ambrogio. Ambrogio's letter had brought him greetings from Tito Valli, the Nomana soldier repatriated from Susdal in the autumn of the previous year. *So,* Michele told himself as the train pulled slowly into the station, *they ought to have an idea at home of what's been happening to me.*

But home? What home? Was the apartment in Nova still his, three years after his father's death? He went to the carriage window, joining Father Turla, who moved over to give him room. Michele said, "We're a bit crowded, eh?"

"Nothing like the train car we rode in between Crinovaya and Oranchi. Remember that?" replied Father Turla happily. His health had improved no end.

"Do I remember?!" growled Michele. *When 438 of us started out, and 195 of us arrived alive!* he thought. All the others had been thrown from the cars into the snow, morning after morning. Who knows if and when (and how) they'd eventually been buried . . . and that killing cold, the thirst that drove them mad, the filthy cars covered in sh——, and the disgusting toilet hole in one corner, through which they collected snow to drink. And . . . but enough of that. One ought to know enough not to think of things like that.

Father Turla's thoughts must have run along the same lines. Having caused his companion to remember those events, he now attempted to distract him.

"Well, Milan is . . . as always, the great Milan", he finally said, unable to think of anything else to say.

Michele smiled and thought, *Yes, right, a priest's rhetoric.*

The central station's enormous metal arches still showed bomb damage here and there. At that time of day the station was nearly deserted. There was more light than in wartime, but not much.

"I don't know if my people will be here waiting", murmured the priest. "We're getting here at least two hours late."

"You see those people, the small groups over there, where the platform starts?" Michele said. "I think they're waiting for us." He added, thoughtfully, "Who knows if my uncle and aunt will also be here."

But they weren't. As the train came to a stop with one final jerk, and the waiting relatives ran, clearly excited and emotional, toward the compartment in which the returning soldiers were traveling, he could see that his people weren't among those waiting. "They're not here, they're not here", he repeated in a low voice to both himself and Father Turla. The latter, having spotted his relatives, suddenly backed away from the window and turned to run out into the station. Michele, continuing to look out for his relatives, suddenly saw his friend Ambrogio, who, on seeing him at the train's window, began waving and running toward him, shouting, "Tintori, Michele Tintori!"

Reaching the train's window, Ambrogio reached up and grabbed his friend's hand, shaking it. "You've arrived . . . thank God! Great! Michele, you've arrived, you're back!" Ambrogio had a pretty woman at his side, or was it his wife? (*Has he married already? He didn't write me about that.*) The girl had her face lifted toward Michele, nodding with emotion, tears in her eyes. When she started crying, he recognized her by the youthful way she moved her lips. It was Francesca, sure. And he hadn't recognized her! What a pretty girl she was for sure! Francesca, who no longer braided her hair and now had it swept up in a chignon. Good heavens, if only his Alma could also have been there! In all the journey from Susdal he'd thought of her constantly, with intense emotion—his Alma, his Almina . . .

"Welcome, Michele!" Ambrogio cried out, the emotion of meeting making him too tonguetied to say anything sensible. "Michele!"

"Thanks for having come", Michele said and repeated, leaning down toward them from the window, "Thanks for coming."

"You know, up to just an hour ago, your uncle and aunt were here?" Ambrogio told him. "Then, as they weren't sure you'd be arriving tonight, they decided to catch the last train back to Monza, because your aunt isn't very well. But come on, get down off the train so we can talk . . . talk more calmly."

Already many of the soldiers were leaving the train. Michele pulled a nearly empty bag down from the luggage rack, the bag he'd been given, along with the uniform he wore, by the senior officer at the Udine stop. Then he joined his friends on the station.

"*Omnia mea mecum porto*", he said, showing them the bag. Francesca nodded, smiling, and Ambrogio leaped at him with open arms, holding him close and kissing him. "The main thing is that now you're home. It seems unbelievable!"

"Let me give you a hug, too," said Francesca, "as if you were one of my brothers." She gave him a hug and also kissed him. "Michele," she said gently, "we know you've been ... been very brave."

"What are you saying?" he joked, moved by the affectionate reception.

"Yes, it is true", she insisted. "Just the other day Ambrogio told us again of your behavior during the retreat, when you were the only one maintaining order among the men."

"Me?" Michele turned to Ambrogio. "Are you crazy?"

"Why do you say that?" Ambrogio answered. "The second day when we were trapped in that pocket, in Posnyakoff. Have you forgotten?" (He thought, *The same morning when Bonsaver died ... if only he were here, too.*)

"Oh, you mean that ... that was nothing!" said Michele, remembering at last.

Around each returning soldier little groups had gathered, consisting not only of their friends and relatives but also relatives of still-missing soldiers, mainly mothers and sisters hoping to hear some news.

Ambrogio asked, "Has anyone from my regiment come with you on the train?"

"No, nobody from the Eighth Artillery, nobody."

Next to them was Father Turla, surrounded by relatives—all were blonds and had the same Bergamasco accent as he; in the group were two children, even more light haired—attempting to control his emotions, but without success. Tears ran down his manly, emaciated face.

"You see that chaplain there?" Michele said. "If you only knew the brutish experiences he and I have lived through ... such awful ... but I don't want to talk like this, particularly not tonight. I'm really tired out."

"You're right", Ambrogio said. "It's better not to talk."

Father Turla, although among his people, was not yet to find peace. A frightened-looking older couple, who had been questioning more than one of the arriving soldiers and had later vainly gone inside the empty train to search it, were nearby, holding onto each other's arms. "Lieutenant, Chaplain ... you're the Lieutenant Chaplain Father Turla, is that right?" asked the man. "We've been told to speak to you."

"Yes, please, go ahead", the priest answered, wiping tears away with his hand. "How may I help you?"

"We're the parents of Captain Riccardo Barrel from Milan, who arrived ... who should have arrived with your group, because we received a notice from military headquarters. But we ... we haven't seen him."

"Ah, yes, Lieutenant Riccardo Barrel," Father Turla said, correcting them, "from Milan, yes. Of course he's here. I'll find him for you right away."

797

"No", insisted the man. (The wife, leaning forward slightly, moved her lips as if repeating her husband's words.) "We've seen that officer. Yes, he's called Riccardo Barrel also, but he's a lieutenant. He's not our son. Our son is a captain."

Father Turla thought, *Among the POW officers there wasn't any Barrel other than the lieutenant. There wasn't another Barrel, at least among the officers.*

Turning to the man, he said, "Have you, in these last few months, let's say during the past twelve months, have you received any letters from your son? Or maybe news about him from any returning POWs?"

"No", murmured the husband.

The woman, her mouth barely moving, also whispered an almost inaudible agreement.

"But, that's ... nearly normal, wouldn't you say?" asked the man, clearly distressed. "Isn't that right?"

The priest nodded thoughtfully. "Yes, of course." He looked around for Lieutenant Barrel and gestured for him to come over. "So, essentially, before hearing from the military, you had no news from your son?"

"No, the last letter we had from him was dated in December of '42, the fourteenth of December", explained the husband. God only knew how many times he'd talked about that letter.

"The notification from military HQ, when did that arrive?"

"Yesterday afternoon", the man said, his lips trembling. "For the two of us, you understand, it was like a coming to life. You understand? We didn't sleep all last night. Then today ... for us, it has been impossible to think of anything else!"

Father Turla said, "At the border crossing we were told that our names would immediately be sent to the regional headquarters so that they could advise parents ... let me ask, in the notification you received did they include the rank?"

The old couple looked at each other with anguish. "No. Only the first name and surname."

"Please wait here a moment." The chaplain took Barrel—the lieutenant— aside. "Do you know if your parents were notified of your return? Are any of your people here to meet you?" he asked.

The lieutenant gestured no. "No," he said, "there's nobody here."

"And during your time in prison, did you meet any captain with your name?"

Again the lieutenant, clearly distressed, gestured no. "There was no Captain Barrel. I already told these people earlier."

"Oh, poor souls ...", murmured the priest, returning to the older couple. It was clear now that the coincidence in names had caused a bureaucratic mistake. How to explain it now to the parents ... he felt great pity for them.

"It'll be best to get in touch with the military HQ that sent you the notification", he said. "Listen, I'm staying here overnight, in Milan, and tomorrow" (at these truly heroic words, his family looked at him in consternation), "I'll accompany you to military HQ in the morning. Once there, we'll be able to clear this up."

"No, we can't wait until tomorrow", exclaimed the woman. "If we wait until tomorrow . . . Riccardo will never return, you understand?"

She moved her lips silently and said no more. Then she grasped her husband fiercely by the arm and began a mournful keening.

"She's not well", her husband whispered. Then, helped by the chaplain and his own relatives and followed by Lieutenant Barrel, the man led his wife to a stone bench on the platform and made her sit, keeping hold of her hands. "Riccardo won't be coming back." Her husband protested. "No, what are you saying, no . . ." He looked into the chaplain's face, mutely seeking some confirmation or support.

Father Turla remained there, tired out. He asked himself what he could do for these poor people, but nothing occurred to him.

Soon the man lifted a finger, as if an idea had just occurred to him. The chaplain noticed a change in his mournful expression; he had brightened up. "The car in front", the man said. "Maybe Riccardo came in the car in front, and we haven't looked for him there."

"But . . .", said the chaplain. "No, listen . . ."

The man released his wife's hand. One of Father Turla's relatives hurried forward to hold it. "Look after her, please, will you?" he said, "while I go and look. I'll be back soon." He got up from the bench and walked toward the train, as if in a trance.

The chaplain followed him. "No, listen, Signor Barrel, listen to me for a moment." He detained the man when he already had one foot on the train's step; he put an arm around the man's shoulders and started talking to him.

Ambrogio looked at Michele. "Now, you come along", he said. "Enough, you can't continue." But after having said that, he searched in his pocket. "Just a moment, look, did you have Bersaglieri from the Third on the train?"

"Yes, a few, three or four."

"Introduce me, please." He had taken a postcard-sized photograph of Stefano from his pocket. "Which ones are they?"

"That one, over there, to start with; come on."

"It's a picture of Stefano, Giovenzana, Stefano, my comrade from Nomana, who was in the Third Bersaglieri", said Ambrogio, indicating the photograph. "He's still missing."

"Yes, I see", said Michele.

It turned out that none of the Bersaglieri of the train remembered ever having seen Stefano in prison.

Ambrogio wasn't the only one showing pictures of missing soldiers. Various of the returned soldiers were here and there examining photographs in the poor light. One or two asked for some additional detail of the missing soldier, but all returned the circulating pictures with a negative shake of the head.

The missing captain's mother had meanwhile calmed down in her grief, though she continued crying wordlessly. Father Turla and his relatives went with her and her husband toward the station's pharmacy. The other soldiers also began moving out, some toward the exit, others, who were connecting with other trains, toward the station's main hall.

9

Michele, between Ambrogio—who carried his bag slung from one shoulder—and Francesca, went slowly down the stairway toward the exit.

They left through the tall doorway leading to the street. The summer evening was pleasant, not too warm. The houses surrounding the vast piazza illuminated by lampposts looked exactly the same to the returning soldier. *Milan,* he thought with new emotion, and, *Home!* and also, *My father is no longer here,* but he said not a word.

"The car is over there." Ambrogio pointed, taking note of his friend's mood. "Come on, let's go!"

In the brief time they'd been together, he'd already given Michele some of the news. The house in Nova was still his, even though his father had died intestate, and was presently occupied by homeless evacuees. He told Michele that his aunt and uncle wanted him to go and live with them in Monza, at least until his own house became available ("which will take months, perhaps years") and that they had prepared a room for him and expected him to go to Monza as soon as he arrived. ("They're mad; we explained to them that it wouldn't be possible. Back in Nomana everyone is expecting you; if we arrived without you, we'd get lynched." Francesca smiled in agreement.) He told him of Manno's death. ("In my letters I didn't say anything because . . . you know . . .")

"How many letters did you write me?"

"Three, exactly three."

"I only received one."

The car traveled through Milan's streets toward the piazza Loreto. Although his thoughts were mainly on Manno, Michele was also aware of the sights around him. The bomb damage had been unbelievably severe, and much of the destruction could still be seen. Despite the darkness, there was also evidence of the resumption by the people of their daily activities. They passed a Jeep. "Those are Americans, right?"

"Right", Ambrogio confirmed.

"What a blessing, the Americans!" Michele said. "I don't know yet how you regard them here, but if a few of us came through alive, it was because of the soy beans they sent to Russia, specifically for us POWs, even though our countries were still at war. Do people here in Italy know about the consignments of soy beans?"

"No, I don't think so . . ."

"In Austria it was clear that the Americans take the Russians seriously; we only felt we'd been freed when we reached the American zone there."

"They're a marvelous people", Ambrogio agreed. "You know, if they weren't here . . . It's a fact; excluding the local Reds, everyone here likes them. Some even admire them to such an extent that in my opinion it is excessive."

Leaving Milan, they reached Sesto San Giovanni, where here and there the walls were splotched with untidy Communist and Socialist slogans and drawings of hammers and sickles. Michele felt ashamed by these, even though Ambrogio, noticing his reaction, took the trouble to explain. "You shouldn't be worried. They won't make it. While the Americans are here, and the English, and they'll stay here for as long as they're needed. Besides, after the June elections, it's clear that they are a minority."

"They're wretches who haven't the faintest idea of what communism really is", Michele murmured. "Just . . . when was it . . . just four days ago, in Galicia, we were stopped for more than an hour next to a sealed freight train, overloaded with men and women, Polish men and women, being deported. You should have heard the way the children cried out, asking for something to drink. If people in Italy were aware of these deportations . . . but I'll tell you more later", Michele said, his voice betraying his tiredness.

"The Reds in the factories try to intimidate the other workmen, to make them toe the line," Ambrogio explained, "but most do not remain passive and generally oppose the Reds. Particularly the members of Azione Cattolica and the ACLI; it's magnificent. You don't know about the ACLI? It's the new organization for Christian laborers; the Pope himself supports it. But we'll talk more calmly later."

"Well, you can be sure that I'll become involved in confronting these murderers and dupes," said Michele determinedly, "and I'll do all I can."

10

After leaving Sesto, they passed through Monza. Here the ambiance—traditional and peaceful—was different, relaxed. The same was the case with the countryside and the villages in Brianza, farther on. Now Michele's thoughts were concentrated on Alma, and the thoughts brought to mind the two verses—pronounced to the cadence of the train wheels—which had kept up his spirits during the unending journey from Susdal to Milan: "*Signor che volesti creare—per me questo amore lontano . . .*" Lord, you who have willed the creation—of this distant love for me ... Soon he'd see the real Alma! In just a matter of minutes ... incredible!

They arrived at a Nomana that was quiet in sleep. The gate to the garden, however, was open, and the car went up the drive, its headlights fanning out flickeringly to illuminate the grass, then cutting a path to the front door. When Ambrogio switched off the motor and the three of them stepped out, it was nearly 2:00 in the morning.

Through the windows they saw the inside staircase light come on, and then the lights in the lobby.

The thirteen-year-old Rodolfo, in pajamas and slippers, had come down to open the door. "Did Michele arrive or not? Ah, look, there you are, hello, hello, Michele!" he nearly shouted. "When midnight came and went, we gave up waiting and went to bed. How are you, Michele?"

The young officer shook the boy's hand. "If I'm not mistaken, you're Rodolfo ..."

"Yes." The boy looked him up and down with curiosity. Their guest wore a new Italian army uniform, the same khaki color as the English; even so, he understood that Michele must have gone through hard times. In one hand he held the nearly empty new bag; he looked like a poor man who had been outfitted from head to toe. Turning toward the stairs, Rodolfo shouted upstairs, "People, you folks up there, come on down, everybody come down! Michele has arrived!"

"Don't shout like that", Francesca scolded him. "Are you mad?"

But the boy, still facing up the stairs, kept shouting, "Wake up, everyone, it's Michele, Michele is here, come on down!"

The three of them followed Rodolfo into the house, while from upstairs there were sounds of movement. "The only ones not here are Fortunato and Pino", Ambrogio told his guest. "Everyone else is here."

"I'll make you a sandwich or something right away", Francesca said, slipping out of her coat. "In the meantime, if you want to freshen up, you remember where the bathroom is, right?"

Michele smiled his thanks. "Yes, right."

But before he left the reception area, Alma appeared at the top of the stairs; she wore a sky blue wool housecoat, her braided chestnut hair ran down to her breast, just as he remembered it, and she was smiling in her usual enigmatic way. "Oh, Michele, dear Michele!" she said in her charming voice. She held out her hand and stood, still as a statue.

"Alma!" exclaimed Michele, whose heart was beating fast enough nearly to jump out of his chest. "Almina!"

"Come on!" Rodolfo shouted at his sister. "Come down. Don't stand there struck dumb."

Behind Alma Giudittina appeared. The eleven-year-old was in pajamas and looked sleepy. Her hair was down her back in a single braid, and, instead of greeting Michele, she shouted down at Rodolfo, "People, folks, come down!" she mimicked him, adding, "Monkey!" Then she turned to Michele and, standing demurely, greeted him.

But Michele had eyes only for Alma. Look at her, she's real, she's part of the world, she really exists, and she's here. *My God, thank you! God, that you should grant me this!* he thought to himself emotionally. He remembered the crazy times during which he'd thought about her, but this wasn't the time to return to the past, to dramatize what happened back there. He had to behave well and leave her with a good impression, but how was it best to do so? He felt his face had gone pale, that all his blood had flooded his heart. What was happening to him?

"Alma", he repeated, frozen to the spot. He felt that if he took just one step he could lose his balance and fall down.

Alma started to come down the stairs, unaware of the internal tumult she was causing him. Wearing satin slippers and with the collar of her light blue housecoat turned up around her slim neck, she approached smiling and offered her hand, which Michele took. "We meet again, Alma."

"God knows how many troubles you've lived through, Michele," she said, "since that day, you remember, when you were here, the last time."

He nodded. "I've certainly experienced many . . ."

"Ambrogio told us you're alive not because of one miracle, but due to many miracles, one after the other."

"That's right, for sure. But now . . ." He stopped.

"But now?"

"Now . . . I've seen you again."

She smiled at the effusiveness and went quiet for a moment, then, "You still intend to write?" she asked.

"Well, what else could I do?"

"That's true." The girl smiled again; to her, this explained his somewhat strange behavior. Her adolescent mind also thought, "I should feel inhibited talking to a writer, but it's funny, I'm not."

How charming she was! To tell the truth, Michele didn't find her exactly as he'd remembered her—not entirely—yet, despite that, she fulfilled his expectations more than ever. *God knows very well how to make his masterpieces,* he thought, *not like us, with our imaginings!* and felt like saying so out loud. But all he could think of were panegyrics, hymns of praise rather than words, the saying of which would have been an open declaration of love, madness. "How old are you now?" he asked.

"I'm nineteen."

"Hey, hello!" Giudittina called out. Having arrived from the stairs down to their level, and having been silent so far, she felt that it was her turn to welcome their guest. "Welcome!" she shouted and made as if about to leap up to grab Michele around the neck, but Rodolfo held her back, grabbing her braided hair and pulling. "Who's a monkey now, hey? Who but you?"

"You two", said Alma. "Is this any way to behave?" Then, easing Rodolfo out of the way with one hand, she turned to Giudittina. "Come, Giudittina, say hello properly."

Giudittina held her hand out to the returning soldier, bowed slightly, and said, "Good evening, that's to say, good morning."

"Good morning or good evening?" Michele said, keeping hold of her hand. "What's the idea of being so formal with me?"

"Well," she said, "I have to show good manners. If not, I get shouted at." The young officer smiled, amused.

Ambrogio had gone out to park the car. Francesca was in the kitchen. "Come," Alma said to Michele, "let's go to the dining room and sit down."

She went ahead of him and put on the lights. Michele followed, as if under a spell. He noticed the girl's waist, held close by the robe's belt. It made her look very slim, virginal.

They sat at either side of the table. Michele wished time would stand still, that they could stay there like that, both together in the dining room, looking at each other in silence, relieved only by the ticking of the clock. What a marvelous, incredible moment—he told himself—he was really living this. One of those moments in life that come as a real compensation for other, more tragic times.

Giudittina and Rodolfo followed them into the dining room. The soldier smiled at them, but it was difficult for him to think of anything other than Alma, who looked at him with her honest brown eyes, a little surprised by his behavior. She explained it out loud with the thought that had come to her shortly before. "You writers are all a little strange."

Michele nodded at her, then smiled and shrugged his shoulders, as if silently saying, "What can we do about it?"

"Listen," Alma suggested, "why don't you tell me about a . . . a miracle? I mean to say, one of these experiences you've had." Then she immediately added, "Oh, of course, not now. What am I saying? It's not the right time."

Michele said, "Why not? If it . . ." He turned to include the two youngsters. "If it interests you. Let's see, now, a miracle . . ." he said, while thinking. "But why look any farther back? Isn't it enough that you're here? Who has ever seen a prettier miracle?" then continued. "All right, let's see . . . well, a kind of miracle—and I'm not joking—was what we had from Saint Anthony. A priest from Bergamo, a Father Turla—he arrived in Milan tonight on the same train—experienced it. Ambrogio and Francesca also met him tonight."

"Yes, it's true", Francesca said, having come into the room to fetch some plates. "Maybe he's still there at the central station, helping console those two poor people."

"Which poor people?" Alma asked.

Rodolfo and Giudittina, awaiting Michele's tale, had also seated themselves, and now both looked at their older sisters with impatience, showing they didn't want interruptions.

"The parents of a missing soldier", Michele said to Alma and left it there; he didn't want her saddened. Life went on, even when death took a hand. The two youngsters had their arms folded on the table, their chins resting on their little fists, looking at him expectantly.

"To tell the truth, I didn't witness this miracle myself," Michele qualified, "because I wasn't in that particular marching column. They were nearly all Alpine troops. Father Turla told me about it and repeated it more than once. Even when we were suffering terribly from hunger, I've heard him say, 'Ah, if Saint Anthony would only repeat the miracle of the bread!'"

"Well, to keep the story short, what happened was this. The marching column of Alpine prisoners had been going for fifteen days, more or less, without having eaten, heading for a horrible place called Crinovaya. It was in winter, in February, and many people had already died from the cold, exhaustion, or more probably from hunger, because the Alpine soldiers could usually put up with the fatigue and the cold. Well, Father Turla was at the rear of the column, with the tired people who had dropped back, dragging themselves along. If someone dropped out, nobody had the strength to help them along, and the guard would . . ."

"Would what?!?" a frightened Giudittina asked, her hands over her mouth.

"Well, it was a very tough situation, very tough indeed, and Father Turla was thinking, *If we only had a piece of bread.* A vision of Saint Anthony of Padua had been in his mind, the miracle of multiplying the loaves for the poor. *And who could be poorer than ourselves,* he thought. *Here we are, hanging on to life by a thread, no more, that's all we have . . .* He directed his thoughts to Saint Anthony, you understand? *Saint Anthony, answer me; who could be poorer than we are, eh, who?* He was almost angry. *You know what? I think you should repeat your miracle for us, here and now, to be fair.* He kept repeating the thought. It was one of those situations when one single thought gets stuck in your mind and then becomes a sort of obsession."

"You mind what Michele tells you. He's not just talking for the sake of it", Ambrogio said as he came into the room. "This is the kind of thing that has happened to me also."

"Me, too", Giudittina said.

"Oh, you . . .", Rodolfo said, disdainfully.

"Well, the column had reached a small town with isbas all around. They're sort of small houses with thatched roofs—nearly all small towns in Russia are like that—and the priest started praying again: *Look, Saint Anthony, why don't you bring us some bread. Just place it over there in the snow, where that shadow is, in the shape of a big loaf of bread. Poor me,* he thought, *here I am seeing bread everywhere I look!*" Michele continued, "and yet, the shadow in the snow looked just like a round loaf; could it be true?"

Father Turla rubbed his eyes. *Now I've even got to where I'm seeing mirages*, he thought, but without taking his eyes off the shape in the snow. The vision was just a step or two away from the path; the entire column of men had gone right past it. When he got near enough, he bent down and reached out and picked it up. It was, in fact, a loaf, a great big Russian loaf, only slightly dusted with snow."

Giudittina slapped an open hand on the table.

"To make sure he wasn't mistaken, the chaplain broke the loaf in two; there was no mistake, it was bread, and it was freshly baked, not frozen. He said, 'Hey, look. Saint Anthony's made us a miracle', and showed it to the other exhausted soldiers, who also couldn't believe their own eyes. Then he divided the bread and ate with them."

Michele had been talking more to the children than to Alma; when he finished, he looked at her, nodded, and said seriously, "I know that it sounds like a fairy tale, one of those fables, the 'flowers' of Saint Francis, but just as sure as there's a God, that's what happened. Not only did Father Turla tell me, others also repeated the story, including an Alpine soldier of the Cuneense Brigade who had himself eaten some of the bread. Later, when we tried to reconstruct what had happened, we figured that some Russian woman must surely have left the loaf near to where the column passed. The country women of Russia still have good Christian souls, yet they had to be careful, because it was forbidden to help POWs. Saint Anthony must have inspired her to do it, and whatever happened, Father Turla found the bread, having sent the invocation to the saint."

"Why a Russian woman?" Giudittina cut in. "It wasn't necessary. Saint Anthony could have put it there himself, just like that."

"But then it wouldn't have been a Russian loaf", her brother Rodolfo explained amiably. "Do you see? It would have been Italian bread, what with Saint Anthony coming from Padua."

"Oh, right, that's true."

Michele was looking at Alma's beautiful, attentive face. How natural it seemed to talk about these things to her! "With her, I seem to go back to relive those wonderful Middle Ages."

From upstairs they heard Francesca's voice, telling her mother and father of Michele's arrival.

"Oh, I'm sorry", Michele said, coming back to the present with a bump. "Sorry I've awakened everybody. I . . . I really shouldn't have agreed to come here at this time of night."

"No, don't mention it again", Alma pleaded with him, then added, "With us, you've no need to stand on ceremony, please. We all really love you."

"Yes, I know", replied Michele. "I'm beginning to realize . . ." then went silent and resumed gazing at her.

But his contemplation of Alma was quickly interrupted by the arrival in the dining room of Gerardo and Giulia, followed by the customary greetings. Michele really liked Alma's parents: Giulia, because of the impression he had of her as mother not only to her own offspring but to everybody. (Before he'd shipped out Michele had noticed this, and now he remembered.) Gerardo he liked for his steadfast work as a manufacturer; he'd seen in Russia the results of a lack of enterprising people. *These bosses are essential in the constant battle of man against miserable conditions*, he thought, contrary to the analyses in most of the Marxist texts. He was totally convinced of this.

Soon after they'd all sat down at the table, Alma went to the kitchen accompanied by Francesca and Noemi (who had also come downstairs, her hair uncombed); the "little statue" began to take over the arrangements in the kitchen, to the point where the other two understood that she was going to serve Michele with her own two hands and probably wouldn't allow anyone to help.

I I

After they had eaten a generous snack—in which they were joined by the thirteen-year-old Rodolfo—they all went upstairs. Manno's room had been prepared for Michele. "And it's your room not only for the next few months, but for the whole year and beyond, for as long as you like", Giulia told him. "Have I made myself clear? You do understand? You've been through some terrible experiences, my own boy, and on top of that you've returned to find your father no longer with us. All of us—not just Ambrogio—but all of us want you to feel our friendship."

There were pajamas on the bed. "They're new. Nobody has used them", Giulia told him. "They're a little big for Ambrogio but should fit you. I had them made for when we were expecting Manno's return . . ." She stopped, her eyes filling with tears, then left the room, pausing only to bless him by making the sign of the Cross with her right hand. It was done humbly and with discretion, not like the great and solemn blessing Gerardo traced every night over his children's heads.

Michele couldn't fall asleep right away; he was too fatigued and too overwrought to be able to relax. His father came to mind; if he were still alive, no doubt they would have spent hours and hours talking together. And yet . . . there flashed into his mind the horrible vision of his poor father's face as it would be now, devastated by three years in the grave. (But his father, his spirit, wouldn't be like this, corrupt: he was in the glory of God, happy forever, together with Michele's mother.) Thinking dolefully about his father, there came into his mind the dead people cannibalized in Crinovaya, now all re-united in the valley (an enormous tangle of twenty-seven thousand bodies!), and he thought about those people in Oranchi who had been carried outside the tented infirmary when they showed the red skin eruptions of typhus. Virtually only the dead ever left the infirmary. One terrible night the men suffering from typhus—all of them convinced they were about to die—had raised up the only chaplain available there, dying on his cot, his eyes large and vague, looking grotesque in just a shirt and his underpants. A soldier had guided the priest's inert hand to grant final absolutions; the chaplain, with those staring eyes, started mumbling the formula for the rites, absolving all of them *in articulo mortis*. Later, once more placed on his own cot, the priest had continued mumbling words of absolution, yet didn't himself die. It was that priest, Father Brevi, who later . . . well, enough. Poor Father Brevi hadn't been repatriated; now he would be somewhere in Siberia, along with the other untameables who had strongly resisted conversion to the Communist doctrine. Who knows where he'd be at this moment? He was paying dearly for his courage, very dearly. Who knew if one day he'd come home . . . but, enough, enough. At least for a while . . . enough of these atrocious memories.

To rid his mind of such thoughts—here in Nomana, just as he'd done so, so many times while in prison—Michele's thoughts turned to Alma. (He'd fallen in love with her like that, evoking her memory this way. More than falling for a real girl, he'd fallen for her image. He didn't for the moment consider how unusual and a marvel it was that his meeting with the flesh-and-blood Alma hadn't disappointed him. He continued to think that she was the embodiment of that old antiphon: *Lord who created for me this distant love* . . . , and he found the thing quite natural, or nearly so.) The unbelievable part, if one thought about it, was really that Alma was now just steps away, separated by only a few walls . . . and here he was, inert, as he'd been when she had indeed been distant by thousands of miles. He turned over several times, unsettled in the bed, until, *Leave it, stop, try to relax*, he told himself. *What do you want? To knock on her door* . . . (he'd noticed which was the bedroom Alma shared with Francesca) *and tell her . . . tell her what?* "*Sorry to disturb you, Alma, I just want a little favor. Just continue sleeping peacefully, while I gaze at you.*" *Was that what you wanted to tell her? Enough, better try to sleep and not lie here awake until dawn.* With the coming of morning he'd see her and could gaze at her as much as he liked, become elated and . . . sing of her—he turned over in bed restlessly—that's it; sing to her as Dante had done with Beatrice and . . . He had already started to idealize Alma. Through his mind also flitted a practical side of the situation. *Careful! Almina belongs to a rich family, manufacturers* . . . While he, he was truly poor, without even a university degree, without a trade, without anything . . . how did the saying go? "Neither money nor talent", that was it. He was nearly asleep, but this last thought jerked him awake. Once more he was sleepless. Well, even so, "talent" he did have, most certainly. The possibility of writing was in him like a state of singular power, like his at times overwhelming power as a man, the possibility to procreate, which he had never yet used. What was more, the Lord had given him not only talent to write, but also, look here . . . here he was, only twenty-five years old and with a really extraordinary experience of men and life. Objectively, it was an enormous store of raw material.

Finally he slept, and soon sleep took away his tension. Outside his open window was the auspicious September nighttime of Lombardy, to which Manno, Stefano, and so many other youths had not returned. He, on the other hand, had come back, his long wanderings, backward and forward between the shores of life and the shades of fetid death, had come to an end. Life had been granted to him.

12

On the following day he awoke later than the rest of the household, all of whom had been careful not to disturb him with noise (especially Giudittina, who knew the importance of caring for someone who, even if indirectly, shared things with Saint Anthony).

When Michele went downstairs, Alma came up to him happily and hurried him into the dining room for breakfast. Ambrogio had already gone out (after having breakfasted standing up, a practice followed by farm and working people like his father, who had once been a laborer and to whom it seemed inappropriate to sit down to breakfast, enjoying the luxury of being surrounded by milk and coffee jugs). Almina made Michele sit down and brought him coffee ("Sorry, we're still using ersatz") and bread ("The bread is good; it's fresh") and, a surprise, fried eggs. (How long had it been since he'd tasted fried eggs? It was beyond his memory.) And she stayed with him to keep him company while he breakfasted, wearing an apron, her lovely smile framed by the chestnut braids resting on her breast.

"I've brought you the newspaper, if you want to see it later. Who knows how long it's been since you read one?"

"Yes, really, I'm very interested in seeing a paper."

Francesca and her mother, Giulia, also came during his breakfast to make sure their guest lacked for nothing. Before he'd finished eating Ambrogio came in, having gone to the mill to resolve some pressing matters. (Despite his father's instructions, he had not entirely ignored the factory in favor of his studies.) "Today I'm free," he announced, "and I can take you in the car to Monza and to Nova, wherever you like."

Michele demurred. "Please, no; no cars. Just lend me a bicycle."

"No, forget bicycles. By now you'll have forgotten how to ride one."

"No, Ambrogio, please find a bicycle I can use. I'll need one in any case to come and go when I visit you these days."

"Are you crazy? You're talking of moving out?! Well, here you are and here you stay, you hear me?"

"No, Ambrogio, listen . . ."

Finally Ambrogio loaned him his own bicycle—his old sporty bluish bike, with the strange flat handlebars—on which Michele, still wearing his uniform, rode to Monza. He had promised to return the next day, although they all begged him to come back that same night. The three females said, "Dinner will be ready for you. We'll be unhappy if you don't come." But even though he was moved by their pleas, he insisted, shaking his head.

When he left Almina felt extraordinarily alone, a horrible sensation that she had rarely experienced in her short life. She retired thoughtfully to the kitchen. Before returning to the factory, Ambrogio went to the kitchen and asked her for half a cup of coffee. "Do you know how many exams Michele has left to take?" Alma asked him, offering the coffee.

"At the university, you mean?"

"Yes."

"Oh, the poor fellow! It's as if he had all of them left to take. He took only a couple of minor exams, you know, and those he took only as reasons to get some leave from the army. But he's a good active fellow, so . . ."

He drank his ersatz coffee and smiled at his sister. *What a gentle being. With those braids and her apron she looks like a child at play,* he thought, then said, "Well, little statue, I'm going, goodbye", and left.

What a marvelous fellow Michele was, thought Alma, as she washed dishes in the sink. And, incredible as it seemed, there was no doubt; he'd shown he was interested in her; yes, more in herself than in Francesca. No one had done that so far. *And not only last night, when he might have been upset and tired, but this morning also, minutes ago. No doubt he's very happy to see me again, and . . . yes, that's it, even though it seems unbelievable . . . with happiness. All the time he was here, he showed his happiness at seeing me. I'm sure I'm not mistaken.*

Her mother came to her side, unaware of her feelings, of which as usual she gave no outward sign.

"You know, Mama," she said after a while, "I was thinking about what I must decide . . . I mean about whether or not to continue studying."

"Yes?"

Following her father's wishes, Alma had a few months ago graduated as a teacher. It was Gerardo's aim to have his boys graduate successfully from the university and his daughters at least to qualify as teachers, to ensure their daily bread.

"So?" her mother asked.

"Maybe the other day you gathered I had decided not to continue, but now I'm thinking of going ahead."

"Well, you still have time to make up your mind."

810

"Yes, but I'm having second thoughts. I mean, although I've not decided, I think I'll register at the university for a higher degree in teaching."

"Your father will be pleased."

"What about you?"

"If you enjoy doing it, why not? I'll also be pleased."

Alma thought to herself, *Michele isn't rich; if he chooses a useless kitten like me for his wife, I'd better not be a burden to him. And so I'd better be ready; I shall be ready.*

She continued fantasizing after leaving the kitchen while helping Noemi with tidying the bedrooms. *He'll be a writer, and I'll teach. During my spare time, for example, in the afternoons—if he agrees—I'll be his secretary. I'll go to the library in Milan and fetch the books he needs and save him wasting his time.* There was a fundamental practicality in her thoughts, a disposition toward efficiency, but, as always, this was in contrast with her outward appearance, the family's statuette.

If he doesn't want me (because really it's almost impossible that he really wants me as his wife, that would be too wonderful), well then, with a literature degree, I'll be able, if nothing else, to be in a position better to understand his books, which will be . . . I'm sure they'll be marvelous.

13

Over the next few days Michele returned to Nomana several times but stayed only a few hours. To his sincere regret, because—even without thinking about Alma—he felt most naturally connected to Nomana, with its atmosphere full of life, and not to Monza, in the depressing apartment occupied by his aunt and uncle. His poor relatives were inevitably under a strain just from the problems of daily life. Besides, his aunt was nearly always grumbling, also because of her health. Yet, at some sacrifice to themselves, they had given him the best-lit room in the apartment, and they had equipped it with an ancient bed and a table, over by the window.

Michele had busied himself in moving his few civilian suits (now adolescent looking and too small to fit) from the house at Nova, along with his law books and the work desk his father had given him when he had gone off to the university. He planned to take the remaining university exams one by one, as soon as possible. *I ought to put them behind me and graduate. I should do it in no more than a year, as it's absolutely necessary that I support myself.*

Meanwhile he would start a draft of the book that he had in outline in his mind.

When he had set up a desk in place of the table in his new room in Monza, he stopped and looked at and was amazed. It was for him, a desk just for him! Who would have thought back at the POW camp? Now nothing could stop him from writing his book; the only obstacles would be fatigue and sleep, or exhaustion from too much work. *Mere details, laughable! What's a little fatigue if you're not forced to sleep in the snow at tens of degrees below zero, and above all, if you have enough to eat? So what if you get a little tired? You can laugh that off!*

At the same time it wouldn't be difficult to meet Alma, speak to her, gaze at her. The possibilities for meeting Alma were without doubt the most important of things. She had brought something very close to happiness into his life. He relished the thought of her, but why was all of this happening to him, while so many others . . . Right, those others, their bruised bodies in the courtyard at Crinovaya, each of them a human soul with a destiny. And the screams from that poor soul from Pavia as he was brutishly pushed into the cauldron of hot soup, and . . . but enough. He'd have to learn how to suppress such thoughts. *Give them eternal peace, Lord, and let them gaze on your face, wherein all good lies, I beseech you.* Maybe happiness wasn't yet within reach, for him. *Well, cheer up, let's go to the Rivas'. They offer sympathetic company, and there one doesn't have time to think about these things. Come, on the bike, I'll be in Nomana in under an hour.*

He wouldn't stay long at Nomana, because when he was there he would think about his university plans, and he might, for example, find it necessary to ask some classmate about the examination arrangements at the faculty. Ambrogio would help, after protesting ("Why don't you take my word on this?" "No, you're taking economics, and I need to know exactly how things are being done in the law course."), and would introduce Michele to some colleague nearing graduation, who, after talking to him on the telephone and explaining, would suddenly offer to lend him textbooks . . . books covering second-, third-, and fourth-year law . . . a real gift! Then Michele would be impatient to go to the fellow student's house to collect the books.

Just the sight of Alma was an inspiration for him. *Lord, don't let me lose her, don't permit it. Well, but what am I doing here dawdling? As if waiting for someone else, someone who's finished studying, to take over and . . . No, Lord, don't let that happen.*

True, the Lord wouldn't let it happen. Besides, looking at things calmly, Michele himself was given to thinking that if in fact the Lord's providential plans called for him to be a writer (*Had it been otherwise, why was I saved that way in Arbusov and all the rest of it?*), and since he couldn't write without Alma at his side . . .

With Alma he didn't want to push too hard. *There's no need to rush things,* he would tell himself when he felt a particularly strong wish to declare his feelings. *This splendid love must last a lifetime.*

On her side, Alma asked him nothing, but it was clear to him in various ways that she was attracted. For example, when she noted his interest in the newspapers, she had collected the papers that were here and there in drawers and on tables around the house and had even gone to the town's fruit dealer, who also sold newspapers, to buy old copies. (These were still the small, single-page papers.) She'd given them to him with a smile. "They're not much, but I noticed you were interested . . . look, in this one there's a list of the election results from June 2, with boxed analyses, you see? My father had forgotten this one in a desk drawer, and now it is of some use."

Later, when the time came for her to leave Nomana to spend the last ten days of September at her school's camp at Varenna, on Lake Como, she simply decided not to go.

"But it's something that was decided months ago", a perplexed Francesca reminded her.

"You two go. I don't feel like going", she answered. "It doesn't appeal to me."

In the end her mother intervened. "Alma, you're already nineteen. You're not going to start having whims?"

"It's not a whim."

"All right, what is it?"

"It's that . . . well, I'm afraid of the snakes." (This was an old story, nearly a family joke. How many times had her brothers kidded her about snakes? Some years ago "by a hair"—as they emphasized—a snake in Varenna missed biting her . . .)

"But back then you didn't fear snakes", said Francesca, who had witnessed the event. Alma had inadvertently sat on a snake in the meadow at the summer place. Feeling it move under her weight, she had taken hold of it and held it up. There she was, the little statue, holding the snake up in the air, not letting go or running off screaming like the other girls. Luckily the gardener had been nearby and with one stroke of his sickle had killed it. White with fright, the Marcelline nuns had taken all the students to the chapel to give thanks for having come safely through the danger. "But then you were less afraid than I was . . . I was really frightened, so much so that Sister Tobietta made me drink down a Fernet, you remember? And you didn't want to have one because you weren't at all affected. And now . . ."

"Well, now, on the other hand, I feel afraid. And no, I'm not going to Varenna. Please don't insist, I beg you."

Francesca and Giudittina had to go without her.

14

So it was that during that last small part of the summer vacations, only Alma and Ambrogio were around to keep Michele company when he dropped by Nomana. (The other university students in the family—facing examinations in the autumn—spent their time closeted in their rooms, studying.)

Both Michele and Ambrogio had many experiences and much news to exchange. Whenever they sat down to talk, Alma would join them, doing some sewing but contributing little to the conversation. If they went out in the garden to stretch their legs, she would keep them company, sometimes not saying a word.

"What are you doing here?" her brother once asked her, a little surprised at her presence. "Have you decided to follow us like a pet dog?"

"Oh, no, come on", Michele said quickly. "It's our fault, not talking about things that interest her. Even so, Alma is . . . just her being here is . . . a celebration, better than all the flowers in the garden together."

Ambrogio looked at him with surprise, then shook his head. "Sometimes I forget you're a poet", he said. He started chuckling. "But have you noticed that you poets are sometimes quite funny?"

He turned to his sister, sure that she would agree with him. "Eh, Alma?"

"No", she replied. "I'd say Michele is the opposite of funny", and continued walking calmly at his side, charming with her two chestnut braids falling on her chest.

"Ho, what kind of answer is that, little statue?" Ambrogio said, laughing. "You know what I say? I say that not only poets are comic, but you women also." Then, turning to Michele, he said, "Well, good, let's talk about something serious. You were telling me about the Russian working man's way of looking at the regime."

Michele continued; the subject interested him, but what he thought about more than anything, as always, was the presence of Alma, and right then it was obvious to him from her attitude and presence there that *she also loves me, I've no doubts any more; it's a case of "love, which every lover loves to have returned", as Dante says . . . that's it, and it's very beautiful to live it.*

At mealtimes Fortunato and Pino would show up and would also keep Michele company. He often asked Pino for details of his experiences with the partisans; he wanted to catch the essential facts, seemed never to get enough of the subject. He'd always wind up by saying, "We'll talk more about this."

Pino had commented, "Look, it seems to me you're giving more importance to this partisan business than it deserves."

Michele shook his head. "What is most certain is that—right or wrong—as time goes by this will become more and more important. You'll see, I've no doubts."

Exams behind him and without worries, the thirteen-year-old Rodolfo would come directly from the villa *I dragoni*, where, with the old caretaker, he was setting traps for the migrating birds. As this meant his hands were usually sticky with birdlime, he would need to wash his hands several times, often arriving at the table late.

"Folks," he would say, his mind still completely occupied with the bird traps, "you should have seen my decoy woodpecker. He not only attracted other woodpeckers but even brought over some sparrows." Then, while tying his napkin around his neck, "He hammered away. He sounded like a carpenter. There were times I thought I'd go deaf."

"What's this about 'hammering'?" his mother asked him, shaking her head. "Is that the proper word? Why don't you speak nicely?"

"Well, Mother, because the exact word doesn't exist for what a woodpecker does—there's hammering for driving home nails, of course—he has a big beak, this big. When he wants to call other woodpeckers he uses that beak to make this noise, which I call hammering because that's what it sounds like."

"He hammers with his beak, you say?" Pino spoke, starting to giggle. "Do you hear him hammering on?"

"Well, look at you. It's you that's got the big beak," Rodolfo muttered, sticking his fork into his pasta and being rewarded by smiles from all around the table.

After eating and taking a walk with the others around the garden, Fortunato and Pino would return to their books. Even this made Michele reflect to himself, *And I, what am I waiting for? Can I afford to waste time?* Of course, he wasn't exactly on vacation. A little relaxation, some rest for his nerves would do him good, but . . . until he got down to work he would have no peace. In the end he pushed forward with a program of study that forced him to reduce the number of his visits to Nomana.

15

When the university classes started up again, Gerardo's three oldest children, now including Alma, went back to commuting between Nomana and Milan. Michele, however, went less often to the university, going almost exclusively in order to take exams. As a former combatant he was able to convene special sittings of the examining committee and made immediate use of this privilege. (This privilege surprised him every time he used it. *There are undeniably good things in the spirit of democracy*, he noted.) He passed his first set of exams—he had chosen the easiest—without difficulty. Next he prepared for a harder exam, and this was also successful. After these results he was able—by looking at the thickness of his textbooks—to estimate more or less the number of days he needed to study to prepare for each exam. The time periods went from one week for the easiest to two or three weeks for those—as he called them—of "medium caliber", and up to a month or more for major exams.

"How do you do it?" Ambrogio would sometimes ask him, amazed. "How do you knock off these exams so fast? I know that Gemellone had you spotted right from the start as a phenomenon, but I'd like you to tell me how you do it. You weren't this spirited at the lyceum."

"Well, as time goes by one gets better", he would answer. But once he said, "Don't be fooled. How much do you think I'll retain, studying like this? The fact is, I've got to get a pass and graduate, and for this reason I don't get into details. It's enough to start each exam with page-by-page data stuck in my brain so I can give the needed answers. It's a kind of memory game, but the memories won't last."

"You don't mean to tell me that you study, but not in order to learn?"

"That's it. I study for the exam, not for afterward. It's exactly the reverse of how it should be."

"Well, now, there's no need to exaggerate."

"I have to be frank, Ambrogio. I realize I've made a mistake in going in for law. I haven't the right mind for it, the juridical approach, not at all, and—if you discount the philosophy of laws—all these things I have to stuff into my head are of no importance to me at all. So my plan is to forget all of this stuff in the end, and this in no way disappoints me. What's more, it's the only plan that appears sensible. What use would it be to retain all this detail in my head?"

"But maybe you should change your major, study something else that interests you."

"I haven't the time. If I change to another major, I won't be able to graduate within the year. I'd need about four years, right?"

"Yes, that's right."

As used to happen when he dealt with his cousin Manno, now, in dealing with Michele, Ambrogio sometimes had the impression he was less equipped, but still definitely he was more constructive. "Is there not another way? Maybe being intelligent equips one to behave in a silly way?" He would have liked to help Michele, but how?

In the event, it was the rapid rhythm with which Michele took his exams that helped Ambrogio. He soon cut back on attending classes and concentrated on preparing for exams. He also, as a former combatant, could choose his dates for examinations. He realized that going from exam to exam, he could graduate within one year and decided to aim for it.

In the meantime—following his study plan—Michele had also started to write a book about his experiences in Russia. However, this almost immediately absorbed him to such an extent that against his will he started seriously neglecting his studies, the exams, everything.

After a while he came back to his original idea. *What am I doing? I need to graduate as soon as possible. I have to qualify however I can. There's no arguing about that.* He decided to recommence taking his exams. *Right away, tomorrow, I'll go to the university and convene the examiners.*

16

Spring was coming. It was even noticeable in the old antiquated streetcar that took Michele, nodding—and over the longer stretches, nearly pitching—to Milan.

Between Monza and Sesto San Giovanni, and between Sesto and Milan, the tracks went through flat land on the town's outskirts where here and there were heaps of refuse and junk and several uncultivated pieces of land covered in thick dry bushes killed off in winter. This was the place, more than anywhere else in Italy, that brought to his mind the tattered desolation of the POW camp. *With those heaps of rags between the barracks, I mustn't forget to mention that in the book. Just outside the fence there were these same bushes, what did that fellow the botanist call them? Artemisia. The Lombardy soldiers, on the other hand, called it "Saint Charles' bush"; if it was crushed while still green it gave off a strong smell . . . it would be as well to remember those bushes in the book.* He took pencil and paper from his pocket and added to the existing notes, "Rags on the ground around the barracks, the Saint Charles and other bushes, desolation, etc."

A middle-aged lady with her handbag in her lap was sitting across from him, curiously observing his note making while pretending not to do so; the other passengers were absorbed in their own thoughts. Michele returned the paper and pencil to his pocket and resumed watching the passing scenery. He could see that new tender green shoots were beginning to show in between the clumps of tumbled dry bushes. *Look at the miracle of spring, even here in this desolation, as elsewhere! One has to recognize that nature doesn't fail its duty, doesn't relax from its work. In order to ruin things, here as elsewhere, man will always be ready.* He reflected, *Here, as if one was necessary, is another manifestation of the destruction inside man. In truth, if one didn't remember the original sin (it was vague enough: God only knew what really had happened!) one would never be able to understand human behavior.*

The poet in him prevailed over these reflections, however, and soon he was contemplating the prompt arrival of spring. In a few weeks—he told himself—the violets would be blooming, violets that in Nova appeared on banks exposed to the noon sun, sometimes as early as mid-March. What a spectacle! When he was a child, he would pick the first violets, pushing his small fingers into the dry herbage, picking two or three at a time, taking pleasure in giving them to the old lady who watched over him. "Look, what a nice smell, Ersilia." (He thought, *What if I slip over to Nova and pick some violets for Alma?*) Ersilia would sigh and pin the untidy bunch of violets to her chest. (How much was expressed in that sigh, if one thought about it now!) Violets would look good in Alma's hair, around her graceful head. *Shaped into a crown, like this or perhaps this other shape.* In his mind's eye he saw Alma's hair decorated in various ways; his vision of her was so strong that it was almost as if he had her before him.

For a few moments the gray outskirts of Milan lost their hold on his mood. He no longer saw the people packed into the streetcar, the poor townspeople. In the swinging car with him, traveling at his side, Almina . . . and spring.

Poor Alma, whom I haven't yet told of my love. Although surely she must have noticed that I'm madly in love with her. How many days without seeing her . . . it had been quite a while, at least ten days without seeing her. *Well, first it was the book; I had to finish that chapter at all costs. Then when Sunday came and I'd intended to go to Nomana, it was Father Turla.* He'd received a note from the priest: "What should I think of your ignoring me? It's been six months since we've been back home, and we've seen neither hide nor hair of you." Those had been his words. Michele felt he owed him a debt; without hesitation he went that Sunday to see him in the mountains near Brescia. That dear old chaplain! It appeared he was also finding it hard to adapt to a normal life. Well, in any case, almost certainly he would see Alma today. She assiduously attended her classes, a serious student, and so almost surely he would meet her at the university.

The streetcar finally reached Milan, rocking its way through the Piazza Loreto, leaving behind the dismal gas station where Mussolini, his unhappy mistress, and several fellow chiefs had been strung up upside down, kept company, so it was said, by some luckless unknown who had been lynched by mistake.

Michele's mind left thoughts of spring, Alma, and Father Turla's country parish, shifting to the vociferous multitude—even though he had not seen them—milling around the suspended corpses. Certainly those lynched men had been responsible for many other deaths, and yet how awful to think of the macabre pleasure felt by the crowd around those hanging bodies, even for him, with his experience of so many similar horrors! He imagined their faces, the repulsive mouths open, rejoicing ... Wild beasts don't go as far; only man, only a human being can reach those extremes. Once again, original sin ... He would have to show in the book the tremendous reality of original sin. Perhaps by naming it explicitly, or perhaps not, maybe only putting it on display from the perspective of its consequences?

Well, referring to it wouldn't be wrong, even doing so several times, because people should be familiar with it, ought to be accustomed to its influence. In any case, it was something he didn't need to decide now. He would have to ponder the point, give it much consideration. *There it is anyway, it exists,* he told himself, *so to exclude it from the whole related force for destruction which man carries with him—a destructive impulse present in everything—would leave man's history unexplained.*

House façades and more façades, not a few with broken windows, heaps of rubble but also several areas of repair and reconstruction; every now and then American or English trucks going along the street; some modest merchandise in shop windows of the via Buenos Aires.

At the Venice Arch the local service streetcar line ended, and Michele got out, walking under an old banner and along beside the threatening red painted hammers and sickles on the walls. (And Marxism, this enormous trick aimed at the immature, continued gathering adherents. *Idiots, if you only knew what is really hiding behind those symbols!*). More than one poster, however, showed a first tentative offer of commercial products, which appeared to Michele as a moving contrast to the political messages. *It's a little like those green shoots show-*

ing above ground out there on the outskirts. Soon we'll see how once again life will triumph over death.

He boarded an inner-city streetcar, shorter than the other multicar vehicle, and somehow less powerful, and, after crossing half the city, got off at the Catholic University.

17

On arriving at the university, after passing an arch crowned by a statue of Christ the Redeemer, there stood a slab of stone that commemorated in Latin the damage wrought by war: *ignivomis globis ab Anglis e caelo temere coniectis.* Now, all the damage having been repaired, the destruction remained in the memory, represented by these stones. A little farther on, the double doors of the chapel were on the right. Michele knew that inside at least two people would be kneeling before the Blessed Sacrament, praying and praising the Lord, right around the clock. Michele went inside; it was agreeably warm. He knelt at the nearest pew (the benches were furnished with comfortable padded leather kneelers: *it's clear that Gemellone is a psychologist*) and prayed intensively for a few minutes. After having given thanks to God, he gave thanks, as he usually did, to his own guardian angel, from whom this time he asked particular vigilance for Alma. *This young girl, Alma, who will be my life's companion: Can I ask you to care for her as efficiently as you've looked after me? Look . . . as I see it, you'd have to come to some sort of . . . agreement with her own guardian angel.* He began day-dreaming. *I'd like to see your form, at least see what you look like, mystic creature made of light. Especially I'd like to see you, my splendid companion, who in certain moments helped me out in a truly daring way. I don't believe Almina's angel can be as strong as you, so . . .* He realized this wasn't properly a prayer. *Well, good,* he said to his angel, *in any case, you understand what I mean.* He got to his feet, genu-flected deeply toward the Blessed Sacrament, turned his head in a sort of nod to his guardian angel, and left the chapel.

He reached the first internal cloister, intending to go along to the left, to-ward the office. He would first arrange the convocation of the examining com-mittee for the next exam and afterward go to the teacher training and literature department in search of Alma. Based on his knowledge of her methodical class attendance, he expected to find her there. How like her to study so intensely! And with her long plaits, she even looked like a young beginning schoolgirl.

Once in the cloister, however, Michele (whether pushed there by his own guardian angel or perhaps by Alma's—we cannot tell which), instead of con-tinuing left, turned straight toward the right, toward the humanities depart-ment; he would go to the office later, he thought.

On the teacher training bulletin board he checked the class schedule and looked at his watch. (*Almost 10:00!*). The first-course students should be in the Toniolo Auditorium, no, in the Salvadori, where Apollonio was teaching Italian literature. (*Apollonio, no less. Well, what luck, at last I'll see him.*)

As he climbed the stairs, he recalled the silly expeditions he and Ambrogio had made in these precincts just after they'd registered as new students. Where would that girl from Emilia, Nilde, be teaching now? (*Brunilde or Leonilde? Who would know?*) What a strange girl, with her bulging forehead and always a ready answer. He shook his head, smiling. And as far as Father Bertrando (the tall, good-looking fellow who wrote rhymes about Mussolini), well, it was generally known he had become a partisan in the war, not in the mountains, though. Of course he'd done his resisting right here at the university. The Crinovaya veteran laughed out loud.

The Salvadori Auditorium, on the second floor, had its door open, and, class over, the students were coming outside. Apollonio, and Alma also, had already gone. The students—mostly girls, wearing their black robes—milled around in the hallway; some started out for other classes. "Riva? Riva?" the girls he asked about Alma's whereabouts shook their heads or frowned in thought; nobody seemed to know her, but when he explained, "She has braids and looks like a high-schooler", they immediately knew whom he sought.

"Oh, yes, right", a couple said.

"She was in the row in front of mine", a girl with glasses and a southern accent said.

"Where could she have gone?" he asked.

But none of the girls seemed to know.

Could she have decided to miss the next class? If so, he'd have time to catch up to her in the locker room. He set off running. But when he reached the female locker room—halfway between the humanities and law faculties—Alma wasn't there either.

Michele, concerned, finally headed toward his own department, law. *How dumb of me not to have rung her*, he thought, *really dumb*. Maybe, being in her first year, Alma had decided to skip a class. He and Ambrogio had often done the same thing in their first year. Or maybe, unthinking kitten that she was, she had left the campus with a classmate. Maybe she was with a fellow about whom she would, with time, feel seriously. Or perhaps she was with a shameless guy, one of those pigs who ... Yes, even that was a possibility. Michele walked along, unthinkingly looking for stones to kick, a habit he'd acquired in the exercise yard at Susdal whenever he was nervous; here, however, there were no stones. He was walking along the long corridor in which, before the war, Gemellone had answered his greeting using his surname, "Hello, Tintori", but, he told himself, this is no time to think about that. His mind was full of something else: jealousy—something not normal with him—it was a depressing sensation. *What a beast I am for leaving Alma alone!* he scolded himself. *What a dumb, stupid thing to do! And yet I can't stop thinking about her. I think about her every hour of the day, yet what do I do? I concentrate on my books, exams, a heap of stuff, but not on her, who is far more important than all the rest.*

Halfway down the corridor there was a small turnoff that led to the library and where there was a bulletin board with class schedules for the law department. Instinctively Michele thought he ought to go and look at these. But no, why do that? But in any case passing the end of the turnoff, he glanced toward the bulletin board and saw Alma standing in front of it.

18

She had her back to him. Like all the other female students she wore a black robe, but it was unmistakably her: the parting in her hair, the plaits, and when she moved, her slimness and narrow waist. Leaning forward a little, she was checking the class schedules. Perhaps, being new, she had got lost.

Michele's heart beat harder. *What's happening to me now? What is it I feel?* He swallowed; had Alma come here, to his area, to the law department . . . *just to . . . just to look for me, be in my world? Yes, absolutely. Why else would she be here? And here I was, dumb idiot, with doubts in my mind about her!*

"Alma", he half called out, noticing he had trouble talking.

Alma turned suddenly, saw him, and her face lit up, blushing to the roots of her hair. "Michele, great, at last!" she blurted out.

Michele drew near to her. "What are you doing here in law country, eh?" he tried to say jokingly, but his voice was a croak.

She blushed deeper. She seemed unable to reply, then said, "A writer like you, can't you imagine why I'd be here?"

"Yes, this writer can . . .", he replied.

Once more she looked unable to say more. Then, in an admonitory tone, she complained, "Why don't you show yourself now and then?"

"You won't believe me. I was asking myself the same thing. And you know how I answered? Because I'm stupid."

"Oh, no . . .", she protested.

"Listen, I was looking for you, too, and . . ." He was going to say, "You had me worried", but couldn't get it out. "I've just come from your department, from the Salvadori Auditorium, where your class with Apollonio just ended. Am I right?"

"Yes", she answered him, with as always no outward sign of the happiness in her heart. "But how did you know? Who told you I was in that class?"

"Your classmates, the other first-year girls, they told me."

"Ah."

"But as you'd already left there, I went looking for you in the locker rooms."

"What?! The female locker rooms? Don't you know fellows aren't allowed?"

"Of course I know", Michele smiled. "That's why I went in with my eyes closed, and only long enough to ask for you, but you weren't there either. Then I didn't know where to look next. I started thinking of things that . . . dumb ideas, of course."

"But what are you saying?" murmured Alma. She could read those thoughts still on his face.

"Well, good; enough of that. Now we can be together a while", he said, putting an arm around her shoulders.

They walked down the corridor; she lifted her head to look at him in the eyes, happy and contented as a young lamb. "If we were seen by the rector", she murmured.

The touch of his hand and arm gave her an indescribable and strange sensation of fulfillment. She thought, *Why don't you do this more often, why?* Michele also felt strong emotions, caused by the close contact between them.

"What were these things you were thinking about?" she suddenly asked. "Don't you want to tell me?"

"I'd look like a fool, that's the thing."

"Please, Michele."

"As I said, these were dumb ideas." But as she continued waiting, "Well, I . . . I confess . . . I, well, I had a feeling of jealousy."

Alma stopped, then looked him in the eyes. "Jealousy?" She felt extraordinarily happy. "If you're jealous, I mean jealous about me, that means . . . that I . . . that for you I . . ."

"Yes, for you I. That's it", Michele replied.

"Oh, I'm sorry, forgive me", Alma said. "How indiscreet of me!"

"No, why?" he replied. "Why indiscreet? Not in any sense of the word."

"But if you've felt, let's say, even only a very little bit jealous . . . oh, that's enough!" she interrupted herself. "You only want to make fun."

"No, Alma, I'm not joking."

"Really jealous? You mean worried that I maybe . . ."

"Exactly," he said, "that you maybe."

"But don't you realize that there is no reason to be jealous about me?" Alma exclaimed. "I'm not saying this to tell you off. Don't get me wrong. It's just that you'll have to realize that it doesn't make sense. There's no reason for it. When I promise to be true to somebody, I'll be true to him for life, each moment of my life, and with joy! People could cut me to bits; they'd get nowhere. I wouldn't even think about being untrue."

"When you promise to be true to somebody?" said Michele, sounding a little stupid. "What does that 'somebody' mean?"

Oh, why don't you just tell me you love me? Why don't you demand my fidelity? Alma asked him mentally, looking fixedly at him. But then she became shy.

I must not ask a man like him, an artist, to behave in a . . . in such a middle-class way.
He's telling me in his own way that he loves me, sort of. They started walking again.

"Please let me explain", Alma said, "what I was trying to tell you. What you ought to realize is that there's no reason for you to be jealous about me. That would be hurting yourself unnecessarily, really absurd."

Ah, good, that sounds a little better, Michele thought.

"Maybe I'm not expressing myself well", Alma continued. "That is, that I . . . that I'll be true to the man I'll love, always. Since I was a little girl I've held myself true to him, even in my thoughts, which . . ."

"But what does this mean . . . 'the man I'll love' mean?" Michele said, once more concerned. "You've gone back to talking in the abstract. Why do you say 'the man I'll love'?"

Alma lifted her head once more and looked him in the eyes. "The man I love", she said in a low voice. And then, stopping again, "The man with whom I'm in love . . . whom I couldn't love more." She hid her face in his shoulder, leaning into his chest.

"If you knew how much I'm in love with you . . .", Michele murmured, and, not trusting himself to continue, he kissed her hair.

For a while neither spoke. Michele put his hand under her chin and lifted her face till he could look into her beautiful, honest, chestnut eyes, innocent and young. "Alma!"

They moved off again. As luck would have it classes had resumed, and the corridor was empty of people. Michele squeezed her shoulders within his arm. "I should have told you right from the start that I love you, on the night I arrived back; should have shouted it out when you appeared at the top of the stairs in your light blue housecoat. You've no idea, you don't have the faintest idea how many times I thought about you in the POW camp. You've no idea how much, how indescribably that helped me."

"Me?"

"Yes, you. Your beautiful face, your graceful figure, Alma. How many times I remembered, thought about you! I wanted to tell you when I arrived, tell you everything that very night", he repeated. He nodded his head, very moved. "And yet I had to control myself, you understand? And later on, when I could see you also cared for me . . ." He became excited. "But by all means you had to feel the same; God himself made it happen." He interrupted himself. "Praise be to God, blessed be the Lord!" he exclaimed in a strong voice. "Let's say it together, Alma: blessed forever!"

"Yes, yes. It was truly the Lord. Oh, Michele!" Alma murmured.

"I had to thank God", he exclaimed. "What's more, I should thank God on my knees, and it still wouldn't be enough. It'll never be enough. But what I wanted to tell you . . ." He hesitated slightly. "When I saw you returned my feelings, I thought, 'If I speak to her, if I tell her everything, about how many times I've thought about her when I was a prisoner, with how much love and happiness, and I let her know my feelings; in short, if I say all this, then if we had to live apart, it would be awful, much more difficult than before.'" He nodded. "And it'll be like that starting from today, I'm afraid. We still have to wait years before we can get married. But how could we have remained silent and not tell each other we feel this love? It would have been impossible, simply out of the question."

"What a marvelous feeling!" Alma murmured. "It's such a beautiful thing! You love me, you're telling me you love me, in love with me . . . you!"

Michele gazed into her eyes again. "You're one of God's works of art", he murmured. They were walking down the long corridor slowly when two students entered the far end and walked in their direction; they looked new to the university. Michele took his arm away from Alma's shoulders. "We have to remember we're in a public place," he observed, then added, "unfortunately", and then was silent. When the two students had gone past, pretending to be at ease, he asked, "You know where they're headed?"

Alma, busy with emotional thoughts to the exclusion of everything else, looked at him questioningly.

"They'll be going to the teacher training department, for 'undisclosed reasons' I'd say."

"Oh, yes, how do you know?"

Other students, coming from the law department, were now also coming into the corridor. Michele said, "When I say for 'undisclosed reasons', it means that they are going to meet the girls there." He laughed, throwing his head back. "It was a phrase used by Gemellone in a notice to students, some five, no, maybe six years ago. It was a proclamation to students about time wasting; it was posted on the main bulletin board by the entrance. Your brother and I also did the same, did you know? We would also go to meet the girls at the teacher training department. In those days we didn't think time could be lost."

"But how do you remember an expression like that, something on the bulletin board, after six years?"

"I've been at the university such a short time that I remember practically everything about those days. Do you feel you've been at the university for a long time?"

"But I've just started here."

"Right. And we're at the end of February. We two, your brother and I, at this same time, we were already in the army."

"Oh, you poor boys", Alma murmured, suddenly aware of how brief their carefree university days had really been.

"Don't feel sorry for me. Or at least not today. Today I'm incomparably the happiest man in the world!" He nodded while gazing at her. "Today, when we've declared our love; good Lord, how good you are!" he exclaimed helplessly.

Alma felt her heart would burst with happiness.

19

They went down to stroll in the beautiful ground floor cloisters, then ate frugally at the university restaurant, and then—as they both wanted to remain together—decided to take a walk around the center of Milan. Michele escorted Alma to the entrance of the female locker rooms, from which she emerged almost immediately, carrying her coat and holding her handbag under an arm. She didn't want to be apart from him for even a minute, so she hadn't even taken off her black student's gown—this she took off as they went toward the exit, balling it up into a small size and putting it into her bag. "What are you doing? Do you always treat your gown that way?"

"Why do you ask? Yes, sometimes."

Michele laughed. Without the gown Alma's slim, very virginal waist became visible. *God in heaven, what a marvelous creature!* Michele thought. As a writer, he was beginning to be perhaps a bit repetitive, but he wasn't aware of it. And for the rest of his life he remained unaware of it, continuing to repeat his observation (out loud or to himself), delighted ever again at this masterpiece of God.

The sun, still almost wintry, was beating down on the city, damp from several days of misty weather, but the onset of spring could be felt in the gusts of cool air, no longer cold, a new breath of the coming spring, which brought Michele memories of childhood violets. They strolled through the afternoon, careless of where they were going, because their happiness accompanied them everywhere. They didn't feel attracted to any one place, as neither of the two lovers—unlike Fanny—knew about the fashionable places to be. (And they were happy in their ignorance. As country people deep down, they had a spiritual wealth that couldn't be enhanced but only diminished by outside forces.)

Later, as light faded and Almina's legs began to feel tired (but she wouldn't for anything mention it, not wanting to interrupt a walk like that or such a spell), their conversation slowly became an outpouring of memories from Michele. He spoke about many things, such as the time in the hell of the Arbusov Valley, when he had gone down into the earth cellar, where instead of thinking about Ambrogio's tragic situation, he had thought of how well she would think of him if he saved his friend. "In the POW camp I felt ashamed when I thought about it, not knowing whether Ambrogio was safe or not. But he was all right." With the same simple words he told her of other terrible events. He remembered life and death, the unending days and nights in the camp, the despair at the beginning and then the weary wait for repatriation. He told her, in the middle of this, there had been the memory of her in his heart, that young girl in Italy with whom he had fallen forever in love, sustaining him like an unquenchable light in the darkness around him. He spoke of these things in his past in words that made a strong impression on Alma. She felt an urgent desire to embrace him, to become as one with him.

The lights had been switched on. The windows in Milan's streets created squares of golden light on the wet sidewalks.

20

Arm in arm they reached the central station and traveled together on the train to Monza. It seemed absurd to both of them that they should part now, although each thought from time to time of a need to be alone for a while, to reflect over what was happening to them, to recall the marvelous hours they had spent together and to finally realize that it had not all been a dream. Neither of the two lovers had ever had a dream as beautiful as this reality.

Having left the train at Monza, Michele once again thanked God from the bottom of his heart; he thanked him as he left the station, as he walked down the street and when he boarded the small local bus; with extraordinary enthusiasm, he gave thanks as he climbed the unpretentious stairs at home. The next day he would need to return to the university to arrange the convocation of the examining committee, not having had time to do so all day, but he had agreed with Alma that they would meet on the little train from Nomana and ride together between Monza and Milan. After having eaten dinner—during which he exchanged desultory conversation with his uncle and aunt (they found day by day an increasing need to talk with him), his mind kept wandering back to the day's event (her face, above all he kept seeing her beautiful face) and to his meeting, doubtless momentous, something to look forward to, on the following day.

Alma, continuing on the train to Nomana, was listening to the conversation (she really barely followed the words) from Miss Quadri Dodini, who on boarding the train at Monza had taken the seat vacated by Michele, a broad satisfied smile on her face. Her beautiful alabaster face hiding the feelings inside her, Alma as usual showed no outward sign of excitement, but she relived in waves the marvelous discoveries of her day. Not only was it without doubt certain that Michele loved her. It was also certain that his love was great, the kind of love given by a real man who had held himself ready for an only love. And the unusual fact that in the truly enormous adventures he had gone through, she had somehow taken a part had been, as he put it, like one of those little red votive lights in the icon corner of some isbas. His wonderful profile! His looks, those intelligent black eyes, very intelligent, and . . . *Lord, it's too much. I thank you, thank you, thank you!* Miss Quadri Dodini was talking about the boredom that took hold of a teacher, obliged to repeated the same classes year after year.

"If you take up teaching, you'll see what I mean. But for sure you'll not be a teacher. You'll get married first."

"But what are you saying? Even if I do get married, I intend to qualify and teach class in any case", Alma declared, finding it hard not to add that the wife of a writer would need to concern herself in order not to be a financial problem to her husband, and she thought, *And not only for myself, but I also have to work to care for the children yet to be born.* Of course, Michele would not approve her plans and would probably have been surprised, but in putting her plans together for the future, she demonstrated how she had her feet on the ground, a true daughter of Gerardo.

While the Quadri Dodini woman carried on talking, Alma with increasing curiosity tried to think of the children she would give to Michele. She didn't consider the physical relationship with Michele—pleasing, for sure, and perhaps the better part of their love—from which the children would issue. Her Christian morals at present forbade that, and she would obey that in her docile way, realizing that her so splendid love was in no small way brought about by her faithful acceptance of the moral code. Without these morals as taught directly by God, even Michele's love for her would have been less, perhaps limping along, spent. So she thought of the children she would one day give to Michele, trying to imagine their looks, their little faces. She loved them already, even though she was not yet able to see them clearly. She found it impossible to roll back time and imagine Michele's face as a child. One thing seemed certain to her: all these children, boys and girls, would have Michele's black intelligent eyes. *I'll bring new tender beings into the world, perpetuating his intelligence.* This seemed to her a lovely thought, fitting of a great writer's wife, and she felt happy inside.

Once off the train, while walking under the leafless oak trees of memory lane, she continued thinking of her loved one. The darkness, the low horizontal tree branches, gave her the lonely feeling—the feeling he had described—felt by Michele in his cell when night fell in that terrible POW camp, surrounded by large forests. She continued thinking about Michele later, during dinner, throughout which she was silent, saying not a word. She continued thinking about him even later until she slept.

The next day, and many others to follow, the two lovers spent together in Milan. Then Alma realized—even with her meekness—that it was up to her to organize her days with Michele, keeping in mind his studies, and she did so rapidly, with a determination that surprised even her.

Michele went back to taking his exams regularly and systematically; after a few months, however, he turned his attention once more to his book, in which he again became totally involved. If this interest caused him to miss a couple of exams, he never forgot Alma and didn't let a week go by without seeing her. Every few days after dinner he would go to Nomana on his bicycle, which obliged him—once he was back home—to stay up rather late in order to make up the time allocated to work.

21

By summer Ambrogio was ready to defend his thesis for his degree, for which occasion his brothers and sisters, parents, and also Michele traveled to Milan. Michele was very concerned about the precarious state of his own finances. On the streetcar taking him to Milan, he thought to himself, *I made a mistake in electing to pay the inheritance tax on the house. That was a real mistake.*

Since it was the month of June and very hot, people on the streetcar wore shirtsleeves. From the open windows, apart from fresh air, wafted the smell of tar, from the paving work to new stretches of road between Monza and Sesto, parallel to the streetcar lines.

The car slowed when passing some road workers. Michele looked absently out the window at workmen with shovels and handcarts. A metal tripod held a tar-smeared sign announcing the contractor's name, on which was visible "ate, Brianza" only. A shiny road roller moved slowly, rolling the newly laid surface, smoke issuing from its chimney. The driver, a youth with a dark-skinned face resembling a bird of prey, lifted his eyes to the streetcar and gave a passing glance at Michele. Another man with the same facial features stood beside the road, hands on hips, supervising the work. Michele noticed how much the two men looked alike. *They must be brothers.* He thought for a moment about the "ate, Brianza". *Agrate, maybe? Or Usmate? Who knows?* (The two men were in fact the Vigano brothers, from Merate. These were the brothers who had traveled with Manno from Tunis to Sicily and who had found him space on the boat. "Who knows if we did the right thing", they had asked themselves when later they learned of the young officer's death. "If he'd stayed in Tunis he might not have died." They had not, in any case, gone to visit his home. And neither of them knew Michele, nor he them.)

The streetcar picked up speed, and the Vigano brothers' work site was left behind. *If my uncle and aunt hadn't advised me to pay that tax . . .* Michele was very worried about his financial situation. They had insisted for his own good. "If you decide to pay the inheritance tax, then the house can be put in your name officially", they had told him. His poor uncle and aunt; both attached a lot of importance to their own property, the apartment for which they had saved for decades. *But I made a mistake in using what little money I got from the army when I left it. That was a total mistake. Maybe if I had asked Ambrogio for his advice, or perhaps better yet, his father, before paying the tax. Now with my aunt being ill, I could have done with the money.* His uncle now had little money for himself, let alone his nephew, given the galloping inflation, which had reduced the value of his savings. Now he hadn't enough even for his own needs; the clinic took most of it. *And at the end of the day, I'll have to help Uncle,* thought Michele, *and not receive help from him. I have to start teaching private classes right away, finding teaching work however I can; if not, I'll soon have serious problems.*

In fact, he already had financial problems, to the extent that he even worried about spending a few coins for car fare. *I'm very nearly touching bottom!* After having been able to face tremendous difficulties during the war, he now discovered that civilian life, too, can have worrying difficulties. Less spectacular for sure, but no less worrisome, and without comparison much more widespread and faced by a majority of the people, every day. He felt less prepared to face these ordinary problems than the problems, the extraordinary problems, of combat in the military, now just a memory.

He met the Rivas—Alma was with them—at the university doorway. They all shook hands, standing near the memorial stone erected after the reconstruction following the bombing: *ignivomis globis e caelo temere coniectis.* Glancing at the memorial, Michele thought that the bombing raids were now really part of the past, and even—though it was close to blasphemy to think that way—almost, perhaps, better times, since money problems in those far-off days were of secondary importance and didn't have the power (*Filthy money!*) to cause distress, as now.

All the members of the Riva family showed their pleasure at seeing him again; Ambrogio, the man of the hour, a little nervous, held Michele's elbow. "So you've come to laugh at me, eh?" he said. "A super brain like you, you want to see how a poor fellow like me will go forward under a cross fire, right?"

"What do you mean by 'super brain'?!" Michele answered. "If there's one thing I'll surely mess up, it'll be my thesis, you'll see." Then, smiling encouragingly, "Ambrogio, forget this business of cross fire. You'll see that these orals are just like a ceremony, a formality."

"That's not true", Ambrogio objected. "Yesterday morning I watched some thesis discussions, and I saw how there are some professors—not the chairmen, but some of those with theses on related subjects—who appear to enjoy making life difficult for the candidate."

Michele shook his head, thinking, *Ambrogio is a real friend. All his family likes me. If they knew the extent of my problems, they'd soon help me, lend me what I need without my having to ask. But as they're Alma's family, I can't tell them my problems. It would be too humiliating.* Alma, his Alma, had placed herself next to him, holding a copy of Ambrogio's thesis under one arm, and gazed at him adoringly, as at an oracle. *No, I'd rather die first.*

Being young and having the girl he loved nearby, his problems would shortly get tucked away in a corner of his mind; although they wouldn't disappear, they would bother him less for a while.

22

The group entered the lobby.

Once inside Ambrogio's mother asked him, "How do you feel?" She was slightly concerned. "I hope you're not nervous?"

"No, I don't think so", he reassured her.

"There's never a reason to be nervous", pronounced Pino, the ex-partisan. "When you're facing that pack of professors, Ambrogio, try to think how they looked this morning, sitting on the toilet, with all that stink."

"Pig", Alma said, upset that her brother should speak that way in Michele's hearing.

Pino's father, Gerardo, bit his lower lip with annoyance. It was clear that if Pino had been a few years younger, he'd have received a smack that would have rocked his blond head on his shoulders.

"Let's go!" Ambrogio exclaimed. "Why all the reassurances? A little thing like this doesn't frighten me. I've been through worse in life, right?"

"Eh! I'd say that's the truth", Michele agreed, and then changed the subject. "But look, where's Fortunato? How come he's not here?"

"This morning he had a call from Busto Arsizio; he went there to negotiate for some looms. We hope this time it'll work out."

"I hope . . .", said the father, forgetting Pino's remark.

Farther into the lobby Fanny was waiting. For some time now she and Ambrogio had resumed their walks together in downtown Milan. (And he had stopped thinking about Colomba once he had heard of her engagement to a young professional in Novara.) Pino saw Fanny first and went toward her. "Here's that Fanny-tastic female! What's her name?"

"Epifania, please", Fanny said, smiling, and with natural grace she shook the hand that Pino stretched out to her.

"Isn't that even worse?" Pino replied.

His father, annoyed once more, started biting his lower lip. But Fanny was far from offended; quite the reverse. She gave the impression of a hostess welcoming her guests. "Welcome. Happy to see you all", she said. She shook everyone's hand, saying something appropriate to each of them, then looked with pleasure at Ambrogio. "How are things with you, Ambrogio?"

"You, too, are you trying to make me nervous?" he said.

"No, I know, we all know, that even cannon fire couldn't make much of an impression on you." She smiled winningly, intentionally, at Ambrogio's mother, who had known her since the times at Stresa.

This Fanny, she's not bad at all, the others were thinking, and Michele also, who before this had seen her only a couple of times; not bad at all. They found her pageboy hairstyle and unusually green eyes attractive and liked her self-confident manner, so much more decided than their own country ways.

She paid close interest to Giulia. "Did your trip here go well, Signora Giulia? Are you tired? But, come along, let's go. By the way, Signora, do you want to have a coffee before going to the assembly hall?"

But no, Giulia didn't want coffee. On the other hand, as they were near the entrance to the chapel, she almost shyly drew the young girl's attention to it. "Before the . . . before going into the exam, perhaps . . . what do you think?"

Fanny, understanding, agreed. They all went into the chapel, and for a few moments they seriously communed with their God. The only one among them who didn't know what to specify in her prayers was Fanny, who finally asked, "Well, Lord help me make a good impression."

By the altar, as always, were two persons praying—right then they were two young nuns—on their knees in praise of the Lord. *These are the columns that support the Catholic University*, thought Gerardo, who had heard the words in a speech by Father Gemelli years before.

They left the chapel together, and Fanny led them toward the great hall. Gerardo continued looking around at the building admiringly. "What a beauty. What a magnificent building!" he said to Fanny. "Father Gemelli knew how to put things, eh, young miss? Do you happen to know if he will be here, too?"

"For the theses? I don't know, but I don't believe so."

"My father was among those people who fought to found this Catholic University, gathering funds and all that", Ambrogio explained to her.

"Ah, yes, I understand."

At the great hall entrance was a group of people. The examination candidates were easily recognized by the newly bound folders they held. Almina handed Ambrogio's folder to him. "Ambrogio, your thesis."

He took the folder and nodded thanks to his sister, ". . . kitten." Then saluting them all with a gesture, he went off, leaving the family to be organized by Fanny ("Let's go in and sit down. There are others here, and we don't want them to take the best seats."), who herded them inside.

After getting the family seated, the decisive Fanny went out again for a moment to see Ambrogio. "How are you feeling?" she asked him fondly. It was clear she would have preferred to stay with him for a while.

Ambrogio jokingly came to attention. "Today I feel a lot better thank you, Sister Mayer", he answered her, parroting the military hospital's form of address. Then, with great tenderness, he caressed her face with a hand. "I guess you'd like to keep me company?"

"Yes," Fanny said, "but I understand that for you, it's better that you be alone."

"Also, you can't help me rehearse; this thing is too long." He held up the folder containing his thesis.

Fanny nodded, understanding. "So, see you later, Ambrogio."

"If you're sitting with the family," he advised her sensibly, "it could be a good time to get to know my father a bit."

"Yes, right."

23

Fanny went back into the hall, which was gradually filling. There were no seats next to Gerardo or Giulia, who were sitting surrounded by the family. In order to be near them Fanny talked the easygoing Pino into giving up his seat. On the Riva parents' other side Michele and Almina were in a world of their own.

With her usual easy style, Fanny set about entertaining the Rivas and Francesca. Occasionally she had to come up with less well-known facts of the university's history: details about the size of the hall, for example, or the date on which it was dedicated, being urged along by Gerardo's questions, which stemmed from his unconditional admiration for everything Father Gemelli had managed to put together. Seeking help, Fanny thought to involve Alma, but when taken away from the ethereal regions she was now inhabiting, Ambrogio's young sister showed her marble statue face, pleading total ignorance. Upon being asked specific questions, she looked blank or pushed out her lower lip, as if to say, "Who cares about these things? I've never thought about questions like these." Fanny decided to leave her alone.

Having been brought back to earth, even though briefly, Alma looked around her and thought she recognized a figure walking calmly down the center aisle. "Oh, look who I see, it's Colomba! How come she's here?" she murmured.

Only Michele heard her, and he looked at the girl as she neared them. Tall and elegant, she had the beautiful face that poor Manno had imagined seeing in the labyrinth of the Cassino stones (surrounded by the rattle of the German Spandaus and the artillery shells exploding nearby; but who thought of these things now?). Colomba, whom nobody had thought to invite, had also come along to witness Ambrogio's oral defense of his thesis.

"Who are you talking about, that girl there in the aisle?" asked Michele, who had never before seen Colomba.

"Yes."

"You know her?"

"It's Colomba, Manno's fiancée, the one to whom he wrote his last letters."

"Ah, well, clearly she found out about today."

Alma turned instinctively to advise the others of Colomba's arrival, but then thought better of it. "I don't know whether to tell the others", she murmured.

"Why ever would you not tell them?" Michele asked.

Just at that moment a file of robed academics came in through a far door, wearing gowns and mortarboards. Walking solemnly one behind the other, they took their seats on the upstage side of the long tribunal table, accompanied by an increase in murmuring from the crowd, who soon after were silent. People who were still standing hurried to sit, as did Colomba, who continued looking around, doubtless for the Rivas.

"Why shouldn't you tell the others?" Michele asked again in a whisper. Alma shrugged her shoulders. "Well, you know, because Fanny is here." Michele thought, *Fanny? So what?* but decided it was none of his business.

After a few moments Francesca also spotted Colomba. Their eyes had met, and they waved happily at each other. Right away Francesca advised her family of Colomba's presence and explained to Fanny, "That girl was Manno's fiancée. You knew Manno, is that right?"

"Yes, in Stresa", said Fanny, nodding. And until the time came for Ambrogio to take his oral, Colomba was the Riva group's center of attention.

The oral examinations, in which candidates defended their theses, proved to be boring to the uninitiated. Not only was it hard to understand what was happening at the large table, but it was also occasionally impossible even to hear what was being said.

Ambrogio was the fifth in the economics discipline. He came on stage—like the other candidates before him—through a small door. When he reached the lone seat before the examiners' table, he nodded over at his family and, on seeing Colomba, greeted her, too.

He answered the examiners' questions with his usual calm air. His mother, Giulia, despite this, felt worried for him, forced as he was to go through that ceremony alone, facing the imposing row of important-looking professors.

His oral exam over, a younger professor made some sharply worded comment to Ambrogio about the "casualness" with which he had got round one question. "Contemptuous type!" Pino commented in a low voice. "Stinking snake!" But it soon became clear that the young examiner's intention had been not to embarrass Ambrogio but rather to take advantage of the opportunity presented to him by this gathering of illustrious colleagues in order to show off his sharp intellectual ability. (The occasion of the discussion of theses, even at the Catholic University, was an opportunity to shine one's light. In fact, it was as well that Gerardo, who—like many other uneducated people—had made great efforts in his direct way to establish the university, wasn't aware of the apple-polishing aspect of the exercise.)

Once the economics orals were over, the examining committee stood and left the hall in procession. The chairman had previously announced that they would return in about ten minutes for the proclamations of the degrees and levels of achievement.

Ambrogio immediately went toward his family, where Colomba joined them. "It went well, congratulations, you were very good", they all spoke at once. Ambrogio joked modestly, but was clearly satisfied that the long periods of studying were behind him. It took him a while to realize that he should ask Colomba about herself and her studies. "I'm hoping to take as many exams as I can," she replied, "because I'm getting married in the spring, and then I'll have to say goodbye to any spare time for studies."

Ambrogio wondered if she said it in a tone of regret. *Maybe I feel that because she's now someone else's*, he thought and, as usual with him, tried not to overestimate his own importance.

It was clear that Colomba was prettier than Fanny and probably prettier than any of the other girls here in the big hall. She said goodbye before the examiners returned for the proclamations. "I'm sorry, please forgive me, but I'm pressed for time."

Watching her leave, Michele said to Alma, "Want to know what I think? That girl will be beautiful until the day she dies. Just like you. Well, we'll talk about that again thirty or forty years from now."

"What funny ideas you have", Alma said.

"That's a fact", Michele agreed.

"Later you'll have to explain", whispered Alma. Smiling, Michele nodded agreement.

The examiners returned to the stage, and their chairman called each of the candidates back to the table, each to receive his parchment, at which time the chief examiner announced the marks awarded to each. Ambrogio was given 105 points out of a possible 110, a great score.

When all the degrees for economics had been handed out, the examiners once again left the hall, giving way to the literature examiners. The Rivas also stood and went toward the exit. "Listen, do you see the man leading the literature professors, their chairman?" Almina said to Michele, pausing for a moment. "That's Apollonio!"

"That man? Well, at last I've seen him!" (Mario Apollonio, dean of the faculty of literature and philosophy, writer, well-known theatrical and literary critic, was smiling a bit at the festive atmosphere surrounding the defense of theses but, all the same, as if the exercise were a game that he enjoyed; he had an extraordinarily human face.) "I like his face", Michele observed.

"Papa, do you see that man?" Alma then said to Gerardo, pointing. "That's Professor Apollonio, dean of literature. He's one of the most important teachers of literature in Italy."

"Ah, yes, I see him, I see him", commented Gerardo, pleased that the Catholic University had as professor such an important scholar.

When the group had left the hall, Fanny once more took charge. She got them moving, walking in directions that would enable Gerardo to see other areas of the university. ("I saw this", he said at each turn, "during the inauguration back in '26." In any case, he continued to be as delighted as he obviously had been twenty years before.)

When they left the university, they followed Fanny to a very chic pastry shop in the via Borgonuovo. Giulia would really have preferred to concentrate on Ambrogio without extraneous distractions, to share his enjoyment at his success in the examination. Michele and Alma, on the other hand, would have preferred to go off alone, but it would have been discourteous not to go along with Fanny, who was so efficiently showing them Milan (which she treated as if it were her own home), and besides, Ambrogio had specifically invited Michele to join the group.

The pastry shop had the rather unusual name of Terza Gallia, which puzzled Pino. "Whatever does it mean? What a strange name!" He turned to Michele. "Hey, author, doesn't it seem a bit extravagant?" Michele held back any comment. Having Almina so near, walking alongside him like a lamb, had him in a state of enchantment to the extent that he didn't want to involve himself in mundane matters, even if it was an amusing philological exercise. He just mumbled something incomprehensible.

"Folks," Fanny called out, intent on sharing information with the provincial family, "this place we're going into is perhaps one of the best cafés in all Europe, do you understand?" She turned to a distracted Michele, thinking this of interest to him. "Here you'll often see people from Milan's world of culture, such as the writer Piovene, professors Andrea Guerritore and Carlo Felice Manara from the state university, plus Zezi Locatelli and Liliana Grassi from architecture."

And so the celebration for Ambrogio's degree took place in that very refined pastry shop.

PART THREE

I

In the fall of that same year of 1947 Michele's book was published. Because of the subject matter, it had been accepted by the first publisher who saw it. Two years after the end of the war, there still weren't many eyewitness accounts of the Italian military tragedy that had occurred in Russia. The professional "readers" for the publishing house (it was one of Italy's most important) didn't recognize, though, the book's unique style, which owed little to contemporary literary schools but was remarkably appropriate to the tragic events it described. With their limited vision as "creatures of habit", they attributed the impression of freshness that emanated from the book to the fact that it had been written by someone outside their "milieu". In any case, as soon as it was published, it began to receive wide distribution.

However, the young author—more than ever struggling with his financial problems—wasn't in good enough spirits as to enjoy the book's success. After selling for next to nothing the furniture from the house at Nova, he didn't have enough hours in the twenty-four to study, to take turns with his uncle caring for his aunt, and to try by any means available to earn some money. He had decided not to ask the Rivas for a loan, not even when his uncle had come out openly and asked him. "You only have to let them see what problems you have. They'll offer to help straight away. And, of course, a loan isn't a gift. You'd be paying them back, with interest." He just couldn't do anything like that. Michele preferred to stick to his frustrating attempts to teach privately, largely unsuccessful because of the large number of other students doing the same. Besides, there was the fact that no one in Monza knew him well.

It was Almina who took pleasure in the book's success and who closely followed the progress of its sale in the bookshops. She had received the first copy. The budding author had taken it to the university; he had arrived in a great hurry one afternoon and found her—her braids lying on her chest and her face as mysterious as always—between classes, going from one classroom to another with her friends.

"Where are you going, young student? You'll find it hard to believe, but I've got a present for you." Then, steering her out of her group, "Guess where I've just been? I came here directly from the publishing house, and I admit I'm a little excited. At this very moment my book is being distributed around Milan, so tomorrow we'll see it displayed in the bookshop windows!" He had opened his briefcase. "They gave me six copies, as agreed; the first one is for you." He handed her the book. "Here, see, it has a dedication."

Receiving it from him, she had at first simply turned the book over and over in her hands, feeling it; soon she read the dedication and then turned to him with a look of indescribable emotion, without saying a word.

That's it, that's what makes her such a beautiful statue; great, she's acting just as I thought she would. It's when she's the most beautiful to look at. He very nearly reached out to caress her, but hesitated due to the presence of so many other people. His face, his whole being, projected a sense of his endless love. "It looks as if books will be the only presents I'll be able to give you, Alma. Well . . .", he said, steadying his voice, "take this other copy of the book for Ambrogio and the family."

She tried to decline. "No, no, one is enough."

"What, with this dedication?" he had commented. "It's better that this one be a gift just for you." He took his leave. "It would be nice now to be together for a while, right? But unfortunately I have to say goodbye, because I have something urgent to do. I'm sorry. Goodbye, Almina." (The urgent task was a meeting with a fellow POW, also a student like himself, but attending the state university, the faculty of chemistry, who produced homemade soap. As rationing was still in force, the black market in essentials also continued to operate. In the next few months Michele would manage to make and sell a few cases of soap, but for a modest return.)

The following day, instead of going to the university on the streetcar, Almina went downtown, getting off at the La Scala stop, and gingerly entered the shopping galleria. She walked quickly inside (the flooring was still only partially repaired, with large cement patches) toward the publisher's own bookshop. In the main window was Michele's new book. It occupied the center of the showcase, so that the author's name on the cover could be clearly seen . . . Michele's name, her Michele. She was able to see to her great happiness that the book was also in the other bookshops of the galleria and those in the neighborhood. On that morning Alma arrived late at the university.

On the following afternoon and for days thereafter, instead of boarding the streetcar to the rail station as usual, she went on foot to the center of town. She first went directly to the publisher's bookshop, her heart beating fast. The book continued to occupy the place of honor in the main window, with ten or twelve other copies arranged around it. The arrangement changed daily, with the books sometimes being in a circle, sometimes stacked like a staircase or in some other imaginative way. Alma would count and check the number of Michele's books, noticing with some concern as the days went past that the number of copies of the book remaining was reduced, yet there were still some of them. Other books had been placed in the windows and had disappeared entirely within a week or less (this upset her, she felt a sort of solidarity with these books' authors), while the remaining copies of Michele's book were still keeping their place.

After thoroughly checking the window, Alma—in her own charming way, with her braids swinging to the movement of her head—would check the windows of the other three bookshops in the galleria and then go on to another fourth bookshop, located outside under the northern arcade of the Piazza del Duomo. The book remained in all their front windows, although reduced to one or two copies only. (On one occasion she couldn't see the book in the Duomo bookshop; her heart turned over, and she reached for the door handle. She intended to ask for the book as if intending to purchase a copy and then show surprise that "that book, the one everybody is talking about", wasn't to be seen in the window. Looking again, she spotted the book just in time and didn't go inside.)

As the nearest streetcar stop for the central station was in the Piazza della Scala, Alma, after inspecting this bookshop, would follow on and walk through the galleria, making sure she stopped to gaze silently into the publisher's window. In the rush hours when the streetcar filled up to the point where some riders would need to cling to the outside, Alma would hurry. But just the same, sometimes before leaving the window she would go inside and in her clear tone of voice ask for a copy of the book, emphasizing ("It's written by Michele Tintori") the author's name, so that others could hear and (why not?) become interested enough to buy the book. Once or twice she gave in to the urge to ask, low voiced, while the clerk wrapped the book for her, "And how is the book going? Is it selling well?"

"Yes, right, it's a success, it keeps right on selling", the clerk would invariably reply.

"And so do you think it'll continue selling as time goes by?"

The clerk shrugged his shoulders. "If you like, I'll take you to see the manager so you can speak to him. Come this way", and although reluctant to go along, Alma, obeying the man's urging, followed him as he zigzagged between the tall bookshelves, arriving at a corner desk. "Commendatore, this young lady wants to talk to you."

The commendatore, a kindhearted shortish man with a prodigious memory about anything to do with books, finally recognized her. "Oh, our young lady! Have you come to buy another copy of the Tintori? How nice." They talked and became acquainted, and some days later he asked her, "Tell me, do you know the author personally?"

"I . . . yes."

Looking at Alma's braided hair and her restrained manners, he thought her younger than her actual age. "Are you perhaps a niece of his?"

Blushing in embarrassment, she had replied, "No, I'm a friend of his."

"Well then, in that case", the commendatore said vaguely, far from thinking that the author might be in love with this girl, "we'll give this young lady a discount." Then, turning to the cashier, "Ten percent discount for the young lady."

Even after this exchange, Alma couldn't prevent herself from continuing to visit the shop and, following the manager's decision—being of a female and practical mind—always got her 10 percent discount.

Michele's financial difficulties peaked at year's end. He understood the need to help his uncle defray the costs incurred by his living in the apartment (food, and the light bill, inflated by his long nights of studying); he also urgently needed to buy a new suit and an overcoat. However, the small amounts of money he was able to earn barely covered his university costs (the local streetcar, the college's restaurant, and the study fees). Additionally, there was the cost of cigarettes, which he was unable to give up due to his nervous state.

On some days he despaired and even asked himself if it was worth it all. Sometimes—when he was particularly despondent—it seemed to him that among man's freedoms, one of the drawbacks was the inability to choose whether or not to exist. Then he would scold himself and recall that, despite everything, his life was shared by Alma too, a considerable advantage. *But what's the use of my being in love, and having her love me, when I don't even have a decent suit to meet her in?* In any case there was no avoiding any of it. As a man, he was forced to fight the despondency and the rest, just as he had had to in combat during the war—when he had had the substantial and useful help of his guardian angel and namesake, Archangel Saint Michael—so he had also to fight these continuing skirmishes against the daily misery. *When one is buried in filth and the sh—— that life always brings, there's no alternative but to fight, fight until one is in the clear.*

2

He graduated in the following spring of 1948, just before the April 18 general elections. It was just a year and a half since he had been repatriated.

Only Ambrogio was present for his oral examination, and Michele would have preferred it if even he hadn't been there, having chosen an uninteresting theme for his thesis and convinced that he had prepared it inadequately. He had particularly objected to Alma being there. "I beg you, don't insist. I don't want you to see me in this, let's say, painful situation. You're too important to me, and I'd rather have you think of me as a successful man. For as long as that can be, do you understand?" So Alma stayed in Nomana on that Saturday, preparing a dinner with which to celebrate the graduation.

The two young men—Ambrogio and Michele—left the university together straight after the results were announced. Both were tired: Ambrogio, because of his work at the factory, felt the tiredness brought about by a week of heavy responsibilities, and Michele was tired due to the prolonged nervous pressure. The new graduate wore a dark camel-colored overcoat, apparently new, but in fact converted out of an old blanket from home.

It was getting dark; in the streets and squares of Milan very few cars were parked. They both got into the Rivas' sporty Millecento, which Ambrogio drove toward downtown.

"So?" Ambrogio said, for something to say.

"Nothing", Michele murmured. Neither really wanted to talk any more about the newly awarded degree.

"I haven't yet asked you, and I'm sorry, but I've been telling myself to do so since this morning. How is it going with the second printing of your book?"

"It just came out", Michele smiled. "Oh, how long now? Maybe ten days ago."

"That's a good sign, a second printing, right?"

"Yes, right."

"And what's more, I see the book is selling. People are reading it with interest. I've heard lots of people talking about it."

Michele nodded. "Even though it brings me little or nothing. Did you know I didn't get even one lira out of the first printing?"

"How come?"

"It was part of the contract. I was supposed to be happy with the fame of being published by such an important firm. They started giving me a small percentage just now from the second printing."

"Good, well, there'll be many more printings", Ambrogio said confidently. "By the way, have you been to see Apollonio?"

"Didn't Alma tell you? Yes, I've seen him."

"Well, it was about time. Better late than never, eh, Michele?" Ambrogio commented.

They both laughed. Despite his determination in their first year at the university, Michele hadn't been to see the famous critic. Recently, when his book was published, Michele had decided to take him a personal copy, but before he could put this decision—one of many he had to make around this time—into action, Apollonio had written a review of the book in Milan's Catholic newspaper. It was a splendid criticism that enthusiastically praised the book. Apollonio had never before written in this way about a living author.

When Alma had read the article (having had it pointed out to her by her father, who had spotted it while reading the paper at breakfast) she had cried out with happiness, unusual behavior for the marble statue. She then danced in circles between the dining room and the kitchen, holding the newspaper up in the air, showing a rare enthusiasm. "Have you seen this? Do you know what it means? There's no other critic as important as Apollonio in all Italy; nobody has better judgment."

"You mean among Catholic critics?" asked her brother Fortunato, who, like his father, was having his morning coffee.

"No, not at all! Among all the other critics. There isn't a more profound expert in literary matters, nobody better qualified than he." Alma didn't stop here; she felt a great need to talk about the matter. "I'll give you an example. When Alfredo Galletti, probably the best of the old school critics, left the chair of Italian literature at the state university, everyone wanted Apollonio to take his place, you understand? Because he had more qualifications than anyone else and for his prestige. But by good fortune he didn't want to leave the Catholic University."

"So," Ambrogio asked Michele, "at last you did go and see him?"

"Yes, but not at the university. I went to his house. And there I found Grassi and Strehler visiting him. You've heard of them, I suppose?" At Ambrogio's shake of the head, he continued. "They're both avid followers of the theater; they're our age, maybe a little older. Their love for the stage is impressive. And when Apollonio talks with them about the stage, he seems as youthful as they. All three of them want to found a regular theater here in Milan or something of that nature. But I don't know if they'll manage; it would need a lot of money."

His face went somber. *Always the lack of money, damned money*, he thought and grimaced. In truth, for a while now (since the vice rector at his old college, the one nicknamed Indigenous Clergy, had found him a job as substitute teacher at a Milan high school) his financial situation had been less precarious, to the extent that he had been able to buy a suit, which he was now wearing. Moreover, for some time now, since the general election had been announced for the next April 18, money problems had become of secondary importance for everyone. What was at stake in these elections was no less than their recently acquired freedoms, and perhaps for some their very lives.

"Well, what exactly did Apollonio tell you?"

"You know, he's not only a teacher. He's also a gentleman. He made me welcome. As far as my plans for the future, however," Michele shook his head, "he said in effect that I must make my way alone. He wants us to remain friends, that was clear, and he invited me to visit him as often as I like, but not as one of his assistants or like the other people in his circle. Because, according to him, I can't develop my own methods of expression except on my own, and also . . . well, he said that I shouldn't associate myself with anyone or any group, not even with him." He grimaced, puzzled looking.

"I don't understand. How do you feel? Are you happy or not?"

"I don't know. At first it made me proud, as you can imagine, given our general inclination toward original sin."

Ambrogio burst out laughing.

"What's so funny? Isn't that the way it is?"

"I can't deny it. It's just that you refer to original sin as if you were commenting on a truck going by."

"That's how I see it."

"Very well, go on."

"Well, after that, first sinful pride", Michele, too, smiled, "I must admit I felt a certain disquiet, which has remained with me, which I still feel. The truth is I am really a loner, you understand? Outside the mainstream, without the least idea of the craft. But that's not all. If you talk about a project you have in mind with other people, I mean with people who are really qualified to give you a valid opinion, you know how much time you can save? It's not only that people can add to your thoughts; your own ideas become clearer, better defined."

"I understand."

"Well, good", Michele concluded. "Anyway, there's always the fact that I can talk to Alma."

"With Alma?! What are you saying? About your work? But she's just . . . a child. Intelligent, granted, but how far can she help you?"

"You're mistaken", Michele retorted abruptly. "Talking to her is a little like rethinking a project while gazing at . . . for example . . . at one of those paintings dating back to the fourteenth or fifteenth century. Whatever is superfluous or inappropriate in your project gets shaken out, falls down, as . . . irreconcilable with what is before you. So, just by being herself, she helps me enormously. Have I explained it well?"

Seeing Ambrogio's silent disbelief, Michele finally nodded to himself, agreeing with his own view, as he habitually had done while under imprisonment as a POW.

"Well, my word, what a crush!" Ambrogio commented. "You're really gone, poor Michele! Let's be clear. I'm in no way responsible!" he laughed. "I haven't the slightest responsibility for your crush on Alma."

They reached the Piazza della Scala. As they'd expected, they were able to park without problem and walked to the nearby provincial headquarters of the Christian Democratic party, where Ambrogio was due to pick up some material for the election campaign.

3

At the Christian Democrat HQ—the old Clerici palace—there was much coming and going. Employees, laborers, and students, volunteering at the end of their workday, would come by and help before going back out of town, carrying out errands on behalf of the several provincial party branches. Some would be shouldering heavy rolls of posters or packages of brochures; others would be there to go upstairs to the offices to seek approval for dates for local meetings or to receive instructions. Those picking up material went to the basement, where the advertising material was stored.

Ambrogio and Michele also went downstairs. On his first visit, Michele looked around curiously. Down in the basement fliers and posters were stacked everywhere; behind a counter the walls of the large open space were labeled with cards identifying piles of promotional material for the several municipalities, neatly stacked below each sign. Five or six students—some wearing the Catholic Action badge—were responsible for issuing the material. The leader of the group, a pale youth wearing a beret and moving around with typical Milanese efficiency, was referred to by his companions as "Bookkeeper".

Hearing this, Ambrogio called out, "Hey, Bookkeeper!" Then, smiling at the man, he said, "The material for Nomana, please."

The bookkeeper had been involved in a discussion with an old laborer; he turned away from the man and came over to Ambrogio. He looked very annoyed.

"What's up?" asked Ambrogio. "Some problem?"

"No, it's just that some thoughtless guy from Limito seems to have taken the posters meant for Cernusco", the bookkeeper replied. (He must have qualified recently, as he couldn't have been any older than eighteen or nineteen.) "Now the fellow from Cernusco will give me what for", he complained. "You see what happens when you're in a hurry? It's always something!"

"Look, I'm sorry", said Ambrogio.

The elderly laborer had come closer. "Come on, Bookkeeper", he pleaded in dialect. "Be a good fellow. There are piles of posters here. Why short Cernusco sul Naviglio?"

Another young man, this one from Gorgonzola, also joined in. "Don't you know that if he arrives in Cernusco without the posters, they'll take and throw him into the canal?"

"Quiet, you, great curse of Gorgonzola", immediately retorted the Cernusco man.

"Gorgonzola and Cernusco together, both from the same stable", interrupted someone else, laughing. (Ambrogio recognized the youth—he was from Incastigo, an industrial area, which would be why he equated the two agricultural towns out on the plain.)

The bookkeeper raised his eyes to the roof, sighed, and then became businesslike. "Come on, let's not waste time", he said, and to Ambrogio, "Will you take just the stuff for Nomana, or will you also take the material for the periphery?"

"I don't know . . . if there's anything for Raperio, give it to me; I'll drop it off on the way by."

One of the students helping with distributing the material advised the book-keeper that the material for Raperio had already been collected half an hour before by a redhead.

"Ah, yes, I know who that would be", Ambrogio said.

The bookkeeper turned to the student. "Look, do me a favor. Put together some posters for Cernusco. Check the distribution list and give the man what's listed. Don't do it just any old way."

"Do I also give him the ones with the skeleton?"

"No!" the bookkeeper came near to shouting. "The posters drawn by Guareschi are meant to be distributed the day after tomorrow, not before. How many times do I have to repeat it?"

Shrugging his shoulders, he said to Ambrogio, "You'll have your material right away." Then, with the other youth's help, he brought the material over. Ambrogio and Michele picked it up and headed for the exit. Just before leaving the basement Ambrogio turned for another look. The people working there, preparing for the very important upcoming election, were all volunteers. People from all levels of society, but joined together—as was Ambrogio—as members of Catholic Action, whose popular straightforward attitude could be felt in the air.

4

After putting the material in the car's trunk, the two young men got in and headed down the via Manzoni, unaware that some hours before the secretary of the Italian Communist party, Palmiro Togliatti, had been in one of the street's big hotels, visiting the town on one of his campaign trips.

Leaving via Manzoni, they passed the Venezia gate and the Piazza Loreto on the way to Sesto. The surface of the streets along the way was broken, but along many stretches they were being repaired with either asphalt or paving stones. Michele noticed that along the sidewalk edge there were wooden barriers covered with jute sacking, placed there by the stonemasons, as usual, to prevent stone chips from their rock splitting from hitting passersby. He thought of his father, the stone-chipping sculptor. He would like to come back here and watch the stonemasons while they worked.

Like many other streets, the walls along this one were covered with election posters. On the whole the anti-Communist party's posters seemed to prevail. This was not so in the streets of the surrounding areas, and particularly in Sesto, which they reached in the car after having passed through a stretch of open country. In this big industrial area there was a palpable impression that something was bubbling up. It was from here that impressive worker's rallies organized by the Reds would march through the streets of Milan, intimidating the population. The walls carried this party's threatening posters, some hand painted, showing the hammer and sickle. Among all that Red propaganda the two youths felt themselves strangely alien.

On one wall they saw a poster that sang the praises of Tito. "Talking of Tito," Michele said, "not the political gorilla across the Adriatic, but the chap in Nomana. Tito, who was with me in Susdal—he lives on that farm out there. What's it called?"

"Casaretto?"

"Right. How is he; is he better?"

Ambrogio shook his head. "Not yet. I've heard that he's gone to another sanitarium and that he's gaining weight slowly, even though he's still quite sick. Poor chap. I'd have liked to go and see him at the farm tomorrow." Ambrogio nodded. There came to his mind that other farm, Nomanella, and the sad mother of the house, Mama Lucia. Also the memory of Ferrante, now bent over even more since Giustina's death and Stefano's disappearance. Poor people . . . he had visited them now and then. He no longer tried to speak words of comfort. He just stayed a while with them.

Luca, however, went more frequently, never forgetting he had been Giustina's fiancé. Every Sunday he'd go there to Nomanella at noon, dressed in his church-going suit, as if she were still there. The grandmother, already a bit gone in the head, didn't always recognize Luca. One day she had even confused him with Stefano. "What, Stefano, you're back?!" she had asked. Luca, still with his forelock and as openhearted as ever, would sit with the family in the kitchen in winter and in the open air in the shade of a cherry tree in summertime. He spoke softly and not necessarily about Giustina. In a way it seemed that as long as he was there, Giustina hadn't gone from this world altogether. But, of course, she really wasn't there any more. One day Ferrante had said, "Luca, you have to look for another girl."

Luca had replied, "There's plenty of time, Father."

Having left Sesto behind them, they next came to Monza. Although a bit of a sleepy town, Monza, peaceful and deeply Catholic, gave a sense of relief to the traveler coming from Sesto. *In a place like this, no one thinks about slaughter,* both Ambrogio and Michele thought. They were ignorant of the coincidence that, a half hour before, Pierello had thought the same when going through Monza, heading from Nomana. Monza, in any case, to someone who came from Sesto or Milan, seemed just a small town.

They left the town behind, reaching the countryside, now blooming exuberantly, and then the first few villages of Brianza itself. The highway took them through the centers of each hamlet. "Have you noticed how many posters there are even here for the elections?" Ambrogio commented.

"Right, yes. I'd give a lot to know how all this business now will end up", Michele muttered.

"It'll be all right. You'll see."

"Let's hope . . ."

They left Incastigo behind, having crossed the double arch of the bridge over the dip made by the Lambro; then the road climbed, zigzagging between the hills, passing wooded areas of leafless locust trees.

"Did you notice if the Lambro's water was muddied?" Ambrogio asked.

"No, and frankly, with this darkness . . ."

"I should have checked earlier, on the way into Milan. Because if the river is full at all, we could come tomorrow to fish over there near our new factory. Well, not exactly new, just in a manner of speaking. It's an empty building we bought on the riverside and are fixing up."

"Right, I'd like to see it."

"In that case, we'll go tomorrow, whatever . . ."

"Is it one of the buildings one can see from the bridge?"

"No, you can't see it from the bridge", Ambrogio paused. "We're installing loom after loom, some of them new, but most of them are secondhand, bought all over the place. To tell the truth, sometimes it worries me to be using these older machines, since I was told at the university it could be a dangerous practice. It's something I was thinking about, which went through my mind, back there when I was in the big examination hall."

"How come?"

"It's not so much a question of the cash—and although we haven't much, we're not short either—it's more the way one looks at things. My father doesn't want to waste any time. He says, 'If we don't create jobs in times like these, I fail to see what good we manufacturers are.' He repeats it often and maintains, 'On the other hand, we can soon replace the used looms if it's really necessary.' In his way of looking at things, he's more like the working man he used to be than a businessman. Creating new jobs has always been a fixed idea with him."

"Yes, I know. But you know, I like your old man."

Ambrogio nodded. "Luckily, about ten days ago in Turin we signed the customs union treaty with France."

"With the French? A customs treaty?"

"Didn't you know?"

"No."

"They signed it in Turin. On our side, Sforza the government minister; for the French, Bidault. This business of customs unions with other European countries is one of De Gasperi's obsessions, I guess you know. He looks on them as a first step toward unifying Europe."

"So, now we have a customs union with France?" Michele said. "I didn't know. For weeks now I've been thinking only about graduating and haven't managed to read the newspapers."

"Well, I'll tell you one thing. I'll be surprised if it lasts. I don't know about other industries, but for our textiles it'll be a great windfall. The French can't compete with our prices."

"But if they've signed, presumably they know what they're doing."

"So you would think."

5

Having gone through the entrance, the car stopped in front of the main house door, where Alma had been waiting. As she came out, Giudittina—now thirteen—followed her. Alma's impatient waiting had affected her as well.

"Michele, how did it go? Did you graduate all right? Yes?!" Alma asked, very moved by the occasion. She shook his hand and then continued to hold it in both of hers. "Now you are an honorable doctor? What good news!"

"Doctorate? You have your doctorate, honorable doctor? Oh, what a laugh!" Giudittina shouted.

"Shut up, will you, sillyhead!" Ambrogio told her. Unexpectedly Giudittina jumped on Michele, who had to scramble to regain his balance. Meanwhile Alma, with her marble statue smile as always, continued fondly holding Michele's hand.

"Look at her, the little monkey! How thoughtless!" Ambrogio exclaimed.

"No, leave her", Michele defended, and to Giudittina, "My, what enthusiasm! You must really like me!"

Mimicking Alma, Giudittina held onto Michele's other hand. "So? Tell all, come on", she said, continuing with her tomfoolery. "Now that you're a doctor, have you grown a couple of inches?"

Ambrogio shook his head, then restarted the car. "I'm going to deliver the posters. Then I'll put the car in the woodshed", he said, referring to the garage, which had been converted from the old firewood shed.

Michele and Alma would have preferred to be alone a while, but it was too dark for walking in the garden. When they went inside the house, the others—Pino, Rodolfo, and briefly from the kitchen Giulia and Francesca—like Giudittina, came to Michele to congratulate him. Giulia suggested that until dinnertime he might want to rest a bit. "Even though it'll only be ten or fifteen minutes, that's better than no rest at all. Lord knows you've had a tiring day. Your bedroom is waiting. Why not lie down for a while?"

But Alma's eyes pleaded, "Don't go, stay here", though she didn't say a word.

"Thank you, but I'm really not tired", Michele answered Giulia.

From the kitchen there wafted the smell of soup and roast meat, life's comforting odors. *My bedroom*, Michele thought. *In other words, poor dead Manno's room.* (He still found himself going back to his brush with death, particularly on happy occasions like this one.) *And now he can't enjoy any of these things. Maybe*, he was imagining, *the place Manno's spirit is is on a very different plane of reality from ours at this moment. If only we could find out how things are in the other world, how they live in the hereafter! But we can't. To begin with, in eternity, moments like this don't exist.*

"Come on", Alma said to him, all happiness because he had stayed with her. "Let's go into the parlor."

In my next book I'll talk about Manno, he made a mental note while he followed the others, led by Alma. *I can't let his memory die with his disappearance, now that he has been swallowed by the silence, the terrible silence. Still, even supposing the new book is successful, how long will people continue to read it? Even if it was read for one hundred or even two hundred or three hundred years, it'll still be nothing, really nothing, compared to eternity.*

"Soon Papa and Fortunato will arrive back from the office", Alma was saying to him, "and also Andrea, you know, Andrea Marsavi. He also wants to congratulate you. Are you happy?"

The young author rested his wondering eyes on his girl, her frail face, her chestnut hair. "Yes, of course", he said, smiling.

6

They were all around Michele at the table: Gerardo and Giulia with their six children, then Andrea, who in a few months would be marrying Francesca and who had arrived with an enormous bunch of flowers for her. *What a pity Fanny can't be here, a real pity,* Ambrogio thought. He and Fanny had also decided to get married so that in a few months the house would see two weddings. The women—including Giudittina—were up and down, helping Noemi and each other to bring in the food and later taking away the empty plates. The usual bustling about of mealtime drove Michele's thoughts of death out of his mind.

"So, in the year and a half since you left the POW camp, you've launched a book and a doctorate", observed Pino.

"That's what you call being busy", agreed Fortunato, himself about to graduate from engineering school. "And what a book! I read the review by Apollonio. What good luck, Michele."

"That's true", Francesca added admiringly. "You know, if we weren't friends I'd feel intimidated by a person like you."

Almina, holding the soup tureen, was quietly enjoying these complimentary remarks, not missing a word. She nodded happily.

"All right, cut it out", Michele said. "You can stop pulling my leg", but on seeing Alma's happiness, he was happy himself. *Blessed be this house, so full of life,* he said to himself, speaking from the heart.

"Listen, Michele," Rodolfo asked, "following an article like that, the one by Apollonio (I also read it; it was great), what'll happen?" This was a more thoughtful Rodolfo than he had been one year ago.

Michele turned to Alma. "Hey, have you been leaning on your brothers and sisters so they'll read the article?"

"No", Alma laughed. She still had the tureen in her hands. "I assure you, I haven't."

"I read it of my own accord, of course", Rodolfo confirmed. "Nobody forced me to. But come on, tell me, what'll happen? Will you be listed among works of literature? Then students would have to read your work?"

At this they all laughed, even though Rodolfo's question intrigued them all.

"Answer, answer", Fortunato chanted.

The young writer shook his head, smiling. "In Italy every critic works on his own behalf," he explained, "and in practice they aren't interested in what other critics say, even the more prominent among them. So the work of any individual critic doesn't count for much. It's different when a foreign critic, particularly if he's from France, discovers an Italian book. Obviously, when you think about it, our literature is quite provincial, more even than in other creative fields. Provincial to an extreme degree." He nodded his head thoughtfully. "Fascism prevented many people from seeing this, which was almost merciful." He noticed Gerardo's attentive, almost tense expression and thought, *Maybe I'm talking too much like a highbrow . . .*

Francesca asked, "But are all critics really the same?"

Michele pursed his lips. "Well, there's an exception, one only, and that's Benedetto Croce. He is regarded, at least nowadays, as the chief of them all."

"Croce . . . the Liberal?"

"Yes, he. Although to me, to tell the truth, he doesn't seem to be, strictly speaking, just a critic. Apart from the fact that he's much given to politics nowadays, overall he's . . . too much the philosopher and treats literature as . . . but maybe we're getting into too abstract a subject. In any case, you know the blunders he's capable of making with his ideas, the stupid things he says, for example about Pascoli."

"Listen," Alma remained in charge of the tureen, "have you, that is, either you or the publisher, have you sent Croce a copy of the book?"

"No, why?"

"Why not?" she exclaimed. "You should have sent him a copy. How come you didn't think of it? What a pity." Her faith in Michele's book was so obvious that the family started laughing. Only Giudittina said, "It's true. You ought to have sent him one."

Alma put the tureen down on the nearest surface (the cover on the radiator) and went over to Michele. "Listen," she said in a low voice, "upstairs I have a copy of the book. Tomorrow you dedicate it, and then I'll send it off."

"What dedication? To whom?"

"To Benedetto Croce."

Michele, amused, wagged his head. "Oh, come on now ..." Then, to remove himself from the center of attention, he deliberately changed the subject to the important matter of the day—the elections—which were coming up within two weeks. Conversation about the election became general around the table, and it soon became clear that a Marxist front victory, although a remote possibility, was something that worried them all. "It's a great risk, really; it's tremendous", Gerardo observed.

"It's better not to think about what would happen if they won", Ambrogio said in a low voice. "But soon you'll see. They won't win."

"I believe the same," said Fortunato, "but what's worrying is the disproportion of what is in the balance. If the Christian Democrats win, it'll just be the winning of an election, period, no more than that; and for the Communists there's always the possibility of taking power the next time around, at the next elections. For the Democrats, however, a Communist victory would be the end, the ..." He chopped at the air, as if imitating an ax stroke.

The gesture was so real that it silenced them for a moment. Giudittina stretched out her neck and mimed a throat-cutting movement. This drew Giulia's attention, and she cast a disapproving glance at Fortunato. "There's always providence on our side, no?" she exclaimed. "Therefore ... besides, why would the Communists win? Here in Brianza, even joined together" (she meant the Communists and Socialists, who had joined together for these elections in a popular front), "they won't get a third of the vote."

"Right", added Rodolfo. "Let's remember that two years ago, in Visate's local elections, the Reds didn't even run. Isn't that right, Andrea?"

Andrea agreed. "It's true. They were afraid that not even one of them would be elected, and so they didn't take part."

"Ah, right", said Francesca. "If I remember correctly, in those elections it was your father who gained the most votes, right?"

Andrea nodded. "He was really elected by the working man."

"But how did you run an election with only one list of candidates?" Pino queried.

"No, there were two lists: one from the Christian Democrats, and the other, smaller, as it turned out, from the Catholic Action."

"And which of the two won?" a now less fidgety Giudittina asked.

"The Christian Democrats, of course, because the other list was smaller and had been entered alongside that of the winners just so there wouldn't be an election without choice."

Not far from Visate, in Monticello (Fortunato remembered) in those earlier elections, they had reelected the former Fascist mayor. The man had been neither formerly a Fascist nor later an anti-Fascist; he was simply a Christian.

Because of this he was thought to be the man most fit to run the municipality, and the people gave him a large majority.

"A pity that all of Italy isn't like our Brianza", Alma said worriedly.

"Of course, there are the Red areas, unfortunately," said Fortunato, "around Emilia, and Toscana . . ."

"Right. Before they all seemed to be Fascists there, and now it seems they're all Communists", pointed out Ambrogio, wagging his head.

"Back in 1924, two years after taking power, when the Fascists held elections, their party won votes, not only in Emilia and Toscana but all over Italy", Gerardo noted. "They got more than two-thirds of the votes. Only here, in our area, did they lose; in Monza and Brianza they managed only 19 percent."

"Whereas now, in Emilia", said Ambrogio, "if you just think about those poor priests murdered in that death's triangle." He looked at Michele. "Haven't you read the paper recently? Did you hear that two weeks ago they'd killed another priest?"

"Yes, I'd heard", Michele nodded.

Giulia looked with concern at her youngest. "Giudittina, go and see how Noemi is doing with that zucchini pie. Give her a hand."

"Oh, please", Giudittina pleaded, aware that she was being sent outside so she wouldn't be frightened by the conversation. She got up reluctantly.

"Come on, hurry."

The young girl left, craning her head left and right with each step. Ambrogio was about to make some joking remark, but thought better of it when he had a sudden vision of what might happen if the Communists, once they had won the elections, acted toward Italian industrialists as they had done with the Russians. Perhaps Giudittina would be killed, probably after being raped repeatedly. Or maybe they'd send her into exile along with her parents, in one of those frightening cattle trucks, just as they were now doing to former leaders in Czechoslovakia and Poland. He felt a sharp fear and thought of the machine gun he'd acquired, kept hidden in the attic, and the arms his brothers also had. Before there was any generalized atrocity they'd wipe out those Red butchers. But that wouldn't solve anything, wouldn't ensure the safety of their families, not for sure. *Lord, don't let that happen, I beg you.* He closed his eyes for a moment and prayed.

Francesca was saying, "I don't understand how the people of Emilia, the people you meet at the seaside, for example, they're so pleasant, so happy. How can they just turn around and kill people like that?"

"They have hot blood", Gerardo announced ponderously. But this wasn't an explanation. Being self-taught, Gerardo inevitably mixed sensible and often wise observations—when they were the fruit of his own experience—with commonplace remarks like this one. His children, accustomed to his ways, didn't react to the statement.

"You should see the people's behavior in Emilia", said Andrea. Then, turning to Francesca at his side, "You know that last Thursday I was meeting with a supplier from Faenza." He turned toward the others. "I had to wait more than an hour for a connection at the station in Bologna. Well, you could say that nobody, or nearly nobody, works in the station; it's as if life stood still. They're waiting for the elections, and as they're nearly all Communists, they're convinced their people will be elected. And those that aren't Communists are afraid to admit it out loud. Anyway, it seems to them useless to do any work in a . . . for a society that they think will be finished. That's how the man from Faenza explained it to me. There was a woman getting off a train, she had a baby in her arms, and as none of the porters showed up, I had to take her suitcase for her at the station exit. The woman looked as if she was about to cry, the poor thing."

"Your reason for helping her wouldn't be because she was pretty, would it?" asked Fortunato, a tolerant smile on his face.

"It's no joking matter", said Gerardo gravely.

Ambrogio went along with his father's mood. "If things are getting bad in the Red areas, we'll have to think about what'll happen when they've lost the elections—I'm sure the Reds will lose—how things will end up. Will they just tamely go back to work, or will they try a civil rebellion? Just look at what is happening in Greece."

Michele looked up alertly. This was a real threat. The way the fighting in Greece was going was an example that was very worrisome. There, after having allied themselves alongside other political groups to fight the Germans, as in Italy, the Communists had unleashed their own revolt. A savage civil war had developed and had gone through phases; the previous summer they had proclaimed the parts of the country under their control an "independent republic". But now they were in retreat toward the Yugoslav border, pushed by American troops and by the Greek regular army. As in their war with Italy, the Greek regulars had shown themselves to be hard, loyal fighters.

While the others around the table were commenting on the Greek conflict ("What a frightening perspective . . . what a disaster if it happened!") and its battles and main figures ("That scoundrel Markos"), Michele was wondering whether the Communists in Greece were even now kidnapping children. His mind went over memories of the Spanish children in the Susdal *lager*, dressed in rags, and their pleas. ("This is a sh——ty country, señor . . .") What barbaric, crazy things were being done to human beings in these times!

While the general conversation went on, Rodolfo, having looked at his watch, threw his napkin on the table and got up. His mother asked, "What are you doing?"

"I'm off", he answered. "It's getting near to my time to be at the Oratory." He had been growing recently. He was not only taller and thinner; his face had become more grave.

"To the Oratory tonight? To do what?" his father asked.

"Those of us in the poster teams have to go out tonight."

"What posters?"

"Just like last week; we have to paste up posters in the town."

"Yes, that's true", Ambrogio explained. "The poster groups have to put them up. These are the election posters that I brought from Milan today."

"Before you go, eat your main course", the mother said. "Look at how many vegetables you've left uneaten on your plate. You don't want to waste all that God-given food."

"But . . .", Rodolfo protested. Then he lifted his eyes to the ceiling and opened his arms wide, mimicking Pierello and accepting the inevitable. He sat down again and put a huge forkful of vegetables in his mouth. His mother looked as if she were about to remonstrate, tell him to mind his table manners, but she held herself back. For a while now her son's behavior had been going through a change, a sort of maturing, and, as he had so promptly obeyed and resumed his seat, there was no need to reprimand him any further.

Michele continued thinking about the Greek children. Up to then no definite news had been received, although the fact was that in their retreat the Greek Communists were gathering together the children in the villages and towns. As it turned out those kidnapped children—among whom were many of very young age—didn't reach Russia, as had the Spanish kids at Susdal. The argument between Tito and Stalin prevented it, and as a result the Greek government was able to repatriate them from Yugoslavia by means of a diplomatic negotiation that made all the world's newspapers.

7

They were drinking coffee (real coffee, imported, as before, from Brazil), and conversation had become general, when from the street they heard a confused shouting. Everyone was fairly nervous. Even though the voices from the street sounded as if the shouters were enjoying themselves, Ambrogio got up, but instead of opening the room's street window, he went into the next room, opening the single window to look outside. A group of poster hangers was approaching, a few young fellows. Ambrogio returned to the dining room and called to Michele, "Come and look." They both went to the open window in the next room and looked out.

The young boys joked and laughed among themselves. At their head as leader was Saulo, the oldest of the chauffeur Celeste's seven sons (that Saulo who would become an industrialist and future mayor of Nomana). Behind Saulo came a boy pushing a bicycle on which he carried a six- or seven-step ladder. Another, also pushing a bike, had a glue bucket hanging from the handlebars. After him came others, carrying posters and brushes, being in turn followed by some younger boys, not there to help with the work, but just along to have fun, and these were the source of much of the noise, shouting loudly in their shrill childish voices. The group's chief, Saulo, though a little embarrassed by their noise, contributed to it by shouting refrains, "Forward with the young-sters! Volunteer martyrs, forward!" and "Charge! The Catholics bearing glue!" Those of his troops who were nearest, and particularly the small boy with the glue bucket, shouted in response, "And you at the head! You, more Christian than most!" until they saw the two men at the window, when they became quiet. "Good evening, Doctor", Saulo greeted Ambrogio. Then, to his group, "Halt! Stop here."

He pointed to a section of wall on the house opposite. "Over there we'll put four in a row, two with the shield and two with the symbol of democracy."

"There are more of the posters with the barbed wire", one of them said, as the others prepared to work.

"I know", Saulo answered irritably. "I know. But as I already told you, we'll be putting those up near the Communist office. Come on, don't waste time."

Shortly Saulo again raised his voice. "No, Adeodato, no. How many times do I have to tell you not to put the posters facedown on the ground when putting on the paste? Don't you see that you're dirtying the symbol of democracy?"

"The symbol of democracy", Michele murmured. "I like that."

"Should we go out?" Ambrogio proposed, low voiced. "We could go briefly to the Oratory. That's where these poster squads are coming from."

"The center of operations, do you mean?" said Michele. They both laughed.

"That center is more likely to be at party HQ. Well, if you like we can also go by there. It's on the way to the Oratory. It would be a new experience for you, right?"

"But . . . what about . . . are we going to leave the family here?" Obviously he was thinking more of Almina, not wanting to be separated from her. But at the same time he was attracted by the chance to see with his own eyes the town's political campaign machinery.

"Come on! We've finished dinner," Ambrogio said, "and we won't be out long. We'll be back in a half hour." He closed the window.

From outside came Saulo's voice. "You bunch of idiots, you've spilled the glue! Miserable clowns! Was that your fault, Adeodato, eh?!"

"No", came the reply from Adeodato. "It was that dizzy Beniamino."

8

Party headquarters—with its customary metal sign—was in the via Manzoni just before the entrance to the piazza. It was really the shop of a clock repairer from Incastigo, who—as he opened for business only on market day,

Wednesday—hadn't had any difficulty in subletting it to the party for the other six days. Inside were a few showcases and two empty cabinets, as well as some cane chairs, which were borrowed from the Oratory for the duration of the campaign. In one corner, heaped on chairs and on the floor, were quantities of propaganda material. Ambrogio recognized some of the packages of fliers he and Michele had collected earlier in Milan.

Sitting in a circle were six or seven party members, all laborers, who were talking among themselves. They greeted the two new arrivals cordially, but without rising, in the independent and somewhat rude manner of Brianza.

"So, is this the center of operations?" said Michele, going back to the earlier joke.

Ambrogio smiled and nodded. "It'll do for us." Then, turning to the others, "Isn't that right?" and then, to Michele, "Come, let's sit down for a while."

The others shifted their chairs to accommodate them in the circle. Ambrogio addressed one of the members, a middle-aged ruddy man with a bull neck. "Renzo, where do the fellows putting up the posters get their material, here or at the Oratory?"

"They assemble all over the place, here and the Oratory both", the man replied in dialect, nodding amiably.

Another man added, also in dialect, "For the posters they come here, while for the paste—as it's made by the stationer's son, he's the glue expert—they go to the stationery shop."

"Right, good."

"Have you ever seen such a circus, eh?" the ruddy man looked at Michele. "Three of my kids are in that bunch."

Ambrogio introduced him to Michele. "This is Renzo Crippa, the vice secretary." And to Renzo, "I just saw one of your sons—Adeodato."

The vice secretary nodded, smiling. "Yes, he's only a little fellow, but . . ." (He obviously meant to say that his son could pull his own weight.)

"Eh!" Ambrogio agreed. "Well," he changed the subject, "how about telling me what you were all talking about?"

"As you can imagine, the one main subject there is", Renzo answered, "about the election, naturally."

"That's understood", another man said, waving his hands. He was young and had very short black hair.

"Some imagination we have, eh?" said a bent white-haired man, Felice (Felisen in dialect) by name. "But that's the way it is. We hardly manage to talk of anything else."

"But here in Nomana in any case you're sure of winning, right?" Michele commented.

"Well, Nomana is no problem", Felice agreed.

"But that doesn't mean we can sleep on the job", put in a so-far silent man of indefinable age, his face skinny and fine drawn.

Ambrogio introduced him to Michele. "This is Pio Cavenago. He has a son studying for the priesthood."

Cavenago nodded politely.

The dark-haired man cut in. "Obviously we can't sleep on the job, because the Reds, they really work, and how!"

"You know, it's incredible", the vice secretary, Renzo, had turned to Ambrogio, curiosity in his face. "Do you know there are people among the Reds who are now sure, absolutely sure, that they'll win? I don't mean here in Nomana, obviously, but in all Italy. You should hear them."

"More than anything they're the people who work in Sesto", declared Felice. "For the most part that's where they manage to get them worked up to this extent."

"But it's unusual", Renzo said, still looking quizzically at Ambrogio, "that they should be so certain."

"Well," Ambrogio answered, "there can't be factual reasoning behind their certainty. After all, these are not the first elections we have held. They've probably started believing their own propaganda. It can't be anything else."

"I certainly hope so. Because if not," muttered Renzo Crippa, "we'd be better off dead."

Michele looked at Crippa with interest. He was, like the others, a laborer, although, unlike the others, he still wore his work jacket. Why would he talk this way? What motivated him? It could only be religion, or maybe . . .

Michele thought he would probe a little and said to Crippa, "Doctor Ambrogio here, and Tito Valli: I suppose they've told you about how things are in Russia, eh?"

Renzo nodded. "So, you know Tito Valli, the poor suffering wretch?"

"Of course I know him", Michele answered. "We were prisoners of war together."

"Ah! So you too escaped by a miracle. Well, yes, they've explained everything to us, and also Luca, too. Do you know Luca Sambruna, our branch secretary? He was in Russia, also."

The young dark-haired man cut in, "Alpine trooper, big paunch . . ."

"Yes, I know Luca."

"Well, from time to time he tells us what he saw; just last night he was talking about it," Renzo continued, "but for me, more than all that stuff . . . well, look I have four children of my own. What really frightens me about communism is that it steals your children. I don't mean that if they win the elections they'll be physically kidnapping them—that may or may not happen in Italy—and also this is less likely in the case of my children, as their father is a laborer, but they'll mess with their minds, that's the thing. You see, we're small town people," he went on, still talking in dialect, "and we can't compete with propaganda like theirs, even though we know it's all wrong. We barely had a primary education. They fill the youngsters' heads with daily propaganda and . . . well, I know what I'm talking about. In other words, our children could—to give an example—be like these kids who run around in bad company, you know, with people that turn their heads. Later the children start thinking the way they do. I know of a case like it. They leave their family, then . . . well, anyway, that's how you lose your kids. And I don't want to lose mine for anything in the world."

Michele nodded. (*To the working class, the greatest gifts are their children . . . even my father, in order not to lose touch with me, didn't he make me study in a school that cost him nearly two-thirds of his veteran's pension?*)

Pio interrupted them, trying to lighten the conversation. "Well, come now, let's not become negative. The Reds won't succeed, because Italy still has a lot, really very many people, who still have a head on their shoulders. And besides, we have the Church, right?"

"Countermanded, Comrade!" broke in the youngest of the group, a youngster of about seventeen, speaking for the first time and jokingly a sentence from the Communist newspaper *Unita*. "'All comrades should keep the chamber pot (*pitale*) in mind.' There was a printing error. They meant to say *Capitale* instead of *pitale*—you know, should keep *Das Kapital* in mind."

"What was that?" a surprised Michele asked Ambrogio.

"It's from one of the cartoons in this week's *Candido*, you know, Guareschi's paper; even here in Nomana it gets read quite a lot."

The others all laughed, and Renzo topped the joke in this direct provincial way, with another, in dialect. "*Martell e scighezz, e 'l popul de mezz*—the hammer and sickle, and the people in the middle."

The conversation was becoming more common, to Michele's disappointment.

"And what about Luca?" Ambrogio said, changing the subject. "How come he's not here at headquarters tonight?"

"He went out earlier to check on the poster groups."

"He said that he'd be going by the Oratory first to make some arrangements with Father Mario", said Felice. "He should be there right now."

"Who? What? Father Mario?" exclaimed Michele, then, to Ambrogio, "He's still around, Father Mario?"

"Of course he's around and still stepping into the breach, more than ever."

"Yes", said Pio. "He's never at rest. A real priest, that Father Mario."

The men in the group all nodded, agreeing.

"Do you want to see him?" Ambrogio asked. "If you do, we'll have to hurry," he looked at his watch, "because in a quarter hour the Oratory closes. Of course, we can in any case come back here later. Would you like to take me to the Oratory?"

"Sure, come on, let's go. We can come back here later."

They both got up to go and said their farewells to the group.

"Pity", Michele observed. "We'd just begun to have a talk."

"You really enjoy this type of gossiping?" Ambrogio looked a little baffled. "It's probably because I'm so accustomed that . . . well, in a short while the Oratory closes. On the way back, if you like, we can stop off here again." And after a pause, "I was trying to be careful not to have you too long away from . . . home."

Michele slapped him on the back.

9

The Oratory lay behind the church, surrounded by an old wall, from which could be seen the shadows of some fir trees. Neither the wall nor the trees muffled the kids' shouts.

Entering the courtyard by the light of three or four weak lightbulbs on the walls, they saw several young boys playing tag, a sight they were accustomed to since they themselves had been children. Michele silently asked himself if it was something they'd still be able to see in Italy in the future. What an important game they'd really be playing in the upcoming elections!

They saw Father Mario and Luca from behind, walking together on one side of the courtyard. The priest's ankles were visible under his cassock. Luca walked slowly, suppressing the usual Alpine trooper's pace with which he'd made light of so many kilometers.

"Father Mario, Luca!" Ambrogio called, raising his voice to be heard over the kids' shouting.

The pair turned around—Luca, with his youthful forelock, and Father Mario, with his glasses, brush-cut hair, and frail child's face.

"Here's my friend Michele, who wants to say hello."

They both hurried over to the new arrivals with happy faces.

"We've been strolling around, the two of us, to see how the election machinery is working", Ambrogio joked, while they all shook hands. "So here we are, while meantime you have these gangs outside putting up posters."

"And there's no holding them back. Who can put up with them?" Luca answered, laughing.

As usual, Father Mario took the joking seriously. "One must show trust in the young boys. Then they behave well."

"Well . . . behaving well . . . I'm not so sure", said Ambrogio, half seriously. He was thinking of the spilled paste bucket.

Luca laughed, nodding his head in agreement.

Michele said, "Well, Father Mario, what's new?"

"What would you have me say?"

"How you see the situation, for example."

"It would be more likely that you . . . who are more learned, a writer . . . I know your book is doing a lot of good." He looked at Michele approvingly, a satisfied smile on his face. "How good that is, Michele! But tell me yourself how you think things will go."

"Well, I'm confident."

"Really? Very good, very good."

The four of them began strolling around the courtyard, risking being knocked over by the boys playing tag. Father Mario wanted to know Michele's opinion about certain happenings reported recently in the newspapers and on the radio, but Michele limited himself to half answers without committing himself.

"Today has been a decisive day for Michele", Ambrogio let them know. "He graduated, did you know?"

"Today? Fancy that!" said Father Mario, his eyes opening wide behind his glasses. "I'm sure you wrote an excellent thesis!"

"For heaven's sake ... no, really it wasn't, Father; please don't make me blush", Michele said. "A patchwork thesis, designed only to get me a passing mark; a poor work, really."

The priest stopped and looked at him with surprise.

"Unfortunately it's true", Michele insisted.

Ambrogio interrupted in order to explain. "Michele took law, a subject he's no longer interested in. His head and his heart are now ... elsewhere."

Smiling, Michele thought to himself, *My heart is right here, in Nomana.*

"Did you know", Ambrogio continued, "that he's already gathering material for a second book?"

Father Mario's face lit up. "A second book? Ah, how good." Turning to Michele, he added, "It's the Lord who gives you the inspiration. We need that kind of inspiration nowadays."

"How good you are, Father", murmured Michele, shaking his head.

"Talking about new books," the priest said, resuming his strolling, "have you read the correspondence between Claudel and Gide, just out?"

"I have it at home; it's published by Garzanti, right? But I still haven't read it. These last few weeks I really haven't had the time."

"It's shocking", said the priest. "You'll see. Some people—the writer of the introduction, for example—see many things in the book, but I encounter only a single theme: a soul rejecting grace. It's frightening, a fearful thing. When you've read it, I really want to hear what you think."

"I don't know whether I could be much distressed about the soul of a champion of a new atheist culture," Michele said softly, "after having seen so many wretched people being destroyed by the same culture. But, of course, you're right, no doubt. Each individual soul is important. But I ..." He looked at Father Mario, whose face had gone somber. "I'm sure I'm mistaken", he offered.

"Listen, Father Mario," Ambrogio cut in, "Michele has already done a lot of thinking for today. Now he just wants to have a look at how the town's election campaign is going. We should talk about that."

"What?!" Luca exclaimed, surprised. "He wants to know what we're doing here in town?" Unlike the other three, Luca spoke in dialect. He looked into Michele's eyes. "If you think you're going to find something here in Nomana to stick in your books, you're totally mistaken, I assure you."

The young writer laughed. "Let's not think about books right now."

"The election campaign . . .", Luca went on. "One does the little one can, that's all. The majority of people here think as we do, you know, but we mustn't let ourselves relax. We need to achieve as many votes as possible, because something needs to be done to compensate for the situation in the Red areas, and if we don't take care of it, who will?" He looked at Ambrogio. "That's all. What else can one say?"

Compensate for the situation in the Red areas, thought Michele. *Luca still thinks like an Alpine soldier. He finds it natural to fight as he did on behalf of the strays, stragglers, and noncombatants, to make sure of their safety, too. No more and no less.*

"The truth is that we do too little", sighed a thoughtful Father Mario. "I'm not talking about Luca and Ambrogio, who show great courage by involving themselves now after what they've already done during the war. That's truly generous behavior. But if one thinks about what is at risk, a chance for our people to continue being Christians! Deep inside, when I think of that, I hear the plea by the Pope."

"Yes, just as well we still have the Pope!" Luca agreed.

"When I think of what he has asked of us," the priest continued, "it concerns me. Here we've had two thousand years of Christian faith and civilization, earned with uncounted sacrifice, day by day, do you realize . . . and it is all being put at risk in an election."

Luca nodded gravely. "But please don't talk about how I'm doing my duty. The truth is I'm taking things very easy. Tonight, after all, what am I doing? And we have very few nights left."

"Well, Luca, there's no need to downgrade your efforts", Ambrogio objected. "One has to do what one can without going overboard. As you've said, to do more could in the end produce the wrong result."

"That's also true", Father Mario agreed. "It is as well not to overdo things. In fact, that's exactly what our own parish priest says, and he knows what's what."

He was referring deferentially to his direct superior. Ambrogio remembered that the parish priest was somewhat critical toward Father Mario. He couldn't stand Father Mario's exuberant devotion, which he considered excessive. During Mass he was sometimes seen to puff out his cheeks disapprovingly when his coadjutor lifted the Host before the assembled faithful, with an exaltation he thought exaggerated. Ambrogio smiled at the memory.

Michele, while continuing to follow the conversation, reflected on the enormous challenge undertaken by the Church militant. The Pope, the supreme shepherd, had taken into his own hands the leadership in the fight for Christianity. *He's really a shepherd, in evangelical terms, who exposes himself to danger, to the wolves outside, for the safety of his flock. Woe to us all if we didn't have a Pope like that,* Michele thought, not for the first time. *Woe, too, if instead we had a doubting and feeble shepherd. But in any case that couldn't happen, because at moments of danger the Lord comes to the help of his Church.* Other forces had joined the battle, elements of the democratic citizenry, but what other organization, if not this one—which had shown itself to be a formidable one—the Catholic Church, could have confronted the rising Red tide now threatening to drown all of Europe?"

"Did you read in yesterday's paper", Father Mario was saying, "that the Hungarian government passed a law that enabled them to take over all the Christian schools?"

"What surprises me is that a Communist government should have let these religious schools continue so long", Ambrogio commented. "In Russia there haven't been religious schools for a long time." (And not only the schools, he reflected. One had only to remember what had happened to the churches, those massive churches that the Russians had erected over the centuries in their town centers—for example, along the Don, in Abrossimovo, Monastirskina, Veshenskaya, where their churches had been deconsecrated and converted into warehouses for grain. And there was Michele's experience, the astonished-looking saints hanging on the walls of the Susdal convent, turned into a POW camp, a *religio depopulata* . . .)

From the bell tower came the chiming: one, two, three, nine in total. The children seemed to raise the level of their shouting, conscious it was time to end their games.

"Nine o'clock", said Father Mario. "Excuse me for a moment while I say goodbye to the children. I'll be right back."

"Yes, right, but listen . . . we have to go, too", Ambrogio said. "Right, Michele?"

Michele, still buried in thought, nodded. "Yes, right, it's late."

Luca also started to say goodnight, but Father Mario, not wanting any of them to go, asked them to wait.

Seeing him approach, some of the children came toward him and breathlessly asked, "We'll only be a minute, please let us finish, we're nearly through . . ."

"Every night it's the same", said the priest. "Come on, be good boys. You can finish tomorrow. Tomorrow is Sunday, and you'll have more time to play."

While these few boys continued pleading to stay longer, the rest of the group faded away, their shouting diminishing and dying down. Some quit playing and made their way outside, panting and sweaty; the bigger boys collected their smaller brothers to go home together. "Goodnight, Father Mario, goodnight." They said their farewells. The priest nodded, speaking to them all. "Goodnight, Corrado, Clemente, *ciao*, Fermo." The courtyard slowly emptied.

Father Mario went along to the area where the games were kept. There were two pingpong tables and a small billiard table, along with some other equipment.

Perhaps the kids who normally help him close the Oratory are out pasting up posters, Luca thought to himself and followed the priest. Ambrogio guessed his intentions and followed him.

Michele started out after the both of them, but then stopped. He would wait in the courtyard. From inside he could hear the clatter of chairs being stacked and windows being closed; soon the lights in the courtyard were out.

In the dark the bell tower stood out. There was some moonlight, enabling Michele to make out the outline of the upper part of the church. The church where, God willing, one day soon his marriage would be blessed. What fascinated him now was the vertical solidity of the bell tower, which seemed to radiate a sense of tranquil safety, of peace. Tired as he was, he could feel a sudden yearning for peace. *Why don't these damned Communists leave us alone, here in the shadow of the bell tower? Why do they insist on involving us in another battle?*

In any case the battle had already started, and losing it was unthinkable. While he gazed at the bell tower, his mind started to wander. Who knew if soon there wouldn't be shots, blood, horror all around this bell tower, a civil war? *No, Lord, no, I beg you.* And yet—one had only to think about Greece—these things could well happen. Who knows, in a case like that, whether their side would win, or perhaps this bell tower would be silenced like the ones in Russia?

"Michele, hey, Michele!" Ambrogio called as he came out of the game room. Turning to Father Mario and Luca he continued talking. "I get the impression that he was out here putting together a poetic description . . . 'the town bathed by the light of the moon' or something like that."

Called back to reality, Michele hurried over to join them. They all went out together and stood on the narrow cobbled street. Luca used a large iron key, turning it twice to lock the Oratory's old door, handing the key over to Father Mario. He then said goodbye. "I've got to get going . . . goodnight."

Down the street came a few children, still at play. "That's enough!" shouted Father Mario. "Go home. It's time to go home. Do you hear me?"

The children looked unhappy but went on their way, and soon their cheerful laughter could be heard.

"Now, maybe," Ambrogio said to the priest, "to finish our inspection tour, Michele and I will walk by the enemy's 'operations center', well, their small social club."

Father Mario smiled. "Do you want me to go along with you?"

"No," Ambrogio answered, "because I don't think your work day is finished yet."

"To tell the truth, it isn't. I have to finish the second half of tomorrow's sermon."

"You see? Well, we'll say goodnight."

10

Michele agreed with his friend's idea, so instead of going directly back to the house, they took a detour that took them past the front of the Garibaldi Club, the Reds' headquarters. Not that they could see much. It was set back and with the lowest windows high up over the street level; all that could be seen near the front entrance was a poorly lit, almost unreadable nameplate.

"What's written on the sign?" asked Michele, who, although they had not stopped, had tried to read the nameplate as they went by.

"Something about Garibaldi Proletarian Club. Basically it's just a tavern like all the others."

As the two of them went by, they were spotted by one of the men inside, who happened to be looking out of one of the windows. "What do they want, these two vultures?" he exclaimed. The speaker was a certain Marasca, a laborer who had a hard time remaining one. Loaded with debts, he was always on the verge of becoming a bum.

Foresto looked up from his seat at a nearby table.

"What do those two vultures want?" Marasca repeated, in a louder tone.

Foresto put down the cards he was shuffling. "What's happening?" he asked.

Instead of answering, Marasca just clicked his tongue in annoyance.

"What's up?" Foresto demanded in a harsh voice.

Marasca, now under pressure to explain, didn't know how to express what it was that bothered him. By this time Ambrogio and Michele had walked on past. "Two sh——heads just went by", Marasca said finally.

Sèp, sitting at Foresto's table, exchanged glances with him, then stood and went rapidly to the window. He pulled back a curtain and looked out. "It's Ambrogio Riva with a friend of his ... it seems to me I've seen the friend around town", he said, letting go of the curtain and returning to his table.

"So, it was two friends of yours, eh?" Foresto commented and resumed shuffling the cards.

Sèp answered with a muttered blasphemy. (He was no longer a Communist; his conversations with his cousin Tito and his mother's daily show of anguish had affected him. He'd become a Socialist, which had annoyed Foresto and the other Communists, but given the alliance between Communists and Socialists in the coming election, they had become reconciled to his switch—not, however, to the point where they had stopped making occasional pointed comments.)

"In fact, it's not this Riva, Ambrogio, I was with in the Ossola in the partisans—real partisans, you know . . . there's another brother", Sèp said, having gone back to sit and glad of this opportunity to throw Foresto's imagined struggle as a partisan in his face.

Foresto grunted, not reacting to the thrust.

"But I don't like this. What are two industrialists doing on our street?" sourly commented Pollastri from a neighboring table.

"They're taking a walk. Why not?" replied Foresto.

There was a silence.

"Just as well they enjoy taking walks while they still can," Foresto added in dialect, "because who knows if in a short while they'll still be able to come out on the streets." They relied on this type of comment to feed their hopes for a real turnaround at the elections, despite the forecasts to the contrary.

"Well, I . . .", Marasca said. He'd come closer to the table, but didn't go on with whatever he'd been going to say.

"You . . . what?" said Foresto harshly. "Do you still have that late-model auto in mind?"

The other card players tried to stifle their laughter. That idiot of a Marasca had been going about, saying that after the elections, when the big share-out time came, he would end up with the Rivas' Millecento. He had said it and repeated it to several people in town, to the point where some people even feared for their property, and Foresto had been forced to tell him to be quiet on the subject.

Foresto said, "And who would you take for a ride in the new car, tell me? Perhaps that dressed-up wife of yours?"

More than one of the card players snorted with laughter, because Marasca's wife—unintelligent and inept and the major reason his life was so miserable—was singularly ugly.

Marasca left Foresto's table mumbling curses. Wherever he went, it seemed, he was always being put upon; life was not kind to him.

II

When Ambrogio and Michele reached the house, Andrea was still there, happy just to be near his Francesca. "Hey, you two, you've managed to avoid saying the Rosary", he reproached them, but with a welcoming smile.

"If you like, we can say another right now", Ambrogio proposed jokingly.

"Yes, right, a good idea", Michele joined in.

Andrea shook his head. His expression showing mimicked fright. Then he turned to Francesca and smiled.

On hearing Michele's voice, Alma—who had been tidying the kitchen—took off her colored apron and came into the dining room. She made her new graduate sit at the table and happily placed herself beside him. "What have you seen that's new?" she asked.

Ambrogio once more thought as he had earlier, *What a pity that Fanny isn't here also.*

The conversation was lively again. Giulia served a liqueur, and later Francesca served another round. At 11:00 (the clock on the radiator cover chimed, Michele listened, absorbed, thinking back to the chimes from the bell tower earlier and his thoughts at the time) Andrea reluctantly rose and said goodnight. Giudittina had already gone to bed, as had Rodolfo. (After he came back, he'd given a jumbled account of the work done by the poster squad.)

Later, when it was nearly midnight, Gerardo and Giulia said, "We'll also go up", and went toward the door, where Giulia turned and asked, "Aren't you tired? You especially, Michele, after all the activity and the examination today?"

Michele appeared not to understand; half dizzy in the company of his Alma, he just smiled at Giulia.

"We're being thrown out", said Ambrogio, himself tired. "We'd better make a move." Then, receiving no response, he added, "Come on. You can spend all of tomorrow with your Almina, right from sunrise to sunset."

Alma pouted, "Idiot!"

They all went up the stairs, saying their sleepy goodnights and see-you-tomorrows as they each went to their rooms.

While Michele dawdled through washing and changing for bed, his mind returned once again to the Nomana bell tower, of which the dining room clock had reminded him. Now, without the distraction of the surrounding conversation, he had a strong vision of the bell tower surrounded by civil war. He saw people firing from the church roof and from the bell tower. Others, sheltering at the sides of the piazza, were firing up at the defenders. Behind them, Red squads searched through the neighborhoods for people to arrest. There was no sign of the Americans; who knows where they were. The Reds went into people's houses, even this very house belonging to the Rivas, which—thank goodness!—was deserted, as Ambrogio and his brothers were outside, fighting, each with his machine gun in hand. Almina couldn't be far away, perhaps in some basement with other townswomen. The Reds would be able to get their hands on her if our people—always reluctant to kill their own neighbors— were vanquished. His fevered imagining showed Alma being dragged off by the Reds, barbarically happy to have seized a girl like her, these, the worst murderers and kidnappers in history, more destructive—despite their initial humanitarian claims—even than the Nazis.

He imagined that the Reds threw Alma down on a bed or on the grass outside and . . . They had done so with countless women before deporting them. Why wouldn't they do the same to her? *But enough, stop imagining these things, these fantasies. Leave it, right now!* He calmed down, but . . . how many

865

women, Russians, Romanians, Polish, and so on had had this done to them in reality? *And including right now, this moment, while I'm here, about to go to sleep, how many are suffering now in Greece? Even more in China, where the Communists appear to have won already. Who knows how many? My God, my God, help them, Lord.*

He blinked several times, breathed deeply, and then looked around the peaceful and tidy room, formerly Manno's. *Let it alone once and for all,* he told himself, *or you'll be so full of adrenaline you'll not be able to sleep.*

Ready for bed, he crossed himself and prayed. Then, getting between the fresh-smelling sheets, he put out the light. Who knows if Italy would ever really find itself in such a horrible situation? Perhaps, after all, the Italian Communists weren't so fanatic about doctrine, their heads not so full of dogmatic beliefs, as their comrades in the East. No doubt, if he thought about that hopeless Robotti whom he'd met in the POW camp.

Then he remembered that he'd also seen and heard Togliatti, the secretary of the party, his wide professorlike face, the glasses and his necktie, always worn a little crooked (soon seized upon and made famous by the newspapers). He'd been at Susdal, haranguing the Italian POWs. Of the content of Togliatti's speech, all he could remember were the blasphemies. You could say that Russia was the capital of blasphemies; on the other hand, their use by an intelligent man like Togliatti had disgusted him to the point where—unusual for him—he'd stopped listening to the man's speech. A pity, because it was noticeable that the Communist leader had an uncommon personality that he'd not been able to put his finger on. But what kind of man was Togliatti, really? One day in the chamber of deputies, to everyone's surprise, he had started a discourse about Guido Cavalcanti and the Florentine fourteenth century. Michele had been indignant. It seemed to be a taking of liberty. *How did he get away with it? By what right? A man like him, to talk about medieval Christianity, which he must hate, there can be no doubt.* On another occasion he went so far as to compare the interior minister, Scelba, to ... who was it? ... an obscure fourteenth-, or was it thirteenth-, century Ghibelline: a person whom Michele—for all his passion for the era in question—had never heard of.

What a strange type, Togliatti. In truth, if he's familiar with those medieval times, he can't be such a fanatic of Communist ideology as the others. In fact, back at Susdal, Michele had already noticed he wasn't in any way dumb. *But enough! Who knows if that was why he'd chosen as his companion that girl from the Catholic University.* This was no other than Nilde, with her Emilian accent and her bulging forehead, who in their first year at the university had bumped into Michele and Ambrogio during one of their forays into the faculty of law. *What a small world!*

In any case Togliatti and the Communists were only a means—it shouldn't be forgotten—just instruments for the punishment of man, counterweights. Here he was, half asleep, wanting to face a possible civil war with some sort of orderliness, and here is where he'd have to start, with man's faults, the sins of all levels of Italian society. During the war that had just finished, the Italian dead hadn't been—relatively speaking—many; according to the last count there had been between four and five hundred thousand, including the civilians killed in the bombings and those who had died in the fighting between the partisans and the Fascists. Cold reason said this was not many compared to the butchery in other countries (Russia and Germany particularly).

One had to think, no doubt, that—in the mysterious balance of the *società dei santi*, communion of saints—the influence of all saints had been essential for Italy, that endless and splendid legion starting with Francis, Thomas, Catherine, and others of the Middle Ages (who knew what Togliatti's opinion of them was?) and continuing to the more recent saints: Bosco, Cottolengo, Father Orione (*Father Orione, son of a stone cutter*) and the still-living Father Pio. There must also have been influence from the, so to speak, "unofficial" saints ("We're still talking in terms of 'more or less', eh, Michele?"), that is to say, all the good people of today, such as Father Mario, Luca, Tito Valli, and Gerardo, who didn't spare himself in efforts to create new jobs, and those laborers meeting together in the watchsmith's shop converted into an operations center (although it was a little laughable), and all the innumerable mothers and fathers of families, the cloistered nuns and contemplative monks, who spend their days doing precisely that: atoning for the sins of others through prayer and penitence. In other words, the thing was knowing whether or not the power of the communion of saints would be able to achieve compensation for the guilt of man. *Twenty years ago, at the end of the Great War, the Red insurrection in Italy could be avoided. Will we achieve victory now that there isn't any fascism?* Or, on the other hand, would Italy, this time around, see the start of an age of abandonment by God, the terrifying situation he had witnessed in eastern Europe?

Sleep was gradually taking over. Yes, but he, personally, what could he do to help mankind? That mankind of which Alma was a part? He'd written the book, great, well done, but couldn't he really do more? Now he'd got the exams behind him (thinking of having graduated, he once more experienced a feeling of freedom), now . . . he could, for example, give speeches, speak out . . . that's right, of course . . . he'd go there to the province's party headquarters, where that bookkeeper with the beret . . . he'd suggest to him . . . but sleep finally took over.

He dreamed of the beret-wearing bookkeeper, who in the dream was happy to accept this offer to talk publicly about communism, then dreamed about his friend the chaplain, Father Turla, who, unlike the bookkeeper, showed disapproval. "Why, when you've made a list of the 'unofficial' saints", he said in his Bergamo accent, "have you forgotten me, left me out completely?"

With the passage of years, one can assume that the communion of saints' salvational mechanism played an effective role. One can presume that the new bloodbath didn't happen because the merits of Italian society at that time outweighed its demerits. As far as one can see, society then, while gravely imperfect, yet as a whole was clean and was neither freed of God, as in the scheme of secular beliefs, nor stuck in the mire of carnal sins, as it would later be.

This is, of course, a matter of intuition, and any truth that is created by intuition remains unproved. However, assuming things really happened that way, by what historic process? In other words—fascism having disappeared—what other means actually intervened?

Providence, in its role of savior, guided the choices and in particular the actions of Communist party Secretary General Togliatti. Neither his choices nor his actions could be attributed to saintly designs, obviously, and during that period, despite his knowledge of the Middle Ages, Togliatti was far from realizing his own role. (In the end one could believe that Togliatti was *uomo della Provvidenza*—providential man—in the same way that Mussolini had been before him.)

12

Anybody who writes can put himself at any level he chooses, even at Togliatti's (there are writers who have gone even farther), and so this scribe will stay with Togliatti a while, accompanied, he hopes, by the reader; but no longer than necessary to relate events. The writer regrets it if this detour seems sacrilegious to some readers, in the same way as Togliatti's excursions into the civilizations of the Middle Ages seemed sacrilegious to Michele.

That night in Milan Togliatti had arrived back at his hotel quite late. He was no less tired than Michele, having had to attend two important meetings earlier. The first, in the afternoon, was with the party's provincial cadres. The other—more tiring, attended only by party bosses—was at night, after dinner, and he had just come from this.

Meanwhile his secretary and companion—the young *professoressa* with the Emilia accent—had already gone up to the room they shared, while the head (in a literal sense he was the head who decided everything for the body of the party) of the Italian Communist party sat in the hotel lobby, with a drink beside him, reflecting alone.

That day, as always, he'd had to experience the usual thing. Since he'd been repatriated from Russia he'd been repeating to all, clearly and without ambiguity, that the party had to adhere to democratic rules. He explained that this directive wasn't a smokescreen, didn't cover any disguised purposes. Well, he said it and repeated it to everybody, but what happened? Nobody, or nearly nobody, starting with his own people, believed him. Of course his people pretended to believe and on the surface behaved as if they believed it (the monolithic ways of the party brought this about, and how . . .), but inside he understood they really didn't believe. Especially the former partisans . . . Some of these couldn't even manage to control themselves, and at intervals, every few days, they killed someone. In Emilia, for example, they regularly killed priests, and if by chance the police arrested them, they had the nerve to boast of being the party's benefactors, irresponsible madmen! It was true that, as a whole, the revolutionary rage had recently calmed down.

Only because they have before them the example of the problems that the Greek comrades are facing. Only this holds them back slightly. What's happening in Greece is for me only the most recent motive. Don't any of them know anything? It's because they've not witnessed anything, don't suspect a thing. He certainly had seen, and knew, he and the few survivors of the terrible Russian repressions brought down on the heads of Communist workers from all countries. To be sure, Togliatti still couldn't manage to explain to himself what had happened. The various reasons that he kept trying to give himself—reasons based on the social history of Russia, such as the extremist nature of the Russian character, the backward conditions in Russia, their autocratic traditions—did not in reality explain those immense massacres of loyal comrades. Under the czar—he thought—it had never been proved, there was no shade of proof that those people who had supported the system had been systematically murdered. The verified massacre of Communists in the Bolshevik states was inexplicable, but all the killing had been verified. That was the thing. Not only that, but he knew somehow (*besides, they've never completely stopped*) that the murdering would soon resume on a grand scale. There were too many warning signs.

He went back in memory to those terrible years in Moscow, the nightmare every night in the hellish Hotel Lux, where he and other anti-Fascist leaders, both Italian and foreigners, were staying. The police regularly made nightly sweeps through the building. They would take some defenseless comrade from his own or someone else's room, taking him away silently to torture him or just to kill him outright. After the night arrests, he'd feel the terrified comrades' eyes on him as if it were in his power to do something, while he himself was unspeakably in anguish about his own fate. Elsewhere in Moscow people of even greater importance than he would also be trembling with fear, without exception all the big fish in the party, not only the plain comrades. (As far as the nonparty people, or even worse the opponents of the system, these were of no interest to him. For sure tens or even dozens of millions of these people had been murdered in Russia, but the fact didn't affect him. To his way of seeing things, the famous statement by Lenin remained valid to the effect that communism had meant to be humanitarian toward its enemies, and if this had not been possible, this was the fault of those enemies, the victims.)

During his time at the Hotel Lux, he was interested above all in the survival of his own people. The three hundred or so Italian comrades, who to survive Fascist persecution at home had fled to Russia as political refugees (*All of them faithful people I trust*)—of this number the police had in a few years suppressed no less than two hundred. *Two hundred out of three hundred, without any of them having committed a crime!* If one thought about it, the thing was truly incredible! And how many of them had been close collaborators of his? Costa, to begin with; Bruno Rossi, and Manservigi from Ferrara, one of the most intelligent men he'd known, always precise in his statement. And the Milanese Gorelli and that other tenacious anti-Fascist, Vincenzo Baccala, who had been the first-ever secretary of the party in Rome. These last two transported to find death in the frightening ice of Colima; and Guarnaschelli, from Turin, a young self-educated laborer, and then Calligaris and the Neapolitan Peluso, and Arnaldo Silva. The last three shot in the head, and . . . how could it all have happened? Even now it didn't seem true!

But this was the truth he had to face, the head of the Italian Communist party. *Some head!* He had had to smile agreeably, like some lapdog, put on a fresh face in case Stalin started looking funny at him or his wife, too. (*That unhappy Paulina, Molotov's wife, remember her, deported and reduced to a skeleton.*) To remove his own people from the way of the executioner's ax, he had been forced to be pitiless toward others, particularly those poor party leaders from Poland, whose elimination he had repeatedly been asked to approve. He had approved it, with the maximum of zeal; as compensation he'd managed to rescue only one or two of his people, among them his brother-in-law Paulo Robotti. *By the time I rescued Paolo from the* Cheka, *they'd already permanently damaged his spine.* He remembered that episode now with some annoyance— the torturing of Paolo, which had gone on for nearly two years, although never mentioned in the family, although always kept quiet, had been the beginning of his rupture with his wife, Rita. Her long anguish, day and night, had eventually made her presence unbearable.

He stretched his hand out for his drink. He just ran the tip of his finger on the rim of the glass without picking it up. And Paolo, poor Paolo, he had not complained or asked questions. Like a true Communist he had fervently dedicated himself to the campaign of indoctrination with the POWs to which he had been assigned. Based on this work, he hadn't felt it necessary to prohibit Paolo's return to Italy, which was the fate of other comrades who, either because of the torture they'd suffered or because they had lost comrades to the wave of killings, no longer were thought reliable. What a dreadful thing, he thought, if he'd have had to leave his brother-in-law behind in Russia forever, which he'd had to do with Armando Cocchi. He vaguely recalled—among the waves of memories—Cocchi's querulous face. A Bolognese who was losing his faith in the cause, Cocchi had reached the point of desperation at which he even confessed his doubts to the Italian officers in the POW *lager*. What incredible irresponsibility!

Outside the hotel, occasional traffic noises came from the via Manzoni. The automobile noises, though muffled, managed to echo in the lobby. One car seemed to stop outside; Togliatti heard snatches of conversation in English, followed by the entrance of two American military officers, mature looking and probably important. They paused in the lobby and exchanged a few quiet words—not noisily, like the youthful American soldiers, but still in a joking manner—then entered the elevators.

They had barely gone out of Togliatti's sight when, as he expected, his two bodyguards came in through a side door. They were two trusted former partisans. They strolled with apparent carelessness in the lobby, looking around, and then, satisfied, left again. Well, it was time to go to bed. However, Togliatti didn't yet go upstairs. He shifted around in his seat to be able to look at the hotel employees behind the front desk and on the bellman's bench. His glance fell on one porter, a gray-haired man, *no doubt a brainless type*, who gave himself airs of importance. In the past, when he was still a young revolutionary, he would have described the man's manner as bourgeois, and, of course, he was. But now he realized that this attitude was the same as that of the porters in the hotels in the Soviet Union. If it had been only the hotel staff employees . . . Countless things in the Soviet Union, despite so many years of effort, were still not properly Socialist. Clearly, thinking about it, it wasn't surprising that Comrade Stalin pursued groups and individuals in Soviet society, a society that still hadn't decided to become Socialist. But how far away was all this from all his youthful hopes, when he and his school friends, particularly Gramsci . . . yes, Gramsci, the little hunchback. The Gramsci who while in jail came up with a theoretical plan that might have avoided the massacres. According to him, power could be seized without violence and gunfire simply by systematically taking over all the means of cultural and social communication. Yes, well, supposing this was achievable (the intellectuals would objectively be the easiest people in society to convert into flocks of sheep), how could they then preserve control without resorting to violence? In Italy they'd use modernist Catholics, Gramsci had written, to change the minds of the enemy masses with a primary objective of turning them into healthy atheists. Fairy tales, unfortunately. One could already see where these modern Catholics had ended up: undergoing the violent criticism of this angry Pope of ours. There was no doubt. In Italy, at least, it was so, because if one were to go by the news coming out of France, Catholic ethics there, in the end . . . and thanks over all to this Mounier . . .

Well, enough. Togliatti looked at his watch. Let's recapitulate: soon the killing would start among Communists at all levels, and—he had no doubt—it wouldn't be restricted to Russia. The massacres would extend through all eastern European society. Of the present chiefs in Prague, Warsaw, Budapest, even though currently regarded as divinities, who would be removed first? Which would be hanged or shot first? Some of those chiefs were friends of his from the Hotel Lux days. (*Caution; I have to be prepared to turn my back on them.*) He sighed. Just the same . . . it was not only inexplicable, but barbaric, indescribably barbaric, that this kind of thing should be part of the Communist reality! He shifted in the chair. Well, that didn't absolve him or excuse his inaction. He shouldn't shut his eyes to it like a small child. However, he should adopt a

871

cautious attitude. Given this situation, we shouldn't try to avoid the checks and balances that naturally attach to democracy. In order to avoid that in our party, too, we start devouring each other (that Secchia!). We should agree to coexist with the other parties; their vigilance, their uproar in action, will practically prevent that sort of excesses. Then it was a matter of democracy as understood in the West, reactionary, so to speak, and not like ours? That's all right given the situation. We just need it, that's all.

Luckily the situation in Italy wasn't like that of eastern Europe. Here there was no Red army, only the Americans. Besides, the need to compete openly in elections with the bourgeois parties created even in the most doubtful observers a belief in the legitimacy of our electoral maneuvers. *If everybody, comrades, adversaries, and even our Soviet leaders believe I'm camouflaging myself as a democrat, that's all right. Let them believe it. I'll let them make me a pretend democrat in order to make myself into a real democrat. Or, let's say*, he thought coldly, *nearly real.* He smiled at the thought unashamedly. *I'll play like a corrupted Western democrat, while protecting myself*, he continued, *because the party, to begin with, should remain as it is, with iron discipline and with all the choices made from above. If not, how could we remain in control? At the very least they'll elect someone in their image, similar in outward appearance, an unprepared Markos type, who will immediately stumble into a revolution and all the usual silliness. No, the party should stay as it is: democratic on the outside, but monolithic inside, and it would be useful to continue to bear arms. The possibility of using them in a revolution keeps us united and has a conditioning effect on those outside. What we do, really, is for ourselves and not, naturally, for those outside.* He felt a touch of resentment. *Not for these bastard capitalists. And less, even, for these disgusting priests—who, only because we agreed they might now have power, for reasons of our own, temporary reasons—certainly not for them. But they shouldn't make the mistake of thinking that we'd ever work for their stinking priestly society. What's more, we'll do whatever is necessary to prevent its growth. It'll be enough to prevent them, day after day, from correcting even the smallest of their mistakes. For example, preventing them from replacing public servants who appear to be harmful or thieves. This should be easy for us to do if we always attribute our actions to the defense of freedom, personal freedom, on which they place so much importance. Soon we'll even become the champions of personal freedoms.* He smirked, amused. *Truly a splendid thought.*

He picked up the glass at last and drank. It was late and time for bed, but he continued delaying going upstairs. He heard the elevator doors open and close and thought it would probably be his secretary. Then he heard high heels coming toward him on the marble floor. A young woman approached his armchair. "Do you need anything, Professor?"

(She called him Professor; despite their intimacy, she behaved outwardly as a student with her tutor. *It's inevitable, there are too many sides of me she doesn't understand*, he thought.)

"No, thank you", he said and finally got up from the armchair.

PART FOUR

I

About one month later, that is to say, two weeks after the general elections, Ambrogio and Fanny became officially engaged.

The event took place on a Sunday. Ambrogio went down to Milan in the sporty Millecento, taking with him an engagement ring in a satin-covered box. His thoughts were on the jewel and on the image of Fanny (Fanny, who would joyfully open the door on his arrival; Fanny, with her sweetly smiling green eyes; a Fanny whom he imagined admiring the ring, her pageboy hair half hiding her face), his pleased anticipation in rhythm with the hum of the car's motor.

His route through the villages—their walls still covered in election posters and the cloth banners still stretched across the streets—distracted his thoughts, however, and his happy anticipation was interrupted by thoughts about the elections and particularly by the comments made in Nomana on the previous night. Certain remarks came to mind that had been made by Michele, who was absolutely elated by the triumph of the Christian party.

"Do we realize this or not?" he said. "In all Europe people have placed power in the hands of Christians. It happened in France, Belgium, Holland, and in Germany. Even in Germany! And now in Italy, too. Have you noticed that this hasn't happened for centuries? And what does it mean? It must be that the people, after experiencing the results to which the other routes lead, now understand finally that salvation can come only from Christ, and public order, also."

And he said, "We have to say thanks primarily to the Pope. Rarely in history has a shepherd been so qualified for the task or so efficient in leading his flock."

Michele had to a degree impressed everyone when he emphasized, "For us Christians this is a great occasion. We're faced with the challenge, the possibility of holding back the collapse of a civilization headed toward disaster. Because there now really exists the possibility of preventing the whole of Europe from becoming an immense Crinovaya; the threat really exists." (He was referring—Ambrogio had understood—to an enormous cannibal pit and wasn't merely speaking figuratively.)

"Given this challenge," Michele had reiterated, "we need to organize our action program, and it won't be easy. What awaits us is an enormous cultural task; soon we'll have to make up for whole past generations."

873

When Ambrogio later asked him to name a specific example of what needed to be done, he had answered that, to begin with, it was inadmissible that in Italy there should only be one Catholic university. "We'll need five, ten, and similarly in other European countries."

And he'd talked of the publishing houses and newspapers, at which point everybody had joined in and cut short what had been an interesting dialogue. The young author, however, had described a grand view of things.

Well, we'll achieve it all yet, no doubt, Ambrogio thought, allowing himself to become euphoric. During those days following the great victory (in Nomana, the Christian party had received 71 percent of the votes) everything seemed possible. He enthusiastically increased the car's speed.

In Catholic Monza, it seemed to him—and perhaps it was true—that the people's faces seemed expansive, happier than usual.

(During those days the Catholics did in fact feel as if awakened from a nightmare, while their adversaries' state of mind was demonstrated by the behavior of the poet Saba, later described by the quasi-poet Vittorio Sereni:

> That day, one or two days after the eighteenth of April,
> I saw him wandering from piazza to piazza,
> from one café to another in Milan,
> pursued by the radio news.
> "Bitch!" he kept shouting. "Bitch!" The people
> watched him, astonished.
> He was talking to Italy. Heartbroken,
> as if addressing a woman
> who, unaware or not, has inflicted on us a deathly wound.)

But now his meeting with Fanny was drawing closer, and these other thoughts lost their effect. Ambrogio, having passed through Sesto without noticing his surroundings, sped through Milan's streets to the via Boccaccio, stopped the car in front of the elegant building where Fanny lived, and rode the elevator impatiently up to her door.

2

He had expected to spend the whole day with his fiancée and her parents in their house. But Fanny had other ideas and, after he had hung his overcoat in the hall closet (where he saw his future mother-in-law's curious foot-long walking stick), said to him, "Look, what I want is for you to take me out for a ride."

"Oh, right. Very well. But . . . where to?"

"No idea", she replied. "We'll decide that later, just so long as we have a good long ride out."

First they all—the engaged couple, mother, and father—went to the parlor. Fanny's home was, as she herself had previously described it, a welcoming place, with paintings, *objets d'art*, and knickknacks everywhere, including the corridors.

Ambrogio glanced at his future father-in-law, the *commendatore* Mayer, wondering—as it was clear that he and his wife weren't coming along for the ride—if the father was unhappy with Fanny's suggestion.

The idea didn't seem to disturb him, and he commented, "A ride out? Wonderful. Just look at the good idea our Ninina has had."

Mister Mayer was bald and obese but lively, and his tone and manner seemed to Ambrogio to be the epitome of a *commendatore*. The parlor they'd gone into, overfurnished with plush armchairs, seemed equally suited to a *commendatore*, or at least to Ambrogio's idea of the term. On one of the tables there was a framed photograph of Fanny wearing her Red Cross uniform, a reminder that during the war this family had not been unaffected by the suffering common to all.

Fanny's mother (who for some time now had not dyed her hair blue; she now had chestnut-streaked hair) also approved of her daughter's idea. "A ride? Ah, yes, right, why not?" Unlike her husband, when in Ambrogio's company she showed no uneasiness; on other occasions she had noticed that he was a patient listener and therefore felt she should speak freely with him on a variety of subjects and promised herself to do so as soon as she had an opportunity. Meanwhile, she kept a complaisant smile on her face.

"So?" said Fanny, once they had all sat in the armchairs. "Tell me, have you started on the villa's alterations?"

"At *I dragoni*? Unfortunately, no, I'm sorry to say, not yet", Ambrogio answered, smiling.

Fanny smiled back, although shaking her head disapprovingly. "Oh, but when are you going to move on it?"

"The alterations themselves won't take much time", he answered her. "You'll see. But for these last few months," he continued, explaining more for her parents' sake than for hers, "apart from the elections, at home we've been totally occupied with the new factory." He turned to the *commendatore*. "My father is determined to increase the number of available jobs, to the point where I wonder . . . we may run the risk of ending up with problems."

"Oh, but your father is very able", the *commendatore* said vaguely. "He knows how to run his business."

Ambrogio, a little confused, decided the comment must be complimentary. However, it was clear that the *commendatore* wasn't aware of what the situation was. Maybe because of his middle-class mentality, he couldn't conceive that someone, particularly an industrialist, could be working under the impulse of an ideal.

"The alterations are more than a few", said Fanny. "There's that wall that has to be removed to increase the size of the bedroom; then there's the bathroom, which has to be built from scratch, and we'd decided to repaint the lobby, remember? And also there's ..." She went on with a list of jobs to be done. Jobs they had decided on together some time before, when she had gone to the house for this very reason. They planned to occupy half of the villa for themselves, leaving the other half for one or another of Ambrogio's brothers or sisters when they married. As Fanny listed the jobs to be done, it seemed to the engaged couple they could see their new little nest taking shape; even Ambrogio briefly let himself be overtaken by this sweet imagining.

"Well, look, I've no intention of waiting", Fanny concluded decidedly. "We've said this summer, and that's how it'll have to be."

"I don't want to wait any longer either, you can be sure", Ambrogio told her.

Her parents smiled. "It seems to me that your parents must be remembering the day when he proposed to her", Ambrogio said to Fanny.

Fanny nodded gracefully. (At times like these Ambrogio thought she was really lovely, and he had a powerful urge to take her in his arms.)

"The proposal?" *Commendatore* Mayer seemed surprised and looked at his wife. "But ... we ... did we ever get engaged?"

Fanny started to laugh, her helmet of golden chestnut hair moving. "Papa, please ...", she said.

"Filippo, please, really ...", the mother stammered, then turned to her future son-in-law. "You see how he can be? He doesn't get the joke."

"Joke? I'm not making any joke. I'm talking seriously", the *commendatore* protested. "When was it that we got engaged?"

"Well, at least you both decided to get married, right?" Fanny tried to redirect her father's thoughts. "Although I'm not sure. You may not have exchanged rings."

The *commendatore* searched his memory, continuing to make negative gestures.

"For goodness' sake, Filippo!" said the now-exasperated mother to her husband. Then, turning to her daughter, "What? What are you saying? That we didn't exchange rings? And what about this ring with the diamond, surrounded by brilliants? Where did that come from?"

"Oh, that ring. I suppose I didn't realize ..."

Meanwhile, the *commendatore* had his bald head lowered between raised shoulders and his lips tight shut, and he continued making gestures that no, he couldn't remember anything.

"Oh, Ambrogio," said Fanny's mother, "you see what an impossible man my husband is?"

A maid came in, pushing a cart bearing the aperitifs. She was middle aged and wore a black dress with a white apron and cap. She was clearly more skillful than Noemi and evidently more impersonal. *She can't be as much a part of the family as Noemi*, thought Ambrogio.

"Just a moment, Ines", Fanny said, turning to the others. "Folks, it seems silly to wait any longer. We should go through our little ceremony now, don't you think?" And to Ambrogio, "Do you agree, Ambrogio?"

"I always agree with you", he answered.

"In that case, I'm going to fetch the ring."

"Right, go."

She rose gracefully and left the parlor, her skirt swirling around her youthful legs as she moved, which drew Ambrogio's gaze.

Ines left the cart in a corner ("Leave it there, Ines", the mother told her. "Later we'll help ourselves.") and also left the room.

Fanny was soon back, holding a satin-covered box, similar to the one Ambrogio had with him and that he now took from his pocket. When Fanny stopped in front of him, he tried to get to his feet, but Fanny put her hands on his shoulders, making him sit. Then she sat on the arm of his chair. She opened the ring case, and Ambrogio opened his. Then they each put a ring on the other's finger. They both fit well, because Fanny had had the foresight to measure them carefully for a good fit.

"There", she said.

"Well, and now don't you kiss each other?" the mother asked anxiously.

"Right", Ambrogio answered enthusiastically.

The engaged couple kissed. Signora Mayer came near to crying.

"Oh, Filippo!" she exclaimed. "Our Ninina, our Ninina is leaving us."

"It can't be helped. You aren't going to cry about it, I hope", the *commendatore* replied. To Ambrogio's surprise the father was more affected by the moment than his wife. "What, do you think that our Ninina would stay at home until she became an old spinster? Well, good!" And turning to the young couple, he repeated, "Well, good!" in an unsteady voice and then groped in his pocket for a handkerchief, his eyes getting unbelievably red.

Fanny smiled and said, "My emotional parents." She lifted her hand. "But look, look at this. Goodness, Ambrogio, what a ring, what a marvelous diamond! Oh, thank you!" She leaned forward to kiss her fiancé again, then, turning to her parents, "Don't you want to see this marvelous ring?" and without removing the ring, she went to her mother, her hand held out. This, like all her gestures, was very graceful. "Do you like it?"

"The one you gave me", said Ambrogio, embarrassed, showing his own ring, "is even prettier."

The others had obviously already seen it. Ambrogio withdrew his hand, a little uncomfortable at the parents' unexpected emotion. "Fanny won't be living far away", he thought to remind them. "And you know you have an open invitation to *I dragoni*. You know you'll always be welcome."

"Yes, yes, you're a good boy, Ambrogio", replied the *commendatore*.

"But really, what an elegant ring!" the mother observed. "Let me get a good look at it, Ninina. Look, Filippo, now that's what you call a ring."

"The stone is from a small stock of diamonds my father bought during the war", Ambrogio explained. "He bought them as a matter of prudence, in case he needed to flee if the front ever overran Nomana. Now we're selling them off in order to buy looms. But my father put one diamond aside for each son, to be used when they become engaged."

"Well, what good luck!" the mother exclaimed enthusiastically. "So that without having to spend money now, your father has a diamond kept at home for each engagement. That's really good luck."

The *commendatore* wagged his head as if accustomed to his wife's remarks.

The maid Ines soon returned to announce discreetly that the meal was served.

3

All four of them went to the dining room, a brightly lit room, with large windows and large, golden-framed, nineteenth-century paintings on the walls.

One of these—similar to all the others, it showed a secular scene (*I'm in a house where religion isn't important*, Ambrogio reminded himself)—hung in front of him, and he kept looking at it. It represented Diana and nymphs bathing, and Actaeon tempting them.

While the antipasti was being served, the previous Sunday's elections came to Ambrogio's mind. It was unusual that they'd not referred to them. Without further thought he said, "And what about the elections?"

"Yes, precisely", Fanny exclaimed. "Did you see the last issue of *Italia Illustrata*, the most recent issue?"

Ambrogio nodded. "Alma brought it home a couple of days ago."

"Well! And how about that Michele?!"

"Yes, he's a great man. You should have seen Almina. She was in seventh heaven, showing off the magazine. You'd have laughed."

"What?" Fanny's mother asked. "*Italia Illustrata?*"

"Please, Mama. It was his sister Alma who had people amused, not *Italia Illustrata.*"

"But . . . are you two talking about the magazine?"

"Yes, of course", Fanny answered. "In the last issue is a section with photographs of the twelve people considered to have had the most influence in the election results. And one of the twelve, you understand, is our nearly brother-in-law Michele Tintori, this friend of ours at the university who wrote a book. But I'd already spoken to you about it, Mama, remember?"

"Ah, yes, you did tell me about him. Wait, isn't he the one who returned from Africa on a boat . . . or am I talking nonsense?"

"Mama, the one on the boat from Africa was a cousin of Ambrogio's named Manno. This Michele we're talking about came back home from Russia."

"Oh, poor soul."

"Did you notice that in listing the twelve people," Fanny asked Ambrogio, "Michele is the only one whose photograph wasn't published in *Italia Illustrata*? Instead of his face they put a picture of his book's cover."

"Yes, right, I saw that."

"Why wouldn't they have published his photo?"

"I don't know. Maybe they simply didn't have one handy, or perhaps they thought it out of place to put a young man's face next to De Gasperi and the other big fish."

"Really impressive, our Michele", repeated Fanny. "Isn't there another printing of the book about to come out?"

"Yes, the third printing. It'll come out next month, in June."

"And what about the letter Benedetto Croce wrote to Michele?"

Ambrogio nodded, smiling.

"Who, what?" asked the *commendatore*, not sure he had heard correctly. "Benedetto Croce wrote to this young fellow?"

"Yes", Ambrogio answered, amused. "And the best part of it is that the whole thing was started by my sister, Alma, who is Michele's fiancée. It was her idea to send a copy of the book to Croce. She came out with it one night during dinner about a month ago. You should have seen her. We were poking fun at her, thinking it was a child's way of thinking. Although Almina is a young girl, right, Fanny? Nobody understands how Michele fell for her. Well, on that evening the young girl was right, it has to be said. She had . . . she has a deep belief in Michele's book. According to her, one just had to send a copy of the book to Croce, and everything would naturally follow. It really was just as she said. The book did impress Croce."

The *commendatore* observed that Ambrogio didn't talk of these things in order to impress or to make himself seem important. He wasn't even thinking about that. Once again his future father-in-law could not help noting how different Ambrogio was from most people he knew.

"Well, this friend of yours must really be good", he concluded.

"But tell me, what is he like?" the mother asked. "Is he handsome?"

Fanny nodded affirmatively. "He's not bad. Sort of tall, and he has dark hair", she said concisely. She went on to say more about the young author, and the mother—to Ambrogio's amusement—accompanied the commentary with little admiring gasps ("Oh, how charming, a charming man . . . but he must really be a darling"), with interjections by Fanny, who could see Ambrogio's amusement ("Mama, please don't be so silly") and played to it. Gradually the conversation turned to other things.

Fanny's closeness—although Fanny was very different from his adolescent imaginings of his ideal fiancée—caused a growing excitement in Ambrogio. This feeling was added to by the excellent wine and the sight of the figures in the painting. He was particularly attracted by one of the nymphs, whose half-revealed nude body was pretty enough to distract him from the food.

"Just now you mentioned the Sunday elections of two weeks ago", said the *commendatore*. "Have you seen Togliatti and Nenni and that crowd, how hard it was for them to admit they'd lost? Poor fellows, I understand how it must have been for them, hesitating for at least three days. You must have seen, it was three days before their own newspaper mentioned the loss. Only after the definitive results had been announced did they relinquish their hopes. Do you know, I didn't know whether to sympathize with them or whether I should be afraid?"

"Sympathetic ... with them?" asked Ambrogio. "And yet ... no, never seriously; although they had to swallow the defeat, really, especially in those constituencies where they'd been so sure of winning. Did you read about those partisans in Tuscany who picked up and left town? There must be a few of them still hiding out in the mountains. Who knows what they had planned in the event they had won?"

"Now", said the *commendatore*, "all that is needed is for the people who won" (unlike Ambrogio, he didn't identify with the newly elected group) "to get busy on increasing production. In order for the house of cards not to come tumbling down, there's no other way: produce and produce again. We've got to ensure that the people have a good life. There's no other way", he repeated.

Ambrogio thought back to Michele's—very different—analysis. In any case, the *commendatore*'s views seemed to be well based. "Yes, I believe that now we have the possibility of being able to produce", he said. "The biggest obstacle to reconstruction to date has been the social disorder, which the Reds haven't stopped provoking: unjustified strikes, pickets in the streets, rows, and the interminable public protests over there between Sesto and Milan. All of which has put a halt to everything. But now this should all stop. Did you see that the last march on Milan was broken up by the police without ceremony? I believe it's possible now for everyone to get to work; then, no doubt, we'll leave these problems behind."

"But the workers also have justification", said the *commendatore*. (And Ambrogio, without being surprised, had the impression that the *commendatore* wasn't entirely pleased with the Christian party's victory.) "They have their reasons. If they protest, nobody can say they don't have good reasons."

Ambrogio said, "They have every reason not to want to live in misery with diminutive salaries. Of course they have rights! It's the disorder, the continual confusion, and the systematic opposition to any of the steps that have to be taken. That's what keeps them in misery, and it's not the workers who're responsible. It's the Communists and the Socialists. They want a system of order in which they are the people who do the ordering. Otherwise they'll cause trouble." He repeated, "It's not the workers who want this disorder, except for a small minority, you understand? The others go along because of fear or ignorance. Besides, the majority of workers don't support them. This is clear from the elections. You only have to check the figures for the popular voting."

"That seems to be what is happening, right enough", said the *commendatore*, almost showing disappointment.

He's Fanny's father, and I shouldn't sit in judgment, Ambrogio told himself, slightly irritated. *But these chic bourgeois people are all the same. First they were nearly petrified at the thought of the Reds winning, and now that the Reds have been swept aside, they don't like the fact that the Christian party has charge of society. They joined up with us to save their skins, but their hearts and minds—here Michele was right—are nearer to the Reds than to us.*

"All right, that's enough of political talk", Fanny interrupted, having sensed the tension between her father and Ambrogio.

"You're right, that is enough, particularly on a day like this", Ambrogio agreed immediately.

The *commendatore* also agreed. "One thing is for sure," he said, evidently trying to make peace with Ambrogio, "if in a reasonable amount of time the winners start seriously to create jobs for people, jobs that pay enough money in wages, in other words, if the people start having a good life, soon nobody will think about communism."

Ambrogio tried to go along with the older man's argument. "Yes, I also think that. During studies for exams (for example, statistics, right, Fanny?) one sees things that at first seem incredible. One time for an exercise I ran some comparisons, and you know what I found? Well, this wasn't detailed research, just some work for an exam. Well, I deduced that within fifteen years, more or less, each family in Italy will be so well off that they'll own, for example, an automobile."

"That's impossible", said the mother.

"That's also what I thought. When you think that today we still need American charity in order to eat ... it sounds like a madman's idea," Ambrogio agreed, "but since the study of economy at the university is a science ... well, I'd say it can't fail."

"But then do you realize that in that case we don't have enough highways?" objected Fanny, the economics graduate.

"Exactly. And it won't just be highways we'll need to build."

"Does your analysis take into account the fact that, three years after the end of the war, our national income is still less than it was prewar?" asked the *commendatore*.

"Yes, that was one of my bases. But I also took into account the upward development curve we experienced just after the end of the previous war. And another parameter: the relationship in America between rising national income and automobile sales. Also ... but maybe these things aren't interesting to the ladies." He looked toward his future mother-in-law.

881

Fanny's mother had been talking to her daughter in a low voice, but paused, as if caught.

Ambrogio hurried to conclude his argument. "To sum it up, I also think that when every family owns a car and a matching level of life, communism will no longer be attractive to anyone."

"Even without the car", added the *commendatore*. "It'll be enough if people are reasonably well off and have enough ...", and he rubbed his finger and thumb together to indicate money.

Ambrogio agreed, nodding. Neither man realized how far from the truth their forecasts would prove to be.

The meal continued, with the talk being less serious. Ambrogio, still facing the nymphs in the painting, felt an increasing desire to reach out and touch one of their bodies. Better still, he wanted to reach out to Fanny, this real Fanny next to him, no painted image. His feelings disturbed him more and more. *What is happening to me? Am I so debauched? This is really something!* This feeling was something he felt now with growing frequency. Simply a normal young man, he was far from being debauched. *It really is time for me to marry. Really the time has come*, he finally told himself. Here he was, twenty-seven years old. Well, there were just a few more months to wait. In a few months he'd be married.

4

At that very moment Almina and Michele were strolling together in the garden at Nomana.

They had every reason to be happy. There was the approval of Michele's book by Croce, the recognition received from *Italia Illustrata*; then they were young (the mere fact of being young is in itself a blessing), in love with one another, and they were together. Michele had one arm around Alma's waist. They exchanged a word every now and then, but mostly they were silent, walking along the paths lined with lilies of the valley under the big trees. When they reached the balcony they were faced with the view of the mountains curving before them.

"Look, Alma, what a marvel God achieved with his work!" They ought to have been happy and to live in peace during these hours that providence had brought them. Instead, the young author felt, though he kept rejecting, the many things that he'd left hanging when he came to Nomana. Duties that he felt he should complete as soon as possible if he wanted to be available to take his part soon in the great fight against the gathering barbarism. First, there was the research he needed to do for his new book; then there was the systematic reading he had to do if he wanted to bring himself up to date with the last few decades of French Catholic writings, *Particularly these two who are so popular, Maritain and Mounier (although I don't like Mounier . . . but what have I read by him? Not much). And to get myself up to date with French Catholic writers, how long will that take me? Let's say at least one hundred evenings of reading, and that right now, without letting any more time slip by.* And at the same time, obviously, he shouldn't ignore works by non-Catholic authors, starting with Proust and books by the Irishman, Joyce, which were—in a unique way—according to some people, the initiators of a new type of literature. (*But "new" in what sense? Not new in the way of Crinovaya and Maidanek, one hopes.*) Besides, there were those important American and English authors (*Eliot!*) whom he'd have to read as soon as possible, which he couldn't ignore any longer. Yet, when he really thought about it, it wasn't the urgency of this reading plan that caused him anguish but the fact that in June, when the summer holidays began, he'd be facing four months without money. He had to find work. It was his first priority. Not only that, but in order to earn his daily bread and to be able to marry, he had to get another degree, this time in literature, since teaching seemed an occupation more compatible with his work as a writer. He half sighed.

Alma raised her enigmatic face to him, a statuette in plaits. "What are you thinking about now?"

"It's not important."

"But you should tell me."

Michele smiled, saying nothing.

"Besides, I already know", she said. "You're thinking about all the things you have to do."

"Exactly."

"Listen," she proposed, "why don't we talk?" She wanted to be able to help. In a confused way she understood the peculiar lack of practicality Michele had demonstrated in taking a degree that was almost of no help at all, even though he had displayed great intelligence in getting it. Of course, she was in no position to be able to lead him, nor did she have the least desire to do so, but neither was she prepared to be just an ornament for him. She loved him indescribably and wanted to be of help. "Michele, do you want us to talk?"

"I was thinking of the things I can't put off, among them certain French books that I should read as soon as possible."

"Those by Catholic writers?"

"Yes."

"We talked about this once before, do you remember? Before you graduated. Well, I haven't told you, but I've taken a look through the university library's catalogue. There are many titles, a lot, even just the most recent. And they have a complete collection of *Esprit* magazine."

"You've checked already? Well, how about that!" Michele commented, shaking his head.

"If you want, I can take out the books you want to read one by one. In other words, if you like, I can be your secretary."

"I don't want to be a burden to you", said Michele, after having thought for a moment about the unexpected offer.

"But what are you saying? A burden? No work I do for you is a burden. Look, listen." Alma gave the impression she was going to launch into a discourse that she had rehearsed for some time. "It seems to me you should go into this new phase of study with the intention of putting it to practical use."

"What do you mean?"

"For example, you could produce articles and have them published in the university's various publications. For you, having published a book, and a well-received one, it won't be difficult to achieve. Articles like that would make you better known among specialists, among those who teach at the university, and prepare the ground for you to become an assistant and then, if you want, a full professor."

"A professor at the university, me?" Michele shook his head negatively. "No, Alma, I'd say not. I've decided to teach, but only young kids, as I do now, because it doesn't clutter my brain. I don't want to give myself to teaching. I don't want to waste one moment more than the required nineteen or twenty hours a week, the bare essential. That way I'll be left with lots of free time and, above all, a free brain for my real work. If I get involved in a university career, I'll be in a fix, don't you see? I'd end up not being able to do anything else." He had a sudden suspicion. "Listen, it isn't that you prefer to see me as a university professor instead of as a secondary teacher? Would that be it?"

"No, please, I'm far removed from all that. I just thought you'd have greater ... possibilities in your battle against the barbarians. And also, it seems to me you ought not so definitely to separate your studies, your reading about these French authors, for example—which in any case you'll be doing—from a practical application of your knowledge."

"And so?"

"Michele, this manner of thinking, this is a bit your ... weakness." Alma couldn't clearly see what she wanted to say, but intuitively tried to be more precise. "You don't face the problems that arise in a practical way, one at a time; you always look at the wider picture. Now, for example, you want to write another book and at the same time take on the studies for another degree, and in that way ..."

"What?"

"In other words, in that case you'll kill yourself with work, while the everyday problems won't be solved practically."

But instead of giving consideration to what Alma said, as it deserved, Michele just shook his head, smiling. Years would have to pass before he came to realize that his statuette with braids was more farsighted about such things than he.

"Well, I was speaking . . . generally", she finally said, no longer insistent.

"It's clear that writing in Italy is not something . . . clearly authors can't live from their books", Michele said. "When you think that in France and in America many of them get to be rich . . . look at the American Burns. He can afford to live in Europe's best hotels, only on the basis of his earnings from his first book, while he gets on with writing his second." (John Horne Burns, a former soldier like Michele, had written a book based on his war experiences on the Italian front and had become well known. Some people in America—among them John Steinbeck—saw in him one of the greatest hopes in recent American literature.)

Lately Burns had returned from America to Italy. Michele had asked his own publisher, who had also published the Italian translation of Burns' book, to introduce him. The two young men—so different from one another—had immediately got along well. For several weeks they would meet every few days and wander together around Milan, discussing life and literature. The one, the irascible John Burns, master of knock-them-down-and-drag-them-out literature, verbally destroying the world with his cynical criticism. The other, Michele, systematically reassembling the pieces, being just as forceful, because when his positive intelligence was unchained, he enjoyed facing obstacles, the more difficult the better.

"Here, on the other hand, there's no writer who can live off book earnings; the publishers themselves will assure you of that. Just take, as an example, B——." (Michele named one of Italy's most notable writers.) "Did you know his work is published by my own publisher? Well, he's also forced to do other work, without which he'd be unable to continue. That's a given situation", he had repeated.

"The Lord will help us", Alma concluded. "Now that's enough. Let's not think any more about these things, which only worry us. Worry you, more than anyone else. After what you've been through, you need to live a little, right?" She gazed at him with infinite love. "Let's thank God for being here, we two together. Why should we worry about all the rest?"

"You're right, very right. When I think about . . ." There had come to mind, like a blow, the memory of those who had remained behind on the long journey, piled up on the prairie outside Crinovaya: twenty-seven thousand corpses. So much for his book's earnings! *Who knows what state their poor bones are in now?* he asked himself. Having come through the sloughs of death, he couldn't help having gloomy thoughts like these every now and then.

Almina intuitively sensed the hurt in him and put a hand to his forehead. "Don't think of those things any more, Michele, please. My love, don't think about those horrible things any more. Think only that life is meant to be better."

Almost as if confirming the thought, a nightingale started singing in the trees, just a stone's throw away. The song was clear and beautiful. The bird sang one long melody, then tried it again with variations. The green space among the trees was filled with a surprising enchantment.

"You hear it?" Alma had stopped and smiled at Michele, her eyes a mixture of sadness and joy.

Michele nodded. The two of them remained still, listening. The nightingale sang on, in crescendo. Then suddenly, just as he had started singing, he stopped.

"Oh, what a pity, he's stopped!" Alma said, after having waited hopefully for a while.

"He'll soon start again. You'll see", Michele assured her. "He can't help himself. He's a little like me. Only he hasn't got anything else to think of, lucky thing. He sang all last night, did you hear him?"

"No."

They resumed their stroll.

"Listen, Michele, I've had an idea", Alma exclaimed.

"An idea?"

"Yes, something to show the Americans that we, too, are thankful."

"Thankful? But . . . what about the Americans?"

"I'm talking about that French ship, with the *Merci America* banners, the ship we were talking about at the table."

"Did we talk about a French ship at the table?"

"Of course we did. Fortunato did; he'd seen it at the movies in a newsreel."

"I didn't hear him. It must have been when I was talking to your father."

"He said that in order to show their gratitude to the Americans for all their help, the Marshall Plan and so on, the French had sent over a ship loaded with French specialties, such as fashions, perfumes, things like that. And on the sides of the ship they'd written *Merci America*. Right now the ship is sailing to various seaports in America."

"Ah, yes, I understand. And?"

"We, on the other hand, have done nothing. And we look ridiculous, according to Fortunato."

"Well, we have done some things ourselves, stopping the Communists at the polls, for example. Did you know that there were people in America who went out in the streets and danced to celebrate our results?"

"Yes, I'd heard that. Well, in any case, I just had this idea. Do you know what we Italians could give the Americans?"

"Go ahead, tell me."

"We could give them the nightingale."

"But . . . how?"

"We'd have to send a certain number, in order to turn them loose in their gardens and woods, so that they could breed and propagate over there also. I don't think—given the climate, nearly the same as here—the difficulties would be insuperable or the costs prohibitive."

"But . . . aren't there nightingales in America?"

"No, there aren't. I'm pretty sure. I remember Manno saying so. If we sent them, say . . . some thousands, we'd get them to propagate . . . it would be a marvelous present, don't you think? Particularly for . . ." She lowered her voice. "For those people like us, for the lovers over there."

"Almina," Michele exclaimed, moved, "do you know that it's a stupendous idea? That would be a really great thing! It's such a wonderfully womanly idea! Good for you, my little marble statue!" He reflected a bit. "I could speak to John Burns . . . no, he would be one of the gift's recipients. I could speak to Apollonio. He'd be amused, at least."

"Wouldn't it be better if you spoke with, I don't know, some specialist in natural science?"

"Well, yes, but I don't know any", Michele objected. "If I were working for one of the newspapers, I could launch the idea in a column . . ."

"That's right."

"I know the editor of *Italia*. He invited me to write for it, and I didn't accept, because I can't send articles in on a regular basis. It's no good my writing just when I have free time. There are basic rules to follow, and where would I find the time for a serious contribution? Later, yes, of course, because *Italia* is a paper that needs to be backed. But now . . ."

"It doesn't matter", Alma said. "Try to speak to Apollonio, then. When will you go and see him?"

"I was thinking of seeing him within a few weeks. But why don't you see him too?"

"Me? No, oh, no. Just think, I'd look like a fool!"

5

The elections of April 18 in 1948 had repercussions that ended up affecting the lives of every person in Italy. In a real way they enabled the completion of reconstruction (which took just over one year) and permitted the systematic development of the country's productive capacity. Even more important was the start of the spiritual renewal among the people. The people now had the right of self-determination since they had a freely elected government, while the prospect of falling back into the hands of a deviationist minority—Red or any other color—slowly disappeared. It meant Italy could rediscover her own identity, go back to being herself, and everybody made efforts to do so. The country was unaware that in only five years' time, with the collapse of a homogeneous political majority, the new government wouldn't be able to exercise true authority. In the next decades Italy would live on the credit of those five years; going still forward at first impetuously, pressing ahead in a disorganized way, with the production of the tools and materials at first advancing and then falling back again in disorder. At the time, however, nobody suspected these things would happen, and the people set to work with great commitment.

For the Rivas, the happy year of 1948 was a wedding year. In June Francesca married in the Nomana church festively decorated with flowers (Andrea had a passion for flowers); in August Ambrogio got married.

For Ambrogio's wedding the whole family traveled to Milan, arriving at the same time as the other close relatives; among whom were the two aunts from Monza who for a while had been evacuated to Nomana. There was Uncle Ettore, his habitual pince-nez perched raffishly on his nose, arriving on foot from his house, walking to the church of San Pietro in Gessate, chosen by Fanny for the ceremony, even though the church wasn't in her own parish. Fanny had picked the church "because I like it immensely". (In other words, a caprice. She thought it a suitable venue because of the church's wall frescoes, in which some of the personages had their hair cut pageboy style, like her own. "But to be sure, eh, we've made a donation to our own parish priest just the same", the *commendatore* informed.) They all met there, relatives and friends, including—as witnesses for the groom—Michele and Luca, the latter wearing the blue ribbon of his medal in his lapel. Celeste had gone to fetch him, and in the short car journey between Catafame and Nomana, the two had talked about Manno, Luca's friend and contemporary, "who would have been here at the party today". Celeste recalled his last journey in Manno's company, to Piacenza. ("I so insisted that he not put himself in danger!") Luca in turn told of his casual encounter with Manno at the little station in Puglia.

The church of San Pietro in Gessate—dominated, almost squashed by the enormous, indigestible mass of the palace of justice across the street—built of brick, is serene, built during the time of the Sforza, when Milan was a city of canals and tranquillity; its floor is lower than the street level.

Look how time passes. Michele, inside the church, let his mind wander while waiting for the bride with the other witnesses. *The centuries, the years that go by, disappearing without pause, and of each of them, what's left behind? A little dust . . . how much . . . one can measure it.* He made an arbitrary calculation of how much the floor had sunk in relation to the street. *One or two millimeters per year, that's about what's left of passing time.*

Suddenly he saw the figure of Alma enter the church and approach happily. As usual she was indescribably attractive to him, wearing a new dress for the occasion. *It's incredible how a dress can enhance a woman's beauty*, he surprised himself by thinking. With Almina at his side, his bad thoughts couldn't last; the ideas about the passing of time left him.

Fanny's friends and relatives—far less numerous than Ambrogio's—could be identified from the Riva group not only by their style of dress (although some of the women down from Brianza were also dressed by fashion houses or Milanese boutiques), but also by a certain something, a free and easy manner, an irreverence, a less constrained behavior. They were, in any case, Fanny's relatives, less attractive than Ambrogio's townspeople, particularly the men.

Following tradition, everyone was standing in his place to await the arrival of the bride inside the church, with the bridegroom near the altar, next to the red velvet-covered hassock, whose upright was covered in flowers. Behind him, next to their own red velvet armchairs, were the four witnesses, including Michele, who was accompanied by Alma, trembling like a dove.

Fanny's two witnesses weren't young, as were Ambrogio's; they were two uncles, one maternal, the other paternal. The maternal uncle (a doctor and head of a hospital department, a "well-off socialist", as described by Fanny a few days before, with her usual careless elegance) was, according to her, "one of these high-society types, very close to the municipal administration at city hall". It was hard to tell which was which; they were both in their sixties, looked faintly sad, and had several gold teeth.

The other invited guests occupied the rest of the pews, all of which were covered in red cloth and decorated with flowers. The women and girls were in dresses of a rich diversity of form and color, with hats decorated with lace and ribbons, and many wore long gloves over their bare forearms. They seemed torn between paying attention to the ceremony and being preoccupied (far more important) with their own outfits. At their sides, the men wore suits in different shades of dark gray, some of the country people with suede gloves poking out of a jacket pocket; waiting, smiling, a bit uneasy. They felt happy and satisfied with their women's outfits.

Fortunato—given the job of usher—came and went inside the church, keeping an eye open for he knew not what, wondering which of Fanny's two witnesses was the rich socialist, whom he had been told to look after specially. *Which of the two of them can be dumb enough to be a socialist?* he asked himself, like the true polemic liberal he was.

Pino, also, was asking himself which man could be the socialist, but without any aggressive intentions, although as far as socialists were concerned—starting with Sèp—he'd received nothing but blows and kicks. All the same, it seemed to him that as a former partisan he still had something to share with them.

After the appropriate wait, Fanny arrived, as beautiful as any woman present, in a white dress with tight long sleeves emphasizing the soft slimness of her arms, her face framed by her thick chestnut-gold hair. She came forward gracefully on her father's arm, walking down the red carpeted aisle. The bridegroom, unnoticed, looked back at her with strong emotions. He tried to look calm, but the thought that within a few hours he could feel this splendid creature in his arms unfettered by clothing made his heart beat strongly. Although twenty-seven, he'd never had physical relations with a woman, and the prospect of the imminent embrace was accompanied by a sensation of mystery that he was prepared to face with a ready virility of which he was clearly conscious.

Fanny also felt emotionally stirred, though not as deeply as Ambrogio, and partly distracted by the commonplace. "Goodness," she said to Ambrogio in an aside once she had joined him, "have you seen my aunt Fiorenza's dress? That mad designer!" Then, shortly after, "If you only knew, my Ambrogio, the effort it took to dissuade Papa from wearing an opera hat." She found herself unable to concentrate and in consequence forced herself to think of unimportant details.

Father Carlo Gnocchi emerged from the sacristy and moved toward the altar. Soon after the end of the war Father Gnocchi had funded various schools for mutilated children. He wore a white surplice embroidered in gold and had an agreeable handsome face. On seeing him Luca stiffened and remembered the face and how it had been during that terrible night battle in Arnautovo, with yellowed skin under a bristly beard, the sunken eyes. He remembered how Father Carlo, kneeling among the wounded in front of the isba aid station, had recognized him despite the darkness and had blessed him, making the sign of the Cross over him.

Afterward there had been that senseless attack when, with Pedrana and the others, they attempted to move the Russians from a fold in the ground ("Now and at the hour of our death . . .") and then the great march to Nicolaievca, during which Captain Grandi had died to the tune of his Alpine troop's mournful singing.

The wedding took place before the celebration of Mass. At the moment of saying a definitive yes, his solemn promise joining him to Fanny for life, Ambrogio once more rapidly took stock—just as he'd done when swearing allegiance in the military—and decided he was acting freely and according to his conscience. He solemnly promised himself to remain faithful, even at the cost of his life, to the trusting creature beside him. Fanny wasn't such a complicated person; she had made her decision some time ago (before him), and now what she wished more than anything was for these formalities to be over.

After the photographer's flashes, the reading of the rites, and the other complementary formalities required of the couple and priest, it was time to start the Mass. A high point of the Mass was Father Carlo's homily: an extraordinarily affectionate and simple felicitation to the couple, avoiding formalisms. So unaffected as to be perfect, Pino recorded it, or rather thought he had recorded it. (Just recently tape recorders had become available in the stores.) Unfortunately, the apparatus he'd placed on the handrail near the priest, although the tape was seen to be running—Pino was a bit clumsy about these things—hadn't had the appropriate button pressed, so that not one word of the priest's felicitous speech was saved. (Which he noticed only later, when the newlyweds had gone, and the most annoying part was that there were perfect recordings of the somewhat silly toasts and vapid speeches, captured at the lunch in the hotel.)

890

Unaware of all this, Fanny, seated, listened to the homily, acting as she would describe it "like a goody two-shoes", and afterward thanked Father Carlo—whom she was seeing for the first time—demurely bowing her head.

We leave out details of the Mass, and of the lunch afterward, organized with great care by Fanny at a first-class hotel. During the lunch the doctor-witness-socialist so well connected at city hall snubbed the young medical student Pino, who was hanging around him. He was also somewhat short with Gerardo, who—respectful, as always, with anybody of importance or even just giving the appearance of being so—showed him courtesy and deference. Beyond this, faithful to the great humanist tradition among Italian medical men, and once he'd warmed himself with some wine, the friend of city hall thought it an opportune time to deliver himself of one of his literary-esthetic lectures, giving his fellow witness Michele the benefit of his ponderous thoughts. Michele, unmoving and without a change of expression on his face, absorbed all the man's trite and boring pronouncements.

Later, well into the afternoon, the two newlyweds—after changing—were able to leave, while the youngsters (only because one of them started it) shouted, "Alone at last! Alone at last!", throwing handfuls of candies at the automobile. (Michele suddenly had a flashback to the shouts, "*Confites, Señor, confites—* candy, Mister, candy" by the Spanish children in Susdal. The war was still close. He still couldn't free himself of the memories; and probably those children were still, at this moment, over there, behind the barbed wire.)

6

The two newlyweds spent their so-called honeymoon in Naples and its enchanting environs: Amalfi, Positano, and Capri.

On their return trip, which they made in stages, they stopped at Perugia. Having arrived at night, Ambrogio went the next morning in the car to visit his ex-orderly Paccoi, whom he hadn't seen for five years, since the faraway day when they had been repatriated. (Fanny lazily remained in bed in the sunny hotel room. They'd agreed she would later go out alone, shopping around town.)

Though usually not so aware of the surrounding beauty, it gradually dawned on Ambrogio, as he went along the streets of Perugia, that he was surrounded by remarkable sights. There wasn't a road or building or even—on examination—a plain wall that didn't evince some trace of beauty. More than once he exclaimed, "Darn, what a beautiful city!" He thought, *Michele was right when he insisted that Perugia was the handsomest of cities . . . and in fact not even Florence is as pretty. Who knows how the people's lives must have been here when they built in this fashion.* The overall beauty, he noticed, wasn't limited just to architecture.

It was part of everything he saw, even—he noticed—in the names of the streets and the town's gateways. Instead of interchangeable labels, seen everywhere else, every one (at least the ancient ones) truly expressed the characteristics of the area in a concise and poetic way.

The strongest impression he felt was when arriving at the northern edge of town. Here the hills on which Perugia is built create undulations in the landscape, which led to the construction of the city walls along wavy, irregular lines (it was not unusual to see the city's history in the wall's stratifications: Etruscan, Roman, and medieval), which gave glimpses of the fields, with their little ravines, a bright green, dotted with wildflowers and silver olive trees. Twice Ambrogio stopped the car to get out and gaze admiringly at the views. The circumstances no doubt conspired to impress. Everything looked to him newly created. *It's not possible*, he said to himself, *that there could be another place so beautiful in the whole world. Whatever happens, I have to come back here with Fanny.* (He would have been amazed if he had known the thoughts of so many of the town's natives, who, as they went about their business at their own calm pace, noticed his car's license and thought, *What good fortune this fellow has, to live in Milan, city of industries, where one can earn real money.*)

Having left the city walls, he took the via Tramontana, a dirt road that took him north to a well-cultivated countryside, running first along the hill's ridges (no doubt these open, windy places had given the road its name, North Wind), then dropping to the foothills, with a group of pine trees crowning the hilltops here, and long lines or clusters of cypresses on the hillsides there. On the less steep stretches wheat, olives, or vines were planted, and, on the steeper parts, just olives, whose tranquil silver-green color imparted a special character to the landscape.

The car went through a few villages, then along a brief stretch of the Tiber national highway lined with cypresses, and passed a few small farmer's houses flanked by neat golden haystacks. Ambrogio stopped several times to ask the way from farm workers, finally arriving at a treed area divided by a narrow road, which gave out onto a big, well-cultivated bowl. Here someone pointed out the distant small farmhouse where Giovanni Paccoi's family lived.

At that moment Paccoi was placidly breaking open the earth in a small field just a stone's throw away from the small road. As soon as Ambrogio spotted the plowman, he recognized Paccoi. Feeling very emotional, he drove the car forward, stopping it behind some lines of grapevines, from which he could observe him without leaving the car. Short and strong, with his left arm somewhat shrunken from the wound he'd suffered in Cerkovo, the former artilleryman's face was sunburned, a little fatter, retaining his usual surprised look, hair wet with sweat as he followed the plow being pulled by two enormous white cows. Here he was in his own environment. Increasingly moved, Ambrogio—aware that he owed him his life—remembered how he had been six years before; the day Bonsaver had visited his battery, for example, when he had been dedicated to ensuring the small table was well laid (*A box covered with a napkin between two stools!*), or during the long walk of the retreat, when his face had been covered in frozen snow. And the dreaded morning when he himself had been wounded. He'd told Paccoi he was free to keep going on his own. *If he'd really left me behind, I'd be dead now.* Yet there had been his reply: "You shouldn't say that to me, agreed, Lieutenant? I know what my duty is." And now, seeing him here in his own Umbrian environment, Ambrogio better understood the great dignity of Paccoi's reply. "Giovanni Paccoi," he murmured, "I'll never be able to thank you enough."

The field Paccoi was preparing for sowing was so small that the plow had to be turned around frequently. Reaching the end of each short furrow, the two yoked cows would halt at his command while he lifted the plow for the turn. On his next cry they would shuffle and stumble into position, snorting while making the turn, and resume pulling as soon as the plow was positioned. It was almost noiseless work (only Paccoi heard the noise of the earth being opened at his feet); however, from a nearby fig tree there came the song of an unidentified bird, a strange, loud, almost ritual song.

As the intruder on this scene, Ambrogio was uncertain as to whether he should show himself and interrupt the work, which he instinctively didn't want to do. Paccoi himself solved the problem. Having noticed the car's arrival but not having seen it emerge from behind the vine-covered stretch of road, he stopped the plow and, shading his eyes with a hand, looked over in that direction. Seeing this, Ambrogio moved the car forward into sight. Stopping the car and getting out, he went with big steps toward his friend. At that moment the bird—it was an oriole—stopped its song.

Ambrogio having written of his impending visit, Paccoi recognized him immediately and almost came to attention, but then, remembering he was no longer in the army, he turned to the cows and told them to rest, then hurried toward his former chief. At his movement the oriole erupted in flight from the fig tree, flashing past in the sunshine. Ambrogio had time to notice its intensely gold color. It looked like a flying golden chip.

"Giovanni, at last, it was time I saw you!"

"Lieutenant!" said Paccoi, returning his ex-chief's embrace with his usual shyness. "Why didn't you tell me in your letter what day you'd be here? I would have waited for you at home, even gone to Perugia to meet you."

"When I wrote you I wasn't sure of the date", Ambrogio answered. "How are you, Giovanni? How's your arm?"

"Well, my lieutenant, I'm all well now." He lifted the wounded arm and moved his hand back and forth. "After all we went through, we have to give thanks to God. And your wounds?"

"I'm also well, thank God. I spent quite some time in the hospitals, but now that's all just a memory. Time flies, and I've even got married; I'm on my honeymoon, as I said in my letter."

"Yes, the letter, of course, you told me." Paccoi went quiet, affected by his emotions. "Eh, my lieutenant," he murmured, "you recall?"

Ambrogio nodded affirmatively; kept nodding.

"But what am I doing?" said Paccoi, remembering something. "I have to thank you for all the presents you've sent."

"Come on, don't make me laugh."

"Those two suit lengths particularly. They were really useful, you know?"

"I owe you my life, which is much more than cloth for a couple of suits", Ambrogio replied. Then, taking him by the arm, he said, "Good, now show me how you do your work. I'm interested."

They went together toward the plow. "Now, go on, finish the end of this field while I wait. This is a nice place to be, here in this pretty field."

"But . . . no, what are you saying? Let's go home straight away. My family is also expecting you, waiting for you just like me. They want to get to know you."

"Would you leave your work half done? Later you'd have to start all over again. No, there's little left to do, I'll wait."

"There's not much left, that's true, but . . ."

"In that case, go ahead. That way I'll also learn how to manage a plow."

Paccoi still hesitated. It seemed impolite not to dedicate himself immediately to his guest. In the end he agreed—or rather obeyed—as was ingrained in him.

Ambrogio walked alongside him up and down the field for the first and second furrows, walking slowly, at the hard-breathing pace set by the cows, then noticed he was disturbing Paccoi's work. He decided to wait in the shade of a small oak. "I'll watch you work from here. Otherwise I'll bother you", he said.

His sunburned face once more shining with sweat, Paccoi walked back and forth under the bright sun, slowly plowing until the small field was completely done. The scene was peaceful. A tangible tranquillity reigned. The now distant war, the tensions of his work at the factory, all faded away. *And I offered him a job with us, back there. He'd have been stupid to accept!*

Finally Paccoi halted and, before turning the cows loose, looked over at his visitor, who hurried over to join him.

They followed behind the two great white cows, still yoked together, on their way to Paccoi's small farmhouse.

7

Soon the guest was enjoying the sober welcome (this was Umbria, where every excess is regarded as bad form) offered by the women of the house, Paccoi's mother and sister-in-law. Having put the two cows in the barn, Giovanni went up to his attic room, where he washed his head, neck, and upper body, afterward putting on a freshly washed shirt before going downstairs. Their guest was seated in the kitchen, and he was served a wooden platter of ham and sheep's milk cheese and a glass of straw-colored wine. *The country folk back home won't have seen a wine so good even in their dreams*, he thought.

He noticed that the women were busying themselves preparing what undoubtedly was to be a sizable meal. "Are you getting lunch ready for more people coming in from the fields?" he asked.

"Yes, and also for you, Mr. Lieutenant, if it pleases you", replied the mother.

"But ... I've left my wife in Perugia ... she's alone, and ..."

Giovanni looked startled. "Can't you go and fetch her with the car? Surely you don't mean you can't stay here with us?"

The mother and sister-in-law also looked concerned. Ambrogio thought about the traditionally plentiful hospitality that was practiced in the Homeric era. "I would be delighted to stay, but ...", he said, "it wasn't something that ... I'd planned."

"What does that mean, that you hadn't planned?" Paccoi asked.

"I mean that I hadn't thought about it. Otherwise I'd have brought my wife and would have come at a better time. I mean, you're very kind, but I'm giving you too much trouble."

"But ... what do you mean, really? What are you thinking about?"

"Oh, please", said the mother. "Don't stand on ceremony", and waved at her daughter-in-law as if to say come, let's get on with it.

Finally, after having studied his watch and figured out how long it would take, Ambrogio decided to go back for Fanny. The wine he'd had made him slightly euphoric; during his drive to Perugia he planned to quote to his wife the old Umbrian saying that he'd learned in Russia from Paccoi: "In the country where one eats well, there will the Lord lead us."

Fanny was delighted to receive the invitation. During the meal, inevitably abundant, she talked to the women and put them at ease, offering them compliments Ambrogio didn't know how to make. She displayed an interest in everything, and she charmed the whole family, which now also included Giovanni's father and brother, who had returned from the fields at noon.

They learned that Giovanni was also planning to marry and that in the new growing season he would start sharecropping a nearby piece of land. "The owners are the same landlords as for this land. They know he's a good man and a hard worker", said his mother in a pleased tone. "Our family and theirs have known each other for many generations."

The men talked about many things, and it was clear that unfortunately even here peacetime had not done away with life's uncertainties. True, the local country people were against violence and bloodletting. In this regard things were different from Lombardy. Here an ancient civility permeated society and softened people's hearts, even those who had voted for the Communists. "They aren't bad people, believe me. They just want land." It was for this reason, to the evident disgust of the men of the house—opponents of communism and, as if this were an inevitable corollary, supporters of fascism (surprising discoveries didn't seem to cease)—that almost all the sharecropping farmers had voted Communist.

Ambrogio protested, "But ownership of land by country people isn't part of communism's doctrine. In fact, it's completely the reverse!" No matter: the Red propaganda in Umbria and its surrounding region was based directly on this lying promise.

In the end, here, too, the only answer eventually will be to industrialize, thought Ambrogio. *But if factories and industry arise in places like this, everything will change, maybe turn everything upside down.* (He was a much better forecaster than he imagined.) *What then?* He didn't really know what to hope for, knowing how impossible it was to confine people to a way of life with which they were no longer content.

The cart in which Giovanni's father and brother had arrived back from work was parked out on the threshing floor. It was incredibly ancient in design, low and square, with a single shaft and two solid wheels. *It looks like a Roman chariot,* Ambrogio thought. (He was right. It was a style of cart that had been used thereabouts for more than two thousand years.)

From time to time Ambrogio's glance fell on the cart just outside the open kitchen door. In the end he experienced a true sense of regret at the idea that maybe soon this attractively designed working implement, a living part of the heritage of the past, would become an antique relic.

8

On the way back to Perugia late in the day, Fanny pulled the Touring Club's guide from the glove compartment (it was the section covering central Italy) and started skimming it. "You know, I really liked those people, really a lot", she said. "It's hard to explain why ... how can I explain? I really liked them."

"And with good reason", murmured Ambrogio.

"They're poor people, but really enchanting! So, here just above Perugia is Gubbio. Let's see what it says about Gubbio. Oh, a mysterious town, look!"

She read a while in silence. "Oh, yes, right ... the Eugubian tablets. I'd almost forgotten."

"The ... Gubbio tablets? What are they?"

"What? You mean you didn't learn about them in school?"

"No. So what are they?"

"They're carved instructions for how to read the future by analyzing the way birds fly. Listen to this: 'They comprise seven slabs of greenish bronze dating back to the third century B.C. The first two are covered with Etruscan characters, and the rest have Latin writing. The text describes how one can arrive at the omens using the flight pattern of the woodpecker.'"

"The ... woodpecker, did you say woodpecker?"

"Yes, why? That's what is written here."

"It's just that this morning when I arrived, the first thing I saw was a woodpecker. At least I think it was. It was as big as a blackbird, and a pretty golden color, greenish-gold. What else could it be? I wondered then, and maybe I was right. I'd never seen a woodpecker before in my life."

"Ambrogio, are you pulling my leg?"

"No, I'm serious."

Fanny decided he wasn't jesting with her. (However, he was indeed mistaken in what he said. He hadn't seen a woodpecker, but an oriole. The two birds look alike, and the oriole is more plentiful in those parts than is the woodpecker and is more striking in appearance. Who can state unequivocally, after all, that a mistake hadn't been made by the Gubbio tablets' translators and that the bird mentioned in the ancient Etruscan wasn't really an oriole instead of a woodpecker?) "Maybe I've married an oracle", Fanny said. "In which case, tell me, what omens should we deduce from this? Come on, tell me."

"How would I know?" Ambrogio was amused. "What does the tour guide book say about the flight patterns? The one I saw this morning was flying from left to right for about fifty yards, rather like an arrow's flight. Then it was out of sight. But before it took off, it sang, too."

"Too? It sang? What nerve, this woodpecker! But the guide doesn't say anything about that. What a shame, it doesn't say anything else. What will we do?"

"In that case, take it easy. It means all is well. Around these parts the people are well mannered, right? So this morning's bird quite simply wished us good luck, just as they all do when they come across a honeymooning couple."

"Oh, what an intelligent oracle my husband is!" and after a while, she burst out eagerly, "What a marvelous place you've brought me to! Where even the woodpeckers take the trouble to wish us luck." She ran her hand lightly over his cheek. "My Ambrogio", she said.

"You're asking to be taken in my arms, right?" (This was the phrase they used in those first days of conjugal lovemaking.)

"Oh, yes", Fanny answered in a low voice.

"We'll soon be at the hotel", Ambrogio said. "I imagine you don't want to go down to dinner tonight either."

"Yes, you're right, after all they gave us to eat."

"Right. So we'll go to bed early, and the night will seem twice as long as the ones we've had up to now."

His young wife smiled her thanks over to him.

Today's great highways didn't then exist, but neither were there many auto-mobiles using the roads, so the national routes were suitable for fairly high speeds. Ambrogio took advantage of this on their last day, once again mentally involved with his duties back in Nomana. He was thinking of work and of his father, and his brother Fortunato, at that very moment taking on his own work. What if, while he was away, there had arisen some serious problem at the mill? Two days before, when he rang up, they'd assured him that he shouldn't worry, not even to think about it, but an industrialist's job is surrounded by unexpected problems. There's no let-up. Seen from outside this isn't apparent, but he knew from experience.

Fanny noticed the increase in the car's speed and smiled.

Ambrogio looked at her. "Forgive me if I'm hurrying, all right?" he finally said.

She replied, "All I know is that I've married an energetic man."

Back in Nomana the newly married couple started living a regular life. Getting up early to get to the factory (the old building) at the same time as his father, Ambrogio would arrive just before the factory workers got there. His lunch break should have lasted two hours, but over time this became shorter as Ambrogio attended to suppliers or clients who dropped by around noon. His late arrivals annoyed Fanny, who liked, after lunch, to walk in *I dragoni's* garden with him, listening to the blackcap's call (the voice of summer in Brianza), which from time to time would cascade from between the leaves overhead. ("What do we have an expensively maintained garden for if we're not going to use it a little? Can you tell me that?")

In the evening Ambrogio normally should have been back home at 7:00, but as he started spending the afternoons at the new factory over on the Lam-bro, and because of related business trips to Milan or Monza, he did not ac-tually have a fixed afternoon timetable. At the beginning Fanny tried to get him to stick to fixed times, reminding him—something of which he was very conscious—of his family duties. Then, bit by bit, she adapted herself. She was not worried because as time went by she noted that Ambrogio loved her more and more. Her married life was not only without problems (the occasional spat about timekeeping could not be counted), but also with respect to their inti-mate feelings, she felt safe and secure. Only during Ambrogio's long absences did she get a little bored. Then she would spend some afternoons with her mother-in-law, Giulia, attending to the needy, although not in a regular pat-tern. On the other hand, it wasn't the kind of work one programmed, as men did theirs (even if—because the work was subject to sudden and urgent needs—it was of itself pretty demanding). Her mother-in-law didn't pressure her.

"You've just got married", she would say. "Soon the babies will start to arrive, and you'll see that you'll barely have time to care for them. That's in the beginning, you understand, because you'll soon get organized. So take it calmly. The important thing about the poor people is that they should know from the start that you are truly interested, that you wish them well. Then they'll start to trust you, and they'll soon ensure you're busy, you'll see. But it's as well this happens after you have practice being a mother."

Giulia seemed to assume that Fanny wanted to have lots of children, seven or eight, maybe ten, as did Francesca, who was already nurturing her first in her womb. As far as this was concerned, however, her daughter-in-law—who unlike the Rivas didn't come from a practicing Catholic family—had her own ideas. After the first few months of married life had gone by without her getting pregnant, she had convinced her husband to practice the Ogino-Knaus method of contraception. *There's nothing immoral about it. Even the Church permits it. Why shouldn't we use it, at least for a few short years?* After some initial resistance, Ambrogio agreed.

10

The happy year of 1948 also saw Rodolfo's entry into a missionary order as a novice. He went in October, when classes began, and he was fifteen years old. The boy, who had become more serene and decided with each passing day, left home one rainy day, headed for the novitiate in Vicenza, the same country from which Manno's mother had come as a newlywed years before.

Giulia and Gerardo were happy at his decision ("to give a son to God!") and didn't try to hide it. But in any case when the moment came for him to leave, when, under the drizzling rain, he entered the car driven by Celeste, Giulia burst into tears, dismayed at his departure. She knew that, just as Ambrogio had gone to be a soldier at Italy's entry in the war, this son would also not hesitate or turn back when face to face with his duty, even though it be the least attractive posting, and she already imagined him, who knows, carrying out his calling in some leper colony, forgetting himself in his service toward souls stricken by sickness.

Ambrogio, too, was reminded in a way of his own departure into the service as he got into the car to accompany his brother to the seminary. The memory prompted him to make a military-flavored joke for the benefit of the family group seeing them off. "Please don't let Luca or Father Carlo know that Rodolfo is going close to the Julia Division recruitment center. As former members of the Tridentina, it could upset them."

Without fully understanding the joke, Giulia sobbed even louder, being joined by Noemi and unexpectedly by Fanny. There were also tears in Alma's and Francesca's eyes (she had come over from Visate in order to be present at the farewells), and the emotional Pino also cried. All of this soon caused Rodolfo's eyes to redden.

For the Riva family the happy year of 1948 finished with two graduations, Fortunato's and Pino's. Autumn had arrived, and the the Riva factories had seen an increase in the number of employees to over seven hundred. They had more than doubled and looked as if they'd catch up with the number of employees at the Marsavi sausage factory, which was also continuing to grow bit by bit.

11

The number of employees at the two textile mills grew even higher in the next few years.

"But the way we're going isn't right", Ambrogio sometimes protested to his father. "There's not enough financial base to carry this kind of expansion."

"But the banks will continue to lend us what we need," Gerardo would say, "just look at the way they increase our credit whenever we ask."

"Because their management has confidence in you. And precisely for this reason we should be cautious. Of course, you are the one who has to decide and not I, but . . . then there's the question of the proportion of supervisors to workers. We don't have a proper balance at our mills."

Fortunato backed his brother on the subject. "Ambrogio is talking sense. Soon we'll have one thousand workers, whereas how many supervisors are there? Some twenty?"

"Today, right now, there are twenty-four", retorted Gerardo.

"And does that seem a proper balance to you? Look, it's all out of proportion, not smart", said Fortunato.

"Precisely", emphasized Ambrogio. "That is another part of the equation that we need to study seriously and thoroughly."

"Even worse," Fortunato insisted, "among our twenty-four supervisors, there isn't one graduate and not even one with a high school diploma, not one. What does it mean? It means that the management is in the hands of self-taught people or a few perhaps who have taken a technical school course."

"But what use do we have for graduates and diplomas in our factory? Will you please tell me?" their father would object, motivated by his own elementary education. "In any case, the two of you are there, both of you graduates, right?"

Ambrogio and Fortunato shook their heads. "Papa, it's not that we just want to debate this with you. It's a problem we have to discuss seriously."

"We can discuss it, no problem. What I don't understand is what you could have against the people supervising. For example, don't you think that Serafino can do his job? Or that maybe Rina's son isn't up to his responsibilities?"

(Rina was one of the firm's master weavers, an older woman. Serafino was one of their best technicians. Gerardo would promote to section chief—when the need was felt—those factory workers who seemed most capable, or, after some specialized training, one of their offspring, more recent employees.)

"Papa, both Serafino and Rina's son are well qualified", Ambrogio said. "They even do miracles, but . . . that's not what we're talking about."

"And they do everything willingly", Gerardo agreed. "In a way, they even serve as an example for us in how to tackle the work. Even though they're not graduates. In any case, boys, I'm not here to place obstacles; you want to study this problem in depth? Perhaps we can set aside, let's say, three consecutive half days? Right, let's do it."

"Look at the Marsavis", Ambrogio went on, knowing from experience that the best argument to convince Gerardo was to put forward a practical case. "In their factory they have dozens of graduates, qualified technicians, did you know?"

"It means that for this sort of work they are a requirement. In any case, I've already told you we can look into the problem."

"The other thing that needs to be looked at", Ambrogio sometimes said, "is how to separate the accounting for industrial activity from those for commercial activity—that is, the ongoing purchases and sales you make, Papa."

Fortunato would add, "Right, like that load of Brazilian cotton that you bought and resold last week. You saw, Ambrogio, what a masterly piece of business that was? Just with that transaction we can pay off half the cost of the last batch of looms we bought. Papa, you did very well", he went on.

"Yes," agreed Ambrogio, "but these are separate and distinct activities. Each year when we give Dr. Mascheroni" (he was referring to the family firm's outside accountant) "our figures for the financial statement, he asks that we give him the figures separately. He says—and he's right—that as things are now, we're not in a position to know if our manufacturing activity makes a profit or not, or by how much."

"That Dr. Pino Mascheroni is a strange bird", their father would come back and say. "I've explained to him many times that for us it's impossible to give him the figures separately as he would like. And both of you also know that sometimes we buy raw material intending to resell it, then we go ahead and use it ourselves, or we use a part of it; and we do this more often than not."

"But if we had a good bookkeeper on the spot, even if it were only one person, with instructions to do this type of accounting, we could keep the figures separately. All that is needed is that someone separate the activities when posting the figures."

"All right, we can also look into that, although . . ." Although, Gerardo wanted to say, and his sons well knew it, that he wasn't attracted to the idea of employing someone to account for activities already past. He believed in using only employees who produced something.

Eventually they devoted three consecutive afternoons to the problem of a more rational organization of the mills' operations. On the last day Fortunato—who had recently taken a business administration course at the Milan Polytechnic—got one of his lecturers to come along and give advice. He showed surprise about the current ratio between supervisors and workers and at the same time felt favorably impressed by Gerardo's intuitive management qualities, to the point where he advised them to be very careful about introducing changes that might counteract his management style. From his analytical remarks, what in particular impressed itself upon their minds and made Gerardo especially thoughtful was his warning, "Take note. It's quite possible that manufacturers with antiquated machinery, which yours certainly is, will find themselves facing a crisis not too many years from now as a result of competition with the new machinery now coming along."

In the end Gerardo made his decision. The capital on hand, although not plentiful, would be used to proceed on a substantial renovation of the production area. This money was at the time invested—as a hedge against inflation—in real estate in Milan and Monza (houses and land they had been able to hang on to despite their recent efforts to expand). "This money", he told his sons, "should be treated as a permanent reserve fund, while you two carry on working during the next two years, say, until the middle of 1952, all right? Later, when you have a sufficiently clear vision of what's needed, we can sell these properties, and based on a feasibility study we'll work on together, we'll go ahead and use the funds for plant renewal."

So this was the plan that Ambrogio, Fortunato, and others with responsibility used as a point of reference over the next few months. However, and as expressed in the ancient proverb "man proposes and God disposes", the crisis, the tempest, arrived ahead of their forecast and was not due to the advanced age of their machinery or because of an imbalance in employees' qualifications or any other internal shortcoming, but in fact, and unexpectedly, it came at them from an outside source. The origin of the crisis was political.

12

One morning in February 1952—while Noemi made their breakfast—Fortunato spotted a heading in the newspaper: France's minister of finance, Pinay, had without prior notice issued a decree canceling the customs agreement with Italy.

He read the report carefully. He was aware that the firm had signed contracts the previous year that had turned over two-thirds of their current production to work eventually destined for France. The production under these contracts didn't go directly to France (*How fortunate*, he thought immediately) but went first to the buyers, an industrial group in Milan that owned factories in Piedmont and Liguria in addition to those in Lombardy. These factories cut and sewed the hemp cloth and rolls of hemp belting that the Riva factory sent them by the carload. The finished product was then exported under a series of contracts that the Milan group had with French railways and shipping lines.

After reading the few vague details in the article, Fortunato turned to Giudittina, already down, half awake, for breakfast. He took the folded newspaper so that the article was on top and gave it to her, saying, "Go upstairs. Papa is getting up. Show him this report. This one, see? Ask him to read it right away."

He remained standing as he usually did while drinking his coffee, thinking, until his father came downstairs.

Hit hard by the news, Gerardo forced himself not to show it. "No doubt we are facing serious problems," he told Fortunato, "but we shouldn't bandage our head before we've cracked our skull. When you get down to the factory, call Ambrogio and try to draw up a balance sheet of our current situation. The material ready for shipping, what is already in production, what material is in the warehouse, what we've ordered but not yet received, et cetera. Also the production we've shipped but not yet been paid for. Then there are the promissory notes from the Brusascas, which we've passed on to the suppliers and banks. I want a quick list of all that. Well, we'll soon see, and I'll contact Brusasca to arrange a meeting." The Brusascas were the Milan owners of the exporting factories.

But that first meeting with the Brusascas wasn't enough. A second and subsequent meetings were necessary. Meanwhile, one of the Milan group's executives started the first of repeated trips to Paris, and eventually old man Brusasca had to go himself.

The most difficult decision to make—because of its potential consequences for both the Brusascas and the Rivas—was to decide whether to suspend or to complete the work under the contracts in effect. The first option—and the best from the financial point of view—would have had the effect of throwing hundreds of people out of work, both in their own as well as at the Brusasca factories and would also have meant holding in the warehouses an enormous amount of raw material not easily switched to alternative use. The second possibility, to deliver work under the current contracts, would give them breathing space for a few months to use in seeking new work and probably allow them to keep the mills open. There remained the threat that the finished products might not be able to enter France. The specifications and specialized form of the finished product would make it nearly impossible to sell in Italy.

The management of the Brusasca group (at their headquarters in Foro Bonaparte in Milan) repeatedly reassured Gerardo. "You mustn't worry. Your promissory notes all were signed by *Commendatore* Brusasca, which you formally specified during negotiations, and you were right, as a signature like that is worth millions, so why worry?"

"Eh", an unconvinced Gerardo would mutter, "eh . . ." He thought to himself, *I keep remembering that in order to produce these big orders I've had to push aside older clients!*

The politicians in Rome, interested in and urged by the Brusascas (who, however, didn't have their own representative in Rome), let them know that the leader of the cabinet, De Gasperi himself, was busy trying to reestablish the customs agreement with France, which had originally been signed at his insistence. There was talk of actual and planned diplomatic meetings, and there were vague assurances. In Milan and Nomana the mood ranged from scepticism (the most frequent reaction) to optimism and even euphoria. (Ambrogio was reminded of those first hours after having been surrounded on the Russian front.)

When a meeting was held to make binding decisions, old man Brusasca said to Gerardo, "Listen, I can see the questions in your eyes. I want to tell you only one thing, that since I've been in this world I've honored my signature and have every intention of backing the signatures on the promissory notes you hold, too."

"Yes, but allow me a question. Suppose the goods don't enter France after all. In that case, do you have enough cash to settle the outstanding debts? Or at least capital reserves in houses or land that you can liquidate at short notice?"

In a low voice Brusasca said, "All my money is in my companies." He was quiet for a moment, then added, "But they're companies that many people want, and it wouldn't be difficult to sell them." He shook his head repeatedly, trying to push the possibility away, and his face became tense. "Look, Riva, let's not allow ourselves to get panicky."

Finally Brusasca said he felt inclined to follow the second of the two options and finish the manufacture of the work in hand. "Always assuming that you, Riva, let me have the fabric to work on."

"Let me talk to my sons", Gerardo replied, needing time to think. "I'll give you the answer tomorrow."

But when faced with the problem, Ambrogio and Fortunato found themselves as ill equipped as children, and once again Gerardo had to use his inborn intuition, backed by his elementary education, in order to make the decision. The idea of idling hundreds of workers overnight was unthinkable, more than anything, and not only because of the agitation, protests, and shouting the Reds would immediately organize. "I put myself in some of the weavers' shoes. We will continue to have bread on our table, but what about them? And there are some like Gatti, with his daughter so ill that it's costing him an arm and a leg . . . and a number of others, each with a problem. Well, when all is said and done, Brusasca is an honest man, so listen, boys, we'll let him have the material."

The merchandise dispatched by Brusasca—first on one train, then another and others—were held up at the frontier by French customs and unloaded. While making every effort to find a way to get the goods into France, Brusasca found out that the customs storage charge alone would cost him a million lire daily. He therefore wasn't able to redeem his promissory notes when they came up for payment and asked the Rivas to agree to extend their expiration date, "just for the time necessary to find a solution to the situation".

As a result, the spring of 1952 involved the Riva family in a new conflict, different but in some ways just as exhausting as that other war that had ended seven years before.

13

They had to negotiate first of all with the suppliers and banks to whom they had endorsed Brusasca's letters of credit, either in full payment or at a discount (in which case they paid the balance in cash). At the same time they had to pursue new business hurriedly in order to keep the looms going, not an easy task. They found themselves pressed to accept jobs at marginal profitability and from some clients of dubious solvency. At the same time they had to try to get rid of the raw materials stored in their warehouses, material they couldn't use for any of the new work. And since the barely manageable financial situation could at any time worsen, they got busy trying to sell some of their properties in Milan and Monza, originally earmarked to finance the firm's expansion.

Neither Gerardo nor his sons had fixed office hours any more. In theory Gerardo would have preferred to do everything himself. (Without mentioning it, he never forgot the tough fight for the survival of his factory that he'd had to face alone during the depression crisis of 1929, and, although irrationally, he would have preferred not to confront his sons with a similar trial.) The two sons, untried as they were, at first let Gerardo handle things, but soon, each according to his own talent, they started tacitly substituting for him in the various jobs that needed to be done. Fortunato principally made himself responsible for sales, and Ambrogio took over the negotiation for the renewals of credits besides the operation of the factories; looking for new work was something Gerardo took care of. Every now and then there would come from Milan vague assurances from the Brusasca group about negotiations that would allow their goods into France. The total of these repeated assurances helped keep their spirits up (just like the time during the retreat when there would be rumors about the proximity of the Allied lines).

After four months of crisis—the letters of credit were valid for four months—Ambrogio personally calculated the total of successfully renewed credits. He entered Gerardo's office with the figures in hand. "Do you know, Papa, the amount of the letters we're renewed for the Brusascas these last four months?"

"Tell me."

"Nearly one billion lire, all separate credits renewed one by one, as you can imagine."

"I'll be . . ." Gerardo murmured, concerned at the figure. "It hardly seems possible we've managed to do it."

"That's right. But the hard part is that now they'll be asking for the renewal of the renewals."

"With some luck they won't ask us to renew all of them. Only the credits that mature during the next few weeks. Well, those we'll just be forced to renew. We can't demand those notes right now when Brusasca is so sure that a good sized *tranche* of his merchandise will get released into France from the customs-bonded warehouse." (It was Brusasca who had used the French word for installment, so now Gerardo repeated it.) "As he begins to deliver, he'll start settling his notes. You'll see. He gave me his word."

"Let's hope so. If it doesn't come through I don't know how long we'll be able to bear it."

14

Three months later, in September, not a thing had changed. At the end of the month Michele and Alma were married; both now taught classes. Alma, a licensed teacher, worked at the same gymnasium as the Quadri Dodini woman. They hadn't married in June—the start of school holidays—only because Michele had wanted first to finish and deliver the manuscript of his second book (a fictional essay) to his publisher. In contrast to his first work, it had proved quite difficult to finish. Having gone through an experience up to now unknown among Italian writers (he had seen with his own eyes and personally experienced the fruit of the total negation of Christianity), he had tried in this second work to weave—using events, discoveries, the statements of the characters—all the threads of the de-Christianization process that had started even before the modern age and had led to the ovens at Auschwitz and the cannibalism in Crinovaya and in other places in Russia. In his work, apart from Catholic historiography, he'd also used the other side of the coin, the secular works, above all the writings of Marx, with which he was familiar from his time in POW camps. Along with many other Catholic specialists, Michele saw the start of the de-Christianization in the passage from Christian humanism to humanism per se, a passage—begun in Italy—that had ended in the creation of a first and perfect—even though on a small scale—Hitler or Stalin, in the person of Grand Duke Valentino, Machiavelli's famous prince. A man admitted to papal circles, into which a rediscovered paganism had infiltrated and where Christian customs had begun to be corrupted throughout society by an incipient immorality.

Later this tragic process had been slowed and then stopped (a sign, according to Michele, that Christ is always alongside the heirs to his apostles, though they be sinners and unworthy) by the great Catholic reformation, called the

Counter-Reformation, which, however, didn't affect all Christianity and even in the Catholic countries didn't reach all cultural sectors. Marx—in Michele's opinion—hadn't given enough importance to this first stage of de-Christianization. He had, however, captured successfully and enthusiastically praised the next phase, that is, the cleavage in Christian society produced by the emergence of Protestantism.

Starting from an assumption that "criticism of religion is the premise of all criticism", Marx had named Luther as the deliverer of man from "exterior slavery to Christ" and had shown how German philosophy soon completed Luther's work, also delivering man from "interior slavery to Christ". Once freed from God—in practice, free from his morality—the different human group-ings with the qualifications to aspire to predominance (first of all the state, then the class, then the race) had, each one—following Michele's explanation—theorized its own supremacy and the enslavement of all other groups and in such a radical form that the existing sense of Christian morals had progressively weakened.

The two culminating points of this process up to now had been the exter-mination of six million defenseless Jews by the Nazi racial aims and ten million (as was thought at the time; in reality there had been double that number of deaths: twenty million) just as defenseless Russian peasants in the Communist class fight. The young writer had tried to convey without equivocation this enormous phenomenon of the annihilation of man, the true outcome of the "liberation from God", but realized the difficulty of the enterprise given the innumerable prejudices that secularization and de-Christianization had planted in nearly everyone's mind. He was aware that, although the analyses that sup-ported his writing had been rigorously arrived at, there would be clashes with many obstacles, which was why he had made an effort to make each page as incisive as possible. He would have been more completely satisfied with the work if he'd had more time, time during which, however, his voice wouldn't have been added to the choir of current culture in a period during which the apocalyptic butcheries—caused by the Communists in government—had be-gun to take place in Asia. Therefore, had he decided to publish the book with-out the finishing touches, with the intention of returning to the work at some later time.

Also, he had noticed that—even given the firm vigilance of Pope Pius XII—a serious error originating in France, a tendency to present the Marxist "truth" as a "Christian truth deranged" (in any case, still Christian), was surreptitiously infiltrating itself into the Catholic society, running the risk of creating im-mense confusion; this had made him impatient to publish.

The marriage of the author to Alma was blessed in Nomana's church by Father Turla, the former military chaplain, who was then completely occupied with a project of his own: the construction in the mountains of a small sanc-tuary in memory of the POWs who had died in Russia, and principally his own Alpine soldiers. "Everything in the sanctuary, the frescoes on the walls, the mosaics on the flooring, the windows, should visually represent those soldiers, how they lived in the *lager*. So that within ten years, or even fifty years from now, the priest officiating at each Mass will be reminded of them. They died consigned to oblivion, far too forgotten."

After the ceremony the guests all went out to the Hotel Villa Olmo on Lake Como. On this September day the lake offered its most beautiful colors. The vistas of water, sky, and hills seen from the hotel's big gardens were truly enchanting. However, the sense of the beauty in things can produce pain if the observer has anguish in his soul.

Ambrogio, for example, didn't have eyes for the view. Although visually aware of the scene before him, his mind kept going back to thoughts of the Brusasca line of credit, which was to expire within two days. There was a lot of money involved. *Last week after extending the credits we managed to come out ahead by a pure miracle, but this coming week I really don't see how we can succeed. And now we have this perfidious bank in Monza, which not only won't extend its note, but has even demanded immediate settlement of the overdraft. There has to be a way of covering that particular hole, but how?*

Fortunato was pondering the sale of one of the properties in Milan. Almost certainly he wouldn't be able to get more for it than the truly low offer made by one possible buyer. Would he really have to sell or not?

Gerardo—who had that day decided not to think about business (*At least on my daughter's wedding day, the devil take it!*)—felt badly about not being able to help Father Turla, with whom he had shared a car from Nomana to Lake Como, to build his little church. *If we manage to climb out of this deep hole we're in without being totally destroyed, I'll help him. I promise I'll help him, if we climb out and when we've climbed out. Well, it'll be the will of God.*

His feeling of being at the bottom of a deep dark well, with a little circle of light way high up, like a small patch of unreachable blue sky, was a feeling he often lived with. This image summed up well his feelings about their situation, to the point where he even lived it in his dreams. Of course, he didn't talk about his state of mind, which today of all days would have sounded inexplicable since—considering it his duty as a father (no more and no less than he considered it his duty as a businessman to redeem the credit notes no matter what the difficulty)—he had taken care of the needs of the young couple, not only buying them their bedroom furniture, as was the custom, but also several other indispensable items and also an automobile, which he'd presented to his son-in-law. "It'll save you a lot of time, time that you can spend on your real work, which is more important."

Only the others, therefore—that is to say, the guests and among the family the young fellows and the ladies, less aware of the gravity of the situation—could give themselves over to the pleasure of the delicate ripples of the water, the dark green of the surrounding hills, and the deep blue of the Lombardy sky overhead. Giudittina in particular was ecstatic; for some time now the seventeen-year-old had become a dreamer—as Michele recently said to Alma—with a penchant for giving languid glances. Alma also—at the very least, she—was totally lost in happiness. It seemed to her that God, giving her this much happiness, was giving more than anyone deserved. With her white bride's dress, her chestnut braids resting on her delicately molded breast, she looked from time to time, enchanted and wordless, at her Michele.

At last, after having changed into another dress, she left at his side. They went in the new auto, with a hail of candies raining down ("Susdal!"), while everyone else around laughed and made jokes, and the young ones—at Fortunato's suggestion—ran toward the car in order to lift the wheels off the ground and so prevent their departure. Noticing the move, Michele stopped the prank by accelerating fast, leaving behind a spray of gravel and skid marks in the driveway.

15

In the spring of the following year, 1953, the crisis continued to fester. *For more than a year we've been fighting like this, mostly on a stop-and-start basis,* Ambrogio would reflect. *How long will this story go on? Certainly this war can't be as long as the previous one, I hope.*

The prospect dismayed him, and he would finish by telling himself that no, the possibility was neither forecast nor possible, and he would grab for one argument or another to reassure himself.

At the elections on June 6 of 1953, the second general elections of the republic, the Christian-inspired party lost the absolute majority it had won five years before. The consequences were to be very serious, although no one or nearly no one in Italy at the time realized it. As far as the Rivas were concerned, they hardly had time to notice. The only one who concerned himself was Michele, who went with his Alma to Nomana every Saturday night. In this dinner Ambrogio would try to participate too, dragging along a reluctant Fanny. "Tomorrow we'll go out wherever you choose", he would say to soften her up. "We'll go and visit your family in Milan if you like."

"Visit my family? Is that the sort of thing you'd enjoy? Well, not I."

"Well, in that case we'll go for a drive." (Tired as he was, he would rather have spent Sunday in the garden or even just asleep in bed.)

"Listen, Ambrogio, I'll go along with you this time, but wouldn't it be better to lengthen next week's outing to include Saturday?"

"On Saturday I'll be too busy. You know that."

"How boring."

During dinner Gerardo would unfailingly push Michele into commenting on the current political happenings. He enjoyed hearing about the historical details that Michele included to support his analysis, and he liked the depth of his son-in-law's reasoning.

Following the elections of 1953, Michele had become a pessimist. "De Gasperi kept saying it before the elections, quite clearly: with a constitution like ours, which prides itself on giving guarantees to everyone, even a clear and homogeneous majority, such as we then had, found serious difficulties in passing laws. Imagine what'll happen now."

"But didn't the Christian Democrats contribute, maybe even more than the others, when it came to writing the constitution?"

"Yes, of course. But don't let us forget that the Christian Democrats had only a relative majority at the time. In practice they, and the Reds as well, each fearing the other's victory, competed with one another to insert into the body of the constitution phrases, cautions, and clauses of all kinds to guarantee the rights of the minorities. And the outcome is that the majority now has too many difficulties in trying to govern. And if the majority isn't homogeneous, it can't govern at all. That's the reason why De Gasperi for many months has been pressuring for the passage of the new electoral law."

"Which one, the 'tricky law'?"

"Right. It was designed to allow parliament to be run by a majority of democratic parties in order to get the more important bills passed. But you saw how that came out ... both the Communists and Socialists made such a fuss over it that even we ourselves call it the 'tricky law'."

"So what now?"

"Now a democracy without a working majority isn't a democracy. And to make any progress the Christian Democrats will see themselves forced into ever more delaying compromises with the Reds."

With Michele gone, neither Gerardo nor his sons had time to think about politics. None of them had even read De Gasperi's so-called political last will. It was Michele again who referred to it some days after the statesman's unexpected death, a man to whom had to be credited Italy's reconstruction and even the sadly failed customs union agreement with France. "The 'last will' left by De Gasperi included a complete analysis of the country's situation. He held that, in fact, for the majority to be able to govern, an indispensable modification of the constitution would be needed. But who could now obtain agreement of two-thirds of the votes required to change the constitution?"

Inevitably their meetings weren't confined to talk of politics. They tried to avoid talking about business or about work. They were left with general talk about daily events, family talk; either Pino or the women in the family would steer the conversation that way.

Pino had been back for some months after a year in England, where he had been taking a course in specialized medicine. One evening soon after he returned he'd gone to see his father in his office at home (Gerardo regularly brought work home and occupied himself with it after dinner) in order to talk to him. His father, in order to start things off, asked him about his specialized course in England, and Pino answered, "Well, I took tropical diseases and improved my English."

"English? Tropical diseases? Why, are you also thinking of going to Africa like your brother Rodolfo?"

"Yes, Papa."

"But you've said nothing about it to your mother or me?"

"I wasn't too sure whether I'd persist with this." (His father remembered the time when Pino was always unsure of himself, when he used to say, "I'm just a poor miserable fellow." Being a partisan had cured him of that, in large part because of the trust that chief of his had put in him, what was his name? Beltrami, whom no one remembered any longer.)

"But now is the time to advise you that you'll soon have two missionary sons in Africa: one a priest and the other a doctor. Always assuming that I'm able to stand it in Africa."

In order to prepare himself better for general practice, he had recently been going to the small hospital in Nomana (the same hospital to which Giustina and Tito Valli had been admitted) and from where he brought occasional news. "Today we admitted so-and-so . . . we've let so-and-so go home . . ." In the town, everybody knew everybody else.

One evening he reported that Foresto had come in; he was still the chief of Nomana's Communists. A few days later, upset, he told them that Foresto's complaint was terminal. He had leukemia, cancer of the blood, an illness that was then incurable. The news saddened them all, because nothing could be done, nothing at all for this man, who although a political opponent was well known. Foresto wanted the doctor to tell him all the truth and found himself suddenly facing a death that already had an implacable hold on him. Everything he believed in, everything he'd worked for up to now, was of no use to him, related as these things were to this world and not to the beyond. For some weeks the unfortunate man distanced himself from everybody, silently thinking, and no one could fathom how it would end; Father Mario visited him daily and tried to gain his interest through conversation, always being careful not to touch on religious themes, being unwilling to take advantage of the man's tragic situation. The sick Foresto never asked him about the beyond, and for his part the priest avoided questioning him; he'd let him talk and listened.

One day, after having stared silently at Father Mario, Foresto asked him to send Luca to him, "assuming he wants to come and see me".

Soon Luca, still secretary of the Christian Democrats and a little surprised at the call, went to visit the Communist boss. Over the next days he was seen to return to visit Foresto without disclosing a single word of their conversation, but what was happening to the sick Communist—who for years had not involved himself in anything except politics—was an awakening of interest in the Christian ethic and its effect on politics. Above all, he was interested to know why so many of Nomana's Christian Democrats were prepared to sacrifice their earthly interests in favor of the Great Beyond. "This attitude has always struck me as a great idiocy, but I have to admit that now I don't see it that way."

Luca, with the help of his sound good sense and using his authentic faith, patiently discussed this with Foresto, helping him as best he could to feel his way among the great questions: life, death, eternal destiny. Eventually Luca suggested he also talk of these things with Father Mario. "He knows infinitely more than I about this, so much so that when I was on the front line, I'd think about his teachings in order to understand what was going on." Foresto ended up agreeing to do so.

Father Mario talked about Christ crucified to this man under sentence of death. It was hard for Foresto to understand the salvational reality of the Cross. It took him weeks to reflect on it all before he finally accepted and asked to confess himself. After this, the dark side of man, the devil who never admits defeat, returned to the attack, making of his soul a battleground. Foresto had to go through exhausting spiritual battles, getting help from Luca and Father Mario. The priest would give him Communion daily, and one afternoon, after a serious crisis, Foresto asked for and was given extreme unction.

As Pino related it at home, "It seems to me that Father Mario pleads daily with the Lord to take him to his side: 'Take him now, while he's at peace with you, take him soon.'"

And one day the Lord did take him. When the bell sounded at the end of his agony, everyone knew it sounded for Foresto—the stranger, as his name suggested—stranger no more. And his body was taken to sacred ground and laid alongside all the others, awaiting the resurrection.

Finally the day for Pino's departure arrived. Still giving the appearance of a helpless child, from time to time he put on a mischievous expression as if about to spring a trick. His brother Rodolfo, having received permission from his superiors, went along with him, Ambrogio, and Fortunato in the car to Milan's Linate Airport. Rodolfo now wore a friar's habit, being close to taking his vows. "So, you'll be clearing the way, eh? You'll be in Africa before me."

"Am I not your older brother? Even though not wiser, perhaps."

16

Rodolfo in his turn left for Africa at the end of 1955. He was nearly twenty-three years old, tall and thin, and even if his face had slightly irregular features, he was really a handsome youth, the handsomest of Gerardo's sons. Along with the evident sense of serious responsibility for his new calling ("I'm one of God's priests forever!"), a restrained happiness could be seen in his eyes. Providence had permitted him to enter into the Lord's field—after years of work and penitence and a deep desire to succeed—as a laborer sent by him to work on the immense harvest.

The doings of his family seemed less important to him ("*After having laid hands on the plow, no one destined for the kingdom of God should ever look back*"), yet before leaving the house to get into the car that would take him to the airport, he couldn't help noticing the anxiety that affected his family, particularly his mother. The continuous effort to be supportive to her husband and help him in the long hard fight, which so far had gone on for three years (a fight that hadn't let up, and it even seemed to become more seriously dramatic with the delivery of a message just before his departure), had imprinted itself visibly on Giulia's features. It was more noticeable to Rodolfo, who didn't see his mother regularly but only occasionally. *Look at how Mama has lost weight, poor woman, as if she has shrunk.*

When he was about to leave, he took his parents to one side. "I'm absolutely convinced about one thing," he told them, "and that is that this punishment, this stewing, as you called it earlier at the table, which the Lord has sent us—or rather, sent you—isn't by chance."

"We hope that you're right", Gerardo said with a sigh.

Earlier he had handed his son a roll of high-denomination French francs, which he had sacrificed to acquire. "I've given the others a gift when they got married, and it's fair that I give you something today as well. You'll not have problems about the money at customs—I've looked into this—because the franc is legal tender in French Equatorial Africa, where you're going."

And when his son tried not to accept the gift, "But why, Papa, what for? I don't need it."

"It'll be useful to you. You'll see. Even if only to give the poor people down there something to eat. The question of providing their daily bread must still be the number one problem for many of them."

Then Rodolfo said, "I'm convinced that this great trial that the Lord has confronted you with is something he wants for you for your own good. It'll probably stop you all from getting rich, which you were in danger of becoming."

His father nearly objected. "But don't you know that to create one job nowadays costs around five million? If one doesn't accumulate the necessary capital, how can one create new jobs? And if we industrialists don't offer jobs, what else do we do in this world?" He wanted to come out with these and other protestations, but said nothing. In his son's—the new priest's—argument there seemed to be a new authority. He sensed a depth of truth. He behaved toward his son as he would in church to his confessor.

"I know", his son said. "I know, Papa, that you've never worked for the money and that all your life has been devoted to service. I've seen that since I was a small child. Even more if today I'm going where I'm going, it is because I've learned from you. For the same reason, it seems to me, Pino went to be a missionary doctor in Tanganyika. But there was the risk, not for you probably, but certainly in some degree for us youngsters, that we would acquire a taste for wealth, take richness and abundance to our hearts. I wish you'd keep that in mind."

He turned to his mother. "Mama, if that's the way it is, we've no need to become worn out by this trial; let us not allow ourselves be anguished about it. That's all I wanted to say. Nothing else." He lifted his young priestly hand, very moved, and blessed them.

17

What had caused the Rivas to worry that the firm's crisis was about to worsen had been a message from Brusasca. The old businessman had advised that he was in no condition, like it or not, to pay his debts in cash. For this reason he'd proposed that they accept settlement by taking over some of his factories.

As they needed to give him a reply, Gerardo and his two older sons met in the office at home on the same evening that Rodolfo left. (It was the same office in which Ambrogio used to study, where Colomba would interrupt him with her jocular, "Eh, fount of knowledge . . ." How distant those days now seemed! Now he'd need to be firm, to concentrate and not let himself be distracted, not even by the memory.)

The two young Rivas soon became concerned when they considered the situation. "Why has Brusasca waited so long, up to today, before offering us his factories? Why didn't he offer them earlier, when we weren't up to our necks in water, as we are now?"

Gerardo answered, "Probably because he did not think he would be forced to do so; and if he had offered us the factories earlier, we would have been reluctant to take them on."

"If we take them now, how long will it take for us to sell them? Months, years?"

"Who can tell?"

"And meantime? He won't let us continue to hold his letters of credit."

"Exactly," Gerardo said, now pale in the face, "and as they come due, we'll be forced to exchange them for new letters of our own."

"And if the new letters of credit can't be settled on time, it'll be our firm and not his that will owe the debt."

"Precisely."

"Ah, no! That's too easy on him."

"He can't do any more. He's already lost too much", said Fortunato, pushing himself upright in his chair. "If we think about the enormous sums we've lost, you have to realize that he's lost much more."

"And after all, by giving us warning, and by making this proposal, old Brusasca proves that he is still a gentleman."

"But how could we take these factories on our shoulders? How many are there?"

"Three. We'll need to be careful assessing their value."

"Three factories, on top of the two we already own? There's no question of our having the funds to operate them, not even to start them working."

"Of that there's no doubt. And in fact he proposes to hand them over closed, stopped, and locked. What's more, the fact is he's closing them now because he hasn't even the money to keep them going. You should also know that for some time he's not paid his workers—all they have for their work are advances on their salary."

"So here we are closing down factories all the same", said Fortunato, who during the past few months had been critical of his father's obsessive attention to improving social conditions, finding jobs, and so on, all of which had worsened their situation.

"Yes", Gerardo agreed. "That's the point we've reached, even if we've done everything possible to avoid getting to this."

"That's it, all right! Everything possible. That's the truth. And we've not reached bottom even now!" Ambrogio said.

"Right. So, boys, what shall we decide on?"

"What happens if we don't accept the offer?"

"In that case I fear that in a short time Brusasca won't even be able to hand over the factories any more."

"Mmm. What a choice!"

"Papa, if this is the point we've reached, there's really no more to say. All that's left is to ask God to get us out of this."

So, once again obliged by outside forces to do something they wished to avoid, the Rivas accepted the three factories in payment and immediately started making efforts to sell them off. This was a task that the Brusasca group had already tried without success, so their work was particularly difficult. Gerardo decided to relieve Fortunato of any other duties, giving him sole responsibility for finding a buyer. In practice the young engineer only nominally gave up his other jobs as his father intended, but in any case dedicated so much effort and talent to this task that he gained the attention of other industrialists. It was essential that the Rivas find some liquidity in order to replace Brusasca's credits with notes of their own. In practical terms they needed to sell at least one of the factories immediately. Fortunato somehow managed this. ("No doubt due to Mama's prayers", as some in the family, including Gerardo, believed.) He sold the factory located in Lombardy, and for a reasonably high price.

Old man Brusasca, having heard the news, and also being aware of the competence with which Fortunato had handled the deal, did something unusual for him; he personally rang to speak to Gerardo. "Your company's future is now safe because of that young fellow", he said. "Congratulations." He too was happy—as was evident in his tone of voice—to see that even the most worrying obstacles could be surpassed.

Having sold the first factory, Fortunato started coming and going between Piedmont and Liguria—the locations of the other two factories—trying to sell these quickly as well, but despite all of his efforts, he wasn't able to succeed again.

18

A few months later, early in 1956, local newspapers carried a report that the Alpine regiment's former chaplain, Father Carlo Gnocchi, had been taken to the hospital because of serious ill health. It had been some time since he had been seen around Nomana. The doctors caring for him wouldn't allow any visitors, so even his friends the Rivas had to get their news about him from the newspapers. Father Carlo was by that time well known all over Italy. His associations to aid wounded children had spread through the central and southern parts of the country; even the president of the republic had inaugurated one of them.

(At the time Fanny remembered the lovely sermon that the celebrated priest had pronounced on her wedding day—the now-lost sermon, much to her regret, all because of Pino's clumsiness in the operation of the tape recorder. She had lamented it with Ambrogio. "Your dear brother! That day he behaved like a true partisan." Ambrogio had smiled. "Now is that reasonable? What do the partisans have to do with tape recorders? Besides, you've always regarded the partisans with approval." "Enough! That's enough of that, drop it! I know what I'm saying." Because of the continuing financial crisis, Fanny would occasionally show her resentment with bitter words.)

On February 28, Father Carlo understood that his end was near. The cancer that had consumed his flesh had left his frame spare and skeletal, and he felt a paralysis stretching from his stomach to his feet. His eyes would occasionally rest on the Crucifix on his bedside table, a Crucifix his mother had given him on the day of his priestly ordination. Gazing at it, he prayed silently. Perhaps he asked God to cut short those hours of suffering; from time to time he would pass a hand over his eyes with great effort. At last, as death approached, he began to have the death rattle. A few minutes before dying, he became lucid and opened his eyes for a last time; with a supreme effort he grasped the Crucifix and placed it on his own chest. Who could know how many Alpine soldiers whose eyes he had closed in the cold snows would now be impatiently awaiting him in the beyond?

His funeral cortège in Milan gathered an enormous multitude of people. There were large numbers of former Alpine soldiers, all wearing their distinctive military headgear, and there were hundreds of his mutilated children. During the sad procession the Alpine veterans carried the crippled children on their shoulders. This was something they had become accustomed to doing, and it was a practice that had pleased Father Carlo a lot.

Walking in the crowd alongside Michele, Ambrogio silently intoned a requiem, the prayer for the dead; but at times he couldn't help wondering why God would have taken Father Carlo from this earth when he was so much needed here and when he was still so young, only fifty-four years old. His mind turned over the basic arguments used by so many people in similar situations. *The scoundrels who create all the problems and all the useless people, those God leaves here with us. Yet he takes the useful people, people who can do good right here. Why?* Many people have been led to conclude that God is not concerned with human affairs or that God doesn't exist. Ambrogio wasn't disposed to get into that line of thought, but would in any case have appreciated receiving an answer to his question. He turned to Michele, putting the question to him in a low voice. Michele, who had been less close to Father Carlo, looked at the Alpine hats in the procession and thought of all the dead men who had been buried without a funeral service, who had been unceremoniously thrown into common graves at the POW camp. (Right now, today, how many were being buried the same way in Russia, in China?) He spent a few moments thinking about the question his brother-in-law had posed. "Why does God take the people who are needed, people who are doing good? Is that what you're asking?"

"Yes. In the meantime he doesn't take the scoundrels, the people who create evil. It makes people wonder if there is a God, you know?"

"Yes, I know. But for this very reason—I'd say—he guides us toward an answer. If God systematically intervened, punishing the evildoers and encouraging the good people, he would be obliging all men to do only good. That's the same as saying that he would be taking away man's free will."

"Ah, yes, I see."

"Of course, when death comes to someone we love, all the arguments and logic get pushed to one side."

"That's true; it's what I'm going through."

"Right. What we don't seem to be able to accept is man's death. I'm talking about death itself", said Michele. He had seen countless deaths and still continued having the same reflections. "This reminds us that we weren't originally meant for this. At each individual death we are given fresh proof."

"Are you still thinking, perhaps, about . . . original sin?"

Michele nodded.

Ambrogio smiled. "But what an obsession."

Michele thought, *Without this belief there's no explanation for history in general or for each person's life in particular,* but he said nothing.

But Father Carlo had died. They would never again hear him talk about God or about the Alpine troops. They'd never again see his smile. At this discouraging reality all the reasonings are truly pushed aside.

19

The family firm's crisis went on increasing and worsening; apart from the usual difficulties, there was now a new and greatly disturbing event. One of their less reliable clients, from whom the Rivas had initially accepted only limited orders, which they had later allowed to become bigger in order not to interrupt the work of their looms, had come to them and asked for their intervention in his letters of credit when they came due. This wasn't an honorable gentleman like old Brusasca but a wily individual who found himself worried about his business and didn't scruple to lie about his financial situation, falsely inducing suppliers to extend credit to his clothing business. He pushed the extension of credit, particularly with companies that were too busy to keep an eye on his activities.

In truth, during those times, while new companies continually opened up, not a few of the older firms were experiencing crises like the one Gerardo and his sons had feared and which they had tried to avoid by a timely renovation of their machinery. (It should be said that despite the terrible problems facing them, the Rivas hadn't entirely forgotten their modernization plan. Ambrogio particularly took the initiative, twisting his father's arm when they sold some property in Milan. He used part of the proceeds to buy some automatic looms based on new technological advances. "We also have to survive, Papa", he'd said in his hardheaded way.)

In the meantime, due to the wily client's insolvency, they had to go through another round of rolling over credits, amounting to a third of the value of the original Brusasca shortages. "So here we are up to our necks in more water than before," the Rivas sourly reflected, "and paying the interest on moving all these credits around is going to fall on our shoulders. Those costs alone could ruin us."

Shortly thereafter another client—who had been a client from way back and a close friend of everybody's, including the Rivas—found himself short of funds and unable to redeem some credits. Their answer to this client—who of all people deserved another chance—was that they weren't able to carry him. His letters of credit (which fortunately for the Rivas didn't amount to an excessive sum) had to be pursued. The old client, whose problems were compounded by other serious misjudgments, became despondent and some months later killed himself. The tragedy of this death caused brief consternation in Nomana, but there was little time available to devote to it. It really felt as if war had returned.

The Rivas' negotiations with the banks had reached the point of humiliation. Some of their bankers, clearly basing their decisions on Gerardo's known integrity, did their best to accede to the repeated requests for credit renewals without adding the many *buts* and *howevers*, but others declared that "very much against their will" they would need new guarantees, which for the Rivas became a nearly tragic problem. There were also true friends like the old manager of one bank, who, on hearing of another bank's action, had on his own initiative increased the Rivas' credit by the exact amount of the problem created by his competitors. This action gave the three Rivas some relief, although it wasn't enough to resolve all their problems.

During this period of crisis, a Milan chemical group offered to buy the factory on the banks of the Lambro, just this one, and only the property. The looms and other textile machinery were of no use to them. For Gerardo this was probably the time of his greatest suffering, and he wouldn't have gone ahead with the sale—despite the desperate need for cash—if Fortunato hadn't taken over, decisively negotiating the sale and facing his father with a substantially completed deal, to which Gerardo responded simply by signing the documents.

Soon after this they had to fire all the workers in the sold factory, and even though in recent years they had been reducing the totals (not a few had found jobs in other factories, particularly in the new glass factory in Nomana, which was rapidly growing), there remained some two hundred who lost their jobs.

The Communists immediately intervened, trying to make as much noise as possible. They announced the "occupation" of the factory and sent along one of their parliamentary deputies to make an "inspection", during which he was followed about by some of his own people. In this tour of the factory the deputy was accompanied by only one Riva employee, a supervising technician (he was one of the oldest of the self-taught people to whom Gerardo had given responsible posts), who tried—as he later explained—to convince the deputy to work toward a refinancing of the company by the government. The deputy (a self-satisfied scalawag who clearly wasn't worried about his own financially secure future) walked up and down the rows of sad-looking inoperative looms, berating the Riva technician (in a loud voice, so that all those in the group could hear him) and pretending great surprise at the antiquity of the machinery.

"Where have these capitalists hidden the money? In Saint-Moritz, at the casino? Why didn't they buy new machinery instead?" The firm's technician soon understood that any attempt on his part to defend the company would be pointless; he followed the deputy for the rest of the tour without speaking.

The Communist newspapers echoed the same questions. "Where have these capitalists hidden the money? Why haven't they invested in new machinery?" and they used all their resources to spread the rumor that the police intended to intervene and expel the workers "occupying" the factory, with baton charges if necessary. They used every effort to create a climate of disorder. The police, however, did not get involved, primarily because the workmen—despite the posters outside the factory walls—hadn't occupied the place. They preferred to wait and see if anything came of Gerardo's assurance that he would make efforts to convince the new owners to hire them.

One morning Nomana woke to find large chalked slogans on the town's walls: "Riva, pay the workers, not the police", along with drawings of hammers and sickles. Everyone in the town knew that the Rivas had paid the workers' wages right down to the last lira and that the police hadn't intervened in any way. But for Gerardo to see his own name being misused in this hateful way made him experience personally the hatred used as an instrument of power by these provincial antichrists, and he suffered silently.

Soon after a majority of the factory's workers were in fact taken on by the chemical group. The older employees remained at home until they were gradually taken on again by the Rivas' factory in Nomana.

20

The firm's crisis, which had started in 1952, ended only in 1958, when the Rivas managed to sell the two factories received three years earlier from Brusasca within a few months of each other. Meanwhile, the other insolvent client had died, and the Rivas saw themselves obliged to settle his credits, which had been endorsed by them over to third parties.

After receiving payment for the last of the Brusasca factories, paying off all the letters of credit, and repaying the loans from relatives (principally those from Uncle Ettore and the Marsavis) and friends, the Rivas found themselves without readily available funds. Gone were the properties in Milan and Monza, but the Nomana factory was still functioning. "At last we're clear; we're alive and well and willing to work", Gerardo (the poor man was already over seventy) would say to his sons.

It would take the Rivas a few more years to regain fully the balance of a normal production rhythm. To reach that point, the most significant factor was the partially complete renovation of the looms, stubbornly carried out by Ambrogio throughout their difficult cash-poor period. Meanwhile Fortunato— who had got married and now lived in Milan, from where he found it easier to keep in touch with clients and suppliers—had begun to tire of being an industrialist. He said nothing to his father at first, but said and repeated to Ambrogio, "This is no job for a man. How come you don't feel the same? The crisis we went through was caused by the French. It was based on politics, I agree, but it's a fact that practically all branches of industry—without exception— find themselves, every few years, say, on a cycle of every twenty or thirty years, faced with the possibility of closing down."

"Well, up to now that hasn't been the case with the Marsavis."

"No, Ambrogio, they also went through bad times during the global depression in 1929, and then again in 1944. Just give them some time, and we'll see what happens."

"But in 1944, it was due to the war, when they couldn't buy their raw materials."

"For one reason or for another, but it happened. And now, let some more time pass and we'll see what happens; I say it again."

To cast doubt on the Marsavis' success at that point seemed senseless. They had not only doubled in size since the end of the war, but, facing up to the shortage of living space for their work force (a serious problem in Brianza at the time), they'd built modern houses in a hillside district and were about to start construction in another area, also on the outskirts of Visate.

"And the periodical risk of failure, of losing everything, that's not the only problem", Fortunato would go on. "There's also the bitter fact that the price that goes with success is to be considered an exploiter, practically a professional burglar."

"Not by our people in Nomana, though, or in Brianza generally."

"But what is Brianza? A tiny part of the country. At most we have fewer than a million people here, compared with the fifty million in all Italy. No, Ambrogio, just look at the television, run by the government. How do they portray us industrialists? They just put up with us because one way or another we are needed, but it's clear they regard us as exploiters, and it's all they can do to speak civilly when they refer to us."

"All right, but if we retreat, throw in the towel, it'd be admitting those rogues are right, and also the Communists—the ones who hold their reins."

This was a fact. The new medium of television had started broadcasting in Italy in 1953, and as time passed it showed itself more and more influenced by Marxists and their followers. In order to get along, the Christians, who had worked for this state enterprise for a long time, did not speak up for themselves, but rather limited themselves to compromise proposals that gradually became institutionalized, so to speak. (This led to protests by the writer Michele Tintori, who warned of the enormous influence of the new medium on the public. "It's more effective than newspapers and the rest of the press put together", he would say. "It'll inevitably influence the coming generations, particularly as it doesn't promote the Italian model, which proved to be the best in time of war. The Alpine solider, for example, or popular Christianity. On the contrary, television continually promotes the so-called progressive model, the potential revolutionary, and the attractiveness of Roman-style layabouts and scroungers, our worst examples of citizenship. Haven't you noticed that the light, uncommitted Roman dialect and attitude are becoming more and more popular?")

Up until then, involved in the fight to survive, the Rivas hadn't noticed the changes despite Michele's warnings. And now, emerging from the nightmare, out of the dark well of the crisis, they still couldn't see it clearly.

They saw that the Italian way of life, although somewhat improved by the industrial expansion, remained under threat from the continuing Red menace.

The presence in the country's fabric of such a large and organized Communist party was felt more and more. The efforts of Marxist ideologues were such that their beliefs hadn't lost any appeal, not even after the fall of the Stalin personality cult in 1956, when the Russian bosses themselves revealed the immeasurable damage that had taken place there. The duty of making people aware of these revelations should have been undertaken by the Christians working in television, but afraid of being called Fascists by the very powerful Communist political apparatus and also pushed to show they were anti-Fascists (as at the time of the mythical resistance), they ended up—in order to enjoy a quiet life—not letting an opportunity go by to call attention—monotonous as parrots—to past Nazi and Fascist crimes, to the extent that—just as intended by the parrots' trainers—public attention ended in being selectively diverted from the Communists' crimes, even the most colossal. The constant horror at the abominable extermination of six million Jews (put into effect by the now-disappeared Nazis) had been used to erect a smokescreen over the disclosure of the extermination of some twenty million farmers and small-holders by the Communists. And the Germans' crimes were also used to conceal the massacres—even greater than the Russians'—that were taking place in China at that time.

Also, the secularist intellectuals (who, although not Communist, ended up holding the view that man's purpose on Earth is to achieve happiness) began discovering, as time went by, their own affinity with the Communists' ideals. More, even, they began noticing that, as the most left wing of the materialists, the Communists were also—at least in their intentions—the more coherent group. This tended to exert more and more influence on the secularist camp and particularly affected the newspapers, which in any case have always been in secular hands in Italy.

It was in this context—although increasingly isolated for lack of media support—that Pope Pius XII continued to his last breath to repeat his tenacious and praiseworthy teachings. And due to his teachings, both the Marxists and the secularists attacked the Pope particularly. In this atmosphere the Gospel was relived. The times of praise, "hosanna", toward the Pope were gone, and now had come the time of the cries of "*crucifige!*" in a sea of increasingly loud slander, more and more foolish. The Pope's people left him so alone that one night, when he was ill in bed and deeply depressed, Christ appeared to him to give him comfort. (In connection with this episode it can be said that, even twenty years later, the Gospel is relived to this day. The very Christians who were at the time made blind and indolent by sloth during the agony and blood sweating of Pius XII now prefer not to talk about this miracle. A sort of conspiracy of silence has grown around this uplifting event, which is spoken about only now and then when some unbeliever brings it up in order to snigger at it.)

PART FIVE

I

Time went by and, with it, life. Michele hadn't even tried to get involved in television (he thought, with good reason, that the Christian Democrats responsible for the medium would never accept someone like him in order not to make enemies of the Reds) and had just finished another work, a stage tragedy. Having presented it to his publisher and while awaiting his reaction to the play, he had made one hundred or so copies of it and sent them off to people in the world of theater. Carrying the first of these copies under one arm, he headed for the Catholic University to deliver it personally to Mario Apollonio, feeling a little nervous. Apollonio was then held, even outside Catholic circles, to be the greatest of theater critics, and so his opinion would certainly be crucial for the new playwright.

The distinguished scholar received the play's text with a warm smile (having just emerged from a classroom, he stood in a surrounding sea of departing students, who eyed with curiosity the new visitor, who by now was about forty). "I'll read your play with great interest", he declared. As he was going to attend a seminar, Michele walked along with him, keeping step.

"You didn't want to give me instruction on the ins and outs of stage writing", he said in a friendly way. "You preferred not to teach me, talk about it in depth, as I asked you to. I suppose you realize what an effort I had to expend as a result?"

"Personal effort in developing a work, or did you go researching in manuals? What I mean is, did you develop a technical style taken from how-to books, texts, or did you discover them for yourself?"

"I've acquired what style I have as I've gone along writing, which was the advice you gave me. But what a gargantuan task! I would never have thought that writing for the stage would be so very different from writing for a reader. It's hugely different. It's another thing altogether."

Apollonio nodded. "An original author like you has to invent or develop techniques. There's no other way", he said. "Then later it's up to us—the people who give the great public the bread of knowledge piece by piece—to study them and make them known."

It was a renewal of earlier praise. To show his gratitude Michele was unable to do other than smile shyly. (On these occasions he remained a youth.) "In the meantime, however, instead of taking me five or six months to write," he commented, "this work has taken me . . . well, let's say a lot longer."

Apollonio replied, "What you are saying makes me want to read it even more. I'll do it with great interest, and afterward I'll phone you."

But it wasn't he who telephoned. His wife called a few days later. Alma answered and recognized the caller's voice from having visited Apollonio's house a few times with Michele.

"But it was you I was calling, signora", she said. "I wanted to tell you that never in my life have I seen my husband so thrilled while reading a work for the stage. I've never seen him like this. He said it was a masterpiece, an extraordinary work. I'm happy for you, believe me."

Just as had happened fourteen years before, when Michele's first book was published (his subsequent works had been received with increasing hostility due to the gradual prevalence of Marxist and pro-Marxists in Italian culture), Alma felt as if she'd felt heaven with a touch. She thanked Apollonio's wife with her usual courteous manner and then ran to Michele's office to advise him of the great news.

"Do you know who just called? Apollonio's wife. Do you know what she said? She said she'd never ever seen her husband so emotional at reading anything as he has been in reading yours ... and ... well, that your tragedy is a masterpiece!"

Michele's whole face lit up. *So it looks like we made it*, he thought. *Perhaps at last my time's come. This time I, too, am a contender.* "But listen, what did she say exactly? Come on, tell me again", he said to his wife.

"She said that according to Apollonio it's an extraordinary work, a real masterpiece."

"Ah, really ..."

Alma was still pretty, particularly so at this moment, when her face blushed with the emotion she felt inside and yet of which, as usual, she didn't make an outward show.

"You're the masterpiece", her husband told her. He pushed his chair back from his work table and said, "Come here." He pulled his marble statue onto his knee. "Tell me how things are going?"

"But I've already told you everything", she said and kissed him.

"Yes, it's great news, really. Let's see now ..." They hugged each other and kissed repeatedly, like happy children.

"Just a moment", he said. "Did the signora tell you it was Apollonio who had asked her to call you?"

"No, she didn't say that. My impression is that she called on her own, impelled by ... friendship. You've no idea how happy she was."

"She's a great lady. And she's shown us she is before, right? Well, it must mean that tomorrow or the day after Apollonio himself will call."

"Yes. Oh, my Michele!" Almina rested her forehead against her husband's cheek. "What happiness to be your wife!"

"Even though you don't get many opportunities like this one to be proud of me. I've given you very few."

"But what are you saying!?" But inside she was thinking, *The thing is that in practical things you just want to do things your way. As when you wouldn't show Croce's letter to your publisher because you thought that Catholics ought not to lean on others, shouldn't sell themselves to others, and rather just rely on themselves.* But as always, true to her marble statue ways, she said nothing.

"Well, it's just as well. Better a thing well done every now and then than never at all", he ended.

The show of affection between them wasn't infrequent, despite their ten years of married life. When on waking Michele saw his wife alongside him in bed, he was still surprised, as at a great gift from God, and would gaze at her in the half light. At times he would lightly stroke her face (it felt to him as if his fingers touched the perfection of a statue), her elegant neck, a shoulder, a breast. *It's not a dream, absolutely not, she's real . . . and she's here, right here with me!* he would tell himself. At times he would kiss her furiously. "You're here, Alma, you're here with me!"

"But . . . what's the matter? Of course . . . I'm your wife", she would mumble, still not quite awake. "What did you expect? That I'd not be here?" Later, when she was awake, she would return his outpourings of love, transported. They remained bewitched with one another despite the fact that their ten years together had put them through repeated testing and, though they would have liked children, hadn't been able to have any. They had witnessed, unable to do anything, the tragic fight for economic survival by Alma's parents, who now were Michele's only parents. And although his style of writing had managed to influence other narrators and even successful journalists, his name didn't figure among the literary Olympians. Nobody formally recognized his influence. He continued working alone, not well known and making no claims.

Professor Apollonio called him some days later. He not only repeated the earlier opinion passed on by his wife, but also stated that work like this had to be staged as soon as possible. He suggested Michele send copies quickly to some men in the world of theater, to whom he would also write at the same time. "What a pity I can no longer recommend the work to my friends Grassi and Strehler."

"What do you mean?"

"Well, the thing is that I'm no longer part of the Piccolo Theater", Apollonio replied, softly chuckling. "I've been replaced through a policy of *alternating* people in management, you understand?"

But no, Michele didn't understand the irony implied in the statement, although he didn't question Apollonio.

2

A few months went by. Bit by bit Michele began to understand that had his work been apolitical it wouldn't have encountered difficulties in being staged. On the contrary, given the shortage of newly written works, its undoubted dramatic value would have caused it to be received with open arms. But as it was a piece of political theater . . . In fact, it was a tragedy, staged in Russia and populated by characters involved in the tremendous happenings there. It depicted in strong and heartbreaking terms the impossibility of using materialist methods to effect a change in the nature and conscience of man, and therefore—no more and no less—the impossibility of constructing communism. It was without any doubt very political theater.

To anyone who pointed this out, he would report, "Is politics today the central preoccupation of the people or not? Well, for this reason theater cannot avoid being—to a greater or lesser extent—political. In the same way that plays in the Middle Ages couldn't avoid being religious, or anything of the Greeks mythical." He would add other solid examples that backed his argument. "Look at Brecht and the extraordinary success he is experiencing in Germany and everywhere else. There is no dramatic writer today who is more on the crest of a wave than Brecht. Is it possible for theater to be more political than his work?"

"Well, yes, that's true, but . . ."

Nobody would develop on that "but", it was too obvious. "But Brecht is a Marxist. He's on the side of those people—critics, reporters, theater managers, all that cultural crowd—who are drifting toward Marxism. Without doubt Brecht is Marxism's poet."

Michele intuitively and obviously sensed these objections, but would silently think, *Brecht, above everything, is a desperately miserable person. In order to maintain his Communist beliefs, he stood by silently and allowed the authorities to take his lover, Carola Neher, to Stalin's prison camps, where she died in who knows what suffering, after who knows what humiliating treatment by the agents of the Cheka. And to think that she had been the principal actress in his "Threepenny Opera". What must Brecht go through nowadays when he happens to watch a performance of his work? Does he feel like a worm, remorseful, or has he converted his thinking and conscience to the point where he no longer feels any emotion?*

One afternoon, having called Apollonio to find out if there were any definitive offers for the play, Michele decided to express his perplexity.

"I find it hard to believe that things have deteriorated to the point that the Marxists have taken over as masters", Apollonio replied somewhat hesitantly. He thought for a moment, then said, "Listen, Tintori, Milan will be getting a visit in a few days from the director, De Ponti, whose theatrical company is to appear next week at the Goldoni Theater. He's a man from a Catholic background, so . . . let's do the following. I'll phone him and try to fix an interview. We'll go and see him together."

The Goldoni, one of the city's major theaters, is not far from the Duomo. Michele and the professor went there on foot, leaving the Piazza del Duomo, where they had agreed to meet. (Passing under the arch in the northern portico, as if placed there on purpose, there was the announcement of upcoming works to be produced by Grassi and Strehler in the Municipal Piccolo Theater. These were all or nearly all Brecht's works, rabid Communist propaganda. They pretended not to notice.)

Once out of the piazza they walked by a restaurant where Michele had eaten several times just after the war with John Burns, that great hope of American literature, now cruelly forgotten. He wanted to remind Apollonio about Burns, but was unable to do so because the professor was talking to him about the director they were about to meet. "His father is the former Senator De Ponti, who above all else is very rich." Apollonio rubbed a finger and thumb together. "A millionaire. This man, the director De Ponti, is also a nephew of the government minister, Tiziano."

"Ah, that I didn't know."

"Both the former senator and the minister are important personalities in the Christian Democratic party, you know, particularly Tiziano. De Ponti—the director we're meeting—is more or less your own age, Tintori. His ability to reach the heights is due not only to his talent as a director, although he has much merit, I assure you, but also to his family connections, or in other words, the party. A person who has been so well treated by the Christians wouldn't dare become in any way involved with the Marxists. Don't you think so? It would be to behave like a . . . something like . . ."

"Yes", Michele agreed.

"Exactly. I don't even want to consider it. It would be to talk badly of the man", Apollonio said. "And besides, I'm convinced that De Ponti won't let this occasion slip past to show that the people who've put their faith in him were right. You'll see." Evidently Apollonio expected people's behavior to be in line with his own. Michele—equally ingenuous—easily agreed with him.

They entered the great building of the Goldoni Theater through a side door. They were expected and were escorted behind the stage to a room with odd and badly put together furniture. Michele stared at everything with lively interest. *This is my first look at the holy theater precincts*, he thought, beginning to enjoy the occasion.

Soon De Ponti arrived. He was dressed with affected carelessness, wearing a polo neck sweater and a checked jacket. His forehead was high, intellectual looking. In one hand he held Michele's script, which Apollonio had sent to him.

"My dear professor. You've no idea how much I've looked forward to seeing you. How are you? How are you?"

After they all sat, De Ponti continued, addressing himself to Apollonio only. "I've always admired you, you know? And in particular your philippic in the latest issue of *Drammaturgia* against these dumb hypocrites in the ministry of tourism and recreation. A masterly dissertation; you skinned them very stylishly."

"Oh", said Apollonio, smiling. "It was just a diversion, *nugae.*"

They went on talking, joking a little; then De Ponti gestured with the script on his hand. "But let's get down to the subject of this meeting", he said. Then, almost without a change in his tone of voice, he said, "First of all, unfortunately I can't put this work into my program, because this year, and even all next year, I find myself like this." He passed his hand over his head to indicate that he was drowning. "My program is full, superfilled."

The statement sounded so improbable that the two visitors looked their surprise at each other. Michele thought, *Well, here we go again.*

Apollonio said, "But this is an objectively important work", his voice low. "Somebody like you, in the vanguard, oughtn't to let it slip through your hands."

"I believe it because it is you who are saying so", De Ponti replied. (*Just make a note of that*, thought Michele, *the way he's saying 'because it is you who are saying so'.*) "I don't doubt it is important, but what can I do? My program of work is completely filled, as I said, for the next two years. I just can't add another item."

After this statement there was a brief silence.

"Forgive me", Michele then said, having hardly spoken at all so far. "May I ask if you've read the piece?"

"Have I read it? Of course I've read it. Yes, of course."

"And how did you find it yourself?"

"But you ask me? And here we have the master! There's no better judgment than his."

Michele noticed the avoidance of his question and thought, *He just doesn't want to commit himself, not even verbally.* He looked at Apollonio and shook his head slightly, as if to say, "We're just wasting our time."

"De Ponti intercepted the look and became annoyed; his face took on a pink tinge. "Look, my dear sir", he said to Michele. "Were you aware that I participated in the resistance?"

"The resistance?" Michele asked. "And what has that to do with this?"

"Oh, so in your view it's not important?"

Apollonio quickly intervened, trying to halt the argument. "You know that Tintori here also suffered during the war. He's one of the few survivors of the Russian concentration camps, which can more properly be called extermination camps, a fact that became public knowledge precisely because of his writings." He smiled, trying to disarm the tension, and immediately showed courteous interest in the director's statement. "So, you took part in the resistance? I'm sure I've read about it somewhere, yes. Where was that? I've forgotten."

"At Urbino."

"At Urbino?"

"Yes, at the university", De Ponti continued, clearly resentful. "Of course it wasn't one of the greatest actions in the national resistance. I wouldn't want to claim to that. The episode at Urbino, well ... after all, it's only a small university. But we contributed, we did something there," he defended himself tensely, "naturally."

Apollonio nodded repeatedly, silently urging him on. Michele felt like telling the man to take his resistance and go take a one-way running jump when his eye fell on a scar on the professor's forehead. Not many people knew how he had acquired the scar. It had been given to him by one of the SS striking him with his rifle's metal butt one day in one of Milan's small squares, when Apollonio saw a few parked trucks filled with deportees and went to help. He hurried to buy something for them and could find only fruit in a nearby shop. When he tried to give the food to the people being shipped east, he was knocked down. He had been carried away unconscious, his head bleeding. For him, resistance to the Nazis had been a lived experience, something authentic. He had suffered—Michele thought—but had never talked about it and specifically never boasted.

Michele decided then and there not to miss this opportunity, and suddenly interrupting De Ponti, who was already a little less vexed, said, "Listen, it seems to me there has been a misunderstanding. You've talked about resistance. Why, I ask myself, did you oppose the Nazis? Because of their erroneous beliefs, I imagine, their overbearing arrogance, and above all the victims they made. In this I'm totally in accord with you. But communism also makes mistakes that cause tragic consequences; and in fact, as far as numbers of victims are concerned, communism has caused incomparably many more, and it hasn't disappeared as have the Nazis. It's causing a slaughter even today, right now, in China, as you know. So in effect when we talk about resistance, you should be in agreement with me on this: that the Communist phenomenon should at least be investigated. The process of Stalinism can't be left solely to the Stalinists, don't you think? And so it's exactly this that my piece looks into."

De Ponti, who had been listening and getting redder in the face, interrupted Michele, almost hysterically. "No, my dear sir! No, no! I was in the resistance", he repeated, raising his voice. "Don't you want to understand? And you can't make me behave as if I hadn't done so."

Michele stopped talking. It was abundantly clear that this man attached no importance to the resistance movement and was interested only in himself, his reputation. *He isn't thinking about anything else. With a father and an uncle so superbly placed, he obviously backs the government, and yet now he expends energy in trying to be on good terms with the other side, the Communists. He doesn't care a bit for the Reds' victims in China. That's the sum of it. Disgusting!*

Apollonio once more spoke, trying patiently to recover the thread of the conversation, but he spoke with less enthusiasm, just restoring the tone of politeness to enable Michele and himself to leave without further outbursts. Then he stood, and the two visitors said goodbye. As Michele retraced his steps through the backstage area, the theater seemed to him to have lost the fascination it had imparted when they arrived.

3

"Urbino", Michele said once they were back on the street. "Wasn't Urbino liberated by regular Italian troops?"

"I don't know", the professor replied, looking at him with curiosity.

"That's how it seems to me. Or maybe it was Anders' Polish troops, which would amount to the same thing. I say that because in Nomana—my wife's hometown—there's a fellow, a former officer in the Alpine regiment in the Italian Corps attached to the Allies, and one afternoon, just talking, he said, 'Our battalion relieved the Poles at the entrance to Urbino: we had the town right before us.' Something like that, but I remember I was reminded of a quotation from Pascoli: 'We have before us windy Urbino.' Yes, I'm not mistaken. I don't believe it was the university people in the resistance who liberated Urbino."

They walked on in silence. After a while, Apollonio said, "Maybe things are worse than I thought."

"I'm sorry for you", Michele said. What he meant was: I'm sorry that a man like you exposed himself to a rejection because of me.

The professor shook his head in a kindly way. In his turn mortified, he hadn't for a moment lost the paternal and intelligently handsome smile that had comforted so many.

The streets of central Milan showed their usual action and movement, as of a working day, enough to encourage the two walking men not to overemphasize or be discouraged by the meeting.

"Maybe the thing that should worry us most", Apollonio said, "is the confusion that seems to be seeping in everywhere. Now everyone applauds holy Pope John, and with good cause; but the unusual thing, illogical even, is that he is also being praised by people who shouldn't, the Communists, in the first place."

"To them what is more important is just one thing: that in his love for all men without exception the Pope is lowering his guard, particularly against them."

"Right. But of course implicit in his openness is his plea that they convert to Catholicism."

"Yes, no doubt. But meantime he lowers his guard, and that's all they consider important."

"As I said, there's a lot of confusion. I'd not like to see the profiteers among us, like the gentleman we just met, end up making too much trouble."

Once more they were silent.

"Well," Michele soon said, "if in two thousands years we Catholics haven't managed to shipwreck the Church, we won't manage to do so now."

They both smiled. It was a joke, but also an established fact. Why worry excessively? At the time the Catholic world still clearly benefited from the enlightening effects of Pius XII's leadership. The Church's doctrine was still unequivocal and clear, and her truths so rooted in the hearts of the faithful that the idea of an approaching crisis seemed truly out of place. And yet . . .

"You know, Professor, last month my publisher returned the script of this tragedy? Along with excuses and nice words, of course, but he won't publish it. I believe that even there, at my publishing house, they dare not upset the Marxists."

"I understand."

Near the Piazza del Duomo they once more passed before the restaurant where Michele used to eat with John Burns. This time Michele reminded the professor. "You see this restaurant, Professor? I came here with John Burns several times, the American writer, you remember? You did read his *Galleria*?"

"Yes, of course. But then I read nothing else of his. John Burns . . . I think he died."

"Yes. His second novel, *Lucifer with a Book*, wasn't a success, and in his misery he drank himself to death."

"Here in Italy?"

"Yes. But not in Milan, in Rome. He found himself unable to leave Italy, poor soul. He died without one lira to his name. The publisher even had to pay for his funeral."

"That's too bad."

Michele unsuccessfully tried to get a look inside the restaurant through the windows. Maybe that waiter still worked there, the Communist whom he—under John Burns' initially amused but increasingly approving eye—had tried to convert to Christianity and democracy. Almost unexpectedly the waiter had ended up a true convert. "My only apostolic and political success to date", he now thought. "I wonder if with the passing of time he has remained firm in the faith."

Entering the Piazza del Duomo, the two bid each other goodbye without having reached the northern portico with the triumphal Marxist program at the Municipal Little Theater. "The experience we've had today is at least a symptom", said Apollonio. (He was unaware that for him, too, there would

931

come a time of ostracism. To make life difficult for Christian culture, the Communists and above all the so-called Christian spokesmen, like this De Ponti, would untiringly criticize him to the point where he lost effective influence. Apollonio would some time later be excluded from the mass media and in the end even from the Catholic media.) "Following this experience, because of it, we now need to motivate ourselves to work more than ever", he continued. "Especially you, now that you've taken on the task of spreading the truth about communism. Even providence itself, it seems to me, has singled you out, preparing you through your terrible experiences." And as Michele remained silent, "Are we agreed?"

"Yes", the writer answered. "On the other hand I can't stop working. And also, well, as you've said, I've seen worse things than this."

When the professor had gone, Michele wandered the streets around the cathedral. Just as in other times, when strolling with John Burns . . . Now that he couldn't discuss things with Burns, he had a sudden wish to say a prayer for the dead in his behalf, at least to help him now after death as he hadn't been able to during life. From time to time he would lift his eyes to the top of the Duomo, looking at it from different angles. All the Gothic spires were decorated with statues, hundreds of them, all carved from the same marble as the Duomo's walls. He thought about the artists who had sculpted them— unknown men who here and elsewhere had given their whole lives, particularly during the Middle Ages, to sculpting patiently and always with admirable talent these cathedral statues, even when aware that once in place nobody would admire them except God.

And hadn't he always thought of himself as a worker in marble? Though he sculpted pages instead of stone. So to what could he attribute this pain he felt because people wouldn't ever know his own work? Of course, as the Gospel teaches, you shouldn't hide your light under a bushel. However, his duty was to continue writing without letting himself be upset, whether successful or not. No doubt his work would please God, and also his own father, the marble sculptor, up there beside God.

4

Some weeks went by. The new playwright had also sent his script to other theater people as well as to a few students of Russian affairs. One of the latter—a well-known journalist and parliamentary deputy—unexpectedly wrote a letter that wasn't evasive; it came from Rome. It read: "Dear Tintori, I started to read your work with caution and mistrust. Soon, as I turned the pages, I was caught up in reading it. It is an original work, very alive, useful, even important. It deserves to be put on stage as soon as possible. Of course it also has flaws, but these are only on the surface." And then, after a short list of these flaws, it continued, "I've telephoned Lucio Ferri, who has also read it and shares my opinion. He thinks it deserves putting on soon and says he'll take care of it. Much good fortune with it. Yours, Ludovico Zarbini."

Michele became very excited. Sitting at his desk carefully rereading the letter, he got up and started pacing up and down. Zarbini was one of the intelligent and sensible journalists in Italy. In any case his opinion of the play was important. Pity Alma wasn't here; he'd have preferred to discuss the letter immediately with her, but she was teaching her girls at the convent school. As for Lucio Ferri, he was a very well-known personality in the theater, and he had liked the work as well as Apollonio. Both were well versed in the theatrical world. What had been said about Ferri in the letter? Michele reopened the letter and read, "Ferri, who has also read it and shares my opinion. He thinks it deserves putting on soon and says he'll take care of it."

But how come Ferri hadn't put himself in touch by now? Ferri, a playwright and actor-manager of a well-known successful theatrical company, openly Christian, had been sent one of the first copies of his work by Michele. Well, it wasn't important. The essential point was that now it seemed Ferri had decided to take charge of the work. "Take care of it." What exactly did that mean? *But what a fellow, this Zarbini. He has wasted no time. He's gone straight to the essential. He's a liberal; in a way I'm not on good terms with them. I find it hard to forgive the near-family arrangement they have with the Marxists. They, on the other hand, just look, first Croce and now Zarbini. Their actions show they're more generous than I!* But what exactly was it that Lucio Ferri wanted to do? This was now the most important thing. Michele had a sudden inspiration. He had to call Apollonio now, without delay! Without doubt he'd know Ferri personally. *And Apollonio can give him a little push.* The telephone was on his desk. He sat again, opened his address book, and looked up Apollonio's number. He took the phone off the hook, then paused. Alma! It wasn't fair to leave her out of this. This would be one of the few moments of joy he'd give her with his writings. He'd await her return, and they'd phone together so she could take part. *On the other hand, if I wait until dinnertime, it's more likely I'll find Apollonio at home.*

5

That same day Apollonio himself telephoned Ferri in Rome and then called Michele. "He's decided to stage the play. Just today he applied for a state subsidy."

"State subsidy?"

"Yes. There's a law that assigns funds to the work of new authors—three million for each work—and he's going to try for a subvention. I have every confidence this time the thing is going forward." In case it was needed, he gave Ferri's telephone number to Michele.

During the following weeks, in the absence of news from Rome, Michele and Alma went from patiently waiting (full of fascinating rich imaginings) to moments of unquiet, until one night when, unable to put up with the uncertainty any more, Michele decided to ring Ferri. Ferri himself answered the call.

"But didn't Apollonio tell you?" he asked as soon as he heard the name Tintori. "We're taking it onto the stage for sure. It's all been decided. Right now I'm casting the actors. We're putting on two plays; one is yours. Just a moment . . . copies . . . have you got more copies of the script? Yes? Well, why haven't you sent them to me? Come, send them to me right away. To my house? No, better send them to the theater. Make a note of the address and phone number. From now on call me there."

I made a mistake calling his house . . . in any case, it's done, he thought as he wrote down the address and number: Stella Theater, *via del teatro di Marcello.* "Two theaters in the same street?" he asked.

"Yes", Ferri replied, laughing. "Only the *teatro di Marcello* is two thousand years old and looks it, being a ruin, a great ruin." He realized that Michele didn't know that part of Rome. "You don't know where the *teatro di Marcello* is? It's near the Campidoglio. You remember the famous slope of Campidoglio, Michelangelo's Campidoglio? Well, it starts right in front of our little *Teatro della Stella.*"

Michele asked if the director had been chosen yet. "No, no, I haven't decided on one yet," Ferri replied, "and to tell the truth, I'm thinking of directing it myself. It would be my first time as a director. What do you think? But I don't know. I haven't decided yet."

More and more excited (at his side, Alma had her face close to his, following the conversation, her heart nearly bursting with happiness), Michele, having totally and temporarily lost his imagination, said, "I . . . I don't know how to thank you."

"It's clear you are new to these things!" said Ferri, starting to laugh. To his two listeners he gave the impression of being not only a person who knew his job, but also a good man.

When the call was over, "Of course there's a providence, don't you see?" Michele exclaimed, getting to his feet. "And to think that after my meeting with De Ponti I thought my play would never be staged, at least during my lifetime. And here, on the other hand . . ."

Alma, unspeakably happy, caressed him. To Michele suddenly came the thought that he was too lucky, so fortunate that it gave him pause, and he reflected that the possibility of not having their play published and seen was a reality for many other writers; it was what was happening to many.

Over the next few days the tension became overpowering for Michele; he felt it during the day each time he lifted his eyes from his current work. Immediately the only thing he could think of was to imagine the stupendous adventure through which he was about to live. He would go to Rome, would see his imagined characters take on flesh, given personality by actors who had prepared themselves to express the events, the feelings, the world imagined by him in the best way possible. Each one of those actors—whose names he didn't yet know—would transform his invented character a bit, even though it was just by a change in external appearance, in order to give it the actor's own interpretation. What would the resulting effect be?

In truth, Michele decided, *it's one thing to write for reading and another, very different, to write for the stage.*

If he woke during the night, he could think of nothing else. He would imagine the theater, the people, the actors, declaiming, and finally the applause; then the newspaper articles, the judgment of the critics and interviews with people unknown to but imagined by him. His unchallengable exposition (so he thought) of the impossibility of building with communism—which amounted to a historic confirmation (in a contrary sense) of the Church's social doctrine—would be absorbed in the tenets of culture, would blossom. Perhaps it would create doubts, if not among Communists, at least among the lay intellectuals who gave them support. Perhaps deep doubts . . . After Rome— why not?—the play, given its enormous success, would go on in other cities, and everywhere the papers would talk about it. Michele's fantasizing was unbridled. Perhaps even the foreign press, which is more influential than ours in world affairs, perhaps they would be interested. His tragedy (*like those of the ancient Greek theater*, he thought, getting excited, *which had been true schools of life*) could become a concrete obstacle against the barbarism that was spreading, could prevent the terrible Communist massacres—as in Russia and China— from spreading to other countries.

6

Some weeks after the telephone conversation with Ferri, when Michele heard (also by telephone) that rehearsals of his tragedy had begun, he could hardly contain himself.

Having obtained a short leave from his school, he went to Rome by road, using as far as he could—Bologna—the new great freeway being constructed to cover all of Italy. Since the war's end the number of cars had increased enormously, but not yet to the extent of making progress difficult on main highways during the working week, so that as he was driving along with few problems, even after leaving the freeway, Michele was free to fantasize. He felt a great euphoria. He didn't think about the proclivity of so many men in the theater toward Marxism (and even critics and reviewers who would also be judging his work). It was enough for him that the few free and impartial individuals like Apollonio, Ferri, and Zarbini had managed to get the work onto a stage. *When the people get to know my work is being shown, they'll go and see it, and it'll go forward on its own.*

He met Ferri that same afternoon. The celebrated dramatist and actor-manager looked a normal, modest man. Despite being tired from the journey, Michele couldn't avoid studying him attentively. He saw that Ferri was examining him with equal interest. They both noticed the strangeness of the situation, and their gestures revealed their knowledge. Immediately their attitudes changed, and they turned to a more open behavior, as if they were old friends. At Ferri's invitation—he was some ten years older than Michele—they started addressing each other informally.

Michele learned that Ferri had decided not to direct the tragedy, having entrusted the job to Pavi Austeri, a well-known director and among the best in Italy. Michele met him the next morning at the rehearsals. He was a stiff man, overwhelmingly intellectual, who greeted him with a strange coldness; Michele was surprised. Immediately afterward he was left open mouthed—he almost couldn't believe his eyes—when he saw that the actors weren't playing their parts while moving around and acting as they usually would (even though at this stage of rehearsals, the scripts were still in hand) but read their lines from fixed positions, standing at lecterns.

At the first natural interruption, he asked the director, "What does this mean, this immobility?"

"Didn't Ferri explain it to you?"

"No."

"We intend to try a truly new experiment. The illusion of movement will be created with lighting; the actors won't move."

"And each will act out his part . . . or rather, read it?"

Pavi Austeri shook his head at "act out" and nodded at "read". "You saw it for yourself", he said dryly.

Michele thought, *It's madness!* but didn't reply. *Just wait and observe,* he told himself.

The rehearsals went ahead. Nobody talked to him, the author who was there with them, to ask him for an explanation or interpretation of the script; they asked him nothing.

The actors (except two or three chosen by Ferri, as Michele would later find out) were very young and consequently unsuited for their roles. *They probably picked young actors to save money,* Michele thought. *Then later they'll have to disguise them with makeup.*

Farther into the rehearsal he was forced to make a judgment. *That one won't be able to play his part. And maybe that one over there and probably that other. Even worse, youngsters made up as older people (and also the reverse) confuse the audience, which will give an ambiguous message. But why are they doing it this way? Why does Pavi Austeri have to make things so difficult? How can such a mishmash ever be a success?*

He couldn't stand the torture of watching for long. Getting to his feet and mumbling some low-voiced excuse, he left the rehearsal. He walked the few paces over toward Lucio Ferri's office.

"The *Dottore* isn't here. He'll be away for at least two days", Michele was told by Ferri's secretary.

"But . . . I was with him yesterday afternoon, and he said nothing about not being here."

"Yes, but this morning he had to leave unexpectedly for Florence, where we're putting on *Un uomo lo sa Dio*" (this was Ferri's most recent work) "because the director is sick."

The mystified Lombard playwright, unaccustomed to these sorts of surprises, was left with the impression that someone was pulling the wool over his eyes. But it couldn't be that Ferri would pull such a stunt. Besides, whatever for? Nobody was forcing Ferri to put on this play.

He left the theater pensively.

The streets outside were too pretty for words. On the opposite side of the street from the theater (the road dropped down to the right, toward the ruins of the Teatro di Marcello and the Tiber) rose the hill of Campidoglio, lined with laurel and pines, followed by the pure stone staircase "which appears to lead to heaven" built by Michelangelo.

Michele remembered the feelings he'd experienced some time before on leaving Milan's Teatro Goldoni after the disappointing interview with De Ponti: that incitement to carry on working, not to give way, which came from the Milanese atmosphere, so overflowing with activity. *Here the atmosphere is totally different*, he thought. And yet he seemed to feel as much at home here; he belonged to this as well as to that other world. It was his culture, his civilization.

Right. But now he needed to reflect. He started walking up and along the Tiber, thinking over the situation. He didn't need much time to realize what was hidden behind Pavi Austeri's actions. The director was behaving toward the play in his hands as if he'd suddenly discovered himself holding a hot potato. He hadn't refused to direct it (Why? probably because of his professional relations with Ferri), but at the same time he must have been afraid and uncomfortable. Of course, it was natural that he'd react unfavorably, just as would the majority of the people in the theater. It was, after all, his world. He had to live in it. Yes, it was no more than that which explained his strange actions. Even here in Rome, according to what Ferri had told him the day before, the majority of critics and theatrical reviewers pretended for their own interest to be favorable to Marxism—that is, if they hadn't already joined the Marxist party. (*But what a lot of cowardice there is in Italy!*) It was this reality to which Pavi Austeri had to adapt. This was the reason why he was so cool toward Michele, why he didn't want competent actors in the cast. Good actors would have contributed toward the success of the play. And that was also the reason why he was turning the play, not into what he had called a truly new experiment, but into a dry dramatic reading, no more and no less, something lifeless, neutral, and untheatrical.

Once he had realized all of this, Michele's first impulse was to return to the theater. He'd ask the director to suspend rehearsals. If he refused—he thought—he'd ask for an intervention by the national authors' rights society to stop the opening of the play.

After pacing furiously for a while, he had second thoughts. Was it worth getting into an argument with somebody he didn't really know? Wouldn't it be better to put the situation to Ferri? Clearly that was best. But his teaching duties (he now gave classes at the lyceum) wouldn't allow him to await Ferri's return to Rome. So what? Talk to him on the telephone from home? No, not like that. What could he possibly settle by phone? He thought it better to go to Florence and see Ferri. *Right now, today, why not? Yes, that's best. I haven't time to waste.* He decided to drive there right away. *Then, if for some reason I don't manage to find him, I'll get out of teaching for the rest of the week, come back here to Rome, and not move until this damned problem is solved.*

He went back to his pensive pacing. He thought he saw something on the other side of the road. It looked like a birdcage hanging among some climbing plants on the rock walls of the Campidoglio. Although absorbed by his own problem, Michele crossed the road to find out what it was, and in fact it was a large cage that held a live but rather shabby eagle. Eagle and writer, both surprised, stared at each other fixedly for a while, without movement. *Who'd have been so wicked as to think of locking you up in there?* Michele thought. *How could he not appreciate that to preserve its symbolic value, an eagle must be free and not in a cage?*

The eagle's beady eyes, fixed on his own, seemed by the very steadiness of their gaze to transmit a message: "Look after yourself first, look after yourself." The strange, half-understood message perturbed him.

See what they've brought you down to, poor bird! Michele remembered that the only other eagles he'd seen had been free, over there in the high Valtellina, Alpine country. A pair of eagles had their nest on a high rock above the valley of the Bormio. From way up there, first one and then the other would launch themselves to soar over the valley on their wide wingspread, searching the ground with their penetrating eyes, occasionally swooping past the rock wall, beautiful to watch. They were at their most breathtaking when together—not looking for prey, just for the pleasure of flying—they would rise above the hilltops, seen from below only as tiny crosses tracing magnificent circles in the clear sky. Any hunter and any idiot would covet and want to own them, but—as he had said to Alma—it was enough for these birds to maintain their distance from man in order to remain safe without in any way ceasing to be part of the beauty of the scene.

Michele came closer and examined the cage, seriously intending to open it and let the eagle fly to freedom, perhaps to the mountains of the Abruzzo, another mountain scene, but he began to have doubts that in its present state the eagle could fly. In any case he found the cage door held closed by a strong lock. He once again looked the eagle in the eye. *It's clear that even if whoever has you locked up doesn't understand anything about living free, he's certainly an expert when it comes to padlocks.*

The eagle's eyes held his gaze fixedly. *What are you trying to tell me? That this could also happen to me; could they lock me up also? Or that I am already in good hands?*

7

He was unable to find Ferri in Florence and could only talk to him on the phone some days later from home. (Alma wasn't there to share the conversation, and although he kept her informed of everything, this time he deliberately telephoned when she wasn't there.) Making a show of not attaching much importance to the matter, Ferri admitted that the choice of director had not been entirely happy. But what could be done now? In particular when the expenses already incurred were taken into consideration.

During those days Michele had pondered at length what he should do in the event that he couldn't get Ferri to agree to a true staging of his script. Should he upset the whole thing, or would it be better to close his eyes and give in to the director Pavi Austeri's manipulations? Of course, if Ferri wasn't up to putting on an honest version of his work, he would have difficulty in finding someone else ready to do so.

Reasoning coldly, he ended up realizing that the dramatized reading of the play would be, after all, better than nothing. A sense of rage and humiliation weighed him down. How powerful was the demon, and how easily he made himself felt here, just as when in the East he had put all those people into POW camps and forced others into cannibalism! But was it possible that such an objectively important work—important in the judgment of Apollonio, Zarbini, and Ferri himself—had to remain dormant, as if it had never been written? Was this how life was? (Yes, this was also life, a voice inside him said: these difficulties and also the impossibility for many people of achieving their goals.) The situation, however, was repugnant to him to the point where he decided to make his decision later.

Now, with Ferri on the phone, he tried to convince him of the magnitude of the error they were going to commit ("Also there's the financial aspect: Who would buy a ticket to watch a dramatized reading?") and that the real solution was to return to the project as originally written ("You have to agree to directing it yourself; it's the only way to straighten this out.").

But Ferri told him that no, this option was no longer possible, unthinkable even. He only promised under pressure by Michele that he would ask Pavi

Austeri to stage the play's key points in the traditional way. Then—showing his theatricality with a *coup de scène*—he gave Michele a piece of important news in a neutral voice: "Didn't I tell you yet that the play would be filmed and shown on television? Everything is arranged. Are you satisfied?"

Michele was struck dumb for a moment. Being on television meant an audience of millions, which changed things, even if—maybe—it made more painful the fact that the work would not be seen as written.

"Did I hear right?" he asked. "They'll show the tragedy on television?"

"Yes, that's right. It'll be shown at a later date; they'll film it at the theater and then put it on afterward. Everything is arranged." Ferri spoke about television with the ease of an insider, which he undoubtedly was.

"Listen, will you at least promise me the major points of the script will be acted out normally?"

"I promise you that I'll ask Pavi."

The prospect of television was received by Alma with enthusiasm, which also affected the rest of the family in Nomana, who all decided to be there for the premiere of such an important work. The only one not interested was Fanny, who since the years of crisis with the family business had felt nothing but annoyance at anything involving Ambrogio's family. "I'm not excited about it, dear", she said to her husband when he suggested going to Rome. She had become a bit neurotic and often addressed her husband in a manner that was brusque and sometimes worse than brusque.

So Ambrogio decided to go to Rome without her, joining his father and his sister Francesca, who in order to go had decided to leave her nestful of children in Visate. (There were already seven, after fourteen years of marriage, every one having the distinctive sharp Marsavi nose.) Giuditta, about to give birth (she had married a few years before), had to give up, albeit reluctantly, the idea of going along. Fortunato (who for some time hadn't been involved in the family business, having become a real estate agent) and his wife, along with Alma, were going to Rome by air and were due to arrive just in time for the premiere.

Michele arrived in Rome a few days ahead of time in order to watch the last rehearsals. As expected, the director Pavi Austeri hadn't accepted the suggestion to perform the key points of the play in a traditional way. It was easy for him to argue that it would make for a confusing mixture. The day before Michele arrived in Rome, however, Austeri had tried something else. He went to the printer responsible for the posters and programs and told them to remove his own name from the proofs and to substitute the name of his assistant, a young man who had helped him intermittently during the preparations.

It was by pure chance that Michele—who had gone to the print works to see the proofs—found out about the switch. He told the printer to hold up the work and immediately called on Ferri to take action, openly threatening him this time with stopping the play altogether. Understanding Michele's objections, Ferri became indignant with Pavi Austeri's behavior; having manipulated the play to his own vision, he now tried to distance himself. Ferri made him put his name back. "But do you see what kind of people you have to work with in this world of theater? Do you realize? And Pavi, I assure you, isn't one of the worst. On the contrary!"

The dress rehearsal was attended by the head of the company, Ferri, Tintori the author, the journalist and Deputy Ludovico Zarbini, a couple of critic friends of his, and an older reviewer from the *Osservatore Romano*, which years earlier had commented favorably on Tintori's books.

Despite the absurdity of the actors, all dressed identically and stuck behind lecterns, having been reduced to simple voices, somehow the strength of the script turned the performance into an exciting event. The insiders who had previously read the script could imagine the missing movement and action and feel moved by it, Zarbini and Ferri especially. Ferri, almost as if deflecting the author's objections, would say every now and then, "If this isn't real theater, I don't know what is!" to the point where Michele let himself be taken along by the general enthusiasm and started looking forward to a successful run, against all reason. They were all being observed by Pavi Austeri (the only person there who maintained his distance, as if because of modesty), who became even more worried than before.

8

On the evening of the first night the Teatro della Stella was filled to capacity. Michele went inside in company with the senior Rivas, with whom he'd dined. At his side was Almina, who for the occasion had made herself a beautiful evening gown in light blue silk: the prettiest dress Michele had ever seen (or would ever see) on her. She was so confident that she appeared to radiate light, with her statuesque looks and hair pulled back into a chignon, her appearance—a true-born Lombard—fitting perfectly into the Roman surroundings. Her husband was so proud of her appearance he would have preferred not to spend time with anybody but her. But he had to give time to other things. To start with, he had to introduce the famous journalist Zarbini—who came toward him in the lobby—to Gerardo and the other in-laws, who knew of his fame and were excited to exchange a few words with him. Michele also asked an usher if any Roman personalities had arrived. (Yes, a few well-known politicians were there.) He had to check with the elderly journalist from the *Osservatore Romano*, who was pacing up and down in the lobby, if he had managed to bring a certain influential critic. (No, the man had an appointment elsewhere, but had promised to come tomorrow.) To compensate, the theater critics from all the Roman newspapers were present.

"And they're all a little nervous", Zarbini told him. "Naturally they don't expect from you a panegyric on communism, yet they hope that in any case your disapproval of it won't go too far. They'll see, eh?" he smiled. "But careful, they can also bite." He pointed out a man seated on a nearby divan. He was a strange individual, with a hard face and streaked white and dark hair, evocative of a zebra's skin. "You know him? He's . . ." Zarbini gave the man's name.

"Ah, yes, the ho . . . no, I've never met him."

"If he decides to be so, he can be implacable."

The play, or rather the reading, started punctually. As in the final rehearsals the lighting—controlled by an experienced technician—was used expertly, giving at first an effect of providing what looked like movement on stage; but it was a passing impression. After about ten minutes Michele noticed that the relationship between actors and audience wasn't the usual theatrical participatory interaction.

This isn't the energy that Apollonio is always referring to. This is different, a sort of . . . attitude of attention, yes, but more like the relationship between a man making a speech and his audience. Was this what Pavi intended? Yes, no doubt about it, and he found the easy way. He's experienced enough not to take risks.

Alma, at his side, and most of the others there were obviously not equipped to make a judgment, but they vaguely noticed that something was missing. Maybe it was too little movement on stage; in any case people listened attentively in order not to miss the thread of conversation on stage. (Because conversation it was.)

There wasn't much applause except when the curtain came down for the intermission, which—Michele noticed, surprised—came down early, before the performance of several more speeches included in the first act. *Why would they do that? What do we owe this to?* But he hadn't the time to ponder over it.

While accompanying Alma toward the lobby, Zarbini waved happily for him to come closer. He wanted to introduce him to an important person, a former cabinet president from Piedmont, still an influential parliamentarian. This politician greeted Michele with simple good manners and engaged him in cordial conversation.

"Do you know that just last year I met some of your characters in Moscow? Khrushchev, for example. I drank vodka with him, and it's a strange feeling to see him as a part of your play, I'll tell you."

Although he had occupied important posts, the politician was still a genuine person, even a little rustic. He seemed to be a real Christian. Michele, who at first behaved toward him with reserve, soon found himself so relaxed and enjoying his company so much that he neglected to do a few of the things he had wanted to do during the intermission. The fact was that this conversation was already becoming new poetry inside his head. He took care to include the man's wife in the conversation—helped in this by Zarbini—who was, like her husband, a woman without pretensions. (She wore a nice fur coat. "Well, more than just nice, it was sen-sa-tion-al", as Almina later commented. "Who knows how much it cost?") The old president also chatted gracefully with Alma; time passed by.

Gerardo and Ambrogio, since the women had stayed in the theater with Fortunato, walked around the lobby, keeping the small group in view. Gerardo found it difficult to believe what he saw, his son-in-law and daughter calmly talking with the former president and with Zarbini! Michele saw Gerardo glance over and immediately looked for a means to bring him into the conversation. Given that the politician came from the world of Piedmontese textiles, he tried to move the conversation to this subject. With genuine pleasure the older man started talking about his own country. Michele brought up the textile business in Brianza ("my own country") and talked in broad terms about the industry. The politician asked if the textile activity in Brianza didn't specialize in cotton. Saying he wasn't an expert, Michele passed the question on to his wife, "Who is the daughter of a textile manufacturer", he explained.

When Almina also couldn't adequately answer his questions, Michele said, "We need your father here", and, enjoying his polite ploy, he waved to Gerardo and Ambrogio, who came over to be presented and answer the politician's questions.

Zarbini, in his role of journalist, wondered a little at Michele's not occupying himself in finding out what the critics thought of the work so far and suddenly decided to do so. "I'm going over to see what the various critics and journalists have to say." Michele was brought back to reality by this; he would have wanted to accompany Zarbini, but clearly it would have taken time to say his courteous goodbyes, so Zarbini went alone.

He was soon back, after Gerardo had finished explaining the characteristics of Brianza's textile industry. "There are differing opinions", he told Michele in answer to his questioning look. "Some discussion."

"Much difference of opinion?" Michele asked and got a nod, yes.

"Won't these gentlemen come along with us and have something in the bar?" the former president's wife suggested.

"Well, yes, I'd be delighted", Alma answered gracefully.

The gentlemen bowed and politely escorted the ladies toward the bar, while Gerardo and Ambrogio went their way.

At the bar there was some crowding. Michele—the youngest of the men—asked what each would have and thrust himself into the crowd at the bar; it took quite some time. When at last they had their drinks, they noticed that some of the people were hurrying out of the bar to return to their seats. "Is it possible they're starting already?" a surprised Zarbini asked.

"No, it can't be. They haven't flashed the lights to advise people", Michele observed. Most of the people were in any case still in the lobby.

With good judgment, the old president let them go, saying, "Go ahead, better check it. I don't want to hold you back."

Approaching the entrance to the theater, Zarbini, Michele, and Alma could hear the actors' voices; the play's reading had already started. Having sat down, Michele guessed they had missed about ten minutes of the resumed performance. How could this be? How could it have happened? Why did they start again without dimming the lobby lights?

He had no more time for these questions, becoming once again absorbed by the actors' reading, standing still behind their lecterns. The playwright again felt that missing relationship that normally operates in theater between actors and spectators.

Finally the reading was over. There was prolonged applause. There were calls for the director and the actors to take a bow, leading Gerardo, Ambrogio, Fortunato, and Alma to think they had just witnessed a greatly successful work. They were unaware (unlike Michele) that the many friends of Ferri and Pavi Austeri alone would have been enough to give the impression of a great premiere.

While the applause was still going on, someone started shouting, "Author . . . we want the author!" so that Michele—though unwillingly—had to take a bow on stage, thanking and smiling at the audience with the others.

9

The applause died down, and the audience started to leave. Among the group from Nomana there were warm comments about what they thought was a great success; they were complimentary toward Michele as they walked up the aisle toward the exit.

Near the door, an usher was waiting for Michele. "*Dottore*, there are two foreign gentlemen who wish to talk to you."

"Two foreigners?"

"Yes sir, two Russians, they said."

"And they want to talk to me?"

The usher nodded. "Yes, sir. One of them had a press card."

"Ah . . ."

"What'll I tell them? Are you going to see them?"

Surprised, Michele nevertheless said, "Why not? Let's hear what they want." Then, turning to his family, "Do you mind waiting for a moment in the lobby? I'll find you over by the exit."

Ambrogio said, "I'm coming with you."

"Yes, let's go."

The usher led the way to an alcove in the lobby where two middle-aged men waited. One was red faced and burly and had a bristly mustache and a big lock of hair tumbled over his forehead. The other was tall and spare, with thinning blond hair and very bright eyes.

"They're Russians all right", Ambrogio murmured as soon as he saw them. "There's no doubt about that." He thought, *In any case, they're not policemen. They look beaten down.* (He had followed his brother-in-law, intending to give him a hand in case it was needed.)

Michele nodded, agreeing. The tall blond somehow reminded him of the unknown Russian infantry lieutenant who twenty years before had inexplicably saved his life at Arbusov. (That was Lieutenant Larichev, whose name Michele never knew. Since that time he hadn't been able to enjoy a play premiere or any other artistic event—how he would have enjoyed it, being an artist himself—for he had been buried, along with the others, Italians, Russians, Germans, who remained forever in that terrible valley.)

"You are Russians?" Michele held out his hand to the burly man.

They both agreed. "Russian exiles", they specified, shaking hands with the two Italians. The robust one with the bristly mustache emotionally explained why they had wanted to greet the author. "What we wanted to tell you is that we found your tragedy full of truth. You seem to have understood well. You're one of the few people in Italy who shows understanding."

Michele, also emotionally affected by this, decided to risk a quip in Russian—the poor Russian picked up by POWs—but it wasn't understood by the two men. He repeated the joke, trying in vain for a better pronunciation, then let it drop.

The burly man recalled a few of the passages from the play they'd just seen acted, or rather read. "How did you manage to get such a play on stage?" he asked. "We were convinced that we were going to see one of these usual pro-Communist works so fashionable in Italy now. We intended to attack it in our magazine. That's what we do—try to fight and explain things without giving up, and yet ... for us, your play was a marvelous surprise."

"Right", the tall one agreed (after having been introduced he had adopted an expression of mute sadness, which seemed to be his usual manner). "Yes, it's true."

"When I was a prisoner of war in Oranchi I was able to talk to nonconforming Russian intellectuals, people like yourselves, unwilling to yield to the dictatorship", Michele said. "For me those were very important meetings, conversations in which I learned many things. The fight for freedom in Russia was incomparably harder than the struggle in Italy during the Fascist era. Don't you agree?"

The burly Russian nodded. "In our prisons it is not possible to write anti-regime ideological treatises the way Gramsci did here in Italy. From what you say you've had an opportunity to talk with Russian internal exiles?"

"Yes, the *zek*, yes. I talked to a few. Among them were some cultured people."

"Ah, if only there were a way of showing your play to our compatriots to show them something from another perspective!" sighed the Russian. "It would be an immensely eye-opening experience for them, too", he smiled. "In any case you're a brave man. Tomorrow all the Italian newspapers will come out attacking you. You know that, right?"

"I hope not", Michele replied. "I hope the Catholic newspapers at least will be on my side."

"Oh, don't count on that", the Russian said bitterly. "Up to a few years ago they were fair, but now even they, all of them, follow the line."

"But no, why do you say that? Agreed, there's some general confusion," Michele insisted, "but things will become clear. We'll recover ground, you'll see."

Most of the people had left the theater. The four of them also moved toward the exit, talking. "Is your magazine published in Italian?"

"Yes, we try to tell people here how things really are in the Soviet Union."

"I'm surprised that I haven't heard of it."

"Unfortunately it has a very small distribution."

"Well, at least now we can keep in touch with each other."

"Agreed", the Russian said. He stopped and took a card from his pocket; Michele did the same, and they exchanged cards.

Next to the exit waited the family from Nomana, Alma among them, happiness in her face as always and enchanting in her sky-blue gown. Michele didn't introduce the Russians. He offered them his hand. They both shook hands with Michele and Ambrogio, bowed, and left. Alma hurried to her husband's side and took his arm.

"Poor souls", Ambrogio said in a low voice, responding to the questioning looks from the family. "They look like Dostoyevski's 'humiliated and offended', don't they?"

Michele, shaking his head, murmured, "A country like Russia with enormous resources, and look at how she treats her sons!"

"They're refugees, right?" asked Fortunato.

"Yes, they publish an anti-Communist magazine here in Rome."

The whole Riva group left the theater just as the marquee lights went out, turning the area around them suddenly dark.

Dark though it was, the surroundings were very attractive. The rocky slope up to Campidoglio seemed to radiate a bluish light, created by well-placed spotlights on the trees around them. At the top the two equestrian statues of the Dioscuri radiated the same light and, beyond at the summit, the fabulous sight of the Michaelangelesque buildings. While the group walked toward the nearby public parking lot, Michele looked briefly at the eagle's cage, but could only see its profile. *Just over there, a few steps away from here, they'll always keep that poor bird prisoner. There it is, and nobody thinks or worries about it*, he reflected.

Behind him Fortunato was commenting on the mishap of the early resumption after the intermission. "I've no idea how a thing like that could happen ... I don't understand how they could restart the reading when nearly all the seats were still empty. And why didn't they advise people by dimming the lights?" He turned to Michele. "Was much lost to the audience during the five or ten minutes?"

"Yes, unfortunately. It was one of the most outstanding and dramatic moments at the end of the first part. Without giving any reason, Pavi Austeri moved it into the beginning of the second part, to be seen after the break." He thought, *Without any reason? Well, just a moment, wait . . .*

Ambrogio asked, "It wouldn't be that he did it on purpose?"

It was only now that Michele realized. He nodded. "Yes, it must be that. That's the reason. I didn't even consider it, but it must be so. Furthermore, I'm convinced that must be it. The director did it out of fear that he'd be the target of Communist criticism. And for sure he at least created some confusion."

"But why would he do that?" Fortunato's wife asked. She was, like the others, unaware of Pavi Austeri's behavior.

Briefly Michele explained. "To him the success or failure of my play isn't important. What is important to him is not to alienate the progressive media, having them against him in the future." He described the director's attempt to expunge his name from the poster and program credits.

"Why, the son of a . . .", Fortunato said between clenched teeth.

The others absorbed the events without excitement. The man was a coward, agreed, but essentially, as they saw it, he hadn't succeeded in stopping the triumph of the play, about which they had no doubts.

"That may be how you see it," Michele said, "but it's not like that. The way things happened, it's clear that the play hasn't been well received. You'll see that in tomorrow's newspapers."

They all expressed their disagreement with this. Nobody believed his forecast.

10

The following morning the light shining through the venetian blinds woke Michele. He realized he wasn't at home. He was in Rome . . . *The newspapers!* he thought. *I have to go out and buy the papers.*

At his side lay a sleeping Alma, her hair partially hiding her face, moist with perspiration. Michele, as usual, spent a moment gazing at her in the half dark. *May God bless you, Alma, for being the way you are.* Today, as every morning, the spell was repeated, the incomparable joy of finding her at his side.

Hanging from a wall sconce was a coat hanger holding her evening gown. *You made yourself a pretty gown, my love, for the successful play that never was.* He shook his head, looking tenderly at her. What a wonderful companion God had given him! Yes, God . . . suddenly he remembered him! He once again put his head on the pillow, blessed himself on the forehead with the sign of the

Cross, and as he did every morning, he prayed, praising God. God, who had not only created him, brought him from nothing, made him in the resemblance of his image, intelligent and able to love. With his creation God had placed him immeasurably higher than a million glazing suns and the other splendid things that it had pleased him to create. Michele recited the prayer in the form he had for years given to it: *Glory be to God, the uncreated and everlasting Being. Glory be to the Son, ever in your mind, expression of your Being. Glory be to the Holy Spirit and love everlasting. Glory be to this Trinity, as it was in the beginning, now and for always. Amen.*

The prayer of praise to God was followed—as it was every morning, with great spiritual intensity—by that entreaty for the dead (his brothers in Christ, who after the fall of man rescued them with infinite love, spilling his own blood) of which he tried to remember especially the ones nearest to him by kinship or friendship.

But he had to get up, trying not to make any noise, wash, and get dressed in a hurry without waking Alma. His Alma! He turned again to look at her; she was beautiful lying there in the half light. What enchantment to be able to remain like this. This contemplation was in a way (the contemplation of a beauty made by the hands of God!) a sort of anticipation of paradise. What loveliness! Why interrupt her sleep? Why should he go outside and fill his head with . . . what? With the volley of insults from the small-minded Communist and Socialist journalists and from the little cowards who for reasons of self-interest pretended to be commentators. People who no doubt had arrogated the mantle—he could almost see their writings in his mind—of spokesmen of the real culture. *What culture? A culture that does damage, has created the greatest massacres in history, and no one even notices!*

But it was April, Rome's particular month, and he was here in Rome, next to this beautiful creature, to whom he was also physically attracted, so why not . . . *Come on, Michele, hurry up, don't waste time.* He swung his legs out of the covers, felt with his feet for his slippers, got up, and went to the bathroom, closing the door quietly. (Nearly all the hotels now offered rooms with a private bathroom. People had begun to forget the poverty of other times.)

When he emerged, washed and shaved, it was to find Alma sitting on the bed.

She greeted him brightly. "Saint Michael the Archangel, good morning!"

"Hello, God's little gift."

"Why didn't you wake me?"

"I wanted to let you sleep on."

"Well, I never . . . this morning instead of sleeping, we need to go running to buy the newspapers! Have you forgotten?" She pushed back the covers and stood on the rug. "I won't make you late, you'll see. I'll get ready in a moment."

"No, take your time. I'll go for the papers."

"But what are you saying? We have to go for them together."

11

They left the hotel without having breakfast and went quickly to the nearest newsstand, where during the previous days Michele had bought newspapers to check on advertisements for the play. They walked past a woman standing quietly by a gate. She was middle aged. At her feet was a bulging suitcase, with a wrapped parcel perched on top. She looked like a maid recently arrived in town and waiting for a bus. As he passed, Michele examined her out of the corner of an eye. She looked tired and out of place. Who knew where she had come from? Maybe she had traveled all night. Michele felt almost ashamed at his own growing impatience to find out what the newspapers had to say about his play. *She, poor thing,* he thought, *won't be reading her own name in the papers, never, ever.* He looked thoughtful.

"Do you want me to get the newspapers?" Alma asked.

"Let's get them together." They bought one of each, and although the news-stand was busy with customers coming and going, they stood there and opened each newspaper to the theater section. All of them had a report, short or long, on the play's first night. They raced through the articles just to get an impression of whether the reports were good or bad. Then Michele said, "Come on, let's go somewhere quiet." The patiently waiting servant with her suitcase, apparently down on her luck, had already slipped his mind.

They walked back toward the hotel, but on the way paused again at a traffic-free street, one of those sloping shady Roman roads lined with severely pruned poplars, their branches angled. "I'll read this one first," said Michele, "and you take this one. Come on, let's see what they say."

They read, then exchanged the first two newspapers, and then went on to read the rest, reading phrases or portions of text out loud.

As expected, the Marxist press dripped bile and hatred. "Have you seen this in *Unità*?" asked Alma.

"Right, yes. What did you expect?"

"They're really unkind to this Pavi Austeri. And did you read this paragraph? It says you are a sort of corrupter of youth. Whatever does he mean? Has the man gone crazy?"

Michele laughed.

"But what does it mean?"

"Put yourself in his shoes. I suppose you know some of the young actors, more or less Communist at the start of rehearsals, began to doubt their political faith after a while. Well, as you can see, even that hasn't escaped the eye of that particular critic."

"But to speak about you this way ... the miserable ..."

"Come on, think about Socrates!" Michele laughed again.

Alma didn't laugh; she became more annoyed. "But look at this snake in *Avanti!*" she exclaimed after a while. "He does nothing but throw insults at you."

"Mmm."

"He says that rather than being a tragedy, it's a farce, because 'the facts about Marxism and communism given by the playwright are no more than the vague ramblings in *Domenica del Corriere'*."

"Pretty good, eh? The premise is that only the people on the left know anything about the Soviet Union. Look, they don't even know that over there a—— lickers like themselves, once their usefulness was over, were sent to the labor camps in large numbers. And if you simply report it, as I did, they don't know how to react except by hurling insults. They're trying to reassure themselves, do you see?"

"What idiots."

"Yes, not much in the way of brains. You saw what Nenni did when Khrushchev revealed what had been done? He showed his indignation by returning his Lenin prize. He had accepted it without realizing—it would seem—what he was doing, poor donkey. And he's the boss. And besides, even after the Khrushchev revelations—at least up to now—they haven't mounted an investigation into what has gone on in Russia, not even the slightest inquiry, nothing."

They went on reading silently.

"What worries me the most", Michele said in a strange voice, "is this!" He became annoyed, shaking the newspaper he held. "Have you seen it?"

"No. Is it *Il Popolo*?"

"Yes, the Christian Democrats' newspaper. They say almost the same as the Marxist paper. It's very strange."

He continued reading. "Evidently the theater column in *Il Popolo* has fallen into the hands of someone like De Ponti. Yes, that must be it." (Those bitter words spoken by those two Russian exiles about the Catholic press, which simply parrots the leftist press!) "Who knows, yesterday in the theater what this little whore of a critic may have said to make sure to disassociate himself from me in order to look good to the Reds." He looked at the foot of the article. "There's no signature. Who could it be? But in any case an article like this is a bad sign."

"And the Catholic paper, does it say the same sort of thing?" asked Alma. "Which one is it? I still haven't seen it."

"No, thank God, *Il Quotidiano* writes favorably, here, look. They have a small circulation, unfortunately." Michele was silent for a while. He remembered the strength of his faith at the time of the great election victory in 1948, fourteen years before. What dreams he had had of great developments in the Catholic newspapers! What a disappointment! His wife watched him worriedly. "Read it, Alma. It quotes Apollonio and ... well, it says nice things. Although it doesn't adopt a firm stand, because ... look, let me see it a moment." He looked at the text and read out loud. "Here it is: 'The first night was marred by accidental inconveniences'—it hints at Pavi Austeri's little games, only we know they weren't casual—'marred by accidental inconveniences that prevented the critics from exercising a clear judgment'. You understand? It's a favorable article, even quite insightful, but they avoid making a definitive judgment."

"Fortunately the *Osservatore Romano* . . ."

"Yes, luckily. They don't go in for ambiguity. Have you read it? It's a long article—not like the party newspapers—serious, reasoned, a well-written article, very favorable."

Also favorable were the independent newspapers, with the exception of one of Rome's largest circulation papers, whose critic praised Ferri and Austeri, then went on to take a swipe at the playwright's defect: a lack of modesty. This same immodest author, standing reading the newspaper under the street poplars, went over the comment that most affected—and baffled—him. "And to think", he said to his wife, "that this fellow is a friend of Ferri's and was one of the few people present at the dress rehearsal. Whatever could have happened to him? I'd like to know what the problem was. Well, enough . . ." He put the newspapers under his arm. "We shouldn't forget that we've yet to have breakfast. Come, let's go back to the hotel."

Alma took his arm and commented in a low voice, "What bad people there are in this world."

Michele smiled at her. "Darling, I've seen worse. And over here, after all, there's nobody shooting into the back of your neck. At least right now they don't, nor is anyone dying from hunger. You have to admit that no one is trying to stop us eating breakfast, right? That's something not to be ignored. Compared to many, many people, we're leading a privileged life; I'm serious." He frowned. "Just think about the number of people who right now are fighting for salvation without any hope of achieving it, destroyed by anguish and condemned to death. All those poor Chinese farmers, small landowners—maybe owning just a few yards of earth—who are being systematically killed."

12

That same day the Riva family left Rome for Lombardy, and Alma went with them, as she had to return to her teaching. Michele stayed behind in order to attend some more performances of his play. He wanted to ascertain more closely the transformation undergone by the text at the moment when it was taken from the written script and turned into the spoken word.

One of those nights Lucio Ferri went looking for him and sat down in the seat next to his. He was interested in Michele's problems, problems he had resolved for himself long before. "The script, for me, is a simple guide, a general indication, you understand. To me the script is translated in my imagination into the actions that will appear on the stage. Of course the process needs experience and long practice."

They remained in their seats during the intermission, and Michele asked, "Look, can you explain to me why the critic from"—he named the large-circulation newspaper—"was so offended?"

"Easily", Ferri replied. "Simple. This fellow is upset with you because you didn't go and talk to him during the rehearsals. He probably wanted you to soft-soap him and personally explain your play to him. That's it, really. He took offense, unreasonable though it may be."

"But ... I even personally handed him a copy of the script. What more could I have done? It seemed to me not right to do any more."

"And you're right. And I have to say I admire you for that, and I even said it to him. I reminded him that in America an author would carefully avoid any attempt to push his work until it had seen its first night; to do otherwise would be seen as unethical. But here we are, in Italy and not America." He shook his head. "Listen, as long as we are talking of unfortunate events, I have some bad news. I didn't know how to tell it to you, and ... you remember the filming of the play for television?" he paused.

"Yes."

"They've canceled it on me. I must admit I sort of expected it after the row caused by all the left-wing newspapers. In any case they called me this morning. The television director called me personally. He told me 'not even to think' it might go on television. He gave the impression of being upset with me, as if I'd given him wrong advice and was making him run a 'serious risk', as he put it." Ferri laughed bitterly. "And just to think that if, instead of dealing with a serious theme such as this, which really affects everyone's future, you had written some unimportant frothy little play, they would have shown it on television; no question about it. And everything had been prepared. All was ready for the broadcast, as you know."

Michele just nodded. After a moment he said, "I'm reminded of that fellow—what's his name?—the director of *Unità*, who turned from Fascist to Communist. You saw how the television people behaved with him? Not only did they repeatedly mention the book in which he described the uplifting experience of his conversion, but they also took the book and staged its contents in two parts. You remember that? It was five or six months ago."

"Yes, of course, I remember."

"Well, in any case the imprisoned writers in Russia, held in work camps and lunatic asylums, they don't have an opportunity to appear on television, and yet they don't whine about it. Well, I won't be whining, either."

Ferri looked at him with interest. It was clear that the playwright had no intention of adapting himself to fashion, wouldn't be bending in any way. He didn't even consider it.

"Don't you need money to live?" he asked.

"No, thank God. I'm teaching at a lyceum, and that puts the bread on the table. And my wife makes a living. She teaches and doesn't need me to get by. In other words . . ."

"I see. Is that how you see things?"

Michele answered quietly, "Yes."

When the performance was finished, Ferri said, "Look, tomorrow I have some spare time, and I'd like to talk with you some more."

"I'd like that, too", Michele answered.

The next morning they talked, first in Ferri's office and later strolling through the streets of Rome. The manager was frank and sincere with Michele, answering all his questions, even the more searching ones about the world of theater ("Have you heard this one? He's only been a homosexual for a year, and already he's a director") and television, where everything was done on the basis of shady deals.

"Listen," Ferri asked, "doesn't this Roman world make you feel like vomiting?"

The Lombard playwright shook his head. "I'm more interested in understanding how this basic corruption spreads, even here in the nation's capital."

Being with him Ferri had the feeling of breathing in pure oxygen. *Like a mountain breeze*, he thought. He asked himself if he could use Michele's personality—so true to his own self—to draw a character for his new play, but finally told himself that, no, *it would be too unbelievable*, he thought, *even though completely true.*

Later, in the afternoon—his last day in Rome—Michele met with the two Russian refugees in the very poor offices in which they produced their small magazine. He agreed to their translating the play into Russian and told them that there would be no copyrights on his part. Despite this, he noted that the cost of publishing it would be more than they could afford and offered to contribute something toward it. *As I travel overseas every couple of years to see the world*, he thought, *with the money I've been saving to go to the USA I'll help this project along. Besides, America will still be there when I want to go.*

So that is what happened, and the tragedy—translated into Russian by the tall blond refugee who looked like Lieutenant Larichev from Arbusov—was published and on sale within the year, being distributed in Russian refugee circles in Europe and America, and was even mailed to the USSR. The method used to send the work to Russia was to send a few copies at a time, week after week, using different-looking envelopes and wrappings. In Italy copies were placed in the rooms of the Rome hotel used by the Soviet government to lodge the Russian intellectuals who came on their highly organized fact-finding tours. The message about the play went from mouth to mouth, and more than one of the visitors asked for copies from the interpreters or from the hotel's employees. In this way, without being aware of it, Michele became a part of the clandestine publishing phenomenon named *samizdat*. Not long after this some Polish intellectuals asked to be put in touch with Michele, and with them he agreed to the same conditions for a translation into Polish. Exactly like the Russian translation, all of the copies sold out quickly.

At about this time came the beginning of the Second Vatican Council—Vatican II—in Rome. The Church—thanks to the efforts of past Pontiffs—was like a well-defended city. For this very reason, though, the Church's voice and teachings didn't reach the people who had left the protection of her walls in the past. In a praiseworthy effort to prevent a further distancing of these people from a Church under siege, the Catholic Church showed a willingness to speak to these people in their own language (sometimes—one had the impression—beyond what was reasonable or possible), which was obviously not the language used by Michele and by all those who had remained faithful across the centuries.

PART SIX

I

Time went on. Time, which cannot be held back and of which some say, "How time drags by!" and others, "My how time flies, and the years go by." But time cannot be delayed. It goes on to its mysterious conclusion.

"After death ... who knows what circumstances we'll find ourselves in? I often ask myself how the Great Beyond must be." Gerardo was talking to his son, Father Rodolfo, back in Nomana from Africa to spend a vacation.

It was August of 1968, and Gerardo was near eighty. He was much thinner, and his clothes—even though Giulia, she too an old woman, made alterations from time to time, and he also had new clothes made occasionally—were big on him. He had lost many of his teeth, so that it was an unpleasant sight when he laughed. He was also going deaf. But he had not stopped working. "I have to be near the sound of the looms", he would say. (His pronouncements, at one time taken seriously by everybody, could give the impression—erroneously most of the time—that they were the babblings of senility, and some even smiled kindly.) He had recently found himself several times questioning Ambrogio about decisions that needed to be made in the factory. In most cases he was mistaken and quickly acknowledged the fact. After these episodes, having thought it out and without being asked, he had handed over the entire management of the factory to Ambrogio, maintaining for himself only a remotely situated small office. He had his old desk taken there and a telephone installed, and he could sit and have the sound of the looms as a background, in fact even less faint here than in the main office.

There, in his own office, he could buy and sell small batches of yarn and fabric, just as he had done when starting out in the business, independently of the firm's routine. "This way I'm not idle", as he would say to the representatives who would call on him (generally older men with whom he had worked for many years, but also a few novices in the business to whom Gerardo's name sounded important). In order to avoid being idle, he also occupied himself with the affairs of his two missionary sons, Father Rodolfo—now visiting Nomana and walking alongside his father—and the doctor, Pino, whose necessities he more or less supplied, sending him regular batches of supplies, which Gerardo would collect from various factories and warehouses. Medicines and more medicines, surgical instruments, agricultural and irrigation machinery, teaching materials, food and clothing. More than once he had been able to take advantage of military flights for his deliveries (the air force then worked under instructions to operate some of their training flights each year to destinations in "especially needy zones"). Dealing with missionaries and with the military, the older Riva had discovered with some surprise the affinity existing between the two professions. Although not all their usages coincided, Gerardo was able to see the same tendency to give, to volunteer, and the ability to manage with poor resources plus other curiously similar habits.

Gerardo, talking to his son now about the Great Beyond, walked along the small path in the garden that led to the old yew tree and the south-facing balcony. The yew tree in which long ago the nightingale sang (no longer, since the opening of the glass factory, whose never-ceasing whistles had driven them away; it had been years since the nightingale had been heard in Nomana). Running alongside the path was still the hedge where Manno on his last leave (before disappearing forever) had held a conversation with one of the nightingales. On the other side of the wall there still grew the wild chamomile, with its calming dry smell. As it was daylight and there were other sounds in the air, the hissing from the glassworks was half drowned out.

"If one could get an idea about the world beyond", Gerardo said. "When I was younger I thought I had a good idea, but now . . ."

"It's not easy to know for sure", agreed his son, feeling pity at the deterioration he saw in his father. (*He is obsessed with thoughts of death*, he thought. *Who knows how many physical deficiencies remind him of that each day, poor Father.*) "But why do you want to know exactly how the Great Beyond is?" he asked his father.

"Well, because . . .", Gerardo muttered.

"We mere men can't understand a reality built only by the spirit", said the priest. "I'm afraid that there's no solution to the question."

"Yet I sometimes ask myself why nobody has ever come back to tell us how things are on the other side."

"For sure somebody did come back", said the son. "Lazarus, for example, who was resurrected by our Lord." He had spoken in a normal tone but noticed that his father, opening his mouth with his bad teeth, had leaned over, closer, offering his ear to the younger man. *I have to remember that he is a little deaf*, Rodolfo thought. *I keep forgetting.* He raised his voice. "Lazarus, the one from the Gospel, for example. Without doubt he must have told about what he saw on the other side, because on leaving the sepulcher he didn't go off and hide. In fact, if you remember, he offered dinner at his house to Christ and his apostles."

"Doesn't the Gospel say what he revealed?"

"No. But this just means that what he said was in agreement with what Christ was teaching daily. That much is clear."

"But what is it exactly that Christ teaches?"

"The same things the Church teaches us nowadays: substantially, that those who seek salvation will enjoy the holy vision of Christ forevermore."

"Right . . . but what does that mean, exactly? The beatific vision . . . we aren't able to imagine it, you say." The old man thought, then, "In any case, more important than anything else, what I want to know is whether over there we'll still truly love the people we loved here on Earth, and whether we'll be together again."

"I believe so. Think of the privileged position to which Christ raised his Mother, higher than the saints, and angels. Besides, the love man has is undoubtedly good. In other words, as all good is found in Christ, over there we'll find our love again. In any case, Papa, remember that over there we won't find a lesser reality than here. It'll be exactly the opposite; we'll find a lasting happiness. The happiness we're always seeking here on Earth, because that is the whole reason for our creation."

"Right," muttered Gerardo, "right." He reflected, using a brain that soon would run down with the ravages of age and molder, like all fleshly organs. "But . . ."

"But?"

"But things over there surely can't be compared to the things of this life. They must be different, very different."

"Yes, for sure." He looked at his father with pity. "Papa, I agree that things here have their value. Just think about Saint Francis and the rock of Mount la Verna. He, I mean Saint Francis, more than most, had a feeling for earthly things: air, water, fire, the flowers, the grass . . . think about his canticle of the creatures. And what is more, as opposed to ourselves he had knowledge of the world over there from having had repeated ecstatic visions. In other words he was, in a way, in a position to compare. Well, at the time of his leaving his hermitage at Verna for Assisi, there to die (he knew he would die and spoke of it, because God had advised him of it), even though impatient to reach heaven, he wept when he took leave of the rock he had so loved, from having so often meditated and prayed in its shade. And that's it: earthly things are also of value. The same with Lazarus . . . It's not that after having experienced the Great Beyond he felt that everything there is and happens here on Earth was reduced to nothing—so much so that he buried himself with preparing that dinner for the Lord, a dinner prepared with great care and zeal, just as a dinner we would offer here in our house."

"Yes", Gerardo nodded repeatedly. "Right. So that the things over there on the other side, I . . . well, I'm not attracted by them. A place where there are billions and billions of souls and, after the resurrection of the bodies, billions of people. Who knows how many billions, you realize? That's without counting the angels, which also reach infinity . . . how could such a place be attractive? I've even asked myself if it is a place where one can feel at ease?"

"Well, these things always were unknown, but not nowadays. To repeat what I said: of course we can't imagine the Great Beyond. But the Creator can certainly create an . . . adequate paradise." Father Rodolfo smiled. "As he has shown us, in abundance, with his created universe. Papa, I'm not a scientist, but I have read in magazines that in our galaxy alone there are more or less one hundred billion stars, and that in the universe, within reach of modern means of research, there are some one hundred billion galaxies. That means one hundred billion multiplied by one hundred billion stars, or suns ... what would that total? In other words, the One who has been able to create that number of suns wouldn't have any difficulty in creating a place where all the billions of men and angels will be magnificently at ease."

"That's also true, yes."

In order to change the subject and take his father's mind off the question of death, Rodolfo went on talking about the stars. "No one knows if—as some say—other stars are inhabited. But if they are not, well, it seems to me that this immense universe would not still be there without a reason, because it would serve to give us an idea of the Creator's power."

"What, to us men? Do you mean to say we're that important?" Gerardo murmured.

"We have had revealed to us that we were made in the image and likeness of God; there's the thing. And we see clearly that there is a profound difference between man and the other animals. Think of this, for example. We are the only creatures able to leave the planet in which we were born, this earth from which we were made (the clay described in the Bible). Did you know that around Christmastime the Americans have planned a flight around the moon?"

Gerardo nodded, looking at his son with his faded, wasted blue eyes. He wouldn't have to wait long—Rodolfo thought, feeling sad again—until he was able to see for himself everything in the Beyond.

2

Noemi came out from the house. (She was over seventy, had put on weight, and walked bent over. Her hair was gray, and she had several teeth missing. In any case, she was still active. She had a few million in a bank account and a well-furnished room and kitchen over the porter's quarters at *I dragoni*. On Sundays she went over to clean it. "That room of mine will be useful when I get old", she used to say.) She shielded her eyes from the sun with one hand and looked around the garden. When she spotted the two men strolling in the vegetable garden, she called out, as she had years ago with the children, "*Signore*, Gerardo, Father Rodolfo, *e pronto*."

"We'll be right there", the priest called back solicitously, meaning to stop her repeating her call, a thing she unfailingly would have done with children. Reversing their steps, Gerardo and his son went toward the house.

In the dining room—always the same, tidy and unchanged—were Giulia and Ambrogio; this last had just arrived from the factory. (His wife and children were at the seaside. For this reason, and because his brother Rodolfo was visiting, he was eating at his parents' home.)

Giulia was tidying a drawer in the sideboard; for some time now she had acquired the habit of tidying things, as if she felt a need to leave everything in its place before herself leaving forever. During the last few years she had carefully reread the letters, checked the books, school exercise books, things used by her children when younger, and had been giving this to one and that to another. "They are things that belong to you. Maybe with time you'll find an interest in them. Take it." In her motherly way, to her daughters and daughters-in-law she had distributed almost all her jewelry piece by piece, valuable knick-knacks, silver and crystal plates and vases. (Some of these had never been used, but the children were accustomed to seeing one or another of them in fixed places around the house and would have preferred to leave them in place, but Giulia would say, "Why wait until my death? Come, take it, enjoy these things while you're still young.") With the years she had become bent over and smaller. *But Mama remains the same*, Father Rodolfo thought when he saw her, automatically thanking God for looking after her.

After having washed their hands (in a new washroom, built out of what had been a larder), the men sat at the table. Giulia still remained bent over the drawer, straightening things out. Her husband joked gently with her. "Before, it was always I who was never on time to eat, but now . . ."

"Coming, I'll be right there", Giulia exclaimed. "While I finish here, you start eating. Just a minute and I'll be through."

"No, Mama, I'm not saying grace until you sit down", Rodolfo said.

Giulia half closed the drawer that she'd been tidying and hurried to the table, where she devoutly participated in the family blessing. Then she got up and hurried out of the dining room. "I'm going to wash my hands, and I'll be right back."

Ambrogio commented, "Mama doesn't seem able to rest." He turned to Rodolfo. "You see how she is?"

Rodolfo nodded. "I'd already noticed."

"Francesca tries to keep her company", Gerardo said. He had leaned his head over to hear Rodolfo's comment. "She comes over from Visate especially every day, despite the fact that they're having problems there, poor devils."

"Yes, I'd heard about that", Rodolfo said.

Ambrogio explained. "The Marsavi family is in trouble, almost as much as we at the time of the Brusasca deal and the exports to France. They try and they try just to stay on their feet from day to day, and they need sums of money much greater than we needed, back then . . . poor Andrea, he never stops battling with the banks."

"And to think their products are so good—at least on the pharmaceutical side, their new activity. Their patented medicine for use against leprosy is very useful. We've been using it for years, and they've never let us pay for it, as you know. We just have to write them, and straight away they send us more. What excellent people!"

Gerardo shook his head thoughtfully. "It's really a shame about their parish priest", he said.

"Their priest?" asked Father Rodolfo with surprise. "What do you mean?"

"The present parish priest in Visate", Ambrogio explained, "is one of these new-style priests who . . . well, as far as their workers are concerned, the Marsavi family's greatest problems were created by him. Just imagine that the man went so far as to say in a sermon that if they're not being paid fairly, the workers have the right to steal; that in the circumstances this wouldn't be stealing. But who's to say they are or aren't underpaid? All I see is that they all own a car, and many of them own an apartment, and many other things."

"And the workers, what have they to say?"

"The older men do as they have always done, the same as always, but many of the younger men are a real calamity", Ambrogio said. "They may not steal, but they do sometimes ruin the products on purpose. This is made worse by the ACLI and the CISL (you know they have a lot of influence here in Brianza), who repeat the crazy speeches made by the priest." He shook his head. "I simply don't understand what's come over our Christian union members. After Vatican II, having the freedom to choose their own course, they didn't seem to know any better than to follow the Reds, and they don't seem to care that this gives the lie to all they said and did before. To deal with them now, I mean the CISL people, is worse than having to negotiate with the Reds themselves. I've lived through this recently, with the start of negotiations with the union for a new work contract. So you can imagine with the Marsavis."

"Did you know that two older working men were beaten up by youngsters in Visate because the older men had shouted at them for doing some vandalism or other?" said Gerardo.

"But what the devil are you doing here in Italy?" Father Rodolfo exclaimed. He saw things from his own point of view. Italians, and Europeans in general—even the working men—to him seemed extraordinarily rich. And they were, when compared with the Africans among whom he lived. These events he was hearing about—like the great student rebellions, news of which had been received at his African mission—looked to him like rich men's games, rich people's whims.

Before anyone said more, Giulia returned to the table. After having washed her hands she had lingered over some other task. The men changed the subject (these things made her anxious). Ambrogio commented on the Americans' plans, of how on the previous night's television he had been reminded that within a year they would be sending three men in a spacecraft to the moon. "They've been talking about it for a while, and we've already seen how unmanned craft have been there about three times. I suppose a manned flight should get there and back without problems."

"But ... will they really walk on the moon?" Gerardo asked. "It seems impossible to me."

"Well, you'll soon see it, Papa", said his son the priest. "Within a year, two at the most, they'll get there, just as they've planned."

"Yet, if one thinks about it, it seems something impossible," remarked Ambrogio, "to land on the moon!"

His mother listened silently, marveling.

Rodolfo said, "It'll really be a great victory for man! Earlier, in the garden, Papa and I were talking about this sort of thing. It'll be an extraordinary demonstration of the superiority of man over the world's other creatures."

"Yes", said Gerardo. "And yet you've seen how some of the television commentators have been behaving? It's as if the moon trip made them angry; they keep talking about the cost."

"Hard to understand, given that we Italians aren't spending even one penny on it", Ambrogio noted.

At the time, sitting around the family table, they couldn't yet understand that all over the world there were mean-spirited people who would denigrate the undertaking, so that just a few years after the event, a sort of veil of silence would descend on the great enterprise. Man would thus find a way to spoil this incomparable adventure ... however, the flight and landing did take place.

3

When the meal ended, Ambrogio had a hurried cup of coffee and returned alone to the mill. Gerardo planned to spend the rest of the day with his son Rodolfo, to catch up on what the young priest had been doing in Africa.

As he approached the factory, Ambrogio could already hear the thrumming noise of the looms. Now they were all automatic, not only faster than the earlier models but also able to change the shuttles when they ran short of thread. (Marietta, the "shuttle queen"—with her extravagant ways, her awful hair, and black, sheeplike eyes—had died, and the shuttle slides and their attendant apprentice girls had all gone.) The modern looms were also able to stop themselves automatically when a thread broke. Each weaver no longer watched over her two to four looms as before (when Giustina was still there) but took care of eight, ten, or more. The walls of the mill were now painted and had new aluminum doors. The new offices now were accessible through a small garden, which had been planted where before there had been a storehouse. The garden was planted in linden trees, still new and frail, contrasting with the superpruned older lindens in the other courtyards.

Ambrogio went to his ground-level office and sat at his desk. On the opposite side of the room (which held no other desks except his own) was a large open window, through which came the clacking noise from the looms and the hot August air. He had a half hour before the "informal" (*Informal! One of those bureaucrat's words*) meeting that had been requested by the worker's committee and started preparing for it. On his desk were files relating to the meeting and also a chart showing the essential factors of production. There were three snaking lines on divergent tracks. One showed the number of employees (about two hundred), which for years hadn't changed much. Another line showed attendance, the line plunging into serious absenteeism, a new phenomenon that was also starting to be felt in Nomana. The third line denoted the cost of labor, and this one ran upward, almost off the graph. These figures particularly worried Ambrogio, not that he needed the graph to tell him the story. He was perfectly aware of the figures, but the graph served as a visual reminder, urging him on to find an answer to the problem.

He had to decide on the elimination of some lines of production that were negative contributors (or marginally loss makers; some of the files on the desk told the story), because who could know what type of blow was about to descend with the new labor contract. Since the time the Socialists came into government, the unions had managed to have laws passed that made the manufacturers' lives more difficult, even though they produced marginal or even zero advantage to the workers. This was particularly felt after the Soviet Union's authorities had decided to award Italian industrialists the job of building the largest automobile plant in Russia, at Togliattigrad on the Volga. (This was a terrible setback for the unions.) During the current year of 1968 came the student uprisings, which further complicated things. According to his brother-in-law Michele, a specialist on communism, these demonstrations were caused by waves of discontent originating in China. Students in the West (pushed toward change and revolution by incessant pressure from "progressive" teachers everywhere) had recently been greatly deluded by events in China. They had really believed that the Chinese students were committed to the so-called Cultural Revolution (while in truth they were being manipulated like puppets by the most ferocious wing of the Chinese Communist party), that they were changing their country with greatly inspired idealism. Students in the West had been convinced of the honesty of this movement and had thrown themselves wholeheartedly into the same battle. In several Western countries the student revolt produced different effects. (They were particularly serious in the United States.) In Italy the confrontations in the streets created a resignation on the part of the political parties. The power vacuum this produced, however, wasn't filled by the student movement—this agglomeration only seemed fit to make noise—but by the labor unions, who were strong and organized. Afterward the unions used their growing power to make increasingly unreasonable demands for raises in pay and social benefits. The few men of culture—like Ambrogio's brother-in-law Michele—writing for the Milanese Catholic newspaper—who made efforts to expose the truth of events in China, trying to counteract the collective blindness on the subject, were rarely listened to, didn't even attract criticism.

Ambrogio thought, *We've reached the point where even the people who know the facts don't see that they should be concerned.* He shook his head. Sometimes he felt that the only people in Italy who retained any common sense, who behaved like adults, were the industrialists. *It makes you feel like letting the majority take over, watch them reach a blank wall . . . Fortunato did well to leave the world of industry!* But had he really done well? Ambrogio had his doubts. *No, there has to be someone keeping up the fight. Things simply can't go on like this. People will be forced to reconsider things one of these days.*

But enough of all that. He had to concentrate on the immediate problem. He started reading the files.

The telephone rang. Ambrogio automatically answered. "Yes? *Pronto?*"

"*Pronto, pronto.* Is that you, Ambrogio? It's Fanny here."

"Ah, good morning, *cara*; how are you?"

"Sorry I'm calling you there instead of at home", Fanny said and giggled.

"That's all right, but how come you're calling me at this time?" Fanny was at the seaside in the Gargano with their two sons (Manno, fifteen, and Filippo, whom they called Popi, fourteen) and their daughter, Orsetta, eleven. During their vacation Ambrogio missed his two sons, particularly the older, so much like himself. Manno had a straight character and a willingness to help, similar in this also to his grandfather Gerardo. "But look, where are you calling from, the hotel?"

"Of course, Ambrogio, naturally. Did you think I'd be at the beach, with this heat? One would be foolish to be there."

"Mmm." Ambrogio smiled. Despite everything he liked hearing Fanny's style of speech, as it reminded him of their earlier days. He thought that he'd be seeing her and the children the next day, Saturday. The prospect of a couple of days away from work felt good at the moment. "So tell me, why have you called? What's the good news?" He expected his wife to ask him to bring an item of clothing or something else that she had forgotten to pack.

"I didn't want to bother you," Fanny said, "particularly as we'd agreed you'd be here on Sunday or, better yet, perhaps on Saturday afternoon."

"That's right. It's going to be tomorrow afternoon. No perhaps about it. Why?" The smile had left his face.

"Well, about your coming tomorrow, you weren't very sure."

"That's true, but later I managed to get free."

"Well, if that's the case, it doesn't matter."

Ambrogio had a vision of his wife's no-longer-handsome face, with its sharp angles and protruding teeth, looking annoyed. He felt a mixture of pity and annoyance, which lasted only a few seconds. "What's up? Tell me." he said, making his tone warm. "Maybe you planned something also down there?"

"The boys insist on going to the Tremiti islands, you see?"

"And can't we all go together on Sunday?"

"No. The only seats left on the boat are for tomorrow's sailing, that's the problem. We've phoned the port, believe me, but the Sunday sailing is hopeless, all sold out."

"I understand."

"Anyway, forget it. Pretend I never called; leave it."

Ambrogio said, "No, wait, why forget it? I'm sure the boys are looking forward to going, right?"

"Well, yes. Just imagine, Manno is determined to look for turtles there."

"That's all right. I can put off my trip until next Saturday. Let's see . . . let me look at my diary . . . yes, we could do that."

"But . . . if it doesn't suit you to put if off . . ."

"Why would that be? It doesn't matter. The trip in the plane, then driving a rental car . . . it's tiring and . . . right, let's do that. I'll come on Saturday, one week from tomorrow."

"Do you want to talk to the children?"

"Yes . . . that is, no, not right now. Any moment now I'm expecting the worker's committee, and I'm still getting prepared for the meeting. Give them a big hug from me. Enjoy the day out, have fun."

"Goodbye, *caro*. Don't be mad at me." Her voice sounded clearly relieved.

"Why would I be? I don't know what you mean. Be careful on the boat. Look after Filippo particularly."

"Right, *ciao*. Look after yourself."

Hanging up the telephone, Ambrogio asked himself whatever could have become of that "Green Eyes" Fanny he had known at the university, who as a Red Cross nurse had taken care of him (how graceful she was then!) and whom he'd later married. She still had those green eyes, of course, but now they had become hard and estranged. *Poor Fanny. I brought her into a world she didn't understand, that didn't fit her.* At the start she had tried to adapt herself, even showing a certain verve, but that interminable trial of the financial crisis came too soon for her, and it had made her disillusioned. There had been days when he was sure he would lose her; a couple of times Fanny had left home (what bad memories!), but had at least gone to shelter at her parents' house and luckily after a few days had returned. As time went by they had arrived at a modus vivendi: her frivolous silliness (her insistence on buying clothes only from fashionable boutiques, her passion for playing canasta, the constant attendance at chic parties, which he disliked) was something to which he adapted without complaint. He had been happy that all these distractions had at least kept her resignedly faithful. On the other hand, her constancy as a wife had been shored up by the presence of her children.

But he had to put distractions aside and get ready for the meeting, had to decide how much he could yield to reach an agreement over the union's demands. He rearranged the files on his desk and noticed there were some missing. He rang for his secretary, a middle-aged woman; she came in and efficiently found the needed files, putting them on his desk. She asked Ambrogio if there would be anything else. She had an air of responsibility and was clearly concerned that the approaching meeting should be beneficial to the running of the factory. *Now here's a woman who remains faithful.* Ambrogio smiled at the thought. The heat and noise continued coming through the open window. What a life, continually interrupted by stumbling blocks! As many as you manage to surmount, more appear. Is it really worthwhile to keep at this weary game? Ambrogio turned once again to his files.

The phone rang again, and Ambrogio answered mechanically. "Hello, Riva here."

"Could I please speak to the *Dottore* Ambrogio Riva?" (It was a hesitant female voice. Who could it be? The voice sounded familiar.)

"Yes, this is he. Who's calling?"

"Is that you, Ambrogio, really you?" the voice exclaimed happily. "What a pleasure it is to hear you again after all this time. Is it really you?"

"Yes, it's me, really. Who's this?"

"You'll have to guess ..."

"It's Colomba, isn't that you, Colomba?" Ambrogio said, feeling unusually emotional. He had not seen Colomba since the day of his examination, when he graduated—how many years ago? "Colomba! How nice to hear from you! How are you? Did you receive my birthday card? Is that why you're calling?"

"Yes, that's right. I received it today. Imagine, it took three weeks to get here! From Novara it was forwarded to me here in Alagna, where we're on holiday. And I said to myself, 'This incredible Ambrogio, sending me a birthday card after all these years!' It's the second birthday card you've sent, isn't it? There was a card last year."

"Yes, you're right."

"Well, I told myself that this time I would call. And here I am ..."

"I'm glad you did."

"If you knew how strange I feel just to hear you after all this time ..."

"Me, too", Ambrogio replied. (It was the truth. He felt an absurd, intense longing, almost like an adolescent's first infatuations.) "We haven't seen each other since the day I graduated, you remember? In other words, back in 1947. That's ... let's see ... twenty-one years ago. Imagine!"

"Exactly, Ambrogio."

Back then, all that time ago, out of loyalty to Fanny, he had promised himself not to see Colomba again. True to his character, he had believed in his own promise and had never broken it.

"How strange you are ...", Colomba said. (Her voice was still young and fresh, making him think of her as she had been. *But that can't be*, he thought.)

"Why do you say that? Is it because I've sprung up after all these years with my card for your birthday? Well, tell me about yourself. How are you? What are you doing? What about your children. There are two, right? They'll be getting on ..."

"Oh, yes, the older, the girl, is engaged to be married. The years go by, dear Ambrogio. The boy is still young. He's at the gymnasium, and . . ." Colomba gave details about her family. Her voice really hadn't changed. Ambrogio felt he could see her suddenly before him as she had been, as a girl with her lithe figure, blue-gray eyes, and handsome Grecian head. "Well, why don't we decide to see each other sometime, I asked myself . . ."

"Ah, yes, I'd be enchanted to see you", agreed Ambrogio.

"We'll be back in Novara at the end of September. Could you come and see us soon after that? And don't let months or even years go by. You have the address."

"Yes," Ambrogio said, "but where did you say you are now? In Alagna?"

"Yes, in Valsesia. I have a villa here, a small wooden cottage, not much, but I've worked hard for it. I bought it after my husband died. For the children, it's ideal."

"Good for you", Ambrogio said, thinking, *Why wait until September? After so many years . . . and we're both mature people. It's true that hearing her voice has moved me, but it's ridiculous to imagine I could now fail in my promise to be faithful to Fanny; I couldn't even think of it.* He said to her, "Let me work this out, Colombina. How long would it take to get to Alagna—two or three hours, I suppose?"

"Yes, something like that. When we come from Novara it takes us just over two hours. Why do you ask? Are you thinking of taking a trip here?"

"Well, perhaps, I don't know . . ."

"Are you serious? What great news, it's like a dream!"

"Tomorrow . . . will you be home? Or maybe you've planned some trip?"

"No, we'll be here. Will you come tomorrow?"

"If I'm invited."

"Of course, but what determination! You're still the same, right? So we'll expect you here tomorrow. No going back on your word now." She sounded surprised and slightly moved. "What time will you arrive?"

"Let's say around four. Does that suit you?"

"Marvelous. This is too good to be true. Look, let me tell you how to find our little cottage. There's a road that leaves Alagna toward . . .", and she started to give him directions.

There came the sound of his secretary's knock on his door, which then opened. Ambrogio covered the phone with his hand and lifted his jaw toward the woman interrogatively.

"The worker's committee is here", she said in a low voice.

"Right, just a minute."

The woman closed the door.

Going back to his call, Ambrogio heard Colomba say, "Well, then I'll see you tomorrow. Now I'll be here waiting, so don't forget." She hung up.

Ambrogio felt surprised at himself. *What on earth am I doing? How far do I want to go? Let's see, it won't be out of spite, coming after Fanny's call?* He could faintly hear a typewriter coming from the other room, and the heat and noise still came through the window. *My life is always the same,* Ambrogio thought. *And the course of my life is cast!* He felt dismay, but immediately brought himself back abruptly, with his usual energy. *Well, but didn't I myself choose this life? And in any case, what else could I do?* He had no more time for reflections. Outside in the other room the worker's representatives were waiting. He reached out for the buzzer . . .

From problem to problem; it'll always be like this. And what for? What were all these questions about? He held his hand, didn't press the buzzer. Tomorrow, without having planned it ahead of time, he'd see Colomba. It was really strange. He shook his head, yet the prospect of seeing her brought back those first feelings of teenage love. *Perhaps I'm attaching more importance to all this than it's worth? And in any case, Colomba's name should have been on the birthday card list some time ago; not just two years ago, but ten or twelve.* But no. Ten years ago it would have seemed to him a disloyalty toward Fanny, particularly as it involved Colomba, toward whom he had felt such a strong attraction before—even more serious in his case, his feelings normally being so constant. Now, thinking it over, what an extraordinary enchantment back there at war's end! She had put a spell on him! It had been his memories of poor Manno, his distaste at the idea of taking his recently dead cousin's girl, that had prevented him from courting her, from telling her he loved her. Then it had seemed like a sort of sacrilege. *What really incredible things we do when we're young!* Well, what was the use of going around in circles about it now? *But remember: then Colomba (Andromache, as Manno called her when talking about her: childish things) was twenty years old, while now she'll be about forty-three or forty-four, not a few of those years having been spent as a widow, working hard to keep house and home together. She also has a daughter about to get married . . . God only knows how she'll look now, the poor thing.* He had an odd feeling of sadness, thinking about how Colomba could have changed since back then. (It was enough to look at Fanny now as compared with years ago.) He felt sympathy, even though in truth her voice on the phone wasn't the voice of a broken woman. *But what sort of nonsense am I imagining? I'm a married man, and . . . well, enough of this fantasizing.*

Finally he pressed the buzzer.

4

But not even on the following day, when he left *I dragoni* for the drive to Alagna, did he rid himself of those foolish adolescent and absurd feelings. What was worse, as he increased speed along the road, these feelings became stronger.

Nomana and its familiar surroundings were soon left behind as he headed west (a direction he didn't often take). He passed fields, villages, and less-known country, which excited him in a sense of living an adventure. Perhaps right now Colomba would be sitting at her mirror getting ready for his arrival (*That's the way it is with women; they regard these things as important*), or maybe she was tidying the living room of the villa. ("Wood-built", she had said. *Poor Colombina. She bought the place with her savings. She graduated in biology; presumably she worked for some chemical or pharmaceutical company, earning a living for herself and her children . . . and even managed to get herself a small villa for their vacations. She's been very brave.*)

He increased his speed, leaving behind the rumbling sound of his crossing the Ticino by the Sesto Calende iron bridge, from which there was a glimpse toward Stresa on the right, toward the lake. (*What sort of condition would that old hotel be in now, the one I stayed at when it was a hospital? Who would be the guests there now?*) Farther in the distance were the mountains where Pino had been with the partisans; these also took his mind back into the past, making him feel young again.

Ambrogio kept an eye on the gas needle, which was slowly moving into the red. *I'll have to stop at the next gas station*, but oddly enough when he saw the first one he went on by without slowing down, and then he also passed by the next, and the one after that. In fact, although he wasn't clearly aware of it—if someone had drawn his attention to it, he would have been very surprised—he didn't manage to make up his mind to interrupt his journey, even for so short a time.

A little over an hour into his trip he started seeing the first signs pointing toward the Valsesia; then he saw a signpost to Alagna, which was still some distance away. At the start the valley was very wide and dotted with villages, appearing to be a continuation of the plain. The car was now traveling faster than was sensible. Going up hills, passing Varallo and a few more gas stations (Ambrogio hardly glanced at these), farther on, a few miles more, and he came to a small isolated gas station, valley walls now rising steeply on either side. Really the sensible thing to do was to stop and fill up with gasoline, but still Ambrogio didn't stop. *At the next one, the next gas station and I'll stop, for sure*, and passed on by. But he didn't get far, because shortly after the motor coughed a couple of times and then stopped. He had no choice but to steer the car over to the right, bringing it to a stop with two wheels up on the grassy bank. *What a mess, what a mess! But what an idiot I've been, how stupid!* The small gas station was over a mile back, and there wasn't a village or any sign of life in sight.

Locking the car, Ambrogio hurried back along the road toward the gas station. He walked fast, but avoided running. *I can't arrive at Alagna in a sweat, like a teenager.* He looked around, seeking anyone who could help. He even tried, embarrassed, to stop one or two of the cars that passed him, without success. There was heavier traffic going the other way, into the valley. *It's Saturday afternoon, that's why. Maybe I'd be better off stopping one of them, and I could be dropped at an auto-club rescue station. Then I can come back . . .* He tried again to stop the next car, then the one behind and a third, but none stopped, so he gave up.

Meanwhile, he hadn't covered more than half a mile, and the gas station was still out of sight. Realizing this, Ambrogio made another, more determined effort to wave down several cars. They all passed without slowing, and finally he sped the last one on its way with a rude gesture. He was immediately surprised at it. *But what the devil am I doing? It isn't as if I had the smallest intention of making . . . well, who knows what with Colomba. I'm just paying a visit to an old friend, that's all.* He repeated the phrase out loud, wagging an admonitory finger at himself. *An old friend. So why am I so excited? It's laughable,* and he laughed out loud, then thought, *I'm talking to myself! I must be mad.*

He stopped gesticulating and tried to behave normally. When he reached the gas station there was no car available to take him back with the gasoline to his car, nor was there a telephone to call Colomba to advise her of his delay. It was already four o'clock, the time he was supposed to arrive in Alagna. In the absence of a can, he carried a bottle of gasoline as he set out to walk back to the car. He had given up the possibility that someone would give him a lift along the way. He couldn't prevent himself from thinking about Colomba, waiting for him. He pictured her as he had last seen her, when she was twenty. He tried to be sensible in his picture of her, adding a bit of gray to her hair, adding girth to her hips, but the picture insisted on remaining that of a young girl.

Above all his thoughts (who could tell what conjectures Colomba would be making about him as she waited), one fixed idea took over. Come what might, he would shortly see her once more. He'd be seeing Colomba! He found it hard to conquer his excitement, and despite himself his nervousness made him walk faster. What the devil was happening to him? He thought, *There are more things in heaven and earth than are dreamt of in our philosophy.* He was unable to account for whatever it was that had taken him over, caught him by surprise . . . When he reached the car, he hurriedly poured the gasoline into the tank, then—with a theatricality foreign to him—threw the empty bottle across the road, where it shattered against a low wall.

It took a while for the gasoline to flow to the motor, but once the engine started, Ambrogio headed for the next gas station and filled his tank, then, *Faster, let's go faster, let's not waste time . . .* He accelerated, still agitated, and sped along the twenty miles that still separated him from Alagna. On at least two occasions he nearly skidded off the road. (*What would they say at home if I ended up in the hospital? Or maybe, if I just smashed the car . . . what sort of double life would people think I'd been living? Lord help me!*) But could he reasonably expect the Lord to help him in these circumstances? Having in any case asked for God's help, he soon found that he was indeed under protection from above. Having gone too fast around a bend where the road needed repairs, the car slid into the middle of the road, cutting in on the central space where one car was passing another. He missed hitting them by yanking the wheel into a sort of zigzag maneuver. Driving away from the incident, Ambrogio experienced a

969

heavy heartbeat. It felt as if someone had punched him in the chest. An accident had been avoided by a sheer miracle! He checked in the rearview mirror and saw that the two cars he'd cut off had stopped and both drivers had left their cars, amazed. God had intervened, but he'd behaved like an animal, putting other people's lives at risk like that and his own as well. After all, he was the head of a family and was also responsible for many people's jobs. Why? Why had he done such a stupid thing? But reflecting on it, he couldn't explain it to himself.

He cut back on his speed. So far clearly God had helped him despite his carelessness. God had (he felt this intimately) shown himself indulgent, merciful. *What could that mean?* he asked himself, trying as usual to grasp the truth of what he had experienced. *Perhaps God wanted to indicate that I should be less rigid than I usually am. Times change, and sensitivity along with it . . . perhaps it was a hint that I should change my ways? Sometimes I feel that it would be my duty to correct the rigid mentality I have inside. God is forbearing. We have a good God, infinitely good toward us, even when we err, that's the truth. I've just experienced it. What right then do I have to consider him above all a God who punishes? That was the way of it during the war, but that was a time for punishment, and . . .* Well, how far did he have to go in changing himself? More than thoughts now, he was having fragments of thought; he decided, as in the past, to leave the question unresolved. Once again his earlier feelings of excitement took over, although he concentrated on maintaining a moderate speed. The road through the valley now went through rocky mountainous stretches, flanked by magnificent fir trees.

Alagna. Before entering the town, Ambrogio stopped the car by a wide grassy patch and changed his shirt (he had carried a spare shirt, one of the things in which Fanny had trained him) and combed his hair. As he resumed his journey he looked at his watch; he was running an hour and a half late.

He went through the town without stopping. The church clock—in a typically Alpine needlelike belltower—confirmed his lateness. Where was the road Colomba had told him about? Was this it? Consulting a young boy, he found it necessary to turn around. In his impatience he had passed the street he sought. Finally he turned into the right street and drove along it slowly until he saw Colomba's villa. On the gateway was a sign bearing her married name.

5

In front of the villa there was a bit of a lawn, with a multicolored umbrella and several lawn chairs. Rising from one of these was Colomba, who took a few steps toward the car. Ambrogio saw her, and his heart started beating strongly. *You miserable . . .* , he thought to himself, as he quickly stopped and opened the car door. *You poor idiot. You're only paying a visit to an old acquaintance, that's all.*

Like a normal civilized person, you're visiting someone. And remember that a woman over forty isn't a young girl of twenty. Understand? Striding from the car to the gate and grasping the rusty handle, almost not looking at the woman, he entered the small garden.

Colomba welcomed him with a happy cry. "Oh, Ambrogio, it's you, you've arrived!" She came to meet him and held her hand out, smiling. "Ambrogio! You know, I'd about given you up? What happened? But first, tell me, how are you? Let me look at you." And then, smiling happily, "You know, you look very well."

So much for reflections or warnings! Colomba was splendid! No less attractive than when she was twenty, although naturally she was not the same person as back then. "You also look very well to me", Ambrogio said. "How do you do it? You're ... you're ...", but he stammered to a stop like a young boy.

Colomba laughed, amused. Her wedding ring flashed on her hand. "Well, tell me, what happened to you?"

"You mean, why am I late, eh?"

Colomba nodded. "Yes, you know, I didn't know whether to wait for you or what."

"I should have phoned you, sorry. But first I couldn't find a phone; my engine stopped in the middle of the country, far from any houses, and it took time to get it going again. After that I didn't stop to phone so as not to waste more time."

"So you had a problem. I'm sorry."

"No, it wasn't serious."

"Thank you for coming. I'm happy you're here."

"Yes", Ambrogio replied. "I'm happy, too."

"After twenty years—twenty-one!"

Ambrogio nodded.

"The children have gone to play tennis with some friends, but they'll soon be back."

They had walked back to the umbrella. "What shall we do? Shall we sit down here, or do you want to see my little chalet first?"

"The house is very pretty", he said politely.

"Oh, it's made of wood, as I told you, very modest."

"In any case, I like it."

"But you've hardly seen it yet", Colomba laughed, her lovely head moving her hair around her face. She still looked like a Grecian carving.

"Well, at least I've seen the outside, right?"

She stood still briefly and looked at the outside of the house. "Yes, from the outside it's not too bad", she agreed. "It looks all right. But come along, and I'll show you the inside."

The chalet consisted of only one level and was built of fir logs supported on a stone base, covered in moss and lichen, which served as a reminder of the hard mountain winters. Next to the house's wall were some wild-looking climbing roses.

The inside was not very comfortable but clean and pretty. It showed good taste and was half villa and half-weekend chalet. In the living room there was a solid-looking stone fireplace with a motto carved on the mantel in Latin: *Nec procul nec adhuc.*

"Where did that saying come from?"

"My father. He suggested it."

"Ah, yes. Tell me about your father. How is he? And how is your mother?"

They exchanged the latest news about mutual friends and acquaintances, about Nomana, about *I dragoni*, the house that had belonged to Eleonora, Colomba's distant aunt.

In a separate room there were trophies in a glass front cabinet. There were about twenty of them.

"What are these for?" Ambrogio asked, surprised. "Who won them, your children?"

"No", Colomba answered. "I won them, most of them, playing tennis. You know, I can still manage to win."

"Ah."

"Do you remember those times we played in Visate? We'd go there by bike. Do you still remember?"

Ambrogio smiled and nodded. "Of course."

"Well, I never stopped playing, even though sometimes it was just to keep busy, to keep in shape." She seemed to be excusing herself, justifying her interest in tennis.

"I understand, and I envy you. I wish I'd done the same."

Her clothes now made sense to Ambrogio. She was wearing a white pleated skirt, belted at the waist. It reminded him of a woman's tennis outfit, although not as short. *So Andromache took up tennis*, he thought. *That's why, despite her widowhood and the passing of years, this glorious creature doesn't get old at all.*

They left the interior of the house and returned to the sunshade out on the lawn. Colomba's delicate feet stepped just as lightly as before (when he was doing his studying in the garden at Nomana). She walked gracefully on the grass, and her figure was as attractive as ever.

"You know something?" Ambrogio couldn't keep it inside. He had adopted a stubborn set to his features, the result of the internal fight with his scruples. "Let me say this before your children return: you're as pretty as ever, Colomba. You've remained a lovely creature."

Her eyes shone with pleasure. "Oh, I'm happy to hear you say that!" she exclaimed happily. "How nice you are, Ambrogio, thank you. The more so because our meeting today, in fact, well . . . for me it was like passing a test, and . . . well, and so I thank you."

"How right Manno was when he used to say that you were a sort of miracle", he went on. "How very right he was!" He shook his head, almost in longing.

Colomba regarded him as if surprised. "But . . . Ambrogio, I remember you as a quiet type, without strong passions. That's how you were always. And surely now, as a businessman you still . . ."

"Are you trying to remind me that I'm the 'chief', eh? Well, perhaps it's just as well you do."

"No, what are you saying? Why would I do that? No, I didn't mean to do that at all. I just observed that you're an industrialist, always have been. You were, even as a youth. It doesn't mean you're one of those businessmen with a pot belly. On the contrary, let me tell you, I've always thought of you as a soldier, you and your cousin", she said, lowering her gaze. "In my eyes, you and he, who didn't return, you were both soldiers."

She went quiet.

Ambrogio thought, *Manno . . . who knows if right now he's watching us, or maybe it no longer means anything to him. Even if he can look down, he doesn't bother.* Without realizing it, he was going back to the thoughts he had had as a young man; he nodded to himself repeatedly.

"Come, let's sit down here. At this time of day it's nice out here", she said.

The strange atmosphere of tension between them was broken when a fifteen-year-old boy came into the garden from the street. He shouted, "Mama, we're back!" Instead of using the gate, he put both hands on the low wall and vaulted over it.

"Giulio, you know I don't like you to do that!" Colomba shouted to him. Behind Giulio came his sister, a pretty twenty-year-old, who came through the gate. They both approached to greet their visitor. While shaking hands, the two youngsters gazed curiously at him. To them Ambrogio was simply the cousin of their mother's first fiancé, a faceless person, remote as the people in their history books. The cousin of a man who, before he died in the war, had written their mother strange letters—which they hadn't read—which referred to the motherland and things of that sort, improbable stuff. The person of Manno was so remote that they never had considered the possibility of having news about him, certainly not as a real person. Once they'd shaken Ambrogio's hand they both sat on the grass before him, shy and a little embarrassed.

They soon relaxed, however, and started talking about everything from school and exams—which, in that year of widespread student protests, weren't to be feared—to the daughter's upcoming marriage. There was no mention of Manno, the conversation turning to Giulio's motorcycle, on which the gearbox was broken and needed replacing. "Which means spending nearly 15,000 lire", the boy said, rubbing his thumb and forefinger together. "In other words I'll have to use the pocket money Mama pays me for a month and a half." His mother made gestures that told him she didn't want to talk about money in the presence of their visitor. He asked himself if maybe this shouldn't be the right time to get to the root of his motorcycle problem. (It wouldn't be the first time that he'd put forward the necessity of buying a new bike. "One of those motorcycles with a license, not an unregistered old wreck like mine . . .") Colomba tried several times to divert the conversation, and for that very reason he kept at it, to the point where Colomba came near to showing her annoyance.

Soon after the part-time maid arrived. She was followed shortly afterward by the daughter's fiancé, a tall youth with glasses, about to graduate. He sat on the grass next to his fiancée and entered into an earnest conversation with their distinguished guest.

Very quickly, it seemed, it was seven o'clock, time for Ambrogio to leave. He didn't feel like cutting the visit short without having had a chance to linger a while longer with Colomba. To talk about what? He didn't know, but he knew he didn't want to leave so soon. Colomba also seemed to indicate that she would rather he stay. "What a pity the problem with your car delayed you so", she said more than once, clearly worried at the possibility of his going.

"Look, there's no sense in my having driven some ninety miles to be here such a short time, don't you think? What would you say if we went out to dinner together?"

"Go out to dinner?" Colomba said. "Oh, what a pity I didn't get anything ready here at home!"

"You weren't to know that I'd be late", Ambrogio said, happy as a child that at least she hadn't turned the idea down out of hand. "Well, in that case, what do you say we do go out to dinner?"

"Out to dinner?" Colomba said again, not accustomed to such invitations. She turned to her daughter as if asking for permission. "What do you say?"

"Mama, if you want to go, why not?"

"In that case, you two come over to my house", the girl's fiancé said quickly to his fiancée and her brother. "Come on, we'll use the barbecue out in the back . . . we'll eat outside together, eh, what do you think?"

The girl was enthusiastic. "Yes, right, I'll make you dinner!" At this show of eagerness Giulio started a sort of red-Indian chant, ululating by tapping his open hand over his mouth.

6

So, when the youngsters had left, Ambrogio and Colomba followed them shortly after, Colomba first having changed her dress. Her daughter had telephoned to book a table at a restaurant outside town that offered a panoramic view of the surrounding country. They reached the place in ten minutes, and the view was impressive from the hilltop location. The area was thick with walnut trees and looked out over the mass of Monte Rosa.

"Why don't we talk to each other for a while before going to our table?" Ambrogio suggested.

"Fine," Colomba agreed, then added, "what should we talk about?" She smiled, although feeling vaguely uneasy.

"About everything, about all that we would like to know about one another. Don't you have questions to ask me?"

"Yes, a few, provided we are both prepared to talk freely, as if at confession." She looked him in the eyes. Once again Ambrogio found himself marveling at her beauty. How long could she go on looking like this? How much longer could this Andromache continue pushing time backward by tenaciously playing tennis? "Let's go", he said. "We can walk along this pathway."

The setting sun bathed everything in red, the pathway along the hillside, the walnut trees, and the fields down below. Colomba unaffectedly took Ambrogio's arm, causing him to wonder if he was in the here-and-now or whether this was all taking place during his student days after the war.

He shook his head as if to bring himself awake. "Would you like to start with your questions?" he proposed.

"If you like", Colomba replied. She was silent for a while, trying to organize her thoughts. "Back then, I mean just after the war when we were young, you liked me quite a lot. It was something I was aware of."

"Yes," Ambrogio confirmed, "although I made every effort not to show it."

"Exactly. That's it. Was it because of the idea ... how can I say ... was it because of the memory of Manno that you didn't say something to me?"

"Yes ... only because of that. It felt to me like sneaking behind his back."

"It wasn't by chance because of ... physical reasons? Back then, I asked myself, you know, if maybe I didn't attract you physically ..."

"How could you have thought that?" exclaimed Ambrogio. "You're very far from the truth." He looked into her eyes. "I won't go any farther, but you were completely wrong if that's what you thought."

Colomba gave a sigh, at the same time showing a perplexed smile.

"Try to think of this", Ambrogio went on. "Haven't you ever asked yourself why you haven't heard from me until now, or rather, last year, when I wrote? For twenty years I've scrupulously kept away from you."

"Really, to be quite truthful, I have to say that it baffled me completely", Colomba answered.

"Well, that's it. We're no longer children, so I can say this. It was because you attracted me too much. That's why I stayed away from you. It wouldn't have been loyal to my wife. I would otherwise have put myself in danger of betraying my wife, even if only in my thoughts."

Colomba half turned to look directly at him, her beautiful face calm and her eyes wide. "I understand. And I believe you. It's your way. It's the kind of thing you'd do."

"It was even worse after you were widowed", Ambrogio went on. "I thought it must have been very hard for you in an emotional sense, let's say, and I didn't want to expose you unnecessarily to temptation."

"It was really very difficult. I was accustomed to enjoying normal physical relations, if that's what you mean. I missed that love terribly at first. It was hard to maintain my loyalty to my departed husband's memory." Colomba nodded, as if agreeing with herself. "Also, perhaps you've some idea of how many men at work tried . . . that's to say, offered to . . . give me comfort. It really hasn't been easy, but with God's help I managed. I never gave in."

"You've been very strong", Ambrogio said, moved by her words.

They continued walking arm in arm, silently.

"So, last year," she resumed, "you thought that with the passing of twenty years we both would have matured enough. It was then that you sent me that birthday card."

"That was more or less it, yes."

"And do you feel totally free from temptation now?"

Ambrogio shook his head. "No. I have to confess it", he said frankly.

"Look, Ambrogio, may I ask you what you feel right now, this instant? You needn't answer if . . ."

"Why wouldn't I? Starting tomorrow I'll have to go back to being silent again for a number of years, but now, here . . . we're no longer adolescents. I don't want to hide anything from you . . ." He paused. "Well, you want to know how I feel inside? To start with, I feel extraordinarily mixed up. While I was on my way here—shall I tell you?—I behaved like a young boy, or better yet, like someone crazy."

"But . . . Ambrogio, what do you mean?"

"It was as if I'd gone off my head, and I still don't understand what happened." He told her how, due to his reluctance to stop, he'd let the car run out of gas, hadn't filled up when he could have done so. It hadn't been a mechanical problem that had delayed him, as he'd earlier led her to believe. He told her of how he'd stupidly cut off those two cars on that bad stretch of road, how he'd risked skidding into the ditch. "I don't understand what took hold of me, because on the outside I feel—and felt at the time—quite normal. That's the funny thing. I don't even know if maybe I'm mistaken in telling you all this. I wouldn't want—forgive my presumption—I wouldn't want to . . . provoke feelings in you that . . . well, I wouldn't want to cause you problems."

"No, don't worry about it", Colomba said almost wearily.

"There's more, as long as I'm confessing everything. Yesterday, after I'd spoken to you on the phone, I had the feeling that I'd played all of my life's cards badly. And yet it's not as if I've wasted my life. I've always done what I saw to be my duty. In my own small circle I've been useful to others. My workers, for example, and their families, even though now it's fashionable to say that one has been hard in business."

"Of course," Colomba said with conviction, "but if things are as you say they are, I have to believe that from tomorrow you'll truly go back to your silence."

"What else could we do? You see it also."

"Well, we could simply decide to remain loyal: you to your wife and I to the memory of my husband, and then, also, friendship is a good feeling . . . and besides, we're mature people. We have grown children of our own."

"I don't know what you feel," Ambrogio said, "but for me it is as if tonight those twenty years had disappeared. I feel as if I've gone back to my youth. This very moment being with you is like being alive twenty years ago."

Colomba shook her head, then reached out and caressed him on the cheek.

"Look, perhaps it's the same with you?" Ambrogio asked.

"Perhaps. Yes, a little."

"You see!" he exclaimed.

Having slowly walked around the path under the walnut trees—the sun-bathed trunks the color of blood—and back the other way, they found themselves back at the restaurant. Ambrogio said decidedly, "Come on, let's go inside."

They went in and sat at their reserved table and started their dinner, but although they tried to talk normally, as they would have liked and as the circumstances called for, they didn't succeed.

Then, by coincidence, a family known to Colomba sat at a nearby table, and Ambrogio finally asserted himself, going into scrupulous detail about his boys' good school marks and about their activities, including the fact that one, the oldest, was named after Manno, while the other had Fanny's late father's name. He talked about his brother-in-law Michele, the writer, who was now involved in a widespread debate about divorce in Italy, held to be a turning point of an era in history. He reminded her of his house, *I dragoni*, including the not very interesting subject of the high cost of house maintenance. When Colomba asked him if this year the swallows had once again built their nest in the porch, he had to admit that he didn't know. "I don't really notice the birds. It was Manno who . . . well, in any case, I'll check and let you know, right?"

Colomba spoke about her own children and about her daughter's upcoming marriage, about the problems involved in planning the wedding. She spoke of her own work—and about tennis.

When supper was over Ambrogio took Colomba back to her house. It had become dark, night already, and the cool clear sky was full of stars. On the ride homeward Colomba was silent. Ambrogio half turned to her and thought that her eyes—so beautiful—were even more beautiful. Finally he realized she was crying.

An almost overwhelming temptation came to him. Simply not to stop, to take her with him somewhere. In a flash several things passed through his mind: the tales he'd heard and read, of the relative unimportance with which the things of the flesh were now regarded, even in Catholic circles. There were priests who practically approved of premarital sexual relations. Why not, in that case, relations outside of marriage? There were many women, he'd heard, serious Catholic women, who on finding out about the "new ethics" had acted as if they'd repented their former stubborn religiosity and thrown all to the winds in an attempt to make up for lost time. Besides, hadn't God himself shown (even right here, today) that he understood Ambrogio's state of mind by helping him survive those crazy moments on his drive over? Right, God! But one couldn't take him lightly. Let the new priests say what they liked: "But I say unto you, if you look at a woman with desire you already commit a sin with her." Well, "I say unto you" was something quite different from the chatter of the latest fashionable theologians, who'd say that "as long as love is there" it is justification for everything. Then one had only to think of old Father Mario, now chaplain at the Monza hospital, and of Father Carlo Gnocchi when he was still alive, and of the true priests, all of whom spoke the same word as two thousand years ago. They were the spokesmen of God and not the permissive priests of today.

He stopped the car at the villa, and they both got out. There were no lights showing at the windows, so Colomba's children must still be out. He took her hand, bringing it to his lips, and kissed it. Colomba continued weeping in silence, not sobbing. Who knew, since she was widowed, how many times she had wept like this. Ambrogio pressed his lips to the back of her hand several times, then left her and drove off.

His return journey was not as eventful as his outward trip had been. It was quiet and tranquil on the surface, but for Ambrogio there were moments of near desolation. Of course the evening could not have ended in any other way than it did. Would he have let his Fanny give herself to another man? The prospect seemed intolerable to him; man cannot live like animals; that was obvious. And the new morality simply wasn't a morality at all. There remained his suffering and, even more, her grief and their destiny—and there remained the great unanswered questions: why, back then when it was possible, didn't they decide to stay together, when their mutual attraction was so strong that it still returned with just as much power as twenty years ago? What was more, why had Manno, who had fallen in love with Colomba before he had, been taken away? These two turning points had completely changed her life. Why had these events come about? He couldn't come up with an answer.

Every now and then he'd say to himself, *Andromache took up tennis*, and, as compared with before, there seemed to him to be something poignant about this fact. This young woman—who had seen her emotional life cut short (and

978

not just once) had not been intimidated. On the contrary, she had made a wager with her own destiny. She didn't intend to let herself go, to decline. And she battled on admirably, almost surprisingly, but how long could she last? What was a woman's strength when compared to the force of time, which turns everything to dust? Thinking about this unequal comparison, Ambrogio was overcome by an anguished sense of inanity. He was far from realizing that his disturbed state of today and the previous day, that adolescent manner in which he'd behaved, was a rebellion against the beginning of his own decline, against the long process of decay, into which each of us, while there is still life, must expect to fall. He was also unaware that not a few people his age had gone or were going through similar inexplicable experiences, of which normally most were ashamed to speak.

After he had reached home and gone to bed, he didn't manage to sleep. He kept turning and had to fight off fantasies about what might have happened if these waking hours had been spent instead with Colomba. Imperfect Christian that he was—as all Christians are—he tried to help himself through prayer and also by imagining the pain and stunned disapproval of his children, particularly his oldest, who was so severe and tenacious in his views. When the time to get up finally came, he rose without having slept for even a minute, an experience he'd not gone through since his war service.

PART SEVEN

I

It was early evening, six years later.

Ambrogio's two sons, Manno and Filippo (called Popi), were driving out of Milan in a Fiat 127, heading for Nomana. The younger, Popi, twenty years old, with dark eyes and hair, an extrovert, whistled as he drove. Manno, twenty-one, with blond hair and blue eyes (like his grandfather Gerardo and his late *zio* Manno), was quiet and serious. It was starting to get dark. In the *viale* Fulvio Testi—the new multilane *superstrada* leaving Milan toward the north—there was the usual heavy traffic. "And yet this evening, at least it's moving well," observed Popi, "because the rush hour is already over. On the other hand, you remember what a mess, yesterday ..."

Manno nodded.

"Listen," Popi continued, "we have to remember: when we can't leave Milan before six, we'll be better off waiting until seven, when the worst of the traffic has gone, eh?"

It was the sort of comment that Popi constantly threw out. He looked over at his older brother, who again nodded absently.

"Besides, even though class is over at the university by five, we won't have a chance of leaving Milan before six, certainly not while the referendum campaign is on, don't forget. Not that *zio* Michele would let us forget the campaign."

Again Manno didn't answer; Popi laughed alone. Uncle Michele, the writer and member of a committee of militant Catholics ("reactionary" in the opinion of many lay people), had promoted the idea of a referendum against legalizing divorce. As the day to vote approached Uncle Michele took no rest and allowed none to his nephews, especially Manno, who like his uncle was a confirmed enemy of divorce. That very day, for example, the uncle had asked Manno to deliver an article to a magazine's editorial office, to collect some brochures at the Christian Democratic party headquarters and also some newspapers from somewhere else, which the uncle would take with him to the Valtellina the next day. Their uncle didn't ever rest, Popi thought. Poor man, he's been working for years on a big book, without any assurance that it would be accepted for publication, now that the Reds and atheists influenced the selection of books in almost every publishing house. Despite this, Uncle Michele didn't rest and now, in the battle against divorce, didn't give any rest to others, at least those who paid him heed, like Manno.

Popi shrugged and went back to whistling. The traffic was moving without serious bottlenecks. Each red traffic light at major junctions collected some thirty or forty cars. There were none of the jams caused by furiously impatient drivers ("Italians at war", as they were called) normally seen at rush hours. Yet despite all this, it wasn't free-flowing traffic.

"Milan's traffic will never flow smoothly", Popi declared, speaking his thoughts out loud. "Listen, do you remember that rainy day in February when there was a sudden general strike? What a mess! And it even happened last year, too. All it takes is for all the cars—not even all the cars—to travel together, and the city becomes blocked, paralyzed. What a joke!"

Manno remained silent. The Fiat 127 was gaining ground on the line in which it had been when it had stopped for the last red light. Driving skillfully, Popi tried to reach the head of the line. "Luckily this year they've doubled the price of gas", he continued, undaunted by his brother's silence. "By charging higher prices the Arabs are putting some order in our traffic . . . those thieves."

Having passed several cars—even a Millecento: although no longer manufactured, they could still be seen—the 127 reached the head of the line. Only another 127 had kept pace with them. It was driven by a young man with fashionably long hair, which the two brothers noticed because they kept their hair traditionally short.

Immediately taking up an imagined challenge, short-haired Popi started racing the other 127's long-haired driver. The 127, Popi thought, then repeated the slogan that had been widely used to sell the model: "The 127, a new way of traveling by automobile". "There's no denying it", he said, still talking to himself. "You see how it goes? With only 900 cubic centimeters under the hood, here we are, leaving the rest of the world behind. It can't be denied!"

Up ahead the traffic lights turned red. They had to slow down from eighty mph to seventy, sixty. Their speed diminished, and so did the Millecento's, which was now beside them. Finally they had to stop for the light.

Popi sighed deeply, then turned to his brother. "Give up! Stop worrying about it!" he exclaimed. "Are you still brooding? You're behaving like an idiot. Why should you worry about whether or not classes are held? You should know by now that in the architecture school there's always a mess, so leave it alone. Wasn't it the same last year?"

"Don't be so fast to laugh about it", Manno growled softly. "At the *Cattolica* at least, both in good times and bad, everything gets done. You should try to do any serious studying surrounded by so much racket."

"Oh, don't worry, we also have problems . . . the days when Gemellone had prayers day and night in the chapel have gone. Now the Reds have their own meeting place, where the walls are covered by posters showing Ho Chi Minh, along with pornographic photos. What do you think?"

Manno shook his blond head and puffed out his cheeks, as if to say, "Don't be ridiculous trying to compare your conditions with ours." In fact, the cause of his bad mood wasn't so much the constant disorder at the architecture school. What bothered him were some of the things he'd seen and heard a few hours earlier, when he'd gone to get brochures at the headquarters of the Christian Democrats. On arrival he'd been received with bad manners and poor grace and had found out that most Milanese Christian Democrats (for some years now part of an opportunist group run by an oil magnate who tried to influence the party's policies) were very annoyed with the divorce referendum committee, which pushed them into open confrontation with the established left. Under these conditions, how could they win in Milan? To make things worse, he'd learned that one of the section chiefs who had been particularly rude to him had been given a nickname that inferred that he was in collusion with big business, acting as a collector of money to finance these same businessmen.

An old fellow in charge of handing out brochures had been the one to tell him about it, apparently to brighten his outlook. "It's really not the way it used to be . . .", he'd said bitterly, shaking his head. Manno couldn't now stop thinking about it. As a counterpoint there came to mind the bookkeeper with the beret and his assistants, all volunteers, about whom his father and Uncle Michele sometimes talked. How could things have reached the stage at which they were today? But he preferred not to discuss this with his brother, who in any case was already critical enough of the Christian Democrats.

Popi didn't take his eyes off the traffic light, and as soon as it turned green he drove off at great speed. Sadly for him, the long-haired driver of the other 127 didn't do the same, calmly making the turnoff to the right, toward Sesto San Giovanni, so that his own rubber-burning start was completely unnecessary.

The major highway going through Milan's industrial northern zone nowadays went past few open fields. Everywhere buildings had been put up, great extensions of housing belonging to one or another municipality. At the Monza turnoff, where the traffic was always heavy, the walls were covered with advertisements and large slogans aimed at inattentive drivers: "Remember that God loves you, remember that God loves you." This was a reminder that they'd reached Brianza. Without paying attention Popi (who had moderated his speed once his race with the longhair was over) resumed his whistling, then said, "So much for the architecture school."

Manno shook his head. "You people at the *Cattolica* should give thanks to poor Apollonio", he said. "Because even over there at the *Cattolica* things are very serious, even worse than at the state university. But Apollonio had backbone enough to expel that female professor, what's-her-name, the one who went to write for the extreme left-wing people, *Manifesto*; from then on the *Cattolica* went back to normal. As the head of the faculty, Apollonio had the power to expel her, so he did so. I once heard him talk about it during dinner at Uncle Michele's. He said everyone at the *Cattolica* was intimidated. What'll happen now, they were all asking; this woman extremist has her rabid followers both inside and outside the university. But he just stood firm and did what he thought was right. And so the rector took heart and soon after got rid of the ten or fifteen worst student troublemakers. In fact there were scarcely twenty of them out of twenty thousand students, but it was enough. Getting rid of them restored order."

"Yes, I know. But it's like a fireplace; under the dead ashes there are still coals glowing", Popi replied.

"But in the meantime your professors can give lectures every day, and when examinations come due, you'll be able to take them calmly. At architecture, on the other hand, we go for months without any real classes, and the professors either go along and talk about revolution, communism, all that drivel, or they have to leave. If just one of them goes into class to talk sensibly about serious things, he's finished. Do you know that just this morning some students were using Professor X for target practice? 'Jump to the right', they'd shout and throw a wooden protractor aimed at his head, forcing him to duck, then 'Go to the left again', and they'd throw something else. He ended up unnerved. Inevitably the professors who are worthwhile, who don't want to give in, don't give lectures any more. I just don't know how it'll all end."

"It'll end up with the Christian Democratic minister for education throwing all the serious professors out of the university, you'll see." Popi was chuckling. "That's how it'll end up."

"The problem is that at our school we didn't have an Apollonio to deal with things at the start", said Manno, puffing out his cheeks. "Unfortunately. Poor Apollonio, what a man he was!" There came to Manno's mind a disconsolate phrase about the weakened state of the Catholic world that Apollonio had written just before his death. "When he died two years ago, I saw Uncle Michele cry like a baby. It was the first and only time I saw him cry", he murmured.

"You'll see him cry one more time when the referendum results are announced", said Popi, half jokingly.

"That's a stupid thing to say", his brother said, but without heat. "God willing, Italy isn't yet composed of spineless weaklings. This time we won't lose. In fact, this is exactly the time to . . ." He stopped and nodded energetically.

"Uncle Michele and you work like donkeys for this referendum, and meantime—you've seen them—there are even priests who suck up to 'the people' by saying it's all right to vote in favor of divorce. The way things are now at the Catholic University, the people in favor of divorce make all the speeches they like, while the people against divorce, like you, aren't allowed to speak. And this in the Catholic University!"

Manno nodded in agreement, a defiant look on his face. "Judas, swine, and superswine have always been with us," he said, "yet Christianity keeps on going, the same as it has for two thousand years."

Popi decided to quit joking. When you had a brother as serious as this, it wasn't any fun trying to get a rise out of him. He switched on his low beams. In the half light of dusk there were already little bonfires along the side of the highway—in this stretch it was down to four lanes—their smoke and warm orange light advertising the presence and availability of the roadside prostitutes.

"Here they are again", Popi said. "Tonight again, the p's." He pronounced only the first letter of the word. Despite the modern customs and widespread foul language at the universities and among young people in general, the two brothers—particularly when speaking to each other—tended to use no off-color terms.

Manno glanced at the roadside fires, kept burning with old auto tires. In the smoky half light of each fire there were one, two, or more prostitutes, most wearing miniskirts that barely covered the crotch. (The miniskirt had come from across the other side of the Alps some years before, and the fashion had taken hold nationwide. Then they'd gone out of fashion, but had been adopted by whores, who dressed in them as an announcement and convenience in their profession.) Around some of the fires, apart from women, there would be the odd man in parley with them. These men's autos parked by the curb blocked the free flow of traffic.

"We have the Socialists to thank for this", Manno observed. "Since they entered into government they've turned our roadsides into whorehouses."

"But it was your Christian Democrats who took them into the government", Popi commented. In his disgust for all of Italy's political parties, he didn't consider himself a part of any of them. (According to his "committed" companions—committed to what?—he was a *qualunquista*, a type of nonpartisan populist.)

"Not all of our people wanted them in", Manno objected, wounded by the accusation. "People like Uncle Michele and our father, in other words the majority of our people—they didn't want them, and you know it."

"But what else could they do if they hadn't enough votes to run a government? Besides, with respect to the Socialists, they had even the Pope and Kennedy and all the other lot against them", Popi said. "Yes, and don't tell me again how Uncle Michele had predicted from the beginning that things would end up in this mire, and that he even wrote about it. I know that, but so what? The fact is nobody paid him any mind, and now we're all up to our necks in it."

"Well, the time has arrived when we can pull ourselves out of this sh—— we're in", Manno said. "That's just exactly what Gabrio Lombardi is aiming at. And this time we'll get out of it, you'll see."

Showing good judgment, neither of them had been looking at the roadside sinners in order not to fall into temptation, as they'd learned from the Lord's Prayer. In fact, neither of them had yet been with a woman. The family's traditions held out against the social pressures.

Abreast of Incastigo the highway bore off to the right into a secondary road—also newly built and lined with poplars—which led to the old bridge over the Lambro. Here, at the turn, was a last bonfire, right next to the spot where the

127 stopped at a traffic light. Here a prostitute was talking to a youth who couldn't have been more than fourteen, who had presumably just made a jesting proposition. The whore reacted by chasing after him, wielding her handbag like a club, pursuing him outside the circle of firelight. A dirty-looking truck driver with checkered trousers was standing nearby laughing and seemed to be calling to the woman, interceding for the boy.

"You've just seen . . .", declaimed Popi, imitating the television announcers; they didn't see any more, as the light turned green and they drove off on the road to the bridge. "Pretty revolting, eh?"

"Yes, revolting", murmured Manno. Then he thought that this sort of spectacle with prostitutes was shoved daily under their noses. It was enough to cause the fall of God knows how many boys from the Brianza area. "It's just as well that one doesn't see spectacles like this in Nomana."

"Poor Italy!" Popi sighed. "Add to what we've just seen the kidnappers, thieves, and delinquents all over the place. Meanwhile the Reds try to tie the hands of the police even more, and the government does everything except govern. It's not just the universities. All of Italy is falling apart."

"Right. And that's just why they have to be opposed. Why we have to make every effort to spoil their plans."

"Using what? Your referendum?"

"Haven't you noticed that all the people who are dragging the country down are in favor of divorce? Well, if we manage to give them one big crack on the head, make them see that they're just a minority, maybe there'll be a reversal."

"The advertising and propaganda they put out in favor of divorce are ten times as great as what you're doing", Popi said. "Almost all the banners in Milan are theirs, and for every one of your posters they have eight or ten. To say nothing of the newspapers."

"Of course, the middle class and their Red allies have more resources than we do." Manno stopped and shook his head. "Naturally . . . I don't know whether to laugh or cry, to see the middle class mixed up with the Reds and looking enthusiastic about it!"

"I don't understand how you can seriously think about winning under these circumstances", said Popi.

The 127 crossed the twin arches of the bridge over the deep bed of the Lambro, a river that over the years had been turned into an open sewer by indiscriminate dumping. (Gone from the river were the green weeds that used to wave in the current. The brilliant golden jumping fish had also disappeared. Now, according to the newspaper articles, all that lived in these waters were the bacilli and bacteria coming from the sewers, which were themselves, in a sense, symbolic.) Past the bridge the road climbed wooded hills where locust trees still flourished, seeming to add to the evening's coolness.

Raperio, a small village forming part of Nomana: here was where Praga's Communists at the war's end had captured that unhappy woman hiding in the piazza's haberdashery. The two youths passed by, unaware of the episode. Just like Incastigo, Nomana, or any other town in Lombardy, Raperio had doubled in size even if not in the population of the town center. The newly constructed houses had multiplied around the periphery of the heart of the village. They were incomparably richer and more comfortable than the old houses, but built, as had happened elsewhere, with a surprising lack of planning. Although following a general line, houses faced in different directions, some at higher levels than others. There were different colors and styles, an extravagant jumble. The overall effect was to ruin a previously beautiful landscape.

At this time of day darkness hid much of this, and in any case the two brothers had barely known the earlier landscape, in which nature and man had created a comfortable harmony. The thought of dinner being prepared gave them an appetite. The 127 quickly went through the new area south of Nomana, consisting of a few streets built with villas and large apartment blocks, some nearly tall enough to be called skyscrapers (via Father Gnocchi, via Kennedy, via Manno Riva, all flowing into the piazzetta Quinto Alpini). The car climbed the older via Santa Caterina, cobblestone now replaced by asphalt. They stopped in front of the gate to *I dragoni*. Popi opened his driver's side door and said, "How about you going to see Uncle Michele, eh, and take him the brochures?"

"Yes, all right."

Popi pushed the door open and got out of the car.

2

Manno swung his long legs (like his brother and many of his generation, he was tall and athletic) over the gear lever, slid into the 127's driver seat, and promptly drove off. He went through the town's center, noisy with cars and motorcycles at this time of evening. Here and there on the old walls could be seen slogans painted with spray cans (replacing the chalk used years ago): "Long live the class of '54. Our class is gone, so weep and wail, now all the sluts will take the veil." Undeniably, in this secularized atmosphere, the recruits had lost their verbal inhibitions.

In front of Sansone's courtyard he had to stop at a red light. Manno glanced into the courtyard framed by the arch bearing the inscription "A.D. 1777"; in place of the hay carts of days gone by, the courtyard was full of parked cars (some families had more than one), some under the arches and others in the former stable or in the chickenhouses, now walled with corrugated iron. Up ahead the piazza was patrolled by an urban guard (Nomana now had three of these guards, equipped with the same black uniform used by the Milan guards; they all carried two-way radios), and Manno had to reduce his speed to walking pace due to the crowds heading for the church. *Of course, we're in May*, he recalled, *and there'll be Benediction*. Still thinking, he told himself, *But until the twelfth I won't be able to attend the evening Mass.* (The twelfth was the day set for the general referendum.) He then passed by the Piper Bar (the "scientist's" bar, as the locals called it), usually frequented by the town's intellectuals. He glimpsed some activists, people his own age, so busy these days with the prodivorce campaign. "Sh——faces", he muttered.

The garden gates at his uncle's were open (it was years since there had been a gateman), and he drove in, announcing his arrival with the car's horn. Next to the house was his uncle's Alfa Romero 1300, with a door open and the interior lights on. "Well, it looks like Uncle Michele is about to go somewhere, most likely to make a speech."

He met his uncle in the lobby, about to leave. "Oh, Manno, how are you? I have to speak shortly in Lomazzo, so I should hurry. Have you brought me everything?"

Manno nodded toward the armful of brochures and newspapers he was bringing inside, the material he'd collected in Milan. In the lobby with his uncle were his Aunt Alma and Luca. Despite his protests, Luca took the material from Manno and went over to put it on a desktop, alongside other propaganda material.

"Our Manno!" said the smiling uncle. "Here's a real 'son of the law'." This literal translation into colloquial Italian from the dialect not only meant "legitimate son", referring to bloodline, but also inferred "man of good habits". "I've made you work today, eh? Sorry. Well, within ten days all this will be over." His tone became grave. "No, not ten days, nine days. So few, really so little time. There's little we can do in nine days."

"Uncle, I read the article you had me take to the office of *Studi Cattolici* magazine", said his nephew. "It's simply tremendous. It hits the bull's-eye. I think it'll be very successful."

Michele waved negatively with one hand. He wanted to explain that the people who would vote for divorce didn't read *Studi Cattolici*. Aunt Alma, on the other hand, smiled her thanks to her nephew. She was busy brushing her husband's jacket. Manno noticed the gratitude in his aunt's smile. *How she loves him*, he thought. *It's incredible! I wish the Lord would give me a woman who loved me as much. A woman like that I'd love the same way, for all my life—more, for all eternity.* It wasn't the first time he'd had the thought.

"Is the jacket all right? I wouldn't want to make people wait", Michele told his wife; then, turning to Luca, "As far as what we talked about, I agree. Don't forget those packages of brochures", he pointed. "They need to be distributed. Then the proof of the poster needs to go to the printer, Corbetta, before tomorrow afternoon. What are you planning? Will you have someone take them or do it yourself?"

Luca replied, "It'd be better if I took them myself."

"Right. Tell him the two lines about the aims of the conference, where it says 'Referendum—a decision for civilization', should be emphasized. Tell him to make the letters three to four inches tall. No, at least four."

Aunt Alma helped her husband into the freshly brushed jacket. "It's as if you thought Luca didn't know what to do", she commented.

"No, it's just as well to remind me", said Luca.

Michele smiled. "I'm well aware how valuable Luca is. He was in the Fifth."

"What Fifth?" asked Manno.

"The Fifth Alpines, right?" Aunt Alma said. "Don't go thinking your uncle can talk about anything else when he and Luca are together. Fifth Battalion, or Fifth, something like that."

"Fifth Regiment", Michele said. "You see how you don't know? That means I don't speak enough about the Alpines. In other words, starting tomorrow we'll talk more of it, eh, Luca?"

Luca laughed, his honest face lighting up, the lock of hair resting on his forehead now thinner and grayer. "Eh, the Alpines", he murmured and made a vague gesture, as if referring to a reality now gone, lost.

"Come, I have to hurry", Michele said. "If not, I'll arrive late, and the people in Lomazzo will complain." He turned to Manno. "Do you need a ride home?"

"No thanks, Uncle, I have my car outside."

"Oh, of course. In that case, listen. In Milan tomorrow you should call at committee headquarters in the via San Marco. Ask for the secretary, and they'll give you three or four typed articles written by volunteer helpers. I want to see them before they go into print. All right?"

"Right, Uncle."

"And once the referendum is behind us, we'll put up a small statue for you."

Manno replied, "It's for you they should erect a statue, a monument."

Smiling, Michele wagged his head, "Well, goodbye." He held out his hand for Luca to shake. "Goodbye, Fifth Alpine", he said, looking sideways at his wife. Turning again to Manno, he said, "In practice, the committee here in Nomana *is* Luca. He does everything."

"Yes, that's the truth, I'm sure", Manno agreed.

"Go on, we'll be all right. There are others working, too", Luca protested, shyly.

"Well, you're doing a great job as always", Michele said, turning toward the doorway. But at that moment they heard his father-in-law's voice coming from the dining room, calling to him. Michele turned again and went toward the dining room door. "Papa, I'm running late. I have to go." Both Gerardo and Giulia could be seen dimly by the light of the television screen.

"Just a moment before you go. Listen!" Gerardo said excitedly. "They're talking about you. Didn't you hear? They've just mentioned your name."

Michele went farther into the room, followed by Alma and the other two. On the screen a commentator was saying, "And in his opinion the rights of the dissenting spouse are infringed by the law, assuming that spouse objects to the divorce. The writer Michele Tintori" (it wasn't the first time during the referendum campaign that Michele had been referred to) "has concluded asserting that the rights of the children to an integral family are also affected by the divorce law." The commentator didn't pause. "On the other hand, the Honorable Such-and-Such, speaking for the Liberal party, has made a case for defending the law, saying that divorce ..."

"Well, my part received a mention, so I'd better go", Michele said happily. "Otherwise I'll really be late."

"When was it that you said those things?" asked Giulia. Like most older people with time on their hands, she wanted to prolong the exchange.

"It'll be part of the written material sent out to the media by the party secretariat or from our committee, something I wrote in my office. Mama, I'll tell you about it tomorrow. Now I have to go. Good night. Good night to you too, Papa", and he left.

His wife, Alma, followed him. "How really important you are, Michele, mine, how brave!" she joked affectionately.

"For sure, for sure", Michele went along with the joke. "Perhaps we'd better not think how important I am, or else I'll end up being impressed myself. Well, goodbye", and putting his arms around her, he pulled her tight and kissed that still-handsome statue's face.

Manno noticed the eagerness in his uncle's face and his aunt's happiness. *What great love they have for each other!* he thought.

"*Ciao*, son of the law", the uncle said to Manno with a smile. Then, followed by Luca carrying the packages of brochures under both arms, he went out.

But the others, including Alma's parents, followed them outside and stood by the car as he started it up. "Just a moment", Alma called to him. "Did you remember to take the key to the garden gate?"

Michele rolled down the window. "Eh, what?"

His wife repeated the question. Michele gestured yes, smiling, and drove off, scattering gravel as he left the garden.

The two older Rivas turned to go back inside with Almina. Giulia said, "I'm happy that finally they've mentioned Michele on television. It was time he was recognized."

Manno was aware that the mention on television wasn't recognition. They mentioned Michele because they had a duty to read out statements made by the committee and by the various parties. He also knew (as his uncle had told him) that as soon as the referendum was over, they wouldn't continue mentioning his name. But he said nothing of this to his grandparents. He offered Luca a ride. "It's no problem. I'm happy to take you."

"No, really, thank you, but I have my own car parked out in the street", Luca told him.

"Well, in that case, please say hello to my colleague, your son Tarcisio."

"Thank you, I'll do that."

989

"I saw him in Milan yesterday at a CL meeting. He knows, doesn't he, that insofar as we can we're also fighting against this divorce law?" (CL, Communion and Liberation, was a young Christian's association to which people were turning, now that Catholic Action seemed increasingly paralyzed.)

Luca nodded cordially. Manno got in his 127 and drove off.

3

Leaving the garden, Luca placed the packages of brochures on the rear seat of his car (a Millecento still in good condition; like many working men from Brianza, he had a small crucifix hanging from his rearview mirror) and sat at the wheel.

He went first to the printer Corbetta's house. Like Luca himself, Corbetta was an old Christian Democrat activist, so he felt easy about bothering him at any time of the night or day. As he opened the car's door in front of the printer and stationery shop, he nearly knocked down Farirö, who was coming down the narrow sidewalk. Farirö was the metalworker who had opened the carabineri barracks for the partisans in times gone by. Jumping from the car, Luca apologized for the near collision, and they exchanged a joke about the incident. (For some years now Farirö had been walking around in clean clothes, in contrast with his rusty work clothing, because his son had become a successful industrialist—an important one, even—but for all that the metalworker hadn't changed his style. Among other things, he still lit a match by striking it across the rear end of his trousers, especially since nowadays his trousers were made from excellent pure wool.)

Behind Farirö, striding down the narrow sidewalk, came Pierello and his young daughter. He had on a peaked cap and carried his lunch bag. He must have been coming from the train, Luca thought (Pierello still worked at the iron foundry in Sesto); but if that was so, why would his daughter be with him?

"*Ciao*, Piero", he greeted him.

Pierello replied dryly, "*Ciao.*"

"Always working, eh?"

Pierello made no reply. He looked very dejected, Luca thought.

"Listen, is something the matter?"

Piero shook his head negatively and continued walking past.

Luca felt perplexed. *What the devil could have happened to him?*

Having delivered the poster proofs to the printer and spent a half hour with him (Corbetta, a great talker, wouldn't let him go), Luca reached home. No longer living in Catafame (although his parents had remained there, renting out the space left empty—even the bird loft—to some migrant workers from down south), he now lived in Nomana in an apartment block in the new part of town. Like many workmen of his age—like Pierello, for example, who lived nearby—he owned a pretty apartment with four rooms and central heating, with furniture comparable in comfort to those at the Riva house. His twenty-one-year-old son, Tarcisio, came to open the door. He was an architecture student, and when he saw his father's burden, relieved him of the packages. "Do you want me to take them to party headquarters, Papa?"

"No, let's go there together after dinner."

"Good, all right, Papa." They both spoke in dialect.

"Your friend Manno sends his regards. I just saw him a while ago."

"Ah, thank you."

He was a good son, Tarcisio, Luca thought. Another "son of the law", the same as Manno, despite that hellhole of a school they both attended in Milan. Luca thought that he couldn't complain about his four other children either. Not one of them had gone astray. He knew that this made him a fortunate man, because things weren't really going so smoothly for other working-class parents, many of whom had argumentative children who answered back cheekily and drove them out of their minds. And in Nomana recently, even drugs had been seen.

"Oh, listen. That boy your age, what's-his-name, Taddeo, Pierello and Luisina's son, who was studying for the priesthood, has he been up to any of his tricks today?"

"Ah, you've already heard? Did one of the Rivas tell you?"

"No, but I saw his father, and he looked very worried."

"I can well believe it. This afternoon the carabinieri called him down to their barracks again. It's probably because of the auto he set on fire in Milan."

"He set fire to a car? Oh, yes, I remember, you already told me about it."

"During a demonstration about Vietnam."

"Yes, right. But what a wrongheaded kid! Whatever did his father do wrong to deserve a boy like that?"

4

At that moment Pierello was at home eating dinner, a dinner that was making him gag. Every now and then he shook his head in disgust (although over fifty, his light brown hair still matched the color of his eyes, having hardly any gray in it). Also sitting at the table were his wife, Luisina, and his two younger daughters. They sat at the kitchen table, as the family never ate at the dining room table, which was kept polished like a mirror.

The three women spoke almost not at all in the face of Pierello's obvious displeasure. From time to time his wife—now aging, but still retaining the charm that had once conquered Pierello—would rise from the table to fetch something or to take a used plate to the garbage pail in the corner, first to scrape it and then to drop it in the dishwasher. Soon she would once more be on her feet for something else; her constant movement betrayed her disquiet. Eventually she removed the espresso pot from the stove and brought the cups and saucers, spoon, and sugar bowl. The older daughter rose and went for some item her mother had not brought. Luisina looked at her questioningly (as the two girls went out to work all day at office jobs, and despite their repeated offers, she didn't normally let them help serve the table).

"Mama, let me, at least today", the girl asked. Luisina remained silent. The girl served the steaming fragrant coffee, giving her father the first cup. "You expect me to have coffee, too?" Pierello protested.

"We have it every night, Papa", the girl replied.

"Yes, but . . ."

"Piero, everything will come out all right", said Luisina. She spoke in dialect, as did her husband. The two girls used Italian.

He nodded and started stirring his coffee. After the girl had served them all with coffee, Luisina rose again to take the coffee pot and put in on another table, next to two covered plates, her son's dinner. Pierello followed her with his eyes, noticed the two plates, and pushed his coffee away. "Tonight I don't want any", he said, depressed.

"Piero, please."

"Leave me alone."

His wife took two sips of her own coffee, then also pushed it away.

The older girl said, "Mama!" Then, turning to her father, "After all, nothing new happened today. It's not as if Taddeo had pulled another dumb trick. The carabinieri only asked him to give some answers about that car, you know?"

"And that doesn't seem important to you?" exclaimed her father, frowning.

"No, it's not that it seems unimportant," the girl sighed, "but what is past is past. Think about that."

"And why did it happen, eh? What would you say if some dumb . . . if someone set fire to our car?" Then, turning to his wife, "More important, the owner of the car too is a working man, right?"

"He's an employee," said the daughter, "but, as it happens . . ."

"That's it, right there. He's an employee, like you," her father said, "and even if he weren't . . . why do some miserable kids have to set fire to cars parked along the street?"

"When there are demonstrations, that's what they do. I'm not saying they do the right thing. They're mindless people. I agree with you, you know that!"

"They're thieves," declared Piero, "because the owner of the burned car ends up without it, and no one pays for it."

"We agree with you, Papa. But after all, these things happen every day. Our Taddeo was just more stupid than the others with him, setting fire to the car in front of witnesses, students who knew who he was and turned him in. And when the police interviewed him, he admitted doing it, didn't deny it. At least in this he was honorable. He didn't lie."

"Oh! Honorable! Burning other people's cars is honorable?"

"How can you say that?" a pained Luisina asked her daughter.

"No, listen . . . what I mean to say is that you shouldn't let it get you down, because for sure they'll call Taddeo again, and maybe he'll even have to go to court. You can't keep reacting like this every time something happens. You'll only make yourselves sick. Don't you see?"

"So it's come to this!" Pierello said and was quiet. He remembered how proud he had been some years back, when his only son was studying for the priesthood (the son whom he'd named after his unforgettable friend Tadeusz, the Polish prisoner). Then, God knows how, the boy had turned, changed.

"It must have been those two friends of his who made him go wild", he said, following his train of thought. "Those two with him in the seminary, principally Consonni's son. That's what happened. And behind them the new coadjutant, Father Vittorio."

"If one listens to the Consonni boy's mother, it was our son who led hers astray", Luisina observed.

"Our son? Well, who knows, maybe she's right. Who can be sure one way or another? But what could have happened to these boys, that's what I ask, that would make no fewer than three of them abandon the seminary . . . and before that, those three were great boys, the best in town, and then they got ruined. And what about some of these young priests? What's happened to them? Can someone tell me?"

"You shouldn't talk that way about people who have been consecrated", Luisina said, gravely, looking sideways at her two girls. "It's not up to us to sit in judgment on them."

"Yes, but you remember Father Mario last year when he came to Nomana for the feast of the Cross? When I was telling him about our son and the bad example he was getting from Father Vittorio, tears came to his eyes. He said nothing, but he's in agreement about all this—and how!"

The mother threw another anguished look at her girls. "Not all young priests are like that. Only some."

The older girl, who had good common sense, got up. "Ermelinda," she said to her younger sister, "let's not forget, Mike Bongiorno is on television tonight. Let's go. It's nearly time."

Ermelinda (named for her paternal grandmother) also got up hesitantly. "Mike Bongiorno, yes, you're right."

"Come", said the older sister, leading the way to the other room, where the family kept the television set. The younger sister hung back. "But wouldn't it be best if tonight we helped Mama to clear the table?"

"Leave it", her sister said quietly. "Mama is concerned that we'll be shocked, don't you see? Poor Mama, if she only knew what we have to listen to in the office every day."

Pierello continued the conversation with his wife. "I agree that all young priests aren't like that. Otherwise it would mean there would be no religion left. That'd be all we need!"

Her daughters no longer being within earshot, Luisina now spoke freely. "When their heads get turned around like that, these young men leave the priesthood. Like that Father ———, the coadjutor in L——, for example. Well, in the end it's a blessing that our son left his religious studies before, while there was time; otherwise I'd have died of grief."

"I agree with that! But don't talk about blessings", Pierello paused. "What a scoundrel!"

He got to his feet, unable to remain still. "Where could he be at this hour?"

"I'll give you one guess he'll be at that little newspaper."

"So, here I am back from work on the 8:00 train, and to talk to him I have to wait till midnight, or even later, eh? And in the end it'll be up to me, up to us, to pay for the car he burned. Because he, the gentleman student, doesn't earn even one lira, and on top we have to pay for his education."

Luisina gestured, as if to say, "Leave it alone."

"Listen, did he tell you what the carabineri asked him, in other words, where do things stand right now?"

She gestured negatively. "He said nothing to me, but he did talk to his sister."

"Ah!" Now standing by the kitchen table, Pierello thought things out. "So here I am, his own father, and to find out the extent of his problem, I'll have to wait until after midnight, eh?" he repeated.

His wife regarded him silently.

"Well, I'm not waiting!" he exclaimed. He went to the coatrack and put on the peaked cap he'd worn from work. "I'm not going to wait", he repeated and headed for the door.

"Piero, this son of ours ... we ought to try not to lose him completely", Luisina said, her eyes becoming red.

Her husband looked at her for a few moments. "Don't be afraid. I won't let my temper take over", he half muttered and left.

5

The office of the little magazine *Brianza Nuova* was located inside the Libreria Don Milani, a small stationery business in a newly constructed building. Its single window looked out on the road close to the piazza. The building had been built in front of a big factory (erected during the "economic miracle"), and together they totally blocked what had been a panoramic view of the countryside and mountains.

Taddeo and the other writer-publishers were in the next-door Piper Bar, the so-called scientist's bar at the corner of the Piazza Victoria. They had gone in one after another, seeing Father Vittorio, the Red coadjutor, sitting at one of the tables, while Benediction took place in the nearby church. He had greeted each youth with some sarcastic comment. "What, you're here instead of in church, where you can hear the story of the chosen people escaping from Pharaoh between two walls of water? Aren't you interested in the story of Saint Peter, who made the wicked people fall down dead?"

The few people walking around the piazza (now nearly entirely paved and used in large part as a parking lot) looked much like the people of war times; better dressed than before, though, particularly the women, and even the young girls, who, under the influence of television and the new ways all dressed in a somewhat sexy manner (to the extent that Michele referred to them as "vampirettes"). It was precisely for the ease with which these young girls could be seen going by that Father Vittorio had become a regular of the bar on the piazza. He wasn't a hypocrite and didn't hide his interest, but the way his personal crisis was evolving he didn't place much importance on this type of temptation. Inside, he also had a measure of noble and just aspirations, but with the passing of time, these feelings were losing ground to the greater attraction he felt for the theories of Karl Marx. Several years before, like so many others, the priest had taken the new path of "progress", truly believing he was following a direction that had originated on high. Then there came a series of doubts, tormenting him, even though his reading of the Gospel had gradually diverged from the tridentine and bourgeois interpretation. Even his recent and growing inclination toward women had at first surprised him, but not to the point of giving him second thoughts.

The progressive youth admired him for his openminded attitude when faced with any objections raised by orthodox Catholics (especially the parish priest, also young, but of a more traditional mentality). This admiration led him to more extreme nonconformist attitudes. That evening a youthful group had come to sit with him. Young men and women, most of them with a background of Christian schooling (some were former seminarians), but also the elite of the handful of young Nomana Communists, nowadays better indoctrinated and open. The savage times of Stalinist communism were long past. This group of leftists was lumped together with the "questioning" Catholics.

Each new arrival was greeted by the same jokes, but soon they moved on to commenting on recent events. Evidently the hero of the day was Pirello's son, Taddeo, who had problems because of his role in the battle for the Communist victory in Indochina. The group of youths was proud that their support for the Communist war of liberation should involve a real sacrifice like this one. The fact that the people of Indochina—Vietnamese, Cambodians, and Laotians—didn't want anything to do with the Communist liberation (and showed it by fleeing before each of their advances, retreating, nine out of ten of them, along with their own national armies or infiltrating the rear area in massive numbers) was unknown to them. When they were told about it, they refused to believe the reports, judging them to be at best due to the population's political ignorance. The Americans' motives (having gone to war to free these people—as they had done years before in Europe against the Nazis— they had, two years before in 1972, pulled back their own troops and now limited their involvement to sending supplies to the national armies) were drowned out by the volume of contrary opinion in nearly all of Italy's newspapers, radio, and television.

The Americans' "imperialism" had been part of the evening's conversation: "Those American swine have to stop sending help to their serfs left behind in Vietnam and Cambodia."

"They have their own students, as well as the rest of the world's public opinion, against them, so they were forced to pull out, but they just can't seem to let go completely."

"And now only the people here in Nomana still want them to win."

"Right, it's because they don't understand anything. How can it be possible not to be aware that a thorough defeat of the Americans would represent an incredible victory for liberty all over the world?"

"Maybe that's the exact thing they don't want."

"What pathetic idiots! How can it not be important to them? All this suffering, all these dead people?" The words came from Tecla, a young girl in blue jeans with burning eyes.

"You're right. And shouldn't we then make bonfires with cars to wake up these hypocrites?" another of the hard-liners asked.

Taddeo, looking serious and modest all at once, nodded. As he was the center of attention, he tried to look a little bashful.

"The people in Nomana will keep on not understanding a thing until they themselves are absorbed by capitalism." The speaker was Consonni, a former seminarian, close to graduating in philosophy from the state university and editor of the magazine. "As proof of this we only need to see the way our own families think, right?"

"That's the way to talk; well done, boys and girls!" the priest said, and the others nodded.

Michele had unsuccessfully tried to have discussions with these youths. For their part, considering themselves to be liberators of whole peoples, they had made sacrifices in order to produce their magazine *Brianza Nuova* and organize their small "progressive" library. They couldn't see, and wouldn't consider, the fact that instead of being liberators they were duped supporters of slave makers, something unthinkable to them even as a hypothesis. Only years later would some of them see it. To Michele they were a living example to his followers of how to win power—not by a violent Leninist revolution but by a sort of kid-napping, a gradual conditioning of people's minds through a takeover of the media—magazines, newspapers, radio, television—and of the social institutions—schools, publishing houses, theater, and cinema. With extraordinary foresight, Gramsci had seen that once these objectives had been achieved and the con-ditioning process was in place, the task of surmounting the great obstacle—the Christian view of the world—would be carried forward spontaneously by Chris-tians themselves. They would gradually convert themselves to atheism once they had accepted the (apparently) neutral and scientific view of things adopted by Marxism. What effectively had put these youths—and countless others spread throughout Italy and all over Europe—on this course had been the fact that once Pius XII had died, Catholic culture had not battled against the Marxist line but had insisted on trying to reach a meeting point with it. Added to this was the fact that European culture—particularly because of the analogous sit-uation created in France, its central point—had declined with incredible ra-pidity, taking great strides backward toward a condition of precivilization. In this respect it seemed to Michele that a statement by Picasso that had been widely disseminated—"If Raphael were born nowadays, he wouldn't sell even one of his paintings, and the world would ignore him"—was symbolic of the general mood, was effectively how things stood. Now that an appreciation for art was lost, it was not unusual to see in some exhibitions, for example, rows of bottles containing the artist's feces instead of a selection of his paintings.

"Well, of course Vietnam is very important", Consonni once more seized their attention, "but we have to remember that this next issue of the paper is aimed at the freedom to divorce. As far as Indochina is concerned, we'll not be able to give it more than half a page."

"Right."

"Of course."

"Yes, we're all agreed."

"Did you write the articles about divorce the way we decided during our last meeting?" Consonni asked them.

"Yes, mine is along those lines."

"And mine."

"Mine isn't ready, although I've drafted it; I wanted to hear what you thought about it."

"Good, well, we'll see them back at the office. Between now and tomorrow you'll have to deliver them to me. This issue can't come out late."

"Right, for sure."

"That's all we'd need."

"Well, in that case, isn't it time we went back to the office?" asked the writer of the drafted article.

"But Elvira hasn't arrived yet." (Elvira was Igino's second daughter, studying literature at the Catholic University.)

"Oh, right."

"She's always arriving late."

"That's true."

They remained there a while longer, waiting for the missing girl.

In the ensuing pause, Father Vittorio turned to Taddeo. "Well, do you want to tell us what questions the carabineri had for you?"

"What should I tell you? Do you want a blow-by-blow report of what happened?" Taddeo smiled, then started recounting his experience in his serious way.

It was then that Pierello arrived outside the bar on his way to the editorial office next door.

6

Through the window he saw his son speaking to his friends. *There he is. Now what's that miserable wretch preaching? He's probably talking about his adventure today. What else? Well, I suppose I also have a right to hear it; after all, I'm his father.*

However, he hadn't forgotten his wife's anguished warning: "Piero, this son of ours . . . we ought to try not to lose him completely!" To lose his only son now! He realized that if he went inside the bar he wouldn't be able to listen to his son's story without interrupting, and there would be an argument—in front of all those people—much worse than a private discussion alone with his son. Being a simple man, Piero loved his son—his only son—with all his soul and had done so ever since the day he was born. So he was aware, despite being so upset, that it would be easy to provoke a break with his son.

Standing there, outside the bar window, irresolute, he saw the priest warmly congratulate Taddeo, looking around at the others for approval. Piero concentrated on a thought. If his son deserved condemnation, how much more was called for in the case of the priest? He backed away from the window in order to give himself time to reflect and thought, *A priest who behaves this way!* To a pious working man like himself, it was a genuine scandal, so much so that he preferred not even to think about the priest. A man of Christ's priesthood, always surrounded by those adoring young girls! With an example like this before them, how could these young men go along the paths of righteousness? It was true that even without this priest, times had changed, and even here in Nomana the correct relations between boys and girls wasn't what it used to be, as when he himself had been young, when the majority of males managed to go into marriage without having known a woman. Ah, yes, things really had changed from those days. Even here now that old saying went around, previously heard only out on the plains, in Sesto, for example, where he worked in the iron foundry: "If the Lord won't pardon the sin of the panties, may he end up there alone playing his pipe." At this thought Pierello smiled, with a certain indulgence, although down deep the reality saddened him. How long would it take for a Christian people to go back to the old ways? Well, with an ordinary person, what could one expect, but a priest? Could it be possible that this priest wasn't aware of the impropriety (if nothing else) of his promiscuous behavior? No wonder many Red priests left the priesthood under pressure, no wonder that the seminaries were being emptied. He'd even heard that in their diocese the last few years the number of men wanting to be priests had dwindled to half. Was it possible that such a serious occurrence wasn't important to Father Vittorio? Didn't he ever think about it? Pierello shook his round head disapprovingly. God only knew how this priest would end up! There came to his mind the case of Father X, the coadjutor of L, a village near Nomana, who—obsessed with desire for a woman—not long ago had petitioned to be released from his vows in order to marry. Then, during one of his first nights as a married man, he had died of a heart attack. Of course, Piero didn't want to elect himself judge and jury, but wasn't this an example to everybody, perhaps? And if so, what an example!

Turning these things over in his mind, Piero had gradually been distancing himself from the Piper Bar; the ambient noise and excessive lighting slowly caused him to leave the piazza altogether. As he left the piazza, he passed the new Oratory. (Made of reinforced concrete, it had a great hall and a theater with velvet-covered seats; there was a large courtyard for games. For the children it offered door-to-door bus service—what a difference from the old days! But of what use was all of this—he thought—if nowadays many parents didn't send their children here, afraid of what damaging beliefs they might acquire from these self-doubting priests?) Good Lord, if one just thought of the situation that had been allowed to arise!

Piero turned down a dark alley. What was happening exactly? After all, since the war, everybody's welfare had improved. The town, the workers, had managed—by hard work, of course, and by making sacrifices—to acquire an apartment, a car. They could send their children to the university, all sorts of things that had been unthinkable up to now. Of course, these things hadn't been achieved by all but certainly by the majority. And by keeping at it along the straight and narrow path, after some years everyone could get there. You'd think that after all this the people would be contented, would have peace of mind, and yet . . . It wasn't only the children who rebelled against their parents and the institutions—like his Taddeo—but the greater part of the people, instead of being happy, seemed to be furious, wanted more and more, faster, and by working less. The unions had also mercilessly become involved. Since the Reds and the Christians had become allied, they grabbed companies by the throat in such a way that things could only end badly, inevitably. And in fact many factories, even when they kept putting their prices up in order to pay the ever-increasing wages, no longer managed to keep afloat and had to ask the government for money to keep going. More than one had already closed, like the old spinning mill on the Lambro where his Luisina used to work, and also the sausage factory in Nomana, and meantime others, like the Motta plant in Milan, were permanently under occupation by the workers, who continued with their demonstrations. *They should have thought about it when there was still time instead of constantly holding protest marches now,* Pierello thought. But what was happening, really? Was it possible that man would never ever live in peace?

After walking aimlessly through various streets, Piero found himself back in the piazza, pulled toward the Piper Bar as if by a magnet. There he found that his son and his companions had left; they'd have returned to the newspaper office for sure. He debated following them there, his first intention. He'd call Taddeo outside and . . . and what? Was it possible that he hadn't yet absorbed the fact that discussions resolve nothing . . . nothing at all? So, yes, so? Feeling a renewal of his frustration, he turned around and walked slowly back toward home. *Tomorrow morning, early, I have to get on the train to Sesto.* The work on the furnaces wasn't as hard as it used to be, thanks to automation, but neither was he as young as he used to be.

7

On the afternoon of the following day, totally unaware of how this trip would end, Michele left for Valtellina. He had an organization meeting at Sondrio, after which he dined with the local committee men in a small restaurant, listening to their concerns. "We'd have a peaceful victory here," they assured him, "if it weren't for our union members and the people from the ACLI."

"Are they working to make divorce easier?"

"Not exactly, but when they get a chance they defend the right to divorce, and the people—accustomed to trusting them—end up not understanding how some of the bishops and Christians are saying the opposite. Our own clergy is very concerned, and they've reached the point where they want to avoid taking a stand."

"But surely since the ACLI people have joined with the Marxists, we can't call them Christians. How can the Christian faithful still regard them as a point of reference?"

"Exactly, it's the way you just explained it", said the committee's president, a solid and sensible administrator, with the usual mountain dweller's ways. "That's exactly the question. Our people are believers and therefore don't change easily."

"I understand", Michele agreed, feeling a pang in his heart. He thought of the great years of Pius XII's pontificate. How could Catholics afterward have been scattered so far? No doubt meaning well, to put themselves closer to errant believers, trying to be the yeast, the leaven in the dough, no doubt about it. And there was another excuse. In her historic progress the Church comes up against not only good and evil but also human stupidity. One only had to think about the tragic defections suffered—even among the common people—by her just fight against the mistakes of the French Revolution. There's no doubt that in the turmoil of some battles, the people's stupidity is so unbeatable that even when the cause is just, it's better to avoid involvement in order not to lose too many adherents. Michele thought himself that perhaps in the end the mistakes and irresponsible actions could have had positive results if they had remained in God's own hands. Yes, but while waiting, stupidities were stupidities . . . Take, now, the outcome of the positions taken by Maritain and Mounier and others who had opened the way to the modernists and Communists. There's the pretty end to that path! He remembered how he had opposed the new ways right from the start. Later—after Vatican II—he felt as if he were pulling against the deliberations of the Church's shepherds and had retreated (and he wasn't alone). He had published almost nothing again, although he kept up his writing "for after the deluge", as he would sadly describe it. Among other projects, he had started a great narrative work that would epitomize his generation's experiences "for use by those who in the future will dedicate themselves to reconstruction". Year after year the news from the East confirmed how accurate his analyses had been. Now it was generally known that the number of communism's victims in the Soviet Union had surpassed several tens of millions. According to the Kurganov-Solzhenitsyn statistics, it had reached sixty-six million, and without the slightest increase in the quality of life for the survivors. A new society, with justice and happiness! Sixty-six million human beings sacrificed in a futile attempt to change man's nature and conscience.

In China there had been even more victims, although there weren't yet any statistics from there, but there had been that terrifying estimate by Walker on behalf of the U.S. Senate (of between thirty-four and sixty-four million victims up to 1970), and—more recently—there were estimates by experts in demographics in Paris who pointed to a "shortfall", in official Chinese statistics, of 150 million souls. And in Indochina? The Communist victory was only a matter of months. Despite the idiotic hopes held by fanatic leftists who were constantly in the streets demonstrating their support for the "liberty" of the Indochinese peoples, how many victims would there be over there? How many millions and millions more? Never, absolutely never in the entire course of history had there been seen such a large-scale slaughter, or so mendacious a defense of it, because while killing an inconceivable number of human beings, communism continued presenting itself as the redeemer of man. (This was made possible, above all, by the constant support received from the world's lay culture that ran the mass media, which although antitotalitarian had much in its lineage comparable with Marxism. It had to be said that without the untiring zeal of so many champions of democratic "enlightenment" to conceal—with all good intentions—first, the slaughters by Lenin and Stalin and then those by Mao, and finally the present happenings in Indochina, it would have been impossible for the Communists to go ahead with such immeasurable massacres and the enslavement of countless human beings.)

Fortunately, for some time now Church authorities hadn't been able to conceal their own anguish about the way things were going. As soon as he noticed the change, Michele returned to the debate, with essays and articles in those few newspapers and magazines that would still publish his writings. "Who knows, however, if there's still time to correct the situations?" he sometimes asked himself. That same night he asked it again in Sondrio.

After dinner Michele went with a few members of the committee to the small town of Tirano, where he made a speech at the *Italia* movie theater, speaking to the fifty or so people there. In the audience was a group of five or six prodivorce activists, including a young Christian union man, there tonight—as he himself announced—to expose the speaker's argument by quoting the workers' thesis. He did so by quoting the Marxist view about divorce; evidently he had no Christian prodivorce arguments. Michele, who had a thorough knowledge of the Marxist views on the matter, could have quoted them to the young man, and in exactly the same order in which they were being delivered. He listened patiently, though, and after refuting these theories point by point, he had clearly shown the plainly Marxist beliefs on which they were based. He then firmly explained the incompatibility between Christianity and Marxist communism.

The prodivorce man tried in various ways to deny this incompatibility, demonstrating to Michele his almost complete ignorance of communism, both in theory and in practice. This saddened the author. Wasn't this the job he'd chosen from the start, to teach—at least in a circle of the faithful—the reality of the Communist world? What a failure he'd been! Even the largest of the Catholic newspapers—the one based in Milan—had finally started to refuse his work (they had also pushed aside Apollonio and others, also fighting for the truth) at the same time that they were asking card-carrying Communists for contributions to the paper. Almost inevitably much of the country's Christian youth, in Nomana and elsewhere, were so ignorant and so unbelievably fascinated by the anti-Christian forces. The left, with this kind of help, had bit by bit taken Italy to a prerevolutionary stage, but—witnessing the failures in the East and knowing that the road to power by the control of the mass media predicted by Gramsci would be a winning strategy—no longer thought about violent revolution. This, in a situation in which they could easily bring the state's organization—already weakened—crashing down . . . If the Christian side couldn't obtain a clear majority in this referendum in order to change the situation, how long could this present phase of disintegration and paralysis go on? This phase in which many of the pro-Communists were Christian youths like the union man in the audience, invincibly ignorant and working against Christianity.

After the meeting the organizers asked Michele to stay with them for a while, hoping he would bring them up to date on the progress of the campaign in the rest of Lombardy and at the same time stay and enjoy a drink in the spirit of the local Alpine hospitality. At first Michele tried to leave ("It's late, and tomorrow morning I have a meeting in Milan"), but he ended up going with them to a bar, because he liked these people. A people without verbal excess, but who nevertheless showed their solid loyalty. They reminded him of his old friend Father Turla. (He was now the parish priest in a village in the Camonica Valley—parallel to this one—where he had at last built the sanctuary in remembrance of the fallen. "Father Turla, I haven't seen you for some time, but the fault isn't only mine, but yours, too. May the Lord forgive this procrastinator.") Apart from Father Turla, these people also reminded Michele of his other companions in the former stable at Crinovaya. And it made no difference that the accents of those old friends were from Piedmont, from the valleys of Maira and Varaita, as opposed to his present companions' Lombardy accent. They were all Alpine people.

8

When he got into his car, the clocktower in Tirano had already chimed midnight. Looking at the tower, it appeared to him to be a giant sentinel put there to mount guard in the darkness.

Good Lord in heaven, how he felt at home in these places! As the car ran through the solitude of the dark roads in the valley bottom, he sorted through memories, filling his heart.

As he drove through Sondrio, the last lights in the town were winking out. Soon he passed by the foot of an already asleep Morbegno. Above the tops of the highest roofs was the small illuminated monument, a stubborn reminder, in the Italy of strikes, divorce, and all the cowardly capitulations, of the heroic loyalty of this area's Alpine soldiers.

"*Ciao*, Morbegno Battalion, with your white tassels", Michele murmured, half declaiming. "*Ciao*, Tirano Battalion, red tassels, *ciao*."

Luca's battalion, the Morbegno, which during the retreat from the Don, now thirty years in the past, had been annihilated during the terrible night in Varvarovca. They had fought alone against the great Russian column driving forward to cut the Tridentina Division in two. It had been the Morbegno's way to help the scattered mass of disbanded soldiers the Alpine troops were dragging behind them. They had fought valiantly to the death, which was why later no white tassels could be seen on the repatriation convoys delivering the Tridentina's survivors to the motherland. Those famed convoys, which came to be called "Rosary convoys", of which Father Carlo Gnocchi and Luca so often spoke. And to think that the prayer itself, the Rosary, had later . . . and yet it was the prayer of the poor, as Father Turla used to say. How could some prominent Catholics have criticized and later proscribed the Rosary? Father

Bertrando, his priest friend at the university, that incurable exhibitionist, had done his part right here in this area at the poplar-planted sanctuary of our Lady of Tirano when at the end of a sermon he'd torn apart a Rosary with great theatricality before the astonished eyes of the villagers. Worse, at the seminary at F, the priests had burned their Rosaries!

They should burn in . . . no, Michele, don't damn them, calm yourself. And slow down; can't you see you're going too fast?

He slowed down. Nowadays Father Bertrando continued more than ever with his exhibitionism, making speeches in favor of divorce, to the applause of both the middle class and the Reds. He'd never stopped being a showoff since his university days, when he wrote poetry dedicated to Mussolini. But he'd never been as much in demand as he was right now. The largest prodivorce national newspaper had recently featured him on the front page, and most of the media seeking to weaken Christian values also gave him praise. Michele thought, *What a shame! how low some Italian papers have gone!* Eight or nine out of ten had closed ranks in favor of divorce, and what was worse, they wrote boorishly and intolerantly! The situation was so bitter that, as the antidivorce committee's press relations man in Milan—publishing capital of Italy—he had managed to establish contact with only a few small newspapers.

In order to be effective, while not forgetting these smaller papers, he had turned to holding public meetings and making speeches. Michele was reminded of those highly trained German military pilots (he'd met some in the Russian POW camp) who, late in the war, were used as foot soldiers due to the shortage of aircraft. It was a memory that disturbed him. This fight about marriage—whose indissolubility had been established in Italy by Christianity over 1,500 years ago—seemed to him to be the last possibility to delay the de-Christianization of customs and laws. This was why—suspending all other activities for four months—he had dedicated himself to it with all his energy and time, without being paid for it. Oh, if this battle were lost! Following the introduction of divorce, no doubt there'd be a law that would permit abortions, meaning the butchering of innocent unborn . . .

Being by nature stubbornly against any utopian beliefs and influenced fundamentally in his understanding of life by his war experiences, Michele thought—as the car ran through the dark countryside—*Unfortunately there'll always be wars. It's not something we can get rid of by wishing it weren't so, but it's one thing to have wars between Christian people and another entirely when they are fought between de-Christianized people, as I saw in the East.* In his imagination he pictured the new means of annihilation that man had invented. In particular he saw those tall nuclear mushroom clouds. Maybe one day even Italy would suffer the same penalty for the production-line extermination of unborn babies. Milan, Monza, Nova, even Nomana, attacked by those balls of fire . . . At the thought he felt the hair on his arms stand on end. What else could he do but fight as he was now doing against the general de-Christianization?

Well, enough, let's just wait and see what we achieve this time. After all, even if in this fight the Christians had the moneyed middle class (owners of the mass media) allied with Marxists of various persuasions against them, at least they had on their side the majority of the wholesome population, clean-thinking people. *And that's quite a lot.* Besides, the faithful had found a real guide in Gabrio Lombardi, the president of the antidivorce committee, who had mustered them for the fight. Michele knew him well, could even call him a friend. Apart from being an exemplary Christian, the man was a real leader, something rare in Italy, where everybody thinks himself a general. Why not, then, maintain a reasonable hope?

(A small start at reversing opinions, not foreseen by Michele, was made a few years later, after the tough slave state installed by the Communist winners in Vietnam—revealed to the world by the mass escape of the "boat people"—and after the huge massacres of helpless people in Cambodia by their own countrymen, as well as the wars among the Communists of Vietnam, Cambodia, and China. These events would cause much rethinking in Italy, not only among the laity who had defended them but also among the proper Communist militants themselves, which soon led to a lessening of Marxist pressure on society. In this way there was a return—who knew for how long—to a situation of relative freedom of thought. As for the Christians, it would be their panic after their defeat in the divorce referendum that would shake them awake. Later God would present his Church with the enormous asset of his Polish Pope, at last a Pope who was once again a "stone" and a "rock".)

The long straight stretches by Valtellina were left behind. On the right was the turnoff to the Spluga valley. Above, between those mountains, was Madesimo, where Michele had sometimes gone skiing as a boy. He recalled that during the awful night when he had fallen prisoner to the Russians, he had in his delirium thought himself to be there in Madesimo. He thought he was wandering through its icy streets looking for Ambrogio. Above the mountain chain on his left was Tartano, perched like an eagle's nest. This was the town where Luca's Alpine troops mainly came from, the members of the squad Luca led in Arnautovo and Nicolaievca. Who knows—Michele asked himself— how many people in a so-typically-Alpine town like Tartano would vote for the indissolubility of marriage? (Later he was to discover that the figure had been 89 percent of the town's voters.)

The first signs of the approach to Lake Como could already be seen— geometric-looking streams in the plains of the valley bottom and some gloomy mirrors of waters surrounded by grass. The road hugged to the left, twisting and turning against the mountainside, sometimes going right through its rock wall. Reaching the side of the lake, the road turned away from it for a while, then once again ran parallel to it, descending to run alongside the promontories that fell precipitously to the water.

The writer reduced speed, although not enough to prevent the rear wheels squealing on the curves. In the darkness the lake surface could hardly be seen except for the opposite side, where the lines of light from villages were reflected in the water. But Michele spent no time admiring the view. He had suddenly remembered that he had not said his prayers that day. *Instead of criticizing the people who want to do away with the Rosary, you'd be better off saying yours!* Being too tired to pray properly, he decided to say a simple Angele Dei: *Angels of God, who watch over us,* he prayed silently, addressing not only his own guardian angel but also his wife Alma's, as was his habit, *care for us who were delivered to you by heaven's mercy . . .* What a charming prayer this was! Men and angels hand in hand to fight together. *You two guardian angels,* Michele prayed, *don't only look after me because I'm on a journey, but also look after her, Alma, who at this hour is sleeping defenselessly.*

Finished with his prayer, he let his mind wander. The car ran along the nearly deserted lakeside road, and at times Michele had to shake his head and open his eyes wide to avoid falling asleep.

He noticed a sudden noise; he couldn't tell if from the motor or the wheels. "Eh, what's happening?" he muttered. He was going through a town, Dervio. He hoped the noise had been caused by some roughness in the road. *Because if not . . . it would be real trouble to get stuck on the road at this time of night.*

As he was leaving the town, the engine coughed once more, then died. Without using the brakes, Michele searched the road ahead. He was coming toward a gas station on the right, the lake side. A building next to it was still lit and looked as if it might be a store. (It turned out to be a bar.) He steered the car at an increasingly slow pace toward the little open space and parked in front of the bar. "What bad luck", he said, then repeated, "what bad luck."

9

He twisted the ignition key several times with lessening conviction, trying to restart the engine. Finally he gave up and considered his situation. It was almost 1:30, and most likely the bar would close soon. He would need to telephone Alma quickly to advise her he wouldn't be home, and then he'd have to find somewhere to sleep. *Just as well that these little towns usually have hotels and pensioni for tourists coming to see the lake.* He would take care of getting the car repaired as soon as the service station opened in the morning. *I'll have to get up bright and early, before 8:00 . . . because at 10:00 I have that meeting in Milan that I can't afford to miss.*

Opening the door, he got out and went up some steps into the bar, a one-story construction furnished with chromed tubular chairs and tables. There were still some late customers, who looked silently at Michele as he entered. He went over to a sleepy-looking girl behind the counter who had raised her head questioningly when he opened the door and asked, "Do you have tokens for the telephone, please?"

She nodded and walked over to the cash register.

"Give me ten of them, please." He handed over a five hundred-lire bill.

The girl opened the drawer and gave him the ten tokens. "We close at 1:30, in five minutes", she advised him.

"Right", he answered. "Can you tell me if I'll find a place to sleep around here?"

The girl nodded and gestured yes; she barely concealed a yawn.

"We'll talk in a minute", Michele said, going to the glassed-in phone booth in a corner and closing the door.

Alma picked up the phone after only a couple of rings. "Eh, what's happening, are you still awake?" he asked, using a jokey voice so that she wouldn't be alarmed. "That's good, that's the way it should be—you should be wide awake when I'm out and about."

"Where are you?"

"Oh, just out and about", he repeated, smiling, "like the colored sails wandering the ocean seeking good fortune". (It was a quotation that Alma and he had heard some ten or fifteen years previously, declaimed by a speaker inaugurating a seaside monument in Romagna. Every now and then he would come up with a quotation like that, so his wife was used to it.)

But this time she didn't understand. "Eh, what . . . what did you say about the sea?" she asked.

"Not sea, lake", he corrected, and when she still didn't seem to understand, he went on. "So, can you tell me why you haven't gone to bed as I've asked you to do whenever I'm out late?"

"But I was asleep. What do you think?" she said. "I have the telephone here by the bed, as we agreed."

"Oh, and you answered the first ring? Where did you get such fast reflexes?" (He was going to add "my little marble statue", but held back, fearing his voice would carry into the silence of the bar.)

"But tell me, what's happened? Where are you?" his wife asked.

"I'm in Dervio, still at the start of the lake, on the Valtellina side. The car doesn't want to keep going, and as it's 1:30 . . ."

"One-thirty already?" exclaimed Alma. "Oh, *mama mia* . . . surely you . . . let me see . . ." Her voice was becoming more alert.

Michele imagined her putting on the light and looking at the alarm clock at the bedside. He smiled tenderly, shaking his head. Alma, who in so many things continued to admire her husband unconditionally, didn't trust him in little things like telling the time, knowing him to be absentminded.

"So, you won't believe me even in such a small thing as the time of night?" he protested, smiling.

"Yes, it's 1:30 all right! Oh, poor us . . .", he heard her say. "Now what do we do?"

"We do the following", said Michele, jokingly using a voice with which one would speak to a child. "Here in this town there are lots of places where I can get some sleep, so you know what I'm going to do? I'll lock the car and go to sleep somewhere. In the morning at 8:00 I'll go and get the car fixed and be on my way, because at 10:00 I have that meeting in Milan. I just rang so that you shouldn't worry."

"Are you joking?" she exclaimed, sounding wide awake. "In Milan you have to go to a meeting with press people, the editors of those Catholic magazines, right? And Cesare Cavalleri will also be there, won't he? This is an important meeting."

"You're right, but ..."

"And you want to go to it without having shaved, and you don't even have a clean shirt or your shaving things?"

"You're right. Well, in the morning I'll come by there first in order to shave and change clothes, right?"

"No, I don't agree", said Alma, who was by now thinking clearly. "It's a problem of time. From where you are to get to Milan would take two hours, right? And how much time do you think the repairs to the car will take? Another hour, more perhaps?" Then she went off on a tangent. "At least the committee will pay for these costs, right?"

"Come on, Almina, let's not be stingy."

"In any case the repair shops won't be open before 8:00, and in that lake area where everyone takes life easy, maybe even later. So, how are you going to be in Milan at 10:00?"

"Well, if the repair looks like it will take a long time, I'll get someone to run me over to Lecco to catch the next Milan train. What else can I do? And even if I only get there in time to greet them and explain the reason I'm late ..."

"No. Don't you see that it's a very important meeting for you, something that could be useful for you, even after the referendum?"

He laughed. "How practical you are!"

"Of course I'm practical", Almina replied. "Any woman who has a writer for a husband has to be practical. What else do you expect?"

"Well, I'll do what I can", Michele promised. "I just wanted you to know where I was. Now, *ciao*, a big hug. They're about to close down here."

"Just a moment, where did you say you were, Dervio? Where are you exactly, in the town center?"

"A little way out of town, going toward Lecco. There's a Shell station. I'm parked in the square, off the road and out of danger. Now you know where I am, and you can take it easy."

"All right, I've written it down: 'Dervio—Shell'. Easy, just the town name and the gas station. I can't forget that. Oh, well, you just wait for me there and relax. I'll come for you. Just give me time to dress and drive there, let's say just over an hour."

"No!" he exclaimed, startled. "Whatever are you thinking about? Are you mad? Driving alone at night? And when you get here—what? Are you going to give me a tow in your little 500? No, listen ..."

"Please don't argue."

"But it's too dangerous. What if you had an accident? Or what if someone comes after you, and he has a more powerful car than yours, and . . ."

"Listen, I'll use Papa's 125. I'll do that, at least, right?"

"By no means, Alma. Think about this, let me . . ."

Alma interrupted. "Please, Michele, let's not waste more time. And of course we won't try to tow your car. I wouldn't know how. You can go and see what can be done . . . I don't know . . . find out the phone number of a repair shop nearby or something. Make some arrangement, see to it yourself. You're an important man . . . *Ciao*, see you soon."

"No, Alma, I don't want this. It's dangerous!" He raised his voice. "I don't want you to do this. Don't do it. Do you understand?"

"I'll be there in a little while, but meantime think about this. We'll be coming back here together like newlyweds. And another thing. It's useless your calling back to make me change my mind, because I'm going to hang up the phone." She paused. "*Ciao*, my love, my sweetest love. You know that being able to help you in your fight against half the world fills me with happiness?" Her voice deepened, became more affectionate. "And if I don't help you, who will?" Click, she was gone.

Michele wagged his head, affected emotionally by the intimate tenderness in his wife's last words. Then he sighed and pressed the button to recover any unused tokens; only one came clinking back.

10

Alma dressed hurriedly, left the room, and went past her parents' door, whispering a fleeting "*Ciao*, Papa, *ciao*, Mama", unaware that this would be her last earthly greeting to her parents. Then she went down the stairs, trying to make no noise. She went outside, closed the house door quietly, and went to get the Fiat 125 from the garage (which had been built where the old woodshed had been). She opened the garden gates, drove out, and then returned to close them again.

There was an incessant and oppressive noise in the night air, coming from the furnaces at the glass factory. It was an annoyance every night in Nomana and seemed to be without a solution. (With the gradual erosion of authority, anybody could now cause harm to the community, thinking only of his own self-interest, and with total impunity.) Alma, still affected by the tenderness of her last words to her husband, remembered the long-gone singing of the nightingale. *Poor little birds, here we are in May. It used to be the best time*, she thought.

Driving through the empty town streets, brightly lit by the tall neon lampposts, Alma thought, *Maybe the nightingale also left because of all these bright lights.* She recalled that day before her marriage when she'd thought to thank the

Americans for their economic aid to Italy by sending them nightingales as gifts and how Michele had liked her idea! How much meaning he had found in her idea . . . her own Michele! What strength of purpose he had, much more than she ever realized at the start, and yet, in so many ways, what a child he could be! There were areas of his life in which he really couldn't organize things for himself, things that any average person would take in his stride (like the usefulness to a writer of making a good impression tomorrow on these editors, and particularly on Cesare Cavalleri). But he didn't notice or didn't consider things important enough to plan ahead for. By good luck, here she was, to help him make his way. She at least hoped that tomorrow, after all this trouble, Michele would be pleasant with these men, the best-disposed of the media representatives, as far as he was concerned, and not get excited and argue with them for any reason. She could imagine him doing so; it was the kind of thing he'd do. Alma hit the steering wheel in exasperation. Then she shook her head and smiled. He was even capable of going to this important meeting wearing his polo-neck sweater with the tassel! How funny he was! She had recently knit him the sweater and, as a joke, had put a tassel on the neck. Michele had worn the sweater calmly and naturally, without saying a word. *My Lord, what a dreamer he is!*

Once outside Nomana she accelerated. The car climbed the rise to Visate (that same stretch that Ambrogio and Colomba had traveled so many times on their bicycles and by which Pino and Sèp had walked down toward home on the day they were both repatriated from Switzerland). Down below on the left, against the hardly visible background of the mountains, was the Nomanella farmhouse. She looked for it by the light of the moon but couldn't see it. She thought that probably old Mama Lucia (widowed for some years now) would already be at the farm to spend the summer, although she might also be staying in town with her married daughter. Wherever she was, she would be constantly saying prayers for her lost ones, poor Lucia . . . Alma checked the fuel gauge; more than she'd need, no problem.

She started leaving towns and villages behind. She felt no fear, despite her husband's concern. *Whenever he's dealing with me, he's always the same. He loses his nerve, becomes emotional. He thinks I'm a shrinking flower . . . and yet in his time it's true, he has seen such terrible things!* She smiled. Michele loved her so intensely he lost all sense of objectivity where she was involved. And yet they'd been married for more than twenty years, and he still loved her like nothing else in his life . . . the thing was incredible . . . and the most incredible thing was that he loved her with the intensity of a boy's love. Didn't ever tire of paying court to her, praising her with those special words of his, simple and poetic. "Don't you believe that one day you'll look at me and see an old woman?" she sometimes asked him, herself a little frightened by the passage of time. "Even I will inevitably grow old and won't be the same. What will you do then? You have to be prepared."

Instead of answering, "But I'll also be old", or something similar, her husband would say, "No, darling, absolutely not, no way, you can't get old! You're a little marble statue, so ..."

He also loved her in the physical sense, with a frequency that sometimes surprised her. "And do other couples also do it so frequently?" she used to ask him. "So very frequently?" He used to joke, "Well, the reason is that we writers are better equipped for certain purposes ... but, seriously, why worry about it? The Lord gave us this. Let's enjoy it." Sometimes Alma would ask herself if maybe it wasn't really too much ... well, enough. In a short while she'd see him again. She'd have to listen to him scolding her for coming out at this time. Then she'd let him do the driving on the return journey and curl up at his side (she already felt the need) and rest her head on his shoulder. *Let's go faster here,* she urged, thinking to herself, *because tomorrow at 8:00 I have to be in class. This referendum is a real pain; why couldn't they have held it during the vacations?*

Although the Lecco road ran through hilly country, some recent engineering work had smoothed out parts of it so that it was possible to maintain an even speed. A few miles before Lecco, at the foothills, the road joined a major highway with several lanes, which in one direction came from Milan. Alma joined this *superstrada* cautiously; she noticed there was still some traffic, and she was pleased because it would help her stay alert while driving. Here was the bridge over the Adda, with Lecco—and its suburb of Pescarenico—on the other side, where the Adda was born, issuing from the lake. The mirrorlike lake of Lucia's flight, from Alessandro Manzoni's novel, in which this stretch was "smooth and flat and would have looked motionless if it weren't for the light ripple and quivering of the moonlight mirrored in the water from the center of the sky". *Just as it is now,* thought Alma, remembering that beautiful page by heart. (She unfailingly made each generation of her school pupils study it.) She reduced speed and looked over the parapet of the bridge, intrigued, then recited a few lines from memory: "Farewell, you hills surging from the waters, rising up to the sky." *Look at them! These are the same uneven summits, known to those raised in your sight, engraved on the mind, no less than the faces of those closest ... farewell!* "Sad is the step of he who grew up near you and leaves you behind!" At hearing her own words, Alma felt a knot in her throat, as if that painful farewell were also for herself. *Farewell, native hearth ...* She tried to go on, but had to stop due to the increasingly unbearable emotion she felt. "Whatever is happening to me?" she muttered, moved.

On the other side of the river, the road went around Lecco running alongside the lake's edge to stay next to it while going north, cut into the rocky mountain. After the bridge the road once more separated into two lanes, but in stretches became reduced to one double lane, the other being incomplete or under repair, probably due to fallen rocks. It had been built over the last two or three years, the period of time when things in Italy had begun to work imperfectly, and this road was an example of the malaise.

After about six miles the double highway ran into the original road built in the nineteenth century, full of tight curves and narrow stretches. This meandered through villages and hamlets, across fields sloping down to the lake and delicate olive trees. Alma looked at the dashboard clock—it was well past 2:00. *I'll have to hurry up,* she told herself and put on more speed, although not to the point where the wheels squealed at the curves. Recovered from her emotional episode (*What funny things happen when you're tired!*), she was calm again and not concerned by the absence of people and traffic, which, however, she couldn't help noticing, far away as she was from her usual places.

I I

The only people concerned with her well-being at that moment were the two guardian angels, hers and Michele's. Her husband was peacefully asleep inside the Alfa 1300. Before the lakeside bar had closed, he'd made arrangements for the car to be repaired at daylight, then had gone to wait for Alma, sitting in the driver's seat. He once more recited the prayer to the two guardian angels, unaware of how important and timely it was at that moment, then thought, *In a while I'll have to keep an eye on the road so that Alma doesn't drive right past and miss seeing me.* He checked his view of the road, following with his eyes the few cars going down the road out of Lecco. Soon his tiredness and mental exhaustion took over, and he rested his forearms on the wheel and laid his head on them. *But stay alert. I can't sleep,* he told himself, *and I'd better be careful . . . don't lean on the horn . . . the horn . . .* Soon he was asleep.

So that the only beings awake and on watch as the time of Alma's death approached were the two guardian angels—the robust angel responsible for Michele and the delicate angel whom God had put alongside Alma before she was born, in her mother's womb, to be her guardian from then on. It was they who caused Alma to say a prayer of her own and—as if aware of the origin of the inspiration—which she directed at both of them. *Angels of God, who are our guardians . . .* How many times had she prayed this, while in the car and elsewhere, at Michele's side . . . but it had been a while since . . . *And even today, I didn't pray all day,* she thought. *Apart from those few minutes this morning on the way to work, I haven't prayed at all. This has been happening often. Yes, I'm spending too little time with God. And yet one must always be ready, as Sister Anna used to tell us in school. She even said the same here in Varenna when I came close to being bitten by that snake when I was a young girl:* "You must always be prepared, as if each day of your life were the last." *Poor Sister Anna . . . what a laugh we all had when, right here in Varenna (it must be very close to here) the Camusso girl had said to her,* "But Sister Anna, don't you think you're being a bit of a wet blanket?" Alma smiled at the memory. *But Sister Anna was right. That's how we should live. Well, let's see, what I did today that I ought to be ashamed of . . .* She ran rapidly through a self-examination. The quick anger with Ivana in class, over the girl behaving like a precocious shopkeeper. Sometimes she let herself get too easily annoyed by Ivana's harmless vulgarity or by the radical chic pretensions of other students, especially the young Bassetti girl, which were equally unbearable to Alma. *But I oughtn't to be like that. I'm required to be patient with them all.*

She remembered an important statement, often quoted by Michele: "We ought to be very careful that our fight against evil doesn't become a persecution of others." She sighed and continued examining her behavior since the morning, forward up until tonight, picking out each negative action that she regretted. *Even yesterday evening, when Michele's statements were quoted on television and his name was mentioned, how silly I was to let myself become vainglorious . . . Michele says that the way his theories have been set aside by the people who control what is and what is not acceptable, the lay intellectuals, in itself helps us avoid being seized by the temptation to vanity, after all. And yet look at me, for just a piece of nonsense—Michele's name being quoted on television—I've let myself puff up with vainglory, just like a peacock. How weak I am in spirit!* she concluded. *How far away from the ideal strong Christian woman pointed out to us by the sisters at school. And, Good Lord, what an abyss when compared to the perfection demanded by the Gospel:* "Be ye therefore perfect, even as your Father which is in heaven is perfect."

She realized (an inner voice insisted) that she ought to repent seriously, not just superficially. *Of course I repent,* she told herself, *and seriously. From now on I'll try not to lapse into these defects.* But she wasn't to have a "from now on", not on Earth in any case, where she would have been able to fall into sins (but could also have spread much happiness).

For some minutes now a battered car had been ahead of the 125, going slowly, not letting Alma pass and slowing her down. With her usual good manners, she didn't blow the horn or flash the lights to demand room to pass. She twice attempted to pass without success and finally did flash her lights in order to try again to pass. The driver of the car ahead, who seemed to be a young man, reacted strangely, slowly moving over to the right, where he remained for a few moments. When Alma attempted to pass him, he slowly drifted back to the middle of the road.

Alma began to get impatient and decided that as soon as a long straight stretch appeared she would indicate her intention to pass with more resolution. Both cars continued in this way for over one mile, then came to a piece of straight road running flush with the mountain on one side and with a few yards' drop to the lake on the other. Alma flashed her bright lights several times and tapped on the horn. Once more the dilapidated car in front moved lazily to the right, apparently even more indecisively than before. What was this? Whatever was the matter with this fellow? Alma wasn't aware that the man was drugged. In such a bad state—even though he wasn't refusing to let her pass—he was reacting to external stimuli as if they came from afar and were happening to someone else. He was, in his confused state, substituting intention for action.

In any case, there was now space enough to pass him. After having once more flashed her lights, Alma accelerated decidedly. She had nearly completed the maneuver when the other car lightly touched the rear of her 125. It was just a small collision, but the rear of the 125 skidded to the right, then to the left, and went on to hit a wheel against the lefthand curb, at which point the car leapt upward. Alma tried with all her strength to maintain control, but in vain. Everything happened in seconds. She heard a grating metallic noise as the car scraped over the stone parapet, and then her head was struck violently. She only had a faraway sensation of pain and didn't feel the car break through the barrier and fall into the black water. Already unconscious, she felt the sudden chill of the cold water, her last sensation here below.

Two guardian angels came down on her soul, diving like benevolent hawks. These were her and Michele's angels, ensuring no harm came to her soul on its way to the world of the spirit. But there were no incidents to cause a delay.

Meanwhile the car, with Alma's senseless body inside, slowly rolled over underwater, sinking to the depths of the lake. Alma's soul, accompanied by the two angels, soared up to the Great Beyond, an unimaginable place to living mortals, composed solely of spirits. Smiling at her without smiling, talking to her without using words, the angels—splendid beings seeming to be half light and half soldier—bade her welcome. "Here you are, marble statue, at last", her own angel greeted her familiarly. (And who if not her own angel would have been more familiar with her, this invisible angel placed at her side by God even before she was born?) The angel saw in her no-longer-earthly eyes a question: "And Michele? What'll happen to Michele without me?" The angel smiled, trying to lighten her pain at the separation.

"His own time will come", the other angel answered in a very soldierlike manner. "It'll just be a few decades, which for us here is the same as nothing."

With one last earthly reaction Alma sighed once.

Meanwhile, all around her, other spiritual beings were materializing, and she saw that one of these was coming to meet her. It was the spirit of an incomparably beautiful woman. Almina's new eyes widened. "Marietta!" she exclaimed. "Oh, Marietta, is that you?"

It was Marietta, the "shuttle queen" from the Riva mill, who so many times had accompanied Alma to church or on walks down Nomana's cobblestoned streets, holding her by the hand. She no longer had that terrible wild hair and yellow skin or the bent legs. However—even though not in a material sense—she still retained the beautiful dark lamb's eyes, which on Earth had always seemed out of place in her poor face. But now they fit perfectly with the rest of her—insubstantial—figure, which had in some way become in harmony with her eyes.

"Welcome, Almina!" Marietta greeted her happily. "Welcome!"

Alma murmured, almost as if to herself, ecstatically, "If I think about it, nobody was more deserving of paradise than you . . ."

"Oh, don't worry about it. Here there are lots of us, really lots of us", Marietta said in an angelic voice (which still bore a trace of her regular voice, as if a little startled), "because not one of those for whom Christ died ever gets lost, Alma dear, not one, if they themselves don't wish it. You'll see your cousin Manno, Giustina, and Stefano, with his father, Ferrante; you'll see Foresto, Sister Candida, and Romualdo, and also Praga, from Incastigo, whom—thanks to the tireless prayers by Father Mario—the devil didn't manage to get hold of, right at the end."

Then Michele's guardian angel waved goodbye with a circular gesture. "Good, well, I have to return below." He gave a half sigh. "My place is still down there." Then, opening his wings, he launched himself back toward man's tragic world.

The End

See, now they vanish,
the faces and places,
with the self which as it could, loved them,
to become renewed, transfigured in another pattern.

T. S. Eliot
Four Quartets
Little Gidding